EVERYMAN,
I WILL GO WITH THEE,
AND BE THY GUIDE,
IN THY MOST NEED
TO GO BY THY SIDE

HENRY JAMES

Collected Stories

Volume 1 (1866–91)
Selected and introduced by John Bayley

—

EVERYMAN'S LIBRARY

244

This book is one of 250 volumes in Everyman's Library
which have been distributed to 4500 state schools
throughout the United Kingdom.
The project has been supported by a grant of £4 million
from the Millennium Commission.

First included in Everyman's Library, 1999
Selection © David Campbell Publishers Ltd., 1999
Introduction, Bibliography and Chronology © David Campbell
Publishers Ltd., 1999
Typography by Peter B. Willberg

ISBN 1-85715-785-0

A CIP catalogue record for this book is available from the
British Library

Published by David Campbell Publishers Ltd.,
Gloucester Mansions, 140A Shaftesbury Avenue,
London WC2H 8HD

Distributed by Random House (UK) Ltd.,
20 Vauxhall Bridge Road, London SW1V 2SA

HENRY JAMES

CONTENTS

INTRODUCTION

In his stories James reveals himself more deeply and comprehensively than he does anywhere in his novels. That is necessarily a bold generalization, but I believe it to be true. By way of example and of contrast let us select two of the earliest stories in this volume, one of them, 'A Landscape-Painter', only the third that the young author wrote. Both are little masterpieces, as good in their own way as anything by the mature master. The editor of the *Atlantic Monthly* must have been pleased to receive stories of this quality. And yet both these tales carry all the signs of an apprentice – a highly skilful and promising apprentice – who is still feeling his way. That is precisely the reason for their freshness and their charm. James is still too uncertain of himself and his craft not to be direct – almost touchingly direct. He cannot help but give away both himself and his method. And that imparts to these two very contrasting tales their *timbre*, as James himself would have put it, and their vividness.

Of the two – 'A Landscape-Painter' and 'A Light Man' – I myself prefer the former. The plot is almost comically artificial, but James was always to like the diary form and the story makes a perfect companion to his sense of place, already so well developed – his sense here of the sea, the islands, the little New England fishing town, the heroine herself as a figure in the landscape. All are seen just as a painter might see them, and remind us that James himself, when young, had the idea of becoming a painter, and studied for a while at Newport on the Atlantic coast. Newport was a much more fashionable place than Chowderville, a point James makes a joke of in the story, but the choice of setting indicates the engaging fact that the stories in bulk can be seen to form a kind of biography of James's own changing moods and his intentions, his likes and dislikes, his boredom and his enthusiasms – his enthusiasms above all. They cover the whole span of his creative life; and some of the last that he wrote, when he revisited New York in the twentieth century and found it horribly changed, remind us by contrast of his wonderful early and, as it were, innocent sense of the pristine beauty of the American scene, as revealed in 'A Landscape-Painter'.

This is the same enthusiasm which James exaggerates almost to the point of parody when describing the charms of English scenery in 'A Passionate Pilgrim', or when, in a later story, he gives us what must be one of the most passionately vivid accounts ever written of the splendours of the Venetian Duomo where 'I wandered beneath these reverted cups of scintillating darkness, stumbling on the great stony swells of the pavement ... where a thousand once-bright fragments glimmer through the long attrition of idle feet and devoted knees.' (Those two adjectives confer with each other brilliantly, and surely Venetian mosaic has never been better described.)

To return briefly to that pioneer tale, 'A Landscape-Painter'. It is an idyll with a dark ending, a formula in which James's stories may be said to specialize, but one never done more subtly, or in a sense more disquietingly. Locksley's innocence, a kind of innocence in which harmless vanity plays a decided part, is disillusioned for the second time. No girl can love so rich a man, even so quietly and obscurely rich a man, for himself alone, and as she apparently expects him to love her. 'If you really love me,' says Miriam after she has secretly read his diary and discovered how rich he is – 'and I think you do – you will not let this make any difference.' She has never said she loved him: she said she would be his wife, and 'I am incapable of more than one deception.'

This has the appearance of a happy ending, but it is also an ending from which the real life of the story has significantly departed, just as vitality has departed from Locksley's own life with the realization that he will never write any more in his diary, and perhaps never paint any more either. This apparently unmotivated decision takes us deep into James's own heart and mind. Locksley has made the irrevocable decision: he has found himself committed to 'normal' life, instead of to the life of imagination and creation represented by his diary and his painting. His painting has earned respect from the anonymous narrator of the tale, into whose hands the diary has passed. Locksley, we learn from this 'narrator', is dead.

Life as a married man – even as a man married to the once bewitching Miriam – offers no more for him it seems, and so he dies. The story ends on an appropriate note of solution, and yet nothing but emptiness and failure appear to lie ahead.

Miriam too has changed, although the shift in tone abruptly fixed up by the young author in his concluding paragraphs must seem an artificial one. From the beautifully observed and naturalistically recorded rustic maiden with whom Locksley gradually falls in love, she has suddenly become like the word-perfect heroine at the close of a play – a Restoration comedy, or the type of neat *Comédie française* production with which the young James was already familiar. But artificial as it is, this change exactly suits what has occurred. Miriam is now a rich married woman. She has changed just as her new husband has changed, and neither can ever be the same again. Young as he was, James already had the obscure horror of marriage and domesticity which in time became, so to speak, natural to him. He can never bear the young men in his stories to get married, and indeed Locksley is almost the only one who does. It is a far far better thing to forbear, to renounce, to remain celibate, and James sees to it that this is the fate to befall most of his heroes, and very often his heroines too. He arranges the matter by means of a plot, and yet the stories get their characteristic resonance and meaning from his own much deeper and more personal instincts.

There is something engaging, touching too, in the oblique way the young James reveals himself in such tales. He was extremely aware of youthful female charm, possibly susceptible to it as well: he may well have been half in love with his cousin Minny Temple, who was to die young, in the fashion in which Locksley fell in love with his picture of Miriam in her seaside setting. But James no doubt knew too, at an early age, that to see and admire and record the picture, to love it even, was one thing: to marry the picture and settle down with it into domesticity was quite another, and not for him.

All these matters are compressed in a sense into one remarkable story, a story with all the lyric tone and freshness of enthusiasm so attractive in the best of James's early tales. 'A Light Man' is equally remarkable in a very different way. It is the first story which hints at the theme of homosexuality, as today we can hardly avoid seeing and recognizing; and it is significant that the author expressed in later life a special affection for the work, and for the way he had composed it – 'done' it, in his own later phrase. A diary is again used, and used with an equal amount of subtlety. As James's biographer Leon Edel remarks, it is the kind of tale in which 'the hero provides one picture of himself while the reader forms another'. James developed a great fondness for this technique, which he was to use superbly in one of the most famous of all his tales and *nouvelles*, 'The Aspern Papers'.

Like every cultured late Victorian James was steeped in the works of Browning, whose skill as a narrator influenced him deeply. He takes as epigraph to 'A Light Man' a verse from Browning's poem 'A Light Woman', whose narrator tells how he stole his friend's mistress just to see how easy the feat would be. The friend accuses him of disloyalty, a charge he does not accept given the woman in question. What will she herself come to think of him? – how will the story end?

> Well anyhow here the story stays,
> So far at least as I understand:
> And Robert Browning, you writer of plays,
> Here's a subject made to your hand!

The final verse is not the one James quotes, but it may have determined something important to his own narrative technique. 'Here the story stays' – not ends: James will become adept at suggesting the possibilities in this, for, as he was later to put it, 'relations ... stop nowhere, and the eternal problem of the artist is but to draw the circle in which they will happily appear to do so'. In early days he could be comparatively clumsy at this, but the fascination of the earlier tales for the reader consists partly in perceiving how the author is creating his own way of doing it.

Brilliant as it is, the tone of 'A Light Man' is appropriately worldly and cynical: his diary makes the greatest possible contrast with that of the landscape-painter. But in the short space of the tale the characters of Theodore and old Mr Sloane come abundantly alive, as alive as that of the 'light man' himself.

The three are locked in a contest in which sex and personality are as ambiguous as money, and as important. It is a theme made not only for James but for writers like Somerset Maugham and Christopher Isherwood, and for a film like Joseph Losey's 'The Servant'. Like 'A Landscape-Painter', James's tale changes its note at the end, and gives us an example of his preference, not perhaps quite satisfactorily managed here, for leaving the future unresolved and the characters' purpose unrequited – a type of ending that achieves maximum effectiveness in 'The Aspern Papers'.

I have dwelt at some length on the first two stories in our selection because they illustrate so well and with such comparative clarity the ways in which James approaches and will ultimately perfect his instincts for story form and narrative method. And so it seems more helpful to concentrate on this in the case of a few revealing examples than to pass the whole collection rapidly in review. What these stories demonstrate above all is James's power of suggestibility: how he brings all manner of considerations, those from his own inner life very much included, into the overall presentation of what might at first appear quite a simple and straightforward narrative.

He soon begins to bring the same sort of technique to bear on social and national as well as on personal issues. In terms of popularity and financial reward 'Daisy Miller' was the most successful story he ever wrote, although it is difficult to think of it today as one of his best, or one that deeply engaged his truest talent and his own most characteristic kinds of awareness. But we should always remember that James, though he might give the impression of leading a secluded aesthetic life, out of the world, was in fact deeply interested in everything worldly from money-making and high society to the national character and the state of the poor. Not for nothing did he learn what he described as 'the lesson of Balzac'; not for nothing had he been an assiduous reader of Carlyle and Dickens. Dickens's London and Balzac's Paris of the great *Comédie humaine* novels were the twin centres of civilization which, together with his American heritage, helped to make him the most comprehensive of late nineteenth-century novelists and story-tellers.

As his art developed, a main subject was turning out to be those many contrasts between burgeoning young America, and ancient, decaying but still infinitely seductive Europe, of which he was to have so varied and so rich an experience. After his first 'passionate pilgrimage' to Europe as a young man he paid a more businesslike extended visit from 1872 to 1874, making the discovery as he travelled that he could practise his art more cheaply and profitably in Europe than in America. It was during this period that he obtained the material for stories like 'The Madonna of the Future', 'Madame de Mauves', 'Benvolio' and 'The Last of the Valerii', stories which verge on allegory and the tradition of American Gothic. Edgar Allen Poe is in the background, as is the Hawthorne who wrote *The House of the Seven Gables* and *The Marble Faun*. Remarkable as these stories are – 'Benvolio' and the more worldly 'Madame de Mauves' in particular – the reader may come to feel that even the most sophisticated and urbane type of allegory is not a genre that really suits James. As 'A Landscape-Painter' demonstrated, he best approaches meaning in a tale by more subtle paths: there is something by James's standards a trifle crude and schematic in the contrast in 'Benvolio' between the Countess, who breathes so seductively the decadent breath of Europe, and the pure-souled, high-minded Scholastica, who is Benvolio's ultimate choice. We may feel, again by James's standards, that neither Benvolio himself nor the two women are really – as he would later have put it – 'there'.

But Daisy Miller emphatically *is* – that is her great strength. James caught the reading public's fancy with this tale of an All-American girl whose instincts were as pure and wholesome as those of Scholastica herself, but who was wholly oblivious of the conventions which governed a nice young girl's conduct in Europe. Europe loved the story in consequence: for a time there were even 'Daisy Miller' hats to be bought there, and 'Daisy Miller' dresses. There is something ironical about success coming to James by such means, and through the invention of such a character, but such success was always important to him, financially dependent as he was on his writing. The many stories and articles he turned out at every period of his long creative life were always much more profitable than his novels.

There followed a period which can be conveniently labelled by the title of one of James's most lively tales, 'The Siege of London'. And not London only, although James was soon to decide that neither Paris nor Rome suited him so well, either as literary headquarters or source of inspiration. In 'Daisy Miller' he had been an interested spectator, as he now was in London society: the time had passed for those franker symbolic examinations of his own provenance and destiny which we found in 'Benvolio'. He had made his decisions, which were very unlike those of Benvolio, and committed himself to the lonely vocation of the dedicated artist. But that did not mean any loss of vivacity and humour, in which all his tales in their different ways abound. James could be as worldly in pursuit of his goals as his hero in 'The Aspern Papers'; and there is something irresistibly comic, as the author is well aware, in the predicament of that hero, condemned to choose, as he gradually comes to realize, between marrying poor Tita in order to obtain the papers, or giving up his whole mission as a bad job. In fact he fatally dithers, and the loss that ensues will always be 'intolerable' to him.

This is not black humour: it is genuine comedy, but it is mixed in the tale with the true flavour of pathos, even of tragedy. Like so many things in James's stories the germ of 'The Aspern Papers' was close, even uncomfortably close, to his own experience. Venice was the city he loved most in Italy, and it was there that he had dedicated himself to the monkish life of a hard-working and solitary author. The very stones of Venice, her churches and statues and incomparable pictures, seemed to inspire and confirm his own resolve. In one of the most haunting scenes in any of his tales his hero gazes up at the great equestrian statue of the warrior Colleoni, feeling through that contemplation, the all-importance of a ruthless will, a will to seize without scruple on what it desires and aspires to.

James saw in the soldier his own very different but equal determination, and his will was, in a bizarre sense, put to the test when an American maiden lady who had become a close friend began to show signs of yearning for a more intimate relation, perhaps even for marriage. James took fright: but he showed his usual determination. He detached himself, as cordially and as coldly as he could manage, and poor Constance Fenimore, who had presumed too far on the pleasure he had undoubtedly experienced in her company, retired chastened to an apartment in Venice where she died, possibly by suicide. The news appalled James, who hastened to Venice to possess himself of any compromising correspondence. He was filled with remorse, perhaps more so even than the occasion required; he could not help feeling that he had behaved heartlessly and like a cad, just as the hero of 'The Aspern Papers' was to do. The story was in a sense a kind of penance, as well as a way of exorcizing what had been for its author a deeply painful experience.

There is no doubt a further element of James's own hidden experience in another and briefer *nouvelle* of this period, 'The Pupil'. (James never knew what length of tale the *donnée* of an idea would yield him, and what had started as a short story sometimes swelled, as he pondered its implications, into a whole novel, as the idea of *The Ambassadors* was to do.) 'The Pupil' has a love theme, of a sort that James understood well, and the touching pathos of pupil and tutor, with their hopeless but mutually needful relationship, is set against the hard grotesque of Morgan's parents, who want to do an affectionate best for their son, but only if it costs them nothing. It seems likely that James has taken a hint here from the case of Dickens's parents – there is something decidedly Dickensian and Micawberish in the setting of the tale – but with his usual refinement of intelligence he has added and explored the idea by perceiving that the parents might genuinely dote on the boy ('Morgan was dear to his mother') without the will, or the love, to abate their selfish pursuits in his interest.

James was becoming interested in the very young, and Morgan is observed with the same tender attention as is Nanda in *The Awkward Age* and young Miles in 'The Turn of the Screw', a story to be met with in the second volume of this selection. James was also interested in heroism, of the quiet unassuming sort, and in a similarly unadvertised sense of honour, of the kind that makes Morgan blush so painfully for his parents at the end of the tale. Relations here indeed 'stop nowhere', for James has left his ending most suggestively but movingly unclear. How much does the boy 'know'? Is he haunted by the thought that his tutor may not want him, or is he upset by the suspicion that the tutor may want him too much? His place, his honourable place, is surely with his own parents, awful as they may be. James resolves the problem, as he does in other stories, by a convenient heart-attack; but the reader's interest has been effectively tempted – satisfied too – by the craftsmanship that displays a climax in the last few pages.

Honour of the unpretentious sort is the theme of other Jamesian tales of the middle period, but it begins to give place to stories which themselves explore the theme of 'story', of hidden meaning, of the true and the false, and how the artist must reconcile them in obtaining his overall effect. Stories like 'The Author of "Beltraffio" ', The Lesson of the Master' and 'The Real Thing' examine the psychology of the artist and the relation between the selves of artist and human being: what he can make use of and what he can't. An anecdote she thought might interest him was once told to James by a neighbour at a dinner party. He stopped her in the middle, thanking her for the idea of it but preferring not to know how, in real life, it ended. Endings in life are merely banal. This truth for the artist makes a painful comedy in 'The Real Thing' (in volume two of this selection), where an all too genuine lady and gent who have fallen on hard times make the dolorous discovery that their very gentility tells against them when they seek to play for the painter the part of the gentlefolk they genuinely are.

As creator and craftsman James was never an experimentalist in the modern sense. His Diaries show his interest in narrative, and in what would today be called the theory of the story, but his instinct was to let a tale grow naturally in his mind and on the page, rather than to try to manipulate it. Sometimes he can remind us of Chekhov; sometimes even, in his sudden economies of effect, of Kipling, de Maupassant, or his fellow-American Ernest Hemingway. Stories like 'The Patagonia' and 'The Marriages' – the former in particular – have a degree of sudden violence about them which the reader may hardly expect, but which is entirely justified by the logic of events and the skill of the narration. What may strike us most is the rich variety of the tales and the amount of ground they cover, in terms not only of geography – the European and transatlantic scenes – but of nationality and society. James is emphatically not a story-writer in the mode, say, of Somerset Maugham, with a single tone and a limited range of theme. He varies; he alters; he reminds us, by the unobtrusive way he gets inside his subjects and characters, of Keats's definition of the true artist as a man of 'negative capability', who does not impose his own outlook and personality on the worlds of which he becomes a part.

That is not to say – to return to my first point – that James's own history and personality are not vividly revealed by many of the stories. The steely determination that lurks in 'The Aspern Papers' was James's own, as are the hidden will, and the secret urge to independence and self-sufficiency, which appear in so many of the stories, in the guise of various sorts of sacrifice or renunciation. The bulk and variety of the stories themselves attest to that need for independence, for in the middle period of James's London life they were his principal source of income, many not included in this volume being what he called 'potboilers', written in comparative haste and solely for money. Short story magazines, of which there were many both in New York and London, paid well in those days; and an experienced and reasonably well-known writer like James could make a regular if still comparatively modest income out of them.

But there was no question of undue haste about the composition of such a masterpiece as 'The Pupil'. It illustrates admirably the way in which an anecdote casually told him by a friend or dinner-table acquaintance could fuse in James's creative process with memories and experiences of his own – memories which would not otherwise have been brought out into the light. An American doctor from Florence happened to mention to James, when they took an Italian railway journey together, the case of a young boy with a weak heart, dragged about the continent by pretentious shabby-genteel parents. 'Here was a thumping windfall', as James was later to recall, and one that incongruously brought back his own peripatetic childhood, carried round Europe by parents whose finances, although never as precarious as those of the Moreens, fluctuated sufficiently to alarm a sensitive small boy, all too conscious of the anxiety in his parents' voices when the dollar dropped during the American depression of 1857, and it became expedient to move in haste from Paris to more frugal lodgings in Boulogne-sur-Mer.

Here was the ideal combination for James: something he had been told, something that he had experienced, coming together in what most readers or writers would hardly recognize as the modest beginnings of a story. But then, as is shown by the title of one of the tales in the second volume of this collection, for James there could always be in every episode of life, somehow and somewhere, 'The Story in It.'

John Bayley

SELECT BIBLIOGRAPHY

Biographically, the five-volume *Life* by Leon Edel, Hart-Davis, 1953–72, is unchallenged in comprehensiveness. F. W. Dupee's *Henry James: His Life and Writings*, Methuen, 1951, rev. ed. 1965, remains an excellent short biography. Miranda Seymour's *A Ring of Foreign Correspondents: Henry James and his English Circle 1897–1916*, Hodder & Stoughton, 1988, offers a charming account of the writer's domestic life and friendships.

There are various collections of letters, including four volumes edited by Edel and published by Harvard University Press in the US and Macmillan in the UK, 1974–84. James's *Complete Notebooks*, edited by Edel and L. H. Powers, Oxford University Press, 1987, throw light on the fiction, including many of the longer tales.

There is a vast quantity of James criticism, much of it excellent. Complete listings can be found in the *Bibliography of Henry James* by Edel and D. H. Laurence, Hart-Davis, 1961, though this is probably only of use to the advanced student. Among accessible short surveys of James's fictions are Dupee (see above), D. W. Jefferson, *Henry James*, Oliver and Boyd, 1960, and Tony Tanner, *Henry James: The Writer and his Work*, University of Massachusetts Press, 1985, which includes a helpful brief bibliography and a chronological listing of James's books. While there are no good studies devoted specifically to the short stories, John Bayley's *The Short Story: Henry James to Elizabeth Bowen*, Harvester Press, 1988, is a useful starting point.

CHRONOLOGY

DATE	AUTHOR'S LIFE	LITERARY CONTEXT
1842	Birth of William James.	
1843	Henry James born in New York City.	
1846		Balzac: *La Cousine Bette*.
1847		Thackeray: *Vanity Fair*.
		Charlotte Brontë: *Jane Eyre*.
		Emily Brontë: *Wuthering Heights*.
1848		
1850		Dickens: *David Copperfield*.
		Hawthorne: *The Scarlet Letter*.
		Turgenev: *A Month in the Country*.
		Death of Balzac.
1851		Melville: *Moby-Dick*.
1852		
1854–6		
1855		Trollope: *The Warden*.
1855–9	Extensive travels and education abroad.	
1856		Flaubert: *Madame Bovary*.
		Turgenev: *Rudin*.
1857		
1858		George Eliot: *Scenes of Clerical Life*.
1859		Eliot: *Adam Bede*.
1860	Return to America.	Eliot: *The Mill on the Floss*.
		Turgenev: *On the Eve*.
		Hawthorne: *The Marble Faun*.
1861		Dickens: *Great Expectations*.
		Eliot: *Silas Marner*.
		Turgenev: *Fathers and Children*.
1861–5		
1862–3	Harvard Law School.	Flaubert: *Salammbô*.
1864	First story ('A Tragedy of Error') published anonymously.	Trollope: *Can You Forgive Her?*
1865	First signed story ('The Story of a Year') published in *Atlantic Monthly*.	Dickens: *Our Mutual Friend*.
1866		Dostoevsky: *Crime and Punishment*.
		Eliot: *Felix Holt*.
1867		Zola: *Thérèse Raquin*.

European revolutions. Californian Gold Rush.

Great Exhibition.
Louis Napoleon proclaimed Emperor of France.
Crimean War.

Indian Mutiny.

Darwin: *The Origin of Species*.

Ten states secede from Union, American Civil war begins.

Presidency of Lincoln.

End of Civil War. Assassination of Lincoln.

Marx: *Das Kapital* I.

DATE	AUTHOR'S LIFE	LITERARY CONTEXT
1869	First adult travels in Europe (to 1870).	Flaubert: *L'Education sentimentale.* Tolstoy: *War and Peace.*
1870	Death of Minny Temple. *Watch and Ward* – first novel – serialized in *Atlantic Monthly.*	
1871		Eliot: *Middlemarch* (to 1872). Zola: *La Fortune des Rougon.*
1872–4	Further travels in Europe.	
1874–5	Returns to America on completion of his first large novel, *Roderick Hudson.*	Hardy: *Far from the Madding Crowd.*
1875	*Transatlantic Sketches, A Passionate Pilgrim* (first collection of stories) and *Roderick Hudson* published.	Trollope: *The Way We Live Now.*
1875–6	Visits Paris, where he meets Turgenev, Zola and Flaubert. Settles in London.	Eliot: *Daniel Deronda.* Twain: *Tom Sawyer.*
1877	*The American.*	
1878	'Daisy Miller' establishes his international reputation. Publishes first volume of essays (*French Poets and Novelists*).	Hardy: *The Return of the Native.*
1879	*Hawthorne.*	Ibsen: *A Doll's House.*
1880		Dostoevsky: *The Brothers Karamazov.* Death of George Eliot and Flaubert.
1881	*Washington Square. The Portrait of a Lady.*	
1882–3	Visits America. Death of his parents.	
1883		Maupassant: *Une Vie.*
1884	Returns to London with his sister Alice.	Mark Twain: *The Adventures of Huckleberry Finn.* Maupassant: *Miss Harriet.*
1885		Howells: *The Rise of Silas Lapham.* Zola: *Germinal.* Maupassant: *Bel Ami.*
1886	*The Bostonians. The Princess Casamassima.*	Stevenson: *Dr Jekyll and Mr Hyde.* Tolstoy: 'The Death of Ivan Illych'.
1887	Living in Italy. Friendship with Constance Fenimore Woolson.	Chekhov: 'The Kiss'.
1888	'The Aspern Papers'.	Kipling: *Plain Tales from the Hills.* Chekhov: 'The Steppe'.

CHRONOLOGY

DATE	AUTHOR'S LIFE	LITERARY CONTEXT
1889		Tolstoy: 'The Kreutzer Sonata'.
1890	*The Tragic Muse*. Dramatizes *The American*, which has a short run.	William James: *Principles of Psychology*. Kipling: *Soldiers Three*.
1891	Writing for the theatre.	Hardy: *Tess of the d'Urbervilles*. Gissing: *New Grub Street*.
1892	Death of Alice James.	Wilde: *Lady Windermere's Fan*. Conan Doyle: *The Adventures of Sherlock Holmes*.
1895	Booed off stage at première of *Guy Domville*. Gives up writing for theatre.	Crane: *The Red Badge of Courage*. Hardy: *Jude the Obscure*. Wells: *The Time Machine*. Wilde: *The Importance of Being Earnest*. Tolstoy: 'Master and Man'.
1896		Chekhov: *The Seagull*; 'My Life'.
1897	Settles at Lamb House, Rye. *The Spoils of Pynton*. *What Maisie Knew*.	Conrad: *The Nigger of the 'Narcissus'*. Wells: *The Invisible Man*.
1898	'In the Cage'. 'The Turn of the Screw'.	Shaw: *Plays Pleasant and Unpleasant*.
1899	*The Awkward Age*. Friendship with Conrad and Wells.	Chopin: *The Awakening*. Norris: *McTeague*.
1900		Dreiser: *Sister Carrie*. Conrad: *Lord Jim*.
1901	*The Sacred Fount*.	Kipling: *Kim*. Shaw: *Three Plays for Puritans*.
1901–9		
1902	*The Wings of the Dove*.	William James: *Varieties of Religious Experience*.
1903	*The Ambassadors*. 'The Beast in the Jungle'. First meeting with Edith Wharton.	Butler: *The Way of All Flesh*. Chekhov: *The Cherry Orchard*.
1904	*The Golden Bowl*.	Conrad: *Nostromo*. Kipling: *Traffics and Discoveries*.
1905	Visits America for the first time in 20 years.	Wells: *Kipps*. Edith Wharton: *The House of Mirth*.
1906	*The American Scene*.	Sinclair: *The Jungle*.
1906–10	Prepares 'New York Edition' of his work in 24 volumes.	

CHRONOLOGY

DATE	AUTHOR'S LIFE	LITERARY CONTEXT
1907		Adams: *The Education of Henry Adams*.
		Conrad: *The Secret Agent*.
		William James: *Pragmatism*.
1908		Forster: *A Room with a View*.
		Bennett: *The Old Wives' Tale*.
1909		Wells: *Ann Veronica; Tono Bungay*.
		Kipling: *Actions and Reactions*.
1910	Last story, 'A Round of Visits', published. Death of brother, William.	Wells: *Mr Polly*.
		Forster: *Howards End*.
1911		Conrad: *Under Western Eyes*.
		Beerbohm: *Zuleika Dobson*.
1912		Wharton: *Ethan Frome*.
		Mann: *Death in Venice*.
1913	*A Small Boy and Others* (autobiography).	Lawrence: *Sons and Lovers*.
		Wharton: *The Custom of the Country*.
		Proust: *Swann's Way*.
1914	*Notes of a Son and Brother* (autobiography).	Joyce: *Dubliners*.
		Conrad: *Chance*.
1915	Becomes British subject.	Lawrence: *The Rainbow*.
		Ford: *The Good Soldier*.
		Conrad: *Victory*.
		Woolf: *The Voyage Out*.
1916	Dies in London, 28 February.	Joyce: *A Portrait of the Artist as a Young Man*.
1917	*The Ivory Tower* and *The Sense of the Past* (unfinished novels). *The Middle Years* (autobiography).	

HISTORICAL EVENTS

Cubist exhibition in Paris.

First Ford Model T car.

Death of Edward VII. Strikes of dockers, miners, railwaymen, transport
workers in Britain (to 1912). Suffragette riots.
Sinking of the *Titanic*. Woodrow Wilson wins US presidential election.

Outbreak of World War I.

A NOTE ON THE TEXT

The texts of the stories in this collection are taken from their
original publications in various sources, and not from the
amended versions James prepared for the New York edition
of his works.

HENRY JAMES
COLLECTED STORIES

VOLUME I (1866–1891)

·

A LANDSCAPE-PAINTER

Do you remember how, a dozen years ago, a number of our friends were startled by the report of the rupture of young Locksley's engagement with Miss Leary? This event made some noise in its day. Both parties possessed certain claims to distinction: Locksley in his wealth, which was believed to be enormous, and the young lady in her beauty, which was in truth very great. I used to hear that her lover was fond of comparing her to the Venus of Milo; and, indeed, if you can imagine the mutilated goddess with her full complement of limbs, dressed out by Madame de Crinoline, and engaged in small-talk beneath the drawing-room chandelier, you may obtain a vague notion of Miss Josephine Leary. Locksley, you remember, was rather a short man, dark, and not particularly good-looking; and when he walked about with his betrothed it was half a matter of surprise that he should have ventured to propose to a young lady of such heroic proportions. Miss Leary had the grey eyes and auburn hair which I have always attributed to the famous statue. The one defect in her face, in spite of an expression of great candour and sweetness, was a certain lack of animation. What it was besides her beauty that attracted Locksley I never discovered; perhaps, since his attachment was so short-lived, it was her beauty alone. I say that his attachment was of brief duration, because the break was understood to have come from him. Both he and Miss Leary very wisely held their tongues on the matter; but among their friends and enemies it of course received a hundred explanations. That most popular with Locksley's well-wishers was, that he had backed out (these events are discussed, you know, in fashionable circles very much as an expected prize-fight which has miscarried is canvassed in reunions of another kind) only on flagrant evidence of the lady's – what, faithlessness? – on overwhelming proof of the most *mercenary* spirit on the part of Miss Leary. You see, our friend was held capable of doing battle for

an 'idea'. It must be owned that this was a novel charge; but, for
myself, having long known Mrs Leary, the mother, who was a
widow with four daughters, to be an inveterate old screw, it was
not impossible for me to believe that her first-born had also
shown the cloven foot. I suppose that the young lady's family
had, on their own side, a very plausible version of their disappointment. It was, however, soon made up to them by Josephine's marriage with a gentleman of expectations very nearly as
brilliant as those of her old suitor. And what was *his* compensation? That is precisely my story.

Locksley disappeared, as you will remember, from public
view. The events above alluded to happened in March. On
calling at his lodgings in April I was told he had gone to the
country. But toward the last of May I met him. He told me that
he was on the look-out for a quiet, unfrequented place at the
seaside, where he might rusticate and sketch. He was looking
very poorly. I suggested Newport, and I remember he hardly
had the energy to smile at the simple joke. We parted without
my having been able to satisfy him, and for a very long time
I quite lost sight of him. He died seven years ago, at the age of
thirty-five. For five years, accordingly, he managed to shield his
life from the eyes of men. Through circumstances which I need
not go into, a good many of his personal belongings have
become mine. You will remember that he was a man of what
are called cultivated tastes; that is, he was fond of reading,
wrote a little, and painted a good deal. He wrote some rather
amateurish verse, but he produced a number of remarkable
paintings. He left a mass of papers, on many subjects, few of
which are calculated to be generally interesting. A few of them,
however, I highly prize – that portion which constitutes his
private diary. It extends from his twenty-fifth to his thirtieth
year, at which period it breaks off suddenly. If you will come to
my house I will show you such of his pictures and sketches as
I possess, and, I trust, convert you to my opinion that he had in
him the stuff of a charming artist. Meanwhile I will place before
you the last hundred pages of his diary, as an answer to your
inquiry regarding the ultimate view taken by the great Nemesis
of his treatment of Miss Leary – his scorn of the magnificent

Venus Victrix. The recent passing away of the one person who had a voice paramount to mine in the disposal of Locksley's effects enables me to act without reserve.

Chowderville, June 9th. – I have been sitting some minutes, pen in hand, wondering whether on this new earth, beneath this new sky, I had better resume this occasional history of nothing at all. I think I will at all events make the experiment. If we fail, as Lady Macbeth remarks, we fail. I find my entries have been longest when I have had least to say. I doubt not, therefore, that, once I have had a sufficient dose of dullness, I shall sit scribbling from morning till night. If nothing happens — But my prophetic soul tells me that something *will* happen. I am determined that something shall – if it be nothing else than that I paint a picture.

When I came up to bed half-an-hour ago I was deadly sleepy. Now, after looking out of the window a little, my brain is immensely refreshed, and I feel as if I could write till morning. But, unfortunately, I have nothing to write about. And then, if I expect to rise early, I must turn in betimes. The whole village is asleep, godless metropolitan that I am! The lamps on the square, outside, flicker in the wind; there is nothing abroad but the blue darkness and the smell of the rising tide. I have spent the whole day on my legs, trudging from one side of the peninsula to the other. What a trump is old Mrs Monkhouse, to have thought of this place! I must write her a letter of passionate thanks. Never before have I seen such a pretty little coast – never before have I been so taken with wave and rock and cloud. I am filled with ecstasy at the life, light, and transparency of the air. I am enamoured of all the moods and tenses of the ocean; and as yet, I suppose, I have not seen half of them. I came in to supper hungry, weary, footsore, sunburnt, dirty – happier, in short, than I have been for a twelvemonth. And now, if you please, for the prodigies of the brush!

June 11th. – Another day afoot, and also afloat. I resolved this morning to leave this abominable little tavern; I can't stand my feather-bed another night. I determined to find some other prospect than the town-pump and the 'drug-store'. I questioned my host, after breakfast, as to the possibility of getting lodgings in any of the outlying farms and cottages. But my host either did not or would not know anything about the matter. So I resolved to wander forth and seek my fortune – to roam inquisitive through the neighbourhood and appeal to the indigenous sentiment of hospitality. But never have I seen a folk so devoid of this amiable quality. By dinner-time I had given up in despair. After dinner I strolled down to the harbour, which is close at hand. The brightness and breeziness of the water tempted me to hire a boat and resume my explorations. I procured an old tub, with a short stump of a mast, which, being planted quite in the centre, gave the craft much the appearance of an inverted mushroom. I made for what I took to be, and what is, an island, lying long and low, some four or five miles over against the town. I sailed for half-an-hour directly before the wind, and at last found myself a ground on the shelving beach of a quiet little cove. Such a dear little cove – so bright, so still, so warm, so remote from Chowderville, which lay in the distance, white and semi-circular! I leaped ashore, and dropped my anchor. Before me rose a steep cliff, crowned with an old ruined fort or tower. I made my way up, and round to the landward entrance. The fort is a hollow old shell; looking upwards, from the beach, you see the harmless blue sky through the gaping loopholes. Its interior is choked with rocks and brambles and masses of fallen masonry. I scrambled up to the parapet, and obtained a noble sea-view. Beyond the broad bay I saw the miniature town and country mapped out before me; and on the other hand, I saw the infinite Atlantic – over which, by the by, all the pretty things are brought from Paris. I spent the whole afternoon in wandering hither and thither on the hills that encircle the little cove in which I had landed, heedless of the minutes and the miles, watching the sailing clouds and the flitting, gleaming sails, listening to the musical attrition of the tidal pebbles, passing the time anyhow. The only particular sensation I remember was that of being ten years old again, together with a general impression of Saturday afternoon, of the liberty to go in wading or even swimming, and of the prospect of limping home in the dusk with a wondrous story of having almost caught a turtle.

When I returned I found – but I know very well what I found, and I need hardly repeat it here for my mortification. Heaven knows I never was a practical character. What thought I about the tide? There lay the old tub, high and dry, with the rusty anchor protruding from the flat green stones and the shallow puddles left by the receding wave. Moving the boat an inch, much more a dozen yards, was quite beyond my strength. I slowly reascended the cliff, to see if from its summit any help was discernible. None was within sight, and I was about to go down again, in profound dejection, when I saw a trim little sail-boat shoot out from behind a neighbouring bluff, and advance along the shore. I quickened pace. On reaching the beach I found the newcomer standing out about a hundred yards. The man at the helm appeared to regard me with some interest. With a mute prayer that his disposition might not be hostile – he didn't look like a wild islander – I invited him by voice and gesture to make for a little point of rocks a short distance above us, where I proceeded to join him. I told him my story, and he readily took me aboard. He was a civil old gentleman, of the seafaring sort, who appeared to be cruising about in the evening-breeze for his pleasure. On landing I visited the proprietor of my old tub, related my misadventure, and offered to pay damages if the boat shall turn out in the morning to have sustained any. Meanwhile, I suppose, it is held secure against the next tidal revolution, however violent.

But for my old gentleman. I have decidedly picked up an acquaintance, if not made a friend. I gave him a very good cigar, and before we reached home we had become thoroughly intimate. In exchange for my cigar he gave me his name; and there was that in his tone which seemed to imply that I had by no means the worst of the exchange. His name is Richard Quarterman, 'though most people', he added, 'call me Cap'n, for respect'. He then proceeded to inquire my own titles and pretensions. I told him no lies, but I told him only half the truth; and if he chooses to indulge mentally in any romantic under-statements, why, he is welcome, and bless his simple heart! The fact is, I have simply broken with the past. I have decided, coolly and calmly, as I believe, that it is necessary to my success, or, at any rate, to my happiness, to abjure for a while my conventional self, and to assume a simple, natural character. How can a man be simple and natural who is known to have a large income? That is the supreme curse. It's bad enough to have it; to be known to have it, to be known only because you have it, is most damnable. I suppose I am too proud to be successfully rich. Let me see how poverty will serve my turn. I have taken a fresh start – I have determined to stand upon my merits. If they fail me I shall fall back upon my dollars, but with God's help I will test them, and see what kind of stuff I am made of. To be young, strong and poor – such in this blessed nineteenth century, is the great basis of solid success. I have resolved to take at least one brief draught from the founts of inspiration of my time. I replied to Captain Quarterman with such reservations as a brief survey of these principles dictated. What a luxury to pass in a poor man's mind for his brother! I begin to respect myself. Thus much the Captain knows: that I am an educated man, with a taste for painting; that I have come hither for the purpose of studying and sketching coast-scenery; toning myself up with the sea air. I have reason to believe, moreover, that he suspects me of limited means and of being of a very frugal mind. Amen! *Vogue la galère!* But the point of my story is in his very hospitable offer of lodgings – I had been telling him of my want of success in the morning in the pursuit of the same. He is a queer mixture of the gentleman of the old school and the hot-headed merchant-captain.

'Young man,' said he, after taking several meditative puffs of his cigar, 'I don't see the point of your living in a tavern when there are folks about you with more house-room than they know what to do with. A tavern is only half a house, just as one of these new-fashioned screw-propellers is only half a ship. Suppose you walk round and take a look at my place. I own quite a respectable tenement over yonder to the left of the town. Do you see that old wharf with the tumble-down warehouses, and the long row of elms behind it? I live right in the midst of the elms. We have the sweetest little garden in the world, stretching down to the water's edge. It's all as quiet as anything can be, short of a churchyard. The back windows, you know, overlook the harbour; and you can see twenty miles up the bay, and fifty miles out to sea. You can paint to yourself there the livelong day, with no more fear of intrusion than if you were out yonder at the light-ship. There's no one but myself and my daughter, who's a perfect lady, sir. She teaches music in a young ladies' school. You see, money's an object, as they say. We have never taken boarders yet, because none ever came in our track; but I guess we can learn the ways. I suppose you've boarded before; you can put us up to a thing or two.'

There was something so kindly and honest in the old man's weather-beaten face, something so friendly in his address, that I forthwith struck a bargain with him, subject to his daughter's approval. I am to have her answer to-morrow. This same daughter strikes me as rather a dark spot in the picture. Teacher in a young ladies' school – probably the establishment of which Mrs Monkhouse spoke to me. I suppose she's over thirty. I think I know the species.

June 12th, A.M. – I have really nothing to do but to scribble. 'Barkis is willing.' Captain Quarterman brought me word this morning that his daughter makes no objection. I am to report this evening; but I shall send my slender baggage in an hour or two.

P.M. – Here I am, domiciled, almost domesticated. The house is less than a mile from the inn, and reached by a very pleasant road, which skirts the harbour. At about six o'clock I presented myself; Captain Quarterman had described the place. A very civil old negress admitted me, and ushered me into the garden, where I found my friends watering their flowers. The old man was in his house-coat and slippers – he gave me a cordial welcome. There is something delightfully easy in his manners – and in Miss Quarterman's, too for that matter. She received me very nicely. The late Mrs Quarterman was probably a superior being. As for the young lady's being thirty, she is about twenty-four. She wore a fresh white dress, with a blue ribbon on her neck, and a rosebud in her button-hole – or whatever corresponds to the button-hole on the feminine bosom. I thought I discerned in this costume, a vague intention of courtesy, of gaiety, of celebrating my arrival. I don't believe

Miss Quarterman wears white muslin every day. She shook hands with me, and made me a pleasing little speech about their taking me in. 'We have never had any inmates before,' said she; 'and we are consequently new to the business. I don't know what you expect. I hope you don't expect a great deal. You must ask for anything you want. If we can give it, we shall be very glad to do so; if we can't, I give you warning that we shall simply tell you so.' Brava, Miss Quarterman! The best of it is, that she is decidedly beautiful – and in the grand manner; tall, and with roundness in her lines. What is the orthodox description of a pretty girl? – white and red? Miss Quarterman is not a pretty girl, she is a handsome woman. She leaves an impression of black and red; that is, she is a brunette with colour. She has a great deal of wavy black hair, which encircles her head like a dusky glory, a smoky halo. Her eyebrows, too, are black, but her eyes themselves are of a rich blue grey, the colour of those slate-cliffs which I saw yesterday, weltering under the tide. She has perfect teeth, and her smile is almost unnaturally brilliant. Her chin is surpassingly round. She has a capital movement, too, and looked uncommonly well as she strolled in the garden-path with a big spray of geranium lifted to her nose. She has very little to say, apparently; but when she speaks, it is to the point, and if the point suggests it, she doesn't hesitate to laugh very musically. Indeed, if she is not talkative, it is not from timidity. Is it from indifference? Time will elucidate this, as well as other mysteries. I cling to the hypothesis that she is amiable. She is, moreover, intelligent; she is probably fond of keeping herself *to* herself, as the phrase is, and is even, possibly, very proud. She is, in short, a woman of character. There you are, Miss Quarterman, at as full length as I can paint you. After tea she gave us some music in the parlour. I confess that I was more taken with the picture of the dusky little room, lighted by the single candle on the piano, and by her stately way of sitting at the instrument, than by the quality of her playing, though that is evidently high.

June 18*th*. – I have now been here almost a week. I occupy two very pleasant rooms. My painting-room is a large and rather bare apartment, with a very good north-light. I have decked it out with a few old prints and sketches, and have already grown very fond of it. When I had disposed my artistic odds and ends so as to make it look as much like a studio as possible, I called in my hosts. The Captain snuffed about, silently, for some moments, and then inquired hopefully if I had ever tried my hand at a ship. On learning that I had not yet got to ships, he relapsed into a prudent reserve. His daughter smiled and questioned, very graciously, and called everything beautiful and delightful; which rather disappointed me, as I had taken her to be a woman of some originality. She is rather a puzzle. Or is she, indeed, a very commonplace person, and the fault in me, who am for ever taking women to mean a great deal more than their Maker intended? Regarding Miss Quarterman I have collected a few facts. She is not twenty-four, but twenty-seven years old. She has taught music ever since she was twenty, in a large boarding-school just out of the town, where she originally obtained her education. Her salary in this establishment, which is, I believe, a tolerably flourishing one, and the proceeds of a few additional lessons, constitute the chief revenues of the household. But the Captain fortunately owns his house, and his needs and habits are of the simplest kind. What does he or his daughter know of the great worldly theory of necessities, the great worldly scale of pleasures? The young lady's only luxuries are a subscription to the circulating library, and an occasional walk on the beach, which, like one of Miss Brontë's heroines, she paces in company with an old Newfoundland dog. I am afraid she is sadly ignorant. She reads nothing but novels. I am bound to believe, however, that she has derived from the perusal of these works a certain second-hand acquaintance with life. 'I read all the novels I can get,' she said yesterday; 'but I only like the good ones. I do so like *The Missing Bride*, which I have just finished.' I must set her to work at some of the masters. I should like some of those fretful daughters of gold, in New York, to see how this woman lives. I wish, too, that half a dozen of *ces messieurs* of the clubs might take a peep at the present way of life of their humble servant. We breakfast at eight o'clock. Immediately afterwards Miss Quarterman, in a shabby old bonnet and shawl, starts off to school. If the weather is fine the Captain goes a-fishing, and I am left quite to my own devices. Twice I have accompanied the old man. The second time I was lucky enough to catch a big blue-fish, which we had for dinner. The Captain is an excellent specimen of the pure navigator, with his loose blue clothes, his ultra-divergent legs, his crisp white hair, his jolly thick-skinned visage. He comes of a sea-faring English race. There is more or less of the ship's cabin in the general aspect of this antiquated house. I have heard the wind whistle about its walls, on two or three occasions, in true mid-ocean style. And then the illusion is heightened, somehow or other, by the extraordinary intensity of the light. My painting-room is a grand observatory of the clouds. I sit by the half-hour watching them sail past my high uncurtained windows. At the back part of the room something tells you that they belong to an ocean-sky; and there, in truth, as you draw nearer, you behold the vast grey complement of sea. This quarter of the town is perfectly quiet. Human activity seems to have passed over it, never again to return, and to have left a deposit of melancholy resignation. The streets are clean, bright and airy; but this fact only deepens the impression of vanished uses. It seems to say that the protecting heavens look down on their decline and can't help them. There is something ghostly in the perpetual stillness. We frequently hear the rattling of the yards and the issuing of orders on the barks and schooners anchored out in the harbour.

June 28*th*. – My experiment works far better than I had hoped. I am thoroughly at my ease; my peace of mind quite passeth understanding. I work diligently; I have none but pleasant thoughts. The past has almost lost its bitterness. For a week, now, I have been out sketching daily. The Captain carries me to a certain point on the shore of the bay, I disembark and strike across the uplands to a spot where I have taken a kind of tryst with a particular effect of rock and shadow, which has been tolerably faithful to its appointment. Here I set up my easel, and paint till sunset. Then I retrace my steps and meet the boat. I am in every way much encouraged; the horizon of my work grows perceptibly wider. And then I am inexpressibly happy in the conviction that I am not wholly unfit for a life of (moderate) industry and (comparative) privation. I am quite in love with my poverty, if I may call it so. And why should I not? At this rate I don't spend eight hundred a year.

July 12*th*. – We have been having a week of bad weather: constant rain, night and day. This is certainly at once the brightest and the blackest spot in New England. The skies can smile, assuredly, but they have also lachrymal moods. I have been painting rather languidly, and at a great disadvantage, at my window... Through all this pouring and pattering Miss Miriam – her name is Miriam, and it exactly fits her – sallies forth to her pupils. She envelops her beautiful head in a great woollen hood, her beautiful figure in a kind of feminine mackintosh; her feet she puts into heavy clogs, and over the whole she balances a cotton umbrella. When she comes home, with the rain-drops glistening on her rich cheeks and her dark lashes, her cloak bespattered with mud and her hands red with the cool damp, she is a very honourable figure. I never fail to make her a very low bow, for which she repays me with a familiar, but not a vulgar, nod. The working-day side of her character is what especially pleases me in Miss Quarterman. This holy working-dress sits upon her with the fine effect of an antique drapery. Little use has she for whale-bones and furbelows. What a poetry there is, after all, in red hands! I kiss yours, Mademoiselle. I do so because you are self-helpful; because you earn your living; because you are honest, simple, and ignorant (for a sensible woman, that is); because you speak and act to the point; because, in short, you are so unlike – certain of your sisters.

July 16*th*. – On Monday it cleared up generously. When I went to my window, on rising, I found sky and sea looking, for their brightness and freshness, like a clever English water-colour. The ocean is of a deep purple blue; above it, the pure, bright sky looks pale, though it hangs over the island horizon a canopy of denser tissue. Here and there on the dark, breezy water gleams the white cap of a wave, or flaps the white cloak of a fishing-boat. I have been sketching sedulously; I have discovered, within a couple of miles' walk, a large, lonely pond, set in a really grand landscape of barren rocks and grassy slopes. At one extremity is a broad outlook on the open sea; at the other, buried in the foliage of an apple-orchard, stands an old haunted-looking farm-house. To the west of the pond is a wide expanse of rock and grass, of sand and marsh. The sheep browse over it – poorly – as they might upon a High-land moor. Except a few stunted firs and cedars, there is not a tree in sight. When I want shade I have to look for it in the shelter of one of the large stones which hold up to the sun a shoulder coated with delicate grey, figured over with fine, pale, sea-green moss, or else in one of the long, shallow dells where a tangle of blackberry-bushes hedges about a pool that reflects the sky. I am giving my best attention to a plain brown hillside, and trying to make it look like something in nature; and as we have now had the same clear sky for several days, I have almost finished quite a satisfactory little study. I go forth immediately after breakfast. Miss Quarterman supplies me with a little parcel of bread and cold meat, which at the noonday hour, in my sunny solitude, within sight of the slumbering ocean, I voraciously convey to my lips with my discoloured fingers. At seven o'clock I return to tea, at which repast we each tell the story of our day's work. For poor Miss Quarterman it is always the same story: a wearisome round of visits to the school, and to the houses of the mayor, the parson, the butcher, the baker, whose young ladies, of course, all receive instruction on the piano. But she doesn't complain, nor, indeed, does she look very weary. When she has put on a fresh light dress for tea, and arranged her hair anew, and with these improvements flits about with the quiet hither and thither of her gentle footstep, preparing our evening meal, peeping into the teapot, cutting the solid loaf – or when, sitting down on the low door-step, she reads out select scraps from the evening-paper – or else, when tea being over, she folds her arms (an attitude which becomes her mightily) and, still sitting on the door-step, gossips away the evening in comfortable idleness, while her father and I indulge in the fragrant pipe and watch the lights shining out, one by one, in different quarters of the darkening bay: at these moments she is as pretty, as cheerful, as careless as it becomes a sensible woman to be. What a pride the Captain takes in his daughter, and she, in return, how perfect is her devotion to the old man! He is proud of her grace, of her tact, of her good sense, of her wit, such as it is. He believes her to be the most accomplished of women. He waits upon her as if, instead of his old familiar Miriam, she were some new arrival – say a daughter-in-law lately brought home. And *à propos* of daughters-in-law, if I were his own son he could not be kinder to me. They are certainly – nay, why should I not say it? – *we* are certainly a very happy little household. Will it last for ever? I say *we*, because both father and daughter have given me a hundred assurances – he direct, and she, if I don't flatter myself, after the manner of her sex, indirect – that I am already a valued friend. It is natural enough that they should like me, because I have tried to please them. The way to the old man's heart is through a studied consideration of his daughter. He knows, I imagine, that I admire Miss Quarterman, but if I should at any time fall below the mark of ceremony, I should have an account to settle with him. All this is as it should be. When people have to economise with the dollars and cents, they have a right to be splendid in their feelings. I have done my best to be nice to the stately Miriam without making love to her. That I haven't done *that*, however, is a fact which I do not, in any degree, set down here to my credit; for I would defy the most impertinent of men (whoever he is) to forget himself with this young lady. Those animated eyes have a power to keep people in their place. I mention the circumstance simply because in future years, when my charming friend shall have become a distant shadow, it will be pleasant, in turning over these pages, to find written testimony to a number of points which I shall be apt to charge solely upon my imagination. I wonder whether Miss Quarterman, in days to come, referring to the tables of her memory for some trivial matter-of-fact, some prosaic date or half-buried landmark, will also encounter this little secret of ours, as I may call it – will decipher an old faint note to this effect, overlaid with the memoranda of intervening years. Of course she will. Sentiment aside, she is a woman of a retentive faculty. Whether she forgives or not I know not; but she certainly doesn't forget. Doubtless, virtue is its own reward; but there is a double satisfaction in being polite to a person on whom it tells!

Another reason for my pleasant relations with the Captain is, that I afford him a chance to rub up his rusty worldly lore and trot out his little scraps of old-fashioned reading, some of which are very curious. It is a great treat for him to spin his threadbare yarns over again to a submissive listener. These warm July evenings, in the sweet-smelling garden, are just the proper setting for his traveller's tales. An odd enough understanding subsists between us on this point. Like many gentlemen of his calling, the Captain is harassed by an irresistible desire to romance, even on the least promising themes; and it is vastly amusing to observe how he will auscultate, as it were, his auditor's inmost mood, to ascertain whether it is in condition to be practised upon. Sometimes his artless fables don't 'take' at all: they are very pretty, I conceive, in the deep and briny well of the Captain's fancy, but they won't bear being transplanted into the dry climate of my land-bred mind. At other times, the auditor being in a dreamy, sentimental, and altogether unprincipled mood, he will drink the old man's saltwater by the bucketful and feel none the worse for it. Which is the worse, wilfully to tell, or wilfully to believe, a pretty little falsehood which will not hurt any one? I suppose you can't believe wilfully; you only pretend to believe. My part of the game, therefore, is certainly as bad as the Captain's. Perhaps I take kindly to his beautiful perversions of fact because I am myself engaged in one, because I am sailing under false colours of the deepest dye. I wonder whether my friends have any suspicion of the real state of the case. How should they? I take for granted that I play my little part pretty well. I am delighted to find it comes so easy. I do not mean that I find little difficulty in forgoing my old luxuries and pleasures – for to these, thank heaven, I was not so indissolubly wedded that one wholesome shock could not loosen my bonds – but that I manage more cleverly than I expected to stifle those innumerable tacit allusions which might serve effectually to belie my character.

Sunday, July 20th. – This has been a very pleasant day for me; although in it, of course, I have done no manner of work. I had this morning a delightful *tête-à-tête* with my hostess. She had sprained her ankle coming down stairs, and so, instead of going forth to Sunday-school and to meeting, she was obliged to remain at home on the sofa. The Captain, who is of a very punctilious piety, went off alone. When I came into the parlour, as the church-bells were ringing, Miss Quarterman asked me if I never went to a place of worship.

'Never when there is anything better to do at home,' said I.

'What is better than going to church?' she asked, with charming simplicity.

She was reclining on the sofa, with her foot on a pillow and her Bible in her lap. She looked by no means afflicted at having to be absent from divine service; and, instead of answering her question, I took the liberty of telling her so.

'I *am* sorry to be absent,' said she. 'You know it's my only festival in the week.'

'So you look upon it as a festival.'

'Isn't it a pleasure to meet one's acquaintance? I confess I am never deeply interested in the sermon, and I very much dislike teaching the children; but I like wearing my best bonnet, and singing in the choir, and walking part of the way home with——'

'With whom?'

'With anyone who offers to walk with me.'

'With Mr Prendergast, for instance,' said I.

Mr Prendergast is a young lawyer in the village, who calls here once a week, and whose attentions to Miss Quarterman have been remarked.

'Yes,' she answered, 'Mr Prendergast will do as an instance.'

'How he will miss you!'

'I suppose he will. We sing off the same book. What are you laughing at? He kindly permits me to hold the book, while he stands with his hands in his pockets. Last Sunday I quite lost patience. "Mr Prendergast," said I, "do hold the book! Where are your manners?" He burst out laughing in the midst of the reading. He will certainly have to hold the book to-day.'

'What a masterful soul he is! I suppose he will call after meeting.'

'Perhaps he will. I hope so.'

'I hope he won't,' said I, frankly. 'I am going to sit down here and talk to you, and I wish our conversation not to be interrupted.'

'Have you anything particular to say?'

'Nothing so particular as Mr Prendergast, perhaps.'

Miss Quarterman has a very pretty affectation of being more matter-of-fact than she really is.

'His rights, then,' she remarked, 'are paramount to yours.'

'Ah, you admit that he has rights?'

'Not at all. I simply assert that you have none.'

'I beg your pardon. I have claims which I mean to enforce. I have a claim upon your undivided attention when I pay you a morning-call.'

'You have had all the attention I am capable of. Have I been so very rude?'

'Not so very rude, perhaps, but rather inconsiderate. You have been sighing for the company of a third person, whom you can't expect me to care much about.'

'Why not, pray? If I, a lady, can put up with Mr Prendergast's society, why shouldn't you, one of his own sex?'

'Because he is so outrageously conceited. You, as a lady, or at any rate as a woman, like conceited men.'

'Ah, yes; I have no doubt that I, as a woman, have all kinds of weak tastes. That's a very old story.'

'Admit, at any rate, that our friend is conceited.'

'Admit it! Why, I have said so a hundred times. I have told him so.'

'Indeed, it has come to that, then?'

'To what, pray?'

'To that critical point in the friendship of a lady and gentleman when they bring against each other all kinds of delightful accusations and rebukes. Take care, Miss Quarterman! A couple of intelligent New-Englanders, of opposite sexes, young, unmarried, are pretty far gone, when they begin to scan each other's faults. So you told Mr Prendergast that he is conceited? And I suppose you added that he was also dreadfully satirical and sceptical? What was his rejoinder? Let me see. Did he ever tell you that you were a wee bit affected?'

'No; he left that for you to say, in this very ingenious manner. Thank you, sir.'

'He left it for me to deny, which is a great deal prettier. Do you think the manner ingenious?'

'I think the matter, considering the day and hour, very profane, Mr Locksley. Suppose you go away and let me peruse my Bible.'

'Meanwhile what shall I do?'

'Go and read yours, if you have one.'

'My Bible,' I said, 'is the female mind.'

I was nevertheless compelled to retire, with the promise of a second audience in half-an-hour. Poor Miss Quarterman owes it to her conscience to read a certain number of chapters. In what a terrible tradition she has been reared, and what an edifying spectacle is the piety of women! Women find a place for everything in their commodious little minds, just as they do in their wonderfully sub-divided trunks when they go on a journey. I have no doubt that this young lady stows away her religion in a corner, just as she does her Sunday-bonnet – and, when the proper moment comes, draws it forth, and reflects, while she puts it on before the glass and blows away the strictly imaginary dust (for what worldly impurity can penetrate through half a dozen layers of cambric and tissue-paper?): 'Dear me, what a comfort it is to have a nice, fresh holiday-creed!' – When I returned to the parlour Miriam was still sitting with her Bible in her lap. Somehow or other I no longer felt in the mood for jesting; so I asked her, without chaffing, what she had been reading, and she answered me in the same tone. She inquired how I had spent my half-hour.

'In thinking good Sabbath thoughts,' I said. 'I have been walking in the garden.' And then I spoke my mind. 'I have been thanking heaven that it has led me, a poor friend-less wanderer, into so peaceful an anchorage.'

'Are you so very poor and friendless?'

'Did you ever hear of an art-student who was not poor? Upon my word, I have yet to sell my first picture. Then, as for being friendless, there are not five people in the world who really care for me.'

'*Really* care? I am afraid you look too close. And then I think five good friends is a very large number. I think myself very well-off with half-a-one. But if you are friendless, it's probably your own fault.'

'Perhaps it is,' said I, sitting down in the rocking-chair; 'and also, perhaps it isn't. Have you found me so very difficult to live with? Haven't you, on the contrary, found me rather sociable?'

She folded her arms, and quietly looked at me for a moment, before answering. I shouldn't wonder if I blushed a little.

'You want a lump of sugar, Mr Locksley; that's the long and short of it. I haven't given you one since you have been here. How you must have suffered! But it's a pity you couldn't have waited a little longer, instead of beginning to put out your paws and bark. For an artist, you are very slap-dash. Men never know how to wait. "Have I found you very difficult to live with? haven't I found you sociable?" Perhaps, after all, considering what I have in my mind, it is as well that you asked for your lump of sugar. I have found you very indulgent. You let us off easily, but you wouldn't like us a bit if you didn't pity us. Don't I go deep? Sociable? ah, well, no – decidedly not! You are entirely too particular. You are considerate of me, because you know that I know that you are so. There's the rub, you see: I know that you know that I know it! Don't interrupt me; I am going to be striking. I want you to understand why I don't consider you sociable. You call poor Mr Prendergast conceited; but, really, I believe he has more humility than you. He envies my father and me – thinks us so cultivated. You don't envy any one, and yet I don't think you're a saint. You treat us kindly because you think virtue in a lowly station ought to be encouraged. Would you take the same amount of pains for a person you thought your equal, a person equally averse with yourself to being under an obligation? There are differences. Of course it's very delightful to fascinate people. Who wouldn't? There is no harm in it, as long as the fascinator doesn't set up for a public benefactor. If I were a man, a clever man like yourself, who had seen the world, who was not to be dazzled and encouraged, but to be listened to, counted with, would you be equally amiable? It will perhaps seem absurd to you, and it will certainly seem egotistical, but I consider myself sociable, for all that I have only a couple of friends – my father and Miss Blankenberg. That is, I mingle with people without any *arrière-pensée*. Of course the people I see are mainly women. Not that I wish you to do so: on the contrary, if the contrary is agreeable to you. But I don't believe you mingle in the same way with men. You may ask me what I know about it! Of course I know nothing; I simply guess. When I have done, indeed, I mean to beg your pardon for all I have said; but until then, give me a chance. You are incapable of exposing yourself to be bored, whereas I take it as my waterproof takes the rain. You have no idea what heroism I show in the exercise of my profession! Every day I have occasion to pocket my pride and to stifle my sense of the ridiculous – of which of course you think I haven't a bit. It is for instance a constant vexation to me to be poor. It makes me frequently hate rich women; it makes me despise poor ones. I don't know whether you suffer acutely from the smallness of your own means; but if you do, I dare say you shun rich men. I don't, I like to bleed; to go into rich people's houses, and to be very polite to the ladies, especially if they are very much dressed, very ignorant and vulgar. All women are like me in this respect, and all men more or less like you. That is, after all, the text of my sermon. Compared with us it has always seemed to me that you are arrant cowards – that we alone are brave. To be sociable you must have a great deal of patience. You are too fine a gentleman. Go and teach school, or open a corner-grocery, or sit in a law-office all day, waiting for clients: then you will be sociable. As yet you are only selfish. It *is* your own fault if people don't care for you; you don't care for them. That you should be indifferent to their good opinion is all very well; but you don't care for their indifference. You are amiable, you are very kind, and you are also very lazy. You consider that you are working now, don't you? Many persons would not call it work.'

It was now certainly my turn to fold my arms.

'And now,' added my companion, as I did so, 'be so good as to excuse me.'

'This was certainly worth waiting for,' said I. 'I don't know what answer to make. My head swims. Sugar, did you say? I don't know whether you have been giving me sugar or vitriol. So you advise me to open a corner-grocery, do you?'

'I advise you to do something that will make you a little less satirical. You had better marry, for instance.'

'*Je ne demande pas mieux*. Will you have me? I can't afford it.'

'Marry a rich woman.'

I shook my head.

'Why not?' asked Miss Quarterman. 'Because people would accuse you of being mercenary? What of that? I mean to marry the first rich man who offers. Do you know that I am tired of living alone in this weary old way, teaching little girls their scales, and turning and patching my dresses? I mean to marry the first man who offers.'

'Even if he is poor?'

'Even if he is poor and has a hump.'

'I am your man, then. Would you take me if I were to offer?'

'Try and see.'

'Must I get upon my knees?'

'No, you needn't even do that. Am I not on mine? It would be too fine an irony. Remain as you are, lounging back in your chair, with your thumbs in your waistcoat.'

If I were writing a romance now, instead of transcribing facts, I would say that I knew not what might have happened at this juncture had not the door opened and admitted the Captain and Mr Prendergast. The latter was in the highest spirits.

'How are you, Miss Miriam? So you have been breaking your leg, eh? How are you, Mr Locksley? I wish I were a doctor now. Which is it, right or left?'

In this simple fashion he made himself agreeable to Miss Miriam. He stopped to dinner and talked without ceasing.

Whether our hostess had talked herself out in her very animated address to myself an hour before, or whether she preferred to oppose no obstacle to Mr Prendergast's fluency, or whether she was indifferent to him, I know not; but she held her tongue with that easy grace, that charming tacit intimation of 'We could if we would', of which she is so perfect a mistress. This very interesting woman has a number of pretty traits in common with her town-bred sisters; only, whereas in these they are laboriously acquired, in her they are richly natural. I am sure that, if I were to plant her in Madison Square to-morrow, she would, after one quick, all-compassing glance, assume the *nil admirari* in a manner to drive the finest lady of them all to despair. Prendergast is a man of excellent intentions but no taste. Two or three times I looked at Miss Quarterman to see what impression his sallies were making upon her. They seemed to produce none whatever. But I know better, *moi*. Not one of them escaped her. But I suppose she said to herself that her impressions on this point were no business of mine. Perhaps she was right. It is a disagreeable word to use of a woman you admire; but I can't help fancying that she has been a little soured. By what? Who shall say? By some old love-affair, perhaps.

July 24th. – This evening the Captain and I took a half-hour's turn about the port. I asked him frankly, as a friend, whether Prendergast wants to marry his daughter.

'I guess he does,' said the old man, 'and yet I hope he don't. You know what he is: he's smart, promising, and already sufficiently well-off. But somehow he isn't for a man what my Miriam is for a female.'

'That he isn't!' said I; 'and honestly, Captain Quarterman, I don't know who is—'

'Unless it be yourself,' said the Captain.

'Thank you. I know a great many ways in which Mr Prendergast is more worthy of her than I.'

'And I know one in which you are more worthy of her than he – that is in being what we used to call one of the old sort.'

'Miss Quarterman made him sufficiently welcome in her quiet way on Sunday,' I rejoined.

'Oh, she respects him,' said Quarterman. 'As she's situated, she might marry him on that. You see, she's weary of hearing little girls drum on the piano. With her ear for music,' added the Captain, 'I wonder she has borne it so long.'

'She is certainly meant for better things,' said I.

'Well,' answered the Captain, who has an honest habit of deprecating your agreement when it occurs to him that he has obtained it for sentiments which fall somewhat short of the stoical – 'well,' said he, with a very dry, edifying expression, 'she's born to do her duty. We are all of us born for that.'

'Sometimes our duty is rather dismal,' said I.

'So it be; but what's the help for it? I don't want to die without seeing my daughter provided for. What she makes by teaching is a pretty slim subsistence. There was a time when I thought she was going to be fixed for life, but it all blew over. There was a young fellow here, from down Boston way, who came about as near to it as you can come when you actually don't. He and Miriam were excellent friends. One day Miriam came up to me, and looked me in the face, and told me she had passed her word.

' "Who to?" says I, though of course I knew, and Miriam told me as much. "When do you expect to marry?" I asked.

' "When Alfred" – his name was Alfred – "grows rich enough," says she.

' "When will that be?"

' "It may not be for years," said poor Miriam.

'A whole year passed, and, so far as I could see, the young man hadn't accumulated very much. He was for ever running to and fro between this place and Boston. I asked no questions, because I knew that my poor girl wished it so. But at last, one day, I began to think it was time to take an observation, and see whereabouts we stood.

' "Has Alfred made his little pile yet?" I asked.

' "I don't know, father," said Miriam.

' "When are you to be married?"

' "Never!" said my poor little girl, and burst into tears. "Please ask me no questions," said she. "Our engagement is over. Ask me no questions."

' "Tell me one thing," said I: "Where is that d—d scoundrel who has broken my daughter's heart?"

'You should have seen the look she gave me.

' "Broken my heart, sir? You are very much mistaken. I don't know who you mean."

' "I mean Alfred Bannister," said I. That was his name.

' "I believe Mr Bannister is in China," says Miriam, as grand as the Queen of Sheba. And there was an end of it. I never learnt the ins and outs of it. I have been told that Bannister is amassing considerable wealth in the China-trade.'

August 7th. – I have made no entry for more than a fortnight. They tell me I have been very ill; and I find no difficulty in believing them. I suppose I took cold, sitting out so late, sketching. At all events, I have had a mild intermittent fever. I have slept so much, however, that the time has seemed rather short. I have been tenderly nursed by this kind old mariner, his daughter, and his black domestic. God bless them, one and all! I say his daughter, because old Cynthia informs me that for half-an-hour one morning, at dawn, after a night during which I had been very feeble, Miss Quarterman relieved guard at my bedside, while I lay sleeping like a log. It is very jolly to see sky and ocean once again. I have got myself into my easy-chair, by the best window, with my shutters closed and the lattice open; and here I sit with my book on my knee, scratching away feebly enough. Now and then I peep from my cool, dark sick-chamber out into the world of light. High noon at midsummer – what a spectacle! There are no clouds in the sky, no waves on the ocean, the sun has it all to himself. To look long at the garden makes the eyes water. And we – 'Hobbs, Nobbs, Stokes and Nokes' – propose to paint that luminosity. *Allons donc!*

The handsomest of women has just tapped, and come in with a plate of early peaches. The peaches are of a gorgeous colour and plumpness; but Miss Quarterman looks pale and thin. The hot weather doesn't agree with her, and besides she is over-worked. Damn her drudgery! Of course I thanked her warmly for her attentions during my illness. She disclaims all gratitude, and refers me to her father and the dusky Cynthia.

'I allude more especially,' I said, 'to that little hour at the end of a weary night when you stole in, like a kind of moral Aurora, and drove away the shadows from my brain. That morning, you know, I began to get better.'

'It was indeed a very little hour,' said Miss Quarterman, colouring. 'It was about ten minutes.' And then she began to scold me for presuming to touch a pen during my convalescence. She laughs at me, indeed, for keeping a diary at all. 'Of all things, a sentimental man is the most despicable!' she exclaimed.

I confess I was somewhat nettled – the thrust seemed gratuitous.

'Of all things a woman without sentiment is the most wanting in sweetness.'

'Sentiment and sweetness are all very well when you have time for them,' said Miss Quarterman. 'I haven't. I am not rich enough. Good morning!'

Speaking of another woman, I would say that she flounced out of the room. But such was the gait of Juno when she moved stiffly over the grass from where Paris stood with Venus holding the apple, gathering up her divine vestment and leaving the others to guess at her face.

Juno has just come back to say that she forgot what she came for half-an-hour ago. What will I be pleased to like for dinner?

'I have just been writing in my diary that you flounced out of the room,' said I.

'Have you, indeed? Now you can write that I have bounced in. There's a nice cold chicken downstairs,' etc. etc.

August 14*th*. – This afternoon I sent for a light vehicle, and treated Miss Quarterman to a drive. We went successively over the three beaches. What a spin we had coming home! I shall never forget that breezy trot over Weston's Beach. The tide was very low, and we had the whole glittering, weltering strand to ourselves. There was a heavy blow last night, which has not yet subsided, and the waves have been lashed into a magnificent fury. Trot, trot, trot, trot, we trundled over the hard sand. The sound of the horse's hoofs rang out sharp against the monotone of the thunderous surf, as we drew nearer and nearer to the long line of the cliffs. At our left, almost from the zenith of the pale evening-sky to the high western horizon of the tumultuous dark-green sea, was suspended, so to speak, one of those gorgeous vertical sunsets that Turner sometimes painted. It was a splendid confusion of purple and green and gold – the clouds flying and floating in the wind like the folds of a mighty banner borne by some triumphal fleet which had rounded the curve of the globe. As we reached the point where the cliffs begin I pulled up, and we remained for some time looking at their long, diminishing, crooked perspective, blue and dun as it receded, with the white surge playing at their feet.

August 17*th*. – This evening, as I lighted my bedroom-candle, I saw that the Captain had something to say to me. So I waited below until my host and his daughter had performed their usual osculation, and the latter had given me that confiding hand-shake which I never fail to extract.

'Prendergast has got his discharge,' said the old man, when he heard his daughter's door close.

'What do you mean?'

He pointed with his thumb to the room above, where we heard, through the thin partition, the movement of Miss Quarterman's light step.

'You mean that he has proposed to Miss Miriam?'

The Captain nodded.

'And has been refused?'

'Flat.'

'Poor fellow!' said I, very honestly. 'Did he tell you himself?'

'Yes, with tears in his eyes. He wanted me to speak for him. I told him it was no use. Then he began to say hard things of my poor girl.'

'What kind of things?'

'A pack of falsehoods. He says she has no heart. She has promised always to regard him as a friend; it's more than I will, hang him!'

'Poor fellow!' said I; and now, as I write, I can only repeat, considering what a hope was here disappointed, Poor fellow!

August 23*rd*. – I have been lounging about all day, thinking of it, dreaming of it, spooning over it, as they say. This is a decided waste of time. I think, accordingly, the best thing for me to do is to sit down and lay the ghost by writing out my little story.

On Thursday evening, Miss Quarterman happened to intimate that she had a holiday on the morrow, it being the birthday of the lady in whose establishment she teaches.

'There is to be a tea-party at four o'clock in the afternoon for the resident pupils and teachers,' Miriam said. 'Tea at four! what do you think of that? And then there is to be a speech-making by the smartest young lady. As my services are not required I propose to be absent. Suppose, father, you take us out in your boat. Will you come, Mr Locksley? We shall have a neat little picnic. Let us go over to old Fort Plunkett, across the bay. We will take our dinner with us, and send Cynthia to spend the day with her sister, and put the house-key in our pocket, and not come home till we please.'

I entered into the project with passion, and it was accordingly carried into execution the next morning, when – about ten o'clock – we pushed off from our little wharf at the garden-foot. It was a perfect summer's day; I can say no more for it; and we made a quiet run over to the point of our destination. I shall never forget the wondrous stillness which brooded over earth and water as we weighed anchor in the lee of my old friend – or old enemy – the ruined fort. The deep, translucent water reposed at the base of the warm sunlit cliff like a great basin of glass, which I half expected to hear shiver and crack as our keel ploughed through it. And how colour and sound stood out in the transparent air! How audibly the little ripples on the beach whispered to the open sky. How our irreverent voices seemed to jar upon the privacy of the little cove! The delicate rocks doubled themselves without a flaw in the clear, dark water. The gleaming white beach lay fringed with its deep deposits of odorous sea-weed, which looked like masses of black lace. The steep, straggling sides of the cliffs lifted their rugged angles against the burning blue of the sky. I remember, when Miss Quarterman stepped ashore and stood upon the beach, relieved against the cool darkness of a recess in the cliff, while her father and I busied ourselves with gathering up our baskets and fastening the anchor – I remember, I say, what a picture she made. There is a certain purity in the air of this place which I have never seen surpassed – a lightness, a brilliancy, a crudity, which allows perfect liberty of self-assertion to each individual object in the landscape. The prospect is ever more or less like a picture which lacks its final process, its reduction to unity. Miss Quarterman's figure, as she stood there on the beach, was almost *criarde*; but how it animated the whole scene! Her light muslin dress, gathered up over her white petticoat, her little black mantilla, the blue veil which she had knotted about her neck, the little silken dome which she poised over her head in one gloved hand, while the other retained her crisp draperies, and which cast down upon her face a sharp circle of shade, where her cheerful eyes shone darkly and her parted lips said things I lost – these are some of the points I hastily noted.

'Young woman,' I cried out, over the water, 'I do wish you might know how pretty you look!'

'How do you know I don't?' she answered. 'I should think I might. You don't look so badly yourself. But it's not I; it's the aerial perspective.'

'Hang it – I am going to become profane!' I called out again.

'Swear ahead,' said the Captain.

'I am going to say you are infernally handsome.'

'Dear me! is that all?' cried Miss Quarterman, with a little light laugh which must have made the tutelar sirens of the cove ready to die with jealousy down in their submarine bowers.

By the time the Captain and I had landed our effects our companion had tripped lightly up the forehead of the cliff – in one place it is very retreating – and disappeared over its crown. She soon returned, with an intensely white pocket-handkerchief added to her other provocations, which she waved to us, as we trudged upward, carrying our baskets. When we stopped to take breath on the summit and wipe our foreheads, we of course rebuked her for roaming about idly with her parasol and gloves.

'Do you think I am going to take any trouble or do any work?' cried Miss Miriam, in the greatest good-humour. 'Is not this my holiday? I am not going to raise a finger, nor soil these beautiful gloves, for which I paid so much at Mr Dawson's at Chowderville. After you have found a shady place for your provisions, I should like you to look for a spring. I am very thirsty.'

'Find the spring yourself, miss,' said her father. 'Mr Locksley and I have a spring in this basket. Take a pull, sir.'

And the Captain drew forth a stout black bottle.

'Give me a cup, and I will look for some water,' said Miriam. 'Only I'm so afraid of the snakes! If you hear a scream you may know it's a snake.'

'Screaming snakes!' said I; 'that's a new species.'

What cheap fun it all sounds now! As we looked about us shade seemed scarce, as it generally is in this region. But Miss Quarterman, like the very adroit and practical young person she is, for all that she would have me believe the contrary, immediately discovered flowing water in the shelter of a pleasant little dell, beneath a clump of firs. Hither, as one of the young gentlemen who imitate Tennyson would say, we brought our basket, he and I; while Miriam dipped the cup, and held it dripping to our thirsty lips, and laid the cloth, and on the grass disposed the platters round. I should have to be a poet, indeed, to describe half the happiness and the silly sweetness and artless revelry of this interminable summer's day. We ate and drank and talked; we ate occasionally with our fingers, we drank out of the necks of our bottles, and we talked with our mouths full, as befits (and excuses) those who talk perfect nonsense. We told stories without the least point. The Captain and I made atrocious puns. I believe, indeed, that Miss Quarterman herself made one little punkin, as I called it. If there had been any superfluous representative of humanity present to notice the fact, I should say that we made fools of ourselves. But as there was no one to criticise us we were brilliant enough. I am conscious myself of having said several witty things, which Miss Quarterman understood: *in vino veritas*. The dear old Captain twanged the long bow indefatigably. The bright high sun dawdled above us, in the same place, and drowned the prospect with light and warmth. One of these days I mean to paint a picture which, in future ages, when my dear native land shall boast a national school of art, will hang in the Salon Carré of the great central museum (located, let us say, in Chicago) and recall to folks – or rather make them forget – Giorgione, Bordone, and Veronese: A Rural Festival; three persons feasting under some trees; scene, nowhere in particular; time and hour, problematical. Female figure, a rich *brune*; young man reclining on his elbow; old man drinking. An empty sky, with no end of expression. The whole stupendous in colour, drawing, feeling. Artist uncertain; supposed to be Robinson, 1900.

After dinner the Captain began to look out across the bay, and, noticing the uprising of a little breeze, expressed a wish to cruise about for an hour or two. He proposed to us to walk along the shore to a point a couple of miles northward, and there meet the boat. His daughter having agreed to this proposition, he set off with the lightened hamper, and in less than half-an-hour we saw him standing out from shore. Miss Quarterman and I did not begin our walk for a long, long time. We sat and talked beneath the trees. At our feet a wide cleft in the hills – almost a glen – stretched down to the silent beach; beyond lay the familiar ocean-line. But, as many philosophers have observed, there is an end to all things. At last we got up. My companion remarked that, as the air was freshening, she supposed she ought to put on her shawl. I helped her to fold it into the proper shape, and then I placed it on her shoulders; it being an old shawl of faded red (Canton crape, I believe they call it), which I have seen very often. And then she tied her veil once more about her neck, and gave me her hat to hold, while she effected a partial redistribution of her hair-pins. By way of being humorous, I spun her hat round on my stick; at which she was kind enough to smile, as with downcast face and uplifted elbows she fumbled among her braids. And then she shook out the creases of her dress and drew on her gloves; and finally she said 'Well!' – that inevitable tribute to time and morality which follows upon even the mildest forms of dissipation. Very slowly it was that we wandered down the little glen. Slowly, too, we followed the course of the narrow and sinuous beach, as it keeps to the foot of the low cliffs. We encountered no sign of human life. Our conversation I need hardly repeat. I think I may trust it to the keeping of my memory; it was the sort of thing that comes back to one – after. If something ever happens which I think *may*, that apparently idle hour will seem, as one looks back, very symptomatic, and what we didn't say be perceived to have been more significant than what we did. There was something between us – there *is* something between us – and we listened to its impalpable presence – I liken it to the hum (very faint) of an unseen insect – in the golden stillness of the afternoon. I must add that if she expects, foresees, if she waits, she does so with a supreme serenity. If she is my fate (and she has the air of it), she is conscious that it's *her* fate to be so.

September 1*st*. – I have been working steadily for a week. This is the first day of autumn. Read aloud to Miss Quarterman a little Wordsworth.

September 10*th. Midnight*. – Worked without interruption – until yesterday, inclusive, that is. But with the day now closing – or opening – begins a new era. My poor vapid old diary, at last you shall hold a *fact*.

For three days past we have been having damp, autumnal weather; dusk has gathered early. This evening, after tea, the Captain went into town – on business, as he said: I believe, to attend some Poorhouse or Hospital Board. Miriam and I went into the parlour. The place seemed cold; she brought in the lamp from the dining-room, and proposed we should have a little fire. I went into the kitchen, procured half-a-dozen logs, and, while she drew the curtains and wheeled up the table, I kindled a lively, crackling blaze. A fortnight ago she would not have allowed me to do this without a protest. She would not have offered to do it herself – not she! – but she would have said that I was not here to serve, but to be served, and would at least have made a show of calling the negress. I should have had my own way, but we have changed all that. Miriam went to her piano, and I sat down to a book. I read not a word, but sat considering my fate and watching it come nearer and nearer. For the first time since I have known her (my fate) she had put on a dark, warm dress; I think it was of the material called alpaca. The first time I saw her (I remember such things) she wore a white dress with a blue neck-ribbon; now she wore a black dress with the same ribbon. That is, I remember wondering, as I sat there eyeing her, whether it *was* the same ribbon, or merely another like it. My heart was in my throat; and yet I thought of a number of trivialities of the same kind. At last I spoke.

'Miss Quarterman,' I said, 'do you remember the first evening I passed beneath your roof, last June?'

'Perfectly,' she replied, without stopping.

'You played that same piece.'

'Yes; I played it very badly, too. I only half knew it. But it is a showy piece, and I wished to produce an effect. I didn't know then how indifferent you are to music.'

'I paid no particular attention to the piece. I was intent upon the performer.'

'So the performer supposed.'

'What reason had you to suppose so?'

'I am sure I don't know. Did you ever know a woman to be able to give a reason when she has guessed aright?'

'I think they generally contrive to make up a reason afterwards. Come, what was yours?'

'Well, you stared so hard.'

'Fie! I don't believe it. That's unkind.'

'You said you wished me to invent a reason. If I really had one, I don't remember it.'

'You told me you remembered the occasion in question perfectly.'

'I meant the circumstances. I remember what we had for tea; I remember what dress I wore. But I don't remember my feelings. They were naturally not very memorable.'

'What did you say when your father proposed that I should come here?'

'I asked how much you would be willing to pay.'

'And then?'

'And then, if you looked respectable.'

'And then?'

'That was all. I told my father to do as he pleased.'

She continued to play, and leaning back in my chair I continued to look at her. There was a considerable pause.

'Miss Quarterman,' said I, at last.

'Well, sir?'

'Excuse me for interrupting you so often. But' – and I got up and went to the piano – 'but, you know, I thank heaven that it has brought you and me together.'

She looked up at me and bowed her head with a little smile, as her hands still wandered over the keys.

'Heaven has certainly been very good to us,' said she.

'How much longer are you going to play?' I asked.

'I'm sure I don't know. As long as you like.'

'If you want to do as I like, you will stop immediately.'

She let her hands rest on the keys a moment, and gave me a rapid, questioning look. Whether she found a sufficient answer in my face I know not; but she slowly rose, and, with a very pretty affectation of obedience, began to close the instrument. I helped her to do so.

'Perhaps you would like to be quite alone,' she said. 'I suppose your own room is too cold.'

'Yes,' I answered, 'you have hit it exactly. I wish to be alone. I wish to monopolise this cheerful blaze. Hadn't you better go into the kitchen and sit with the cook? It takes you women to make such cruel speeches.'

'When we women are cruel, Mr Locksley, it is the merest accident. We are not wilfully so. When we learn that we have been unkind we very humbly ask pardon, without even knowing what our crime has been.' And she made me a very low curtsey.

'I will tell you what your crime has been,' said I. 'Come and sit by the fire. It's rather a long story.'

'A long story? Then let me get my work.'

'Confound your work! Excuse me, but you exasperate me. I want you to listen to me. Believe me, you will need all your attention.'

She looked at me steadily a moment, and I returned her glance. During that moment I was reflecting whether I might put my arm round her waist and kiss her; but I decided that I might do nothing of the sort. She walked over and quietly seated herself in a low chair by the fire. Here she patiently folded her arms. I sat down before her.

'With you, Miss Quarterman,' said I, 'one must be very explicit. You are not in the habit of taking things for granted. You have a great deal of imagination, but you rarely exercise it on behalf of other people.'

'Is that my crime?' asked my companion.

'It's not so much a crime as a vice, and perhaps not so much a vice as a virtue. Your crime is, that you are so stone-cold to a poor devil who loves you.'

She burst into a rather shrill laugh. I wonder whether she thought I meant Prendergast.

'Who are you speaking for, Mr Locksley?' she asked.

'Are there so many? For myself.'

'Honestly?'

'Do you think me capable of deceiving you?'

'What is that French phrase that you are for ever using? I think I may say "*Allons donc!*"'

'Let us speak plain English, Miss Quarterman.'

'"Stone-cold" is certainly very plain English. I don't see the relative importance of the two branches of your proposition. Which is the principal, and which the subordinate clause – that I am stone-cold, as you call it, or that you love me, as you call it?'

'As I call it? What would you have me call it? For pity's sake, Miss Quarterman, be serious, or I shall call it something else. Yes, I love you. Don't you believe it?'

'How can I help believing what you tell me?'

'Dearest, bravest of women,' said I.

And I attempted to take her hand.

'No, no, Mr Locksley,' said she – 'not just yet, if you please.'

'Actions speak louder than words,' said I.

'There is no need of speaking loud. I hear you perfectly.'

'I certainly shall not whisper,' said I; 'although it is the custom, I believe, for lovers to do so. Will you be my wife?'

I don't know whether *she* whispered or not, but before I left her she consented.

September 12*th*. – We are to be married in about three weeks.

September 19*th*. – I have been in New York a week, transacting business. I got back yesterday. I find everyone here talking about our engagement. Miriam tells me that it was talked about a month ago, and that there is a very general feeling of disappointment that I am so very poor.

'Really, if you don't mind it,' I remarked, 'I don't see why others should.'

'I don't know whether you are poor or not,' says Miriam, 'but I know that I am rich.'

'Indeed! I was not aware that you had a private fortune,' etc. etc.

This little farce is repeated in some shape every day. I am very idle. I smoke a great deal, and lounge about all day, with my hands in my pockets. I am free from that ineffable weariness of ceaseless *buying* which I suffered from six months ago. That intercourse was conducted by means of little parcels, and I have resolved that this engagement, at all events, shall have no connection with the shops. I was cheated of my poetry once; I shan't be a second time. Fortunately there is not much danger of this, for my mistress is positively lyrical. She takes an enthusiastic interest in her simple outfit – showing me triumphantly certain of her purchases, and making a great mystery about others, which she is pleased to denominate table-cloths and napkins. Last evening I found her sewing buttons on a table-cloth. I had heard a great deal of a certain pink silk dress, and this morning, accordingly, she marched up to me, arrayed in this garment, upon which all the art and taste and eyesight, and all the velvet and lace, of Chowderville have been lavished.

'There is only one objection to it,' said Miriam, parading before the glass in my painting-room: 'I am afraid it is above our station.'

'By Jove! I will paint your portrait in it and make our fortune,' said I. 'All the other men who have handsome wives will bring them to be painted.'

'You mean all the women who have handsome dresses,' Miriam replied, with great humility.

Our wedding is fixed for next Thursday. I tell Miriam that it will be as little of a wedding, and as much of a marriage, as possible. Her father and her good friend Miss Blankenberg (the schoolmistress) alone are to be present. My secret oppresses me considerably; but I have resolved to keep it for the honey-moon, when it may leak out as occasion helps it. I am harassed with a dismal apprehension that if Miriam were to discover it now, the whole thing would have to be done over again. I have taken rooms at a romantic little watering-place called Crag-thorpe, ten miles off. The hotel is already quite purged of cockneys, and we shall be almost alone.

September 28th. – We have been here two days. The little transaction in the church went off smoothly. I am truly sorry for the Captain. We drove directly over here, and reached the place at dusk. It was a raw, black day. We have a couple of good rooms, close to the savage sea. I am nevertheless afraid I have made a mistake. It would perhaps have been wiser to go to New York. These things are not immaterial; we make our own heaven, but we scarcely make our own earth. I am writing at a little table by the window, looking out on the rocks, the gather-ing dusk, the rising fog. My wife has wandered down to the rocky platform in front of the house. I can see her from here, bareheaded, in that old crimson shawl, talking to one of the landlord's little boys. She has just given the infant a kiss, bless her tender heart! I remember her telling me once that she was very fond of little boys; and, indeed, I have noticed that they are seldom too dirty for her to take on her knee. I have been reading over these pages for the first time in – I don't know when. They are filled with *her* – even more in thought than in word. I believe I will show them to her when she comes in. I will give her the book to read, and sit by her, watching her face – watching the great secret dawn upon her.

Later. – Somehow or other, I can write this quietly enough; but I hardly think I shall ever write any more. When Miriam came in I handed her this book.

'I want you to read it,' said I.

She turned very pale, and laid it on the table, shaking her head.

'I know it,' she said.

'What do you know?'

'That you have ever so much money. But believe me, Mr Locksley, I am none the worse for the knowledge. You intimated in one place in your book that I am fitted by nature for wealth and splendour. I verily believe I am. You pretend to hate your money; but you would not have had me without it. If you really love me – and I think you do – you will not let this make any difference. I am not such a fool as to attempt to talk now about what passed through me when you asked me to – to do *this*. But I remember what I said.'

'What do you expect me to do?' I asked. 'Shall I call you some horrible name and cast you off?'

'I expect you to show the same courage that I am showing. I never said I loved you. I never deceived you in that. I said I would be your wife. So I will, faithfully. I haven't so much heart as you think; and yet, too, I have a great deal more. I am incapable of more than one deception. – Mercy! didn't you see it? didn't you know it? see that I saw it? know that I knew it? It was diamond cut diamond. You cheated me and I mystified you. Now that you tell me your secret I can tell you mine. *Now* we are free, with the fortune that you know. Excuse me, but it sometimes comes over me! *Now* we can be good and honest and true. It was all a make-believe virtue before.'

'So you read that thing?' I asked: actually – strange as it may seem – for something to say.

'Yes, while you were ill. It was lying with your pen in it, on the table. I read it because I suspected. Otherwise I wouldn't have done so.'

'It was the act of a false woman,' said I.

'A false woman? No, it was the act of any woman – placed as I was placed. You don't believe it?' And she began to smile. 'Come, you may abuse me in your diary if you like – I shall never peep into it again!'

A LIGHT MAN

'And I – what I seem to my friend, you see –
What I soon shall seem to his love, you guess.
What I seem to myself, do you ask of me?
No hero, I confess.'

A Light Woman – Browning's Men and Women

APRIL 4, 1857 – I have changed my sky without changing my
mind. I resume these old notes in a new world. I hardly know of
what use they are; but it's easier to stick to the habit than to
drop it. I have been at home now a week – at home, forsooth!
And yet, after all, it is home. I am dejected, I am bored, I am
blue. How can a man be more at home than that? Nevertheless,
I am the citizen of a great country, and for that matter, of a great
city. I walked to-day some ten miles or so along Broadway, and
on the whole I don't blush for my native land. We are a capable
race and a good-looking withal; and I don't see why we
shouldn't prosper as well as another. This, by the way, ought
to be a very encouraging reflection. A capable fellow and a
good-looking withal; I don't see why he shouldn't die a million-
aire. At all events he must do something. When a man has, at
thirty-two, a net income of considerably less than nothing, he
can scarcely hope to overtake a fortune before he himself is
overtaken by age and philosophy – two deplorable obstructions. I am afraid that one of them has already planted itself
in my path. What am I? What do I wish? Whither do I tend?
What do I believe? I am constantly beset by these impertinent
whisperings. Formerly it was enough that I was Maximus Austin; that I was endowed with a cheerful mind and a good
digestion; that one day or another, when I had come to the
end, I should return to America and begin at the beginning;
that, meanwhile, existence was sweet in – in the Rue Tronchet.
But now? Has the sweetness really passed out of life? Have
I eaten the plums and left nothing but the bread and milk and
corn-starch, or whatever the horrible concoction is? – I had it
to-day for dinner. Pleasure, at least, I imagine – pleasure pure

39

and simple, pleasure crude, brutal and vulgar – this poor flimsy delusion has lost all its charm. I shall never again care for certain things – and indeed for certain persons. Of such things, of such persons, I firmly maintain, however, that I was never an enthusiastic votary. It would be more to my credit, I suppose, if I had been. More would be forgiven me if I had loved a little more, if into all my folly and egotism I had put a little more *naïveté* and sincerity. Well, I did the best I could, I was at once too bad and too good for it all. At present, it's far enough off; I have put the sea between us; I am stranded. I sit high and dry, scanning the horizon for a friendly sail, or waiting for a high tide to set me afloat. The wave of pleasure has deposited me here in the sand. Shall I owe my rescue to the wave of pain? At moments I feel a kind of longing to expiate my stupid little sins. I see, as through a glass, darkly, the beauty of labour and love. Decidedly, I am willing to work. It's written.

7th – My sail is in sight; it's at hand; I have all but boarded the vessel. I received this morning a letter from the best man in the world. Here it is:

DEAR MAX: I see this very moment, in an old newspaper which had already passed through my hands without yielding up its most precious item, the announcement of your arrival in New York. To think of your having perhaps missed the welcome you had a right to expect from me! Here it is dear Max – as cordial as you please. When I say I have just read of your arrival, I mean that twenty minutes have elapsed by the clock. These have been spent in conversation with my excellent friend Mr Sloane – we having taken the liberty of making you the topic. I haven't time to say more about Frederick Sloane than that he is very anxious to make your acquaintance, and that, if your time is not otherwise engaged, he would like you very much to spend a month with him. He is an excellent host, or I shouldn't be here myself. It appears that he knew your mother very intimately, and he has a taste for visiting the amenities of the parents upon the children; the original ground of my own connection with him was that he had been a particular friend of my father. You may have heard your mother speak of him. He is

a very strange old fellow, but you will like him. Whether or no
you come for his sake, come for mine.

Yours always,
THEODORE LISLE

Theodore's letter is of course very kind, but it's remarkably
obscure. My mother may have had the highest regard for
Mr Sloane, but she never mentioned his name in my
hearing. Who is he, what is he, and what is the nature of his
relations with Theodore? I shall learn betimes. I have written to
Theodore that I gladly accept (I believe I suppressed the
'gladly' though) his friend's invitation, and that I shall
immediately present myself. What can I do that is better?
Speaking sordidly, I shall obtain food and lodging while I look
about me. I shall have a base of operations. D–, it appears, is a
long day's journey, but enchanting when you reach it. I am
curious to see an enchanting American town. And to stay a
month! Mr Frederick Sloane, whoever you are, *vous faites
bien les choses*, and the little that I know of you is very much
to your credit. You enjoyed the friendship of my dear mother,
you possess the esteem of the virtuous Theodore, you commend yourself to my own affection. At this rate, I shall not
grudge it.

D–, 14th. – I have been here since Thursday evening – three
days. As we rattled up to the tavern in the village, I perceived
from the top of the coach, in the twilight, Theodore beneath the
porch, scanning the vehicle, with all his amiable disposition in
his eyes. He has grown older, of course, in these five years, but
less so than I had expected. His is one of those smooth,
unwrinkled souls that keep their bodies fair and fresh. As tall
as ever, moreover, and as lean and clean. How short and fat and
dark and debauched he makes one feel! By nothing he says or
means, of course, but merely by his old unconscious purity and
simplicity – that slender straightness which makes him remind
you of the spire of an English abbey. He greeted me with smiles,
and stares, and alarming blushes. He assures me that he never
would have known me, and that five years have altered me –
sehr! I asked him if it were for the better? He looked at me hard

for a moment, with his eyes of blue, and then, for an answer, he blushed again.

On my arrival we agreed to walk over from the village. He dismissed his waggon with my luggage, and we went arm-in-arm through the dusk. The town is seated at the foot of certain mountains, whose names I have yet to learn, and at the head of a big sheet of water, which, as yet, too, I know only as 'the Lake'. The road hitherward soon leaves the village and wanders in rural loveliness by the margin of this expanse. Sometimes the water is hidden by clumps of trees, behind which we heard it lapping and gurgling in the darkness; sometimes it stretches out from your feet in shining vagueness, as if it were tired of making, all day, a million little eyes at the great stupid hills. The walk from the tavern takes some half an hour, and in this interval Theodore made his position a little more clear. Mr Sloane is a rich old widower; his age is seventy-two, and as his health is thoroughly broken, is practically even greater; and his fortune – Theodore, characteristically, doesn't know anything definite about that. It's probably about a million. He has lived much in Europe, and in the 'great world'; he has had adventures and passions and all that sort of thing; and now, in the evening of his days, like an old French diplomatist, he takes it into his head to write his memoirs. To this end he has lured poor Theodore to his gruesome side, to mend his pens for him. He has been a great scribbler, says Theodore, all his days, and he proposes to incorporate a large amount of promiscuous literary matter into these *souvenirs intimes*. Theodore's principal function seems to be to get him to leave things out. In fact, the poor youth seems troubled in conscience. His patron's lucubrations have taken the turn of many other memoirs, and have ceased to address themselves *virginibus puerisque*. On the whole, he declares they are a very odd mixture – a medley of gold and tinsel, of bad taste and a good sense. I can readily understand it. The old man bores me, puzzles me, and amuses me.

He was in waiting to receive me. We found him in his library – which, by the way, is simply the most delightful apartment that I ever smoked a cigar in – a room arranged for a lifetime. At one end stands a great fireplace, with a florid, fantastic mantelpiece in carved white marble – an importation, of course, and, as one may say, an interpolation; the groundwork of the house, the 'fixtures', being throughout plain, solid and domestic. Over the mantel-shelf is a large landscape, a fine Gainsborough, full of the complicated harmonies of an English summer. Beneath it stands a row of bronzes of the Renaissance and potteries of the Orient. Facing the door, as you enter, is an immense window set in a recess, with cushioned seats and large clear panes, stationed as it were at the very apex of the lake (which forms an almost perfect oval) and commanding a view of its whole extent. At the other end, opposite the fireplace, the wall is studded, from floor to ceiling, with choice foreign paintings, placed in relief against the orthodox crimson screen. Elsewhere the walls are covered with books, arranged neither in formal regularity nor quite helter-skelter, but in a sort of genial incongruity, which tells that sooner or later each volume feels sure of leaving the ranks and returning into different company. Mr Sloane makes use of his books. His two passions, according to Theodore, are reading and talking; but to talk he must have a book in his hand. The charm of the room lies in the absence of certain pedantic tones – the browns, blacks and greys – which distinguish most libraries. The apartment is of the feminine gender. There are half a dozen light colours scattered about – pink in the carpet, tender blue in the curtains, yellow in the chairs. The result is a general look of brightness and lightness; it expresses even a certain cynicism. You perceive the place to be the home, not of a man of learning, but of a man of fancy.

He rose from his chair – the man of fancy, to greet me – the man of fact. As I looked at him, in the lamplight, it seemed to me, for the first five minutes, that I had seldom seen an uglier little person. It took me five minutes to get the point of view; then I began to admire. He is diminutive, or at best of my own moderate stature, and bent and contracted with his seventy years; lean and delicate, moreover, and very highly finished. He is curiously pale, with a kind of opaque yellow pallor. Literally, it's a magnificent yellow. His skin is of just the hue and apparent texture of some old crumpled Oriental scroll. I know a dozen painters who would give more than they have to arrive at the exact 'tone' of his thick-veined, bloodless hands, his polished ivory knuckles. His eyes are circled with red, but in the battered little setting of their orbits they have the lustre of old sapphires. His nose, owing to the falling away of other portions of his face, has assumed a grotesque, unnatural prominence; it describes an immense arch, gleaming like a piece of parchment stretched on ivory. He has, apparently, all his teeth, but has muffled his cranium in a dead black wig; of course he's clean shaven. In his dress he has a muffled, wadded look and an apparent aversion to linen, inasmuch as none is visible on his person. He seems neat enough, but not fastidious. At first, as I say, I fancied him monstrously ugly; but on further acquaintance I perceived that what I had taken for ugliness is nothing but the incomplete remains of remarkable good looks. The line of his features is pure; his nose, *cœteris paribus*, would be extremely handsome; his eyes are the oldest eyes I ever saw, and yet they are wonderfully living. He has something remarkably insinuating.

He offered his two hands, as Theodore introduced me; I gave him my own, and he stood smiling at me like some quaint old image in ivory and ebony, scanning my face with a curiosity which he took no pains to conceal. 'God bless me,' he said, at last, 'how much you look like your father!' I sat down, and for half an hour we talked of many things – of my journey, of my impressions of America, of my reminiscences of Europe, and, by implication, of my prospects. His voice is weak and cracked, but he makes it express everything. Mr Sloane is not yet in his dotage – oh no! He nevertheless makes himself out a poor creature. In reply to an inquiry of mine about his health, he favoured me with a long list of his infirmities (some of which are very trying, certainly) and assured me that he was quite finished.

'I live out of mere curiosity,' he said.

'I have heard of people dying from the same motive.'

He looked at me a moment, as if to ascertain whether I were laughing at him. And then, after a pause, 'Perhaps you don't know that I disbelieve in a future life,' he remarked, blandly.

At these words Theodore got up and walked to the fire.

'Well, we shan't quarrel about that,' said I. Theodore turned round, staring.

'Do you mean that you agree with me?' the old man asked.

'I certainly haven't come here to talk theology! Don't ask me to disbelieve, and I'll never ask you to believe.'

'Come,' cried Mr Sloane, rubbing his hands, 'you'll not persuade me you are a Christian – like your friend Theodore there.'

'Like Theodore – assuredly not.' And then, somehow, I don't know why, at the thought of Theodore's Christianity I burst into a laugh. 'Excuse me, my dear fellow,' I said, 'you know, for the last ten years I have lived in pagan lands.'

'What do you call pagan?' asked Theodore, smiling.

I saw the old man, with his hands locked, eyeing me shrewdly, and waiting for my answer. I hesitated a moment, and then I said, 'Everything that makes life tolerable!'

Hereupon Mr Sloane began to laugh till he coughed. Verily, I thought, if he lives for curiosity, he's easily satisfied.

We went into dinner, and this repast showed me that some of his curiosity is culinary. I observed, by the way, that for a victim of neuralgia, dyspepsia, and a thousand other ills, Mr Sloane plies a most inconsequential knife and fork. Sauces and spices and condiments seem to be the chief of his diet. After dinner he dismissed us, in consideration of my natural desire to see my friend in private. Theodore has capital quarters – a downy bedroom and a snug little *salon*. We talked till near midnight – of ourselves, of each other, and of the author of the memoirs, down stairs. That is, I spoke of myself, and Theodore listened; and then Theodore descanted upon Mr Sloane, and I listened. His commerce with the old man has sharpened his wits. Sloane has taught him to observe and judge, and Theodore turns round, observes, judges – him! He has become quite the critic and analyst. There is something very pleasant in the discrimi-nations of a conscientious mind, in which criticism is tempered by an angelic charity. Only, it may easily end by acting on one's nerves. At midnight we repaired to the library, to take leave of our host till the morrow – an attention which, under all circumstances, he rigidly exacts. As I gave him my hand he held it again and looked at me as he had done on my arrival. 'Bless my soul,' he said, at last, 'how much you look like your mother!'

To-night, at the end of my third day, I begin to feel decidedly at home. The fact is, I am remarkably comfortable. The house is pervaded by an indefinable, irresistible love of luxury and privacy. Mr Frederick Sloane is a horribly corrupt old mortal. Already in his relaxing presence I have become heartily reconciled to doing nothing. But with Theodore on one side – standing there like a tall interrogation-point – I honestly believe I can defy Mr Sloane on the other. The former asked me this morning, with visible solicitude, in allusion to the bit of dialogue I have quoted above on matters of faith, whether I am really a materialist – whether I don't believe something? I told him I would believe anything he liked. He looked at me a while, in friendly sadness. 'I hardly know whether you are not worse than Mr Sloane,' he said.

But Theodore is, after all, in duty bound to give a man a long rope in these matters. His own rope is one of the longest. He reads Voltaire with Mr Sloane, and Emerson in his own room. He is the stronger man of the two; he has the larger stomach. Mr Sloane delights, of course, in Voltaire, but he can't read a line of Emerson. Theodore delights in Emerson, and enjoys Voltaire, though he thinks him superficial. It appears that since we parted in Paris, five years ago, his conscience has dwelt in many lands. *C'est tout une histoire* – which he tells very prettily. He left college determined to enter the church, and came abroad with his mind full of theology and Tübingen. He appears to have studied, not wisely but too well. Instead of faith full-armed and serene, there sprang from the labour of his brain a myriad sickly questions, piping for answers. He went for a winter to Italy, where, I take it, he was not quite so much afflicted as he ought to have been at the sight of the beautiful spiritual repose that he had missed. It was after this that we spent those three months together in Brittany – the best-spent months of my long residence in Europe. Theodore inoculated me, I think, with some of his seriousness, and I just touched him with my profanity; and we agreed together that there were a few good things left – health, friendship, a summer sky, and the lovely byways of an old French province. He came home, searched the Scriptures once more, accepted a 'call', and made an attempt to respond to it. But the inner voice failed him. His outlook was cheerless enough. During his absence his married sister, the elder one, had taken the other to live with her, relieving Theodore of the charge of contribution to her support. But suddenly, behold the husband, the brother-in-law, dies, leaving a mere figment of property; and the two ladies, with their two little girls, are afloat in the wide world. Theodore finds himself at twenty-six without an income, without a profession, and with a family of four females to support. Well, in his quiet way he draws on his courage. The history of the two years that passed before he came to Mr Sloane is really absolutely edifying. He rescued his sisters and nieces from the deep waters, placed them high and dry, established them somewhere in decent gentility – and then found at last that his strength had left him – had dropped dead like an overridden horse. In short, he had worked himself to the bone. It was now his sisters' turn. They nursed him with all the added tenderness of gratitude for the past and terror of the future, and brought him safely through a grievous malady. Meanwhile Mr Sloane, having decided to treat himself to a private secretary and suffered dreadful mischance in three successive experiments, had heard of Theodore's situation and his merits; had furthermore recognised in him the son of an early and intimate friend, and had finally offered him the very comfortable position he now occupies. There is a decided incongruity between Theodore as a man – as Theodore, in fine – and the dear fellow as the intellectual agent, confidant, complaisant, purveyor, pander – what you will – of a battered old cynic and dilettante – a worldling if there ever was one. There seems at first sight a perfect want of agreement between his character and his function. One is gold and the other brass, or something very like it. But on reflection I can enter into it – his having, under the circumstances, accepted Mr Sloane's offer and been content to do his duties. *Ce que c'est de nous!* Theodore's contentment in such a case is a theme for the moralist – a better moralist than I. The best and purest mortals are an odd mixture, and in none of us does honesty exist on its own terms. Ideally, Theodore hasn't the smallest business *dans cette galère*. It offends my sense of propriety to find him here. I feel that I ought to notify him as a friend that he has knocked at the wrong door, and that he had better retreat before he is brought to the blush. However, I suppose he might as well be here as reading Emerson 'evenings' in the back parlour, to those two very plain sisters – judging from their photographs. Practically it hurts no one not to be too much of a prig. Poor Theodore was weak, depressed, out of work. Mr Sloane offers him a lodging and a salary in return for – after all, merely a little tact. All he has to do is to read to the old man, lay down the book a while, with his finger in the place, and let him talk; take it up again, read another dozen pages and submit to another commentary. Then to write a dozen pages under his dictation – to suggest a word, polish off a period, or help him out with a complicated idea or a half-remembered fact. This is all, I say; and yet this is much. Theodore's apparent success proves it to be much, as well as the old man's satisfaction. It is a part; he has to simulate. He has to 'make believe' a little – a good deal; he has to put his pride in his pocket and send his conscience to the wash. He has to be accommodating – to listen and pretend and flatter; and he does it as well as many a worse man – does it far better than I. I might bully the old man, but I don't think I could humour him. After all, however, it is not a matter of comparative merit. In every son of woman there are two men – the practical man and the dreamer. We live for our dreams – but, meanwhile, we live by our wits. When the dreamer is a poet, the other fellow is an artist. Theodore, at bottom, is only a man of taste. If he were not destined to become a high priest among moralists, he might be a prince among connoisseurs. He plays his part, therefore, artistically, with spirit, with originality, with all his native refinement. How can Mr Sloane fail to believe that he possesses a paragon? He is no such fool as not to appreciate a *nature distinguée* when it comes in his way. He confidentially assured me this morning that Theodore has the most charming mind in the world, but that it's a pity he's so simple as not to suspect it. If he only doesn't ruin him with his flattery!

19th. – I am certainly fortunate among men. This morning when, tentatively, I spoke of going away, Mr Sloane rose from his seat in horror and declared that for the present I must regard his house as my home. 'Come, come,' he said, 'when you leave this place where do you intend to go?' Where, indeed? I graciously allowed Mr Sloane to have the best of the argument. Theodore assures me that he appreciates these and other affabilities, and that I have made what he calls a 'conquest' of his venerable heart. Poor, battered, bamboozled old organ! he would have one believe that it has a most tragical record of capture and recapture. At all events, it appears that I am master of the citadel. For the present I have no wish to evacuate. I feel, nevertheless, in some far-off corner of my soul, that I ought to shoulder my victorious banner and advance to more fruitful triumphs.

I blush for my beastly laziness. It isn't that I am willing to stay here a month, but that I am willing to stay here six. Such is the charming, disgusting truth. Have I really outlived the age of energy? Have I survived my ambition, my integrity, my self-respect? Verily, I ought to have survived the habit of asking myself silly questions. I made up my mind long ago to go in for nothing but present success; and I don't care for that sufficiently to secure it at the cost of temporary suffering. I have a passion for nothing – not even for life. I know very well the appearance I make in the world. I pass for a clever, accomplished, capable, good-natured fellow, who can do anything if he would only try. I am supposed to be rather cultivated, to have latent talents. When I was younger I used to find a certain entertainment in the spectacle of human affairs. I liked to see men and women hurrying on each other's heels across the stage. But I am sick and tired of them now; not that I am a misanthrope, God forbid! They are not worth hating. I never knew but one creature who was, and her I went and loved. To be consistent, I ought to have hated my mother, and now I ought to detest Theodore. But I don't – truly, on the whole, I don't – any more than I dote on him. I firmly believe that it makes a difference to him, his idea that I *am* fond of him. He believes in that, as he believes in all the rest of it – in my culture, my latent talents, my underlying 'earnestness', my sense of beauty and love of truth. Oh, for a *man* among them all – a fellow with eyes in his head – eyes that would know me for what I am and let me see they had guessed it. Possibly such a fellow as that might get a 'rise' out of me.

In the name of bread and butter, what am I to do? (I was obliged this morning to borrow fifty dollars from Theodore, who remembered gleefully that he has been owing me a trifling sum for the past four years, and in fact has preserved a note to this effect.) Within the last week I have hatched a desperate plan: I have made up my mind to take a wife – a rich one, *bien entendu*. Why not accept the goods of the gods? It is not my fault, after all, if I pass for a good fellow. Why not admit that practically, mechanically – as I may say – maritally, I *may* be a good fellow? I warrant myself kind. I should never beat my wife; I don't think I should even contradict her. Assume that her fortune has the proper number of zeros and that she herself is one of them, and I can even imagine her adoring me. I really think this is my only way. Curiously, as I look back upon my brief career, it all seems to tend to this consummation. It has its graceful curves and crooks, indeed, and here and there a passionate tangent; but on the whole, if I were to unfold it here *à la* Hogarth, what better legend could I scrawl beneath the series of pictures than So-and-So's Progress to a Mercenary Marriage?

Coming events do what we all know with their shadows. My noble fate is, perhaps, not far off. I already feel throughout my person a magnificent languor – as from the possession of many dollars. Or is it simply my sense of well-being in this perfectly appointed house? Is it simply the contact of the highest civilisation I have known? At all events, the place is of velvet, and my only complaint of Mr Sloane is that, instead of an old widower, he's not an old widow (or a young maid), so that I might marry him, survive him, and dwell for ever in this rich and mellow home. As I write here, at my bedroom table, I have only to stretch out an arm and raise the window-curtain to see the thick-planted garden budding and breathing and growing in the silvery silence. Far above in the liquid darkness rolls the brilliant ball of the moon; beneath, in its light, lies the lake, in murmuring, troubled sleep; round about, the mountains, look-ing strange and blanched, seem to bare their heads and undrape their shoulders. So much for midnight. To-morrow the scene will be lovely with the beauty of day. Under one aspect or another I have it always before me. At the end of the garden is moored a boat, in which Theodore and I have indulged in an immense deal of irregular navigation. What lovely landward coves and bays – what alder-smothered creeks – what lily-sheeted pools – what sheer steep hillsides, making the water dark and quiet where they hang. I confess that in these excursions Theodore looks after the boat and I after the scenery. Mr Sloane avoids the water – on account of the damp-ness, he says; because he's afraid of drowning, I suspect.

22nd. – Theodore is right. The *bonhomme* has taken me into his favour. I protest I don't see how he was to escape it. *Je l'ai bien soigné*, as they say in Paris. I don't blush for it. In one coin or another I must repay his hospitality – which is certainly very liberal. Theodore dots his *i*'s, crosses his *t*'s, verifies his quota-tions; while I set traps for that famous 'curiosity'. This speaks vastly well for my powers. He pretends to be surprised at nothing, and to possess in perfection – poor, pitiable old fop – the art of keeping his countenance; but repeatedly, I know, I have made him stare. As for his corruption, which I spoke of above, it's a very pretty piece of wickedness, but it strikes me as a purely intellectual matter. I imagine him never to have had any real senses. He may have been unclean; morally, he's not very tidy now; but he never can have been what the French call a *viveur*. He's too delicate, he's of a feminine turn; and what woman was ever a *viveur*? He likes to sit in his chair and read scandal, talk scandal, make scandal, so far as he may without catching a cold or bringing on a headache. I already feel as if I had known him a lifetime. I read him as clearly as if I had. I know the type to which he belongs; I have encountered, first and last, a good many specimens of it. He's neither more nor less than a gossip – a gossip flanked by a coxcomb and an egotist. He's shallow, vain, cold, superstitious, timid, pretentious, capricious; a pretty list of foibles! And yet, for all this, he has his good points. His caprices are sometimes generous, and his rebellion against the ugliness of life frequently makes him do kind things. His memory (for trifles) is remarkable, and (where his own performances are not involved) his taste is excellent. He has no courage for evil more than for good. He is the victim, however, of more illusions with regard to himself than I ever knew a single brain to shelter. At the age of twenty, poor, ignorant and remarkably handsome, he married a woman of immense wealth, many years his senior. At the end of three years she very considerately took herself off and left him to the enjoyment of his freedom and riches. If he had remained poor he might from time to time have rubbed at random against the truth, and would be able to recognise the touch of it. But he wraps himself in his money as in a wadded dressing-gown, and goes trundling through life on his little gold wheels. The greater part of his career, from the time of his marriage till about ten years ago, was spent in Europe, which, superficially, he knows very well. He has lived in fifty places, known thousands of people, and spent a very large fortune. At one time, I believe, he spent considerably too much, trembled for an instant on the verge of a pecuniary crash, but recovered himself, and found himself more frightened than hurt, yet audibly recommended to lower his pitch. He passed five years in a species of penitent seclusion on the lake of – I forget what (his genius seems to be partial to lakes), and laid the basis of his present magnificent taste for literature. I can't call him anything but magnificent in this respect, so long as he must have his punctuation done by a *nature distinguée*. At the close of this period, by economy, he had made up his losses. His turning the screw during those relatively impecunious years represents, I am pretty sure, the only act of resolution of his life. It was rendered possible by his morbid, his actually pusillanimous dread of poverty; he doesn't feel safe without half a million between him and starvation. Meanwhile he had turned from a young man into an old man; his health was broken, his spirit was jaded, and I imagine, to do him justice, that he began to feel certain natural, filial longings for this dear American mother of us all. They say the most hopeless truants and triflers have come to it. He came to it, at all events; he packed up his books and pictures and gimcracks, and bade farewell to Europe. This house which he now occupies belonged to his wife's estate. She had, for sentimental reasons of her own, commended it to his particular care. On his return he came to see it, liked it, turned a parcel of carpenters and upholsterers into it, and by inhabiting it for nine years transformed it into the perfect dwelling which I find it. Here he has spent all his time, with the exception of a usual winter's visit to New York – a practice recently discontinued, owing to the increase of his ailments and the projection of these famous memoirs. His life has finally come to be passed in comparative solitude. He tells of various distant relatives, as well as intimate friends of both sexes, who used formerly to be entertained at his cost; but with each of them, in the course of time, he seems to have succeeded in quarrelling. Throughout life, evidently, he has had capital fingers for plucking off parasites. Rich, lonely, and vain, he must have been fair game for the race of social sycophants and cormorants; and it's much to the credit of his sharpness and that instinct of self-defence which nature bestows even on the weak, that he has not been despoiled and *exploité*. Apparently they have all been bunglers. I maintain that something is to be done with him still. But one must work in obedience to certain definite laws. Doctor Jones, his physician, tells me that in point of fact he has had for the past ten years an unbroken series of favourites, *protégés*, heirs presumptive; but that each, in turn, by some fatally false movement, has spilled his pottage. The doctor declares, moreover, that they were mostly very common people. Gradually the old man seems to have developed a preference for two or three strictly exquisite intimates, over a throng of your vulgar pensioners. His tardy literary schemes, too – fruit of his all but sapless senility – have absorbed more and more of his time and attention. The end of it all is, therefore, that Theodore and I have him quite to ourselves, and that it behooves us to hold our porringers straight.

Poor, pretentious old simpleton! It's not his fault, after all, that he fancies himself a great little man. How are you to judge of the stature of mankind when men have forever addressed you on their knees? Peace and joy to his innocent fatuity! He believes himself the most rational of men; in fact, he's the most superstitious. He fancies himself a philosopher, an inquirer, a discoverer. He has not yet discovered that he is a humbug, that Theodore is a prig, and that I am an adventurer. He prides himself on his good manners, his urbanity, his knowing a rule of conduct for every occasion in life. My private impression is that his skinny old bosom contains unsuspected treasures of impertinence. He takes his stand on his speculative audacity – his direct, undaunted gaze at the universe; in truth, his mind is haunted by a hundred dingy old-world spectres and theological phantasms. He imagines himself one of the most solid of men; he is essentially one of the hollowest. He thinks himself ardent, impulsive, passionate, magnanimous – capable of boundless enthusiasm for an idea or a sentiment. It is clear to me that on no occasion of disinterested action can he ever have done anything in time. He believes, finally, that he has drained the cup of life to the dregs; that he has known, in its bitterest intensity, every emotion of which the human spirit is capable; that he has loved, struggled, suffered. Mere vanity, all of it. He has never loved any one but himself; he has never suffered from anything but an undigested supper or an exploded pretension; he has never touched with the end of his lips the vulgar bowl from which the mass of mankind quaffs its floods of joy and sorrow. Well, the long and short of it all is, that I honestly pity him. He may have given sly knocks in his life, but he can't hurt any one now. I pity his ignorance, his weakness, his pusillanimity. He has tasted the real sweetness of life no more than its bitterness; he has never dreamed, nor experimented, nor dared; he has never known any but mercenary affection; neither men nor women have risked aught for *him* – for his good spirits, his good looks, his empty pockets. How I should like to give him, for once, a real sensation!

26th. – I took a row this morning with Theodore a couple of miles along the lake, to a point where we went ashore and lounged away an hour in the sunshine, which is still very comfortable. Poor Theodore seems troubled about many things. For one, he is troubled about me; he is actually more anxious about my future than I myself; he thinks better of me than I do of myself; he is so deucedly conscientious, so scrupulous, so averse to giving offence or to *brusquer* any situation before it has played itself out, that he shrinks from betraying his apprehensions or asking direct questions. But I know that he would like very much to extract from me some intimation that there is something under the sun I should like to do. I catch myself in the act of taking – heaven forgive me! – a half-malignant joy in confounding his expectations – leading his generous sympathies off the scent by giving him momentary glimpses of my latent wickedness. But in Theodore I have so firm a friend that I shall have a considerable job if I ever find it needful to make him change his mind about me. He admires me – that's absolute; he takes my low moral tone for an eccentricity of genius, and it only imparts an extra flavour – a *haut goût* – to the charm of my intercourse. Nevertheless, I can see that he is disappointed. I have even less to show, after all these years, than he had hoped. Heaven help us! little enough it must strike him as being. What a contradiction there is in our being friends at all! I believe we shall end with hating each other. It's all very well now – our agreeing to differ, for we haven't opposed interests. But if we should *really* clash, the situation would be warm! I wonder, as it is, that Theodore keeps his patience with me. His education since we parted should tend logically to make him despise me. He has studied, thought, suffered, loved – loved those very plain sisters and nieces. Poor me! how should I be virtuous? I have no sisters, plain or pretty! – nothing to love, work for, live for. My dear Theodore, if you are going one of these days to despise me and drop me – in the name of comfort, come to the point at once, and make an end of our state of tension.

He is troubled, too, about Mr Sloane. His attitude toward the *bonhomme* quite passes my comprehension. It's the queerest jumble of contraries. He penetrates him, disapproves of him – yet respects and admires him. It all comes of the poor boy's shrinking New England conscience. He's afraid to give his perceptions a fair chance, lest, forsooth, they should look over his neighbour's wall. He'll not understand that he may as well sacrifice the old reprobate for a lamb as for a sheep. His view of the gentleman, therefore, is a perfect tissue of cobwebs – a jumble of half-way sorrows, and wire-drawn charities, and hair-breadth 'scapes from utter damnation, and sudden platitudes of generosity – fit, all of it, to make an angel curse!

'The man's a perfect egotist and fool,' say I, 'but I like him.' Now Theodore likes him – or rather wants to like him; but he can't reconcile it to his self-respect – fastidious deity! – to like a fool. Why the deuce can't he leave it alone altogether? It's a purely practical matter. He ought to do the duties of his place all the better for having his head clear of officious sentiment. I don't believe in disinterested service; and Theodore is too desperately bent on preserving his disinterestedness. With me it's different. I am perfectly free to love the *bonhomme* – for a fool. I'm neither a scribe nor a Pharisee; I am simply a student of the art of life.

And then, Theodore is troubled about his sisters. He's afraid he's not doing his duty by them. He thinks he ought to be with them – to be getting a larger salary – to be teaching his nieces. I am not versed in such questions. Perhaps he ought.

May 3rd. – This morning Theodore sent me word that he was ill and unable to get up; upon which I immediately went in to see him. He had caught cold, was sick and a little feverish. I urged him to make no attempt to leave his room, and assured him that I would do what I could to reconcile Mr Sloane to his absence. This I found an easy matter. I read to him for a couple of hours, wrote four letters – one in French – and then talked for a while – a good while. I have done more talking, by the way, in the last fortnight, than in any previous twelve months – much of it, too, none of the wisest, nor, I may add, of the most superstitiously veracious. In a little discussion, two or three days ago, with Theodore, I came to the point and let him know that in gossiping with Mr Sloane I made no scruple, for our common satisfaction, of 'colouring' more or less. My confession gave him 'that turn', as Mrs Gamp would say, that his present illness may be the result of it. Nevertheless, poor dear fellow, I trust he will be on his legs to-morrow. This afternoon, somehow, I found myself really in the humour of talking. There was something propitious in the circumstances; a hard, cold rain without, a wood-fire in the library, the *bonhomme* puffing cigarettes in his arm-chair, beside him a portfolio of newly imported prints and photographs, and – Theodore tucked safely away in bed. Finally, when I brought our *tête-à-tête* to a close (taking good care not to overstay my welcome) Mr Sloane seized me by both hands and honoured me with one of his venerable grins. 'Max,' he said – 'you must let me call you Max – you are the most delightful man I ever knew.'

Verily, there's some virtue left in me yet. I believe I almost blushed.

'Why didn't I know you ten years ago?' the old man went on. 'There are ten years lost.'

'Ten years ago I was not worth your knowing,' Max remarked.

'But I did know you!' cried the *bonhomme*. 'I knew you in knowing your mother.'

Ah! my mother again. When the old man begins that chapter I feel like telling him to blow out his candle and go to bed.

'At all events,' he continued, 'we must make the most of the years that remain. I am a rotten old carcase, but I have no intention of dying. You won't get tired of me and want to go away?'

'I am devoted to you, sir,' I said. 'But I must be looking for some occupation, you know.'

'Occupation? bother! I'll give you occupation. I'll give you wages.'

'I am afraid that you will want to give me the wages without the work.' And then I declared that I must go up and look at poor Theodore.

The *bonhomme* still kept my hands. 'I wish very much that I could get you to be as fond of me as you are of poor Theodore.'

'Ah, don't talk about fondness, Mr Sloane. I don't deal much in that article.'

'Don't you like my secretary?'

'Not as he deserves.'

'Nor as he likes you, perhaps?'

'He likes me more than I deserve.'

'Well, Max,' my host pursued, 'we can be good friends all the same. We don't need a hocus-pocus of false sentiment. We are *men*, aren't we? – men of sublime good sense.' And just here, as the old man looked at me, the pressure of his hands deepend to a convulsive grasp, and the bloodless mask of his countenance was suddenly distorted with a nameless fear. 'Ah, my dear young man!' he cried, 'come and be a son to me – the son of my age and desolation! For God's sake, don't leave me to pine and die alone!'

I was greatly surprised – and I may add I was moved. Is it true, then, that this dilapidated organism contains such measureless depths of horror and longing? He has evidently a mortal fear of death. I assured him on my honour that he may henceforth call upon me for any service.

8th. – Theodore's little turn proved more serious than I expected. He has been confined to his room till to-day. This evening he came down to the library in his dressing-gown. Decidedly, Mr Sloane is an eccentric, but hardly, as Theodore thinks, a 'charming' one. There is something extremely curious in his humours and fancies – the incongruous fits and starts, as it were, of his taste. For some reason, best known to himself, he took it into his head to regard it as a want of delicacy, of respect, of *savoir-vivre* – of heaven knows what – that poor Theodore, who is still weak and languid, should enter the sacred precinct of his study in the vulgar drapery of a dressing-gown. The sovereign trouble with the *bonhomme* is an absolute lack of the instinct of justice. He's of the real feminine turn – I believe I have written it before – without the redeeming fidelity of the sex. I honestly believe that I might come into his study in my night-shirt and he would smile at it as a picturesque *déshabillé*. But for poor Theodore to-night there was nothing but scowls and frowns, and barely a civil inquiry about his health. But poor

Theodore is not such a fool, either; he will not die of a snub-bing; I never said he was a weakling. Once he fairly saw from what quarter the wind blew, he bore the master's brutality with the utmost coolness and gallantry. Can it be that Mr Sloane really wishes to drop him? The delicious old brute! He under-stands favour and friendship only as a selfish rapture – a reac-tion, an infatuation, an act of aggressive, exclusive patronage. It's not a bestowal, with him, but a transfer, and half his plea-sure in causing his sun to shine is that – being woefully near its setting – it will produce certain long fantastic shadows. He wants to cast my shadow, I suppose, over Theodore; but for-tunately I am not altogether an opaque body. Since Theodore was taken ill he has been into his room but once, and has sent him none but a dry little message or two. I, too, have been much less attentive than I should have wished to be; but my time has not been my own. It has been, every moment of it, at the disposal of my host. He actually runs after me; he devours me; he makes a fool of himself, and is trying hard to make one of me. I find that he will bear – that, in fact, he actually enjoys – a sort of unexpected contradiction. He likes anything that will tickle his fancy, give an unusual tone to our relations, remind him of certain historical characters whom he thinks he resem-bles. I have stepped into Theodore's shoes, and done – with what I feel in my bones to be very inferior skill and taste – all the reading, writing, condensing, transcribing and advising that he has been accustomed to do. I have driven with the *bonhomme*; played chess and cribbage with him; beaten him, bullied him, contradicted him; forced him into going out on the water under my charge. Who shall say, after this, that I haven't done my best to discourage his advances, put myself in a bad light? As yet, my efforts are vain; in fact they quite turn to my own confusion. Mr Sloane is so thankful at having escaped from the lake with his life that he looks upon me as a preserver and protector. Con-found it all; it's a bore! But one thing is certain, it can't last for ever. Admit that he *has* cast Theodore out and taken me in. He will speedily discover that he has made a pretty mess of it, and he had much better have left well enough alone. He likes my reading and writing now, but in a month he will begin to hate them. He will miss Theodore's better temper and better knowledge – his healthy impersonal judgement. What an advantage that well-regulated youth has over me, after all! I am for days, he is for years; he for the long run, I for the short. I, perhaps, am intended for success, but he is adapted for happiness. He has in his heart a tiny sacred particle which leavens his whole being and keeps it pure and sound – a faculty of admiration and respect. For him human nature is still a wonder and mystery; it bears a divine stamp – Mr Sloane's tawdry composition as well as the rest.

13th. – I have refused, of course, to supplant Theodore further, in the exercise of his functions, and he has resumed his morning labours with Mr Sloane. I, on my side, have spent these morning hours in scouring the country on that capital black mare, the use of which is one of the perquisites of Theodore's place. The days have been magnificent – the heat of the sun tempered by a murmuring, wandering wind, the whole north a mighty ecstasy of sound and verdure, the sky a far-away vault of bended blue. Not far from the mill at M–, the other end of the lake, I met, for the third time, that very pretty young girl who reminds me so forcibly of A. L. She makes so lavish a use of her eyes that I ventured to stop and bid her good-morning. She seems nothing loath to an acquaintance. She's a pure barbarian in speech, but her eyes are quite articulate. These rides do me good; I was growing too pensive.

There is something the matter with Theodore; his illness seems to have left him strangely affected. He has fits of silent stiffness, alternating with spasms of extravagant gaiety. He avoids me at times for hours together, and then he comes and looks at me with an inscrutable smile, as if he were on the verge of a burst of confidence – which again is swallowed up in the immensity of his dumbness. Is he hatching some astounding benefit to his species? Is he working to bring about my removal to a higher sphere of action? *Nous verrons bien.*

18th. – Theodore threatens departure. He received this morning a letter from one of his sisters – the young widow – announcing her engagement to a clergyman whose acquaintance she has recently made, and intimating her expectation of an immediate union with the gentleman – a ceremony which would require Theodore's attendance. Theodore, in high good humour, read the letter aloud at breakfast – and, to tell the truth, it was a charming epistle. He then spoke of his having to go on to the wedding, a proposition to which Mr Sloane graciously assented – much more than assented. 'I shall be sorry to lose you, after so happy a connection,' said the old man. Theodore turned pale, stared a moment, and then, recovering his colour and his composure, declared that he should have no objection in life to coming back.

'Bless your soul!' cried the *bonhomme*, 'you don't mean to say you will leave your other sister all alone?'

To which Theodore replied that he would arrange for her and her little girl to live with the married pair. 'It's the only proper thing,' he remarked, as if it were quite settled. Has it come to this, then, that Mr Sloane actually wants to turn him out of the house? The shameless old villain! He keeps smiling an uncanny smile, which means, as I read it, that if the poor young man once departs he shall never return on the old footing – for all his impudence!

20th. – This morning, at breakfast, we had a terrific scene. A letter arrives for Theodore; he opens it, turns white and red, frowns, falters, and then informs us that the clever widow has broken off her engagement. No wedding, therefore, and no departure for Theodore. The *bonhomme* was furious. In his fury he took the liberty of calling poor Mrs Parker (the sister) a very uncivil name. Theodore rebuked him, with perfect good taste, and kept his temper.

'If my opinions don't suit you, Mr Lisle,' the old man broke out, 'and my mode of expressing them displeases you, you know you can easily protect yourself.'

'My dear Mr Sloane,' said Theodore, 'your opinions, as a general thing, interest me deeply, and have never ceased to act beneficially upon the formation of my own. Your mode of expressing them is always brilliant, and I wouldn't for the world, after all our pleasant intercourse, separate from you in bitterness. Only, I repeat, your qualification of my sister's conduct is perfectly uncalled for. If you knew her, you would be the first to admit it.'

There was something in Theodore's look and manner, as he said these words, which puzzled me all the morning. After dinner, finding myself alone with him, I told him I was glad he was not obliged to go away. He looked at me with the mysterious smile I have mentioned, thanked me, and fell into meditation. As this bescribbled chronicle is the record of my follies as well of my *hauts faits*, I needn't hesitate to say that for a moment I was a good deal vexed. What business has this angel of candour to deal in signs and portents, to look unutterable things? What right has he to do so with me especially, in whom he has always professed an absolute confidence? Just as I was about to cry out, 'Come, my dear fellow, this affectation of mystery has lasted quite long enough – favour me at last with the result of your cogitations!' – as I was on the point of thus expressing my impatience of his ominous behaviour, the oracle at last addressed itself to utterance.

'You see, my dear Max,' he said, 'I can't, in justice to myself, go away in obedience to the sort of notice that was served on me this morning. What do you think of my actual footing here?'

Theodore's actual footing here seems to me impossible; of course I said so.

'No, I assure you it's not,' he answered. 'I should, on the contrary, feel very uncomfortable to think that I had come away, except by my own choice. You see a man can't afford to cheapen himself. What are you laughing at?'

'I am laughing, in the first place, my dear fellow, to hear on your lips the language of cold calculation; and in the second place, at your odd notion of the process by which a man keeps himself up in the market.'

'I assure you it's the correct notion. I came here as a particular favour to Mr Sloane; it was expressly understood so. The sort of work was odious to me; I had regularly to break myself in. I had to trample on my convictions, preferences, prejudices. I don't take such things easily; I take them hard; and when once the effort has been made, I can't consent to have it wasted. If Mr Sloane needed me then, he needs me still. I am ignorant of any change having taken place in his intentions, or in his means of satisfying them. I came, not to amuse him, but to do a certain work; I hope to remain until the work is completed. To go away sooner is to make a confession of incapacity which, I protest, costs me too much. I am too conceited, if you like.'

Theodore spoke these words with a face which I have never seen him wear – a fixed, mechanical smile; a hard, dry glitter in his eyes; a harsh, strident tone in his voice – in his whole physiognomy a gleam, as it were, a note of defiance. Now I confess that for defiance I have never been conscious of an especial relish. When I am defied I am beastly. 'My dear man,' I replied, 'your sentiments do you prodigious credit. Your very ingenious theory of your present situation, as well as your extremely pronounced sense of your personal value, are calculated to ensure you a degree of practical success which can very well dispense with the furtherance of my poor good wishes.' Oh, the grimness of his visage as he listened to this, and, I suppose I may add, the grimness of mine! But I have ceased to be puzzled. Theodore's conduct for the past ten days is suddenly illumined with a backward, lurid ray. I will note down here a few plain truths which it behooves me to take to heart – commit to memory. Theodore is jealous of Maximus Austin. Theodore hates the said Maximus. Theodore has been seeking for the past three months to see his name written, last but not least, in a certain testamentary document: 'Finally, I bequeath to my dear young friend, Theodore Lisle, in return for invaluable services and unfailing devotion, the bulk of my property, real and personal, consisting of – ' (hereupon follows an exhaustive enumeration of houses, lands, public securities, books, pictures, horses, and dogs). It is for this that he has toiled, and watched, and prayed; submitted to intellectual weariness and spiritual torture; accommodated himself to levity, blasphemy, and insult. For this he sets his teeth and tightens his grasp; for this he'll fight. Dear me, it's an immense weight off one's mind! There are nothing, then, but vulgar, common laws; no sublime exceptions, no transcendent anomalies. Theodore's a knave, a hypo– nay, nay; stay, irreverent hand! – Theodore's a *man*! Well, that's all I want. *He* wants fight – he shall have it. Have I got, at last, my simple, natural emotion?

21st. – I have lost no time. This evening, late, after I had heard Theodore go to his room (I had left the library early, on the pretext of having letters to write), I repaired to Mr Sloane, who had not yet gone to bed, and informed him I should be obliged to leave him at once, and pick up a subsistence some-how in New York. He felt the blow; it brought him straight down on his marrow-bones. He went through the whole gamut of his arts and graces; he blustered, whimpered, entreated, flattered. He tried to drag in Theodore's name; but this I, of course, prevented. But, finally, why, *why*, WHY, after all my promises of fidelity, must I thus cruelly desert him? Then came my trump card: I have spent my last penny; while I stay, I'm a beggar. The remainder of this extraordinary scene I have no power to describe: how the *bonhomme*, touched, inflamed, inspired, by the thought of my destitution, and at the same time annoyed, perplexed, bewildered at having to commit himself to doing anything for me, worked himself into a ner-vous frenzy which deprived him of a clear sense of the value of his words and his actions; how I, prompted by the irresistible spirit of my desire to leap astride of his weakness and ride it hard to the goal of my dreams, cunningly contrived to keep his spirit at the fever-point, so that strength and reason and resist-ance should burn themselves out. I shall probably never again have such a sensation as I enjoyed to-night – actually feel a heated human heart throbbing and turning and struggling in my grasp; know its pants, its spasms, its convulsions, and its final senseless quiescence. At half-past one o'clock Mr Sloane got out of his chair, went to his secretary, opened a private drawer, and took out a folded paper. 'This is my will,' he said, 'made some seven weeks ago. If you will stay with me I will destroy it.'

'Really, Mr Sloane,' I said, 'if you think my purpose is to exert any pressure upon your testamentary inclinations – '

'I will tear it in pieces,' he cried; 'I will burn it up! I shall be as sick as a dog to-morrow; but I will do it. A-a-h!'

He clapped his hand to his side, as if in sudden, overwhelming pain, and sank back fainting into his chair. A single glance assured me that he was unconscious. I possessed myself of the paper, opened it, and perceived that he had left everything to his saintly secretary. For an instant a savage, puerile feeling of hate popped up in my bosom, and I came within a hair's-breadth of obeying my foremost impulse – that of stuffing the document into the fire. Fortunately, my reason overtook my passion, though for a moment it was an even race. I put the paper back into the bureau, closed it, and rang the bell for Robert (the old man's servant). Before he came I stood watching the poor, pale remnant of mortality before me, and wondering whether those feeble life-gasps were numbered. He was as white as a sheet, grimacing with pain – horribly ugly. Suddenly he opened his eyes; they met my own; I fell on my knees and took his hands. They closed on mine with a grasp strangely akin to the rigidity of death. Nevertheless, since then he has revived, and has relapsed again into a comparatively healthy sleep. Robert seems to know how to deal with him.

22nd. – Mr Sloane is seriously ill – out of his mind and unconscious of people's identity. The doctor has been here, off and on, all day, but this evening reports improvement. I have kept out of the old man's room, and confined myself to my own, reflecting largely upon the chance of his immediate death. Does Theodore know of the will? Would it occur to him to divide the property? Would it occur to me, in his place? We met at dinner, and talked in a grave, desultory, friendly fashion. After all, he's an excellent fellow. I don't hate him. I don't even dislike him. He jars on me, *il m'agace*; but that's no reason why I should do him an evil turn. Nor shall I. The property is a fixed idea, that's all. I shall get it if I can. We are fairly matched. Before heaven, no, we are not fairly matched! Theodore has a conscience.

23rd. – I am restless and nervous – and for good reasons. Scribbling here keeps me quiet. This morning Mr Sloane is better; feeble and uncertain in mind, but unmistakably on the rise. I may confess now that I feel relieved of a horrid burden. Last night I hardly slept a wink. I lay awake listening to the

pendulum of my clock. It seemed to say, 'He lives – he dies.'
I fully expected to hear it stop suddenly at *dies*. But it kept going
all the morning, and to a decidedly more lively tune. In the
afternoon the old man sent for me. I found him in his great
muffled bed, with his face the colour of damp chalk, and his
eyes glowing faintly, like torches half stamped out. I was forcibly
struck with the utter loneliness of his lot. For all human attendance, my villainous self grinning at his bedside and old Robert
without, listening, doubtless, at the keyhole. The *bonhomme*
stared at me stupidly; then seemed to know me, and greeted
me with a sickly smile. It was some moments before he was able
to speak. At last he faintly bade me to descend into the library,
open the secret drawer of the secretary (which he contrived to
direct me how to do), possess myself of his will, and burn it up.
He appears to have forgotten his having taken it out the night
before last. I told him that I had an insurmountable aversion to
any personal dealings with the document. He smiled, patted the
back of my hand, and requested me, in that case, to get it, at least,
and bring it to him. I couldn't deny him that favour? No,
I couldn't, indeed. I went down to the library, therefore, and
on entering the room found Theodore standing by the fireplace
with a bundle of papers. The secretary was open. I stood still,
looking from the violated cabinet to the documents in his hand.
Among them I recognised, by its shape and size, the paper of
which I had intended to possess myself. Without delay I walked
straight up to him. He looked surprised, but not confused. 'I am
afraid I shall have to trouble you to surrender one of those
papers,' I said.

'Surrender, Maximus? To anything of your own you are
perfectly welcome. I didn't know that you made use of Mr
Sloane's secretary. I was looking for some pages of notes
which I have made myself and in which I conceive I have a
property.'

'This is what I want, Theodore,' I said; and I drew the will,
unfolded, from between his hands. As I did so his eyes fell upon
the superscription, 'Last Will and Testament. March. F.S.' He
flushed an extraordinary crimson. Our eyes met. Somehow –
I don't know how or why, or for that matter why not – I burst

into a violent peal of laughter. Theodore stood staring, with two hot, bitter tears in his eyes.

'Of course you think I came to ferret out that thing,' he said.

I shrugged my shoulders – those of my body only. I confess, morally, I was on my knees with contrition, but there was a fascination in it – a fatality. I remembered that in the hurry of my movements the other evening I had slipped the will simply into one of the outer drawers of the cabinet, among Theodore's own papers. 'Mr Sloane sent me for it,' I remarked.

'Very good; I am glad to hear he's well enough to think of such things.'

'He means to destroy it.'

'I hope, then, he has another made.'

'Mentally, I suppose he has.'

'Unfortunately, his weakness isn't mental – or exclusively so.'

'Oh, he will live to make a dozen more,' I said. 'Do you know the purport of this one?'

Theodore's colour, by this time, had died away into plain white. He shook his head. The doggedness of the movement provoked me, and I wished to arouse his curiosity. 'I have his commission to destroy it.'

Theodore smiled very grandly. 'It's not a task I envy you,' he said.

'I should think not – especially if you knew the import of the will.' He stood with folded arms, regarding me with his cold, detached eyes. I couldn't stand it. 'Come, it's your property! You are sole legatee. I give it to you.' And I thrust the paper into his hand.

He received it mechanically; but after a pause, bethinking himself, he unfolded it and cast his eyes over the contents. Then he slowly smoothed it together and held it a moment with a tremulous hand. 'You say that Mr Sloane directed you to destroy it?' he finally inquired.

'I say so.'

'And that you know the contents?'

'Exactly.'

'And that you were about to do what he asked you?'

'On the contrary, I declined.'

Theodore fixed his eyes for a moment on the superscription and then raised them again to my face. 'Thank you, Max,' he said. 'You have left me a real satisfaction.' He tore the sheet across and threw the bits into the fire. We stood watching them burn. 'Now he can make another,' said Theodore.

'Twenty others,' I replied.

'No,' said Theodore, 'you will take care of that.'

'You are very bitter,' I said, sharply enough.

'No, I am perfectly indifferent. Farewell.' And he put out his hand.

'Are you going away?'

'Of course I am. Good-by.'

'Good-by, then. But isn't your departure rather sudden?'

'I ought to have gone three weeks ago – three weeks ago.' I had taken his hand, he pulled it away; his voice was trembling – there were tears in it.

'Is *that* indifference?' I asked.

'It's something you will never know!' he cried. 'It's shame! I am not sorry you should see what I feel. It will suggest to you, perhaps, that my heart had never been in this filthy contest. Let me assure you, at any rate, that it hasn't; that it has had nothing but scorn for the base perversion of my pride and my ambition. I could easily shed tears of joy at their return – the return of the prodigals! Tears of sorrow – sorrow –'

He was unable to go on. He sank into a chair, covering his face with his hands.

'For God's sake, stick to the joy!' I exclaimed.

He rose to his feet again. 'Well,' he said, 'it was for your sake that I parted with my self-respect; with your assistance I recover it.'

'How for my sake?'

'For whom but you would I have gone as far as I did? For what other purpose than that of keeping our friendship whole would I have borne your company into this narrow pass? A man whom I cared for less I would long since have parted with. You were needed – you and something you have about you that always takes me so – to bring me to this. You ennobled, exalted,

enchanted the struggle. I *did* value my prospect of coming into
Mr Sloane's property. I valued it for my poor sister's sake as
well as for my own, so long as it was the natural reward of
conscientious service, and not the prize of hypocrisy and cunning. With another man than you I never would have contested
such a prize. But you fascinated me, even as my rival. You
played with me, deceived me, betrayed me. I held my ground,
hoping you would see that what you were doing was not fair.
But if you have seen it, it has made no difference with you. For
Mr Sloane, from the moment that, under your magical influence, he revealed his nasty little nature, I had nothing but
contempt.'

'And for me now?'

'Don't ask me. I don't trust myself.'

'Hate, I suppose.'

'Is that the best you can imagine? Farewell.'

'Is it a serious farewell – farewell for ever?'

'How can there be any other?'

'I am sorry this should be your point of view. It's characteristic. All the more reason then that I should say a word in self-
defence. You accuse me of having "played with you, deceived
you, betrayed you". It seems to me that you are quite beside the
mark. You say you were such a friend of mine; if so, you ought
to be one still. It was not to my fine sentiments you attached
yourself, for I never had any or pretended to any. In anything
I have done recently, therefore, there has been no inconsistency. I never pretended to take one's friendship so seriously.
I don't understand the word in the sense you attach to it. I don't
understand the feeling of affection between men. To me it
means quite another thing. You give it a meaning of your
own; you enjoy the profit of your invention; it's no more than
just that you should pay the penalty. Only it seems to me rather
hard that *I* should pay it.' Theodore remained silent, but he
looked quite sick. 'Is it still a "serious farewell"?' I went on. 'It
seems a pity. After this clearing up, it appears to me that I shall
be on better terms with you. No man can have a deeper appreciation of your excellent parts, a keener enjoyment of your
society. I should very much regret the loss of it.'

'Have we, then, all this while understood each other so little?' said Theodore.

'Don't say "we" and "each other". I think I have understood you.'

'Very likely. It's not for my having kept anything back.'

'Well, I do you justice. To me you have always been over-generous. Try now and be just.'

Still he stood silent, with his cold, hard frown. It was plain that, if he was to come back to me, it would be from the other world – if there be one! What he was going to answer I know not. The door opened, and Robert appeared, pale, trembling, his eyes starting in his head.

'I verily believe that poor Mr Sloane is dead in his bed!' he cried.

There was a moment's perfect silence. 'Amen,' said I. 'Yes, old boy, try and be just.' Mr Sloane had quietly died in my absence.

24th. – Theodore went up to town this morning, having shaken hands with me in silence before he started. Doctor Jones, and Brooks the attorney, have been very officious, and, by their advice, I have telegraphed to a certain Miss Meredith, a maiden lady, by their account the nearest of kin; or, in other words, simply a discarded niece of the defunct. She telegraphs back that she will arrive in person for the funeral. I shall remain till she comes. I have lost a fortune, but have I irretrievably lost a friend? I am sure I can't say. Yes, I shall wait for Miss Meredith.

A PASSIONATE PILGRIM

I

INTENDING to sail for America in the early part of June, I determined to spend the interval of six weeks in England, of which I had dreamed much but as yet knew nothing. I had formed in Italy and France a resolute preference for old inns, deeming that what they sometimes cost the ungratified body they repay the delighted mind. On my arrival in London, therefore, I lodged at a certain antique hostelry far to the east of Temple Bar, deep in what I used to denominate the Johnsonian city. Here, on the first evening of my stay, I descended to the little coffee-room and bespoke my dinner of the genius of decorum, in the person of the solitary waiter. No sooner had I crossed the threshold of this apartment than I felt I had mown the first swath in my golden-ripe crop of British 'impressions'. The coffee-room of the Red-Lion, like so many other places and things I was destined to see in England, seemed to have been waiting for long years, with just that sturdy sufferance of time written on its visage, for me to come and gaze, ravished but unamazed.

The latent preparedness of the American mind for even the most delectable features of English life is a fact which I never fairly probed to its depths. The roots of it are so deeply buried in the virgin soil of our primary culture, that, without some great upheaval of experience, it would be hard to say exactly when and where and how it begins. It makes an American's enjoyment of England an emotion more fatal and sacred than his enjoyment, say, of Italy or Spain. I had seen the coffee-room of the Red-Lion years ago, at home, – at Saragossa, Illinois, – in books, in visions, in dreams, in Dickens, in Smollett, and Boswell. It was small, and subdivided into six small compartments by a series of perpendicular screens of mahogany, something higher than a man's stature, furnished on either side with a narrow uncushioned ledge, denominated in ancient Britain a seat. In each of the little dining-boxes thus immutably constituted was a small table, which in crowded seasons was expected to accommodate the several agents of a fourfold British hungriness. But crowded seasons had passed away from the Red-Lion for ever. It was crowded only with memories and ghosts and atmosphere. Round the room there marched, breast-high, a magnificent panelling of mahogany, so dark with time and so polished with unremitted friction, that by gazing awhile into its lucid blackness I fancied I could discern the lingering images of a party of gentlemen in periwigs and short-clothes, just arrived from York by the coach. On the dark yellow walls, coated by the fumes of English coal, of English mutton, of Scotch whisky, were a dozen melancholy prints, sallow-toned with age, – the Derby favourite of the year 1807, the Bank of England, her Majesty the Queen. On the floor was a Turkey carpet – as old as the mahogany, almost, as the Bank of England, as the Queen, – into which the waiter in his lonely revolutions had trodden so many massive soot-flakes and drops of overflowing beer, that the glowing looms of Smyrna would certainly not have recognised it. To say that I ordered my dinner of this superior being would be altogether to misrepresent the process, owing to which, having dreamed of lamb and spinach, and a charlotte-russe, I sat down in penitence to a mutton-chop and a rice pudding. Bracing my feet against the cross-beam of my little oaken table, I opposed to the mahogany partition behind me that vigorous dorsal resistance which expresses the old-English idea of repose. The sturdy screen refused even to creak; but my poor Yankee joints made up the deficiency. While I was waiting for my chop there came into the room a person whom I took to be my sole fellow-lodger. He seemed, like myself, to have submitted to proposals for dinner; the table on the other side of my partition had been prepared to receive him. He walked up to the fire, exposed his back to it, consulted his watch, and looked apparently out of the window, but really at me. He was a man of something less than middle age and more than middle stature, though indeed you would have called him neither young nor tall. He was chiefly remarkable for his exaggerated leanness. His hair, very thin on the summit of his head, was dark, short, and fine. His eye was of a pale, turbid grey, unsuited, perhaps, to his dark hair and brow, but not altogether out of harmony with his colourless, bilious complexion. His nose was aquiline and delicate; beneath it hung a thin, comely, dark moustache. His mouth and chin were meagre and uncertain of outline; not vulgar, perhaps, but weak. A cold, fatal, gentlemanly weakness, indeed, seemed expressed in his attentuated person. His eye was restless and deprecating; his whole physiognomy, his manner of shifting his weight from foot to foot, the spiritless droop of his head, told of exhausted purpose, of a will relaxed. His dress was neat and careful, with an air of half-mourning. I made up my mind on three points: he was unmarried, he was ill, he was not an Englishman. The waiter approached him, and they murmured momentarily in barely audible tones. I heard the words 'claret', 'sherry', with a tentative inflection, and finally 'beer', with a gentle affirmative. Perhaps he was a Russian in reduced circumstances; he reminded me of a certain type of Russian which I had met on the Continent. While I was weighing this hypothesis, – for you see I was interested, – there appeared a short, brisk man with reddish-brown hair, a vulgar nose, a sharp blue eye, and a red beard, confined to his lower jaw and chin. My impecunious Russian was still standing on the rug, with his mild gaze bent on vacancy; the other marched up to him, and with his umbrella gave him a playful poke in the concave frontage of his melancholy waistcoat. 'A penny-ha'penny for your thoughts!' said the new-comer.

His companion uttered an exclamation, stared, then laid his two hands on the other's shoulders. The latter looked round at me keenly, compassing me in a momentary glance. I read in its own high light that this was an American eye-beam; and with such confidence that I hardly needed to see its owner, as he prepared, with his friend, to seat himself at the table adjoining my own, take from his overcoat-pocket three New York papers and lay them beside his plate. As my neighbours proceeded to dine, I became conscious that, through no indiscretion of my own, a large portion of their conversation made its way over the top of our dividing partition and mingled its savour with that of my simple repast. Occasionally their tone was lowered, as with the intention of secrecy; but I heard a phrase here and a phrase there distinctly enough to grow very curious as to the burden of the whole, and, in fact, to succeed at last in guessing it. The two voices were pitched in an unforgotten key, and equally native to our Cisatlantic air; they seemed to fall upon the muffled medium of surrounding parlance as the rattle of pease on the face of a drum. They were American, however, with a difference; and I had no hesitation in assigning the lighter and softer of the two to the pale, thin gentleman, whom I decidedly preferred to his comrade. The latter began to question him about his voyage.

'Horrible, horrible! I was deadly sick from the hour we left New York.'

'Well, you do look considerably reduced,' his friend affirmed.

'Reduced! I've been on the verge of the grave. I haven't slept six hours in three weeks.' This was said with great gravity. 'Well, I have made the voyage for the last time.'

'The deuce you have! You mean to stay here for ever?'

'Here, or somewhere! It's likely to be a short for ever.'

There was a pause; after which: 'You're the same cheerful old boy, Searle. Going to die to-morrow, eh?'

'I almost wish I were.'

'You're not in love with England, then? I've heard people say at home that you dressed and talked and acted like an Englishman. But I know Englishmen, and I know you. You're not one of them, Searle, not you. You'll go under here, sir; you'll go under as sure as my name is Simmons.'

Following this, I heard a sudden clatter, as of the dropping of a knife and fork. 'Well, you're a delicate sort of creature, Simmons! I have been wandering about all day in this accursed city, ready to cry with home-sickness and heart-sickness and every possible sort of sickness, and thinking, in the absence of anything better, of meeting you here this evening, and of your uttering some syllable of cheer and comfort, and giving me some feeble ray of hope. Go under? Am I not under now? I can't sink lower, except to sink into my grave!'

Mr Simmons seems to have staggered a moment under this outbreak of passion. But the next, 'Don't cry, Searle,' I heard him say. 'Remember the waiter. I've grown Englishman enough for that. For heaven's sake, don't let us have any feelings. Feelings will do nothing for you here. It's best to come to the point. Tell me in three words what you expect of me.'

I heard another movement, as if poor Searle had collapsed in his chair. 'Upon my word, Simmons, you are inconceivable. You got my letter?'

'Yes, I got your letter. I was never sorrier to get anything in my life.'

At this declaration Mr Searle rattled out an oath, which it was well perhaps that I but partially heard. 'John Simmons,' he cried, 'what devil possesses you? Are you going to betray me here in a foreign land, to turn out a false friend, a heartless rogue?'

'Go on, sir,' said sturdy Simmons. 'Pour it all out. I'll wait till you have done. – Your beer is very bad,' to the waiter. 'I'll have some more.'

'For God's sake, explain yourself!' cried Searle.

There was a pause, at the end of which I heard Mr Simmons set down his empty tankard with emphasis. 'You poor morbid man,' he resumed, 'I don't want to say anything to make you feel sore. I pity you. But you must allow me to say that you have acted like a blasted fool!'

Mr Searle seemed to have made an effort to compose himself. 'Be so good as to tell me what was the meaning of your letter.'

'I was a fool, myself, to have written that letter. It came of my infernal meddlesome benevolence. I had much better have let you alone. To tell you the plain truth, I never was so horrified in my life as when I found that on the strength of that letter you had come out here to seek your fortune.'

'What did you expect me to do?'

'I expected you to wait patiently till I had made further inquiries and had written to you again.'

'You have made further inquiries now?'

'Inquiries! I have made assaults.'

'And you find I have no claim?'

'No claim to call a claim. It looked at first as if you had a very pretty one. I confess the idea took hold of me –'

'Thanks to your preposterous benevolence!'

Mr Simmons seemed for a moment to experience a difficulty in swallowing. 'Your beer is undrinkable,' he said to the waiter. 'I'll have some brandy. – Come, Searle,' he resumed, 'don't challenge me to the arts of debate, or I'll settle right down on you. Benevolence, as I say, was part of it. The reflection that if I put the thing through it would be a very pretty feather in my cap and a very pretty penny in my purse was part of it. And the satisfaction of seeing a poor nobody of a Yankee walk right into an old English estate was a good deal of it. Upon my word, Searle, when I think of it, I wish with all my heart that, erratic genius as you are, you had a claim, for the very beauty of it! I should hardly care what you did with the confounded property when you got it. I could leave you alone to turn it into Yankee notions, – into ducks and drakes, as they call it here. I should like to see you stamping over it and kicking up its sacred dust in their very faces!'

'You don't know me, Simmons!' said Searle, for all response to this untender benediction.

'I should be very glad to think I didn't, Searle. I have been to no small amount of trouble for you. I have consulted by main force three first-rate men. They smile at the idea. I should like you to see the smile negative of one of these London big-wigs. If your title were written in letters of fire, it wouldn't stand being sniffed at in that fashion. I sounded in person the solicitor of your distinguished kinsman. He seemed to have been in a manner forewarned and forearmed. It seems your brother George, some twenty years ago, put forth a feeler. So you are not to have the glory of even frightening them.'

'I never frightened any one,' said Searle, 'I shouldn't begin at this time of day. I should approach the subject like a gentleman.'

'Well, if you want very much to do something like a gentleman, you've got a capital chance. Take your disappointment like a gentleman.'

I had finished my dinner, and I had become keenly interested in poor Mr Searle's mysterious claim; so interested that it was vexatious to hear his emotions reflected in his voice without noting them in his face. I left my place, went over to the fire, took up the evening paper, and established a post of observation behind it.

Lawyer Simmons was in the act of choosing a soft chop from the dish, – an act accompanied by a great deal of prying and poking with his own personal fork. My disillusioned compatriot had pushed away his plate; he sat with his elbows on the table, gloomily nursing his head with his hands. His companion stared at him a moment, I fancied half tenderly; I am not sure whether it was pity or whether it was beer and brandy. 'I say, Searle,' – and for my benefit, I think, taking me for an impressible native, he attuned his voice to something of a pompous pitch, – 'in this country it is the inestimable privilege of a loyal citizen, under whatsoever stress of pleasure or of pain, to make a point of eating his dinner.'

Searle disgustedly gave his plate another push. 'Anything may happen, now!' he said. 'I don't care a straw.'

'You ought to care. Have another chop, and you *will* care. Have some brandy. Take my advice!'

Searle from between his two hands looked at him. 'I have had enough of your advice!' he said.

'A little more,' said Simmons, mildly; 'I sha'n't trouble you again. What do you mean to do?'

'Nothing.'

'O, come!'

'Nothing, nothing, nothing!'

'Nothing but starve. How about your money?'

'Why do you ask? You don't care.'

'My dear fellow, if you want to make me offer you twenty pounds, you set most clumsily about it. You said just now I don't know you. Possibly! There is, perhaps, no such enormous difference between knowing you and not knowing you. At any rate, you don't know me. I expect you to go home.'

'I won't go home! I have crossed the ocean for the last time.'

'What is the matter? Are you afraid?'

'Yes, I'm afraid! "I thank thee, Jew, for teaching me that word!"'

'You're more afraid to go than to stay?'

'I sha'n't stay. I shall die.'

'O, are you sure of that?'

'One can always be sure of that.'

Mr Simmons started and stared: his mild cynic had turned grim stoic. 'Upon my soul,' he said, 'one would think that Death had named the day!'

'We have named it, between us.'

This was too much even for Mr Simmons's easy morality. 'I say, Searle,' he cried, 'I'm not more of a stickler than the next man, but if you are going to blaspheme, I shall wash my hands of you. If you'll consent to return home with me by the steamer of the 23rd, I'll pay your passage down. More than that, I'll pay your wine bill.'

Searle meditated. 'I believe I never willed anything in my life,' he said; 'but I feel sure that I have willed this, that I stay here till I take my leave for a newer world than that poor old New World of ours. It's an odd feeling, – I rather like it! What should I do at home?'

'You said just now you were homesick.'

'So I was – for a morning. But haven't I been all my life long sick for Europe? And now that I've got it, am I to cast it off again? I'm much obliged to you for your offer. I have enough for the present. I have about my person some forty pounds' worth of British gold and the same amount, say, of Yankee vitality. They'll last me out together! After they are gone, I shall lay my head in some English churchyard, beside some ivied tower, beneath an English yew.'

I had thus far distinctly followed the dialogue; but at this point the landlord came in, and, begging my pardon, would suggest that No. 12, a most superior apartment, having now been vacated, it would give him pleasure, etc. The fate of No. 12 having been decreed, I transferred my attention back to my friends. They had risen to their feet; Simmons had put on his overcoat; he stood polishing his rusty black hat with his napkin. 'Do you mean to go down to the place?' he asked.

'Possibly. I have dreamed of it so much I should like to see it.'

'Shall you call on Mr Searle?'

'Heaven forbid!'

'Something has just occurred to me,' Simmons pursued, with an unhandsome grin, as if Mephistopheles were playing at malice. 'There's a Miss Searle, the old man's sister.'

'Well?' said the other, frowning.

'Well, sir! suppose, instead of dying, you should marry!'

Mr Searle frowned in silence. Simmons gave him a tap on the stomach. 'Line those ribs a bit first!' The poor gentleman blushed crimson and his eyes filled with tears. 'You *are* a coarse brute,' he said. The scene was pathetic. I was prevented from seeing the conclusion of it by the reappearance of the landlord, on behalf of No. 12. He insisted on my coming to inspect the premises. Half an hour afterwards I was rattling along in a Hansom toward Covent Garden, where I heard Madame Bosio in the Barber of Seville. On my return from the opera I went into the coffee-room, vaguely fancying I might catch another glimpse of Mr Searle. I was not disappointed. I found him sitting before the fire, with his head fallen on his breast, sunk in the merciful stupor of tardy sleep. I looked at him for some moments. His face, pale and refined in the dim lamplight, impressed me with an air of helpless, ineffective delicacy. They say fortune comes while we sleep. Standing there I felt benignant enough to be poor Mr Searle's fortune. As I walked away, I perceived amid the shadows of one of the little dining-stalls which I have described the lonely ever-dressed waiter, dozing attendance on my friend, and shifting aside for a while the burden of waiterhood. I lingered a moment beside the old inn-yard, in which, upon a time, the coaches and postchaises found space to turn and disgorge. Above the upward vista of the enclosing galleries, from which lounging lodgers and crumpled chambermaids and all the picturesque domesticity of an antique tavern must have watched the great entrances and exits of the posting and coaching drama, I descried the distant lurid twinkle of the London constellations. At the foot of the stairs, enshrined in the glittering niche of her well-appointed bar, the landlady sat napping like some solemn idol amid votive brass and plate.

The next morning, not finding the innocent object of my benevolent curiosity in the coffee-room, I learned from the waiter that he had ordered breakfast in bed. Into this asylum I was not yet prepared to pursue him. I spent the morning running about London, chiefly on business, but snatching by the way many a vivid impression of its huge metropolitan interest. Beneath the sullen black and grey of that hoary civic world the hungry American mind detects the magic colours of association. As the afternoon approached, however, my impatient heart began to babble of green fields; it was of English meadows I had chiefly dreamed. Thinking over the suburban lions, I fixed upon Hampton Court. The day was the more propitious that it yielded just that dim, subaqueous light which sleeps so fondly upon the English landscape.

At the end of an hour I found myself wandering through the multitudinous rooms of the great palace. They follow each other in infinite succession, with no great variety of interest or aspect, but with a sort of regal monotony, and a fine specific flavour. They are most exactly of their various times. You pass from great painted and panelled bedchambers and closets, anterooms, drawing-rooms, council-rooms, through king's suite, queen's suite, and prince's suite, until you feel as if you were strolling through the appointed hours and stages of some decorous monarchical day. On one side are the old monumental upholsteries, the vast cold tarnished beds and canopies, with the circumference of disapparelled royalty attested by a gilded balustrade, and the great carved and yawning chimney-places, where dukes-in-waiting may have warmed their weary heels; on the other side, in deep recesses, the immense windows, the framed and draped embrasures where the sovereign whispered and favourites smiled, looking out on the terraced gardens and the misty glades of Bushey Park. The dark walls are gravely decorated by innumerable dark portraits of persons attached to Court and State, more especially with various members of the Dutch-looking *entourage* of William of Orange, the restorer of the palace; with good store, too, of the lily-bosomed models of Lely and Kneller. The whole tone of this long-drawn interior is immensely sombre, prosaic, and sad. The tints of all things have sunk to a cold and melancholy brown, and the great palatial void seems to hold no stouter tenantry than a sort of pungent odorous chill. I seemed to be the only visitor. I held ungrudged communion with the formal genius of the spot. Poor mortalised kings! ineffective lure of royalty! This, or something like it, was the murmured burden of my musings. They were interrupted suddenly by my coming upon a person standing in devout contemplation before a simpering countess of Sir Peter Lely's creation. On hearing my footstep this person turned his head, and I recognised my fellow-lodger at the Red-Lion. I was apparently recognised as well; I detected an air of overture in his glance. In a few moments, seeing I had a catalogue, he asked the name of the portrait. On my ascertaining it, he inquired, timidly, how I liked the lady.

'Well,' said I, not quite timidly enough, perhaps, 'I confess she seems to me rather a light piece of work.'

He remained silent, and a little abashed, I think. As we strolled away he stole a sidelong glance of farewell at his leering shepherdess. To speak with him face to face was to feel keenly that he was weak and interesting. We talked of our inn, of London, of the palace; he uttered his mind freely, but he seemed to struggle with a weight of depression. It was a simple mind enough, with no great culture, I fancied, but with a certain appealing native grace. I foresaw that I should find him a true American, full of that perplexing interfusion of refinement and crudity which marks the American mind. His perceptions, I divined, were delicate; his opinions, possibly, gross. On my telling him that I too was an American, he stopped short and seemed overcome with emotion: then silently passing his arm into my own, he suffered me to lead him through the rest of the palace and down into the gardens. A vast gravelled platform stretches itself before the basement of the palace, taking the afternoon sun. A portion of the edifice is reserved as a series of private apartments, occupied by state pensioners, reduced gentlewomen in receipt of the

Queen's bounty, and other deserving persons. Many of these apartments have their little private gardens; and here and there, between their verdure-coated walls, you catch a glimpse of these dim horticultural closets. My companion and I took many a turn up and down this spacious level, looking down on the antique geometry of the lower garden and on the stoutly woven tapestry of vine and blossom which muffles the foundations of the huge red pile. I thought of the various images of old-world gentility, which, early and late, must have strolled upon that ancient terrace and felt the great protecting quietude of the solemn palace. We looked through an antique grating into one of the little private gardens, and saw an old lady with a black mantilla on her head, a decanter of water in one hand and a crutch in the other, come forth, followed by three little dogs and a cat, to sprinkle a plant. She had an opinion, I fancied, on the virtue of Queen Caroline. There are few sensations so exquisite in life as to stand with a companion in a foreign land and inhale to the depths of your consciousness the alien savour of the air and the tonic picturesqueness of things. This common relish of local colour makes comrades of strangers. My companion seemed oppressed with vague amazement. He stared and lingered and scanned the scene with a gentle scowl. His enjoyment appeared to give him pain. I proposed, at last, that we should dine in the neighbourhood and take a late train to town. We made our way out of the gardens into the adjoining village, where we found an excellent inn. Mr Searle sat down to table with small apparent interest in the repast, but gradually warming to his work, he declared at the end of half an hour that for the first time in a month he felt an appetite.

'You're an invalid?' I said.

'Yes,' he answered. 'A hopeless one!'

The little village of Hampton Court stands clustered about the broad entrance of Bushey Park. After we had dined we lounged along into the hazy vista of the great avenue of horse-chestnuts. There is a rare emotion, familiar to every intelligent traveller, in which the mind, with a great passionate throb, achieves a magical synthesis of its impressions. You feel England; you feel Italy. The reflection for the moment has an extraordinary poignancy. I had known it from time to time in Italy, and had opened my soul to it as to the spirit of the Lord. Since my arrival in England I had been waiting for it to come. A bottle of excellent Burgundy at dinner had perhaps unlocked to it the gates of sense; it came now with a conquering tread. Just the scene around me was the England of my visions. Over against us, amid the deep-hued bloom of its ordered gardens, the dark red palace, with its formal copings and its vacant windows, seemed to tell of a proud and splendid past; the little village nestling between park and palace, around a patch of turfy common, with its tavern of gentility, its ivy-towered church, its parsonage, retained to my modernised fancy the lurking semblance of a feudal hamlet. It was in this dark composite light that I had read all English prose; it was this mild moist air that had blown from the verses of English poets; beneath these broad acres of rain-deepened greenness a thousand honoured dead lay buried.

'Well,' I said to my friend, 'I think there is no mistake about this being England. We may like it or not, it's positive! No more dense and stubborn fact ever settled down on an expectant tourist. It brings my heart into my throat.'

Searle was silent. I looked at him; he was looking up at the sky, as if he were watching some visible descent of the elements. 'On me too,' he said, 'it's settling down!' Then with a forced smile: 'Heaven give me strength to bear it!'

'O mighty world,' I cried, 'to hold at once so rare an Italy and so brave an England!'

'To say nothing of America,' added Searle.

'O,' I answered, 'America has a world to herself!'

'You have the advantage over me,' my companion resumed, after a pause, 'in coming to all this with an educated eye. You already know the old. I have never known it but by report. I have always fancied I should like it. In a small way at home, you know, I have tried to stick to the old. I must be a conservative by nature. People at home – a few people – used to call me a snob.'

'I don't believe you were a snob,' I cried. 'You look too amiable.'

He smiled sadly. 'There it is,' he said. 'It's the old story! I'm amiable! I know what that means! I was too great a fool to be even a snob! If I had been I should probably have come abroad earlier in life – before – before –' He paused, and his head dropped sadly on his breast.

The bottle of Burgundy had loosened his tongue. I felt that my learning his story was merely a question of time. Something told me that I had gained his confidence and he would unfold himself. 'Before you lost your health,' I said.

'Before I lost my health,' he answered. 'And my property, – the little I had. And my ambition. And my self-esteem.'

'Come!' I said. 'You shall get them all back. This tonic English climate will wind you up in a month. And with the return of health, all the rest will return.'

He sat musing, with his eyes fixed on the distant palace. 'They are too far gone, – self-esteem, especially! I should like to be an old genteel pensioner, lodged over there in the palace, and spending my days in maundering about these classic haunts. I should go every morning, at the hour when it gets the sun, into that long gallery where all those pretty women of Lely's are hung, – I know you despise them! – and stroll up and down and pay them compliments. Poor, precious, forsaken creatures! So flattered and courted in their day, so neglected now! Offering up their shoulders and ringlets and smiles to that inexorable solitude!'

I patted my friend on the shoulder. 'You shall be yourself again yet,' I said.

Just at this moment there came cantering down the shallow glade of the avenue a young girl on a fine black horse, – one of those lovely budding gentlewomen, perfectly mounted and equipped, who form to American eyes the sweetest incident of English scenery. She had distanced her servant, and, as she came abreast of us, turned slightly in her saddle and looked back at him. In the movement she dropped her whip. Drawing in her horse, she cast upon the ground a glance of maidenly alarm. 'This is something better than a Lely,' I said. Searle hastened forward, picked up the whip, and removing his hat with an air of great devotion, presented it to the young girl.

Fluttered and blushing, she reached forward, took it with softly murmured gratitude, and the next moment was bounding over the elastic turf. Searle stood watching her; the servant, as he passed us, touched his hat. When Searle turned toward me again, I saw that his face was glowing with a violent blush. 'I doubt of your having come abroad too late!' I said, laughing.

A short distance from where we had stopped was an old stone bench. We went and sat down on it and watched the light mist turning to sullen gold in the rays of the evening sun. 'We ought to be thinking of the train back to London, I suppose,' I said at last.

'O, hang the train!' said Searle.

'Willingly! There could be no better spot than this to feel the magic of an English twilight.' So we lingered, and the twilight lingered around us, – a light and not a darkness. As we sat, there came trudging along the road an individual whom, from afar, I recognised as a member of the genus 'tramp'. I had read of the British tramp, but I had never yet encountered him, and I brought my historic consciousness to bear upon the present specimen. As he approached us he slackened pace and finally halted, touching his cap. He was a man of middle age, clad in a greasy bonnet, with greasy earlocks depending from its sides. Round his neck was a grimy red scarf, tucked into his waistcoat; his coat and trousers had a remote affinity with those of a reduced hostler. In one hand he had a stick; on his arm he bore a tattered basket, with a handful of withered green stuff in the bottom. His face was pale, haggard, and degraded beyond description, – a singular mixture of brutality and finesse. He had a history. From what height had he fallen, from what depth had he risen? Never was a form of rascally beggarhood more complete. There was a merciless fixedness of outline about him which filled me with a kind of awe. I felt as if I were in the presence of a personage, – an artist in vagrancy.

'For God's sake, gentlemen,' he said, in that raucous tone of weather-beaten poverty suggestive of chronic sore-throat exacerbated by perpetual gin, – 'for God's sake, gentlemen, have pity on a poor fern-collector!' – turning up his stale dandelions. 'Food hasn't passed my lips, gentlemen, in the last three days.'

We gaped responsive, in the precious pity of guileless Yankeeism. 'I wonder,' thought I, 'if half a crown would be enough?' And our fasting botanist went limping away through the park with a mystery of satirical gratitude super-added to his general mystery.

'I feel as if I had seen my *doppel-ganger*,' said Searle. 'He reminds me of myself. What am I but a tramp?'

Upon this hint I spoke. 'What are you, my friend?' I asked. 'Who are you?'

A sudden blush rose to his pale face, so that I feared I had offended him. He poked a moment at the sod with the point of his umbrella, before answering. 'Who am I?' he said at last. 'My name is Clement Searle. I was born in New York. I have lived in New York. What am I? That's easily told. Nothing! I assure you, nothing.'

'A very good fellow, apparently,' I protested.

'A very good fellow! Ah, there it is! You've said more than you mean. It's by having been a very good fellow all my days that I've come to this. I have drifted through life. I'm a failure, sir, – a failure as hopeless and helpless as any that ever swallowed up the slender investments of the widow and the orphan. I don't pay five cents on the dollar. Of what I was to begin with no memory remains. I have been ebbing away, from the start, in a steady current which, at forty, has left this arid sand-bank behind. To begin with, certainly, I was not a fountain of wisdom. All the more reason for a definite channel, – for will and purpose and direction. I walked by chance and sympathy and sentiment. Take a turn through New York and you'll find my tattered sympathies and sentiments dangling on every bush and fluttering in every breeze; the men to whom I lent money, the women to whom I made love, the friends I trusted, the dreams I cherished, the poisonous fumes of pleasure, amid which nothing was sweet or precious but the manhood they stifled! It was my fault that I believed in pleasure here below. I believe in it still, but as I believe in God and not in man! I believed in eating your cake and having it. I respected Pleasure, and she made a fool of me. Other men, treating her like the arrant strumpet she is, enjoyed her for the hour, but kept their good manners for plain-faced Business, with the larger dowry, to whom they are now lawfully married. My taste was to be delicate; well, perhaps I was so! I had a little money; it went the way of my little wit. Here in my pocket I have forty pounds of it left. The only thing I have to show for my money and my wit is a little volume of verses, printed at my own expense, in which fifteen years ago I made bold to sing the charms of love and idleness. Six months since I got hold of the volume; it reads like the poetry of fifty years ago. The form is incredible. I hadn't seen Hampton Court then. When I was thirty I married. It was a sad mistake, but a generous one. The young girl was poor and obscure, but beautiful and proud. I fancied she would make an incomparable woman. It was a sad mistake! She died at the end of three years, leaving no children. Since then I have idled long. I have had bad habits. To this impalpable thread of existence the current of my life has shrunk. To-morrow I shall be high and dry. Was I meant to come to this? Upon my soul I wasn't! If I say what I feel, you'll fancy my vanity quite equal to my folly, and set me down as one of those dreary theorisers after the fact, who draw any moral from their misfortunes but the damning moral that vice is vice and that's an end of it. Take it for what it's worth. I have always fancied that I was meant for a gentler world. Before heaven, sir, – whoever you are, – I'm in practice so absurdly tender-hearted that I can afford to say it, – I came into the world an aristocrat. I was born with a soul for the picturesque. It condemns me, I confess; but in a measure, too, it absolves me. I found it nowhere. I found a world all hard lines and harsh lights, without shade, without composition, as they say of pictures, without the lovely mystery of colour. To furnish colour, I melted down the very substance of my own soul. I went about with my brush, touching up and toning down; a very pretty chiaroscuro you'll find in my track! Sitting here, in this old park, in this old land, I feel – I feel that I hover on the misty verge of what might have been! I should have been born here and not there; here my vulgar idleness would have been – don't laugh now! – would have been elegant leisure. How it was that I never came abroad is more than I can say. It might have cut the knot; but the knot was too tight. I was always unwell or in debt or entangled. Besides, I had a horror of the sea – with reason, heaven knows! A year ago I was reminded of the existence of an old claim to a portion of an English estate, cherished off and on by various members of my family for the past eighty years. It's undeniably slender and desperately hard to define. I am by no means sure that to this hour I have mastered it. You look as if you had a clear head. Some other time, if you'll consent, we'll puzzle it out, such as it is, together. Poverty was staring me in the face; I sat down and got my claim by heart, as I used to get nine times nine as a boy. I dreamed about it for six months, half expecting to wake up some fine morning to hear through a latticed casement the cawing of an English rookery. A couple of months since there came out here on business of his own a sort of half-friend of mine, a sharp New York lawyer, an extremely common fellow, but a man with an eye for the weak point and the strong point. It was with him yesterday that you saw me dining. He undertook, as he expressed it, to "nose round" and see if anything could be made of this pretended right. The matter had never seriously been taken up. A month later I got a letter from Simmons, assuring me that things looked mighty well, that he should be vastly amased if I hadn't a case. I took fire in a humid sort of way; I acted, for the first time in my life; I sailed for England. I have been here three days: it seems three months. After keeping me waiting for thirty-six hours, last evening my precious Simmons makes his appearance, and informs me, with his mouth full of mutton, that I was a blasted fool to have taken him at his word; that he had been precipitate; that I had been precipitate; that my claim was moonshine; and that I must do penance and take a ticket for another fortnight of seasickness in his agreeable society. My friend, my friend! Shall I say I was disappointed? I'm already resigned. I doubted the practicability of my claim. I felt in my deeper consciousness that it was the crowning illusion of a life of illusions. Well, it was a pretty one. Poor Simmons! I forgive him with all my heart. But for him I shouldn't be sitting in this place, in this air, with these thoughts. This is a world I could have loved. There's a great fitness in its having been kept for the last. After this nothing would have been tolerable. I shall now have a month of it, I hope, and I shall not have a chance to be disenchanted. There's one thing!' – and here, pausing, he laid his hand on mine; I rose and stood before him, – 'I wish it were possible you should be with me to the end.'

'I promise you,' I said, 'to leave you only at your own request. But it must be on condition of your omitting from your conversation this intolerable flavour of mortality. The end! Perhaps it's the beginning.'

He shook his head. 'You don't know me. It's a long story. I'm incurably ill.'

'I know you a little. I have a strong suspicion that your illness is in great measure a matter of mind and spirits. All that you've told me is but another way of saying that you have lived hitherto in yourself. The tenement's haunted! Live abroad! Take an interest!'

He looked at me for a moment with his sad weak eyes. Then with a faint smile: 'Don't cut down a man you find hanging. He has had a reason for it. I'm bankrupt.'

'O, health is money!' I said. 'Get well, and the rest will take care of itself. I'm interested in your claim.'

'Don't ask me to expound it now! It's a sad muddle. Let it alone. I know nothing of business. If I myself were to take the matter in hand, I should break short off the poor little silken thread of my expectancy. In a better world than this I think I should be listened to. But in this hard world there's small bestowal of ideal justice. There is no doubt, I fancy, that, a hundred years ago, we suffered a palpable wrong. But we made no appeal at the time, and the dust of a century now lies heaped upon our silence. Let it rest!'

'What is the estimated value of your interest?'

'We were instructed from the first to accept a compromise. Compared with the whole property, our utmost right is extremely small. Simmons talked of eighty-five thousand dollars. Why eighty-five I'm sure I don't know. Don't beguile me into figures.'

'Allow me one more question. Who is actually in possession?'

'A certain Mr Richard Searle. I know nothing about him.'

'He is in some way related to you?'

'Our great-grandfathers were half-brothers. What does that make?'

'Twentieth cousins, say. And where does your twentieth cousin live?'

'At Lockley Park, Herefordshire.'

I pondered awhile. 'I'm interested in you, Mr Searle,' I said. 'In your story, in your title, such as it is, and in this Lockley Park, Herefordshire. Suppose we go down and see it.'

He rose to his feet with a certain alertness. 'I shall make a sound man of him, yet,' I said to myself.

'I shouldn't have the heart,' he said, 'to accomplish the melancholy pilgrimage alone. But with you I'll go anywhere.'

On our return to London we determined to spend three days there together, and then to go into the country. We felt to excellent purpose the sombre charm of London, the mighty mother-city of our mighty race, the great distributing heart of our traditional life. Certain London characteristics – monuments, relics, hints of history, local moods and memories – are more deeply suggestive to an American soul than anything else in Europe. With an equal attentive piety my friend and I glanced at these things. Their influence on Searle was deep and singular. His observation I soon perceived to be extremely acute. His almost passionate relish for the old, the artificial, and social, wellnigh extinct from its long inanition, began now to tremble and thrill with a tardy vitality. I watched in silent wonderment this strange metaphysical renascence.

Between the fair boundaries of the counties of Hereford and Worcester rise in a long undulation the sloping pastures of the Malvern Hills. Consulting a big red book on the castles and manors of England, we found Lockley Park to be seated near the base of this grassy range, – though in which county I forget. In the pages of this genial volume, Lockley Park and its appurtenances made a very handsome figure. We took up our abode at a certain little wayside inn, at which in the days of leisure the coach must have stopped for lunch, and burnished pewters of rustic ale been tenderly exalted to 'outsides' athirst with breezy progression. Here we stopped, for sheer admiration of its steep thatched roof, its latticed windows, and its homely porch. We allowed a couple of days to elapse in vague, undirected strolls and sweet sentimental observance of the land, before we prepared to execute the especial purpose of our journey. This admirable region is a compendium of the general physiognomy of England. The noble friendliness of the scenery, its subtle old-friendliness, the magical familiarity of multitudinous details, appealed to us at every step and at every glance. Deep in our souls a natural affection answered. The whole land, in the full, warm rains of the last of April, had burst into sudden perfect spring. The dark walls of the hedgerows had turned into blooming screens; the sodden verdure of lawn and meadow was streaked with a ranker freshness. We went forth without loss of time for a long walk on the hills. Reaching their summits, you find half England unrolled at your feet. A dozen broad counties, within the vast range of your vision, commingle their green exhalations. Closely beneath us lay the dark, rich flats of hedgy Worcestershire and the copse-chequered slopes of rolling Hereford, white with the blossom of apples. At widely opposite points of the large expanse two great cathedral towers rise sharply, taking the light, from the settled shadow of their circling towns, – the light, the ineffable English light! 'Out of England,' cried Searle, 'it's but a garish world!'

The whole vast sweep of our surrounding prospect lay answering in a myriad fleeting shades the cloudy process of the tremendous sky. The English heaven is a fit antithesis to the complex English earth. We possess in America the infinite beauty of the blue; England possesses the splendour of combined and animated clouds. Over against us, from our station on the hills, we saw them piled and dissolved, compacted and shifted, blotting the azure with sullen rain spots, stretching, breeze-fretted, into dappled fields of grey, bursting into a storm of light or melting into a drizzle of silver. We made our way along the rounded summits of these well-grazed heights, – mild, breezy inland downs, – and descended through long-drawn slopes of fields, green to cottage doors, to where a rural village beckoned us from its seat among the meadows. Close beside it, I admit, the railway shoots fiercely from its tunnel in the hills; and yet there broods upon this charming hamlet an old-time quietude and privacy, which seems to make it a violation of confidence to tell its name so far away. We struck through a narrow lane, a green lane, dim with its height of hedges; it led us to a superb old farm-house, now jostled by the multiplied lanes and roads which have curtailed its ancient appanage. It stands in stubborn picturesqueness, at the receipt of sad-eyed contemplation and the sufferance of 'sketches'. I doubt whether out of Nuremberg – or Pompeii! – you may find so forcible an image of the domiciliary genius of the past. It is cruelly complete; its bended beams and joists, beneath the burden of its gables, seem to ache and groan with memories and regrets. The short, low windows, where lead and glass combine in equal proportions to hint to the wondering stranger of the mediaeval gloom within, still prefer their darksome office to the grace of modern day. Such an old house fills an American with an indefinable feeling of respect. So propped and patched and tinkered with clumsy tenderness, clustered so richly about its central English sturdiness, its oaken vertebrations, so humanised with ages of use and touches of beneficent affection, it seemed to offer to our grateful eyes a small, rude synthesis of the great English social order. Passing out upon the high-road, we came to the common browsing-patch, the 'village green' of the tales of our youth. Nothing was wanting; the shaggy, mouse-coloured donkey, nosing the turf with his mild and huge proboscis, the geese, the old woman – *the* old woman, in person, with her red cloak and her black bonnet, frilled about the face and double-frilled beside her decent, placid cheeks, – the towering ploughman with his white smock-frock, puckered on chest and back, his short corduroys, his mighty calves, his big, red, rural face. We greeted these things as children greet the loved pictures in a story-book, lost and mourned and found again. It was marvellous how well we knew them. Beside the road we saw a ploughboy straddle, whistling, on a stile. Gainsborough might have painted him. Beyond the stile, across the level velvet of a meadow, a footpath lay, like a thread of darker woof. We followed it from field to field and from stile to stile. It was the way to church. At the church we finally arrived, lost in its rook-haunted churchyard, hidden from the work-day world by the broad stillness of pastures, – a grey, grey tower, a huge black yew, a cluster of village graves, with crooked headstones, in grassy, low relief. The whole scene was deeply ecclesiastical. My companion was overcome.

'You must bury me here,' he cried. 'It's the first church I have seen in my life. How it makes a Sunday where it stands!'

The next day we saw a church of statelier proportions. We walked over to Worcester, through such a mist of local colour, that I felt like one of Smollett's pedestrian heroes, faring tavern-ward for a night of adventures. As we neared the provincial city we saw the steepled mass of the cathedral, long and high, rise far into the cloud-freckled blue. And as we came nearer still, we stopped on the bridge and viewed the solid minster reflected in the yellow Severn. And going farther yet we entered the town, – where surely Miss Austen's heroines, in chariots and curricles, must often have come a shopping for swan's-down boas and high lace mittens; – we lounged about the gentle close and gased insatiably at that most soul-soothing sight, the waning, wasting afternoon light, the visible ether which feels the voices of the chimes, far aloft on the broad perpendicular field of the cathedral tower; saw it linger and nestle and abide, as it loves to do on all bold architectural spaces, converting them graciously into registers and witnesses of nature; tasted, too, as deeply of the peculiar stillness of this clerical precinct; saw a rosy English lad come forth and lock the door of the old foundation school, which marries its hoary basement to the soaring Gothic of the church, and carry his big responsible key into one of the quiet canonical houses; and then stood musing together on the effect on one's mind of having in one's boyhood haunted such cathedral shades as a King's scholar, and yet kept ruddy with much cricket in misty meadows by the Severn. On the third morning we betook ourselves to Lockley Park, having learned that the greater part of it was open to visitors, and that, indeed, on application, the house was occasionally shown.

Within its broad enclosure many a declining spur of the great hills melted into parklike slopes and dells. A long avenue wound and circled from the outermost gate through an untrimmed woodland, whence you glanced at further slopes and glades and copses and bosky recesses, – at everything except the limits of the place. It was as free and wild and untended as the villa of an Italian prince; and I have never seen the stern English fact of property put on such an air of innocence. The weather had just become perfect; it was one of the dozen exquisite days of the English year, – days stamped with a refinement of purity unknown in more liberal climes. It was as if the mellow brightness, as tender as that of the prim-roses which starred the dark waysides like petals wind-scattered over beds of moss, had been meted out to us by the cubic foot, – tempered, refined, recorded! From this external region we passed into the heart of the park, through a second lodge-gate, with weather-worn gilding on its twisted bars, to the smooth slopes where the great trees stood singly and the tame deer browsed along the bed of a woodland stream. Hence, before us, we perceived the dark Elizabethan manor among its blooming parterres and terraces.

'Here you can wander all day,' I said to Searle, 'like a proscribed and exiled prince, hovering about the dominion of the usurper.'

'To think,' he answered, 'of people having enjoyed this all these years! I know what I am, – what might I have been? What does all this make of you?'

'That it makes you happy,' I said, 'I should hesitate to believe. But it's hard to suppose that such a place has not some beneficent action of its own.'

'What a perfect scene and background it forms!' Searle went on. 'What legends, what histories it knows! My heart is break-ing with unutterable visions. There's Tennyson's Talking Oak. What summer days one could spend here! How I could lounge my bit of life away on this shady stretch of turf! Haven't I some maiden-cousin in yon moated grange who would give me kind leave?' And then turning almost fiercely upon me: 'Why did you bring me here? Why did you drag me into this torment of vain regrets?'

At this moment there passed near us a servant who had emerged from the gardens of the great house. I hailed him and inquired whether we should be likely to gain admittance. He answered that Mr Searle was away from home, and that he thought it probable the housekeeper would consent to do the honours of the mansion. I passed my arm into Searle's. 'Come,' I said. 'Drain the cup, bitter-sweet though it be. We shall go in.' We passed another lodge-gate and entered the gardens. The house was an admirable specimen of complete Elizabethan, a multitudinous cluster of gables and porches, oriels and turrets, screens of ivy and pinnacles of slate. Two broad terraces commanded the great wooded horizon of the adjacent domain. Our summons was answered by the butler in person, solemn and *tout de noir habillé*. He repeated the statement that Mr Searle was away from home, and that he would present our petition to the housekeeper. We would be so good, however, as to give him our cards. This request, following so directly on the assertion that Mr Searle was absent, seemed to my companion not distinctly pertinent. 'Surely not for the housekeeper,' he said.

The butler gave a deferential cough. 'Miss Searle is at home.'

'Yours alone will suffice,' said Searle. I took out a card and pencil, and wrote beneath my name, *New York*. Standing with the pencil in my hand I felt a sudden impulse. Without in the least weighing proprieties or results, I yielded to it. I added above my name, *Mr Clement Searle*. What would come of it?

Before many minutes the housekeeper attended us – a fresh rosy little old woman in a dowdy clean cap and a scanty calico gown; an exquisite specimen of refined and venerable servility. She had the accent of the country, but the manners of the house. Under her guidance we passed through a dozen apartments, duly stocked with old pictures, old tapestry, old carvings, old armour, with all the constituent properties of an English manor. The pictures were especially valuable. The two Vandykes, the trio of rosy Rubenses, the sole and sombre Rembrandt, glowed with conscious authenticity. A Claude, a Murillo, a Greuze, and a Gainsborough hung gracious in their chosen places. Searle strolled about silent, pale, and grave, with bloodshot eyes and lips compressed. He uttered no comment and asked no question. Missing him, at last, from my side,

I retraced my steps and found him in a room we had just left, on a tarnished silken divan, with his face buried in his hands. Before him, ranged on an antique buffet, was a magnificent collection of old Italian majolica; huge platters radiant with their steady colours, jugs and vases nobly bellied and embossed. There came to me, as I looked, a sudden vision of the young English gentleman, who, eighty years ago, had travelled by slow stages to Italy and been waited on at his inn by persuasive toymen. 'What is it, Searle?' I asked. 'Are you unwell?'

He uncovered his haggard face and showed a burning blush. Then smiling in hot irony: 'A memory of the past! I was thinking of a china vase that used to stand on the parlour mantel-shelf while I was a boy, with the portrait of General Jackson painted on one side and a bunch of flowers on the other. How long do you suppose that majolica has been in the family?'

'A long time probably. It was brought hither in the last century, into old, old England, out of old, old Italy, by some old young buck of this excellent house with a taste for *chinoiseries*. Here it has stood for a hundred years, keeping its clear, firm hues in this aristocratic twilight.'

Searle sprang to his feet. 'I say,' he cried, 'in heaven's name take me away! I can't stand this. Before I know it I shall do something I shall be ashamed of. I shall steal one of their d–d majolicas. I shall proclaim my identity and assert my rights! I shall go blubbering to Miss Searle and ask her in pity's name to keep me here for a month!'

If poor Searle could ever have been said to look 'dangerous', he looked so now. I began to regret my officious presentation of his name, and prepared without delay to lead him out of the house. We overtook the housekeeper in the last room of the suite, a small, unused boudoir, over the chimney-piece of which hung a noble portrait of a young man in a powdered wig and a brocaded waistcoat. I was immediately struck with his resemblance to my companion.

'This is Mr Clement Searle, Mr Searle's great-uncle, by Sir Joshua Reynolds,' quoth the housekeeper. 'He died young, poor gentleman. He perished at sea, going to America.'

'He's the young buck,' I said, 'who brought the majolica out of Italy.'

'Indeed, sir, I believe he did,' said the housekeeper, staring.

'He's the image of you, Searle,' I murmured.

'He's wonderfully like the gentleman, saving his presence,' said the housekeeper.

My friend stood gazing. 'Clement Searle – at sea – going to America – ' he muttered. Then harshly, to the housekeeper, 'Why the deuce did he go to America?'

'Why, indeed, sir? You may well ask. I believe he had kins-folk there. It was for them to come to him.'

Searle broke into a laugh. 'It was for them to have come to him! Well, well,' he said, fixing his eyes on the little old woman, 'they have come to him at last!'

She blushed like a wrinkled rose-leaf. 'Indeed, sir,' she said, 'I verily believe that you are one of *us*!'

'My name is the name of that lovely youth,' Searle went on. 'Kinsman, I salute you! Attend!' And he grasped me by the arm. 'I have an idea! He perished at sea. His spirit came ashore and wandered forlorn till it got lodgement again in my poor body. In my poor body it has lived, homesick, these forty years, shaking its rickety cage, urging me, stupid, to carry it back to the scenes of its youth. And I never knew what was the matter with me! Let me exhale my spirit here!'

The housekeeper essayed a timorous smile. The scene was embarrassing. My confusion was not allayed when I suddenly perceived in the doorway the figure of a lady. 'Miss Searle!' whispered the housekeeper. My first impression of Miss Searle was that she was neither young nor beautiful. She stood with a timid air on the threshold, pale, trying to smile, and twirling my card in her fingers. I immediately bowed. Searle, I think, gazed marvelling.

'If I am not mistaken,' said the lady, 'one of you gentlemen is Mr Clement Searle.'

'My friend is Mr Clement Searle,' I replied. 'Allow me to add that I alone am responsible for your having received his name.'

'I should have been sorry not to receive it,' said Miss Searle, beginning to blush. 'Your being from America has led me to – to interrupt you.'

'The interruption, madam, has been on our part. And with just that excuse, – that we are from America.'

Miss Searle, while I spoke, had fixed her eyes on my friend, as he stood silent beneath Sir Joshua's portrait. The house-keeper, amazed and mystified, took a liberty. 'Heaven preserve us, Miss! It's your great-uncle's picture come to life.'

'I'm not mistaken, then,' said Miss Searle. 'We are distantly related.' She had the aspect of an extremely modest woman. She was evidently embarrassed at having to proceed unassisted in her overture. Searle eyed her with gentle wonder from head to foot. I fancied I read his thoughts. This, then, was Miss Searle, his maiden-cousin, prospective heiress of these manor-ial acres and treasures. She was a person of about thirty-three years of age, taller than most women, with health and strength in the rounded amplitude of her shape. She had a small blue eye, a massive chignon of yellow hair, and a mouth at once broad and comely. She was dressed in a lustreless black satin gown, with a short train. Around her neck she wore a blue silk handkerchief, and over this handkerchief, in many con-volutions, a string of amber beads. Her appearance was singu-lar; she was large, yet not imposing; girlish, yet mature. Her glance and accent, in addressing us, were simple, too simple. Searle, I think, had been fancying some proud cold beauty of five-and-twenty; he was relieved at finding the lady timid and plain. His person was suddenly illumined with an old disused gallantry.

'We are distant cousins, I believe. I am happy to claim a relationship which you are so good as to remember. I had not in the least counted on your doing so.'

'Perhaps I have done wrong,' and Miss Searle blushed anew and smiled. 'But I have always known of there being people of our blood in America, and I have often wondered and asked about them; without learning much, however. To-day, when this card was brought me and I knew of a Clement Searle wandering about the house like a stranger, I felt as if I ought to do something. I hardly knew what! My brother is in London. I have done what I think he would have done. Welcome, as a cousin.' And with a gesture at once frank and shy, she put out her hand.

'I'm welcome indeed,' said Searle, taking it, 'if he would have done it half as graciously.'

'You've seen the show,' Miss Searle went on. 'Perhaps now you'll have some lunch.' We followed her into a small breakfast-room, where a deep bay-window opened on the mossy flags of the great terrace. Here, for some moments, she remained silent and shy, in the manner of a person resting from a great effort. Searle, too, was formal and reticent, so that I had to busy myself with providing small-talk. It was of course easy to descant on the beauties of park and mansion. Meanwhile I observed our hostess. She had small beauty and scanty grace; her dress was out of taste and out of season; yet she pleased me well. There was about her a sturdy sweetness, a homely flavour of the sequestered *châtelaine* of feudal days. To be so simple amid this massive luxury, so mellow and yet so fresh, so modest and yet so placid, told of just the spacious leisure in which I had fancied human life to be steeped in many a park-circled home. Miss Searle was to the Belle au Bois Dormant what a fact is to a fairy-tale, an interpretation to a myth. We, on our side, were to our hostess objects of no light scrutiny. The best possible English breeding still marvels visibly at the native American. Miss Searle's wonderment was guileless enough to have been more overt and yet inoffensive; there was no taint of offence indeed in her utterance of the unvarying amenity that she had met an American family on the Lake of Como whom she would have almost taken to be English.

'If I lived here,' I said, 'I think I should hardly need to go away, even to the Lake of Como.'

'You might perhaps get tired of it. And then the Lake of Como! If I could only go abroad again!'

'You have been but once?'

'Only once. Three years ago my brother took me to Switzerland. We thought it extremely beautiful. Except for this journey, I have always lived here. Here I was born. It's a dear old place, indeed, and I know it well. Sometimes I fancy I'm a little tired.' And on my asking her how she spent her time and what society she saw, 'It's extremely quiet,' she went on, proceeding by short steps and simple statements, in the manner of a person summoned for the first time to define her situation and enumerate the elements of her life. 'We see very few people. I don't think there are many nice people hereabouts. At least we don't know them. Our own family is very small. My brother cares for little else but riding and books. He had a great sorrow ten years ago. He lost his wife and his only son, a dear little boy, who would have succeeded him in the estates. Do you know that I'm likely to have them now? Poor me! Since his loss my brother has preferred to be quite alone. I'm sorry he's away. But you must wait till he comes back. I expect him in a day or two.' She talked more and more, with a rambling, earnest vapidity, about her circumstances, her solitude, her bad eyes, so that she couldn't read, her flowers, her ferns, her dogs, and the curate, recently inducted by her brother and warranted sound orthodox, who had lately begun to light his altar candles; pausing every now and then to blush in self-surprise, and yet moving steadily from point to point in the deepening excitement of temptation and occasion. Of all the old things I had seen in England, this mind of Miss Searle's seemed to me the oldest, the quaintest, the most ripely verdant; so fenced and protected by convention and precedent and usage; so passive and mild and docile. I felt as if I were talking with a potential heroine of Miss Burney. As she talked, she rested her dull, kind eyes upon her kinsman with a sort of fascinated stare. At last, 'Did you mean to go away,' she demanded, 'without asking for us?'

'I had thought it over, Miss Searle, and had determined not to trouble you. You have shown me how unfriendly I should have been.'

'But you knew of the place being ours and of our relationship?'

'Just so. It was because of these things that I came down here – because of them, almost, that I came to England. I have always liked to think of them.'

'You merely wished to look, then? We don't pretend to be much to look at.'

'You don't know what you are, Miss Searle,' said my friend, gravely.

'You like the old place, then?'

Searle looked at her in silence. 'If I could only tell you,' he said at last.

'Do tell me! You must come and stay with us.'

Searle began to laugh. 'Take care, take care,' he cried. 'I should surprise you. At least I should bore you. I should never leave you.'

'O, you'd get homesick for America!'

At this Searle laughed the more. 'By the way,' he cried to me, 'tell Miss Searle about America!' And he stepped through the window out upon the terrace, followed by two beautiful dogs, a pointer and a young stag-hound, who from the moment we came in had established the fondest relation with him. Miss Searle looked at him as he went, with a certain tender wonder in her eye. I read in her glance, methought, that she was interested. I suddenly recalled the last words I had heard spoken by my friend's adviser in London: 'Instead of dying you'd better marry.' If Miss Searle could be gently manipulated. O for a certain divine tact! Something assured me that her heart was virgin soil; that sentiment had never bloomed there. If I could but sow the seed! There lurked within her the perfect image of one of the patient wives of old.

'He has lost his heart to England,' I said. 'He ought to have been born here.'

'And yet,' said Miss Searle, 'he's not in the least an Englishman.'

'How do you know that?'

'I hardly know how. I never talked with a foreigner before; but he looks and talks as I have fancied foreigners.'

'Yes, he's foreign enough!'

'Is he married?'

'He's a widower, – without children.'

'Has he property?'

'Very little.'

'But enough to travel?'

I meditated. 'He has not expected to travel far,' I said at last. 'You know he's in poor health.'

'Poor gentleman! So I fancied.'

'He's better, though, than he thinks. He came here because he wanted to see your place before he dies.'

'Poor fellow!' And I fancied I perceived in her eye the lustre of a rising tear. 'And he was going off without my seeing him?'

'He's a modest man, you see.'

'He's very much of a gentleman.'

'Assuredly!'

At this moment we heard on the terrace a loud, harsh cry. 'It's the great peacock!' said Miss Searle, stepping to the window and passing out. I followed her. Below us on the terrace, leaning on the parapet, stood our friend, with his arm round the neck of the pointer. Before him, on the grand walk, strutted a splendid peacock, with ruffled neck and expanded tail. The other dog had apparently indulged in a momentary attempt to abash the gorgeous fowl; but at Searle's voice he had bounded back to the terrace and leaped upon the parapet, where he now stood licking his new friend's face. The scene had a beautiful old-time air; the peacock flaunting in the foreground, like the very genius of antique gardenry; the broad terrace, which flattered an innate taste of mine for all deserted promenades to which people may have adjourned from formal dinners, to drink coffee in old Sèvres, and where the stiff brocade of women's dresses may have rustled autumnal leaves; and far around us, with one leafy circle melting into another, the timbered acres of the park. 'The very beasts have made him welcome,' I said, as we rejoined our companion.

'The peacock has done for you, Mr Searle,' said his cousin, 'what he does only for very great people. A year ago there came here a duchess to see my brother. I don't think that since then he has spread his tail as wide for any one else by a dozen feathers.'

'It's not alone the peacock,' said Searle. 'Just now there came slipping across my path a little green lizard, the first

I ever saw, the lizard of literature! And if you have a ghost, broad daylight though it be, I expect to see him here. Do you know the annals of your house, Miss Searle?'

'O dear, no! You must ask my brother for all those things.'

'You ought to have a book full of legends and traditions. You ought to have loves and murders and mysteries by the roomful. I count upon it.'

'O Mr Searle! We have always been a very well-behaved family. Nothing out of the way has ever happened, I think.'

'Nothing out of the way? O horrors! We have done better than that in America. Why, I myself!' – and he gazed at her a moment with a gleam of malice, and then broke into a laugh. 'Suppose I should turn out a better Searle than you? Better than you, nursed here in romance and picturesqueness. Come, don't disappoint me. You have some history among you all, you have some poetry. I have been famished all my days for these things. Do you understand? Ah, you can't understand! Tell me something! When I think of what must have happened here! when I think of the lovers who must have strolled on this terrace and wandered through those glades! of all the figures and passions and purposes that must have haunted these walls! of the births and deaths, the joys and sufferings, the young hopes and the old regrets, the intense experience –' And here he faltered a moment, with the increase of his vehemence. The gleam in his eye, which I have called a gleam of malice, had settled into a deep unnatural light. I began to fear he had become over-excited. But he went on with redoubled passion. 'To see it all evoked before me,' he cried, 'if the Devil alone could do it, I'd make a bargain with the Devil! O Miss Searle, I'm a most unhappy man!'

'O dear, O dear!' said Miss Searle.

'Look at that window, that blessed oriel!' And he pointed to a small, protruding casement above us, relieved against the purple brick-work, framed in chiselled stone, and curtained with ivy.

'It's my room,' said Miss Searle.

'Of course it's a woman's room. Think of the forgotten loveliness which has peeped from that window; think of the old-time women's lives which have known chiefly that outlook on this bosky world. O gentle cousins! And you, Miss Searle, you're one of them yet.' And he marched towards her and took her great white hand. She surrendered it, blushing to her eyes, and pressing her other hand to her breast. 'You're a woman of the past. You're nobly simple. It has been a romance to see you. It doesn't matter what I say to you. You didn't know me yesterday, you'll not know me to-morrow. Let me to-day do a mad, sweet thing. Let me fancy you the soul of all the dead women who have trod these terrace-flags, which lie here like sepulchral tablets in the pavement of a church. Let me say I worship you!' And he raised her hand to his lips. She gently withdrew it, and for a moment averted her face. Meeting her eyes the next moment, I saw that they were filled with tears. The Belle au Bois Dormant was awake.

There followed an embarrassed pause. An issue was suddenly presented by the appearance of the butler bearing a letter. 'A telegram, Miss,' he said.

'Dear me!' cried Miss Searle, 'I can't open a telegram. Cousin, help me.'

Searle took the missive, opened it, and read aloud: '*I shall be home to dinner. Keep the American.*'

II

'KEEP the American!' Miss Searle, in compliance with the injunction conveyed in her brother's telegram (with something certainly of telegraphic curtness), lost no time in expressing the pleasure it would give her to have my companion remain. 'Really you must,' she said; and forthwith repaired to the housekeeper, to give orders for the preparation of a room.

'How in the world,' asked Searle, 'did he know of my being here?'

'He learned, probably,' I expounded, 'from his solicitor of the visit of your friend Simmons. Simmons and the solicitor must have had another interview since your arrival in England. Simmons, for reasons of his own, has communicated to the solicitor your journey to this neighbourhood, and

Mr Searle, learning this, has immediately taken for granted that you have formally presented yourself to his sister. He's hospitably inclined, and he wishes her to do the proper thing by you. More, perhaps! I have my little theory that he is the very Phœnix of usurpers, that his nobler sense has been captivated by the exposition of the men of law, and that he means gracefully to surrender you your fractional interest in the estate.'

'I give it up!' said my friend, musing. 'Come what come will!'

'You of course,' said Miss Searle, reappearing and turning to me, 'are included in my brother's invitation. I have bespoken your lodging as well. Your luggage shall immediately be sent for.'

It was arranged that I in person should be driven over to our little inn, and that I should return with our effects in time to meet Mr Searle at dinner. On my arrival, several hours later, I was immediately conducted to my room. The servant pointed out to me that it communicated by a door and a private passage with that of my companion. I made my way along this passage, – a low, narrow corridor, with a long latticed casement, through which there streamed, upon a series of grotesquely sculptured oaken closets and cupboards, the lurid animating glow of the western sun, – knocked at his door, and, getting no answer, opened it. In an arm-chair by the open window sat my friend, sleeping, with arms and legs relaxed and head placidly reverted. It was a great relief to find him resting from his rhapsodies, and I watched him for some moments before waking him. There was a faint glow of colour in his cheek and a light parting of his lips, as in a smile; something nearer to mental soundness than I had yet seen in him. It was almost happiness, it was almost health. I laid my hand on his arm and gently shook it. He opened his eyes, gazed at me a moment, vaguely recognised me, then closed them again. 'Let me dream, let me dream!' he said.

'What are you dreaming about?'

A moment passed before his answer came. 'About a tall woman in a quaint black dress, with yellow hair, and a sweet,

sweet smile, and a soft, low, delicious voice! I'm in love with her.'

'It's better to see her,' I said, 'than to dream about her. Get up and dress, and we shall go down to dinner and meet her.'

'Dinner – dinner –' And he gradually opened his eyes again. 'Yes, upon my word, I shall dine!'

'You're a well man!' I said, as he rose to his feet. 'You'll live to bury Mr Simmons.' He had spent the hours of my absence, he told me, with Miss Searle. They had strolled together over the park and through the gardens and greenhouses. 'You must already be intimate!' I said, smiling.

'She is intimate with me,' he answered. 'Heaven knows what rigmarole I've treated her to!' They had parted an hour ago, since when, he believed, her brother had arrived.

The slow-fading twilight still abode in the great drawing-room as we entered it. The housekeeper had told us that this apartment was rarely used, there being a smaller and more convenient one for the same needs. It seemed now, however, to be occupied in my comrade's honour. At the farther end of it, rising to the roof, like a ducal tomb in a cathedral, was a great chimney-piece of chiselled white marble, yellowed by time, in which a light fire was crackling. Before the fire stood a small short man with his hands behind him; near him stood Miss Searle, so transformed by her dress that at first I scarcely knew her. There was in our entrance and reception something profoundly chilling and solemn. We moved in silence up the long room. Mr Searle advanced slowly a dozen steps to meet us. His sister stood motionless. I was conscious of her masking her visage with a large white tinselled fan, and of her eyes, grave and expanded, watching us intently over the top of it. The master of Lockley Park grasped in silence the proffered hand of his kinsman, and eyed him from head to foot, suppressing, I think, a start of surprise at his resemblance to Sir Joshua's portrait. 'This is a happy day!' he said. And then turning to me with a bow, 'My cousin's friend is my friend.' Miss Searle lowered her fan.

The first thing that struck me in Mr Searle's appearance was his short and meagre stature, which was less by half a head than that of his sister. The second was the preternatural redness of his hair and beard. They intermingled over his ears and surrounded his head like a huge lurid nimbus. His face was pale and attenuated, like the face of a scholar, a dilettante, a man who lives in a library, bending over books and prints and medals. At a distance it had an oddly innocent and youthful look; but on a nearer view it revealed a number of finely etched and scratched wrinkles, of a singularly aged and cunning effect. It was the complexion of a man of sixty. His nose was arched and delicate, identical almost with the nose of my friend. In harmony with the effect of his hair was that of his eyes, which were large and deep-set, with a sort of vulpine keenness and redness, but full of temper and spirit. Imagine this physiognomy – grave and solemn in aspect, grotesquely solemn, almost, in spite of the bushy brightness in which it was encased – set in motion by a smile which seemed to whisper terribly, 'I am *the* smile, the sole and official, the grin to command,' and you will have an imperfect notion of the remarkable presence of our host; something better worth seeing and knowing, I fancied as I covertly scrutinised him, than anything our excursion had yet introduced us to. Of how thoroughly I had entered into sympathy with my companion and how effectually I had associated my sensibilities with his, I had small suspicion until, within the short five minutes which preceded the announcement of dinner, I distinctly perceived him place himself, morally speaking, on the defensive. To neither of us was Mr Searle, as the Italians would say, sympathetic. I might have fancied from her attitude that Miss Searle apprehended our thoughts. A signal change had been wrought in her since the morning; during the hour, indeed (as I read in the light of the wondering glance he cast at her), that had elapsed since her parting with her cousin. She had not yet recovered from some great agitation. Her face was pale and her eyes red with weeping. These tragic betrayals gave an unexpected dignity to her aspect, which was further enhanced by the rare picturesqueness of her dress.

Whether it was taste or whether it was accident, I know not; but Miss Searle, as she stood there, half in the cool twilight, half

in the arrested glow of the fire as it spent itself in the vastness of
its marble cave, was a figure for a cunning painter. She was
dressed in the faded splendour of a beautiful tissue of combined
and blended silk and crape of a tender sea-green colour, festooned and garnished and puffed into a massive *bouillonnement*;
a piece of millinery which, though it must have witnessed a
number of stately dinners, preserved still an air of admirable
elegance. Over her white shoulders she wore an ancient web of
the most precious and venerable lace, and about her rounded
throat a necklace of heavy pearls. I went with her in to dinner,
and Mr Searle, following with my friend, took his arm (as the
latter afterwards told me) and pretended sportively to conduct
him. As dinner proceeded, the feeling grew within me that a
drama had begun to be played in which the three persons
before me were actors, each of a most exacting part. The part
of my friend, however, seemed the most heavily charged, and
I was filled with a strong desire that he should acquit himself
with honour. I seemed to see him summon his shadowy faculties to obey his shadowy will. The poor fellow sat playing
solemnly at self-esteem. With Miss Searle, credulous, passive,
and pitying, he had finally flung aside all vanity and propriety,
and shown her the bottom of his fantastic heart. But with our
host there might be no talking of nonsense nor taking of liberties; there and then, if ever, sat a double-distilled conservative,
breathing the fumes of hereditary privilege and security. For an
hour, then, I saw my poor friend turn faithfully about to speak
graciously of barren things. He was to prove himself a sound
American, so that his relish of this elder world might seem
purely disinterested. What his kinsman had expected to find
him, I know not; but, with all his finely adjusted urbanity, he
was unable to repress a shade of annoyance at finding him likely
to speak graciously at all. Mr Searle was not the man to show his
hand, but I think his best card had been a certain implicit
confidence that this exotic parasite would hardly have good
manners. Our host, with great decency, led the conversation to
America, talking of it rather as if it were some fabled planet,
alien to the British orbit, lately proclaimed indeed to have the
proportion of atmospheric gases required to support animal

life, but not, save under cover of a liberal afterthought, to be admitted into one's regular conception of things. I, for my part, felt nothing but regret that the spheric smoothness of his universe should be strained to cracking by the intrusion of our square shoulders.

'I knew in a general way,' said Mr Searle, 'of my having relations in America; but you know one hardly realises those things. I could hardly more have imagined people of our blood there, than I could have imagined being there myself. There was a man I knew at college, a very odd fellow, a nice fellow too; he and I were rather cronies; I think he afterwards went to America; to the Argentine Republic, I believe. Do you know the Argentine Republic? What an extraordinary name, by the way! And then, you know, there was that great-uncle of mine whom Sir Joshua painted. He went to America, but he never got there. He was lost at sea. You look enough like him to have one fancy he *did* get there, and that he has lived along till now. If you are he, you've not done a wise thing to show yourself here. He left a bad name behind him. There's a ghost who comes sobbing about the house every now and then, the ghost of one against whom he wrought a great evil!'

'O brother!' cried Miss Searle, in simple horror.

'Of course you know nothing of such things,' said Mr Searle. 'You're too sound a sleeper to hear the sobbing of ghosts.'

'I'm sure I should like immensely to hear the sobbing of a ghost!' said my friend, with the light of his previous eagerness playing up into his eyes. 'Why does it sob? Unfold the wondrous tale.'

Mr Searle eyed his audience for a moment gaugingly; and then, as the French say, *se recueillit*, as if he were measuring his own imaginative force.

He wished to do justice to his theme. With the five fingernails of his left hand nervously playing against the tinkling crystal of his wineglass, and his bright eye telling of a gleeful sense that, small and grotesque as he sat there, he was for the moment profoundly impressive, he distilled into our untutored minds the sombre legend of his house. 'Mr Clement Searle, from all I gather, was a young man of great talents but a weak disposition. His mother was left a widow early in life, with two sons, of whom he was the older and the more promising. She educated him with the utmost fondness and care. Of course, when he came to manhood she wished him to marry well. His means were quite sufficient to enable him to overlook the want of means in his wife; and Mrs Searle selected a young lady who possessed, as she conceived, every good gift save a fortune, – a fine, proud, handsome girl, the daughter of an old friend, – an old lover, I fancy, of her own. Clement, however, as it appeared, had either chosen otherwise or was as yet unprepared to choose. The young lady discharged upon him in vain the battery of her attractions; in vain his mother urged her cause. Clement remained cold, insensible, inflexible. Mrs Searle possessed a native force of which in its feminine branch the family seems to have lost trick. A proud, passionate, imperious woman, she had had great cares and a number of lawsuits; they had given her a great will. She suspected that her son's affections were lodged elsewhere, and lodged amiss. Irritated by his stubborn defiance of her wishes, she persisted in her urgency. The more she watched him the more she believed that he loved in secret. If he loved in secret, of course he loved beneath him. He went about sombre, sullen, and preoccupied. At last, with the fatal indiscretion of an angry woman, she threatened to bring the young lady of her choice – who, by the way, seems to have been no shrinking blossom – to stay in the house. A stormy scene was the result. He threatened that if she did so, he would leave the country and sail for America. She probably disbelieved him; she knew him to be weak, but she overrated his weakness. At all events, the fair rejected arrived and Clement departed. On a dark December day he took ship at Southampton. The two women, desperate with rage and sorrow, sat alone in this great house, mingling their tears and imprecations. A fortnight later, on Christmas eve, in the midst of a great snow-storm, long famous in the country, there came to them a mighty quickening of their bitterness. A young woman, soaked and chilled by the storm, gained entrance to the house and made her way into the presence of the mistress and her guest. She poured out her tale. She was a poor curate's daughter of Hereford. Clement Searle had loved her; loved her all too well. She had been turned out in wrath from her father's house; his mother, at least, might pity her; if not for herself, then for the child she was soon to bring forth. The poor girl had been a second time too trustful. The women, in scorn, in horror, with blows, possibly, turned her forth again into the storm. In the storm she wandered, and in the deep snow she died. Her lover, as you know, perished in that hard winter weather at sea; the news came to his mother late, but soon enough. We are haunted by the curate's daughter!'

There was a pause of some moments. 'Ah, well we may be!' said Miss Searle, with great pity.

Searle blazed up into enthusiasm. 'Of course you know,' – and suddenly he began to blush violently, – 'I should be sorry to claim any identity with my faithless namesake, poor fellow. But I shall be hugely tickled if this poor ghost should be deceived by my resemblance and mistake me for her cruel lover. She's welcome to the comfort of it. What one can do in the case I shall be glad to do. But can a ghost haunt a ghost? I *am* a ghost!'

Mr Searle stared a moment, and then smiling superbly: 'I could almost believe you are!' he said.

'Oh brother – cousin!' cried Miss Searle, with the gentlest, yet most appealing dignity, 'how can you talk so horribly?'

This horrible talk, however, evidently possessed a potent magic for my friend; and his imagination, chilled for a while by the frigid contact of his kinsman, began to glow again with its earlier fire. From this moment he ceased to steer his cockle-shell, to care what he said or how he said it, so long as he expressed his passionate satisfaction in the scene about him. As he talked I ceased even mentally to protest. I have wondered since that I should not have resented the exhibition of so rank and florid an egotism. But a great frankness for the time makes its own law, and a great passion its own channel. There was, moreover, an immense sweetness in the manner of my friend's speech. Free alike from either adulation or envy, the very soul of it was a divine apprehension, an imaginative mastery, free as the flight of Ariel, of the poetry of his companions' situation and of the contrasted prosiness of their attitude.

'How does the look of age come?' he demanded, at dessert. 'Does it come of itself, unobserved, unrecorded, unmeasured? Or do you woo it and set baits and traps for it, and watch it like the dawning brownness of a meerschaum pipe, and nail it down when it appears, just where it peeps out, and light a votive taper beneath it and give thanks to it daily? Or do you forbid it and fight it and resist it, and yet feel it settling and deepening about you, as irresistible as fate?'

'What the deuce is the man talking about?' said the smile of our host.

'I found a grey hair this morning,' said Miss Searle.

'Good heavens! I hope you respected it,' cried Searle.

'I looked at it for a long time in my little glass,' said his cousin, simply.

'Miss Searle, for many years to come, can afford to be amused at grey hairs,' I said.

'Ten years hence I shall be forty-three,' she answered.

'That's my age,' said Searle. 'If I had only come here ten years ago! I should have had more time to enjoy the feast, but I should have had less of an appetite. I needed to get famished for it.'

'Why did you wait for the starving point?' asked Mr Searle. 'To think of these ten years that we might have been enjoying you!' And at the thought of these wasted ten years Mr Searle broke into a violent nervous laugh.

'I always had a notion, – a stupid, vulgar notion, if there ever was one, – that to come abroad properly one ought to have a pot of money. My pot was too nearly empty. At last I came with my empty pot!'

Mr Searle coughed with an air of hesitation. 'You're a – you're in limited circumstances?'

My friend apparently was vastly tickled to have his bleak situation called by so soft a name. 'Limited circumstances!' he cried with a long, light laugh; 'I'm in no circumstances at all!'

'Upon my word!' murmured Mr Searle, with an air of being divided between his sense of the indecency and his sense of the rarity of a gentleman taking just that tone about his affairs. 'Well – well – well!' he added, in a voice which might have meant everything or nothing; and proceeded, with a twinkle in his eye, to finish a glass of wine. His sparkling eye, as he drank, encountered mine over the top of his glass, and, for a moment, we exchanged a long deep glance, – a glance so keen as to leave a slight embarrassment on the face of each. 'And you,' said Mr Searle, by way of carrying it off, 'how about your circumstances?'

'O, his,' said my friend, 'his are unlimited! He could buy up Lockley Park!' He had drunk, I think, a rather greater number of glasses of port – I admit that the port was infinitely drinkable – than was to have been desired in the interest of perfect self-control. He was rapidly drifting beyond any tacit dissuasion of mine. A certain feverish harshness in his glance and voice warned me that to attempt to direct him would simply irritate him. As we rose from the table he caught my troubled look. Passing his arm for a moment into mine, 'This is the great night!' he whispered. 'The night of fatality, the night of destiny!'

Mr Searle had caused the whole lower region of the house to be thrown open and a multitude of lights to be placed in convenient and effective positions. Such a marshalled wealth of ancient candlesticks and flambeaux I had never beheld. Niched against the dark panellings, casting great luminous circles upon the pendent stiffness of sombre tapestries, enhancing and completing with admirable effect the vastness and mystery of the ancient house, they seemed to people the great rooms, as our little group passed slowly from one to another, with a dim, expectant presence. We had a delightful hour of it. Mr Searle at once assumed the part of cicerone, and – I had not hitherto done him justice – Mr Searle became agreeable. While I lingered behind with Miss Searle, he walked in advance with his kinsman. It was as if he had said, 'Well, if you want the old place, you shall have it – metaphysically!' To speak vulgarly, he rubbed it in. Carrying a great silver candlestick in his left hand, he raised it and lowered it and cast the light hither and thither, upon pictures and hangings and bits of carving and a hundred lurking architectural treasures. Mr Searle knew his house. He hinted at innumerable traditions and memories, and evoked with a very pretty wit the figures of its earlier occupants. He told a dozen anecdotes with an almost reverential gravity and neatness. His companion attended, with a sort of brooding intelligence. Miss Searle and I, meanwhile, were not wholly silent.

'I suppose that by this time,' I said, 'you and your cousin are almost old friends.'

She trifled a moment with her fan, and then raising her homely candid gaze: 'Old friends, and at the same time strangely new! My cousin, – my cousin,' – and her voice lingered on the word, – 'it seems so strange to call him my cousin, after thinking these many years that I had no cousin! He's a most singular man.'

'It's not so much he as his circumstances that are singular,' I ventured to say.

'I'm so sorry for his circumstances. I wish I could help him in some way. He interests me so much.' And here Miss Searle gave a rich, mellow sigh. 'I wish I had known him a long time ago. He told me that he is but the shadow of what he was.'

I wondered whether Searle had been consciously playing upon the fancy of this gentle creature. If he had, I believed he had gained his point. But in fact, his position had become to my sense so charged with opposing forces, that I hardly ventured wholly to rejoice. 'His better self just now,' I said, 'seems again to be taking shape. It will have been a good deed on your part, Miss Searle, if you help to restore him to soundness and serenity.'

'Ah, what can I do?'

'Be a friend to him. Let him like you, let him love you! You see in him now, doubtless, much to pity and to wonder at. But let him simply enjoy awhile the grateful sense of your nearness and dearness. He will be a better and stronger man for it, and then you can love him, you can respect him without restriction.'

Miss Searle listened with a puzzled tenderness of gaze. 'It's a hard part for poor me to play!'

Her almost infantine gentleness left me no choice but to be absolutely frank. 'Did you ever play any part at all?' I asked.

Her eyes met mine, wonderingly; she blushed, as with a sudden sense of my meaning. 'Never! I think I have hardly lived.'

'You've begun now, perhaps. You have begun to care for something outside the narrow circle of habit and duty. (Excuse me if I am rather too outspoken: you know I'm a foreigner.) It's a great moment: I wish you joy!'

'I could almost fancy you are laughing at me. I feel more trouble than joy.'

'Why do you feel trouble?'

She paused, with her eyes fixed on our two companions. 'My cousin's arrival,' she said at last, 'is a great disturbance.'

'You mean that you did wrong in recognising him? In that case the fault is mine. He had no intention of giving you the opportunity.'

'I did wrong, after a fashion! But I can't find it in my heart to regret it. I never shall regret it! I did what I thought proper. Heaven forgive me!'

'Heaven bless you, Miss Searle! Is any harm to come of it? I did the evil; let me bear the brunt!'

She shook her head gravely. 'You don't know my brother!'

'The sooner I do know him, then, the better!' And hereupon I felt a dull irritation which had been gathering force for more than an hour explode into sudden wrath. 'What on earth *is* your brother?' I demanded. She turned away. 'Are you afraid of him?' I asked.

She gave me a tearful sidelong glance. 'He's looking at me!' she murmured.

I looked at him. He was standing with his back to us, holding a large Venetian hand-mirror, framed in rococo silver, which he had taken from a shelf of antiquities, in just such a position that he caught the reflection of his sister's person. Shall I confess it? Something in this performance so tickled my sense of the picturesque, that it was with a sort of blunted anger that I muttered, 'The sneak!' Yet I felt passion enough to urge me forward. It seemed to me that by implication I, too, was being covertly watched. I should not be watched for nothing! 'Miss Searle,' I said, insisting upon her attention, 'promise me something.'

She turned upon me with a start and the glance of one appealing from some great pain. 'O, don't ask me!' she cried. It was as if she were standing on the verge of some sudden lapse of familiar ground and had been summoned to make a leap. I felt that retreat was impossible, and that it was the greater kindness to beckon her forward.

'Promise me,' I repeated.

Still with her eyes she protested. 'O, dreadful day!' she cried, at last.

'Promise me to let him speak to you, if he should ask you, any wish you may suspect on your brother's part notwithstanding.'

She coloured deeply. 'You mean,' she said, – 'you mean that he – has something particular to say.'

'Something most particular!'

'Poor cousin!'

I gave her a deeply questioning look. 'Well, poor cousin! But promise me.'

'I promise,' she said, and moved away across the long room and out of the door.

'You're in time to hear the most delightful story!' said my friend, as I rejoined the two gentlemen. They were standing before an old sombre portrait of a lady in the dress of Queen Anne's time, with her ill-painted flesh-tints showing livid in the candlelight against her dark drapery and background. 'This is Mistress Margaret Searle, – a sort of Beatrix Esmond, – who did as she pleased. She married a paltry Frenchman, a penniless fiddler, in the teeth of her whole family. Fair Margaret, my compliments! Upon my soul, she looks like Miss Searle! Pray go on. What came of it all?'

Mr Searle looked at his kinsman for a moment with an air of distaste for his boisterous homage, and of pity for his crude imagination. Then resuming, with a very effective dryness of tone: 'I found a year ago, in a box of very old papers, a letter from Mistress Margaret to Cynthia Searle, her elder sister. It was dated from Paris and dreadfully ill-spelled. It contained a most passionate appeal for – a – for pecuniary assistance. She had just been confined, she was starving, and neglected by her husband; she cursed the day she left England. It was a most dismal effusion. I never heard that she found means to return.'

'So much for marrying a Frenchman!' I said, sententiously.

Mr Searle was silent for some moments. 'This was the first,' he said finally, 'and the last of the family who has been so d–d un-English!'

'Does Miss Searle know her history?' asked my friend, staring at the rounded whiteness of the lady's heavy cheek.

'Miss Searle knows nothing!' said our host, with zeal.

This utterance seemed to kindle in my friend a generous opposing zeal. 'She shall know at least the tale of Mistress Margaret,' he cried, and walked rapidly away in search of her.

Mr Searle and I pursued our march through the lighted rooms. 'You've found a cousin,' I said, 'with a vengeance.'

'Ah, a vengeance?' said my host, stiffly.

'I mean that he takes as keen an interest in your annals and possessions as yourself.'

'O, exactly so!' and Mr Searle burst into resounding laughter. 'He tells me,' he resumed, in a moment, 'that he is an invalid. I should never have fancied it.'

'Within the past few hours,' I said, 'he's a changed man. Your place and your kindness have refreshed him immensely.'

Mr Searle uttered the little shapeless ejaculation with which many an Englishman is apt to announce the concussion of any especial courtesy of speech. He bent his eyes on the floor frowningly, and then, to my surprise, he suddenly stopped and looked at me with a penetrating eye. 'I'm an honest man!' he said. I was quite prepared to assent; but he went on, with a sort of fury of frankness, as if it was the first time in his life that he had been prompted to expound himself, as if the process was mightily unpleasant to him and he was hurrying through it as a task. 'An honest man, mind you! I know nothing about Mr Clement Searle! I never expected to see him. He has been to me a – a –' And here Mr Searle paused to select a word which should vividly enough express what, for good or for ill, his kinsman had been to him. 'He has been to me an *amazement*! I have no doubt he is a most amiable man! You'll not deny, however, that he's a very odd style of person. I'm sorry he's ill!

I'm sorry he's poor! He's my fiftieth cousin! Well and good! I'm an honest man. He shall not have it to say that he was not received at my house.'

'He, too, thank heaven! is an honest man!' I said, smiling.

'Why the deuce, then,' cried Mr Searle, turning almost fiercely upon me, 'has he established this underhand claim to my property?'

This startling utterance flashed backward a gleam of light upon the demeanour of our host and the suppressed agitation of his sister. In an instant the jealous soul of the unhappy gentleman revealed itself. For a moment I was so amazed and scandalised at the directness of his attack that I lacked words to respond. As soon as he had spoken, Mr Searle appeared to feel that he had struck too hard a blow. 'Excuse me, sir,' he hurried on, 'if I speak of this matter with heat. But I have seldom suffered so grievous a shock as on learning, as I learned this morning from my solicitor, the monstrous proceedings of Mr Clement Searle. Great heaven, sir, for what does the man take me? He pretends to the Lord knows what fantastic passion for my place. Let him respect it, then. Let him, with his tawdry parade of imagination, imagine a tithe of what I feel. I love my estate; it's my passion, my life, myself! Am I to make a great hole in it for a beggarly foreigner, a man without means, without proof, a stranger, an adventurer, a Bohemian? I thought America boasted that she had land for all men! Upon my soul, sir, I have never been so shocked in my life.'

I paused for some moments before speaking, to allow his passion fully to expend itself and to flicker up again if it chose; for on my own part it seemed well that I should answer him once for all. 'Your really absurd apprehensions, Mr Searle,' I said at last, – 'your terrors, I may call them, – have fairly overmastered your common-sense. You are attacking a man of straw, a creature of base illusion; though I'm sadly afraid you have wounded a man of spirit and of conscience. Either my friend has no valid claim on your estate, in which case your agitation is superfluous; or he *has* a valid claim –'

Mr Searle seised my arm and glared at me, as I may say; his pale face paler still with the horror of my suggestion, his great keen eyes flashing, and his flamboyant hair erect and quivering.

'A valid claim!' he whispered. 'Let him try it!'

We had emerged into the great hall of the mansion and stood facing the main doorway. The door stood open into the porch, through whose stone archway I saw the garden glittering in the blue light of a full moon. As Mr Searle uttered the words I have just repeated, I beheld my companion come slowly up into the porch from without, bare-headed, bright in the outer moonlight, dark then in the shadow of the archway, and bright again in the lamplight on the threshold of the hall. As he crossed the threshold the butler made his appearance at the head of the staircase on our left, faltered visibly a moment on seeing Mr Searle; but then, perceiving my friend, he gravely descended. He bore in his hand a small plated salver. On the salver, gleaming in the light of the suspended lamp, lay a folded note. Clement Searle came forward, staring a little and startled, I think, by some fine sense of a near explosion. The butler applied the match. He advanced toward my friend, extending salver and note. Mr Searle made a movement as if to spring forward, but controlled himself. 'Tottenham!' he shouted, in strident voice.

'Yes, sir!' said Tottenham, halting.

'Stand where you are. For whom is that note?'

'For Mr Clement Searle,' said the butler, staring straight before him as if to discredit a suspicion of his having read the direction.

'Who gave it to you?'

'Mrs Horridge, sir.' (The housekeeper.)

'Who gave it Mrs Horridge?'

There was on Tottenham's part just an infinitesimal pause before replying.

'My dear sir,' broke in Searle, completely sobered by the sense of violated courtesy, 'isn't that rather my business?'

'What happens in my house is my business; and mighty strange things seem to be happening.' Mr Searle had become exasperated to that point that, a rare thing for an Englishman, he compromised himself before a servant.

'Bring me the note!' he cried. The butler obeyed.

'Really, this is too much!' cried my companion, affronted and helpless.

I was disgusted. Before Mr Searle had time to take the note, I possessed myself of it. 'If you have no regard for your sister,' I said, 'let a stranger, at least, act for her.' And I tore the disputed thing into a dozen pieces.

'In the name of decency,' cried Searle, 'what does this horrid business mean?'

Mr Searle was about to break out upon him; but at this moment his sister appeared on the staircase, summoned evidently by our high-pitched and angry voices. She had exchanged her dinner-dress for a dark dressing-gown, removed her ornaments, and begun to disarrange her hair, a heavy truss of which escaped from the comb. She hurried downward, with a pale, questioning face. Feeling distinctly that, for ourselves, immediate departure was in the air, and divining Mr Tottenham to be a butler of remarkable intuitions and extreme celerity, I seized the opportunity to request him, *sotto voce*, to send a carriage to the door without delay. 'And put up our things,' I added.

Our host rushed at his sister and seized the white wrist which escaped from the loose sleeve of her dress. 'What was in that note?' he demanded.

Miss Searle looked first at its scattered fragments and then at her cousin. 'Did you read it?' she asked.

'No, but I thank you for it!' said Searle.

Her eyes for an instant communed brightly with his own; then she transferred them to her brother's face, where the light went out of them and left a dull, sad patience. An inexorable patience he seemed to find it; he flushed crimson with rage and the sense of his unhandsomeness, and flung her away. 'You're a child!' he cried. 'Go to bed.'

In poor Searle's face as well the gathered serenity was twisted into a sickened frown, and the reflected brightness of his happy day turned to blank confusion. 'Have I been dealing these three hours with a madman?' he asked plaintively.

'A madman, yes, if you will! A man mad with the love of his home and the sense of its stability. I have held my tongue till now, but you have been too much for me. Who are you, what are you? From what paradise of fools do you come, that you fancy I shall cut off a piece of my land, my home, my heart, to toss to you? Forsooth, I shall share my land with you? Prove your infernal claim! There isn't *that* in it!' And he kicked one of the bits of paper on the floor.

Searle received this broadside gaping. Then turning away, he went and seated himself on a bench against the wall and rubbed his forehead amazedly. I looked at my watch, and listened for the wheels of our carriage.

Mr Searle went on. 'Wasn't it enough that you should have practised against my property? Need you have come into my very house to practise against my sister?'

Searle put his two hands to his face. 'Oh, oh, oh!' he softly roared.

Miss Searle crossed rapidly and dropped on her knees at his side.

'Go to bed, you fool!' shrieked her brother.

'Dear cousin,' said Miss Searle, 'it's cruel that you are to have to think of us so!'

'O, I shall think of you!' he said. And he laid a hand on her head.

'I believe you have done nothing wrong!' she murmured.

'I've done what I could,' her brother pursued. 'But it's arrant folly to pretend to friendship when this abomination lies between us. You were welcome to my meat and my wine, but I wonder you could swallow them. The sight spoiled my appetite!' cried the furious little man, with a laugh. 'Proceed with your case! My people in London are instructed and prepared.'

'I have a fancy,' I said to Searle, 'that your case has vastly improved since you gave it up.'

'Oho! you don't feign ignorance, then?' and he shook his flaming *chevelure* at me. 'It is very kind of you to give it up!' And he laughed resoundingly. 'Perhaps you will also give up my sister!'

Searle sat in his chair in a species of collapse, staring at his adversary. 'O miserable man!' he moaned at last. 'I fancied we had become such friends!'

'Boh! you imbecile!' cried our host.

Searle seemed not to hear him. 'Am I seriously expected,' he pursued, slowly and painfully – 'am I seriously expected – to – to sit here and defend myself – to prove I have done nothing wrong? Think what you please.' And he rose, with an effort, to his feet. 'I know what *you* think!' he added, to Miss Searle.

The carriage wheels resounded on the gravel, and at the same moment the footman descended with our two portmanteaus. Mr Tottenham followed him with our hats and coats.

'Good God!' cried Mr Searle; 'you are not going away!' This ejaculation, under the circumstances, had a grand comicality which prompted me to violent laughter. 'Bless my soul!' he added; 'of course you are going.'

'It's perhaps well,' said Miss Searle, with a great effort, inexpressibly touching in one for whom great efforts were visibly new and strange, 'that I should tell you what my poor little note contained.'

'That matter of your note, madam,' said her brother, 'you and I will settle together!'

'Let me imagine its contents,' said Searle.

'Ah! they have been too much imagined!' she answered simply. 'It was only a word of warning. I knew something painful was coming.'

Searle took his hat. 'The pains and the pleasures of this day,' he said to his kinsman, 'I shall equally never forget. Knowing you,' and he offered his hand to Miss Searle, 'has been the pleasure of pleasures. I hoped something more was to come of it.'

'A deal too much has come of it!' cried our host, irrepressibly.

Searle looked at him mildly, almost benignantly, from head to foot; and then closing his eyes with an air of sudden physical distress: 'I'm afraid so! I can't stand more of this.' I gave him my arm, and crossed the threshold. As we passed out I heard Miss Searle burst into a torrent of sobs.

'We shall hear from each other yet, I take it!' cried her brother, harassing our retreat.

Searle stopped and turned round on him sharply, almost fiercely. 'O ridiculous man!' he cried.

'Do you mean to say you shall not prosecute?' screamed the other. 'I shall force you to prosecute! I shall drag you into court, and you shall be beaten – beaten – beaten!' And this soft vocable continued to ring in our ears as we drove away.

We drove, of course, to the little wayside inn whence we had departed in the morning so unencumbered, in all broad England, with either enemies or friends. My companion, as the carriage rolled along, seemed utterly overwhelmed and exhausted. 'What a dream!' he murmured stupidly. 'What an awakening! What a long, long day! What a hideous scene! Poor me! Poor woman!' When we had resumed possession of our two little neighbouring rooms, I asked him if Miss Searle's note had been the result of anything that had passed between them on his going to rejoin her. 'I found her on the terrace,' he said, 'walking a restless walk in the moonlight. I was greatly excited; I hardly know what I said. I asked her, I think, if she knew the story of Margaret Searle. She seemed frightened and troubled, and she used just the words her brother had used, "I know nothing". For the moment, somehow, I felt as a man drunk. I stood before her and told her, with great emphasis, how sweet Margaret Searle had married a beggarly foreigner, in obedience to her heart and in defiance of her family. As I talked the sheeted moonlight seemed to close about us, and we stood in a dream, in a solitude, in a romance. She grew younger, fairer, more gracious. I trembled with a divine loquacity. Before I knew it I had gone far. I was taking her hand and calling her "Margaret!" She had said that it was impossible; that she could do nothing; that she was a fool, a child, a slave. Then, with a sudden huge conviction, I spoke of my claim against the estate. "It exists, then?" she said. "It exists," I answered, "but I have forgone it. Be generous! Pay it from your heart!" For an instant her face was radiant. "If I marry you," she cried, "it will repair the trouble." "In our marriage," I affirmed, "the trouble will melt away like a rain-drop in the ocean." "Our marriage!" she repeated, wonderingly; and the deep, deep ring of her voice seemed to shatter the crystal walls of our illusion. "I must think, I must think!'' she said; and she hurried away with her face in her hands. I walked up and down the terrace for some moments, and then came in and met you. This is the only witchcraft I have used!'

The poor fellow was at once so excited and so exhausted by the day's events, that I fancied he would get little sleep. Conscious, on my own part, of a stubborn wakefulness, I but partly undressed, set my fire a blazing, and sat down to do some writing. I heard the great clock in the little parlour below strike twelve, one, half past one. Just as the vibration of this last stroke was dying on the air the door of communication into Searle's room was flung open, and my companion stood on the threshold, pale as a corpse, in his nightshirt, standing like a phantom against the darkness behind him. 'Look at me!' he said, in a low voice, 'touch me, embrace me, revere me! You see a man who has seen a ghost!'

'Great heaven, what do you mean?'

'Write it down!' he went on. 'There, take your pen. Put it into dreadful words. Make it of all ghost-stories the ghostliest, the truest! How do I look? Am I human? Am I pale? Am I red? Am I speaking English? A ghost, sir! Do you understand?'

I confess, there came upon me, by contact, a great supernatural shock. I shall always feel that I, too, have seen a ghost. My first movement – I can't smile at it even now – was to spring to the door, close it with a great blow, and then turn the key upon the gaping blackness from which Searle had emerged. I seized his two hands; they were wet with perspiration. I pushed my chair to the fire and forced him to sit down in it. I kneeled down before him and held his hands as firmly as possible. They trembled and quivered; his eyes were fixed, save that the pupil dilated and contracted with extraordinary force. I asked no questions, but waited with my heart in my throat. At last he spoke. 'I'm not frightened, but I'm – O, EXCITED! This is life! This is living! My nerves – my heart – my brain! They are throbbing with the wildness of a myriad lives! Do you feel it? Do you tingle? Are you hot? Are you cold? Hold me tight – tight – tight! I shall tremble away into waves – waves – waves, and know the universe and approach my

Maker!' He paused a moment and then went on: 'A woman – as clear as that candle. – No, far clearer! In a blue dress, with a black mantle on her head, and a little black muff. Young, dreadfully pretty, pale and ill, with the sadness of all the women who ever loved and suffered pleading and accusing in her dead dark eyes. God knows I never did any such thing! But she took me for my elder, for the other Clement. She came to me here as she would have come to me there. She wrung her hands and spoke to me. "Marry me!" she moaned; "marry me and right me!" I sat up in bed just as I sit here, looked at her, heard her, – heard her voice melt away, watched her figure fade away. Heaven and earth! Here I am!'

I made no attempt either to explain my friend's vision or to discredit it. It is enough that I felt for the hour the irresistible contagion of his own agitation. On the whole, I think my own vision was the more interesting of the two. He beheld but the transient, irresponsible spectre: I beheld the human subject, hot from the spectral presence. Nevertheless, I soon recovered my wits sufficiently to feel the necessity of guarding my friend's health against the evil results of excitement and exposure. It was tacitly established that, for the night, he was not to return to his room; and I soon made him fairly comfortable in his place by the fire. Wishing especially to obviate a chill, I removed my bedding and wrapped him about with multitudinous blankets and counterpanes. I had no nerves either for writing or sleep; so I put out my lights, renewed the fire, and sat down on the opposite side of the hearth. I found a kind of solemn entertainment in watching my friend. Silent, swathed and muffled to his chin, he sat rigid and erect with the dignity of his great adventure. For the most part his eyes were closed; though from time to time he would open them with a vast steady expansion and gaze unblinking into the firelight, as if he again beheld, without terror, the image of that blighted maid. With his cadaverous, emaciated face, his tragic wrinkles, intensified by the upward glow from the hearth, his drooping black moustache, his transcendent gravity, and a certain high fantastical air in the flickering alternations of his brow, he looked like the vision-haunted knight of La Mancha, nursed by the Duke and Duchess. The night passed wholly without speech. Towards its close I slept for half an hour. When I awoke the awakened birds had begun to twitter. Searle sat unperturbed, staring at me. We exchanged a long look; I felt with a pang that his glittering eyes had tasted their last of natural sleep. 'How is it? are you comfortable?' I asked.

He gazed for some time without replying. Then he spoke with a strange, innocent grandiloquence, and with pauses between his words, as if an inner voice were slowly prompting him. 'You asked me, when you first knew me, what I was. "Nothing," I said, – "nothing." Nothing I have always deemed myself. But I have wronged myself. I'm a personage! I'm rare among men! I'm a haunted man!'

Sleep had passed out of his eyes: I felt with a deeper pang that perfect sanity had passed out of his voice. From this moment I prepared myself for the worst. There was in my friend, however, such an essential gentleness and conservative patience, that to persons surrounding him the worst was likely to come without hurry or violence. He had so confirmed a habit of good manners that, at the core of reason, the process of disorder might have been long at work without finding an issue. As morning began fully to dawn upon us, I brought our grotesque vigil to an end. Searle appeared so weak that I gave him my hands to help him to rise from his chair; he retained them for some moments after rising to his feet, from an apparent inability to keep his balance. 'Well,' he said, 'I've seen one ghost, but I doubt of my living to see another. I shall soon be myself as brave a ghost as the best of them. I shall haunt Mr Searle! It can only mean one thing, – my near, dear death.'

On my proposing breakfast, 'This shall be my breakfast!' he said; and he drew from his travelling-sack a phial of morphine. He took a strong dose and went to bed. At noon I found him on foot again, dressed, shaved, and apparently refreshed. 'Poor fellow!' he said, 'you have got more than you bargained for, – a ghost-encumbered comrade. But it won't be for long.' It imme-diately became a question, of course, whither we should now direct our steps.

'As I have so little time,' said Searle, 'I should like to see the best, the best alone.' I answered that, either for time or eternity, I had imagined Oxford to be the best thing in England; and for Oxford in the course of an hour we accordingly departed.

Of Oxford I feel small vocation to speak in detail. It must long remain for an American one of the supreme gratifications of travel. The impression it produces, the emotions it stirs, in an American mind, are too large and various to be compassed by words. It seems to embody with undreamed completeness a kind of dim and sacred ideal of the Western intellect, – a scholastic city, an appointed home of contemplation. No other spot in Europe, I imagine, extorts from our barbarous hearts so passionate an admiration. A finer pen than mine must enumerate the splendid devices by which it performs this great office; I can bear testimony only to the dominant tone of its effect. Passing through the various streets in which the obverse longitude of the hoary college walls seems to maintain an antique stillness, you feel this to be the most dignified of towns. Over all, through all, the great corporate fact of the University prevails and penetrates, like some steady bass in a symphony of lighter chords, like the mediaeval and mystical presence of the Empire in the linked dispersion of lesser states. The plain Gothic of the long street-fronts of the colleges – blessed seraglios of culture and leisure – irritate the fancy like the blank harem-walls of Eastern towns. Within their arching portals, however, you perceive more sacred and sunless courts, and the dark verdure grateful and restful to bookish eyes. The grey-green quadrangles stand forever open with a noble and trustful hospitality. The seat of the humanities is stronger in the admonitory shadow of her great name than in a marshalled host of wardens and beadles. Directly after our arrival my friend and I strolled eagerly forth in the luminous early dusk. We reached the bridge which passes beneath the walls of Magdalen and saw the eight-spired tower, embossed with its slender shaftings, rise in temperate beauty, – the perfect prose of Gothic, – wooing the eyes to the sky, as it was slowly drained of day. We entered the little monkish doorway and stood in that dim, fantastic outer court, made narrow by the dominant presence of the great tower, in which the heart beats faster, and the swallows niche more lovingly in the tangled ivy, I fancied, than elsewhere in Oxford. We passed thence into the great cloister, and studied the little sculptured monsters along the entablature of the arcade. I was pleased to see that Searle became extremely interested; but I very soon began to fear that the influence of the place would prove too potent for his unbalanced imagination. I may say that from this time forward, with my unhappy friend, I found it hard to distinguish between the play of fancy and the labour of thought, and to fix the balance between perception and illusion. He had already taken a fancy to confound his identity with that of the earlier Clement Searle; he now began to speak almost wholly as from the imagined consciousness of his old-time kinsman.

'This was my college, you know,' he said, 'the noblest in all Oxford. How often I have paced this gentle cloister, side by side with a friend of the hour! My friends are all dead, but many a young fellow as we meet him, dark or fair, tall or short, reminds me of them. Even Oxford, they say, feels about its massive base the murmurs of the tide of time; there are things eliminated, things insinuated! Mine was ancient Oxford, – the fine old haunt of rank abuses, of precedent and privilege. What cared I, who was a perfect gentleman, with my pockets full of money? I had an allowance of two thousand a year.'

It became evident to me, on the following day, that his strength had begun to ebb, and that he was unequal to the labour of regular sight-seeing. He read my apprehension in my eyes, and took pains to assure me that I was right. 'I am going down hill. Thank heaven it's an easy slope, coated with English turf and with an English churchyard at the foot.' The almost hysterical emotion produced by our adventure at Lockley Park had given place to a broad, calm satisfaction, in which the scene around us was reflected as in the depths of a lucid lake. We took an afternoon walk through Christ-Church Meadow, and at the river-bank procured a boat, which I pulled up the stream to Iffley and to the slanting woods of Nuneham, – the sweetest, flattest, reediest stream-side landscape that the heart need demand. Here, of course, we encountered in hundreds the mighty lads of England, clad in white flannel and blue, immense, fair-haired, magnificent in their youth, lounging down the current in their idle punts, in friendly couples or in solitude possibly portentous of scholastic honours; or pulling in straining crews and hoarsely exhorted from the near bank. When, in conjunction with all this magnificent sport, you think of the verdant quietude and the silvery sanctities of the college gardens, you cannot but consider that the youth of England have their porridge well salted. As my companion found himself less and less able to walk, we repaired on three successive days to these scholastic domains, and spent long hours sitting in their greenest places. They seemed to us the fairest things in England and the ripest and sweetest fruits of the English system. Locked in their antique verdure, guarded (as in the case of New College) by gentle battlements of silver-grey, outshouldering the matted leafage of centenary vines, filled with perfumes and privacy and memories, with students lounging bookishly on the turf (as if tenderly to spare it the pressure of their boot-heels), and with the great conservative presence of the college front appealing gravely from the restless outer world, they seem places to lie down on the grass in for ever, in the happy faith that life is all a vast old English garden, and time an endless English afternoon. This charmed seclusion was especially grateful to my friend, and his sense of it reached its climax, I remember, on the last afternoon of our three, as we sat dreaming in the spacious garden of St John's. The long college façade here, perhaps, broods over the lawn with a more effective air of property than elsewhere. Searle fell into unceasing talk and exhaled his swarming impressions with a tender felicity, compounded of the oddest mixture of wisdom and folly. Every student who passed us was the subject of an extemporised romance, and every feature of the place the theme of a lyric rhapsody.

'Isn't it all,' he demanded, 'a delightful lie? Mightn't one fancy this the very central point of the world's heart, where all the echoes of the world's life arrive only to falter and die? Listen! The air is thick with arrested voices. It is well there should be such places, shaped in the interest of factitious needs;

framed to minister to the book-begotten longing for a medium
in which one may dream unwaked, and believe unconfuted; to
foster the sweet illusion that all is well in this weary world, all
perfect and rounded, mellow and complete in this sphere of the
pitiful unachieved and the dreadful uncommenced. The
world's made! Work's over! Now for leisure! England's safe!
Now for Theocritus and Horace, for lawn and sky! What a
sense it all gives one of the composite life of England, and
how essential a factor of the educated, British consciousness
one omits in not thinking of Oxford! Thank heaven they had
the wit to send me here in the other time. I'm not much with it,
perhaps; but what should I have been without it? The misty
spires and towers of Oxford seen far off on the level have been
all these years one of the constant things of memory. Seriously,
what does Oxford do for these people? Are they wiser, gentler,
richer, deeper? At moments when its massive influence surges
into my mind like a tidal wave, I take it as a sort of affront to my
dignity. My soul reverts to the naked background of our own
education, the dead white wall before which we played our
parts. I assent to it all with a sort of desperate calmness; I bow
to it with a dogged pride. We are nursed at the opposite pole.
Naked come we into a naked world. There is a certain grandeur
in the absence of a *mise en scène*, a certain heroic strain in those
young imaginations of the West, which find nothing made to
their hands, which have to concoct their own mysteries, and
raise high into our morning air, with a ringing hammer and
nails, the castles in which they dwell. *Noblesse oblige*: Oxford
obliges. What a horrible thing not to respond to such obligations. If you pay the pious debt to the last farthing of interest,
you may go through life with her blessing; but if you let it stand
unhonoured, you are a worse barbarian than we! But for better
or worse, in a myriad private hearts, think how she must be
loved! How the youthful sentiment of mankind seems visibly to
brood upon her! Think of the young lives now taking colour in
her corridors and cloisters. Think of the centuries' tale of dead
lads, – dead alike with the close of the young days to which
these haunts were a present world and the ending of the larger
lives which a sterner mother-scene has gathered into her

massive history! What are those two young fellows kicking their
heels over on the grass there? One of them has the Saturday
Review; the other – upon my soul – the other has Artemus
Ward! Where do they live, how do they live, to what end do
they live? Miserable boys! How can they read Artemus Ward
under those windows of Elizabeth? What do you think loveliest
in all Oxford? The poetry of certain windows. Do you see that
one yonder, the second of those lesser bays, with the broken
mullion and open casement? That used to be the window of my
fidus Achates, a hundred years ago. Remind me to tell you the
story of that broken mullion. Don't tell me it's not a common
thing to have one's *fidus Achates* at another college. Pray, was
I pledged to common things? He was a charming fellow. By the
way, he was a good deal like you. Of course his cocked hat, his
long hair in a black ribbon, his cinnamon velvet suit, and his
flowered waistcoat made a difference! We gentlemen used to
wear swords.'

There was something surprising and impressive in my
friend's gushing magniloquence. The poor disheartened loafer
had turned rhapsodist and seer. I was particularly struck with
his having laid aside the diffidence and shy self-consciousness
which had marked him during the first days of our acquaintance. He was becoming more and more a disembodied observer and critic; the shell of sense, growing daily thinner and more
transparent, transmitted the tremor of his quickened spirit. He
revealed an unexpected faculty for becoming acquainted with
the lounging gownsmen whom we met in our vague peregrina-
tions. If I left him for ten minutes, I was sure to find him, on my
return, in earnest conversation with some affable wandering
scholar. Several young men with whom he had thus established
relations invited him to their rooms and entertained him, as
I gathered, with boisterous hospitality. For myself, I chose not
to be present on these occasions; I shrunk partly from being
held in any degree responsible for his vagaries, and partly from
witnessing that painful aggravation of them which I feared
might be induced by champagne and youthful society. He
reported these adventures with less eloquence than I had
fancied he might use; but, on the whole, I suspect that a certain

method in his madness, a certain firmness in his most melting *bonhomie*, had ensured him perfect respect. Two things, however, became evident, – that he drank more champagne than was good for him, and that the boyish grossness of his entertainers tended rather, on reflection, to disturb in his mind the pure image of Oxford. At the same time it completed his knowledge of the place. Making the acquaintance of several tutors and fellows, he dined in Hall in half a dozen colleges, and alluded afterwards to these banquets with a sort of religious unction. One evening, at the close of one of these entertainments, he came back to the hotel in a cab, accompanied by a friendly student, and a physician, looking deadly pale. He had swooned away on leaving table, and had remained so stubbornly unconscious as to excite great alarm among his companions. The following twenty-four hours, of course, he spent in bed; but on the third day he declared himself strong enough to go out. On reaching the street his strength again forsook him, and I insisted upon his returning to his room. He besought me with tears in his eyes not to shut him up. 'It's my last chance,' he said. 'I want to go back for an hour to that garden of St John's. Let me look and feel; to-morrow I die.' It seemed to me possible that with a Bath-chair the expedition might be accomplished. The hotel, it appeared, possessed such a convenience: it was immediately produced. It became necessary hereupon that we should have a person to propel the chair. As there was no one available on the spot, I prepared to perform the office; but just as Searle had got seated and wrapped (he had come to suffer acutely from cold), an elderly man emerged from a lurking-place near the door, and, with a formal salute, offered to wait upon the gentleman. We assented, and he proceeded solemnly to trundle the chair before him. I recognised him as an individual whom I had seen lounging shyly about the hotel doors, at intervals during our stay, with a depressed air of wanting employment and a hopeless doubt of finding any. He had once, indeed, in a half-hearted way, proposed himself as an amateur cicerone for a tour through the colleges; and I now, as I looked at him, remembered with a pang that I had declined his services with untender curtness. Since then, his shyness, apparently, had grown less or his misery greater; for it was with a strange, grim avidity that he now attached himself to our service. He was a pitiful image of shabby gentility and the dinginess of 'reduced circumstances'. He imparted an original force to the term 'seedy'. He was, I suppose, some fifty years of age; but his pale, haggard, unwholesome visage, his plaintive, drooping carriage, and the irremediable decay of his apparel, seemed to add to the burden of his days and experience. His eyes were bloodshot and weak-looking, his handsome nose had turned to purple, and his sandy beard, largely streaked with grey, bristled with a month's desperate indifference to the razor. In all this rusty forlornness there lurked a visible assurance of our friend's having known better days. Obviously, he was the victim of some fatal depreciation in the market value of pure gentility. There had been something terribly pathetic in the way he fiercely merged the attempt to touch the greasy rim of his antiquated hat into a rounded and sweeping bow, as from jaunty equal to equal. Exchanging a few words with him as we went along, I was struck with the refinement of his tone.

'Take me by some long roundabout way,' said Searle, 'so that I may see as many college walls as possible.'

'You can wander without losing your way?' I asked of our attendant.

'I ought to be able to, sir,' he said, after a moment, with pregnant gravity. And as we were passing Wadham College, 'That's my college, sir,' he added.

At these words, Searle commanded him to stop and come and stand in front of him. 'You say that is *your* college?' he demanded.

'Wadham might deny me, sir; but Heaven forbid I should deny Wadham. If you'll allow me to take you into the quad, I'll show you my windows, thirty years ago!'

Searle sat staring, with his huge, pale eyes, which now had come to usurp the greatest place in his wasted visage, filled with wonder and pity. 'If you'll be so kind,' he said, with immense politeness. But just as this degenerate son of Wadham was about to propel him across the threshold of the court, he turned about, disengaged his hands, with his own hand, from the back of the chair, drew him alongside of him and turned to me. 'While we are here, my dear fellow,' he said, 'be so good as to perform this service. You understand?' I smiled sufferance at our companion, and we resumed our way. The latter showed us his window of thirty years ago, where now a rosy youth in a scarlet smoking-fez was puffing a cigarette in the open lattice. Thence we proceeded into the little garden, the smallest, I believe, and certainly the sweetest of all the bosky resorts in Oxford. I pushed the chair along to a bench on the lawn, wheeled it about toward the façade of the college, and sat down on the grass. Our attendant shifted himself mournfully from one foot to the other. Searle eyed him open-mouthed. At length he broke out: 'God bless my soul, sir, you don't suppose that I expect you to stand! There's an empty bench.'

'Thank you,' said our friend, bending his joints to sit.

'You English,' said Searle, 'are really fabulous! I don't know whether I most admire you or despise you! Now tell me: who are you? what are you? what brought you to this?'

The poor fellow blushed up to his eyes, took off his hat, and wiped his forehead with a ragged handkerchief. 'My name is Rawson, sir. Beyond that, it's a long story.'

'I ask out of sympathy,' said Searle. 'I have a fellow-feeling! You're a poor devil; I'm a poor devil too.'

'I'm the poorer devil of the two,' said the stranger, with a little emphatic nod of the head.

'Possibly. I suppose an English poor devil is the poorest of all poor devils. And then, you have fallen from a height. From Wadham College as a gentleman commoner (is that what they call you?) to Wadham College as a Bath-chair man! Good heavens, man, the fall's enough to kill you!'

'I didn't take it all at once, sir. I dropped a bit one time and a bit another.'

'That's me, that's me!' cried Searle, clapping his hands.

'And now,' said our friend, 'I believe I can't drop further.'

'My dear fellow,' and Searle clasped his hand and shook it, 'there's a perfect similarity in our lot.'

Mr Rawson lifted his eyebrows. 'Save for the difference of sitting in a Bath-chair and walking behind it!'

'O, I'm at my last gasp, Mr Rawson.'

'I'm at my last penny, sir.'

'Literally, Mr Rawson?'

Mr Rawson shook his head, with a world of vague bitterness. 'I have almost come to the point,' he said, 'of drinking my beer and buttoning my coat figuratively; but I don't talk in figures.'

Fearing that the conversation had taken a turn which might seem to cast a rather fantastic light upon Mr Rawson's troubles, I took the liberty of asking him with great gravity how he made a living.

'I don't make a living,' he answered, with tearful eyes, 'I can't make a living. I have a wife and three children, starving, sir. You wouldn't believe what I have come to. I sent my wife to her mother's, who can ill afford to keep her, and came to Oxford a week ago, thinking I might pick up a few half-crowns by showing people about the colleges. But it's no use. I haven't the assurance. I don't look decent. They want a nice little old man with black gloves, and a clean shirt, and a silver-headed stick. What do I look as if I knew about Oxford, sir?'

'Dear me,' cried Searle, 'why didn't you speak to us before?'

'I wanted to; half a dozen times I have been on the point of it. I knew you were Americans.'

'And Americans are rich!' cried Searle, laughing. 'My dear Mr Rawson, American as I am, I'm living on charity.'

'And I'm not, sir! There it is. I'm dying for the want of charity. You say you're a pauper; it takes an American pauper to go bowling about in a Bath-chair. America's an easy country.'

'Ah, me!' groaned Searle. 'Have I come to Wadham gardens to hear the praise of America?'

'Wadham gardens are very well!' said Mr Rawson; 'but one may sit here hungry and shabby, so long as one isn't too shabby, as well as elsewhere. You'll not persuade me that it's not an easier thing to keep afloat yonder than here. I wish I were there, that's all!' added Mr Rawson, with a sort of feeble-minded energy. Then brooding for a moment on his wrongs: 'Have you a brother? or you, sir? It matters little to you. But it has mattered to me with a vengeance! Shabby as I sit here, I have a brother with his five thousand a year. Being a couple of years my senior, he gorges while I starve. There's England for you! A very pretty place for *him*!'

'Poor England!' said Searle, softly.

'Has your brother never helped you?' I asked.

'A twenty-pound note now and then! I don't say that there have not been times when I have sorely tried his generosity. I have not been what I should. I married dreadfully amiss. But the devil of it is that he started fair and I started foul; with the tastes, the desires, the needs, the sensibilities of a gentleman, – and nothing else! I can't afford to live in England.'

'This poor gentleman,' said I, 'fancied a couple of months ago that he couldn't afford to live in America.'

'I'd change chances with him!' And Mr Rawson gave a passionate slap to his knee.

Searle reclined in his chair with his eyes closed and his face twitching with violent emotion. Suddenly he opened his eyes with a look of awful gravity. 'My friend,' he said, 'you're a failure! Be judged! Don't talk about chances. Don't talk about fair starts and foul starts. I'm at that point myself that I have a right to speak. It lies neither in one's chance nor one's start to make one a success; nor in anything one's brother can do or can undo. It lies in one's own will! You and I, sir, have had none; that's very plain! We have been weak, sir; as weak as water. Here we are, sitting staring in each other's faces and reading our weakness in each other's eyes. We are of no account!'

Mr Rawson received this address with a countenance in which heartfelt conviction was oddly mingled with a vague suspicion that a proper self-respect required him to resent its unflattering candour. In the course of a minute a proper self-respect yielded to the warm, comfortable sense of his being understood, even to his light dishonour. 'Go on, sir, go on,' he said. 'It's wholesome truth.' And he wiped his eyes with his dingy handkerchief.

'Dear me!' cried Searle. 'I've made you cry. Well! we speak as from man to man. I should be glad to think that you had felt for a moment the side-light of that great undarkening of the spirit which precedes – which precedes the grand illumination of death.'

Mr Rawson sat silent for a moment, with his eyes fixed on the ground and his well-cut nose more deeply tinged by the force of emotion. Then at last, looking up: 'You're a very good-natured man, sir; and you'll not persuade me that you don't come of a good-natured race. Say what you please about a chance; when a man's fifty, – degraded, penniless, a husband and father, – a chance to get on his legs again is not to be despised. Something tells me that my chance is in your country, – that great home of chances. I can starve here, of course; but I don't want to starve. Hang it, sir, I want to live. I see thirty years of life before me yet. If only, by God's help, I could spend them there! It's a fixed idea of mine. I've had it for the last ten years. It's not that I'm a radical. I've no ideas! Old England's good enough for me, but I'm not good enough for old England. I'm a shabby man that wants to get out of a room full of staring gentlefolks. I'm forever put to the blush. It's a perfect agony of spirit. Everything reminds me of my younger and better self. O, for a cooling, cleansing plunge into the unknowing and the unknown! I lie awake thinking of it.'

Searle closed his eyes and shivered with a long-drawn tremor which I hardly knew whether to take for an expression of physical or of mental pain. In a moment I perceived it was neither. 'O my country, my country, my country!' he murmured in a broken voice; and then sat for some time abstracted and depressed. I intimated to our companion that it was time we should bring our *séance* to a close, and he, without hesitating, possessed himself of the little handrail of the Bath-chair and pushed it before him. We had got half-way home before Searle spoke or moved. Suddenly in the High Street, as we were passing in front of a chop-house, from whose open doors there proceeded a potent suggestion of juicy joints and suet puddings, he motioned us to halt. 'This is my last five pounds,' he said, drawing a note from his pocket-book. 'Do me the favour, Mr Rawson, to accept it. Go in there and order a colossal dinner. Order a bottle of Burgundy and drink it to my immortal health!' Mr Rawson stiffened himself up and received the gift with momentarily irresponsive fingers. Bur Mr Rawson had the nerves of a gentleman. I saw the titillation of his pointed finger-tips as they closed upon the crisp paper; I noted the fine tremor in his empurpled nostril as it became more deeply conscious of the succulent flavour of the spot. He crushed the crackling note in his palm with a convulsive pressure.

'It shall be Chambertin!' he said, jerking a spasmodic bow. The next moment the door swung behind him.

Searle relapsed into his feeble stupor, and on reaching the hotel I helped him to get to bed. For the rest of the day he lay in a half-somnolent state, without motion or speech. The doctor, whom I had constantly in attendance, declared that his end was near. He expressed great surprise that he should have lasted so long; he must have been living for a month on a cruelly extorted strength. Toward evening, as I sat by his bedside in the deepening dusk, he aroused himself with a purpose which I had vaguely felt gathering beneath his quietude. 'My cousin, my cousin,' he said, confusedly. 'Is she here?' It was the first time he had spoken of Miss Searle since our exit from her brother's house. 'I was to have married her,' he went on. 'What a dream! That day was like a string of verses – rhymed hours. But the last verse is bad measure. What's the rhyme to "love"? *Above!* Was she a simple person, a sweet person? Or have I dreamed it? She had the healing gift; her touch would have cured my madness. I want you to do something. Write three lines, three words: "Good-bye; remember me; be happy." And then, after a long pause: 'It's strange a man in my condition should have a wish. Need a man eat his breakfast before his hanging? What a creature is man! what a farce is life! Here I lie, worn down to a mere throbbing fever-point; I breathe and nothing more, and yet I *desire*! My desire lives. If I could see her! Help me out with it and let me die.'

Half an hour later, at a venture, I despatched a note to Miss Searle: '*Your cousin is rapidly dying. He asks to see you.*' I was conscious of a certain unkindness in doing so. It would bring a great trouble, and no power to face the trouble. But out of her distress I fondly hoped a sufficient energy might be born. On the following day my friend's exhaustion had become so total that I began to fear that his intelligence was altogether gone. But towards evening he rallied awhile, and talked in a maundering way about many things, confounding in a ghastly jumble the memories of the past weeks and those of bygone years. 'By the way,' he said suddenly, 'I have made no will. I haven't much to bequeath. Yet I've something.' He had been playing listlessly with a large signet-ring on his left hand, which he now tried to draw off. 'I leave you this,' working it round and round vainly. 'If you can get it off. What mighty knuckles! There must be such knuckles in the mummies of the Pharaohs. Well, when I'm gone! Nay, I leave you something more precious than gold, – the sense of a great kindness. But I have a little gold left. Bring me those trinkets.' I placed on the bed before him several articles of jewelry, relics of early elegance: his watch and chain, of great value, a locket and seal, some shirt-buttons and scarf-pins. He trifled with them feebly for some moments, murmuring various names and dates associated with them. At last, looking up with a sudden energy, 'What's become of Mr Rawson?'

'You want to see him?'

'How much are these things worth?' he asked, without heeding me. 'How much would they bring?' And he held them up in his weak hands. 'They have a great weight. Two hundred pounds? I am richer than I thought! Rawson – Rawson – you want to get out of this awful England.'

I stepped to the door and requested the servant, whom I kept in constant attendance in the adjoining sitting-room, to send and ascertain if Mr Rawson was on the premises. He returned in a few moments, introducing our shabby friend. Mr Rawson was pale, even to his nose, and, with his suppressed agitation, had an air of great distinction. I led him up to the bed. In Searle's eyes, as they fell on him, there shone for a moment the light of a high fraternal greeting.

'Great God!' said Mr Rawson, fervently.

'My friend,' said Searle, 'there is to be one American the less. Let there be one the more. At the worst, you'll be as good a one as I. Foolish me! Take these trinkets; let them help you on your way. They are gifts and memories, but this is a better use. Heaven speed you! May America be kind to you. Be kind, at the last, to your own country!'

'Really, this is too much; I can't,' our friend protested in a tremulous voice. 'Do get well, and I'll stop here!'

'Nay; I'm booked for my journey, you for yours. I hope you don't suffer at sea.'

Mr Rawson exhaled a groan of helpless gratitude, appealing piteously from so awful a good fortune. 'It's like the angel of the Lord,' he said, 'who bids people in the Bible to rise and flee!'

Searle had sunk back upon his pillow, exhausted: I led Mr Rawson back into the sitting-room, where in three words I proposed to him a rough valuation of our friend's trinkets. He assented with perfect good breeding; they passed into my possession and a second bank-note into his.

From the collapse into which this beneficent interview had plunged him, Searle gave few signs of being likely to emerge. He breathed, as he had said, and nothing more. The twilight deepened: I lit the night-lamp. The doctor sat silent and official at the foot of the bed; I resumed my constant place near the head. Suddenly Searle opened his eyes widely. 'She'll not come,' he murmured. 'Amen! she's an English sister.' Five minutes passed. He started forward. 'She has come, she is here!' he whispered. His words conveyed to my mind so absolute an assurance, that I lightly rose and passed into the sitting-room. At the same moment, through the opposite door, the servant introduced a lady. A lady, I say; for an instant she was simply such; tall, pale, dressed in deep mourning. The next moment I had uttered her name – 'Miss Searle!' She looked ten years older.

She met me, with both hands extended, and an immense question in her face. 'He has just spoken your name,' I said. And then, with a fuller consciousness of the change in her dress and countenance: 'What has happened?'

'O death, death!' said Miss Searle. 'You and I are left.'

There came to me with her words a sort of sickening shock, the sense of poetic justice having been grimly shuffled away. 'Your brother?' I demanded.

She laid her hand on my arm, and I felt its pressure deepen as she spoke. 'He was thrown from his horse in the park. He died on the spot. Six days have passed. – Six months!'

She took my arm. A moment later we had entered the room and approached the bedside. The doctor withdrew. Searle opened his eyes and looked at her from head to foot. Suddenly he seemed to perceive her mourning. 'Already!' he cried, audibly; with a smile, as I believe, of pleasure.

She dropped on her knees and took his hand. 'Not for you, cousin,' she whispered. 'For my poor brother.'

He started in all his deathly longitude as with a galvanic shock. 'Dead! *he* dead! Life itself!' And then, after a moment, with a slight rising inflection: 'You are free?'

'Free, cousin. Sadly free. And now – *now* – with what use for freedom?'

He looked steadily a moment into her eyes, dark in the heavy shadow of her musty mourning veil. 'For me,' he said, 'wear colours!'

In a moment more death had come, the doctor had silently attested it, and Miss Searle had burst into sobs.

We buried him in the little churchyard in which he had expressed the wish to lie; beneath one of the mightiest of English yews and the little tower than which none in all England has a softer and hoarier grey. A year has passed. Miss Searle, I believe, has begun to wear colours.

THE MADONNA OF THE FUTURE

WE had been talking about the masters who had achieved but a single masterpiece, – the artists and poets who but once in their lives had known the divine afflatus, and touched the high level of the best. Our host had been showing us a charming little cabinet picture by a painter whose name we had never heard, and who, after this one spasmodic bid for fame, had apparently relapsed into fatal mediocrity. There was some discussion as to the frequency of this phenomenon; during which, I observed, H— sat silent, finishing his cigar with a meditative air, and looking at the picture, which was being handed round the table. 'I don't know how common a case it is,' he said at last, 'but I've seen it. I've known a poor fellow who painted his one masterpiece, and' – he added with a smile – 'he didn't even paint that. He made his bid for fame, and missed it.' We all knew H— for a clever man who had seen much of men and manners, and had a great stock of reminiscences. Some one immediately questioned him further, and while I was engrossed with the raptures of my neighbour over the little picture, he was induced to tell his tale. If I were to doubt whether it would bear repeating, I should only have to remember how that charming woman, our hostess, who had left the table, ventured back in rustling rose-colour, to pronounce our lingering a want of gallantry, and, finding us a listening circle, had sunk into her chair in spite of our cigars, and heard the story out so graciously, that when the catastrophe was reached she glanced across at me, and showed me a tender tear in each of her beautiful eyes.

It relates to my youth, and to Italy: two fine things! (H— began). I had arrived late in the evening at Florence, and while I finished my bottle of wine at supper, had fancied that, tired traveller though I was, I might pay the city a finer compliment than by going vulgarly to bed. A narrow passage wandered darkly away out of the little square before my hotel, and looked as if it bored into the heart of Florence. I followed it, and at the end of ten minutes emerged upon a great piazza, filled only with the mild autumn moonlight. Opposite rose the Palazzo Vecchio, like some huge civic fortress, with the great bell-tower springing from its embattled verge like a mountain-pine from the edge of a cliff. At its base, in its projected shadow, gleamed certain dim sculptures which I wonderingly approached. One of the images, on the left of the palace door, was a magnificent colossus, shining through the dusky air like some embodied Defiance. In a moment I recognised him as Michael Angelo's David. I turned with a certain relief from his sinister strength to a slender figure in bronze, stationed beneath the high, light loggia, which opposes the free and elegant span of its arches to the dead masonry of the palace; a figure supremely shapely and graceful; gentle, almost, in spite of his holding out with his light nervous arm the snaky head of the slaughtered Gorgon. His name is Perseus, and you may read his story, not in the Greek mythology, but in memoirs of Benvenuto Cellini. Glancing from one of these fine fellows to the other, I probably uttered some irrepressible commonplace of praise, for, as if provoked by my voice, a man rose from the steps of the loggia, where he had been sitting in the shadow, and addressed me in good English, – a small, slim personage, clad in a sort of black velvet tunic (as it seemed), and with a mass of auburn hair, which gleamed in the moonlight, escaping from a little mediaeval berretta. In a tone of the most insinuating deference, he asked me for my 'impressions'. He seemed picturesque, fantastic, slightly unreal. Hovering there in this consecrated neighbourhood, he might have passed for the genius of aesthetic hospitality, – if the genius of aesthetic hospitality were not commonly some shabby little custode, flourishing a calico pocket-handkerchief, and openly resentful of the divided franc. This fantasy was made none the less plausible by the brilliant tirade with which he greeted my embarrassed silence.

'I've known Florence long, sir, but I've never known her so lovely as to-night. It's as if the ghosts of her past were abroad in the empty streets. The present is sleeping; the past hovers about us like a dream made visible. Fancy the old Florentines strolling up in couples to pass judgement on the last performance of Michael, of Benvenuto! We should come in for a precious lesson if we might overhear what they say. The plainest burgher of them, in his cap and gown, had a taste in the matter! That was the prime of art, sir. The sun stood high in heaven, and his broad and equal blaze made the darkest places bright and the dullest eyes clear. We live in the evening of time! We grope in the grey dusk, carrying each our poor little taper of selfish and painful wisdom, holding it up to the great models and to the dim idea, and seeing nothing but overwhelming greatness and dimness. The days of illumination are gone! But do you know I fancy – I fancy,' – and he grew suddenly almost familiar in this visionary fervour, – 'I fancy the light of that time rests upon us here for an hour! I have never seen the David so grand, the Perseus so fair! Even the inferior productions of John of Bologna and of Baccio Bandinelli seem to realise the artist's dream. I feel as if the moonlit air were charged with the secrets of the masters, and as if, standing here in religious contemplation, we might – we might witness a revelation!' Perceiving at this moment, I suppose, my halting comprehension reflected in my puzzled face, this interesting rhapsodist paused and blushed. Then with a melancholy smile, 'You think me a moonstruck charlatan, I suppose. It's not my habit to hang about the piazza and pounce upon innocent tourists. But to-night, I confess, I'm under the charm. And then, somehow, I fancied you, too, were an artist!'

'I'm not an artist, I'm sorry to say, as you must understand the term. But pray make no apologies. I am also under the charm; your eloquent reflections have only deepened it.'

'If you're not an artist, you're worthy to be one!' he rejoined, with a bow. 'A young man who arrives at Florence late in the evening, and, instead of going prosaically to bed, or hanging over the travellers' book at his hotel, walks forth without loss of time to pay his devoirs to the beautiful, is a young man after my own heart!'

The mystery was suddenly solved; my friend was an American! He must have been, to take the picturesque so prodigiously to heart. 'None the less so, I trust,' I answered, 'if the young man is a sordid New-Yorker.'

'New-Yorkers,' he solemnly proclaimed, 'have been munificent patrons of art!'

For a moment I was alarmed. Was this midnight reverie mere Yankee enterprise, and was he simply a desperate brother of the brush who had posted himself here to extort an 'order' from a sauntering tourist? But I was not called to defend myself. A great brazen note broke suddenly from the far-off summit of the bell-tower above us and sounded the first stroke of midnight. My companion started, apologised for detaining me, and prepared to retire. But he seemed to offer so lively a promise of further entertainment, that I was indisposed to part with him, and suggested that we should stroll homeward together. He cordially assented, so we turned out of the Piazza, passed down before the statued arcade of the Uffizi, and came out upon the Arno. What course we took I hardly remember, but we roamed slowly about for an hour, my companion delivering by snatches a sort of moon-touched aesthetic lecture. I listened in puzzled fascination, and wondered who the deuce he was. He confessed with a melancholy but all-respectful head-shake to his American origin. 'We are the disinherited of Art!' he cried. 'We are condemned to be superficial! We are excluded from the magic circle. The soil of American perception is a poor little barren, artificial deposit. Yes! we are wedded to imperfection. An American, to excel, has just ten times as much to learn as a European. We lack the deeper sense. We have neither taste, nor tact, nor force. How should we have them? Our crude and garish climate, our silent past, our deafening present, the constant pressure about us of unlovely circumstance, are as void of all that nourishes and prompts and inspires the artist, as my sad heart is void of bitterness in saying so! We poor aspirants must live in perpetual exile.'

'You seem fairly at home in exile,' I answered, 'and Florence seems to me a very pretty Siberia. But do you know my own thought? Nothing is so idle as to talk about our want of a nutritive soil, of opportunity, of inspiration, and all the rest of it. The worthy part is to do something fine! There's no law in our glorious Constitution against that. Invent, create, achieve! No matter if you've to study fifty times as much as one of these! What else are you an artist for? Be you our Moses,' I added, laughing, and laying my hand on his shoulder, 'and lead us out of the house of bondage!'

'Golden words, – golden words, young man!' he cried, with a tender smile. ' "Invent, create, achieve!" Yes, that's our business: I know it well. Don't take me, in Heaven's name, for one of your barren complainers, – querulous cynics, who have neither talent nor faith! I'm at work!' – and he glanced about him and lowered his voice as if this were a quite peculiar secret, – 'I'm at work night and day. I've undertaken a *creation*! I'm no Moses; I'm only a poor, patient artist; but it would be a fine thing if I were to cause some slender stream of beauty to flow in our thirsty land! Don't think me a monster of conceit,' he went on, as he saw me smile at the avidity with which he adopted my fantasy; 'I confess that I'm in one of those moods when great things seem possible! This is one of my nervous nights, – I dream waking! When the south-wind blows over Florence at midnight, it seems to coax the soul from all the fair things locked away in her churches and galleries; it comes into my own little studio with the moonlight, and sets my heart beating too deeply for rest. You see I am always adding a thought to my conception! This evening I felt that I couldn't sleep unless I had communed with the genius of Michael!'

He seemed deeply versed in local history and tradition, and he expatiated *con amore* on the charms of Florence. I gathered that he was an old resident, and that he had taken the lovely city into his heart. 'I owe her everything,' he declared. 'It's only since I came here that I have really lived, intellectually. One by one, all profane desires, all mere worldly aims, have dropped away from me, and left me nothing but my pencil, my little note-book' (and he tapped his breast-pocket), 'and the worship of the pure masters, – those who were pure because they were innocent, and those who were pure because they were strong!'

'And have you been very productive all this time?' I asked, with amenity.

He was silent awhile before replying. 'Not in the vulgar sense!' he said, at last. 'I have chosen never to manifest myself by imperfection. The good in every performance I have reabsorbed into the generative force of new creations; the bad – there's always plenty of that – I have religiously destroyed. I may say, with some satisfaction, that I have not added a mite to the rubbish of the world. As a proof of my conscientiousness,' – and he stopped short, and eyed me with extraordinary candour, as if the proof were to be overwhelming, – 'I've never sold a picture! "At least no merchant traffics in my heart!" Do you remember the line in Browning? My little studio has never been profaned by superficial, feverish, mercenary work. It's a temple of labour, but of leisure! Art is long. If we work for ourselves, of course we must hurry. If we work for her, we must often pause. She can wait!'

This had brought us to my hotel door, somewhat to my relief, I confess, for I had begun to feel unequal to the society of a genius of this heroic strain. I left him, however, not without expressing a friendly hope that we should meet again. The next morning my curiosity had not abated; I was anxious to see him by common daylight. I counted upon meeting him in one of the many aesthetic haunts of Florence, and I was gratified without delay. I found him in the course of the morning in the Tribune of the Uffizi, – that little treasure-chamber of perfect works. He had turned his back on the Venus de' Medici, and with his arms resting on the railing which protects the pictures, and his head buried in his hands, he was lost in the contemplation of that superb triptych of Andrea Mantegna, – a work which has neither the material splendour nor the commanding force of some of its neighbours, but which, glowing there with the loveliness of patient labour, suits possibly a more constant need of the soul. I looked at the picture for some time over his shoulder; at last, with a heavy sigh, he turned away and our eyes met. As he recognised me a deep blush rose to his face; he fancied, perhaps, that he had made a fool of himself overnight. But I offered him my hand with a frankness which assured him I was not a scoffer. I knew him by his ardent *chevelure*; otherwise he was much altered. His midnight mood was over, and he

looked as haggard as an actor by daylight. He was far older than
I had supposed, and he had less bravery of costume and
gesture. He seemed the quite poor, patient artist he had proclaimed himself, and the fact that he had never sold a picture
was more obvious than glorious. His velvet coat was threadbare, and his short slouched hat, of an antique pattern, revealed
a rustiness which marked it an 'original', and not one of the
picturesque reproductions which brethren of his craft affect.
His eye was mild and heavy, and his expression singularly
gentle and acquiescent; the more so for a certain pallid leanness
of visage which I hardly knew whether to refer to the consuming
fire of genius or to a meagre diet. A very little talk, however,
cleared his brow and brought back his eloquence.

'And this is your first visit to these enchanted halls?' he cried.
'Happy, thrice happy youth!' And taking me by the arm, he
prepared to lead me to each of the pre-eminent works in turn
and show me the cream of the gallery. But before we left the
Mantegna, he pressed my arm and gave it a loving look. '*He* was
not in a hurry,' he murmured. 'He knew nothing of "raw Haste,
half-sister to Delay"!' How sound a critic my friend was I am
unable to say, but he was an extremely amusing one; overflowing with opinions, theories, and sympathies, with disquisi-
tion and gossip and anecdote. He was a shade too sentimental
for my own sympathies, and I fancied he was rather too fond of
superfine discriminations and of discovering subtle intentions
in the shallow felicities of chance. At moments, too, he plunged
into the sea of metaphysics and floundered awhile in waters too
deep for intellectual security. But his abounding knowledge
and happy judgement told a touching story of long attentive
hours in this worshipful company; there was a reproach to my
wasteful saunterings in so devoted a culture of opportunity.
'There are two moods,' I remember his saying, 'in which we
may walk through galleries, – the critical and the ideal. They
seize us at their pleasure, and we can never tell which is to take
its turn. The critical mood, oddly, is the genial one, the friendly,
the condescending. It relishes the pretty trivialities of art, its
vulgar clevernesses, its conscious graces. It has a kindly greeting for anything which looks as if, according to his light, the

painter had enjoyed doing it, – for the little Dutch cabbages and kettles, for the taper fingers and breezy mantles of late-coming Madonnas, for the little blue-hilled pastoral, sceptical Italian landscapes. Then there are the days of fierce, fastidious longing, – solemn church-feasts of the intellect, – when all vulgar effort and all petty success is a weariness, and everything but the best – the best of the best – disgusts. In these hours we are relentless aristocrats of taste. We'll not take Michael for granted, we'll not swallow Raphael whole!'

The gallery of the Uffizi is not only rich in its possessions, but peculiarly fortunate in that fine architectural accident, as one may call it, which unites it – with the breadth of river and city between them – to those princely chambers of the Pitti Palace. The Louvre and the Vatican hardly give you such a sense of sustained enclosure as those long passages projected over street and stream to establish a sort of inviolate transition between the two palaces of art. We passed along the gallery in which those precious drawings by eminent hands hang chaste and grey above the swirl and murmur of the yellow Arno, and reached the ducal saloons of the Pitti. Ducal as they are, it must be confessed that they are imperfect as show-rooms, and that with their deep-set windows and their massive mouldings, it is rather a broken light that reaches the pictured walls. But here the masterpieces hang thick, and you seem to see them in a luminous atmosphere of their own. And the great saloons, with their superb dim ceilings, their outer wall in splendid shadow, and the sombre opposite glow of mellow canvas and dusky gilding, make, themselves, almost as fine a picture as the Titians and Raphaels they imperfectly reveal. We lingered briefly before many a Raphael and Titian; but I saw my friend was impatient, and I suffered him at last to lead me directly to the goal of our journey, – the most tenderly fair of Raphael's Virgins, the Madonna in the Chair. Of all the fine pictures of the world, it seemed to me this is the one with which criticism has least to do. None betrays less effort, less of the mechanism of effect and of the irrepressible discord between conception and result, which shows dimly in so many consummate works. Graceful, human, near to our sympathies as it is, it has nothing of manner, of method, nothing, almost, of style; it blooms there in rounded softness, as instinct with harmony as if it were an immediate exhalation of genius. The figure melts away the spectator's mind into a sort of passionate tenderness which he knows not whether he has given to heavenly purity or to earthly charm. He is intoxicated with the fragrance of the tenderest blossom of maternity that ever bloomed on earth.

'That's what I call a fine picture,' said my companion, after we had gazed awhile in silence. 'I have a right to say so, for I've copied it so often and so carefully that I could repeat it now with my eyes shut. Other works are of Raphael: this *is* Raphael himself. Others you can praise, you can qualify, you can measure, explain, account for: this you can only love and admire. I don't know in what seeming he walked among men, while this divine mood was upon him; but after it, surely, he could do nothing but die; this world had nothing more to teach him. Think of it awhile, my friend, and you'll admit that I'm not raving. Think of his seeing that spotless image, not for a moment, for a day, in a happy dream, as a restless fever-fit, not as a poet in a five minutes' frenzy, time to snatch his phrase and scribble his immortal stanza, but for days together, while the slow labour of the brush went on, while the foul vapours of life interposed, and the fancy ached with tension, fixed, radiant, distinct, as we see it now! What a master, certainly! But ah, what a seer!'

'Don't you imagine,' I answered, 'that he had a model, and that some pretty young woman –'

'As pretty a young woman as you please! It doesn't diminish the miracle! He took his hint, of course, and the young woman, possibly, sat smiling before his canvas. But, meanwhile, the painter's idea had taken wings. No lovely human outline could charm it to vulgar fact. He saw the fair form made perfect; he rose to the vision without tremor, without effort of wing; he communed with it face to face, and resolved into finer and lovelier truth the purity which completes it as the perfume completes the rose. That's what they call idealism; the word's vastly abused, but the thing is good. It's my own creed, at any rate. Lovely Madonna, model at once and muse, I call you to witness that I too am an idealist!'

'An idealist, then,' I said, half jocosely, wishing to provoke him to further utterance, 'is a gentleman who says to Nature in the person of a beautiful girl, "Go to, you're all wrong! Your fine is coarse, your bright is dim, your grace is *gaucherie*. This is the way you should have done it!" Isn't the chance against him?'

He turned upon me almost angrily, but perceiving the genial flavour of my sarcasm, he smiled gravely. 'Look at that picture,' he said, 'and cease your irreverent mockery! Idealism is *that*! There's no explaining it; one must feel the flame! It says nothing to Nature, or to any beautiful girl, that they'll not both forgive! It says to the fair woman, "Accept me as your artist-friend, lend me your beautiful face, trust me, help me, and your eyes shall be half my masterpiece!" No one so loves and respects the rich realities of nature as the artist whose imagination caresses and flatters them. He knows what a fact may hold (whether Raphael knew, you may judge by his portrait behind us there, of Tommaso Inghirami); but his fancy hovers above it, as Ariel above the sleeping prince. There is only one Raphael, but an artist may still be an artist. As I said last night, the days of illumination are gone; visions are rare; we have to look long to see them. But in meditation we may still woo the ideal; round it, smooth it, perfect it. The result – the result' (here his voice faltered suddenly, and he fixed his eyes for a moment on the picture; when they met my own again they were full of tears) – 'the result may be less than this; but still it may be good, it may be *great*!' he cried with vehemence. 'It may hang somewhere, in after years, in goodly company, and keep the artist's memory warm. Think of being known to mankind after some such fashion as this! of hanging here through the slow centuries in the gaze of an altered world, living on and on in the cunning of an eye and hand that are part of the dust of ages, a delight and a law to remote generations; making beauty a force and purity an example!'

'Heaven forbid!' I said, smiling, 'that I should take the wind out of your sails; but doesn't it occur to you that beside being strong in his genius, Raphael was happy in a certain good faith of which we have lost the trick? There are people, I know, who deny that his spotless Madonnas are anything more than pretty blondes of that period, enhanced by the Raphaelesque touch, which they declare is a profane touch. Be that as it may, people's religious and aesthetic needs went hand in hand, and there was, as I may say, a demand for the Blessed Virgin, visible and adorable, which must have given firmness to the artist's hand. I'm afraid there is no demand now.'

My companion seemed painfully puzzled; he shivered, as it were, in this chilling blast of scepticism. Then shaking his head with sublime confidence: 'There is always a demand!' he cried; 'that ineffable type is one of the eternal needs of man's heart; but pious souls long for it in silence, almost in shame. Let it appear, and this faith grows brave. How *should* it appear in this corrupt generation? It can't be made to order. It could, indeed, when the order came, trumpet-toned, from the lips of the Church herself, and was addressed to genius panting with inspiration. But it can spring now only from the soil of passionate labour and culture. Do you really fancy that while, from time to time, a man of complete artistic vision is born into the world, that image can perish? The man who paints it has painted everything. The subject admits of every perfection, – form, colour, expression, composition. It can be as simple as you please, and yet as rich, as broad and pure, and yet as full of delicate detail. Think of the chance for flesh in the little naked, nestling child, irradiating divinity; of the chance for drapery in the chaste and ample garment of the mother! Think of the great story you compress into that simple theme! Think, above all, of the mother's face and its ineffable suggestiveness, of the mingled burden of joy and trouble, the tenderness turned to worship, and the worship turned to far-seeing pity! Then look at it all in perfect line and lovely colour, breathing truth and beauty and mastery!'

'Anch' io son pittore!' I cried. 'Unless I'm mistaken, you've a masterpiece on the stocks. If you put all that in, you'll do more than Raphael himself did. Let me know when your picture is finished, and wherever in the wide world I may be, I'll post back to Florence and make my bow to – the *Madonna of the future*!'

He blushed vividly and gave a heavy sigh, half of protest, half of resignation. 'I don't often mention my picture, in so many words. I detest this modern custom of premature publicity.

A great work needs silence, privacy, mystery even. And then, do you know, people are so cruel, so frivolous, so unable to imagine a man's wishing to paint a Madonna at this time of day, that I've been laughed at, – laughed at, sir!' And his blush deepened to crimson. 'I don't know what has prompted me to be so frank and trustful with you. You look as if you wouldn't laugh at me. My dear young man,' – and he laid his hand on my arm, – 'I'm worthy of respect. Whatever my talents may be, I'm honest. There's nothing grotesque in a pure ambition, or in a life devoted to it!'

There was something so sternly sincere in his look and tone, that further questions seemed impertinent. I had repeated opportunity to ask them, however; for after this we spent much time together. Daily, for a fortnight, we met by appointment, to see the sights. He knew the city so well, he had strolled and lounged so often through its streets and churches and galleries, he was so deeply versed in its greater and lesser memories, so imbued with the local genius, that he was an altogether ideal *valet de place*, and I was glad enough to leave my Murray at home, and gather facts and opinions alike from his gossiping commentary. He talked of Florence like a lover, and admitted that it was a very old affair; he had lost his heart to her at first sight. 'It's the fashion to talk of all cities as feminine,' he said, 'but, as a rule, it's a monstrous mistake. Is Florence of the same sex as New York, as Chicago? She's the sole true woman of them all; one feels towards her as a lad in his teens feels to some beautiful older woman with a "history". It's a sort of aspiring gallantry she creates.' This disinterested passion seemed to stand my friend in stead of the common social ties; he led a lonely life, apparently, and cared for nothing but his work. I was duly flattered by his having taken my frivolous self into his favour, and by his generous sacrifice of precious hours, as they must have been, to my society. We spent many of these hours among those early paintings in which Florence is so rich, returning ever and anon with restless sympathies to wonder whether these tender blossoms of art had not a vital fragrance and savour more precious than the full-fruited knowledge of the later works. We lingered often in the sepulchral chapel of

San Lorenzo, and watched Michael Angelo's dim-visaged warrior sitting there like some awful Genius of Doubt and brooding behind his eternal mask upon the mysteries of life. We stood more than once in the little convent chambers where Fra Angelico wrought as if an angel indeed had held his hand, and gathered that sense of scattered dews and early bird-notes which makes an hour among his relics seem like a morning stroll in some monkish garden. We did all this and much more, – wandered into dark chapels, damp courts, and dusty palace-rooms, in quest of lingering hints of fresco and lurking treasures of carving.

I was more and more impressed with my companion's prodigious singleness of purpose. Everything was a pretext for some wildly idealistic rhapsody or reverie. Nothing could be seen or said that did not end sooner or later in a glowing discourse on the true, the beautiful, and the good. If my friend was not a genius, he was certainly a monomaniac; and I found as great a fascination in watching the odd lights and shades of his character as if he had been a creature from another planet. He seemed, indeed, to know very little of this one, and lived and moved altogether in his own little province of art. A creature more unsullied by the world it is impossible to conceive, and I often thought it a flaw in his artistic character that he hadn't a harmless vice or two. It amused me vastly at times to think that he was of our shrewd Yankee race; but, after all, there could be no better token of his American origin than this high aesthetic fever. The very heat of his devotion was a sign of conversion; those born to European opportunity manage better to reconcile enthusiasm with comfort. He had, moreover, all our native mistrust for intellectual discretion and our native relish for sonorous superlatives. As a critic he was vastly more generous than just, and his mildest terms of approbation were 'stupendous', 'transcendent', and 'incomparable'. The small change of admiration seemed to him no coin for a gentleman to handle; and yet, frank as he was intellectually, he was, personally, altogether a mystery. His professions, somehow, were all half-professions, and his allusions to his work and circumstances left something dimly ambiguous in the background. He was modest and proud, and never spoke of his domestic matters. He was evidently poor; yet he must have had some slender independence, since he could afford to make so merry over the fact that his culture of ideal beauty had never brought him a penny. His poverty, I supposed, was his motive for neither inviting me to his lodging nor mentioning its whereabouts. We met either in some public place or at my hotel, where I entertained him as freely as I might without appearing to be prompted by charity. He seemed always hungry, which was his nearest approach to a 'redeeming vice'. I made a point of asking no impertinent questions, but, each time we met, I ventured to make some respectful allusion to the *magnum opus*, to inquire, as it were, as to its health and progress. 'We're getting on, with the Lord's help,' he would say with a grave smile. 'We're doing well. You see I have the grand advantage that I lose no time. These hours I spend with you are pure profit. They're *suggestive*! Just as the truly religious soul is always at worship, the genuine artist is always in labour. He takes his property wherever he finds it, and learns some precious secret from every object that stands up in the light. If you but knew the rapture of observation! I gather with every glance some hint for light, for colour or relief! When I get home, I pour out my treasures into the lap of my Madonna. O, I'm not idle! *Nulla dies sine linea.*'

I was introduced in Florence to an American lady whose drawing-room had long formed an attractive place of reunion for the foreign residents. She lived on a fourth floor, and she was not rich; but she offered her visitors very good tea, little cakes at option, and conversation not quite to match. Her conversation had mainly an aesthetic flavour, for Mrs Coventry was famously 'artistic'. Her apartment was a sort of Pitti Palace *au petit pied*. She possessed 'early masters' by the dozen, – a cluster of Peruginos in her dining-room, a Giotto in her boudoir, an Andrea del Sarto over her parlour chimney-piece. Backed by these treasures, and by innumerable bronzes, mosaics, majolica dishes, and little worm-eaten diptychs showing angular saints on gilded panels, our hostess enjoyed the dignity of a sort of high-priestess of the arts. She always wore on her bosom a huge miniature copy of the Madonna della Seggiola. Gaining her ear quietly one evening I asked her whether she knew that remarkable man, Mr Theobald.

'Know him!' she exclaimed; 'know poor Theobald! All Florence knows him, his flame-coloured locks, his black velvet coat, his interminable harangues on the beautiful, and his wondrous Madonna that mortal eye has never seen, and that mortal patience has quite given up expecting.'

'Really,' I cried, 'you don't believe in his Madonna?'

'My dear ingenuous youth,' rejoined my shrewd friend, 'has he made a convert of you? Well, we all believed in him once; he came down upon Florence and took the town by storm. Another Raphael, at the very least, had been born among men, and poor, dear America was to have the credit of him. Hadn't he the very hair of Raphael flowing down on his shoulders? The hair, alas, but not the head! We swallowed him whole, however; we hung upon his lips and proclaimed his genius on the house-tops. The women were all dying to sit to him for their portraits and be made immortal, like Leonardo's Joconde. We decided that his manner was a good deal like Leonardo's, – mysterious and inscrutable and fascinating. Mysterious it certainly was; mystery was the beginning and the end of it. The months passed by, and the miracle hung fire; our master never produced his masterpiece. He passed hours in the galleries and churches, posturing, musing, and gazing; he talked more than ever about the beautiful, but he never put brush to canvas. We had all subscribed, as it were, to the great performance; but as it never came off, people began to ask for their money again. I was one of the last of the faithful; I carried devotion so far as to sit to him for my head. If you could have seen the horrible creature he made of me, you would admit that even a woman with no more vanity than will tie her bonnet straight must have cooled off then. The man didn't know the very alphabet of drawing! His strong point, he intimated, was his sentiment; but is it a consolation, when one has been painted a fright, to know it has been done with peculiar gusto? One by one, I confess, we fell away from the faith, and Mr Theobald didn't lift his little finger to preserve us. At the

first hint that we were tired of waiting and that we should like
the show to begin, he was off in a huff. "Great work requires
time, contemplation, privacy, mystery! O ye of little faith!" We
answered that we didn't insist on a great work; that the five-act
tragedy might come at his convenience; that we merely asked
for something to keep us from yawning, some inexpensive little
lever de rideau. Hereupon the poor man took his stand as a
genius misconceived and persecuted, an *âme méconnue*, and
washed his hands of us from that hour! No, I believe he does
me the honour to consider me the head and front of the conspiracy formed to nip his glory in the bud, – a bud that has taken
twenty years to blossom. Ask him if he knows me, and he'd tell
you I'm a horribly ugly old woman who has vowed his destruction because he wouldn't paint her portrait as a pendant to
Titian's Flora. I fancy that since then he has had none but
chance followers, innocent strangers like yourself, who have
taken him at his word. The mountain's still in labour; I've not
heard that the mouse has been born. I pass him once in a while
in the galleries, and he fixes his great dark eyes on me with a
sublimity of indifference, as if I were a bad copy of a Sassofer-
rato! It is a long time ago now that I heard that he was making
studies for a Madonna who was to be a *résumé* of all the other
Madonnas of the Italian school, – like that antique Venus who
borrowed a nose from one great image and an ankle from
another. It's certainly a masterly idea. The parts may be fine,
but when I think of my unhappy portrait I tremble for the
whole. He has communicated this striking idea under the
pledge of solemn secrecy to fifty chosen spirits, to every one
he has ever been able to buttonhole for five minutes. I suppose
he wants to get an order for it, and he's not to blame; for
Heaven knows how he lives. I see by your blush,' my hostess
frankly continued, 'that you have been honoured with his confidence. You needn't be ashamed, my dear young man; a man
of your age is none the worse for a certain generous credulity.
Only allow me to give you a word of advice: keep your credulity
out of your pockets! Don't pay for the picture till it's delivered.
You've not been treated to a peep at it, I imagine. No more have
your fifty predecessors in the faith. There are people who doubt

whether there is any picture to be seen. I fancy, myself, that if one were to get into his studio, one would find something very like the picture in that tale of Balzac's, – a mere mass of incoherent scratches and daubs, a jumble of dead paint!'

I listened to this pungent recital in silent wonder. It had a painfully plausible sound, and was not inconsistent with certain shy suspicions of my own. My hostess was a clever woman, and presumably a generous one. I determined to let my judgement wait upon events. Possibly she was right; but if she was wrong, she was cruelly wrong! Her version of my friend's eccentricities made me impatient to see him again and examine him in the light of public opinion. On our next meeting, I immediately asked him if he knew Mrs Coventry. He laid his hand on my arm and gave me a sad smile. 'Has she taxed *your* gallantry at last?' he asked. 'She's a foolish woman. She's frivolous and heartless, and she pretends to be serious and kind. She prattles about Giotto's second manner and Vittoria Colonna's liaison with "Michael", – one would think that Michael lived across the way and was expected in to take a hand at whist, – but she knows as little about art, and about the conditions of production, as I know about Buddhism. She profanes sacred words,' he added more vehemently, after a pause. 'She cares for you only as some one to hand teacups in that horrible mendacious little parlour of hers, with its trumpery Peruginos! If you can't dash off a new picture every three days, and let her hand it round among her guests, she tells them in plain English you're an impostor!'

This attempt of mine to test Mrs Coventry's accuracy was made in the course of a late afternoon walk to the quiet old church of San Miniato, on one of the hill-tops which directly overlook the city, from whose gate you are guided to it by a stony and cypress-bordered walk, which seems a most fitting avenue to a shrine. No spot is more propitious to lingering repose than the broad terrace in front of the church, where, lounging against the parapet, you may glance in slow alternation from the black and yellow marbles of the church façade, seamed and cracked with time and wind-sown with a tender flora of its own, down to the full domes and slender towers of

Florence and over to the blue sweep of the wide-mouthed cup of mountains into whose hollow the little treasure-city has been dropped. I had proposed, as a diversion from the painful memories evoked by Mrs Coventry's name, that Theobald should go with me the next evening to the opera, where some rarely played work was to be given. He declined, as I had half expected, for I had observed that he regularly kept his evenings in reserve, and never alluded to his manner of passing them. 'You have reminded me before,' I said, smiling, 'of that charming speech of the Florentine painter in Alfred de Musset's Lorenzaccio: "*I do no harm to any one. I pass my days in my studio. On Sunday, I go to the Annunziata or to Santa Maria; the monks think I have a voice; they dress me in a white gown and a red cap, and I take a share in the choruses, sometimes I do a little solo: these are the only times I go into public. In the evening, I visit my sweetheart; when the night is fine, we pass it on her balcony.*" I don't know whether you have a sweetheart, or whether she has a balcony. But if you're so happy, it's certainly better than trying to find a charm in a third-rate *prima donna*.'

He made no immediate response, but at last he turned to me solemnly. 'Can you look upon a beautiful woman with reverent eyes?'

'Really,' I said, 'I don't pretend to be sheepish, but I should be sorry to think I was impudent.' And I asked him what in the world he meant. When at last I had assured him that I could undertake to temper admiration with respect, he informed me, with an air of religious mystery, that it was in his power to introduce me to the most beautiful woman in Italy. 'A beauty with a soul!'

'Upon my word,' I cried, 'you're extremely fortunate. I shall rejoice to witness the conjunction.'

'This woman's beauty,' he answered, 'is a lesson, a morality, a poem! It's my daily study.'

Of course, after this, I lost no time in reminding him of what, before we parted, had taken the shape of a promise. 'I feel somehow,' he had said, 'as if it were a sort of violation of that privacy in which I have always contemplated her beauty. This is friendship, my friend. No hint of her existence has ever fallen from my lips. But with too great a familiarity we are apt to lose a sense of the real value of things, and you perhaps will throw some new light upon it and offer a fresher interpretation.' We went accordingly by appointment to a certain ancient house in the heart of Florence, – the precinct of the Mercato Vecchio, – and climbed a dark, steep staircase to the very summit of the edifice. Theobald's beauty seemed as jealously exalted above the line of common vision as the Belle aux Cheveux d'Or in her tower-top. He passed without knocking into the dark vestibule of a small apartment, and, flinging open an inner door, ushered me into a small saloon. The room seemed mean and sombre, though I caught a glimpse of white curtains swaying gently at an open window. At a table, near a lamp, sat a woman dressed in black, working at a piece of embroidery. As Theobald entered, she looked up calmly, with a smile; but seeing me, she made a movement of surprise, and rose with a kind of stately grace. Theobald stepped forward, took her hand and kissed it, with an indescribable air of immemorial usage. As he bent his head, she looked at me askance, and I thought she blushed.

'Behold the Serafina!' said Theobald, frankly, waving me forward. 'This is a friend, and a lover of the arts,' he added, introducing me. I received a smile, a courtesy, and a request to be seated.

The most beautiful woman in Italy was a person of a generous Italian type and of a great simplicity of demeanour. Seated again at her lamp, with her embroidery, she seemed to have nothing whatever to say. Theobald, bending towards her in a sort of Platonic ecstasy, asked her a dozen paternally tender questions as to her health, her state of mind, her occupations, and the progress of her embroidery, which he examined minutely and summoned me to admire. It was some portion of an ecclesiastical vestment, – yellow satin wrought with an elabourate design of silver and gold. She made answer in a full, rich voice, but with a brevity which I hesitated whether to attribute to native reserve or to the profane constraint of my presence. She had been that morning to confession; she had also been to market, and had bought a chicken for dinner. She felt very happy; she had nothing to complain of, except that the people for whom she was making her vestment, and who furnished her materials, should be willing to put such rotten silver thread into the garment, as one might say, of the Lord. From time to time, as she took her slow stitches, she raised her eyes and covered me with a glance which seemed at first to denote a placid curiosity, but in which, as I saw it repeated, I thought I perceived the dim glimmer of an attempt to establish an understanding with me at the expense of our companion. Meanwhile, as mindful as possible of Theobald's injunction of reverence, I considered the lady's personal claims to the fine compliment he had paid her.

That she was indeed a beautiful woman I perceived, after recovering from the surprise of finding her without the freshness of youth. Her beauty was of a sort which, in losing youth, loses little of its essential charm, expressed for the most part as it was in form and structure, and, as Theobald would have said, in 'composition'. She was broad and ample, low-browed and large-eyed, dark and pale. Her thick brown hair hung low beside her cheek and ear, and seemed to drape her head with a covering as chaste and formal as the veil of a nun. The poise and carriage of her head was admirably free and noble, and the more effective that their freedom was at moments discreetly corrected by a little sanctimonious droop, which harmonised admirably with the level gaze of her dark and quiet eye. A strong, serene physical nature and the placid temper which comes of no nerves and no troubles seemed this lady's comfortable portion. She was dressed in plain dull black, save for a sort of dark blue kerchief which was folded across her bosom and exposed a glimpse of her massive throat. Over this kerchief was suspended a little silver cross. I admired her greatly, and yet with a large reserve. A certain mild intellectual apathy belonged properly to her type of beauty, and had always seemed to round and enrich it; but this *bourgeoise* Egeria, if I viewed her right, betrayed a rather vulgar stagnation of mind. There might have been once a dim, spiritual light in her face; but it had long since begun to wane. And furthermore, in plain prose, she was growing stout. My disappointment amounted very nearly to complete disenchantment when Theobald, as if to facilitate my covert inspection, declaring that the lamp was very dim and that she would ruin her eyes without more light, rose and fetched a couple of candles from the mantelpiece, which he placed lighted on the table. In this brighter illumination I perceived that our hostess was decidedly an elderly woman. She was neither haggard nor worn nor grey; she was simply coarse. The 'soul' which Theobald had promised seemed scarcely worth making such a point of; it was no deeper mystery than a sort of matronly mildness of lip and brow. I would have been ready even to declare that that sanctified bend of the head was nothing more than the trick of a person constantly working at embroidery. It occurred to me even that it was a trick of a less innocent sort; for, in spite of the mellow quietude of her wits, this stately needlewoman dropped a hint that she took the situation rather less *au sérieux* than her friend. When he rose to light the candles, she looked across at me with a quick, intelligent smile and tapped her forehead with her forefinger; then, as from a sudden feeling of compassionate loyalty to poor Theobald, I preserved a blank face, she gave a little shrug and resumed her work.

What was the relation of this singular couple? Was he the most ardent of friends or the most reverent of lovers? Did she regard him as an eccentric youth whose benevolent admiration of her beauty she was not ill-pleased to humour at this small cost of having him climb into her little parlour and gossip of summer nights? With her decent and sombre dress, her simple gravity, and that fine piece of priestly needlework, she looked like some pious lay-member of a sisterhood, living by special permission outside her convent walls. Or was she maintained here aloft by her friend in comfortable leisure, so that he might have before him the perfect, eternal type, uncorrupted and untarnished by the struggle for existence? Her shapely hands, I observed, were very fair and white; they lacked the traces of what is called 'honest toil'.

'And the pictures, how do they come on?' she asked of Theobald, after a long pause.

'Finely, finely! I have here a friend whose sympathy and encouragement give me new faith and ardour.'

Our hostess turned to me, gazed at me a moment rather inscrutably, and then tapping her forehead with the gesture she had used a minute before, 'He has a magnificent genius!' she said, with perfect gravity.

'I'm inclined to think so,' I answered, with a smile.

'Eh, why do you smile?' she cried. 'If you doubt it, you must see the *bambino*!' And she took the lamp and conducted me to the other side of the room, where on the wall, in a plain black frame, hung a large drawing in red chalk. Beneath it was festooned a little bowl for holy-water. The drawing represented a very young child, entirely naked, half nestling back against his mother's gown, but with his two little arms outstretched, as if in the act of benediction. It was executed with singular freedom and power, and yet seemed vivid with the sacred bloom of infancy. A sort of dimpled elegance and grace, mingled with its boldness, recalled the touch of Correggio. 'That's what he can do!' said my hostess. 'It's the blessed little boy whom I lost. It's his very image, and the Signor Teobaldo gave it me as a gift. He has given me many things beside!'

I looked at the picture for some time and admired it vastly. Turning back to Theobald, I assured him that if it were hung among the drawings in the Uffizi and labelled with a glorious name, it would hold its own. My praise seemed to give him extreme pleasure; he pressed my hands, and his eyes filled with tears. It moved him apparently with the desire to expatiate on the history of the drawing, for he rose and made his adieux to our companion, kissing her hand with the same mild ardour as before. It occurred to me that the offer of a similar piece of gallantry on my own part might help me to know what manner of woman she was. When she perceived my intention, she withdrew her hand, dropped her eyes solemnly, and made me a severe courtesy. Theobald took my arm and led me rapidly into the street.

'And what do you think of the divine Serafina?' he cried with fervour.

'It's certainly good solid beauty!' I answered.

He eyed me an instant askance, and then seemed hurried along by the current of remembrance. 'You should have seen the mother and the child together, seen them as I first saw them, – the mother with her head draped in a shawl, a divine trouble in her face, and the bambino pressed to her bosom. You would have said, I think, that Raphael had found his match in common chance. I was coming in, one summer night, from a long walk in the country, when I met this apparition at the city gate. The woman held out her hand. I hardly knew whether to say, "What do you want?" or to fall down and worship. She asked for a little money. I saw that she was beautiful and pale. She might have stepped out of the stable of Bethlehem! I gave her money and helped her on her way into the town. I had guessed her story. She, too, was a maiden mother, and she had been turned out into the world in her shame. I felt in all my pulses that here was my subject marvellously realised. I felt like one of the old convent artists who had had a vision. I rescued the poor creatures, cherished them, watched them as I would have done some precious work of art, some lovely fragment of fresco discovered in a mouldering cloister. In a month – as if to deepen and consecrate the pathos of it all – the poor little child died. When she felt that he was going, she held him up to me for ten minutes, and I made that sketch. You saw a feverish haste in it, I suppose; I wanted to spare the poor little mortal the pain of his position. After that, I doubly valued the mother. She is the simplest, sweetest, most natural creature that ever bloomed in this brave old land of Italy. She lives in the memory of her child, in her gratitude for the scanty kindness I have been able to show her, and in her simple religion! She's not even conscious of her beauty; my admiration has never made her vain. Heaven knows I've made no secret of it. You must have observed the singular transparency of her expression, the lovely modesty of her glance. And was there ever such a truly virginal brow, such a natural classic elegance in the wave of the hair and the arch of the forehead? I've studied her; I may say I know her. I've absorbed her little by little; my mind is stamped and imbued, and I have determined now to clinch the impression; I shall at last invite her to sit for me!'

'"At last, – at last"?' I repeated, in much amazement. 'Do you mean that she has never done so yet?'

'I've not really had – a – a sitting,' said Theobald, speaking very slowly. 'I've taken notes, you know; I've got my grand fundamental impression. That's the great thing! But I've not actually had her as a model, posed and draped and lighted, before my easel.'

What had become for the moment of my perception and my tact I am at a loss to say; in their absence, I was unable to repress headlong exclamation. I was destined to regret it. We had stopped at a turning, beneath a lamp. 'My poor friend,' I exclaimed, laying my hand on his shoulder, 'you've *dawdled*! She's an old, old woman – for a Madonna!'

It was as if I had brutally struck him; I shall never forget the long, slow, almost ghastly look of pain with which he answered me. 'Dawdled – old, old!' he stammered. 'Are you joking?'

'Why, my dear fellow, I suppose you don't take the woman for twenty?'

He drew a long breath and leaned against a house, looking at me with questioning, protesting, reproachful eyes. At last, starting forward, and grasping my arm: 'Answer me solemnly: does she seem to you truly old? Is she wrinkled, is she faded, am I blind?'

Then at last I understood the immensity of his illusion; how, one by one, the noiseless years had ebbed away, and left him brooding in charmed inaction, forever preparing for a work forever deferred. It seemed to me almost a kindness now to tell him the plain truth. 'I should be sorry to say you're blind,' I answered, 'but I think you're deceived. You've lost time in effortless contemplation. Your friend was once young and fresh and virginal; but, I protest, that was some years ago. Still, she has *de beaux restes*? By all means make her sit for you!' I broke down; his face was too horribly reproachful.

He took off his hat and stood passing his handkerchief mechanically over his forehead. '*De beaux restes?* I thank you for sparing me the plain English. I must make up my Madonna out of *de beaux restes*! What a masterpiece she'll be! Old – old! Old – old!' he murmured.

'Never mind her age,' I cried, revolted at what I had done, 'never mind my impression of her! You have your memory, your notes, your genius. Finish your picture in a month. I proclaim it beforehand a masterpiece, and I hereby offer you for it any sum you may choose to ask.'

He stared, but he seemed scarcely to understand me. 'Old – old!' he kept stupidly repeating. 'If she is old, what am I? If her beauty has faded, where – where is my strength? Has life been a dream? Have I worshipped too long, – have I loved too well?' The charm, in truth, was broken. That the chord of illusion should have snapped at my light, accidental touch showed how it had been weakened by excessive tension. The poor fellow's sense of wasted time, of vanished opportunity, seemed to roll in upon his soul in waves of darkness. He suddenly dropped his head and burst into tears.

I led him homeward with all possible tenderness, but I attempted neither to check his grief, to restore his equanimity, nor to unsay the hard truth. When we reached my hotel I tried to induce him to come in. 'We'll drink a glass of wine,' I said, smiling, 'to the completion of the Madonna.'

With a violent effort he held up his head, mused for a moment with a formidably sombre frown, and then giving me his hand, 'I'll finish it,' he cried, 'in a month! No, in a fortnight! After all, I have it *here*!' And he tapped his forehead. 'Of course she's old! She can afford to have it said of her, – a woman who has made twenty years pass like a twelvemonth! Old – old! Why, sir, she shall be eternal!'

I wished to see him safely to his own door, but he waved me back and walked away with an air of resolution, whistling and swinging his cane. I waited a moment, and then followed him at a distance, and saw him proceed to cross the Santa Trinità Bridge. When he reached the middle, he suddenly paused, as if his strength had deserted him, and leaned upon the parapet gazing over into the river. I was careful to keep him in sight; I confess that I passed ten very nervous minutes. He recovered himself at last, and went his way, slowly and with hanging head.

That I should have really startled poor Theobald into a bolder use of his long-garnered stores of knowledge and taste, into the vulgar effort and hazard of production, seemed at first reason enough for his continued silence, and absence; but as day followed day without his either calling or sending me a line, and without my meeting him in his customary haunts, in the galleries, in the chapel at San Lorenzo, or strolling between the Arno-side and the great hedge-screen of verdure which, along the drive of the Cascine, throws the fair occupants of barouche and phaeton into such becoming relief, – as for more than a week I got neither tidings nor sight of him, I began to fear that I had fatally offended him, and that, instead of giving wholesome impetus to his talent, I had brutally paralysed it. I had a wretched suspicion that I had made him ill. My stay at Florence was drawing to a close, and it was important that, before resuming my journey, I should assure myself of the truth. Theobald, to the last, had kept his lodging a mystery, and I was altogether at a loss where to look for him. The simplest course was to make inquiry of the beauty of the Mercato Vecchio, and I confess that unsatisfied curiosity as to the lady herself counselled it as well. Perhaps I had done her injustice, and she was as immortally fresh and fair as he conceived her. I was, at any rate, anxious to behold once more the ripe enchantress who had made twenty years pass as a twelvemonth. I repaired accordingly, one morning, to her abode, climbed the interminable staircase, and reached her door. It stood ajar, and as I hesitated whether to enter, a little serving-maid came clattering out with an empty kettle, as if she had just performed some savoury errand. The inner door, too, was open; so I crossed the little vestibule and entered the room in which I had formerly been received. It had not its evening aspect. The table, or one end of it, was spread for a late breakfast, and before it sat a gentleman, – an individual, at least, of the male sex, – dealing justice upon a beefsteak and onions, and a bottle of wine. At his elbow, in friendly proximity, was placed the lady of the house. Her attitude, as I entered, was not that of an enchantress. With one hand she held in her lap a plate of smoking maccaroni; with the other she had lifted high in air one of the pendulous filaments of this succulent compound, and was in the act of slipping it gently down her throat. On the uncovered end of the table, facing her companion, were ranged half a dozen small statuettes, of some snuff-coloured substance resembling terra-cotta. He, brandishing his knife with ardour, was apparently descanting on their merits.

Evidently I darkened the door. My hostess dropped her maccaroni – into her mouth, and rose hastily with a harsh exclamation and a flushed face. I immediately perceived that the Signora Serafina's secret was even better worth knowing than I had supposed, and that the way to learn it was to take it for granted. I summoned my best Italian, I smiled and bowed and apologised for my intrusion; and in a moment, whether or no I had dispelled the lady's irritation, I had, at least, stimulated her prudence. I was welcome, she said; I must take a seat. This was another friend of hers, – also an artist, she declared with a smile which was almost amiable. Her companion wiped his moustache and bowed with great civility. I saw at a glance that he was equal to the situation. He was presumably the author of the statuettes on the table, and he knew a money-spending *forestiere* when he saw one. He was a small, wiry man, with a clever, impudent, tossed-up nose, a sharp little black eye, and waxed ends to his moustache. On the side of his head he wore jauntily a little crimson velvet smoking-cap, and I observed that his feet were encased in brilliant slippers. On Serafina's remarking with dignity that I was the friend of Mr Theobald, he broke out into that fantastic French of which Italians are so insistently lavish, and declared with fervour that Mr Theobald was a magnificent genius.

'I'm sure I don't know,' I answered with a shrug. 'If you're in a position to affirm it, you have the advantage of me. I've seen nothing from his hand but the bambino yonder, which certainly is fine.'

He declared that the bambino was a masterpiece, a pure Correggio. It was only a pity, he added, with a knowing laugh, that the sketch had not been made on some good bit of honey-combed old panel. The stately Serafina hereupon protested that Mr Theobald was the soul of honour, and that he would never lend himself to a deceit. 'I'm not a judge of genius,' she said, 'and I know nothing of pictures. I'm but a poor simple widow; but I know that the Signor Teobaldo has the heart of an angel and the virtue of a saint. He's my benefactor,' she added sententiously. The after-glow of the somewhat sinister flush with which she had greeted me still lingered in her cheek, and perhaps did not favour her beauty; I could not but fancy it a wise custom of Theobald's to visit her only by candlelight. She was coarse, and her poor adorer was a poet.

'I have the greatest esteem for him,' I said; 'it is for this reason that I have been uneasy at not seeing him for ten days. Have you seen him? Is he perhaps ill?'

'Ill! Heaven forbid!' cried Serafina, with genuine vehemence.

Her companion uttered a rapid expletive, and reproached her with not having been to see him. She hesitated a moment; then she simpered the least bit and bridled. 'He comes to see me – without reproach! But it would not be the same for me to go to him, though, indeed, you may almost call him a man of holy life.'

'He has the greatest admiration for you,' I said. 'He would have been honoured by your visit.'

She looked at me a moment sharply. 'More admiration than you. Admit that!' Of course I protested with all the eloquence at my command, and my mysterious hostess then confessed that she had taken no fancy to me on my former visit, and that, Theobald not having returned, she believed I had poisoned his mind against her. 'It would be no kindness to the poor gentleman, I can tell you that,' she said. 'He has come to see me every evening for years. It's a long friendship! No one knows him as well as I.'

'I don't pretend to know him, or to understand him,' I said. 'He's a mystery! Nevertheless, he seems to me a little –' And I touched my forehead and waved my hand in the air.

Serafina glanced at her companion a moment, as if for inspiration. He contented himself with shrugging his shoulders, as he filled his glass again. The *padrona* hereupon gave me a more softly insinuating smile than would have seemed likely to bloom on so candid a brow. 'It's for that that I love him!' she said. 'The world has so little kindness for such persons. It laughs at them, and despises them, and cheats them. He is too good for this wicked life! It's his fancy that he finds a little Paradise up here in my poor apartment. If he thinks so, how can I help it? He has a strange belief – really, I ought to be ashamed to tell you – that I resemble the Blessed Virgin: Heaven forgive me! I let him think what he pleases, so long as it makes him happy. He was very kind to me once, and I am not one that forgets a favour. So I receive him every evening civilly, and ask after his health, and let him look at me on this side and that! For that matter, I may say it without vanity, I was worth looking at once! And he's not always amusing, poor man! He sits sometimes for an hour without speaking a word, or else he talks away, without stopping, on art and nature, and beauty and duty, and fifty fine things that are all so much Latin to me. I beg you to understand that he has never said a word to me that I mightn't decently listen to. He may be a little cracked, but he's one of the saints.'

'Eh!' cried the man, 'the saints were all a little cracked!'

Serafina, I fancied, left part of her story untold; but she told enough of it to make poor Theobald's own statement seem intensely pathetic in its exalted simplicity. 'It's a strange fortune, certainly,' she went on, 'to have such a friend as this dear man, – a friend who's less than a lover and more than a friend.' I glanced at her companion, who preserved an impenetrable smile, twisted the end of his moustache, and disposed of a copious mouthful. Was *he* less than a lover? 'But what will you have?' Serafina pursued. 'In this hard world one mustn't ask too many questions; one must take what comes and keep what one gets. I've kept my good friend for twenty years, and I do hope that, at this time of day, Signore, you've not come to turn him against me!'

I assured her that I had no such design, and that I should vastly regret disturbing Mr Theobald's habits or convictions. On the contrary, I was alarmed about him, and I should immediately go in search of him. She gave me his address and a florid account of her sufferings at his non-appearance. She had not been to him, for various reasons; chiefly because she was afraid of displeasing him, as he had always made such a mystery of his home. 'You might have sent this gentleman!' I ventured to suggest.

'Ah,' cried the gentleman, 'he admires the Signora Serafina, but he wouldn't admire me.' And then, confidentially, with his finger on his nose, 'He's a purist!'

I was about to withdraw, on the promise that I would inform the Signora Serafina of my friend's condition, when her companion, who had risen from table and girded his loins apparently for the onset, grasped me gently by the arm, and led me before the row of statuettes. 'I perceive by your conversation, signore, that you are a patron of the arts. Allow me to request your honourable attention for these modest products of my own ingenuity. They are brand-new, fresh from my atelier, and have never been exhibited in public. I have brought them here to receive the verdict of this dear lady, who is a good critic, for all she may pretend to the contrary. I am the inventor of this peculiar style of statuette, – of subject, manner, material, everything. Touch them, I pray you; handle them; you needn't fear. Delicate as they look, it is impossible they should break! My various creations have met with great success. They are especially admired by Americans. I have sent them all over Europe, – to London, Paris, Vienna! You may have observed some little specimens in Paris, on the Boulevard, in a shop of which they constitute the speciality. There is always a crowd about the window. They form a very pleasing ornament for the mantelshelf of a gay young bachelor, for the boudoir of a pretty woman. You couldn't make a prettier present to a person with whom you wished to exchange a harmless joke. It is not classic art, signore, of course; but, between ourselves, isn't classic art sometimes rather a bore? Caricature, burlesque, *la charge*, as the French say, has hitherto been confined to paper, to the pen and pencil. Now, it has been my inspiration to introduce it into statuary. For this purpose I have invented a peculiar plastic compound which you will permit me not to divulge. That's my secret, signore! It's as light, you perceive, as cork, and yet as firm as alabaster! I frankly confess that I really pride myself as much on this little stroke of chemical ingenuity as upon the other element of novelty in my creations, – my types. What do you say to my types, signore? The idea is bold; does it strike you as happy? Cats and monkeys, – monkeys and cats, – all human life is there! Human life, of course, I mean, viewed with the eye of the satirist! To combine sculpture and satire, signore, has been my unprecedented ambition. I flatter myself that I have not egregiously failed.'

As this jaunty Juvenal of the chimney-piece delivered himself of his persuasive allocution, he took up his little groups successively from the table, held them aloft, turned them about, rapped them with his knuckles, and gazed at them lovingly with his head on one side. They consisted each of a cat and a monkey, fantastically draped, in some preposterously sentimental conjunction. They exhibited a certain sameness of motive, and illustrated chiefly the different phases of what, in delicate terms, may be called gallantry and coquetry; but they were strikingly clever and expressive, and were at once very perfect cats and monkeys and very natural men and women. I confess, however, that they failed to amuse me. I was doubtless not in a mood to enjoy them, for they seemed to me peculiarly cynical and vulgar. Their imitative felicity was revolting. As I looked askance at the complacent little artist, brandishing them between finger and thumb, and caressing them with an amorous eye, he seemed to me himself little more than an exceptionally intelligent ape. I mustered an admiring grin, however, and he blew another blast. 'My figures are studied from life! I have a little menagerie of monkeys whose frolics I contemplate by the hour. As for the cats, one has only to look out of one's back window! Since I have begun to examine these expressive little brutes, I have made many profound observations. Speaking, signore, to a man of imagination, I may say that my little designs are not without a philosophy of their own. Truly, I don't know whether the cats and monkeys imitate us, or whether it's we who imitate them.' I congratulated him on his philosophy, and he resumed: 'You will do me the honour to admit that I have handled my subjects with delicacy. Eh, it was needed, signore! I have been free, but not too free – eh? Just a hint, you know! You may see as much or as little as you please. These little groups, however, are no measure of my invention. If you will favour me with a call at my studio, I think that you will admit that my combinations are really infinite. I likewise execute figures to command. You have perhaps some little motive, – the fruit of your philosophy of life, signore, – which you would like to have interpreted. I can promise to work it up to your satisfaction; it shall be as malicious as you please! Allow me to present you with my card, and to remind you that my prices are moderate. Only sixty francs for a little group like that. My statuettes are as durable as bronze, – *ære perennius*, signore, – and, between ourselves, I think they are more amusing!'

As I pocketed his card, I glanced at Madonna Serafina, wondering whether she had an eye for contrasts. She had picked up one of the little couples and was tenderly dusting it with a feather broom.

What I had just seen and heard had so deepened my compassionate interest in my deluded friend, that I took a summary leave, and made my way directly to the house designated by this remarkable woman. It was in an obscure corner of the opposite side of the town, and presented a sombre and squalid appearance. An old woman in the doorway, on my inquiring for Theobald, ushered me in with a mumbled blessing and an expression of relief at the poor gentleman having a friend. His lodging seemed to consist of a single room at the top of the house. On getting no answer to my knock, I opened the door, supposing that he was absent; so that it gave me a certain shock to find him sitting there helpless and dumb. He was seated near the single window, facing an easel which supported a large canvas. On my entering, he looked up at me blankly, without changing his position, which was that of absolute lassitude and dejection, his arms loosely folded, his legs stretched before him, his head hanging on his breast. Advancing into the room, I perceived that his face vividly corresponded with his attitude. He was pale, haggard, and unshaven, and his dull and sunken eye gazed at me without a spark of recognition. I had been afraid that he would greet me with fierce reproaches, as the cruelly officious patron who had turned his peace to bitterness, and I was relieved to find that my appearance awakened no visible resentment. 'Don't you know me?' I asked, as I put out my hand. 'Have you already forgotten me?'

He made no response, kept his position stupidly, and left me staring about the room. It spoke most plaintively for itself. Shabby, sordid, naked, it contained, beyond the wretched bed, but the scantiest provision for personal comfort. It was bedroom at once and studio, – a grim ghost of a studio. A few dusty casts and prints on the walls, three or four old canvases turned face inward, and a rusty-looking colour-box formed, with the easel at the window, the sum of its appurtenances. The place savoured horribly of poverty. Its only wealth was the picture on the easel, presumably the famous Madonna. Averted as this was from the door, I was unable to see its face; but at last, sickened by the vacant misery of the spot, I passed behind Theobald, eagerly and tenderly. I can hardly say that I was surprised at what I found, – a canvas that was a mere dead blank, cracked and discoloured by time. This was his immortal work! Though not surprised, I confess I was powerfully moved, and I think that for five minutes I could not have trusted myself to speak. At last, my silent nearness affected him; he stirred and turned, and then rose and looked at me with a slowly kindling eye. I murmured some kind, ineffective nothings about his being ill and needing advice and care, but he seemed absorbed in the effort to recall distinctly what had last passed between us. 'You were right,' he said with a pitiful smile, 'I'm a dawdler! I'm a failure! I shall do nothing more in this world. You opened my eyes; and, though the truth is bitter, I bear you no grudge. Amen! I've been sitting here for a week, face to face with the truth, with the past, with my weakness and poverty and nullity. I shall never touch a brush! I believe I've neither eaten nor slept. Look at that canvas!' he went on, as I relieved my emotion in the urgent request that he would come home with me and dine. 'That was to have contained my masterpiece! Isn't it a promising foundation? The elements of it are all *here*.' And he tapped his forehead with that mystic confidence which had marked the gesture before. 'If I could only transpose them into some brain that had the hand, the will! Since I've been sitting here taking stock of my intellects, I've come to believe that I have the material for a hundred masterpieces. But my hand is paralysed now, and they'll never be painted. I never began! I waited and waited to be worthier to begin, and wasted my life in preparation. While I fancied my creation was growing, it was dying. I've taken it all too hard! Michael Angelo didn't when he went at the Lorenzo! He did his best at a venture, and his venture is immortal. *That*'s mine!' And he pointed with a gesture I shall never forget at the empty canvas. 'I suppose we're a genus by ourselves in the providential scheme, – we talents that can't act, that can't do nor dare! We take it out in talk, in plans and promises, in study, in visions! But our visions, let me tell you,' he cried, with a toss of his head, 'have a way of being brilliant, and a man hasn't lived in vain who has seen the things I have! Of course you'll not believe in them when that bit of worm-eaten cloth is all I have to show for them; but to convince you, to enchant and astound the world, I need only the hand of Raphael. I have his brain. A pity, you'll say, I haven't his modesty! Ah, let me babble now; it's all I have left! I'm the half of a genius! Where in the wide world is my other half? Lodged perhaps in the vulgar soul, the cunning, ready fingers of some dull copyist or some trivial artisan who turns out by the dozen his easy prodigies of touch! But it's not for me to sneer at him; he at least does something. He's not a dawdler! Well for me if I had been vulgar and clever and reckless, if I could have shut my eyes and dealt my stroke!'

What to say to the poor fellow, what to do for him, seemed hard to determine; I chiefly felt that I must break the spell of his present inaction, and remove him from the haunted atmosphere of the little room it seemed such cruel irony to call a studio. I cannot say I persuaded him to come out with me; he simply suffered himself to be led, and when we began to walk in the open air I was able to measure his pitifully weakened condition. Nevertheless, he seemed in a certain way to revive, and murmured at last that he would like to go to the Pitti Gallery. I shall never forget our melancholy stroll through those gorgeous halls, every picture on whose walls seemed, even to my own sympathetic vision, to glow with a sort of insolent renewal of strength and lustre. The eyes and lips of the great portraits seemed to smile in ineffable scorn of the dejected pretender who had dreamed of competing with their triumphant authors; the celestial candour, even, of the Madonna in the Chair, as we paused in perfect silence before her, was tinged with the sinister irony of the women of Leonardo. Perfect silence indeed marked our whole progress, – the silence of a deep farewell; for I felt in all my pulses, as Theobald, leaning on my arm, dragged one heavy foot after the other, that he was looking his last. When we came out, he was so exhausted that, instead of taking him to my hotel to dine, I called a carriage and drove him straight to his own poor lodging. He had sunk into an extraordinary lethargy; he lay back in the carriage, with his eyes closed, as pale as death, his faint breathing interrupted at intervals by a sudden gasp, like a smothered sob or a vain attempt to speak. With the help of the old woman who had admitted me before, and who emerged from a dark back court, I contrived to lead him up the long steep staircase and lay him on his wretched bed. To her I gave him in charge, while I prepared in all haste to seek a physician. But she followed me out of the room with a pitiful clasping of her hands.

'Poor, dear, blessed gentleman,' she murmured; 'is he dying?'

'Possibly. How long has he been thus?'

'Since a night he passed ten days ago. I came up in the morning to make his poor bed, and found him sitting up in his clothes before that great canvas he keeps there. Poor, dear, strange man, he says his prayers to it! He had not been to bed, nor since then properly! What has happened to him? Has he found out about the Serafina?' she whispered with a glittering eye and a toothless grin.

'Prove at least that one old woman can be faithful,' I said, 'and watch him well till I come back.' My return was delayed, through the absence of the English physician on a round of visits, and my vainly pursuing him from house to house before I overtook him. I brought him to Theobald's bedside none too soon. A violent fever had seized our patient, and the case was evidently grave. A couple of hours later I knew that he had brain-fever. From this moment I was with him constantly, but

I am far from wishing to describe his illness. Excessively painful to witness, it was happily brief. Life burned out in delirium. A certain night that I passed at his pillow, listening to his wild snatches of regret, of aspiration, of rapture and awe at the phantasmal pictures with which his brain seemed to swarm, recurs to my memory now like some stray page from a lost masterpiece of tragedy. Before a week was over we had buried him in the little Protestant cemetery on the way to Fiesole. The Signora Serafina, whom I had caused to be informed of his illness, had come in person, I was told, to inquire about its progress; but she was absent from his funeral, which was attended by but a scanty concourse of mourners. Half a dozen old Florentine sojourners, in spite of the prolonged estrangement which had preceded his death, had felt the kindly impulse to honour his grave. Among them was my friend Mrs Coventry, whom I found, on my departure, waiting at her carriage door at the gate of the cemetery.

'Well,' she said, relieving at last with a significant smile the solemnity of our immediate greeting, 'and the great Madonna? Have you seen her, after all?'

'I've seen her,' I said; 'she's mine, – by request. But I shall never show her to you.'

'And why not, pray?'

'My dear Mrs Coventry, you'd not understand her!'

'Upon my word, you're polite.'

'Excuse me; I'm sad and vexed and bitter.' And with reprehensible rudeness, I marched away. I was excessively impatient to leave Florence; my friend's dark spirit seemed diffused through all things. I had packed my trunk to start for Rome that night, and meanwhile, to beguile my unrest, I aimlessly paced the streets. Chance led me at last to the church of San Lorenzo. Remembering poor Theobald's phrase about Michael Angelo, – 'He did his best at a venture,' – I went in and turned my steps to the chapel of the tombs. Viewing in sadness the sadness of its immortal treasures, I fancied, while I stood there, that the scene demanded no ampler commentary. As I passed through the church again to depart, a woman, turning away from one of the side-altars, met me face to face.

The black shawl depending from her head draped pictur-esquely the handsome visage of Madonna Serafina. She stopped as she recognised me, and I saw that she wished to speak. Her eye was bright and her ample bosom heaved in a way that seemed to portend a certain sharpness of reproach. But the expression of my own face, apparently, drew the sting from her resentment, and she addressed me in a tone in which bitterness was tempered by a sort of dogged resignation. 'I know it was you, now, that separated us,' she said. 'It was a pity he ever brought you to see me! Of course, you couldn't think of me as he did. Well, the Lord gave him, the Lord has taken him. I've just paid for a nine days' mass for his soul. And I can tell you this, signore, I never deceived him. Who put it into his head that I was made to live on holy thoughts and fine phrases? It was his own fancy, and it pleased him to think so. Did he suffer much?' she added more softly, after a pause.

'His sufferings were great, but they were short.'

'And did he speak of me?' She had hesitated and dropped her eyes; she raised them with her question, and revealed in their sombre stillness a gleam of feminine confidence which, for the moment, revived and illumined her beauty. Poor Theo-bald! Whatever name he had given his passion, it was still her fine eyes that had charmed him.

'Be contented, madam,' I answered, gravely.

She dropped her eyes again and was silent. Then exhaling a full, rich sigh, as she gathered her shawl together: 'He was a magnificent genius!'

I bowed, and we separated.

Passing through a narrow side-street on my way back to my hotel, I perceived above a doorway a sign which it seemed to me I had read before. I suddenly remembered that it was identical with the superscription of a card that I had carried for an hour in my waistcoat-pocket. On the threshold stood the ingenious artist whose claims to public favour were thus distinctly signal-ised, smoking a pipe in the evening air, and giving the finishing polish with a bit of rag to one of his inimitable 'combinations'. I caught the expressive curl of a couple of tails. He recognised me, removed his little red cap with a most obsequious bow, and motioned me to enter his studio. I returned his bow and passed on, vexed with the apparition. For a week afterwards, whenever I was seized among the ruins of triumphant Rome with some peculiarly poignant memory of Theobald's transcendent illusions and deplorable failure, I seemed to hear a fantastic, impertinent murmur, 'Cats and monkeys, monkeys and cats; all human life is there!'

MADAME DE MAUVES

I

THE view from the terrace at Saint-Germain-en-Laye is immense and famous. Paris lies spread before you in dusky vastness, domed and fortified, glittering here and there through her light vapours, and girdled with her silver Seine. Behind you is a park of stately symmetry, and behind that a forest, where you may lounge through turfy avenues and light-chequered glades, and quite forget that you are within half an hour of the boulevards. One afternoon, however, in mid-spring, some five years ago, a young man seated on the terrace had chosen not to forget this. His eyes were fixed in idle wistfulness on the mighty human hive before him. He was fond of rural things, and he had come to Saint-Germain a week before to meet the spring half-way; but though he could boast of a six months' acquaintance with the great city, he never looked at it from his present standpoint without a feeling of painfully unsatisfied curiosity. There were moments when it seemed to him that not to be there just then was to miss some thrilling chapter of experience. And yet his winter's experience had been rather fruitless, and he had closed the book almost with a yawn. Though not in the least a cynic, he was what one may call a disappointed observer; and he never chose the right-hand road without beginning to suspect after an hour's wayfaring that the left would have been the interesting one. He now had a dozen minds to go to Paris for the evening, to dine at the Café Brébant, and to repair afterwards to the Gymnase and listen to the latest exposition of the duties of the injured husband. He would probably have risen to execute this project, if he had not observed a little girl who, wandering along the terrace, had suddenly stopped short and begun to gaze at him with round-eyed frankness. For a moment he was simply amused, for the child's face denoted helpless wonderment; the next he was agreeably surprised. 'Why, this is my friend Maggie,' he said; 'I see you have not forgotten me.'

Maggie, after a short parley, was induced to seal her remembrance with a kiss. Invited then to explain her appearance at Saint-Germain, she embarked on a recital in which the general, according to the infantine method, was so fatally sacrificed to the particular, that Longmore looked about him for a superior source of information. He found it in Maggie's mamma, who was seated with another lady at the opposite end of the terrace; so, taking the child by the hand, he led her back to her companions.

Maggie's mamma was a young American lady, as you would immediately have perceived, with a pretty and friendly face and an expensive spring toilet. She greeted Longmore with surprised cordiality, mentioned his name to her friend, and bade him bring a chair and sit with them. The other lady, who, though equally young and perhaps even prettier, was dressed more soberly, remained silent, stroking the hair of the little girl, whom she had drawn against her knee. She had never heard of Longmore, but she now perceived that her companion had crossed the ocean with him, had met him afterwards in travelling, and (having left her husband in Wall Street) was indebted to him for various small services.

Maggie's mamma turned from time to time and smiled at her friend with an air of invitation; the latter smiled back, and continued gracefully to say nothing.

For ten minutes Longmore felt a revival of interest in his interlocutress; then (as riddles are more amusing than commonplaces) it gave way to curiosity about her friend. His eyes wandered; her volubility was less suggestive than the latter's silence.

The stranger was perhaps not obviously a beauty nor obviously an American, but essentially both, on a closer scrutiny. She was slight and fair, and, though naturally pale, delicately flushed, apparently with recent excitement. What chiefly struck Longmore in her face was the union of a pair of beautifully gentle, almost languid grey eyes, with a mouth peculiarly expressive and firm. Her forehead was a trifle more expansive than belongs to classic types, and her thick brown hair was dressed out of the fashion, which was just then very ugly. Her throat and bust were slender, but all the more in harmony with certain rapid, charming movements of the head, which she had a way of throwing back every now and then, with an air of attention and a sidelong glance from her dove-like eyes. She seemed at once alert and indifferent, contemplative and restless; and Longmore very soon discovered that if she was not a brilliant beauty, she was at least an extremely interesting one. This very impression made him magnanimous. He perceived that he had interrupted a confidential conversation, and he judged it discreet to withdraw, having first learned from Maggie's mamma – Mrs Draper – that she was to take the six-o'clock train back to Paris. He promised to meet her at the station.

He kept his appointment, and Mrs Draper arrived betimes, accompanied by her friend. The latter, however, made her farewells at the door and drove away again, giving Longmore time only to raise his hat. 'Who is she?' he asked with visible ardour, as he brought Mrs Draper her tickets.

'Come and see me to-morrow at the Hôtel de l'Empire,' she answered, 'and I will tell you all about her.' The force of this offer in making him punctual at the Hôtel de l'Empire Longmore doubtless never exactly measured; and it was perhaps well that he did not, for he found his friend, who was on the point of leaving Paris, so distracted by procrastinating milliners and perjured lingères that she had no wits left for disinterested narrative. 'You must find Saint-Germain dreadfully dull,' she said, as he was going. 'Why won't you come with me to London?'

'Introduce me to Madame de Mauves,' he answered, 'and Saint-Germain will satisfy me.' All he had learned was the lady's name and residence.

'Ah! she, poor woman, will not make Saint-Germain cheerful for you. She's very unhappy.'

Longmore's further inquiries were arrested by the arrival of a young lady with a bandbox; but he went away with the promise of a note of introduction, to be immediately despatched to him at Saint-Germain.

He waited a week, but the note never came; and he declared that it was not for Mrs Draper to complain of her milliner's treachery. He lounged on the terrace and walked in the forest, studied suburban street life, and made a languid attempt to investigate the records of the court of the exiled Stuarts; but he spent most of his time in wondering where Madame de Mauves lived, and whether she never walked on the terrace. Sometimes, he finally discovered; for one afternoon toward dusk he perceived her leaning against the parapet, alone. In his momentary hesitation to approach her, it seemed to him that there was almost a shade of trepidation; but his curiosity was not diminished by the consciousness of this result of a quarter of an hour's acquaintance. She immediately recognised him on his drawing near, with the manner of a person unaccustomed to encounter a confusing variety of faces. Her dress, her expression, were the same as before; her charm was there, like that of sweet music on a second hearing. She soon made conversation easy by asking him for news of Mrs Draper. Longmore told her that he was daily expecting news, and, after a pause, mentioned the promised note of introduction.

'It seems less necessary now,' he said – 'for me, at least. But for you – I should have liked you to know the flattering things Mrs Draper would probably have said about me.'

'If it arrives at last,' she answered, 'you must come and see me and bring it. If it doesn't, you must come without it.'

Then, as she continued to linger in spite of the thickening twilight, she explained that she was waiting for her husband, who was to arrive in the train from Paris, and who often passed along the terrace on his way home. Longmore well remembered that Mrs Draper had pronounced her unhappy, and he found it convenient to suppose that this same husband made her so. Edified by his six months in Paris – 'What else is possible,' he asked himself, 'for a sweet American girl who marries an unclean Frenchman?'

But this tender expectancy of her lord's return undermined his hypothesis, and it received a further check from the gentle eagerness with which she turned and greeted an approaching figure. Longmore beheld in the fading light a stoutish gentleman, on the fair side of forty, in a high light hat, whose countenance, indistinct against the sky, was adorned by a fantastically

pointed moustache. M. de Mauves saluted his wife with punctilious gallantry, and having bowed to Longmore, asked her
several questions in French. Before taking his proffered arm to
walk to their carriage, which was in waiting at the terrace gate,
she introduced our hero as a friend of Mrs Draper, and a fellow-
countryman, whom she hoped to see at home. M. de Mauves
responded briefly, but civilly, in very fair English, and led his
wife away.

Longmore watched him as he went, twisting his picturesque
moustache, with a feeling of irritation which he certainly would
have been at a loss to account for. The only conceivable cause
was the light which M. de Mauves's good English cast upon his
own bad French. For reasons involved apparently in the very
structure of his being, Longmore found himself unable to speak
the language tolerably. He admired and enjoyed it, but the very
genius of awkwardness controlled his phraseology. But he
reflected with satisfaction that Madame de Mauves and he
had a common idiom, and his vexation was effectually dispelled
by his finding on his table that evening a letter from Mrs
Draper. It enclosed a short, formal missive to Madame de
Mauves, but the epistle itself was copious and confidential.
She had deferred writing till she reached London, where for a
week, of course, she had found other amusements.

'I think it is these distracting Englishwomen,' she wrote,
'with their green barege gowns and their white-stitched boots,
who have reminded me in self-defence of my graceful friend at
Saint-Germain and my promise to introduce you to her.
I believe I told you that she was unhappy, and I wondered afterwards whether I had not been guilty of a breach of confidence.
But you would have found it out for yourself, and besides, she
told me no secrets. She declared she was the happiest creature
in the world, and then, poor thing, she burst into tears, and
I prayed to be delivered from such happiness. It's the miserable
story of an American girl, born to be neither a slave nor a toy,
marrying a profligate Frenchman, who believes that a woman
must be one or the other. The silliest American woman is too
good for the best foreigner, and the poorest of us have moral
needs a Frenchman can't appreciate. She was romantic and

wilful, and thought Americans were vulgar. Matrimonial felicity perhaps *is* vulgar; but I think nowadays she wishes she were
a little less elegant. M. de Mauves cared, of course, for nothing
but her money, which he's spending royally on his *menus plai-
sirs*. I hope you appreciate the compliment I pay you when
I recommend you to go and console an unhappy wife. I have
never given a man such a proof of esteem, and if you were to
disappoint me I should renounce the world. Prove to Madame
de Mauves that an American friend may mingle admiration and
respect better than a French husband. She avoids society and
lives quite alone, seeing no one but a horrible French sister-in-
law. Do let me hear that you have drawn some of the sadness
from that desperate smile of hers. Make her smile with a good
conscience.'

These zealous admonitions left Longmore slightly disturbed. He found himself on the edge of a domestic tragedy
from which he instinctively recoiled. To call upon Madame de
Mauves with his present knowledge seemed a sort of fishing in
troubled waters. He was a modest man, and yet he asked
himself whether the effect of his attentions might not be to
add to her tribulation. A flattering sense of unwonted opportunity, however, made him, with the lapse of time, more confident, – possibly more reckless. It seemed a very inspiring idea
to draw the sadness from his fair countrywoman's smile, and at
least he hoped to persuade her that there was such a thing as an
agreeable American. He immediately called upon her.

II

SHE had been placed for her education, fourteen years before,
in a Parisian convent, by a widowed mamma, fonder of Homburg and Nice than of letting out tucks in the frocks of a
vigorously growing daughter. Here, besides various elegant
accomplishments, – the art of wearing a train, of composing a
bouquet, of presenting a cup of tea, – she acquired a certain
turn of the imagination which might have passed for a sign of
precocious worldliness. She dreamed of marrying a title, – not
for the pleasure of hearing herself called Mme la Vicomtesse

(for which it seemed to her that she should never greatly care), but because she had a romantic belief that the best birth is the guaranty of an ideal delicacy of feeling. Romances are rarely shaped in such perfect good faith, and Euphemia's excuse was in the radical purity of her imagination. She was profoundly incorruptible, and she cherished this pernicious conceit as if it had been a dogma revealed by a white-winged angel. Even after experience had given her a hundred rude hints, she found it easier to believe in fables, when they had a certain nobleness of meaning, than in well-attested but sordid facts. She believed that a gentleman with a long pedigree must be of necessity a very fine fellow, and that the consciousness of a picturesque family tradition imparts an exquisite tone to the character. *Noblesse oblige*, she thought, as regards yourself, and insures, as regards your wife. She had never spoken to a nobleman in her life, and these convictions were but a matter of transcendent theory. They were the fruit, in part, of the perusal of various ultramontane works of fiction – the only ones admitted to the convent library – in which the hero was always a legitimist vicomte who fought duels by the dozen, but went twice a month to confession; and in part of the perfumed gossip of her companions, many of them *filles de haut lieu*, who in the convent garden, after Sundays at home, depicted their brothers and cousins as Prince Charmings and young Paladins. Euphemia listened and said nothing; she shrouded her visions of matrimony under a coronet in religious mystery. She was not of that type of young lady who is easily induced to declare that her husband must be six feet high and a little near-sighted, part his hair in the middle, and have amber lights in his beard. To her companions she seemed to have a very pallid fancy; and even the fact that she was a sprig of the transatlantic democracy never sufficiently explained her apathy on social questions. She had a mental image of that son of the Crusaders who was to suffer her to adore him, but like many an artist who has produced a masterpiece of idealisation, she shrank from exposing it to public criticism. It was the portrait of a gentleman rather ugly than handsome, and rather poor than rich. But his ugliness was to be nobly expressive, and his poverty delicately proud. Euphemia had a fortune of her own, which, at the proper time, after fixing on her in eloquent silence those fine eyes which were to soften the feudal severity of his visage, he was to accept with a world of stifled protestations. One condition alone she was to make, – that his blood should be of the very finest strain. On this she would stake her happiness.

It so chanced that circumstances were to give convincing colour to this primitive logic.

Though little of a talker, Euphemia was an ardent listener, and there were moments when she fairly hung upon the lips of Mademoiselle Marie de Mauves. Her intimacy with this chosen schoolmate was, like most intimacies, based on their points of difference. Mademoiselle de Mauves was very positive, very shrewd, very ironical, very French, – everything that Euphemia felt herself unpardonable in not being. During her Sundays *en ville* she had examined the world and judged it, and she imparted her impressions to our attentive heroine with an agreeable mixture of enthusiasm and scepticism. She was moreover a handsome and well-grown person, on whom Euphemia's ribbons and trinkets had a trick of looking better than on their slender proprietress. She had, finally, the supreme merit of being a rigorous example of the virtue of exalted birth, having, as she did, ancestors honourably mentioned by Joinville and Commines, and a stately grandmother with a hooked nose, who came up with her after the holidays from a veritable *castel* in Auvergne. It seemed to Euphemia that these attributes made her friend more at home in the world than if she had been the daughter of even the most prosperous grocer. A certain aristocratic impudence Mademoiselle de Mauves abundantly possessed, and her raids among her friend's finery were quite in the spirit of her baronial ancestors in the twelfth century, – a spirit which Euphemia considered but a large way of understanding friendship, – a freedom from small deference to the world's opinions which would sooner or later justify itself in acts of surprising magnanimity. Mademoiselle de Mauves perhaps enjoyed but slightly that easy attitude toward society which Euphemia envied her. She proved herself later in life such an

accomplished schemer that her sense of having further heights
to scale must have awakened early. Our heroine's ribbons and
trinkets had much to do with the other's sisterly patronage, and
her appealing pliancy of character even more; but the concluding motive of Marie's writing to her grandmamma to invite
Euphemia for a three weeks' holiday to the *castel* in Auvergne,
involved altogether superior considerations. Mademoiselle de
Mauves was indeed at this time seventeen years of age, and
presumably capable of general views; and Euphemia, who was
hardly less, was a very well-grown subject for experiment,
besides being pretty enough almost to pre-assure success. It is
a proof of the sincerity of Euphemia's aspirations that the *castel*
was not a shock to her faith. It was neither a cheerful nor a
luxurious abode, but the young girl found it as delightful as a
play. It had battered towers and an empty moat, a rusty draw-
bridge and a court paved with crooked, grass-grown slabs, over
which the antique coach-wheels of the old lady with the hooked
nose seemed to awaken the echoes of the seventeenth century.
Euphemia was not frightened out of her dream; she had the
pleasure of seeing it assume the consistency of a flattering
presentiment. She had a taste for old servants, old anecdotes,
old furniture, faded household colours, and sweetly stale
odours, – musty treasures in which the Château de Mauves
abounded. She made a dozen sketches in water-colours, after
her conventual pattern; but sentimentally, as one may say, she
was forever sketching with a freer hand.

Old Madame de Mauves had nothing severe but her nose,
and she seemed to Euphemia, as indeed she was, a graciously
venerable relic of a historic order of things. She took a great
fancy to the young American, who was ready to sit all day at her
feet and listen to anecdotes of the *bon temps* and quotations
from the family chronicles. Madame de Mauves was a very
honest old woman, and uttered her thoughts with antique
plainness. One day, after pushing back Euphemia's shining
locks and blinking at her with some tenderness from under
her spectacles, she declared, with an energetic shake of the
head, that she didn't know what to make of her. And in answer
to the young girl's startled blush, – 'I should like to advise you,'

she said, 'but you seem to me so all of a piece that I am afraid that if I advise you, I shall spoil you. It's easy to see that you're not one of us. I don't know whether you're better, but you seem to me to listen to the murmur of your own young spirit, rather than to the voice from behind the confessional or to the whisper of opportunity. Young girls, in my day, when they were stupid, were very docile, but when they were clever, were very sly. You're clever enough, I imagine, and yet if I guessed all your secrets at this moment, is there one I should have to frown at? I can tell you a wickeder one than any you have discovered for yourself. If you expect to live in France, and you want to be happy, don't listen too hard to that little voice I just spoke of, – the voice that is neither the curé's nor the world's. You'll fancy it saying things that it won't help your case to hear. They'll make you sad, and when you're sad you'll grow plain, and when you're plain you'll grow bitter, and when you're bitter you'll be very disagreeable. I was brought up to think that a woman's first duty was to please, and the happiest women I've known have been the ones who performed this duty faithfully. As you're not a Catholic, I suppose you can't be a dévote; and if you don't take life as a fifty years' mass, the only way to take it is as a game of skill. Listen: not to lose, you must, – I don't say cheat; but don't be too sure your neighbour won't, and don't be shocked out of your self-possession if he does. Don't lose, my dear; I beseech you, don't lose. Be neither suspicious nor credulous; but if you find your neighbour peeping, don't cry out, but very politely wait your own chance. I've had my *revanche* more than once in my day, but I'm not sure that the sweetest I could take against life as a whole would be to have your blessed innocence profit by my experience.'

This was rather awful advice, but Euphemia understood it too little to be either edified or frightened. She sat listening to it very much as she would have listened to the speeches of an old lady in a comedy, whose diction should picturesquely correspond to the pattern of her mantilla and the fashion of her head-dress. Her indifference was doubly dangerous, for Madame de Mauves spoke at the prompting of coming events, and her words were the result of a somewhat troubled conscience, – a conscience which told her at once that Euphemia was too tender a victim to be sacrificed to an ambition, and that the prosperity of her house was too precious a heritage to be sacrificed to a scruple. The prosperity in question had suffered repeated and grievous breaches, and the house of De Mauves had been pervaded by the cold comfort of an establishment in which people were obliged to balance dinner-table allusions to feudal ancestors against the absence of side dishes; a state of things the more regrettable as the family was now mainly represented by a gentleman whose appetite was large, and who justly maintained that its historic glories were not established by underfed heroes.

Three days after Euphemia's arrival, Richard de Mauves came down from Paris to pay his respects to his grandmother, and treated our heroine to her first encounter with a gentilhomme in the flesh. On coming in he kissed his grandmother's hand, with a smile which caused her to draw it away with dignity, and set Euphemia, who was standing by, wondering what had happened between them. Her unanswered wonder was but the beginning of a life of bitter perplexity, but the reader is free to know that the smile of M. de Mauves was a reply to a certain postscript affixed by the old lady to a letter promptly addressed to him by her granddaughter, after Euphemia had been admitted to justify the latter's promises. Mademoiselle de Mauves brought her letter to her grandmother for approval, but obtained no more than was expressed in a frigid nod. The old lady watched her with a sombre glance as she proceeded to seal the letter, and suddenly bade her open it again and bring her a pen.

'Your sister's flatteries are all nonsense,' she wrote; 'the young lady is far too good for you, *mauvais sujet*. If you have a conscience you'll not come and take possession of an angel of innocence.'

The young girl, who had read these lines, made up a little face as she redirected the letter; but she laid down her pen with a confident nod, which might have seemed to mean that, to the best of her belief, her brother had not a conscience.

'If you meant what you said,' the young man whispered to his grandmother on the first opportunity, 'it would have been simpler not to let her send the letter!'

It was perhaps because she was wounded by this cynical insinuation, that Madame de Mauves remained in her own apartment during a greater part of Euphemia's stay, so that the latter's angelic innocence was left entirely to the Baron's mercy. It suffered no worse mischance, however, than to be prompted to intenser communion with itself. M. de Mauves was the hero of the young girl's romance made real, and so completely accordant with this creature of her imagination, that she felt afraid of him, very much as she would have been of a supernatural apparition. He was thirty-five years old, – young enough to suggest possibilities of ardent activity, and old enough to have formed opinions which a simple woman might deem it an intellectual privilege to listen to. He was perhaps a trifle handsomer than Euphemia's rather grim, Quixotic ideal, but a very few days reconciled her to his good looks, as they would have reconciled her to his ugliness. He was quiet, grave, and eminently distinguished. He spoke little, but his speeches, without being sententious, had a certain noble-ness of tone which caused them to re-echo in the young girl's ears at the end of the day. He paid her very little direct atten-tion, but his chance words – if he only asked her if she objected to his cigarette – were accompanied by a smile of extraordinary kindness.

It happened that shortly after his arrival, riding an unruly horse, which Euphemia with shy admiration had watched him mount in the castle yard, he was thrown with a violence which, without disparaging his skill, made him for a fortnight an interesting invalid, lounging in the library with a bandaged knee. To beguile his confinement, Euphemia was repeatedly induced to sing to him, which she did with a little natural tremor in her voice, which might have passed for an exquisite refinement of art. He never overwhelmed her with com-pliments, but he listened with unwandering attention, remembered all her melodies, and sat humming them to him-self. While his imprisonment lasted, indeed, he passed hours in

her company, and made her feel not unlike some unfriended
artist who has suddenly gained the opportunity to devote a
fortnight to the study of a great model. Euphemia studied
with noiseless diligence what she supposed to be the 'character'
of M. de Mauves, and the more she looked the more fine lights
and shades she seemed to behold in this masterpiece of nature.
M. de Mauves's character indeed, whether from a sense of
being generously scrutinised, or for reasons which bid graceful
defiance to analysis, had never been so amiable; it seemed really
to reflect the purity of Euphemia's interpretation of it. There
had been nothing especially to admire in the state of mind in
which he left Paris, – a hard determination to marry a young girl
whose charms might or might not justify his sister's account of
them, but who was mistress, at the worst, of a couple of hundred thousand francs a year. He had not counted out sentiment; if she pleased him, so much the better; but he had left a
meagre margin for it, and he would hardly have admitted that
so excellent a match could be improved by it. He was a placid
sceptic, and it was a singular fate for a man who believed in
nothing to be so tenderly believed in. What his original faith
had been he could hardly have told you; for as he came back to
his childhood's home to mend his fortunes by pretending to fall
in love, he was a thoroughly perverted creature, and overlaid
with more corruptions than a summer day's questioning of his
conscience would have released him from. Ten years' pursuit of
pleasure, which a bureau full of unpaid bills was all he had to
show for, had pretty well stifled the natural lad, whose violent
will and generous temper might have been shaped by other
circumstances to a result which a romantic imagination might
fairly accept as a late-blooming flower of hereditary honour.
The Baron's violence had been subdued, and he had learned to
be irreproachably polite; but he had lost the edge of his generosity, and his politeness, which in the long run society paid for,
was hardly more than a form of luxurious egotism, like his
fondness for cambric handkerchiefs, lavender gloves, and
other fopperies by which shopkeepers remained out of pocket.
In after years he was terribly polite to his wife. He had formed
himself, as the phrase was, and the form prescribed to him by

the society into which his birth and his tastes introduced him was marked by some peculiar features. That which mainly concerns us is its classification of the fairer half of humanity as objects not essentially different – say from the light gloves one soils in an evening and throws away. To do M. de Mauves justice, he had in the course of time encountered such plentiful evidence of this pliant, glove-like quality in the feminine character, that idealism naturally seemed to him a losing game.

Euphemia, as he lay on his sofa, seemed by no means a refutation; she simply reminded him that very young women are generally innocent, and that this, on the whole, was the most charming stage of their development. Her innocence inspired him with profound respect, and it seemed to him that if he shortly became her husband it would be exposed to a danger the less. Old Madame de Mauves, who flattered herself that in this whole matter she was being laudably rigid, might have learned a lesson from his gallant consideration. For a fortnight the Baron was almost a blushing boy again. He watched from behind the 'Figaro', and admired, and held his tongue. He was not in the least disposed toward a flirtation; he had no desire to trouble the waters he proposed to transfuse into the golden cup of matrimony. Sometimes a word, a look, a movement of Euphemia's, gave him the oddest sense of being, or of seeming at least, almost bashful; for she had a way of not dropping her eyes, according to the mysterious virginal mechanism, of not fluttering out of the room when she found him there alone, of treating him rather as a benignant than as a pernicious influence, – a radiant frankness of demeanour, in fine, in spite of an evident natural reserve, which it seemed equally graceless not to make the subject of a compliment and indelicate not to take for granted. In this way there was wrought in the Baron's mind a vague, unwonted resonance of soft impressions, as we may call it, which indicated the transmutation of 'sentiment' from a contingency into a fact. His imagination enjoyed it; he was very fond of music, and this reminded him of some of the best he had ever heard. In spite of the bore of being laid up with a lame knee, he was in a better humour than he had known for months; he lay smoking cigarettes and listening to the nightingales, with the comfortable smile of one of his country neighbours whose big ox should have taken the prize at a fair. Every now and then, with an impatient suspicion of the resemblance, he declared that he was pitifully *bête*; but he was under a charm which braved even the supreme penalty of seeming ridiculous. One morning he had half an hour's tête-à-tête with his grandmother's confessor, a soft-voiced old abbé, whom, for reasons of her own, Madame de Mauves had suddenly summoned, and had left waiting in the drawing-room while she rearranged her curls. His reverence, going up to the old lady, assured her that M. le Baron was in a most edifying state of mind, and a promising subject for the operation of grace. This was a pious interpretation of the Baron's momentary good-humour. He had always lazily wondered what priests were good for, and he now remembered, with a sense of especial obligation to the abbé, that they were excellent for marrying people.

A day or two after this he left off his bandages, and tried to walk. He made his way into the garden and hobbled successfully along one of the alleys; but in the midst of his progress he was seized with a spasm of pain which forced him to stop and call for help. In an instant Euphemia came tripping along the path and offered him her arm with the frankest solicitude.

'Not to the house,' he said, taking it; 'farther on, to the bosquet.' This choice was prompted by her having immediately confessed that she had seen him leave the house, had feared an accident, and had followed him on tiptoe.

'Why didn't you join me?' he had asked, giving her a look in which admiration was no longer disguised, and yet felt itself half at the mercy of her replying that a *jeune fille* should not be seen following a gentleman. But it drew a breath which filled its lungs for a long time afterward, when she replied simply that if she had overtaken him he might have accepted her arm out of politeness, whereas she wished to have the pleasure of seeing him walk alone.

The bosquet was covered with an odorous tangle of blossoming vines, and a nightingale overhead was shaking out love-notes with a profuseness which made the Baron consider his own conduct the perfection of propriety.

'In America,' he said, 'I have always heard that when a man wishes to marry a young girl, he offers himself simply, face to face, without any ceremony, – without parents, and uncles, and cousins sitting round in a circle.'

'Why, I believe so,' said Euphemia, staring, and too surprised to be alarmed.

'Very well, then,' said the Baron, 'suppose our bosquet here to be America. I offer you my hand, à l'Américaine. It will make me intensely happy to have you accept it.'

Whether Euphemia's acceptance was in the American manner is more than I can say; I incline to think that for fluttering, grateful, trustful, softly-amazed young hearts, there is only one manner all over the world.

That evening, in the little turret chamber which it was her happiness to inhabit, she wrote a dutiful letter to her mamma, and had just sealed it when she was sent for by Madame de Mauves. She found this ancient lady seated in her boudoir, in a lavender satin gown, with all her candles lighted, as if to celebrate her grandson's betrothal. 'Are you very happy?' Madame de Mauves demanded, making Euphemia sit down before her.

'I'm almost afraid to say so,' said the young girl, 'lest I should wake myself up,'

'May you never wake up, *belle enfant*,' said the old lady, solemnly. 'This is the first marriage ever made in our family in this way, – by a Baron de Mauves proposing to a young girl in an arbour, like Jeannot and Jeannette. It has not been our way of doing things, and people may say it wants frankness. My grandson tells me he considers it the perfection of frankness. Very good. I'm a very old woman, and if your differences should ever be as frank as your agreement, I shouldn't like to see them. But I should be sorry to die and think you were going to be unhappy. You can't be, beyond a certain point; because, though in this world the Lord sometimes makes light of our expectations, he never altogether ignores our deserts. But you're very young and innocent, and easy to deceive. There never was a man in the world – among the saints themselves – as good as you believe the Baron. But he's a *galant homme* and a gentleman, and I've been talking to him to-night. To you I want to say this, – that you're to forget the worldly rubbish I talked the other day about frivolous women being happy. It's not the kind of happiness that would suit you. Whatever befalls you, promise me this: to be yourself. The Baronne de Mauves will be none the worse for it. Yourself, understand, in spite of everything, – bad precepts and bad examples, bad usage even. Be persistently and patiently yourself, and a De Mauves will do you justice!'

Euphemia remembered this speech in after years, and more than once, wearily closing her eyes, she seemed to see the old woman sitting upright in her faded finery and smiling grimly, like one of the Fates who sees the wheel of fortune turning up her favourite event. But at the moment it seemed to her simply to have the proper gravity of the occasion; this was the way, she supposed, in which lucky young girls were addressed on their engagement by wise old women of quality.

At her convent, to which she immediately returned, she found a letter from her mother, which shocked her far more than the remarks of Madame de Mauves. Who were these people, Mrs Cleve demanded, who had presumed to talk to her daughter of marriage without asking her leave? Questionable gentlefolk, plainly; the best French people never did such things. Euphemia would return straightway to her convent, shut herself up, and await her own arrival.

It took Mrs Cleve three weeks to travel from Nice to Paris, and during this time the young girl had no communication with her lover beyond accepting a bouquet of violets, marked with his initials and left by a female friend. 'I've not brought you up with such devoted care,' she declared to her daughter at their first interview, 'to marry a penniless Frenchman. I will take you straight home, and you will please to forget M. de Mauves.'

Mrs Cleve received that evening at her hotel a visit from the Baron which mitigated her wrath, but failed to modify her decision. He had very good manners, but she was sure he had horrible morals; and Mrs Cleve, who had been a very good-natured censor on her own account, felt a genuine spiritual need to sacrifice her daughter to propriety. She belonged to that large class of Americans who make light of America in familiar discourse, but are startled back into a sense of moral responsibility when they find Europeans taking them at their word. 'I know the type, my dear,' she said to her daughter with a sagacious nod. 'He'll not beat you; sometimes you'll wish he would.'

Euphemia remained solemnly silent; for the only answer she felt capable of making her mother was that her mind was too small a measure of things, and that the Baron's 'type' was one which it took some mystical illumination to appreciate. A person who confounded him with the common throng of her watering-place acquaintance was not a person to argue with. It seemed to Euphemia that she had no cause to plead; her cause was in the Lord's hands and her lover's.

M. de Mauves had been irritated and mortified by Mrs Cleve's opposition, and hardly knew how to handle an adversary who failed to perceive that a De Mauves of necessity gave more than he received. But he had obtained information on his return to Paris which exalted the uses of humility. Euphemia's fortune, wonderful to say, was greater than its fame, and in view of such a prize, even a De Mauves could afford to take a snubbing.

The young man's tact, his deference, his urbane insistence, won a concession from Mrs Cleve. The engagement was to be suspended and her daughter was to return home, be brought out and receive the homage she was entitled to, and which would but too surely take a form dangerous to the Baron's suit. They were to exchange neither letters, nor mementos, nor messages; but if at the end of two years Euphemia had refused offers enough to attest the permanence of her attachment, he should receive an invitation to address her again.

This decision was promulgated in the presence of the parties interested. The Baron bore himself gallantly, and looked at the young girl, expecting some tender protestation. But she only looked at him silently in return, neither weeping, nor smiling, nor putting out her hand. On this they separated; but as the Baron walked away, he declared to himself that, in spite of the confounded two years, he was a very happy fellow, – to have a fiancée who, to several millions of francs, added such strangely beautiful eyes.

How many offers Euphemia refused but scantily concerns us, – and how the Baron wore his two years away. He found that he needed pastimes, and, as pastimes were expensive, he added heavily to the list of debts to be cancelled by Euphemia's millions. Sometimes, in the thick of what he had once called pleasure with a keener conviction than now, he put to himself the case of their failing him after all; and then he remembered that last mute assurance of her eyes, and drew a long breath of such confidence as he felt in nothing else in the world save his own punctuality in an affair of honour.

At last, one morning, he took the express to Havre with a letter of Mrs Cleve's in his pocket, and ten days later made his bow to mother and daughter in New York. His stay was brief, and he was apparently unable to bring himself to view what Euphemia's uncle, Mr Butterworth, who gave her away at the altar, called our great experiment in democratic self-govern-ment in a serious light. He smiled at everything, and seemed to regard the New World as a colossal *plaisanterie*. It is true that a perpetual smile was the most natural expression of counten-ance for a man about to marry Euphemia Cleve.

III

LONGMORE's first visit seemed to open to him so large an opportunity for tranquil enjoyment, that he very soon paid a second, and, at the end of a fortnight, had spent a great many hours in the little drawing-room which Madame de Mauves rarely quitted except to drive or walk in the forest. She lived in an old-fashioned pavilion, between a high-walled court and an excessively artificial garden, beyond whose enclosure you saw a long line of tree-tops. Longmore liked the garden, and in the mild afternoons used to move his chair through the open win-dow to the little terrace which overlooked it, while his hostess sat just within. After a while she came out and wandered through the narrow alleys and beside the thin-spouting foun-tain, and last introduced him to a little gate in the garden wall, opening upon a lane which led into the forest. Hitherward, more than once, she wandered with him, bare-headed and meaning to go but twenty rods, but always strolling good-naturedly farther, and often taking a generous walk. They discovered a vast deal to talk about, and to the pleasure of finding the hours tread inaudibly away, Longmore was able to add the satisfaction of suspecting that he was a 'resource' for Madame de Mauves. He had made her acquaintance with the sense, not altogether comfortable, that she was a woman with a painful secret, and that seeking her acquaintance would be like visiting at a house where there was an invalid who could bear no noise. But he very soon perceived that her sorrow, since sorrow it was, was not an aggressive one; that it was not fond of attitudes and ceremonies, and that her earnest wish was to forget it. He felt that even if Mrs Draper had not told him she was unhappy, he would have guessed it; and yet he could hardly have pointed to his evidence. It was chiefly negative, – she never alluded to her husband. Beyond this it seemed to him simply that her whole being was pitched on a lower key than harmonious Nature meant; she was like a powerful singer who had lost her high notes. She never drooped nor sighed nor looked unutterable things; she indulged in no dusky sarcasms against fate; she had, in short, none of the coquetry of unhappiness. But Longmore was sure that her gentle gaiety was the result of strenuous effort, and that she was trying to interest herself in his thoughts to escape from her own. If she had wished to irritate his curiosity and lead him to take her confidence by storm, nothing could have served her purpose better than this ingenuous reserve. He declared to himself that there was a rare magnanimity in such ardent self-effacement, and that but one woman in ten thousand was capable of merging an intensely personal grief in thankless outward contemplation. Madame de Mauves, he instinctively felt, was not sweeping the horizon for a compensation or a consoler; she had suffered a personal deception which had disgusted her with persons. She was not striving to balance her sorrow with some strongly flavoured joy; for the present, she was trying to live with it, peaceably, reputably, and without scandal, – turning the key on it occasionally, as you would on a companion liable to attacks of insanity. Longmore was a man of fine senses and of an active imagination, whose leading-strings had never been slipped. He began to regard his hostess as a figure haunted by a shadow which was somehow her intenser, more authentic self. This hovering mystery came to have for him an extraordinary charm. Her delicate beauty acquired to his eye the serious cast of certain blank-browed Greek statues, and sometimes, when his imagination, more than his ear, detected a vague tremor in the tone in which she attempted to make a friendly question seem to have behind it none of the hollow resonance of absent-mindedness, his marvelling eyes gave her an answer more eloquent, though much less to the point, than the one she demanded.

She gave him indeed much to wonder about, and, in his ignorance, he formed a dozen experimental theories upon the history of her marriage. She had married for love and staked her whole soul on it; of that he was convinced. She had not married a Frenchman to be near Paris and her base of supplies of millinery; he was sure she had seen conjugal happiness in a light of which her present life, with its conveniences for shopping and its moral aridity, was the absolute negation. But by what extraordinary process of the heart – through what mysterious intermission of that moral instinct which may keep pace with the heart, even when that organ is making unprecedented time – had she fixed her affections on an arrogantly frivolous Frenchman? Longmore needed no telling; he knew M. de Mauves was frivolous; it was stamped on his eyes, his nose, his mouth, his carriage. For French women Longmore had but a scanty kindness, or at least (what with him was very much the same thing) but a scanty gallantry; they all seemed to belong to the type of a certain fine lady to whom he had ventured to present a letter of introduction, and whom, directly after his first visit to her, he had set down in his note-book as 'metallic'. Why should Madame de Mauves have chosen a French woman's lot, – she whose character had a perfume which doesn't belong to even the brightest metals? He asked her one day frankly if it had cost her nothing to transplant herself, – if she was not oppressed with a sense of irreconcilable difference from 'all these people'. She was silent awhile, and he fancied that she was hesitating as to whether she should resent so unceremonious an allusion to her husband. He almost wished she would; it would seem a proof that her deep reserve of sorrow had a limit.

'I almost grew up here,' she said at last, 'and it was here for me that those dreams of the future took shape that we all have when we cease to be very young. As matters stand, one may be very American and yet arrange it with one's conscience to live in Europe. My imagination perhaps – I had a little when I was younger – helped me to think I should find happiness here. And after all, for a woman, what does it signify? This is not America, perhaps, about me, but it's quite as little France. France is out there, beyond the garden, in the town, in the forest; but here, close about me, in my room and' – she paused a moment – 'in my mind, it's a nameless country of my own. It's not her country,' she added, 'that makes a woman happy or unhappy.'

Madame Clairin, Euphemia's sister-in-law, might have been supposed to have undertaken the graceful task of making Longmore ashamed of his uncivil jottings about her sex and nation. Mademoiselle de Mauves, bringing example to the confirmation of precept, had made a remunerative match and sacrificed her name to the millions of a prosperous and aspiring wholesale druggist, – a gentleman liberal enough to consider his fortune a moderate price for being towed into circles unpervaded by pharmaceutic odours. His system, possibly, was sound, but his own application of it was unfortunate. M. Clairin's head was turned by his good luck. Having secured an aristocratic wife, he adopted an aristocratic vice and began to gamble at the Bourse. In an evil hour he lost heavily and staked heavily to recover himself. But he overtook his loss only by a greater one. Then he let everything go, – his wits, his courage, his probity, – everything that had made him what his ridiculous marriage had so promptly unmade. He walked up the Rue Vivienne one day with his hands in his empty pockets, and stood for half an hour staring confusedly up and down the glittering boulevard. People brushed against him, and half a dozen carriages almost ran over him, until at last a policeman, who had been watching him for some time, took him by the arm and led him gently away. He looked at the man's cocked hat and sword with tears in his eyes; he hoped he was going to interpret to him the wrath of Heaven, – to execute the penalty of his dead-weight of self-abhorrence. But the sergent de ville only stationed him in the embrasure of a door, out of harm's way, and walked away to supervise a financial contest between an old lady and a cabman. Poor M. Clairin had only been married a year, but he had had time to measure the lofty spirit of a De Mauves. When night had fallen, he repaired to the house of a friend and asked for a night's lodging; and as his friend, who was simply his old head book-keeper and lived in a small way, was put to some trouble to accommodate him, – 'You must excuse me,' Clairin said, 'but I can't go home. I'm afraid of my wife!' Toward morning he blew his brains out. His widow turned the remnants of his property to better account than could have been expected, and wore the very handsomest mourning. It was for this latter reason, perhaps, that she was obliged to retrench at other points and accept a temporary home under her brother's roof.

Fortune had played Madame Clairin a terrible trick, but had found an adversary and not a victim. Though quite without beauty, she had always had what is called the grand air, and her air from this time forward was grander than ever. As she trailed about in her sable furbelows, tossing back her well-dressed head, and holding up her vigilant eye-glass, she seemed to be sweeping the whole field of society and asking herself where she should pluck her revenge. Suddenly she espied it, ready made to her hand, in poor Longmore's wealth and amiability. American dollars and American complaisance had made her brother's fortune; why shouldn't they make hers? She overestimated Longmore's wealth and misinterpreted his amiability; for she was sure that a man could not be so contented without being rich, nor so unassuming without being weak. He encountered her advances with a formal politeness which covered a great deal of unflattering discomposure. She made him feel acutely uncomfortable; and though he was at a loss to conceive how he could be an object of interest to a shrewd Parisienne, he had an indefinable sense of being enclosed in a magnetic circle, like the victim of an incantation. If Madame Clairin could have fathomed his Puritanic soul, she would have laid by her wand

and her book and admitted that he was an impossible subject. She gave him a kind of moral chill, and he never mentally alluded to her save as that dreadful woman, – that terrible woman. He did justice to her grand air, but for his pleasure he preferred the small air of Madame de Mauves; and he never made her his bow, after standing frigidly passive for five minutes to one of her gracious overtures to intimacy, without feeling a peculiar desire to ramble away into the forest, fling himself down on the warm grass, and, staring up at the blue sky, forget that there were any women in nature who didn't please like the swaying tree-tops. One day, on his arrival, she met him in the court and told him that her sister-in-law was shut up with a headache, and that his visit must be for her. He followed her into the drawing-room with the best grace at his command, and sat twirling his hat for half an hour. Suddenly he understood her; the caressing cadence of her voice was a distinct invitation to solicit the incomparable honour of her hand. He blushed to the roots of his hair and jumped up with uncontrollable alacrity; then, dropping a glance at Madame Clairin, who sat watching him with hard eyes over the edge of her smile, as it were, perceived on her brow a flash of unforgiving wrath. It was not becoming, but his eyes lingered a moment, for it seemed to illuminate her character. What he saw there frightened him, and he felt himself murmuring, 'Poor Madame de Mauves!' His departure was abrupt, and this time he really went into the forest and lay down on the grass.

After this he admired Madame de Mauves more than ever; she seemed a brighter figure, dogged by a darker shadow. At the end of a month he received a letter from a friend with whom he had arranged a tour through the Low Countries, reminding him of his promise to meet him promptly at Brussels. It was only after his answer was posted that he fully measured the zeal with which he had declared that the journey must either be deferred or abandoned, – that he could not possibly leave Saint-Germain. He took a walk in the forest, and asked himself if this was irrevocably true. If it was, surely his duty was to march straight home and pack his trunk. Poor Webster, who, he knew, had counted ardently on this excursion, was an excellent fellow;

six weeks ago he would have gone through fire and water to join Webster. It had never been in his books to throw overboard a friend whom he had loved for ten years for a married woman whom for six weeks he had – admired. It was certainly beyond question that he was lingering at Saint-Germain because this admirable married woman was there; but in the midst of all this admiration what had become of prudence? This was the conduct of a man prepared to fall utterly in love. If she was as unhappy as he believed, the love of such a man would help her very little more than his indifference; if she was less so, she needed no help and could dispense with his friendly offices. He was sure, moreover, that if she knew he was staying on her account, she would be extremely annoyed. But this very feeling had much to do with making it hard to go; her displeasure would only enhance the gentle stoicism which touched him to the heart. At moments, indeed, he assured himself that to linger was simply impertinent; it was indelicate to make a daily study of such a shrinking grief. But inclination answered that some day her self-support would fail, and he had a vision of this admirable creature calling vainly for help. He would be her friend, to any length; it was unworthy of both of them to think about consequences. But he was a friend who carried about with him a muttering resentment that he had not known her five years earlier, and a brooding hostility to those who had anticipated him. It seemed one of fortune's most mocking strokes, that she should be surrounded by persons whose only merit was that they threw the charm of her character into radiant relief.

Longmore's growing irritation made it more and more difficult for him to see any other merit than this in the Baron de Mauves. And yet, disinterestedly, it would have been hard to give a name to the portentous vices which such an estimate implied, and there were times when our hero was almost persuaded against his finer judgement that he was really the most considerate of husbands, and that his wife liked melancholy for melancholy's sake. His manners were perfect, his urbanity was unbounded, and he seemed never to address her but, sentimentally speaking, hat in hand. His tone to Longmore (as the latter was perfectly aware) was that of a man of the world to a man not quite of the world; but what it lacked in deference it made up in easy friendliness. 'I can't thank you enough for having overcome my wife's shyness,' he more than once declared. 'If we left her to do as she pleased, she would bury herself alive. Come often, and bring some one else. She'll have nothing to do with my friends, but perhaps she'll accept yours.'

The Baron made these speeches with a remorseless placidity very amazing to our hero, who had an innocent belief that a man's head may point out to him the shortcomings of his heart and make him ashamed of them. He could not fancy him capable both of neglecting his wife and taking an almost humourous view of her suffering. Longmore had, at any rate, an exasperating sense that the Baron thought rather less of his wife than more, for that very same fine difference of nature which so deeply stirred his own sympathies. He was rarely present during Longmore's visits, and made a daily journey to Paris, where he had 'business', as he once mentioned, – not in the least with a tone of apology. When he appeared, it was late in the evening, and with an imperturbable air of being on the best of terms with every one and everything, which was peculiarly annoying if you happened to have a tacit quarrel with him. If he was a good fellow, he was surely a good fellow spoiled. Something he had, however, which Longmore vaguely envied – a kind of superb positiveness – a manner rounded and polished by the traditions of centuries – an amenity exercised for his own sake and not his neighbours' – which seemed the result of something better than a good conscience – of a vigorous and unscrupulous temperament. The Baron was plainly not a moral man, and poor Longmore, who was, would have been glad to learn the secret of his luxurious serenity. What was it that enabled him, without being a monster with visibly cloven feet, exhaling brimstone, to misprise so cruelly a lovely wife, and to walk about the world with a smile under his moustache? It was the essential grossness of his imagination, which had nevertheless helped him to turn so many neat compliments. He could be very polite, and he could doubtless be supremely impertinent; but he was as unable to draw a moral inference of the finer strain, as a schoolboy who has been playing truant for a week to solve a problem in algebra. It was ten to one he didn't know his wife was unhappy; he and his brilliant sister had doubtless agreed to consider their companion a Puritanical little person, of meagre aspirations and slender accomplishments, contented with looking at Paris from the terrace, and, as an especial treat, having a countryman very much like herself to supply her with homely transatlantic gossip. M. de Mauves was tired of his companion: he relished a higher flavour in female society. She was too modest, too simple, too delicate; she had too few arts, too little coquetry, too much charity. M. de Mauves, some day, lighting a cigar, had probably decided she was stupid. It was the same sort of taste, Longmore moralised, as the taste for Gérôme in painting, and for M. Gustave Flaubert in literature. The Baron was a pagan and his wife was a Christian, and between them, accordingly, was a gulf. He was by race and instinct a *grand seigneur.* Longmore had often heard of this distinguished social type, and was properly grateful for an opportunity to examine it closely. It had certainly a picturesque boldness of outline, but it was fed from spiritual sources so remote from those of which he felt the living gush in his own soul, that he found himself gazing at it, in irreconcilable antipathy, across a dim historic mist. 'I'm a modern *bourgeois,*' he said, 'and not perhaps so good a judge of how far a pretty woman's tongue may go at supper without prejudice to her reputation. But I've not met one of the sweetest of women without recognising her and discovering that a certain sort of character offers better entertainment than Thérésa's songs, sung by a dissipated duchess. Wit for wit, I think mine carries me further.' It was easy indeed to perceive that, as became a *grand seigneur,* M. de Mauves had a stock of rigid notions. He would not especially have desired, perhaps, that his wife should compete in amateur operettas with the duchesses in question, chiefly of recent origin; but he held that a gentleman may take his amusement where he finds it, that he is quite at liberty not to find it at home; and that the wife of a De Mauves who should hang her head and have red eyes, and allow herself to make any other response to officious condolence than that her husband's amusements were his own affair, would have forfeited every claim to having her finger-tips bowed over and kissed. And yet

in spite of these sound principles, Longmore fancied that the
Baron was more irritated than gratified by his wife's irreproachable reserve. Did it dimly occur to him that it was self-control
and not self-effacement? She was a model to all the inferior
matrons of his line, past and to come, and an occasional
'scene' from her at a convenient moment would have something
reassuring, – would attest her stupidity a trifle more forcibly
than her inscrutable tranquillity.

Longmore would have given much to know the principle of
her submissiveness, and he tried more than once, but with
rather awkward timidity, to sound the mystery. She seemed to
him to have been long resisting the force of cruel evidence, and,
though she had succumbed to it at last, to have denied herself
the right to complain, because if faith was gone her heroic
generosity remained. He believed even that she was capable
of reproaching herself with having expected too much, and of
trying to persuade herself out of her bitterness by saying that
her hopes had been illusions and that this was simply – life.
'I hate tragedy,' she once said to him; 'I have a really pusillanimous dread of moral suffering. I believe that – without base
concessions – there is always some way of escaping from it. I had
almost rather never smile all my life than have a single violent
explosion of grief.' She lived evidently in nervous apprehension
of being fatally convinced, – of seeing to the end of her deception. Longmore, when he thought of this, felt an immense
longing to offer her something of which she could be as sure
as of the sun in heaven.

IV

HIS friend Webster lost no time in accusing him of the basest
infidelity, and asking him what he found at Saint-Germain to
prefer to Van Eyck and Memling, Rubens and Rembrandt. A
day or two after the receipt of Webster's letter, he took a walk
with Madame de Mauves in the forest. They sat down on a
fallen log, and she began to arrange into a bouquet the ane-
mones and violets she had gathered. 'I have a letter,' he said at
last, 'from a friend whom I some time ago promised to join at

Brussels. The time has come, – it has passed. It finds me terribly unwilling to leave Saint-Germain.'

She looked up with the candid interest which she always displayed in his affairs, but with no disposition, apparently, to make a personal application of his words. 'Saint-Germain is pleasant enough,' she said; 'but are you doing yourself justice? Won't you regret in future days that instead of travelling and seeing cities and monuments and museums and improving your mind, you sat here – for instance – on a log, pulling my flowers to pieces?'

'What I shall regret in future days,' he answered after some hesitation, 'is that I should have sat here and not spoken the truth on the matter. I am fond of museums and monuments and of improving my mind, and I'm particularly fond of my friend Webster. But I can't bring myself to leave Saint-Germain without asking you a question. You must forgive me if it's unfortunate, and be assured that curiosity was never more respectful. Are you really as unhappy as I imagine you to be?'

She had evidently not expected his question, and she greeted it with a startled blush. 'If I strike you as unhappy,' she said, 'I have been a poorer friend to you than I wished to be.'

'I, perhaps, have been a better friend of yours than you have supposed. I've admired your reserve, your courage, your studied gaiety. But I have felt the existence of something beneath them that was more *you* – more you as I wished to know you – than they were; something that I have believed to be a constant sorrow.'

She listened with great gravity, but without an air of offence, and he felt that while he had been timorously calculating the last consequences of friendship, she had placidly accepted them. 'You surprise me,' she said slowly, and her blush still lingered. 'But to refuse to answer you would confirm an impression which is evidently already too strong. An unhappiness that one can sit comfortably talking about, is an unhappiness with distinct limitations. If I were examined before a board of commissioners for investigating the felicity of mankind, I'm sure I should be pronounced a very fortunate woman.'

There was something delightfully gentle to him in her tone, and its softness seemed to deepen as she continued: 'But let me add, with all gratitude for your sympathy, that it's my own affair altogether. It needn't disturb you, Mr Longmore, for I have often found myself in your company a very contented person.'

'You're a wonderful woman,' he said, 'and I admire you as I never have admired any one. You're wiser than anything I, for one, can say to you; and what I ask of you is not to let me advise or console you, but simply thank you for letting me know you.' He had intended no such outburst as this, but his voice rang loud, and he felt a kind of unfamiliar joy as he uttered it.

She shook her head with some impatience. 'Let us be friends, – as I supposed we were going to be, – without protestations and fine words. To have you making bows to my wisdom, – that would be real wretchedness. I can dispense with your admiration better than the Flemish painters can, – better than Van Eyck and Rubens, in spite of all their worshippers. Go join your friend, – see everything, enjoy everything, learn everything, and write me an excellent letter, brimming over with your impressions. I'm extremely fond of the Dutch painters,' she added with a slight faltering of the voice, which Longmore had noticed once before, and which he had interpreted as the sudden weariness of a spirit self-condemned to play a part.

'I don't believe you care about the Dutch painters at all,' he said with an unhesitating laugh. 'But I shall certainly write you a letter.'

She rose and turned homeward, thoughtfully rearranging her flowers as she walked. Little was said; Longmore was asking himself, with a tremor in the unspoken words, whether all this meant simply that he was in love. He looked at the rooks wheeling against the golden-hued sky, between the tree-tops, but not at his companion, whose personal presence seemed lost in the felicity she had created. Madame de Mauves was silent and grave, because she was painfully disappointed. A sentimental friendship she had not desired; her scheme had been to pass with Longmore as a placid creature with a good deal of leisure, which she was disposed to devote to profitable conversation of an impersonal sort. She liked him extremely, and felt that there was something in him to which, when she made up her girlish mind, that a needy French baron was the ripest fruit of time, she had done very scanty justice. They went through the little gate in the garden wall and approached the house. On the terrace Madame Clairin was entertaining a friend, – a little elderly gentleman with a white moustache, and an order in his button-hole. Madame de Mauves chose to pass round the house into the court; whereupon her sister-in-law, greeting Longmore with a commanding nod, lifted her eye-glass and stared at them as they went by. Longmore heard the little old gentleman uttering some old-fashioned epigram about 'la vieille galanterie Française', and then, by a sudden impulse, he looked at Madame de Mauves and wondered what she was doing in such a world. She stopped before the house, without asking him to come in. 'I hope,' she said, 'you'll consider my advice, and waste no more time at Saint-Germain.'

For an instant there rose to his lips some faded compliment about his time not being wasted, but it expired before the simple sincerity of her look. She stood there as gently serious as the angel of disinterestedness, and Longmore felt as if he should insult her by treating her words as a bait for flattery. 'I shall start in a day or two,' he answered, 'but I won't promise you not to come back.'

'I hope not,' she said simply. 'I expect to be here a long time.'

'I shall come and say good-by,' he rejoined; on which she nodded with a smile, and went in.

He turned away, and walked slowly homeward by the terrace. It seemed to him that to leave her thus, for a gain on which she herself insisted, was to know her better and admire her more. But he was in a vague ferment of feeling which her evasion of his question half an hour before had done more to deepen than to allay. Suddenly, on the terrace, he encountered M. de Mauves, who was leaning against the parapet finishing a cigar. The Baron, who, he fancied, had an air of peculiar affability, offered him his fair, plump hand. Longmore stopped; he felt a sudden angry desire to cry out to him that he had the loveliest wife in the world; that he ought to be ashamed of himself not to know it; and that for all his shrewdness he had never looked into the depths of her eyes. The Baron, we know, considered that he had; but there was something in Euphemia's eyes now that was not there five years before. They talked for a while about various things, and M. de Mauves gave a humourous account of his visit to America. His tone was not soothing to Longmore's excited sensibilities. He seemed to consider the country a gigantic joke, and his urbanity only went so far as to admit that it was not a bad one. Longmore was not, by habit, an aggressive apologist for our institutions; but the Baron's narrative confirmed his worst impressions of French superficiality. He had understood nothing, he had felt nothing, he had learned nothing; and our hero, glancing askance at his aristocratic profile, declared that if the chief merit of a long pedigree was to leave one so vaingloriously stupid, he thanked his stars that the Longmores had emerged from obscurity in the present century, in the person of an enterprising lumber merchant. M. de Mauves dwelt of course on that prime oddity of ours, – the liberty allowed to young girls; and related the history of his researches into the 'opportunities' it presented to French noblemen, – researches in which, during a fortnight's stay, he seemed to have spent many agreeable hours. 'I am bound to admit,' he said, 'that in every case I was disarmed by the extreme candour of the young lady, and that they took care of themselves to better purpose than I have seen some mammas in France take care of them.' Longmore greeted this handsome concession with the grimmest of smiles, and damned his impertinent patronage.

Mentioning at last that he was about to leave Saint-Germain, he was surprised, without exactly being flattered, by the Baron's quickened attention. 'I'm very sorry,' the latter cried. 'I hoped we had you for the summer.' Longmore murmured something civil, and wondered why M. de Mauves should care whether he stayed or went. 'You were a diversion to Madame de Mauves,' the Baron added. 'I assure you I mentally blessed your visits.'

'They were a great pleasure to me,' Longmore said gravely. 'Some day I expect to come back.'

'Pray do,' and the Baron laid his hand urgently on his arm. 'You see I have confidence in you!' Longmore was silent for a moment, and the Baron puffed his cigar reflectively and watched the smoke. 'Madame de Mauves,' he said at last, 'is a rather singular person.'

Longmore shifted his position, and wondered whether he was going to 'explain' Madame de Mauves.

'Being as you are her fellow-countryman,' the Baron went on, 'I don't mind speaking frankly. She's just a little morbid, – the most charming woman in the world, as you see, but a little fanciful, – a little *exaltée*. Now you see she has taken this extraordinary fancy for solitude. I can't get her to go anywhere, – to see any one. When my friends present themselves she's polite, but she's freezing. She doesn't do herself justice, and I expect every day to hear two or three of them say to me, "Your wife's *jolie à croquer*: what a pity she hasn't a little *esprit*." You must have found out that she has really a great deal. But to tell the whole truth, what she needs is to forget herself. She sits alone for hours poring over her English books and looking at life through that terrible brown fog which they always seem to me to fling over the world. I doubt if your English authors,' the Baron continued, with a serenity which Longmore afterwards characterised as sublime, 'are very sound reading for young married women. I don't pretend to know much about them; but I remember that, not long after our marriage, Madame de Mauves undertook to read me one day a certain Wordsworth, – a poet highly esteemed, it appears, *chez vous*. It seemed to me that she took me by the nape of the neck and forced my head for half an hour over a basin of *soupe aux choux*, and that one ought to ventilate the drawing-room before any one called. But I suppose you know him, – *ce génie là*. I think my wife never forgave me, and that it was a real shock to her to find she had married a man who had very much the same taste in literature as in cookery. But you're a man of general culture,' said the Baron, turning to Longmore and fixing his eyes on the seal on his watch-guard. 'You can talk about everything, and I'm sure you like Alfred de Musset as well as Wordsworth. Talk to her about everything, Alfred de Musset included. Bah! I forgot you're going. Come back then as soon as possible and talk about your travels. If Madame de Mauves too would travel for a couple of months, it would do her good. It would enlarge her horizon,' – and M. de Mauves made a series of short nervous jerks with his stick in the air, – 'it would wake up her imagination. She's too rigid, you know, – it would show her that one may bend a trifle without breaking.' He paused a moment and gave two or three vigorous puffs. Then turning to his companion again, with a little nod and a confidential smile: – 'I hope you admire my candour. I wouldn't say all this to one of *us*.'

Evening was coming on, and the lingering light seemed to float in the air in faintly golden motes. Longmore stood gazing at these luminous particles; he could almost have fancied them a swarm of humming insects, murmuring as a refrain, 'She has a great deal of *esprit*, – she has a great deal of *esprit*.' 'Yes, she has a great deal,' he said mechanically, turning to the Baron. M. de Mauves glanced at him sharply, as if to ask what the deuce he was talking about. 'She has a great deal of intelligence,' said Longmore, deliberately, 'a great deal of beauty, a great many virtues.'

M. de Mauves busied himself for a moment in lighting another cigar, and when he had finished, with a return of his confidential smile, 'I suspect you of thinking,' he said, 'that I don't do my wife justice. Take care, – take care, young man; that's a dangerous assumption. In general, a man always does his wife justice. More than justice,' cried the Baron with a laugh, – 'that we keep for the wives of other men!'

Longmore afterwards remembered it in favour of the Baron's grace of address that he had not measured at this moment the dusky abyss over which it hovered. But a sort of deepening subterranean echo lingered on his spiritual ear. For the present his keenest sensation was a desire to get away and cry aloud that M. de Mauves was an arrogant fool. He bade him an abrupt good-night, which must serve also, he said, as good-by.

'Decidedly, then, you go?' said M. de Mauves, almost peremptorily.

'Decidedly.'

'Of course you'll come and say good-by to Madame de Mauves.' His tone implied that the omission would be most uncivil; but there seemed to Longmore something so ludicrous in his taking a lesson in consideration from M. de Mauves, that he burst into a laugh. The Baron frowned, like a man for whom it was a new and most unpleasant sensation to be perplexed. 'You're a queer fellow,' he murmured, as Longmore turned away, not foreseeing that he would think him a very queer fellow indeed before he had done with him.

Longmore sat down to dinner at his hotel with his usual good intentions; but as he was lifting his first glass of wine to his lips, he suddenly fell to musing and set down his wine untasted. His reverie lasted long, and when he emerged from it, his fish was cold; but this mattered little, for his appetite was gone. That evening he packed his trunk with a kind of indignant energy. This was so effective that the operation was accomplished before bedtime, and as he was not in the least sleepy, he devoted the interval to writing two letters; one was a short note to Madame de Mauves, which he entrusted to a servant, to be delivered the next morning. He had found it best, he said, to leave Saint-Germain immediately, but he expected to be back in Paris in the early autumn. The other letter was the result of his having remembered a day or two before that he had not yet complied with Mrs Draper's injunction to give her an account of his impressions of her friend. The present occasion seemed propitious, and he wrote half a dozen pages. His tone, however, was grave, and Mrs Draper, on receiving them, was slightly disappointed, – she would have preferred a stronger flavour of rhapsody. But what chiefly concerns us is the concluding sentences.

'The only time she ever spoke to me of her marriage,' he wrote, 'she intimated that it had been a perfect love-match. With all abatements, I suppose most marriages are; but in her case this would mean more, I think, than in that of most women; for her love was an absolute idealisation. She believed her husband was a hero of rose-coloured romance, and he turns out to be not even a hero of very sad-coloured reality. For some time now she has been sounding her mistake, but I don't

believe she has touched the bottom of it yet. She strikes me as a
person who is begging off from full knowledge, – who has struck
a truce with painful truth, and is trying awhile the experiment of
living with closed eyes. In the dark she tries to see again the
gilding on her idol. Illusion of course is illusion, and one must
always pay for it; but there is something truly tragical in seeing
an earthly penalty levied on such divine folly as this. As for M.
de Mauves, he's a Frenchman to his fingers' ends; and I confess
I should dislike him for this if he were a much better man. He
can't forgive his wife for having married him too sentimentally
and loved him too well; for in some uncorrupted corner of his
being he feels, I suppose, that as she saw him, so he ought to
have been. It's a perpetual vexation to him that a little American bourgeoise should have fancied him a finer fellow than he
is, or than he at all wants to be. He hasn't a glimmering of real
acquaintance with his wife; he can't understand the stream of
passion flowing so clear and still. To tell the truth, I hardly can
myself; but when I see the spectacle I can admire it furiously.
M. de Mauves, at any rate, would like to have the comfort of
feeling that his wife was as corruptible as himself; and you'll
hardly believe me when I tell you that he goes about intimating
to gentlemen whom he deems worthy of the knowledge, that it
would be a convenience to him to have them make love to her.'

V

ON reaching Paris, Longmore straightway purchased a
Murray's 'Belgium', to help himself to believe that he would
start on the morrow for Brussels; but when the morrow came, it
occurred to him that, by way of preparation, he ought to
acquaint himself more intimately with the Flemish painters in
the Louvre. This took a whole morning, but it did little to
hasten his departure. He had abruptly left Saint-Germain,
because it seemed to him that respect for Madame de Mauves
demanded that he should allow her husband no reason to
suppose that he had understood him; but now that he had
satisfied this immediate need of delicacy, he found himself
thinking more and more ardently of Euphemia. It was a poor

expression of ardour to be lingering irresolutely on the deserted
boulevards, but he detested the idea of leaving Saint-Germain
five hundred miles behind him. He felt very foolish, nevertheless, and wandered about nervously, promising himself to take
the next train; but a dozen trains started, and Longmore was
still in Paris. This sentimental tumult was more than he had
bargained for, and, as he looked in the shop windows, he
wondered whether it was a 'passion'. He had never been fond
of the word, and had grown up with a kind of horror of what it
represented. He had hoped that when he fell in love, he should
do it with an excellent conscience, with no greater agitation
than a mild general glow of satisfaction. But here was a sentiment compounded of pity and anger, as well as admiration, and
bristling with scruples and doubts. He had come abroad to
enjoy the Flemish painters and all others; but what fair-tressed
saint of Van Eyck or Memling was so appealing a figure as
Madame de Mauves? His restless steps carried him at last out
of the long villa-bordered avenue which leads to the Bois de
Boulogne.

Summer had fairly begun, and the drive beside the lake was
empty, but there were various loungers on the benches and
chairs, and the great café had an air of animation. Longmore's
walk had given him an appetite, and he went into the establishment and demanded a dinner, remarking for the hundredth
time, as he observed the smart little tables disposed in the open
air, how much better they ordered this matter in France.

'Will monsieur dine in the garden, or in the salon?' asked the
waiter. Longmore chose the garden; and observing that a great
vine of June roses was trained over the wall of the house, placed
himself at a table near by, where the best of dinners was served
him on the whitest of linen, in the most shining of porcelain. It
so happened that his table was near a window, and that as he sat
he could look into a corner of the salon. So it was that his
attention rested on a lady seated just within the window,
which was open, face to face apparently to a companion who
was concealed by the curtain. She was a very pretty woman,
and Longmore looked at her as often as was consistent with
good manners. After a while he even began to wonder who she

was, and to suspect that she was one of those ladies whom it is no breach of good manners to look at as often as you like. Longmore, too, if he had been so disposed, would have been the more free to give her all his attention, that her own was fixed upon the person opposite to her. She was what the French call a *belle brune*, and though our hero, who had rather a conservative taste in such matters, had no great relish for her bold outlines and even bolder colouring, he could not help admiring her expression of basking contentment.

She was evidently very happy, and her happiness gave her an air of innocence. The talk of her friend, whoever he was, abundantly suited her humour, for she sat listening to him with a broad, lazy smile, and interrupted him occasionally, while she crunched her bon-bons, with a murmured response, presumably as broad, which seemed to deepen his eloquence. She drank a great deal of champagne and ate an immense number of strawberries, and was plainly altogether a person with an impartial relish for strawberries, champagne, and what she would have called *bêtises*.

They had half finished dinner when Longmore sat down, and he was still in his place when they rose. She had hung her bonnet on a nail above her chair, and her companion passed round the table to take it down for her. As he did so, she bent her head to look at a wine stain on her dress, and in the movement exposed the greater part of the back of a very handsome neck. The gentleman observed it, and observed also, apparently, that the room beyond them was empty; that he stood within eyeshot of Longmore, he failed to observe. He stooped suddenly and imprinted a gallant kiss on the fair expanse. Longmore then recognised M. de Mauves. The recipient of this vigorous tribute put on her bonnet, using his flushed smile as a mirror, and in a moment they passed through the garden on their way to their carriage.

Then, for the first time, M. de Mauves perceived Longmore. He measured with a rapid glance the young man's relation to the open window, and checked himself in the impulse to stop and speak to him. He contented himself with bowing with great gravity as he opened the gate for his companion.

That evening Longmore made a railway journey, but not to Brussels. He had effectually ceased to care about Brussels; the only thing he now cared about was Madame de Mauves. The atmosphere of his mind had had a sudden clearing up; pity and anger were still throbbing there, but they had space to rage at their pleasure, for doubts and scruples had abruptly departed. It was little, he felt, that he could interpose between her resignation and the unsparing harshness of her position; but that little, if it involved the sacrifice of everything that bound him to the tranquil past, it seemed to him that he could offer her with a rapture which at last made reflection a woefully halting substitute for faith. Nothing in his tranquil past had given such a zest to consciousness as the sense of tending with all his being to a single aim which bore him company on his journey to Saint-Germain. How to justify his return, how to explain his ardour, troubled him little. He was not sure, even, that he wished to be understood; he wished only to feel that it was by no fault of his that Madame de Mauves was alone with the ugliness of fate. He was conscious of no distinct desire to 'make love' to her; if he could have uttered the essence of his longing, he would have said that he wished her to remember that in a world coloured grey to her vision by disappointment, there was one vividly honest man. She might certainly have remembered it, however, without his coming back to remind her; and it is not to be denied that, as he packed his valise that evening, he wished immensely to hear the sound of her voice.

He waited the next day till his usual hour of calling, – the late afternoon; but he learned at the door that Madame de Mauves was not at home. The servant offered the information that she was walking in the forest. Longmore went through the garden and out of the little door into the lane, and, after half an hour's vain exploration, saw her coming toward him at the end of a green by-path. As he appeared, she stopped for a moment, as if to turn aside; then recognising him, she slowly advanced, and he was soon shaking hands with her.

'Nothing has happened,' she said, looking at him fixedly. 'You're not ill?'

'Nothing, except that when I got to Paris I found how fond I had grown of Saint-Germain.'

She neither smiled nor looked flattered; it seemed indeed to Longmore that she was annoyed. But he was uncertain, for he immediately perceived that in his absence the whole character of her face had altered. It told him that something momentous had happened. It was no longer self-contained melancholy that he read in her eyes, but grief and agitation which had lately struggled with that passionate love of peace of which she had spoken to him, and forced it to know that deep experience is never peaceful. She was pale, and she had evidently been shedding tears. He felt his heart beating hard; he seemed now to know her secrets. She continued to look at him with a contracted brow, as if his return had given her a sense of responsibility too great to be disguised by a commonplace welcome. For some moments, as he turned and walked beside her, neither spoke; then abruptly, – 'Tell me truly, Mr Longmore,' she said, 'why you have come back.'

He turned and looked at her with an air which startled her into a certainty of what she had feared. 'Because I've learned the real answer to the question I asked you the other day. You're not happy, – you're too good to be happy on the terms offered you. Madame de Mauves,' he went on with a gesture which protested against a gesture of her own, 'I can't be happy if you're not. I don't care for anything so long as I see such a depth of unconquerable sadness in your eyes. I found during three dreary days in Paris that the thing in the world I most care for is this daily privilege of seeing you. I know it's absolutely brutal to tell you I admire you; it's an insult to you to treat you as if you had complained to me or appealed to me. But such a friendship as I waked up to there,' – and he tossed his head toward the distant city – 'is a potent force, I assure you; and when forces are compressed they explode. But if you had told me every trouble in your heart, it would have mattered little; I couldn't say more than I must say now, – that if that in life from which you've hoped most has given you least, *my* devoted respect will refuse no service and betray no trust.'

She had begun to make marks in the earth with the point of her parasol; but she stopped and listened to him in perfect immobility. Rather, her immobility was not perfect; for when he stopped speaking a faint flush had stolen into her cheek. It told Longmore that she was moved, and his first perceiving it was the happiest instant of his life. She raised her eyes at last, and looked at him with what at first seemed a pleading dread of excessive emotion.

'Thank you – thank you!' she said, calmly enough; but the next moment her own emotion overcame her calmness, and she burst into tears. Her tears vanished as quickly as they came, but they did Longmore a world of good. He had always felt indefinably afraid of her; her being had somehow seemed fed by a deeper faith and a stronger will than his own; but her half-dozen smothered sobs showed him the bottom of her heart, and assured him that she was weak enough to be grateful.

'Excuse me,' she said; 'I'm too nervous to listen to you. I believe I could have faced an enemy to-day, but I can't endure a friend.'

'You're killing yourself with stoicism, – that's my belief,' he cried. 'Listen to a friend for his own sake, if not for yours. I have never ventured to offer you an atom of compassion, and you can't accuse yourself of an abuse of charity.'

She looked about her with a kind of weary confusion which promised a reluctant attention. But suddenly perceiving by the wayside the fallen log on which they had rested a few evenings before, she went and sat down on it in impatient resignation, and looked at Longmore, as he stood silent, watching her, with a glance which seemed to urge that, if she was charitable now, he must be very wise.

'Something came to my knowledge yesterday,' he said as he sat down beside her, 'which gave me a supreme sense of your moral isolation. You are truth itself, and there is no truth about you. You believe in purity and duty and dignity, and you live in a world in which they are daily belied. I sometimes ask myself with a kind of rage how you ever came into such a world, – and why the perversity of fate never let me know you before.'

'I like my "world" no better than you do, and it was not for its own sake I came into it. But what particular group of people is worth pinning one's faith upon? I confess it sometimes seems to me that men and women are very poor creatures. I suppose I'm romantic. I have a most unfortunate taste for poetic fitness. Life is hard prose, which one must learn to read contentedly. I believe I once thought that all the prose was in America, which was very foolish. What I thought, what I believed, what I expected, when I was an ignorant girl, fatally addicted to falling in love with my own theories, is more than I can begin to tell you now. Sometimes, when I remember certain impulses, certain illusions of those days, they take away my breath, and I wonder my bedazzled visions didn't lead me into troubles greater than any I have now to lament. I had a conviction which you would probably smile at if I were to attempt to express it to you. It was a singular form for passionate faith to take, but it had all of the sweetness and the ardour of passionate faith. It led me to take a great step, and it lies behind me now in the distance like a shadow melting slowly in the light of experience. It has faded, but it has not vanished. Some feelings, I am sure, die only with ourselves; some illusions are as much the condition of our life as our heart-beats. They say that life itself is an illusion, – that this world is a shadow of which the reality is yet to come. Life is all of a piece, then, and there is no shame in being miserably human. As for my "isolation", it doesn't greatly matter; it's the fault, in part, of my obstinacy. There have been times when I have been frantically distressed, and, to tell you the truth, wretchedly homesick, because my maid – a jewel of a maid – lied to me with every second breath. There have been moments when I have wished I was the daughter of a poor New England minister, living in a little white house under a couple of elms, and doing all the housework.'

She had begun to speak slowly, with an air of effort; but she went on quickly, as if talking were a relief. 'My marriage introduced me to people and things which seemed to me at first very strange and then very horrible, and then, to tell the truth, very contemptible. At first I expended a great deal of sorrow and dismay and pity on it all; but there soon came a time when

I began to wonder whether it was worth one's tears. If I could tell you the eternal friendships I've seen broken, the inconsolable woes consoled, the jealousies and vanities leading off the dance, you would agree with me that tempers like yours and mine can understand neither such losses nor such compensations. A year ago, while I was in the country, a friend of mine was in despair at the infidelity of her husband; she wrote me a most tragical letter, and on my return to Paris I went immediately to see her. A week had elapsed, and, as I had seen stranger things, I thought she might have recovered her spirits. Not at all; she was still in despair, – but at what? At the conduct, the abandoned, shameless conduct of Mme de T. You'll imagine, of course, that Mme de T. was the lady whom my friend's husband preferred to his wife. Far from it; he had never seen her. Who, then, was Mme de T.? Mme de T. was cruelly devoted to M. de V. And who was M. de V.? M. de V. – in two words, my friend was cultivating two jealousies at once. I hardly know what I said to her; something, at any rate, that she found unpardonable, for she quite gave me up. Shortly afterward my husband proposed we should cease to live in Paris, and I gladly assented, for I believe I was falling into a state of mind that made me a detestable companion. I should have preferred to go quite into the country, into Auvergne, where my husband has a place. But to him Paris, in some degree, is necessary, and Saint-Germain has been a sort of compromise.'

'A sort of compromise!' Longmore repeated. 'That's your whole life.'

'It's the life of many people, of most people of quiet tastes, and it is certainly better than acute distress. One is at loss theoretically to defend a compromise; but if I found a poor creature clinging to one from day to day, I should think it poor friendship to make him lose his hold.' Madame de Mauves had no sooner uttered these words than she smiled faintly, as if to mitigate their personal application.

'Heaven forbid,' said Longmore, 'that one should do that unless one has something better to offer. And yet I am haunted by a vision of a life in which you should have found no compromises, for they are a perversion of natures that tend only to goodness and rectitude. As I see it, you should have found happiness serene, profound, complete; a *femme de chambre* not a jewel perhaps, but warranted to tell but one fib a day; a society possibly rather provincial, but (in spite of your poor opinion of mankind) a good deal of solid virtue; jealousies and vanities very tame, and no particular inquities and adulteries. A husband,' he added after a moment, – 'a husband of your own faith and race and spiritual substance, who would have loved you well.'

She rose to her feet, shaking her head. 'You are very kind to go to the expense of visions for me. Visions are vain things; we must make the best of the reality.'

'And yet,' said Longmore, provoked by what seemed the very wantonness of her patience, 'the reality, if I'm not mistaken, has very recently taken a shape that keenly tests your philosophy.'

She seemed on the point of replying that his sympathy was too zealous; but a couple of impatient tears in his eyes proved that it was founded on a devotion to which it was impossible not to defer. 'Philosophy?' she said. 'I have none. Thank Heaven!' she cried, with vehemence, 'I have none. I believe, Mr Longmore,' she added in a moment, 'that I have nothing on earth but a conscience, – it's a good time to tell you so, – nothing but a dogged, clinging, inexpugnable conscience. Does that prove me to be indeed of your faith and race, and have you one for which you can say as much? I don't say it in vanity, for I believe that if my conscience will prevent me from doing anything very base, it will effectually prevent me from doing anything very fine.'

'I am delighted to hear it,' cried Longmore. 'We are made for each other. It's very certain I too shall never do anything fine. And yet I have fancied that in my case this inexpugnable organ you so eloquently describe might be blinded and gagged awhile, in a fine cause, if not turned out of doors. In yours,' he went on with the same appealing irony, 'is it absolutely invincible?'

But her fancy made no concession to his sarcasm. 'Don't laugh at your conscience,' she answered gravely; 'that's the only blasphemy I know.'

She had hardly spoken when she turned suddenly at an unexpected sound, and at the same moment Longmore heard a footstep in an adjacent by-path which crossed their own at a short distance from where they stood.

'It's M. de Mauves,' said Euphemia directly, and moved slowly forward. Longmore, wondering how she knew it, had overtaken her by the time her husband advanced into sight. A solitary walk in the forest was a pastime to which M. de Mauves was not addicted, but he seemed on this occasion to have resorted to it with some equanimity. He was smoking a fragrant cigar, and his thumb was thrust into the armhole of his waistcoat, with an air of contemplative serenity. He stopped short with surprise on seeing his wife and her companion, and Longmore considered his surprise impertinent. He glanced rapidly from one to the other, fixed Longmore's eye sharply for a single instant, and then lifted his hat with formal politeness.

'I was not aware,' he said, turning to Madame de Mauves, 'that I might congratulate you on the return of monsieur.'

'You should have known it,' she answered gravely, 'if I had expected Mr Longmore's return.'

She had become very pale, and Longmore felt that this was a first meeting after a stormy parting. 'My return was unexpected to myself,' he said. 'I came last evening.'

M. de Mauves smiled with extreme urbanity. 'It's needless for me to welcome you. Madame de Mauves knows the duties of hospitality.' And with another bow he continued his walk.

Madame de Mauves and her companion returned slowly home, with few words, but, on Longmore's part at least, many thoughts. The Baron's appearance had given him an angry chill; it was a dusky cloud reabsorbing the light which had begun to shine between himself and his companion.

He watched Euphemia narrowly as they went, and wondered what she had last had to suffer. Her husband's presence had checked her frankness, but nothing indicated that she had accepted the insulting meaning of his words. Matters were evidently at a crisis between them, and Longmore wondered vainly what it was on Euphemia's part that prevented an absolute rupture. What did she suspect? – how much did she know? To what was she resigned? – how much had she forgiven? How, above all, did she reconcile with knowledge, or with suspicion, that ineradicable tenderness of which she had just now all but assured him? 'She has loved him once,' Longmore said with a sinking of the heart, 'and with her to love once is to commit one's being for ever. Her husband thinks her too rigid! What would a poet call it?'

He relapsed with a kind of aching impotence into the sense of her being somehow beyond him, unattainable, immeasurable by his own fretful spirit. Suddenly he gave three passionate switches in the air with his cane, which made Madame de Mauves look round. She could hardly have guessed that they meant that where ambition was so vain, it was an innocent compensation to plunge into worship.

Madame de Mauves found in her drawing-room the little elderly Frenchman, M. de Chalumeau, whom Longmore had observed a few days before on the terrace. On this occasion, too, Madame Clairin was entertaining him, but as her sister-in-law came in she surrendered her post and addressed herself to our hero. Longmore, at thirty, was still an ingenuous youth, and there was something in this lady's large coquetry which had the power of making him blush. He was surprised at finding he had not absolutely forfeited her favour by his deportment at their last interview, and a suspicion of her meaning to approach him on another line completed his uneasiness.

'So you've returned from Brussels,' she said, 'by way of the forest.'

'I've not been to Brussels. I returned yesterday from Paris by the only way, – by the train.'

Madame Clairin stared and laughed. 'I've never known a young man to be so fond of Saint-Germain. They generally declare it's horribly dull.'

'That's not very polite to you,' said Longmore, who was vexed at his blushes, and determined not to be abashed.

'Ah, what am I?' demanded Madame Clairin, swinging open her fan. 'I'm the dullest thing here. They've not had your success with my sister-in-law.'

'It would have been very easy to have it. Madame de Mauves is kindness itself.'

'To her own countrymen!'

Longmore remained silent; he hated the talk. Madame Clairin looked at him a moment, and then turned her head and surveyed Euphemia, to whom M. de Chalumeau was serving up another epigram, which she was receiving with a slight droop of the head and her eyes absently wandering through the window. 'Don't pretend to tell me,' she murmured suddenly, 'that you're not in love with that pretty woman.'

'*Allons donc!*' cried Longmore, in the best French he had ever uttered. He rose the next minute, and took a hasty farewell.

VI

HE allowed several days to pass without going back; it seemed delicate not to appear to regard his friend's frankness during their last interview as a general invitation. This cost him a great effort, for hopeless passions are not the most deferential; and he had, moreover, a constant fear, that if, as he believed, the hour of supreme 'explanations' had come, the magic of her magnanimity might convert M. de Mauves. Vicious men, it was abundantly recorded, had been so converted as to be acceptable to God, and the something divine in Euphemia's temper would sanctify any means she should choose to employ. Her means, he kept repeating, were no business of his, and the essence of his admiration ought to be to respect her freedom; but he felt as if he should turn away into a world out of which most of the joy had departed, if her freedom, after all, should spare him only a murmured 'Thank you.'

When he called again he found to his vexation that he was to run the gantlet of Madame Clairin's officious hospitality. It was one of the first mornings of perfect summer, and the drawing-room, through the open windows, was flooded with a sweet confusion of odours and bird-notes which filled him with the hope that Madame de Mauves would come out and spend half the day in the forest. But Madame Clairin, with her hair not yet dressed, emerged like a brassy discord in a maze of melody.

At the same moment the servant returned with Euphemia's regrets; she was indisposed and unable to see Mr Longmore. The young man knew that he looked disappointed, and that Madame Clairin was observing him, and this consciousness impelled her to give him a glance of almost aggressive frigidity. This was apparently what she desired. She wished to throw him off his balance, and, if he was not mistaken, she had the means.

'Put down your hat, Mr Longmore,' she said, 'and be polite for once. You were not at all polite the other day when I asked you that friendly question about the state of your heart.'

'I have no heart – to talk about,' said Longmore, uncompromisingly.

'As well say you've none at all. I advise you to cultivate a little eloquence; you may have use for it. That was not an idle question of mine; I don't ask idle questions. For a couple of months now that you've been coming and going among us, it seems to me that you have had very few to answer of any sort.'

'I have certainly been very well treated,' said Longmore.

Madame Clairin was silent a moment, and then – 'Have you never felt disposed to ask any?' she demanded.

Her look, her tone, were so charged with roundabout meanings that it seemed to Longmore as if even to understand her would savour of dishonest complicity. 'What is it you have to tell me?' he asked, frowning and blushing.

Madame Clairin flushed. It is rather hard, when you come bearing yourself very much as the sibyl when she came to the Roman king, to be treated as something worse than a vulgar gossip. 'I might tell you, Mr Longmore,' she said, 'that you have as bad a *ton* as any young man I ever met. Where have you lived, – what are your ideas? I wish to call your attention to a fact which it takes some delicacy to touch upon. You have noticed, I supposed, that my sister-in-law is not the happiest woman in the world.'

Longmore assented with a gesture.

Madame Clairin looked slightly disappointed at his want of enthusiasm. Nevertheless – 'You have formed, I suppose,' she continued, 'your conjectures on the causes of her – dissatisfaction.'

'Conjecture has been superfluous. I have seen the causes – or at least a specimen of them – with my own eyes.'

'I know perfectly what you mean. My brother, in a single word, is in love with another woman. I don't judge him; I don't judge my sister-in-law. I permit myself to say that in her position I would have managed otherwise. I would have kept my husband's affection, or I would have frankly done without it, before this. But my sister is an odd compound; I don't profess to understand her. Therefore it is, in a measure, that I appeal to you, her fellow-countryman. Of course you'll be surprised at my way of looking at the matter, and I admit that it's a way in use only among people whose family traditions compel them to take a superior view of things.' Madame Clairin paused, and Longmore wondered where her family traditions were going to lead her.

'Listen,' she went on. 'There has never been a De Mauves who has not given his wife the right to be jealous. We know our history for ages back, and the fact is established. It's a shame if you like, but it's something to have a shame with such a pedigree. The De Mauves are real Frenchmen, and their wives – I may say it – have been worthy of them. You may see all their portraits in our Château de Mauves; every one of them an "injured" beauty, but not one of them hanging her head. Not one of them had the bad taste to be jealous, and yet not one in a dozen was guilty of an escapade, – not one of them was talked about. There's good sense for you! How they managed – go and look at the dusky, faded canvases and pastels, and ask. They were femmes d'esprit. When they had a headache, they put on a little rouge and came to supper as usual; and when they had a heart-ache, they put a little rouge on their hearts. These are fine traditions, and it doesn't seem to me fair that a little American bourgeoise should come in and interrupt them, and should hang her photograph, with her obstinate little *air penché*, in the gallery of our shrewd fine ladies. A De Mauves must be a De Mauves. When she married my brother, I don't suppose she took him for a member of a *societé de bonnes œuvres*. I don't say we're right; who is right? But we're as history has made us, and if any one is to change, it had better be Madame de Mauves herself.' Again Madame Clairin paused and opened and closed her fan. 'Let her conform!' she said, with amazing audacity.

Longmore's reply was ambiguous; he simply said, 'Ah!'

Madame Clairin's pious retrospect had apparently imparted an honest zeal to her indignation. 'For a long time,' she continued, 'my sister has been taking the attitude of an injured woman, affecting a disgust with the world, and shutting herself up to read the "Imitation". I've never remarked on her conduct, but I've quite lost patience with it. When a woman with her prettiness lets her husband wander, she deserves her fate. I don't wish you to agree with me – on the contrary; but I call such a woman a goose. She must have bored him to death. What has passed between them for many months needn't concern us; what provocation my sister has had – monstrous, if you wish – what ennui my brother has suffered. It's enough that a week ago, just after you had ostensibly gone to Brussels, something happened to produce an explosion. She found a letter in his pocket – a photograph – a trinket – *que sais-je?* At any rate, the scene was terrible. I didn't listen at the keyhole, and I don't know what was said; but I have reason to believe that my brother was called to account as I fancy none of his ancestors have ever been, – even by injured sweethearts.'

Longmore had leaned forward in silent attention with his elbows on his knees, and instinctively he dropped his face into his hands. 'Ah, poor woman!' he groaned.

'Voilà!' said Madame Clairin. 'You pity her.'

'Pity her?' cried Longmore, looking up with ardent eyes and forgetting the spirit of Madame Clairin's narrative in the miserable facts. 'Don't you?'

'A little. But I'm not acting sentimentally; I'm acting politically. I wish to arrange things, – to see my brother free to do as he chooses, – to see Euphemia contented. Do you understand me?'

'Very well, I think. You're the most immoral person I've lately had the privilege of conversing with.'

Madame Clairin shrugged her shoulders. 'Possibly. When was there a great politician who was not immoral?'

'Nay,' said Longmore in the same tone. 'You're too superficial to be a great politician. You don't begin to know anything about Madame de Mauves.'

Madame Clairin inclined her head to one side, eyed Longmore sharply, mused a moment, and then smiled with an excellent imitation of intelligent compassion. 'It's not in my interest to contradict you.'

'It would be in your interest to learn, Madame Clairin,' the young man went on with unceremonious candour, 'what honest men most admire in a woman, – and to recognise it when you see it.'

Longmore certainly did injustice to her talents for diplomacy, for she covered her natural annoyance at this sally with a pretty piece of irony. 'So you *are* in love!' she quietly exclaimed.

Longmore was silent awhile. 'I wonder if you would understand me,' he said at last, 'if I were to tell you that I have for Madame de Mauves the most devoted friendship?'

'You underrate my intelligence. But in that case you ought to exert your influence to put an end to these painful domestic scenes.'

'Do you suppose,' cried Longmore, 'that she talks to me about her domestic scenes?'

Madame Clairin stared. 'Then your friendship isn't returned?' And as Longmore turned away, shaking his head, – 'Now, at least,' she added, 'she will have something to tell you. I happen to know the upshot of my brother's last interview with his wife.' Longmore rose to his feet as a sort of protest against the indelicacy of the position into which he was being forced; but all that made him tender made him curious, and she caught in his averted eyes an expression which prompted her to strike her blow. 'My brother is monstrously in love with a certain person in Paris; of course he ought not to be; but he wouldn't be a De Mauves if he were not. It was this unsanctified passion that spoke. "Listen, madam," he cried at last: "let us live like people who understand life! It's unpleasant to be forced to say such things outright, but you have a way of bringing one down to the rudiments. I'm faithless, I'm heartless, I'm brutal, I'm everything horrible, – it's understood. Take your revenge, console yourself; you're too pretty a woman to have anything to complain of. Here's a handsome young man sighing himself into a consumption for you. Listen to the poor fellow, and you'll find that virtue is none the less becoming for being good-natured. You'll see that it's not after all such a doleful world, and that there is even an advantage in having the most impudent of husbands."' Madame Clairin paused; Longmore had turned very pale. 'You may believe it,' she said; 'the speech took place in my presence; things were done in order. And now, Mr Longmore,' – this with a smile which he was too troubled at the moment to appreciate, but which he remembered later with a kind of awe, – 'we count upon you!'

'He said this to her, face to face, as you say it to me now?' Longmore asked slowly, after a silence.

'Word for word, and with the greatest politeness.'

'And Madame de Mauves – what did she say?'

Madame Clairin smiled again. 'To such a speech as that a woman says – nothing. She had been sitting with a piece of needlework, and I think she had not seen her husband since their quarrel the day before. He came in with the gravity of an ambassador, and I'm sure that when he made his *demande en mariage* his manner was not more respectful. He only wanted white gloves!' said Madame Clairin. 'Euphemia sat silent a few moments drawing her stitches, and then without a word, without a glance, she walked out of the room. It was just what she should have done!'

'Yes,' Longmore repeated, 'it was just what she should have done.'

'And I, left alone with my brother, do you know what I said?'

Longmore shook his head. '*Mauvais sujet!*' he suggested.

' "You've done me the honour," I said, "to take this step in my presence. I don't pretend to qualify it. You know what you're about, and it's your own affair. But you may confide in my discretion." Do you think he has had reason to complain of it?' She received no answer; Longmore was slowly turning away and passing his gloves mechanically round the band of his hat. 'I hope,' she cried, 'you're not going to start for Brussels!'

Plainly, Longmore was deeply disturbed, and Madame Clairin might flatter herself on the success of her plea for old-fashioned manners. And yet there was something that left her more puzzled than satisfied in the reflective tone with which he answered, 'No, I shall remain here for the present.' The processes of his mind seemed provokingly subterranean, and she would have fancied for a moment that he was linked with her sister in some monstrous conspiracy of asceticism.

'Come this evening,' she boldly resumed. 'The rest will take care of itself. Meanwhile I shall take the liberty of telling my sister-in-law that I have repeated – in short, that I have put you *au fait*.'

Longmore started and coloured, and she hardly knew whether he was going to assent or demur. 'Tell her what you please. Nothing you can tell her will affect her conduct.'

'Voyons! Do you mean to tell me that a woman, young, pretty, sentimental, neglected – insulted, if you will – ? I see you don't believe it. Believe simply in your own opportunity! But for heaven's sake, if it's to lead anywhere, don't come back with that *visage de croquemort*. You look as if you were going to bury your heart, – not to offer it to a pretty woman. You're much better when you smile. Come, do yourself justice.'

'Yes,' he said, 'I must do myself justice.' And abruptly, with a bow, he took his departure.

VII

HE felt, when he found himself unobserved, in the open air, that he must plunge into violent action, walk fast and far, and defer the opportunity for thought. He strode away into the forest, swinging his cane, throwing back his head, gazing away into the verdurous vistas, and following the road without a purpose. He felt immensely excited, but he could hardly have said whether his emotion was a pain or a joy. It was joyous as all increase of freedom is joyous; something seemed to have been knocked down across his path; his destiny appeared to have rounded a cape and brought him into sight of an open sea. But his freedom resolved itself somehow into the need of despising all mankind, with a single exception; and the fact of Madame de Mauves inhabiting a planet contaminated by the presence of this baser multitude kept his elation from seeming a pledge of ideal bliss.

But she was there, and circumstance now forced them to be intimate. She had ceased to have what men call a secret for him, and this fact itself brought with it a sort of rapture. He had no prevision that he should 'profit', in the vulgar sense, by the extraordinary position into which they had been thrown; it might be but a cruel trick of destiny to make hope a harsher mockery and renunciation a keener suffering. But above all this rose the conviction that she could do nothing that would not deepen his admiration.

It was this feeling that circumstance – unlovely as it was in itself – was to force the beauty of her character into more perfect relief, that made him stride along as if he were celebrating a kind of spiritual festival. He rambled at random for a couple of hours, and found at last that he had left the forest behind him and had wandered into an unfamiliar region. It was a perfectly rural scene, and the still summer day gave it a charm for which its meagre elements but half accounted.

Longmore thought he had never seen anything so characteristically French; all the French novels seemed to have described it, all the French landscapists to have painted it. The fields and trees were of a cool metallic green; the grass looked as if it might stain your trousers, and the foliage your hands. The clear light had a sort of mild greyness; the sunbeams were of silver rather than gold. A great red-roofed, high-stacked farm-house, with whitewashed walls and a straggling yard, surveyed the high road, on one side, from behind a transparent curtain of poplars. A narrow stream, half choked with emerald rushes and edged with grey aspens, occupied the opposite quarter. The meadows rolled and sloped away gently to the low horizon, which was barely concealed by the continuous line of clipped and marshalled trees. The prospect was not rich, but it had a frank homeliness which touched the young man's fancy. It was full of light atmosphere and diffused sunshine, and if it was prosaic, it was soothing.

Longmore was disposed to walk further, and he advanced along the road beneath the poplars. In twenty minutes he came to a village which straggled away to the right, among orchards and *potagers*. On the left, at a stone's throw from the road, stood a little pink-faced inn, which reminded him that he had not breakfasted, having left home with a prevision of hospitality from Madame de Mauves. In the inn he found a brick-tiled parlour and a hostess in sabots and a white cap, whom, over the omelette she speedily served him, – borrowing licence from the bottle of sound red wine which accompanied it, – he assured that she was a true artist. To reward his compliment, she invited him to smoke his cigar in her little garden behind the house.

Here he found a *tonnelle* and a view of ripening crops, stretching down to the stream. The tonnelle was rather close, and he preferred to lounge on a bench against the pink wall, in the sun, which was not too hot. Here, as he rested and gazed and mused, he fell into a train of thought which, in an indefinable fashion, was a soft influence from the scene about him. His heart, which had been beating fast for the past three hours, gradually checked its pulses and left him looking at life with a rather more level gaze. The homely tavern sounds coming out through the open windows, the sunny stillness of the fields and crops, which covered so much vigorous natural life, suggested very little that was transcendental, had very little to say about renunciation, – nothing at all about spiritual zeal. They seemed to utter a message from plain ripe nature, to express the unperverted reality of things, to say that the common lot is not brilliantly amusing, and that the part of wisdom is to grasp frankly at experience, lest you miss it altogether. What reason there was for his falling a-wondering after this whether a deeply wounded heart might be soothed and healed by such a scene, it would be difficult to explain; certain it is that, as he sat there, he had a waking dream of an unhappy woman strolling by the slow-flowing stream before him, and pulling down the blossoming boughs in the orchards. He mused and mused, and at last found himself feeling angry that he could not somehow think worse of Madame de Mauves, – or at any rate think otherwise. He could fairly claim that in a sentimental way he asked very little of life, – he made modest demands on passion; why then should his only passion be born to ill-fortune? why should his first – his last – glimpse of positive happiness be so indissolubly linked with renunciation?

It is perhaps because, like many spirits of the same stock, he had in his composition a lurking principle of asceticism to whose authority he had ever paid an unquestioning respect, that he now felt all the vehemence of rebellion. To renounce – to renounce again – to renounce for ever – was this all that youth and longing and resolve were meant for? Was experience to be muffled and mutilated, like an indecent picture? Was a man to sit and deliberately condemn his future to be the blank memory of a regret, rather than the long reverberation of a joy? Sacrifice? The word was a trap for minds muddled by fear, an ignoble refuge of weakness. To insist now seemed not to dare, but simply to be, to live on possible terms.

His hostess came out to hang a cloth to dry on the hedge, and, though her guest was sitting quietly enough, she seemed to see in his kindled eyes a flattering testimony to the quality of her wine.

As she turned back into the house, she was met by a young man whom Longmore observed in spite of his preoccupation. He was evidently a member of that jovial fraternity of artists whose very shabbiness has an affinity with the element of picturesqueness and unexpectedness in life which provokes a great deal of unformulated envy among people foredoomed to be respectable.

Longmore was struck first with his looking like a very clever man, and then with his looking like a very happy one. The combination, as it was expressed in his face, might have arrested the attention of even a less cynical philosopher. He had a slouched hat and a blond beard, a light easel under one arm, and an unfinished sketch in oils under the other.

He stopped and stood talking for some moments to the landlady with a peculiarly good-humoured smile. They were discussing the possibilities of dinner; the hostess enumerated some very savoury ones, and he nodded briskly, assenting to everything. It couldn't be, Longmore thought, that he found such soft contentment in the prospect of lamb chops and spinach and a *tarte à la crême*. When the dinner had been ordered, he turned up his sketch, and the good woman fell a-wondering and looking off at the spot by the stream-side where he had made it.

Was it his work, Longmore wondered, that made him so happy? Was a strong talent the best thing in the world? The landlady went back to her kitchen, and the young painter stood as if he were waiting for something, beside the gate which opened upon the path across the fields. Longmore sat brooding and asking himself whether it was better to cultivate an art than to cultivate a passion. Before he had answered the question the painter had grown tired of waiting. He picked up a pebble, tossed it lightly into an upper window, and called, 'Claudine!'

Claudine appeared; Longmore heard her at the window, bidding the young man to have patience. 'But I'm losing my light,' he said; 'I must have my shadows in the same place as yesterday.'

'Go without me, then,' Claudine answered; 'I will join you in ten minutes.' Her voice was fresh and young; it seemed to say to Longmore that she was as happy as her companion.

'Don't forget the Chénier,' cried the young man; and turning away, he passed out of the gate and followed the path across the fields until he disappeared among the trees by the side of the stream. Who was Claudine? Longmore vaguely wondered; and was she as pretty as her voice? Before long he had a chance to satisfy himself; she came out of the house with her hat and parasol, prepared to follow her companion. She had on a pink muslin dress and a little white hat, and she was as pretty as a Frenchwoman needs to be to be pleasing. She had a clear brown skin and a bright dark eye, and a step which seemed to keep time to some slow music, heard only by herself. Her hands were encumbered with various articles which she seemed to intend to carry with her. In one arm she held her parasol and a large roll of needlework, and in the other a shawl and a heavy white umbrella, such as painters use for sketching. Meanwhile she was trying to thrust into her pocket a paper-covered volume which Longmore saw to be the Poems of André Chénier; but in the effort she dropped the large umbrella, and uttered a half-smiling exclamation of disgust. Longmore stepped forward with a bow and picked up the umbrella, and as she, protesting her gratitude, put out her hand to take it, it seemed to him that she was unbecomingly overburdened.

'You have too much to carry,' he said; 'you must let me help you.'

'You're very good, monsieur,' she answered. 'My husband always forgets something. He can do nothing without his umbrella. He is *d'une étourderie*–'

'You must allow me to carry the umbrella,' Longmore said. 'It's too heavy for a lady.'

She assented, after many compliments to his politeness; and he walked by her side into the meadow. She went lightly and rapidly, picking her steps and glancing forward to catch a glimpse of her husband. She was graceful, she was charming, she had an air of decision and yet of sweetness, and it seemed to Longmore that a young artist would work none the worse for having her seated at his side, reading Chénier's iambics. They were newly married, he supposed, and evidently their path of life had none of the mocking crookedness of some others. They asked little; but what need one ask more than such quiet summer days, with the creature one loves, by a shady stream, with art and books and a wide, unshadowed horizon? To spend such a morning, to stroll back to dinner in the red-tiled parlour of the inn, to ramble away again as the sun got low, – all this was a vision of bliss which floated before him, only to torture him with a sense of the impossible. All Frenchwomen are not coquettes, he remarked, as he kept pace with his companion. She uttered a word now and then, for politeness' sake, but she never looked at him, and seemed not in the least to care that he was a well-favoured young man. She cared for nothing but the young artist in the shabby coat and the slouched hat, and for discovering where he had set up his easel.

This was soon done. He was encamped under the trees, close to the stream, and, in the diffused green shade of the little wood, seemed to be in no immediate need of his umbrella. He received a vivacious rebuke, however, for forgetting it, and was informed of what he owed to Longmore's complaisance. He was duly grateful; he thanked our hero warmly, and offered him a seat on the grass. But Longmore felt like a marplot, and lingered only long enough to glance at the young man's sketch, and to see it was a very clever rendering of the silvery stream and the vivid green rushes. The young wife had spread her shawl on the grass at the base of a tree, and meant to seat herself when Longmore had gone, and murmur Chénier's verses to the music of the gurgling river. Longmore looked awhile from one to the other, barely stifled a sigh, bade them good morning, and took his departure.

He knew neither where to go nor what to do; he seemed afloat on the sea of ineffectual longing. He strolled slowly back to the inn, and in the doorway met the landlady coming back from the butcher's with the lamb chops for the dinner of her lodgers.

'Monsieur has made the acquaintance of the *dame* of our young painter,' she said with a broad smile, – a smile too broad for malicious meanings. 'Monsieur has perhaps seen the young man's picture. It appears that he has a great deal of talent.'

'His picture was very pretty,' said Longmore, 'but his *dame* was prettier still.'

'She's a very nice little woman; but I pity her all the more.'

'I don't see why she's to be pitied,' said Longmore; 'they seem a very happy couple.'

The landlady gave a knowing nod.

'Don't trust to it, monsieur! Those artists, – *ça n'a pas de principes*! From one day to another he can plant her there! I know them, *allez*. I've had them here very often; one year with one, another year with another.'

Longmore was puzzled for a moment. Then, 'You mean she's not his wife?' he asked.

She shrugged her shoulders. 'What shall I tell you? They are not *des hommes sérieux*, those gentlemen! They don't engage themselves for an eternity. It's none of my business, and I've no wish to speak ill of madame. She's a very nice little woman, and she loves her *jeune homme* to distraction.'

'Who is she?' asked Longmore. 'What do you know about her?'

'Nothing for certain; but it's my belief that she's better than he. I've even gone so far as to believe that she's a lady, – a true lady, – and that she has given up a great many things for him. I do the best I can for them, but I don't believe she's been obliged all her life to content herself with a dinner of two courses.' And she turned over her lamb chops tenderly, as if to say that though a good cook could imagine better things, yet if you could have but one course, lamb chops had much in their favour. 'I shall cook them with bread crumbs. *Voilà les femmes, monsieur!*'

Longmore turned away with the feeling that women were indeed a measureless mystery, and that it was hard to say whether there was greater beauty in their strength or in their weakness. He walked back to Saint-Germain, more slowly than he had come, with less philosophic resignation to any event, and more of the urgent egotism of the passion which philosophers call the supremely selfish one. Every now and then the episode of the happy young painter and the charming woman who had given up a great many things for him rose vividly in his mind, and seemed to mock his moral unrest like some obtrusive vision of unattainable bliss.

The landlady's gossip cast no shadow on its brightness; her voice seemed that of the vulgar chorus of the uninitiated, which stands always ready with its gross prose rendering of the inspired passages in human action. Was it possible a man could take *that* from a woman, – take all that lent lightness to that other woman's footstep and intensity to her glance, – and not give her the absolute certainty of a devotion as unalterable as the process of the sun? Was it possible that such a rapturous union had the seeds of trouble, – that the charm of such a perfect accord could be broken by anything but death? Longmore felt an immense desire to cry out a thousand times 'No!' for it seemed to him at last that he was somehow spiritually the same as the young painter, and that the latter's companion had the soul of Euphemia de Mauves.

The heat of the sun, as he walked along, became oppressive and when he re-entered the forest he turned aside into the deepest shade he could find, and stretched himself on the mossy ground at the foot of a great beech. He lay for a while staring up into the verdurous dusk overhead, and trying to conceive Madame de Mauves hastening toward some quiet stream-side where he waited, as he had seen that trusting creature do an hour before. It would be hard to say how well he succeeded; but the effort soothed him rather than excited him, and as he had had a good deal both of moral and physical fatigue, he sank at last into a quiet sleep.

While he slept he had a strange, vivid dream. He seemed to be in a wood, very much like the one on which his eyes had lately closed; but the wood was divided by the murmuring stream he had left an hour before. He was walking up and down, he thought, restlessly and in intense expectation of some momentous event. Suddenly, at a distance, through the trees, he saw the gleam of a woman's dress, and hurried forward to meet her. As he advanced he recognised her, but he saw at the same time that she was on the opposite bank of the river. She seemed at first not to notice him, but when they were opposite each other she stopped and looked at him very gravely and pityingly. She made him no motion that he should cross the stream, but he wished greatly to stand by her side. He knew the water was deep, and it seemed to him that he knew that he should have to plunge, and that he feared that when he rose to the surface she would have disappeared. Nevertheless, he was going to plunge, when a boat turned into the current from above and came swiftly toward them, guided by an oarsman,

who was sitting so that they could not see his face. He brought
the boat to the bank where Longmore stood; the latter stepped
in, and with a few strokes they touched the opposite shore.
Longmore got out, and, though he was sure he had crossed the
stream, Madame de Mauves was not there. He turned with a
kind of agony and saw that now she was on the other bank, – the
one he had left. She gave him a grave, silent glance, and walked
away up the stream. The boat and the boatman resumed their
course, but after going a short distance they stopped, and the
boatman turned back and looked at the still divided couple.
Then Longmore recognised him, – just as he had recognised
him a few days before at the café in the Bois de Boulogne.

VIII

HE must have slept some time after he ceased dreaming, for he
had no immediate memory of his dream. It came back to him
later, after he had roused himself and had walked nearly home.
No great ingenuity was needed to make it seem a rather striking
allegory, and it haunted and oppressed him for the rest of the
day. He took refuge, however, in his quickened conviction that
the only sound policy in life is to grasp unsparingly at happiness; and it seemed no more than one of the vigorous measures
dictated by such a policy, to return that evening to Madame de
Mauves. And yet when he had decided to do so, and had carefully dressed himself, he felt an irresistible nervous tremor
which made it easier to linger at his open window, wondering,
with a strange mixture of dread and desire, whether Madame
Clairin had told her sister-in-law that she had told him . . .
His presence now might be simply a gratuitous cause of suffering; and yet his absence might seem to imply that it was in the
power of circumstances to make them ashamed to meet each
other's eyes. He sat a long time with his head in his hands,
lost in a painful confusion of hopes and questionings. He
felt at moments as if he could throttle Madame Clairin, and
yet he could not help asking himself whether it was not
possible that she might have done him a service. It was late
when he left the hotel, and as he entered the gate of the other

house his heart was beating so that he was sure his voice would show it.

The servant ushered him into the drawing-room, which was empty, with the lamp burning low. But the long windows were open, and their light curtains swaying in a soft, warm wind, and Longmore stepped out upon the terrace. There he found Madame de Mauves alone, slowly pacing up and down. She was dressed in white, very simply, and her hair was arranged, not as she usually wore it, but in a single loose coil, like that of a person unprepared for company.

She stopped when she saw Longmore, seemed slightly startled, uttered an exclamation, and stood waiting for him to speak. He looked at her, tried to say something, but found no words. He knew it was awkward, it was offensive, to stand silent, gazing; but he could not say what was suitable, and he dared not say what he wished.

Her face was indistinct in the dim light, but he could see that her eyes were fixed on him, and he wondered what they expressed. Did they warn him, did they plead or did they confess to a sense of provocation? For an instant his head swam; he felt as if it would make all things clear to stride forward and fold her in his arms. But a moment later he was still standing looking at her; he had not moved; he knew that she had spoken, but he had not understood her.

'You were here this morning,' she continued, and now, slowly, the meaning of her words came to him. 'I had a bad headache and had to shut myself up.' She spoke in her usual voice.

Longmore mastered his agitation and answered her without betraying himself: 'I hope you are better now.'

'Yes, thank you, I'm better – much better.'

He was silent a moment, and she moved away to a chair and seated herself. After a pause he followed her and stood before her, leaning against the balustrade of the terrace. 'I hoped you might have been able to come out for the morning into the forest. I went alone; it was a lovely day, and I took a long walk.'

'It was a lovely day,' she said absently, and sat with her eyes lowered, slowly opening and closing her fan. Longmore, as he watched her, felt more and more sure that her sister-in-law had seen her since her interview with him; that her attitude toward him was changed. It was this same something that chilled the ardour with which he had come, or at least converted the dozen passionate speeches which kept rising to his lips into a kind of reverential silence. No, certainly, he could not clasp her to his arms now, any more than some early worshipper could have clasped the marble statue in his temple. But Longmore's statue spoke at last, with a full human voice, and even with a shade of human hesitation. She looked up, and it seemed to him that her eyes shone through the dusk.

'I'm very glad you came this evening,' she said. 'I have a particular reason for being glad. I half expected you, and yet I thought it possible you might not come.'

'As I have been feeling all day,' Longmore answered, 'it was impossible I should not come. I have spent the day in thinking of you.'

She made no immediate reply, but continued to open and close her fan thoughtfully. At last, – 'I have something to say to you,' she said abruptly. 'I want you to know to a certainty that I have a very high opinion of you.' Longmore started and shifted his position. To what was she coming? But he said nothing, and she went on.

'I take a great interest in you; there's no reason why I should not say it, – I have a great friendship for you.'

He began to laugh; he hardly knew why, unless that this seemed the very mockery of coldness. But she continued without heeding him.

'You know, I suppose, that a great disappointment always implies a great confidence – a great hope?'

'I have hoped,' he said, 'hoped strongly; but doubtless never rationally enough to have a right to bemoan my disappointment.'

'You do yourself injustice. I have such confidence in your reason, that I should be greatly disappointed if I were to find it wanting.'

'I really almost believe that you are amusing yourself at my expense,' cried Longmore. 'My reason? Reason is a mere word! The only reality in the world is *feeling*!'

She rose to her feet and looked at him gravely. His eyes by this time were accustomed to the imperfect light, and he could see that her look was reproachful, and yet that it was beseechingly kind. She shook her head impatiently, and laid her fan upon his arm with a strong pressure.

'If that were so, it would be a weary world. I know your feeling, however, nearly enough. You needn't try to express it. It's enough that it gives me the right to ask a favour of you, – to make an urgent, a solemn request.'

'Make it; I listen.'

'*Don't disappoint me*. If you don't understand me now, you will to-morrow, or very soon. When I said just now that I had a very high opinion of you, I meant it very seriously. It was not a vain compliment. I believe that there is no appeal one may make to your generosity which can remain long unanswered. If this were to happen, – if I were to find you selfish where I thought you generous, narrow where I thought you large,' – and she spoke slowly, with her voice lingering with emphasis on each of these words, – 'vulgar where I thought you rare, – I should think worse of human nature. I should suffer, – I should suffer keenly. I should say to myself in the dull days of the future, "There was one man who might have done so and so; and he, too, failed." But this shall not be. You have made too good an impression on me not to make the very best. If you wish to please me for ever, there's a way.'

She was standing close to him, with her dress touching him, her eyes fixed on his. As she went on her manner grew strangely intense, and she had the singular appearance of a woman preaching reason with a kind of passion. Longmore was confused, dazzled, almost bewildered. The intention of her words was all remonstrance, refusal, dismissal; but her presence there, so close, so urgent, so personal, seemed a distracting contradiction of it. She had never been so lovely. In her white dress, with her pale face and deeply lighted eyes, she seemed the very spirit of the summer night. When she had ceased speaking, she drew a long breath; Longmore felt it on his cheek, and it stirred in his whole being a sudden, rapturous conjecture. Were her words in their soft severity a mere delusive spell, meant to throw into relief her almost ghostly beauty, and was this the only truth, the only reality, the only law?

He closed his eyes and felt that she was watching him, not without pain and perplexity herself. He looked at her again, met her own eyes, and saw a tear in each of them. Then this last suggestion of his desire seemed to die away with a stifled murmur, and her beauty, more and more radiant in the darkness, rose before him as a symbol of something vague which was yet more beautiful than itself.

'I may understand you to-morrow,' he said, 'but I don't understand you now.'

'And yet I took counsel with myself to-day and asked myself how I had best speak to you. On one side, I might have refused to see you at all.' Longmore made a violent movement, and she added: 'In that case I should have written to you. I might see you, I thought, and simply say to you that there were excellent reasons why we should part, and that I begged this visit should be your last. This I inclined to do; what made me decide otherwise was – simply friendship! I said to myself that I should be glad to remember in future days, not that I had dismissed you, but that you had gone away out of the fullness of your own wisdom.'

'The fullness – the fullness!' cried Longmore.

'I'm prepared, if necessary,' Madame de Mauves continued after a pause, 'to fall back upon my strict right. But, as I said before, I shall be greatly disappointed, if I am obliged to.'

'When I hear you say that,' Longmore answered, 'I feel so angry, so horribly irritated, that I wonder it is not easy to leave you without more words.'

'If you should go away in anger, this idea of mine about our parting would be but half realised. No, I don't want to think of you as angry; I don't want even to think of you as making a serious sacrifice. I want to think of you as –'

'As a creature who never has existed, – who never can exist! A creature who knew you without loving you, – who left you without regretting you!'

She turned impatiently away and walked to the other end of the terrace. When she came back, he saw that her impatience had become a cold sternness. She stood before him again, looking at him from head to foot, in deep reproachfulness, almost in scorn. Beneath her glance he felt a kind of shame. He coloured; she observed it and withheld something she was about to say. She turned away again, walked to the other end of the terrace, and stood there looking away into the garden. It seemed to him that she had guessed he understood her, and slowly – slowly – half as the fruit of his vague self-reproach, – he did understand her. She was giving him a chance to do gallantly what it seemed unworthy of both of them he should do meanly.

She liked him, she must have liked him greatly, to wish so to spare him, to go to the trouble of conceiving an ideal of conduct for him. With this sense of her friendship, – her strong friendship she had just called it, – Longmore's soul rose with a new flight, and suddenly felt itself breathing a clearer air. The words ceased to seem a mere bribe to his ardour; they were charged with ardour themselves; they were a present happiness. He moved rapidly toward her with a feeling that this was something he might immediately enjoy.

They were separated by two-thirds of the length of the terrace, and he had to pass the drawing-room window. As he did so he started with an exclamation. Madame Clairin stood posted there, watching him. Conscious, apparently, that she might be suspected of eavesdropping, she stepped forward with a smile and looked from Longmore to his hostess.

'Such a tête-à-tête as that,' she said, 'one owes no apology for interrupting. One ought to come in for good manners.'

Madame de Mauves turned round, but she answered nothing. She looked straight at Longmore, and her eyes had extra-ordinary eloquence. He was not exactly sure, indeed, what she meant them to say; but they seemed to say plainly something of this kind; 'Call it what you will, what you have to urge upon me is the thing which this woman can best conceive. What I ask of you is something she can't!' They seemed, somehow, to beg him to suffer her to be herself, and to intimate that that self was as little as possible like Madame Clairin. He felt an immense answering desire not to do anything which would seem natural to this lady. He had laid his hat and cane on the parapet of the terrace. He took them up, offered his hand to Madame de Mauves with a simple good night, bowed silently to Madame Clairin, and departed.

IX

HE went home and without lighting his candle flung himself on his bed. But he got no sleep till morning; he lay hour after hour tossing, thinking, wondering; his mind had never been so active. It seemed to him that Euphemia had laid on him in those last moments an inspiring commission, and that she had expressed herself almost as largely as if she had listened assentingly to an assurance of his love. It was neither easy nor delightful thoroughly to understand her; but little by little her perfect meaning sank into his mind and soothed it with a sense of opportunity, which somehow stifled his sense of loss. For, to begin with, she meant that she could love him in no degree nor contingency, in no imaginable future. This was absolute; he felt that he could alter it no more than he could transpose the constellations he lay gazing at through his open window. He wondered what it was, in the background of her life, that she grasped so closely: a sense of duty, unquenchable to the end? a love that no offence could trample out? 'Good Heavens!' he thought, 'is the world so rich in the purest pearls of passion, that such tenderness as that can be wasted for ever, – poured away without a sigh into bottomless darkness?' Had she, in spite of the detestable present, some precious memory which contained the germ of a shrinking hope? Was she prepared to submit to everything and yet to believe? Was it strength, was it weakness, was it a vulgar fear, was it conviction, conscience, constancy?

Longmore sank back with a sigh and an oppressive feeling that it was vain to guess at such a woman's motives. He only felt that those of Madame de Mauves were buried deep in her soul, and that they must be of some fine temper, not of a base

one. He had a dim, overwhelming sense of a sort of invulner-
able constancy being the supreme law of her character, – a
constancy which still found a foothold among crumbling
ruins. 'She has loved once,' he said to himself as he rose and
wandered to his window; 'that's for ever. Yes, yes, – if she loved
again she would be *common*.' He stood for a long time looking
out into the starlit silence of the town and the forest, and
thinking of what life would have been if *his* constancy had met
hers unpledged. But life was this, now, and he must live. It was
living keenly to stand there with a petition from such a woman
to revolve. He was not to disappoint her, he was to justify a
conception which it had beguiled her weariness to shape. Longmore's imagination swelled; he threw back his head and
seemed to be looking for Madame de Mauves's conception
among the blinking, mocking stars. But it came to him rather
on the mild night-wind, as it wandered in over the house-tops
which covered the rest of so many heavy human hearts. What
she asked he felt that she was asking, not for her own sake (she
feared nothing, she needed nothing), but for that of his own
happiness and his own character. He must assent to destiny.
Why else was he young and strong, intelligent and resolute? He
must not give it to her to reproach him with thinking that she
had a moment's attention for his love, – to plead, to argue, to
break off in bitterness; he must see everything from above, her
indifference and his own ardour; he must prove his strength, he
must do the handsome thing; he must decide that the handsome thing was to submit to the inevitable, to be supremely
delicate, to spare her all pain, to stifle his passion, to ask no
compensation, to depart without delay and try to believe that
wisdom is its own reward. All this, neither more nor less, it was
a matter of friendship with Madame de Mauves to expect of
him. And what should he gain by it? He should have pleased
her! . . . He flung himself on his bed again, fell asleep at last, and
slept till morning.

Before noon the next day he had made up his mind that he
would leave Saint-Germain at once. It seemed easier to leave
without seeing her, and yet if he might ask a grain of 'compensation', it would be five minutes face to face with her. He passed

a restless day. Wherever he went he seemed to see her standing before him in the dusky halo of evening, and looking at him with an air of still negation more intoxicating than the most passionate self-surrender. He must certainly go, and yet it was hideously hard. He compromised and went to Paris to spend the rest of the day. He strolled along the boulevards and looked at the shops, sat awhile in the Tuileries gardens and looked at the shabby unfortunates for whom this only was nature and summer; but simply felt, as a result of it all, that it was a very dusty, dreary, lonely world into which Madame de Mauves was turning him away.

In a sombre mood he made his way back to the boulevards and sat down at a table on the great plain of hot asphalt, before a café. Night came on, the lamps were lighted, the tables near him found occupants, and Paris began to wear that peculiar evening look of hers which seems to say, in the flare of windows and theatre doors, and the muffled rumble of swift-rolling carriages, that this is no world for you unless you have your pockets lined and your scruples drugged. Longmore, however, had neither scruples nor desires; he looked at the swarming city for the first time with an easy sense of repaying its indifference. Before long a carriage drove up to the pavement directly in front of him, and remained standing for several minutes without its occupant getting out. It was one of those neat, plain coupés, drawn by a single powerful horse, in which one is apt to imagine a pale, handsome woman, buried among silk cushions, and yawning as she sees the gas-lamps glittering in the gutters. At last the door opened and out stepped M. de Mauves. He stopped and leaned on the window for some time, talking in an excited manner to a person within. At last he gave a nod and the carriage rolled away. He stood swinging his cane and looking up and down the boulevard, with the air of a man fumbling, as one may say, with the loose change of time. He turned toward the café and was apparently, for want of anything better worth his attention, about to seat himself at one of the tables, when he perceived Longmore. He wavered an instant, and then, without a change in his nonchalant gait, strolled toward him with a bow and a vague smile.

It was the first time they had met since their encounter in the forest after Longmore's false start for Brussels. Madame Clairin's revelations, as we may call them, had not made the Baron especially present to his mind; he had another office for his emotions than disgust. But as M. de Mauves came toward him he felt deep in his heart that he abhorred him. He noticed, however, for the first time, a shadow upon the Baron's cool placidity, and his delight at finding that somewhere at last the shoe pinched *him*, mingled with his impulse to be as exasperatingly impenetrable as possible, enabled him to return the other's greeting with all his own self-possession.

M. de Mauves sat down, and the two men looked at each other across the table, exchanging formal greetings which did little to make their mutual scrutiny seem gracious. Longmore had no reason to suppose that the Baron knew of his sister's revelations. He was sure that M. de Mauves cared very little about his opinions, and yet he had a sense that there was that in his eyes which would have made the Baron change colour if keener suspicion had helped him to read it. M. de Mauves did not change colour, but he looked at Longmore with a half-defiant intentness, which betrayed at once an irritating memory of the episode in the Bois de Boulogne, and such vigilant curiosity as was natural to a gentleman who had entrusted his 'honour' to another gentleman's magnanimity, – or to his artlessness. It would appear that Longmore seemed to the Baron to possess these virtues in rather scantier measure than a few days before; for the cloud deepened on his face, and he turned away and frowned as he lighted a cigar.

The person in the coupé, Longmore thought, whether or no the same person as the heroine of the episode of the Bois de Boulogne, was not a source of unalloyed delight. Longmore had dark blue eyes, of admirable lucidity, – truth-telling eyes which had in his childhood always made his harshest taskmasters smile at his nursery fibs. An observer watching the two men, and knowing something of their relations, would certainly have said that what he saw in those eyes must not a little have puzzled and tormented M. de Mauves. They judged him, they mocked him, they eluded him, they threatened him, they triumphed over him, they treated him as no pair of eyes had ever treated him. The Baron's scheme had been to make no one happy but himself, and here was Longmore already, if looks were to be trusted, primed for an enterprise more inspiring than the finest of his own achievements. Was this candid young barbarian but a *faux bonhomme* after all? He had puzzled the Baron before, and this was once too often.

M. de Mauves hated to seem preoccupied, and he took up the evening paper to help himself to look indifferent. As he glanced over it he uttered some cold commonplace on the political situation, which gave Longmore an easy opportunity of replying by an ironical sally which made him seem for the moment aggressively at his ease. And yet our hero was far from being master of the situation. The Baron's ill-humour did him good, so far as it pointed to a want of harmony with the lady in the coupé; but it disturbed him sorely as he began to suspect that it possibly meant jealousy of himself. It passed through his mind that jealousy is a passion with a double face, and that in some of its moods it bears a plausible likeness to affection. It recurred to him painfully that the Baron might grow ashamed of his political compact with his wife, and he felt that it would be far more tolerable in the future to think of his continued turpitude than of his repentance. The two men sat for half an hour exchanging stinted small-talk, the Baron feeling a nervous need of playing the spy, and Longmore indulging a ferocious relish of his discomfort. These rigid courtesies were interrupted however by the arrival of a friend of M. de Mauves, – a tall, pale, consumptive-looking dandy, who filled the air with the odour of heliotrope. He looked up and down the boulevard wearily, examined the Baron's toilet from head to foot, then surveyed his own in the same fashion, and at last announced languidly that the Duchess was in town! M. de Mauves must come with him to call; she had abused him dreadfully a couple of evenings before, – a sure sign she wanted to see him.

'I depend upon you,' said M. de Mauves's friend with an infantine drawl, 'to put her *en train*.'

M. de Mauves resisted, and protested that he was *d'une humeur massacrante*; but at last he allowed himself to be drawn to his feet, and stood looking awkwardly – awkwardly for M. de Mauves – at Longmore. 'You'll excuse me,' he said dryly; 'you, too, probably, have occupation for the evening?'

'None but to catch my train,' Longmore answered, looking at his watch.

'Ah, you go back to Saint-Germain?'

'In half an hour.'

M. de Mauves seemed on the point of disengaging himself from his companion's arm, which was locked in his own; but on the latter uttering some persuasive murmur, he lifted his hat stiffly and turned away.

Longmore packed his trunk the next day with dogged hero-ism and wandered off to the terrace, to try and beguile the restlessness with which he waited for evening; for he wished to see Madame de Mauves for the last time at the hour of long shadows and pale pink-reflected lights, as he had almost always seen her. Destiny, however, took no account of this humble plea for poetic justice; it was his fortune to meet her on the terrace sitting under a tree, alone. It was an hour when the place was almost empty; the day was warm, but as he took his place beside her a light breeze stirred the leafy edges on the broad circle of shadow in which she sat. She looked at him with candid anxiety, and he immediately told her that he should leave Saint-Germain that evening, – that he must bid her fare-well. Her eye expanded and brightened for a moment as he spoke; but she said nothing and turned her glance away toward distant Paris, as it lay twinkling and flashing through its hot exhalations. 'I have a request to make of you,' he added. 'That you think of me as a man who has felt much and claimed little.'

She drew a long breath, which almost suggested pain. 'I can't think of you as unhappy. It's impossible. You have a life to lead, you have duties, talents, and interests. I shall hear of your career. And then,' she continued after a pause and with the deepest seriousness, 'one can't be unhappy through having a better opinion of a friend, instead of a worse.'

For a moment he failed to understand her. 'Do you mean that there can be varying degrees in my opinion of you?'

She rose and pushed away her chair. 'I mean,' she said quickly, 'that it's better to have done nothing in bitterness, – nothing in passion.' And she began to walk.

Longmore followed her, without answering. But he took off his hat and with his pocket-handkerchief wiped his forehead. 'Where shall you go? what shall you do?' he asked at last, abruptly.

'Do? I shall do as I've always done, – except perhaps that I shall go for a while to Auvergne.'

'I shall go to America. I have done with Europe for the present.'

She glanced at him as he walked beside her after he had spoken these words, and then bent her eyes for a long time on the ground. At last, seeing that she was going far, she stopped and put out her hand. 'Good-by,' she said; 'may you have all the happiness you deserve!'

He took her hand and looked at her, but something was passing in him that made it impossible to return her hand's light pressure. Something of infinite value was floating past him, and he had taken an oath not to raise a finger to stop it. It was borne by the strong current of the world's great life and not of his own small one. Madame de Mauves disengaged her hand, gathered her shawl, and smiled at him almost as you would do at a child you should wish to encourage. Several moments later he was still standing watching her receding figure. When it had disappeared, he shook himself, walked rapidly back to his hotel, and without waiting for the evening train paid his bill and departed.

Later in the day M. de Mauves came into his wife's drawing-room, where she sat waiting to be summoned to dinner. He was dressed with a scrupulous freshness which seemed to indicate an intention of dining out. He walked up and down for some moments in silence, then rang the bell for a servant, and went out into the hall to meet him. He ordered the carriage to take him to the station, paused a moment with his hand on the knob of the door, dismissed the servant angrily as the latter lingered observing him, re-entered the drawing-room, resumed his restless walk, and at last stepped abruptly before his wife, who had taken up a book. 'May I ask the favour,' he said with evident effort, in spite of a forced smile of easy courtesy, 'of having a question answered?'

'It's a favour I never refused,' Madame de Mauves replied.

'Very true. Do you expect this evening a visit from Mr Longmore?'

'Mr Longmore,' said his wife, 'has left Saint-Germain.' M. de Mauve started and his smile expired. 'Mr Longmore,' his wife continued, 'has gone to America.'

M. de Mauves stared a moment, flushed deeply, and turned away. Then recovering himself, – 'Had anything happened?' he asked, 'Had he a sudden call?'

But his question received no answer. At the same moment the servant threw open the door and announced dinner; Madame Clairin rustled in, rubbing her white hands, Madame de Mauves passed silently into the dining-room, and he stood frowning and wondering. Before long he went out upon the terrace and continued his uneasy walk. At the end of a quarter of an hour the servant came to inform him that the carriage was at the door. 'Send it away,' he said curtly. 'I shall not use it.' When the ladies had half finished dinner he went in and joined them, with a formal apology to his wife for his tardiness.

The dishes were brought back, but he hardly tasted them; on the other hand, he drank a great deal of wine. There was little talk; what there was, was supplied by Madame Clairin. Twice she saw her brother's eyes fixed on her own, over his wineglass, with a piercing, questioning glance. She replied by an elevation of the eyebrows, which did the office of a shrug of the shoulders. M. de Mauves was left alone to finish his wine; he sat over it for more than an hour, and let the darkness gather about him. At last the servant came in with a letter and lighted a candle. The letter was a telegram, which M. de Mauves, when he had read it, burnt at the candle. After five minutes' meditation, he wrote a message on the back of a visiting-card and gave it to the servant to carry to the office. The man knew quite as much as his master suspected about the lady to whom the telegram was addressed; but its contents puzzled him; they consisted of the single word, '*Impossible*.' As the evening passed without her

brother reappearing in the drawing-room, Madame Clairin
came to him where he sat, by his solitary candle. He took no
notice of her presence for some time; but he was the one person
to whom she allowed this licence. At last, speaking in a peremptory tone, 'The American has gone home at an hour's
notice,' he said. 'What does it mean?'

Madame Clairin now gave free play to the shrug she had
been obliged to suppress at the table. 'It means that I have a
sister-in-law whom I haven't the honour to understand.'

He said nothing more, and silently allowed her to depart, as
if it had been her duty to provide him with an explanation and
he was disgusted with her levity. When she had gone, he went
into the garden and walked up and down, smoking. He saw his
wife sitting alone on the terrace, but remained below strolling
along the narrow paths. He remained a long time. It became
late and Madame de Mauves disappeared. Toward midnight
he dropped upon a bench, tired, with a kind of angry sigh. It
was sinking into his mind that he, too, did not understand
Madame Clairin's sister-in-law.

Longmore was obliged to wait a week in London for a ship.
It was very hot, and he went out for a day to Richmond. In the
garden of the hotel at which he dined he met his friend Mrs
Draper, who was staying there. She made eager inquiry about
Madame de Mauves, but Longmore at first, as they sat looking
out at the famous view of the Thames, parried her questions
and confined himself to small-talk. At last she said she was
afraid he had something to conceal; whereupon, after a pause,
he asked her if she remembered recommending him, in the
letter she sent to him at Saint-Germain, to draw the sadness
from her friend's smile. 'The last I saw of her was her smile,'
said he, – 'when I bade her good-by.'

'I remember urging you to "console" her,' Mrs Draper
answered, 'and I wondered afterwards whether – a model of
discretion as you are – I hadn't given you rather foolish advice.'

'She has her consolation in herself,' he said; 'she needs none
that any one else can offer her. That's for troubles for which – be
it more, be it less – our own folly has to answer. Madame de
Mauves has not a grain of folly left.'

'Ah, don't say that!' murmured Mrs Draper. 'Just a little folly is very graceful.'

Longmore rose to go, with a quick nervous movement. 'Don't talk of grace,' he said, 'till you have measured her reason.'

For two years after his return to America he heard nothing of Madame de Mauves. That he thought of her intently, constantly, I need hardly say: most people wondered why such a clever young man should not 'devote' himself to something; but to himself he seemed absorbingly occupied. He never wrote to her; he believed that she preferred it. At last he heard that Mrs Draper had come home, and he immediately called on her. 'Of course,' she said after the first greetings, 'you are dying for news of Madame de Mauves. Prepare yourself for something strange. I heard from her two or three times during the year after your return. She left Saint-Germain and went to live in the country, on some old property of her husband's. She wrote me very kind little notes, but I felt somehow that – in spite of what you said about "consolation" – they were the notes of a very sad woman. The only advice I could have given her was to leave her wretch of a husband and come back to her own land and her own people. But this I didn't feel free to do, and yet it made me so miserable not to be able to help her that I preferred to let our correspondence die a natural death. I had no news of her for a year. Last summer, however, I met at Vichy a clever young Frenchman whom I accidentally learned to be a friend of Euphemia's lovely sister-in-law, Madame Clairin. I lost no time in asking him what he knew about Madame de Mauves, – a countrywoman of mine and an old friend. "I congratulate you on possessing her friendship," he answered. "That's the charming little woman who killed her husband." You may imagine that I promptly asked for an explanation, and he proceeded to relate to me what he called the whole story. M. de Mauves had *fait quelques folies*, which his wife had taken absurdly to heart. He had repented and asked her forgiveness, which she had inexorably refused. She was very pretty, and severity, apparently, suited her style; for whether or no her husband had been in love with her before, he fell madly in love with her now. He was the proudest man in France, but he had begged her on his knees to be readmitted to favour. All in vain! She was stone, she was ice, she was outraged virtue. People noticed a great change in him: he gave up society, ceased to care for anything, looked shockingly. One fine day they learned that he had blown out his brains. My friend had the story of course from Madame Clairin.'

Longmore was strongly moved, and his first impulse after he had recovered his composure was to return immediately to Europe. But several years have passed, and he still lingers at home. The truth is, that in the midst of all the ardent tenderness of his memory of Madame de Mauves, he has become conscious of a singular feeling, – a feeling for which awe would be hardly too strong a name.

BENVOLIO

I

ONCE upon a time (as if he had lived in a fairy-tale) there was a very interesting young man. This is not a fairy-tale, and yet our young man was in some respects as pretty a fellow as any fairy prince. I call him interesting because his type of character is one I have always found it profitable to observe. If you fail to consider him so, I shall be willing to confess that the fault is mine and not his; I shall have told my story with too little skill.

His name was Benvolio; that is, it was not; but we shall call him so for the sake both of convenience and of picturesqueness. He was about to enter upon the third decade of our mortal span; he had a little property, and he followed no regular profession. His personal appearance was in the highest degree prepossessing. Having said this, it were perhaps well that I should let you – you especially, madam – suppose that he exactly corresponded to your ideal of manly beauty; but I am bound to explain definitely wherein it was that he resembled a fairy prince, and I need furthermore to make a record of certain little peculiarities and anomalies in which it is probable that your brilliant conception would be deficient. Benvolio was slim and fair, with clustering locks, remarkably fine eyes, and such a frank, expressive smile that on the journey through life it was almost as serviceable to its owner as the magic key, or the enchanted ring, or the wishing-cap, or any other bauble of necromantic properties. Unfortunately this charming smile was not always at his command, and its place was sometimes occupied by a very perverse and dusky frown, which rendered the young man no service whatever – not even that of frightening people; for though it expressed extreme irritation and impatience, it was characterised by the brevity of contempt, and the only revenge upon disagreeable things and offensive people that it seemed to express a desire for on Benvolio's part was that of forgetting and ignoring them with the utmost possible celerity. It never made any one tremble, though now and then it perhaps made irritable people murmur an imprecation or two. You might have supposed from Benvolio's manner, when he was in good humour (which was the greater part of the time), from his brilliant, intelligent glance, from his easy, irresponsible step, and in especial from the sweet, clear, lingering, caressing tone of his voice – the voice as it were of a man whose fortune has been made for him, and who assumes, a trifle egotistically, that the rest of the world is equally at leisure to share with him the sweets of life, to pluck the wayside flowers, and chase the butterflies afield – you might have supposed, I say, from all this luxurious assurance of demeanour, that our hero really had the wishing-cap sitting invisible on his handsome brow, or was obliged only to close his knuckles together a moment to exert an effective pressure upon the magic ring. The young man, I have said, was a mixture of inconsistencies; I may say more exactly that he was a tissue of contradictions. He did possess the magic ring, in a certain fashion; he possessed in other words the poetic imagination. Everything that fancy could do for him was done in perfection. It gave him immense satisfactions; it transfigured the world; it made very common objects sometimes seem radiantly beautiful, and it converted beautiful ones into infinite sources of intoxication. Benvolio had what is called the poetic temperament. It is rather out of fashion to describe a man in these terms; but I believe, in spite of much evidence to the contrary, that there are poets still; and if we may call a spade a spade, why should we not call such a person as Benvolio a poet?

These contradictions that I speak of ran through his whole nature, and they were perfectly apparent in his habits, in his manners, in his conversation, and even in his physiognomy. It was as if the souls of two very different men had been placed together to make the voyage of life in the same boat, and had agreed for convenience' sake to take the helm in alternation. The helm, with Benvolio, was always the imagination; but in his different moods it worked very differently. To an acute observer his face itself would have betrayed these variations; and it is certain that his dress, his talk, his way of spending his

time, one day and another, abundantly indicated them. Sometimes he looked very young – rosy, radiant, blooming, younger
than his years. Then suddenly, as the light struck his head in a
particular manner, you would see that his golden locks contained a surprising number of silver threads; and with your
attention quickened by this discovery, you would proceed to
detect something grave and discreet in his smile – something
vague and ghostly, like the dim adumbration of the darker half
of the lunar disc. You might have met Benvolio, in certain states
of mind, dressed like a man of the highest fashion – wearing his
hat on his ear, a rose in his button-hole, a wonderful intaglio or
an antique Syracusan coin, by way of a pin, in his cravat. Then,
on the morrow, you would have espied him braving the sunshine in a rusty scholar's coat, with his hat pulled over his brow
– a costume wholly at odds with flowers and gems. It was all a
matter of fancy; but his fancy was a weather-cock, and faced
east or west as the wind blew. His conversation matched his
coat and breeches; he talked one day the talk of the town; he
chattered, he gossiped, he asked questions and told stories; you
would have said that he was a charming fellow for a dinner-
party or the pauses of a cotillion. The next he either talked
philosophy or politics, or said nothing at all; he was absent and
indifferent; he was thinking his own thoughts; he had a book in
his pocket, and evidently he was composing one in his head. At
home he lived in two chambers. One was an immense room,
hung with pictures, lined with books, draped with rugs and
tapestries, decorated with a multitude of ingenious devices (for
of all these things he was very fond); the other, his sleeping-
room, was almost as bare as a monastic cell. It had a meagre
little strip of carpet on the floor, and a dozen well-thumbed
volumes of classic poets and sages on the mantel-shelf. On the
wall hung three or four coarsely engraved portraits of the most
exemplary of these worthies; these were the only ornaments.
But the room had the charm of a great window, in a deep
embrasure, looking out upon a tangled, silent, moss-grown
garden, and in the embrasure stood the little ink-blotted table
at which Benvolio did most of his poetic scribbling. The
windows of his sumptuous sitting-room commanded a wide

public square, where people were always passing and lounging, where military music used to play on vernal nights, and half the life of the great town went forward. At the risk of your thinking our hero a sad idler, I will say that he spent an inordinate amount of time in gazing out of these windows (in either direction) with his elbows on the sill. The garden did not belong to the house which he inhabited, but to a neighbouring one, and the proprietor, a graceless old miser, was very chary of permits to visit his domain. But Benvolio's fancy used to wander through the alleys without stirring the long arms of the untended plants, and to bend over the heavy-headed flowers without leaving a footprint on their beds. It was here that his happiest thoughts came to him – that inspiration (as we may say, speaking of a man of the poetic temperament) descended upon him in silence, and for certain divine, appreciable moments stood poised along the course of his scratching quill. It was not, however, that he had not spent some very charming hours in the larger, richer apartment. He used to receive his friends there – sometimes in great numbers, sometimes at boisterous, many-voiced suppers, which lasted far into the night. When these entertainments were over he never made a direct transition to his little scholar's cell. He went out and wandered for an hour through the dark, sleeping streets of the town, ridding himself of the fumes of wine, and feeling not at all tipsy, but intensely, portentously sober. More than once, when he had come back and prepared to go to bed, he saw the first faint glow of dawn trembling upward over the tree-tops of his garden. His friends, coming to see him, often found the greater room empty, and advancing, rapped at the door of his chamber. But he frequently kept quiet, not desiring in the least to see them, knowing exactly what they were going to say, and not thinking it worth hearing. Then, hearing them stride away, and the outer door close behind them, he would come forth and take a turn in his slippers, over his Persian carpets, and glance out of the window and see his defeated visitant stand scratching his chin in the sunny square. After this he would laugh lightly to himself – as is said to be the habit of the scribbling tribe in moments of production.

Although he had many relatives he enjoyed extreme liberty. His family was so large, his brothers and sisters were so numerous, that he could absent himself and be little missed. Sometimes he used this privilege freely; he tired of people whom he had seen very often, and he had seen, of course, a great deal of his family. At other moments he was extremely domestic; he suddenly found solitude depressing, and it seemed to him that if one sought society as a refuge, one needed to be on familiar terms with it, and that with no one was familiarity so natural as among people who had grown up at a common fireside. Nevertheless it frequently occurred to him – for sooner or later everything occurred to him – that he was too independent and irresponsible; that he would be happier if he had a little golden ball and chain tied to his ankle. His curiosity about all things – life and love and art and truth – was great, and his theory was to satisfy it as freely as might be; but as the years went by this pursuit of impartial science appeared to produce a singular result. He became conscious of an intellectual condition similar to that of a palate which has lost its relish. To a man with a disordered appetite all things taste alike, and so it seemed to Benvolio that the gustatory faculty of his mind was losing its keenness. It had still its savoury moments, its feasts and its holidays; but, on the whole, the spectacle of human life was growing flat and stale. This is simply a wordy way of expressing that comprehensive fact – Benvolio was *blasé*. He knew it, he knew it betimes, and he regretted it acutely. He believed that the mind can keep its freshness to the last, and that it is only fools that are overbored. There was a way of never being bored, and the wise man's duty was to find it out. One of its rudiments, he believed, was that one grows tired of one's self sooner than of anything else in the world. Idleness, every one admitted, was the greatest of follies; but idleness was subtle, and exacted tribute under a hundred plausible disguises. One was often idle when one seemed to be ardently occupied; one was always idle when one's occupation had not a high aim. One was idle therefore when one was working simply for one's self. Curiosity for curiosity's sake, art for art's sake, these were essentially broken-winded steeds. Ennui was at the end of everything that did not multiply our relations with life. To multiply his relations, therefore, Benvolio reflected, should be the wise man's aim. Poor Benvolio had to reflect on this, because, as I say, he was a poet and not a man of action. A fine fellow of the latter stamp would have solved the problem without knowing it, and bequeathed to his fellow men not frigid formulas but vivid examples. But Benvolio had often said to himself that he was born to imagine great things – not to do them; and he had said this by no means sadly, for on the whole he was very well content with his portion. Imagine them he determined he would, and on a magnificent scale. He would multiply his labours at least, and they should be very serious ones. He would cultivate great ideas, he would enunciate great truths, he would write immortal verses. In all this there was a large amount of talent and a liberal share of ambition. I will not say that Benvolio was a man of genius; it may seem to make the distinction too cheap; but he was at any rate a man with an intellectual passion; and if, being near him, you had been able to listen intently enough, he would, like the great people of his craft, have seemed to emit something of that vague magical murmur – the voice of the infinite – which lurks in the involutions of a sea-shell. He himself, by the way, had once made use of this little simile, and had written a poem in which it was melodiously set forth that the poetic minds scattered about the world correspond to the little shells one picks up on the beach, all resonant with the echo of ocean. The whole thing was of course rounded off with the sands of time, the waves of history, and other harmonious conceits.

II

BUT (as you are naturally expecting to hear), Benvolio knew perfectly well that there is one relation with life which is a better antidote to ennui than any other – the relation established with a charming woman. Benvolio was of course in love. Who was his mistress, you ask (I flatter myself with some impatience), and was she pretty, was she kind, was he successful? Hereby hangs my tale, which I must relate in due form.

Benvolio's mistress was a lady whom (as I cannot tell you her real name) it will be quite in keeping to speak of as the Countess. The Countess was a young widow, who had some time since divested herself of her mourning weeds – which indeed she had never worn but very lightly. She was rich, extremely pretty, and free to do as she listed. She was passionately fond of pleasure and admiration, and they gushed forth at her feet in unceasing streams. Her beauty was not of the conventional type, but it was dazzlingly brilliant; few faces were more expressive, more fascinating. Hers was never the same for two days together; it reflected her momentary circumstances with extraordinary vividness, and in knowing her you had the advantage of knowing a dozen different women. She was clever and accomplished, and had the credit of being perfectly amiable; indeed it was difficult to imagine a person combining a greater number of the precious gifts of nature and fortune. She represented felicity, gaiety, success; she was made to charm, to play a part, to exert a sway. She lived in a great house, behind high verdure-muffled walls, where other Countesses, in other years, had played a part no less brilliant. It was an antiquated quarter, into which the tide of commerce had lately begun to roll heavily; but the turbid wave of trade broke in vain against the Countess's enclosure, and if in her garden and her drawing-room you heard the deep uproar of the city, it was only as a vague undertone to sweeter things – to music, and witty talk, and tender colloquy. There was something very striking in this little oasis of luxury and privacy, in the midst of common toil and traffic.

Benvolio was a great deal at this lady's house; he rarely desired better entertainment. I spoke just now of privacy; but privacy was not what he found there, nor what he wished to find. He went there when he wished to learn with the least trouble what was going on in the world; for the talk of the people the Countess generally had about her was an epitome of the gossip, the rumours, the interests, the hopes and fears, of polite society. She was a thoroughly liberal hostess; all she asked was to be entertained; if you would contribute to the common fund of amusement, of discussion, you were a welcome guest. Sooner or later, among your fellow-guests, you encountered every one of consequence. There were frivolous people and wise people; people whose fortune was in their pockets and people whose fortune was in their brains; people deeply concerned in public affairs and people concerned only with the fit of their garments or with the effect upon the company of the announcement of their names. Benvolio, with his taste for a large and various social spectacle, appreciated all this; but he was best pleased, as a general thing, when he found the Countess alone. This was often his fortune, for the simple reason that when the Countess expected him she invariably caused herself to be refused to every one else. This is almost an answer to your inquiry whether Benvolio was successful in his suit. As yet, strictly speaking, there was no suit; Benvolio had never made love to the Countess. This sounds very strange, but it is nevertheless true. He was in love with her; he thought her the most charming creature conceivable; he spent hours with her alone by her own orders; he had had opportunity – he had been up to his neck in opportunity – and yet he had never said to her, as would have seemed so natural, 'Dear Countess, I beseech you to be my wife.' If you are surprised, I may also confide to you that the Countess was; and surprise under the circumstances very easily became displeasure. It is by no means certain that if Benvolio had made the little speech we have just imagined, the Countess would have fallen into his arms, confessed to an answering flame, and rung in *finis* to our tale, with the wedding-bells. But she nevertheless expected him in civility to pay her this supreme compliment. Her answer would be – what it might be; but his silence was a permanent offence. Every man, roughly speaking, had asked the Countess to marry him, and every man had been told that she was much obliged, but had not been thinking of changing her condition. But here, with the one man who failed to ask her, she was perpetually thinking of it, and this negative quality in Benvolio was more present to her mind, gave her more to think about, than all the positiveness of her other suitors. The truth was she liked Benvolio extremely, and his independence rendered him excellent service. The Countess had a very lively fancy, and she had fingered, nimbly enough, the volume of the young man's merits. She was by nature a trifle cold; she rarely lost her head; she measured each step as she took it; she had had little fancies and incipient passions; but on the whole she had thought much more about love than felt it. She had often tried to form an image of the sort of man it would be well for her to love – for so it was she expressed it. She had succeeded but indifferently, and her imagination had never found a pair of wings until the day she met Benvolio. Then it seemed to her that her quest was ended – her prize gained. This nervous, ardent, deep-eyed youth struck her as the harmonious counterpart of her own facile personality. This conviction rested with the Countess on a fine sense of propriety which it would be vain to attempt to analyse; he was different from herself and from the other men who surrounded her, and she valued him as a specimen of a rare and distinguished type. In the old days she would have appointed him to be her minstrel or her jester – it is to be feared that poor Benvolio would have figured rather dismally in the latter capacity; and at present a woman who was in her own right a considerable social figure, might give such a man a place in her train as an illustrious husband. I don't know how good a judge the Countess was of such matters, but she believed that the world would hear of Benvolio. She had beauty, ancestry, money, luxury, but she had not genius; and if genius was to be had, why not secure it, and complete the list? This is doubtless a rather coarse statement of the Countess's argument; but you have it thrown in gratis, as it were; for all I am bound to tell you is that this charming young woman took a fancy to this clever young man, and that she used to cry sometimes for a quarter of a minute when she imagined he was indifferent to her. Her tears were wasted, because he really cared for her – more even than she would have imagined if she had taken a favourable view of the case. But Benvolio, I cannot too much repeat, was an exceedingly complex character, and there was many a lapse in the logic of his conduct. The Countess charmed him, excited him, interested him; he did her abundant justice – more than justice; but at the end of all he felt that she failed to satisfy him. If a man could have half a dozen wives – and Benvolio had once maintained, poetically, that he ought to have – the Countess would do very well for one of them – possibly even for the best of them. But she would not serve for all seasons and all moods; she needed a complement, an alternative – what the French call a *repoussoir*. One day he was going to see her, knowing that he was expected. There was to be a number of other people – in fact, a very brilliant assembly; but Benvolio knew that a certain touch of the hand, a certain glance of the eye, a certain caress of the voice, would be reserved for him alone. Happy Benvolio, you will say, to be going about the world with such charming secrets as this locked up in his young heart! Happy Benvolio indeed; but mark how he trifled with his happiness. He went to the Countess's gate, but he went no further; he stopped, stood there a moment, frowning intensely, and biting the finger of his glove; then suddenly he turned and strode away in the opposite direction. He walked and walked and left the town behind him. He went his way till he reached the country, and here he bent his steps toward a little wood which he knew very well, and whither indeed, on a spring afternoon, when she had taken a fancy to play at shepherd and shepherdess, he had once come with the Countess. He flung himself on the grass, on the edge of the wood – not in the same place where he had lain at the Countess's feet, pulling sonnets out of his pocket and reading them one by one; a little stream flowed beside him; opposite, the sun was declining; the distant city lay before him, lifting its towers and chimneys against the reddening western sky. The twilight fell and deepened and the stars came out. Benvolio lay there thinking that he preferred them to the Countess's wax candles. He went back to town in a farmer's waggon, talking with the honest rustic who drove it.

Very much in this way, when he had been on the point of knocking at the gate of the Countess's heart and asking ardently to be admitted, he had paused, stood frowning, and then turned short and rambled away into solitude. She never knew how near, two or three times, he had come. Two or three times she had accused him of being rude, and this was nothing but the backward swing of the pendulum. One day it seemed to her that he was altogether too vexatious, and she reproached herself with her good nature. She had made herself too cheap; such conduct was beneath her dignity; she would take another tone. She closed her door to him, and bade her people say, whenever he came, that she was engaged. At first Benvolio only wondered. Oddly enough, he was not what is commonly called sensitive; he never supposed you meant to offend him; not being at all impertinent himself, he was not on the watch for impertinence in others. Only, when he fairly caught you in the act he was immensely disgusted. Therefore, as I say, he simply wondered what had suddenly made the Countess so busy; then he remembered certain other charming persons whom he knew, and went to see how the world wagged with them. But they rendered the Countess eminent service; she gained by comparison, and Benvolio began to miss her. All that other charming women were who led the life of the world (as it is called) the Countess was in a superior, in a perfect degree; she was the ripest fruit of a high civilisation; her companions and rivals, beside her, had but a pallid bloom, an acrid savour. Benvolio had a relish in all things for the best, and he found himself breathing sighs under the Countess's darkened windows. He wrote to her, asking why in the world she treated him so cruelly, and then she knew that her charm was working. She was careful not to answer his letter, and to see that he was refused at her gate as inexorably as ever. It is an ill wind that blows nobody good, and Benvolio, one night after his dismissal, wandered about the moonlit streets till nearly morning, composing the finest verses he had ever produced. The subscribers to the magazine to which he sent them were at least the gainers. But unlike many poets, Benvolio did not on this occasion bury his passion in his poem; or if he did, its ghost was stalking abroad the very next night. He went again to the Countess's gate, and again it was closed in his face. So, after a very moderate amount of hesitation, he bravely (and with a dexterity which surprised him) scaled her garden wall and dropped down in the moonshine, upon her lawn. I don't know whether she was expecting him, but if she had been, the matter could not have been better arranged. She was sitting in a little niche of shrubbery, with no protector, but a microscopic lap-dog. She pretended to be scandalised at his audacity, but his audacity carried the hour. 'This time certainly,' thought the Countess, 'he will make his declaration. He didn't jump that wall, at the risk of his neck, simply to ask me for a cup of tea.' Not a bit of it; Benvolio was devoted, but he was not more explicit than before. He declared that this was the happiest hour of his life; that there was a charming air of romance in his position; that, honestly, he thanked the Countess for having made him desperate; that he would never come to see her again but by the garden wall; that something, to-night – what was it? – was vastly becoming to her; that he devoutly hoped she would receive no one else; that his admiration for her was unbounded; that the stars, finally, had a curious pink light! He looked at her, through the flower-scented dusk, with admiring eyes; but he looked at the stars as well; he threw back his head and folded his arms, and let the conversation flag while he examined the firmament. He observed also the long shafts of light proceeding from the windows of the house, as they fell upon the lawn and played among the shrubbery. The Countess had always thought him a singular man, but to-night she thought him more singular than ever. She became satirical, and the point of her satire was that he was after all but a dull fellow; that his admiration was a poor compliment; that he would do well to turn his attention to astronomy! In answer to this he came perhaps (to the Countess's sense) as near as he had ever come to making a declaration.

'Dear lady,' he said, 'you don't begin to know how much I admire you!'

She left her place at this, and walked about her lawn, looking at him askance while he talked, trailing her embroidered robe over the grass and fingering the folded petals of her flowers. He made a sort of sentimental profession of faith; he assured her that she represented his ideal of a certain sort of woman. This last phrase made her pause a moment and stare at him wide-eyed. 'Oh, I mean the finest sort,' he cried – 'the sort that exerts the widest sway! You represent the world and everything that the world can give, and you represent them at their best – in their most generous, most graceful, most inspiring form. If a man were a revolutionist, you would reconcile him to society. You are a divine embodiment of all the amenities, the refinements, the complexities of life! You are the flower of urbanity, of culture, of tradition! You are the product of so many influences that it widens one's horizon to know you; of you too it is true that to admire you is a liberal education! Your charm is irresistible; I assure you I don't resist it!'

Compliments agreed with the Countess, as we may say; they not only made her happier, but they made her better. It became a matter of conscience with her to deserve them. These were magnificent ones, and she was by no means indifferent to them. Her cheek faintly flushed, her eyes vaguely glowed, and though her beauty, in the literal sense, was questionable, all that Benvolio said of her had never seemed more true. He said more in the same strain, and she listened without interrupting him. But at last she suddenly became impatient; it seemed to her that this was after all a tolerably inexpensive sort of wooing. But she did not betray her impatience with any petulance; she simply shook her finger a moment, to enjoin silence, and then she said, in a voice of extreme gentleness – 'You have too much imagination!' He answered that, to do her perfect justice, he had too little. To this she replied that it was not of her any longer he was talking; he had left her far behind. He was spinning fancies about some highly subtilised figment of his brain. The best answer to this, it seemed to Benvolio, was to seize her hand and kiss it. I don't know what the Countess thought of this form of argument; I incline to think it both pleased and vexed her; it was at once too much and too little. She snatched her hand away and went rapidly into the house. Although Benvolio immediately followed her, he was unable to overtake her; she had retired into impenetrable seclusion. A short time afterwards she left town and went for the summer to an estate which she possessed in a distant part of the country.

III

BENVOLIO was extremely fond of the country, but he remained in town after all his friends had departed. Many of them made him promise that he would come and see them. He promised, or half promised, but when he reflected that in almost every case he would find a house full of fellow-guests, to whose pursuits he would have to conform, and that if he rambled away with a valued duodecimo in his pocket to spend the morning alone in the woods, he would be denounced as a marplot and a selfish brute, he felt no great desire to pay visits. He had, as we know, his moods of expansion and of contraction; he had been tolerably inflated for many months past, and now he had begun to take in sail. And then I suspect the foolish fellow had no money to travel withal. He had lately put all his available funds into the purchase of a picture – an estimable work of the Venetian school, which had been suddenly thrown into the market. It was offered for a moderate sum, and Benvolio, who was one of the first to see it, secured it, and hung it triumphantly in his room. It had all the classic Venetian glow, and he used to lie on his divan by the hour, gazing at it. It had, indeed, a peculiar property, of which I have known no other example. Most pictures that are remarkable for their colour (especially if they have been painted for a couple of centuries), need a flood of sunshine on the canvas to bring it out. But this remarkable work seemed to have a hidden radiance of its own, which showed brightest when the room was half darkened. When Benvolio wished especially to enjoy his treasure he dropped his Venetian blinds, and the picture bloomed out into the cool dusk with enchanting effect. It represented, in a fantastic way, the story of Perseus and Andromeda – the beautiful naked maiden chained to a rock, on which, with picturesque incongruity, a wild fig-tree was growing; the green Adriatic tumbling at her feet, and a splendid brown-limbed youth in a curious helmet hovering near her on a winged horse. The journey his fancy made as he lay and looked at his picture Benvolio preferred to any journey he might make by the public conveyances.

But he resorted for entertainment, as he had often done before, to the windows overlooking the old garden behind his house. As the summer deepened, of course the charm of the garden increased. It grew more tangled and bosky and mossy, and sent forth sweeter and heavier odours into the neighbouring air. It was a perfect solitude; Benvolio had never seen a visitor there. One day, therefore, at this time, it puzzled him most agreeably to perceive a young girl sitting under one of the trees. She sat there a long time, and though she was at a distance, he managed, by looking long enough, to make out that she was pretty. She was dressed in black, and when she left her place her step had a kind of nun-like gentleness and demureness. Although she was alone, there was something timid and tentative in her movements. She wandered away and disappeared from sight, save that here and there he saw her white parasol gleaming in the gaps of the foliage. Then she came back to her seat under the great tree, and remained there for some time, arranging in her lap certain flowers that she had gathered. Then she rose again and vanished, and Benvolio waited in vain for her return. She had evidently gone into the house. The next day he saw her again, and the next, and the next. On these occasions she had a book in her hand, and she sat in her former place a long time, and read it with an air of great attention. Now and then she raised her head and glanced toward the house, as if to keep something in sight which divided her care; and once or twice she laid down her book and tripped away to her hidden duties with a lighter step than she had shown the first day. Benvolio formed a theory that she had an invalid parent, or a relation of some kind, who was unable to walk, and had been moved into a window overlooking the garden. She always took up her book again when she came back, and bent her pretty head over it with charming earnestness. Benvolio had already discovered that her head was pretty. He fancied it resembled a certain exquisite little head on a Greek silver coin which lay, with several others, in an agate cup on his table. You see he had also already taken to fancying, and I offer this as the excuse for his staring at his modest neighbour by the hour. But he was not during these hours idle, because he was – I can't say falling in love with her; he knew her too little for that, and besides, he was in love with the Countess – but because he was at any rate cudgelling his brains about her. Who was she? what was she? why had he never seen her before? The house in which she apparently lived was in

another street from Benvolio's own, but he went out of his way
on purpose to look at it. It was an ancient, grizzled, sad-faced
structure, with grated windows on the ground floor; it looked
like a convent or a prison. Over a wall, beside it, there tumbled
into the street some stray tendrils of a wild creeper from Benvolio's garden. Suddenly Benvolio began to suspect that the
book the young girl in the garden was reading was none other
than a volume of his own, put forth some six months before.
His volume had a white cover and so had this; white covers are
rather rare, and there was nothing impossible either in this
young lady's reading his book or in her finding it interesting.
Very many other women had done the same. Benvolio's neighbour had a pencil in her pocket, which she every now and then
drew forth, to make with it a little mark on her page. This quiet
gesture gave the young man an exquisite pleasure.

I am ashamed to say how much time he spent, for a week, at
his window. Every day the young girl came into the garden. At
last there occurred a rainy day – a long, warm summer's rain –
and she stayed within doors. He missed her quite acutely, and
wondered, half-smiling, half-frowning, that her absence should
make such a difference for him. He actually depended upon
her. He was ignorant of her name; he knew neither the colour of
her eyes nor the shade of her hair, nor the sound of her voice; it
was very likely that if he were to meet her face to face, elsewhere, he would not recognise her. But she interested him; he
liked her; he found her little indefinite, black-dressed figure
sympathetic. He used to find the Countess sympathetic, and
certainly the Countess was as unlike this quiet garden-nymph
as she could very well be and be yet a charming woman.
Benvolio's sympathies, as we know, were large. After the rain
the young girl came out again, and now she had another book,
having apparently finished Benvolio's. He was gratified to
observe that she bestowed upon this one a much more
wandering attention. Sometimes she let it drop listlessly at
her side, and seemed to lose herself in maidenly reverie. Was
she thinking how much more beautiful Benvolio's verses were
than others of the day? Was she perhaps repeating them to
herself? It charmed Benvolio to suppose she might be; for he

was not spoiled in this respect. The Countess knew none of his poetry by heart; she was nothing of a reader. She had his book on her table, but he once noticed that half the leaves were uncut.

After a couple of days of sunshine the rain came back again, to our hero's infinite annoyance, and this time it lasted several days. The garden lay dripping and desolate; its charm had quite departed. These days passed gloomily for Benvolio; he decided that rainy weather, in summer, in town, was intolerable. He began to think of the Countess again – he was sure that over her broad lands the summer sun was shining. He saw them, in envious fancy, studded with joyous Watteau-groups, feasting and making music under the shade of ancestral beeches. What a charming life! he thought – what brilliant, enchanted, memorable days! He had said the very reverse of all this, as you remember, three weeks before. I don't know that he had ever devoted a formula to the idea that men of imagination are not bound to be consistent, but he certainly conformed to its spirit. We are not, however, by any means at the end of his inconsistencies. He immediately wrote a letter to the Countess, asking her if he might pay her a visit.

Shortly after he had sent his letter the weather mended, and he went out for a walk. The sun was near setting; the streets were all ruddy and golden with its light, and the scattered rain-clouds, broken into a thousand little particles, were flecking the sky like a shower of opals and amethysts. Benvolio stopped, as he sauntered along, to gossip a while with his friend the book-seller. The bookseller was a foreigner and a man of taste; his shop was in the arcade of the great square. When Benvolio went in he was serving a lady, and the lady was dressed in black. Benvolio just now found it natural to notice a lady who was dressed in black, and the fact that this lady's face was averted made observation at once more easy and more fruitless. But at last her errand was finished; she had been ordering several books, and the bookseller was writing down their names. Then she turned round, and Benvolio saw her face. He stood staring at her most inconsiderately, for he felt an immediate certainty that she was the bookish damsel of the garden. She gave a glance round the shop, at the books on the walls, at the prints and busts, the apparatus of learning, in various forms, that it contained, and then, with the soundless, half-furtive step which Benvolio now knew so well, she took her departure. Benvolio seized the startled bookseller by the two hands and besieged him with questions. The bookseller, however, was able to answer but few of them. The young girl had been in his shop but once before, and had simply left an address, without any name. It was the address of which Benvolio had assured himself. The books she had ordered were all learned works – disquisitions on philosophy, on history, on the natural sciences, matters, all of them, in which she seemed an expert. For some of the volumes that she had just bespoken the bookseller was to send to foreign countries; the others were to be despatched that evening to the address which the young girl had left. As Benvolio stood there the old bibliophile gathered these latter together, and while he was so engaged he uttered a little cry of distress: one of the volumes of a set was missing. The work was a rare one, and it would be hard to repair the loss. Benvolio on the instant had an inspiration; he demanded leave of his friend to act as messenger: he himself would carry the books, as if he came from the shop, and he would explain the absence of the lost volume, and the bookseller's views about replacing it, far better than one of the hirelings. He asked leave, I say, but he did not wait till it was given; he snatched up the pile of books and strode triumphantly away!

IV

As there was no name on the parcel, Benvolio, on reaching the old grey house over the wall of whose court an adventurous tendril stretched its long arm into the street, found himself wondering in what terms he should ask to have speech of the person for whom the books were intended. At any hazard he was determined not to retreat until he had caught a glimpse of the interior and its inhabitants; for this was the same man, you must remember, who had scaled the moonlit wall of the Countess's garden. An old serving-woman in a quaint cap answered his summons, and stood blinking out at the fading daylight from a little wrinkled white face, as if she had never been compelled to take so direct a look at it before. He informed her that he had come from the bookseller's, and that he had been charged with a personal message for the venerable gentleman who had bespoken the parcel. Might he crave licence to speak with him? This obsequious phrase was an improvisation of the moment – he had shaped it on the chance. But Benvolio had an indefinable conviction that it would fit the case; the only thing that surprised him was the quiet complaisance of the old woman.

'If it's on a bookish errand you come, sir,' she said, with a little wheezy sigh, 'I suppose I only do my duty in admitting you!'

She led him into the house, through various dusky chambers, and at last ushered him into an apartment of which the side opposite to the door was occupied by a broad, low casement. Through its small old panes there came a green dim light – the light of the low western sun shining through the wet trees of the famous garden. Everything else was ancient and brown; the walls were covered with tiers upon tiers of books. Near the window, in the still twilight, sat two persons, one of whom rose as Benvolio came in. This was the young girl of the garden – the young girl who had been an hour since at the bookseller's. The other was an old man, who turned his head, but otherwise sat motionless.

Both his movement and his stillness immediately announced to Benvolio's quick perception that he was blind. In his quality of poet Benvolio was inventive; a brain that is constantly tapped for rhymes is tolerably alert. In a few moments, therefore, he had given a vigorous push to the wheel of fortune. Various things had happened. He had made a soft, respectful speech, he hardly knew about what; and the old man had told him he had a delectable voice – a voice that seemed to belong rather to a person of education than to a tradesman's porter. Benvolio confessed to having picked up an education, and the old man had thereupon bidden the young girl offer him a seat. Benvolio chose his seat where he could see her, as she sat at the low-browed casement. The bookseller in the square thought it likely Benvolio would come back that evening and give him an account of his errand, and before he closed his shop he looked up and down the street, to see whether the young man was approaching. Benvolio came, but the shop was closed. This he never noticed, however; he walked three times round all the arcades, without noticing it. He was thinking of something else. He had sat all the evening with the blind old scholar and his daughter, and he was thinking intently, ardently of them. When I say of them, of course I mean of the daughter.

A few days afterwards he got a note from the Countess, saying it would give her pleasure to receive his visit. He immediately wrote to her that, with a thousand regrets, he found himself urgently occupied in town and must beg leave to defer his departure for a day or two. The regrets were perfectly sincere, but the plea was none the less valid. Benvolio had become deeply interested in his tranquil neighbours, and, for the moment, a certain way the young girl had of looking at him – fixing her eyes, first, with a little vague, half-absent smile, on an imaginary point above his head, and then slowly dropping them till they met his own – was quite sufficient to make him happy. He had called once more on her father, and once more, and yet once more, and he had a vivid prevision that he should often call again. He had been in the garden and found its mild mouldiness even more delightful on a nearer view. He had pulled off his very ill-fitting mask, and let his neighbours know that his trade was not to carry parcels, but to scribble verses. The old man had never heard of his verses; he read nothing that had been published later than the sixth century; and nowadays he could read only with his daughter's eyes. Benvolio had seen the little white volume on the table, and assured himself it was his own; and he noted the fact that in spite of its well-thumbed air, the young girl had never given her father a hint of its contents. I said just now that several things had happened in the first half hour of Benvolio's first visit. One of them was that this modest maiden fell in love with our young man. What happened when she learned that he was the author

of the little white volume, I hardly know how to express; her
innocent passion began to throb and flutter. Benvolio possessed an old quarto volume bound in Russia leather, about
which there clung an agreeable pungent odour. In this old
quarto he kept a sort of diary – if that can be called a diary in
which a whole year had sometimes been allowed to pass without an entry. On the other hand, there were some interminable
records of a single day. Turning it over you would have
chanced, not infrequently, upon the name of the Countess;
and at this time you would have observed on every page some
mention of 'the Professor' and of a certain person named
Scholastica. Scholastica, you will immediately guess, was the
Professor's daughter. Probably this was not her own name, but
it was the name by which Benvolio preferred to know her, and
we need not be more exact than he. By this time of course he
knew a great deal about her, and about her venerable sire. The
Professor, before the loss of his eyesight and his health, had
been one of the stateliest pillars of the University. He was now
an old man; he had married late in life. When his infirmities
came upon him he gave up his chair and his classes and buried
himself in his library. He made his daughter his reader and his
secretary, and his prodigious memory assisted her clear young
voice and her softly-moving pen. He was held in great honour
in the scholastic world; learned men came from afar to consult
the blind sage and to appeal to his wisdom as to the ultimate
law. The University settled a pension upon him, and he dwelt
in a dusky corner, among the academic shades. The pension
was small, but the old scholar and the young girl lived with
conventual simplicity. It so happened, however, that he had a
brother, or rather a half-brother, who was not a bookish man,
save as regarded his ledger and day-book. This personage had
made money in trade, and had retired, wifeless and childless,
into the old grey house attached to Benvolio's garden. He had
the reputation of skinflint, a curmudgeon, a bloodless old miser
who spent his days in shuffling about his mouldy mansion,
making his pockets jingle, and his nights in lifting his money-
bags out of trapdoors and counting over his hoard. He was
nothing but a chilling shadow, an evil name, a pretext for a

curse; no one had ever seen him, much less crossed his threshold. But it seemed that he had a soft spot in his heart. He wrote
one day to his brother, whom he had not seen for years, that the
rumour had come to him that he was blind, infirm, and poor;
that he himself had a large house with a garden behind it; and
that if the Professor were not too proud, he was welcome to
come and lodge there. The Professor had come, in this way, a
few weeks before, and though it would seem that to a sightless
old ascetic all lodgings might be the same, he took a great
satisfaction in his new abode. His daughter found it a paradise,
compared with their two narrow chambers under the old gable
of the University, where, amid the constant coming and going
of students, a young girl was compelled to lead a cloistered life.

Benvolio had assigned as his motive for intrusion, when he
had been obliged to acknowledge his real character, an irresistible desire to ask the old man's opinion on certain knotty points
of philosophy. This was a pardonable fiction, for the event, at
any rate, justified it. Benvolio, when he was fairly launched in a
philosophical discussion, was capable of forgetting that there
was anything in the world but metaphysics; he revelled in transcendent abstractions and became unconscious of all concrete
things – even of that most brilliant of concrete things, the
Countess. He longed to embark on a voyage of discovery on
the great sea of pure reason. He knew that from such voyages
the deep-browed adventurer rarely returns; but if he were to
find an El Dorado of thought, why should he regret the dusky
world of fact? Benvolio had high colloquies with the Professor,
who was a devout Neo-Platonist, and whose venerable wit had
spun to subtler tenuity the ethereal speculations of the Alexan-
drian school. Benvolio at this season declared that study and
science were the only game in life worth the candle, and wondered how he could ever for an instant have cared for more
vulgar exercises. He turned off a little poem in the style of
Milton's *Penseroso*, which, if it had not quite the merit of that
famous effusion, was at least the young man's own happiest
performance. When Benvolio liked a thing he liked it as a whole
– it appealed to all his senses. He relished its accidents, its
accessories, its material envelope. In the satisfaction he took

in his visits to the Professor it would have been hard to say where the charm of philosophy began or ended. If it began with a glimpse of the old man's mild, sightless blue eyes, sitting fixed beneath his shaggy white brows like patches of pale winter sky under a high-piled cloud, it hardly ended before it reached the little black bow on Scholastica's slipper; and certainly it had taken a comprehensive sweep in the interval. There was nothing in his friends that had not a charm, an interest, a character, for his appreciative mind. Their seclusion, their stillness, their super-simple notions of the world and the world's ways, the faint, musty perfume of the University which hovered about them, their brown old apartment, impenetrable to the rumours of the town – all these things were part of his entertainment. Then the essence of it perhaps was that in this silent, simple life the intellectual key, if you touched it, was so finely resonant. In the way of thought there was nothing into which his friends were not initiated – nothing they could not understand. The mellow light of their low-browed room, streaked with the moted rays that slanted past the dusky book-shelves, was the atmosphere of intelligence. All this made them, humble folk as they were, not so simple as they at first appeared. They, too, in their own fashion, knew the world; they were not people to be patronised; to visit them was not a condescension, but a privilege.

In the Professor this was not surprising. He had passed fifty years in arduous study, and it was proper to his character and his office that he should be erudite and venerable. But his devoted little daughter seemed to Benvolio at first almost grotesquely wise. She was an anomaly, a prodigy, a charming monstrosity. Charming, at any rate, she was, and as pretty, I must lose no more time in saying, as had seemed likely to Benvolio at his window. And yet, even on a nearer view, her prettiness shone forth slowly. It was as if it had been covered with a series of film-like veils, which had to be successively drawn aside. And then it was such a homely, shrinking, subtle prettiness, that Benvolio, in the private record I have mentioned, never thought of calling it by the arrogant name of beauty. He called it by no name at all; he contented himself with enjoying it – with looking into the young girl's mild grey

eyes and saying things, on purpose, that caused her candid
smile to deepen until (like the broadening ripple of a lake) it
reached a particular dimple in her left cheek. This was its
maximum; no smile could do more, and Benvolio desired
nothing better. Yet I cannot say he was in love with the young
girl; he only liked her. But he liked her, no doubt, as a man likes
a thing but once in his life. As he knew her better, the oddity of
her great learning quite faded away; it seemed delightfully
natural, and he only wondered why there were not more
women of the same pattern. Scholastica had imbibed the
wine of science instead of her mother's milk. Her mother had
died in her infancy, leaving her cradled in an old folio, three-
quarters opened, like a wide V. Her father had been her nurse,
her playmate, her teacher, her life-long companion, her only
friend. He taught her the Greek alphabet before she knew her
own, and fed her with crumbs from his scholastic revels. She
had taken submissively what was given her, and, without knowing it, she grew up a little handmaid of science.

Benvolio perceived that she was not in the least a woman of
genius. The passion for knowledge, of its own motion, would
never have carried her far. But she had a perfect understanding
– a mind as clear and still and natural as a woodland pool,
giving back an exact and definite image of everything that was
presented to it. And then she was so teachable, so diligent, so
indefatigable. Slender and meagre as she was, and rather pale
too, with being much within doors, she was never tired, she
never had a headache, she never closed her book or laid down a
pen with a sigh. Benvolio said to himself that she was exquisitely constituted for helping a man. What a work he might do on
summer mornings and winter nights, with that brightly demure
little creature at his side, transcribing, recollecting, sympathis-
ing! He wondered how much she cared for these things herself;
whether a woman could care for them without being dry and
harsh. It was in a great measure for information on this point
that he used to question her eyes with the frequency that I have
mentioned. But they never gave him a perfectly direct answer,
and this was why he came and came again. They seemed to him
to say, 'If you could lead a student's life for my sake, I could be a

life-long household scribe for yours.' Was it divine philosophy that made Scholastica charming, or was it she that made philosophy divine? I cannot relate everything that came to pass between these young people, and I must leave a great deal to your imagination. The summer waned, and when the autumn afternoons began to grow vague, the quiet couple in the old grey house had expanded to a talkative trio. For Benvolio the days had passed very fast; the trio had talked of so many things. He had spent many an hour in the garden with the young girl, strolling in the weedy paths, or resting on a moss-grown bench. She was a delightful listener, because she not only attended, but she followed. Benvolio had known women to fix very beautiful eyes upon him, and watch with an air of ecstasy the movement of his lips, and yet had found them three minutes afterwards quite incapable of saying what he was talking about. Scholastica gazed at him, but she understood him too.

V

YOU will say that my description of Benvolio has done him injustice, and that, far from being the sentimental weathercock I have depicted, he is proving himself a model of constancy. But mark the sequel! It was at this moment precisely, that, one morning, having gone to bed the night before singing paeans to divine philosophy, he woke up with a headache, and in the worst of humours with abstract science. He remembered Scholastica telling him that she never had headaches, and the memory quite annoyed him. He suddenly found himself thinking of her as a neat little mechanical toy, wound up to turn pages and write a pretty hand, but with neither a head nor a heart that was capable of human ailments. He fell asleep again, and in one of those brief but vivid dreams that sometimes occur in the morning hours, he had a brilliant vision of the Countess. *She* was human beyond a doubt, and duly familiar with headaches and heart-aches. He felt an irresistible desire to see her and to tell her that he adored her. This satisfaction was not unattainable, and before the day was over he was well on his way toward enjoying it. He left town and made his pilgrimage to her estate, where he found her holding her usual court and leading a merry life. He had meant to stay with her a week; he stayed two months – the most entertaining months he had ever known. I cannot pretend of course to enumerate the diversions of this fortunate circle, or to say just how Benvolio spent every hour of his time. But if the summer had passed quickly with him, the autumn moved with a tread as light. He thought once in a while of Scholastica and her father – once in a while, I say, when present occupations suffered his thoughts to wander. This was not often, for the Countess had always, as the phrase is, a hundred arrows in her quiver. You see, the negative, with Benvolio, always implied as distinct a positive, and his excuse for being inconstant on one side was that he was at such a time very assiduous on another. He developed at this period a talent as yet untried and unsuspected; he proved himself capable of writing brilliant dramatic poetry. The long autumn evenings, in a great country house, were a natural occasion for the much-abused pastime known as private theatricals. The Countess had a theatre, and abundant material for a troupe of amateur players; all that was lacking was a play exactly adapted to her resources. She proposed to Benvolio to write one; the idea took his fancy; he shut himself up in the library, and in a week produced a masterpiece. He had found the subject, one day when he was pulling over the Countess's books, in an old MS. chronicle written by the chaplain of one of her late husband's ancestors. It was the germ of an admirable drama, and Benvolio greatly enjoyed his attempt to make a work of art of it. All his genius, all his imagination went into it. This was the proper mission of his faculties, he cried to himself – the study of warm human passions, the painting of rich dramatic pictures, not the dry chopping of logic. His play was acted with brilliant success, the Countess herself representing the heroine. Benvolio had never seen her don the buskin, and had no idea of her aptitude for the stage; but she was inimitable, she was a natural artist. What gives charm to life, Benvolio hereupon said to himself, is the element of the unexpected; and this one finds only in women of the Countess's type. And I should do wrong to imply that he here made an invidious comparison, for he did not even think of Scholastica. His play was repeated several times, and people were invited to see it from all the country round. There was a great bivouac of servants in the castle-court; in the cold November nights a bonfire was lighted to keep the servants warm. It was a great triumph for Benvolio, and he frankly enjoyed it. He knew he enjoyed it, and how great a triumph it was, and he felt every disposition to drain the cup to the last drop. He relished his own elation, and found himself excellent company. He began immediately another drama – a comedy this time – and he was greatly interested to observe that when his work was on the stocks he found himself regarding all the people about him as types and available figures. Everything he saw or heard was grist to his mill; everything presented itself as possible material. Life on these terms became really very interesting, and for several nights the laurels of Molière kept Benvolio awake.

Delightful as this was, however, it could not last for ever. When the winter nights had begun, the Countess returned to town, and Benvolio came back with her, his unfinished comedy in his pocket. During much of the journey he was silent and abstracted, and the Countess supposed he was thinking of how he should make the most of that capital situation in his third act. The Countess's perspicacity was just sufficient to carry her so far – to lead her, in other words, into plausible mistakes. Benvolio was really wondering what in the name of mystery had suddenly become of his inspiration, and why the witticisms in his play and his comedy had begun to seem as mechanical as the cracking of the post-boy's whip. He looked out at the scrubby fields, the rusty woods, the sullen sky, and asked himself whether *that* was the world to which it had been but yesterday his high ambition to hold up the mirror. The Countess's *dame de compagnie* sat opposite to him in the carriage. Yesterday he thought her, with her pale, discreet face, and her eager movements that pretended to be indifferent, a finished specimen of an entertaining genus. To-day he could only say that if there was a whole genus it was a thousand pities, for the poor lady struck him as miserably false and servile. The real seemed hideous; he felt homesick for his dear familiar rooms between the garden and the square, and he longed to get into them and bolt his door and bury himself in his old arm-chair and cultivate idealism for evermore. The first thing he actually did on getting into them was to go to the window and look out into the garden. It had greatly changed in his absence, and the old maimed statues, which all the summer had been comfortably muffled in verdure, were now, by an odd contradiction of propriety, standing white and naked in the cold. I don't exactly know how soon it was that Benvolio went back to see his neighbours. It was after no great interval, and yet it was not immediately. He had a bad conscience, and he was wondering what he should say to them. It seemed to him now (though he had not thought of it sooner) that they might accuse him of neglecting them. He had appealed to their friendship, he had professed the highest esteem for them, and then he had turned his back on them without farewell, and without a word of explanation. He had not written to them; in truth during his sojourn with the Countess, it would not have been hard for him to persuade himself that they were people he had only dreamed about, or read about, at most, in some old volume of memoirs. People of their value, he could now imagine them saying, were not to be taken up and dropped for a fancy; and if friendship was not to be friendship as they themselves understood it, it was better that he should forget them at once and for ever. It is perhaps too much to affirm that he imagined them saying all this; they were too mild and civil, too unused to acting in self-defence. But they might easily receive him in a way that would imply a delicate resentment. Benvolio felt profaned, dishonoured, almost contaminated; so that perhaps when he did at last return to his friends, it was because that was the simplest way to be purified. How did they receive him? I told you a good way back that Scholastica was in love with him, and you may arrange the scene in any manner that best accords with this circumstance. Her forgiveness, of course, when once that chord was touched, was proportionate to her displeasure. But Benvolio took refuge both from his own compunction and from the young girl's reproaches, in whatever form these were conveyed, in making a full confession of what he was pleased to call his frivolity. As he walked through the naked garden with Scholastica, kicking the wrinkled leaves, he told her the whole story of his sojourn with the Countess. The young girl listened with bright intentness, as she would have listened to some thrilling passage in a romance; but she neither sighed, nor looked wistful, nor seemed to envy the Countess or to repine at her own ignorance of the great world. It was all too remote for comparison; it was not, for Scholastica, among the things that might have been. Benvolio talked to her very freely about the Countess. If she liked it, he found on his side that it eased his mind; and as he said nothing that the Countess would not have been flattered by, there was no harm done. Although, however, Benvolio uttered nothing but praise of this distinguished lady, he was very frank in saying that she and her way of life always left him at the end in a worse humour than when they found him. They were very well in their way, he said, but their way was not his way – it only seemed so at moments. For him, he was convinced, the only real felicity was in the pleasures of study! Scholastica answered that it gave her high satisfaction to hear this, for it was her father's belief that Benvolio had a great aptitude for philosophical research, and that it was a sacred duty to cultivate so rare a faculty.

'And what is your belief?' Benvolio asked, remembering that the young girl knew several of his poems by heart.

Her answer was very simple. 'I believe you are a poet.'

'And a poet oughtn't to run the risk of turning pedant?'

'No,' she answered; 'a poet ought to run all risks – even that one which for a poet is perhaps most cruel. But he ought to escape them all!'

Benvolio took great satisfaction in hearing that the Professor deemed that he had in him the making of a philosopher, and it gave an impetus to the zeal with which he returned to work.

VI

OF course even the most zealous student cannot work always, and often, after a very philosophic day, Benvolio spent with the Countess a very sentimental evening. It is my duty as a veracious historian not to conceal the fact that he discoursed to the Countess about Scholastica. He gave such a puzzling description of her that the Countess declared that she must be a delightfully quaint creature and that it would be vastly amusing to know her. She hardly supposed Benvolio was in love with this little bookworm in petticoats, but to make sure – if that might be called making sure – she deliberately asked him. He said No; he hardly saw how he could be, since he was in love with the Countess herself! For a while this answer satisfied her, but as the winter went by she began to wonder whether there were not such a thing as a man being in love with two women at once. During many months that followed, Benvolio led a kind of double life. Sometimes it charmed him and gave him an inspiring sense of personal power. He haunted the domicile of his gentle neighbours, and drank deep of the garnered wisdom of the ages; and he made appearances as frequent in the Countess's drawing-room, where he played his part with magnificent zest and ardour. It was a life of alternation and contrast, and it really demanded a vigorous and elastic temperament. Sometimes his own seemed to him quite inadequate to the occasion – he felt fevered, bewildered, exhausted. But when it came to the point of choosing one thing or the other, it was impossible to give up either his worldly habits or his studious aspirations. Benvolio raged inwardly at the cruel limitations of the human mind, and declared it was a great outrage that a man should not be personally able to do everything he could imagine doing. I hardly know how she contrived it, but the Countess was at this time a more engaging woman than she had ever been. Her beauty acquired an ampler and richer cast, and she had a manner of looking at you as she slowly turned away with a vague reproachfulness that was at the same time an encouragement, which had lighted a hopeless flame in many a youthful breast. Benvolio one day felt in the mood for finishing his comedy, and the Countess and her friends acted it. Its success was no less brilliant than that of its predecessor, and the manager of the theatre immediately demanded the privilege of producing it. You will hardly believe me, however, when I tell you that on the night that his comedy was introduced to the public, its eccentric author sat discussing the absolute and the relative with the Professor and his daughter. Benvolio had all winter been observing that Scholastica never looked so pretty as when she sat, of a winter's night, plying a quiet needle in the mellow circle of a certain antique brass lamp. On the night in question he happened to fall a-thinking of this picture, and he tramped out across the snow for the express purpose of looking at it. It was sweeter even than his memory promised, and it banished every thought of his theatrical honours from his head. Scholastica gave him some tea, and her tea, for mysterious reasons, was delicious; better, strange to say, than that of the Countess, who, however, it must be added, recovered her ground in coffee. The Professor's parsimonious brother owned a ship which made voyages to China and brought him goodly chests of the incomparable plant. He sold the cargo for great sums, but he kept a chest for himself. It was always the best one, and he had at this time carefully measured out a part of his annual dole, made it into a little parcel, and presented it to Scholastica. This is the secret history of Benvolio's fragrant cups. While he was drinking them on the night I speak of – I am ashamed to say how many he drank – his name, at the theatre, was being tossed across the footlights to a brilliant, clamorous multitude, who hailed him as the redeemer of the national stage. But I am not sure that he even told his friends that his play was being acted. Indeed, this was hardly possible, for I meant to say just now that he had forgotten it.

It is very certain, however, that he enjoyed the criticisms the next day in the newspapers. Radiant and jubilant, he went to see the Countess, with half a dozen of them in his pocket. He found her looking terribly dark. She had been at the theatre, prepared to revel in his triumph – to place on his head with her own hand, as it were, the laurel awarded by the public; and his absence had seemed to her a sort of personal slight. Yet his triumph had nevertheless given her an exceeding pleasure, for it had been the seal of her secret hopes of him. Decidedly he was to be a great man, and this was not the moment for letting him go! At the same time there was something noble in his indifference, his want of eagerness, his finding it so easy to forget his honours. It was only an intellectual Croesus, the Countess said to herself, who could afford to keep so loose an account with fame. But she insisted on knowing where he had been, and he told her he had been discussing philosophy and tea with the Professor.

'And was not the daughter there?' the Countess demanded.

'Most sensibly!' he cried. And then he added in a moment – 'I don't know whether I ever told you, but she's almost as pretty as you.'

The Countess resented the compliment to Scholastica much more than she enjoyed the compliment to herself. She felt an extreme curiosity to see this inky-fingered siren, and as she seldom failed, sooner or later, to compass her desires, she succeeded at last in catching a glimpse of her innocent rival. To do so she was obliged to set a great deal of machinery in motion. She induced Benvolio to give a lunch, in his rooms, to some ladies who professed a desire to see his works of art, and of whom she constituted herself the chaperone. She took care that he threw open a certain vestibule that looked into the garden, and here, at the window, she spent much of her time. There was but a chance that Scholastica would come forth into the garden, but it was a chance worth staking something upon. The Countess gave to it time and temper, and she was finally rewarded. Scholastica came out. The poor girl strolled about for half an hour, in profound unconsciousness that the Countess's fine eyes were devouring her. The impression she made was singular. The Countess found her both pretty and ugly: she did not admire her herself, but she understood that Benvolio might. For herself, personally, she detested her, and when Scholastica went in and she turned away from the window, her first movement was to pass before a mirror, which showed her something that, impartially considered, seemed to her a thousand times more beautiful. The Countess made no comments, and took good care Benvolio did not suspect the trick she had played him. There was something more she promised herself to do, and she impatiently awaited her opportunity.

In the middle of the winter she announced to him that she was going to spend ten days in the country; she had received the most attractive accounts of the state of things on her domain. There had been great snow-falls, and the sleighing was magnificent; the lakes and streams were solidly frozen, there was an unclouded moon, and the resident gentry were skating, half the night, by torch-light. The Countess was passionately fond both of sleighing and skating, and she found this picture irresistible. And then she was charitable, and observed that it would be a kindness to the poor resident gentry, whose usual pleasures were of a frugal sort, to throw open her house and give a ball or two, with the village fiddlers. Perhaps even they might organise a bear-hunt – an entertainment at which, if properly conducted, a lady might be present as spectator. The Countess told Benvolio all this one day as he sat with her in her boudoir, in the fire-light, during the hour that precedes dinner. She had said more than once that he must decamp – that she must go and dress; but neither of them had moved. She did not invite him to go with her to the country; she only watched him as he sat gazing with a frown at the fire-light – the crackling blaze of the great logs which had been cut in the Countess's bear-haunted forests. At last she rose impatiently, and fairly turned him out. After he had gone she stood for a moment looking at the fire, with the tip of her foot on the fender. She had not to wait long; he came back within the minute – came back and begged her leave to go with her to the country – to skate with her in the crystal moonlight and dance with her to the sound of the village violins. It hardly matters in what terms his request was granted; the notable point is that he made it. He was her only companion, and when they were established in the castle the hospitality extended to the resident gentry was less abundant than had been promised. Benvolio, however, did not complain of the absence of it, because, for the week or so, he was passionately in love with his hostess. They took long sleigh-rides and drank deep of the poetry of winter. The blue shadows on the snow, the cold amber lights in the west, the leafless twigs against the snow-charged sky, all gave them extraordinary pleasure. The nights were even better, when the great silver stars, before the moonrise, glittered on the polished ice, and the young Countess and her lover, firmly joining hands, launched

themselves into motion and into the darkness and went skim-
ming for miles with their winged steps. On their return, before
the great chimney-place in the old library, they lingered a while
and drank little cups of wine heated with spices. It was perhaps
here, cup in hand – this point is uncertain – that Benvolio broke
through the last bond of his reserve, and told the Countess that
he loved her, in a manner to satisfy her. To be his in all solemnity, his only and his for ever – this he explicitly, passionately,
imperiously demanded of her. After this she gave her ball to her
country neighbours, and Benvolio danced, to a boisterous,
swinging measure, with a dozen ruddy beauties dressed in the
fashions of the year before last. The Countess danced with the
lusty male counterparts of these damsels, but she found plenty
of chances to watch Benvolio. Toward the end of the evening
she saw him looking grave and bored, with very much such a
frown in his forehead as when he had sat staring at the fire that
last day in her boudoir. She said to herself for the hundredth
time that he was the strangest of mortals.

On their return to the city she had frequent occasions to say
it again. He looked at moments as if he had repented of his
bargain – as if it did not at all suit him that his being the
Countess's only lover should involve her being his only mistress. She deemed now that she had acquired the right to make
him give an account of his time, and he did not conceal the fact
that the first thing he had done on reaching town was to go to
see his eccentric neighbours. She treated him hereupon to a
passionate outburst of jealousy; called Scholastica a dozen
harsh names – a little dingy blue-stocking, a little underhand,
hypocritical Puritan; demanded he should promise never to
speak to her again, and summoned him to make a choice
once for all. Would he belong to her, or to that odious little
schoolmistress? It must be one thing or the other; he must take
her or leave her; it was impossible she should have a lover who
was so little to be depended upon. The Countess did not say
this made her unhappy, but she repeated a dozen times that it
made her ridiculous. Benvolio turned very pale; she had never
seen him so before; a great struggle was evidently taking place
within him. A terrible scene was the consequence. He broke

out into reproaches and imprecations; he accused the Countess of being his bad angel, of making him neglect his best faculties, mutilate his genius, squander his life; and yet he confessed that he was committed to her, that she fascinated him beyond resistance, and that, at any sacrifice, he must still be her slave. This confession gave the Countess uncommon satisfaction, and made up in a measure for the unflattering remarks that accompanied it. She on her side confessed – what she had always been too proud to acknowledge hitherto – that she cared vastly for him, and that she had waited for long months for him to say something of this kind. They parted on terms which it would be hard to define – full of mutual resentment and devotion, at once adoring and hating each other. All this was deep and stirring emotion, and Benvolio, as an artist, always in one way or another found his profit in emotion, even when it lacerated or suffocated him. There was, moreover, a sort of elation in having burnt his ships behind him, and he vowed to seek his fortune, his intellectual fortune, in the tumult of life and action. He did no work; his power of work, for the time at least, was paralysed. Sometimes this frightened him; it seemed as if his genius were dead, his career cut short; at other moments his faith soared supreme; he heard, in broken murmurs, the voice of the muse, and said to himself that he was only resting, waiting, storing up knowledge. Before long he felt tolerably tranquil again; ideas began to come to him, and the world to seem entertaining. He demanded of the Countess that, without further delay, their union should be solemnised. But the Countess, at that interview I have just related, had, in spite of her high spirit, received a great fright. Benvolio, stalking up and down with clenched hands and angry eyes, had seemed to her a terrible man to marry; and though she was conscious of a strong will of her own, as well as of robust nerves, she had shuddered at the thought that such scenes might often occur. She had hitherto seen little but the mild and genial, or at most the joyous and fantastic side of her friend's disposition; but it now appeared that there was another side to be taken into account, and that if Benvolio had talked of sacrifices, these were not all to be made by him. They say the world likes its master – that a horse of high spirit likes being well ridden. This may be true in the long run; but the Countess, who was essentially a woman of the world, was not yet prepared to pay our young man the tribute of her luxurious liberty. She admired him more, now that she was afraid of him, but at the same time she liked him a trifle less. She answered that marriage was a very serious matter; that they had lately had a taste of each other's tempers; that they had better wait a while longer; that she had made up her mind to travel for a year, and that she strongly recommended him to come with her, for travelling was notoriously an excellent test of friendship.

VII

SHE went to Italy, and Benvolio went with her; but before he went he paid a visit to his other mistress. He flattered himself that he had burned his ships behind him, but the fire was still visibly smouldering. It is true, nevertheless, that he passed a very strange half-hour with Scholastica and her father. The young girl had greatly changed; she barely greeted him; she looked at him coldly. He had no idea her face could wear that look; it vexed him to find it there. He had not been to see her for many weeks, and he now came to tell her that he was going away for a year; it is true these were not conciliatory facts. But she had taught him to think that she possessed in perfection the art of trustful resignation, of unprotesting, cheerful patience – virtues that sat so gracefully on her bended brow that the thought of their being at any rate supremely becoming took the edge from his remorse at making them necessary. But now Scholastica looked older as well as sadder, and decidedly not so pretty. Her figure was meagre, her movements were angular, her charming eye was dull. After the first minute he avoided this charming eye; it made him uncomfortable. Her voice she scarcely allowed him to hear. The Professor, as usual, was serene and frigid, impartial and transcendental. There was a chill in the air, a shadow between them. Benvolio went so far as to wonder that he had ever found a great attraction in the young girl, and his present disillusionment gave him even more anger than pain. He took leave abruptly and coldly, and puzzled his brain for a long time afterward over the mystery of Scholastica's reserve.

The Countess had said that travelling was a test of friendship; in this case friendship (or whatever the passion was to be called) promised for some time to resist the test. Benvolio passed six months of the liveliest felicity. The world has nothing better to offer to a man of sensibility than a first visit to Italy during those years of life when perception is at its keenest, when knowledge has arrived, and yet youth has not departed. He made with the Countess a long, slow progress through the lovely land, from the Alps to the Sicilian sea; and it seemed to him that his imagination, his intellect, his genius, expanded with every breath and rejoiced in every glance. The Countess was in an almost equal ecstasy, and their sympathy was perfect in all points save the lady's somewhat indiscriminate predilection for assemblies and receptions. She had a thousand letters of introduction to deliver, which entailed a vast deal of social exertion. Often, on balmy nights when he would have preferred to meditate among the ruins of the Forum, or to listen to the moonlit ripple of the Adriatic, Benvolio found himself dragged away to kiss the hand of a decayed princess, or to take a pinch from the snuff-box of an epicurean cardinal. But the cardinals, the princesses, the ruins, the warm southern tides which seemed the voice of history itself – these and a thousand other things resolved themselves into an immense pictorial spectacle – the very stuff that inspiration is made of. Everything Benvolio had written before coming to Italy now appeared to him worthless; this was the needful stamp, the consecration of talent. One day, however, his felicity was clouded; by a trifle you will say, possibly; but you must remember that in men of Benvolio's disposition primary impulses are almost always produced by small accidents. The Countess, speaking of the tone of voice of some one they had met, happened to say that it reminded her of the voice of that queer little woman at home – the daughter of the blind professor. Was this pure inadvertence, or was it malicious design? Benvolio never knew, though he immediately demanded of her, in surprise, when and where she had heard

Scholastica's voice. His whole attention was aroused; the Countess perceived it, and for a moment she hesitated. Then she bravely replied that she had seen the young girl in the musty old book-room where she spent her dreary life. At these words, uttered in a profoundly mocking tone, Benvolio had an extraordinary sensation. He was walking with the Countess in the garden of a palace, and they had just approached the low balustrade of a terrace which commanded a magnificent view. On one side were violet Apennines, dotted here and there with a gleaming castle or convent; on the other stood the great palace through whose galleries the two had just been strolling, with its walls encrusted with medallions and its cornice charged with statues. But Benvolio's heart began to beat; the tears sprang to his eyes; the perfect landscape around him faded away and turned to blankness, and there rose before him, distinctly, vividly present, the old brown room that looked into the dull northern garden, tenanted by the quiet figures he had once told himself that he loved. He had a choking sensation and a sudden overwhelming desire to return to his own country.

The Countess would say nothing more than that the fancy had taken her one day to go and see Scholastica. 'I suppose I may go where I please!' she cried in the tone of the great lady who is accustomed to believe that her glance confers honour wherever it falls. 'I am sure I did her no harm. She's a good little creature, and it's not her fault if she's so ridiculously plain.' Benvolio looked at her intently, but he saw that he should learn nothing from her that she did not choose to tell. As he stood there he was amazed to find how natural, or at least how easy, it was to disbelieve her. She had been with the young girl; that accounted for anything; it accounted abundantly for Scholastica's painful constraint. What had the Countess said and done? what infernal trick had she played upon the poor girl's simplicity? He helplessly wondered, but he felt that she could be trusted to hit her mark. She had done him the honour to be jealous, and in order to alienate Scholastica she had invented some ingenious calumny against himself. He felt sick and angry, and for a week he treated his companion with grim indifference. The charm was broken, the cup of pleasure was drained. This remained no secret to the Countess, who was furious at the mistake she had made. At last she abruptly told Benvolio that the test had failed; they must separate; he would gratify her by taking his leave. He asked no second permission, but bade her farewell in the midst of her little retinue, and went journeying out of Italy with no other company than his thick-swarming memories and projects.

The first thing he did on reaching home was to repair to the Professor's abode. The old man's chair, for the first time, was empty, and Scholastica was not in the room. He went out into the garden, where, after wandering hither and thither, he found the young girl seated in a dusky arbour. She was dressed, as usual, in black; but her head was drooping, her empty hands were folded, and her sweet face was more joyless even than when he had last seen it. If she had been changed then, she was doubly changed now. Benvolio looked round, and as the Professor was nowhere visible, he immediately guessed the cause of her mourning aspect. The good old man had gone to join his immortal brothers, the classic sages, and Scholastica was utterly alone. She seemed frightened at seeing him, but he took her hand, and she let him sit down beside her. 'Whatever you were once told that made you think ill of me is detestably false,' he said. 'I have the tenderest friendship for you, and now more than ever I should like to show it.' She slowly gathered courage to meet his eyes; she found them reassuring, and at last, though she never told him in what way her mind had been poisoned, she suffered him to believe that her old confidence had come back. She told him how her father had died, and how, in spite of the philosophic maxims he had bequeathed to her for her consolation, she felt very lonely and helpless. Her uncle had offered her a maintenance, meagre but sufficient; she had the old serving-woman to keep her company, and she meant to live in her present abode and occupy herself with collecting her father's papers and giving them to the world according to a plan for which he had left particular directions. She seemed irresistibly tender and touching, and yet full of dignity and self-support. Benvolio fell in love with her again on the spot, and only abstained from telling her so because he remembered just in time that he had an engagement to be married to the Countess, and that this understanding had not yet been formally rescinded. He paid Scholastica a long visit, and they went in together and rummaged over her father's books and papers. The old scholar's literary memoranda proved to be extremely valuable; it would be a useful and interesting task to give them to the world. When Scholastica heard Benvolio's high estimate of them her cheek began to glow and her spirit to revive. The present then was secure, she seemed to say to herself, and she would have occupation for many a month. He offered to give her every assistance in his power, and in consequence he came daily to see her. Scholastica lived so much out of the world that she was not obliged to trouble herself about vulgar gossip. Whatever jests were aimed at the young man for his visible devotion to a mysterious charmer, he was very sure that her ear was never wounded by base insinuations. The old serving-woman sat in a corner, nodding over her distaff, and the two friends held long confabulations over yellow manuscripts in which the commentary, it must be confessed, did not always adhere very closely to the text. Six months elapsed, and Benvolio found an ineffable charm in this mild mixture of sentiment and study. He had never in his life been so long of the same mind; it really seemed as if, as the phrase is, the fold were taken for ever – as if he had done with the world and were ready to live henceforth in the closet. He hardly thought of the Countess, and they had no correspondence. She was in Italy, in Greece, in the East, in the Holy Land, in places and situations that taxed the imagination.

One day, in the darkness of the vestibule, after he had left Scholastica, he was arrested by a little old man of sordid aspect, of whom he could make out hardly more than a pair of sharply glowing eyes and an immense bald head, polished like a ball of ivory. He was a quite terrible little figure in his way, and Benvolio at first was frightened. 'Mr Poet,' said the old man, 'let me say a single word. I give my niece a maintenance. She may do what she likes. But she forfeits every penny of her allowance and her expectations if she is fool enough to marry a fellow who scribbles rhymes. I am told they are sometimes an hour finding two that will match! Good evening, Mr Poet!' Benvolio heard a sound like the faint jingle of loose coin in a breeches pocket, and the old man abruptly retreated into his domiciliary gloom. Benvolio had never seen him before, and he had no wish ever to see him again. He had not proposed to himself to marry Scholastica, and even if he had, I am pretty sure he would now have taken the modest view of the matter and decided that his hand and heart were an insufficient compensation for the relinquishment of a miser's fortune. The young girl never spoke of her uncle; he lived quite alone, apparently, haunting his upper chambers like a restless ghost, and sending her, by the old serving-woman, her slender monthly allowance, wrapped up in a piece of old newspaper. It was shortly after this that the Countess at last came back. Benvolio had been taking one of those long walks to which he had always been addicted, and passing through the public gardens on his way home, he had sat down on a bench to rest. In a few moments a carriage came rolling by; in it sat the Countess – beautiful, sombre, solitary. He rose with a ceremonious salute, and she went her way. But in five minutes she passed back again, and this time her carriage stopped. She gave him a single glance, and he got in. For a week afterward Scholastica vainly awaited him. What had happened? It had happened that though she had proved herself both false and cruel, the Countess again asserted her charm, and our precious hero again succumbed to it. But he resumed his visits to Scholastica after an interval of neglect not long enough to be unpardonable; the only difference was that now they were not so frequent.

My story draws to a close, for I am afraid you have already lost patience with the history of this amiable weathercock. Another year ran its course, and the Professor's manuscripts were arranged in great piles and almost ready for the printer. Benvolio had had a constant hand in the work, and had found it exceedingly interesting; it involved inquiries and researches of the most stimulating and profitable kind. Scholastica was very happy. Her friend was often absent for many days, during which she knew he was leading the great world's life; but she had learned that if she patiently waited, the pendulum would swing back, and he would reappear and bury himself in their books and papers and talk. And their talk, you may be sure, was not all technical; they touched on everything that came into their heads, and Benvolio by no means felt obliged to be silent about those mundane matters as to which a vow of personal ignorance had been taken for his companion. He took her into his poetic confidence, and read her everything he had written since his return from Italy. The more he worked the more he desired to work; and so, at this time, occupied as he was with editing the Professor's manuscripts, he had never been so productive on his own account. He wrote another drama, on an Italian subject, which was performed with magnificent success; and this production he discussed with Scholastica scene by scene and speech by speech. He proposed to her to come and see it acted from a covered box, where her seclusion would be complete. She seemed for an instant to feel the force of the temptation; then she shook her head with a frank smile, and said it was better not. The play was dedicated to the Countess, who had suggested the subject to him in Italy, where it had been imparted to her, as a family anecdote, by one of her old princesses. This easy, fruitful, complex life might have lasted for ever, but for two most regrettable events. *Might* have lasted I say; you observe I do not affirm it positively. Scholastica lost her peace of mind; she was suffering a secret annoyance. She concealed it as far as she might from her friend, and with some success; for although he suspected something and questioned her, she persuaded him that it was his own fancy. In reality it was no fancy at all, but the very uncomfortable fact that her shabby old uncle, the miser, was a terrible thorn in her side. He had told Benvolio that she might do as she liked, but he had recently revoked this amiable concession. He informed her one day, by means of an illegible note, scrawled with a blunt pencil, on the back of an old letter, that her beggarly friend the Poet came to see her altogether too often; that he was determined she never should marry a crack-brained rhymester; and that he requested that before the sacrifice became too painful she would be so good as to dismiss Mr Benvolio. This was accompanied by an intimation, more explicit than gracious, that he opened his money-bags only for those who deferred to his incomparable wisdom. Scholastica was poor, and simple, and lonely; but she was proud, for all that, with a shrinking and unexpressed pride of her own, and her uncle's charity, proffered on these terms, became intolerably bitter to her soul. She sent him word that she thanked him for his past liberality, but she would no longer be a charge upon him. She said to herself that she could work; she had a superior education; many women, she knew, supported themselves. She even found something inspiring in the idea of going out into the world of which she knew so little, to seek her fortune. Her great desire, however, was to keep her situation a secret from Benvolio, and to prevent his knowing the sacrifice she was making for him. This it is especially that proves she was proud. It so happened that circumstances made secrecy possible. I don't know whether the Countess had always an idea of marrying Benvolio, but her imperious vanity still suffered from the spectacle of his divided allegiance, and it suggested to her a truly malignant revenge. A brilliant political mission, to treat of a special question, was about to be despatched to a neighbouring government, and half a dozen young men of eminence were to be attached to it. The Countess had influence at Court, and without saying anything to Benvolio, she immediately urged his claim to a post on the ground of his distinguished services to literature. She pulled her wires so cleverly that in a very short time she had the pleasure of presenting him his appointment on a great sheet of parchment, from which the royal seal dangled by a blue ribbon. It involved an exile of but a few weeks, and to this, with her eye on the sequel of her project, she was able to resign herself. Benvolio's imagination took fire at the thought of spending a month at a foreign court, in the very hotbed of consummate diplomacy; this was a phase of experience with which he was as yet unacquainted. He departed, and no sooner had he gone than the Countess, at a venture, waited upon Scholastica. She knew the girl was poor, and she believed that in spite of her homely virtues she would not, if the opportunity were placed before her in a certain light, prove implacably indisposed to better her fortunes. She knew nothing of the young girl's contingent expectations from her uncle, and her interference at this juncture was simply a remarkable coincidence. She laid before her a proposal from a certain great lady, whose husband, an eminent general, had just been dubbed governor of an island on the other side of the globe. This lady desired a preceptress for her children; she had heard of Scholastica's merit, and she ventured to hope that she might persuade her to accompany her to the Antipodes and reside in her family. The offer was brilliant; to Scholastica it seemed mysteriously and providentially opportune. Nevertheless she hesitated, and demanded time for reflection; without telling herself why, she wished to wait till Benvolio should return. He wrote her two or three letters, full of the echoes of his brilliant actual life, and without a word about the things that were nearer her own experience. The month elapsed, but he was still absent. Scholastica, who was in correspondence with the governor's wife, delayed her decision from week to week. She had sold her father's manuscripts to a publisher, for a very small sum, and gone, meanwhile, to live in a convent. At last the governor's lady demanded her ultimatum. The poor girl scanned the horizon, and saw no rescuing friend; Benvolio was still at the court of Illyria! What she saw was the Countess's fine eyes eagerly watching her over the top of her fan. They seemed to contain a horrible menace, and to hold somehow her happiness at their mercy. Her heart sank; she gathered up her few possessions and set sail, with her illustrious protectors, for the Antipodes. Shortly after her departure Benvolio returned. He felt a terrible pang of rage and grief when he learned that she had gone; he went to the Countess, prepared to accuse her of the basest treachery. But she checked his reproaches by arts that she had never gone so far as to use before, and promised him that, if he would trust her, he should never miss that pale-eyed little governess. It can hardly be supposed that he believed her; but he appears to have been guilty of letting himself be persuaded without belief. For some time after this he almost lived with the Countess. He had, with infinite pains, purchased from his neighbour, the miser, the right of occupancy of the late

Professor's apartment. This repulsive proprietor, in spite of his constitutional aversion to rhymesters, had not resisted the financial argument, and seemed greatly amazed that a poet should have a dollar to spend. Scholastica had left all things in their old places, but Benvolio, for the present, never went into the room. He turned the key in the door, and kept it in his waistcoat-pocket, where, while he was with the Countess, his fingers fumbled with it. Several months rolled by, and the Countess's promise was not verified. He missed Scholastica woefully, and missed her more as time elapsed. He began at last to go to the old brown room and to try to do some work there. He only half succeeded in a fashion; it seemed dark and empty; doubly empty when he remembered what it might have been. Suddenly he ceased to visit the Countess; a long time passed without her seeing him. She met him at another house, and had some remarkable words with him. She covered him with reproaches that were doubtless deserved, but he made her an answer that caused her to open her eyes and flush, and admit afterward that, for a clever woman, she had been a great fool. 'Don't you see,' he said, 'can't you imagine, that I cared for you only by contrast? You took the trouble to kill the contrast, and with it you killed everything else. For a constancy I prefer *this*!' And he tapped his poetic brow. He never saw the Countess again.

I rather regret now that I said at the beginning of my story that it was not to be a fairy-tale; otherwise I should be at liberty to relate, with harmonious geniality, that if Benvolio missed Scholastica, he missed the Countess also, and led an extremely fretful and unproductive life, until one day he sailed for the Antipodes and brought Scholastica home. After this he began to produce again; only, many people said that his poetry had become dismally dull. But excuse me; I am writing as if it *were* a fairy-tale!

DAISY MILLER: A STUDY

I

AT the little town of Vevey, in Switzerland, there is a particularly comfortable hotel. There are, indeed, many hotels; for the entertainment of tourists is the business of the place, which, as many travellers will remember, is seated upon the edge of a remarkably blue lake – a lake that it behooves every tourist to visit. The shore of the lake presents an unbroken array of establishments of this order, of every category, from the 'grand hotel' of the newest fashion, with a chalk-white front, a hundred balconies, and a dozen flags flying from its roof, to the little Swiss *pension* of an elder day, with its name inscribed in German-looking lettering upon a pink or yellow wall, and an awkward summer-house in the angle of the garden. One of the hotels at Vevey, however, is famous, even classical, being distinguished from many of its upstart neighbours by an air both of luxury and of maturity. In this region, in the month of June, American travellers are extremely numerous; it may be said, indeed, that Vevey assumes at this period some of the characteristics of an American watering-place. There are sights and sounds which evoke a vision, an echo, of Newport and Saratoga. There is a flitting hither and thither of 'stylish' young girls, a rustling of muslin flounces, a rattle of dance-music in the morning hours, a sound of high-pitched voices at all times. You receive an impression of these things at the excellent inn of the 'Trois Couronnes', and are transported in fancy to the Ocean House or to Congress Hall. But at the 'Trois Couronnes', it must be added, there are other features that are much at variance with these suggestions: neat German waiters, who look like secretaries of legation; Russian princesses sitting in the garden; little Polish boys walking about, held by the hand, with their governors; a view of the snowy crest of the Dent du Midi and the picturesque towers of the Castle of Chillon.

I hardly know whether it was the analogies or the differences that were uppermost in the mind of a young American, who,

two or three years ago, sat in the garden of the 'Trois Couronnes', looking about him, rather idly, at some of the graceful
objects I have mentioned. It was a beautiful summer morning,
and in whatever fashion the young American looked at
things, they must have seemed to him charming. He had
come from Geneva the day before, by the little steamer, to
see his aunt, who was staying at the hotel – Geneva having
been for a long time his place of residence. But his aunt had a
headache – his aunt had almost always a headache – and
now she was shut up in her room, smelling camphor, so that
he was at liberty to wander about. He was some seven-and-
twenty years of age; when his friends spoke of him, they usually
said that he was at Geneva, 'studying'. When his enemies
spoke of him they said – but, after all, he had no enemies; he
was an extremely amiable fellow, and universally liked. What
I should say is, simply, that when certain persons spoke of him
they affirmed that the reason of his spending so much time at
Geneva was that he was extremely devoted to a lady who lived
there – a foreign lady – a person older than himself. Very
few Americans – indeed I think none – had ever seen this
lady, about whom there were some singular stories. But
Winterbourne had an old attachment for the little metropolis
of Calvinism; he had been put to school there as a boy, and
he had afterwards gone to college there – circumstances which
had led to his forming a great many youthful friendships.
Many of these he had kept, and they were a source of great
satisfaction to him.

After knocking at his aunt's door and learning that she was
indisposed, he had taken a walk about the town, and then he
had come in to his breakfast. He had now finished his breakfast;
but he was drinking a small cup of coffee, which had been
served to him on a little table in the garden by one of the waiters
who looked like an *attaché*. At last he finished his coffee and lit a
cigarette. Presently a small boy came walking along the path –
an urchin of nine or ten. The child, who was diminutive for
his years, had an aged expression of countenance, a pale
complexion, and sharp little features. He was dressed in knickerbockers, with red stockings, which displayed his poor little

spindleshanks; he also wore a brilliant red cravat. He carried in his hand a long alpenstock, the sharp point of which he thrust into everything that he approached – the flower-beds, the garden-benches, the trains of the ladies' dresses. In front of Winterbourne he paused, looking at him with a pair of bright, penetrating little eyes.

'Will you give me a lump of sugar?' he asked, in a sharp, hard little voice – a voice immature, and yet, somehow, not young.

Winterbourne glanced at the small table near him, on which his coffee-service rested, and saw that several morsels of sugar remained. 'Yes, you may take one,' he answered; 'but I don't think sugar is good for little boys.'

This little boy stepped forward and carefully selected three of the coveted fragments, two of which he buried in the pocket of his knickerbockers, depositing the other as promptly in another place. He poked his alpenstock, lance-fashion, into Winterbourne's bench, and tried to crack the lump of sugar with his teeth.

'Oh, blazes; it's har-r-d!' he exclaimed, pronouncing the adjective in a peculiar manner.

Winterbourne had immediately perceived that he might have the honour of claiming him as a fellow-countryman. 'Take care you don't hurt your teeth,' he said, paternally.

'I haven't got any teeth to hurt. They have all come out. I have only got seven teeth. My mother counted them last night, and one came out right afterwards. She said she'd slap me if any more came out. I can't help it. It's this old Europe. It's the climate that makes them come out. In America they didn't come out. It's these hotels.'

Winterbourne was much amused. 'If you eat three lumps of sugar, your mother will certainly slap you,' he said.

'She's got to give me some candy, then,' rejoined his young interlocutor. 'I can't get any candy here – any American candy. American candy's the best candy.'

'And are American little boys the best little boys?' asked Winterbourne.

'I don't know. I'm an American boy,' said the child.

'I see you are one of the best!' laughed Winterbourne.

'Are you an American man?' pursued this vivacious infant. And then, on Winterbourne's affirmative reply – 'American men are the best,' he declared.

His companion thanked him for the compliment; and the child, who had now got astride of his alpenstock, stood looking about him, while he attacked a second lump of sugar. Winterbourne wondered if he himself had been like this in his infancy, for he had been brought to Europe at about this age.

'Here comes my sister!' cried the child, in a moment. 'She's an American girl.'

Winterbourne looked along the path and saw a beautiful young lady advancing. 'American girls are the best girls,' he said, cheerfully, to his young companion.

'My sister ain't the best!' the child declared. 'She's always blowing at me.'

'I imagine that is your fault, not hers,' said Winterbourne. The young lady meanwhile had drawn near. She was dressed in white muslin, with a hundred frills and flounces, and knots of pale-coloured ribbon. She was bare-headed; but she balanced in her hand a large parasol, with a deep border of embroidery; and she was strikingly, admirably pretty. 'How pretty they are!' thought Winterbourne, straightening himself in his seat, as if he were prepared to rise.

The young lady paused in front of his bench, near the parapet of the garden, which overlooked the lake. The little boy had now converted his alpenstock into a vaulting-pole, by the aid of which he was springing about in the gravel, and kicking it up not a little.

'Randolph,' said the young lady, 'what *are* you doing?'

'I'm going up the Alps,' replied Randolph. 'This is the way!' And he gave another little jump, scattering the pebbles about Winterbourne's ears.

'That's the way they come down,' said Winterbourne.

'He's an American man!' cried Randolph, in his little hard voice.

The young lady gave no heed to this announcement, but looked straight at her brother. 'Well, I guess you had better be quiet,' she simply observed.

It seemed to Winterbourne that he had been in a manner presented. He got up and stepped slowly towards the young girl, throwing away his cigarette. 'This little boy and I have made acquaintance,' he said, with great civility. In Geneva, as he had been perfectly aware, a young man was not at liberty to speak to a young unmarried lady except under certain rarely-occurring conditions; but here at Vevey, what conditions could be better than these? – a pretty American girl coming and standing in front of you in a garden. This pretty American girl, however, on hearing Winterbourne's observation, simply glanced at him; she then turned her head and looked over the parapet, at the lake and the opposite mountains. He wondered whether he had gone too far; but he decided that he must advance farther, rather than retreat. While he was thinking of something else to say, the young lady turned to the little boy again.

'I should like to know where you got that pole,' she said.

'I bought it!' responded Randolph.

'You don't mean to say you're going to take it to Italy.'

'Yes, I am going to take it to Italy!' the child declared.

The young girl glanced over the front of her dress, and smoothed out a knot or two of ribbon. Then she rested her eyes upon the prospect again. 'Well, I guess you had better leave it somewhere,' she said, after a moment.

'Are you going to Italy?' Winterbourne inquired, in a tone of great respect.

The young lady glanced at him again. 'Yes, sir,' she replied. And she said nothing more.

'Are you – a – going over the Simplon?' Winterbourne pursued, a little embarrassed.

'I don't know,' she said. 'I suppose it's some mountain. Randolph, what mountain are we going over?'

'Going where?' the child demanded.

'To Italy,' Winterbourne explained.

'I don't know,' said Randolph. 'I don't want to go to Italy. I want to go to America.'

'Oh, Italy is a beautiful place!' rejoined the young man.

'Can you get candy there?' Randolph loudly inquired.

'I hope not,' said his sister. 'I guess you have had enough candy, and mother thinks so too.'

'I haven't had any for ever so long – for a hundred weeks!' cried the boy, still jumping about.

The young lady inspected her flounces and smoothed her ribbons again; and Winterbourne presently risked an observation upon the beauty of the view. He was ceasing to be embarrassed, for he had begun to perceive that she was not in the least embarrassed herself. There had not been the slightest alteration in her charming complexion; she was evidently neither offended nor fluttered. If she looked another way when he spoke to her, and seemed not particularly to hear him, this was simply her habit, her manner. Yet, as he talked a little more, and pointed out some of the objects of interest in the view, with which she appeared quite unacquainted, she gradually gave him more of the benefit of her glance; and then he saw that this glance was perfectly direct and unshrinking. It was not, however, what would have been called an immodest glance, for the young girl's eyes were singularly honest and fresh. They were wonderfully pretty eyes; and, indeed, Winterbourne had not seen for a long time anything prettier than his fair countrywoman's various features – her complexion, her nose, her ears, her teeth. He had a great relish for feminine beauty; he was addicted to observing and analysing it; and as regards this young lady's face he made several observations. It was not at all insipid, but it was not exactly expressive; and though it was eminently delicate Winterbourne mentally accused it – very forgivingly – of a want of finish. He thought it very possible that Master Randolph's sister was a coquette; he was sure she had a spirit of her own; but in her bright, sweet, superficial little visage there was no mockery, no irony. Before long it became obvious that she was much disposed towards conversation. She told him that they were going to Rome for the winter – she and her mother and Randolph. She asked him if he was a 'real American'; she wouldn't have taken him for one; he seemed more like a German – this was said after a little hesitation, especially when he spoke. Winterbourne, laughing, answered that he had met Germans who spoke like Americans;

but that he had not, so far as he remembered, met an American who spoke like a German. Then he asked her if she would not be more comfortable in sitting upon the bench which he had just quitted. She answered that she liked standing up and walking about; but she presently sat down. She told him she was from New York State – 'if you know where that is'. Winterbourne learned more about her by catching hold of her small, slippery brother and making him stand a few minutes by his side.

'Tell me your name, my boy,' he said.

'Randolph C. Miller,' said the boy, sharply. 'And I'll tell you her name'; and he levelled his alpenstock at his sister.

'You had better wait till you are asked!' said this young lady, calmly.

'I should like very much to know your name,' said Winterbourne.

'Her name is Daisy Miller!' cried the child. 'But that isn't her real name; that isn't her name on her cards.'

'It's a pity you haven't got one of my cards!' said Miss Miller.

'Her real name is Annie P. Miller,' the boy went on.

'Ask him *his* name,' said his sister, indicating Winterbourne.

But on this point Randolph seemed perfectly indifferent; he continued to supply information with regard to his own family. 'My father's name is Ezra B. Miller,' he announced. 'My father ain't in Europe; my father's in a better place than Europe.'

Winterbourne imagined for a moment that this was the manner in which the child had been taught to intimate that Mr Miller had been removed to the sphere of celestial rewards. But Randolph immediately added, 'My father's in Schenectady. He's got a big business. My father's rich, you bet.'

'Well!' ejaculated Miss Miller, lowering her parasol and looking at the embroidered border. Winterbourne presently released the child, who departed, dragging his alpenstock along the path. 'He doesn't like Europe,' said the young girl. 'He wants to go back.'

'To Schenectady, you mean?'

'Yes; he wants to go right home. He hasn't got any boys here. There is one boy here, but he always goes round with a teacher; they won't let him play.'

'And your brother hasn't any teacher?' Winterbourne inquired.

'Mother thought of getting him one, to travel round with us. There was a lady told her of a very good teacher; an American lady – perhaps you know her – Mrs Sanders. I think she came from Boston. She told her of this teacher, and we thought of getting him to travel round with us. But Randolph said he didn't want a teacher travelling round with us. He said he wouldn't have lessons when he was in the cars. And we *are* in the cars about half the time. There was an English lady we met in the cars – I think her name was Miss Featherstone; perhaps you know her. She wanted to know why I didn't give Randolph lessons – give him "instruction", she called it. I guess he could give me more instruction than I could give him. He's very smart.'

'Yes,' said Winterbourne; 'he seems very smart.'

'Mother's going to get a teacher for him as soon as we get to Italy. Can you get good teachers in Italy?'

'Very good, I should think,' said Winterbourne.

'Or else she's going to find some school. He ought to learn some more. He's only nine. He's going to college.' And in this way Miss Miller continued to converse upon the affairs of her family, and upon other topics. She sat there with her extremely pretty hands, ornamented with very brilliant rings, folded in her lap, and with her pretty eyes now resting upon those of Winterbourne, now wandering over the garden, the people who passed by, and the beautiful view. She talked to Winterbourne as if she had known him a long time. He found it very pleasant. It was many years since he had heard a young girl talk so much. It might have been said of this unknown young lady, who had come and sat down beside him upon a bench, that she chattered. She was very quiet, she sat in a charming tranquil attitude; but her lips and her eyes were constantly moving. She had a soft, slender, agreeable voice, and her tone was decidedly sociable. She gave Winterbourne a history of her movements and intentions, and those of her mother and brother, in Europe, and enumerated, in particular, the various hotels at which they had stopped. 'That English lady in the cars,' she said – 'Miss Featherstone – asked me if we didn't all live in hotels in

America. I told her I had never been in so many hotels in my life as since I came to Europe. I have never seen so many – it's nothing but hotels.' But Miss Miller did not make this remark with a querulous accent; she appeared to be in the best humour with everything. She declared that the hotels were very good, when once you got used to their ways, and that Europe was perfectly sweet. She was not disappointed – not a bit. Perhaps it was because she had heard so much about it before. She had ever so many intimate friends that had been there ever so many times. And then she had had ever so many dresses and things from Paris. Whenever she put on a Paris dress she felt as if she were in Europe.

'It was a kind of a wishing-cap,' said Winterbourne.

'Yes,' said Miss Miller, without examining this analogy; 'it always made me wish I was here. But I needn't have done that for dresses. I am sure they send all the pretty ones to America; you see the most frightful things here. The only thing I don't like,' she proceeded, 'is the society. There isn't any society; or, if there is, I don't know where it keeps itself. Do you? I suppose there is some society somewhere, but I haven't seen anything of it. I'm very fond of society, and I have always had a great deal of it. I don't mean only in Schenectady, but in New York. I used to go to New York every winter. In New York I had lots of society. Last winter I had seventeen dinners given me; and three of them were by gentlemen,' added Daisy Miller. 'I have more friends in New York than in Schenectady – more gentle-men friends; and more young lady friends too,' she resumed in a moment. She paused again for an instant; she was looking at Winterbourne with all her prettiness in her lively eyes and in her light, slightly monotonous smile. 'I have always had,' she said, 'a great deal of gentlemen's society.'

Poor Winterbourne was amused, perplexed, and decidedly charmed. He had never yet heard a young girl express herself in just this fashion; never, at least, save in cases where to say such things seemed a kind of demonstrative evidence of a certain laxity of deportment. And yet was he to accuse Miss Daisy Miller of actual or potential *inconduite*, as they said at Geneva? He felt that he had lived at Geneva so long that he had lost a good deal; he had become dishabituated to the American tone. Never, indeed, since he had grown old enough to appreciate things, had he encountered a young American girl of so pronounced a type as this. Certainly she was very charming; but how deucedly sociable! Was she simply a pretty girl from New York State – were they all like that, the pretty girls who had a good deal of gentlemen's society? Or was she also a designing, an audacious, an unscrupulous young person? Winterbourne had lost his instinct in this matter, and his reason could not help him. Miss Daisy Miller looked extremely innocent. Some people had told him that, after all, American girls were exceedingly innocent; and others had told him that, after all, they were not. He was inclined to think Miss Daisy Miller was a flirt – a pretty American flirt. He had never, as yet, had any relations with young ladies of this category. He had known, here in Europe, two or three women – persons older than Miss Daisy Miller, and provided, for respectability's sake, with husbands – who were great coquettes – dangerous, terrible women, with whom one's relations were liable to take a serious turn. But this young girl was not a coquette in that sense; she was very unsophisticated; she was only a pretty American flirt. Winterbourne was almost grateful for having found the formula that applied to Miss Daisy Miller. He leaned back in his seat; he remarked to himself that she had the most charming nose he had ever seen; he wondered what were the regular conditions and limitations of one's intercourse with a pretty American flirt. It presently became apparent that he was on the way to learn.

'Have you been to that old castle?' asked the young girl, pointing with her parasol to the far-gleaming walls of the Château de Chillon.

'Yes, formerly, more than once,' said Winterbourne. 'You too, I suppose, have seen it?'

'No; we haven't been there. I want to go there dreadfully. Of course I mean to go there. I wouldn't go away from here without having seen that old castle.'

'It's a very pretty excursion,' said Winterbourne, 'and very easy to make. You can drive, you know, or you can go by the little steamer.'

'You can go in the cars,' said Miss Miller.

'Yes; you can go in the cars,' Winterbourne assented.

'Our courier says they take you right up to the castle,' the young girl continued. 'We were going last week; but my mother gave out. She suffers dreadfully from dyspepsia. She said she couldn't go. Randolph wouldn't go either; he says he doesn't think much of old castles. But I guess we'll go this week, if we can get Randolph.'

'Your brother is not interested in ancient monuments?' Winterbourne inquired, smiling.

'He says he don't care much about old castles. He's only nine. He wants to stay at the hotel. Mother's afraid to leave him alone, and the courier won't stay with him; so we haven't been to many places. But it will be too bad if we don't go up there.' And Miss Miller pointed again at the Château de Chillon.

'I should think it might be arranged,' said Winterbourne. 'Couldn't you get some one to stay – for the afternoon – with Randolph?'

Miss Miller looked at him a moment; and then, very placidly – 'I wish *you* would stay with him!' she said.

Winterbourne hesitated a moment. 'I would much rather go to Chillon with you.'

'With me?' asked the young girl, with the same placidity.

She didn't rise, blushing, as a young girl at Geneva would have done; and yet Winterbourne, conscious that he had been very bold, thought it possible she was offended. 'With your mother,' he answered very respectfully.

But it seemed that both his audacity and his respect were lost upon Miss Daisy Miller. 'I guess my mother won't go, after all,' she said. 'She don't like to ride round in the afternoon. But did you really mean what you said just now; that you would like to go up there?'

'Most earnestly,' Winterbourne declared.

'Then we may arrange it. If mother will stay with Randolph, I guess Eugenio will.'

'Eugenio?' the young man inquired.

'Eugenio's our courier. He doesn't like to stay with Randolph; he's the most fastidious man I ever saw. But he's a splendid courier. I guess he'll stay at home with Randolph if mother does, and then we can go to the castle.'

Winterbourne reflected for an instant as lucidly as possible – 'we' could only mean Miss Daisy Miller and himself. This programme seemed almost too agreeable for credence; he felt as if he ought to kiss the young lady's hand. Possibly he would have done so – and quite spoiled the project; but at this moment another person – presumably Eugenio – appeared. A tall, handsome man, with superb whiskers, wearing a velvet morning-coat and a brilliant watch-chain, approached Miss Miller, looking sharply at her companion. 'Oh, Eugenio!' said Miss Miller, with the friendliest accent.

Eugenio had looked at Winterbourne from head to foot; he now bowed gravely to the young lady. 'I have the honour to inform mademoiselle that luncheon is upon the table.'

Miss Miller slowly rose. 'See here, Eugenio,' she said. 'I'm going to that old castle, any way.'

'To the Château de Chillon, mademoiselle?' the courier inquired. 'Mademoiselle has made arrangements?' he added, in a tone which struck Winterbourne as very impertinent.

Eugenio's tone apparently threw, even to Miss Miller's own apprehension, a slightly ironical light upon the young girl's situation. She turned to Winterbourne, blushing a little – a very little. 'You won't back out?' she said.

'I shall not be happy till we go!' he protested.

'And you are staying in this hotel?' she went on. 'And you are really an American?'

The courier stood looking at Winterbourne, offensively. The young man, at least, thought his manner of looking an offence to Miss Miller; it conveyed an imputation that she 'picked up' acquaintances. 'I shall have the honour of presenting to you a person who will tell you all about me,' he said smiling, and referring to his aunt.

'Oh, well, we'll go some day,' said Miss Miller. And she gave him a smile and turned away. She put up her parasol and walked back to the inn beside Eugenio. Winterbourne stood looking after her; and as she moved away, drawing her muslin furbelows over the gravel, said to himself that she had the *tournure* of a princess.

II

HE had, however, engaged to do more than proved feasible, in promising to present his aunt, Mrs Costello, to Miss Daisy Miller. As soon as the former lady had got better of her headache he waited upon her in her apartment; and, after the proper inquiries in regard to her health, he asked her if she had observed, in the hotel, an American family – a mamma, a daughter, and a little boy.

'And a courier?' said Mrs Costello. 'Oh, yes, I have observed them. Seen them – heard them – and kept out of their way.' Mrs Costello was a widow with a fortune; a person of much distinction, who frequently intimated that, if she were not so dreadfully liable to sick-headaches, she would probably have left a deeper impress upon her time. She had a long pale face, a high nose, and a great deal of very striking white hair, which she wore in large puffs and *rouleaux* over the top of her head. She had two sons married in New York, and another who was now in Europe. This young man was amusing himself at Homburg, and, though he was on his travels, was rarely perceived to visit any particular city at the moment selected by his mother for her own appearance there. Her nephew, who had come up to Vevey expressly to see her, was therefore more attentive than those who, as she said, were nearer to her. He had imbibed at Geneva the idea that one must always be attentive to one's aunt. Mrs Costello had not seen him for many years, and she was greatly pleased with him, manifesting her approbation by initiating him into many of the secrets of that social sway which, as she gave him to understand, she exerted in the American capital. She admitted that she was very exclusive; but, if he were acquainted with New York, he would see that one had to be. And her picture of the minutely hierarchical constitution of the society of that city, which she presented to him in many different lights, was, to Winterbourne's imagination, almost oppressively striking.

He immediately perceived, from her tone, that Miss Daisy Miller's place in the social scale was low. 'I am afraid you don't approve of them,' he said.

'They are very common,' Mrs Costello declared. 'They are the sort of Americans that one does one's duty by not – not accepting.'

'Ah, you don't accept them?' said the young man.

'I can't, my dear Frederick. I would if I could, but I can't.'

'The young girl is very pretty,' said Winterbourne, in a moment.

'Of course she's pretty. But she is very common.'

'I see what you mean, of course,' said Winterbourne, after another pause.

'She has that charming look that they all have,' his aunt resumed. 'I can't think where they pick it up; and she dresses in perfection – no, you don't know how well she dresses. I can't think where they get their taste.'

'But, my dear aunt, she is not, after all, a Comanche savage.'

'She is a young lady,' said Mrs Costello, 'who has an intimacy with her mamma's courier.'

'An intimacy with the courier?' the young man demanded.

'Oh, the mother is just as bad! They treat the courier like a familiar friend – like a gentleman. I shouldn't wonder if he dines with them. Very likely they have never seen a man with such good manners, such fine clothes, so like a gentleman. He probably corresponds to the young lady's idea of a Count. He sits with them in the garden, in the evening. I think he smokes.'

Winterbourne listened with interest to these disclosures; they helped him to make up his mind about Miss Daisy. Evidently she was rather wild. 'Well,' he said, 'I am not a courier, and yet she was very charming to me.'

'You had better have said at first,' said Mrs Costello, with dignity, 'that you had made her acquaintance.'

'We simply met in the garden, and we talked a bit.'

'*Tout bonnement!* And pray what did you say?'

'I said I should take the liberty of introducing her to my admirable aunt.'

'I am much obliged to you.'

'It was to guarantee my respectability,' said Winterbourne.

'And pray who is to guarantee hers?'

'Ah, you are cruel!' said the young man. 'She's a very nice girl.'

'You don't say that as if you believed it,' Mrs Costello observed.

'She is completely uncultivated,' Winterbourne went on. 'But she is wonderfully pretty, and, in short, she is very nice. To prove that I believe it, I am going to take her to the Château de Chillon.'

'You two are going off there together? I should say it proved just the contrary. How long had you known her, may I ask, when this interesting project was formed? You haven't been twenty-fours in the house.'

'I had known her half-an-hour!' said Winterbourne, smiling.

'Dear me!' cried Mrs Costello. 'What a dreadful girl!'

Her nephew was silent for some moments. 'You really think, then,' he began, earnestly, and with a desire for trust-worthy information – 'you really think that —' But he paused again.

'Think what, sir?' said his aunt.

'That she is the sort of young lady who expects a man – sooner or later – to carry her off?'

'I haven't the least idea what such young ladies expect a man to do. But I really think that you had better not meddle with little American girls that are uncultivated, as you call them. You have lived too long out of the country. You will be sure to make some great mistake. You are too innocent.'

'My dear aunt, I am not so innocent,' said Winterbourne, smiling and curling his moustache.

'You are too guilty, then!'

Winterbourne continued to curl his moustache, medita-tively. 'You won't let the poor girl know you then?' he asked at last.

'Is it literally true that she is going to the Château de Chillon with you?'

'I think that she fully intends it.'

'Then, my dear Frederick,' said Mrs Costello, 'I must decline the honour of her acquaintance. I am an old woman, but I am not too old – thank Heaven – to be shocked!'

'But don't they all do these things – the young girls in America?' Winterbourne inquired.

Mrs Costello stared a moment. 'I should like to see my granddaughters do them!' she declared, grimly.

This seemed to throw some light upon the matter, for Winterbourne remembered to have heard that his pretty cousins in New York were 'tremendous flirts'. If, therefore, Miss Daisy Miller exceeded the liberal licence allowed to these young ladies, it was probable that anything might be expected of her. Winterbourne was impatient to see her again, and he was vexed with himself that, by instinct, he should not appreciate her justly.

Though he was impatient to see her, he hardly knew what he should say to her about his aunt's refusal to become acquainted with her; but he discovered, promptly enough, that with Miss Daisy Miller there was no great need of walking on tiptoe. He found her that evening in the garden, wandering about in the warm starlight, like an indolent sylph, and swinging to and fro the largest fan he had ever beheld. It was ten o'clock. He had dined with his aunt, had been sitting with her since dinner, and had just taken leave of her till the morrow. Miss Daisy Miller seemed very glad to see him; she declared it was the longest evening she had ever passed.

'Have you been all alone?' he asked.

'I have been walking round with mother. But mother gets tired walking round,' she answered.

'Has she gone to bed?'

'No; she doesn't like to go to bed,' said the young girl. 'She doesn't sleep – not three hours. She says she doesn't know how she lives. She's dreadfully nervous. I guess she sleeps more than she thinks. She's gone somewhere after Randolph; she wants to try to get him to go to bed. He doesn't like to go to bed.'

'Let us hope she will persuade him,' observed Winterbourne.

'She will talk to him all she can; but he doesn't like her to talk to him,' said Miss Daisy, opening her fan. 'She's going to try to get Eugenio to talk to him. But he isn't afraid of Eugenio. Eugenio's a splendid courier, but he can't make much impression on Randolph! I don't believe he'll go to bed before eleven.' It appeared that Randolph's vigil was in fact triumphantly prolonged, for Winterbourne strolled about with the young girl for some time without meeting her mother. 'I have been looking round for that lady you want to introduce me to,' his companion resumed. 'She's your aunt.' Then, on Winterbourne's admitting the fact, and expressing some curiosity as to how she had learned it, she said she had heard all about Mrs Costello from the chambermaid. She was very quiet and very *comme il faut*; she wore white puffs; she spoke to no one, and she never dined at the *table d'hôte*. Every two days she had a headache. 'I think that's a lovely description, headache and all!' said Miss Daisy, chattering along in her thin, gay voice. 'I want to know her ever so much. I know just what *your* aunt would be; I know I should like her. She would be very exclusive. I like a lady to be exclusive; I'm dying to be exclusive myself. Well, we *are* exclusive, mother and I. We don't speak to every one – or they don't speak to us. I suppose it's about the same thing. Anyway, I shall be ever so glad to know your aunt.'

Winterbourne was embarrassed. 'She would be most happy,' he said; 'but I am afraid those headaches will interfere.'

The young girl looked at him through the dusk. 'But I suppose she doesn't have a headache every day,' she said, sympathetically.

Winterbourne was silent a moment. 'She tells me she does,' he answered at last – not knowing what to say.

Miss Daisy Miller stopped and stood looking at him. Her prettiness was still visible in the darkness; she was opening and closing her enormous fan. 'She doesn't want to know me!' she said, suddenly. 'Why don't you say so? You needn't be afraid. I'm not afraid!' And she gave a little laugh.

Winterbourne fancied there was a tremor in her voice; he was touched, shocked, mortified by it. 'My dear young lady,' he protested, 'she knows no one. It's her wretched health.'

The young girl walked on a few steps, laughing still. 'You needn't be afraid,' she repeated. 'Why should she want to know me?' Then she paused again; she was close to the parapet of the garden, and in front of her was the starlit lake. There was a vague sheen upon its surface, and in the distance were dimly-seen mountain forms. Daisy Miller looked out upon the mysterious prospect, and then she gave another little laugh. 'Gracious! she *is* exclusive!' she said. Winterbourne wondered whether she was seriously wounded, and for a moment almost wished that her sense of injury might be such as to make it becoming in him to attempt to reassure and comfort her. He had a pleasant sense that she would be very approachable for consolatory purposes. He felt then, for the instant, quite ready to sacrifice his aunt, conversationally; to admit that she was a proud, rude woman, and to declare that they needn't mind her. But before he had time to commit himself to this perilous mixture of gallantry and impiety, the young lady, resuming her walk, gave an exclamation in quite another tone. 'Well; here's mother! I guess she hasn't got Randolph to go to bed.' The figure of a lady appeared, at a distance, very indistinct in the darkness, and advancing with a slow and wavering movement. Suddenly it seemed to pause.

'Are you sure it is your mother? Can you distinguish her in this thick dusk?' Winterbourne asked.

'Well!' cried Miss Daisy Miller, with a laugh, 'I guess I know my own mother. And when she has got on my shawl, too! She is always wearing my things.'

The lady in question, ceasing to advance, hovered vaguely about the spot at which she had checked her steps.

'I am afraid your mother doesn't see you,' said Winterbourne. 'Or perhaps,' he added – thinking, with Miss Miller, the joke permissible – 'perhaps she feels guilty about your shawl.'

'Oh, it's a fearful old thing!' the young girl replied, serenely. 'I told her she could wear it. She won't come here, because she sees you.'

'Ah, then,' said Winterbourne, 'I had better leave you.'

'Oh no; come on!' urged Miss Daisy Miller.

'I'm afraid your mother doesn't approve of my walking with you.'

Miss Miller gave him a serious glance. 'It isn't for me; it's for you – that is, it's for *her*. Well; I don't know who it's for! But mother doesn't like any of my gentlemen friends. She's right down timid. She always makes a fuss if I introduce a gentleman. But I *do* introduce them – almost always. If I didn't introduce my gentlemen friends to mother,' the young girl added, in her little soft, flat monotone, 'I shouldn't think I was natural.'

'To introduce me,' said Winterbourne, 'you must know my name.' And he proceeded to pronounce it.

'Oh, dear; I can't say all that!' said his companion, with a laugh. But by this time they had come up to Mrs Miller, who, as they drew near, walked to the parapet of the garden and leaned upon it, looking intently at the lake and turning her back upon them. 'Mother!' said the young girl, in a tone of decision. Upon this the elder lady turned round. 'Mr Winterbourne,' said Miss Daisy Miller, introducing the young man very frankly and prettily. 'Common', she was, as Mrs Costello had pronounced her; yet it was a wonder to Winterbourne that, with her commonness, she had a singularly delicate grace.

Her mother was a small, spare, light person, with a wandering eye, a very exiguous nose, and a large forehead, decorated with a certain amount of thin, much-frizzled hair. Like her daughter, Mrs Miller was dressed with extreme elegance; she had enormous diamonds in her ears. So far as Winterbourne could observe, she gave him no greeting – she certainly was not looking at him. Daisy was near her, pulling her shawl straight. 'What are you doing, poking round here?' this young lady inquired; but by no means with that harshness of accent which her choice of words may imply.

'I don't know,' said her mother, turning towards the lake again.

'I shouldn't think you'd want that shawl!' Daisy exclaimed.

'Well – I do!' her mother answered, with a little laugh.

'Did you get Randolph to go to bed?' asked the young girl.

'No; I couldn't induce him,' said Mrs Miller, very gently. 'He wants to talk to the waiter. He likes to talk to that waiter.'

'I was telling Mr Winterbourne,' the young girl went on; and to the young man's ear her tone might have indicated that she had been uttering his name all her life.

'Oh, yes!' said Winterbourne; 'I have the pleasure of knowing your son.'

Randolph's mamma was silent; she turned her attention to the lake. But at last she spoke. 'Well, I don't see how he lives!'

'Anyhow, it isn't so bad as it was at Dover,' said Daisy Miller.

'And what occurred at Dover?' Winterbourne asked.

'He wouldn't go to bed at all. I guess he sat up all night – in the public parlour. He wasn't in bed at twelve o'clock: I know that.'

'It was half-past twelve,' declared Mrs Miller, with mild emphasis.

'Does he sleep much during the day?' Winterbourne demanded.

'I guess he doesn't sleep much,' Daisy rejoined.

'I wish he would!' said her mother. 'It seems as if he couldn't.'

'I think he's real tiresome,' Daisy pursued.

Then, for some moments, there was silence. 'Well, Daisy Miller,' said the elder lady, presently, 'I shouldn't think you'd want to talk against your own brother!'

'Well, he *is* tiresome, mother,' said Daisy, quite without the asperity of a retort.

'He's only nine,' urged Mrs Miller.

'Well, he wouldn't go to that castle,' said the young girl. 'I'm going there with Mr Winterbourne.'

To this announcement, very placidly made, Daisy's mamma offered no response. Winterbourne took for granted that she deeply disapproved of the projected excursion; but he said to himself that she was a simple, easily-managed person, and that a few deferential protestations would take the edge from her displeasure. 'Yes,' he began; 'your daughter has kindly allowed me the honour of being her guide.'

Mrs Miller's wandering eyes attached themselves, with a sort of appealing air, to Daisy, who, however, strolled a few steps farther, gently humming to herself. 'I presume you will go in the cars,' said her mother.

'Yes; or in the boat,' said Winterbourne.

'Well, of course, I don't know,' Mrs Miller rejoined. 'I have never been to that castle.'

'It is a pity you shouldn't go,' said Winterbourne, beginning to feel reassured as to her opposition. And yet he was quite prepared to find that, as a matter of course, she meant to accompany her daughter.

'We've been thinking ever so much about going,' she pursued; 'but it seems as if we couldn't. Of course Daisy – she wants to go round. But there's a lady here – I don't know her name – she says she shouldn't think we'd want to go to see castles *here*; she should think we'd want to wait till we got to Italy. It seems as if there would be so many there,' continued Mrs Miller, with an air of increasing confidence. 'Of course, we only want to see the principal ones. We visited several in England,' she presently added.

'Ah, yes! in England there are beautiful castles,' said Winterbourne. 'But Chillon, here, is very well worth seeing.'

'Well, if Daisy feels up to it —,' said Mrs Miller, in a tone impregnated with a sense of the magnitude of the enterprise. 'It seems as if there was nothing she wouldn't undertake.'

'Oh, I think she'll enjoy it!' Winterbourne declared. And he desired more and more to make it a certainty that he was to have the privilege of a *tête-à-tête* with the young lady, who was still strolling along in front of them, softly vocalising. 'You are not disposed, madam,' he inquired, 'to undertake it yourself?'

Daisy's mother looked at him, an instant, askance, and then walked forward in silence. Then – 'I guess she had better go alone,' she said, simply.

Winterbourne observed to himself that this was a very different type of maternity from that of the vigilant matrons who massed themselves in the forefront of social intercourse in the dark old city at the other end of the lake. But his meditations were interrupted by hearing his name very distinctly pronounced by Mrs Miller's unprotected daughter.

'Mr Winterbourne!' murmured Daisy.

'Mademoiselle!' said the young man.

'Don't you want to take me out in a boat?'

'At present?' he asked.

'Of course!' said Daisy.

'Well, Annie Miller!' exclaimed her mother.

'I beg you, madam, to let her go,' said Winterbourne, ardently; for he had never yet enjoyed the sensation of guiding through the summer starlight a skiff freighted with a fresh and beautiful young girl.

'I shouldn't think she'd want to,' said her mother. 'I should think she'd rather go indoors.'

'I'm sure Mr Winterbourne wants to take me,' Daisy declared. 'He's so awfully devoted!'

'I will row you over to Chillon, in the starlight.'

'I don't believe it!' said Daisy.

'Well!' ejaculated the elder lady again.

'You haven't spoken to me for half-an-hour,' her daughter went on.

'I have been having some very pleasant conversation with your mother,' said Winterbourne.

'Well; I want you to take me out in a boat!' Daisy repeated. They had all stopped, and she had turned round and was looking at Winterbourne. Her face wore a charming smile, her pretty eyes were gleaming, she was swinging her great fan about. No; it's impossible to be prettier than that, thought Winterbourne.

'There are half-a-dozen boats moored at that landing-place,' he said, pointing to certain steps which descended from the garden to the lake. 'If you will do me the honour to accept my arm, we will go and select one of them.'

Daisy stood there smiling; she threw back her head and gave a little light laugh. 'I like a gentleman to be formal!' she declared.

'I assure you it's a formal offer.'

'I was bound I would make you say something,' Daisy went on.

'You see it's not very difficult,' said Winterbourne. 'But I am afraid you are chaffing me.'

'I think not, sir,' remarked Mrs Miller, very gently.

'Do, then, let me give you a row,' he said to the young girl.

'It's quite lovely, the way you say that!' cried Daisy.

'It will be still more lovely to do it.'

'Yes, it would be lovely!' said Daisy. But she made no movement to accompany him; she only stood there laughing.

'I should think you had better find out what time it is,' interposed her mother.

'It is eleven o'clock, madam,' said a voice, with a foreign accent, out of the neighbouring darkness; and Winterbourne, turning, perceived the florid personage who was in attendance upon the two ladies. He had apparently just approached.

'Oh, Eugenio,' said Daisy, 'I am going out in a boat!' Eugenio bowed. 'At eleven o'clock, mademoiselle?'

'I am going with Mr Winterbourne. This very minute.'

'Do tell her she can't,' said Mrs Miller to the courier.

'I think you had better not go out in a boat, mademoiselle,' Eugenio declared.

Winterbourne wished to Heaven this pretty girl were not so familiar with her courier; but he said nothing.

'I suppose you don't think it's proper!' Daisy exclaimed. 'Eugenio doesn't think anything's proper.'

'I am at your service,' said Winterbourne.

'Does mademoiselle propose to go alone?' asked Eugenio of Mrs Miller.

'Oh, no; with this gentleman!' answered Daisy's mamma.

The courier looked for a moment at Winterbourne – the latter thought he was smiling – and then, solemnly, with a bow, 'As mademoiselle pleases!' he said.

'Oh, I hoped you would make a fuss!' said Daisy. 'I don't care to go now.'

'I myself shall make a fuss if you don't go,' said Winterbourne.

'That's all I want – a little fuss!' And the young girl began to laugh again.

'Mr Randolph has gone to bed!' the courier announced, frigidly.

'Oh, Daisy; now we can go!' said Mrs Miller.

Daisy turned away from Winterbourne, looking at him, smiling and fanning herself. 'Good night,' she said; 'I hope you are disappointed, or disgusted, or something!'

He looked at her, taking the hand she offered him. 'I am puzzled,' he answered.

'Well; I hope it won't keep you awake!' she said, very smartly; and, under the escort of the privileged Eugenio, the two ladies passed towards the house.

Winterbourne stood looking after them; he was indeed puzzled. He lingered beside the lake for a quarter of an hour, turning over the mystery of the young girl's sudden familiarities and caprices. But the only very definite conclusion he came to was that he should enjoy deucedly 'going off' with her somewhere.

Two days afterwards he went off with her to the Castle of Chillon. He waited for her in the large hall of the hotel, where the couriers, the servants, the foreign tourists were lounging about and staring. It was not the place he would have chosen, but she had appointed it. She came tripping downstairs, buttoning her long gloves, squeezing her folded parasol against her pretty figure, dressed in the perfection of a soberly elegant travelling-costume. Winterbourne was a man of imagination and, as our ancestors used to say, of sensibility; as he looked at her dress and, on the great staircase, her little rapid, confiding step, he felt as if there were something romantic going forward. He could have believed he was going to elope with her. He passed out with her among all the idle people that were assembled there; they were all looking at her very hard; she had begun to chatter as soon as she joined him. Winterbourne's preference had been that they should be conveyed to Chillon in a carriage; but she expressed a lively wish to go in the little steamer; she declared that she had a passion for steamboats. There was always such a lovely breeze upon the water, and you saw such lots of people. The sail was not long, but Winterbourne's companion found time to say a great many things. To the young man himself their little excursion was so much of an escapade – an adventure – that, even allowing for her habitual sense of freedom, he had some expectation of seeing her regard it in the same way. But it must be confessed that, in this particular, he was disappointed. Daisy Miller was extremely animated, she was in charming spirits; but she was apparently not at all excited; she was not fluttered; she avoided neither his eyes nor those of any one else; she blushed neither when she looked at him nor when she saw that people were looking at her. People continued to look at her a great deal, and Winterbourne took much satisfaction in his pretty companion's distinguished air. He had been a little afraid that she would talk loud, laugh overmuch, and even, perhaps, desire to move about the boat a good deal. But he quite forgot his fears; he sat smiling, with his eyes upon her face, while, without moving from her place, she delivered herself of a great number of original reflections. It was the most charming garrulity he had ever heard. He had assented to the idea that she was 'common'; but was she so, after all, or was he simply getting used to her commonness? Her conversation was chiefly of what metaphysicians term the objective cast; but every now and then it took a subjective turn.

'What on *earth* are you so grave about?' she suddenly demanded, fixing her agreeable eyes upon Winterbourne's.

'Am I grave?' he asked. 'I had an idea I was grinning from ear to ear.'

'You look as if you were taking me to a funeral. If that's a grin, your ears are very near together.'

'Should you like me to dance a hornpipe on the deck?'

'Pray do, and I'll carry round your hat. It will pay the expenses of our journey.'

'I never was better pleased in my life,' murmured Winterbourne.

She looked at him a moment, and then burst into a little laugh. 'I like to make you say those things! You're a queer mixture!'

In the castle, after they had landed, the subjective element decidedly prevailed. Daisy tripped about the vaulted chambers, rustled her skirts in the corkscrew staircases, flirted back with a pretty little cry and a shudder from the edge of the *oubliettes*, and turned a singularly well-shaped ear to everything that Winterbourne told her about the place. But he saw that she

cared very little for feudal antiquities, and that the dusky traditions of Chillon made but a slight impression upon her. They
had the good fortune to have been able to walk about without
other companionship than that of the custodian; and Winterbourne arranged with this functionary that they should not be
hurried – that they should linger and pause wherever they
chose. The custodian interpreted the bargain generously –
Winterbourne, on his side, had been generous – and ended by
leaving them quite to themselves. Miss Miller's observations
were not remarkable for logical consistency; for anything she
wanted to say she was sure to find a pretext. She found a great
many pretexts in the rugged embrasures of Chillon for asking
Winterbourne sudden questions about himself – his family, his
previous history, his tastes, his habits, his intentions – and for
supplying information upon corresponding points in her own
personality. Of her own tastes, habits and intentions Miss
Miller was prepared to give the most definite, and indeed the
most favourable, account.

'Well; I hope you know enough!' she said to her companion,
after he had told her the history of the unhappy Bonivard.
'I never saw a man that knew so much!' The history of Bonivard
had evidently, as they say, gone into one ear and out of the
other. But Daisy went on to say that she wished Winterbourne
would travel with them and 'go round' with them; they might
know something, in that case. 'Don't you want to come and
teach Randolph?' she asked. Winterbourne said that nothing
could possibly please him so much; but that he had unfortunately other occupations. 'Other occupations? I don't believe
it!' said Miss Daisy. 'What do you mean? You are not in business.' The young man admitted that he was not in business; but
he had engagements which, even within a day or two, would
force him to go back to Geneva. 'Oh, bother!' she said, 'I don't
believe it!' and she began to talk about something else. But a
few moments later, when he was pointing out to her the pretty
design of an antique fireplace, she broke out irrelevantly, 'You
don't mean to say you are going back to Geneva?'

'It is a melancholy fact that I shall have to return to Geneva
to-morrow.'

'Well, Mr Winterbourne,' said Daisy; 'I think you're horrid!'

'Oh, don't say such dreadful things!' said Winterbourne – 'just at the last.'

'The last!' cried the young girl; 'I call it the first. I have half a mind to leave you here and go straight back to the hotel alone.' And for the next ten minutes she did nothing but call him horrid. Poor Winterbourne was fairly bewildered; no young lady had as yet done him the honour to be so agitated by the announcement of his movements. His companion, after this, ceased to pay any attention to the curiosities of Chillon or the beauties of the lake; she opened fire upon the mysterious charmer in Geneva, whom she appeared to have instantly taken it for granted that he was hurrying back to see. How did Miss Daisy Miller know that there was a charmer in Geneva? Winterbourne, who denied the existence of such a person, was quite unable to discover; and he was divided between amazement at the rapidity of her induction and amusement at the frankness of her *persiflage*. She seemed to him, in all this, an extraordinary mixture of innocence and crudity. 'Does she never allow you more than three days at a time?' asked Daisy, ironically. 'Doesn't she give you a vacation in summer? There's no one so hard worked but they can get leave to go off somewhere at this season. I suppose, if you stay another day, she'll come after you in the boat. Do wait over till Friday, and I will go down to the landing to see her arrive!' Winterbourne began to think he had been wrong to feel disappointed in the temper in which the young lady had embarked. If he had missed the personal accent, the personal accent was now making its appearance. It sounded very distinctly, at last, in her telling him she would stop 'teasing' him if he would promise her solemnly to come down to Rome in the winter.

'That's not a difficult promise to make,' said Winterbourne. 'My aunt has taken an apartment in Rome for the winter, and has already asked me to come and see her.'

'I don't want you to come for your aunt,' said Daisy; 'I want you to come for me.' And this was the only allusion that the young man was ever to hear her make to his invidious kinswoman. He declared that, at any rate, he would certainly come.

After this Daisy stopped teasing. Winterbourne took a carriage, and they drove back to Vevey in the dusk; the young girl was very quiet.

In the evening Winterbourne mentioned to Mrs Costello that he had spent the afternoon at Chillon, with Miss Daisy Miller.

'The Americans – of the courier?' asked this lady.

'Ah, happily,' said Winterbourne, 'the courier stayed at home.'

'She went with you all alone?'

'All alone.'

Mrs Costello sniffed a little at her smelling-bottle. 'And that,' she exclaimed, 'is the young person you wanted me to know!'

III

WINTERBOURNE, who had returned to Geneva the day after his excursion to Chillon, went to Rome towards the end of January. His aunt had been established there for several weeks, and he had received a couple of letters from her. 'Those people you were so devoted to last summer at Vevey have turned up here, courier and all,' she wrote. 'They seem to have made several acquaintances, but the courier continues to be the most *intime*. The young lady, however, is also very intimate with some third-rate Italians, with whom she rackets about in a way that makes much talk. Bring me that pretty novel of Cherbuliez's – "Paule Méré" – and don't come later than the 23rd.'

In the natural course of events, Winterbourne, on arriving in Rome, would presently have ascertained Mrs Miller's address at the American banker's and have gone to pay his compliments to Miss Daisy. 'After what happened at Vevey I certainly think I may call upon them,' he said to Mrs Costello.

'If, after what happens – at Vevey and everywhere – you desire to keep up the acquaintance, you are very welcome. Of course a man may know every one. Men are welcome to the privilege!'

'Pray what is it that happens – here, for instance?' Winterbourne demanded.

'The girl goes about alone with her foreigners. As to what happens farther, you must apply elsewhere for information. She has picked up half-a-dozen of the regular Roman fortune-hunters, and she takes them about to people's houses. When she comes to a party she brings with her a gentleman with a good deal of manner and a wonderful moustache.'

'And where is the mother?'

'I haven't the least idea. They are very dreadful people.'

Winterbourne meditated a moment. 'They are very ignorant – very innocent only. Depend upon it they are not bad.'

'They are hopelessly vulgar,' said Mrs Costello. 'Whether or no being hopelessly vulgar is being "bad" is a question for the metaphysicians. They are bad enough to dislike, at any rate; and for this short life that is quite enough.'

The news that Daisy Miller was surrounded by half-a-dozen wonderful moustaches checked Winterbourne's impulse to go straightway to see her. He had perhaps not definitely flattered himself that he had made an ineffaceable impression upon her heart, but he was annoyed at hearing of a state of affairs so little in harmony with an image that had lately flitted in and out of his own meditations; the image of a very pretty girl looking out of an old Roman window and asking herself urgently when Mr Winterbourne would arrive. If, however, he determined to wait a little before reminding Miss Miller of his claims to her consideration, he went very soon to call upon two or three other friends. One of these friends was an American lady who had spent several winters at Geneva, where she had placed her children at school. She was a very accomplished woman and she lived in the Via Gregoriana. Winterbourne found her in a little crimson drawing-room, on a third floor; the room was filled with southern sunshine. He had not been there ten minutes when the servant came in, announcing 'Madame Mila!' This announcement was presently followed by the entrance of little Randolph Miller, who stopped in the middle of the room and stood staring at Winterbourne. An instant later his pretty sister crossed the threshold; and then, after a considerable interval, Mrs Miller slowly advanced.

'I know you!' said Randolph.

'I'm sure you know a great many things,' exclaimed Winterbourne, taking him by the hand. 'How is your education coming on?'

Daisy was exchanging greetings very prettily with her hostess; but when she heard Winterbourne's voice she quickly turned her head. 'Well, I declare!' she said.

'I told you I should come, you know,' Winterbourne rejoined, smiling.

'Well – I didn't believe it,' said Miss Daisy.

'I am much obliged to you,' laughed the young man.

'You might have come to see me!' said Daisy.

'I arrived only yesterday.'

'I don't believe that!' the young girl declared.

Winterbourne turned with a protesting smile to her mother; but this lady evaded his glance, and seating herself, fixed her eyes upon her son. 'We've got a bigger place than this,' said Randolph. 'It's all gold on the walls.'

Mrs Miller turned uneasily in her chair. 'I told you if I were to bring you, you would say something!' she murmured.

'I told *you*!' Randolph exclaimed. 'I tell *you*, sir!' he added jocosely, giving Winterbourne a thump on the knee. 'It *is* bigger, too!'

Daisy had entered upon a lively conversation with her hostess; Winterbourne judged it becoming to address a few words to her mother. 'I hope you have been well since we parted at Vevey,' he said.

Mrs Miller now certainly looked at him – at his chin. 'Not very well, sir,' she answered.

'She's got the dyspepsia,' said Randolph. 'I've got it too. Father's got it. I've got it worst!'

This announcement, instead of embarrassing Mrs Miller, seemed to relieve her. 'I suffer from the liver,' she said. 'I think it's this climate; it's less bracing than Schenectady, especially in the winter season. I don't know whether you know we reside at Schenectady. I was saying to Daisy that I certainly hadn't found any one like Dr Davis, and I didn't believe I should. Oh, at Schenectady, he stands first; they think everything of him. He has so much to do, and yet there was nothing he wouldn't do for me. He said he never saw anything like my dyspepsia, but he was bound to cure it. I'm sure there was nothing he wouldn't try. He was just going to try something new when we came off. Mr Miller wanted Daisy to see Europe for herself. But I wrote to Mr Miller that it seems as if I couldn't get on without Dr Davis. At Schenectady he stands at the very top; and there's a great deal of sickness there, too. It affects my sleep.'

Winterbourne had a good deal of pathological gossip with Dr Davis's patient, during which Daisy chattered unremittingly to her own companion. The young man asked Mrs Miller how she was pleased with Rome. 'Well, I must say I am disappointed,' she answered. 'We had heard so much about it; I suppose we had heard too much. But we couldn't help that. We had been led to expect something different.'

'Ah, wait a little, and you will become very fond of it,' said Winterbourne.

'I hate it worse and worse every day!' cried Randolph.

'You are like the infant Hannibal,' said Winterbourne.

'No, I ain't!' Randolph declared, at a venture.

'You are not much like an infant,' said his mother. 'But we have seen places,' she resumed, 'that I should put a long way before Rome.' And in reply to Winterbourne's interrogation, 'There's Zurich,' she observed; 'I think Zurich is lovely; and we hadn't heard half so much about it.'

'The best place we've seen is the City of Richmond!' said Randolph.

'He means the ship,' his mother explained. 'We crossed in that ship. Randolph had a good time on the City of Richmond.'

'It's the best place I've seen,' the child repeated. 'Only it was turned the wrong way.'

'Well, we've got to turn the right way some time,' said Mrs Miller, with a little laugh. Winterbourne expressed the hope that her daughter at least found some gratification in Rome, and she declared that Daisy was quite carried away. 'It's on account of the society – the society's splendid. She goes round everywhere; she has made a great number of acquaintances. Of course she goes round more than I do. I must say they have been very sociable; they have taken her right in. And then she knows a great many gentlemen. Oh, she thinks there's nothing like Rome. Of course, it's a great deal pleasanter for a young lady if she knows plenty of gentlemen.'

By this time Daisy had turned her attention again to Winterbourne. 'I've been telling Mrs Walker how mean you were!' the young girl announced.

'And what is the evidence you have offered?' asked Winterbourne, rather annoyed at Miss Miller's want of appreciation of the zeal of an admirer who on his way down to Rome had stopped neither at Bologna nor at Florence, simply because of a certain sentimental impatience. He remembered that a cynical compatriot had once told him that American women – the pretty ones, and this gave a largeness to the axiom – were at once the most exacting in the world and the least endowed with a sense of indebtedness.

'Why, you were awfully mean at Vevey,' said Daisy. 'You wouldn't do anything. You wouldn't stay there when I asked you.'

'My dearest young lady,' cried Winterbourne, with eloquence, 'have I come all the way to Rome to encounter your reproaches?'

'Just hear him say that!' said Daisy to her hostess, giving a twist to a bow on this lady's dress. 'Did you ever hear anything so quaint?'

'So quaint, my dear?' murmured Mrs Walker, in the tone of a partisan of Winterbourne.

'Well, I don't know,' said Daisy, fingering Mrs Walker's ribbons. 'Mrs Walker, I want to tell you something.'

'Mother,' interposed Randolph, with his rough ends to his words, 'I tell you you've got to go. Eugenio'll raise something!'

'I'm not afraid of Eugenio,' said Daisy, with a toss of her head. 'Look here, Mrs Walker,' she went on, 'you know I'm coming to your party.'

'I am delighted to hear it.'

'I've got a lovely dress.'

'I am very sure of that.'

'But I want to ask a favour – permission to bring a friend.'

'I shall be happy to see any of your friends,' said Mrs Walker, turning with a smile to Mrs Miller.

'Oh, they are not my friends,' answered Daisy's mamma, smiling shyly, in her own fashion. 'I never spoke to them!'

'It's an intimate friend of mine – Mr Giovanelli,' said Daisy, without a tremor in her clear little voice or a shadow on her brilliant little face.

Mrs Walker was silent a moment, she gave a rapid glance at Winterbourne. 'I shall be glad to see Mr Giovanelli,' she then said.

'He's an Italian,' Daisy pursued, with the prettiest serenity. 'He's a great friend of mine – he's the handsomest man in the world – except Mr Winterbourne! He knows plenty of Italians, but he wants to know some Americans. He thinks ever so much of Americans. He's tremendously clever. He's perfectly lovely!'

It was settled that this brilliant personage should be brought to Mrs Walker's party, and then Mrs Miller prepared to take her leave. 'I guess we'll go back to the hotel,' she said.

'You may go back to the hotel, mother, but I'm going to take a walk,' said Daisy.

'She's going to walk with Mr Giovanelli,' Randolph proclaimed.

'I am going to the Pincio,' said Daisy, smiling.

'Alone, my dear – at this hour?' Mrs Walker asked. The afternoon was drawing to a close – it was the hour for the throng of carriages and of contemplative pedestrians. 'I don't think it's safe, my dear,' said Mrs Walker.

'Neither do I,' subjoined Mrs Miller. 'You'll get the fever as sure as you live. Remember what Dr Davis told you!'

'Give her some medicine before she goes,' said Randolph.

The company had risen to its feet; Daisy, still showing her pretty teeth, bent over and kissed her hostess. 'Mrs Walker, you are too perfect,' she said. 'I'm not going alone; I am going to meet a friend.'

'Your friend won't keep you from getting the fever,' Mrs Miller observed.

'Is it Mr Giovanelli?' asked the hostess.

Winterbourne was watching the young girl; at this question his attention quickened. She stood there smiling and smoothing her bonnet-ribbons; she glanced at Winterbourne. Then, while she glanced and smiled, she answered without a shade of hesitation, 'Mr Giovanelli – the beautiful Giovanelli.'

'My dear young friend,' said Mrs Walker, taking her hand, pleadingly, 'don't walk off to the Pincio at this hour to meet a beautiful Italian.'

'Well, he speaks English,' said Mrs Miller.

'Gracious me!' Daisy exclaimed, 'I don't want to do anything improper. There's an easy way to settle it.' She continued to glance at Winterbourne. 'The Pincio is only a hundred yards distant, and if Mr Winterbourne were as polite as he pretends he would offer to walk with me!'

Winterbourne's politeness hastened to affirm itself, and the young girl gave him gracious leave to accompany her. They passed down-stairs before her mother, and at the door Winterbourne perceived Mrs Miller's carriage drawn up, with the ornamental courier whose acquaintance he had made at Vevey seated within. 'Good-bye, Eugenio!' cried Daisy, 'I'm going to take a walk.' The distance from the Via Gregoriana to the beautiful garden at the other end of the Pincian Hill is, in fact, rapidly traversed. As the day was splendid, however, and the concourse of vehicles, walkers, and loungers numerous, the young Americans found their progress much delayed. This fact was highly agreeable to Winterbourne, in spite of his consciousness of his singular situation. The slow-moving, idly gazing Roman crowd bestowed much attention upon the extremely pretty young foreign lady who was passing through it upon his arm; and he wondered what on earth had been in Daisy's mind when she proposed to expose herself, unattended, to its appreciation. His own mission, to her sense, apparently, was to consign her to the hands of Mr Giovanelli; but Winterbourne, at once annoyed and gratified, resolved that he would do no such thing.

'Why haven't you been to see me?' asked Daisy. 'You can't get out of that.'

'I have had the honour of telling you that I have only just stepped out of the train.'

'You must have stayed in the train a good while after it stopped!' cried the young girl, with her little laugh. 'I suppose you were asleep. You have had time to go to see Mrs Walker.'

'I knew Mrs Walker –' Winterbourne began to explain.

'I knew where you knew her. You knew her at Geneva. She told me so. Well, you knew me at Vevey. That's just as good. So you ought to have come.' She asked him no other question than this; she began to prattle about her own affairs. 'We've got splendid rooms at the hotel; Eugenio says they're the best rooms in Rome. We are going to stay all winter – if we don't die of the fever; and I guess we'll stay then. It's a great deal nicer than I thought; I thought it would be fearfully quiet; I was sure it would be awfully poky. I was sure we should be going round all the time with one of those dreadful old men that explain about the pictures and things. But we only had about a week of that, and now I'm enjoying myself. I know ever so many people, and they are all so charming. The society's extremely select. There are all kinds – English, and Germans, and Italians. I think I like the English best. I like their style of conversation. But there are some lovely Americans. I never saw anything so hospitable. There's something or other every day. There's not much dancing; but I must say I never thought dancing was everything. I was always fond of conversation. I guess I shall have plenty at Mrs Walker's – her rooms are so small.' When they had passed the gate of the Pincian Gardens, Miss Miller began to wonder where Mr Giovanelli might be. 'We had better go straight to that place in front,' she said, 'where you look at the view.'

'I certainly shall not help you to find him,' Winterbourne declared.

'Then I shall find him without you,' said Miss Daisy.

'You certainly won't leave me!' cried Winterbourne.

She burst into her little laugh. 'Are you afraid you'll get lost – or run over? But there's Giovanelli, leaning against that tree. He's staring at the women in the carriages: did you ever see anything so cool?'

Winterbourne perceived at some distance a little man standing with folded arms, nursing his cane. He had a handsome
face, an artfully poised hat, a glass in one eye and a nosegay in
his button-hole. Winterbourne looked at him a moment and
then said, 'Do you mean to speak to that man?'

'Do I mean to speak to him? Why, you don't suppose I mean
to communicate by signs?'

'Pray understand, then,' said Winterbourne, 'that I intend
to remain with you.'

Daisy stopped and looked at him, without a sign of troubled
consciousness in her face; with nothing but the presence of her
charming eyes and her happy dimples. 'Well, she's a cool one!'
thought the young man.

'I don't like the way you say that,' said Daisy. 'It's too
imperious.'

'I beg your pardon if I say it wrong. The main point is to give
you an idea of my meaning.'

The young girl looked at him more gravely, but with eyes
that were prettier than ever. 'I have never allowed a gentleman
to dictate to me, or to interfere with anything I do.'

'I think you have made a mistake,' said Winterbourne. 'You
should sometimes listen to a gentleman – the right one?'

Daisy began to laugh again. 'I do nothing but listen to
gentlemen!' she exclaimed. 'Tell me if Mr Giovanelli is the
right one.'

The gentleman with the nosegay in his bosom had now
perceived our two friends, and was approaching the young
girl with obsequious rapidity. He bowed to Winterbourne as
well as to the latter's companion; he had a brilliant smile, an
intelligent eye; Winterbourne thought him not a bad-looking
fellow. But he nevertheless said to Daisy – 'No, he's not the
right one.'

Daisy evidently had a natural talent for performing introductions; she mentioned the name of each of her companions
to the other. She strolled along with one of them on each side of
her; Mr Giovanelli, who spoke English very cleverly – Winterbourne afterwards learned that he had practised the idiom
upon a great many American heiresses – addressed her a great

deal of very polite nonsense; he was extremely urbane, and the young American, who said nothing, reflected upon that profundity of Italian cleverness which enables people to appear more gracious in proportion as they are more acutely disappointed. Giovanelli, of course, had counted upon something more intimate; he had not bargained for a party of three. But he kept his temper in a manner which suggested far-stretching intentions. Winterbourne flattered himself that he had taken his measure. 'He is not a gentleman,' said the young American; 'he is only a clever imitation of one. He is a music-master, or a penny-a-liner, or a third-rate artist. Damn his good looks!' Mr Giovanelli had certainly a very pretty face; but Winterbourne felt a superior indignation at his own lovely fellow-countrywoman's not knowing the difference between a spurious gentleman and a real one. Giovanelli chattered and jested and made himself wonderfully agreeable. It was true that if he was an imitation the imitation was very skilful. 'Nevertheless,' Winterbourne said to himself, 'a nice girl ought to know!' And then he came back to the question whether this was in fact a nice girl. Would a nice girl – even allowing for her being a little American flirt – make a rendezvous with a presumably low-lived foreigner? The rendezvous in this case, indeed, had been in broad daylight, and in the most crowded corner of Rome; but was it not impossible to regard the choice of these circumstances as a proof of extreme cynicism? Singular though it may seem, Winterbourne was vexed that the young girl, in joining her *amoroso*, should not appear more impatient of his own company, and he was vexed because of his inclination. It was impossible to regard her as a perfectly well-conducted young lady; she was wanting in a certain indispensable delicacy. It would therefore simplify matters greatly to be able to treat her as the object of one of those sentiments which are called by romancers 'lawless passions'. That she should seem to wish to get rid of him would help him to think more lightly of her, and to be able to think more lightly of her would make her much less perplexing. But Daisy, on this occasion, continued to present herself as an inscrutable combination of audacity and innocence.

She had been walking some quarter of an hour, attended by her two cavaliers, and responding in a tone of very childish gaiety, as it seemed to Winterbourne, to the pretty speeches of Mr Giovanelli, when a carriage that had detached itself from the revolving train drew up beside the path. At the same moment Winterbourne perceived that his friend Mrs Walker – the lady whose house he had lately left – was seated in the vehicle and was beckoning to him. Leaving Miss Miller's side, he hastened to obey her summons. Mrs Walker was flushed; she wore an excited air. 'It is really too dreadful,' she said. 'That girl must not do this sort of thing. She must not walk here with you two men. Fifty people have noticed her.'

Winterbourne raised his eyebrows. 'I think it's a pity to make too much fuss about it.'

'It's a pity to let the girl ruin herself!'

'She is very innocent,' said Winterbourne.

'She's very crazy!' cried Mrs Walker. 'Did you ever see anything so imbecile as her mother? After you had all left me, just now, I could not sit still for thinking of it. It seemed too pitiful, not even to attempt to save her. I ordered the carriage and put on my bonnet, and came here as quickly as possible. Thank Heaven I have found you!'

'What do you propose to do with us?' asked Winterbourne, smiling.

'To ask her to get in, to drive her about here for half-an-hour, so that the world may see she is not running absolutely wild, and then to take her safely home.'

'I don't think it's a very happy thought,' said Winterbourne; 'but you can try.'

Mrs Walker tried. The young man went in pursuit of Miss Miller, who had simply nodded and smiled at his interlocutrix in the carriage and had gone her way with her own companion. Daisy, on learning that Mrs Walker wished to speak to her, retraced her steps with a perfect good grace and with Mr Giovanelli at her side. She declared that she was delighted to have a chance to present this gentleman to Mrs Walker. She immediately achieved the introduction, and declared that she had never in her life seen anything so lovely as Mrs Walker's carriage-rug.

'I am glad you admire it,' said this lady, smiling sweetly. 'Will you get in and let me put it over you?'

'Oh, no, thank you,' said Daisy. 'I shall admire it much more as I see you driving round with it.'

'Do get in and drive with me,' said Mrs Walker.

'That would be charming, but it's so enchanting just as I am!' and Daisy gave a brilliant glance at the gentlemen on either side of her.

'It may be enchanting, dear child, but it is not the custom here,' urged Mrs Walker, leaning forward in her victoria with her hands devoutly clasped.

'Well, it ought to be, then!' said Daisy. 'If I didn't walk I should expire.'

'You should walk with your mother, dear,' cried the lady from Geneva, losing patience.

'With my mother dear!' exclaimed the young girl. Winterbourne saw that she scented interference. 'My mother never walked ten steps in her life. And then, you know,' she added with a laugh, 'I am more than five years old.'

'You are old enough to be more reasonable. You are old enough, dear Miss Miller, to be talked about.'

Daisy looked at Mrs Walker, smiling intensely. 'Talked about? What do you mean?'

'Come into my carriage and I will tell you.'

Daisy turned her quickened glance again from one of the gentlemen beside her to the other. Mr Giovanelli was bowing to and fro, rubbing down his gloves and laughing very agreeably; Winterbourne thought it a most unpleasant scene. 'I don't think I want to know what you mean,' said Daisy presently. 'I don't think I should like it.'

Winterbourne wished that Mrs Walker would tuck in her carriage-rug and drive away; but this lady did not enjoy being defied, as she afterwards told him. 'Should you prefer being thought a very reckless girl?' she demanded.

'Gracious me!' exclaimed Daisy. She looked again at Mr Giovanelli, then she turned to Winterbourne. There was a little pink flush in her cheek; she was tremendously pretty. 'Does Mr Winterbourne think,' she asked slowly, smiling, throwing back her head and glancing at him from head to foot, 'that – to save my reputation – I ought to get into the carriage?'

Winterbourne coloured; for an instant he hesitated greatly. It seemed so strange to hear her speak that way of her 'reputation'. But he himself, in fact, must speak in accordance with gallantry. The finest gallantry, here, was simply to tell her the truth; and the truth, for Winterbourne, as the few indications I have been able to give have made him known to the reader, was that Daisy Miller should take Mrs Walker's advice. He looked at her exquisite prettiness; and then he said very gently, 'I think you should get into the carriage.'

Daisy gave a violent laugh. 'I never heard anything so stiff! If this is improper, Mrs Walker,' she pursued, 'then I am all improper, and you must give me up. Good-bye; I hope you'll have a lovely ride!' and, with Mr Giovanelli, who made a triumphantly obsequious salute, she turned away.

Mrs Walker sat looking after her, and there were tears in Mrs Walker's eyes. 'Get in here, sir,' she said to Winterbourne, indicating the place beside her. The young man answered that he felt bound to accompany Miss Miller; whereupon Mrs Walker declared that if he refused her this favour she would never speak to him again. She was evidently in earnest. Winterbourne overtook Daisy and her companion, and, offering the young girl his hand, told her that Mrs Walker had made an imperious claim upon his society. He expected that in answer she would say something rather free, something to commit herself still farther to that 'recklessness' from which Mrs Walker had so charitably endeavoured to dissuade her. But she only shook his hand, hardly looking at him, while Mr Giovanelli bade him farewell with a too emphatic flourish of the hat.

Winterbourne was not in the best possible humour as he took his seat in Mrs Walker's victoria. 'That was not clever of you,' he said candidly, while the vehicle mingled again with the throng of carriages.

'In such a case,' his companion answered, 'I don't wish to be clever, I wish to be *earnest!*'

'Well, your earnestness has only offended her and put her off.'

'It has happened very well,' said Mrs Walker. 'If she is so perfectly determined to compromise herself, the sooner one knows it the better; one can act accordingly.'

'I suspect she meant no harm,' Winterbourne rejoined.

'So I thought a month ago. But she has been going too far.'

'What has she been doing?'

'Everything that is not done here. Flirting with any man she could pick up; sitting in corners with mysterious Italians; dancing all the evening with the same partners; receiving visits at eleven o'clock at night. Her mother goes away when visitors come.'

'But her brother,' said Winterbourne, laughing, 'sits up till midnight.'

'He must be edified by what he sees. I'm told that at their hotel every one is talking about her, and that a smile goes round among the servants when a gentleman comes and asks for Miss Miller.'

'The servants be hanged!' said Winterbourne angrily. 'The poor girl's only fault,' he presently added, 'is that she is very uncultivated.'

'She is naturally indelicate,' Mrs Walker declared. 'Take that example this morning. How long had you known her at Vevey?'

'A couple of days.'

'Fancy, then, her making it a personal matter that you should have left the place!'

Winterbourne was silent for some moments; then he said, 'I suspect, Mrs Walker, that you and I have lived too long at Geneva!' And he added a request that she should inform him with what particular design she had made him enter her carriage.

'I wished to beg you to cease your relations with Miss Miller – not to flirt with her – to give her no farther opportunity to expose herself – to let her alone, in short.'

'I'm afraid I can't do that,' said Winterbourne. 'I like her extremely.'

'All the more reason that you shouldn't help her to make a scandal.'

'There shall be nothing scandalous in my attentions to her.'

'There certainly will be in the way she takes them. But I have said what I had on my conscience,' Mrs Walker pursued. 'If you wish to rejoin the young lady I will put you down. Here, by-the-way, you have a chance.'

The carriage was traversing that part of the Pincian Garden which overhangs the wall of Rome and overlooks the beautiful Villa Borghese. It is bordered by a large parapet, near which there are several seats. One of the seats, at a distance, was occupied by a gentleman and a lady, towards whom Mrs Walker gave a toss of her head. At the same moment these persons rose and walked towards the parapet. Winterbourne had asked the coachman to stop; he now descended from the carriage. His companion looked at him a moment in silence; then, while he raised his hat, she drove majestically away. Winterbourne stood there; he had turned his eyes towards Daisy and her cavalier. They evidently saw no one; they were too deeply occupied with each other. When they reached the low garden-wall they stood a moment looking off at the great flat-topped pine-clusters of the Villa Borghese; then Giovanelli seated himself familiarly upon the broad ledge of the wall. The western sun in the opposite sky sent out a brilliant shaft through a couple of cloud-bars; whereupon Daisy's companion took her parasol out of her hands and opened it. She came a little nearer and he held the parasol over her; then, still holding it, he let it rest upon her shoulder, so that both of their heads were hidden from Winterbourne. This young man lingered a moment, then he began to walk. But he walked – not towards the couple with the parasol; towards the residence of his aunt, Mrs Costello.

IV

HE flattered himself on the following day that there was no smiling among the servants when he, at least, asked for Mrs Miller at her hotel. This lady and her daughter, however, were not at home; and on the next day after, repeating his visit,

Winterbourne again had the misfortune not to find them. Mrs Walker's party took place on the evening of the third day, and in spite of the frigidity of his last interview with the hostess Winterbourne was among the guests. Mrs Walker was one of those American ladies who, while residing abroad, make a point, in their own phrase, of studying European society; and she had on this occasion collected several specimens of her diversely-born fellow-mortals to serve, as it were, as text-books. When Winterbourne arrived Daisy Miller was not there; but in a few moments he saw her mother come in alone, very shyly and ruefully. Mrs Miller's hair, above her exposed-looking temples, was more frizzled than ever. As she approached Mrs Walker, Winterbourne also drew near.

'You see I've come all alone,' said poor Mrs Miller. 'I'm so frightened; I don't know what to do; it's the first time I've ever been to a party alone – especially in this country. I wanted to bring Randolph or Eugenio, or some one, but Daisy just pushed me off by myself. I ain't used to going round alone.'

'And does not your daughter intend to favour us with her society?' demanded Mrs Walker, impressively.

'Well, Daisy's all dressed,' said Mrs Miller, with that accent of the dispassionate, if not of the philosophic, historian with which she always recorded the current incidents of her daughter's career. 'She got dressed on purpose before dinner. But she's got a friend of hers there; that gentleman – the Italian – that she wanted to bring. They've got going at the piano; it seems as if they couldn't leave off. Mr Giovanelli sings splendidly. But I guess they'll come before very long,' concluded Mrs Miller hopefully.

'I'm sorry she should come – in that way,' said Mrs Walker.

'Well, I told her that there was no use in her getting dressed before dinner if she was going to wait three hours,' responded Daisy's mamma. 'I didn't see the use of her putting on such a dress as that to sit round with Mr Giovanelli.'

'This is most horrible!' said Mrs Walker, turning away and addressing herself to Winterbourne. '*Elle s'affiche*. It's her revenge for my having ventured to remonstrate with her. When she comes I shall not speak to her.'

Daisy came after eleven o'clock, but she was not, on such an occasion, a young lady to wait to be spoken to. She rustled forward in radiant loveliness, smiling and chattering, carrying a large bouquet and attended by Mr Giovanelli. Every one stopped talking, and turned and looked at her. She came straight to Mrs Walker. 'I'm afraid you thought I never was coming, so I sent mother off to tell you. I wanted to make Mr Giovanelli practise some things before he came; you know he sings beautifully, and I want you to ask him to sing. This is Mr Giovanelli; you know I introduced him to you; he's got the most lovely voice and he knows the most charming set of songs. I made him go over them this evening, on purpose; we had the greatest time at the hotel.' Of all this Daisy delivered herself with the sweetest, brightest audibleness, looking now at her hostess and now round the room, while she gave a series of little pats, round her shoulders, to the edges of her dress. 'Is there any one I know?' she asked.

'I think every one knows you!' said Mrs Walker pregnantly, and she gave a very cursory greeting to Mr Giovanelli. This gentleman bore himself gallantly. He smiled and bowed and showed his white teeth, he curled his moustaches and rolled his eyes, and performed all the proper functions of a handsome Italian at an evening party. He sang, very prettily, half-a-dozen songs, though Mrs Walker afterwards declared that she had been quite unable to find out who asked him. It was apparently not Daisy who had given him his orders. Daisy sat at a distance from the piano, and though she had publicly, as it were, professed a high admiration for his singing, talked, not inaudibly, while it was going on.

'It's a pity these rooms are so small; we can't dance,' she said to Winterbourne, as if she had seen him five minutes before.

'I am not sorry we can't dance,' Winterbourne answered; 'I don't dance.'

'Of course you don't dance; you're too stiff,' said Miss Daisy. 'I hope you enjoyed your drive with Mrs Walker.'

'No, I didn't enjoy it; I preferred walking with you.'

'We paired off, that was much better,' said Daisy. 'But did you ever hear anything so cool as Mrs Walker's wanting me to get into her carriage and drop poor Mr Giovanelli; and under the pretext that it was proper? People have different ideas! It would have been most unkind; he had been talking about that walk for ten days.'

'He should not have talked about it at all,' said Winterbourne; 'he would never have proposed to a young lady of this country to walk about the streets with him.'

'About the streets?' cried Daisy, with her pretty stare. 'Where then would he have proposed to her to walk? The Pincio is not the streets, either; and I, thank goodness, am not a young lady of this country. The young ladies of this country have a dreadfully poky time of it, so far as I can learn; I don't see why I should change my habits for *them*.'

'I am afraid your habits are those of a flirt,' said Winterbourne gravely.

'Of course they are,' she cried, giving him her little smiling stare again. 'I'm a fearful, frightful flirt! Did you ever hear of a nice girl that was not? But I suppose you will tell me now that I am not a nice girl.'

'You're a very nice girl, but I wish you would flirt with me, and me only,' said Winterbourne.

'Ah! thank you, thank you very much; you are the last man I should think of flirting with. As I have had the pleasure of informing you, you are too stiff.'

'You say that too often,' said Winterbourne.

Daisy gave a delighted laugh. 'If I could have the sweet hope of making you angry, I would say it again.'

'Don't do that; when I am angry I'm stiffer than ever. But if you won't flirt with me, do cease at least to flirt with your friend at the piano; they don't understand that sort of thing here.'

'I thought they understood nothing else!' exclaimed Daisy.

'Not in young unmarried women.'

'It seems to me much more proper in young unmarried women than in old married ones,' Daisy declared.

'Well,' said Winterbourne, 'when you deal with natives you must go by the custom of the place. Flirting is a purely American custom; it doesn't exist here. So when you show yourself in public with Mr Giovanelli and without your mother —'

'Gracious! poor mother!' interposed Daisy.

'Though you may be flirting, Mr Giovanelli is not; he means something else.'

'He isn't preaching, at any rate,' said Daisy with vivacity. 'And if you want very much to know, we are neither of us flirting; we are too good friends for that; we are very intimate friends.'

'Ah!' rejoined Winterbourne, 'if you are in love with each other it is another affair.'

She had allowed him up to this point to talk so frankly that he had no expectation of shocking her by this ejaculation; but she immediately got up, blushing visibly, and leaving him to exclaim mentally that little American flirts were the queerest creatures in the world. 'Mr Giovanelli, at least,' she said, giving her interlocutor a single glance, 'never says such very disagreeable things to me.'

Winterbourne was bewildered; he stood staring. Mr Giovanelli had finished singing; he left the piano and came over to Daisy. 'Won't you come into the other room and have some tea?' he asked, bending before her with his decorative smile.

Daisy turned to Winterbourne, beginning to smile again. He was still more perplexed, for this inconsequent smile made nothing clear, though it seemed to prove, indeed, that she had a sweetness and softness that reverted instinctively to the pardon of offences. 'It has never occurred to Mr Winterbourne to offer me any tea,' she said, with her little tormenting manner.

'I have offered you advice,' Winterbourne rejoined.

'I prefer weak tea!' cried Daisy, and she went off with the brilliant Giovanelli. She sat with him in the adjoining room, in the embrasure of the window, for the rest of the evening. There was an interesting performance at the piano, but neither of these young people gave heed to it. When Daisy came to take leave of Mrs Walker, this lady conscientiously repaired the weakness of which she had been guilty at the moment of the young girl's arrival. She turned her back straight upon Miss Miller and left her to depart with what grace she might. Winterbourne was standing near the door; he saw it all. Daisy turned very pale and looked at her mother, but Mrs Miller was humbly unconscious of any violation of the usual social forms. She appeared, indeed, to have felt an incongruous impulse to draw attention to her own striking observance of them. 'Good night, Mrs Walker,' she said; 'we've had a beautiful evening. You see if I let Daisy come to parties without me, I don't want her to go away without me.' Daisy turned away, looking with a pale, grave face at the circle near the door; Winterbourne saw that, for the first moment, she was too much shocked and puzzled even for indignation. He on his side was greatly touched.

'That was very cruel,' he said to Mrs Walker.

'She never enters my drawing-room again,' replied his hostess.

Since Winterbourne was not to meet her in Mrs Walker's drawing-room, he went as often as possible to Mrs Miller's hotel. The ladies were rarely at home, but when he found them the devoted Giovanelli was always present. Very often the polished little Roman was in the drawing-room with Daisy alone, Mrs Miller being apparently constantly of the opinion that discretion is the better part of surveillance. Winterbourne noted, at first with surprise, that Daisy on these occasions was never embarrassed or annoyed by his own entrance; but he very presently began to feel that she had no more surprises for him; the unexpected in her behaviour was the only thing to expect. She showed no displeasure at her *tête-à-tête* with Giovanelli being interrupted; she could chatter as freshly and freely with two gentlemen as with one; there was always in her conversation, the same odd mixture of audacity and puerility. Winterbourne remarked to himself that if she was seriously interested in Giovanelli it was very singular that she should not take more trouble to preserve the sanctity of their interviews, and he liked her the more for her innocent-looking indifference and her apparently inexhaustible good humour. He could hardly have said why, but she seemed to him a girl who would never be jealous. At the risk of exciting a somewhat derisive smile on the reader's part, I may affirm that with regard to the women who had hitherto interested him it very often seemed to Winterbourne among the possibilities that, given certain contingencies, he should be afraid – literally afraid – of these ladies. He had a pleasant sense that he should never be afraid of Daisy Miller. It must be added that this sentiment was not altogether flattering to Daisy; it was part of his conviction, or rather of his apprehension, that she would prove a very light young person.

But she was evidently very much interested in Giovanelli. She looked at him whenever he spoke; she was perpetually telling him to do this and to do that; she was constantly 'chaffing' and abusing him. She appeared completely to have forgotten that Winterbourne had said anything to displease her at Mrs Walker's little party. One Sunday afternoon, having gone to St Peter's with his aunt, Winterbourne perceived Daisy strolling about the great church in company with the inevitable Giovanelli. Presently he pointed out the young girl and her cavalier to Mrs Costello. This lady looked at them a moment through her eyeglass, and then she said:

'That's what makes you so pensive in these days, eh?'

'I had not the least idea I was pensive,' said the young man.

'You are very much pre-occupied, you are thinking of something.'

'And what is it,' he asked, 'that you accuse me of thinking of?'

'Of that young lady's – Miss Baker's, Miss Chandler's – what's her name? – Miss Miller's intrigue with that little barber's block.'

'Do you call it an intrigue,' Winterbourne asked – 'an affair that goes on with such peculiar publicity?'

'That's their folly,' said Mrs Costello, 'it's not their merit.'

'No,' rejoined Winterbourne, with something of that pensiveness to which his aunt had alluded. 'I don't believe that there is anything to be called an intrigue.'

'I have heard a dozen people speak of it; they say she is quite carried away by him.'

'They are certainly very intimate,' said Winterbourne.

Mrs Costello inspected the young couple again with her optical instrument. 'He is very handsome. One easily sees how it is. She thinks him the most elegant man in the world, the finest gentleman. She has never seen anything like him; he is better even than the courier. It was the courier probably who introduced him, and if he succeeds in marrying the young lady, the courier will come in for a magnificent commission.'

'I don't believe she thinks of marrying him,' said Winterbourne, 'and I don't believe he hopes to marry her.'

'You may be very sure she thinks of nothing. She goes on from day to day, from hour to hour, as they did in the Golden Age. I can imagine nothing more vulgar. And at the same time,' added Mrs Costello, 'depend upon it that she may tell you any moment that she is "engaged".'

'I think that is more than Giovanelli expects,' said Winterbourne.

'Who is Giovanelli?'

'The little Italian. I have asked questions about him and learned something. He is apparently a perfectly respectable little man. I believe he is in a small way a *cavaliere avvocato*. But he doesn't move in what are called the first circles. I think it is really not absolutely impossible that the courier introduced him. He is evidently immensely charmed with Miss Miller. If she thinks him the finest gentleman in the world, he, on his side, has never found himself in personal contact with such splendour, such opulence, such expensiveness, as this young lady's. And then she must seem to him wonderfully pretty and interesting. I rather doubt whether he dreams of marrying her. That must appear to him too impossible a piece of luck. He has nothing but his handsome face to offer, and there is a substantial Mr Miller in that mysterious land of dollars. Giovanelli knows that he hasn't a title to offer. If he were only a count or a *marchese*! He must wonder at his luck at the way they have taken him up.'

'He accounts for it by his handsome face, and thinks Miss Miller a young lady *qui se passe ses fantaisies*!' said Mrs Costello.

'It is very true,' Winterbourne pursued, 'that Daisy and her mamma have not yet risen to that stage of – what shall I call it? – of culture, at which the idea of catching a count or a *marchese* begins. I believe that they are intellectually incapable of that conception.'

'Ah! but the *cavaliere* can't believe it,' said Mrs Costello.

Of the observation excited by Daisy's 'intrigue', Winterbourne gathered that day at St Peter's sufficient evidence. A dozen of the American colonists in Rome came to talk with Mrs Costello, who sat on a little portable stool at the base of one of the great pilasters. The vesper-service was going forward in splendid chants and organ-tones in the adjacent choir, and meanwhile, between Mrs Costello and her friends, there was a great deal said about poor little Miss Miller's going really 'too far'. Winterbourne was not pleased with what he heard; but when, coming out upon the great steps of the church, he saw Daisy, who had emerged before him, get into an open cab with her accomplice and roll away through the cynical streets of Rome, he could not deny to himself that she was going very far indeed. He felt very sorry for her – not exactly that he believed that she had completely lost her head, but because it was painful to hear so much that was pretty and undefended and natural assigned to a vulgar place among the categories of disorder. He made an attempt after this to give a hint to Mrs Miller. He met one day in the Corso a friend – a tourist like himself – who had just come out of the Doria Palace, where he had been walking through the beautiful gallery. His friend talked for a moment about the superb portrait of Innocent X. by Velasquez, which hangs in one of the cabinets of the palace, and then said, 'And in the same cabinet, by-the-way, I had the pleasure of contemplating a picture of a different kind – that pretty American girl whom you pointed out to me last week.' In answer to Winterbourne's inquiries, his friend narrated that the pretty American girl – prettier than ever – was seated with a companion in the secluded nook in which the great papal portrait is enshrined.

'Who was her companion?' asked Winterbourne.

'A little Italian with a bouquet in his button-hole. The girl is delightfully pretty, but I thought I understood from you the other day that she was a young lady *du meilleur monde*.'

'So she is!' answered Winterbourne; and having assured himself that his informant had seen Daisy and her companion but five minutes before, he jumped into a cab and went to call on Mrs Miller. She was at home; but she apologised to him for receiving him in Daisy's absence.

'She's gone out somewhere with Mr Giovanelli,' said Mrs Miller. 'She's always going round with Mr Giovanelli.'

'I have noticed that they are very intimate,' Winterbourne observed.

'Oh! it seems as if they couldn't live without each other!' said Mrs Miller. 'Well, he's a real gentleman, anyhow. I keep telling Daisy she's engaged!'

'And what does Daisy say?'

'Oh, she says she isn't engaged. But she might as well be!' this impartial parent resumed. 'She goes on as if she was. But I've made Mr Giovanelli promise to tell me, if *she* doesn't. I should want to write to Mr Miller about it – shouldn't you?'

Winterbourne replied that he certainly should; and the state of mind of Daisy's mamma struck him as so unprecedented in the annals of parental vigilance that he gave up as utterly irrelevant the attempt to place her upon her guard.

After this Daisy was never at home, and Winterbourne ceased to meet her at the houses of their common acquaintance, because, as he perceived, these shrewd people had quite made up their minds that she was going too far. They ceased to invite her, and they intimated that they desired to express to observant Europeans the great truth that, though Miss Daisy Miller was a young American lady, her behaviour was not representative – was regarded by her compatriots as abnormal. Winterbourne wondered how she felt about all the cold shoulders that were turned towards her, and sometimes it annoyed him to suspect that she did not feel at all. He said to himself that she was too light and childish, too uncultivated and unreasoning, too provincial, to have reflected upon her ostracism or even to have perceived it. Then at other moments he believed that she carried about in her elegant and irresponsible little organism a defiant, passionate, perfectly observant consciousness of the impression she produced. He asked himself whether Daisy's defiance came from the consciousness of innocence or from her being, essentially, a young person of the reckless class. It must be admitted that holding oneself to a belief in Daisy's 'innocence' came to seem to Winterbourne more and more a matter of fine-spun gallantry. As I have already had occasion to relate, he was angry at finding himself reduced to chopping logic about this young lady; he was vexed at his want of instinctive certitude as to how far her eccentricities were generic, national, and how far they were personal. From either view of them he had somehow missed her, and now it was too late. She was 'carried away' by Mr Giovanelli.

A few days after his brief interview with her mother, he encountered her in that beautiful abode of flowering desolation known as the Palace of the Caesars. The early Roman spring had filled the air with bloom and perfume, and the rugged surface of the Palatine was muffled with tender verdure. Daisy was strolling along the top of one of those great mounds of ruin that are embanked with mossy marble and paved with monumental inscriptions. It seemed to him that Rome had never been so lovely as just then. He stood looking off at the enchanting harmony of line and colour that remotely encircles the city, inhaling the softly humid odours and feeling the freshness of the year and the antiquity of the place reaffirm themselves in mysterious interfusion. It seemed to him also that Daisy had never looked so pretty; but this had been an observation of his whenever he met her. Giovanelli was at her side, and Giovanelli, too, wore an aspect of even unwonted brilliancy.

'Well,' said Daisy, 'I should think you would be lonesome!'

'Lonesome?' asked Winterbourne.

'You are always going round by yourself. Can't you get any one to walk with you?'

'I am not so fortunate,' said Winterbourne, 'as your companion.'

Giovanelli, from the first, had treated Winterbourne with distinguished politeness; he listened with a deferential air to his remarks; he laughed, punctiliously, at his pleasantries; he seemed disposed to testify to his belief that Winterbourne was a superior young man. He carried himself in no degree like a jealous wooer; he had obviously a great deal of tact; he had no objection to your expecting a little humility of him. It even seemed to Winterbourne at times that Giovanelli would find

a certain mental relief in being able to have a private understanding with him – to say to him, as an intelligent man, that,
bless you, *he* knew how extraordinary was this young lady, and
didn't flatter himself with delusive – or at least *too* delusive –
hopes of matrimony and dollars. On this occasion he strolled
away from his companion to pluck a sprig of almond-blossom,
which he carefully arranged in his button-hole.

'I know why you say that,' said Daisy, watching Giovanelli.
'Because you think I go round too much with *him*!' And she
nodded at her attendant.

'Every one thinks so – if you care to know,' said Winterbourne.

'Of course I care to know!' Daisy exclaimed seriously. 'But
I don't believe it. They are only pretending to be shocked. They
don't really care a straw what I do. Besides, I don't go round so
much.'

'I think you will find they do care. They will show it –
disagreeably.'

Daisy looked at him a moment. 'How – disagreeably?'

'Haven't you noticed anything?' Winterbourne asked.

'I have noticed you. But I noticed you were as stiff as an
umbrella the first time I saw you.'

'You will find I am not so stiff as several others,' said Winterbourne, smiling.

'How shall I find it?'

'By going to see the others.'

'What will they do to me?'

'They will give you the cold shoulder. Do you know what
that means?'

Daisy was looking at him intently; she began to colour. 'Do
you mean as Mrs Walker did the other night?'

'Exactly!' said Winterbourne.

She looked away at Giovanelli, who was decorating himself
with his almond-blossom. Then looking back at Winterbourne
– 'I shouldn't think you would let people be so unkind!' she
said.

'How can I help it?' he asked.

'I should think you would say something.'

'I do say something.' And he paused a moment. 'I say that your mother tells me that she believes you are engaged.'

'Well, she does,' said Daisy very simply.

Winterbourne began to laugh. 'And does Randolph believe it?' he asked.

'I guess Randolph doesn't believe anything,' said Daisy. Randolph's scepticism excited Winterbourne to farther hilarity, and he observed that Giovanelli was coming back to them. Daisy, observing it too, addressed herself again to her countryman. 'Since you have mentioned it,' she said, 'I *am* engaged.' . . . Winterbourne looked at her; he had stopped laughing. 'You don't believe it!' she added.

He was silent a moment; and then, 'Yes, I believe it!' he said.

'Oh, no, you don't,' she answered. 'Well, then – I am not!'

The young girl and her cicerone were on their way to the gate of the enclosure, so that Winterbourne, who had but lately entered, presently took leave of them. A week afterwards he went to dine at a beautiful villa on the Caelian Hill, and, on arriving, dismissed his hired vehicle. The evening was charming, and he promised himself the satisfaction of walking home beneath the Arch of Constantine and past the vaguely lighted monuments of the Forum. There was a waning moon in the sky, and her radiance was not brilliant, but she was veiled in a thin cloud-curtain which seemed to diffuse and equalise it. When, on his return from the villa (it was eleven o'clock), Winterbourne approached the dusky circle of the Colosseum, it occurred to him, as a lover of the picturesque, that the interior, in the pale moonshine, would be well worth a glance. He turned aside and walked to one of the empty arches, near which, as he observed, an open carriage – one of the little Roman street-cabs – was stationed. Then he passed in among the cavernous shadows of the great structure, and emerged upon the clear and silent arena. The place had never seemed to him more impressive. One-half of the gigantic circus was in deep shade; the other was sleeping in the luminous dusk. As he stood there he began to murmur Byron's famous lines, out of 'Manfred'; but before he had finished his quotation he remembered that if nocturnal meditations in the Colosseum are recommended by the poets, they are deprecated by the doctors. The historic atmosphere was there, certainly; but the historic atmosphere, scientifically considered, was no better than a villainous miasma. Winterbourne walked to the middle of the arena, to take a more general glance, intending thereafter to make a hasty retreat. The great cross in the centre was covered with shadow; it was only as he drew near it that he made it out distinctly. Then he saw that two persons were stationed upon the low steps which formed its base. One of these was a woman, seated; her companion was standing in front of her.

Presently the sound of the woman's voice came to him distinctly in the warm night-air. 'Well, he looks at us as one of the old lions or tigers may have looked at the Christian martyrs!' These were the words he heard, in the familiar accent of Miss Daisy Miller.

'Let us hope he is not very hungry,' responded the ingenious Giovanelli. 'He will have to take me first; you will serve for dessert!'

Winterbourne stopped, with a sort of horror; and, it must be added, with a sort of relief. It was as if a sudden illumination had been flashed upon the ambiguity of Daisy's behaviour and the riddle had become easy to read. She was a young lady whom a gentleman need no longer be at pains to respect. He stood there looking at her – looking at her companion, and not reflecting that though he saw them vaguely, he himself must have been more brightly visible. He felt angry with himself that he had bothered so much about the right way of regarding Miss Daisy Miller. Then, as he was going to advance again, he checked himself; not from the fear that he was doing her injustice, but from a sense of the danger of appearing unbecomingly exhilarated by this sudden revulsion from cautious criticism. He turned away towards the entrance of the place; but as he did so he heard Daisy speak again.

'Why, it was Mr Winterbourne! He saw me – and he cuts me!'

What a clever little reprobate she was, and how smartly she played an injured innocence! But he wouldn't cut her. Winterbourne came forward again, and went towards the great cross.

Daisy had got up; Giovanelli lifted his hat. Winterbourne had now begun to think simply of the craziness, from a sanitary point of view, of a delicate young girl lounging away the evening in this nest of malaria. What if she *were* a clever little reprobate? that was no reason for her dying of the *perniciosa*. 'How long have you been here?' he asked, almost brutally.

Daisy, lovely in the flattering moonlight, looked at him a moment. Then – 'All the evening,' she answered gently... 'I never saw anything so pretty.'

'I am afraid,' said Winterbourne, 'that you will not think Roman fever very pretty. This is the way people catch it. I wonder,' he added, turning to Giovanelli, 'that you, a native Roman, should countenance such a terrible indiscretion.'

'Ah,' said the handsome native, 'for myself, I am not afraid.'

'Neither am I – for you! I am speaking for this young lady.'

Giovanelli lifted his well-shaped eyebrows and showed his brilliant teeth. But he took Winterbourne's rebuke with docility. 'I told the Signorina it was a grave indiscretion; but when was the Signorina ever prudent?'

'I never was sick, and I don't mean to be!' the Signorina declared. 'I don't look like much, but I'm healthy! I was bound to see the Colosseum by moonlight; I shouldn't have wanted to go home without that; and we have had the most beautiful time, haven't we, Mr Giovanelli? If there has been any danger, Eugenio can give me some pills. He has got some splendid pills.'

'I should advise you,' said Winterbourne, 'to drive home as fast as possible and take one!'

'What you say is very wise,' Giovanelli rejoined. 'I will go and make sure the carriage is at hand.' And he went forward rapidly.

Daisy followed with Winterbourne. He kept looking at her; she seemed not in the least embarrassed. Winterbourne said nothing; Daisy chattered about the beauty of the place. 'Well, I *have* seen the Colosseum by moonlight!' she exclaimed. 'That's one good thing.' Then, noticing Winterbourne's silence, she asked him why he didn't speak. He made no answer; he only began to laugh. They passed under one of the dark archways; Giovanelli was in front with the carriage. Here

Daisy stopped a moment, looking at the young American. '*Did* you believe I was engaged the other day?' she asked.

'It doesn't matter what I believed the other day,' said Winterbourne, still laughing.

'Well, what do you believe now?'

'I believe that it makes very little difference whether you are engaged or not!'

He felt the young girl's pretty eyes fixed upon him through the thick gloom of the archway; she was apparently going to answer. But Giovanelli hurried her forward. 'Quick, quick,' he said; 'if we get in by midnight we are quite safe.'

Daisy took her seat in the carriage, and the fortunate Italian placed himself beside her. 'Don't forget Eugenio's pills!' said Winterbourne, as he lifted his hat.

'I don't care,' said Daisy, in a little strange tone, 'whether I have Roman fever or not!' Upon this the cab-driver cracked his whip, and they rolled away over the desultory patches of the antique pavement.

Winterbourne – to do him justice, as it were – mentioned to no one that he had encountered Miss Miller, at midnight, in the Colosseum with a gentleman; but nevertheless, a couple of days later, the fact of her having been there under these circumstances was known to every member of the little American circle, and commented on accordingly. Winterbourne reflected that they had of course known it at the hotel, and that, after Daisy's return, there had been an exchange of jokes between the porter and the cab-driver. But the young man was conscious at the same moment that it had ceased to be a matter of serious regret to him that the little American flirt should be 'talked about' by low-minded menials. These people, a day or two later, had serious information to give: the little American flirt was alarmingly ill. Winterbourne, when the rumour came to him, immediately went to the hotel for more news. He found that two or three charitable friends had preceded him, and that they were being entertained in Mrs Miller's salon by Randolph.

'It's going round at night,' said Randolph – 'that's what made her sick. She's always going round at night. I shouldn't think she'd want to – it's so plaguey dark. You can't see anything here at night, except when there's a moon. In America there's always a moon!' Mrs Miller was invisible; she was now, at least, giving her daughter the advantage of her society. It was evident that Daisy was dangerously ill.

Winterbourne went often to ask for news of her, and once he saw Mrs Miller, who, though deeply alarmed, was – rather to his surprise – perfectly composed, and, as it appeared, a most efficient and judicious nurse. She talked a good deal about Dr Davis, but Winterbourne paid her the compliment of saying to himself that she was not, after all, such a monstrous goose. 'Daisy spoke of you the other day,' she said to him. 'Half the time she doesn't know what she's saying, but that time I think she did. She gave me a message; she told me to tell you. She told me to tell you that she never was engaged to that handsome Italian. I am sure I am very glad; Mr Giovanelli hasn't been near us since she was taken ill. I thought he was so much of a gentleman; but I don't call that very polite! A lady told me that he was afraid I was angry with him for taking Daisy round at night. Well, so I am; but I suppose he knows I'm a lady. I would scorn to scold him. Anyway, she says she's not engaged. I don't know why she wanted you to know; but she said to me three times – "Mind you tell Mr Winterbourne." And then she told me to ask if you remembered the time you went to that castle, in Switzerland. But I said I wouldn't give any such messages as that. Only, if she is not engaged, I'm sure I'm glad to know it.'

But, as Winterbourne had said, it mattered very little. A week after this the poor girl died; it had been a terrible case of the fever. Daisy's grave was in the little Protestant cemetery, in an angle of the wall of imperial Rome, beneath the cypresses and the thick spring-flowers. Winterbourne stood there beside it, with a number of other mourners; a number larger than the scandal excited by the young lady's career would have led you to expect. Near him stood Giovanelli, who came nearer still before Winterbourne turned away. Giovanelli was very pale; on this occasion he had no flower in his button-hole; he seemed to wish to say something. At last he said, 'She was the most beautiful young lady I ever saw, and the most amiable.' And then he added in a moment, 'And she was the most innocent.'

Winterbourne looked at him and presently repeated his words, 'And the most innocent?'

'The most innocent!'

Winterbourne felt sore and angry. 'Why the devil,' he asked, 'did you take her to that fatal place?'

Mr Giovanelli's urbanity was apparently imperturbable. He looked on the ground a moment, and then he said, 'For myself, I had no fear; and she wanted to go.'

'That was no reason!' Winterbourne declared.

The subtle Roman again dropped his eyes. 'If she had lived, I should have got nothing. She would never have married me, I am sure.'

'She would never have married you?'

'For a moment I hoped so. But no. I am sure.'

Winterbourne listened to him; he stood staring at the raw protuberance among the April daisies. When he turned away again Mr Giovanelli, with his light slow step, had retired.

Winterbourne almost immediately left Rome; but the following summer he again met his aunt, Mrs Costello, at Vevey. Mrs Costello was fond of Vevey. In the interval Winterbourne had often thought of Daisy Miller and her mystifying manners. One day he spoke of her to his aunt – said it was on his conscience that he had done her injustice.

'I am sure I don't know,' said Mrs Costello. 'How did your injustice affect her?'

'She sent me a message before her death which I didn't understand at the time. But I have understood it since. She would have appreciated one's esteem.'

'Is that a modest way,' asked Mrs Costello, 'of saying that she would have reciprocated one's affection?'

Winterbourne offered no answer to this question; but he presently said, 'You were right in that remark that you made last summer. I was booked to make a mistake. I have lived too long in foreign parts.'

Nevertheless, he went back to live at Geneva, whence there continue to come the most contradictory accounts of his motives of sojourn: a report that he is 'studying' hard – an intimation that he is much interested in a very clever foreign lady.

AN INTERNATIONAL EPISODE

I

FOUR years ago – in 1874 – two young Englishmen had occasion to go to the United States. They crossed the ocean at midsummer, and, arriving in New York on the first day of August, were much struck with the fervid temperature of that city. Disembarking upon the wharf, they climbed into one of those huge high-hung coaches which convey passengers to the hotels, and with a great deal of bouncing and bumping, took their course through Broadway. The midsummer aspect of New York is not perhaps the most favourable one; still, it is not without its picturesque and even brilliant side. Nothing could well resemble less a typical English street than the interminable avenue, rich in incongruities, through which our two travellers advanced – looking out on each side of them at the comfortable animation of the sidewalks, the high-coloured, heterogeneous architecture, the huge white marble façades, glittering in the strong, crude light and bedizened with gilded lettering, the multifarious awnings, banners and streamers, the extraordinary number of omnibuses, horse-cars and other democratic vehicles, the vendors of cooling fluids, the white trousers and big straw-hats of the policemen, the tripping gait of the modish young persons on the pavement, the general brightness, newness, juvenility, both of people and things. The young men had exchanged few observations; but in crossing Union Square, in front of the monument to Washington – in the very shadow, indeed, projected by the image of the *pater patriae* – one of them remarked to the other, 'It seems a rum-looking place.'

'Ah, very odd, very odd,' said the other, who was the clever man of the two.

'Pity it's so beastly hot,' resumed the first speaker, after a pause.

'You know we are in a low latitude,' said his friend.

'I daresay,' remarked the other.

'I wonder,' said the second speaker, presently, 'if they can give one a bath.'

'I daresay not,' rejoined the other.

'Oh, I say!' cried his comrade.

This animated discussion was checked by their arrival at the hotel, which had been recommended to them by an American gentleman whose acquaintance they made – with whom, indeed, they became very intimate – on the steamer, and who had proposed to accompany them to the inn and introduce them, in a friendly way, to the proprietor. This plan, however, had been defeated by their friend's finding that his 'partner' was awaiting him on the wharf, and that his commercial associate desired him instantly to come and give his attention to certain telegrams received from St Louis. But the two Englishmen, with nothing but their national prestige and personal graces to recommend them, were very well received at the hotel, which had an air of capacious hospitality. They found that a bath was not unattainable, and were indeed struck with the facilities for prolonged and reiterated immersion with which their apartment was supplied. After bathing a good deal – more indeed than they had ever done before on a single occasion – they made their way into the dining-room of the hotel, which was a spacious restaurant, with a fountain in the middle, a great many tall plants in ornamental tubs, and an array of French waiters. The first dinner on land, after a sea-voyage, is under any circumstances a delightful occasion, and there was something particularly agreeable in the circumstances in which our young Englishmen found themselves. They were extremely good-natured young men; they were more observant than they appeared; in a sort of inarticulate, accidentally dissimulative fashion, they were highly appreciative. This was perhaps especially the case with the elder, who was also, as I have said, the man of talent. They sat down at a little table which was a very different affair from the great clattering see-saw in the saloon of the steamer. The wide doors and windows of the restaurant stood open, beneath large awnings, to a wide pavement, where there were other plants in tubs, and rows of spreading trees, and beyond which there was a large shady square, without any palings and with marble-paved walks. And above the vivid verdure rose other façades of white marble and of pale chocolate-coloured stone, squaring themselves against the deep blue sky. Here, outside, in the light and the shade and the heat, there was a great tinkling of the bells of innumerable street-cars, and a constant strolling and shuffling and rustling of many pedestrians, a large proportion of whom were young women in Pompadour-looking dresses. Within, the place was cool and vaguely-lighted; with the plash of water, the odour of flowers and the flitting of French waiters, as I have said, upon soundless carpets.

'It's rather like Paris, you know,' said the younger of our two travellers.

'It's like Paris – only more so,' his companion rejoined.

'I suppose it's the French waiters,' said the first speaker. 'Why don't they have French waiters in London?'

'Fancy a French waiter at a club,' said his friend.

The young Englishman stared a little, as if he could not fancy it. 'In Paris I'm very apt to dine at a place where there's an English waiter. Don't you know, what's-his-name's, close to the thingumbob? They always set an English waiter at me. I suppose they think I can't speak French.'

'No more you can.' And the elder of the young Englishmen unfolded his napkin.

His companion took no notice whatever of this declaration. 'I say,' he resumed, in a moment, 'I suppose we must learn to speak American. I suppose we must take lessons.'

'I can't understand them,' said the clever man.

'What the deuce is *he* saying?' asked his comrade, appealing from the French waiter.

'He is recommending some soft-shell crabs,' said the clever man.

And so, in desultory observation of the idiosyncrasies of the new society in which they found themselves, the young Englishmen proceeded to dine – going in largely, as the phrase is, for cooling draughts and dishes, of which their attendant offered them a very long list. After dinner they went out and slowly walked about the neighbouring streets. The early dusk

of waning summer was coming on, but the heat was still very
great. The pavements were hot even to the stout boot-soles of
the British travellers, and the trees along the kerb-stone emitted
strange exotic odours. The young men wandered through the
adjoining square – that queer place without palings, and with
marble walks arranged in black and white lozenges. There were
a great many benches, crowded with shabby-looking people,
and the travellers remarked, very justly, that it was not much
like Belgrave Square. On one side was an enormous hotel,
lifting up into the hot darkness an immense array of open,
brightly-lighted windows. At the base of this populous structure was an eternal jangle of horse-cars, and all round it, in the
upper dusk, was a sinister hum of mosquitoes. The ground-
floor of the hotel seemed to be a huge transparent cage, flinging
a wide glare of gaslight into the street, of which it formed a sort
of public adjunct, absorbing and emitting the passers-by pro-
miscuously. The young Englishmen went in with every one
else, from curiosity, and saw a couple of hundred men sitting
on divans along a great marble-paved corridor, with their legs
stretched out, together with several dozen more standing in a
queue, as at the ticket-office of a railway station, before a bril-
liantly-illuminated counter, of vast extent. These latter persons, who carried portmanteaux in their hands, had a
dejected, exhausted look; their garments were not very fresh,
and they seemed to be rendering some mysterious tribute to a
magnificent young man with a waxed moustache and a shirt
front adorned with diamond buttons, who every now and then
dropped an absent glance over their multitudinous patience.
They were American citizens doing homage to an hotel-clerk.

'I'm glad he didn't tell us to go there,' said one of our
Englishmen, alluding to their friend on the steamer, who had
told them so many things. They walked up the Fifth Avenue,
where, for instance, he had told them that all the first families
lived. But the first families were out of town, and our young
travellers had only the satisfaction of seeing some of the second
– or perhaps even the third – taking the evening air upon
balconies and high flights of doorsteps, in the streets which
radiate from the more ornamental thoroughfare. They went a

little way down one of these side-streets, and they saw young ladies in white dresses – charming-looking persons – seated in graceful attitudes on the chocolate-coloured steps. In one or two places these young ladies were conversing across the street with other young ladies seated in similar postures and costumes in front of the opposite houses, and in the warm night air their colloquial tones sounded strange in the ears of the young Englishmen. One of our friends, nevertheless – the younger one – intimated that he felt a disposition to intercept a few of these soft familiarities; but his companion observed, pertinently enough, that he had better be careful. 'We must not begin with making mistakes,' said his companion.

'But he told us, you know – he told us,' urged the young man, alluding again to the friend on the steamer.

'Never mind what he told us!' answered his comrade, who, if he had greater talents, was also apparently more of a moralist.

By bed-time – in their impatience to taste of a terrestrial couch again our seafarers went to bed early – it was still insufferably hot, and the buzz of the mosquitoes at the open windows might have passed for an audible crepitation of the temperature. 'We can't stand this, you know,' the young Englishmen said to each other; and they tossed about all night more boisterously than they had tossed upon the Atlantic billows. On the morrow, their first thought was that they would re-embark that day for England; and then it occurred to them that they might find an asylum nearer at hand. The cave of Æolus became their ideal of comfort, and they wondered where the Americans went when they wished to cool off. They had not the least idea, and they determined to apply for information to Mr J. L. Westgate. This was the name inscribed in a bold hand on the back of a letter carefully preserved in the pocket-book of our junior traveller. Beneath the address, in the left-hand corner of the envelope, were the words, 'Introducing Lord Lambeth and Percy Beaumont, Esq.' The letter had been given to the two Englishmen by a good friend of theirs in London, who had been in America two years previously and had singled out Mr J. L. Westgate from the many friends he had left there as the consignee, as it were, of his compatriots. 'He is a capital fellow,' the

Englishman in London had said, 'and he has got an awfully pretty wife. He's tremendously hospitable – he will do everything in the world for you; and as he knows every one over there, it is quite needless I should give you any other introduction. He will make you see every one; trust to him for putting you into circulation. He has got a tremendously pretty wife.' It was natural that in the hour of tribulation Lord Lambeth and Mr Percy Beaumont should have bethought themselves of a gentleman whose attractions had been thus vividly depicted; all the more so that he lived in the Fifth Avenue and that the Fifth Avenue, as they had ascertained the night before, was contiguous to their hotel. 'Ten to one he'll be out of town,' said Percy Beaumont; 'but we can at least find out where he has gone, and we can immediately start in pursuit. He can't possibly have gone to a hotter place, you know.'

'Oh, there's only one hotter place,' said Lord Lambeth, 'and I hope he hasn't gone there.'

They strolled along the shady side of the street to the number indicated upon the precious letter. The house presented an imposing chocolate-coloured expanse, relieved by facings and window-cornices of florid sculpture, and by a couple of dusty rose-trees, which clambered over the balconies and the portico. This last-mentioned feature was approached by a monumental flight of steps.

'Rather better than a London house,' said Lord Lambeth, looking down from this altitude, after they had rung the bell.

'It depends upon what London house you mean,' replied his companion. 'You have a tremendous chance to get wet between the house-door and your carriage.'

'Well,' said Lord Lambeth, glancing at the burning heavens, 'I "guess" it doesn't rain so much here!'

The door was opened by a long negro in a white jacket, who grinned familiarly when Lord Lambeth asked for Mr Westgate.

'He ain't at home, sir; he's down town at his o'fice.'

'Oh, at his office?' said the visitors. 'And when will he be at home?'

'Well, sir, when he goes out dis way in de mo'ning, he ain't liable to come home all day.'

This was discouraging; but the address of Mr Westgate's office was freely imparted by the intelligent black, and was taken down by Percy Beaumont in his pocket-book. The two gentlemen then returned, languidly, to their hotel, and sent for a hackney-coach; and in this commodious vehicle they rolled comfortably down town. They measured the whole length of Broadway again, and found it a path of fire; and then, deflecting to the left, they were deposited by their conductor before a fresh, light, ornamental structure, ten storeys high, in a street crowded with keen-faced, light-limbed young men, who were running about very quickly and stopping each other eagerly at corners and in doorways. Passing into this brilliant building, they were introduced by one of the keen-faced young men – he was a charming fellow, in wonderful cream-coloured garments and a hat with a blue ribbon, who had evidently perceived them to be aliens and helpless – to a very snug hydraulic elevator, in which they took their place with many other persons, and which, shooting upward in its vertical socket, presently projected them into the seventh horizontal compartment of the edifice. Here, after brief delay, they found themselves face to face with the friend of their friend in London. His office was composed of several different rooms, and they waited very silently in one of these after they had sent in their letter and their cards. The letter was not one which it would take Mr Westgate very long to read, but he came out to speak to them more instantly than they could have expected; he had evidently jumped up from his work. He was a tall, lean personage, and was dressed all in fresh white linen; he had a thin, sharp, familiar face, with an expression that was at one and the same time sociable and business-like, a quick, intelligent eye, and a large brown moustache, which concealed his mouth and made his chin, beneath it, look small. Lord Lambeth thought he looked tremendously clever.

'How do you do, Lord Lambeth – how do you do, sir?' he said, holding the open letter in his hand. 'I'm very glad to see you – I hope you're very well. You had better come in here – I think it's cooler'; and he led the way into another room, where there were law-books and papers, and windows wide open beneath striped awnings. Just opposite one of the windows, on a line with his eyes, Lord Lambeth observed the weather-vane of a church steeple. The uproar of the street sounded infinitely far below, and Lord Lambeth felt very high in the air. 'I say it's cooler,' pursued their host, 'but everything is relative. How do you stand the heat?'

'I can't say we like it,' said Lord Lambeth; 'but Beaumont likes it better than I.'

'Well, it won't last,' Mr Westgate very cheerfully declared; 'nothing unpleasant lasts over here. It was very hot when Captain Littledale was here; he did nothing but drink sherry-cobblers. He expresses some doubt in his letter whether I shall remember him – as if I didn't remember making six sherry-cobblers for him one day, in about twenty minutes. I hope you left him well; two years having elapsed since then.'

'Oh, yes, he's all right,' said Lord Lambeth.

'I am always very glad to see your countrymen,' Mr Westgate pursued. 'I thought it would be time some of you should be coming along. A friend of mine was saying to me only a day or two ago, "It's time for the water-melons and the Englishmen."'

'The Englishmen and the water-melons just now are about the same thing,' Percy Beaumont observed, wiping his dripping forehead.

'Ah, well, we'll put you on ice, as we do the melons. You must go down to Newport.'

'We'll go anywhere!' said Lord Lambeth.

'Yes, you want to go to Newport – that's what you want to do,' Mr Westgate affirmed. 'But let's see – when did you get here?'

'Only yesterday,' said Percy Beaumont.

'Ah, yes, by the "Russia". Where are you staying?'

'At the "Hanover", I think they call it.'

'Pretty comfortable?' inquired Mr Westgate.

'It seems a capital place, but I can't say we like the gnats,' said Lord Lambeth.

Mr Westgate stared and laughed. 'Oh, no, of course you don't like the gnats. We shall expect you to like a good many things over here, but we shan't insist upon your liking the gnats; though certainly you'll admit that, as gnats, they are fine, eh? But you oughtn't to remain in the city.'

'So we think,' said Lord Lambeth. 'If you would kindly suggest something—'

'Suggest something, my dear sir?' – and Mr Westgate looked at him, narrowing his eyelids. 'Open your mouth and shut your eyes! Leave it to me, and I'll put you through. It's a matter of national pride with me that all Englishmen should have a good time; and, as I have had considerable practice, I have learned to minister to their wants. I find they generally want the right thing. So just please to consider yourselves my property; and if any one should try to appropriate you, please to say, "Hands off; too late for the market." But let's see,' continued the American, in his slow, humorous voice, with a distinctness of utterance which appeared to his visitors to be part of a facetious intention – a strangely leisurely, speculative voice for a man evidently so busy and, as they felt, so professional – 'let's see; are you going to make something of a stay, Lord Lambeth?'

'Oh dear no,' said the young Englishman; 'my cousin was coming over on some business, so I just came across, at an hour's notice, for the lark.'

'Is it your first visit to the United States?'

'Oh dear, yes.'

'I was obliged to come on some business,' said Percy Beaumont, 'and I brought Lambeth with me.'

'And *you* have been here before, sir?'

'Never – never.'

'I thought, from your referring to business—' said Mr Westgate.

'Oh, you see I'm by way of being a barrister,' Percy Beaumont answered. 'I know some people that think of bringing a suit against one of your railways, and they asked me to come over and take measures accordingly.'

Mr Westgate gave one of his slow, keen looks again. 'What's your railroad?' he asked.

'The Tennessee Central.'

The American tilted back his chair a little, and poised it an instant. 'Well, I'm sorry you want to attack one of our institutions,' he said, smiling. 'But I guess you had better enjoy yourself *first*!'

'I'm certainly rather afraid I can't work in this weather,' the young barrister confessed.

'Leave that to the natives,' said Mr Westgate. 'Leave the Tennessee Central to me, Mr Beaumont. Some day we'll talk it over, and I guess I can make it square. But I didn't know you Englishmen ever did any work, in the upper classes.'

'Oh, we do a lot of work; don't we, Lambeth?' asked Percy Beaumont.

'I must certainly be at home by the 19th of September,' said the younger Englishman, irrelevantly, but gently.

'For the shooting, eh? or is it the hunting – or the fishing?' inquired his entertainer.

'Oh, I must be in Scotland,' said Lord Lambeth, blushing a little.

'Well then,' rejoined Mr Westgate, 'you had better amuse yourself first, also. You must go down and see Mrs Westgate.'

'We should be so happy – if you would kindly tell us the train,' said Percy Beaumont.

'It isn't a train – it's a boat.'

'Oh, I see. And what is the name of – a – the – a – town?'

'It isn't a town,' said Mr Westgate, laughing. 'It's a – well, what shall I call it? It's a watering-place. In short, it's Newport. You'll see what it is. It's cool; that's the principal thing. You will greatly oblige me by going down there and putting yourself into the hands of Mrs Westgate. It isn't perhaps for me to say it; but you couldn't be in better hands. Also in those of her sister, who is staying with her. She is very fond of Englishmen. She thinks there is nothing like them.'

'Mrs Westgate or – a – her sister?' asked Percy Beaumont, modestly, yet in the tone of an inquiring traveller.

'Oh, I mean my wife,' said Mr Westgate. 'I don't suppose my sister-in-law knows much about them. She has always led a very quiet life; she has lived in Boston.'

Percy Beaumont listened with interest. 'That, I believe,' he said, 'is the most – a – intellectual town?'

'I believe it is very intellectual. I don't go there much,' responded his host.

'I say, we ought to go there,' said Lord Lambeth to his companion.

'Oh, Lord Lambeth, wait till the great heat is over!' Mr Westgate interposed. 'Boston in this weather would be very trying; it's not the temperature for intellectual exertion. At Boston, you know, you have to pass an examination at the city limits; and when you come away they give you a kind of degree.'

Lord Lambeth stared, blushing a little; and Percy Beaumont stared a little also – but only with his fine natural complexion; glancing aside after a moment to see that his companion was not looking too credulous, for he had heard a great deal about American humour. 'I daresay it is very jolly,' said the younger gentleman.

'I daresay it is,' said Mr Westgate. 'Only I must impress upon you that at present – to-morrow morning, at an early hour – you will be expected at Newport. We have a house there; half the people in New York go there for the summer. I am not sure that at this very moment my wife can take you in; she has got a lot of people staying with her; I don't know who they all are; only she may have no room. But you can begin with the hotel, and meanwhile you can live at my house. In that way – simply sleeping at the hotel – you will find it tolerable. For the rest, you must make yourself at home at my place. You mustn't be shy, you know; if you are only here for a month that will be a great waste of time. Mrs Westgate won't neglect you, and you had better not try to resist her. I know something about that. I expect you'll find some pretty girls on the premises. I shall write to my wife by this afternoon's mail, and to-morrow she and Miss Alden will look out for you. Just walk right in and make yourself comfortable. Your steamer leaves from this part of the city, and I will immediately send out and get you a cabin. Then, at half-past four o'clock, just call for me here, and I will go with you and put you on board. It's a big boat; you might get lost. A few days hence, at the end of the week, I will come down to Newport and see how you are getting on.'

The two young Englishmen inaugurated the policy of not resisting Mrs Westgate by submitting, with great docility and thankfulness, to her husband. He was evidently a very good fellow, and he made an impression upon his visitors; his hospitality seemed to recommend itself, consciously – with a friendly wink, as it were – as if it hinted, judicially, that you could not possibly make a better bargain. Lord Lambeth and his cousin left their entertainer to his labours and returned to their hotel, where they spent three or four hours in their respective shower-baths. Percy Beaumont had suggested that they ought to see something of the town; but 'Oh, damn the town!' his noble kinsman had rejoined. They returned to Mr Westgate's office in a carriage, with their luggage, very punctually; but it must be reluctantly recorded that, this time, he kept them waiting so long that they felt themselves missing the steamer and were deterred only by an amiable modesty from dispensing with his attendance and starting on a hasty scramble to the wharf. But when at last he appeared, and the carriage plunged into the purlieus of Broadway, they jolted and jostled to such good purpose that they reached the huge white vessel while the bell for departure was still ringing and the absorption of passengers still active. It was indeed, as Mr Westgate had said, a big boat, and his leadership in the innumerable and interminable corridors and cabins, with which he seemed perfectly acquainted, and of which any one and every one appeared to have the *entrée*, was very grateful to the slightly bewildered voyagers. He showed them their state-room – a spacious apartment, embellished with gaslamps, mirrors *en pied* and sculptured furniture – and then, long after they had been intimately convinced that the steamer was in motion and launched upon the unknown stream that they were about to navigate, he bade them a sociable farewell.

'Well, good-bye, Lord Lambeth,' he said. 'Good-bye, Mr Percy Beaumont; I hope you'll have a good time. Just let them do what they want with you. I'll come down by-and-by and look after you.'

II

THE young Englishmen emerged from their cabin and amused themselves with wandering about the immense labyrinthine steamer, which struck them as an extraordinary mixture of a ship and an hotel. It was densely crowded with passengers, the larger number of whom appeared to be ladies and very young children; and in the big saloons, ornamented in white and gold, which followed each other in surprising succession, beneath the swinging gas-lights and among the small side-passages where the negro domestics of both sexes assembled with an air of philosophic leisure, every one was moving to and fro and exchanging loud and familiar observations. Eventually, at the instance of a discriminating black, our young men went and had some 'supper', in a wonderful place arranged like a theatre, where, in a gilded gallery upon which little boxes appeared to open, a large orchestra was playing operatic selections, and, below, people were handing about bills of fare, as if they had been programmes. All this was sufficiently curious; but the agreeable thing, later, was to sit out on one of the great white decks of the steamer, in the warm, breezy darkness, and, in the vague starlight, to make out the line of low, mysterious coast. The young Englishmen tried American cigars – those of Mr Westgate – and talked together as they usually talked, with many odd silences, lapses of logic and incongruities of transition; like people who have grown old together and learned to supply each other's missing phrases; or, more especially, like people thoroughly conscious of a common point of view, so that a style of conversation superficially lacking in finish might suffice for a reference to a fund of associations in the light of which everything was all right.

'We really seem to be going out to sea,' Percy Beaumont observed. 'Upon my word, we are going back to England. He has shipped us off again. I call that "real mean". '

'I suppose it's all right,' said Lord Lambeth. 'I want to see those pretty girls at Newport. You know he told us the place was an island; and aren't all islands in the sea?'

'Well,' resumed the elder traveller after a while, 'if his house is as good as his cigars, we shall do very well.'

'He seems a very good fellow,' said Lord Lambeth, as if this idea had just occurred to him.

'I say, we had better remain at the inn,' rejoined his companion, presently. 'I don't think I like the way he spoke of his house. I don't like stopping in the house with such a tremendous lot of women.'

'Oh, I don't mind,' said Lord Lambeth. And then they smoked awhile in silence. 'Fancy his thinking we do no work in England!' the young man resumed.

'I daresay he didn't really think so,' said Percy Beaumont.

'Well, I guess they don't know much about England over here!' declared Lord Lambeth, humorously. And then there was another long pause. 'He was devilish civil,' observed the young nobleman.

'Nothing, certainly, could have been more civil,' rejoined his companion.

'Littledale said his wife was great fun,' said Lord Lambeth.

'Whose wife – Littledale's?'

'This American's – Mrs Westgate. What's his name? J. L.'

Beaumont was silent a moment. 'What was fun to Littledale,' he said at last, rather sententiously, 'may be death to us.'

'What do you mean by that?' asked his kinsman. 'I am as good a man as Littledale.'

'My dear boy, I hope you won't begin to flirt,' said Percy Beaumont.

'I don't care. I daresay I shan't begin.'

'With a married woman, if she's bent upon it, it's all very well,' Beaumont expounded. 'But our friend mentioned a young lady – a sister, a sister-in-law. For God's sake, don't get entangled with her.'

'How do you mean, entangled?'

'Depend upon it she will try to hook you.'

'Oh, bother!' said Lord Lambeth.

'American girls are very clever,' urged his companion.

'So much the better,' the young man declared.

'I fancy they are always up to some game of that sort,' Beaumont continued.

'They can't be worse than they are in England,' said Lord Lambeth, judicially.

'Ah, but in England,' replied Beaumont, 'you have got your natural protectors. You have got your mother and sisters.'

'My mother and sisters –' began the young nobleman, with a certain energy. But he stopped in time, puffing at his cigar.

'Your mother spoke to me about it, with tears in her eyes,' said Percy Beaumont. 'She said she felt very nervous. I promised to keep you out of mischief.'

'You had better take care of yourself,' said the object of maternal and ducal solicitude.

'Ah,' rejoined the young barrister, 'I haven't the expectation of a hundred thousand a year – not to mention other attractions.'

'Well,' said Lord Lambeth, 'don't cry out before you're hurt!'

It was certainly very much cooler at Newport, where our travellers found themselves assigned to a couple of diminutive bedrooms in a far-away angle of an immense hotel. They had gone ashore in the early summer twilight, and had very promptly put themselves to bed; thanks to which circumstance and to their having, during the previous hours, in their commodious cabin, slept the sleep of youth and health, they began to feel, towards eleven o'clock, very alert and inquisitive. They looked out of their windows across a row of small green fields, bordered with low stone dykes, of rude construction, and saw a deep blue ocean lying beneath a deep blue sky and flecked now and then with scintillating patches of foam. A strong, fresh breeze came in through the curtainless casements and prompted our young men to observe, generously, that it didn't seem half a bad climate. They made other observations after they had emerged from their rooms in pursuit of breakfast – a meal of which they partook in a huge bare hall, where a hundred negroes, in white jackets, were shuffling about upon an uncarpeted floor; where the flies were superabundant and the tables and dishes covered over with a strange, voluminous integument of coarse blue gauze; and where several little boys and girls, who had risen late, were seated in fastidious solitude at the morning repast. These young persons had not the morning paper before them, but they were engaged in languid perusal of the bill of fare.

This latter document was a great puzzle to our friends, who, on reflecting that its bewildering categories had relation to breakfast alone, had an uneasy prevision of an encyclopaedic dinner-list. They found a great deal of entertainment at the hotel, an enormous wooden structure, for the erection of which it seemed to them that the virgin forests of the West must have been terribly deflowered. It was perforated from end to end with immense bare corridors, through which a strong draught was blowing – bearing along wonderful figures of ladies in white morning-dresses and clouds of Valenciennes lace, who seemed to float down the long vistas with expanded furbelows, like angels spreading their wings. In front was a gigantic verandah, upon which an army might have encamped – a vast wooden terrace, with a roof as lofty as the nave of a cathedral. Here our young Englishmen enjoyed, as they supposed, a glimpse of American society, which was distributed over the measureless expanse in a variety of sedentary attitudes, and appeared to consist largely of pretty young girls, dressed as if for a *fête champêtre*, swaying to and fro in rocking-chairs, fanning themselves with large straw fans, and enjoying an enviable exemption from social cares. Lord Lambeth had a theory, which it might be interesting to trace to its origin, that it would be not only agreeable, but easily possible, to enter into relations with one of these young ladies; and his companion found occasion to check the young nobleman's colloquial impulses.

'You had better take care,' said Percy Beaumont, 'or you will have an offended father or brother pulling out a bowie-knife.'

'I assure you it is all right,' Lord Lambeth replied. 'You know the Americans come to these big hotels to make acquaintances.'

'I know nothing about it, and neither do you,' said his kinsman, who, like a clever man, had begun to perceive that the observation of American society demanded a readjustment of one's standard.

'Hang it, then, let's find out!' cried Lord Lambeth with some impatience. 'You know, I don't want to miss anything.'

'We will find out,' said Percy Beaumont, very reasonably. 'We will go and see Mrs Westgate and make all the proper inquiries.'

And so the two inquiring Englishmen, who had this lady's address inscribed in her husband's hand upon a card, descended from the verandah of the big hotel and took their way, according to direction, along a large straight road, past a series of fresh-looking villas, embosomed in shrubs and flowers and enclosed in an ingenious variety of wooden palings. The morning was brilliant and cool, the villas were smart and snug, and the walk of the young travellers was very entertaining. Everything looked as if it had received a coat of fresh paint the day before – the red roofs, the green shutters, the clean, bright browns and buffs of the house-fronts. The flower-beds on the little lawns seemed to sparkle in the radiant air, and the gravel in the short carriage-sweeps to flash and twinkle. Along the road came a hundred little basket-phaetons, in which, almost always, a couple of ladies were sitting – ladies in white dresses and long white gloves, holding the reins and looking at the two Englishmen, whose nationality was not elusive, through thick blue veils, tied tightly about their faces as if to guard their complexions. At last the young men came within sight of the sea again, and then, having interrogated a gardener over the paling of a villa, they turned into an open gate. Here they found themselves face to face with the ocean and with a very picturesque structure, resembling a magnified *chalet*, which was perched upon a green embankment just above it. The house had a verandah of extraordinary width all around it, and a great many doors and windows standing open to the verandah. These various apertures had, in common, such an accessible, hospitable air, such a breezy flutter, within, of light curtains, such expansive thresholds and reassuring interiors, that our friends hardly knew which was the regular entrance, and, after hesitating a moment, presented themselves at one of the

windows. The room within was dark, but in a moment a graceful figure vaguely shaped itself in the rich-looking gloom, and a
lady came to meet them. Then they saw that she had been
seated at a table, writing, and that she had heard them and
had got up. She stepped out into the light; she wore a frank,
charming smile, with which she held out her hand to Percy
Beaumont.

'Oh, you must be Lord Lambeth and Mr Beaumont,' she
said. 'I have heard from my husband that you would come. I am
extremely glad to see you.' And she shook hands with each of
her visitors. Her visitors were a little shy, but they had very good
manners; they responded with smiles and exclamations, and
they apologised for not knowing the front door. The lady
rejoined, with vivacity, that when she wanted to see people
very much she did not insist upon those distinctions, and that
Mr Westgate had written to her of his English friends in terms
that made her really anxious. 'He said you were so terribly
prostrated,' said Mrs Westgate.

'Oh, you mean by the heat?' replied Percy Beaumont. 'We
were rather knocked up, but we feel wonderfully better. We had
such a jolly – a – voyage down here. It's so very good of you to
mind.'

'Yes, it's so very kind of you,' murmured Lord Lambeth.

Mrs Westgate stood smiling; she was extremely pretty.
'Well, I did mind,' she said; 'and I thought of sending for
you this morning, to the Ocean House. I am very glad you
are better, and I am charmed you have arrived. You must
come round to the other side of the piazza.' And she led the
way, with a light, smooth step, looking back at the young men
and smiling.

The other side of the piazza was, as Lord Lambeth presently
remarked, a very jolly place. It was of the most liberal proportions, and with its awnings, its fanciful chairs, its cushions and
rugs, its view of the ocean, close at hand, tumbling along the
base of the low cliffs whose level tops intervened in lawnlike
smoothness, it formed a charming complement to the drawing-
room. As such it was in course of use at the present moment; it
was occupied by a social circle. There were several ladies and

two or three gentlemen, to whom Mrs Westgate proceeded to introduce the distinguished strangers. She mentioned a great many names, very freely and distinctly: the young Englishmen, shuffling about and bowing, were rather bewildered. But at last they were provided with chairs – low wicker chairs, gilded and tied with a great many ribbons – and one of the ladies (a very young person, with a little snub nose and several dimples) offered Percy Beaumont a fan. The fan was also adorned with pink love-knots; but Percy Beaumont declined it, although he was very hot. Presently, however, it became cooler; the breeze from the sea was delicious, the view was charming, and the people sitting there looked exceedingly fresh and comfortable. Several of the ladies seemed to be young girls, and the gentlemen were slim, fair youths, such as our friends had seen the day before in New York. The ladies were working upon bands of tapestry, and one of the young men had an open book in his lap. Beaumont afterwards learned from one of the ladies that this young man had been reading aloud – that he was from Boston and was very fond of reading aloud. Beaumont said it was a great pity that they had interrupted him; he should like so much (from all he had heard) to hear a Bostonian read. Couldn't the young man be induced to go on?

'Oh no,' said his informant, very freely; 'he wouldn't be able to get the young ladies to attend to him now.'

There was something very friendly, Beaumont perceived, in the attitude of the company; they looked at the young Englishmen with an air of animated sympathy and interest; they smiled, brightly and unanimously, at everything either of the visitors said. Lord Lambeth and his companion felt that they were being made very welcome. Mrs Westgate seated herself between them, and, talking a great deal to each, they had occasion to observe that she was as pretty as their friend Littledale had promised. She was thirty years old, with the eyes and the smile of a girl of seventeen, and she was extremely light and graceful, elegant, exquisite. Mrs Westgate was extremely spontaneous. She was very frank and demonstrative, and appeared always – while she looked at you delightedly with her beautiful

young eyes – to be making sudden confessions and concessions, after momentary hesitations.

'We shall expect to see a great deal of you,' she said to Lord
Lambeth, with a kind of joyous earnestness. 'We are very fond
of Englishmen here; that is, there are a great many we have
been fond of. After a day or two you must come and stay with
us; we hope you will stay a long time. Newport's a very nice
place when you come really to know it, when you know plenty
of people. Of course, you and Mr Beaumont will have no
difficulty about that. Englishmen are very well received here;
there are almost always two or three of them about. I think they
always like it, and I must say I should think they would. They
receive ever so much attention. I must say I think they sometimes get spoiled; but I am sure you and Mr Beaumont are
proof against that. My husband tells me you are a friend of
Captain Littledale; he was such a charming man. He made
himself most agreeable here, and I am sure I wonder he didn't
stay. It couldn't have been pleasanter for him in his own country. Though I suppose it is very pleasant in England, for English
people. I don't know myself; I have been there very little. I have
been a great deal abroad, but I am always on the Continent.
I must say I'm extremely fond of Paris; you know we Americans
always are; we go there when we die. Did you ever hear that
before? that was said by a great wit. I mean the good Americans;
but we are all good; you'll see that for yourself. All I know of
England is London, and all I know of London is that place – on
that little corner, you know, where you buy jackets – jackets
with that coarse braid and those big buttons. They make very
good jackets in London, I will do you the justice to say that.
And some people like the hats; but about the hats I was always a
heretic; I always got my hats in Paris. You can't wear an English
hat – at least, I never could – unless you dress your hair *à
l'Anglaise*; and I must say that is a talent I never possessed. In
Paris they will make things to suit your peculiarities; but in
England I think you like much more to have – how shall I say it?
– one thing for everybody. I mean as regards dress. I don't know
about other things; but I have always supposed that in other
things everything was different. I mean according to the people

– according to the classes, and all that. I am afraid you will think that I don't take a very favourable view; but you know you can't take a very favourable view in Dover Street, in the month of November. That has always been my fate. Do you know Jones's Hotel, in Dover Street? That's all I know of England. Of course, every one admits that the English hotels are your weak point. There was always the most frightful fog; I couldn't see to try my things on. When I got over to America – into the light – I usually found they were twice too big. The next time I mean to go in the season; I think I shall go next year. I want very much to take my sister; she has never been to England. I don't know whether you know what I mean by saying that the Englishmen who come here sometimes get spoiled. I mean that they take things as a matter of course – things that are done for them. Now, naturally, they are only a matter of course when the Englishmen are very nice. But, of course, they are almost always very nice. Of course, this isn't nearly such an interesting country as England; there are not nearly so many things to see, and we haven't your country life. I have never seen anything of your country life; when I am in Europe I am always on the Continent. But I have heard a great deal about it; I know that when you are among yourselves in the country you have the most beautiful time. Of course, we have nothing of that sort, we have nothing on that scale. I don't apologise, Lord Lambeth; some Americans are always apologising; you must have noticed that. We have the reputation of always boasting and bragging and waving the American flag; but I must say that what strikes me is that we are perpetually making excuses and trying to smooth things over. The American flag has quite gone out of fashion; it's very carefully folded up, like an old table-cloth. Why should we apologise? The English never apologise – do they? No, I must say I never apologise. You must take us as we come – with all our imperfections on our heads. Of course we haven't your country life, and your old ruins, and your great estates, and your leisure-class, and all that. But if we haven't, I should think you might find it a pleasant change – I think any country is pleasant where they have pleasant manners. Captain Littledale told me he had never seen such pleasant manners as at Newport; and he had been a great deal in European society. Hadn't he been in the diplomatic service? He told me the dream of his life was to get appointed to a diplomatic post in Washington. But he doesn't seem to have succeeded. I suppose that in England promotion – and all that sort of thing – is fearfully slow. With us, you know, it's a great deal too fast. You see I admit our drawbacks. But I must confess I think Newport is an ideal place. I don't know anything like it any-where. Captain Littledale told me he didn't know anything like it anywhere. It's entirely different from most watering-places; it's a most charming life. I must say I think that when one goes to a foreign country, one ought to enjoy the differences. Of course there are differences; otherwise what did one come abroad for? Look for your pleasure in the differences, Lord Lambeth; that's the way to do it; and then I am sure you will find American society – at least Newport society – most charm-ing and most interesting. I wish very much my husband were here; but he's dreadfully confined to New York. I suppose you think that's very strange – for a gentleman. Only you see we haven't any leisure-class.'

Mrs Westgate's discourse, delivered in a soft, sweet voice, flowed on like a miniature torrent and was interrupted by a hundred little smiles, glances and gestures, which might have figured the irregularities and obstructions of such a stream. Lord Lambeth listened to her with, it must be confessed, a rather ineffectual attention, although he indulged in a good many little murmurs and ejaculations of assent and depreca-tion. He had no great faculty for apprehending generalisations. There were some three or four indeed which, in the play of his own intelligence, he had originated, and which had seemed convenient at the moment; but at the present time he could hardly have been said to follow Mrs Westgate as she darted gracefully about in the sea of speculation. Fortunately she asked for no especial rejoinder, for she looked about at the rest of the company as well, and smiled at Percy Beaumont, on the other side of her, as if he too must understand her and agree with her. He was rather more successful than his com-panion; for besides being, as we know, cleverer, his attention was not vaguely distracted by close vicinity to a remarkably interesting young girl, with dark hair and blue eyes. This was the case with Lord Lambeth, to whom it occurred after a while that the young girl with blue eyes and dark hair was the pretty sister of whom Mrs Westgate had spoken. She presently turned to him with a remark which established her identity.

'It's a great pity you couldn't have brought my brother-in-law with you. It's a great shame he should be in New York in these days.'

'Oh yes; it's so very hot,' said Lord Lambeth.

'It must be dreadful,' said the young girl.

'I daresay he is very busy,' Lord Lambeth observed.

'The gentlemen in America work too much,' the young girl went on.

'Oh, do they? I daresay they like it,' said her interlocutor.

'I don't like it. One never sees them.'

'Don't you, really?' asked Lord Lambeth. 'I shouldn't have fancied that.'

'Have you come to study American manners?' asked the young girl.

'Oh, I don't know. I just came over for a lark. I haven't got long.' Here there was a pause, and Lord Lambeth began again. 'But Mr Westgate will come down here, will not he?'

'I certainly hope he will. He must help to entertain you and Mr Beaumont.'

Lord Lambeth looked at her a little with his handsome brown eyes. 'Do you suppose he would have come down with us, if we had urged him?'

Mr Westgate's sister-in-law was silent a moment, and then – 'I daresay he would,' she answered.

'Really!' said the young Englishman. 'He was immensely civil to Beaumont and me,' he added.

'He is a dear good fellow,' the young lady rejoined. 'And he is a perfect husband. But all Americans are that,' she continued, smiling.

'Really!' Lord Lambeth exclaimed again; and wondered whether all American ladies had such a passion for generalising as these two.

III

HE sat there a good while: there was a great deal of talk; it was all very friendly and lively and jolly. Every one present, sooner or later, said something to him, and seemed to make a particular point of addressing him by name. Two or three other persons came in, and there was a shifting of seats and changing of places; the gentlemen all entered into intimate conversation with the two Englishmen, made them urgent offers of hospitality and hoped they might frequently be of service to them. They were afraid Lord Lambeth and Mr Beaumont were not very comfortable at their hotel – that it was not, as one of them said, 'so private as those dear little English inns of yours'. This last gentlemen went on to say that unfortunately, as yet, perhaps, privacy was not quite so easily obtained in America as might be desired; still, he continued, you could generally get it by paying for it; in fact you could get everything in America nowadays by paying for it. American life was certainly growing a great deal more private; it was growing very much like England. Everything at Newport, for instance, was thoroughly private; Lord Lambeth would probably be struck with that. It was also represented to the strangers that it mattered very little whether their hotel was agreeable, as every one would want them to make visits; they would stay with other people, and, in any case, they would be a great deal at Mrs Westgate's. They would find that very charming; it was the pleasantest house in Newport. It was a pity Mr Westgate was always away; he was a man of the highest ability – very acute, very acute. He worked like a horse and he left his wife – well, to do about as she liked. He liked her to enjoy herself, and she seemed to know how. She was extremely brilliant, and a splendid talker. Some people preferred her sister; but Miss Alden was very different; she was in a different style altogether. Some people even thought her prettier, and, certainly, she was not so sharp. She was more in the Boston style; she had lived a great deal in Boston and she was very highly educated. Boston girls, it was intimated, were more like English young ladies.

Lord Lambeth had presently a chance to test the truth of this proposition; for on the company rising in compliance with a suggestion from their hostess that they should walk down to the rocks and look at the sea, the young Englishman again found himself, as they strolled across the grass, in proximity to Mrs Westgate's sister. Though she was but a girl of twenty, she appeared to feel the obligation to exert an active hospitality; and this was perhaps the more to be noticed as she seemed by nature a reserved and retiring person, and had little of her sister's fraternising quality. She was perhaps rather too thin, and she was a little pale; but as she moved slowly over the grass, with her arms hanging at her sides, looking gravely for a moment at the sea and then brightly, for all her gravity, at him, Lord Lambeth thought her at least as pretty as Mrs Westgate, and reflected that if this was the Boston style the Boston style was very charming. He thought she looked very clever; he could imagine that she was highly educated; but at the same time she seemed gentle and graceful. For all her cleverness, however, he felt that she had to think a little what to say; she didn't say the first thing that came into her head; he had come from a different part of the world and from a different society, and she was trying to adapt her conversation. The others were scattering themselves near the rocks; Mrs Westgate had charge of Percy Beaumont.

'Very jolly place, isn't it?' said Lord Lambeth. 'It's a very jolly place to sit.'

'Very charming,' said the young girl; 'I often sit here; there are all kinds of cosy corners – as if they had been made on purpose.'

'Ah! I suppose you have had some of them made,' said the young man.

Miss Alden looked at him a moment. 'Oh no, we have had nothing made. It's pure nature.'

'I should think you would have a few little benches – rustic seats and that sort of thing. It might be so jolly to sit here, you know,' Lord Lambeth went on.

'I am afraid we haven't so many of those things as you,' said the young girl, thoughtfully.

'I daresay you go in for pure nature as you were saying. Nature, over here, must be so grand, you know.' And Lord Lambeth looked about him.

The little coast-line hereabouts was very pretty, but it was not at all grand; and Miss Alden appeared to rise to a perception of this fact. 'I am afraid it seems to you very rough,' she said. 'It's not like the coast scenery in Kingsley's novels.'

'Ah, the novels always overdo it, you know,' Lord Lambeth rejoined. 'You must not go by the novels.'

They were wandering about a little on the rocks, and they stopped and looked down into a narrow chasm where the rising tide made a curious bellowing sound. It was loud enough to prevent their hearing each other, and they stood there for some moments in silence. The young girl looked at her companion, observing him attentively but covertly, as women, even when very young, know how to do. Lord Lambeth repaid observation; tall, straight and strong, he was handsome as certain young Englishmen, and certain young Englishmen almost alone, are handsome; with a perfect finish of feature and a look of intellectual repose and gentle good temper which seemed somehow to be consequent upon his well-cut nose and chin. And to speak of Lord Lambeth's expression of intellectual repose is not simply a civil way of saying that he looked stupid. He was evidently not a young man of an irritable imagination; he was not, as he would himself have said, tremendously clever; but, though there was a kind of appealing dullness in his eye, he looked thoroughly reasonable and competent, and his appearance proclaimed that to be a nobleman, an athlete, and an excellent fellow, was a sufficiently brilliant combination of qualities. The young girl beside him, it may be attested without farther delay, thought him the handsomest young man she had ever seen; and Bessie Alden's imagination, unlike that of her companion, was irritable. He, however, was also making up his mind that she was uncommonly pretty.

'I daresay it's very gay here – that you have lots of balls and parties,' he said; for, if he was not tremendously clever, he rather prided himself on having, with women, a sufficiency of conversation.

'Oh yes, there is a great deal going on,' Bessie Alden replied. 'There are not so many balls, but there are a good many other things. You will see for yourself; we live rather in the midst of it.'

'It's very kind of you to say that. But I thought you Americans were always dancing.'

'I suppose we dance a good deal; but I have never seen much of it. We don't do it much, at any rate, in summer. And I am sure,' said Bessie Alden, 'that we don't have so many balls as you have in England.'

'Really!' exclaimed Lord Lambeth. 'Ah, in England it all depends, you know.'

'You will not think much of our gaieties,' said the young girl, looking at him with a little mixture of interrogation and decision which was peculiar to her. The interrogation seemed earnest and the decision seemed arch; but the mixture, at any rate, was charming. 'Those things, with us, are much less splendid than in England.'

'I fancy you don't mean that,' said Lord Lambeth, laughing.

'I assure you I mean everything I say,' the young girl declared. 'Certainly, from what I have read about English society, it is very different.'

'Ah, well, you know,' said her companion, 'those things are often described by fellows who know nothing about them. You mustn't mind what you read.'

'Oh, I *shall* mind what I read!' Bessie Alden rejoined. 'When I read Thackeray and George Eliot, how can I help minding them?'

'Ah, well, Thackeray – and George Eliot,' said the young nobleman; 'I haven't read much of them.'

'Don't you suppose they know about society?' asked Bessie Alden.

'Oh, I daresay they know; they were so very clever. But those fashionable novels,' said Lord Lambeth, 'they are awful rot, you know.'

His companion looked at him a moment with her dark blue eyes, and then she looked down into the chasm where the water was tumbling about. 'Do you mean Mrs Gore, for instance?' she said presently, raising her eyes.

'I am afraid I haven't read that either,' was the young man's rejoinder, laughing a little and blushing. 'I am afraid you'll think I am not very intellectual.'

'Reading Mrs Gore is no proof of intellect. But I like reading everything about English life – even poor books. I am so curious about it.'

'Aren't ladies always curious?' asked the young man, jestingly.

But Bessie Alden appeared to desire to answer his question seriously. 'I don't think so – I don't think we are enough so – that we care about many things. So it's all the more of a compliment,' she added, 'that I should want to know so much about England.'

The logic here seemed a little close; but Lord Lambeth, conscious of a compliment, found his natural modesty just at hand. 'I am sure you know a great deal more than I do.'

'I really think I know a great deal – for a person who has never been there.'

'Have you really never been there?' cried Lord Lambeth. 'Fancy!'

'Never – except in imagination,' said the young girl.

'Fancy!' repeated her companion. 'But I daresay you'll go soon, won't you?'

'It's the dream of my life!' declared Bessie Alden, smiling.

'But your sister seems to know a tremendous lot about London,' Lord Lambeth went on.

The young girl was silent a moment. 'My sister and I are two very different persons,' she presently said. 'She has been a great deal in Europe. She has been in England several times. She has known a great many English people.'

'But you must have known some, too,' said Lord Lambeth.

'I don't think that I have ever spoken to one before. You are the first Englishman that – to my knowledge – I have ever talked with.'

Bessie Alden made this statement with a certain gravity – almost, as it seemed to Lord Lambeth, an impressiveness. Attempts at impressiveness always made him feel awkward, and he now began to laugh and swing his stick. 'Ah, you would have been sure to know!' he said. And then he added, after an instant – 'I'm sorry I am not a better specimen.'

The young girl looked away; but she smiled, laying aside her impressiveness. 'You must remember that you are only a beginning,' she said. Then she retraced her steps, leading the way back to the lawn, where they saw Mrs Westgate come towards them with Percy Beaumont still at her side. 'Perhaps I shall go to England next year,' Miss Alden continued; 'I want to, immensely. My sister is going to Europe, and she has asked me to go with her. If we go, I shall make her stay as long as possible in London.'

'Ah, you must come in July,' said Lord Lambeth. 'That's the time when there is most going on.'

'I don't think I can wait till July,' the young girl rejoined. 'By the first of May I shall be very impatient.' They had gone farther, and Mrs Westgate and her companion were near them. 'Kitty,' said Miss Alden, 'I have given out that we are going to London next May. So please to conduct yourself accordingly.'

Percy Beaumont wore a somewhat animated – even a slightly irritated – air. He was by no means so handsome a man as his cousin, although in his cousin's absence he might have passed for a striking specimen of the tall, muscular, fair-bearded, clear-eyed Englishman. Just now Beaumont's clear eyes, which were small and of a pale grey colour, had a rather troubled light, and, after glancing at Bessie Alden while she spoke, he rested them upon his kinsman. Mrs Westgate meanwhile, with her superfluously pretty gaze, looked at every one alike.

'You had better wait till the time comes,' she said to her sister. 'Perhaps next May you won't care so much about London. Mr Beaumont and I,' she went on smiling at her companion, 'have had a tremendous discussion. We don't agree about anything. It's perfectly delightful.'

'Oh, I say, Percy!' exclaimed Lord Lambeth.

'I disagree,' said Beaumont, stroking down his black hair, 'even to the point of not thinking it delightful.'

'Oh, I say!' cried Lord Lambeth again.

'I don't see anything delightful in my disagreeing with Mrs Westgate,' said Percy Beaumont.

'Well, I do!' Mrs Westgate declared; and she turned to her sister. 'You know you have to go to town. The phaeton is there. You had better take Lord Lambeth.'

At this point Percy Beaumont certainly looked straight at his kinsman; he tried to catch his eye. But Lord Lambeth would not look at him; his own eyes were better occupied. 'I shall be very happy,' cried Bessie Alden. 'I am only going to some shops. But I will drive you about and show you the place.'

'An American woman who respects herself,' said Mrs Westgate, turning to Beaumont with her bright expository air, 'must buy something every day of her life. If she cannot do it herself, she must send out some member of her family for the purpose. So Bessie goes forth to fulfil my mission.'

The young girl had walked away, with Lord Lambeth by her side, to whom she was talking still; and Percy Beaumont watched them as they passed towards the house. 'She fulfils her own mission,' he presently said; 'that of being a very attractive young lady.'

'I don't know that I should say very attractive,' Mrs Westgate rejoined. 'She is not so much that as she is charming when you really know her. She is very shy.'

'Oh indeed?' said Percy Beaumont.

'Extremely shy,' Mrs Westgate repeated. 'But she is a dear good girl; she is a charming species of girl. She is not in the least a flirt; that isn't at all her line; she doesn't know the alphabet of that sort of thing. She is very simple – very serious. She has lived a great deal in Boston, with another sister of mine – the eldest of us – who married a Bostonian. She is very cultivated, not at all like me – I am not in the least cultivated. She has studied immensely and read everything; she is what they call in Boston "thoughtful".'

'A rum sort of girl for Lambeth to get hold of!' his lordship's kinsman privately reflected.

'I really believe,' Mrs Westgate continued, 'that the most charming girl in the world is a Boston superstructure upon a New York *fonds*; or perhaps a New York superstructure upon a Boston *fonds*. At any rate it's the mixture,' said Mrs Westgate, who continued to give Percy Beaumont a great deal of information.

Lord Lambeth got into a little basket-phaeton with Bessie Alden, and she drove him down the long avenue, whose extent he had measured on foot a couple of hours before, into the ancient town, as it was called in that part of the world, of Newport. The ancient town was a curious affair – a collection of fresh-looking little wooden houses, painted white, scattered over a hill-side and clustered about a long, straight street, paved with enormous cobble-stones. There were plenty of shops – a large proportion of which appeared to be those of fruit-vendors, with piles of huge water-melons and pumpkins stacked in front of them; and, drawn up before the shops, or bumping about on the cobble-stones, were innumerable other basket-phaetons freighted with ladies of high fashion, who greeted each other from vehicle to vehicle and conversed on the edge of the pavement in a manner that struck Lord Lambeth as demonstrative – with a great many 'Oh, my dears', and little quick exclamations and caresses. His companion went into seventeen shops – he amused himself with counting them – and accumulated, at the bottom of the phaeton, a pile of bundles that hardly left the young Englishman a place for his feet. As she had no groom nor footman, he sat in the phaeton to hold the ponies; where, although he was not a particularly acute observer, he saw much to entertain him – especially the ladies just mentioned, who wandered up and down with the appearance of a kind of aimless intentness, as if they were looking for something to buy, and who, tripping in and out of their vehicles, displayed remarkably pretty feet. It all seemed to Lord Lambeth very odd, and bright, and gay. Of course, before they got back to the villa, he had had a great deal of desultory conversation with Bessie Alden.

The young Englishmen spent the whole of that day and the whole of many successive days in what the French call the *intimité* of their new friends. They agreed that it was extremely jolly – that they had never known anything more agreeable. It is not proposed to narrate minutely the incidents of their sojourn on this charming shore; though if it were convenient I might present a record of impressions none the less delectable that they were not exhaustively analysed. Many of them still linger in the minds of our travellers, attended by a train of harmonious images – images of brilliant mornings on lawns and piazzas that overlooked the sea; of innumerable pretty girls; of infinite lounging and talking and laughing and flirting and lunching and dining; of universal friendliness and frankness; of occasions on which they knew every one and everything and had an extraordinary sense of ease; of drives and rides in the late afternoon, over gleaming beaches, on long sea-roads, beneath a sky lighted up by marvellous sunsets; of tea-tables, on the return, informal, irregular, agreeable; of evenings at open windows or on the perpetual verandahs, in the summer starlight, above the warm Atlantic. The young Englishmen were introduced to everybody, entertained by everybody, intimate with everybody. At the end of three days they had removed their luggage from the hotel, and had gone to stay with Mrs Westgate – a step to which Percy Beaumont at first offered some conscientious opposition. I call his opposition conscientious because it was founded upon some talk that he had had, on the second day, with Bessie Alden. He had indeed had a good deal of talk with her, for she was not literally always in conversation with Lord Lambeth. He had meditated upon Mrs Westgate's account of her sister and he discovered, for himself, that the young lady was clever and appeared to have read a great deal. She seemed very nice, though he could not make out that, as Mrs Westgate had said, she was shy. If she was shy she carried it off very well.

'Mr Beaumont,' she had said, 'please tell me something about Lord Lambeth's family. How would you say it in England? – his position.'

'His position?' Percy Beaumont repeated.

'His rank – or whatever you call it. Unfortunately we haven't got a "Peerage", like the people in Thackeray.'

'That's a great pity,' said Beaumont. 'You would find it all set forth there so much better than I can do it.'

'He is a great noble, then?'

'Oh yes, he is a great noble.'

'Is he a peer?'

'Almost.'

'And has he any other title than Lord Lambeth?'

'His title is the Marquis of Lambeth,' said Beaumont; and then he was silent; Bessie Alden appeared to be looking at him with interest. 'He is the son of the Duke of Bayswater,' he added, presently.

'The eldest son?'

'The only son.'

'And are his parents living?'

'Oh yes; if his father were not living he would be a duke.'

'So that when his father dies,' pursued Bessie Alden, with more simplicity than might have been expected in a clever girl, 'he will become Duke of Bayswater?'

'Of course,' said Percy Beaumont. 'But his father is in excellent health.'

'And his mother?'

Beaumont smiled a little. 'The Duchess is uncommonly robust.'

'And has he any sisters?'

'Yes, there are two.'

'And what are they called?'

'One of them is married. She is the Countess of Pimlico.'

'And the other?'

'The other is unmarried; she is plain Lady Julia.'

Bessie Alden looked at him a moment. 'Is she very plain?'

Beaumont began to laugh again. 'You would not find her so handsome as her brother,' he said; and it was after this that he attempted to dissuade the heir of the Duke of Bayswater from accepting Mrs Westgate's invitation. 'Depend upon it,' he said, 'that girl means to try for you.'

'It seems to me you are doing your best to make a fool of me,' the modest young nobleman answered.

'She has been asking me,' said Beaumont, 'all about your people and your possessions.'

'I am sure it is very good of her!' Lord Lambeth rejoined.

'Well, then,' observed his companion, 'if you go, you go with your eyes open.'

'Damn my eyes!' exclaimed Lord Lambeth. 'If one is to be a dozen times a day at the house, it is a great deal more convenient to sleep there. I am sick of travelling up and down this beastly Avenue.'

Since he had determined to go, Percy Beaumont would of course have been very sorry to allow him to go alone; he was a man of conscience, and he remembered his promise to the Duchess. It was obviously the memory of this promise that made him say to his companion a couple of days later that he rather wondered he should be so fond of that girl.

'In the first place, how do you know how fond I am of her?' asked Lord Lambeth. 'And in the second place, why shouldn't I be fond of her?'

'I shouldn't think she would be in your line.'

'What do you call my "line"? You don't set her down as "fast"?'

'Exactly so. Mrs Westgate tells me that there is no such thing as the "fast girl" in America; that it's an English invention and that the term has no meaning here.'

'All the better. It's an animal I detest.'

'You prefer a blue-stocking.'

'Is that what you call Miss Alden?'

'Her sister tells me,' said Percy Beaumont, 'that she is tremendously literary.'

'I don't know anything about that. She is certainly very clever.'

'Well,' said Beaumont, 'I should have supposed you would have found that sort of thing awfully slow.'

'In point of fact,' Lord Lambeth rejoined, 'I find it uncommonly lively.'

After this, Percy Beaumont held his tongue; but on August 10th he wrote to the Duchess of Bayswater. He was, as I have said, a man of conscience, and he had a strong, incorruptible sense of the proprieties of life. His kinsman, meanwhile, was having a great deal of talk with Bessie Alden – on the red sea-rocks beyond the lawn; in the course of long island rides, with a slow return in the glowing twilight; on the deep verandah, late in the evening. Lord Lambeth, who had stayed at many houses, had never stayed at a house in which it was possible for a young man to converse so frequently with a young lady. This young lady no longer applied to Percy Beaumont for information concerning his lordship. She addressed herself directly to the young nobleman. She asked him a great many questions, some of which bored him a little; for he took no pleasure in talking about himself.

'Lord Lambeth,' said Bessie Alden, 'are you an hereditary legislator?'

'Oh, I say,' cried Lord Lambeth, 'don't make me call myself such names as that.'

'But you are a member of Parliament,' said the young girl.

'I don't like the sound of that either.'

'Doesn't your father sit in the House of Lords?' Bessie Alden went on.

'Very seldom,' said Lord Lambeth.

'Is it an important position?' she asked.

'Oh dear no,' said Lord Lambeth.

'I should think it would be very grand,' said Bessie Alden, 'to possess simply by an accident of birth the right to make laws for a great nation.'

'Ah, but one doesn't make laws. It's a great humbug.'

'I don't believe that,' the young girl declared. 'It must be a great privilege, and I should think that if one thought of it in the right way – from a high point of view – it would be very inspiring.'

'The less one thinks of it the better,' Lord Lambeth affirmed.

'I think it's tremendous,' said Bessie Alden; and on another occasion she asked him if he had any tenantry. Hereupon it was that, as I have said, he was a little bored.

'Do you want to buy up their leases?' he asked.

'Well – have you got any livings?' she demanded.

'Oh, I say!' he cried. 'Have you got a clergyman that is looking out?' But she made him tell her that he had a Castle; he confessed to but one. It was the place in which he had been born and brought up, and, as he had an old-time liking for it, he was beguiled into describing it a little and saying it was really very jolly. Bessie Alden listened with great interest, and declared that she would give the world to see such a place. Whereupon – 'It would be awfully kind of you to come and stay there,' said Lord Lambeth. He took a vague satisfaction in the circumstance that Percy Beaumont had not heard him make the remark I have just recorded.

Mr Westgate, all this time, had not, as they said at Newport, 'come on'. His wife more than once announced that she expected him on the morrow; but on the morrow she wandered about a little, with a telegram in her jewelled fingers, declaring it was very tiresome that his business detained him in New York; that he could only hope the Englishmen were having a good time. 'I must say,' said Mrs Westgate, 'that it is no thanks to him if you are!' And she went on to explain, while she continued that slow-paced promenade which enabled her well-adjusted skirts to display themselves so advantageously, that unfortunately in America there was no leisure-class. It was Lord Lambeth's theory, freely propounded when the young men were together, that Percy Beaumont was having a very good time with Mrs Westgate, and that under the pretext of meeting for the purpose of animated discussion, they were indulging in practices that imparted a shade of hypocrisy to the lady's regret for her husband's absence.

'I assure you we are always discussing and differing,' said Percy Beaumont. 'She is awfully argumentative. American ladies certainly don't mind contradicting you. Upon my word I don't think I was ever treated so by a woman before. She's so devilish positive.'

Mrs Westgate's positive quality, however, evidently had its attractions; for Beaumont was constantly at his hostess's side. He detached himself one day to the extent of going to New York to talk over the Tennessee Central with Mr Westgate; but he was absent only forty-eight hours, during which, with Mr Westgate's assistance, he completely settled this piece of business. 'They certainly do things quickly in New York,' he observed to his cousin; and he added that Mr Westgate had seemed very uneasy lest his wife should miss her visitor – he had been in such an awful hurry to send him back to her. 'I'm afraid you'll never come up to an American husband – if that's what the wives expect,' he said to Lord Lambeth.

Mrs Westgate, however, was not to enjoy much longer the entertainment with which an indulgent husband had desired to keep her provided. On August 21st Lord Lambeth received a telegram from his mother, requesting him to return immediately to England; his father had been taken ill, and it was his filial duty to come to him.

The young Englishman was visibly annoyed. 'What the deuce does it mean?' he asked of his kinsman. 'What am I to do?'

Percy Beaumont was annoyed as well; he had deemed it his duty, as I have narrated, to write to the Duchess, but he had not expected that this distinguished woman would act so promptly upon his hint. 'It means,' he said, 'that your father is laid up. I don't suppose it's anything serious; but you have no option. Take the first steamer; but don't be alarmed.'

Lord Lambeth made his farewells; but the few last words that he exchanged with Bessie Alden are the only ones that have a place in our record. 'Of course I needn't assure you,' he said, 'that if you should come to England next year, I expect to be the first person that you inform of it.'

Bessie Alden looked at him a little and she smiled. 'Oh, if we come to London,' she answered, 'I should think you would hear of it.'

Percy Beaumont returned with his cousin, and his sense of duty compelled him, one windless afternoon, in mid-Atlantic, to say to Lord Lambeth that he suspected that the Duchess's telegram was in part the result of something he himself had written to her. 'I wrote to her – as I explicitly notified you I had promised to do – that you were extremely interested in a little American girl.'

Lord Lambeth was extremely angry, and he indulged for some moments in the simple language of resentment. But I have said that he was a reasonable young man, and I can give no better proof of it than the fact that he remarked to his companion at the end of half-an-hour – 'You were quite right after all. I am very much interested in her. Only, to be fair,' he added, 'you should have told my mother also that she is not – seriously – interested in me.'

Percy Beaumont gave a little laugh. 'There is nothing so charming as modesty in a young man in your position. That speech is a capital proof that you are sweet on her.'

'She is not interested – she is not!' Lord Lambeth repeated.

'My dear fellow,' said his companion, 'you are very far gone.'

IV

IN point of fact, as Percy Beaumont would have said, Mrs Westgate disembarked on the 18th of May on the British coast. She was accompanied by her sister, but she was not attended by any other member of her family. To the deprivation of her husband's society Mrs Westgate was, however, habituated; she had made half-a-dozen journeys to Europe without him, and she now accounted for his absence, to interrogative friends on this side of the Atlantic, by allusion to the regrettable but conspicuous fact that in America there was no leisure-class. The two ladies came up to London and alighted at Jones's Hotel, where Mrs Westgate, who had made on former occasions the most agreeable impression at this establishment, received an obsequious greeting. Bessie Alden had felt much excited about coming to England; she had expected the 'associations' would be very charming, that it would be an infinite pleasure to rest her eyes upon the things she had read about in the poets and historians. She was very fond of the poets and historians, of the picturesque, of the past, of retrospect, of mementos and reverberations of greatness; so that on coming into the great English world, where strangeness and familiarity would go hand in hand, she was prepared for a multitude of fresh emotions. They began very promptly – these tender, fluttering sensations; they began with the sight of the beautiful English landscape, whose dark richness was quickened and brightened by the season; with the carpeted fields and flowering hedge-rows, as she looked at them from the window of the train; with the spires of the rural churches, peeping above the rook-haunted tree-tops; with the oak-studded parks, the ancient homes, the cloudy light, the speech, the manners, the thousand differences. Mrs Westgate's impressions had of course much less novelty and keenness, and she gave but a wandering attention to her sister's ejaculations and rhapsodies.

'You know my enjoyment of England is not so intellectual as Bessie's,' she said to several of her friends in the course of her visit to this country. 'And yet if it is not intellectual, I can't say it is physical. I don't think I can quite say what it is, my enjoyment of England.' When once it was settled that the two ladies should come abroad and should spend a few weeks in England on their way to the Continent, they of course exchanged a good many allusions to their London acquaintance.

'It will certainly be much nicer having friends there,' Bessie Alden had said one day, as she sat on the sunny deck of the steamer, at her sister's feet, on a large blue rug.

'Whom do you mean by friends?' Mrs Westgate asked.

'All those English gentlemen whom you have known and entertained. Captain Littledale, for instance. And Lord Lambeth and Mr Beaumont,' added Bessie Alden.

'Do you expect them to give us a very grand reception?'

Bessie reflected a moment; she was addicted, as we know, to reflection. 'Well, yes.'

'My poor sweet child!' murmured her sister.

'What have I said that is so silly?' asked Bessie.

'You are a little too simple; just a little. It is very becoming, but it pleases people at your expense.'

'I am certainly too simple to understand you,' said Bessie.

'Shall I tell you a story?' asked her sister.

'If you would be so good. That is what they do to amuse simple people.'

Mrs Westgate consulted her memory, while her companion sat gazing at the shining sea. 'Did you ever hear of the Duke of Green-Erin?'

'I think not,' said Bessie.

'Well, it's no matter,' her sister went on.

'It's a proof of my simplicity.'

'My story is meant to illustrate that of some other people,' said Mrs Westgate. 'The Duke of Green-Erin is what they call in England a great swell; and some five years ago he came to America. He spent most of his time in New York, and in New York he spent his days and his nights at the Butterworths'. You have heard at least of the Butterworths. *Bien*. They did everything in the world for him – they turned themselves inside out. They gave him a dozen dinner-parties and balls, and were the means of his being invited to fifty more. At first he used to come into Mrs Butterworth's box at the opera in a tweed travelling-suit; but some one stopped that. At any rate, he had a beautiful time, and they parted the best friends in the world. Two years elapse, and the Butterworths come abroad and go to London. The first thing they see in all the papers – in England those things are in the most prominent place – is that the Duke of Green-Erin has arrived in town for the Season. They wait a little, and then Mr Butterworth – as polite as ever – goes and leaves a card. They wait a little more; the visit is not returned; they wait three weeks – *silence de mort* – the Duke gives no sign. The Butterworths see a lot of other people, put down the Duke of Green-Erin as a rude, ungrateful man, and forget all about him. One fine day they go to Ascot Races, and there they meet him face to face. He stares a moment and then comes up to Mr Butterworth, taking something from his pocket-book – something which proves to be a bank-note. "I'm glad to see you, Mr Butterworth," he says, "so that I can pay you that ten pounds I lost to you in New York. I saw the other day you remembered our bet; here are the ten pounds, Mr Butterworth. Good-bye, Mr Butterworth." And off he goes, and that's the last they see of the Duke of Green-Erin.'

'Is that your story?' asked Bessie Alden.

'Don't you think it's interesting?' her sister replied.

'I don't believe it,' said the young girl.

'Ah!' cried Mrs Westgate, 'you are not so simple after all. Believe it or not as you please; there is no smoke without fire.'

'Is that the way,' asked Bessie after a moment, 'that you expect your friends to treat you?'

'I defy them to treat me very ill, because I shall not give them the opportunity. With the best will in the world, in that case, they can't be very disobliging.'

Bessie Alden was silent a moment. 'I don't see what makes you talk that way,' she said. 'The English are a great people.'

'Exactly; and that is just the way they have grown great – by dropping you when you have ceased to be useful. People say they are not clever; but I think they are very clever.'

'You know you have liked them – all the Englishmen you have seen,' said Bessie.

'They have liked me,' her sister rejoined; 'it would be more correct to say that. And of course one likes that.'

Bessie Alden resumed for some moments her studies in sea-green. 'Well,' she said, 'whether they like me or not, I mean to like them. And happily,' she added, 'Lord Lambeth does not owe me ten pounds.'

During the first few days after their arrival at Jones's Hotel our charming Americans were much occupied with what they would have called looking about them. They found occasion to make a large number of purchases, and their opportunities for conversation were such only as were offered by the deferential London shopmen. Bessie Alden, even in driving from the station, took an immense fancy to the British metropolis, and, at the risk of exhibiting her as a young woman of vulgar tastes, it must be recorded that for a considerable period she desired no higher pleasure than to drive about the crowded streets in a Hansom cab. To her attentive eyes they were full of a strange picturesque life, and it is at least beneath the dignity of our historic muse to enumerate the trivial objects and incidents which this simple young lady from Boston found so entertaining. It may be freely mentioned, however, that whenever, after a round of visits in Bond Street and Regent Street, she was about to return with her sister to Jones's Hotel, she made an earnest request that they should be driven home by way of Westminster Abbey. She had begun by asking whether it would not be possible to take the Tower on the way to their lodgings; but it happened that at a more primitive stage of her culture Mrs Westgate had paid a visit to this venerable monument, which she spoke of ever afterwards, vaguely, as a dreadful disappointment; so that she expressed the liveliest disapproval of any attempt to combine historical researches with the purchase of hair-brushes and note-paper. The most she would consent to do in this line was to spend half-an-hour at Madame Tussaud's, where she saw several dusty wax effigies of members of the Royal Family. She told Bessie that if she wished to go to the Tower she must get some one else to take her. Bessie expressed hereupon an earnest disposition to go alone; but upon this proposal as well Mrs Westgate sprinkled cold water.

'Remember,' she said, 'that you are not in your innocent little Boston. It is not a question of walking up and down Beacon Street.' Then she went on to explain that there were two classes of American girls in Europe – those that walked about alone and those that did not. 'You happen to belong, my dear,' she said to her sister, 'to the class that does not.'

'It is only,' answered Bessie, laughing, 'because you happen to prevent me.' And she devoted much private meditation to this question of effecting a visit to the Tower of London.

Suddenly it seemed as if the problem might be solved; the two ladies at Jones's Hotel received a visit from Willie Woodley. Such was the social appellation of a young American who had sailed from New York a few days after their own departure, and who, having the privilege of intimacy with them in that city, had lost no time, on his arrival in London, in coming to pay them his respects. He had, in fact, gone to see them directly after going to see his tailor; than which there can be no greater exhibition of promptitude on the part of a young American who has just alighted at the Charing Cross Hotel. He was a slim, pale youth, of the most amiable disposition, famous for the skill with which he led the 'German' in New York. Indeed, by the young ladies who habitually figured in this fashionable frolic he was believed to be 'the best dancer in the world'; it was in these terms that he was always spoken of, and that his identity was indicated. He was the gentlest, softest young man it was possible to meet; he was beautifully dressed – 'in the English style' – and he knew an immense deal about London. He had been at Newport during the previous summer, at the time of our young Englishmen's visit, and he took extreme pleasure in the society of Bessie Alden, whom he always addressed as 'Miss Bessie'. She immediately arranged with him, in the presence of her sister, that he should conduct her to the scene of Lady Jane Grey's execution.

'You may do as you please,' said Mrs Westgate. 'Only – if you desire the information – it is not the custom here for young ladies to knock about London with young men.'

'Miss Bessie has waltzed with me so often,' observed Willie Woodley; 'she can surely go out with me in a Hansom.'

'I consider waltzing,' said Mrs Westgate, 'the most innocent pleasure of our time.'

'It's a compliment to our time!' exclaimed the young man, with a little laugh, in spite of himself.

'I don't see why I should regard what is done here,' said Bessie Alden. 'Why should I suffer the restrictions of a society of which I enjoy none of the privileges?'

'That's very good – very good,' murmured Willie Woodley.

'Oh, go to the Tower, and feel the axe, if you like!' said Mrs Westgate. 'I consent to your going with Mr Woodley; but I should not let you go with an Englishman.'

'Miss Bessie wouldn't care to go with an Englishman!' Mr Woodley declared, with a faint asperity that was, perhaps, not unnatural in a young man who, dressing in the manner that I have indicated, and knowing a great deal, as I have said, about London, saw no reason for drawing these sharp distinctions. He agreed upon a day with Miss Bessie – a day of that same week.

An ingenious mind might, perhaps, trace a connection between the young girl's allusion to her destitution of social privileges and a question she asked on the morrow as she sat with her sister at lunch.

'Don't you mean to write to – to any one?' said Bessie.

'I wrote this morning to Captain Littledale,' Mrs Westgate replied.

'But Mr Woodley said that Captain Littledale had gone to India.'

'He said he thought he had heard so; he knew nothing about it.'

For a moment Bessie Alden said nothing more; then, at last, 'And don't you intend to write to – to Mr Beaumont?' she inquired.

'You mean to Lord Lambeth,' said her sister.

'I said Mr Beaumont because he was so good a friend of yours.'

Mrs Westgate looked at the young girl with sisterly candour. 'I don't care two straws for Mr Beaumont.'

'You were certainly very nice to him.'

'I am nice to every one,' said Mrs Westgate, simply.

'To every one but me,' rejoined Bessie, smiling.

Her sister continued to look at her; then, at last, 'Are you in love with Lord Lambeth?' she asked.

The young girl stared a moment, and the question was apparently too humorous even to make her blush. 'Not that I know of,' she answered.

'Because if you are,' Mrs Westgate went on, 'I shall certainly not send for him.'

'That proves what I said,' declared Bessie, smiling – 'that you are not nice to me.'

'It would be a poor service, my dear child,' said her sister.

'In what sense? There is nothing against Lord Lambeth, that I know of.'

Mrs Westgate was silent a moment. 'You *are* in love with him, then?'

Bessie stared again; but this time she blushed a little. 'Ah! if you won't be serious,' she answered, 'we will not mention him again.'

For some moments Lord Lambeth was not mentioned again, and it was Mrs Westgate who, at the end of this period, reverted to him. 'Of course I will let him know we are here; because I think he would be hurt – justly enough – if we should go away without seeing him. It is fair to give him a chance to come and thank me for the kindness we showed him. But I don't want to seem eager.'

'Neither do I,' said Bessie, with a little laugh.

'Though I confess,' added her sister, 'that I am curious to see how he will behave.'

'He behaved very well at Newport.'

'Newport is not London. At Newport he could do as he liked; but here, it is another affair. He has to have an eye to consequences.'

'If he had more freedom, then, at Newport,' argued Bessie, 'it is the more to his credit that he behaved well; and if he has to be so careful here, it is possible he will behave even better.'

'Better – better,' repeated her sister. 'My dear child, what is your point of view?'

'How do you mean – my point of view?'

'Don't you care for Lord Lambeth – a little?'

This time Bessie Alden was displeased; she slowly got up from table, turning her face away from her sister. 'You will oblige me by not talking so,' she said.

Mrs Westgate sat watching her for some moments as she moved slowly about the room and went and stood at the window. 'I will write to him this afternoon,' she said at last.

'Do as you please!' Bessie answered; and presently she turned round. 'I am not afraid to say that I like Lord Lambeth. I like him very much.'

'He is not clever,' Mrs Westgate declared.

'Well, there have been clever people whom I have disliked,' said Bessie Alden; 'so that I suppose I may like a stupid one. Besides, Lord Lambeth is not stupid.'

'Not so stupid as he looks!' exclaimed her sister, smiling.

'If I were in love with Lord Lambeth, as you said just now, it would be bad policy on your part to abuse him.'

'My dear child, don't give me lessons in policy!' cried Mrs Westgate. 'The policy I mean to follow is very deep.'

The young girl began to walk about the room again; then she stopped before her sister. 'I have never heard in the course of five minutes,' she said, 'so many hints and innuendos. I wish you would tell me in plain English what you mean.'

'I mean that you may be much annoyed.'

'That is still only a hint,' said Bessie.

Her sister looked at her, hesitating an instant. 'It will be said of you that you have come after Lord Lambeth – that you followed him.'

Bessie Alden threw back her pretty head like a startled hind, and a look flashed into her face that made Mrs Westgate rise from her chair. 'Who says such things as that?' she demanded.

'People here.'

'I don't believe it,' said Bessie.

'You have a very convenient faculty of doubt. But my policy will be, as I say, very deep. I shall leave you to find out this kind of thing for yourself.'

Bessie fixed her eyes upon her sister, and Mrs Westgate thought for a moment there were tears in them. 'Do they talk that way here?' she asked.

'You will see. I shall leave you alone.'

'Don't leave me alone,' said Bessie Alden. 'Take me away.'

'No; I want to see what you make of it,' her sister continued. 'I don't understand.'

'You will understand after Lord Lambeth has come,' said Mrs Westgate, with a little laugh.

The two ladies had arranged that on this afternoon Willie Woodley should go with them to Hyde Park, where Bessie Alden expected to derive much entertainment from sitting on a little green chair, under the great trees, beside Rotten Row. The want of a suitable escort had hitherto rendered this pleasure inaccessible; but no escort, now, for such an expedition, could have been more suitable than their devoted young countryman, whose mission in life, it might almost be said, was to find chairs for ladies, and who appeared on the stroke of half-past five with a white camellia in his button-hole.

'I have written to Lord Lambeth, my dear,' said Mrs Westgate to her sister, on coming into the room where Bessie Alden, drawing on her long grey gloves, was entertaining their visitor.

Bessie said nothing, but Willie Woodley exclaimed that his lordship was in town; he had seen his name in the *Morning Post*.

'Do you read the *Morning Post*?' asked Mrs Westgate.

'Oh yes; it's great fun,' Willie Woodley affirmed.

'I want so to see it,' said Bessie, 'there is so much about it in Thackeray.'

'I will send it to you every morning,' said Willie Woodley.

He found them what Bessie Alden thought excellent places, under the great trees, beside the famous avenue whose humours had been made familiar to the young girl's childhood by the pictures in *Punch*. The day was bright and warm, and the crowd of riders and spectators and the great procession of carriages were proportionately dense and brilliant. The scene bore the stamp of the London Season at its height, and Bessie Alden found more entertainment in it than she was able to express to her companions. She sat silent, under her parasol, and her imagination, according to its wont, let itself loose into the great changing assemblage of striking and suggestive figures. They stirred up a host of old impressions and preconceptions, and she found herself fitting a history to this person and a theory to that, and making a place for them all in her little private museum of types. But if she said little, her sister on one side and Willie Woodley on the other expressed themselves in lively alternation.

'Look at that green dress with blue flounces,' said Mrs Westgate. '*Quelle toilette!*'

'That's the Marquis of Blackborough,' said the young man – 'the one in the white coat. I heard him speak the other night in the House of Lords; it was something about ramrods; he called them *wamwods*. He's an awful swell.'

'Did you ever see anything like the way they are pinned back?' Mrs Westgate resumed. 'They never know where to stop.'

'They do nothing but stop,' said Willie Woodley. 'It prevents them from walking. Here comes a great celebrity – Lady Beatrice Bellevue. She's awfully fast; see what little steps she takes.'

'Well, my dear,' Mrs Westgate pursued, 'I hope you are getting some ideas for your *couturière*?'

'I am getting plenty of ideas,' said Bessie, 'but I don't know that my *couturière* would appreciate them.'

Willie Woodley presently perceived a friend on horseback, who drove up beside the barrier of the Row and beckoned to him. He went forward and the crowd of pedestrians closed about him, so that for some ten minutes he was hidden from sight. At last he reappeared, bringing a gentleman with him – a gentleman whom Bessie at first supposed to be his friend dismounted. But at a second glance she found herself looking at Lord Lambeth, who was shaking hands with her sister.

'I found him over there,' said Willie Woodley, 'and I told him you were here.'

And then Lord Lambeth, touching his hat a little, shook hands with Bessie. 'Fancy your being here!' he said. He was blushing and smiling; he looked very handsome, and he had a kind of splendour that he had not had in America. Bessie Alden's imagination, as we know, was just then in exercise; so that the tall young Englishman, as he stood there looking down at her, had the benefit of it. 'He is handsomer and more splendid than anything I have ever seen,' she said to herself. And then she remembered that he was a Marquis, and she thought he looked like a Marquis.

'Really, you know,' he cried, 'you ought to have let a man know you were here!'

'I wrote to you an hour ago,' said Mrs Westgate.

'Doesn't all the world know it?' asked Bessie, smiling.

'I assure you I didn't know it!' cried Lord Lambeth. 'Upon my honour I hadn't heard of it. Ask Woodley now; had I, Woodley?'

'Well, I think you are rather a humbug,' said Willie Woodley.

'You don't believe that – do you, Miss Alden?' asked his lordship. 'You don't believe I'm a humbug, eh?'

'No,' said Bessie, 'I don't.'

'You are too tall to stand up, Lord Lambeth,' Mrs Westgate observed. 'You are only tolerable when you sit down. Be so good as to get a chair.'

He found a chair and placed it sidewise, close to the two ladies. 'If I hadn't met Woodley I should never have found you,' he went on. 'Should I, Woodley?'

'Well, I guess not,' said the young American.

'Not even with my letter?' asked Mrs Westgate.

'Ah, well, I haven't got your letter yet; I suppose I shall get it this evening. It was awfully kind of you to write.'

'So I said to Bessie,' observed Mrs Westgate.

'Did she say so, Miss Alden?' Lord Lambeth inquired. 'I daresay you have been here a month.'

'We have been here three,' said Mrs Westgate.

'Have you been here three months?' the young man asked again of Bessie.

'It seems a long time,' Bessie answered.

'I say, after that you had better not call me a humbug!' cried Lord Lambeth. 'I have only been in town three weeks; but you must have been hiding away. I haven't seen you anywhere.'

'Where should you have seen us – where should we have gone?' asked Mrs Westgate.

'You should have gone to Hurlingham,' said Willie Woodley.

'No, let Lord Lambeth tell us,' Mrs Westgate insisted.

'There are plenty of places to go to,' said Lord Lambeth – 'each one stupider than the other. I mean people's houses; they send you cards.'

'No one has sent us cards,' said Bessie.

'We are very quiet,' her sister declared. 'We are here as travellers.'

'We have been to Madame Tussaud's,' Bessie pursued.

'Oh, I say!' cried Lord Lambeth.

'We thought we should find your image there,' said Mrs Westgate – 'yours and Mr Beaumont's.'

'In the Chamber of Horrors?' laughed the young man.

'It did duty very well for a party,' said Mrs Westgate. 'All the women were *décolletées*, and many of the figures looked as if they could speak if they tried.'

'Upon my word,' Lord Lambeth rejoined, 'you see people at London parties that look as if they couldn't speak if they tried.'

'Do you think Mr Woodley could find us Mr Beaumont?' asked Mrs Westgate.

Lord Lambeth stared and looked round him. 'I daresay he could. Beaumont often comes here. Don't you think you could find him, Woodley? Make a dive into the crowd.'

'Thank you; I have had enough diving,' said Willie Woodley. 'I will wait till Mr Beaumont comes to the surface.'

'I will bring him to see you,' said Lord Lambeth; 'where are you staying?'

'You will find the address in my letter – Jones's Hotel.'

'Oh, one of those places just out of Piccadilly? Beastly hole, isn't it?' Lord Lambeth inquired.

'I believe it's the best hotel in London,' said Mrs Westgate.

'But they give you awful rubbish to eat, don't they?' his lordship went on.

'Yes,' said Mrs Westgate.

'I always feel so sorry for the people that come up to town and go to live in those places,' continued the young man. 'They eat nothing but poison.'

'Oh, I say!' cried Willie Woodley.

'Well, how do you like London, Miss Alden?' Lord Lambeth asked, unperturbed by this ejaculation.

'I think it's grand,' said Bessie Alden.

'My sister likes it, in spite of the "poison"!' Mrs Westgate exclaimed.

'I hope you are going to stay a long time.'

'As long as I can,' said Bessie.

'And where is Mr Westgate?' asked Lord Lambeth of this gentleman's wife.

'He's where he always is – in that tiresome New York.'

'He must be tremendously clever,' said the young man.

'I suppose he is,' said Mrs Westgate.

Lord Lambeth sat for nearly an hour with his American friends; but it is not our purpose to relate their conversation in full. He addressed a great many remarks to Bessie Alden, and finally turned towards her altogether, while Willie Woodley entertained Mrs Westgate. Bessie herself said very little; she was on her guard, thinking of what her sister had said to her at lunch. Little by little, however, she interested herself in Lord Lambeth again, as she had done at Newport; only it seemed to her that here he might become more interesting. He would be an unconscious part of the antiquity, the impressiveness, the picturesqueness of England; and poor Bessie

Alden, like many a Yankee maiden, was terribly at the mercy of picturesqueness.

'I have often wished I were at Newport again,' said the young man. 'Those days I spent at your sister's were awfully jolly.'

'We enjoyed them very much; I hope your father is better.'

'Oh dear, yes. When I got to England, he was out grouse-shooting. It was what you call in America a gigantic fraud. My mother had got nervous. My three weeks at Newport seemed like a happy dream.'

'America certainly is very different from England,' said Bessie.

'I hope you like England better, eh?' Lord Lambeth rejoined, almost persuasively.

'No Englishman can ask that seriously of a person of another country.'

Her companion looked at her for a moment. 'You mean it's a matter of course?'

'If I were English,' said Bessie, 'it would certainly seem to me a matter of course that every one should be a good patriot.'

'Oh dear, yes; patriotism is everything,' said Lord Lambeth, not quite following, but very contented. 'Now, what are you going to do here?'

'On Thursday I am going to the Tower.'

'The Tower?'

'The Tower of London. Did you never hear of it?'

'Oh yes, I have been there,' said Lord Lambeth. 'I was taken there by my governess, when I was six years old. It's a rum idea, your going there.'

'Do give me a few more rum ideas,' said Bessie. 'I want to see everything of that sort. I am going to Hampton Court, and to Windsor, and to the Dulwich Gallery.'

Lord Lambeth seemed greatly amused. 'I wonder you don't go to the Rosherville Gardens.'

'Are they interesting?' asked Bessie.

'Oh, wonderful!'

'Are they very old? That's all I care for,' said Bessie.

'They are tremendously old; they are all falling to ruins.'

'I think there is nothing so charming as an old ruinous garden,' said the young girl. 'We must certainly go there.'

Lord Lambeth broke out into merriment. 'I say, Woodley,' he cried, 'here's Miss Alden wants to go to the Rosherville Gardens!'

Willie Woodley looked a little blank; he was caught in the fact of ignorance of an apparently conspicuous feature of London life. But in a moment he turned it off. 'Very well,' he said, 'I'll write for a permit.'

Lord Lambeth's exhilaration increased. ''Gad, I believe you Americans would go anywhere!' he cried.

'We wish to go to Parliament,' said Bessie. 'That's one of the first things.'

'Oh, it would bore you to death!' cried the young man.

'We wish to hear you speak.'

'I never speak – except to young ladies,' said Lord Lambeth, smiling.

Bessie Alden looked at him awhile; smiling, too, in the shadow of her parasol. 'You are very strange,' she murmured. 'I don't think I approve of you.'

'Ah, now, don't be severe, Miss Alden!' said Lord Lambeth, smiling still more. 'Please don't be severe. I want you to like me – awfully.'

'To like you awfully? You must not laugh at me, then, when I make mistakes. I consider it my right – as a free-born American – to make as many mistakes as I choose.'

'Upon my word, I didn't laugh at you,' said Lord Lambeth.

'And not only that,' Bessie went on; 'but I hold that all my mistakes shall be set down to my credit. You must think the better of me for them.'

'I can't think better of you than I do,' the young man declared.

Bessie Alden looked at him a moment again. 'You certainly speak very well to young ladies. But why don't you address the House? – isn't that what they call it?'

'Because I have nothing to say,' said Lord Lambeth.

'Haven't you a great position?' asked Bessie Alden.

He looked a moment at the back of his glove. 'I'll set that down,' he said, 'as one of your mistakes – to your credit.' And, as if he disliked talking about his position, he changed the subject. 'I wish you would let me go with you to the Tower, and to Hampton Court, and to all those other places.'

'We shall be most happy,' said Bessie.

'And of course I shall be delighted to show you the Houses of Parliament – some day that suits you. There are a lot of things I want to do for you. I want you to have a good time. And I should like very much to present some of my friends to you, if it wouldn't bore you. Then it would be awfully kind of you to come down to Branches.'

'We are much obliged to you, Lord Lambeth,' said Bessie. 'What is Branches?'

'It's a house in the country. I think you might like it.'

Willie Woodley and Mrs Westgate, at this moment, were sitting in silence, and the young man's ear caught these last words of Lord Lambeth's. 'He's inviting Miss Bessie to one of his castles,' he murmured to his companion.

Mrs Westgate, foreseeing what she mentally called 'complications', immediately got up; and the two ladies, taking leave of Lord Lambeth, returned, under Mr Woodley's conduct, to Jones's Hotel.

V

LORD LAMBETH came to see them on the morrow, bringing Percy Beaumont with him – the latter having instantly declared his intention of neglecting none of the usual offices of civility. This declaration, however, when his kinsman informed him of the advent of their American friends, had been preceded by another remark.

'Here they are, then, and you are in for it.'

'What am I in for?' demanded Lord Lambeth.

'I will let your mother give it a name. With all respect to whom,' added Percy Beaumont, 'I must decline on this occasion to do any more police duty. Her Grace must look after you herself.'

'I will give her a chance,' said her Grace's son, a trifle grimly. 'I shall make her go and see them.'

'She won't do it, my boy.'

'We'll see if she doesn't,' said Lord Lambeth.

But if Percy Beaumont took a sombre view of the arrival of the two ladies at Jones's Hotel, he was sufficiently a man of the world to offer them a smiling countenance. He fell into animated conversation – conversation, at least, that was animated on her side – with Mrs Westgate, while his companion made himself agreeable to the younger lady. Mrs Westgate began confessing and protesting, declaring and expounding.

'I must say London is a great deal brighter and prettier just now than it was when I was here last – in the month of November. There is evidently a great deal going on, and you seem to have a good many flowers. I have no doubt it is very charming for all you people, and that you amuse yourselves immensely. It is very good of you to let Bessie and me come and sit and look at you. I suppose you will think I am very satirical, but I must confess that that's the feeling I have in London.'

'I am afraid I don't quite understand to what feeling you allude,' said Percy Beaumont.

'The feeling that it's all very well for you English people. Everything is beautifully arranged for you.'

'It seems to me it is very well for some Americans, sometimes,' rejoined Beaumont.

'For some of them, yes – if they like to be patronised. But I must say I don't like to be patronised. I may be very eccentric and undisciplined and unreasonable; but I confess I never was fond of patronage. I like to associate with people on the same terms as I do in my own country; that's a peculiar taste that I have. But here people seem to expect something else – Heaven knows what! I am afraid you will think I am very ungrateful, for I certainly have received a great deal of attention. The last time I was here, a lady sent me a message that I was at liberty to come and see her.'

'Dear me, I hope you didn't go,' observed Percy Beaumont.

'You are deliciously *naïf*, I must say that for you!' Mrs Westgate exclaimed. 'It must be a great advantage to you here in London. I suppose that if I myself had a little more *naïveté*, I should enjoy it more. I should be content to sit on a chair in the Park, and see the people pass, and be told that this is the Duchess of Suffolk, and that is the Lord Chamberlain, and that I must be thankful for the privilege of beholding them. I daresay it is very wicked and critical of me to ask for anything else. But I was always critical, and I freely confess to the sin of being fastidious. I am told there is some remarkably superior second-rate society provided here for strangers. *Merci*! I don't want any superior second-rate society. I want the society that I have been accustomed to.'

'I hope you don't call Lambeth and me second-rate,' Beaumont interposed.

'Oh, I am accustomed to you!' said Mrs Westgate. 'Do you know that you English sometimes make the most wonderful speeches? The first time I came to London, I went out to dine – as I told you, I have received a great deal of attention. After dinner, in the drawing-room, I had some conversation with an old lady; I assure you I had. I forget what we talked about; but she presently said, in allusion to something we were discussing, "Oh, you know, the aristocracy do so-and-so; but in one's own class of life it is very different." In one's own class of life! What is a poor unprotected American woman to do in a country where she is liable to have that sort of thing said to her?'

'You seem to get hold of some very queer old ladies; I compliment you on your acquaintance!' Percy Beaumont exclaimed. 'If you are trying to bring me to admit that London is an odious place, you'll not succeed. I'm extremely fond of it, and I think it the jolliest place in the world.'

'*Pour vous autres*. I never said the contrary,' Mrs Westgate retorted. I make use of this expression because both interlocutors had begun to raise their voices. Percy Beaumont naturally did not like to hear his country abused, and Mrs Westgate, no less naturally, did not like a stubborn debater.

'Hallo!' said Lord Lambeth; 'what are they up to now?' And he came away from the window, where he had been standing with Bessie Alden.

'I quite agree with a very clever countrywoman of mine,' Mrs Westgate continued, with charming ardour, though with imperfect relevancy. She smiled at the two gentlemen for a moment with terrible brightness, as if to toss at their feet – upon their native heath – the gauntlet of defiance. 'For me, there are only two social positions worth speaking of – that of an American lady and that of the Emperor of Russia.'

'And what do you do with the American gentlemen?' asked Lord Lambeth.

'She leaves them in America!' said Percy Beaumont.

On the departure of their visitors, Bessie Alden told her sister that Lord Lambeth would come the next day, to go with them to the Tower, and that he had kindly offered to bring his 'trap', and drive them thither. Mrs Westgate listened in silence to this communication, and for some time afterwards she said nothing. But at last, 'If you had not requested me the other day not to mention it,' she began, 'there is something I should venture to ask you.' Bessie frowned a little; her dark blue eyes were more dark than blue. But her sister went on. 'As it is, I will take the risk. You are not in love with Lord Lambeth: I believe it, perfectly. Very good. But is there, by chance, any danger of your becoming so? It's a very simple question; don't take offence. I have a particular reason,' said Mrs Westgate, 'for wanting to know.'

Bessie Alden for some moments said nothing; she only looked displeased. 'No; there is no danger,' she answered at last, curtly.

'Then I should like to frighten them,' declared Mrs Westgate, clasping her jewelled hands.

'To frighten whom?'

'All these people; Lord Lambeth's family and friends.'

'How should you frighten them?' asked the young girl.

'It wouldn't be I – it would be you. It would frighten them to think that you should absorb his lordship's young affections.'

Bessie Alden, with her clear eyes still overshadowed by her dark brows, continued to interrogate. 'Why should that frighten them?'

Mrs Westgate poised her answer with a smile before delivering it. 'Because they think you are not good enough. You are a charming girl, beautiful and amiable, intelligent and clever, and as *bien-élevée* as it is possible to be; but you are not a fit match for Lord Lambeth.'

Bessie Alden was immensely disgusted. 'Where do you get such extraordinary ideas?' she asked. 'You have said some such strange things lately. My dear Kitty, where do you collect them?'

Kitty was evidently enamoured of her idea. 'Yes, it would put them on pins and needles, and it wouldn't hurt you. Mr Beaumont is already most uneasy; I could soon see that.'

The young girl meditated a moment. 'Do you mean that they spy upon him – that they interfere with him?'

'I don't know what power they have to interfere, but I know that a British mamma may worry her son's life out.'

It has been intimated that, as regards certain disagreeable things, Bessie Alden had a fund of scepticism. She abstained on the present occasion from expressing disbelief, for she wished not to irritate her sister. But she said to herself that Kitty had been misinformed – that this was a traveller's tale. Though she was a girl of a lively imagination, there could in the nature of things be, to her sense, no reality in the idea of her belonging to a vulgar category. What she said aloud was – 'I must say that in that case I am very sorry for Lord Lambeth.'

Mrs Westgate, more and more exhilarated by her scheme, was smiling at her again. 'If I could only believe it was safe!' she exclaimed. 'When you begin to pity him, I, on my side, am afraid.'

'Afraid of what?'

'Of your pitying him too much.'

Bessie Alden turned away impatiently; but at the end of a minute she turned back. 'What if I should pity him too much?' she asked.

Mrs Westgate hereupon turned away, but after a moment's reflection she also faced her sister again. 'It would come, after all, to the same thing,' she said.

Lord Lambeth came the next day with his trap, and the two ladies, attended by Willie Woodley, placed themselves under his guidance and were conveyed eastward, through some of the duskier portions of the metropolis, to the great turreted donjon which overlooks the London shipping. They all descended from their vehicle and entered the famous enclosure; and they secured the services of a venerable beefeater, who, though there were many other claimants for legendary information, made a fine exclusive party of them and marched them through courts and corridors, through armouries and prisons. He delivered his usual peripatetic discourse, and they stopped and stared, and peeped and stopped, according to the official admonitions. Bessie Alden asked the old man in the crimson doublet a great many questions; she thought it a most fascinating place. Lord Lambeth was in high good-humour; he was constantly laughing; he enjoyed what he would have called the lark. Willie Woodley kept looking at the ceilings and tapping the walls with the knuckle of a pearl-grey glove; and Mrs Westgate, asking at frequent intervals to be allowed to sit down and wait till they came back, was as frequently informed that they would never come back. To a great many of Bessie's questions – chiefly on collateral points of English history – the ancient warder was naturally unable to reply; whereupon she always appealed to Lord Lambeth. But his lordship was very ignorant. He declared that he knew nothing about that sort of thing, and he seemed greatly diverted at being treated as an authority.

'You can't expect every one to know as much as you,' he said.

'I should expect you to know a great deal more,' declared Bessie Alden.

'Women always know more than men about names and dates, and that sort of thing,' Lord Lambeth rejoined. 'There was Lady Jane Grey we have just been hearing about, who went in for Latin and Greek and all the learning of her age.'

'*You* have no right to be ignorant, at all events,' said Bessie.

'Why haven't I as good a right as any one else?'

'Because you have lived in the midst of all these things.'

'What things do you mean? Axes and blocks and thumb-screws?'

'All these historical things. You belong to an historical family.'

'Bessie is really too historical,' said Mrs Westgate, catching a word of this dialogue.

'Yes, you are too historical,' said Lord Lambeth, laughing, but thankful for a formula. 'Upon my honour, you are too historical!'

He went with the ladies a couple of days later to Hampton Court, Willie Woodley being also of the party. The afternoon was charming, the famous horse-chestnuts were in blossom, and Lord Lambeth, who quite entered into the spirit of the cockney excursionist, declared that it was a jolly old place. Bessie Alden was in ecstasies; she went about murmuring and exclaiming.

'It's too lovely,' said the young girl, 'it's too enchanting; it's too exactly what it ought to be!'

At Hampton Court the little flocks of visitors are not provided with an official bellwether, but are left to browse at discretion upon the local antiquities. It happened in this manner that, in default of another informant, Bessie Alden, who on doubtful questions was able to suggest a great many alternatives, found herself again applying for intellectual assistance to Lord Lambeth. But he again assured her that he was utterly helpless in such matters – that his education had been sadly neglected.

'And I am sorry it makes you unhappy,' he added in a moment.

'You are very disappointing, Lord Lambeth,' she said.

'Ah, now, don't say that!' he cried. 'That's the worst thing you could possibly say.'

'No,' she rejoined; 'it is not so bad as to say that I had expected nothing of you.'

'I don't know. Give me a notion of the sort of thing you expected.'

'Well,' said Bessie Alden, 'that you would be more what I should like to be – what I should try to be – in your place.'

'Ah, my place!' exclaimed Lord Lambeth; 'you are always talking about my place.'

The young girl looked at him; he thought she coloured a little; and for a moment she made no rejoinder.

'Does it strike you that I am always talking about your place?' she asked.

'I am sure you do it a great honour,' he said, fearing he had been uncivil.

'I have often thought about it,' she went on after a moment. 'I have often thought about your being an hereditary legislator. An hereditary legislator ought to know a great many things.'

'Not if he doesn't legislate.'

'But you will legislate; it's absurd your saying you won't. You are very much looked up to here – I am assured of that.'

'I don't know that I ever noticed it.'

'It is because you are used to it, then. You ought to fill the place.'

'How do you mean, to fill it?' asked Lord Lambeth.

'You ought to be very clever and brilliant, and to know almost everything.'

Lord Lambeth looked at her a moment. 'Shall I tell you something?' he asked. 'A young man in my position, as you call it— '

'I didn't invent the term,' interposed Bessie Alden. 'I have seen it in a great many books.'

'Hang it, you are always at your books! A fellow in my position, then, does very well, whatever he does. That's about what I mean to say.'

'Well, if your own people are content with you,' said Bessie Alden, laughing, 'it is not for me to complain. But I shall always think that, properly, you should have a great mind – a great character.'

'Ah, that's very theoretic!' Lord Lambeth declared. 'Depend upon it, that's a Yankee prejudice.'

'Happy the country,' said Bessie Alden, 'where even people's prejudices are so elevated!'

'Well, after all,' observed Lord Lambeth, 'I don't know that I am such a fool as you are trying to make me out.'

'I said nothing so rude as that; but I must repeat that you are disappointing.'

'My dear Miss Alden,' exclaimed the young man, 'I am the best fellow in the world!'

'Ah, if it were not for that!' said Bessie Alden, with a smile.

Mrs Westgate had a good many more friends in London than she pretended, and before long she had renewed acquaintance with most of them. Their hospitality was extreme, so that, one thing leading to another, she began, as the phrase is, to go out. Bessie Alden, in this way, saw something of what she found it a great satisfaction to call to herself English society. She went to balls and danced, she went to dinners and talked, she went to concerts and listened (at concerts Bessie always listened), she went to exhibitions and wondered. Her enjoyment was keen and her curiosity insatiable, and, grateful in general for all her opportunities, she especially prized the privilege of meeting certain celebrated persons – authors and artists, philosophers and statesmen – of whose renown she had been a humble and distant beholder, and who now, as a part of the habitual furniture of London drawing-rooms, struck her as stars fallen from the firmament and become palpable – revealing also, sometimes, on contact, qualities not to have been predicted of bodies sidereal. Bessie, who knew so many of her contemporaries by reputation, had a good many personal disappointments; but, on the other hand, she had innumerable satisfactions and enthusiasms, and she communicated the emotions of either class to a dear friend, of her own sex, in Boston, with whom she was in voluminous correspondence. Some of her reflections, indeed, she attempted to impart to Lord Lambeth, who came almost every day to Jones's Hotel, and whom Mrs Westgate admitted to be really devoted. Captain Littledale, it appeared, had gone to India; and of several others of Mrs Westgate's ex-pensioners – gentlemen who, as she said, had made, in New York, a club-house of her drawing-room – no tidings were to be obtained; but Lord Lambeth was certainly attentive enough to make up for the accidental absences, the short memories, all the other irregularities, of every one else. He drove them in the Park, he took them to visit private collections of pictures, and having a house of his own, invited them to dinner. Mrs Westgate, following the fashion of many of her compatriots, caused herself and her sister to be presented at the English Court by her diplomatic representative – for it was in this manner that she alluded to the American Minister to England, inquiring what on earth he was put there for, if not to make the proper arrangements for one's going to a Drawing Room.

Lord Lambeth declared that he hated Drawing Rooms, but he participated in the ceremony on the day on which the two ladies at Jones's Hotel repaired to Buckingham Palace in a remarkable coach which his lordship had sent to fetch them. He had on a gorgeous uniform, and Bessie Alden was particularly struck with his appearance – especially when on her asking him, rather foolishly as she felt, if he were a loyal subject, he replied that he was a loyal subject to *her*. This declaration was emphasised by his dancing with her at a royal ball to which the two ladies afterwards went, and was not impaired by the fact that she thought he danced very ill. He seemed to her wonderfully kind; she asked herself, with growing vivacity, why he should be so kind. It was his disposition – that seemed the natural answer. She had told her sister that she liked him very much, and now that she liked him more she wondered why. She liked him for his disposition; to this question as well that seemed the natural answer. When once the impressions of London life began to crowd thickly upon her she completely forgot her sister's warning about the cynicism of public opinion. It had given her great pain at the moment; but there was no particular reason why she should remember it; it corresponded too little with any sensible reality; and it was disagreeable to Bessie to remember disagreeable things. So she was not haunted with the sense of a vulgar imputation. She was not in love with Lord Lambeth – she assured herself of that. It will immediately be observed that when such assurances become necessary the state of a young lady's affections is already ambiguous; and indeed Bessie Alden made no attempt to dissimulate – to herself, of course – a certain tenderness that she felt for the young nobleman. She said to herself that she liked the type to which he belonged – the simple, candid, manly, healthy English temperament. She spoke to herself of him as women speak of young men they like – alluded to his bravery (which she had never in the least seen tested), to his honesty and gentlemanliness; and was not silent upon the subject of his good looks. She was perfectly conscious, moreover, that she liked to think of his more adventitious merits – that her imagination was excited and gratified by the sight of a handsome young man endowed with such large opportunities – opportunities she hardly knew for what, but, as she supposed, for doing great things – for setting an example, for exerting an influence, for conferring happiness, for encouraging the arts. She had a kind of ideal of conduct for a young man who should find himself in this magnificent position, and she tried to adapt it to Lord Lambeth's deportment, as you might attempt to fit a silhouette in cut paper upon a shadow projected upon a wall. But Bessie Alden's silhouette refused to coincide with his lordship's image; and this want of harmony sometimes vexed her more than she thought reasonable. When he was absent it was of course less striking – then he seemed to her a sufficiently graceful combination of high responsibilities and amiable qualities. But when he sat there within sight, laughing and talking with his customary good humour and simplicity, she measured it more accurately, and she felt acutely that if Lord Lambeth's position was heroic, there was but little of the hero in the young man himself. Then her imagination wandered away from him – very far away; for it was an incontestable fact that at such moments he seemed distinctly dull. I am afraid that while Bessie's imagination was thus invidiously roaming, she cannot have been herself a very lively companion; but it may well have been that these occasional fits of indifference seemed to Lord Lambeth a part of the young girl's personal charm. It had been a part of this charm from the first that he felt that she judged him and measured him more freely and irresponsibly – more at her ease and her leisure, as it were – than several young ladies with whom he had been on the whole about as intimate. To feel this, and yet to feel that she also liked him, was very agreeable to Lord Lambeth. He fancied he had compassed that gratification so desirable to young men of title and fortune – being liked for himself. It is true that a cynical counsellor might have whispered to him, 'Liked for yourself? Yes; but not so very much!' He had, at any rate, the constant hope of being liked more.

It may seem, perhaps, a trifle singular – but it is nevertheless true – that Bessie Alden, when he struck her as dull, devoted some time, on grounds of conscience, to trying to like him more. I say on grounds of conscience, because she felt that he had been extremely 'nice' to her sister, and because she reflected that it was no more than fair that she should think as well of him as he thought of her. This effort was possibly sometimes not so successful as it might have been, for the result of it was occasionally a vague irritation, which expressed itself in hostile criticism of several British institutions. Bessie Alden went to some entertainments at which she met Lord Lambeth; but she went to others at which his lordship was neither actually nor potentially present; and it was chiefly on these latter occasions that she encountered those literary and artistic celebrities of whom mention has been made. After a while she reduced the matter to a principle. If Lord Lambeth should appear anywhere, it was a symbol that there would be no poets and philosophers; and in consequence – for it was almost a strict consequence – she used to enumerate to the young man these objects of her admiration.

'You seem to be awfully fond of that sort of people,' said Lord Lambeth one day, as if the idea had just occurred to him.

'They are the people in England I am most curious to see,' Bessie Alden replied.

'I suppose that's because you have read so much,' said Lord Lambeth, gallantly.

'I have not read so much. It is because we think so much of them at home.'

'Oh, I see!' observed the young nobleman. 'In Boston.'

'Not only in Boston; everywhere,' said Bessie. 'We hold them in great honour; they go to the best dinner-parties.'

'I daresay you are right. I can't say I know many of them.'

'It's a pity you don't,' Bessie Alden declared. 'It would do you good.'

'I daresay it would,' said Lord Lambeth, very humbly. 'But I must say I don't like the looks of some of them.'

'Neither do I – of some of them. But there are all kinds, and many of them are charming.'

'I have talked with two or three of them,' the young man went on, 'and I thought they had a kind of fawning manner.'

'Why should they fawn?' Bessie Alden demanded.

'I'm sure I don't know. Why, indeed?'

'Perhaps you only thought so,' said Bessie.

'Well, of course,' rejoined her companion, 'that's a kind of thing that can't be proved.'

'In America they don't fawn,' said Bessie.

'Ah! well, then, they must be better company.'

Bessie was silent a moment. 'That is one of the things I don't like about England,' she said; 'your keeping the distinguished people apart.'

'How do you mean, apart?'

'Why, letting them come only to certain places. You never see them.'

Lord Lambeth looked at her a moment. 'What people do you mean?'

'The eminent people – the authors and artists – the clever people.'

'Oh, there are other eminent people besides those!' said Lord Lambeth.

'Well, you certainly keep them apart,' repeated the young girl.

'And there are other clever people,' added Lord Lambeth, simply.

Bessie Alden looked at him, and she gave a light laugh. 'Not many,' she said.

On another occasion – just after a dinner-party – she told him that there was something else in England she did not like.

'Oh, I say!' he cried; 'haven't you abused us enough?'

'I have never abused you at all,' said Bessie; 'but I don't like your *precedence*.'

'It isn't my precedence!' Lord Lambeth declared, laughing.

'Yes, it is yours – just exactly yours; and I think it's odious,' said Bessie.

'I never saw such a young lady for discussing things! Has some one had the impudence to go before you?' asked his lordship.

'It is not the going before me that I object to,' said Bessie; 'it is their thinking that they have a right to do it – a right that I should recognise.'

'I never saw such a young lady as you are for not "recognising". I have no doubt the thing is beastly, but it saves a lot of trouble.'

'It makes a lot of trouble. It's horrid!' said Bessie.

'But how would you have the first people go?' asked Lord Lambeth. 'They can't go last.'

'Whom do you mean by the first people?'

'Ah, if you mean to question first principles!' said Lord Lambeth.

'If those are your first principles, no wonder some of your arrangements are horrid,' observed Bessie Alden, with a very pretty ferocity. 'I am a young girl, so of course I go last; but imagine what Kitty must feel on being informed that she is not at liberty to budge until certain other ladies have passed out!'

'Oh, I say, she is not "informed"!' cried Lord Lambeth. 'No one would do such a thing as that.'

'She is made to feel it,' the young girl insisted – 'as if they were afraid she would make a rush for the door. No, you have a lovely country,' said Bessie Alden, 'but your precedence is horrid.'

'I certainly shouldn't think your sister would like it,' rejoined Lord Lambeth, with even exaggerated gravity. But Bessie Alden could induce him to enter no formal protest against this repulsive custom, which he seemed to think an extreme convenience.

VI

PERCY BEAUMONT all this time had been a very much less frequent visitor at Jones's Hotel than his noble kinsman; he had in fact called but twice upon the two American ladies. Lord Lambeth, who often saw him, reproached him with his neglect, and declared that although Mrs Westgate had said nothing about it, he was sure that she was secretly wounded by it. 'She suffers too much to speak,' said Lord Lambeth.

'That's all gammon,' said Percy Beaumont; 'there's a limit to what people can suffer!' And, though sending no apologies to Jones's Hotel, he undertook in a manner to explain his absence. 'You are always there,' he said; 'and that's reason enough for my not going.'

'I don't see why. There is enough for both of us.'

'I don't care to be a witness of your – your reckless passion,' said Percy Beaumont.

Lord Lambeth looked at him with a cold eye, and for a moment said nothing. 'It's not so obvious as you might suppose,' he rejoined, dryly, 'considering what a demonstrative beggar I am.'

'I don't want to know anything about it – nothing whatever,' said Beaumont. 'Your mother asks me every time she sees me whether I believe you are really lost – and Lady Pimlico does the same. I prefer to be able to answer that I know nothing about it – that I never go there. I stay away for consistency's sake. As I said the other day, they must look after you themselves.'

'You are devilish considerate,' said Lord Lambeth. 'They never question me.'

'They are afraid of you. They are afraid of irritating you and making you worse. So they go to work very cautiously, and, somewhere or other, they get their information. They know a great deal about you. They know that you have been with those ladies to the dome of St Paul's and – where was the other place? – to the Thames Tunnel.'

'If all their knowledge is as accurate as that, it must be very valuable,' said Lord Lambeth.

'Well, at any rate, they know that you have been visiting the "sights of the metropolis". They think – very naturally, as it seems to me – that when you take to visiting the sights of the metropolis with a little American girl, there is serious cause for alarm.' Lord Lambeth responded to this intimation by scornful laughter, and his companion continued, after a pause: 'I said just now I didn't want to know anything about the affair; but I will confess that I am curious to learn whether you propose to marry Miss Bessie Alden.'

On this point Lord Lambeth gave his interlocutor no immediate satisfaction; he was musing, with a frown. 'By Jove,' he said, 'they go rather too far. They *shall* find me dangerous – I promise them.'

Percy Beaumont began to laugh. 'You don't redeem your promises. You said the other day you would make your mother call.'

Lord Lambeth continued to meditate. 'I asked her to call,' he said, simply.

'And she declined?'

'Yes, but she shall do it yet.'

'Upon my word,' said Percy Beaumont, 'if she gets much more frightened I believe she will.' Lord Lambeth looked at him, and he went on. 'She will go to the girl herself.'

'How do you mean, she will go to her?'

'She will beg her off, or she will bribe her. She will take strong measures.'

Lord Lambeth turned away in silence, and his companion watched him take twenty steps and then slowly return. 'I have invited Mrs Westgate and Miss Alden to Branches,' he said, 'and this evening I shall name a day.'

'And shall you invite your mother and your sisters to meet them?'

'Explicitly!'

'That will set the Duchess off,' said Percy Beaumont. 'I suspect she will come.'

'She may do as she pleases.'

Beaumont looked at Lord Lambeth. 'You do really propose to marry the little sister, then?'

'I like the way you talk about it!' cried the young man. 'She won't gobble me down; don't be afraid.'

'She won't leave you on your knees,' said Percy Beaumont. 'What *is* the inducement?'

'You talk about proposing – wait till I have proposed,' Lord Lambeth went on.

'That's right, my dear fellow; think about it,' said Percy Beaumont.

'She's a charming girl,' pursued his lordship.

'Of course she's a charming girl. I don't know a girl more charming, intrinsically. But there are other charming girls nearer home.'

'I like her spirit,' observed Lord Lambeth, almost as if he were trying to torment his cousin.

'What's the peculiarity of her spirit?'

'She's not afraid, and she says things out, and she thinks herself as good as any one. She is the only girl I have ever seen that was not dying to marry me.'

'How do you know that, if you haven't asked her?'

'I don't know how; but I know it.'

'I am sure she asked me questions enough about your property and your titles,' said Beaumont.

'She has asked me questions, too; no end of them,' Lord Lambeth admitted. 'But she asked for information, don't you know.'

'Information? Ay, I'll warrant she wanted it. Depend upon it that she is dying to marry you just as much and just as little as all the rest of them.'

'I shouldn't like her to refuse me – I shouldn't like that.'

'If the thing would be so disagreeable, then, both to you and to her, in Heaven's name leave it alone,' said Percy Beaumont.

Mrs Westgate, on her side, had plenty to say to her sister about the rarity of Mr Beaumont's visits and the non-appearance of the Duchess of Bayswater. She professed, however, to derive more satisfaction from this latter circumstance than she could have done from the most lavish attentions on the part of this great lady. 'It is most marked,' she said, 'most marked. It is a delicious proof that we have made them miserable. The day we dined with Lord Lambeth I was really sorry for the poor fellow.' It will have been gathered that the entertainment offered by Lord Lambeth to his American friends had not been graced by the presence of his anxious mother. He had invited several choice spirits to meet them; but the ladies of his immediate family were to Mrs Westgate's sense – a sense, possibly, morbidly acute – conspicuous by their absence.

'I don't want to express myself in a manner that you dislike,' said Bessie Alden; 'but I don't know why you should have so many theories about Lord Lambeth's poor mother. You know a great many young men in New York without knowing their mothers.'

Mrs Westgate looked at her sister, and then turned away. 'My dear Bessie, you are superb!' she said.

'One thing is certain,' the young girl continued. 'If I believed I were a cause of annoyance – however unwitting – to Lord Lambeth's family, I should insist—'

'Insist upon my leaving England,' said Mrs Westgate.

'No, not that. I want to go to the National Gallery again; I want to see Stratford-on-Avon and Canterbury Cathedral. But I should insist upon his coming to see us no more.'

'That would be very modest and very pretty of you – but you wouldn't do it now.'

'Why do you say "now"?' asked Bessie Alden. 'Have I ceased to be modest?'

'You care for him too much. A month ago, when you said you didn't, I believe it was quite true. But at present, my dear child,' said Mrs Westgate, 'you wouldn't find it quite so simple a matter never to see Lord Lambeth again. I have seen it coming on.'

'You are mistaken,' said Bessie. 'You don't understand.'

'My dear child, don't be perverse,' rejoined her sister.

'I know him better, certainly, if you mean that,' said Bessie. 'And I like him very much. But I don't like him enough to make trouble for him with his family. However, I don't believe in that.'

'I like the way you say "however"!' Mrs Westgate exclaimed. 'Come, you would not marry him?'

'Oh no,' said the young girl.

Mrs Westgate, for a moment, seemed vexed. 'Why not, pray?' she demanded.

'Because I don't care to,' said Bessie Alden.

The morning after Lord Lambeth had had, with Percy Beaumont, that exchange of ideas which has just been narrated, the ladies at Jones's Hotel received from his lordship a written invitation to pay their projected visit to Branches Castle on the following Tuesday. 'I think I have made up a very pleasant party,' the young nobleman said. 'Several people whom you know, and my mother and sisters, who have so long been regrettably prevented from making your acquaintance.' Bessie Alden lost no time in calling her sister's attention to the injustice she had done the Duchess of Bayswater, whose hostility was now proved to be a vain illusion.

'Wait till you see if she comes,' said Mrs Westgate. 'And if she is to meet us at her son's house the obligation was all the greater for her to call upon us.'

Bessie had not to wait long, and it appeared that Lord Lambeth's mother now accepted Mrs Westgate's view of her duties. On the morrow, early in the afternoon, two cards were brought to the apartment of the American ladies – one of them bearing the name of the Duchess of Bayswater and the other that of the Countess of Pimlico. Mrs Westgate glanced at the clock. 'It is not yet four,' she said; 'they have come early; they wish to see us. We will receive them.' And she gave orders that her visitors should be admitted. A few moments later they were introduced, and there was a solemn exchange of amenities. The Duchess was a large lady, with a fine fresh colour; the Countess of Pimlico was very pretty and elegant.

The Duchess looked about her as she sat down – looked not especially at Mrs Westgate. 'I daresay my son has told you that I have been wanting to come and see you,' she observed.

'You are very kind,' said Mrs Westgate, vaguely – her conscience not allowing her to assent to this proposition – and indeed not permitting her to enunciate her own with any appreciable emphasis.

'He says you were so kind to him in America,' said the Duchess.

'We are very glad,' Mrs Westgate replied, 'to have been able to make him a little more – a little less – a little more comfortable.'

'I think he stayed at your house,' remarked the Duchess of Bayswater, looking at Bessie Alden.

'A very short time,' said Mrs Westgate.

'Oh!' said the Duchess; and she continued to look at Bessie, who was engaged in conversation with her daughter.

'Do you like London?' Lady Pimlico had asked of Bessie, after looking at her a good deal – at her face and her hands, her dress and her hair.

'Very much indeed,' said Bessie.

'Do you like this hotel?'

'It is very comfortable,' said Bessie.

'Do you like stopping at hotels?' inquired Lady Pimlico, after a pause.

'I am very fond of travelling,' Bessie answered, 'and I suppose hotels are a necessary part of it. But they are not the part I am fondest of.'

'Oh, I hate travelling!' said the Countess of Pimlico, and transferred her attention to Mrs Westgate.

'My son tells me you are going to Branches,' the Duchess presently resumed.

'Lord Lambeth has been so good as to ask us,' said Mrs Westgate, who perceived that her visitor had now begun to look at her, and who had her customary happy consciousness of a distinguished appearance. The only mitigation of her felicity on this point was that, having inspected her visitor's own costume, she said to herself, 'She won't know how well I am dressed!'

'He has asked me to go, but I am not sure I shall be able,' murmured the Duchess.

'He had offered us the p— the prospect of meeting you,' said Mrs Westgate.

'I hate the country at this season,' responded the Duchess.

Mrs Westgate gave a little shrug. 'I think it is pleasanter than London.'

But the Duchess's eyes were absent again; she was looking very fixedly at Bessie. In a moment she slowly rose, walked to a chair that stood empty at the young girl's right hand, and silently seated herself. As she was a majestic, voluminous woman, this little transaction had, inevitably, an air of somewhat impressive intention. It diffused a certain awkwardness, which Lady Pimlico, as a sympathetic daughter, perhaps desired to rectify in turning to Mrs Westgate.

'I daresay you go out a great deal,' she observed.

'No, very little. We are strangers, and we didn't come here for society.'

'I see,' said Lady Pimlico. 'It's rather nice in town just now.'

'It's charming,' said Mrs Westgate. 'But we only go to see a few people – whom we like.'

'Of course one can't like every one,' said Lady Pimlico.

'It depends upon one's society,' Mrs Westgate rejoined.

The Duchess, meanwhile, had addressed herself to Bessie. 'My son tells me the young ladies in America are so clever.'

'I am glad they made so good an impression on him,' said Bessie, smiling.

The Duchess was not smiling; her large fresh face was very tranquil. 'He is very susceptible,' she said. 'He thinks every one clever, and sometimes they are.'

'Sometimes,' Bessie assented, smiling still.

The Duchess looked at her a little and then went on – 'Lambeth is very susceptible, but he is very volatile, too.'

'Volatile?' asked Bessie.

'He is very inconstant. It won't do to depend on him.'

'Ah!' said Bessie; 'I don't recognise that description. We have depended on him greatly – my sister and I – and he has never disappointed us.'

'He will disappoint you yet,' said the Duchess.

Bessie gave a little laugh, as if she were amused at the Duchess's persistency. 'I suppose it will depend on what we expect of him.'

'The less you expect the better,' Lord Lambeth's mother declared.

'Well,' said Bessie, 'we expect nothing unreasonable.'

The Duchess, for a moment, was silent, though she appeared to have more to say. 'Lambeth says he has seen so much of you,' she presently began.

'He has been to see us very often – he has been very kind,' said Bessie Alden.

'I daresay you are used to that. I am told there is a great deal of that in America.'

'A great deal of kindness?' the young girl inquired, smiling.

'Is that what you call it? I know you have different expressions.'

'We certainly don't always understand each other,' said Mrs Westgate, the termination of whose interview with Lady Pimlico allowed her to give her attention to their elder visitor.

'I am speaking of the young men calling so much upon the young ladies,' the Duchess explained.

'But surely in England,' said Mrs Westgate, 'the young ladies don't call upon the young men?'

'Some of them do – almost!' Lady Pimlico declared. 'When the young men are a great *parti*.'

'Bessie, you must make a note of that,' said Mrs Westgate. 'My sister,' she added, 'is a model traveller. She writes down all the curious facts she hears, in a little book she keeps for the purpose.'

The Duchess was a little flushed; she looked all about the room, while her daughter turned to Bessie. 'My brother told us you were wonderfully clever,' said Lady Pimlico.

'He should have said my sister,' Bessie answered – 'when she says such things as that.'

'Shall you be long at Branches?' the Duchess asked, abruptly, of the young girl.

'Lord Lambeth has asked us for three days,' said Bessie.

'I shall go,' the Duchess declared, 'and my daughter too.'

'That will be charming!' Bessie rejoined.

'Delightful!' murmured Mrs Westgate.

'I shall expect to see a deal of you,' the Duchess continued. 'When I go to Branches I monopolise my son's guests.'

'They must be most happy,' said Mrs Westgate, very graciously.

'I want immensely to see it – to see the Castle,' said Bessie to the Duchess. 'I have never seen one – in England at least; and you know we have none in America.'

'Ah! you are fond of castles?' inquired her Grace.

'Immensely!' replied the young girl. 'It has been the dream of my life to live in one.'

The Duchess looked at her a moment, as if she hardly knew how to take this assurance, which, from her Grace's point of view, was either very artless or very audacious. 'Well,' she said, rising, 'I will show you Branches myself.' And upon this the two great ladies took their departure.

'What did they mean by it?' asked Mrs Westgate, when they were gone.

'They meant to be polite,' said Bessie, 'because we are going to meet them.'

'It is too late to be polite,' Mrs Westgate replied, almost grimly. 'They meant to overawe us by their fine manners and their grandeur, and to make you *lâcher prise*.'

'*Lâcher prise*? What strange things you say!' murmured Bessie Alden.

'They meant to snub us, so that we shouldn't dare to go to Branches,' Mrs Westgate continued.

'On the contrary,' said Bessie, 'the Duchess offered to show me the place herself.'

'Yes, you may depend upon it she won't let you out of her sight. She will show you the place from morning till night.'

'You have a theory for everything,' said Bessie.

'And you apparently have none for anything.'

'I saw no attempt to "overawe" us,' said the young girl. 'Their manners were not fine.'

'They were not even good!' Mrs Westgate declared.

Bessie was silent awhile, but in a few moments she observed that she had a very good theory. 'They came to look at me!' she said, as if this had been a very ingenious hypothesis. Mrs Westgate did it justice; she greeted it with a smile and pronounced it most brilliant; while in reality she felt that the young girl's scepticism, or her charity, or, as she had sometimes called it, appropriately, her idealism, was proof against irony. Bessie, however, remained meditative all the rest of that day and well on into the morrow.

On the morrow, before lunch, Mrs Westgate had occasion to go out for an hour, and left her sister writing a letter. When she came back she met Lord Lambeth at the door of the hotel, coming away. She thought he looked slightly embarrassed; he was certainly very grave. 'I am sorry to have missed you. Won't you come back?' she asked.

'No,' said the young man, 'I can't. I have seen your sister. I can never come back.' Then he looked at her a moment, and took her hand. 'Good-bye, Mrs Westgate,' he said. 'You have been very kind to me.' And with what she thought a strange, sad look in his handsome young face, he turned away.

She went in and she found Bessie still writing her letter; that is, Mrs Westgate perceived she was sitting at the table with the pen in her hand and not writing. 'Lord Lambeth has been here,' said the elder lady at last.

Then Bessie got up and showed her a pale, serious face. She bent this face upon her sister for some time, confessing silently and, a little, pleading. 'I told him,' she said at last, 'that we could not go to Branches.'

Mrs Westgate displayed just a spark of irritation. 'He might have waited,' she said with a smile, 'till one had seen the Castle.' Later, an hour afterwards, she said, 'Dear Bessie, I wish you might have accepted him.'

'I couldn't,' said Bessie, gently.

'He is a dear good fellow,' said Mrs Westgate.

'I couldn't,' Bessie repeated.

'If it is only,' her sister added, 'because those women will think that they succeeded – that they paralysed us!'

Bessie Alden turned away; but presently she added, 'They were interesting; I should have liked to see them again.'

'So should I!' cried Mrs Westgate, significantly.

'And I should have liked to see the Castle,' said Bessie. 'But now we must leave England,' she added.

Her sister looked at her. 'You will not wait to go to the National Gallery?'

'Not now.'

'Nor to Canterbury Cathedral?'

Bessie reflected a moment. 'We can stop there on our way to Paris,' she said.

Lord Lambeth did not tell Percy Beaumont that the contingency he was not prepared at all to like had occurred; but Percy Beaumont, on hearing that the two ladies had left London, wondered with some intensity what had happened; wondered, that is, until the Duchess of Bayswater came, a little, to his assistance. The two ladies went to Paris, and Mrs Westgate beguiled the journey to that city by repeating several times, 'That's what I regret; they will think they petrified us.' But Bessie Alden seemed to regret nothing.

THE PENSION BEAUREPAS

I

I WAS not rich – on the contrary; and I had been told the Pension Beaurepas was cheap. I had, moreover, been told that a boarding-house is a capital place for the study of human nature. I had a fancy for a literary career, and a friend of mine had said to me, 'If you mean to write you ought to go and live in a boarding-house; there is no other such place to pick up material.' I had read something of this kind in a letter addressed by Stendhal to his sister: 'I have a passionate desire to know human nature, and have a great mind to live in a boarding-house, where people cannot conceal their real char-acters.' I was an admirer of La Chartreuse de Parme, and it appeared to me that one could not do better than follow in the footsteps of its author. I remembered, too, the magnificent boarding-house in Balzac's Père Goriot, – the '*pension bour-geoise des deux sexes et autres*', kept by Madam Vauquer, *née* De Conflans. Magnificent, I mean, as a piece of portraiture; the establishment, as an establishment, was certainly sordid enough, and I hoped for better things from the Pension Beau-repas. This institution was one of the most esteemed in Geneva, and, standing in a little garden of its own, not far from the lake, had a very homely, comfortable, sociable aspect. The regular entrance was, as one might say, at the back, which looked upon the street, or rather upon a little *place*, adorned like every place in Geneva, great or small, with a fountain. This fact was not prepossessing, for on crossing the threshold you found yourself more or less in the kitchen, encompassed with culinary odours. This, however, was no great matter, for at the Pension Beaurepas there was no attempt at gentility or at concealment of the domestic machinery. The latter was of a very simple sort. Madame Beaurepas was an excellent little old woman – she was very far advanced in life, and had been keeping a pension for forty years – whose only faults were that she was slightly deaf, that she was fond of a surreptitious pinch of snuff, and that, at the age of seventy-three, she wore flowers in her cap. There was a tradition in the house that she was not so deaf as she pretended; that she feigned this infirmity in order to possess herself of the secrets of her lodgers. But I never subscribed to this theory; I am convinced that Madame Beaurepas had outlived the period of indiscreet curiosity. She was a philosopher, on a matter-of-fact basis; she had been having lodgers for forty years, and all that she asked of them was that they should pay their bills, make use of the door-mat, and fold their napkins. She cared very little for their secrets. 'J'en ai vus de toutes les couleurs,' she said to me. She had quite ceased to care for individuals; she cared only for types, for categories. Her large observation had made her acquainted with a great number, and her mind was a complete collection of 'heads'. She flattered herself that she knew at a glance where to pigeon-hole a newcomer, and if she made any mistakes her deportment never betrayed them. I think that, as regards individuals, she had neither likes nor dislikes; but she was capable of expressing esteem or contempt for a species. She had her own ways, I suppose, of manifesting her approval, but her manner of indicating the reverse was simple and unvarying. 'Je trouve que c'est déplacé!' – this exhausted her view of the matter. If one of her inmates had put arsenic into the *pot-au-feu*, I believe Madame Beaurepas would have contented herself with remarking that the proceeding was out of place. The line of misconduct to which she most objected was an undue assumption of gentility; she had no patience with boarders who gave themselves airs. 'When people come *chez moi*, it is not to cut a figure in the world; I have never had that illusion,' I remember hearing her say; 'and when you pay seven francs a day, *tout compris*, it comprises everything but the right to look down upon the others. But there are people who, the less they pay, the more they take themselves *au sérieux*. My most difficult boarders have always been those who have had the little rooms.'

Madame Beaurepas had a niece, a young woman of some forty odd years; and the two ladies, with the assistance of a couple of thick-waisted, red-armed peasant women, kept the

house going. If on your exits and entrances you peeped into the
kitchen, it made very little difference; for Célestine, the cook,
had no pretension to be an invisible functionary or to deal in
occult methods. She was always at your service, with a grateful
grin: she blacked your boots; she trudged off to fetch a cab; she
would have carried your baggage, if you had allowed her, on her
broad little back. She was always tramping in and out, between
her kitchen and the fountain in the place, where it often seemed
to me that a large part of the preparation for our dinner went
forward – the wringing out of towels and table-cloths, the
washing of potatoes and cabbages, the scouring of saucepans
and cleansing of water-bottles. You enjoyed, from the door-
step, a perpetual back view of Célestine and of her large, loose,
woollen ankles, as she craned, from the waist, over into the
fountain and dabbled in her various utensils. This sounds as if
life went on in a very make-shift fashion at the Pension Beaurepas – as if the tone of the establishment were sordid. But such
was not at all the case. We were simply very *bourgeois*; we
practised the good old Genevese principle of not sacrificing to
appearances. This is an excellent principle – when you have the
reality. We had the reality at the Pension Beaurepas: we had it in
the shape of soft, short beds, equipped with fluffy *duvets*; of
admirable coffee, served to us in the morning by Célestine in
person, as we lay recumbent on these downy couches; of
copious, wholesome, succulent dinners, conformable to the
best provincial traditions. For myself, I thought the Pension
Beaurepas picturesque, and this, with me, at that time was a
great word. I was young and ingenuous; I had just come from
America. I wished to perfect myself in the French tongue, and
I innocently believed that it flourished by Lake Leman. I used
to go to lectures at the Academy, and come home with a violent
appetite. I always enjoyed my morning walk across the long
bridge (there was only one, just there, in those days) which
spans the deep blue out-gush of the lake, and up the dark, steep
streets of the old Calvinistic city. The garden faced this way,
toward the lake and the old town; and this was the pleasantest
approach to the house. There was a high wall, with a double
gate in the middle, flanked by a couple of ancient massive posts;

the big rusty *grille* contained some old-fashioned iron-work. The garden was rather mouldy and weedy, tangled and untended; but it contained a little thin-flowing fountain, several green benches, a rickety little table of the same complexion, and three orange-trees, in tubs, which were deposited as effectively as possible in front of the windows of the *salon*.

II

As commonly happens in boarding-houses, the rustle of petticoats was, at the Pension Beaurepas, the most familiar form of the human tread. There was the usual allotment of economical widows and old maids, and to maintain the balance of the sexes there were only an old Frenchman and a young American. It hardly made the matter easier that the old Frenchman came from Lausanne. He was a native of that estimable town, but he had once spent six months in Paris, he had tasted of the tree of knowledge; he had got beyond Lausanne, whose resources he pronounced inadequate. Lausanne, as he said, '*manquait d'agréments*'. When obliged, for reasons which he never specified, to bring his residence in Paris to a close, he had fallen back on Geneva; he had broken his fall at the Pension Beaurepas. Geneva was, after all, more like Paris, and at a Genevese boarding-house there was sure to be plenty of Americans with whom one could talk about the French metropolis. M. Pigeonneau was a little lean man, with a large, narrow nose, who sat a great deal in the garden, reading with the aid of a large magnifying glass a volume from the *cabinet de lecture*.

One day, a fortnight after my arrival at the Pension Beaurepas, I came back rather earlier than usual from my academic session; it wanted half an hour of the midday breakfast. I went into the salon with the design of possessing myself of the day's *Galignani* before one of the little English old maids should have removed it to her virginal bower – a privilege to which Madame Beaurepas frequently alluded as one of the attractions of the establishment. In the salon I found a new-comer, a tall gentleman in a high black hat, whom I immediately recognised as a compatriot. I had often seen him, or his equivalent, in the hotel-parlours of my native land. He apparently supposed himself to be at the present moment in a hotel-parlour; his hat was on his head, or, rather, half off it – pushed back from his forehead, and rather suspended than poised. He stood before a table on which old newspapers were scattered, one of which he had taken up and, with his eye-glass on his nose, was holding out at arm's-length. It was that honourable but extremely diminutive sheet, the *Journal de Genève*, a newspaper of about the size of a pocket-handkerchief. As I drew near, looking for my *Galignani*, the tall gentleman gave me, over the top of his eye-glass, a somewhat solemn stare. Presently, however, before I had time to lay my hand on the object of my search, he silently offered me the *Journal de Genève*.

'It appears,' he said, 'to be the paper of the country.'

'Yes,' I answered, 'I believe it's the best.'

He gazed at it again, still holding it at arm's-length, as if it had been a looking-glass. 'Well,' he said, 'I suppose it's natural a small country should have small papers. You could wrap it up, mountains and all, in one of our dailies!'

I found my *Galignani* and went off with it into the garden, where I seated myself on a bench in the shade. Presently I saw the tall gentleman in the hat appear in one of the open windows of the salon, and stand there with his hands in his pockets and his legs a little apart. He looked very much bored, and – I don't know why – I immediately began to feel sorry for him. He was not at all a picturesque personage; he looked like a jaded, faded man of business. But after a little he came into the garden and began to stroll about; and then his restless, unoccupied carriage, and the vague, unacquainted manner in which his eyes wandered over the place seemed to make it proper that, as an older resident, I should exercise a certain hospitality. I said something to him, and he came and sat down beside me on my bench, clasping one of his long knees in his hands.

'When is it this big breakfast of theirs comes off?' he inquired. 'That's what I call it – the little breakfast and the big breakfast. I never thought I should live to see the time when I should care to eat two breakfasts. But a man's glad to do anything, over here.'

'For myself,' I observed, 'I find plenty to do.'

He turned his head and glanced at me with a dry, deliberate, kind-looking eye. 'You're getting used to the life, are you?'

'I like the life very much,' I answered, laughing.

'How long have you tried it?'

'Do you mean in this place?'

'Well, I mean anywhere. It seems to me pretty much the same all over.'

'I have been in this house only a fortnight,' I said.

'Well, what should you say, from what you have seen?' my companion asked.

'Oh,' said I, 'you can see all there is immediately. It's very simple.'

'Sweet simplicity, eh? I'm afraid my two ladies will find it too simple.'

'Everything is very good,' I went on. 'And Madame Beau-repas is a charming old woman. And then it's very cheap.'

'Cheap, is it?' my friend repeated meditatively.

'Doesn't it strike you so?' I asked. I thought it very possible he had not inquired the terms. But he appeared not to have heard me; he sat there, clasping his knee and blinking, in a contemplative manner, at the sunshine.

'Are you from the United States, sir?' he presently demanded, turning his head again.

'Yes, sir,' I replied; and I mentioned the place of my nativity.

'I presumed,' he said, 'that you were American or English. I'm from the United States myself; from New York city. Many of our people here?'

'Not so many as, I believe, there have sometimes been. There are two or three ladies.'

'Well,' my interlocutor declared, 'I am very fond of ladies' society. I think when it's superior there's nothing comes up to it. I've got two ladies here myself; I must make you acquainted with them.'

I rejoined that I should be delighted, and I inquired of my friend whether he had been long in Europe.

'Well, it seems precious long,' he said, 'but my time's not up yet. We have been here fourteen weeks and a half.'

'Are you travelling for pleasure?' I asked.

My companion turned his head again and looked at me – looked at me so long in silence that I at last also turned and met his eyes.

'No, sir,' he said presently. 'No, sir,' he repeated, after a considerable interval.

'Excuse me,' said I, for there was something so solemn in his tone that I feared I had been indiscreet.

He took no notice of my ejaculation; he simply continued to look at me. 'I'm travelling,' he said, at last, 'to please the doctors. They seemed to think they would like it.'

'Ah, they sent you abroad for your health?'

'They sent me abroad because they were so confoundedly muddled they didn't know what else to do.'

'That's often the best thing,' I ventured to remark.

'It was a confession of weakness; they wanted me to stop plaguing them. They didn't know enough to cure me, and that's the way they thought they would get round it. I wanted to be cured – I didn't want to be transported. I hadn't done any harm.'

I assented to the general proposition of the inefficiency of doctors, and asked my companion if he had been seriously ill.

'I didn't sleep,' he said, after some delay.

'Ah, that's very annoying. I suppose you were overworked.'

'I didn't eat; I took no interest in my food.'

'Well, I hope you both eat and sleep now,' I said.

'I couldn't hold a pen,' my neighbour went on. 'I couldn't sit still. I couldn't walk from my house to the cars – and it's only a little way. I lost my interest in business.'

'You needed a holiday,' I observed.

'That's what the doctors said. It wasn't so very smart of them. I had been paying strict attention to business for twenty-three years.'

'In all that time you have never had a holiday?' I exclaimed, with horror.

My companion waited a little. 'Sundays,' he said at last.

'No wonder, then, you were out of sorts.'

'Well, sir,' said my friend, 'I shouldn't have been where I was three years ago if I had spent my time travelling round Europe. I was in a very advantageous position. I did a very large business. I was considerably interested in lumber.' He paused, turned his head, and looked at me a moment. 'Have you any business interests yourself?' I answered that I had none, and he went on again, slowly, softly, deliberately. 'Well, sir, perhaps you are not aware that business in the United States is not what it was a short time since. Business interests are very insecure. There seems to be a general falling-off. Different parties offer different explanations of the fact, but so far as I am aware none of their observations have set things going again.' I ingeniously intimated that if business was dull, the time was good for coming away; whereupon my neighbour threw back his head and stretched his legs a while. 'Well, sir, that's one view of the matter certainly. There's something to be said for that. These things should be looked at all round. That's the ground my wife took. That's the ground,' he added in a moment, 'that a lady would naturally take'; and he gave a little dry laugh.

'You think it's slightly illogical,' I remarked.

'Well, sir, the ground I took was that the worse a man's business is, the more it requires looking after. I shouldn't want to go out to take a walk – not even to go to church – if my house was on fire. My firm is not doing the business it was; it's like a sick child, it requires nursing. What I wanted the doctors to do was to fix me up, so that I could go on at home. I'd have taken anything they'd have given me, and as many times a day. I wanted to be right there; I had my reasons; I have them still. But I came off, all the same,' said my friend, with a melancholy smile.

I was a great deal younger than he, but there was something so simple and communicative in his tone, so expressive of a desire to fraternise, and so exempt from any theory of human differences, that I quite forgot his seniority, and found myself offering him paternal advice. 'Don't think about all that,' said I. 'Simply enjoy yourself, amuse yourself, get well. Travel about and see Europe. At the end of a year, by the time you are ready to go home, things will have improved over there, and you will be quite well and happy.'

My friend laid his hand on my knee; he looked at me for some moments, and I thought he was going to say, 'You are very young!' But he said presently, '*You* have got used to Europe any way!'

III

AT breakfast I encountered his ladies – his wife and daughter. They were placed, however, at a distance from me, and it was not until the *pensionnaires* had dispersed, and some of them, according to custom, had come out into the garden, that he had an opportunity of making me acquainted with them.

'Will you allow me to introduce you to my daughter?' he said, moved apparently by a paternal inclination to provide this young lady with social diversion. She was standing with her mother, in one of the paths, looking about with no great complacency, as I imagined, at the homely characteristics of the place, and old M. Pigeonneau was hovering near, hesitating apparently between the desire to be urbane and the absence of a pretext. 'Mrs Ruck – Miss Sophy Ruck,' said my friend, leading me up.

Mrs Ruck was a large, plump, light coloured person, with a smooth fair face, a somnolent eye, and an elaborate coiffure. Miss Sophy was a girl of one and twenty, very small and very pretty – what I suppose would have been called a lively brunette. Both of these ladies were attired in black silk dresses, very much trimmed; they had an air of the highest elegance.

'Do you think highly of this pension?' inquired Mrs Ruck, after a few preliminaries.

'It's a little rough, but it seems to me comfortable,' I answered.

'Does it take a high rank in Geneva?' Mrs Ruck pursued.

'I imagine it enjoys a very fair fame,' I said, smiling.

'I should never dream of comparing it to a New York boarding-house,' said Mrs Ruck.

'It's quite a different style,' her daughter observed. Miss Ruck had folded her arms; she was holding her elbows with a pair of white little hands, and she was tapping the ground with a pretty little foot.

'We hardly expected to come to a pension,' said Mrs Ruck. 'But we thought we would try; we had heard so much about Swiss pensions. I was saying to Mr Ruck that I wondered whether this was a favourable specimen. I was afraid we might have made a mistake.'

'We knew some people who had been here; they thought everything of Madame Beaurepas,' said Miss Sophy. 'They said she was a real friend.'

'Mr and Mrs Parker – perhaps you have heard her speak of them,' Mrs Ruck pursued.

'Madame Beaurepas has had a great many Americans; she is very fond of Americans,' I replied.

'Well, I must say I should think she would be, if she compares them with some others.'

'Mother is always comparing,' observed Miss Ruck.

'Of course I am always comparing,' rejoined the elder lady. 'I never had a chance till now; I never knew my privileges. Give me an American!' And Mrs Ruck indulged in a little laugh.

'Well, I must say there are some things I like over here,' said Miss Sophy, with courage. And indeed I could see that she was a young woman of great decision.

'You like the shops – that's what you like,' her father affirmed.

The young lady addressed herself to me, without heeding this remark. 'I suppose you feel quite at home here.'

'Oh, he likes it; he has got used to the life!' exclaimed Mr Ruck.

'I wish you'd teach Mr Ruck,' said his wife. 'It seems as if he couldn't get used to anything.'

'I'm used to you, my dear,' the husband retorted, giving me a humorous look.

'He's intensely restless,' continued Mrs Ruck. 'That's what made me want to come to a pension. I thought he would settle down more.'

'I don't think I *am* used to you, after all,' said her husband.

In view of a possible exchange of conjugal repartee I took refuge in conversation with Miss Ruck, who seemed perfectly able to play her part in any colloquy. I learned from this young lady that, with her parents, after visiting the British islands, she had been spending a month in Paris, and that she thought she should have died when she left that city. 'I hung out of the carriage, when we left the hotel,' said Miss Ruck, 'I assure you I did. And mother did, too.'

'Out of the other window, I hope,' said I.

'Yes, one out of each window,' she replied, promptly. 'Father had hard work, I can tell you. We hadn't half finished; there were ever so many places we wanted to go to.'

'Your father insisted on coming away?'

'Yes; after we had been there about a month he said he had enough. He's fearfully restless; he's very much out of health. Mother and I said to him that if he was restless in Paris he needn't hope for peace anywhere. We don't mean to leave him alone till he takes us back.' There was an air of keen resolution in Miss Ruck's pretty face, of lucid apprehension of desirable ends, which made me, as she pronounced these words, direct a glance of covert compassion toward her poor recalcitrant father. He had walked away a little with his wife, and I saw only his back and his stooping, patient-looking shoulders, whose air of acute resignation was thrown into relief by the voluminous tranquillity of Mrs Ruck. 'He will have to take us back in September, any way,' the young girl pursued; 'he will have to take us back to get some things we have ordered.'

'Have you ordered a great many things?' I asked, jocosely.

'Well, I guess we have ordered *some*. Of course we wanted to take advantage of being in Paris – ladies always do. We have left the principal things till we go back. Of course that is the principal interest, for ladies. Mother said she should feel so shabby, if she just passed through. We have promised all the people to be back in September, and I never broke a promise yet. So Mr Ruck has got to make his plans accordingly.'

'And what are his plans?'

'I don't know; he doesn't seem able to make any. His great idea was to get to Geneva; but now that he has got here he doesn't seem to care. It's the effect of ill health. He used to be so bright; but now he is quite subdued. It's about time he should improve, any way. We went out last night to look at the jewellers' windows – in that street behind the hotel. I had always heard of those jewellers' windows. We saw some lovely things, but it didn't seem to rouse father. He'll get tired of Geneva sooner than he did of Paris.'

'Ah,' said I, 'there are finer things here than the jewellers' windows. We are very near some of the most beautiful scenery in Europe.'

'I suppose you mean the mountains. Well, we have seen plenty of mountains at home. We used to go to the mountains every summer. We are familiar enough with the mountains. Aren't we, mother?' the young lady demanded, appealing to Mrs Ruck, who, with her husband, had drawn near again.

'Aren't we what?' inquired the elder lady.

'Aren't we familiar with the mountains?'

'Well, I hope so,' said Mrs Ruck.

Mr Ruck, with his hands in his pockets, gave me a sociable wink. 'There's nothing much you can tell them!' he said.

The two ladies stood face to face a few moments, surveying each other's garments. 'Don't you want to go out?' the young girl at last inquired of her mother.

'Well, I think we had better; we have got to go up to that place.'

'To what place?' asked Mr Ruck.

'To that jeweller's – to that big one.'

'They all seemed big enough; they were too big!' And Mr Ruck gave me another wink.

'That one where we saw the blue cross,' said his daughter.

'Oh, come, what do you want of that blue cross?' poor Mr Ruck demanded.

'She wants to hang it on a black velvet ribbon and tie it round her neck,' said his wife.

'A black velvet ribbon? No, I thank you!' cried the young lady. 'Do you suppose I would wear that cross on a black velvet ribbon? On a nice little gold chain, if you please – a little narrow gold chain, like an old-fashioned watch-chain. That's the proper thing for that blue cross. I know the sort of chain I mean; I'm going to look for one. When I want a thing,' said Miss Ruck, with decision, 'I can generally find it.'

'Look here, Sophy,' her father urged, 'you don't want that blue cross.'

'I do want it – I happen to want it.' And Sophy glanced at me with a little laugh.

Her laugh, which in itself was pretty, suggested that there were various relations in which one might stand to Miss Ruck; but I think I was conscious of a certain satisfaction in not occupying the paternal one. 'Don't worry the poor child,' said her mother.

'Come on, mother,' said Miss Ruck.

'We are going to look about a little,' explained the elder lady to me, by way of taking leave.

'I know what that means,' remarked Mr Ruck, as his companions moved away. He stood looking at them a moment, while he raised his hand to his head, behind, and stood rubbing it a little, with a movement that displaced his hat. (I may remark in parenthesis that I never saw a hat more easily displaced than Mr Ruck's.) I supposed he was going to say something querulous, but I was mistaken. Mr Ruck was unhappy, but he was very good-natured. 'Well, they want to pick up something,' he said. 'That's the principal interest, for ladies.'

IV

MR RUCK distinguished me, as the French say. He honoured me with his esteem, and, as the days elapsed, with a large portion of his confidence. Sometimes he bored me a little, for the tone of his conversation was not cheerful, tending as it did almost exclusively to a melancholy dirge over the financial prostration of our common country. 'No, sir, business in the United States is not what it once was,' he found occasion to remark several times a day. 'There's not the same spring –

there's not the same hopeful feeling. You can see it in all departments.' He used to sit by the hour in the little garden of the pension, with a roll of American newspapers in his lap and his high hat pushed back, swinging one of his long legs and reading the *New York Herald*. He paid a daily visit to the American banker's, on the other side of the Rhône, and remained there a long time, turning over the old papers on the green velvet table in the middle of the Salon des Étrangers and fraternising with chance compatriots. But in spite of these diversions his time hung heavily upon his hands. I used sometimes to propose to him to take a walk; but he had a mortal horror of pedestrianism, and regarded my own taste for it as a morbid form of activity. 'You'll kill yourself, if you don't look out,' he said, 'walking all over the country. I don't want to walk round that way; I ain't a postman!' Briefly speaking, Mr Ruck had few resources. His wife and daughter, on the other hand, it was to be supposed, were possessed of a good many that could not be apparent to an unobtrusive young man. They also sat a great deal in the garden or in the salon, side by side, with folded hands, contemplating material objects, and were remarkably independent of most of the usual feminine aids to idleness – light literature, tapestry, the use of the piano. They were, however, much fonder of locomotion than their companion, and I often met them in the Rue du Rhône and on the quays, loitering in front of the jewellers' windows. They might have had a cavalier in the person of old M. Pigeonneau, who possessed a high appreciation of their charms, but who, owing to the absence of a common idiom, was deprived of the pleasures of intimacy. He knew no English, and Mrs Ruck and her daughter had, as it seemed, an incurable mistrust of the beautiful tongue which, as the old man endeavoured to impress upon them, was pre-eminently the language of conversation.

'They have a *tournure de princesse* – a *distinction suprême*,' he said to me. 'One is surprised to find them in a little pension, at seven francs a day.'

'Oh, they don't come for economy,' I answered. 'They must be rich.'

'They don't come for my *beaux yeux* – for mine,' said M. Pigeonneau, sadly. 'Perhaps it's for yours, young man. Je vous recommande la mère.'

I reflected a moment. 'They came on account of Mr Ruck – because at hotels he's so restless.'

M. Pigeonneau gave me a knowing nod. 'Of course he is, with such a wife as that! – a *femme superbe*. Madame Ruck is preserved in perfection – a miraculous *fraîcheur*. I like those large, fair, quiet women; they are often, *dans l'intimité*, the most agreeable. I'll warrant you that at heart Madame Ruck is a finished coquette.'

'I rather doubt it,' I said.

'You suppose her cold? Ne vous y fiez pas!'

'It is a matter in which I have nothing at stake.'

'You young Americans are droll,' said M. Pigeonneau; 'you never have anything at stake! But the little one, for example; I'll warrant you she's not cold. She is admirably made.'

'She is very pretty.'

' "She is very pretty!" Vous dites cela d'un ton! When you pay compliments to Mademoiselle Ruck, I hope that's not the way you do it.'

'I don't pay compliments to Mademoiselle Ruck.'

'Ah, decidedly,' said M. Pigeonneau, 'you young Americans are droll!'

I should have suspected that these two ladies would not especially commend themselves to Madame Beaurepas; that as a *maîtresse de salon*, which she in some degree aspired to be, she would have found them wanting in a certain flexibility of deportment. But I should have gone quite wrong; Madame Beaurepas had no fault at all to find with her new pension-naires. 'I have no observation whatever to make about them,' she said to me one evening. 'I see nothing in those ladies which is at all *déplacé*. They don't complain of anything; they don't meddle; they take what's given them; they leave me tranquil. The Americans are often like that. Often, but not always,' Madame Beaurepas pursued. 'We are to have a specimen to-morrow of a very different sort.'

'An American?' I inquired.

'Two *Américaines* – a mother and a daughter. There are Americans and Americans: when you are *difficiles*, you are more so than any one, and when you have pretensions – ah, *par exemple*, it's serious. I foresee that with this little lady everything will be serious, beginning with her *café au lait*. She has been staying at the Pension Chamousset – my *concurrent*, you know, farther up the street; but she is coming away because the coffee is bad. She holds to her coffee, it appears. I don't know what liquid Madame Chamousset may have invented, but we will do the best we can for her. Only, I know she will make me *des histoires* about something else. She will demand a new lamp for the salon; *vous allez voir cela*. She wishes to pay but eleven francs a day for herself and her daughter, *tout compris*; and for their eleven francs they expect to be lodged like princesses. But she is very "ladylike" – isn't that what you call it in English? Oh, *pour cela*, she is ladylike!'

I caught a glimpse on the morrow of this ladylike person, who was arriving at her new residence as I came in from a walk. She had come in a cab, with her daughter and her luggage; and, with an air of perfect softness and serenity, she was disputing the fare as she stood among her boxes, on the steps. She addressed her cabman in a very English accent, but with extreme precision and correctness. 'I wish to be perfectly reasonable, but I don't wish to encourage you in exorbitant demands. With a franc and a half you are sufficiently paid. It is not the custom at Geneva to give a *pour-boire* for so short a drive. I have made inquiries, and I find it is not the custom, even in the best families. I am a stranger, yes, but I always adopt the custom of the native families. I think it my duty toward the natives.'

'But I am a native, too, *moi*!' said the cabman, with an angry laugh.

'You seem to me to speak with a German accent,' continued the lady. 'You are probably from Basel. A franc and a half is sufficient. I see you have left behind the little red bag which I asked you to hold between your knees; you will please to go back to the other house and get it. Very well, if you are impolite I will make a complaint of you to-morrow at the

administration. Aurora, you will find a pencil in the outer pocket
of my embroidered satchel; please to write down his number, –
87; do you see it distinctly? – in case we should forget it.'

The young lady addressed as 'Aurora' – a slight, fair girl,
holding a large parcel of umbrellas – stood at hand while this
allocution went forward, but she apparently gave no heed to it.
She stood looking about her, in a listless manner, at the front of
the house, at the corridor, at Célestine tucking up her apron in
the door-way, at me as I passed in amid the disseminated
luggage; her mother's parsimonious attitude seeming to produce in Miss Aurora neither sympathy nor embarrassment. At
dinner the two ladies were placed on the same side of the table
as myself, below Mrs Ruck and her daughter, my own position
being on the right of Mr Ruck. I had therefore little observation
of Mrs Church – such I learned to be her name – but I occasionally heard her soft, distinct voice.

'White wine, if you please; we prefer white wine. There is
none on the table? Then you will please to get some, and to
remember to place a bottle of it always here, between my
daughter and myself.'

'That lady seems to know what she wants,' said Mr Ruck,
'and she speaks so I can understand her. I can't understand
every one, over here. I should like to make that lady's acquaintance. Perhaps she knows what I want, too; it seems hard to find
out. But I don't want any of their sour white wine; that's one of
the things I don't want. I expect she'll be an addition to the
pension.'

Mr Ruck made the acquaintance of Mrs Church that evening in the parlour, being presented to her by his wife, who
presumed on the rights conferred upon herself by the mutual
proximity, at table, of the two ladies. I suspected that in Mrs
Church's view Mrs Ruck presumed too far. The fugitive from
the Pension Chamousset, as M. Pigeonneau called her, was a
little fresh, plump, comely woman, looking less than her age,
with a round, bright, serious face. She was very simply and
frugally dressed, not at all in the manner of Mr Ruck's companions, and she had an air of quiet distinction which was an
excellent defensive weapon. She exhibited a polite disposition

to listen to what Mr Ruck might have to say, but her manner
was equivalent to an intimation that what she valued least in
boarding-house life was its social opportunities. She had placed
herself near a lamp, after carefully screwing it and turning it up,
and she had opened in her lap, with the assistance of a large
embroidered marker, an octavo volume, which I perceived to
be in German. To Mrs Ruck and her daughter she was evidently a puzzle, with her economical attire and her expensive
culture. The two younger ladies, however, had begun to
fraternise very freely, and Miss Ruck presently went wandering
out of the room with her arm round the waist of Miss Church. It
was a very warm evening; the long windows of the salon stood
wide open into the garden, and, inspired by the balmy darkness, M. Pigeonneau and Mademoiselle Beaurepas, a most
obliging little woman, who lisped and always wore a huge
cravat, declared they would organise a *fête de nuit*. They
engaged in this undertaking, and the fête developed itself,
consisting of half a dozen red paper lanterns, hung about on
the trees, and of several glasses of *sirop*, carried on a tray by the
stout-armed Célestine. As the festival deepened to its climax
I went out into the garden, where M. Pigeonneau was master of
ceremonies.

'But where are those charming young ladies,' he cried, 'Miss
Ruck and the new-comer, *l'aimable transfuge*? Their absence
has been remarked, and they are wanting to the brilliancy of the
occasion. *Voyez* I have selected a glass of syrup – a generous
glass – for Mademoiselle Ruck, and I advise you, my young
friend, if you wish to make a good impression, to put aside one
which you may offer to the other young lady. What is her name?
Miss Church. I see; it's a singular name. There is a church in
which I would willingly worship!'

Mr Ruck presently came out of the salon, having concluded
his interview with Mrs Church. Through the open window
I saw the latter lady sitting under the lamp with her German
octavo, while Mrs Ruck, established, empty-handed, in an
arm-chair near her, gazed at her with an air of fascination.

'Well, I told you she would know what I want,' said Mr
Ruck. 'She says I want to go up to Appenzell, wherever that

is; that I want to drink whey and live in a high latitude – what did she call it? – a high altitude. She seemed to think we ought to leave for Appenzell to-morrow; she'd got it all fixed. She says this ain't a high enough lat – a high enough altitude. And she says I mustn't go too high, either; that would be just as bad; she seems to know just the right figure. She says she'll give me a list of the hotels where we must stop, on the way to Appenzell. I asked her if she didn't want to go with us, but she says she'd rather sit still and read. I expect she's a big reader.'

The daughter of this accomplished woman now reappeared, in company with Miss Ruck, with whom she had been strolling through the outlying parts of the garden.

'Well,' said Miss Ruck, glancing at the red paper lanterns, 'are they trying to stick the flower-pots into the trees?'

'It's an illumination in honour of our arrival,' the other young girl rejoined. 'It's a triumph over Madame Chamousset.'

'Meanwhile, at the Pension Chamousset,' I ventured to suggest, 'they have put out their lights; they are sitting in darkness, lamenting your departure.'

She looked at me, smiling; she was standing in the light that came from the house. M. Pigeonneau, meanwhile, who had been awaiting his chance, advanced to Miss Ruck with his glass of syrup. 'I have kept it for you, mademoiselle,' he said; 'I have jealously guarded it. It is very delicious!'

Miss Ruck looked at him and his syrup, without making any motion to take the glass. 'Well, I guess it's sour,' she said in a moment; and she gave a little shake of her head.

M. Pigeonneau stood staring, with his syrup in his hand; then he slowly turned away. He looked about at the rest of us, as if to appeal from Miss Ruck's insensibility, and went to deposit his rejected tribute on a bench.

'Won't you give it to me?' asked Miss Church, in faultless French. 'J'adore le sirop, moi.'

M. Pigeonneau came back with alacrity, and presented the glass with a very low bow. 'I adore good manners,' murmured the old man.

This incident caused me to look at Miss Church with quickened interest. She was not strikingly pretty, but in her charming, irregular face there was something brilliant and ardent. Like her mother, she was very simply dressed.

'She wants to go to America, and her mother won't let her,' said Miss Sophy to me, explaining her companion's situation.

'I am very sorry – for America,' I answered, laughing.

'Well, I don't want to say anything against your mother, but I think it's shameful,' Miss Ruck pursued.

'Mamma has very good reasons; she will tell you them all.'

'Well, I'm sure I don't want to hear them,' said Miss Ruck. 'You have got a right to go to your own country; every one has a right to go to their own country.'

'Mamma is not very patriotic,' said Aurora Church, smiling.

'Well, I call that dreadful,' her companion declared. 'I have heard that there are some Americans like that, but I never believed it.'

'There are all sorts of Americans,' I said, laughing.

'Aurora's one of the right sort,' rejoined Miss Ruck, who had apparently become very intimate with her new friend.

'Are you very patriotic?' I asked of the young girl.

'She's right down homesick,' said Miss Sophy; 'she's dying to go. If I were you my mother would have to take me.'

'Mamma is going to take me to Dresden.'

'Well, I declare I never heard of anything so dreadful!' cried Miss Ruck. 'It's like something in a story.'

'I never heard there was anything very dreadful in Dresden,' I interposed.

Miss Ruck looked at me a moment. 'Well, I don't believe *you* are a good American,' she replied, 'and I never supposed you were. You had better go in there and talk to Mrs Church.'

'Dresden is really very nice, isn't it?' I asked of her companion.

'It isn't nice if you happen to prefer New York,' said Miss Sophy. 'Miss Church prefers New York. Tell him you are dying to see New York; it will make him angry,' she went on.

'I have no desire to make him angry,' said Aurora, smiling.

'It is only Miss Ruck who can do that,' I rejoined. 'Have you been a long time in Europe?'

'Always.'

'I call that wicked!' Miss Sophy declared.

'You might be in a worse place,' I continued. 'I find Europe very interesting.'

Miss Ruck gave a little laugh. 'I was saying that you wanted to pass for a European.'

'Yes, I want to pass for a Dalmatian.'

Miss Ruck looked at me a moment. 'Well, you had better not come home,' she said. 'No one will speak to you.'

'Were you born in these countries?' I asked of her companion.

'Oh, no; I came to Europe when I was a small child. But I remember America a little, and it seems delightful.'

'Wait till you see it again. It's just too lovely,' said Miss Sophy.

'It's the grandest country in the world,' I added.

Miss Ruck began to toss her head. 'Come away, my dear,' she said. 'If there's a creature I despise it's a man that tries to say funny things about his own country.'

'Don't you think one can be tired of Europe?' Aurora asked, lingering.

'Possibly – after many years.'

'Father was tired of it after three weeks,' said Miss Ruck.

'I have been here sixteen years,' her friend went on, looking at me with a charming intentness, as if she had a purpose in speaking. 'It used to be for my education. I don't know what it's for now.'

'She's beautifully educated,' said Miss Ruck. 'She knows four languages.'

'I am not very sure that I know English.'

'You should go to Boston!' cried Miss Sophy. 'They speak splendidly in Boston.'

'C'est mon rêve,' said Aurora, still looking at me.

'Have you been all over Europe,' I asked – 'in all the different countries?'

She hesitated a moment. 'Everywhere that there's a *pension*. Mamma is devoted to *pensions*. We have lived, at one time or another, in every *pension* in Europe.'

'Well, I should think you had seen about enough,' said Miss Ruck.

'It's a delightful way of seeing Europe,' Aurora rejoined, with her brilliant smile. 'You may imagine how it has attached me to the different countries. I have such charming souvenirs! There is a *pension* awaiting us now at Dresden, – eight francs a day, without wine. That's rather dear. Mamma means to make them give us wine. Mamma is a great authority on *pensions;* she is known, that way, all over Europe. Last winter we were in Italy, and she discovered one at Piacenza, – four francs a day. We made economies.'

'Your mother doesn't seem to mingle much,' observed Miss Ruck, glancing through the window at the scholastic attitude of Mrs Church.

'No, she doesn't mingle, except in the native society. Though she lives in *pensions*, she detests them.'

'Why does she live in them, then?' asked Miss Sophy, rather resentfully.

'Oh, because we are so poor; it's the cheapest way to live. We have tried having a cook, but the cook always steals. Mamma used to set me to watch her; that's the way I passed my *jeunesse* – my *belle jeunesse*. We are frightfully poor,' the young girl went on, with the same strange frankness – a curious mixture of girlish grace and conscious cynicism. 'Nous n'avons pas le sou. That's one of the reasons we don't go back to America; mamma says we can't afford to live there.'

'Well, any one can see that you're an American girl,' Miss Ruck remarked, in a consolatory manner. 'I can tell an American girl a mile off. You've got the American style.'

'I'm afraid I haven't the American *toilette*,' said Aurora, looking at the other's superior splendour.

'Well, your dress was cut in France; any one can see that.'

'Yes,' said Aurora, with a laugh, 'my dress was cut in France – at Avranches.'

'Well, you've got a lovely figure, any way,' pursued her companion.

'Ah,' said the young girl, 'at Avranches, too, my figure was admired.' And she looked at me askance, with a certain coquetry. But I was an innocent youth, and I only looked back at her, wondering. She was a great deal nicer than Miss Ruck, and yet Miss Ruck would not have said that. 'I try to be like an American girl,' she continued; 'I do my best, though mamma doesn't at all encourage it. I am very patriotic. I try to copy them, though mamma has brought me up *à la française*; that is, as much as one can in *pensions*. For instance, I have never been out of the house without mamma; oh, never, never. But some-times I despair; American girls are so wonderfully frank. I can't be frank, like that. I am always afraid. But I do what I can, as you see. Excusez du peu!'

I thought this young lady at least as outspoken as most of her unexpatriated sisters; there was something almost comical in her despondency. But she had by no means caught, as it seemed to me, the American tone. Whatever her tone was, however, it had a fascination; there was something dainty about it, and yet it was decidedly audacious.

The young ladies began to stroll about the garden again, and I enjoyed their society until M. Pigeonneau's festival came to an end.

V

MR RUCK did not take his departure to Appenzell on the morrow, in spite of the eagerness to witness such an event which he had attributed to Mrs Church. He continued, on the contrary, for many days after, to hang about the garden, to wander up to the banker's and back again, to engage in desultory conversation with his fellow-boarders, and to endeavour to assuage his constitutional restlessness by perusal of the American journals. But on the morrow I had the honour of making Mrs Church's acquaintance. She came into the salon, after the midday breakfast, with her German octavo under her arm, and she appealed to me for assistance in select-ing a quiet corner.

'Would you very kindly,' she said, 'move that large fauteuil a little more this way? Not the largest; the one with the little cushion. The fauteuils here are very insufficient; I must ask

Madame Beaurepas for another. Thank you; a little more to the left, please; that will do. Are you particularly engaged?' she inquired, after she had seated herself. 'If not, I should like to have some conversation with you. It is some time since I have met a young American of your – what shall I call it? – your affiliations. I have learned your name from Madame Beaurepas; I think I used to know some of your people. I don't know what has become of all my friends. I used to have a charming little circle at home, but now I meet no one I know. Don't you think there is a great difference between the people one meets and the people one would like to meet? Fortunately, sometimes,' added my interlocutress graciously, 'it's quite the same. I suppose you are a specimen, a favourable specimen,' she went on, 'of young America. Tell me, now, what is young America thinking of in these days of ours? What are its feelings, its opinions, its aspirations? What is its *ideal*?' I had seated myself near Mrs Church, and she had pointed this interrogation with the gaze of her bright little eyes. I felt it embarrassing to be treated as a favourable specimen of young America, and to be expected to answer for the great republic. Observing my hesitation, Mrs Church clasped her hands on the open page of her book and gave an intense, melancholy smile. '*Has* it an ideal?' she softly asked. 'Well, we must talk of this,' she went on, without insisting. 'Speak, for the present, for yourself simply. Have you come to Europe with any special design?'

'Nothing to boast of,' I said. 'I am studying a little.'

'Ah, I am glad to hear that. You are gathering up a little European culture; that's what we lack, you know, at home. No individual can do much, of course. But you must not be discouraged; every little counts.'

'I see that you, at least, are doing your part,' I rejoined gallantly, dropping my eyes on my companion's learned volume.

'Yes, I frankly admit that I am fond of study. There is no one, after all, like the Germans. That is, for facts. For opinions I by no means always go with them. I form my opinions myself. I am sorry to say, however,' Mrs Church continued, 'that I can hardly pretend to diffuse my acquisitions. I am afraid I am sadly selfish; I do little to irrigate the soil. I belong – I frankly confess it – to the class of absentees.'

'I had the pleasure, last evening,' I said, 'of making the acquaintance of your daughter. She told me you had been a long time in Europe.'

Mrs Church smiled benignantly. 'Can one ever be too long? We shall never leave it.'

'Your daughter won't like that,' I said, smiling too.

'Has she been taking you into her confidence? She is a more sensible young lady than she sometimes appears. I have taken great pains with her; she is really – I may be permitted to say it – superbly educated.'

'She seemed to me a very charming girl,' I rejoined. 'And I learned that she speaks four languages.'

'It is not only that,' said Mrs Church, in a tone which suggested that this might be a very superficial species of culture. 'She has made what we call *de fortes études* – such as I suppose you are making now. She is familiar with the results of modern science; she keeps pace with the new historical school.'

'Ah,' said I, 'she has gone much farther than I!'

'You doubtless think I exaggerate, and you force me, therefore, to mention the fact that I am able to speak of such matters with a certain intelligence.'

'That is very evident,' I said. 'But your daughter thinks you ought to take her home.' I began to fear, as soon as I had uttered these words, that they savoured of treachery to the young lady, but I was reassured by seeing that they produced on her mother's placid countenance no symptom whatever of irritation.

'My daughter has her little theories,' Mrs Church observed, 'she has, I may say, her illusions. And what wonder! What would youth be without its illusions? Aurora has a theory that she would be happier in New York, in Boston, in Philadelphia, than in one of the charming old cities in which our lot is cast. But she is mistaken, that is all. We must allow our children their illusions, must we not? But we must watch over them.'

Although she herself seemed proof against discomposure, I found something vaguely irritating in her soft, sweet positiveness.

'American cities,' I said, 'are the paradise of young girls.'

'Do you mean,' asked Mrs Church, 'that the young girls who come from those places are angels?'

'Yes,' I said, resolutely.

'This young lady – what is her odd name? – with whom my daughter has formed a somewhat precipitate acquaintance: is Miss Ruck an angel? But I won't force you to say anything uncivil. It would be too cruel to make a single exception.'

'Well,' said I, 'at any rate, in America young girls have an easier lot. They have much more liberty.'

My companion laid her hand for an instant on my arm. 'My dear young friend, I know America, I know the conditions of life there, so well. There is perhaps no subject on which I have reflected more than on our national idiosyncrasies.'

'I am afraid you don't approve of them,' said I, a little brutally.

Brutal indeed my proposition was, and Mrs Church was not prepared to assent to it in this rough shape. She dropped her eyes on her book, with an air of acute meditation. Then, raising them, 'We are very crude,' she softly observed – 'we are very crude.' Lest even this delicately-uttered statement should seem to savour of the vice that she deprecated, she went on to explain. 'There are two classes of minds, you know – those that hold back, and those that push forward. My daughter and I are not pushers; we move with little steps. We like the old, trodden paths; we like the old, old world.'

'Ah,' said I, 'you know what you like; there is a great virtue in that.'

'Yes, we like Europe; we prefer it. We like the opportunities of Europe; we like the *rest*. There is so much in that, you know. The world seems to me to be hurrying, pressing forward so fiercely, without knowing where it is going. "Whither?" I often ask, in my little quiet way. But I have yet to learn that any one can tell me.'

'You're a great conservative,' I observed, while I wondered whether I myself could answer this inquiry.

Mrs Church gave me a smile which was equivalent to a confession. 'I wish to retain a *little* – just a little. Surely, we have done so much, we might rest a while; we might pause. That is all my feeling – just to stop a little, to wait! I have seen so many changes. I wish to draw in, to draw in – to hold back, to hold back.'

'You shouldn't hold your daughter back!' I answered, laughing and getting up. I got up, not by way of terminating our interview, for I perceived Mrs Church's exposition of her views to be by no means complete, but in order to offer a chair to Miss Aurora, who at this moment drew near. She thanked me and remained standing, but without at first, as I noticed, meeting her mother's eye.

'You have been engaged with your new acquaintance, my dear?' this lady inquired.

'Yes, mamma dear,' said the young girl, gently.

'Do you find her very edifying?'

Aurora was silent a moment; then she looked at her mother. 'I don't know, mamma; she is very fresh.'

I ventured to indulge in a respectful laugh. 'Your mother has another word for that. But I must not,' I added, 'be crude.'

'Ah, vous m'en voulez?' inquired Mrs Church. 'And yet I can't pretend I said it in jest. I feel it too much. We have been having a little social discussion,' she said to her daughter. 'There is still so much to be said. And I wish,' she continued, turning to me, 'that I could give you our point of view. Don't you wish, Aurora, that we could give him our point of view?'

'Yes, mamma,' said Aurora.

'We consider ourselves very fortunate in our point of view, don't we dearest?' mamma demanded.

'Very fortunate, indeed, mamma.'

'You see we have acquired an insight into European life,' the elder lady pursued. 'We have our place at many a European fireside. We find so much to esteem – so much to enjoy. Do we not, my daughter?'

'So very much, mamma,' the young girl went on, with a sort of inscrutable submissiveness. I wondered at it; it offered so strange a contrast to the mocking freedom of her tone the night before; but while I wondered, I was careful not to let my perplexity take precedence of my good manners.

'I don't know what you ladies may have found at European firesides,' I said, 'but there can be very little doubt what you have left there.'

Mrs Church got up, to acknowledge my compliment. 'We have spent some charming hours. And that reminds me that we have just now such an occasion in prospect. We are to call upon some Genevese friends – the family of the Pasteur Galopin. They are to go with us to the old library at the Hôtel de Ville, where there are some very interesting documents of the period of the Reformation; we are promised a glimpse of some manuscripts of poor Servetus, the antagonist and victim, you know, of Calvin. Here, of course, one can only speak of Calvin under one's breath, but some day, when we are more private,' and Mrs Church looked round the room, 'I will give you my view of him. I think it has a touch of originality. Aurora is familiar with, are you not, my daughter, familiar with my view of Calvin?'

'Yes, mamma,' said Aurora, with docility, while the two ladies went to prepare for their visit to the Pasteur Galopin.

VI

'She has demanded a new lamp; I told you she would!' This communication was made me by Madame Beaurepas a couple of days later. 'And she has asked for a new *tapis de lit*, and she has requested me to provide Célestine with a pair of light shoes. I told her that, as a general thing, cooks are not shod with satin. That poor Célestine!'

'Mrs Church may be exacting,' I said, 'but she is a clever little woman.'

'A lady who pays but five francs and a half shouldn't be too clever. C'est déplacé. I don't like the type.'

'What type do you call Mrs Church's?'

'Mon Dieu,' said Madame Beaurepas, 'c'est une de ces mamans comme vous en avez, qui promènent leur fille.'

'She is trying to marry her daughter? I don't think she's of that sort.'

But Madame Beaurepas shrewdly held to her idea. 'She is trying it in her own way; she does it very quietly. She doesn't want an American; she wants a foreigner. And she wants a *mari sérieux*. But she is travelling over Europe in search of one. She would like a magistrate.'

'A magistrate?'

'A *gros bonnet* of some kind; a professor or a deputy.'

'I am very sorry for the poor girl,' I said, laughing.

'You needn't pity her too much; she's a sly thing.'

'Ah, for that, no!' I exclaimed. 'She's a charming girl.'

Madame Beaurepas gave an elderly grin. 'She has hooked you, eh? But the mother won't have you.'

I developed my idea, without heeding this insinuation. 'She's a charming girl, but she is a little odd. It's a necessity of her position. She is less submissive to her mother than she has to pretend to be. That's in self-defence; it's to make her life possible.'

'She wishes to get away from her mother,' continued Madame Beaurepas. 'She wishes to *courir les champs*.'

'She wishes to go to America, her native country.'

'Precisely. And she will certainly go.'

'I hope so!' I rejoined.

'Some fine morning – or evening – she will go off with a young man; probably with a young American.'

'Allons donc!' said I, with disgust.

'That will be quite America enough,' pursued my cynical hostess. 'I have kept a boarding-house for forty years. I have seen that type.'

'Have such things as that happened *chez vous*?' I asked.

'Everything has happened *chez moi*. But nothing has happened more than once. Therefore this won't happen here. It will be at the next place they go to, or the next. Besides, here there is no young American *pour la partie* – none except you, monsieur. You are susceptible, but you are too reasonable.'

'It's lucky for you I am reasonable,' I answered. 'It's thanks to that fact that you escape a scolding.'

One morning, about this time, instead of coming back to breakfast at the *pension*, after my lectures at the Academy, I went to partake of this meal with a fellow-student, at an ancient eating-house in the collegiate quarter. On separating from my friend, I took my way along that charming public walk known in Geneva as the Treille, a shady terrace, of immense elevation, overhanging a portion of the lower town. There are spreading trees and well-worn benches, and over the tiles and chimneys of the *ville basse* there is a view of the snow-crested Alps. On the other side, as you turn your back to the view, the promenade is overlooked by a row of tall, sober-faced *hôtels*, the dwellings of the local aristocracy. I was very fond of the place, and often resorted to it to stimulate my sense of the picturesque. Presently, as I lingered there on this occasion, I became aware that a gentleman was seated not far from where I stood, with his back to the Alpine chain, which this morning was brilliant and distinct, and a newspaper, unfolded, in his lap. He was not reading, however; he was staring before him in gloomy contemplation. I don't know whether I recognised first the newspaper or its proprietor; one, in either case, would have helped me to identify the other. One was the *New York Herald*; the other, of course, was Mr Ruck. As I drew nearer, he transferred his eyes from the stony, high-featured masks of the grey old houses on the other side of the terrace, and I knew by the expression of his face just how he had been feeling about these distinguished abodes. He had made up his mind that their proprietors were a dusky, narrow-minded, unsociable company; plunging their roots into a superfluous past. I endeavoured, therefore, as I sat down beside him, to suggest something more impersonal.

'That's a beautiful view of the Alps,' I observed.

'Yes,' said Mr Ruck, without moving, 'I've examined it. Fine thing, in its way – fine thing. Beauties of nature – that sort of thing. We came up on purpose to look at it.'

'Your ladies, then, have been with you?'

'Yes; they are just walking round. They're awfully restless. They keep saying I'm restless, but I'm as quiet as a sleeping child to them. It takes,' he added in a moment, dryly, 'the form of shopping.'

'Are they shopping now?'

'Well, if they ain't, they're trying to. They told me to sit here a while, and they'd just walk round. I generally know what that means. But that's the principal interest for ladies,' he added, retracting his irony. 'We thought we'd come up here and see the cathedral; Mrs Church seemed to think it a dead loss that we shouldn't see the cathedral, especially as we hadn't seen many yet. And I had to come up to the banker's any way. Well, we certainly saw the cathedral. I don't know as we are any the better for it, and I don't know as I should know it again. But we saw it, any way. I don't know as I should want to go there regularly; but I suppose it will give us, in conversation, a kind of hold on Mrs Church, eh? I guess we want something of that kind. Well,' Mr Ruck continued, 'I stepped in at the banker's to see if there wasn't something, and they handed me out a Herald.'

'I hope the Herald is full of good news,' I said.

'Can't say it is. D—d bad news.'

'Political,' I inquired, 'or commercial?'

'Oh, hang politics! It's business, sir. There ain't any business. It's all gone to,' – and Mr Ruck became profane. 'Nine failures in one day. What do you say to that?'

'I hope they haven't injured you,' I said.

'Well, they haven't helped me much. So many houses on fire, that's all. If they happen to take place in your own street, they don't increase the value of your property. When mine catches, I suppose they'll write and tell me – one of these days, when they've got nothing else to do. I didn't get a blessed letter this morning; I suppose they think I'm having such a good time over here it's a pity to disturb me. If I could attend to business for about half an hour, I'd find out something. But I can't, and it's no use talking. The state of my health was never so unsatisfactory as it was about five o'clock this morning.'

'I am very sorry to hear that,' I said, 'and I recommend you strongly not to think of business.'

'I don't,' Mr Ruck replied. 'I'm thinking of cathedrals; I'm thinking of the beauties of nature. Come,' he went on, turning round on the bench and leaning his elbow on the parapet, 'I'll think of those mountains over there; they *are* pretty, certainly. Can't you get over there?'

'Over where?'

'Over to those hills. Don't they run a train right up?'

'You can go to Chamouni,' I said. 'You can go to Grindel-
wald and Zermatt and fifty other places. You can't go by rail,
but you can drive.'

'All right, we'll drive – and not in a one-horse concern,
either. Yes, Chamouni is one of the places we put down.
I hope there are a few nice shops in Chamouni.' Mr Ruck
spoke with a certain quickened emphasis, and in a tone more
explicitly humorous than he commonly employed. I thought he
was excited, and yet he had not the appearance of excitement.
He looked like a man who has simply taken, in the face of
disaster, a sudden, somewhat imaginative, resolution not to
'worry'. He presently twisted himself about on his bench
again and began to watch for his companions. 'Well, they *are*
walking round,' he resumed; 'I guess they've hit on something,
somewhere. And they've got a carriage waiting outside of that
archway, too. They seem to do a big business in archways here,
don't they. They like to have a carriage to carry home the
things – those ladies of mine. Then they're sure they've got
them'. The ladies, after this, to do them justice, were not very
long in appearing. They came toward us, from under the archway to which Mr Ruck had somewhat invidiously alluded,
slowly and with a rather exhausted step and expression. My
companion looked at them a moment, as they advanced.
'They're tired,' he said softly. 'When they're tired, like that,
it's very expensive.'

'Well,' said Mrs Ruck, 'I'm glad you've had some company.'
Her husband looked at her, in silence, through narrowed eyelids, and I suspected that this gracious observation on the lady's
part was prompted by a restless conscience.

Miss Sophy glanced at me with her little straightforward air
of defiance. 'It would have been more proper if *we* had had the
company. Why didn't you come after us, instead of sitting
there?' she asked of Mr Ruck's companion.

'I was told by your father,' I explained, 'that you were
engaged in sacred rites.' Miss Ruck was not gracious, though
I doubt whether it was because her conscience was better than
her mother's.

'Well, for a gentleman there is nothing so sacred as ladies' society,' replied Miss Ruck, in the manner of a person accustomed to giving neat retorts.

'I suppose you refer to the cathedral,' said her mother. 'Well, I must say, we didn't go back there. I don't know what it may be of a Sunday, but it gave me a chill.'

'We discovered the loveliest little lace-shop,' observed the young girl, with a serenity that was superior to bravado.

Her father looked at her a while; then turned about again, leaning on the parapet, and gazed away at the 'hills'.

'Well, it was certainly cheap,' said Mrs Ruck, also contemplating the Alps.

'We are going to Chamouni,' said her husband. 'You haven't any occasion for lace at Chamouni.'

'Well, I'm glad to hear you have decided to go somewhere,' rejoined his wife. 'I don't want to be a fixture at a boarding-house.'

'You can wear lace anywhere,' said Miss Ruck, 'if you put it on right. That's the great thing, with lace. I don't think they know how to wear lace in Europe. I know how I mean to wear mine; but I mean to keep it till I get home.'

Her father transferred his melancholy gaze to her elaborately-appointed little person; there was a great deal of very new-looking detail in Miss Ruck's appearance. Then, in a tone of voice quite out of consonance with his facial despondency, 'Have you purchased a great deal?' he inquired.

'I have purchased enough for you to make a fuss about.'

'He can't make a fuss about that,' said Mrs Ruck.

'Well, you'll see!' declared the young girl with a little sharp laugh.

But her father went on, in the same tone: 'Have you got it in your pocket? Why don't you put it on – why don't you hang it round you?'

'I'll hang it round *you*, if you don't look out!' cried Miss Sophy.

'Don't you want to show it to this gentleman?' Mr Ruck continued.

'Mercy, how you do talk about that lace!' said his wife.

'Well, I want to be lively. There's every reason for it; we're going to Chamouni.'

'You're restless; that's what's the matter with you.' And Mrs Ruck got up.

'No, I ain't,' said her husband. 'I never felt so quiet; I feel as peaceful as a little child.'

Mrs Ruck, who had no sense whatever of humour, looked at her daughter and at me. 'Well, I hope you'll improve,' she said.

'Send in the bills,' Mr Ruck went on, rising to his feet. 'Don't hesitate, Sophy. I don't care what you do now. In for a penny, in for a pound.'

Miss Ruck joined her mother, with a little toss of her head, and we followed the ladies to the carriage. 'In your place,' said Miss Sophy to her father, 'I wouldn't talk so much about pennies and pounds before strangers.'

Poor Mr Ruck appeared to feel the force of this observation, which, in the consciousness of a man who had never been 'mean', could hardly fail to strike a responsive chord. He coloured a little, and he was silent; his companions got into their vehicle, the front seat of which was adorned with a large parcel. Mr Ruck gave the parcel a little poke with his umbrella, and then, turning to me with a rather grimly penitential smile, 'After all,' he said, 'for the ladies that's the principal interest.'

VII

OLD M. Pigeonneau had more than once proposed to me to take a walk, but I had hitherto been unable to respond to so alluring an invitation. It befell, however, one afternoon, that I perceived him going forth upon a desultory stroll, with a certain lonesomeness of demeanour that attracted my sympathy. I hastily overtook him, and passed my hand into his venerable arm, a proceeding which produced in the good old man so jovial a sense of comradeship that he ardently proposed we should bend our steps to the English Garden; no locality less festive was worthy of the occasion. To the English Garden, accordingly, we went; it lay beyond the bridge, beside the lake. It was very pretty and very animated; there was a band playing in the middle, and a considerable number of persons sitting under the small trees, on benches and little chairs, or strolling beside the blue water. We joined the strollers, we observed our companions, and conversed on obvious topics. Some of these last, of course, were the pretty women who embellished the scene, and who, in the light of M. Pigeonneau's comprehensive criticism, appeared surprisingly numerous. He seemed bent upon our making up our minds as to which was the prettiest, and as this was an innocent game I consented to play at it.

Suddenly M. Pigeonneau stopped, pressing my arm with the liveliest emotion. 'La voilà, la voilà, the prettiest!' he quickly murmured, 'coming toward us, in a blue dress, with the other.' It was at the other I was looking, for the other, to my surprise, was our interesting fellow-pensioner, the daughter of a vigilant mother. M. Pigeonneau, meanwhile, had redoubled his exclamations; he had recognised Miss Sophy Ruck. 'Oh, la belle rencontre, nos aimables convives; the prettiest girl in the world, in effect!'

We immediately greeted and joined the young ladies, who, like ourselves, were walking arm in arm and enjoying the scene.

'I was citing you with admiration to my friend, even before I had recognised you,' said M. Pigeonneau to Miss Ruck.

'I don't believe in French compliments,' remarked this young lady, presenting her back to the smiling old man.

'Are you and Miss Ruck walking alone?' I asked of her companion. 'You had better accept of M. Pigeonneau's gallant protection, and of mine.'

Aurora Church had taken her hand out of Miss Ruck's arm; she looked at me, smiling, with her head a little inclined, while, upon her shoulder, she made her open parasol revolve. 'Which is most improper, – to walk alone or to walk with gentlemen? I wish to do what is most improper.'

'What mysterious logic governs your conduct?' I inquired.

'He thinks you can't understand him when he talks like that,' said Miss Ruck. 'But I do understand you, always!'

'So I have always ventured to hope, my dear Miss Ruck.'

'Well, if I didn't, it wouldn't be much loss,' rejoined this young lady.

'Allons, en marche!' cried M. Pigeonneau, smiling still, and undiscouraged by her inhumanity. 'Let us make together the tour of the garden.' And he imposed his society upon Miss Ruck with a respectful, elderly grace which was evidently unable to see anything in her reluctance but modesty, and was sublimely conscious of a mission to place modesty at its ease. This ill-assorted couple walked in front, while Aurora Church and I strolled along together.

'I am sure this is more improper,' said my companion; 'this is delightfully improper. I don't say that as a compliment to you,' she added. 'I would say it to any man, no matter how stupid.'

'Oh, I am very stupid,' I answered, 'but this doesn't seem to me wrong.'

'Not for you, no; only for me. There is nothing that a man can do that is wrong, is there? *En morale*, you know, I mean. Ah, yes, he can steal; but I think there is nothing else, is there?'

'I don't know. One doesn't know those things until after one has done them. Then one is enlightened.'

'And you mean that you have never been enlightened? You make yourself out very good.'

'That is better than making one's self out bad, as you do.'

The young girl glanced at me a moment, and then, with her charming smile, 'That's one of the consequences of a false position.'

'Is your position false?' I inquired, smiling too at this large formula.

'Distinctly so.'

'In what way?'

'Oh, in every way. For instance, I have to pretend to be a *jeune fille*. I am not a jeune fille; no American girl is a jeune fille; an American girl is an intelligent, responsible creature. I have to pretend to be very innocent, but I am not very innocent.'

'You don't pretend to be very innocent; you pretend to be – what shall I call it? – very wise.'

'That's no pretence. I am wise.'

'You are not an American girl,' I ventured to observe.

My companion almost stopped, looking at me; there was a little flush in her cheek. 'Voilà!' she said. 'There's my false position. I want to be an American girl, and I'm not.'

'Do you want me to tell you?' I went on. 'An American girl wouldn't talk as you are talking now.'

'Please tell me,' said Aurora Church, with expressive eagerness. 'How would she talk?'

'I can't tell you all the things an American girl would say, but I think I can tell you the things she wouldn't say. She wouldn't reason out her conduct, as you seem to me to do.'

Aurora gave me the most flattering attention. 'I see. She would be simpler. To do very simple things that are not at all simple – that is the American girl!'

I permitted myself a small explosion of hilarity. 'I don't know whether you are a French girl, or what you are,' I said, 'but you are very witty.'

'Ah, you mean that I strike false notes!' cried Aurora Church, sadly. 'That's just what I want to avoid. I wish you would always tell me.'

The conversational union between Miss Ruck and her neighbour, in front of us, had evidently not become a close one. The young lady suddenly turned round to us with a question: 'Don't you want some ice cream?'

'*She* doesn't strike false notes,' I murmured.

There was a kind of pavilion or kiosk, which served as a café, and at which the delicacies procurable at such an establishment were dispensed. Miss Ruck pointed to the little green tables and chairs which were set out on the gravel; M. Pigeonneau, fluttering with a sense of dissipation, seconded the proposal, and we presently sat down and gave our order to a nimble attendant. I managed again to place myself next to Aurora Church; our companions were on the other side of the table.

My neighbour was delighted with our situation. 'This is best of all,' she said. 'I never believed I should come to a café with two strange men! Now, you can't persuade me this isn't wrong.'

'To make it wrong we ought to see your mother coming down that path.'

'Ah, my mother makes everything wrong,' said the young girl, attacking with a little spoon in the shape of a spade the apex of a pink ice. And then she returned to her idea of a moment before: 'You must promise to tell me – to warn me in some way – whenever I strike a false note. You must give a little cough, like that – ahem!'

'You will keep me very busy, and people will think I am in a consumption.'

'*Voyons*,' she continued, 'why have you never talked to me more? Is that a false note? Why haven't you been "attentive"? That's what American girls call it; that's what Miss Ruck calls it.'

I assured myself that our companions were out of ear-shot, and that Miss Ruck was much occupied with a large vanilla cream. 'Because you are always entwined with that young lady. There is no getting near you.'

Aurora looked at her friend while the latter devoted herself to her ice. 'You wonder why I like her so much, I suppose. So does mamma; elle s'y perd. I don't like her particularly; je n'en suis pas folle. But she gives me information; she tells me about America. Mamma has always tried to prevent my knowing anything about it, and I am all the more curious. And then Miss Ruck is very fresh.'

'I may not be so fresh as Miss Ruck,' I said, 'but in future, when you want information, I recommend you to come to me for it.'

'Our friend offers to take me to America; she invites me to go back with her, to stay with her. You couldn't do that, could you?' And the young girl looked at me a moment. '*Bon*, a false note! I can see it by your face; you remind me of a *maître de piano*.'

'You overdo the character – the poor American girl,' I said. 'Are you going to stay with that delightful family?'

'I will go and stay with any one that will take me or ask me. It's a real *nostalgie*. She says that in New York – in Thirty-Seventh Street – I should have the most lovely time.'

'I have no doubt you would enjoy it.'

'Absolute liberty to begin with.'

'It seems to me you have a certain liberty here,' I rejoined.

'Ah, *this*? Oh, I shall pay for this. I shall be punished by mamma, and I shall be lectured by Madame Galopin.'

'The wife of the pasteur?'

'His *digne épouse*. Madame Galopin, for mamma, is the incarnation of European opinion. That's what vexes me with mamma, her thinking so much of people like Madame Galopin. Going to see Madame Galopin – mamma calls that being in European society. European society! I'm so sick of that expression; I have heard it since I was six years old. Who is Madame Galopin – who thinks anything of her here? She is nobody; she is perfectly third-rate. If I like America better than mamma, I also know Europe better.'

'But your mother, certainly,' I objected, a trifle timidly, for my young lady was excited, and had a charming little passion in her eye – 'your mother has a great many social relations all over the continent.'

'She thinks so, but half the people don't care for us. They are not so good as we, and they know it – I'll do them that justice – and they wonder why we should care for them. When we are polite to them, they think the less of us; there are plenty of people like that. Mamma thinks so much of them simply because they are foreigners. If I could tell you all the dull, stupid, second-rate people I have had to talk to, for no better reason than that they were *de leur pays*! – Germans, French, Italians, Turks, everything. When I complain, mamma always says that at any rate it's practice in the language. And she makes so much of the English, too; I don't know what that's practice in.'

Before I had time to suggest an hypothesis, as regards this latter point, I saw something that made me rise, with a certain solemnity, from my chair. This was nothing less than the neat little figure of Mrs Church – a perfect model of the *femme comme il faut* – approaching our table with an impatient step, and followed most unexpectedly in her advance by the pre-eminent form of Mr Ruck. She had evidently come in quest of her daughter, and if she had commanded this gentleman's attendance, it had been on no softer ground than that of his

unenvied paternity to her guilty child's accomplice. My movement had given the alarm, and Aurora Church and M. Pigeonneau got up; Miss Ruck alone did not, in the local phrase,
derange herself. Mrs Church, beneath her modest little bonnet,
looked very serious, but not at all fluttered; she came straight to
her daughter, who received her with a smile, and then she
looked all round at the rest of us, very fixedly and tranquilly,
without bowing. I must do both these ladies the justice to
mention that neither of them made the least little 'scene'.

'I have come for you, dearest,' said the mother.

'Yes, dear mamma.'

'Come for you – come for you,' Mrs Church repeated,
looking down at the relics of our little feast. 'I was obliged
to ask Mr Ruck's assistance. I was puzzled; I thought a long
time.'

'Well, Mrs Church, I was glad to see you puzzled once
in your life!' said Mr Ruck, with friendly jocosity. 'But you
came pretty straight for all that. I had hard work to keep up
with you.'

'We will take a cab, Aurora,' Mrs Church went on, without
heeding this pleasantry – 'a closed one. Come, my daughter.'

'Yes, dear mamma.' The young girl was blushing, yet she
was still smiling; she looked round at us all, and, as her eyes met
mine, I thought she was beautiful. 'Good-bye,' she said to us.
'I have had a *lovely time*.'

'We must not linger,' said her mother; 'it is five o'clock. We
are to dine, you know, with Madame Galopin.'

'I had quite forgotten,' Aurora declared. 'That will be
charming.'

'Do you want me to assist you to carry her back, ma'am?'
asked Mr Ruck.

Mrs Church hesitated a moment, with her serene little gaze.
'Do you prefer, then, to leave your daughter to finish the
evening with these gentlemen?'

Mr Ruck pushed back his hat and scratched the top of his
head. 'Well, I don't know. How would you like that, Sophy?'

'Well, I never!' exclaimed Sophy, as Mrs Church marched
off with her daughter.

VIII

I HAD half expected that Mrs Church would make me feel the weight of her disapproval of my own share in that little act of revelry in the English Garden. But she maintained her claim to being a highly reasonable woman – I could not but admire the justice of this pretension – by recognising my irresponsibility. I had taken her daughter as I found her, which was, according to Mrs Church's view, in a very equivocal position. The natural instinct of a young man, in such a situation, is not to protest but to profit; and it was clear to Mrs Church that I had had nothing to do with Miss Aurora's appearing in public under the insufficient chaperonage of Miss Ruck. Besides, she liked to converse, and she apparently did me the honour to believe that of all the members of the Pension Beaurepas I had the most cultivated understanding. I found her in the salon a couple of evenings after the incident I have just narrated, and I approached her with a view of making my peace with her, if this should prove necessary. But Mrs Church was as gracious as I could have desired; she put her marker into her book, and folded her plump little hands on the cover. She made no specific allusion to the English Garden; she embarked, rather, upon those general considerations in which her refined intellect was so much at home.

'Always at your studies, Mrs Church,' I ventured to observe.

'Que voulez-vous? To say studies is to say too much; one doesn't study in the parlour of a boarding-house. But I do what I can; I have always done what I can. That is all I have ever claimed.'

'No one can do more, and you seem to have done a great deal.'

'Do you know my secret?' she asked, with an air of brightening confidence. And she paused a moment before she imparted her secret – 'To care only for the *best*! To do the best, to know the best – to have, to desire, to recognise, only the best. That's what I have always done, in my quiet little way. I have gone through Europe on my devoted little errand, seeking, seeing, heeding, only the best. And it has not been for myself alone; it has been for my daughter. My daughter has had the best. We are not rich, but I can say that.'

'She has had you, madam,' I rejoined finely.

'Certainly, such as I am, I have been devoted. We have got something everywhere; a little here, a little there. That's the real secret – to get something everywhere; you always can if you *are* devoted. Sometimes it has been a little music, sometimes a little deeper insight into the history of art; every little counts you know. Sometimes it has been just a glimpse, a view, of a lovely landscape, an impression. We have always been on the look-out. Sometimes it has been a valued friendship, a delightful social tie.'

'Here comes the "European society", the poor daughter's bugbear,' I said to myself. 'Certainly,' I remarked aloud – I admit, rather perversely – 'if you have lived a great deal in *pensions*, you must have got acquainted with lots of people.'

Mrs Church dropped her eyes a moment; and then, with considerable gravity, 'I think the European pension system in many respects remarkable, and in some satisfactory. But of the friendships that we have formed, few have been contracted in establishments of this kind.'

'I am sorry to hear that!' I said, laughing.

'I don't say it for you, though I might say it for some others. We have been interested in European *homes*.'

'Oh, I see!'

'We have the *entrée* of the old Genevese society. I like its tone. I prefer it to that of Mr Ruck,' added Mrs Church, calmly; 'to that of Mrs Ruck and Miss Ruck – of Miss Ruck, especially.'

'Ah, the poor Rucks haven't any tone at all,' I said. 'Don't take them more seriously than they take themselves.'

'Tell me this,' my companion rejoined, 'are they fair examples?'

'Examples of what?'

'Of our American tendencies.'

'"Tendencies" is a big word, dear lady; tendencies are difficult to calculate. And you shouldn't abuse those good Rucks, who have been very kind to your daughter. They have invited her to go and stay with them in Thirty-Seventh Street.'

'Aurora has told me. It might be very serious.'

'It might be very droll,' I said.

'To me,' declared Mrs Church, 'it is simply terrible. I think we shall have to leave the Pension Beaurepas. I shall go back to Madame Chamousset.'

'On account of the Rucks?' I asked.

'Pray, why don't they go themselves? I have given them some excellent addresses – written down the very hours of the trains. They were going to Appenzell; I thought it was arranged.'

'They talk of Chamouni now,' I said; 'but they are very helpless and undecided.'

'I will give them some Chamouni addresses. Mrs Ruck will send for a *chaise à porteurs;* I will give her the name of a man who lets them lower than you get them at the hotels. After that they *must* go.'

'Well, I doubt,' I observed, 'whether Mr Ruck will ever really be seen on the Mer de Glace – in a high hat. He's not like you; he doesn't value his European privileges. He takes no interest. He regrets Wall Street, acutely. As his wife says, he is very restless, but he has no curiosity about Chamouni. So you must not depend too much on the effect of your addresses.'

'Is it a frequent type?' asked Mrs Church, with an air of self-control.

'I am afraid so. Mr Ruck is a broken-down man of business. He is broken-down in health, and I suspect he is broken-down in fortune. He has spent his whole life in buying and selling; he knows how to do nothing else. His wife and daughter have spent their lives, not in selling, but in buying; and they, on their side, know how to do nothing else. To get something in a shop that they can put on their backs – that is their one idea; they haven't another in their heads. Of course they spend no end of money, and they do it with an implacable persistence, with a mixture of audacity and of cunning. They do it in his teeth and they do it behind his back; the mother protects the daughter, and the daughter eggs on the mother. Between them they are bleeding him to death.'

'Ah, what a picture!' murmured Mrs Church. 'I am afraid they are very – uncultivated.'

'I share your fears. They are perfectly ignorant; they have no resources. The vision of fine clothes occupies their whole imagination. They have not an idea – even a worse one – to compete with it. Poor Mr Ruck, who is extremely good-natured and soft, seems to me a really tragic figure. He is getting bad news every day from home; his business is going to the dogs. He is unable to stop it; he has to stand and watch his fortunes ebb. He has been used to doing things in a big way, and he feels "mean" if he makes a fuss about bills. So the ladies keep sending them in.'

'But haven't they common sense? Don't they know they are ruining themselves?'

'They don't believe it. The duty of an American husband and father is to keep them going. If he asks them how, that's his own affair. So, by way of not being mean, of being a good American husband and father, poor Ruck stands staring at bankruptcy.'

Mrs Church looked at me a moment, in quickened meditation. 'Why, if Aurora were to go to stay with them, she might not even be properly fed!'

'I don't, on the whole, recommend,' I said, laughing, 'that your daughter should pay a visit to Thirty-Seventh Street.'

'Why should I be subjected to such trials – so sadly *éprouvée*? Why should a daughter of mine like that dreadful girl?'

'*Does* she like her?'

'Pray, do you mean,' asked my companion, softly, 'that Aurora is a hypocrite?'

I hesitated a moment. 'A little, since you ask me. I think you have forced her to be.'

Mrs Church answered this possibly presumptuous charge with a tranquil, candid exultation. 'I never force my daughter!'

'She is nevertheless in a false position,' I rejoined. 'She hungers and thirsts to go back to her own country; she wants to "come out" in New York, which is certainly, socially speaking, the El Dorado of young ladies. She likes any one, for the moment, who will talk to her of that, and serve as a connecting-link with her native shores. Miss Ruck performs this agreeable office.'

'Your idea is, then, that if she were to go with Miss Ruck to America she would drop her afterwards.'

I complimented Mrs Church upon her logical mind, but I repudiated this cynical supposition. 'I can't imagine her – when it should come to the point – embarking with the famille Ruck. But I wish she might go, nevertheless.'

Mrs Church shook her head serenely, and smiled at my inappropriate zeal. 'I trust my poor child may never be guilty of so fatal a mistake. She is completely in error; she is wholly unadapted to the peculiar conditions of American life. It would not please her. She would not sympathise. My daughter's ideal is not the ideal of the class of young women to which Miss Ruck belongs. I fear they are very numerous; they give the tone – they give the tone.'

'It is you that are mistaken,' I said; 'go home for six months and see.'

'I have not, unfortunately, the means to make costly experiments. My daughter has had great advantages – rare advantages – and I should be very sorry to believe that *au fond* she does not appreciate them. One thing is certain: I must remove her from this pernicious influence. We must part company with this deplorable family. If Mr Ruck and his ladies cannot be induced to go to Chamouni – a journey that no traveller with the smallest self-respect would omit – my daughter and I shall be obliged to retire. We shall go to Dresden.'

'To Dresden?'

'The capital of Saxony. I had arranged to go there for the autumn, but it will be simpler to go immediately. There are several works in the gallery with which my daughter has not, I think, sufficiently familiarised herself; it is especially strong in the seventeenth-century schools.'

As my companion offered me this information I perceived Mr Ruck come lounging in, with his hands in his pockets, and his elbows making acute angles. He had his usual anomalous appearance of both seeking and avoiding society, and he wandered obliquely toward Mrs Church, whose last words he had overheard. 'The seventeenth-century schools,' he said, slowly, as if he were weighing some very small object in a very large pair of scales. 'Now, do you suppose they *had* schools at that period?'

Mrs Church rose with a good deal of precision, making no answer to this incongruous jest. She clasped her large volume to her neat little bosom, and she fixed a gentle, serious eye upon Mr Ruck.

'I had a letter this morning from Chamouni,' she said.

'Well,' replied Mr Ruck, 'I suppose you've got friends all over.'

'I have friends at Chamouni, but they are leaving. To their great regret.' I had got up, too; I listened to this statement, and I wondered. I am almost ashamed to mention the subject of my agitation. I asked myself whether this was a sudden improvisation, consecrated by maternal devotion; but this point has never been elucidated. 'They are giving up some charming rooms; perhaps you would like them. I would suggest your telegraphing. The weather is glorious,' continued Mrs Church, 'and the highest peaks are now perceived with extraordinary distinctness.'

Mr Ruck listened, as he always listened, respectfully. 'Well,' he said, 'I don't know as I want to go up Mount Blank. That's the principal attraction, isn't it?'

'There are many others. I thought I would offer you an – an exceptional opportunity.'

'Well,' said Mr Ruck, 'you're right down friendly. But I seem to have more opportunities than I know what to do with. I don't seem able to take hold.'

'It only needs a little decision,' remarked Mrs Church, with an air which was an admirable example of this virtue. 'I wish you good-night, sir.' And she moved noiselessly away.

Mr Ruck, with his long legs apart, stood staring after her; then he transferred his perfectly quiet eyes to me. 'Does she own a hotel over there?' he asked. 'Has she got any stock in Mount Blank?'

IX

THE next day Madame Beaurepas handed me, with her own elderly fingers, a missive, which proved to be a telegram. After glancing at it, I informed her that it was apparently a signal for my departure; my brother had arrived in England, and proposed to me to meet him there; he had come on business and was to spend but three weeks in Europe. 'But my house empties itself!' cried the old woman. 'The famille Ruck talks of leaving me, and Madame Church *nous fait la révérence*.'

'Mrs Church is going away?'

'She is packing her trunk; she is a very extraordinary person. Do you know what she asked me this morning? To invent some combination by which the famille Ruck should move away. I informed her that I was not an inventor. That poor famille Ruck! "Oblige me by getting rid of them," said Madame Church, as she would have asked Célestine to remove a dish of cabbage. She speaks as if the world were made for Madame Church. I intimated to her that if she objected to the company there was a very simple remedy; and at present *elle fait ses paquets*.'

'She really asked you to get the Rucks out of the house?'

'She asked me to tell them that their rooms had been let, three months ago, to another family. She has an *aplomb*!'

Mrs Church's aplomb caused me considerable diversion; I am not sure that it was not, in some degree, to laugh over it at my leisure that I went out into the garden that evening to smoke a cigar. The night was dark and not particularly balmy, and most of my fellow-pensioners, after dinner, had remained indoors. A long straight walk conducted from the door of the house to the ancient grille that I have described, and I stood here for some time, looking through the iron bars at the silent empty street. The prospect was not entertaining, and I presently turned away. At this moment I saw, in the distance, the door of the house open and throw a shaft of lamplight into the darkness. Into the lamplight there stepped the figure of a female, who presently closed the door behind her. She disappeared in the dusk of the garden, and I had seen her but for an

instant, but I remained under the impression that Aurora
Church, on the eve of her departure, had come out for a
meditative stroll.

I lingered near the gate, keeping the red tip of my cigar
turned toward the house, and before long a young lady
emerged from among the shadows of the trees and encountered
the light of a lamp that stood just outside the gate. It was in fact
Aurora Church, but she seemed more bent upon conversation
than upon meditation. She stood a moment looking at me, and
then she said, –

'Ought I to retire – to return to the house?'

'If you ought, I should be very sorry to tell you so,'
I answered.

'But we are all alone; there is no one else in the garden.'

'It is not the first time that I have been alone with a young
lady. I am not at all terrified.'

'Ah, but I?' said the young girl. 'I have never been alone' –
then, quickly, she interrupted herself. 'Good, there's another
false note!'

'Yes, I am obliged to admit that one is very false.'

She stood looking at me. 'I am going away to-morrow; after
that there will be no one to tell me.'

'That will matter little,' I presently replied. 'Telling you will
do no good.'

'Ah, why do you say that?' murmured Aurora Church.

I said it partly because it was true; but I said it for other
reasons, as well, which it was hard to define. Standing there
bare-headed, in the night air, in the vague light, this young
lady looked extremely interesting; and the interest of her
appearance was not diminished by a suspicion on my own
part that she had come into the garden knowing me to be
there. I thought her a charming girl, and I felt very sorry for
her; but as I looked at her, the terms in which Madame
Beaurepas had ventured to characterise her recurred to me
with a certain force. I had professed a contempt for them at
the time, but it now came into my head that perhaps this
unfortunately situated, this insidiously mutinous, young
creature was looking out for a preserver. She was certainly not

a girl to throw herself at a man's head, but it was possible that in her intense – her almost morbid – desire to put into effect an ideal which was perhaps after all charged with as many fallacies as her mother affirmed, she might do something reckless and irregular – something in which a sympathetic compatriot, as yet unknown, would find his profit. The image, unshaped though it was, of this sympathetic compatriot filled me with a sort of envy. For some moments I was silent, conscious of these things, and then I answered her question. 'Because some things – some differences – are felt, not learned. To you liberty is not natural; you are like a person who has bought a repeater, and, in his satisfaction, is constantly making it sound. To a real American girl her liberty is a very vulgarly-ticking old clock.'

'Ah, you mean, then,' said the poor girl, 'that my mother has ruined me?'

'Ruined you?'

'She has so perverted my mind that when I try to be natural I am necessarily immodest.'

'That again is a false note,' I said, laughing.

She turned away. 'I think you are cruel.'

'By no means,' I declared; 'because, for my own taste, I prefer you as – as—'

I hesitated, and she turned back. 'As what?'

'As you are.'

She looked at me a while again, and then she said, in a little reasoning voice that reminded me of her mother's, only that it was conscious and studied, 'I was not aware that I am under any particular obligation to please you!' And then she gave a clear laugh, quite at variance with her voice.

'Oh, there is no obligation,' I said, 'but one has preferences. I am very sorry you are going away.'

'What does it matter to you? You are going yourself.'

'As I am going in a different direction, that makes all the greater separation.'

She answered nothing; she stood looking through the bars of the tall gate at the empty, dusky street. 'This grille is like a cage,' she said at last.

'Fortunately, it is a cage that will open.' And I laid my hand on the lock.

'Don't open it,' and she pressed the gate back. 'If you should open it I would go out – and never return.'

'Where should you go?'

'To America.'

'Straight away?'

'Somehow or other. I would go to the American consul. I would beg him to give me money – to help me.'

I received this assertion without a smile; I was not in a smiling humour. On the contrary, I felt singularly excited, and I kept my hand on the lock of the gate. I believed (or I thought I believed) what my companion said, and I had – absurd as it may appear – an irritated vision of her throwing herself upon consular sympathy. It seemed to me, for a moment, that to pass out of that gate with this yearning, straining young creature would be to pass into some mysterious felicity. If I were only a hero of romance, I would offer, myself, to take her to America.

In a moment more, perhaps, I should have persuaded myself that I was one, but at this juncture I heard a sound that was not romantic. It proved to be the very realistic tread of Célestine, the cook, who stood grinning at us as we turned about from our colloquy.

'I ask *bien pardon*,' said Célestine. 'The mother of mademoiselle desires that mademoiselle should come in immediately. M. le Pasteur Galopin has come to make his adieux to *ces dames*.'

Aurora gave me only one glance, but it was a touching one. Then she slowly departed with Célestine.

The next morning, on coming into the garden, I found that Mrs Church and her daughter had departed. I was informed of this fact by old M. Pigeonneau, who sat there under a tree, having his coffee at a little green table.

'I have nothing to envy you,' he said; 'I had the last glimpse of that charming Miss Aurora.'

'I had a very late glimpse,' I answered, 'and it was all I could possibly desire.'

'I have always noticed,' rejoined M. Pigeonneau, 'that your desires are more moderate than mine. Que voulez-vous? I am of the old school. Je crois que la race se perd. I regret the departure of that young girl: she had an enchanting smile. Ce sera une femme d'esprit. For the mother, I can console myself. I am not sure that *she* was a femme d'esprit, though she wished to pass for one. Round, rosy, *potelée*, she yet had not the temperament of her appearance; she was a *femme austère*. I have often noticed that contradiction in American ladies. You see a plump little woman, with a speaking eye and the contour and complexion of a ripe peach, and if you venture to conduct yourself in the smallest degree in accordance with these *indices*, you discover a species of Methodist – of what do you call it? – of Quakeress. On the other hand, you encounter a tall, lean, angular person, without colour, without grace, all elbows and knees, and you find it's a nature of the tropics! The women of duty look like coquettes, and the others look like alpenstocks! However, we have still the handsome Madame Ruck – a real *femme de Rubens, celle-là*. It is very true that to talk to her one must know the Flemish tongue!'

I had determined, in accordance with my brother's telegram, to go away in the afternoon; so that, having various duties to perform, I left M. Pigeonneau to his international comparisons. Among other things, I went in the course of the morning to the banker's, to draw money for my journey, and there I found Mr Ruck, with a pile of crumpled letters in his lap, his chair tipped back and his eyes gloomily fixed on the fringe of the green plush table-cloth. I timidly expressed the hope that he had got better news from home; whereupon he gave me a look in which, considering his provocation, the absence of irritation was conspicuous.

He took up his letters in his large hand, and crushing them together held it out to me. 'That epistolary matter,' he said, 'is worth about five cents. But I guess,' he added, rising, 'I have taken it in by this time.' When I had drawn my money, I asked him to come and breakfast with me at the little *brasserie*, much favoured by students, to which I used to resort in the old town. 'I couldn't eat, sir,' he said, 'I couldn't eat. Bad news takes away the appetite. But I guess I'll go with you, so that I needn't go to table down there at the pension. The old woman down there is always accusing me of turning up my nose at her food. Well, I guess I shan't turn up my nose at anything now.'

We went to the little brasserie, where poor Mr Ruck made the lightest possible breakfast. But if he ate very little, he talked a great deal; he talked about business, going into a hundred details in which I was quite unable to follow him. His talk was not angry nor bitter; it was a long, meditative, melancholy monologue; if it had been a trifle less incoherent I should almost have called it philosophic. I was very sorry for him; I wanted to do something for him, but the only thing I could do was, when we had breakfasted, to see him safely back to the Pension Beaurepas. We went across the Treille and down the Corraterie, out of which we turned into the Rue du Rhône. In this latter street, as all the world knows, are many of those brilliant jewellers' shops for which Geneva is famous. I always admired their glittering windows, and never passed them without a lingering glance. Even on this occasion, preoccupied as I was with my impending departure and with my companion's troubles, I suffered my eyes to wander along the precious tiers that flashed and twinkled behind the huge, clear plates of glass. Thanks to this inveterate habit, I made a discovery. In the largest and most brilliant of these establishments I perceived two ladies, seated before the counter with an air of absorption which sufficiently proclaimed their identity. I hoped my companion would not see them, but as we came abreast of the door, a little beyond, we found it open to the warm summer air. Mr Ruck happened to glance in, and he immediately recognised his wife and daughter. He slowly stopped, looking at them; I wondered what he would do. The salesman was holding up a bracelet before them, on its velvet cushion, and flashing it about in an irresistible manner.

Mr Ruck said nothing, but he presently went in, and I did the same.

'It will be an opportunity,' I remarked, as cheerfully as possible, 'for me to bid good-bye to the ladies.'

They turned round when Mr Ruck came in, and looked at him without confusion. 'Well, you had better go home to breakfast,' remarked his wife. Miss Sophy made no remark, but she took the bracelet from the attendant and gazed at it very fixedly. Mr Ruck seated himself on an empty stool and looked round the shop.

'Well, you have been here before,' said his wife; 'you were here the first day we came.'

Miss Ruck extended the precious object in her hands towards me. 'Don't you think that sweet?' she inquired.

I looked at it a moment. 'No, I think it's ugly.'

She glanced at me a moment, incredulous. 'Well, I don't believe you have any taste.'

'Why, sir, it's just lovely,' said Mrs Ruck.

'You'll see it some day on me, any way,' her daughter declared.

'No, he won't,' said Mr Ruck quietly.

'It will be his own fault, then,' Miss Sophy observed.

'Well, if we are going to Chamouni we want to get something here,' said Mrs Ruck. 'We may not have another chance.'

Mr Ruck was still looking round the shop, whistling in a very low tone. 'We ain't going to Chamouni. We are going to New York city, straight.'

'Well, I'm glad to hear that,' said Mrs Ruck. 'Don't you suppose we want to take something home?'

'If we are going straight back I must have that bracelet,' her daughter declared. 'Only I don't want a velvet case; I want a satin case.'

'I must bid you good-bye,' I said to the ladies. 'I am leaving Geneva in an hour or two.'

'Take a good look at that bracelet, so you'll know it when you see it,' said Miss Sophy.

'She's bound to have something,' remarked her mother, almost proudly.

Mr Ruck was still vaguely inspecting the shop; he was still whistling a little. 'I am afraid he is not at all well,' I said, softly, to his wife.

She twisted her head a little, and glanced at him.

'Well, I wish he'd improve!' she exclaimed.

'A satin case, and a nice one!' said Miss Ruck to the shop-man.

I bade Mr Ruck good-bye. 'Don't wait for me,' he said, sitting there on his stool, and not meeting my eye. 'I've got to see this thing through.'

I went back to the Pension Beaurepas, and when, an hour later, I left it with my luggage, the family had not returned.

THE POINT OF VIEW

I

From Miss AURORA CHURCH, *at sea, to* Miss WHITESIDE, *in Paris*

... My dear child, the bromide of sodium (if that's what you call it) proved perfectly useless. I don't mean that it did me no good, but that I never had occasion to take the bottle out of my bag. It might have done wonders for me if I had needed it; but I didn't, simply because I have been a wonder myself. Will you believe that I have spent the whole voyage on deck, in the most animated conversation and exercise? Twelve times round the deck makes a mile, I believe; and by this measurement I have been walking twenty miles a day. And down to every meal, if you please, where I have displayed the appetite of a fish-wife. Of course the weather has been lovely; so there's no great merit. The wicked old Atlantic has been as blue as the sapphire in my only ring (a rather good one), and as smooth as the slippery floor of Madame Galopin's dining-room. We have been for the last three hours in sight of land, and we are soon to enter the Bay of New York, which is said to be exquisitely beautiful. But of course you recall it, though they say that everything changes so fast over here. I find I don't remember anything, for my recollections of our voyage to Europe, so many years ago, are exceedingly dim; I only have a painful impression that mamma shut me up for an hour every day in the state-room, and made me learn by heart some religious poem. I was only five years old, and I believe that as a child I was extremely timid; on the other hand, mamma, as you know, was dreadfully severe. She is severe to this day; only I have become indifferent; I have been so pinched and pushed – morally speaking, *bien entendu*. It is true, however, that there are children of five on the vessel to-day who have been extremely conspicuous, – ranging all over the ship, and always under one's feet. Of course they are little compatriots, which means that they are little barbarians. I don't mean that all our compatriots are barbarous; they seem to improve, somehow, after their first communion. I don't know whether it's that ceremony that improves them, – especially as so few of them go in for it; but the women are certainly nicer than the little girls; I mean, of course, in proportion, you know. You warned me not to generalise, and you see I have already begun, before we have arrived. But I suppose there is no harm in it so long as it is favourable. Isn't it favourable when I say that I have had the most lovely time? I have never had so much liberty in my life, and I have been out alone, as you may say, every day of the voyage. If it is a foretaste of what is to come, I shall take to that very kindly. When I say that I have been out alone, I mean that we have always been two. But we two were alone, so to speak, and it was not like always having mamma, or Madame Galopin, or some lady in the *pension*, or the temporary cook. Mamma has been very poorly; she is so very well on land, it's a wonder to see her at all taken down. She says, however, that it isn't the being at sea; it's, on the contrary, approaching the land. She is not in a hurry to arrive; she says that great disillusions await us. I didn't know that she had any illusions – she's so stern, so philosophic. She is very serious; she sits for hours in perfect silence, with her eyes fixed on the horizon. I heard her say yesterday to an English gentleman – a very odd Mr Antrobus, the only person with whom she converses – that she was afraid she shouldn't like her native land, and that she shouldn't like not liking it. But this is a mistake – she will like that immensely (I mean not liking it). If it should prove at all agreeable, mamma will be furious, for that will go against her system. You know all about mamma's system; I have explained that so often. It goes against her system that we should come back at all; that was *my* system – I have had at last to invent one! She consented to come only because she saw that, having no *dot*, I should never marry in Europe; and I pretended to be immensely preoccupied with this idea, in order to make her start. In reality *cela m'est parfaitement égal*. I am only afraid I shall like it too much (I don't mean marriage, of course, but one's native land). Say what you will, it's a charming thing to go out alone, and I have given notice to mamma that I mean to be always *en course*. When I tell her that, she looks at me in the same silence; her eye dilates, and then she slowly closes it. It's

as if the sea were affecting her a little, though it's so beautifully
calm. I ask her if she will try my bromide, which is there in my
bag; but she motions me off, and I begin to walk again, tapping
my little boot-soles upon the smooth, clean deck. This allusion
to my boot-soles, by the way, is not prompted by vanity; but it's
a fact that at sea one's feet and one's shoes assume the most
extraordinary importance, so that we should take the precaution to have nice ones. They are all you seem to see, as the
people walk about the deck; you get to know them intimately
and to dislike some of them so much. I am afraid you will think
that I have already broken loose; and for aught I know, I am
writing as a *demoiselle bien-élevée* should not write. I don't know
whether it's the American air; if it is, all I can say is that the
American air is very charming. It makes me impatient and
restless, and I sit scribbling here because I am so eager to arrive,
and the time passes better if I occupy myself. I am in the saloon,
where we have our meals, and opposite to me is a big round
port-hole, wide open, to let in the smell of the land. Every now
and then I rise a little and look through it, to see whether we are
arriving. I mean in the Bay, you know, for we shall not come up
to the city till dark. I don't want to lose the Bay; it appears that
it's so wonderful. I don't exactly understand what it contains,
except some beautiful islands; but I suppose you will know all
about that. It is easy to see that these are the last hours, for all
the people about me are writing letters to put into the post as
soon as we come up to the dock. I believe they are dreadful at
the custom-house, and you will remember how many new
things you persuaded mamma that (with my preoccupation of
marriage) I should take to this country, where even the prettiest
girls are expected not to go unadorned. We ruined ourselves in
Paris (that is part of mamma's solemnity); *mais au moins je serai
belle!* Moreover, I believe that mamma is prepared to say or to
do anything that may be necessary for escaping from their
odious duties; as she very justly remarks, she can't afford to
be ruined twice. I don't know how one approaches these
terrible *douaniers*, but I mean to invent something very charming. I mean to say, 'Voyons, Messieurs, a young girl like me,
brought up in the strictest foreign traditions, kept always in the

background by a very superior mother – *la voilà*; you can see for yourself! – what is it possible that she should attempt to smuggle in? Nothing but a few simple relics of her convent!' I won't tell them that my convent was called the *Magasin du Bon Marché*. Mamma began to scold me three days ago for insisting on so many trunks, and the truth is that, between us, we have not fewer than seven. For relics, that's a good many! We are all writing very long letters – or at least we are writing a great number. There is no news of the Bay as yet. Mr Antrobus, mamma's friend, opposite to me, is beginning on his ninth. He is an Honourable, and a Member of Parliament; he has written, during the voyage, about a hundred letters, and he seems greatly alarmed at the number of stamps he will have to buy when he arrives. He is full of information; but he has not enough, for he asks as many questions as mamma when she goes to hire apartments. He is going to 'look into' various things; he speaks as if they had a little hole for the purpose. He walks almost as much as I, and he has very big shoes. He asks questions even of me, and I tell him again and again that I know nothing about America. But it makes no difference; he always begins again, and, indeed, it is not strange that he should find my ignorance incredible. 'Now, how would it be in one of your Southwestern States?' – that's his favourite way of opening conversation. Fancy me giving an account of the Southwestern States! I tell him he had better ask mamma – a little to tease that lady, who knows no more about such places than I. Mr Antrobus is very big and black; he speaks with a sort of brogue; he has a wife and ten children; he is not very romantic. But he has lots of letters to people *là-bas* (I forget that we are just arriving), and mamma, who takes an interest in him in spite of his views (which are dreadfully advanced, and not at all like mamma's own), has promised to give him the *entrée* to the best society. I don't know what she knows about the best society over here to-day, for we have not kept up our connections at all, and no one will know (or, I am afraid, care) anything about us. She has an idea that we shall be immensely recognised; but really, except the poor little Rucks, who are bankrupt, and, I am told, in no society at all, I don't know on whom we can count.

C'est égal. Mamma has an idea that, whether or not we appreciate America ourselves, we shall at least be universally appreciated. It's true that we have begun to be, a little; you would see that by the way that Mr Cockerel and Mr Louis Leverett are always inviting me to walk. Both of these gentlemen, who are Americans, have asked leave to call upon me in New York, and I have said, *Mon Dieu, oui*, if it's the custom of the country. Of course I have not dared to tell this to mamma, who flatters herself that we have brought with us in our trunks a complete set of customs of our own, and that we shall only have to shake them out a little and put them on when we arrive. If only the two gentlemen I just spoke of don't call at the same time, I don't think I shall be too much frightened. If they do, on the other hand, I won't answer for it. They have a particular aversion to each other, and they are ready to fight about poor little me. I am only the pretext, however; for, as Mr Leverett says, it's really the opposition of temperaments. I hope they won't cut each other's throats, for I am not crazy about either of them. They are very well for the deck of a ship, but I shouldn't care about them in a *salon*; they are not at all distinguished. They think they are, but they are not; at least, Mr Louis Leverett does; Mr Cockerel doesn't appear to care so much. They are extremely different (with their opposed temperaments), and each very amusing for a while; but I should get dreadfully tired of passing my life with either. Neither has proposed that, as yet; but it is evidently what they are coming to. It will be in a great measure to spite each other, for I think that *au fond* they don't quite believe in me. If they don't, it's the only point on which they agree. They hate each other awfully; they take such different views. That is, Mr Cockerel hates Mr Leverett – he calls him a sickly little ass; he says that his opinions are half affectation, and the other half dyspepsia. Mr Leverett speaks of Mr Cockerel as a 'strident savage', but he declares he finds him most diverting. He says there is nothing in which we can't find a certain entertainment, if we only look at it in the right way, and that we have no business with either hating or loving; we ought only to strive to understand. To understand is to forgive, he says. That is very pretty, but I don't like the suppression of our affections, though

I have no desire to fix mine upon Mr Leverett. He is very artistic, and talks like an article in some review. He has lived a great deal in Paris, and Mr Cockerel says that is what has made him such an idiot. That is not complimentary to you, dear Louisa, and still less to your brilliant brother; for Mr Cockerel explains that he means it (the bad effect of Paris) chiefly of the men. In fact, he means the bad effect of Europe altogether. This, however, is compromising to mamma; and I am afraid there is no doubt that (from what I have told him) he thinks mamma also an idiot. (I am not responsible, you know, – I have always wanted to go home.) If mamma knew him, which she doesn't, for she always closes her eyes when I pass on his arm, she would think him disgusting. Mr Leverett, however, tells me he is nothing to what we shall see yet. He is from Philadelphia (Mr Cockerel); he insists that we shall go and see Philadelphia, but mamma says she saw it in 1855, and it was then *affreux*. Mr Cockerel says that mamma is evidently not familiar with the march of improvement in this country; he speaks of 1855 as if it were a hundred years ago. Mamma says she knows it goes only too fast – it goes so fast that it has time to do nothing well; and then Mr Cockerel, who, to do him justice, is perfectly good-natured, remarks that she had better wait till she has been ashore and seen the improvements. Mamma rejoins that she sees them from here, the improvements, and that they give her a sinking of the heart. (This little exchange of ideas is carried on through me; they have never spoken to each other.) Mr Cockerel, as I say, is extremely good-natured, and he carries out what I have heard said about the men in America being very considerate of the women. They evidently listen to them a great deal; they don't contradict them, but it seems to me that this is rather negative. There is very little gallantry in not contradicting one; and it strikes me that there are some things the men don't express. There are others on the ship whom I've noticed. It's as if they were all one's brothers or one's cousins. But I promised you not to generalise, and perhaps there will be more expression when we arrive. Mr Cockerel returns to America, after a general tour, with a renewed conviction that this is the only country. I left him on deck an hour ago, looking at the

coast-line with an opera-glass, and saying it was the prettiest
thing he had seen in all his tour. When I remarked that the coast
seemed rather low, he said it would be all the easier to get
ashore. Mr Leverett doesn't seem in a hurry to get ashore; he
is sitting within sight of me in a corner of the saloon – writing
letters, I suppose, but looking, from the way he bites his pen
and rolls his eyes about, as if he were composing a sonnet and
waiting for a rhyme. Perhaps the sonnet is addressed to me; but
I forget that he suppresses the affections! The only person in
whom mamma takes much interest is the great French critic,
M. Lejaune, whom we have the honour to carry with us. We
have read a few of his works, though mamma disapproves of his
tendencies and thinks him a dreadful materialist. We have read
them for the style; you know he is one of the new Academicians.
He is a Frenchman like any other, except that he is rather more
quiet; and he has a grey moustache and the ribbon of the
Legion of Honour. He is the first French writer of distinction
who has been to America since De Tocqueville; the French, in
such matters, are not very enterprising. Also, he has the air of
wondering what he is doing *dans cette galère*. He has come with
his *beau-frère*, who is an engineer, and is looking after some
mines, and he talks with scarcely any one else, as he speaks no
English and appears to take for granted that no one speaks
French. Mamma would be delighted to assure him of the contrary; she has never conversed with an Academician. She
always makes a little vague inclination, with a smile, when he
passes her, and he answers with a most respectful bow; but it
goes no further, to mamma's disappointment. He is always with
the *beau-frère*, a rather untidy, fat, bearded man, – decorated,
too, always smoking and looking at the feet of the ladies, whom
mamma (though she has very good feet) has not the courage to
aborder. I believe M. Lejaune is going to write a book about
America, and Mr Leverett says it will be terrible. Mr Leverett
has made his acquaintance, and says M. Lejaune will put him
into his book; he says the movement of the French intellect is
superb. As a general thing he doesn't care for Academicians,
but he thinks M. Lejaune is an exception, he is so living, so
personal. I asked Mr Cockerel what he thought of M. Lejaune's

plan of writing a book, and he answered that he didn't see what it mattered to him that a Frenchman the more should make a monkey of himself. I asked him why he hadn't written a book about Europe, and he said that, in the first place, Europe isn't worth writing about, and, in the second, if he said what he thought, people would think it was a joke. He said they are very superstitious about Europe over here; he wants people in America to behave as if Europe didn't exist. I told this to Mr Leverett, and he answered that if Europe didn't exist America wouldn't, for Europe keeps us alive by buying our corn. He said, also, that the trouble with America in the future will be that she will produce things in such enormous quantities that there won't be enough people in the rest of the world to buy them, and that we shall be left with our productions – most of them very hideous – on our hands. I asked him if he thought corn a hideous production, and he replied that there is nothing more unbeautiful than too much food. I think that to feed the world too well, however, that will be, after all, a *beau rôle*. Of course I don't understand these things, and I don't believe Mr Leverett does; but Mr Cockerel seems to know what he is talking about, and he says that America is complete in herself. I don't know exactly what he means, but he speaks as if human affairs had somehow moved over to this side of the world. It may be a very good place for them, and Heaven knows I am extremely tired of Europe, which mamma has always insisted so on my appreciating; but I don't think I like the idea of our being so completely cut off. Mr Cockerel says it is not we that are cut off, but Europe, and he seems to think that Europe has deserved it somehow. That may be; our life over there was sometimes extremely tiresome, though mamma says it is now that our real fatigues will begin. I like to abuse those dreadful old countries myself, but I am not sure that I am pleased when others do the same. We had some rather pretty moments there, after all; and at Piacenza we certainly lived on four francs a day. Mamma is already in a terrible state of mind about the expenses here; she is frightened by what people on the ship (the few that she has spoken to) have told her. There is one comfort, at any rate – we have spent so much money in coming here that we

shall have none left to get away. I am scribbling along, as you
see, to occupy me till we get news of the islands. Here comes
Mr Cockerel to bring it. Yes, they are in sight; he tells me that
they are lovelier than ever, and that I must come right up right
away. I suppose you will think that I am already beginning to
use the language of the country. It is certain that at the end of a
month I shall speak nothing else. I have picked up every dialect,
wherever we have travelled; you have heard my Platt-Deutsch
and my Neapolitan. But, *voyons un peu* the Bay! I have just
called to Mr Leverett to remind him of the islands. 'The islands
– the islands? Ah, my dear young lady, I have seen Capri, I have
seen Ischia!' Well, so have I, but that doesn't prevent . . . (*A little
later.*) – I have seen the islands; they are rather queer.

II

Mrs CHURCH, *in New York, to* Madame GALOPIN, *at Geneva*

October 17, 1880

IF I felt far away from you in the middle of that deplorable
Atlantic, *chère* Madame, how do I feel now, in the heart of this
extraordinary city? We have arrived, – we have arrived, dear
friend; but I don't know whether to tell you that I consider that
an advantage. If we had been given our choice of coming safely
to land or going down to the bottom of the sea, I should doubtless have chosen the former course; for I hold, with your noble
husband, and in opposition to the general tendency of modern
thought, that our lives are not our own to dispose of, but a
sacred trust from a higher power, by whom we shall be held
responsible. Nevertheless, if I had foreseen more vividly some
of the impressions that awaited me here, I am not sure that, for
my daughter at least, I should not have preferred on the spot to
hand in our account. Should I not have been less (rather than
more) guilty in presuming to dispose of *her* destiny, than of my
own? There is a nice point for dear M. Galopin to settle – one of
those points which I have heard him discuss in the pulpit with
such elevation. We are safe, however, as I say; by which I mean
that we are physically safe. We have taken up the thread of our
familiar pension-life, but under strikingly different conditions.

We have found a refuge in a boarding-house which has been highly recommended to me, and where the arrangements partake of that barbarous magnificence which in this country is the only alternative from primitive rudeness. The terms, per week, are as magnificent as all the rest. The landlady wears diamond ear-rings; and the drawing-rooms are decorated with marble statues. I should indeed be sorry to let you know how I have allowed myself to be *rançonnée*; and I should be still more sorry that it should come to the ears of any of my good friends in Geneva, who know me less well than you and might judge me more harshly. There is no wine given for dinner, and I have vainly requested the person who conducts the establishment to garnish her table more liberally. She says I may have all the wine I want if I will order it at the merchant's, and settle the matter with him. But I have never, as you know, consented to regard our modest allowance of *eau rougie* as an extra; indeed, I remember that it is largely to your excellent advice that I have owed my habit of being firm on this point. There are, however, greater difficulties than the question of what we shall drink for dinner, *chère* Madame. Still, I have never lost courage, and I shall not lose courage now. At the worst, we can re-embark again, and seek repose and refreshment on the shores of your beautiful lake. (There is absolutely no scenery here!) We shall not, perhaps, in that case have achieved what we desired, but we shall at least have made an honourable retreat. What we desire – I know it is just this that puzzles you, dear friend; I don't think you ever really comprehended my motives in taking this formidable step, though you were good enough, and your magnanimous husband was good enough, to press my hand at parting in a way that seemed to say that you would still be with me, even if I was wrong. To be very brief, I wished to put an end to the reclamations of my daughter. Many Americans had assured her that she was wasting her youth in those historic lands, which it was her privilege to see so intimately, and this unfortunate conviction had taken possession of her. 'Let me at least see for myself,' she used to say; 'if I should dislike it over there as much as you promise me, so much the better for you. In that case we will come back and make a new arrangement at

Stuttgart.' The experiment is a terribly expensive one; but you know that my devotion never has shrunk from an ordeal. There is another point, moreover, which, from a mother to a mother, it would be affectation not to touch upon. I remember the just satisfaction with which you announced to me the betrothal of your charming Cécile. You know with what earnest care my Aurora has been educated, – how thoroughly she is acquainted with the principal results of modern research. We have always studied together; we have always enjoyed together. It will perhaps surprise you to hear that she makes these very advantages a reproach to me, – represents them as an injury to herself. 'In this country,' she says, 'the gentlemen have not those accomplishments; they care nothing for the results of modern research; and it will not help a young person to be sought in marriage that she can give an account of the last German theory of Pessimism.' That is possible; and I have never concealed from her that it was not for this country that I had educated her. If she marries in the United States, it is, of course, my intention that my son-in-law shall accompany us to Europe. But, when she calls my attention more and more to these facts, I feel that we are moving in a different world. This is more and more the country of the many; the few find less and less place for them; and the individual – well, the individual has quite ceased to be recognised. He is recognised as a voter, but he is not recognised as a gentleman – still less as a lady. My daughter and I, of course, can only pretend to constitute a *few*! You know that I have never for a moment remitted my pretensions as an individual, though, among the agitations of pension-life, I have sometimes needed all my energy to uphold them. 'Oh, yes, I may be poor,' I have had occasion to say, 'I may be unprotected, I may be reserved, I may occupy a small apartment in the *quatrième*, and be unable to scatter unscrupulous bribes among the domestics; but at least I am a *person*, with personal rights.' In this country the people have rights, but the person has none. You would have perceived that if you had come with me to make arrangements at this establishment. The very fine lady who condescends to preside over it kept me waiting twenty minutes, and then came sailing in without a word of apology.

I had sat very silent, with my eyes on the clock; Aurora amused herself with a false admiration of the room, – a wonderful drawing-room, with magenta curtains, frescoed walls, and photographs of the landlady's friends – as if one cared anything about her friends! When this exalted personage came in, she simply remarked that she had just been trying on a dress – that it took so long to get a skirt to hang. 'It seems to take very long, indeed!' I answered. 'But I hope the skirt is right at last. You might have sent for us to come up and look at it!' She evidently didn't understand, and when I asked her to show us her rooms, she handed us over to a negro as *dégingandé* as herself. While we looked at them, I heard her sit down to the piano in the drawing-room; she began to sing an air from a comic opera. I began to fear we had gone quite astray; I didn't know in what house we could be, and was only reassured by seeing a Bible in every room. When we came down our musical hostess expressed no hope that the rooms had pleased us, and seemed quite indifferent to our taking them. She would not consent, moreover, to the least diminution, and was inflexible, as I told you, on the subject of wine. When I pushed this point, she was so good as to observe that she didn't keep a *cabaret*. One is not in the least considered; there is no respect for one's privacy, for one's preferences, for one's reserves. The familiarity is without limits, and I have already made a dozen acquaintances, of whom I know, and wish to know, nothing. Aurora tells me that she is the 'belle of the boarding-house'. It appears that this is a great distinction. It brings me back to my poor child and her prospects. She takes a very critical view of them herself; she tells me that I have given her a false education, and that no one will marry her to-day. No American will marry her, because she is too much of a foreigner, and no foreigner will marry her, because she is too much of an American. I remind her that scarcely a day passes that a foreigner, usually of distinction, doesn't select an American bride, and she answers me that in these cases the young lady is not married for her fine eyes. Not always, I reply; and then she declares that she would marry no foreigner who should not be one of the first of the first. You will say, doubtless, that she should content herself with advantages that have not been deemed insufficient for Cécile; but I will not repeat to you the remark she made when I once made use of this argument. You will doubtless be surprised to hear that I have ceased to argue; but it is time I should tell you that I have at last agreed to let her act for herself. She is to live for three months *à l'Américaine*, and I am to be a mere spectator. You will feel with me that this is a cruel position for a *cœur de mère*. I count the days till our three months are over, and I know that you will join with me in my prayers. Aurora walks the streets alone. She goes out in the tramway; a *voiture de place* costs five francs for the least little *course*. (I beseech you not to let it be known that I have sometimes had the weakness . . .) My daughter is sometimes accompanied by a gentleman – by a dozen gentlemen; she remains out for hours, and her conduct excites no surprise in this establishment. I know but too well the emotions it will excite in your quiet home. If you betray us, *chère* Madame, we are lost; and why, after all, should any one know of these things in Geneva? Aurora pretends that she has been able to persuade herself that she doesn't care who knows them; but there is a strange expression in her face, which proves that her conscience is not at rest. I watch her, I let her go, but I sit with my hands clasped. There is a peculiar custom in this country – I shouldn't know how to express it in Genevese – it is called 'being attentive', and young girls are the object of the attention. It has not necessarily anything to do with projects of marriage, – though it is the privilege only of the unmarried, and though, at the same time (fortunately, and this may surprise you), it has no relation to other projects. It is simply an invention by which young persons of the two sexes pass their time together. How shall I muster courage to tell you that Aurora is now engaged in this *délassement*, in company with several gentlemen? Though it has no relation to marriage, it happily does not exclude it, and marriages have been known to take place in consequence (or in spite) of it. It is true that even in this country a young lady may marry but one husband at a time, whereas she may receive at once the attentions of several gentlemen, who are equally entitled 'admirers'. My daughter, then, has admirers to an indefinite number. You will think I am joking, perhaps, when

I tell you that I am unable to be exact – I who was formerly *l'exactitude même*. Two of these gentlemen are, to a certain extent, old friends, having been passengers on the steamer which carried us so far from you. One of them, still young, is typical of the American character, but a respectable person, and a lawyer in considerable practice. Every one in this country follows a profession; but it must be admitted that the professions are more highly remunerated than *chez vous*. Mr Cockerel, even while I write you, is in complete possession of my daughter. He called for her an hour ago in a 'boghey', – a strange, unsafe, rickety vehicle, mounted on enormous wheels, which holds two persons very near together; and I watched her from the window take her place at his side. Then he whirled her away, behind two little horses with terribly thin legs; the whole equipage – and most of all her being in it – was in the most questionable taste. But she will return, and she will return very much as she went. It is the same when she goes down to Mr Louis Leverett, who has no vehicle, and who merely comes and sits with her in the front *salon*. He has lived a great deal in Europe, and is very fond of the arts, and though I am not sure I agree with him in his views of the relation of art to life and life to art, and in his interpretation of some of the great works that Aurora and I have studied together, he seems to me a sufficiently serious and intelligent young man. I do not regard him as intrinsically dangerous; but, on the other hand, he offers absolutely no guarantees. I have no means whatever of ascertaining his pecuniary situation. There is a vagueness on these points which is extremely embarrassing, and it never occurs to young men to offer you a reference. In Geneva I should not be at a loss; I should come to you, *chère* Madame, with my little inquiry, and what you should not be able to tell me would not be worth knowing. But no one in New York can give me the smallest information about the *état de fortune* of Mr Louis Leverett. It is true that he is a native of Boston, where most of his friends reside; I cannot, however, go to the expense of a journey to Boston simply to learn, perhaps, that Mr Leverett (the young Louis) has an income of five thousand francs. As I say, however, he does not strike me as dangerous. When Aurora comes back to me, after having passed an hour with the young Louis, she says that he has described to her his emotions on visiting the home of Shelley, or discussed some of the differences between the Boston Temperament and that of the Italians of the Renaissance. You will not enter into these *rapprochements*, and I can't blame you. But you won't betray me, *chère* Madame?

III

From Miss STURDY, *at Newport, to* Mrs DRAPER, *in Florence*

September 30

I PROMISED to tell you how I like it, but the truth is, I have gone to and fro so often that I have ceased to like and dislike. Nothing strikes me as unexpected; I expect everything in its order. Then, too, you know, I am not a critic; I have no talent for keen analysis, as the magazines say; I don't go into the reasons of things. It is true I have been for a longer time than usual on the wrong side of the water, and I admit that I feel a little out of training for American life. They are breaking me in very fast, however. I don't mean that they bully me; I absolutely decline to be bullied. I say what I think, because I believe that I have, on the whole, the advantage of knowing what I think – when I think anything – which is half the battle. Sometimes, indeed, I think nothing at all. They don't like that over here; they like you to have impressions. That they like these impressions to be favourable appears to me perfectly natural; I don't make a crime to them of that; it seems to me, on the contrary, a very amiable quality. When individuals have it, we call them sympathetic; I don't see why we shouldn't give nations the same benefit. But there are things I haven't the least desire to have an opinion about. The privilege of indifference is the dearest one we possess, and I hold that intelligent people are known by the way they exercise it. Life is full of rubbish, and we have at least our share of it over here. When you wake up in the morning you find that during the night a cartload has been deposited in your front garden. I decline, however, to have any of it in my premises; there are thousands of things I want to

know nothing about. I have outlived the necessity of being
hypocritical; I have nothing to gain and everything to lose.
When one is fifty years old – single, stout, and red in the face
– one has outlived a good many necessities. They tell me over
here that my increase of weight is extremely marked, and
though they don't tell me that I am coarse, I am sure they
think me so. There is very little coarseness here – not quite
enough, I think – though there is plenty of vulgarity, which is a
very different thing. On the whole, the country is becoming
much more agreeable. It isn't that the people are charming, for
that they always were (the best of them, I mean, for it isn't true
of the others), but that places and things as well have acquired
the art of pleasing. The houses are extremely good, and they
look so extraordinarily fresh and clean. European interiors, in
comparison, seem musty and gritty. We have a great deal of
taste; I shouldn't wonder if we should end by inventing something pretty; we only need a little time. Of course, as yet, it's all
imitation, except, by the way, these piazzas. I am sitting on one
now; I am writing to you with my portfolio on my knees. This
broad, light *loggia* surrounds the house with a movement as free
as the expanded wings of a bird, and the wandering airs come
up from the deep sea, which murmurs on the rocks at the end of
the lawn. Newport is more charming even than you remember
it; like everything else over here, it has improved. It is very
exquisite to-day; it is, indeed, I think, in all the world, the
only exquisite watering-place, for I detest the whole genus.
The crowd has left it now, which makes it all the better, though
plenty of talkers remain in these large, light, luxurious houses,
which are planted with a kind of Dutch definiteness all over the
green carpet of the cliff. This carpet is very neatly laid and
wonderfully well swept, and the sea, just at hand, is capable
of prodigies of blue. Here and there a pretty woman strolls over
one of the lawns, which all touch each other, you know, without
hedges or fences; the light looks intense as it plays upon her
brilliant dress; her large parasol shines like a silver dome. The
long lines of the far shores are soft and pure, though they are
places that one hasn't the least desire to visit. Altogether the
effect is very delicate, and anything that is delicate counts

immensely over here; for delicacy, I think, is as rare as coarseness. I am talking to you of the sea, however, without having told you a word of my voyage. It was very comfortable and amusing; I should like to take another next month. You know I am almost offensively well at sea, – that I breast the weather and brave the storm. We had no storm fortunately, and I had brought with me a supply of light literature; so I passed nine days on deck in my sea-chair, with my heels up, reading Tauchnitz novels. There was a great lot of people, but no one in particular, save some fifty American girls. You know all about the American girl, however, having been one yourself. They are, on the whole, very nice, but fifty is too many; there are always too many. There was an inquiring Briton, a radical M.P., by name Mr Antrobus, who entertained me as much as any one else. He is an excellent man; I even asked him to come down here and spend a couple of days. He looked rather frightened, till I told him he shouldn't be alone with me, that the house was my brother's, and that I gave the invitation in his name. He came a week ago; he goes everywhere; we have heard of him in a dozen places. The English are very simple, or at least they seem so over here. Their old measurements and comparisons desert them; they don't know whether it's all a joke, or whether it's too serious by half. We are quicker than they, though we talk so much more slowly. We think fast, and yet we talk as deliberately as if we were speaking a foreign language. They toss off their sentences with an air of easy familiarity with the tongue, and yet they misunderstand two-thirds of what people say to them. Perhaps, after all, it is only *our* thoughts they think slowly; they think their own often to a lively tune enough. Mr Antrobus arrived here at eight o'clock in the morning; I don't know how he managed it; it appears to be his favourite hour; wherever we have heard of him he has come in with the dawn. In England, he would arrive at 5.30 P.M. He asks innumerable questions, but they are easy to answer, for he has a sweet credulity. He made me rather ashamed; he is a better American than so many of us; he takes us more seriously than we take ourselves. He seems to think that an oligarchy of wealth is growing up here, and he advised me to be on my guard against it. I don't know exactly what I can do, but I promised him to look out. He is fearfully energetic; the energy of the people here is nothing to that of the inquiring Briton. If we should devote half the energy to building up our institutions that they devote to obtaining information about them, we should have a very satisfactory country. Mr Antrobus seemed to think very well of us, which surprised me, on the whole, because, say what one will, it's not so agreeable as England. It's very horrid that this should be; and it's delightful, when one thinks of it, that some things in England are, after all, so disagreeable. At the same time, Mr Antrobus appeared to be a good deal preoccupied with our dangers. I don't understand, quite, what they are; they seem to me so few, on a Newport piazza, on this bright, still day. But, after all, what one sees on a Newport piazza is not America; it's the back of Europe! I don't mean to say that I haven't noticed any dangers since my return; there are two or three that seem to me very serious, but they are not those that Mr Antrobus means. One, for instance, is that we shall cease to speak the English language, which I prefer so much to any other. It's less and less spoken; American is crowding it out. All the children speak American, and as a child's language it's dreadfully rough. It's exclusively in use in the schools; all the magazines and newspapers are in American. Of course, a people of fifty millions, who have invented a new civilisation, have a right to a language of their own; that's what they tell me, and I can't quarrel with it. But I wish they had made it as pretty as the mother-tongue, from which, after all, it is more or less derived. We ought to have invented something as noble as our country. They tell me it's more expressive, and yet some admirable things have been said in the Queen's English. There can be no question of the Queen over here, of course, and American no doubt is the music of the future. Poor dear future, how 'expressive' you'll be! For women and children, as I say, it strikes one as very rough; and moreover they don't speak it well, their own though it be. My little nephews, when I first came home, had not gone back to school, and it distressed me to see that, though they are charming children, they had the vocal inflections of little newsboys. My niece is sixteen years old; she has the sweetest nature possible; she is extremely well-bred, and is dressed to perfection. She chatters from morning till night; but it isn't a pleasant sound! These little persons are in the opposite case from so many English girls, who know how to speak, but don't know how to talk. My niece knows how to talk, but doesn't know how to speak. *A propos* of the young people, that is our other danger; the young people are eating us up, – there is nothing in America but the young people. The country is made for the rising generation; life is arranged for them; they are the destruction of society. People talk of them, consider them, defer to them, bow down to them. They are always present, and whenever they are present there is an end to everything else. They are often very pretty; and physically, they are wonderfully looked after; they are scoured and brushed, they wear hygienic clothes, they go every week to the dentist's. But the little boys kick your shins, and the little girls offer to slap your face! There is an immense literature entirely addressed to them, in which the kicking of shins and the slapping of faces is much recommended. As a woman of fifty, I protest. I insist on being judged by my peers. It's too late, however, for several millions of little feet are actively engaged in stamping out conversation, and I don't see how they can long fail to keep it under. The future is theirs; maturity will evidently be at an increasing discount. Longfellow wrote a charming little poem, called 'The Children's Hour', but he ought to have called it 'The Children's Century'. And by children, of course, I don't mean simple infants; I mean everything of less than twenty. The social importance of the young American increases steadily up to that age, and then it suddenly stops. The young girls, of course, are more important than the lads; but the lads are very important too. I am struck with the way they are known and talked about; they are little celebrities; they have reputations and pretensions; they are taken very seriously. As for the young girls, as I said just now, there are too many. You will say, perhaps, that I am jealous of them, with my fifty years and my red face. I don't think so, because I don't suffer; my red face doesn't frighten people away, and I always find plenty of talkers. The young girls themselves, I believe, like me very much;

and as for me, I delight in the young girls. They are often very pretty; not so pretty as people say in the magazines, but pretty enough. The magazines rather overdo that; they make a mistake. I have seen no great beauties, but the level of prettiness is high, and occasionally one sees a woman completely handsome. (As a general thing, a pretty person here means a person with a pretty face. The figure is rarely mentioned, though there are several good ones.) The level of prettiness is high, but the level of conversation is low; that's one of the signs of its being a young ladies' country. There are a good many things young ladies can't talk about; but think of all the things they can, when they are as clever as most of these. Perhaps one ought to content one's self with that measure, but it's difficult if one has lived for a while by a larger one. This one is decidedly narrow; I stretch it sometimes till it cracks. Then it is that they call me coarse, which I undoubtedly am, thank Heaven! People's talk is of course much more *châtiée* over here than in Europe; I am struck with that wherever I go. There are certain things that are never said at all, certain allusions that are never made. There are no light stories, no *propos risqués*. I don't know exactly what people talk about, for the supply of scandal is small, and it's poor in quality. They don't seem, however, to lack topics. The young girls are always there; they keep the gates of conversation; very little passes that is not innocent. I find we do very well without wickedness; and, for myself, as I take my ease, I don't miss my liberties. You remember what I thought of the tone of your table in Florence, and how surprised you were when I asked you why you allowed such things. You said they were like the courses of the seasons; one couldn't prevent them; also that to change the tone of your table you would have to change so many other things. Of course, in your house one never saw a young girl; I was the only spinster, and no one was afraid of me! Of course, too, if talk is more innocent in this country, manners are so, to begin with. The liberty of the young people is the strongest proof of it. The young girls are let loose in the world, and the world gets more good of it than *ces demoiselles* get harm. In your world – excuse me, but you know what I mean – this wouldn't do at all. Your world is a sad affair, and the young ladies would encounter all sorts of horrors. Over here, considering the way they knock about, they remain wonderfully simple, and the reason is that society protects them instead of setting them traps. There is almost no gallantry, as you understand it; the flirtations are child's play. People have no time for making love; the men, in particular, are extremely busy. I am told that sort of thing consumes hours; I have never had any time for it myself. If the leisure class should increase here considerably, there may possibly be a change; but I doubt it, for the women seem to me in all essentials exceedingly reserved. Great superficial frankness, but an extreme dread of complications. The men strike me as very good fellows. I think that at bottom they are better than the women, who are very subtle, but rather hard. They are not so nice to the men as the men are to them; I mean, of course, in proportion, you know. But women are not so nice as men, 'anyhow', as they say here. The men, of course, are professional, commercial; there are very few gentlemen pure and simple. This personage needs to be very well done, however, to be of great utility; and I suppose you won't pretend that he is always well done in your countries. When he's not, the less of him the better. It's very much the same, however, with the system on which the young girls in this country are brought up. (You see, I have to come back to the young girls.) When it succeeds, they are the most charming possible; when it doesn't, the failure is disastrous. If a girl is a very nice girl, the American method brings her to great completeness, – makes all her graces flower; but if she isn't nice, it makes her exceedingly disagreeable, – elaborately and fatally perverts her. In a word, the American girl is rarely negative, and when she isn't a great success she is a great warning. In nineteen cases out of twenty, among the people who know how to live – I won't say what *their* proportion is – the results are highly satisfactory. The girls are not shy, but I don't know why they should be, for there is really nothing here to be afraid of. Manners are very gentle, very humane; the democratic system deprives people of weapons that every one doesn't equally possess. No one is formidable; no one is on stilts; no one has great pretensions or any recognised right to be arrogant. I think

there is not much wickedness, and there is certainly less cruelty
than with you. Every one can sit; no one is kept standing. One is
much less liable to be snubbed, which you will say is a pity.
I think it is, to a certain extent; but, on the other hand, folly is
less fatuous, in form, than in your countries; and as people
generally have fewer revenges to take, there is less need of
their being stamped on in advance. The general good nature,
the social equality, deprive them of triumphs on the one hand,
and of grievances on the other. There is extremely little impertinence; there is almost none. You will say I am describing a
terrible society, – a society without great figures or great social
prizes. You have hit it, my dear; there are no great figures. (The
great prize, of course, in Europe, is the opportunity to be a great
figure.) You would miss these things a good deal, – you who
delight to contemplate greatness; and my advice to you, of
course, is never to come back. You would miss the small people
even more than the great; every one is middle-sized, and you
can never have that momentary sense of tallness which is so
agreeable in Europe. There are no brilliant types; the most
important people seem to lack dignity. They are very *bourgeois*;
they make little jokes; on occasion they make puns; they have
no form; they are too good-natured. The men have no style; the
women, who are fidgety and talk too much, have it only in their
coiffure, where they have it superabundantly. But I console
myself with the greater *bonhomie*. Have you ever arrived at an
English country-house in the dusk of a winter's day? Have you
ever made a call in London, when you knew nobody but the
hostess? People here are more expressive, more demonstrative;
and it is a pleasure, when one comes back (if one happens, like
me, to be no one in particular), to feel one's social value rise.
They attend to you more; they have you on their mind; they talk
to you; they listen to you. That is, the men do; the women listen
very little – not enough. They interrupt; they talk too much;
one feels their presence too much as a sound. I imagine it is
partly because their wits are quick, and they think of a good
many things to say; not that they always say such wonders.
Perfect repose, after all, is not *all* self-control; it is also partly
stupidity. American women, however, make too many vague

exclamations, – say too many indefinite things. In short, they have a great deal of nature. On the whole, I find very little affectation, though we shall probably have more as we improve. As yet, people haven't the assurance that carries those things off; they know too much about each other. The trouble is that over here we have all been brought up together. You will think this a picture of a dreadfully insipid society; but I hasten to add that it's not all so tame as that. I have been speaking of the people that one meets socially; and these are the smallest part of American life. The others – those one meets on a basis of mere convenience – are much more exciting; they keep one's temper in healthy exercise. I mean the people in the shops, and on the railroads; the servants, the hackmen, the labourers, every one of whom you buy anything or have occasion to make an inquiry. With them you need all your best manners, for you must always have enough for two. If you think we are *too* democratic, taste a little of American life in these walks, and you will be reassured. This is the region of inequality, and you will find plenty of people to make your courtesy to. You see it from below – the weight of inequality is on your own back. You asked me to tell you about prices; they are simply dreadful.

IV

From The Honourable EDWARD ANTROBUS, M.P., *in Boston, to* The
Honourable MRS ANTROBUS

October 17

MY DEAR SUSAN,

I sent you a post-card on the 13th and a native newspaper yesterday; I really have had no time to write. I sent you the newspaper partly because it contained a report – extremely incorrect – of some remarks I made at the meeting of the Association of the Teachers of New England; partly because it is so curious that I thought it would interest you and the children. I cut out some portions which I didn't think it would be well for the children to see; the parts remaining contain the most striking features. Please point out to the children the peculiar orthography, which probably will be adopted in

England by the time they are grown up; the amusing oddities of expression, &c. Some of them are intentional; you will have heard of the celebrated American humour, &c. (remind me, by the way, on my return to Thistleton, to give you a few examples of it); others are unconscious, and are perhaps on that account the more diverting. Point out to the children the difference (in so far as you are sure that you yourself perceive it). You must excuse me if these lines are not very legible; I am writing them by the light of a railway-lamp, which rattles above my left ear; it being only at odd moments that I can find time to look into everything that I wish to. You will say that this is a very odd moment, indeed, when I tell you that I am in bed in a sleeping-car. I occupy the upper berth (I will explain to you the arrangement when I return), while the lower forms the couch – the jolts are fearful – of an unknown female. You will be very anxious for my explanation; but I assure you that it is the custom of the country. I myself am assured that a lady may travel in this manner all over the Union (the Union of States) without a loss of consideration. In case of her occupying the upper berth I presume it would be different; but I must make inquiries on this point. Whether it be the fact that a mysterious being of another sex has retired to rest behind the same curtains, or whether it be the swing of the train, which rushes through the air with very much the same movement as the tail of a kite, the situation is, at any rate, so anomalous that I am unable to sleep. A ventilator is open just over my head, and a lively draught, mingled with a drizzle of cinders, pours in through this ingenious orifice. (I will describe to you its form on my return.) If I had occupied the lower berth I should have had a whole window to myself, and by drawing back the blind (a safe proceeding at the dead of night), I should have been able, by the light of an extraordinarily brilliant moon, to see a little better what I write. The question occurs to me, however, – Would the lady below me in that case have ascended to the upper berth? (You know my old taste for contingent inquiries.) I incline to think (from what I have seen) that she would simply have requested me to evacuate my own couch. (The ladies in this country ask for anything they want.) In this case I suppose I should have had an extensive view of the country, which, from what I saw of it before I turned in (while the lady beneath me was going to bed), offered a rather ragged expanse, dotted with little white wooden houses, which looked in the moonshine like paste-board boxes. I have been unable to ascertain as precisely as I should wish by whom these modest residences are occupied; for they are too small to be the homes of country gentlemen, there is no peasantry here, and (in New England, for all the corn comes from the far West) there are no yeomen nor farm-ers. The information that one receives in this country is apt to be rather conflicting, but I am determined to sift the mystery to the bottom. I have already noted down a multitude of facts bearing upon the points that interest me most, – the operation of the school-boards, the co-education of the sexes, the eleva-tion of the tone of the lower classes, the participation of the latter in political life. Political life, indeed, is almost wholly confined to the lower-middle class, and the upper section of the lower class. In some of the large towns, indeed, the lowest order of all participates considerably, – a very interesting phase, to which I shall give more attention. It is very gratifying to see the taste for public affairs pervading so many social strata; but the indifference of the gentry is a fact not to be lightly con-sidered. It may be objected, indeed, that there are no gentry; and it is very true that I have not yet encountered a character of the type of Lord Bottomley, – a type which I am free to confess I should be sorry to see disappear from our English system, if system it may be called, where so much is the growth of blind and incoherent forces. It is nevertheless obvious that an idle and luxurious class exists in this country, and that it is less exempt than in our own from the reproach of preferring inglor-ious ease to the furtherance of liberal ideas. It is rapidly increas-ing, and I am not sure that the indefinite growth of the dilettante spirit, in connection with large and lavishly expended wealth, is an unmixed good, even in a society in which freedom of development has obtained so many interesting triumphs. The fact that this body is not represented in the governing class, is perhaps as much the result of the jealousy with which it is viewed by the more earnest workers as of its own – I dare not, perhaps, apply a harsher term than – levity. Such, at least, is the impression I have gathered in the Middle States and in New England; in the Southwest, the Northwest, and the far West, it will doubtless be liable to correction. These divisions are probably new to you; but they are the general denomination of large and flourishing communities, with which I hope to make myself at least superficially acquainted. The fatigue of traversing, as I habitually do, three or four hundred miles at a bound, is, of course, considerable; but there is usually much to inquire into by the way. The conductors of the trains, with whom I freely converse, are often men of vigorous and original minds, and even of some social eminence. One of them, a few days ago, gave me a letter of introduction to his brother-in-law, who is president of a Western university. Don't have any fear, therefore, that I am not in the best society! The arrangements for travelling are, as a general thing, extremely ingenious, as you will probably have inferred from what I told you above; but it must at the same time be conceded that some of them are more ingenious than happy. Some of the facilities, with regard to luggage, the transmission of parcels, &c., are doubtless very useful when explained, but I have not yet succeeded in mastering the intricacies. There are, on the other hand, no cabs and no porters, and I have calculated that I have myself carried my *impedimenta* – which, you know, are somewhat numerous, and from which I cannot bear to be separated – some seventy or eighty miles. I have sometimes thought it was a great mistake not to bring Plummeridge; he would have been useful on such occasions. On the other hand, the startling question would have presented itself – Who would have carried Plummeridge's portmanteau? He would have been useful, indeed, for brushing and packing my clothes, and getting me my tub; I travel with a large tin one, – there are none to be obtained at the inns, – and the transport of this receptacle often presents the most insoluble difficulties. It is often, too, an object of considerable embarrassment in arriving at private houses, where the servants have less reserve of manner than in England; and, to tell you the truth, I am by no means certain at the present moment that the tub has been placed in the train with me. 'On board' the train is

the consecrated phrase here; it is an allusion to the tossing and
pitching of the concatenation of cars, so similar to that of a
vessel in a storm. As I was about to inquire, however, Who
would get Plummeridge *his* tub, and attend to his little com-
forts? We could not very well make our appearance, on coming
to stay with people, with *two* of the utensils I have named;
though, as regards a single one, I have had the courage, as
I may say, of a life-long habit. It would hardly be expected
that we should both use the same; though there have been
occasions in my travels as to which I see no way of blinking
the fact that Plummeridge would have had to sit down to dinner
with me. Such a contingency would completely have unnerved
him; and, on the whole, it was doubtless the wiser part to leave
him respectfully touching his hat on the tender in the Mersey.
No one touches his hat over here, and though it is doubtless the
sign of a more advanced social order, I confess that when I see
poor Plummeridge again, this familiar little gesture – familiar,
I mean, only in the sense of being often seen – will give me a
measurable satisfaction. You will see from what I tell you that
democracy is not a mere word in this country, and I could give
you many more instances of its universal reign. This, however,
is what we come here to look at, and, in so far as there seems to
be proper occasion, to admire; though I am by no means sure
that we can hope to establish within an appreciable time a
corresponding change in the somewhat rigid fabric of English
manners. I am not even prepared to affirm that such a change is
desirable; you know this is one of the points on which I do not
as yet see my way to going as far as Lord B—. I have always held
that there is a certain social ideal of inequality as well as of
equality, and if I have found the people of this country, as a
general thing, quite equal to each other, I am not sure that I am
prepared to go so far as to say that, as a whole, they are equal to
– excuse that dreadful blot! The movement of the train and the
precarious nature of the light – it is close to my nose, and most
offensive – would, I flatter myself, long since have got the better
of a less resolute diarist! What I was not prepared for was the
very considerable body of aristocratic feeling that lurks beneath
this republican simplicity. I have on several occasions been

made the confidant of these romantic but delusive vagaries, of which the stronghold appears to be the Empire City, – a slang name for New York. I was assured in many quarters that that locality, at least, is ripe for a monarchy, and if one of the Queen's sons would come and talk it over, he would meet with the highest encouragement. This information was given me in strict confidence, with closed doors, as it were; it reminded me a good deal of the dreams of the old Jacobites, when they whispered their messages to the king across the water. I doubt, however, whether these less excusable visionaries will be able to secure the services of a Pretender, for I fear that in such a case he would encounter a still more fatal Culloden. I have given a good deal of time, as I told you, to the educational system, and have visited no fewer than one hundred and forty-three schools and colleges. It is extraordinary, the number of persons who are being educated in this country; and yet, at the same time, the tone of the people is less scholarly than one might expect. A lady, a few days since, described to me her daughter as being always 'on the go', which I take to be a jocular way of saying that the young lady was very fond of paying visits. Another person, the wife of a United States senator, informed me that if I should go to Washington in January, I should be quite 'in the swim'. I inquired the meaning of the phrase, but her explanation made it rather more than less ambiguous. To say that I am on the go describes very accurately my own situation. I went yesterday to the Pognanuc High School, to hear fifty-seven boys and girls recite in unison a most remarkable ode to the American Flag, and shortly afterward attended a ladies' lunch, at which some eighty or ninety of the sex were present. There was only one individual in trousers – his trousers by the way, though he brought a dozen pair, are getting rather seedy. The men in America do not partake of this meal, at which ladies assemble in large numbers to discuss religious, political, and social topics. These immense female symposia (at which every delicacy is provided) are one of the most striking features of American life, and would seem to prove that men are not so indispensable in the scheme of creation as they sometimes suppose. I have been admitted on the footing of an Englishman – 'just to show you some of our bright women', the hostess yesterday remarked. ('Bright' here has the meaning of *intellectual*.) I perceived, indeed, a great many intellectual foreheads. These curious collations are organised according to age. I have also been present as an inquiring stranger at several 'girls' lunches', from which married ladies are rigidly excluded, but where the fair revellers are equally numerous and equally bright. There is a good deal I should like to tell you about my study of the educational question, but my position is somewhat cramped, and I must dismiss it briefly. My leading impression is that the children in this country are better educated than the adults. The position of a child is, on the whole, one of great distinction. There is a popular ballad of which the refrain, if I am not mistaken, is 'Make me a child again, just for to-night!' and which seems to express the sentiment of regret for lost privileges. At all events they are a powerful and independent class, and have organs, of immense circulation, in the press. They are often extremely 'bright'. I have talked with a great many teachers, most of them lady-teachers, as they are called in this country. The phrase does not mean teachers of ladies, as you might suppose, but applies to the sex of the instructress, who often has large classes of young men under her control. I was lately introduced to a young woman of twenty-three, who occupies the chair of Moral Philosophy and Belles-Lettres in a Western college, and who told me with the utmost frankness that she was adored by the undergraduates. This young woman was the daughter of a petty trader in one of the Southwestern States, and had studied at Amanda College, in Missourah, an institution at which young people of the two sexes pursue their education together. She was very pretty and modest, and expressed a great desire to see something of English country-life, in consequence of which I made her promise to come down to Thistleton in the event of her crossing the Atlantic. She is not the least like Gwendolen or Charlotte, and I am not prepared to say how they would get on with her; the boys would probably do better. Still, I think her acquaintance would be of value to Miss Bumpus, and the two might pass their time very pleasantly in the schoolroom. I grant you freely that those I have seen here are much less comfortable than the schoolroom at Thistleton. Has Charlotte, by the way, designed any more texts for the walls? I have been extremely interested in my visit to Philadelphia, where I saw several thousand little red houses with white steps, occupied by intelligent artisans, and arranged (in streets) on the rectangular system. Improved cooking-stoves, rosewood pianos, gas and hot water, aesthetic furniture, and complete sets of the British Essayists. A tramway through every street; every block of equal length; blocks and houses scientifically lettered and numbered. There is absolutely no loss of time, and no need of looking for anything, or, indeed, *at* anything. The mind always on one's object; it is very delightful.

V

From LOUIS LEVERETT, *in Boston, to* HARVARD TREMONT, *in Paris*

November

THE scales have turned, my sympathetic Harvard, and the beam that has lifted you up has dropped me again on this terribly hard spot. I am extremely sorry to have missed you in London, but I received your little note, and took due heed of your injunction to let you know how I got on. I don't get on at all, my dear Harvard – I am consumed with the love of the farther shore. I have been so long away that I have dropped out of my place in this little Boston world, and the shallow tides of New England life have closed over it. I am a stranger here, and I find it hard to believe that I ever was a native. It is very hard, very cold, very vacant. I think of your warm, rich Paris; I think of the Boulevard St Michel on the mild spring evenings. I see the little corner by the window (of the Café de la Jeunesse) where I used to sit; the doors are open, the soft, deep breath of the great city comes in. It is brilliant, yet there is a kind of tone, of body, in the brightness; the mighty murmur of the ripest civilisation in the world comes in; the dear old *peuple de Paris*, the most interesting people in the world, pass by. I have a little book in my pocket; it is exquisitely printed, a modern Elzevir. It is a lyric cry from the heart of young France, and is full of the sentiment of form. There is no form here, dear Harvard; I had no idea how little form there was. I don't know what I shall do; I feel so undraped, so uncurtained, so uncushioned; I feel as if I were sitting in the centre of a mighty 'reflector'. A terrible crude glare is over everything; the earth looks peeled and excoriated; the raw heavens seem to bleed with the quick, hard light. I have not got back my rooms in West Cedar street; they are occupied by a mesmeric healer. I am staying at an hotel, and it is very dreadful. Nothing for one's self; nothing for one's preferences and habits. No one to receive you when you arrive; you push in through a crowd, you edge up to a counter; you write your name in a horrible book, where every one may come and stare at it and finger it. A man behind the counter stares at you in silence; his stare seems to say to you, 'What the devil do *you* want?' But after this stare he never looks at you again. He tosses down a key at you; he presses a bell; a savage Irishman arrives. 'Take him away,' he seems to say to the Irishman; but it is all done in silence; there is no answer to your own speech, – 'What is to be done with me, please?' 'Wait and you will see,' the awful silence seems to say. There is a great crowd around you, but there is also a great stillness; every now and then you hear some one expectorate. There are a thousand people in this huge and hideous structure; they feed together in a big white-walled room. It is lighted by a thousand gas-jets, and heated by cast-iron screens, which vomit forth torrents of scorching air. The temperature is terrible; the atmosphere is more so; the furious light and heat seem to intensify the dreadful definiteness. When things are so ugly, they should not be so definite; and they are terribly ugly here. There is no mystery in the corners; there is no light and shade in the types. The people are haggard and joyless; they look as if they had no passions, no tastes, no senses. They sit feeding in silence, in the dry, hard light; occasionally I hear the high, firm note of a child. The servants are black and familiar; their faces shine as they shuffle about; there are blue tones in their dark masks. They have no manners; they address you, but they don't answer you; they plant themselves at your elbow (it rubs their clothes as you eat), and watch you as if your proceedings were strange. They deluge you with iced water; it's the only thing they will bring you; if you look round to summon them, they have gone for more. If you read the newspaper, – which I don't, gracious Heaven! I can't, – they hang over your shoulder and peruse it also. I always fold it up and present it to them; the newspapers here are indeed for an African taste. There are long corridors defended by gusts of hot air; down the middle swoops a pale little girl on parlourskates. 'Get out of my way!' she shrieks as she passes; she has ribbons in her hair and frills on her dress; she makes the tour of the immense hotel. I think of Puck, who put a girdle round the earth in forty minutes, and wonder what he said as he flitted by. A black waiter marches past me, bearing a tray, which he thrusts into my spine as he goes. It is laden with large white jugs; they tinkle as he moves, and I recognise the unconsoling fluid. We are dying of iced water, of hot air, of gas. I sit in my room thinking of these things – this room of mine which is a chamber of pain. The walls are white and bare, they shine in the rays of a horrible chandelier of imitation bronze, which depends from the middle of the ceiling. It flings a patch of shadow on a small table covered with white marble, of which the genial surface supports at the present moment the sheet of paper on which I address you; and when I go to bed (I like to read in bed, Harvard) it becomes an object of mockery and torment. It dangles at inaccessible heights; it stares me in the face; it flings the light upon the covers of my book, but not upon the page – the little French Elzevir that I love so well. I rise and put out the gas, and then my room becomes even lighter than before. Then a crude illumination from the hall, from the neighbouring room, pours through the glass openings that surmount the two doors of my apartment. It covers my bed, where I toss and groan; it beats in through my closed lids; it is accompanied by the most vulgar, though the most human, sounds. I spring up to call for some help, some remedy; but there is no bell, and I feel desolate and weak. There is only a strange orifice in the wall, through which the traveller in distress may transmit his appeal. I fill it with incoherent sounds, and sounds more incoherent yet come back to me. I gather at last their meaning; they appear to constitute a somewhat stern inquiry. A hollow, impersonal voice wishes to

know what I want, and the very question paralyses me. I want
everything – yet I want nothing, – nothing this hard impersonality can give! I want my little corner of Paris; I want the rich,
the deep, the dark Old World; I want to be out of this horrible
place. Yet I can't confide all this to that mechanical tube; it
would be of no use; a mocking laugh would come up from the
office. Fancy appealing in these sacred, these intimate
moments, to an 'office'; fancy calling out into indifferent
space for a candle, for a curtain! I pay incalculable sums in
this dreadful house, and yet I haven't a servant to wait upon
me. I fling myself back on my couch, and for a long time afterward the orifice in the wall emits strange murmurs and
rumblings. It seems unsatisfied, indignant; it is evidently scolding me for my vagueness. My vagueness, indeed, dear Harvard!
I loathe their horrible arrangements; isn't that definite enough?
You asked me to tell you whom I see, and what I think of
my friends. I haven't very many; I don't feel at all *en rapport*.
The people are very good, very serious, very devoted to their
work; but there is a terrible absence of variety of type. Every one
is Mr Jones, Mr Brown; and every one looks like Mr Jones and
Mr Brown. They are thin; they are diluted in the great tepid
bath of Democracy! They lack completeness of identity;
they are quite without modelling. No, they are not beautiful,
my poor Harvard; it must be whispered that they are not
beautiful. You may say that they are as beautiful as the French,
as the Germans; but I can't agree with you there. The
French, the Germans, have the greatest beauty of all, – the
beauty of their ugliness, – the beauty of the strange, the grotesque. These people are not even ugly; they are only plain.
Many of the girls are pretty; but to be only pretty is (to my
sense) to be plain. Yet I have had some talk. I have seen a
woman. She was on the steamer, and I afterward saw her in
New York, – a peculiar type, a real personality; a great deal of
modelling, a great deal of colour, and yet a great deal of mystery. She was not, however, of this country; she was a compound of far-off things. But she was looking for something here
– like me. We found each other, and for a moment that was
enough. I have lost her now; I am sorry, because she liked to

listen to me. She has passed away; I shall not see her again. She liked to listen to me; she almost understood!

VI
From M. Gustave Lejaune, *of the French Academy, to* M. Adolphe Bouche, *in Paris*

Washington, October 5

I give you my little notes; you must make allowances for haste, for bad inns, for the perpetual scramble, for ill-humour. Everywhere the same impression, – the platitude of unbalanced democracy intensified by the platitude of the spirit of commerce. Everything on an immense scale – everything illustrated by millions of examples. My brother-in-law is always busy; he has appointments, inspections, interviews, disputes. The people, it appears, are incredibly sharp in conversation, in argument; they wait for you in silence at the corner of the road, and then they suddenly discharge their revolver. If you fall, they empty your pockets; the only chance is to shoot them first. With that, no amenities, no preliminaries, no manners, no care for the appearance. I wander about while my brother is occupied; I lounge along the streets; I stop at the corners; I look into the shops; *je regarde passer les femmes*. It's an easy country to see; one sees everything there is; the civilisation is skin deep; you don't have to dig. This positive, practical, pushing *bourgeoisie* is always about its business; it lives in the street, in the hotel, in the train; one is always in a crowd – there are seventy-five people in the tramway. They sit in your lap; they stand on your toes; when they wish to pass, they simply push you. Everything in silence; they know that silence is golden, and they have the worship of gold. When the conductor wishes your fare, he gives you a poke, very serious, without a word. As for the types – but there is only one – they are all variations of the same – the *commis-voyageur* minus the gaiety. The women are often pretty; you meet the young ones in the streets, in the trains, in search of a husband. They look at you frankly, coldly, judicially, to see if you will serve; but they don't want what you might think (*du moins on me l'assure*); they only want the husband.

A Frenchman may mistake; he needs to be sure he is right, and I always make sure. They begin at fifteen; the mother sends them out; it lasts all day (with an interval for dinner at a pastry-cook's); sometimes it goes on for ten years. If they haven't found the husband then, they give it up; they make place for the *cadettes*, as the number of women is enormous. No *salons*, no society, no conversation; people don't receive at home; the young girls have to look for the husband where they can. It is no disgrace not to find him – several have never done so. They continue to go about unmarried – from the force of habit, from the love of movement, without hopes, without regrets – no imagination, no sensibility, no desire for the convent. We have made several journeys, – few of less than three hundred miles. Enormous trains, enormous *wagons*, with beds and lava-tories, and negroes who brush you with a big broom, as if they were grooming a horse. A bounding movement, a roaring noise, a crowd of people who look horribly tired, a boy who passes up and down throwing pamphlets and sweetmeats into your lap – that is an American journey. There are windows in the *wagons* – enormous, like everything else; but there is noth-ing to see. The country is a void – no features, no objects, no details, nothing to show you that you are in one place more than another. *Aussi*, you are not in one place; you are everywhere, anywhere; the train goes a hundred miles an hour. The cities are all the same; little houses ten feet high, or else big ones two hundred; tramways, telegraph-poles, enormous signs, holes in the pavement, oceans of mud, *commis-voyageurs*, young ladies looking for the husband. On the other hand, no beggars and no *cocottes* – none, at least, that you see. A colossal mediocrity, except (my brother-in-law tells me) in the machinery, which is magnificent. Naturally, no architecture (they make houses of wood and of iron), no art, no literature, no theatre. I have opened some of the books; *mais ils ne se laissent pas lire*. No form, no matter, no style, no general ideas; they seem to be written for children and young ladies. The most successful (those that they praise most) are the facetious; they sell in thousands of editions. I have looked into some of the most *vantés*; but you need to be forewarned, to know that they are

amusing; *des plaisanteries de croquemort*. They have a novelist
with pretensions to literature, who writes about the chase for
the husband and the adventures of the rich Americans in
our corrupt old Europe, where their primaeval candour puts
the Europeans to shame. *C'est proprement écrit*; but it's terribly
pale. What isn't pale is the newspapers – enormous, like everything else (fifty columns of advertisements), and full of the *commérages* of a continent. And such a tone, *grand Dieu!*
The amenities, the personalities, the recriminations, are like so
many *coups de revolver*. Headings six inches tall; correspond-
ences from places one never heard of; telegrams from Europe
about Sarah Bernhardt; little paragraphs about nothing at all;
the *menu* of the neighbour's dinner; articles on the European
situation *à pouffer de rire*; all the *tripotage* of local politics. The
reportage is incredible; I am chased up and down by the interviewers. The matrimonial infelicities of M. and Madame X.
(they give the name), *tout au long*, with every detail – not in six
lines, discreetly veiled, with an art of insinuation, as with us; but
with all the facts (or the fictions), the letters, the dates, the
places, the hours. I open a paper at hazard, and I find *au beau
milieu, à propos* of nothing, the announcement – 'Miss
Susan Green has the longest nose in Western New York.'
Miss Susan Green (*je me renseigne*) is a celebrated authoress;
and the Americans have the reputation of spoiling their women.
They spoil them *à coups de poing*. We have seen few interiors (no
one speaks French); but if the newspapers give an idea of the
domestic *mœurs*, the *mœurs* must be curious. The passport is
abolished, but they have printed my *signalement* in these sheets, –
perhaps for the young ladies who look for the husband. We
went one night to the theatre; the piece was French (they are
the only ones), but the acting was American – too American; we
came out in the middle. The want of taste is incredible. An
Englishman whom I met tells me that even the language corrupts itself from day to day; an Englishman ceases to understand. It encourages me to find that I am not the only one. There
are things every day that one can't describe. Such is Washington,
where we arrived this morning, coming from Philadelphia. My
brother-in-law wishes to see the Bureau of Patents, and on our

arrival he went to look at his machines, while I walked about the streets and visited the Capitol! The human machine is what interests me most. I don't even care for the political – for that's what they call their government here – 'the machine'. It operates very roughly, and some day, evidently, it will explode. It is true that you would never suspect that they have a government; this is the principal seat, but, save for three or four big buildings, most of them *affreux*, it looks like a settlement of negroes. No movement, no officials, no authority, no embodiment of the State. Enormous streets, *comme toujours*, lined with little red houses where nothing ever passes but the tramway. The Capitol – a vast structure, false classic, white marble, iron and stucco, which has *assez grand air* – must be seen to be appreciated. The goddess of liberty on the top, dressed in a bear's skin; their liberty over here is the liberty of bears. You go into the Capitol as you would into a railway station; you walk about as you would in the Palais Royal. No functionaries, no door-keepers, no officers, no uniforms, no badges, no restrictions, no authority – nothing but a crowd of shabby people circulating in a labyrinth of spittoons. We are too much governed perhaps in France; but at least we have a certain incarnation of the national conscience, of the national dignity. The dignity is absent here, and I am told that the conscience is an abyss. '*L'état c'est moi*' even – I like that better than the spittoons. These implements are architectural, monumental; they are the only monuments. *En somme*, the country is interesting, now that we too have the Republic; it is the biggest illustration, the biggest warning. It is the last word of democracy, and that word is – flatness. It is very big, very rich, and perfectly ugly. A Frenchman couldn't live here; for life with us, after all, at the worst is a sort of appreciation. Here, there is nothing to appreciate. As for the people, they are the English *minus* the conventions. You can fancy what remains. The women, *pourtant*, are sometimes rather well turned. There was one at Philadelphia – I made her acquaintance by accident – whom it is probable I shall see again. She is not looking for the husband; she has already got one. It was at the hotel; I think the husband doesn't matter. A Frenchman, as I have said, may mistake, and he needs to be sure he is right. *Aussi*, I always make sure!

VII

From MARCELLUS COCKEREL, *in Washington, to* Mrs COOLER, *née* COCKEREL, *at Oakland, California*

October 25

I OUGHT to have written to you long before this, for I have had your last excellent letter for four months in my hands. The first half of that time I was still in Europe; the last I have spent on my native soil. I think, therefore, my silence is owing to the fact that over there I was too miserable to write, and that here I have been too happy. I got back the 1st of September – you will have seen it in the papers. Delightful country, where one sees everything in the papers – the big, familiar, vulgar, good-natured, delightful papers, none of which has any reputation to keep up for anything but getting the news! I really think that has had as much to do as anything else with my satisfaction at getting home – the difference in what they call the 'tone of the press'. In Europe it's too dreary – the sapience, the solemnity, the false respectability, the verbosity, the long disquisitions on superannuated subjects. Here the newspapers are like the rail-road trains, which carry everything that comes to the station, and have only the religion of punctuality. As a woman, however, you probably detest them; you think they are (the great word) vulgar. I admitted it just now, and I am very happy to have an early opportunity to announce to you that that idea has quite ceased to have any terrors for me. There are some conceptions to which the female mind can never rise. Vulgarity is a stupid, superficial, question-begging accusation, which has become to-day the easiest refuge of mediocrity. Better than anything else, it saves people the trouble of thinking, and anything which does that succeeds. You must know that in these last three years in Europe I have become terribly vulgar myself; that's one service my travels have rendered me. By three years in Europe I mean three years in foreign parts altogether, for I spent several months of that time in Japan, India, and the rest of the East. Do you remember when you bade me good-by in San Francisco, the night before I embarked for Yokohama? You foretold that I should take such a fancy to foreign life that America would never see me more, and that if *you* should wish to see me (an event you were good enough to regard as possible), you would have to make a rendezvous in Paris or in Rome. I think we made one (which you never kept), but I shall never make another for those cities. It was in Paris, however, that I got your letter; I remember the moment as well as if it were (to my honour) much more recent. You must know that, among many places I dislike, Paris carries the palm. I am bored to death there; it's the home of every humbug. The life is full of that false comfort which is worse than discomfort, and the small, fat, irritable people give me the shivers. I had been making these reflections even more devoutly than usual one very tiresome evening toward the beginning of last summer, when, as I re-entered my hotel at ten o'clock, the little reptile of a portress handed me your gracious lines. I was in a villainous humour. I had been having an over-dressed dinner in a stuffy restaurant, and had gone from there to a suffocating theatre, where, by way of amusement, I saw a play in which blood and lies were the least of the horrors. The theatres over there are insupportable; the atmosphere is pestilential. People sit with their elbows in your sides; they squeeze past you every half-hour. It was one of my bad moments; I have a great many in Europe. The conventional, perfunctory play, all in falsetto, which I seemed to have seen a thousand times; the horrible faces of the people; the pushing, bullying *ouvreuse*, with her false politeness and her real rapacity, drove me out of the place at the end of an hour; and, as it was too early to go home, I sat down before a *café* on the Boulevard, where they served me a glass of sour, watery beer. There on the Boulevard, in the summer night, life itself was even uglier than the play, and it wouldn't do for me to tell you what I saw. Besides, I was sick of the Boulevard, with its eternal grimace and the deadly sameness of the *article de Paris*, which pretends to be so various – the shop-windows a wilderness of rubbish and the passers-by a procession of manikins. Suddenly it came over me that I was

supposed to be amusing myself – my face was a yard long – and
that you probably at that moment were saying to your husband:
'He stays away so long! What a good time he must be having!'
The idea was the first thing that had made me smile for a
month; I got up and walked home, reflecting, as I went, that
I was 'seeing Europe', and that, after all, one *must* see Europe.
It was because I had been convinced of this that I came out, and
it is because the operation has been brought to a close that
I have been so happy for the last eight weeks. I was very conscientious about it, and, though your letter that night made me
abominably homesick, I held out to the end, knowing it to be
once for all. I sha'n't trouble Europe again; I shall see America
for the rest of my days. My long delay has had the advantage
that now, at least, I can give you my impressions – I don't mean
of Europe; impressions of Europe are easy to get – but of this
country, as it strikes the re-instated exile. Very likely you'll
think them queer; but keep my letter, and twenty years hence
they will be quite commonplace. They won't even be vulgar. It
was very deliberate, my going round the world. I knew that one
ought to see for one's self, and that I should have eternity, so to
speak, to rest. I travelled energetically; I went everywhere and
saw everything; took as many letters as possible, and made as
many acquaintances. In short, I held my nose to the grindstone.
The upshot of it all is that I have got rid of a superstition. We
have so many, that one the less – perhaps the biggest of all –
makes a real difference in one's comfort. The superstition in
question – of course you have it – is that there is no salvation but
through Europe. Our salvation is here, if we have eyes to see it,
and the salvation of Europe into the bargain; that is, if Europe is
to be saved, which I rather doubt. Of course, you'll call me a
bird o' freedom, a braggart, a waver of the stars and stripes; but
I'm in the delightful position of not minding in the least what
any one calls me. I haven't a mission; I don't want to preach;
I have simply arrived at a state of mind; I have got Europe off my
back. You have no idea how it simplifies things, and how jolly it
makes me feel. Now I can live; now I can talk. If we wretched
Americans could only say once for all, 'Oh, Europe be hanged!'
we should attend much better to our proper business. We have

simply to live our life, and the rest will look after itself. You will probably inquire what it is that I like better over here, and I will answer that it's simply – life. Disagreeables for disagreeables, I prefer our own. The way I have been bored and bullied in foreign parts, and the way I have had to say I found it pleasant! For a good while this appeared to be a sort of congenital obligation, but one fine day it occurred to me that there was no obligation at all, and that it would ease me immensely to admit to myself that (for me, at least) all those things had no importance. I mean the things they rub into you in Europe; the tiresome international topics, the petty politics, the stupid social customs, the baby-house scenery. The vastness and freshness of this American world, the great scale and great pace of our development, the good sense and good nature of the people, console me for there being no cathedrals and no Titians. I hear nothing about Prince Bismarck and Gambetta, about the Emperor William and the Czar of Russia, about Lord Beaconsfield and the Prince of Wales. I used to get so tired of their Mumbo-Jumbo of a Bismarck, of his secrets and surprises, his mysterious intentions and oracular words. They revile us for our party politics; but what are all the European jealousies and rivalries, their armaments and their wars, their rapacities and their mutual lies, but the intensity of the spirit of party? what question, what interest, what idea, what need of mankind, is involved in any of these things? Their big, pompous armies, drawn up in great silly rows, their gold lace, their salaams, their hierarchies, seem a pastime for children; there's a sense of humour and of reality over here that laughs at all that. Yes, we are nearer the reality – we are nearer what they will all have to come to. The questions of the future are social questions, which the Bismarcks and Beaconsfields are very much afraid to see settled; and the sight of a row of supercilious potentates holding their peoples like their personal property, and bristling all over, to make a mutual impression, with feathers and sabres, strikes us as a mixture of the grotesque and the abominable. What do we care for the mutual impressions of potentates who amuse themselves with sitting on people? Those things are their own affair, and they ought to be shut up in a dark room to have it out together. Once one feels, over here, that the great questions of the future are social questions, that a mighty tide is sweeping the world to democracy, and that this country is the biggest stage on which the drama can be enacted, the fashionable European topics seem petty and parochial. They talk about things that we have settled ages ago, and the solemnity with which they propound to you their little domestic embarrassments makes a heavy draft on one's good nature. In England they were talking about the Hares and Rabbits Bill, about the extension of the County Franchise, about the Dissenters' Burials, about the Deceased Wife's Sister, about the abolition of the House of Lords, about heaven knows what ridiculous little measure for the propping-up of their ridiculous little country. And they call *us* provincial! It is hard to sit and look respectable while people discuss the utility of the House of Lords and the beauty of a State Church, and it's only in a dowdy, musty civilisation that you'll find them doing such things. The lightness and clearness of the social air, that's the great relief in these parts. The gentility of bishops, the propriety of parsons, even the impressiveness of a restored cathedral, give less of a charm to life than that. I used to be furious with the bishops and parsons, with the humbuggery of the whole affair, which every one was conscious of, but which people agreed not to expose, because they would be compromised all round. The convenience of life over here, the quick and simple arrangements, the absence of the spirit of routine, are a blessed change from the stupid stiffness with which I struggled for two long years. There were people with swords and cockades who used to order me about; for the simplest operation of life I had to kootoo to some bloated official. When it was a question of my doing a little differently from others, the bloated official gasped as if I had given him a blow on the stomach; he needed to take a week to think of it. On the other hand, it's impossible to take an American by surprise; he is ashamed to confess that he has not the wit to do a thing that another man has had the wit to think of. Besides being as good as his neighbour, he must therefore be as clever, – which is an affliction only to people who are afraid he may be cleverer. If this general efficiency and spontaneity of the people – the union of the sense of freedom with the love of knowledge – isn't the very essence of a high civilisation, I don't know what a high civilisation is. I felt this greater ease on my first railroad journey, – felt the blessing of sitting in a train where I could move about, where I could stretch my legs and come and go, where I had a seat and a window to myself, where there were chairs and tables and food and drink. The villainous little boxes on the European trains, in which you are stuck down in a corner, with doubled-up knees, opposite to a row of people – often most offensive types – who stare at you for ten hours on end – these were part of my two years' ordeal. The large, free way of doing things here is everywhere a pleasure. In London, at my hotel, they used to come to me on Saturday to make me order my Sunday's dinner, and when I asked for a sheet of paper, they put it into the bill. The meagreness, the stinginess, the perpetual expectation of a sixpence, used to exasperate me. Of course, I saw a great many people who were pleasant; but as I am writing to you, and not to one of them, I may say that they were dreadfully apt to be dull. The imagination among the people I see here is more flexible; and then they have the advantage of a larger horizon. It's not bounded on the north by the British aristocracy, and on the south by the *scrutin de liste*. (I mix up the countries a little, but they are not worth the keeping apart.) The absence of little conventional measurements, of little cut-and-dried judgements, is an immense refreshment. We are more analytic, more dis-criminating, more familiar with realities. As for manners, there are bad manners everywhere, but an aristocracy is bad manners organised. (I don't mean that they may not be polite among themselves, but they are rude to every one else.) The sight of all these growing millions simply minding their business, is impressive to me, – more so than all the gilt buttons and padded chests of the Old World; and there is a certain powerful type of 'practical' American (you'll find him chiefly in the West), who doesn't brag as I do (I'm not practical), but who quietly feels that he has the Future in his vitals, – a type that strikes me more than any I met in your favourite countries. Of course you'll come back to the cathedrals and Titians, but there's a thought that helps one to do without them, – the thought that though there's an immense deal of plainness, there's little misery, little squalour, little degradation. There is no regular wife-beating class, and there are none of the stultified peasants of whom it takes so many to make a European noble. The people here are more conscious of things; they invent, they act, they answer for themselves; they are not (I speak of social matters) tied up by authority and precedent. We shall have all the Titians by and by, and we shall move over a few cathedrals. You had better stay here if you want to have the best. Of course, I am a roaring Yankee; but you'll call me that if I say the least, so I may as well take my ease and say the most. Washington's a most entertaining place; and here at least, at the seat of government, one isn't overgoverned. In fact, there's no government at all to speak of; it seems too good to be true. The first day I was here I went to the Capitol, and it took me ever so long to figure to myself that I had as good a right there as any one else, – that the whole magnificent pile (it *is* magnificent by the way) was in fact my own. In Europe one doesn't rise to such conceptions, and my spirit had been broken in Europe. The doors were gaping wide – I walked all about; there were no door-keepers, no officers, nor flunkeys, – not even a policeman to be seen. It seemed strange not to see a uniform, if only as a patch of colour. But this isn't government by livery. The absence of these things is odd at first; you seem to miss something, to fancy the machine has stopped. It hasn't, though; it only works without fire and smoke. At the end of three days, this simple negative impression – the fact is that there are no soldiers nor spies, nothing but plain black coats – begins to affect the imagination, becomes vivid, majestic, symbolic. It ends by being more impressive than the biggest review I saw in Germany. Of course, I'm a roaring Yankee; but one has to take a big brush to copy a big model. The future is here, of course; but it isn't only that – the present is here as well. You will complain that I don't give you any personal news; but I am more modest for myself than for my country. I spent a month in New York, and while I was there I saw a good deal of a rather interesting girl who came over with me in the steamer, and whom for a day or two I thought I should like to marry. But I shouldn't. She has been spoiled by Europe!

VIII

From Miss AURORA CHURCH, *in New York, to* Miss WHITESIDE, *in Paris*

January 9

I TOLD you (after we landed) about my agreement with mamma – that I was to have my liberty for three months, and if at the end of this time I shouldn't have made a good use of it, I was to give it back to her. Well, the time is up to-day, and I am very much afraid I haven't made a good use of it. In fact, I haven't made any use of it at all – I haven't got married, for that is what mamma meant by our little bargain. She has been trying to marry me in Europe, for years, without a *dot*, and as she has never (to the best of my knowledge) even come near it, she thought at last that, if she were to leave it to me, I might do better. I couldn't certainly do worse. Well, my dear, I have done very badly – that is, I haven't done at all. I haven't even tried. I had an idea that this affair came of itself over here; but it hasn't come to me. I won't say I am disappointed, for I haven't, on the whole, seen any one I should like to marry. When you marry people over here, they expect you to love them, and I haven't seen any one I should like to love. I don't know what the reason is, but they are none of them what I have thought of. It may be that I have thought of the impossible; and yet I have seen people in Europe whom I should have liked to marry. It is true, they were almost always married to some one else. What I *am* disappointed in is simply having to give back my liberty. I don't wish particularly to be married; and I do wish to do as I like – as I have been doing for the last month. All the same, I am sorry for poor mamma, as nothing has happened that she wished to happen. To begin with, we are not appreciated, not even by the Rucks, who have disappeared, in the strange way in which people over here seem to vanish from the world. We have made no sensation; my new dresses count for nothing (they all have better ones); our philological and historical studies

don't show. We have been told we might do better in Boston;
but, on the other hand, mamma hears that in Boston the people
only marry their cousins. Then mamma is out of sorts because
the country is exceedingly dear and we have spent all our
money. Moreover, I have neither eloped, nor been insulted,
nor been talked about, nor – so far as I know – deteriorated in
manners or character; so that mamma is wrong in all her pre-
visions. I think she would have rather liked me to be insulted.
But I have been insulted as little as I have been adored. They
don't adore you over here; they only make you think they are
going to. Do you remember the two gentlemen who were on the
ship, and who, after we arrived here, came to see me *à tour de
rôle*? At first I never dreamed they were making love to me,
though mamma was sure it must be that; then, as it went on a
good while, I thought perhaps it *was* that; and I ended by seeing
that it wasn't anything! It was simply conversation; they are
very fond of conversation over here. Mr Leverett and
Mr Cockerel disappeared one fine day, without the smallest
pretension to having broken my heart, I am sure, though it only
depended on me to think they had! All the gentlemen are like
that; you can't tell what they mean; everything is very confused;
society appears to consist of a sort of innocent jilting. I think, on
the whole, I *am* a little disappointed – I don't mean about one's
not marrying; I mean about the life generally. It seems so
different at first, that you expect it will be very exciting; and
then you find that, after all, when you have walked out for a
week or two by yourself and driven out with a gentleman in a
buggy, that's about all there is of it, as they say here. Mamma is
very angry at not finding more to dislike; she admitted yesterday that, once one has got a little settled, the country has not
even the merit of being hateful. This has evidently something to
do with her suddenly proposing three days ago that we should
go to the West. Imagine my surprise at such an idea coming
from mamma! The people in the pension – who, as usual, wish
immensely to get rid of her – have talked to her about the West,
and she has taken it up with a kind of desperation. You see, we
must do something; we can't simply remain here. We are
rapidly being ruined, and we are not – so to speak – getting

married. Perhaps it will be easier in the West; at any rate, it will be cheaper, and the country will have the advantage of being more hateful. It is a question between that and returning to Europe, and for the moment mamma is balancing. I say nothing: I am really indifferent; perhaps I shall marry a pioneer. I am just thinking how I shall give back my liberty. It really won't be possible; I haven't got it any more; I have given it away to others. Mamma may recover it, if she can, from *them*! She comes in at this moment to say that we must push farther – she has decided for the West. Wonderful mamma! It appears that my real chance is for a pioneer – they have sometimes millions. But, fancy us in the West!

THE SIEGE OF LONDON

PART I

I

THAT solemn piece of upholstery, the curtain of the Comédie Française, had fallen upon the first act of the piece, and our two Americans had taken advantage of the interval to pass out of the huge, hot theatre, in company with the other occupants of the stalls. But they were among the first to return, and they beguiled the rest of the intermission with looking at the house, which had lately been cleansed of its historic cobwebs and ornamented with frescos illustrative of the classic drama. In the month of September the audience at the Théâtre Français is comparatively thin, and on this occasion the drama – *L'Aventurière* of Emile Augier – had no pretensions to novelty. Many of the boxes were empty, others were occupied by persons of provincial or nomadic appearance. The boxes are far from the stage, near which our spectators were placed; but even at a distance Rupert Waterville was able to appreciate certain details. He was fond of appreciating details, and when he went to the theatre he looked about him a good deal, making use of a dainty but remarkably powerful glass. He knew that such a course was wanting in true distinction, and that it was indelicate to level at a lady an instrument which was often only less injurious in effect than a double-barrelled pistol; but he was always very curious, and he was sure, in any case, that at that moment, at that antiquated play – so he was pleased to qualify the masterpiece of an Academician – he would not be observed by any one he knew. Standing up therefore with his back to the stage, he made the circuit of the boxes, while several other persons, near him, performed the same operation with even greater coolness.

'Not a single pretty woman,' he remarked at last to his friend; an observation which Littlemore, sitting in his place and staring with a bored expression at the new-looking curtain, received in perfect silence. He rarely indulged in these optical excursions; he had been a great deal in Paris and had ceased to care about it, or wonder about it, much; he fancied that the French capital could have no more surprises for him, though it had had a good many in former days. Waterville was still in the stage of surprise; he suddenly expressed this emotion. 'By Jove!' he exclaimed; 'I beg your pardon – I beg *her* pardon – there is, after all, a woman that may be called' – he paused a little, inspecting her – 'a kind of beauty!'

'What kind?' Littlemore asked, vaguely.

'An unusual kind – an indescribable kind.' Littlemore was not heeding his answer, but he presently heard himself appealed to. 'I say, I wish very much you would do me a favour.'

'I did you a favour in coming here,' said Littlemore. 'It's insufferably hot, and the play is like a dinner that has been dressed by the kitchen-maid. The actors are all *doublures*.'

'It's simply to answer me this: is *she* respectable, now?' Waterville rejoined, inattentive to his friend's epigram.

Littlemore gave a groan, without turning his head. 'You are always wanting to know if they are respectable. What on earth can it matter?'

'I have made such mistakes – I have lost all confidence,' said poor Waterville, to whom European civilisation had not ceased to be a novelty, and who during the last six months had found himself confronted with problems long unsuspected. Whenever he encountered a very nice-looking woman, he was sure to discover that she belonged to the class represented by the heroine of M. Augier's drama; and whenever his attention rested upon a person of a florid style of attraction, there was the strongest probability that she would turn out to be a countess. The countesses looked so superficial and the others looked so exclusive. Now Littlemore distinguished at a glance; he never made mistakes.

'Simply for looking at them, it doesn't matter, I suppose,' said Waterville, ingenuously, answering his companion's rather cynical inquiry.

'You stare at them all alike,' Littlemore went on, still without moving; 'except indeed when I tell you that they are not respectable – then your attention acquires a fixedness!'

'If your judgement is against this lady, I promise never to look at her again. I mean the one in the third box from the passage, in white, with the red flowers,' he added, as Littlemore slowly rose and stood beside him. 'The young man is leaning forward. It is the young man that makes me doubt of her. Will you have the glass?'

Littlemore looked about him without concentration. 'No, I thank you, my eyes are good enough. The young man's a very good young man,' he added in a moment.

'Very indeed; but he's several years younger than she. Wait till she turns her head.'

She turned it very soon – she apparently had been speaking to the *ouvreuse*, at the door of the box – and presented her face to the public – a fair, well-drawn face, with smiling eyes, smiling lips, ornamented over the brow with delicate rings of black hair and, in each ear, with the sparkle of a diamond sufficiently large to be seen across the Théâtre Français. Littlemore looked at her; then, abruptly, he gave an exclamation. 'Give me the glass!'

'Do you know her?' his companion asked, as he directed the little instrument.

Littlemore made no answer; he only looked in silence; then he handed back the glass. 'No, she's not respectable,' he said. And he dropped into his seat again. As Waterville remained standing, he added, 'Please sit down; I think she saw me.'

'Don't you want her to see you?' asked Waterville the interrogator, taking his seat.

Littlemore hesitated. 'I don't want to spoil her game.' By this time the *entr'acte* was at an end; the curtain rose again.

It had been Waterville's idea that they should go to the theatre. Littlemore, who was always for not doing a thing, had recommended that, the evening being lovely, they should simply sit and smoke at the door of the Grand Café, in a decent part of the Boulevard. Nevertheless Rupert Waterville enjoyed the second act even less than he had done the first, which he thought heavy. He began to wonder whether his companion would wish to stay to the end; a useless line of speculation, for now that he had got to the theatre, Littlemore's objection to doing things would certainly keep him from going. Waterville also wondered what he knew about the lady in the box. Once or twice he glanced at his friend, and then he saw that Littlemore was not following the play. He was thinking of something else; he was thinking of that woman. When the curtain fell again he sat in his place, making way for his neighbours, as usual, to edge past him, grinding his knees – his legs were long – with their own protuberances. When the two men were alone in the stalls, Littlemore said: 'I think I should like to see her again, after all.' He spoke as if Waterville might have known all about her. Waterville was conscious of not doing so, but as there was evidently a good deal to know, he felt that he should lose nothing by being a little discreet. So, for the moment, he asked no questions; he only said –

'Well, here's the glass.'

Littlemore gave him a glance of good-natured compassion. 'I don't mean that I want to stare at her with that beastly thing. I mean – to see her – as I used to see her.'

'How did you use to see her?' asked Waterville, bidding farewell to discretion.

'On the back piazza, at San Diego.' And as his interlocutor, in receipt of this information, only stared, he went on – 'Come out where we can breathe, and I'll tell you more.'

They made their way to the low and narrow door, more worthy of a rabbit-hutch than of a great theatre, by which you pass from the stalls of the Comédie to the lobby, and as Littlemore went first, his ingenuous friend, behind him, could see that he glanced up at the box in the occupants of which they were interested. The more interesting of these had her back to the house; she was apparently just leaving the box, after her companion; but as she had not put on her mantle it was evident that they were not quitting the theatre. Littlemore's pursuit of fresh air did not lead him into the street; he had passed his arm into Waterville's, and when they reached that fine frigid staircase which ascends to the Foyer, he began silently to mount it. Littlemore was averse to active pleasures, but his friend reflected that now at least he had launched himself – he was going to look for the lady whom, with a monosyllable, he

appeared to have classified. The young man resigned himself
for the moment to asking no questions, and the two strolled
together into the shining saloon where Houdon's admirable
statue of Voltaire, reflected in a dozen mirrors, is gaped at by
visitors obviously less acute than the genius expressed in those
living features. Waterville knew that Voltaire was very witty; he
had read *Candide*, and had already had several opportunities of
appreciating the statue. The Foyer was not crowded; only a
dozen groups were scattered over the polished floor, several
others having passed out to the balcony which overhangs the
square of the Palais Royal. The windows were open, the brilliant lights of Paris made the dull summer evening look like an
anniversary or a revolution; a murmur of voices seemed to
come up from the streets, and even in the Foyer one heard
the slow click of the horses and the rumble of the crookedly-
driven fiacres on the hard, smooth asphalt. A lady and a gentleman, with their backs to our friends, stood before the image of
Voltaire; the lady was dressed in white, including a white bonnet. Littlemore felt, as so many persons feel in that spot, that
the scene was conspicuously Parisian, and he gave a mysterious
laugh.

'It seems comical to see her here! The last time was in New
Mexico.'

'In New Mexico?'

'At San Diego.'

'Oh, on the back piazza,' said Waterville, putting things
together. He had not been aware of the position of San Diego,
for if on the occasion of his lately being appointed to a subordinate diplomatic post in London, he had been paying a good
deal of attention to European geography, he had rather
neglected that of his own country.

They had not spoken loud, and they were not standing near
her; but suddenly, as if she had heard them, the lady in white
turned round. Her eye caught Waterville's first, and in that
glance he saw that if she had heard them it was not because
they were audible but because she had extraordinary quickness
of ear. There was no recognition in it – there was none, at
first, even when it rested lightly upon George Littlemore. But

recognition flashed out a moment later, accompanied with a delicate increase of colour and a quick extension of her apparently constant smile. She had turned completely round; she stood there in sudden friendliness, with parted lips, with a hand, gloved to the elbow, almost imperiously offered. She was even prettier than at a distance. 'Well, I declare!' she exclaimed; so loud that every one in the room appeared to feel personally addressed. Waterville was surprised; he had not been prepared, even after the mention of the back piazza, to find her an American. Her companion turned round as she spoke; he was a fresh, lean young man, in evening dress; he kept his hands in his pockets; Waterville imagined that he at any rate was not an American. He looked very grave – for such a fair, festive young man – and gave Waterville and Littlemore, though his height was not superior to theirs, a narrow, vertical glance. Then he turned back to the statue of Voltaire, as if it had been, after all, among his premonitions that the lady he was attending would recognise people he didn't know, and didn't even, perhaps, care to know. This possibly confirmed slightly Littlemore's assertion that she was not respectable. The young man was, at least; consummately so. 'Where in the world did you drop from?' the lady inquired.

'I have been here some time,' Littlemore said, going forward, rather deliberately, to shake hands with her. He smiled a little, but he was more serious than she; he kept his eye on her own as if she had been just a trifle dangerous; it was the manner in which a duly discreet person would have approached some glossy, graceful animal which had an occasional trick of biting.

'Here in Paris, do you mean?'

'No; here and there – in Europe generally.'

'Well, it's queer I haven't met you.'

'Better late than never!' said Littlemore. His smile was a little fixed.

'Well, you look very natural,' the lady went on.

'So do you – or very charming – it's the same thing,' Littlemore answered, laughing, and evidently wishing to be easy. It was as if, face to face, and after a considerable lapse of time, he had found her more imposing than he expected when, in the stalls below, he determined to come and meet her. As he spoke, the young man who was with her gave up his inspection of Voltaire and faced about, listlessly, without looking either at Littlemore or at Waterville.

'I want to introduce you to my friend,' she went on. 'Sir Arthur Demesne – Mr Littlemore. Mr Littlemore – Sir Arthur Demesne. Sir Arthur Demesne is an Englishman – Mr Littlemore is a countryman of mine, an old friend. I haven't seen him for years. For how long? Don't let's count! – I wonder you knew me,' she continued, addressing Littlemore. 'I'm fearfully changed.' All this was said in a clear, gay tone, which was the more audible as she spoke with a kind of caressing slowness. The two men, to do honour to her introduction, silently exchanged a glance; the Englishman, perhaps, coloured a little. He was very conscious of his companion. 'I haven't introduced you to many people yet,' she remarked.

'Oh, I don't mind,' said Sir Arthur Demesne.

'Well, it's queer to see you!' she exclaimed, looking still at Littlemore. 'You have changed, too – I can see that.'

'Not where you are concerned.'

'That's what I want to find out. Why don't you introduce your friend? I see he's dying to know me!'

Littlemore proceeded to this ceremony; but he reduced it to its simplest elements, merely glancing at Rupert Waterville, and murmuring his name.

'You didn't tell him *my* name,' the lady cried, while Waterville made her a formal salutation. 'I hope you haven't forgotten it!'

Littlemore gave her a glance which was intended to be more penetrating than what he had hitherto permitted himself; if it had been put into words it would have said, 'Ah, but *which* name?'

She answered the unspoken question, putting out her hand, as she had done to Littlemore, 'Happy to make your acquaintance, Mr Waterville. I'm Mrs Headway – perhaps you've heard of me. If you've ever been in America you must have heard of me. Not so much in New York, but in the Western cities. You *are* an American? Well, then, we are all compatriots – except Sir

Arthur Demesne. Let me introduce you to Sir Arthur.
Sir Arthur Demesne, Mr Waterville – Mr Waterville, Sir Arthur
Demesne. Sir Arthur Demesne is a member of Parliament;
don't he look young?' She waited for no answer to this question, but suddenly asked another, as she moved her bracelets
back over her long, loose gloves. 'Well, Mr Littlemore, what are
you thinking of?'

He was thinking that he must indeed have forgotten her
name, for the one that she had pronounced awakened no
association. But he could hardly tell her that.

'I'm thinking of San Diego.'

'The back piazza, at my sister's? Oh, don't; it was too horrid.
She has left now. I believe every one has left.'

Sir Arthur Demesne drew out his watch with the air of a man
who could take no part in these domestic reminiscences; he
appeared to combine a generic self-possession with a degree of
individual shyness. He said something about its being time they
should go back to their seats, but Mrs Headway paid no attention to the remark. Waterville wished her to linger; he felt in
looking at her as if he had been looking at a charming picture.
Her low-growing hair, with its fine dense undulations, was of a
shade of blackness that has now become rare; her complexion
had the bloom of a white flower; her profile, when she turned
her head, was as pure and fine as the outline of a cameo.

'You know this is the first theatre,' she said to Waterville, as if
she wished to be sociable. 'And this is Voltaire, the celebrated
writer.'

'I'm devoted to the Comédie Française,' Waterville
answered, smiling.

'Dreadfully bad house; we didn't hear a word,' said Sir
Arthur.

'Ah, yes, the boxes!' murmured Waterville.

'I'm rather disappointed,' Mrs Headway went on. 'But
I want to see what becomes of that woman.'

'Doña Clorinde? Oh, I suppose they'll shoot her; they generally shoot the women, in French plays,' Littlemore said.

'It will remind me of San Diego!' cried Mrs Headway.

'Ah, at San Diego the women did the shooting.'

'They don't seem to have killed you!' Mrs Headway rejoined, archly.

'No, but I am riddled with wounds.'

'Well, this is very remarkable,' the lady went on, turning to Houdon's statue. 'It's beautifully modelled.'

'You are perhaps reading M. de Voltaire,' Littlemore suggested.

'No; but I've purchased his works.'

'They are not proper reading for ladies,' said the young Englishman, severely, offering his arm to Mrs Headway.

'Ah, you might have told me before I had bought them!' she exclaimed, in exaggerated dismay.

'I couldn't imagine you would buy a hundred and fifty volumes.'

'A hundred and fifty? I have only bought two.'

'Perhaps two won't hurt you?' said Littlemore with a smile.

She darted him a reproachful ray. 'I know what you mean, – that I'm too bad already. Well, bad as I am, you must come and see me.' And she threw him the name of her hotel, as she walked away with her Englishman. Waterville looked after the latter with a certain interest; he had heard of him in London, and had seen his portrait in 'Vanity Fair'.

It was not yet time to go down, in spite of this gentleman's saying so, and Littlemore and his friend passed out on the balcony of the Foyer. 'Headway – Headway? Where the deuce did she get that name?' Littlemore asked, as they looked down into the animated dusk.

'From her husband, I suppose,' Waterville suggested.

'From her husband? From which? The last was named Beck.'

'How many has she had?' Waterville inquired, anxious to hear how it was that Mrs Headway was not respectable.

'I haven't the least idea. But it wouldn't be difficult to find out, as I believe they are all living. She was Mrs Beck – Nancy Beck – when I knew her.'

'Nancy Beck!' cried Waterville, aghast. He was thinking of her delicate profile, like that of a pretty Roman empress. There was a great deal to be explained.

Littlemore explained it in a few words before they returned to their places, admitting indeed that he was not yet able to elucidate her present situation. She was a memory of his Western days; he had seen her last some six years before. He had known her very well and in several places; the circle of her activity was chiefly the Southwest. This activity was of a vague character, except in the sense that it was exclusively social. She was supposed to have a husband, one Philadelphus Beck, the editor of a Democratic newspaper, the *Dakotah Sentinel*; but Littlemore had never seen him – the pair were living apart – and it was the impression at San Diego that matrimony, for Mr and Mrs Beck, was about played out. He remembered now to have heard afterwards that she was getting a divorce. She got divorces very easily, she was so taking in court. She had got one or two before from a man whose name he had forgotten, and there was a legend that even these were not the first. She had been exceedingly divorced! When he first met her in California, she called herself Mrs Grenville, which he had been given to understand was not an appellation acquired in matrimony, but her parental name, resumed after the dissolution of an unfortunate union. She had had these episodes – her unions were all unfortunate – and had borne half a dozen names. She was a charming woman, especially for New Mexico; but she had been divorced too often – it was a tax on one's credulity; she must have repudiated more husbands than she had married.

At San Diego she was staying with her sister, whose actual spouse (she, too, had been divorced), the principal man of the place, kept a bank (with the aid of a six-shooter), and who had never suffered Nancy to want for a home during her unattached periods. Nancy had begun very young; she must be about thirty-seven to-day. That was all he meant by her not being respectable. The chronology was rather mixed; her sister at least had once told him that there was one winter when she didn't know herself *who* was Nancy's husband. She had gone in mainly for editors – she esteemed the journalistic profession. They must all have been dreadful ruffians, for her own amiability was manifest. It was well known that whatever she had done she had done in self-defence. In fine, she had done things;

that was the main point now! She was very pretty, good-natured and clever, and quite the best company in those parts. She was a genuine product of the far West – a flower of the Pacific slope; ignorant, audacious, crude, but full of pluck and spirit, of natural intelligence, and of a certain intermittent, haphazard good taste. She used to say that she only wanted a chance – apparently she had found it now. At one time, without her, he didn't see how he could have put up with the life. He had started a cattle-ranch, to which San Diego was the nearest town, and he used to ride over to see her. Sometimes he stayed there for a week; then he went to see her every evening. It was horribly hot; they used to sit on the back piazza. She was always as attractive, and very nearly as well-dressed, as they had just beheld her. As far as appearance went, she might have been transplanted at an hour's notice from that dusty old settlement to the city by the Seine.

'Some of those Western women are wonderful,' Littlemore said. 'Like her, they only want a chance.'

He had not been in love with her – there never was anything of that sort between them. There might have been, of course; but as it happened there was not. Headway apparently was the successor of Beck; perhaps there had been others between. She was in no sort of 'society'; she only had a local reputation ('the elegant and accomplished Mrs Beck', the newspapers called her – the other editors, to whom she wasn't married), though, indeed, in that spacious civilisation the locality was large. She knew nothing of the East, and to the best of his belief at that period had never seen New York. Various things might have happened in those six years, however; no doubt she had 'come up'. The West was sending us everything (Littlemore spoke as a New Yorker); no doubt it would send us at last our brilliant women. This little woman used to look quite over the head of New York; even in those days she thought and talked of Paris, which there was no prospect of her knowing; that was the way she had got on in New Mexico. She had had her ambition, her presentiments; she had known she was meant for better things. Even at San Diego she had prefigured her little Sir Arthur; every now and then a wandering Englishman came within her range. They were not all baronets and M.P.s, but they were usually a change from the editors. What she was doing with her present acquisition he was curious to see. She was certainly – if he had any capacity for that state of mind, which was not too apparent – making him happy. She looked very splendid; Headway had probably made a 'pile', an achievement not to be imputed to any of the others. She didn't accept money – he was sure she didn't accept money.

On their way back to their seats Littlemore, whose tone had been humorous, but with that strain of the pensive which is inseparable from retrospect, suddenly broke into audible laughter.

'The modelling of a statue and the works of Voltaire!' he exclaimed, recurring to two or three things she had said. 'It's comical to hear her attempt those flights, for in New Mexico she knew nothing about modelling.'

'She didn't strike me as affected,' Waterville rejoined, feeling a vague impulse to take a considerate view of her.

'Oh, no; she's only – as she says – fearfully changed.'

They were in their places before the play went on again, and they both gave another glance at Mrs Headway's box. She leaned back, slowly fanning herself, and evidently watching Littlemore, as if she had been waiting to see him come in. Sir Arthur Demesne sat beside her, rather gloomily, resting a round pink chin upon a high stiff collar; neither of them seemed to speak.

'Are you sure she makes him happy?' Waterville asked.

'Yes – that's the way those people show it.'

'But does she go about alone with him that way? Where's her husband?'

'I suppose she has divorced him.'

'And does she want to marry the baronet?' Waterville asked, as if his companion were omniscient.

It amused Littlemore for the moment to appear so. 'He wants to marry her, I guess.'

'And be divorced, like the others?'

'Oh, no; this time she has got what she wants,' said Littlemore, as the curtain rose.

He suffered three days to elapse before he called at the Hôtel Meurice, which she had designated, and we may occupy this interval in adding a few words to the story we have taken from his lips. George Littlemore's residence in the far West had been of the usual tentative sort – he had gone there to replenish a pocket depleted by youthful extravagance. His first attempts had failed; the days were passing away when a fortune was to be picked up even by a young man who might be supposed to have inherited from an honourable father, lately removed, some of those fine abilities, mainly dedicated to the importation of tea, to which the elder Mr Littlemore was indebted for the power of leaving his son well off. Littlemore had dissipated his patrimony, and he was not quick to discover his talents, which, consisting chiefly of an unlimited faculty for smoking and horse-breaking, appeared to lie in the direction of none of the professions called liberal. He had been sent to Harvard to have his aptitudes cultivated, but here they took such a form that repression had been found more necessary than stimulus – repression embodied in an occasional sojourn in one of the lovely villages of the Connecticut valley. Rustication saved him, perhaps, in the sense that it detached him; it destroyed his ambitions, which had been foolish. At the age of thirty, Littlemore had mastered none of the useful arts, unless we include in the number the great art of indifference. He was roused from his indifference by a stroke of good luck. To oblige a friend who was even in more pressing need of cash than himself, he had purchased for a moderate sum (the proceeds of a successful game of poker) a share in a silver-mine which the disposer, with unusual candour, admitted to be destitute of metal. Littlemore looked into his mine and recognised the truth of the contention, which, however, was demolished some two years later by a sudden revival of curiosity on the part of one of the other shareholders. This gentleman, convinced that a silver-mine without silver is as rare as an effect without a cause, discovered the sparkle of the precious element deep down in the reasons of things. The discovery was agreeable to Littlemore, and was the beginning of a fortune which, through several dull years and in many rough places, he had repeatedly despaired of, and which a man whose purpose was never very keen did not perhaps altogether deserve. It was before he saw himself successful that he had made the acquaintance of the lady now established at the Hôtel Meurice. To-day he owned the largest share in his mine, which remained perversely productive, and which enabled him to buy, among other things, in Montana, a cattle-ranch of much finer proportions than the dry acres near San Diego. Ranches and mines encourage security, and the consciousness of not having to watch the sources of his income too anxiously (an obligation which for a man of his disposition spoils everything) now added itself to his usual coolness. It was not that this same coolness had not been considerably tried. To take only one – the principal – instance: he had lost his wife after only a twelvemonth of marriage, some three years before the date at which we meet him. He was more than forty when he encountered and wooed a young girl of twenty-three, who, like himself, had consulted all the probabilities in expecting a succession of happy years. She left him a small daughter, now intrusted to the care of his only sister, the wife of an English squire and mistress of a dull park in Hampshire. This lady, Mrs Dolphin by name, had captivated her landowner during a journey in which Mr Dolphin had promised himself to examine the institutions of the United States. The institution on which he reported most favourably was the pretty girls of the larger towns, and he returned to New York a year or two later to marry Miss Littlemore, who, unlike her brother, had not wasted her patrimony. Her sister-in-law, married many years later, and coming to Europe on this occasion, had died in London – where she flattered herself the doctors were infallible – a week after the birth of her little girl; and poor Littlemore, though relinquishing his child for the moment, remained in these disappointing countries, to be within call of the Hampshire nursery. He was rather a noticeable man, especially since his hair and moustache had turned white. Tall and strong, with a good figure and a bad carriage, he looked capable but indolent, and was usually supposed to have an importance of which he was far from being conscious. His eye was at once keen and quiet, his smile dim

and dilatory, but exceedingly genuine. His principal occupation to-day was doing nothing, and he did it with a sort of
artistic perfection. This faculty excited real envy on the part
of Rupert Waterville, who was ten years younger than he, and
who had too many ambitions and anxieties – none of them very
important, but making collectively a considerable incubus – to
be able to wait for inspiration. He thought it a great accomplishment, he hoped some day to arrive at it; it made a man so
independent; he had his resources within his own breast. Littlemore could sit for a whole evening, without utterance or
movement, smoking cigars and looking absently at his finger-
nails. As every one knew that he was a good fellow and had
made his fortune, this dull behaviour could not well be attributed to stupidity or to moroseness. It seemed to imply a fund of
reminiscence, an experience of life which had left him hundreds of things to think about. Waterville felt that if he could
make a good use of these present years, and keep a sharp look-
out for experience, he too, at forty-five, might have time to look
at his finger-nails. He had an idea that such contemplations –
not of course in their literal, but in their symbolic intensity –
were a sign of a man of the world. Waterville, reckoning
possibly without an ungrateful Department of State, had also
an idea that he had embraced the diplomatic career. He was the
junior of the two Secretaries who render the *personnel* of the
United States Legation in London exceptionally numerous,
and was at present enjoying his annual leave of absence. It
became a diplomatist to be inscrutable, and though he had by
no means, as a whole, taken Littlemore as his model – there
were much better ones in the diplomatic body in London – he
thought he looked inscrutable when of an evening, in Paris,
after he had been asked what he would like to do, he replied that
he should like to do nothing, and simply sat for an interminable
time in front of the Grand Café, on the Boulevard de la Madeleine (he was very fond of cafés), ordering a succession of *demi-
tasses*. It was very rarely that Littlemore cared even to go to the
theatre, and the visit to the Comédie Française, which we
have described, had been undertaken at Waterville's instance.
He had seen *Le Demi-Monde* a few nights before, and had been

told that *L'Aventurière* would show him a particular treatment
of the same subject – the justice to be meted out to unscrupulous women who attempt to thrust themselves into honourable
families. It seemed to him that in both of these cases the ladies
had deserved their fate, but he wished it might have been
brought about by a little less lying on the part of the represent-
atives of honour. Littlemore and he, without being intimate,
were very good friends, and spent much of their time together.
As it turned out, Littlemore was very glad he had gone to the
theatre, for he found himself much interested in this new
incarnation of Nancy Beck.

II

HIS delay in going to see her was nevertheless calculated; there
were more reasons for it than it is necessary to mention. But
when he went, Mrs Headway was at home, and Littlemore was
not surprised to see Sir Arthur Demesne in her sitting-room.
There was something in the air which seemed to indicate that
this gentleman's visit had already lasted a certain time. Littlemore thought it probable that, given the circumstances, he
would now bring it to a close; he must have learned from
their hostess that Littlemore was an old and familiar friend.
He might of course have definite rights – he had every appearance of it; but the more definite they were the more gracefully
he could afford to waive them. Littlemore made these reflections while Sir Arthur Demesne sat there looking at him without giving any sign of departure. Mrs Headway was very
gracious – she had the manner of having known you a hundred
years; she scolded Littlemore extravagantly for not having been
to see her sooner, but this was only a form of the gracious. By
daylight she looked a little faded; but she had an expression
which could never fade. She had the best rooms in the hotel,
and an air of extreme opulence and prosperity; her courier sat
outside, in the ante-chamber, and she evidently knew how to
live. She attempted to include Sir Arthur in the conversation,
but though the young man remained in his place, he declined to
be included. He smiled, in silence; but he was evidently

uncomfortable. The conversation, therefore, remained super-ficial – a quality that, of old, had by no means belonged to Mrs Headway's interviews with her friends. The Englishman looked at Littlemore with a strange, perverse expression which Littlemore, at first, with a good deal of private amuse-ment, simply attributed to jealousy.

'My dear Sir Arthur, I wish very much you would go,' Mrs Headway remarked, at the end of a quarter of an hour.

Sir Arthur got up and took his hat. 'I thought I should oblige you by staying.'

'To defend me against Mr Littlemore? I've known him since I was a baby – I know the worst he can do.' She fixed her charming smile for a moment on her retreating visitor, and she added, with much unexpectedness, 'I want to talk to him about my past!'

'That's just what I want to hear,' said Sir Arthur, with his hand on the door.

'We are going to talk American; you wouldn't understand us! – He speaks in the English style,' she explained, in her little sufficient way, as the baronet, who announced that at all events he would come back in the evening, let himself out.

'He doesn't know about your past?' Littlemore inquired, trying not to make the question sound impertinent.

'Oh, yes; I've told him everything; but he doesn't under-stand. The English are so peculiar; I think they are rather stupid. He has never heard of a woman being –' But here Mrs Headway checked herself, while Littlemore filled out the blank. 'What are you laughing at? It doesn't matter,' she went on; 'there are more things in the world than those people have heard of. However, I like them very much; at least I like him. He's such a gentleman; do you know what I mean? Only, he stays too long, and he isn't amusing. I'm very glad to see you, for a change.'

'Do you mean I'm not a gentleman?' Littlemore asked.

'No indeed; you used to be, in New Mexico. I think you were the only one – and I hope you are still. That's why I recognised you the other night; I might have cut you, you know.'

'You can still, if you like. It's not too late.'

'Oh, no; that's not what I want. I want you to help me.'

'To help you?'

Mrs Headway fixed her eyes for a moment on the door. 'Do you suppose that man is there still?'

'That young man – your poor Englishman?'

'No; I mean Max. Max is my courier,' said Mrs Headway, with a certain impressiveness.

'I haven't the least idea. I'll see, if you like.'

'No; in that case I should have to give him an order, and I don't know what in the world to ask him to do. He sits there for hours; with my simple habits I afford him no employment. I am afraid I have no imagination.'

'The burden of grandeur,' said Littlemore.

'Oh yes, I'm very grand. But on the whole I like it. I'm only afraid he'll hear. I talk so very loud; that's another thing I'm trying to get over.'

'Why do you want to be different?'

'Well, because everything else is different,' Mrs Headway rejoined, with a little sigh. 'Did you hear that I'd lost my husband?' she went on, abruptly.

'Do you mean – a – Mr—?' and Littlemore paused, with an effect that did not seem to come home to her.

'I mean Mr Headway,' she said, with dignity. 'I've been through a good deal since you saw me last: marriage, and death, and trouble, and all sorts of things.'

'You had been through a good deal of marriage before that,' Littlemore ventured to observe.

She rested her eyes on him with soft brightness, and without a change of colour. 'Not so much – not so much –'

'Not so much as might have been thought.'

'Not so much as was reported. I forget whether I was married when I saw you last.'

'It was one of the reports,' said Littlemore. 'But I never saw Mr Beck.'

'You didn't lose much; he was a simple *wretch*! I have done certain things in my life which I have never understood; no wonder others can't understand them. But that's all over! Are you sure Max doesn't hear?' she asked, quickly.

'Not at all sure. But if you suspect him of listening at the keyhole, I would send him away.'

'I don't think he does that. I am always rushing to the door.'

'Then he doesn't hear. I had no idea you had so many secrets. When I parted with you, Mr Headway was in the future.'

'Well, now he's in the past. He was a pleasant man – I can understand my doing that. But he only lived a year. He had neuralgia of the heart; he left me very well off.' She mentioned these various facts as if they were quite of the same order.

'I'm glad to hear it; you used to have expensive tastes.'

'I have plenty of money,' said Mrs Headway. 'Mr Headway had property at Denver, which has increased immensely in value. After his death I tried New York. But I don't like New York.' Littlemore's hostess uttered this last sentence in a tone which was the *résumé* of a social episode. 'I mean to live in Europe – I like Europe,' she announced; and the manner of the announcement had a touch of prophecy, as the other words had had a reverberation of history.

Littlemore was very much struck with all this, and he was greatly entertained with Mrs Headway. 'Are you travelling with that young man?' he inquired, with the coolness of a person who wishes to make his entertainment go as far as possible.

She folded her arms as she leaned back in her chair. 'Look here, Mr Littlemore,' she said; 'I'm about as good-natured as I used to be in America, but I know a great deal more. Of course I ain't travelling with that young man; he's only a friend.'

'He isn't a lover?' asked Littlemore, rather cruelly.

'Do people travel with their lovers? I don't want you to laugh at me – I want you to help me.' She fixed her eyes on him with an air of tender remonstrance that might have touched him; she looked so gentle and reasonable. 'As I tell you, I have taken a great fancy to this old Europe; I feel as if I should never go back. But I want to see something of the life. I think it would suit me – if I could get started a little. Mr Littlemore,' she added, in a moment – 'I may as well be frank, for I ain't at all ashamed. I want to get into society. That's what I'm after!'

Littlemore settled himself in his chair, with the feeling of a man who, knowing that he will have to pull, seeks to obtain a certain leverage. It was in a tone of light jocosity, almost of encouragement, however, that he repeated: 'Into society? It seems to me you are in it already, with baronets for your adorers.'

'That's just what I want to know!' she said, with a certain eagerness. 'Is a baronet much?'

'So they are apt to think. But I know very little about it.'

'Ain't you in society yourself?'

'I? Never in the world! Where did you get that idea? I care no more about society than about that copy of the *Figaro*.'

Mrs Headway's countenance assumed for a moment a look of extreme disappointment, and Littlemore could see that, having heard of his silver-mine and his cattle-ranch, and knowing that he was living in Europe, she had hoped to find him immersed in the world of fashion. But she speedily recovered herself. 'I don't believe a word of it. You know you're a gentleman – you can't help yourself.'

'I may be a gentleman, but I have none of the habits of one.' Littlemore hesitated a moment, and then he added – 'I lived too long in the great Southwest.'

She flushed quickly; she instantly understood – understood even more that he had meant to say. But she wished to make use of him, and it was of more importance that she should appear forgiving – especially as she had the happy consciousness of being so, than that she should punish a cruel speech. She could afford, however, to be lightly ironical. 'That makes no difference – a gentleman is always a gentleman.'

'Not always,' said Littlemore, laughing.

'It's impossible that, through your sister, you shouldn't know something about European society,' said Mrs Headway.

At the mention of his sister, made with a studied lightness of reference which he caught as it passed, Littlemore was unable to repress a start. 'What in the world have you got to do with my sister?' he would have liked to say. The introduction of this lady was disagreeable to him; she belonged to quite another order of ideas, and it was out of the question that Mrs Headway should ever make her acquaintance – if this was what, as that lady would have said – she was 'after'. But he took advantage of a side-issue. 'What do you mean by European society? One can't talk about that. It's a very vague phrase.'

'Well, I mean English society – I mean the society your sister lives in – that's what I mean,' said Mrs Headway, who was quite prepared to be definite. 'I mean the people I saw in London last May – the people I saw at the opera and in the park, the people who go to the Queen's drawing-rooms. When I was in London I stayed at that hotel on the corner of Piccadilly – that looking straight down St James's Street – and I spent hours together at the window looking at the people in the carriages. I had a carriage of my own, and when I was not at my window I was driving all round. I was all alone; I saw every one, but I knew no one – I had no one to tell me. I didn't know Sir Arthur then – I only met him a month ago at Homburg. He followed me to Paris – that's how he came to be my guest.' Serenely, prosaically, without any of the inflation of vanity, Mrs Headway made this last assertion; it was as if she were used to being followed, or as if a gentleman one met at Homburg would inevitably follow. In the same tone she went on: 'I attracted a good deal of attention in London – I could easily see that.'

'You'll do that wherever you go,' Littlemore said, insufficiently enough, as he felt.

'I don't want to attract so much; I think it's vulgar,' Mrs Headway rejoined, with a certain soft sweetness which seemed to denote the enjoyment of a new idea. She was evidently open to new ideas.

'Every one was looking at you the other night at the theatre,' Littlemore continued. 'How can you hope to escape notice?'

'I don't want to escape notice – people have always looked at me, and I suppose they always will. But there are different ways of being looked at, and I know the way I want. I mean to have it, too!' Mrs Headway exclaimed. Yes, she was very definite.

Littlemore sat there, face to face with her, and for some time he said nothing. He had a mixture of feelings, and the memory of other places, other hours, was stealing over him. There had

been of old a very considerable absence of interposing surfaces
between these two – he had known her as one knew people only
in the great Southwest. He had liked her extremely, in a town
where it would have been ridiculous to be difficult to please.
But his sense of this fact was somehow connected with Southwestern conditions; his liking for Nancy Beck was an emotion
of which the proper setting was a back piazza. She presented
herself here on a new basis – she appeared to desire to be
classified afresh. Littlemore said to himself that this was too
much trouble; he had taken her in that way – he couldn't begin
at this time of day to take her in another way. He asked himself
whether she were going to be a bore. It was not easy to suppose
Mrs Headway capable of this offence; but she might become
tiresome if she were bent upon being different. It made him
rather afraid when she began to talk about European society,
about his sister, about things being vulgar. Littlemore was a
very good fellow, and he had at least the average human love of
justice; but there was in his composition an element of the
indolent, the sceptical, perhaps even the brutal, which made
him desire to preserve the simplicity of their former terms of
intercourse. He had no particular desire to see a woman rise
again, as the mystic process was called; he didn't believe in
women's rising again. He believed in their not going down;
thought it perfectly possible and eminently desirable, but held
it was much better for society that they should not endeavour,
as the French say, to *mêler les genres*. In general, he didn't
pretend to say what was good for society – society seemed to
him in rather a bad way; but he had a conviction on this
particular point. Nancy Beck going in for the great prizes,
that spectacle might be entertaining for a simple spectator;
but it would be a nuisance, an embarrassment, from the
moment anything more than contemplation should be
expected of him. He had no wish to be rough, but it might be
well to show her that he was not to be humbugged.

'Oh, if there's anything you want you'll have it,' he said in
answer to her last remark. 'You have always had what you
want.'

'Well, I want something new this time. Does your sister reside in London?'

'My dear lady, what do you know about my sister?' Littlemore asked. 'She's not a woman you would care for.'

Mrs Headway was silent a moment. 'You don't respect me!' she exclaimed suddenly in a loud, almost gay tone of voice. If Littlemore wished, as I say, to preserve the simplicity of their old terms of intercourse, she was apparently willing to humour him.

'Ah, my dear Mrs Beck . . . !' he cried, vaguely, protestingly, and using her former name quite by accident. At San Diego he had never thought whether he respected her or not; that never came up.

'That's a proof of it – calling me by that hateful name! Don't you believe I'm married? I haven't been fortunate in my names,' she added, pensively.

'You make it very awkward when you say such mad things. My sister lives most of the year in the country; she is very simple, rather dull, perhaps a trifle narrow-minded. You are very clever, very lively, and as wide as all creation. That's why I think you wouldn't like her.'

'You ought to be ashamed to run down your sister!' cried Mrs Headway. 'You told me once – at San Diego – that she was the nicest woman you knew. I made a note of that, you see. And you told me she was just my age. So that makes it rather uncomfortable for you, if you won't introduce me!' And Littlemore's hostess gave a pitiless laugh. 'I'm not in the least afraid of her being dull. It's very distinguished to be dull. I'm ever so much too lively.'

'You are indeed, ever so much! But nothing is more easy than to know my sister,' said Littlemore, who knew perfectly that what he said was untrue. And then, as a diversion from this delicate topic, he suddenly asked, 'Are you going to marry Sir Arthur?'

'Don't you think I've been married about enough?'

'Possibly; but this is a new line, it would be different. An Englishman – that's a new sensation.'

'If I should marry, it would be a European,' said Mrs Headway calmly.

'Your chance is very good; they are all marrying Americans.'

'He would have to be some one fine, the man I should marry now. I have a good deal to make up for! That's what I want to know about Sir Arthur; all this time you haven't told me.'

'I have nothing in the world to tell – I have never heard of him. Hasn't he told you himself?'

'Nothing at all; he is very modest. He doesn't brag, nor make himself out anything great. That's what I like him for: I think it's in such good taste. I like good taste!' exclaimed Mrs Headway. 'But all this time,' she added, 'you haven't told me you would help me.'

'How can I help you? I'm no one, I have no power.'

'You can help me by not preventing me. I want you to promise not to prevent me.' She gave him her fixed, bright gaze again; her eyes seemed to look far into his.

'Good Lord, how could I prevent you?'

'I'm not sure that you could. But you might try.'

'I'm too indolent, and too stupid,' said Littlemore jocosely.

'Yes,' she replied, musing as she still looked at him. 'I think you are too stupid. But I think you are also too kind,' she added more graciously. She was almost irresistible when she said such a thing as that.

They talked for a quarter of an hour longer, and at last – as if she had had scruples – she spoke to him of his own marriage, of the death of his wife, matters to which she alluded more felicitously (as he thought) than to some other points. 'If you have a little girl you ought to be very happy; that's what I should like to have. Lord, I should make her a nice woman! Not like me – in another style!' When he rose to leave her, she told him that he must come and see her very often; she was to be some weeks longer in Paris; he must bring Mr Waterville.

'Your English friend won't like that – our coming very often,' Littlemore said, as he stood with his hand on the door.

'I don't know what he has got to do with it,' she answered, staring.

'Neither do I. Only he must be in love with you.'

'That doesn't give him any right. Mercy, if I had had to put myself out for all the men that have been in love with me!'

'Of course you would have had a terrible life! Even doing as you please, you have had rather an agitated one. But your young Englishman's sentiments appear to give him the right to sit there, after one comes in, looking blighted and bored. That might become very tiresome.'

'The moment he becomes tiresome I send him away. You can trust me for that.'

'Oh,' said Littlemore, 'it doesn't matter, after all.' He remembered that it would be very inconvenient to him to have undisturbed possession of Mrs Headway.

She came out with him into the ante-chamber. Mr Max, the courier, was fortunately not there. She lingered a little; she appeared to have more to say.

'On the contrary, he likes you to come,' she remarked in a moment; 'he wants to study my friends.'

'To study them?'

'He wants to find out about me, and he thinks they may tell him something. Some day he will ask you right out, "What sort of a woman is she, any way?"'

'Hasn't he found out yet?'

'He doesn't understand me,' said Mrs Headway, surveying the front of her dress. 'He has never seen any one like me.'

'I should imagine not!'

'So he will ask you, as I say.'

'I will tell him you are the most charming woman in Europe.'

'That ain't a description! Besides, he knows it. He wants to know if I'm respectable.'

'He's very curious!' Littlemore cried, with a laugh.

She grew a little pale; she seemed to be watching his lips. 'Mind you tell him,' she went on with a smile that brought none of her colour back.

'Respectable? I'll tell him you're adorable!'

Mrs Headway stood a moment longer. 'Ah, you're no use!' she murmured. And she suddenly turned away and passed back into her sitting-room, slowly drawing her far-trailing skirts.

III

'*Elle ne se doute de rien!*' Littlemore said to himself as he walked away from the hotel; and he repeated the phrase in talking about her to Waterville. 'She wants to be right,' he added; 'but she will never really succeed; she has begun too late, she will never be more than half-right. However, she won't know when she's wrong, so it doesn't signify!' And then he proceeded to assert that in some respects she would remain incurable; she had no delicacy; no discretion, no shading; she was a woman who suddenly said to you, 'You don't respect me!' As if that were a thing for a woman to say!

'It depends upon what she meant by it.' Waterville liked to see the meanings of things.

'The more she meant by it the less she ought to say it!' Littlemore declared.

But he returned to the Hôtel Meurice, and on the next occasion he took Waterville with him. The Secretary of Legation, who had not often been in close quarters with a lady of this ambiguous quality, was prepared to regard Mrs Headway as a very curious type. He was afraid she might be dangerous; but, on the whole, he felt secure. The object of his devotion at present was his country, or at least the Department of State; he had no intention of being diverted from that allegiance. Besides, he had his ideal of the attractive woman – a person pitched in a very much lower key than this shining, smiling, rustling, chattering daughter of the Territories. The woman he should care for would have repose, a certain love of privacy – she would sometimes let one alone. Mrs Headway was personal, familiar, intimate; she was always appealing or accusing, demanding explanations and pledges, saying things one had to answer. All this was accompanied with a hundred smiles and radiations and other natural graces, but the general effect of it was slightly fatiguing. She had certainly a great deal of charm, an immense desire to please, and a wonderful collection of dresses and trinkets; but she was eager and preoccupied, and it was impossible that other people should share her eagerness. If she wished to get into society, there was no reason why her

bachelor visitors should wish to see her there; for it was the
absence of the usual social encumbrances which made her
drawing-room attractive. There was no doubt whatever that
she was several women in one, and she ought to content herself
with that sort of numerical triumph. Littlemore said to Waterville that it was stupid of her to wish to scale the heights; she
ought to know how much more she was in her place down
below. She appeared vaguely to irritate him; even her fluttering
attempts at self-culture – she had become a great critic, and
handled many of the productions of the age with a bold, free
touch – constituted a vague invocation, an appeal for sympathy
which was naturally annoying to a man who disliked the trouble
of revising old decisions, consecrated by a certain amount of
reminiscence that might be called tender. She had, however,
one palpable charm; she was full of surprises. Even Waterville
was obliged to confess that an element of the unexpected was
not to be excluded from his conception of the woman who
should have an ideal repose. Of course there were two kinds
of surprises, and only one of them was thoroughly pleasant,
though Mrs Headway dealt impartially in both. She had the
sudden delights, the odd exclamations, the queer curiosities of
a person who has grown up in a country where everything is
new and many things ugly, and who, with a natural turn for the
arts and amenities of life, makes a tardy acquaintance with
some of the finer usages, the higher pleasures. She was provincial – it was easy to see that she was provincial; that took no
great cleverness. But what was Parisian enough – if to be
Parisian was the measure of success – was the way she picked
up ideas and took a hint from every circumstance. 'Only give
me time, and I shall know all I have need of,' she said to
Littlemore, who watched her progress with a mixture of
admiration and sadness. She delighted to speak of herself as a
poor little barbarian who was trying to pick up a few crumbs of
knowledge, and this habit took great effect from her delicate
face, her perfect dress, and the brilliancy of her manners.

One of her surprises was that after that first visit she said no
more to Littlemore about Mrs Dolphin. He did her perhaps the
grossest injustice; but he had quite expected her to bring up this

lady whenever they met. 'If she will only leave Agnes alone, she may do what she will,' he said to Waterville, expressing his relief. 'My sister would never look at her, and it would be very awkward to have to tell her so.' She expected assistance; she made him feel that simply by the way she looked at him; but for the moment she demanded no definite service. She held her tongue, but she waited, and her patience itself was a kind of admonition. In the way of society, it must be confessed, her privileges were meagre, Sir Arthur Demesne and her two compatriots being, so far as the latter could discover, her only visitors. She might have had other friends, but she held her head very high, and liked better to see no one than not to see the best company. It was evident that she flattered herself that she produced the effect of being, not neglected, but fastidious. There were plenty of Americans in Paris, but in this direction she failed to extend her acquaintance; the nice people wouldn't come and see her, and nothing would have induced her to receive the others. She had the most exact conception of the people she wished to see and to avoid. Littlemore expected every day that she would ask him why he didn't bring some of his friends, and he had his answer ready. It was a very poor one, for it consisted simply of a conventional assurance that he wished to keep her for himself. She would be sure to retort that this was very 'thin', as, indeed, it was; but the days went by without her calling him to account. The little American colony in Paris is rich in amiable women, but there were none to whom Littlemore could make up his mind to say that it would be a favour to him to call on Mrs Headway. He shouldn't like them the better for doing so, and he wished to like those of whom he might ask a favour. Except, therefore, that he occasionally spoke of her as a little Western woman, very pretty and rather queer, who had formerly been a great chum of his, she remained unknown in the *salons* of the Avenue Gabriel and the streets that encircle the Arch of Triumph. To ask the men to go and see her, without asking the ladies, would only accentuate the fact that he didn't ask the ladies; so he asked no one at all. Besides, it was true – just a little – that he wished to keep her to himself, and he was fatuous enough to believe that she cared much more for him than for her Englishman. Of course, however, he would never dream of marrying her, whereas the Englishman apparently was immersed in that vision. She hated her past; she used to announce that very often, talking of it as if it were an appendage of the same order as a dishonest courier, or even an inconvenient protrusion of drapery. Therefore, as Littlemore was part of her past, it might have been supposed that she would hate him too, and wish to banish him, with all the images he recalled, from her sight. But she made an exception in his favour, and if she disliked their old relations as a chapter of her own history, she seemed still to like them as a chapter of his. He felt that she clung to him, that she believed he could help her and in the long run would. It was to the long run that she appeared little by little to have attuned herself.

She succeeded perfectly in maintaining harmony between Sir Arthur Demesne and her American visitors, who spent much less time in her drawing-room. She had easily persuaded him that there were no grounds for jealousy, and that they had no wish, as she said, to crowd him out; for it was ridiculous to be jealous of two persons at once, and Rupert Waterville, after he had learned the way to her hospitable apartment, appeared there as often as his friend Littlemore. The two, indeed, usually came together, and they ended by relieving their competitor of a certain sense of responsibility. This amiable and excellent but somewhat limited and slightly pretentious young man, who had not yet made up his mind, was sometimes rather oppressed with the magnitude of his undertaking, and when he was alone with Mrs Headway the tension of his thoughts occasionally became quite painful. He was very slim and straight, and looked taller than his height; he had the prettiest, silkiest hair, which waved away from a large white forehead, and he was endowed with a nose of the so-called Roman model. He looked younger than his years (in spite of those last two attributes), partly on account of the delicacy of his complexion and the almost childlike candour of his round blue eye. He was diffident and self-conscious; there were certain letters he could not pronounce. At the same time he had the manners of a young man who had been brought up to fill a considerable place in the world, with whom a certain correctness had become a habit, and who, though he might occasionally be a little awkward about small things, would be sure to acquit himself honourably in great ones. He was very simple, and he believed himself very serious; he had the blood of a score of Warwickshire squires in his veins; mingled in the last instance with the somewhat paler fluid which animated the long-necked daughter of a banker who had expected an earl for his son-in-law, but who had consented to regard Sir Baldwin Demesne as the least insufficient of baronets. The boy, the only one, had come into his title at five years of age; his mother, who disappointed her auriferous sire a second time when poor Sir Baldwin broke his neck in the hunting field, watched over him with a tenderness that burned as steadily as a candle shaded by a transparent hand. She never admitted, even to herself, that he was not the cleverest of men; but it took all her own cleverness, which was much greater than his, to maintain this appearance. Fortunately he was not wild, so that he would never marry an actress or a governess, like two or three of the young men who had been at Eton with him. With this ground of nervousness the less, Lady Demesne awaited with an air of confidence his promotion to some high office. He represented in Parliament the Conservative instincts and vote of a red-roofed market town, and sent regularly to his bookseller for all the new publications on economical subjects, for he was determined that his political attitude should have a firm statistical basis. He was not conceited; he was only misinformed – misinformed, I mean, about himself. He thought himself indispensable in the scheme of things – not as an individual, but as an institution. This conviction, however, was too sacred to betray itself by vulgar assumptions. If he was a little man in a big place, he never strutted nor talked loud; he merely felt it as a kind of luxury that he had a large social circumference. It was like sleeping in a big bed; one didn't toss about the more, but one felt a greater freshness.

He had never seen anything like Mrs Headway; he hardly knew by what standard to measure her. She was not like an English lady – not like those at least with whom he had been accustomed to converse; and yet it was impossible not to see that she had a standard of her own. He suspected that she was provincial, but as he was very much under the charm he compromised matters by saying to himself that she was only foreign. It was of course provincial to be foreign; but this was, after all, a peculiarity which she shared with a great many nice people. He was not wild, and his mother had flattered herself that in this all-important matter he would not be perverse; but it was all the same most unexpected that he should have taken a fancy to an American widow, five years older than himself, who knew no one and who sometimes didn't appear to understand exactly who he was. Though he disapproved of it, it was precisely her foreignness that pleased him; she seemed to be as little as possible of his own race and creed; there was not a touch of Warwickshire in her composition. She was like an Hungarian or a Pole, with the difference that he could almost understand her language. The unfortunate young man was fascinated, though he had not yet admitted to himself that he was in love. He would be very slow and deliberate in such a position, for he was deeply conscious of its importance. He was a young man who had arranged his life; he had determined to marry at thirty-two. A long line of ancestors was watching him; he hardly knew what they would think of Mrs Headway. He hardly knew what he thought himself; the only thing he was absolutely sure of was that she made the time pass as it passed in no other pursuit. He was vaguely uneasy; he was by no means sure it was right the time should pass like that. There was nothing to show for it but the fragments of Mrs Headway's conversation, the peculiarities of her accent, the sallies of her wit, the audacities of her fancy, her mysterious allusions to her past. Of course he knew that she had a past; she was not a young girl, she was a widow – and widows are essentially an expression of an accomplished fact. He was not jealous of her antecedents, but he wished to understand them, and it was here that the difficulty occurred. The subject was illumined with fitful flashes, but it never placed itself before him as a general picture. He asked her a good many questions, but her answers were so startling that, like sudden luminous points, they seemed to intensify the darkness round their edges. She had apparently

spent her life in an inferior province of an inferior country; but
it didn't follow from this that she herself had been low. She had
been a lily among thistles; and there was something romantic in
a man in his position taking an interest in such a woman. It
pleased Sir Arthur to believe he was romantic; that had been
the case with several of his ancestors, who supplied a precedent
without which he would perhaps not have ventured to trust
himself. He was the victim of perplexities from which a single
spark of direct perception would have saved him. He took
everything in the literal sense; he had not a grain of humour.
He sat there vaguely waiting for something to happen, and not
committing himself by rash declarations. If he was in love, it
was in his own way, reflectively, inexpressively, obstinately. He
was waiting for the formula which would justify his conduct
and Mrs Headway's peculiarities. He hardly knew where it
would come from; you might have thought from his manner
that he would discover it in one of the elaborate *entrées* that
were served to the pair when Mrs Headway consented to dine
with him at Bignon's or the Café Anglais; or in one of the
numerous bandboxes that arrived from the Rue de la Paix,
and from which she often lifted the lid in the presence of her
admirer. There were moments when he got weary of waiting in
vain, and at these moments the arrival of her American friends
(he often wondered that she had so few) seemed to lift
the mystery from his shoulders and give him a chance to rest.
This formula – she herself was not yet able to give it, for she was
not aware how much ground it was expected to cover. She
talked about her past, because she thought it the best thing to
do; she had a shrewd conviction that it was better to make a
good use of it than to attempt to efface it. To efface it was
impossible, though that was what she would have preferred.
She had no objection to telling fibs, but now that she was taking
a new departure, she wished to tell only those that were necessary. She would have been delighted if it had been possible to
tell none at all. A few, however, were indispensable, and we
need not attempt to estimate more closely the ingenious
re-arrangements of fact with which she entertained and mystified Sir Arthur. She knew of course that as a product of

fashionable circles she was nowhere, but she might have great success as a child of nature.

IV

RUPERT WATERVILLE, in the midst of intercourse in which every one perhaps had a good many mental reservations, never forgot that he was in a representative position, that he was responsible, official; and he asked himself more than once how far it was permitted to him to countenance Mrs Headway's pretensions to being an American lady typical even of the newer phases. In his own way he was as puzzled as poor Sir Arthur, and indeed he flattered himself that he was as particular as any Englishman could be. Suppose that after all this free association Mrs Headway should come over to London and ask at the Legation to be presented to the Queen? It would be so awkward to refuse her – of course they would have to refuse her – that he was very careful about making tacit promises. She might construe anything as a tacit promise – he knew how the smallest gestures of diplomatists were studied and interpreted. It was his effort therefore to be really the diplomatist in his relations with this attractive but dangerous woman. The party of four used often to dine together – Sir Arthur pushed his confidence so far – and on these occasions Mrs Headway, availing herself of one of the privileges of a lady, even at the most expensive restaurant – used to wipe her glasses with her napkin. One evening, when after polishing a goblet she held it up to the light, giving it, with her head on one side, the least glimmer of a wink, he said to himself as he watched her that she looked like a modern bacchante. He noticed at this moment that the baronet was gazing at her too, and he wondered if the same idea had come to him. He often wondered what the baronet thought; he had devoted first and last a good deal of speculation to the baronial class. Littlemore, alone, at this moment, was not observing Mrs Headway; he never appeared to observe her, though she often observed him. Waterville asked himself among other things why Sir Arthur had not brought his own friends to see her, for Paris during the several weeks that now elapsed was rich in

English visitors. He wondered whether she had asked him and
he had refused; he would have liked very much to know
whether she had asked him. He explained his curiosity to Littlemore, who, however, took very little interest in it. Littlemore
said, nevertheless, that he had no doubt she had asked him; she
never would be deterred by false delicacy.

'She has been very delicate with you,' Waterville replied.
'She hasn't been at all pressing of late.'

'It is only because she has given me up; she thinks I'm a
brute.'

'I wonder what she thinks of me,' Waterville said, pensively.

'Oh, she counts upon you to introduce her to the Minister.
It's lucky for you that our representative here is absent.'

'Well,' Waterville rejoined, 'the Minister has settled two or
three difficult questions, and I suppose he can settle this one.
I shall do nothing but by the orders of my chief.' He was very
fond of talking about his chief.

'She does me injustice,' Littlemore added in a moment.
'I have spoken to several people about her.'

'Ah; but what have you told them?'

'That she lives at the Hôtel Meurice; and that she wants to
know nice people.'

'They are flattered, I suppose, at your thinking them nice,
but they don't go,' said Waterville.

'I spoke of her to Mrs Bagshaw, and Mrs Bagshaw has
promised to go.'

'Ah,' Waterville murmured; 'you don't call Mrs Bagshaw
nice? Mrs Headway won't see her.'

'That's exactly what she wants, – to be able to cut some one!'

Waterville had a theory that Sir Arthur was keeping Mrs
Headway as a surprise – he meant perhaps to produce her
during the next London season. He presently, however, learned
as much about the matter as he could have desired to know. He
had once offered to accompany his beautiful compatriot to the
Museum of the Luxembourg and tell her a little about the
modern French school. She had not examined this collection,
in spite of her determination to see everything remarkable (she
carried her *Murray* in her lap even when she went to see the

great tailor in the Rue de la Paix, to whom, as she said, she had given no end of points); for she usually went to such places with Sir Arthur, and Sir Arthur was indifferent to the modern painters of France. 'He says there are much better men in England. I must wait for the Royal Academy, next year. He seems to think one can wait for anything, but I'm not so good at waiting as he. I can't afford to wait – I've waited long enough.' So much as this Mrs Headway said on the occasion of her arranging with Rupert Waterville that they should some day visit the Luxembourg together. She alluded to the Englishman as if he were her husband or her brother, her natural protector and companion.

'I wonder if she knows how that sounds?' Waterville said to himself. 'I don't believe she would do it if she knew how it sounds.' And he made the further reflection that when one arrived from San Diego there was no end to the things one had to learn: it took so many things to make a well-bred woman. Clever as she was, Mrs Headway was right in saying that she couldn't afford to wait. She must learn quickly. She wrote to Waterville one day to propose that they should go to the Museum on the morrow; Sir Arthur's mother was in Paris, on her way to Cannes, where she was to spend the winter. She was only passing through, but she would be there three days and he would naturally give himself up to her. She appeared to have the properest ideas as to what a gentleman would propose to do for his mother. She herself, therefore, would be free, and she named the hour at which she should expect him to call for her. He was punctual to the appointment, and they drove across the river in the large high-hung barouche in which she constantly rolled about Paris. With Mr Max on the box – the courier was ornamented with enormous whiskers – this vehicle had an appearance of great respectability, though Sir Arthur assured her – she repeated this to her other friends – that in London, next year, they would do the thing much better for her. It struck her other friends of course that the baronet was prepared to be very consistent, and this on the whole was what Waterville would have expected of him. Littlemore simply remarked that at San Diego she drove herself about in a rickety buggy, with muddy wheels, and with a mule very often in the shafts. Waterville felt something like excitement as he asked himself whether the baronet's mother would now consent to know her. She must of course be aware that it was a woman who was keeping her son in Paris at a season when English gentlemen were most naturally employed in shooting partridges.

'She is staying at the Hôtel du Rhin, and I have made him feel that he mustn't leave her while she is here,' Mrs Headway said, as they drove up the narrow Rue de Seine. 'Her name is Lady Demesne, but her full title is the Honourable Lady Demesne, as she's a Baron's daughter. Her father used to be a banker, but he did something or other for the Government – the Tories, you know, they call them – and so he was raised to the peerage. So you see one *can* be raised! She has a lady with her as a companion.' Waterville's neighbour gave him this information with a seriousness that made him smile; he wondered whether she thought he didn't know how a Baron's daughter was addressed. In that she was very provincial; she had a way of exaggerating the value of her intellectual acquisitions and of assuming that others had been as ignorant as she. He noted, too, that she had ended by suppressing poor Sir Arthur's name altogether, and designating him only by a sort of conjugal pronoun. She had been so much, and so easily, married, that she was full of these misleading references to gentlemen.

V

THEY walked through the gallery of the Luxembourg, and except that Mrs Headway looked at everything at once and at nothing long enough, talked, as usual, rather too loud, and bestowed too much attention on the bad copies that were being made of several indifferent pictures, she was a very agreeable companion and a grateful recipient of knowledge. She was very quick to understand, and Waterville was sure that before she left the gallery she knew something about the French school. She was quite prepared to compare it critically with London exhibitions of the following year. As Littlemore and he had remarked more than once, she was a very odd mixture. Her conversation, her personality, were full of little joints and seams, all of them very visible, where the old and the new had been pieced together. When they had passed through the different rooms of the palace Mrs Headway proposed that instead of returning directly they should take a stroll in the adjoining gardens, which she wished very much to see and was sure she should like. She had quite seized the difference between the old Paris and the new, and felt the force of the romantic associations of the Latin quarter as perfectly as if she had enjoyed all the benefits of modern culture. The autumn sun was warm in the alleys and terraces of the Luxembourg; the masses of foliage above them, clipped and squared, rusty with ruddy patches, shed a thick lacework over the white sky, which was streaked with the palest blue. The beds of flowers near the palace were of the vividest yellow and red, and the sunlight rested on the smooth grey walls of those parts of its basement that looked south; in front of which, on the long green benches, a row of brown-cheeked nurses, in white caps and white aprons, sat offering nutrition to as many bundles of white drapery. There were other white caps wandering in the broad paths, attended by little brown French children; the small, straw-seated chairs were piled and stacked in some places and disseminated in others. An old lady in black, with white hair fastened over each of her temples by a large black comb, sat on the edge of a stone bench (too high for her delicate length), motionless, staring straight before her and holding a large door-key; under a tree a priest was reading – you could see his lips move at a distance; a young soldier, dwarfish and red-legged, strolled past with his hands in his pockets, which were very much distended. Waterville sat down with Mrs Headway on the straw-bottomed chairs, and she presently said, 'I like this; it's even better than the pictures in the gallery. It's more of a picture.'

'Everything in France is a picture – even things that are ugly,' Waterville replied. 'Everything makes a subject.'

'Well, I like France!' Mrs Headway went on, with a little incongruous sigh. Then, suddenly, from an impulse even more inconsequent than her sigh, she added, 'He asked me to go and see her, but I told him I wouldn't. She may come and see me if she likes.' This was so abrupt that Waterville was slightly confounded; but he speedily perceived that she had returned by a short cut to Sir Arthur Demesne and his honourable mother. Waterville liked to know about other people's affairs, but he did not like this taste to be imputed to him; and therefore, though he was curious to see how the old lady, as he called her, would treat his companion, he was rather displeased with the latter for being so confidential. He had never imagined he was so intimate with her as that. Mrs Headway, however, had a manner of taking intimacy for granted; a manner which Sir Arthur's mother at least would be sure not to like. He pretended to wonder a little what she was talking about, but she scarcely explained. She only went on, through untraceable transitions: 'The least she can do is to come. I have been very kind to her son. That's not a reason for my going to her – it's a reason for her coming to me. Besides, if she doesn't like what I've done, she can leave me alone. I want to get into European society, but I want to get in in my own way. I don't want to run after people; I want them to run after me. I guess they will, some day!' Waterville listened to this with his eyes on the ground; he felt himself blushing a little. There was something in Mrs Headway that shocked and mortified him, and Littlemore had been right in saying that she had a deficiency of shading. She was terribly distinct; her motives, her impulses, her desires were absolutely glaring. She needed to see, to hear, her own thoughts. Vehement thought, with Mrs Headway, was inevitably speech, though speech was not always thought, and now she had suddenly become vehement. 'If she does once come – then, ah, then, I shall be too perfect with her; I sha'n't let her go! But she must take the first step. I confess, I hope she'll be nice.'

'Perhaps she won't,' said Waterville perversely.

'Well, I don't care if she isn't. He has never told me anything about her; never a word about any of his own belongings. If I wished, I might believe he's ashamed of them.'

'I don't think it's that.'

'I know it isn't. I know what it is. It's just modesty. He doesn't want to brag – he's too much of a gentleman. He doesn't want to dazzle me – he wants me to like him for himself.

Well, I do like him,' she added in a moment. 'But I shall like him still better if he brings his mother. They shall know that in America.'

'Do you think it will make an impression in America?' Waterville asked, smiling.

'It will show them that I am visited by the British aristocracy. They won't like that.'

'Surely they grudge you no innocent pleasure,' Waterville murmured, smiling still.

'They grudged me common politeness – when I was in New York! Did you ever hear how they treated me, when I came on from the West?'

Waterville stared; this episode was quite new to him. His companion had turned towards him; her pretty head was tossed back like a flower in the wind; there was a flush in her cheek, a sharper light in her eye. 'Ah! my dear New Yorkers, they're incapable of rudeness!' cried the young man.

'You're one of them, I see. But I don't speak of the men. The men were well enough – though they did allow it.'

'Allow what, Mrs Headway?' Waterville was quite in the dark.

She wouldn't answer at once; her eyes, glittering a little, were fixed upon absent images. 'What did you hear about me over there? Don't pretend you heard nothing.'

He had heard nothing at all; there had not been a word about Mrs Headway in New York. He couldn't pretend, and he was obliged to tell her this. 'But I have been away,' he added, 'and in America I didn't go out. There's nothing to go out for in New York – only little boys and girls.'

'There are plenty of old women! They decided I was improper. I'm very well known in the West – I'm known from Chicago to San Francisco – if not personally (in all cases), at least by reputation. People can tell you out there. In New York they decided I wasn't good enough. Not good enough for New York! What do you say to that?' And she gave a sweet little laugh. Whether she had struggled with her pride before making this avowal, Waterville never knew. The crudity of the avowal seemed to indicate that she had no pride, and yet there was a spot in her heart which, as he now perceived, was intensely sore and had suddenly begun to throb. 'I took a house for the winter – one of the handsomest houses in the place – but I sat there all alone. They didn't think me proper. Such as you see me here, I wasn't a success! I tell you the truth, at whatever cost. Not a decent woman came to see me!'

Waterville was embarrassed; diplomatist as he was, he hardly knew what line to take. He could not see what need there was of her telling him the truth, though the incident appeared to have been most curious, and he was glad to know the facts on the best authority. It was the first he knew of this remarkable woman's having spent a winter in his native city – which was virtually a proof of her having come and gone in complete obscurity. It was vain for him to pretend that he had been a good deal away, for he had been appointed to his post in London only six months before, and Mrs Headway's social failure preceded that event. In the midst of these reflections he had an inspiration. He attempted neither to explain, to minimise, nor to apologise; he ventured simply to lay his hand for an instant on her own and to exclaim, as tenderly as possible, 'I wish *I* had known you were there!'

'I had plenty of men – but men don't count. If they are not a positive help, they're a hindrance, and the more you have, the worse it looks. The women simply turned their backs.'

'They were afraid of you – they were jealous,' Waterville said.

'It's very good of you to try and explain it away; all I know is, not one of them crossed my threshold. You needn't try and tone it down; I know perfectly how the case stands. In New York, if you please, I was a failure!'

'So much the worse for New York!' cried Waterville, who, as he afterwards said to Littlemore, had got quite worked up.

'And now you know why I want to get into society over here?' She jumped up and stood before him; with a dry, hard smile she looked down at him. Her smile itself was an answer to her question; it expressed an urgent desire for revenge. There was an abruptness in her movements which left Waterville quite behind; but as he still sat there, returning her glance, he felt that he at last, in the light of that smile, the flash of that almost fierce question, understood Mrs Headway.

She turned away, to walk to the gate of the garden, and he went with her, laughing vaguely, uneasily, at her tragic tone. Of course she expected him to help her to her revenge; but his female relations, his mother and his sisters, his innumerable cousins, had been a party to the slight she suffered, and he reflected as he walked along that after all they had been right. They had been right in not going to see a woman who could chatter that way about her social wrongs; whether Mrs Headway were respectable or not, they had a correct instinct, for at any rate she was vulgar. European society might let her in, but European society would be wrong. New York, Waterville said to himself with a glow of civic pride, was quite capable of taking a higher stand in such a matter than London. They went some distance without speaking; at last he said, expressing honestly the thought which at that moment was uppermost in his mind, 'I hate that phrase, "getting into society". I don't think one ought to attribute to one's self that sort of ambition. One ought to assume that one is in society – that one *is* society – and to hold that if one has good manners, one has, from the social point of view, achieved the great thing. The rest regards others.'

For a moment she appeared not to understand; then she broke out: 'Well, I suppose I haven't good manners; at any rate, I'm not satisfied! Of course, I don't talk right – I know that very well. But let me get where I want to first – then I'll look after my expressions. If I once get there, I shall be perfect!' she cried with a tremor of passion. They reached the gate of the garden and stood a moment outside, opposite to the low arcade of the Odéon, lined with bookstalls at which Waterville cast a slightly wistful glance, waiting for Mrs Headway's carriage, which had drawn up at a short distance. The whiskered Max had seated himself within, and on the tense, elastic cushions had fallen into a doze. The carriage got into motion without his awaking; he came to his senses only as it stopped again. He started up, staring; then, without confusion, he proceeded to descend.

'I have learned it in Italy – they say the *siesta*,' he remarked with an agreeable smile, holding the door open to Mrs Headway.

'Well, I should think you had!' this lady replied, laughing amicably as she got into the vehicle, whither Waterville followed her. It was not a surprise to him to perceive that she spoiled her courier; she naturally would spoil her courier. But civilisation begins at home, said Waterville; and the incident threw an ironical light upon her desire to get into society. It failed, however, to divert her thoughts from the subject she was discussing with Waterville, for as Max ascended the box and the carriage went on its way, she threw out another little note of defiance. 'If once I'm all right over here, I can snap my fingers at New York! You'll see the faces those women will make.'

Waterville was sure his mother and sisters would make no faces; but he felt afresh, as the carriage rolled back to the Hôtel Meurice, that now he understood Mrs Headway. As they were about to enter the court of the hotel a closed carriage passed before them, and while a few moments later he helped his companion to alight, he saw that Sir Arthur Demesne had descended from the other vehicle. Sir Arthur perceived Mrs Headway, and instantly gave his hand to a lady seated in the *coupé*. This lady emerged with a certain slow impressiveness, and as she stood before the door of the hotel – a woman still young and fair, with a good deal of height, gentle, tranquil, plainly dressed, yet distinctly imposing – Waterville saw that the baronet had brought his mother to call upon Nancy Beck. Mrs Headway's triumph had begun; the Dowager Lady Demesne had taken the first step. Waterville wondered whether the ladies in New York, notified by some magnetic wave, were distorting their features. Mrs Headway, quickly conscious of what had happened, was neither too prompt to appropriate the visit, nor too slow to acknowledge it. She just paused, smiling at Sir Arthur.

'I wish to introduce my mother – she wants very much to know you.' He approached Mrs Headway; the lady had taken his arm. She was at once simple and circumspect; she had all the resources of an English matron.

Mrs Headway, without advancing a step, put out her hands as if to draw her visitor quickly closer. 'I declare, you're too sweet!' Waterville heard her say.

He was turning away, as his own business was over; but the young Englishman, who had surrendered his mother to the embrace, as it might now almost be called, of their hostess, just checked him with a friendly gesture. 'I daresay I sha'n't see you again – I'm going away.'

'Good-by, then,' said Waterville. 'You return to England?'

'No; I go to Cannes with my mother.'

'You remain at Cannes?'

'Till Christmas very likely.'

The ladies, escorted by Mr Max, had passed into the hotel, and Waterville presently quitted his interlocutor. He smiled as he walked away reflecting that this personage had obtained a concession from his mother only at the price of a concession.

The next morning he went to see Littlemore, from whom he had a standing invitation to breakfast, and who, as usual, was smoking a cigar and looking through a dozen newspapers. Littlemore had a large apartment and an accomplished cook; he got up late and wandered about his room all the morning, stopping from time to time to look out of his windows which overhung the Place de la Madeleine. They had not been seated many minutes at breakfast when Waterville announced that Mrs Headway was about to be abandoned by Sir Arthur, who was going to Cannes.

'That's no news to me,' Littlemore said. 'He came last night to bid me good-by.'

'To bid you good-by? He was very civil all of a sudden.'

'He didn't come from civility – he came from curiosity. Having dined here, he had a pretext for calling.'

'I hope his curiosity was satisfied,' Waterville remarked, in the manner of a person who could enter into such a sentiment.

Littlemore hesitated. 'Well, I suspect not. He sat here some time, but we talked about everything but what he wanted to know.'

'And what did he want to know?'

'Whether I know anything against Nancy Beck.'

Waterville stared. 'Did he call her Nancy Beck?'

'We never mentioned her; but I saw what he wanted, and that he wanted me to lead up to her – only I wouldn't do it.'

'Ah, poor man!' Waterville murmured.

'I don't see why you pity him,' said Littlemore. 'Mrs Beck's admirers were never pitied.'

'Well, of course he wants to marry her.'

'Let him do it, then. I have nothing to say to it.'

'He believes there's something in her past that's hard to swallow.'

'Let him leave it alone, then.'

'How can he, if he's in love with her?' Waterville asked, in the tone of a man who could enter into that sentiment too.

'Ah, my dear fellow, he must settle it himself. He has no right, at any rate, to ask me such a question. There was a moment, just as he was going, when he had it on his tongue's end. He stood there in the doorway, he couldn't leave me – he was going to plump out with it. He looked at me straight, and I looked straight at him; we remained that way for almost a minute. Then he decided to hold his tongue, and took himself off.'

Waterville listened to this little description with intense interest. 'And if he had asked you, what would you have said?'

'What do you think?'

'Well, I suppose you would have said that his question wasn't fair?'

'That would have been tantamount to admitting the worst.'

'Yes,' said Waterville, thoughtfully, 'you couldn't do that. On the other hand, if he had put it to you on your honour whether she were a woman to marry, it would have been very awkward.'

'Awkward enough. Fortunately, he has no business to put things to me on my honour. Moreover, nothing has passed between us to give him the right to ask me questions about Mrs Headway. As she is a great friend of mine, he can't pretend to expect me to give confidential information about her.'

'You don't think she's a woman to marry, all the same,' Waterville declared. 'And if a man were to ask you that, you might knock him down, but it wouldn't be an answer.'

'It would have to serve,' said Littlemore. He added in a moment, 'There are certain cases where it's a man's duty to commit perjury.'

Waterville looked grave. 'Certain cases?'

'Where a woman's honour is at stake.'

'I see what you mean. That's of course if he has been himself concerned –'

'Himself or another. It doesn't matter.'

'I think it does matter. I don't like perjury,' said Waterville. 'It's a delicate question.'

They were interrupted by the arrival of the servant with a second course, and Littlemore gave a laugh as he helped himself. 'It would be a joke to see her married to that superior being!'

'It would be a great responsibility.'

'Responsibility or not, it would be very amusing.'

'Do you mean to assist her, then?'

'Heaven forbid! But I mean to bet on her.'

Waterville gave his companion a serious glance; he thought him strangely superficial. The situation, however, was difficult, and he laid down his fork with a little sigh.

PART II

VI

THE Easter holidays that year were unusually genial; mild, watery sunshine assisted the progress of the spring. The high, dense hedges, in Warwickshire, were like walls of hawthorn embedded in banks of primrose, and the finest trees in England, springing out of them with a regularity which suggested conservative principles, began to cover themselves with a kind of green downiness. Rupert Waterville, devoted to his duties and faithful in attendance at the Legation, had had little time to enjoy that rural hospitality which is the great invention of the English people and the most perfect expression of their character. He had been invited now and then – for in London he commended himself to many people as a very sensible young man – but he had been obliged to decline more proposals than he accepted. It was still, therefore, rather a novelty to him to stay at one of those fine old houses, surrounded with hereditary acres, which from the first of his coming to England he had thought of with such curiosity and such envy. He proposed to himself to see as many of them as possible, but he disliked to do things in a hurry, or when his mind was preoccupied, as it was so apt to be, with what he believed to be business of importance. He kept the country-houses in reserve; he would take them up in their order, after he should have got a little more used to London. Without hesitation, however, he had accepted the invitation to Longlands; it had come to him in a simple and familiar note, from Lady Demesne, with whom he had no acquaintance. He knew of her return from Cannes, where she had spent the whole winter, for he had seen it related in a Sunday newspaper; yet it was with a certain surprise that he heard from her in these informal terms. 'Dear Mr Waterville,' she wrote, 'my son tells me that you will perhaps be able to come down here on the 17th, to spend two or three days. If you can, it will give us much pleasure. We can promise you the society of your charming countrywoman, Mrs Headway.'

He had seen Mrs Headway; she had written to him a fortnight before from an hotel in Cork Street, to say that she had arrived in London for the season and should be very glad to see him. He had gone to see her, trembling with the fear that she would break ground about her presentation; but he was agreeably surprised to observe that she neglected this topic. She had spent the winter in Rome, travelling directly from that city to England, with just a little stop in Paris, to buy a few clothes. She had taken much satisfaction in Rome, where she made many friends; she assured him that she knew half the Roman nobility. 'They are charming people; they have only one fault, they stay too long,' she said. And, in answer to his inquiring glance, 'I mean when they come to see you,' she explained. 'They used to come every evening, and they wanted to stay till the next day. They were all princes and counts. I used to give them cigars, &c. I knew as many people as I wanted,' she added, in a moment, discovering perhaps in Waterville's eye the traces of that sympathy with which six months before he had listened to her account of her discomfiture in New York. 'There were lots of English; I knew all the English, and I mean to visit them here. The Americans waited to see what the English would do, so as to do the opposite. Thanks to that, I was spared some precious specimens. There are, you know, some fearful ones. Besides, in Rome, society doesn't matter, if you have a feeling for the ruins and the Campagna; I had an immense feeling for the Campagna. I was always mooning round in some damp old temple. It reminded me a good deal of the country round San Diego – if it hadn't been for the temples. I liked to think it all over, when I was driving round; I was always brooding over the past.' At this moment, however, Mrs Headway had dismissed the past; she was prepared to give herself up wholly to the actual. She wished Waterville to advise her as to how she should live – what she should do. Should she stay at an hotel or should she take a house? She guessed she had better take a house, if she could find a nice one. Max wanted to look for one, and she didn't know but she'd let him; he got her such a nice one in Rome. She said nothing about Sir Arthur Demesne, who, it seemed to Waterville, would have been her natural guide and sponsor; he wondered whether her relations with the baronet had come to an end. Waterville had met him a couple of times since the opening of Parliament, and they had exchanged twenty words, none of which, however, had reference to Mrs Headway. Waterville had been recalled to London just after the incident of which he was witness in the court of the Hôtel Meurice; and all he knew of its consequence was what he had learned from Littlemore, who, on his way back to America, where he had suddenly ascertained that there were reasons for his spending the winter, passed through the British capital. Littlemore had reported that Mrs Headway was enchanted with Lady Demesne, and had no words to speak of her kindness and sweetness. 'She told me she liked to know her son's friends, and I told her I liked to know my friends' mothers,' Mrs Headway had related. 'I should be willing to be old if I could be like that,' she had added, oblivious for the moment that she was at least as near to the age of the mother as to that of the son. The mother and son, at any rate, had retired to Cannes together, and at this moment Littlemore had received letters from home which caused him to start for Arizona. Mrs Headway had accordingly been left to her own devices, and he was afraid she had bored herself, though Mrs Bagshaw had called upon her. In November she had travelled to Italy, not by way of Cannes.

'What do you suppose she'll do in Rome?' Waterville had asked; his imagination failing him here, for he had not yet trodden the Seven Hills.

'I haven't the least idea. And I don't care!' Littlemore added in a moment. Before he left London he mentioned to Waterville that Mrs Headway, on his going to take leave of her in Paris, had made another, and a rather unexpected, attack. 'About the society business – she said I must really do something – she couldn't go on in that way. And she appealed to me in the name – I don't think I quite know how to say it.'

'I should be very glad if you would try,' said Waterville, who was constantly reminding himself that Americans in Europe were, after all, in a manner, to a man in his position, as the sheep to the shepherd.

'Well, in the name of the affection that we had formerly entertained for each other.'

'The affection?'

'So she was good enough to call it. But I deny it all. If one had to have an affection for every woman one used to sit up "evenings" with –!' And Littlemore paused, not defining the result of such an obligation. Waterville tried to imagine what it would be; while his friend embarked for New York, without telling him how, after all, he had resisted Mrs Headway's attack.

At Christmas, Waterville knew of Sir Arthur's return to England, and believed that he also knew that the baronet had not gone down to Rome. He had a theory that Lady Demesne was a very clever woman – clever enough to make her son do what she preferred and yet also make him think it his own choice. She had been politic, accommodating, about going to see Mrs Headway; but, having seen her and judged her, she had determined to break the thing off. She had been sweet and kind, as Mrs Headway said, because for the moment that was easiest; but she had made her last visit on the same occasion as her first. She had been sweet and kind, but she had set her face as a stone, and if poor Mrs Headway, arriving in London for the season, expected to find any vague promises redeemed, she would taste of the bitterness of shattered hopes. He had made up his mind that, shepherd as he was, and Mrs Headway one of his sheep, it was none of his present duty to run about after her, especially as she could be trusted not to stray too far. He saw her a second time, and she still said nothing about Sir Arthur. Waterville, who always had a theory, said to himself that she was waiting, that the baronet had not turned up. She was also getting into a house; the courier had found her in Chesterfield Street, Mayfair, a little gem, which was to cost her what jewels cost. After all this, Waterville was greatly surprised at Lady Demesne's note, and he went down to Longlands with much the same impatience with which, in Paris, he would have gone, if he had been able, to the first night of a new comedy. It seemed to him that, through a sudden stroke of good fortune, he had received a *billet d'auteur*.

It was agreeable to him to arrive at an English country-house at the close of the day. He liked the drive from the station in the twilight, the sight of the fields and copses and cottages, vague and lonely in contrast to his definite, lighted goal; the sound of the wheels on the long avenue, which turned and wound repeatedly without bringing him to what he reached however at last – the wide, grey front, with a glow in its scattered windows and a sweep of still firmer gravel up to the door. The front at Longlands, which was of this sober complexion, had a grand, pompous air; it was attributed to the genius of Sir Christopher Wren. There were wings which came forward in a semicircle, with statues placed at intervals on the cornice; so that in the flattering dusk it looked like an Italian palace, erected through some magical evocation in an English park. Waterville had taken a late train, which left him but twenty minutes to dress for dinner. He prided himself considerably on the art of dressing both quickly and well; but this operation left him no time to inquire whether the apartment to which he had been assigned befitted the dignity of a Secretary of Legation. On emerging from his room he found there was an ambassador in the house, and this discovery was a check to uneasy reflections. He tacitly assumed that he would have had a better room if it had not been for the ambassador, who was of course counted first. The large, brilliant house gave an impression of the last century and of foreign taste, of light colours, high, vaulted ceilings, with pale mythological frescos, gilded doors, surmounted by old French panels, faded tapestries and delicate damasks, stores of ancient china, among which great jars of pink roses were conspicuous. The people in the house had assembled for dinner in the principal hall, which was animated by a fire of great logs, and the company was so numerous that Waterville was afraid he was the last. Lady Demesne gave him a smile and a touch of her hand; she was very tranquil, and, saying nothing in particular, treated him as if he had been a constant visitor. Waterville was not sure whether he liked this or hated it; but these alternatives mattered equally little to his hostess, who looked at her guests as if to see whether the number were right. The master of the house was talking to a lady before the fire; when he caught sight of Waterville across the room, he waved him 'how d'ye do', with an air of being delighted to see him. He had never had that air in Paris, and Waterville had a chance to observe, what he had often heard, to how much greater advantage the English appear in their country-houses. Lady Demesne turned to him again, with her sweet vague smile, which looked as if it were the same for everything.

'We are waiting for Mrs Headway,' she said.

'Ah, she has arrived?' Waterville had quite forgotten her.

'She came at half-past five. At six she went to dress. She has had two hours.'

'Let us hope that the results will be proportionate,' said Waterville, smiling.

'Oh, the results; I don't know,' Lady Demesne murmured, without looking at him; and in these simple words Waterville saw the confirmation of his theory that she was playing a deep game. He wondered whether he should sit next to Mrs Headway at dinner, and hoped, with due deference to this lady's charms, that he should have something more novel. The results of a toilet which she had protracted through two hours were presently visible. She appeared on the staircase which descended to the hall, and which, for three minutes, as she came down rather slowly, facing the people beneath, placed her in considerable relief. Waterville, as he looked at her, felt that this was a moment of importance for her: it was virtually her entrance into English society. Mrs Headway entered English society very well, with her charming smile upon her lips and with the trophies of the Rue de la Paix trailing behind her. She made a portentous rustling as she moved. People turned their eyes toward her; there was soon a perceptible diminution of talk, though talk had not been particularly audible. She looked very much alone, and it was rather pretentious of her to come down last, though it was possible that this was simply because, before her glass, she had been unable to please herself. For she evidently felt the importance of the occasion, and Waterville was sure that her heart was beating. She was very valiant, however; she smiled more intensely, and advanced like a woman who was used to being looked at. She had at any rate the support of knowing that she was pretty; for nothing on this occasion was wanting to her prettiness, and the determination to succeed, which might have made her hard, was veiled in the virtuous consciousness that she had neglected nothing. Lady Demesne went forward to meet her; Sir Arthur took no notice of her; and presently Waterville found himself proceeding to dinner with the wife of an ecclesiastic, to whom Lady Demesne had presented him for this purpose when the hall was almost empty. The rank of this ecclesiastic in the hierarchy he learned early on the morrow; but in the mean time it seemed to him strange, somehow, that in England ecclesiastics should have wives. English life, even at the end of a year, was full of those surprises. The lady, however, was very easily accounted for; she was in no sense a violent exception, and there had been no need of the Reformation to produce her. Her name was Mrs April; she was wrapped in a large lace shawl; to eat her dinner she removed but one glove, and the other gave Waterville at moments an odd impression that the whole repast, in spite of its great completeness, was something of the picnic order. Mrs Headway was opposite, at a little distance; she had been taken in, as Waterville learned from his neighbour, by a general, a gentleman with a lean, aquiline face and a cultivated whisker, and she had on the other side a smart young man of an identity less definite. Poor Sir Arthur sat between two ladies much older than himself, whose names, redolent of history, Waterville had often heard, and had associated with figures more romantic. Mrs Headway gave Waterville no greeting; she evidently had not seen him till they were seated at table, when she simply stared at him with a violence of surprise that for a moment almost effaced her smile. It was a copious and well-ordered banquet, but as Waterville looked up and down the table he wondered whether some of its elements might not be a little dull. As he made this reflection he became conscious that he was judging the affair much more from Mrs Headway's point of view than from his own. He knew no one but Mrs April, who, displaying an almost motherly desire to give him information, told him the names of many of their companions; in return for which he explained to her that he was not in that set. Mrs Headway got on in perfection with her general; Waterville watched her more than he appeared to do, and saw that the general, who evidently was a cool hand, was drawing her out. Waterville hoped she would be careful. He was a man of fancy, in his way, and as he compared her with the rest of the company he said to himself that she was a very plucky little woman, and that her present undertaking had a touch of the heroic. She was alone against many, and her opponents were a very serried phalanx; those who were there represented a thousand others. They looked so different from her that to the eye of the imagination she stood very much on her merits. All those people seemed so completely made up, so unconscious of effort, so surrounded with things to rest upon; the men with their clean complexions, their well-hung chins, their cold, pleasant eyes, their shoulders set back, their absence of gesture; the women, several very handsome, half strangled in strings of pearls, with smooth plain tresses, seeming to look at nothing in particular, supporting silence as if it were as becoming as candlelight, yet talking a little, sometimes, in fresh, rich voices. They were all wrapped in a community of ideas, of traditions; they understood each other's accent, even each other's variations. Mrs Headway, with all her prettiness, seemed to transcend these variations; she looked foreign, exaggerated; she had too much expression; she might have been engaged for the evening. Waterville remarked, moreover, that English society was always looking out for amusement and that its transactions were conducted on a cash basis. If Mrs Headway were amusing enough she would probably succeed, and her fortune – if fortune there was – would not be a hindrance.

In the drawing-room, after dinner, he went up to her, but she gave him no greeting. She only looked at him with an expression he had never seen before – a strange, bold expression of displeasure.

'Why have you come down here?' she asked. 'Have you come to watch me?'

Waterville coloured to the roots of his hair. He knew it was terribly little like a diplomatist; but he was unable to control his blushes. Besides, he was shocked, he was angry, and in addition he was mystified. 'I came because I was asked,' he said.

'Who asked you?'

'The same person that asked you, I suppose – Lady Desmesne.'

'She's an old cat!' Mrs Headway exclaimed, turning away from him.

He turned away from her as well. He didn't know what he had done to deserve such treatment. It was a complete surprise; he had never seen her like that before. She was a very vulgar woman; that was the way people talked, he supposed, at San Diego. He threw himself almost passionately into the conversation of the others, who all seemed to him, possibly a little by contrast, extraordinarily genial and friendly. He had not, however, the consolation of seeing Mrs Headway punished for her rudeness, for she was not in the least neglected. On the contrary, in the part of the room where she sat the group was denser, and every now and then it was agitated with unanimous laughter. If she should amuse them, he said to himself, she would succeed, and evidently she was amusing them.

VII

IF she was strange, he had not come to the end of her strangeness. The next day was a Sunday and uncommonly fine; he was down before breakfast, and took a walk in the park, stopping to gaze at the thin-legged deer, scattered like pins on a velvet cushion over some of the remoter slopes, and wandering along the edge of a large sheet of ornamental water, which had a temple, in imitation of that of Vesta, on an island in the middle. He thought at this time no more about Mrs Headway; he only reflected that these stately objects had for more than a hundred years furnished a background to a great deal of family history. A little more reflection would perhaps have suggested to him that Mrs Headway was possibly an incident of some importance in the history of a family. Two or three ladies failed to appear at breakfast; Mrs Headway was one of them.

'She tells me she never leaves her room till noon,' he heard Lady Demesne say to the general, her companion of the previous evening, who had asked about her. 'She takes three hours to dress.'

'She's a monstrous clever woman!' the general exclaimed.

'To do it in three hours?'

'No, I mean the way she keeps her wits about her.'

'Yes; I think she's very clever,' said Lady Demesne, in a tone in which Waterville flattered himself that he saw more meaning than the general could see. There was something in this tall, straight, deliberate woman, who seemed at once benevolent and distant, that Waterville admired. With her delicate surface, her conventional mildness, he could see that she was very strong; she had set her patience upon a height, and she carried it like a diadem. She had very little to say to Waterville, but every now and then she made some inquiry of him that showed she had not forgotten him. Demesne himself was apparently in excellent spirits, though there was nothing bustling in his deportment, and he only went about looking very fresh and fair, as if he took a bath every hour or two, and very secure against the unexpected. Waterville had less conversation with him than with his mother; but the young man had found occasion to say to him the night before, in the smoking-room, that he was delighted Waterville had been able to come, and that if he was fond of real English scenery there were several things about there he should like very much to show him.

'You must give me an hour or two before you go, you know; I really think there are some things you'll like.'

Sir Arthur spoke as if Waterville would be very fastidious; he seemed to wish to attach a vague importance to him. On the Sunday morning after breakfast he asked Waterville if he should care to go to church; most of the ladies and several of the men were going.

'It's just as you please, you know; but it's rather a pretty walk across the fields, and a curious little church of King Stephen's time.'

Waterville knew what this meant; it was already a picture. Besides, he liked going to church, especially when he sat in the Squire's pew, which was sometimes as big as a boudoir. So he replied that he should be delighted. Then he added, without explaining his reason –

'Is Mrs Headway going?'

'I really don't know,' said his host, with an abrupt change of tone – as if Waterville had asked him whether the housekeeper were going.

'The English are awfully queer!' Waterville indulged mentally in this exclamation, to which since his arrival in England he had had recourse whenever he encountered a gap in the

consistency of things. The church was even a better picture
than Sir Arthur's description of it, and Waterville said to
himself that Mrs Headway had been a great fool not to
come. He knew what she was after; she wished to study English
life, so that she might take possession of it, and to pass in among
a hedge of bobbing rustics, and sit among the monuments of
the old Demesnes, would have told her a great deal about
English life. If she wished to fortify herself for the struggle
she had better come to that old church. When he returned
to Longlands – he had walked back across the meadows
with the canon's wife, who was a vigorous pedestrian – it
wanted half an hour of luncheon, and he was unwilling to
go indoors. He remembered that he had not yet seen the
gardens, and he wandered away in search of them. They
were on a scale which enabled him to find them without
difficulty, and they looked as if they had been kept up unremittingly for a century or two. He had not advanced very
far between their blooming borders when he heard a voice
that he recognised, and a moment after, at the turn of an
alley, he came upon Mrs Headway, who was attended by
the master of Longlands. She was bareheaded beneath her
parasol, which she flung back, stopping short, as she beheld
her compatriot.

'Oh, it's Mr Waterville come to spy me out as usual!' It was
with this remark that she greeted the slightly embarrassed
young man.

'Hallo! you've come home from church,' Sir Arthur said,
pulling out his watch.

Waterville was struck with his coolness. He admired it; for,
after all, he said to himself, it must have been disagreeable to
him to be interrupted. He felt a little like a fool, and wished he
had kept Mrs April with him, to give him the air of having come
for her sake.

Mrs Headway looked adorably fresh, in a toilet which
Waterville, who had his ideas on such matters, was sure
would not be regarded as the proper thing for a Sunday morning in an English country-house: a *négligé* of white flounces and
frills, interspersed with yellow ribbons – a garment which

Madame de Pompadour might have worn when she received a visit from Louis XV., but would probably not have worn when she went into the world. The sight of this costume gave the finishing touch to Waterville's impression that Mrs Headway knew, on the whole, what she was about. She would take a line of her own; she would not be too accommodating. She would not come down to breakfast; she would not go to church; she would wear on Sunday mornings little elaborately informal dresses, and look dreadfully un-British and un-Protestant. Perhaps, after all, this was better. She began to talk with a certain volubility.

'Isn't this too lovely? I walked all the way from the house. I'm not much at walking, but the grass in this place is like a parlour. The whole thing is beyond everything. Sir Arthur, you ought to go and look after the Ambassador; it's shameful the way I've kept you. You didn't care about the Ambassador? You said just now you had scarcely spoken to him, and you must make it up. I never saw such a way of neglecting your guests. Is that the usual style over here? Go and take him out for a ride, or make him play a game of billiards. Mr Waterville will take me home; besides, I want to scold him for spying on me.'

Waterville sharply resented this accusation. 'I had no idea you were here,' he declared.

'We weren't hiding,' said Sir Arthur quietly. 'Perhaps you'll see Mrs Headway back to the house. I think I ought to look after old Davidoff. I believe lunch is at two.'

He left them, and Waterville wandered through the gardens with Mrs Headway. She immediately wished to know if he had come there to look after her; but this inquiry was accompanied, to his surprise, with the acrimony she had displayed the night before. He was determined not to let that pass, however; when people had treated him in that way they should not be allowed to forget it.

'Do you suppose I am always thinking of you?' he asked. 'You're out of my mind sometimes. I came here to look at the gardens, and if you hadn't spoken to me I should have passed on.'

Mrs Headway was perfectly good-natured; she appeared not even to hear his defence. 'He has got two other places,' she simply rejoined. 'That's just what I wanted to know.'

But Waterville would not be turned away from his grievance. That mode of reparation to a person whom you had insulted which consisted in forgetting that you had done so, was doubtless largely in use in New Mexico; but a person of honour demanded something more. 'What did you mean last night by accusing me of having come down here to watch you? You must excuse me if I tell you that I think you were rather rude.' The sting of this accusation lay in the fact that there was a certain amount of truth in it; yet for a moment Mrs Headway, looking very blank, failed to recognise the allusion. 'She's a barbarian, after all,' thought Waterville. 'She thinks a woman may slap a man's face and run away!'

'Oh!' cried Mrs Headway, suddenly, 'I remember, I was angry with you; I didn't expect to see you. But I didn't really care about it at all. Every now and then I am angry, like that, and I work it off on any one that's handy. But it's over in three minutes, and I never think of it again. I was angry last night; I was furious with the old woman.'

'With the old woman?'

'With Sir Arthur's mother. She has no business here, any way. In this country, when the husband dies, they're expected to clear out. She has a house of her own, ten miles from here, and she has another in Portman Square; so she's got plenty of places to live. But she sticks – she sticks to him like a plaster. All of a sudden it came over me that she didn't invite me here because she liked me, but because she suspects me. She's afraid we'll make a match, and she thinks I ain't good enough for her son. She must think I'm in a great hurry to get hold of him. I never went after him, he came after me. I should never have thought of anything if it hadn't been for him. He began it last summer at Homburg; he wanted to know why I didn't come to England; he told me I should have great success. He doesn't know much about it, any way; he hasn't got much gumption. But he's a very nice man, all the same; it's very pleasant to see him surrounded by his – ' And Mrs Headway paused a moment, looking admiringly about her – 'Surrounded by all his old heirlooms. I like the old place,' she went on; 'it's beautifully mounted; I'm quite satisfied with what I've seen. I thought Lady Demesne was very friendly; she left a card on me in London, and very soon after, she wrote to me to ask me here. But I'm very quick; I sometimes see things in a flash. I saw something yesterday, when she came to speak to me at dinner-time. She saw I looked pretty, and it made her blue with rage; she hoped I would be ugly. I should like very much to oblige her; but what can one do? Then I saw that she had asked me here only because he insisted. He didn't come to see me when I first arrived – he never came near me for ten days. She managed to prevent him; she got him to make some promise. But he changed his mind after a little, and then he had to do something really polite. He called three days in succession, and he made her come. She's one of those women that resists as long as she can, and then seems to give in, while she's really resisting more than ever. She hates me like poison; I don't know what she thinks I've done. She's very underhand; she's a regular old cat. When I saw you last night at dinner, I thought she had got you here to help her.'

'To help her?' Waterville asked.

'To tell her about me. To give her information, that she can make use of against me. You may tell her what you like!'

Waterville was almost breathless with the attention he had given this extraordinary burst of confidence, and now he really felt faint. He stopped short; Mrs Headway went on a few steps, and then, stopping too, turned and looked at him. 'You're the most unspeakable woman!' he exclaimed. She seemed to him indeed a barbarian.

She laughed at him – he felt she was laughing at his expression of face – and her laugh rang through the stately gardens. 'What sort of a woman is that?'

'You've got no delicacy,' said Waterville, resolutely.

She coloured quickly, though, strange to say, she appeared not to be angry. 'No delicacy?' she repeated.

'You ought to keep those things to yourself.'

'Oh, I know what you mean; I talk about everything. When I'm excited I've got to talk. But I must do things in my own way. I've got plenty of delicacy, when people are nice to me. Ask Arthur Demesne if I ain't delicate – ask George Littlemore if I ain't. Don't stand there all day; come in to lunch!' And Mrs Headway resumed her walk, while Rupert Waterville, raising his eyes for a moment, slowly overtook her. 'Wait till I get settled; then I'll be delicate,' she pursued. 'You can't be delicate when you're trying to save your life. It's very well for *you* to talk, with the whole American Legation to back you. Of course I'm excited. I've got hold of this thing, and I don't mean to let go!' Before they reached the house she told him why he had been invited to Longlands at the same time as herself. Waterville would have liked to believe that his personal attractions sufficiently explained the fact; but she took no account of this supposition. Mrs Headway preferred to think that she lived in an element of ingenious machination, and that most things that happened had reference to herself. Waterville had been asked because he represented, however modestly, the American Legation, and their host had a friendly desire to make it appear that this pretty American visitor, of whom no one knew anything, was under the protection of that establishment. 'It would start me better,' said Mrs Headway, serenely. 'You can't help yourself – you've helped to start me. If he had known the Minister he would have asked him – or the first secretary. But he don't know them.'

They reached the house by the time Mrs Headway had developed this idea, which gave Waterville a pretext more than sufficient for detaining her in the portico. 'Do you mean to say Sir Arthur told you this?' he inquired, almost sternly.

'Told me? Of course not! Do you suppose I would let him take the tone with me that I need any favours? I should like to hear him tell me that I'm in want of assistance!'

'I don't see why he shouldn't – at the pace you go yourself. You say it to every one.'

'To every one? I say it to you, and to George Littlemore – when I'm nervous. I say it to you because I like you, and to him because I'm afraid of him. I'm not in the least afraid of you, by the way. I'm all alone – I haven't got any one. I must have some comfort, mustn't I? Sir Arthur scolded me for putting you off last night – he noticed it; and that was what made me guess his idea.'

'I'm much obliged to him,' said Waterville, rather bewildered.

'So mind you answer for me. Don't you want to give me your arm, to go in?'

'You're a most extraordinary combination,' he murmured, as she stood smiling at him.

'Oh, come, don't *you* fall in love with me!' she cried, with a laugh; and, without taking his arm, passed in before him.

That evening, before he went to dress for dinner, Waterville wandered into the library, where he felt sure that he should find some superior bindings. There was no one in the room, and he spent a happy half-hour among the treasures of literature and the triumphs of old morocco. He had a great esteem for good literature; he held that it should have handsome covers. The daylight had begun to wane, but whenever, in the rich-looking dimness, he made out the glimmer of a well-gilded back, he took down the volume and carried it to one of the deep-set windows. He had just finished the inspection of a delightfully fragrant folio, and was about to carry it back to its niche, when he found himself standing face to face with Lady Demesne. He was startled for a moment, for her tall, slim figure, her fair visage, which looked white in the high, brown room, and the air of serious intention with which she presented herself, gave something spectral to her presence. He saw her smile, however, and heard her say, in that tone of hers which was sweet almost to sadness, 'Are you looking at our books? I'm afraid they are rather dull.'

'Dull? Why, they are as bright as the day they were bound.' And he turned the glittering panels of his folio towards her.

'I'm afraid I haven't looked at them for a long time,' she murmured, going nearer to the window, where she stood looking out. Beyond the clear pane the park stretched away, with the greyness of evening beginning to hang itself on the great limbs of the oaks. The place appeared cold and empty, and the trees had an air of conscious importance, as if nature herself had been bribed somehow to take the side of country families. Lady Demesne was not an easy person to talk with; she was neither spontaneous nor abundant; she was conscious of herself, conscious of many things. Her very simplicity was conventional, though it was rather a noble convention. You might have pitied her, if you had seen that she lived in constant unrelaxed communion with certain rigid ideals. This made her at times seem tired, like a person who has undertaken too much. She gave an impression of still brightness, which was not at all brilliancy, but a carefully preserved purity. She said nothing for a moment, and there was an appearance of design in her silence, as if she wished to let him know that she had a certain business with him, without taking the trouble to announce it. She had been accustomed to expect that people would suppose things, and to be saved the trouble of explanations. Waterville made some haphazard remark about the beauty of the evening (in point of fact, the weather had changed for the worse), to which she vouchsafed no reply. Then, presently, she said, with her usual gentleness, 'I hoped I should find you here – I wish to ask you something.'

'Anything I can tell you – I shall be delighted!' Waterville exclaimed.

She gave him a look, not imperious, almost appealing, which seemed to say – 'Please be very simple – very simple indeed.' Then she glanced about her, as if there had been other people in the room; she didn't wish to appear closeted with him, or to have come on purpose. There she was, at any rate, and she went on. 'When my son told me he should ask you to come down, I was very glad. I mean, of course, that we were delighted – ' And she paused a moment. Then she added, simply, 'I want to ask you about Mrs Headway.'

'Ah, here it is!' cried Waterville within himself. More super-ficially, he smiled, as agreeably as possible, and said, 'Ah yes, I see!'

'Do you mind my asking you? I hope you don't mind. I haven't any one else to ask.'

'Your son knows her much better than I do.' Waterville said this without an intention of malice, simply to escape from the difficulties of his situation; but after he had said it, he was almost frightened by its mocking sound.

'I don't think he knows her. She knows him, which is very different. When I ask him about her, he merely tells me she is fascinating. She *is* fascinating,' said her ladyship, with inimit-able dryness.

'So I think, myself. I like her very much,' Waterville rejoined, cheerfully.

'You are in all the better position to speak of her, then.'

'To speak well of her,' said Waterville, smiling.

'Of course, if you can. I should be delighted to hear you do that. That's what I wish – to hear some good of her.'

It might have seemed, after this, that nothing would have remained but for Waterville to launch himself in a panegyric of his mysterious countrywoman; but he was no more to be tempted into that danger than into another. 'I can only say I like her,' he repeated. 'She has been very kind to me.'

'Every one seems to like her,' said Lady Demesne, with an unstudied effect of pathos. 'She is certainly very amusing.'

'She is very good-natured; she has lots of good intentions.'

'What do you call good intentions?' asked Lady Demesne, very sweetly.

'Well, I mean that she wants to be friendly and pleasant.'

'Of course you have to defend her. She's your country-woman.'

'To defend her – I must wait till she's attacked,' said Water-ville, laughing.

'That's very true. I needn't call your attention to the fact that I am not attacking her. I should never attack a person staying in this house. I only want to know something about her, and if you can't tell me, perhaps at least you can mention some one who will.'

'She'll tell you herself. Tell you by the hour!'

'What she has told my son? I shouldn't understand it. My son doesn't understand it. It's very strange. I rather hoped you might explain it.'

Waterville was silent a moment. 'I'm afraid I can't explain Mrs Headway,' he remarked at last.

'I see you admit she is very peculiar.'

Waterville hesitated again. 'It's too great a responsibility to answer you.' He felt that he was very disobliging; he knew exactly what Lady Demesne wished him to say. He was unprepared to blight the reputation of Mrs Headway to accommodate Lady Demesne; and yet, with his active little imagination, he could enter perfectly into the feelings of this tender, formal, serious woman, who – it was easy to see – had looked for her own happiness in the cultivation of duty and in extreme constancy to two or three objects of devotion chosen once for all. She must, indeed, have had a vision of things which would represent Mrs Headway as both displeasing and dangerous. But he presently became aware that she had taken his last words as a concession in which she might find help.

'You know why I ask you these things, then?'

'I think I have an idea,' said Waterville, persisting in irrelevant laughter. His laugh sounded foolish in his own ears.

'If you know that, I think you ought to assist me.' Her tone changed as she spoke these words; there was a quick tremor in it; he could see it was a confession of distress. Her distress was deep; he immediately felt that it must have been, before she made up her mind to speak to him. He was sorry for her, and determined to be very serious.

'If I could help you I would. But my position is very difficult.'

'It's not so difficult as mine!' She was going all lengths; she was really appealing to him. 'I don't imagine that you are under any obligation to Mrs Headway – you seem to me very different,' she added.

Waterville was not insensible to any discrimination that told in his favour; but these words gave him a slight shock, as if they had been an attempt at bribery. 'I am surprised that you don't like her,' he ventured to observe.

Lady Demesne looked out of the window a little. 'I don't think you are really surprised, though possibly you try to be. I don't like her, at any rate, and I can't fancy why my son should. She's very pretty, and she appears to be very clever; but I don't trust her. I don't know what has taken possession of him; it is not usual in his family to marry people like that. I don't think she's a lady. The person I should wish for him would be so very different – perhaps you can see what I mean. There's something in her history that we don't understand. My son understands it no better than I. If you could only explain to us, that might be a help. I treat you with great confidence the first time I see you; it's because I don't know where to turn. I am exceedingly anxious.'

It was very plain that she was anxious; her manner had become more vehement; her eyes seemed to shine in the thickening dusk. 'Are you very sure there is danger?' Waterville asked. 'Has he asked her to marry him, and has she consented?'

'If I wait till they settle it all, it will be too late. I have reason to believe that my son is not engaged, but he is terribly entangled. At the same time he is very uneasy, and that may save him yet. He has a great sense of honour. He is not satisfied about her past life; he doesn't know what to think of what we have been told. Even what she admits is so strange. She has been married four or five times – she has been divorced again and again – it seems so extraordinary. She tells him that in America it is different, and I daresay you have not our ideas; but really there is a limit to everything. There must have been some great irregularities – I am afraid some great scandals. It's dreadful to have to accept such things. He has not told me all this; but it's not necessary he should tell me; I know him well enough to guess.'

'Does he know that you have spoken to me?' Waterville asked.

'Not in the least. But I must tell you that I shall repeat to him anything that you may say against her.'

'I had better say nothing, then. It's very delicate. Mrs Headway is quite undefended. One may like her or not, of course. I have seen nothing of her that is not perfectly correct.'

'And you have heard nothing?'

Waterville remembered Littlemore's assertion that there were cases in which a man was bound in honour to tell an untruth, and he wondered whether this were such a case. Lady Demesne imposed herself, she made him believe in the reality of her grievance, and he saw the gulf that divided her from a pushing little woman who had lived with Western editors. She was right to wish not to be connected with Mrs Headway. After all, there had been nothing in his relations with that lady to make it incumbent on him to lie for her. He had not sought her acquaintance, she had sought his; she had sent for him to come and see her. And yet he couldn't give her away, as they said in New York; that stuck in his throat. 'I am afraid I really can't say anything. And it wouldn't matter. Your son won't give her up because I happen not to like her.'

'If he were to believe she has done wrong, he would give her up.'

'Well, I have no right to say so,' said Waterville.

Lady Demesne turned away; she was much disappointed in him. He was afraid she was going to break out – 'Why, then, do you suppose I asked you here?' She quitted her place near the window and was apparently about to leave the room. But she stopped short. 'You know something against her, but you won't say it.'

Waterville hugged his folio and looked awkward. 'You attribute things to me. I shall never say anything.'

'Of course you are perfectly free. There is some one else who knows, I think – another American – a gentleman who was in Paris when my son was there. I have forgotten his name.'

'A friend of Mrs Headway's? I suppose you mean George Littlemore.'

'Yes – Mr Littlemore. He has a sister, whom I have met; I didn't know she was his sister till to-day. Mrs Headway spoke of her, but I find she doesn't know her. That itself is a proof, I think. Do you think *he* would help me?' Lady Demesne asked, very simply.

'I doubt it, but you can try.'

'I wish he had come with you. Do you think he would come?'

'He is in America at this moment, but I believe he soon comes back.'

'I shall go to his sister; I will ask her to bring him to see me. She is extremely nice; I think she will understand. Unfortunately there is very little time.'

'Don't count too much on Littlemore,' said Waterville, gravely.

'You men have no pity.'

'Why should we pity you? How can Mrs Headway hurt such a person as you?'

Lady Demesne hesitated a moment. 'It hurts me to hear her voice.'

'Her voice is very sweet.'

'Possibly. But she's horrible!'

This was too much, it seemed to Waterville; poor Mrs Headway was extremely open to criticism, and he himself had declared she was a barbarian. Yet she was not horrible. 'It's for your son to pity you. If he doesn't, how can you expect it of others?'

'Oh, but he does!' And with a majesty that was more striking even than her logic, Lady Demesne moved towards the door.

Waterville advanced to open it for her, and as she passed out he said, 'There's one thing you can do – try to like her!'

She shot him a terrible glance. 'That would be worst of all!'

VIII

GEORGE LITTLEMORE arrived in London on the twentieth of May, and one of the first things he did was to go and see Waterville at the Legation, where he made known to him that he had taken for the rest of the season a house at Queen Anne's Gate, so that his sister and her husband, who, under the pressure of diminished rents, had let their own town-residence, might come up and spend a couple of months with him.

'One of the consequences of your having a house will be that you will have to entertain Mrs Headway,' Waterville said.

Littlemore sat there with his hands crossed upon his stick; he looked at Waterville with an eye that failed to kindle at the mention of this lady's name. 'Has she got into European society?' he asked, rather languidly.

'Very much, I should say. She has a house, and a carriage, and diamonds, and everything handsome. She seems already to know a lot of people; they put her name in the *Morning Post*. She has come up very quickly; she's almost famous. Every one is asking about her – you'll be plied with questions.'

Littlemore listened gravely. 'How did she get in?'

'She met a large party at Longlands, and made them all think her great fun. They must have taken her up; she only wanted a start.'

Littlemore seemed suddenly to be struck with the grotesqueness of this news, to which his first response was a burst of quick laughter. 'To think of Nancy Beck! The people here are queer people. There's no one they won't go after. They wouldn't touch her in New York.'

'Oh, New York's old-fashioned,' said Waterville; and he announced to his friend that Lady Demesne was very eager for his arrival, and wanted to make him help her prevent her son's bringing such a person into the family. Littlemore apparently was not alarmed at her ladyship's projects, and intimated, in the manner of a man who thought them rather impertinent, that he could trust himself to keep out of her way. 'It isn't a proper marriage, at any rate,' Waterville declared.

'Why not, if he loves her?'

'Oh, if that's all you want!' cried Waterville, with a degree of cynicism that rather surprised his companion. 'Would you marry her yourself?'

'Certainly, if I were in love with her.'

'You took care not to be that.'

'Yes, I did – and so Demesne had better have done. But since he's bitten – !' and Littlemore terminated his sentence in a suppressed yawn.

Waterville presently asked him how he would manage, in view of his sister's advent, about asking Mrs Headway to his house; and he replied that he would manage by simply not asking her. Upon this, Waterville declared that he was very inconsistent; to which Littlemore rejoined that it was very possible. But he asked whether they couldn't talk about something else than Mrs Headway. He couldn't enter into the young man's interest in her, and was sure to have enough of her later.

Waterville would have been sorry to give a false idea of his interest in Mrs Headway; for he flattered himself the feeling had definite limits. He had been two or three times to see her; but it was a relief to think that she was now quite independent of him. There had been no revival of that intimate intercourse which occurred during the visit to Longlands. She could dispense with assistance now; she knew herself that she was in the current of success. She pretended to be surprised at her good fortune, especially at its rapidity; but she was really surprised at nothing. She took things as they came, and, being essentially a woman of action, wasted almost as little time in elation as she would have done in despondence. She talked a great deal about Lord Edward and Lady Margaret, and about such other members of the nobility as had shown a desire to cultivate her acquaintance; professing to understand perfectly the sources of a popularity which apparently was destined to increase. 'They come to laugh at me,' she said; 'they come simply to get things to repeat. I can't open my mouth but they burst into fits. It's a settled thing that I'm an American humorist; if I say the simplest things, they begin to roar. I must express myself somehow; and indeed when I hold my tongue they think me funnier than ever. They repeat what I say to a great person, and a great person told some of them the other night that he wanted to hear me for himself. I'll do for him what I do for the others; no better and no worse. I don't know how I do it; I talk the only way I can. They tell me it isn't so much the things I say as the way I say them. Well, they're very easy to please. They don't care for me; it's only to be able to repeat Mrs Headway's "last". Every one wants to have it first; it's a regular race.' When she found what was expected of her, she undertook to supply the article in abundance; and the poor little woman really worked hard at her Americanisms. If the taste of London lay that way, she would do her best to gratify it; it was only a pity she hadn't known it before; she would have made more extensive preparations. She thought it a disadvantage, of old, to live in Arizona, in Dakotah, in the newly admitted States; but now she perceived that, as she phrased it to herself, this was the best thing that ever had happened to her. She tried to remember all the queer stories she had heard out there, and keenly regretted that she had not taken them down in writing; she drummed up the echoes of the Rocky Mountains and practised the intonations of the Pacific slope. When she saw her audience in convulsions, she said to herself that this was success, and believed that, if she had only come to London five years sooner, she might have married a duke. That would have been even a more absorbing spectacle for the London world than the actual proceedings of Sir Arthur Demesne, who, however, lived sufficiently in the eye of society to justify the rumour that there were bets about town as to the issue of his already protracted courtship. It was food for curiosity to see a young man of his pattern – one of the few 'earnest' young men of the Tory side, with an income sufficient for tastes more marked than those by which he was known – make up to a lady several years older than himself, whose fund of Californian slang was even larger than her stock of dollars. Mrs Headway had got a good many new ideas since her arrival in London, but she also retained several old ones. The chief of these – it was now a year old – was that Sir Arthur Demesne was the most irreproachable young man in the world. There were, of course, a good many things that he was not. He was not amusing; he was not insinuating; he was not of an absolutely irrepressible ardour. She believed he was constant; but he was certainly not eager. With these things, however, Mrs Headway could perfectly dispense; she had, in particular, quite outlived the need of being amused. She had had a very exciting life, and her vision of happiness at present was to be magnificently bored. The idea of complete and uncriticised respectability filled her soul with satisfaction; her imagination prostrated itself in the presence of this virtue. She was aware that she had achieved it but ill in her own person; but she could now, at least, connect herself with it by sacred ties. She could prove in that way what was her deepest feeling. This was a religious appreciation of Sir Arthur's great quality – his smooth and rounded, his blooming, lily-like exemption from social flaws.

She was at home when Littlemore went to see her, and surrounded by several visitors, to whom she was giving a late cup of tea and to whom she introduced her compatriot. He stayed till they dispersed, in spite of the manoeuvres of a gentleman who evidently desired to outstay him, but who, whatever might have been his happy fortune on former visits, received on this occasion no encouragement from Mrs Headway. He looked at Littlemore slowly, beginning with his boots and travelling upwards, as if to discover the reason of so unexpected a preference, and then, without a salutation, left him face to face with their hostess.

'I'm curious to see what you'll do for me, now that you've got your sister with you,' Mrs Headway presently remarked, having heard of this circumstance from Rupert Waterville. 'I suppose you'll have to do something, you know. I'm sorry for you; but I don't see how you can get off. You might ask me to dine some day when she's dining out. I would come even then, I think, because I want to keep on the right side of you.'

'I call that the wrong side,' said Littlemore.

'Yes, I see. It's your sister that's on the right side. You're in rather an embarrassing position, ain't you? However, you take those things very quietly. There's something in you that exasperates me. What does your sister think of me? Does she hate me?'

'She knows nothing about you.'

'Have you told her nothing?'

'Never a word.'

'Hasn't she asked you? That shows that she hates me. She thinks I ain't creditable to America. I know all that. She wants to show people over here that, however they may be taken in by me, she knows much better. But she'll have to ask you about me; she can't go on for ever. Then what'll you say?'

'That you're the most successful woman in Europe.'

'Oh, bother!' cried Mrs Headway, with irritation.

'Haven't you got into European society?'

'Maybe I have, maybe I haven't. It's too soon to see. I can't tell this season. Every one says I've got to wait till next, to see if it's the same. Sometimes they take you up for a few weeks, and then never know you again. You've got to fasten the thing somehow – to drive in a nail.'

'You speak as if it were your coffin,' said Littlemore.

'Well, it is a kind of coffin. I'm burying my past!'

Littlemore winced at this. He was tired to death of her past. He changed the subject, and made her talk about London, a topic which she treated with a great deal of humour. She entertained him for half an hour, at the expense of most of her new acquaintances and of some of the most venerable features of the great city. He himself looked at England from the out-side, as much as it was possible to do; but in the midst of her familiar allusions to people and things known to her only since yesterday, he was struck with the fact that she would never really be initiated. She buzzed over the surface of things like a fly on a window-pane. She liked it immensely; she was flat-tered, encouraged, excited; she dropped her confident judge-ments as if she were scattering flowers, and talked about her intentions, her prospects, her wishes. But she knew no more about English life than about the molecular theory. The words in which he had described her of old to Waterville came back to him: '*Elle ne se doute de rien*!' Suddenly she jumped up; she was going out to dine, and it was time to dress. 'Before you leave I want you to promise me something,' she said off-hand, but with a look which he had seen before and which meant that the point was important. 'You'll be sure to be questioned about me.' And then she paused.

'How do people know I know you?'

'You haven't bragged about it? Is that what you mean? You can be a brute when you try. They do know it, at any rate. Possibly I may have told them. They'll come to you, to ask about me. I mean from Lady Demesne. She's in an awful state – she's so afraid her son'll marry me.'

Littlemore was unable to control a laugh. 'I'm not, if he hasn't done it yet.'

'He can't make up his mind. He likes me so much, yet he thinks I'm not a woman to marry.' It was positively grotesque, the detachment with which she spoke of herself.

'He must be a poor creature if he won't marry you as you are,' Littlemore said.

This was not a very gallant form of speech; but Mrs Head-way let it pass. She only replied, 'Well, he wants to be very careful, and so he ought to be!'

'If he asks too many questions, he's not worth marrying.'

'I beg your pardon – he's worth marrying whatever he does – he's worth marrying for me. And I want to marry him – that's what I want to do.'

'Is he waiting for me, to settle it?'

'He's waiting for I don't know what – for some one to come and tell him that I'm the sweetest of the sweet. Then he'll believe it. Some one who has been out there and knows all about me. Of course you're the man, you're created on pur-pose. Don't you remember how I told you in Paris that he wanted to ask you? He was ashamed, and he gave it up; he tried to forget me. But now it's all on again; only, meanwhile, his mother has been at him. She works at him night and day, like a weasel in a hole, to persuade him that I'm far beneath him. He's very fond of her, and he's very open to influence – I mean from his mother, not from any one else. Except me, of course. Oh, I've influenced him, I've explained everything fifty times over. But some things are rather complicated, don't you know; and he keeps coming back to them. He wants every little speck explained. He won't come to you himself, but his mother will, or she'll send some of her people. I guess she'll send the lawyer – the family solicitor, they call him. She wanted to send him out to America to make inquiries, only she didn't know where to send. Of course I couldn't be expected to give the places, they've got to find them out for themselves. She knows all about you, and she has made the acquaintance of your sister.

So you see how much I know. She's waiting for you; she means to catch you. She has an idea she can fix you – make you say what'll meet her views. Then she'll lay it before Sir Arthur. So you'll be so good as to deny everything.'

Littlemore listened to this little address attentively, but the conclusion left him staring. 'You don't mean that anything I can say will make a difference?'

'Don't be affected! You know it will as well as I.'

'You make him out a precious idiot.'

'Never mind what I make him out. I want to marry him, that's all. And I appeal to you solemnly. You can save me, as you can lose me. If you lose me, you'll be a coward. And if you say a word against me, I shall be lost.'

'Go and dress for dinner, that's your salvation,' Littlemore answered, separating from her at the head of the stairs.

IX

IT was very well for him to take that tone; but he felt as he walked home that he should scarcely know what to say to people who were determined, as Mrs Headway put it, to catch him. She had worked a certain spell; she had succeeded in making him feel responsible. The sight of her success, however, rather hardened his heart; he was irritated by her ascending movement. He dined alone that evening, while his sister and her husband, who had engagements every day for a month, partook of their repast at the expense of some friends. Mrs Dolphin, however, came home rather early, and immediately sought admittance to the small apartment at the foot of the staircase, which was already spoken of as Littlemore's den. Reginald had gone to a 'squash' somewhere, and she had returned without delay, having something particular to say to her brother. She was too impatient even to wait till the next morning. She looked impatient; she was very unlike George Littlemore. 'I want you to tell me about Mrs Headway,' she said, while he started slightly at the coincidence of this remark with his own thoughts. He was just making up his mind at last to speak to her. She unfastened her cloak and tossed it over a chair, then pulled off her long tight black gloves, which were not so fine as those Mrs Headway wore; all this as if she were preparing herself for an important interview. She was a small, neat woman, who had once been pretty, with a small, thin voice, a sweet, quiet manner, and a perfect knowledge of what it was proper to do on every occasion in life. She always did it, and her conception of it was so definite that failure would have left her without excuse. She was usually not taken for an American, but she made a point of being one, because she flattered herself that she was of a type which, in that nationality, borrowed distinction from its rarity. She was by nature a great conservative, and had ended by being a better Tory than her husband. She was thought by some of her old friends to have changed immensely since her marriage. She knew as much about English society as if she had invented it; had a way, usually, of looking as if she were dressed for a ride; had also thin lips and pretty teeth; and was as positive as she was amiable. She told her brother that Mrs Headway had given out that he was her most intimate friend, and she thought it rather odd he had never spoken of her. He admitted that he had known her a long time, referred to the circumstances in which the acquaintance had sprung up, and added that he had seen her that afternoon. He sat there smoking his cigar and looking at the ceiling, while Mrs Dolphin delivered herself of a series of questions. Was it true that he liked her so much, was it true he thought her a possible woman to marry, was it not true that her antecedents had been most peculiar?

'I may as well tell you that I have a letter from Lady Demesne,' Mrs Dolphin said. 'It came to me just before I went out, and I have it in my pocket.'

She drew forth the missive, which she evidently wished to read to him; but he gave her no invitation to do so. He knew that she had come to him to extract a declaration adverse to Mrs Headway's projects, and however little satisfaction he might take in this lady's upward flight, he hated to be urged and pushed. He had a great esteem for Mrs Dolphin, who, among other Hampshire notions, had picked up that of the preponderance of the male members of a family, so that she treated him with a consideration which made his having an English sister rather a luxury. Nevertheless he was not very encouraging about Mrs Headway. He admitted once for all that she had not behaved properly – it wasn't worth while to split hairs about that – but he couldn't see that she was much worse than many other women, and he couldn't get up much feeling about her marrying or not marrying. Moreover, it was none of his business, and he intimated that it was none of Mrs Dolphin's.

'One surely can't resist the claims of common humanity!' his sister replied; and she added that he was very inconsistent. He didn't respect Mrs Headway, he knew the most dreadful things about her, he didn't think her fit company for his own flesh and blood. And yet he was willing to let poor Arthur Demesne be taken in by her!

'Perfectly willing!' Littlemore exclaimed. 'All I've got to do is not to marry her myself.'

'Don't you think we have any responsibilities, any duties?'

'I don't know what you mean. If she can succeed, she's welcome. It's a splendid sight in its way.'

'How do you mean splendid?'

'Why, she has run up the tree as if she were a squirrel!'

'It's very true that she has an audacity *à toute épreuve*. But English society has become scandalously easy. I never saw anything like the people that are taken up. Mrs Headway has had only to appear to succeed. If they think there's something bad about you they'll be sure to run after you. It's like the decadence of the Roman Empire. You can see to look at Mrs Headway that she's not a lady. She's pretty, very pretty, but she looks like a dissipated dressmaker. She failed absolutely in New York. I have seen her three times – she apparently goes everywhere. I didn't speak of her – I was wanting to see what you would do. I saw that you meant to do nothing, then this letter decided me. It's written on purpose to be shown to you; it's what she wants you to do. She wrote to me before I came to town, and I went to see her as soon as I arrived. I think it very important. I told her that if she would draw up a little statement I would put it before you as soon as we got settled. She's in real distress. I think you ought to feel for her. You ought to communicate the facts exactly as they stand. A woman has no right to do such things and come and ask to be accepted. She may make it up with her conscience, but she can't make it up with society. Last night at Lady Dovedale's I was afraid she would know who I was and come and speak to me. I was so frightened that I went away. If Sir Arthur wishes to marry her for what she is, of course he's welcome. But at least he ought to know.'

Mrs Dolphin was not excited nor voluble; she moved from point to point with a calmness which had all the air of being used to have reason on its side. She deeply desired, however, that Mrs Headway's triumphant career should be checked; she had sufficiently abused the facilities of things. Herself a party to an international marriage, Mrs Dolphin naturally wished that the class to which she belonged should close its ranks and carry its standard high.

'It seems to me that she's quite as good as the little baronet,' said Littlemore, lighting another cigar.

'As good? What do you mean? No one has ever breathed a word against him.'

'Very likely. But he's a nonentity, and she at least is somebody. She's a person, and a very clever one. Besides, she's quite as good as the women that lots of them have married. I never heard that the British gentry were so unspotted.'

'I know nothing about other cases,' Mrs Dolphin said, 'I only know about this one. It so happens that I have been brought near to it, and that an appeal has been made to me. The English are very romantic – the most romantic people in the world, if that's what you mean. They do the strangest things, from the force of passion – even those from whom you would least expect it. They marry their cooks – they marry their coachmen – and their romances always have the most miserable end. I'm sure this one would be most wretched. How can you pretend that such a woman as that is to be trusted? What I see is a fine old race – one of the oldest and most honourable in England, people with every tradition of good conduct and high principle – and a dreadful, disreputable, vulgar little woman, who hasn't an idea of what such things are, trying to force her way into it. I hate to see such things – I want to go to the rescue!'

'I don't – I don't care anything about the fine old race.'

'Not from interested motives, of course, any more than I. But surely, on artistic grounds, on grounds of decency?'

'Mrs Headway isn't indecent – you go too far. You must remember that she's an old friend of mine.' Littlemore had become rather stern; Mrs Dolphin was forgetting the consideration due, from an English point of view, to brothers.

She forgot it even a little more. 'Oh, if you are in love with her, too!' she murmured, turning away.

He made no answer to this, and the words had no sting for him. But at last, to finish the affair, he asked what in the world the old lady wanted him to do. Did she want him to go out into Piccadilly and announce to the passers-by that there was one winter when even Mrs Headway's sister didn't know who was her husband?

Mrs Dolphin answered this inquiry by reading out Lady Demesne's letter, which her brother, as she folded it up again, pronounced one of the most extraordinary letters he had ever heard.

'It's very sad – it's a cry of distress,' said Mrs Dolphin. 'The whole meaning of it is that she wishes you would come and see her. She doesn't say so in so many words, but I can read between the lines. Besides, she told me she would give anything to see you. Let me assure you it's your duty to go.'

'To go and abuse Nancy Beck?'

'Go and praise her, if you like!' This was very clever of Mrs Dolphin, but her brother was not so easily caught. He didn't take that view of his duty, and he declined to cross her ladyship's threshold. 'Then she'll come and see you,' said Mrs Dolphin, with decision.

'If she does, I'll tell her Nancy's an angel.'

'If you can say so conscientiously, she'll be delighted to hear it,' Mrs Dolphin replied, as she gathered up her cloak and gloves.

Meeting Rupert Waterville the next day, as he often did, at the St George's Club, which offers a much-appreciated hospitality to secretaries of legation and to the natives of the countries they assist in representing, Littlemore let him know that his prophecy had been fulfilled and that Lady Demesne had been making proposals for an interview. 'My sister read me a most remarkable letter from her,' he said.

'What sort of a letter?'

'The letter of a woman so scared that she will do anything. I may be a great brute, but her fright amuses me.'

'You're in the position of Olivier de Jalin, in the *Demi-Monde*,' Waterville remarked.

'In the *Demi-Monde*?' Littlemore was not quick at catching literary allusions.

'Don't you remember the play we saw in Paris? Or like Don Fabrice in *L'Aventurière*. A bad woman tries to marry an honourable man, who doesn't know how bad she is, and they who do know step in and push her back.'

'Yes, I remember. There was a good deal of lying, all round.'

'They prevented the marriage, however, which is the great thing.'

'The great thing, if you care about it. One of them was the intimate friend of the fellow, the other was his son. Demesne's nothing to me.'

'He's a very good fellow,' said Waterville.

'Go and tell him, then.'

'Play the part of Olivier de Jalin? Oh, I can't; I'm not Olivier. But I wish he would come along. Mrs Headway oughtn't really to be allowed to pass.'

'I wish to heaven they'd let me alone,' Littlemore murmured, ruefully, staring for a while out of the window.

'Do you still hold to that theory you propounded in Paris? Are you willing to commit perjury?' Waterville asked.

'Of course I can refuse to answer questions – even that one.'

'As I told you before, that will amount to a condemnation.'

'It may amount to what it pleases. I think I will go to Paris.'

'That will be the same as not answering. But it's quite the best thing you can do. I have been thinking a great deal about it, and it seems to me, from the social point of view, that, as I say, she really oughtn't to pass.' Waterville had the air of looking at the thing from a great elevation; his tone, the expression of his face, indicated this lofty flight; the effect of which, as he glanced down at his didactic young friend, Littlemore found peculiarly irritating.

'No, after all, hanged if they shall drive me away!' he exclaimed abruptly; and walked off, while his companion looked after him.

X

THE morning after this Littlemore received a note from Mrs Headway – a short and simple note, consisting merely of the words, 'I shall be at home this afternoon; will you come and see me at five? I have something particular to say to you.' He sent no answer to this inquiry, but he went to the little house in Chesterfield Street at the hour that its mistress had designated.

'I don't believe you know what sort of woman I am!' she exclaimed, as soon as he stood before her.

'Oh, Lord!' Littlemore groaned, dropping into a chair. Then he added, 'Don't begin on that sort of thing!'

'I shall begin – that's what I wanted to say. It's very important. You don't know me – you don't understand me. You think you do – but you don't.'

'It isn't for the want of your having told me – many, many times!' And Littlemore smiled, though he was bored at the prospect that opened before him. The last word of all was, decidedly, that Mrs Headway was a nuisance. She didn't deserve to be spared!

She glared at him a little, at this; her face was no longer the face that smiled. She looked sharp and violent, almost old; the change was complete. But she gave a little angry laugh. 'Yes, I know; men are so stupid. They know nothing about women but what women tell them. And women tell them things on purpose, to see how stupid they can be. I've told you things like that, just for amusement, when it was dull. If you believed them, it was your own fault. But now I am serious, I want you really to know.'

'I don't want to know. I know enough.'

'How do you mean, you know enough?' she cried, with a flushed face. 'What business have you to know anything?' The poor little woman, in her passionate purpose, was not obliged to be consistent, and the loud laugh with which Littlemore greeted this interrogation must have seemed to her unduly harsh. 'You shall know what I want you to know, however. You think me a bad woman – you don't respect me; I told you that in Paris. I have done things I don't understand, myself, to-day; that I admit, as fully as you please. But I've completely changed, and I want to change everything. You ought to enter into that; you ought to see what I want. I hate everything that has happened to me before this; I loathe it, I despise it. I went on that way trying – one thing and another. But now I've got what I want. Do you expect me to go down on my knees to you? I believe I will, I'm so anxious. You can help me – no one else can do a thing – no one can do anything – they are only waiting to see if he'll do it. I told you in Paris you could help me, and it's just as true now. Say a good word for me, for God's sake! You haven't lifted your little finger, or I should know it by this time. It will just make the difference. Or if your sister would come and see me, I should be all right. Women are pitiless, pitiless, and you are pitiless too. It isn't that she's any-thing so great, most of my friends are better than that! – but she's the one woman who *knows*, and people know that she knows. *He* knows that she knows, and he knows she doesn't come. So she kills me – she kills me! I understand perfectly what he wants – I shall do everything, be anything, I shall be the most perfect wife. The old woman will adore me when she knows me – it's too stupid of her not to see. Everything in the past is over; it has all fallen away from me; it's the life of another woman. This was what I wanted; I knew I should find it some day. What could I do in those horrible places? I had to take what I could. But now I've got a nice country. I want you to do me justice; you have never done me justice; that's what I sent for you for.'

Littlemore suddenly ceased to be bored; but a variety of feelings had taken the place of a single one. It was impossible not to be touched; she really meant what she said. People don't change their nature; but they change their desires, their ideal, their effort. This incoherent and passionate protestation was an assurance that she was literally panting to be respectable. But the poor woman, whatever she did, was condemned, as Littlemore had said of old, in Paris, to Waterville, to be only half-right. The colour rose to her visitor's face as he listened to this outpouring of anxiety and egotism; she had not managed her early life very well, but there was no need of her going down on her knees. 'It's very painful to me to hear all this,' he said. 'You are under no obligation to say such things to me. You entirely misconceive my attitude – my influence.'

'Oh yes, you shirk it – you only wish to shirk it!' she cried, flinging away fiercely the sofa-cushion on which she had been resting.

'Marry whom you please!' Littlemore almost shouted, springing to his feet.

He had hardly spoken when the door was thrown open, and the servant announced Sir Arthur Demesne. The baronet entered with a certain briskness, but he stopped short on seeing that Mrs Headway had another visitor. Recognising Littlemore, however, he gave a slight exclamation, which might have passed for a greeting. Mrs Headway, who had risen as he came in, looked with extraordinary earnestness from one of the men to the other; then, like a person who had a sudden inspiration, she clasped her hands together and cried out, 'I'm so glad you've met; if I had arranged it, it couldn't be better!'

'If you had arranged it?' said Sir Arthur, crinkling a little his high, white forehead, while the conviction rose before Littlemore that she had indeed arranged it.

'I'm going to do something very strange,' she went on, and her eye glittered with a light that confirmed her words.

'You're excited, I'm afraid you're ill.' Sir Arthur stood there with his hat and his stick; he was evidently much annoyed.

'It's an excellent opportunity; you must forgive me if I take advantage.' And she flashed a tender, touching ray at the baronet. 'I have wanted this a long time – perhaps you have seen I wanted it. Mr Littlemore has known me a long, long time; he's an old, old friend. I told you that in Paris, don't you remember? Well, he's my only one, and I want him to speak for me.' Her eyes had turned now to Littlemore; they rested upon him with a sweetness that only made the whole proceeding more audacious. She had begun to smile again, though she was visibly trembling. 'He's my only one,' she continued; 'it's a great pity, you ought to have known others. But I'm very much alone, I must make the best of what I have. I want so much that some one else than myself should speak for me. Women usually can ask that service of a relative, or of another woman. I can't; it's a great pity, but it's not my fault, it's my misfortune. None of my people are here; and I'm terribly alone in the world. But Mr Littlemore will tell you; he will say he has known me for years. He will tell you whether he knows any reason – whether he knows anything against me. He's been wanting the chance; but he thought he couldn't begin himself. You see I treat you as an old friend, dear Mr Littlemore. I will leave you with Sir Arthur. You will both excuse me.' The expression of her face, turned towards Littlemore, as she delivered herself of this singular proposal had the intentness of a magician who wishes to work a spell. She gave Sir Arthur another smile, and then she swept out of the room.

The two men remained in the extraordinary position that she had created for them; neither of them moved even to open the door for her. She closed it behind her, and for a moment there was a deep, portentous silence. Sir Arthur Demesne, who was very pale, stared hard at the carpet.

'I am placed in an impossible situation,' Littlemore said at last, 'and I don't imagine that you accept it any more than I do.'

The baronet kept the same attitude; he neither looked up nor answered. Littlemore felt a sudden gush of pity for him. Of course he couldn't accept the situation; but all the same, he was half sick with anxiety to see how this nondescript American, who was both so valuable and so superfluous, so familiar and so inscrutable, would consider Mrs Headway's challenge.

'Have you any question to ask me?' Littlemore went on.

At this Sir Arthur looked up. Littlemore had seen the look before; he had described it to Waterville after the baronet came to call on him in Paris. There were other things mingled with it now – shame, annoyance, pride; but the great thing, the intense desire to *know*, was paramount.

'Good God, how can I tell him?' Littlemore exclaimed to himself.

Sir Arthur's hesitation was probably extremely brief; but Littlemore heard the ticking of the clock while it lasted. 'Certainly, I have no question to ask,' the young man said in a voice of cool, almost insolent surprise.

'Good-day, then.'

'Good-day.'

And Littlemore left Sir Arthur in possession. He expected to find Mrs Headway at the foot of the staircase; but he quitted the house without interruption.

On the morrow, after lunch, as he was leaving the little mansion at Queen Anne's Gate, the postman handed him a letter. Littlemore opened and read it on the steps of his house, an operation which took but a moment. It ran as follows: –

'DEAR MR LITTLEMORE, – It will interest you to know that I am engaged to be married to Sir Arthur Demesne, and that our marriage is to take place as soon as their stupid old Parliament rises. But it's not to come out for some days, and I am sure that I can trust meanwhile to your complete discretion.

'Yours very sincerely,

'NANCY H.

'P.S. – He made me a terrible scene for what I did yesterday, but he came back in the evening and made it up. That's how the thing comes to be settled. He won't tell me what passed between you – he requested me never to allude to the subject. I don't care; I was bound you should speak!'

Littlemore thrust this epistle into his pocket and marched away with it. He had come out to do various things, but he forgot his business for the time, and before he knew it had walked into Hyde Park. He left the carriages and riders to one side of him and followed the Serpentine into Kensington Gardens, of which he made the complete circuit. He felt annoyed, and more disappointed than he understood – than he would have understood if he had tried. Now that Nancy Beck had succeeded, her success seemed offensive, and he was almost sorry he had not said to Sir Arthur – 'Oh, well, she was pretty bad, you know.' However, now the thing was settled, at least they would leave him alone. He walked off his irritation, and before he went about the business he had come out for, had ceased to think about Mrs Headway. He went home at six o'clock, and the servant who admitted him informed him in doing so that Mrs Dolphin had requested he should be told on his return that she wished to see him in the drawing-room. 'It's another trap!' he said to himself, instinctively; but, in spite of this reflection, he went upstairs. On entering the apartment in which Mrs Dolphin was accustomed to sit, he found that she had a visitor. This visitor, who was apparently on the point of departing, was a tall, elderly woman, and the two ladies stood together in the middle of the room.

'I'm so glad you've come back,' said Mrs Dolphin, without meeting her brother's eye. 'I want so much to introduce you to Lady Demesne, and I hoped you would come in. Must you really go – won't you stay a little?' she added, turning to her companion; and without waiting for an answer, went on hastily – 'I must leave you a moment – excuse me. I will come back!' Before he knew it, Littlemore found himself alone with Lady Demesne, and he understood that, since he had not been willing to go and see her, she had taken upon herself to make an advance. It had the queerest effect, all the same, to see his sister playing the same tricks as Nancy Beck!

'Ah, she must be in a fidget!' he said to himself as he stood before Lady Demesne. She looked delicate and modest, even timid, as far as a tall, serene woman who carried her head very well could look so; and she was such a different type from Mrs Headway that his present vision of Nancy's triumph gave her by contrast something of the dignity of the vanquished. It made him feel sorry for her. She lost no time; she went straight to the point. She evidently felt that in the situation in which she had placed herself, her only advantage could consist in being simple and business-like.

'I'm so glad to see you for a moment. I wish so much to ask you if you can give me any information about a person you

know and about whom I have been in correspondence with Mrs
Dolphin. I mean Mrs Headway.'

'Won't you sit down?' asked Littlemore.

'No, I thank you. I have only a moment.'

'May I ask you why you make this inquiry?'

'Of course I must give you my reason. I am afraid my son will
marry her.'

Littlemore was puzzled for a moment; then he felt sure that
she was not yet aware of the fact imparted to him in Mrs
Headway's note. 'You don't like her?' he said, exaggerating in
spite of himself the interrogative inflexion.

'Not at all,' said Lady Demesne, smiling and looking at him.
Her smile was gentle, without rancour; Littlemore thought it
almost beautiful.

'What would you like me to say?' he asked.

'Whether you think her respectable.'

'What good will that do you? How can it possibly affect the
event?'

'It will do me no good, of course, if your opinion is favourable. But if you tell me it is not, I shall be able to say to my son
that the one person in London who has known her more than
six months thinks her a bad woman.'

This epithet, on Lady Demesne's clear lips, evoked no
protest from Littlemore. He had suddenly become conscious
of the need to utter the simple truth with which he
had answered Rupert Waterville's first question at the Théâtre
Français. 'I don't think Mrs Headway respectable,' he said.

'I was sure you would say that.' Lady Demesne seemed to
pant a little.

'I can say nothing more – not a word. That's my opinion.
I don't think it will help you.'

'I think it will. I wished to have it from your own lips. That
makes all the difference,' said Lady Demesne. 'I am exceedingly obliged to you.' And she offered him her hand; after which
he accompanied her in silence to the door.

He felt no discomfort, no remorse, at what he had said; he
only felt relief. Perhaps it was because he believed it would
make no difference. It made a difference only in what was at

the bottom of all things – his own sense of fitness. He only wished he had remarked to Lady Demesne that Mrs Headway would probably make her son a capital wife. But that, at least, would make no difference. He requested his sister, who had wondered greatly at the brevity of his interview with Lady Demesne, to spare him all questions on this subject; and Mrs Dolphin went about for some days in the happy faith that there were to be no dreadful Americans in English society compromising her native land.

Her faith, however, was short-lived. Nothing had made any difference; it was, perhaps, too late. The London world heard in the first days of July, not that Sir Arthur Demesne was to marry Mrs Headway, but that the pair had been privately, and it was to be hoped, as regards Mrs Headway, on this occasion indissolubly, united. Lady Demesne gave neither sign nor sound; she only retired to the country.

'I think you might have done differently,' said Mrs Dolphin, very pale, to her brother. 'But of course everything will come out now.'

'Yes, and make her more the fashion than ever!' Littlemore answered, with cynical laughter. After his little interview with the elder Lady Demesne, he did not feel himself at liberty to call again upon the younger; and he never learned – he never even wished to know – whether in the pride of her success she forgave him.

Waterville – it was very strange – was positively scandalised at this success. He held that Mrs Headway ought never to have been allowed to marry a confiding gentleman; and he used, in speaking to Littlemore, the same words as Mrs Dolphin. He thought Littlemore might have done differently.

He spoke with such vehemence that Littlemore looked at him hard – hard enough to make him blush.

'Did you want to marry her yourself?' his friend inquired. 'My dear fellow, you're in love with her! That's what's the matter with you.'

This, however, blushing still more, Waterville indignantly denied. A little later he heard from New York that people were beginning to ask who in the world was Mrs Headway.

LADY BARBERINA

I

IT is well known that there are few sights in the world more brilliant than the main avenues of Hyde Park of a fine afternoon in June. This was quite the opinion of two persons who, on a beautiful day at the beginning of that month, four years ago, had established themselves under the great trees in a couple of iron chairs (the big ones with arms, for which, if I mistake not, you pay twopence), and sat there with the slow procession of the Drive behind them, while their faces were turned to the more vivid agitation of the Row. They were lost in the multitude of observers, and they belonged, superficially, at least, to that class of persons who, wherever they may be, rank rather with the spectators than with the spectacle. They were quiet, simple, elderly, of aspect somewhat neutral; you would have liked them extremely, but you would scarcely have noticed them. Nevertheless, in all that shining host, it is to them, obscure, that we must give our attention. The reader is begged to have confidence; he is not asked to make vain concessions. There was that in the faces of our friends which indicated that they were growing old together, and that they were fond enough of each other's company not to object (if it was a condition) even to that. The reader will have guessed that they were husband and wife; and perhaps while he is about it he will have guessed that they were of that nationality for which Hyde Park at the height of the season is most completely illustrative. They were familiar strangers, as it were; and people at once so initiated and so detached could only be Americans. This reflection, indeed, you would have made only after some delay; for it must be admitted that they carried few patriotic signs on the surface. They had the American turn of mind, but that was very subtle; and to your eye – if your eye had cared about it – they might have been of English, or even of Continental, parentage. It was as if it suited them to be colourless; their colour was all in their talk. They were not in the least verdant; they were grey, rather, of monotonous hue. If they were interested in the riders, the horses, the walkers, the great exhibition of English wealth and health, beauty, luxury and leisure, it was because all this referred itself to other impressions, because they had the key to almost everything that needed an answer – because, in a word, they were able to compare. They had not arrived, they had only returned; and recognition much more than surprise was expressed in their quiet gaze. It may as well be said outright that Dexter Freer and his wife belonged to that class of Americans who are constantly 'passing through' London. Possessors of a fortune of which, from any standpoint, the limits were plainly visible, they were unable to command that highest of luxuries – a habitation in their own country. They found it much more possible to economise at Dresden or Florence than at Buffalo or Minneapolis. The economy was as great, and the inspiration was greater. From Dresden, from Florence, moreover, they constantly made excursions which would not have been possible in those other cities; and it is even to be feared that they had some rather expensive methods of saving. They came to London to buy their portmanteaus, their tooth-brushes, their writing-paper; they occasionally even crossed the Atlantic to assure themselves that prices over there were still the same. They were eminently a social pair; their interests were mainly personal. Their point of view always was so distinctly human that they passed for being fond of gossip; and they certainly knew a good deal about the affairs of other people. They had friends in every country, in every town; and it was not their fault if people told them their secrets. Dexter Freer was a tall, lean man, with an interested eye, and a nose that rather aspired than drooped, yet was salient withal. He brushed his hair, which was streaked with white, forward over his ears, in those locks which are represented in the portraits of clean-shaven gentlemen who flourished fifty years ago, and wore an old-fashioned neckcloth and gaiters. His wife, a small, plump person, of superficial freshness, with a white face, and hair that was still perfectly black, smiled perpetually, but had never laughed since the death of a son whom she had lost ten years after her marriage.

Her husband, on the other hand, who was usually quite grave, indulged on great occasions in resounding mirth. People confided in her less than in him; but that mattered little, as she confided sufficiently in herself. Her dress, which was always black or dark grey, was so harmoniously simple that you could see she was fond of it; it was never smart by accident. She was full of intentions, of the most judicious sort; and though she was perpetually moving about the world she had the air of being perfectly stationary. She was celebrated for the promptitude with which she made her sitting-room at an inn, where she might be spending a night or two, look like an apartment long inhabited. With books, flowers, photographs, draperies, rapidly distributed – she had even a way, for the most part, of having a piano – the place seemed almost hereditary. The pair were just back from America, where they had spent three months, and now were able to face the world with something of the elation which people feel who have been justified in a prevision. They had found their native land quite ruinous.

'There he is again!' said Mr Freer, following with his eyes a young man who passed along the Row, riding slowly. 'That's a beautiful thoroughbred!'

Mrs Freer asked idle questions only when she wished for time to think. At present she had simply to look and see who it was her husband meant. 'The horse is too big,' she remarked, in a moment.

'You mean that the rider is too small,' her husband rejoined; 'he is mounted on his millions.'

'Is it really millions?'

'Seven or eight, they tell me.'

'How disgusting!' It was in this manner that Mrs Freer usually spoke of the large fortunes of the day. 'I wish he would see us,' she added.

'He does see us, but he doesn't like to look at us. He is too conscious; he isn't easy.'

'Too conscious of his big horse?'

'Yes, and of his big fortune; he is rather ashamed of it.'

'This is an odd place to come, then,' said Mrs Freer.

'I am not sure of that. He will find people here richer than himself, and other big horses in plenty, and that will cheer him up. Perhaps, too, he is looking for that girl.'

'The one we heard about? He can't be such a fool.'

'He isn't a fool,' said Dexter Freer. 'If he is thinking of her, he has some good reason.'

'I wonder what Mary Lemon would say.'

'She would say it was right, if he should do it. She thinks he can do no wrong. He is exceedingly fond of her.'

'I shan't be sure of that if he takes home a wife who will despise her.'

'Why should the girl despise her? She is a delightful woman.'

'The girl will never know it – and if she should, it would make no difference; she will despise everything.'

'I don't believe it, my dear; she will like some things very much. Every one will be very nice to her.'

'She will despise them all the more. But we are speaking as if it were all arranged; I don't believe in it at all,' said Mrs Freer.

'Well, something of the sort – in this case or in some other – is sure to happen sooner or later,' her husband replied, turning round a little toward the part of the delta which is formed, near the entrance to the Park, by the divergence of the two great vistas of the Drive and the Row.

Our friends had turned their backs, as I have said, to the solemn revolution of wheels and the densely-packed mass of spectators who had chosen that part of the show. These spectators were now agitated by a unanimous impulse: the pushing back of chairs, the shuffle of feet, the rustle of garments and the deepening murmur of voices sufficiently expressed it. Royalty was approaching – royalty was passing – royalty had passed. Freer turned his head and his ear a little; but he failed to alter his position further, and his wife took no notice of the flurry. They had seen royalty pass, all over Europe, and they knew that it passed very quickly. Sometimes it came back; sometimes it didn't; for more than once they had seen it pass for the last time. They were veteran tourists, and they knew perfectly when to get up and when to remain seated. Mr Freer went on with his proposition: 'Some young fellow is certain to do it, and one of these girls is certain to take the risk. They must take risks, over here, more and more.'

'The girls, I have no doubt, will be glad enough; they have had very little chance as yet. But I don't want Jackson to begin.'

'Do you know I rather think I do?' said Dexter Freer; 'It will be very amusing.'

'For us, perhaps, but not for him; he will repent of it, and be wretched. He is too good for that.'

'Wretched, never! He has no capacity for wretchedness; and that's why he can afford to risk it.'

'He will have to make great concessions,' Mrs Freer remarked.

'He won't make one.'

'I should like to see.'

'You admit, then, that it will be amusing, which is all I contend for. But, as you say, we are talking as if it were settled, whereas there is probably nothing in it, after all. The best stories always turn out false. I shall be sorry in this case.'

They relapsed into silence, while people passed and repassed them – continuous, successive, mechanical, with strange sequences of faces. They looked at the people, but no one looked at them, though every one was there so admittedly to see what was to be seen. It was all striking, all pictorial, and it made a great composition. The wide, long area of the Row, its red-brown surface dotted with bounding figures, stretched away into the distance and became suffused and misty in the bright, thick air. The deep, dark English verdure that bordered and overhung it, looked rich and old, revived and refreshed though it was by the breath of June. The mild blue of the sky was spotted with great silvery clouds, and the light drizzled down in heavenly shafts over the quieter spaces of the Park, as one saw them beyond the Row. All this, however, was only a background, for the scene was before everything personal; superbly so, and full of the gloss and lustre, the contrasted tones, of a thousand polished surfaces. Certain things were salient, pervasive – the shining flanks of the perfect horses, the twinkle of bits and spurs, the smoothness of fine cloth adjusted to shoulders and limbs, the sheen of hats and boots, the freshness of complexions, the expression of smiling, talking faces, the flash and flutter of rapid gallops. Faces were everywhere, and they were the great effect; above all, the fair faces of women on tall horses, flushed a little under their stiff black hats, with figures stiffened, in spite of much definition of curve, by their tight-fitting habits. Their hard little helmets; their neat, compact heads; their straight necks; their firm, tailor-made armour; their blooming, competent physique, made them look doubly like amazons about to ride a charge. The men, with their eyes before them, with hats of undulating brim, good profiles, high collars, white flowers on their chests, long legs and long feet, had an air more elaboratively decorative, as they jolted beside the ladies, always out of step. These were youthful types; but it was not all youth, for many a saddle was surmounted by a richer rotundity; and ruddy faces, with short white whiskers or with matronly chins, looked down comfortably from an equilibrium which was moral and social as well as physical. The walkers differed from the riders only in being on foot, and in looking at the riders more than these looked at them; for they would have done as well in the saddle and ridden as the others ride. The women had tight little bonnets and still tighter little knots of hair; their round chins rested on a close swathing of lace, or, in some cases, of silver chains and circlets. They had flat backs and small waists; they walked slowly, with their elbows out, carrying vast parasols, and turning their heads very little to the right or the left. They were amazons unmounted, quite ready to spring into the saddle. There was a great deal of beauty and a general look of successful development, which came from clear, quiet eyes, and from well-cut lips, on which syllables were liquid and sentences brief. Some of the young men, as well as the women, had the happiest proportions and oval faces, in which line and colour were pure and fresh and the idea of the moment was not very intense.

'They are very good-looking,' said Mr Freer, at the end of ten minutes; 'they are the finest whites.'

'So long as they remain white they do very well; but when they venture upon colour!' his wife replied. She sat with her eyes on a level with the skirts of the ladies who passed her; and she had been following the progress of a green velvet robe, enriched with ornaments of steel and much gathered up in the hands of its wearer, who, herself apparently in her teens, was accompanied by a young lady draped in scanty pink muslin, embroidered, aesthetically, with flowers that simulated the iris.

'All the same, in a crowd, they are wonderfully well turned out,' Dexter Freer went on; 'take the men, and women, and horses together. Look at that big fellow on the light chestnut: what could be more perfect? By the way, it's Lord Canterville,' he added in a moment, as if the fact were of some importance.

Mrs Freer recognised its importance to the degree of raising her glass to look at Lord Canterville. 'How do you know it's he?' she asked, with her glass still up.

'I heard him say something the night I went to the House of Lords. It was very few words, but I remember him. A man who was near me told me who he was.'

'He is not so handsome as you,' said Mrs Freer, dropping her glass.

'Ah, you're too difficult!' her husband murmured. 'What a pity the girl isn't with him,' he went on; 'we might see something.'

It appeared in a moment that the girl was with him. The nobleman designated had ridden slowly forward from the start, but just opposite our friends he pulled up to look behind him, as if he had been waiting for some one. At the same moment a gentleman in the Walk engaged his attention, so that he advanced to the barrier which protects the pedestrians, and halted there, bending a little from his saddle and talking with his friend, who leaned against the rail. Lord Canterville was indeed perfect, as his American admirer had said. Upwards of sixty, and of great stature and great presence, he was really a splendid apparition. In exquisite preservation, he had the freshness of middle life, and would have been young to the eye if the lapse of years were not needed to account for his considerable girth. He was clad from head to foot in garments of a radiant grey, and his fine florid countenance was surmounted with a white hat, of which the majestic curves were a triumph of good form. Over his mighty chest was spread a beard of the richest growth, and of a colour, in spite of a few streaks, vaguely grizzled, to which the coat of his admirable horse appeared to be a perfect match. It left no opportunity, in his uppermost button-hole, for the customary gardenia; but this was of comparatively little consequence, as the vegetation of the beard itself was tropical. Astride his great steed, with his big fist, gloved in pearl-grey, on his swelling thigh, his face lighted up with good-humoured indifference, and all his magnificent surface reflecting the mild sunshine, he was a very imposing man indeed, and visibly, incontestably, a personage. People almost lingered to look at him as they passed. His halt was brief, however, for he was almost immediately joined by two handsome girls, who were as well turned out, in Dexter Freer's phrase, as himself. They had been detained a moment at the entrance to the Row, and now advanced side by side, their groom close behind them. One was taller and older than the other, and it was apparent at a glance that they were sisters. Between them, with their charming shoulders, contracted waists, and skirts that hung without a wrinkle, like a plate of zinc, they represented in a singularly complete form the pretty English girl in the position in which she is prettiest.

'Of course they are his daughters,' said Dexter Freer, as they rode away with Lord Canterville; 'and in that case one of them must be Jackson Lemon's sweetheart. Probably the bigger; they said it was the eldest. She is evidently a fine creature.'

'She would hate it over there,' Mrs Freer remarked, for all answer to this cluster of inductions.

'You know I don't admit that. But granting she should, it would do her good to have to accommodate herself.'

'She wouldn't accommodate herself.'

'She looks so confoundedly fortunate, perched up on that saddle,' Dexter Freer pursued, without heeding his wife's rejoinder.

'Aren't they supposed to be very poor?'

'Yes, they look it!' And his eyes followed the distinguished trio, as, with the groom, as distinguished in his way as any of them, they started on a canter.

The air was full of sound, but it was low and diffused; and when, near our friends, it became articulate, the words were simple and few.

'It's as good as the circus, isn't it, Mrs Freer?' These words correspond to that description, but they pierced the air more effectually than any our friends had lately heard. They were uttered by a young man who had stopped short in the path, absorbed by the sight of his compatriots. He was short and stout, he had a round, kind face, and short, stiff-looking hair, which was reproduced in a small bristling beard. He wore a double-breasted walking-coat, which was not, however, buttoned, and on the summit of his round head was perched a hat of exceeding smallness, and of the so-called 'pot' category. It evidently fitted him, but a hatter himself would not have known why. His hands were encased in new gloves, of a dark-brown colour, and they hung with an air of unaccustomed inaction at his sides. He sported neither umbrella nor stick. He extended one of his hands, almost with eagerness, to Mrs Freer, blushing a little as he became aware that he had been eager.

'Oh, Doctor Feeder!' she said, smiling at him. Then she repeated to her husband, 'Doctor Feeder, my dear!' and her husband said, 'Oh, Doctor, how d'ye do?' I have spoken of the composition of his appearance; but the items were not perceived by these two. They saw only one thing, his delightful face, which was both simple and clever, and unreservedly good. They had lately made the voyage from New York in his company, and it was plain that he would be very genial at sea. After he had stood in front of them a moment, a chair beside Mrs Freer became vacant, on which he took possession of it, and sat there telling her what he thought of the Park and how he liked London. As she knew every one she had known many of his people at home; and while she listened to him she remembered how large their contribution had been to the virtue and culture of Cincinnati. Mrs Freer's social horizon included even that city; she had been on terms almost familiar with several families from Ohio, and was acquainted with the position of the Feeders there. This family, very numerous, was interwoven into an enormous cousinship. She herself was quite out of such a system, but she could have told you whom Doctor Feeder's great-grandfather had married. Every one, indeed, had heard of the good deeds of the descendants of this worthy, who were generally physicians, excellent ones, and whose name expressed not inaptly their numerous acts of charity. Sidney Feeder, who had several cousins of this name established in the same line at Cincinnati, had transferred himself and his ambition to New York, where his practice, at the end of three years, had begun to grow. He had studied his profession at Vienna, and was impregnated with German science; indeed, if he had only worn spectacles, he might perfectly, as he sat there watching the riders in Rotten Row as if their proceedings were a successful demonstration, have passed for a young German of distinction. He had come over to London to attend a medical congress which met this year in the British capital; for his interest in the healing art was by no means limited to the cure of his patients; it embraced every form of experiment, and the expression of his honest eyes would almost have reconciled you to vivisection. It was the first time he had come to the Park; for social experiments he had little leisure. Being aware, however, that it was a very typical, and as it were symptomatic, sight, he had conscientiously reserved an afternoon, and had dressed himself carefully for the occasion. 'It's quite a brilliant show,' he said to Mrs Freer; 'it makes me wish I had a mount.' Little as he resembled Lord Canterville, he rode very well.

'Wait till Jackson Lemon passes again, and you can stop him and make him let you take a turn.' This was the jocular suggestion of Dexter Freer.

'Why, is he here? I have been looking out for him; I should like to see him.'

'Doesn't he go to your medical congress?' asked Mrs Freer.

'Well, yes, he attends; but he isn't very regular. I guess he goes out a good deal.'

'I guess he does,' said Mr Freer; 'and if he isn't very regular, I guess he has a good reason. A beautiful reason, a charming reason,' he went on, bending forward to look down toward the beginning of the Row. 'Dear me, what a lovely reason!'

Doctor Feeder followed the direction of his eyes, and after a moment understood his allusion. Little Jackson Lemon, on his big horse, passed along the avenue again, riding beside one of the young girls who had come that way shortly before in the company of Lord Canterville. His lordship followed, in conversation with the other, his younger daughter. As they advanced, Jackson Lemon turned his eyes toward the multitude under the trees, and it so happened that they rested upon the Dexter Freers. He smiled, and raised his hat with all possible friendliness; and his three companions turned to see to whom he was bowing with so much cordiality. As he settled his hat on his head he espied the young man from Cincinnati, whom he had at first overlooked; whereupon he smiled still more brightly and waved Sidney Feeder an airy salutation with his hand, reining in a little at the same time just for an instant, as if he half expected the Doctor to come and speak to him. Seeing him with strangers, however, Sidney Feeder hung back, staring a little as he rode away.

It is open to us to know that at this moment the young lady by whose side he was riding said to him, familiarly enough: 'Who are those people you bowed to?'

'Some old friends of mine – Americans,' Jackson Lemon answered.

'Of course they are Americans; there is nothing but Americans nowadays.'

'Oh yes, our turn's coming round!' laughed the young man.

'But that doesn't say who they are,' his companion continued. 'It's so difficult to say who Americans are,' she added, before he had time to answer her.

'Dexter Freer and his wife – there is nothing difficult about that; every one knows them.'

'I never heard of them,' said the English girl.

'Ah, that's your fault. I assure you everybody knows them.'

'And does everybody know the little man with the fat face whom you kissed your hand to?'

'I didn't kiss my hand, but I would if I had thought of it. He is a great chum of mine, – a fellow-student at Vienna.'

'And what's *his* name?'

'Doctor Feeder.'

Jackson Lemon's companion was silent a moment. 'Are *all* your friends doctors?' she presently inquired.

'No; some of them are in other businesses.'

'Are they all in some business?'

'Most of them; save two or three, like Dexter Freer.'

'Dexter Freer? I thought you said Doctor Freer.'

The young man gave a laugh. 'You heard me wrong. You have got doctors on the brain, Lady Barb.'

'I am rather glad,' said Lady Barb, giving the rein to her horse, who bounded away.

'Well, yes, she's very handsome, the reason,' Doctor Feeder remarked, as he sat under the trees.

'Is he going to marry her?' Mrs Freer inquired.

'Marry her? I hope not.'

'Why do you hope not?'

'Because I know nothing about her. I want to know something about the woman that man marries.'

'I suppose you would like him to marry in Cincinnati,' Mrs Freer rejoined lightly.

'Well, I am not particular where it is; but I want to know her first.' Doctor Feeder was very sturdy.

'We were in hopes you would know all about it,' said Mr Freer.

'No; I haven't kept up with him there.'

'We have heard from a dozen people that he has been always with her for the last month; and that kind of thing, in England, is supposed to mean something. Hasn't he spoken of her when you have seen him?'

'No, he has only talked about the new treatment of spinal meningitis. He is very much interested in spinal meningitis.'

'I wonder if he talks about it to Lady Barb,' said Mrs Freer.

'Who is she, any way?' the young man inquired.

'Lady Barberina Clement.'

'And who is Lady Barberina Clement?'

'The daughter of Lord Canterville.'

'And who is Lord Canterville?'

'Dexter must tell you that,' said Mrs Freer.

And Dexter accordingly told him that the Marquis of Canterville had been in his day a great sporting nobleman and an ornament to English society, and had held more than once a high post in her Majesty's household. Dexter Freer knew all these things – how his lordship had married a daughter of Lord Treherne, a very serious, intelligent and beautiful woman, who had redeemed him from the extravagance of his youth and presented him in rapid succession with a dozen little tenants for the nurseries at Pasterns – this being, as Mr Freer also knew, the name of the principal seat of the Cantervilles. The Marquis was a Tory, but very liberal for a Tory, and very popular in society at large; good-natured, good-looking, knowing how to be genial and yet remain a *grand seigneur*, clever enough to make an occasional speech, and much associated with the fine old English pursuits, as well as with many of the new improvements – the purification of the Turf, the opening of the museums on Sunday, the propagation of coffee-taverns, the latest ideas on sanitary reform. He disapproved of the extension of the suffrage, but he positively had drainage on the brain. It had been said of him at least once (and I think in print) that he was just the man to convey to the popular mind the impression that the British aristocracy is still a living force. He was not very rich, unfortunately (for a man who had to exemplify such truths), and of his twelve children no less than seven were daughters. Lady Barberina, Jackson Lemon's friend, was the second; the eldest had married Lord Beauchemin. Mr Freer had caught quite the right pronunciation of this name: he called it Bitumen. Lady Louisa had done very well, for her husband was rich, and she had brought him nothing to speak of; but it was hardly to be expected that the others would do so well. Happily the younger girls were still in the schoolroom; and before they had come up, Lady Canterville, who was a woman of resources, would have worked off the two that were out. It was Lady Agatha's first season; she was not so pretty as her sister, but she was thought to be cleverer. Half a dozen people had spoken to him of Jackson Lemon's being a great deal at the Cantervilles. He was supposed to be enormously rich.

'Well, so he is,' said Sidney Feeder, who had listened to Mr Freer's little recital with attention, with eagerness even, but with an air of imperfect apprehension.

'Yes, but not so rich as they probably think.'

'Do they want his money? Is that what they're after?'

'You go straight to the point,' Mrs Freer murmured.

'I haven't the least idea,' said her husband. 'He is a very nice fellow in himself.'

'Yes, but he's a doctor,' Mrs Freer remarked.

'What have they got against that?' asked Sidney Feeder.

'Why, over here, you know, they only call them in to prescribe,' said Dexter Freer; 'the profession isn't – a – what you'd call aristocratic.'

'Well, I don't know it, and I don't know that I want to know it. How do you mean, aristocratic? What profession is? It would be rather a curious one. Many of the gentlemen at the congress there are quite charming.'

'I like doctors very much,' said Mrs Freer; 'my father was a doctor. But they don't marry the daughters of marquises.'

'I don't believe Jackson wants to marry that one.'

'Very possibly not – people are such asses,' said Dexter Freer. 'But he will have to decide. I wish you would find out, by the way; you can if you will.'

'I will ask him – up at the congress; I can do that. I suppose he has got to marry some one,' Sidney Feeder added, in a moment, 'and she may be a nice girl.'

'She is said to be charming.'

'Very well, then; it won't hurt him. I must say, however, I am not sure I like all that about her family.'

'What I told you? It's all to their honour and glory.'

'Are they quite on the square? It's like those people in Thackeray.'

'Oh, if Thackeray could have done this!' Mrs Freer exclaimed, with a good deal of expression.

'You mean all this scene?' asked the young man.

'No; the marriage of a British noblewoman and an American doctor. It would have been a subject for Thackeray.'

'You see you do want it, my dear,' said Dexter Freer quietly.

'I want it as a story, but I don't want it for Doctor Lemon.'

'Does he call himself "Doctor" still?' Mr Freer asked of young Feeder.

'I suppose he does; I call him so. Of course he doesn't practise. But once a doctor, always a doctor.'

'That's doctrine for Lady Barb!'

Sidney Feeder stared. 'Hasn't she got a title too? What would she expect him to be? President of the United States? He's a man of real ability; he might have stood at the head of his profession. When I think of that, I want to swear. What did his father want to go and make all that money for?'

'It must certainly be odd to them to see a "medical man" with six or eight millions,' Mr Freer observed.

'They use the same term as the Choctaws,' said his wife.

'Why, some of their own physicians make immense fortunes,' Sidney Feeder declared.

'Couldn't he be made a baronet by the Queen?' This suggestion came from Mrs Freer.

'Yes, then he would be aristocratic,' said the young man.

'But I don't see why he should want to marry over here; it seems to me to be going out of his way. However, if he is happy, I don't care. I like him very much; he has got lots of ability. If it hadn't been for his father he would have made a splendid doctor. But, as I say, he takes a great interest in medical science, and I guess he means to promote it all he can – with his fortune. He will always be doing something in the way of research. He thinks we *do* know something, and he is bound we shall know more. I hope she won't prevent him, the young marchioness – is that her rank? And I hope they are really good people. He ought to be very useful. I should want to know a good deal about the family I was going to marry into.'

'He looked to me, as he rode there, as if he knew a good deal about the Clements,' Dexter Freer said, rising, as his wife suggested that they ought to be going; 'and he looked to me pleased with the knowledge. There they come, down on the other side. Will you walk away with us, or will you stay?'

'Stop him and ask him, and then come and tell us – in Jermyn Street.' This was Mrs Freer's parting injunction to Sidney Feeder.

'He ought to come himself – tell him that,' her husband added.

'Well, I guess I'll stay,' said the young man, as his companions merged themselves in the crowd that now was tending toward the gates. He went and stood by the barrier, and saw Doctor Lemon and his friends pull up at the entrance to the Row, where they apparently prepared to separate. The separation took some time, and Sidney Feeder became interested. Lord Canterville and his younger daughter lingered to talk with two gentlemen, also mounted, who looked a good deal at the legs of Lady Agatha's horse. Jackson Lemon and Lady Barberina were face to face, very near each other; and she, leaning forward a little, stroked the overlapping neck of his glossy bay. At a distance he appeared to be talking, and she to be listening and saying nothing. 'Oh yes, he's making love to her,' thought Sidney Feeder. Suddenly her father turned away, to leave the Park, and she joined him and disappeared, while Doctor Lemon came up on the left again, as if for a final gallop. He had not gone far before he perceived his *confrère*, who awaited him at the rail; and he repeated the gesture which Lady Barberina had spoken of as a kissing of his hand, though it must be added that, to his friend's eyes, it had not quite that significance. When he reached the point where Feeder stood he pulled up.

'If I had known you were coming here I would have given you a mount,' he said. There was not in his person that irradiation of wealth and distinction which made Lord Canterville glow like a picture; but as he sat there with his little legs stuck out, he looked very bright and sharp and happy, wearing in his degree the aspect of one of Fortune's favourites. He had a thin, keen, delicate face, a nose very carefully finished, a rapid eye, a trifle hard in expression, and a small moustache, a good deal cultivated. He was not striking, but he was very positive, and it was easy to see that he was full of purpose.

'How many horses have you got – about forty?' his compatriot inquired, in response to his greeting.

'About five hundred,' said Jackson Lemon.

'Did you mount your friends – the three you were riding with?'

'Mount them? They have got the best horses in England.'

'Did they sell you this one?' Sidney Feeder continued in the same humorous strain.

'What do you think of him?' said his friend, not deigning to answer this question.

'He's an awful old screw; I wonder he can carry you.'

'Where did you get your hat?' asked Doctor Lemon, in return.

'I got it in New York. What's the matter with it?'

'It's very beautiful; I wish I had bought one like it.'

'The head's the thing – not the hat. I don't mean yours, but mine. There is something very deep in your question; I must think it over.'

'Don't – don't,' said Jackson Lemon; 'you will never get to the bottom of it. Are you having a good time?'

'A glorious time. Have you been up to-day?'

'Up among the doctors? No; I have had a lot of things to do.'

'We had a very interesting discussion. I made a few remarks.'

'You ought to have told me. What were they about?'

'About the intermarriage of races, from the point of view—' And Sidney Feeder paused a moment, occupied with the attempt to scratch the nose of his friend's horse.

'From the point of view of the progeny, I suppose?'

'Not at all; from the point of view of the old friends.'

'Damn the old friends!' Doctor Lemon exclaimed, with jocular crudity.

'Is it true that you are going to marry a young marchioness?'

The face of the young man in the saddle became just a trifle rigid, and his firm eyes fixed themselves on Doctor Feeder.

'Who has told you that?'

'Mr and Mrs Freer, whom I met just now.'

'Mr and Mrs Freer be hanged! And who told them?'

'Ever so many people; I don't know who.'

'Gad, how things are tattled!' cried Jackson Lemon, with some asperity.

'I can see it's true, by the way you say that.'

'Do Freer and his wife believe it?' Jackson Lemon went on impatiently.

'They want you to go and see them: you can judge for yourself.'

'I will go and see them, and tell them to mind their business.'

'In Jermyn Street; but I forget the number. I am sorry the marchioness isn't American,' Sidney Feeder continued.

'If I should marry her, she would be,' said his friend. 'But I don't see what difference it can make to you.'

'Why, she'll look down on the profession; and I don't like that from your wife.'

'That will touch me more than you.'

'Then it *is* true?' cried Feeder, more seriously looking up at his friend.

'She won't look down; I will answer for that.'

'You won't care; you are out of it all now.'

'No, I am not; I mean to do a great deal of work.'

'I will believe that when I see it,' said Sidney Feeder, who was by no means perfectly incredulous, but who thought it salutary to take that tone. 'I am not sure that you have any right to work – you oughtn't to have everything; you ought to leave the field to us. You must pay the penalty of being so rich. You would have been celebrated if you had continued to practise – more celebrated than any one. But you won't be now – you can't be. Some one else will be, in your place.'

Jackson Lemon listened to this, but without meeting the eyes of the speaker; not, however, as if he were avoiding them, but as if the long stretch of the Ride, now less and less obstructed, invited him and made his companion's talk a little retarding. Nevertheless, he answered, deliberately and kindly enough: 'I hope it will be you'; and he bowed to a lady who rode past.

'Very likely it will. I hope I make you feel badly – that's what I'm trying to do.'

'Oh, awfully!' cried Jackson Lemon; 'all the more that I am not in the least engaged.'

'Well, that's good. Won't you come up to-morrow?' Doctor Feeder went on.

'I'll try, my dear fellow; I can't be sure. By-by!'

'Oh, you're lost anyway!' cried Sidney Feeder, as the other started away.

II

IT was Lady Marmaduke, the wife of Sir Henry Marmaduke, who had introduced Jackson Lemon to Lady Beauchemin; after which Lady Beauchemin had made him acquainted with her mother and sisters. Lady Marmaduke was also transatlantic; she had been for her conjugal baronet the most permanent consequence of a tour in the United States. At present, at the end of ten years, she knew her London as she had never known her New York, so that it had been easy for her to be, as she called herself, Jackson Lemon's social godmother. She had views with regard to his career, and these views fitted into a social scheme which, if our space permitted, I should be glad to lay before the reader in its magnitude. She wished to add an arch or two to the bridge on which she had effected her transit from America, and it was her belief that Jackson Lemon might furnish the materials. This bridge, as yet a somewhat sketchy and rickety structure, she saw (in the future) boldly stretching from one solid pillar to another. It would have to go both ways, for reciprocity was the keynote of Lady Marmaduke's plan. It was her belief that an ultimate fusion was inevitable, and that those who were the first to understand the situation would gain the most. The first time Jackson Lemon had dined with her, he met Lady Beauchemin, who was her intimate friend. Lady Beauchemin was remarkably gracious; she asked him to come and see her as if she really meant it. He presented himself, and in her drawing-room met her mother, who happened to be calling at the same moment. Lady Canterville, not less friendly than her daughter, invited him down to Pasterns for Easter week; and before a month had passed it seemed to him that, though he was not what he would have called intimate at any house in London, the door of the house of Clement opened to

him pretty often. This was a considerable good fortune, for it
always opened upon a charming picture. The inmates were a
blooming and beautiful race, and their interior had an aspect of
the ripest comfort. It was not the splendour of New York (as
New York had lately begun to appear to the young man), but a
splendour in which there was an unpurchasable ingredient of
age. He himself had a great deal of money, and money was
good, even when it was new; but old money was the best. Even
after he learned that Lord Canterville's fortune was more
ancient than abundant, it was still the mellowness of the golden
element that struck him. It was Lady Beauchemin who had told
him that her father was not rich; having told him, besides this,
many surprising things – things that were surprising in themselves or surprising on her lips. This struck him afresh later that
evening – the day he met Sidney Feeder in the Park. He dined
out, in the company of Lady Beauchemin, and afterward, as
she was alone – her husband had gone down to listen to a
debate – she offered to 'take him on'. She was going to several
places, and he must be going to some of them. They compared
notes, and it was settled that they should proceed together to
the Trumpingtons', whither, also, it appeared at eleven o'clock
that all the world was going, the approach to the house being
choked for half a mile with carriages. It was a close, muggy
night; Lady Beauchemin's chariot, in its place in the rank,
stood still for long periods. In his corner beside her, through
the open window, Jackson Lemon, rather hot, rather
oppressed, looked out on the moist, greasy pavement, over
which was flung, a considerable distance up and down, the
flare of a public-house. Lady Beauchemin, however, was not
impatient, for she had a purpose in her mind, and now she
could say what she wished.

'Do you really love her?' That was the first thing she said.

'Well, I guess so,' Jackson Lemon answered, as if he did not
recognise the obligation to be serious.

Lady Beauchemin looked at him a moment in silence; he felt
her gaze, and turning his eyes, saw her face, partly shadowed,
with the aid of a street-lamp. She was not so pretty as Lady
Barberina; her countenance had a certain sharpness; her hair,

very light in colour and wonderfully frizzled, almost covered her eyes, the expression of which, however, together with that of her pointed nose, and the glitter of several diamonds, emerged from the gloom. 'You don't seem to know. I never saw a man in such an odd state,' she presently remarked.

'You push me a little too much; I must have time to think of it,' the young man went on. 'You know in my country they allow us plenty of time.' He had several little oddities of expression, of which he was perfectly conscious, and which he found convenient, for they protected him in a society in which a lonely American was rather exposed; they gave him the advantage which corresponded with certain drawbacks. He had very few natural Americanisms, but the occasional use of one, discreetly chosen, made him appear simpler than he really was, and he had his reasons for wishing this result. He was not simple; he was subtle, circumspect, shrewd, and perfectly aware that he might make mistakes. There was a danger of his making a mistake at present – a mistake which would be immensely grave. He was determined only to succeed. It is true that for a great success he would take a certain risk; but the risk was to be considered, and he gained time while he multiplied his guesses and talked about his country.

'You may take ten years if you like,' said Lady Beauchemin. 'I am in no hurry whatever to make you my brother-in-law. Only you must remember that you spoke to me first.'

'What did I say?'

'You told me that Barberina was the finest girl you had seen in England.'

'Oh, I am willing to stand by that; I like her type.'

'I should think you might!'

'I like her very much – with all her peculiarities.'

'What do you mean by her peculiarities?'

'Well, she has some peculiar ideas,' said Jackson Lemon, in a tone of the sweetest reasonableness; 'and she has a peculiar way of speaking.'

'Ah, you can't expect us to speak as well as you!' cried Lady Beauchemin.

'I don't know why not; you do some things much better.'

'We have our own ways, at any rate, and we think them the best in the world. One of them is not to let a gentleman devote himself to a girl for three or four months without some sense of responsibility. If you don't wish to marry my sister you ought to go away.'

'I ought never to have come,' said Jackson Lemon.

'I can scarcely agree to that; for I should have lost the pleasure of knowing you.'

'It would have spared you this duty, which you dislike very much.'

'Asking you about your intentions? I don't dislike it at all; it amuses me extremely.'

'Should you like your sister to marry me?' asked Jackson Lemon, with great simplicity.

If he expected to take Lady Beauchemin by surprise he was disappointed; for she was perfectly prepared to commit herself. 'I should like it very much. I think English and American society ought to be but one – I mean the best of each – a great whole.'

'Will you allow me to ask whether Lady Marmaduke suggested that to you?'

'We have often talked of it.'

'Oh yes, that's her aim.'

'Well, it's my aim too. I think there's a great deal to be done.'

'And you would like me to do it?'

'To begin it, precisely. Don't you think we ought to see more of each other? – I mean the best in each country.'

Jackson Lemon was silent a moment. 'I am afraid I haven't any general ideas. If I should marry an English girl it wouldn't be for the good of the species.'

'Well, we want to be mixed a little; that I am sure of,' Lady Beauchemin said.

'You certainly got that from Lady Marmaduke.'

'It's too tiresome, your not consenting to be serious! But my father will make you so,' Lady Beauchemin went on. 'I may as well let you know that he intends in a day or two to ask you your intentions. That's all I wished to say to you. I think you ought to be prepared.'

'I am much obliged to you; Lord Canterville will do quite right.'

There was, to Lady Beauchemin, something really unfathomable in this little American doctor, whom she had taken up on grounds of large policy, and who, though he was assumed to have sunk the medical character, was neither handsome nor distinguished, but only immensely rich and quite original, for he was not insignificant. It was unfathomable, to begin with, that a medical man should be so rich, or that so rich a man should be medical; it was even, to an eye which was always gratified by suitability, rather irritating. Jackson Lemon himself could have explained it better than any one else, but this was an explanation that one could scarcely ask for. There were other things; his cool acceptance of certain situations; his general indisposition to explain; his way of taking refuge in jokes which at times had not even the merit of being American; his way, too, of appearing to be a suitor without being an aspirant. Lady Beauchemin, however, was, like Jackson Lemon, prepared to run a certain risk. His reserves made him slippery; but that was only when one pressed. She flattered herself that she could handle people lightly. 'My father will be sure to act with perfect tact,' she said; 'of course, if you shouldn't care to be questioned, you can go out of town.' She had the air of really wishing to make everything easy for him.

'I don't want to go out of town; I am enjoying it far too much here,' her companion answered. 'And wouldn't your father have a right to ask me what I meant by that?'

Lady Beauchemin hesitated; she was slightly perplexed. But in a moment she exclaimed: 'He is incapable of saying anything vulgar!'

She had not really answered his inquiry, and he was conscious of that; but he was quite ready to say to her, a little later, as he guided her steps from the brougham to the strip of carpet which, between a somewhat rickety border of striped cloth and a double row of waiting footmen, policemen and dingy amateurs of both sexes, stretched from the kerbstone to the portal of the Trumpingtons, 'Of course I shall not wait for Lord Canterville to speak to me.'

He had been expecting some such announcement as this from Lady Beauchemin, and he judged that her father would do no more than his duty. He knew that he ought to be prepared with an answer to Lord Canterville, and he wondered at himself for not yet having come to the point. Sidney Feeder's question in the Park had made him feel rather pointless; it was the first allusion that had been made to his possible marriage, except on the part of Lady Beauchemin. None of his own people were in London; he was perfectly independent, and even if his mother had been within reach he could not have consulted her on the subject. He loved her dearly, better than any one; but she was not a woman to consult, for she approved of whatever he did: it was her standard. He was careful not to be too serious when he talked with Lady Beauchemin; but he was very serious indeed as he thought over the matter within himself, which he did even among the diversions of the next half-hour, while he squeezed obliquely and slowly through the crush in Mrs Trumpington's drawing-room. At the end of the half-hour he came away, and at the door he found Lady Beauchemin, from whom he had separated on entering the house, and who, this time with a companion of her own sex, was awaiting her carriage and still 'going on'. He gave her his arm into the street, and as she stepped into the vehicle she repeated that she wished he would go out of town for a few days.

'Who, then, would tell me what to do?' he asked, for answer, looking at her through the window.

She might tell him what to do, but he felt free, all the same; and he was determined this should continue. To prove it to himself he jumped into a hansom and drove back to Brook Street, to his hotel, instead of proceeding to a bright-windowed house in Portland Place, where he knew that after midnight he should find Lady Canterville and her daughters. There had been a reference to the subject between Lady Barberina and himself during their ride, and she would probably expect him; but it made him taste his liberty not to go, and he liked to taste his liberty. He was aware that to taste it in perfection he ought to go to bed; but he did not go to bed, he did not even take off his hat. He walked up and down his sitting-room, with his head surmounted by this ornament, a good deal tipped back, and his hands in his pockets. There were a good many cards stuck into the frame of the mirror, over his chimney-piece, and every time he passed the place he seemed to see what was written on one of them – the name of the mistress of the house in Portland Place, his own name, and, in the lower left-hand corner, the words: 'A small Dance'. Of course, now, he must make up his mind; he would make it up to the next day: that was what he said to himself as he walked up and down; and according to his decision he would speak to Lord Canterville or he would take the night-express to Paris. It was better meanwhile that he should not see Lady Barberina. It was vivid to him, as he paused occasionally, looking vaguely at that card in the chimney-glass, that he had come pretty far; and he had come so far because he was under the charm – yes, he was in love with Lady Barb. There was no doubt whatever of that; he had a faculty for diagnosis, and he knew perfectly well what was the matter with him. He wasted no time in musing upon the mystery of this passion, in wondering whether he might not have escaped it by a little vigilance at first, or whether it would die out if he should go away. He accepted it frankly, for the sake of the pleasure it gave him – the girl was the delight of his eyes – and confined himself to considering whether such a marriage would square with his general situation. This would not at all necessarily follow from the fact that he was in love; too many other things would come in between. The most important of these was the change, not only of the geographical, but of the social, standpoint for his wife, and a certain readjustment that it would involve in his own relation to things. He was not inclined to readjustments, and there was no reason why he should be; his own position was in most respects so advantageous. But the girl tempted him almost irresistibly, satisfying his imagination both as a lover and as a student of the human organism; she was so blooming, so complete, of a type so rarely encountered in that degree of perfection. Jackson Lemon was not an Anglomaniac, but he admired the physical conditions of the English – their complexion, their temperament, their tissue; and Lady Barberina struck him, in flexible, virginal form, as a wonderful compendium of these elements. There was something simple and robust in her beauty; it had the quietness of an old Greek statue, without the vulgarity of the modern simper or of contemporary prettiness. Her head was antique; and though her conversation was quite of the present period, Jackson Lemon had said to himself that there was sure to be in her soul a certain primitive sincerity which would match with her facial mould. He saw her as she might be in the future, the beautiful mother of beautiful children, in whom the look of race should be conspicuous. He should like his children to have the look of race, and he was not unaware that he must take his precautions accordingly. A great many people had it in England; and it was a pleasure to him to see it, especially as no one had it so unmistakably as the second daughter of Lord Canterville. It would be a great luxury to call such a woman one's own; nothing could be more evident than that, because it made no difference that she was not strikingly clever. Striking cleverness was not a part of harmonious form and the English complexion; it was associated with the modern simper, which was a result of modern nerves. If Jackson Lemon had wanted a nervous wife, of course he could have found her at home; but this tall, fair girl, whose character, like her figure, appeared mainly to have been formed by riding across country, was differently put together. All the same, would it suit his book, as they said in London, to marry her and transport her to New York? He came back to this question; came back to it with a persistency which, had she been admitted to a view of it, would have tried the patience of Lady Beauchemin. She had been irritated, more than once, at his appearing to attach himself so exclusively to this horn of the dilemma – as if it could possibly fail to be a good thing for a little American doctor to marry the daughter of an English peer. It would have been more becoming, in her ladyship's eyes, that he should take that for granted a little more, and the consent of her ladyship's – of their ladyship's – family a little less. They looked at the matter so differently! Jackson Lemon was conscious that if he should marry Lady Barberina Clement it would be because it suited him, and not because it suited his possible sisters-in-law. He believed that he acted in all things by his own will – an organ for which he had the highest respect.

It would have seemed, however, that on this occasion it was not working very regularly, for though he had come home to go to bed, the stroke of half-past twelve saw him jump, not into his couch, but into a hansom which the whistle of the porter had summoned to the door of his hotel, and in which he rattled off to Portland Place. Here he found – in a very large house – an assembly of three hundred people, and a band of music concealed in a bower of azaleas. Lady Canterville had not arrived; he wandered through the rooms and assured himself of that. He also discovered a very good conservatory, where there were banks and pyramids of azaleas. He watched the top of the staircase, but it was a long time before he saw what he was looking for, and his impatience at last was extreme. The reward, however, when it came, was all that he could have desired. It was a little smile from Lady Barberina, who stood behind her mother while the latter extended her finger-tips to the hostess. The entrance of this charming woman, with her beautiful daughters – always a noticeable incident – was effected with a certain brilliancy, and just now it was agreeable to Jackson Lemon to think that it concerned him more than any one else in the house. Tall, dazzling, indifferent, looking about her as if she saw very little, Lady Barberina was certainly a figure round which a young man's fancy might revolve. She was very quiet and simple, had little manner and little movement; but her detachment was not a vulgar art. She appeared to efface herself, to wait till, in the natural course, she should be attended to; and in this there was evidently no exaggeration, for she was too proud not to have perfect confidence. Her sister, smaller, slighter, with a little surprised smile, which seemed to say that in her extreme innocence she was yet prepared for anything, having heard, indirectly, such extraordinary things about society, was much more impatient and more expressive, and projected across a threshold the pretty radiance of her eyes and teeth before her mother's name was announced. Lady Canterville was thought by many persons to be very superior to her daughters; she had kept even more beauty than she had given them; and it was a beauty which had been called intellectual. She had extraordinary sweetness, without any definite professions; her manner was mild almost to tenderness; there was even a kind of pity in it. Moreover, her features were perfect, and nothing could be more gently gracious than a way she had of speaking, or rather, of listening, to people, with her head inclined a little to one side. Jackson Lemon liked her very much, and she had certainly been most kind to him. He approached Lady Barberina as soon as he could do so without an appearance of precipitation, and said to her that he hoped very much she would not dance. He was a master of the art which flourishes in New York above every other, and he had guided her through a dozen waltzes with a skill which, as she felt, left absolutely nothing to be desired. But dancing was not his business to-night. She smiled a little at the expression of his hope.

'That is what mamma has brought us here for,' she said; 'she doesn't like it if we don't dance.'

'How does she know whether she likes it or not? You have always danced.'

'Once I didn't,' said Lady Barberina.

He told her that, at any rate, he would settle it with her mother, and persuaded her to wander with him into the conservatory, where there were coloured lights suspended among the plants, and a vault of verdure overhead. In comparison with the other rooms the conservatory was dusky and remote. But they were not alone; half a dozen other couples were in possession. The gloom was rosy with the slopes of azalea, and suffused with mitigated music, which made it possible to talk without consideration of one's neighbours. Nevertheless, though it was only in looking back on the scene later that Lady Barberina perceived this, these dispersed couples were talking very softly. She did not look at them; it seemed to her that, virtually, she was alone with Jackson Lemon. She said something about conservatories, about the fragrance of the air; for all answer to which he asked her, as he stood there before her, a question by which she might have been exceedingly startled.

'How do people who marry in England ever know each other before marriage? They have no chance.'

'I am sure I don't know,' said Lady Barberina; 'I never was married.'

'It's very different in my country. There a man may see much of a girl; he may come and see her, he may be constantly alone with her. I wish you allowed that over here.'

Lady Barberina suddenly examined the less ornamental side of her fan, as if it had never occurred to her before to look at it. 'It must be so very odd, America,' she murmured at last.

'Well, I guess in that matter we are right; over here it's a leap in the dark.'

'I am sure I don't know,' said the girl. She had folded her fan; she stretched out her arm mechanically and plucked a sprig of azalea.

'I guess it doesn't signify, after all,' Jackson Lemon remarked. 'They say that love is blind at the best.' His keen young face was bent upon hers; his thumbs were in the pockets of his trousers; he smiled a little, showing his fine teeth. She said nothing, but only pulled her azalea to pieces. She was usually so quiet that this small movement looked restless.

'This is the first time I have seen you in the least without a lot of people,' he went on.

'Yes, it's very tiresome,' she said.

'I have been sick of it; I didn't want to come here to-night.'

She had not met his eyes, though she knew they were seeking her own. But now she looked at him a moment. She had never objected to his appearance, and in this respect she had no repugnance to overcome. She liked a man to be tall and handsome, and Jackson Lemon was neither; but when she was sixteen, and as tall herself as she was to be at twenty, she had been in love (for three weeks) with one of her cousins, a little fellow in the Hussars, who was shorter even than the American, shorter consequently than herself. This proved that distinction might be independent of stature – not that she ever reasoned it out. Jackson Lemon's facial spareness, his bright little eye, which seemed always to be measuring things, struck her as original, and she thought them very cutting, which would do very well for a husband of hers. As she made this reflection, of course it never occurred to her that she herself might be cut; she was not a sacrificial lamb. She perceived that his features expressed a mind – a mind that would be rather effective. She would never have taken him for a doctor; though, indeed, when all was said, that was very negative and didn't account for the way he imposed himself.

'Why, then, did you come?' she asked, in answer to his last speech.

'Because it seems to me after all better to see you in this way than not to see you at all; I want to know you better.'

'I don't think I ought to stay here,' said Lady Barberina, looking round her.

'Don't go till I have told you I love you,' murmured the young man.

She made no exclamation, indulged in no start; he could not see even that she changed colour. She took his request with a noble simplicity, with her head erect and her eyes lowered.

'I don't think you have a right to tell me that.'

'Why not?' Jackson Lemon demanded. 'I wish to claim the right; I wish you to give it to me.'

'I can't – I don't know you. You have said it yourself.'

'Can't you have a little faith? That will help us to know each other better. It's disgusting, the want of opportunity; even at Pasterns I could scarcely get a walk with you. But I have the greatest faith in you. I feel that I love you, and I couldn't do more than that at the end of six months. I love your beauty – I love you from head to foot. Don't move, please don't move.' He lowered his tone; but it went straight to her ear, and it must be believed that it had a certain eloquence. For himself, after he had heard himself say these words, all his being was in a glow. It was a luxury to speak to her of her beauty; it brought him nearer to her than he had ever been. But the colour had come into her face, and it seemed to remind him that her beauty was not all. 'Everything about you is sweet and noble,' he went on; 'everything is dear to me. I am sure you are good. I don't know what you think of me; I asked Lady Beauchemin to tell me, and she told me to judge for myself. Well, then, I judge you like me.

Haven't I a right to assume that till the contrary is proved? May I speak to your father? That's what I want to know. I have been waiting; but now what should I wait for longer? I want to be able to tell him that you have given me some hope. I suppose I ought to speak to him first. I meant to, to-morrow, but meanwhile, to-night, I thought I would just put this in. In my country it wouldn't matter particularly. You must see all that over there for yourself. If you should tell me not to speak to your father, I wouldn't; I would wait. But I like better to ask your leave to speak to him than to ask his to speak to you.'

His voice had sunk almost to a whisper; but, though it trembled, his emotion gave it peculiar intensity. He had the same attitude, his thumbs in his trousers, his attentive head, his smile, which was a matter of course; no one would have imagined what he was saying. She had listened without moving, and at the end she raised her eyes. They rested on his a moment, and he remembered, a good while later, the look which passed her lids.

'You may say anything that you please to my father, but I don't wish to hear any more. You have said too much, considering how little idea you have given me before.'

'I was watching you,' said Jackson Lemon.

Lady Barberina held her head higher, looking straight at him. Then, quite seriously, 'I don't like to be watched,' she remarked.

'You shouldn't be so beautiful, then. Won't you give me a word of hope?' he added.

'I have never supposed I should marry a foreigner,' said Lady Barberina.

'Do you call me a foreigner?'

'I think your ideas are very different, and your country is different; you have told me so yourself.'

'I should like to show it to you; I would make you like it.'

'I am not sure what you would make me do,' said Lady Barberina, very honestly.

'Nothing that you don't want.'

'I am sure you would try,' she declared, with a smile.

'Well,' said Jackson Lemon, 'after all, I am trying now.'

To this she simply replied she must go to her mother, and he was obliged to lead her out of the conservatory. Lady Canterville was not immediately found, so that he had time to murmur as they went, 'Now that I have spoken, I am very happy.'

'Perhaps you are happy too soon,' said the girl.

'Ah, don't say that, Lady Barb.'

'Of course I must think of it.'

'Of course you must!' said Jackson Lemon. 'I will speak to your father to-morrow.'

'I can't fancy what he will say.'

'How can he dislike me?' the young man asked, in a tone which Lady Beauchemin, if she had heard him, would have been forced to attribute to his general affectation of the jocose. What Lady Beauchemin's sister thought of it is not recorded; but there is perhaps a clue to her opinion in the answer she made him after a moment's silence: 'Really, you know, you *are* a foreigner!' With this she turned her back upon him, for she was already in her mother's hands. Jackson Lemon said a few words to Lady Canterville; they were chiefly about its being very hot. She gave him her vague, sweet attention, as if he were saying something ingenious of which she missed the point. He could see that she was thinking of the doings of her daughter Agatha, whose attitude toward the contemporary young man was wanting in the perception of differences – a madness without method; she was evidently not occupied with Lady Barberina, who was more to be trusted. This young woman never met her suitor's eyes again; she let her own rest, rather ostentatiously, upon other objects. At last he was going away without a glance from her. Lady Canterville had asked him to come to lunch on the morrow, and he had said he would do so if she would promise him he should see his lordship. 'I can't pay you another visit until I have had some talk with him,' he said.

'I don't see why not; but if I speak to him I daresay he will be at home,' she answered.

'It will be worth his while!'

Jackson Lemon left the house reflecting that as he had never proposed to a girl before he could not be expected to know how women demean themselves in this emergency. He had heard,

indeed, that Lady Barb had had no end of offers; and though he
thought it probable that the number was exaggerated, as it
always is, it was to be supposed that her way of appearing
suddenly to have dropped him was but the usual behaviour
for the occasion.

III

At her mother's the next day she was absent from luncheon,
and Lady Canterville mentioned to him (he didn't ask) that she
had gone to see a dear old great-aunt, who was also her godmother, and who lived at Roehampton. Lord Canterville was
not present, but our young man was informed by his hostess
that he had promised her he would come in exactly at three
o'clock. Jackson Lemon lunched with Lady Canterville and the
children, who appeared in force at this repast, all the younger
girls being present, and two little boys, the juniors of the two
sons who were in their teens. Jackson, who was very fond of
children, and thought these absolutely the finest in the world –
magnificent specimens of a magnificent brood, such as it
would be so satisfactory in future days to see about his own
knee – Jackson felt that he was being treated as one of the
family, but was not frightened by what he supposed the privilege to imply. Lady Canterville betrayed no consciousness
whatever of his having mooted the question of becoming her
son-in-law, and he believed that her eldest daughter had not
told her of their talk the night before. This idea gave him
pleasure; he liked to think that Lady Barb was judging him for
herself. Perhaps, indeed, she was taking counsel of the old lady
at Roehampton: he believed that he was the sort of lover of
whom a godmother would approve. Godmothers in his mind
were mainly associated with fairy-tales (he had had no baptismal
sponsors of his own); and that point of view would be favourable to a young man with a great deal of gold who had suddenly
arrived from a foreign country – an apparition, surely, sufficiently elfish. He made up his mind that he should like Lady
Canterville as a mother-in-law; she would be too well-bred to
meddle. Her husband came in at three o'clock, just after they

had left the table, and said to Jackson Lemon that it was very good in him to have waited.

'I haven't waited,' Jackson replied, with his watch in his hand; 'you are punctual to the minute.'

I know not how Lord Canterville may have judged his young friend, but Jackson Lemon had been told more than once in his life that he was a very good fellow, but rather too literal. After he had lighted a cigarette in his lordship's 'den', a large brown apartment on the ground-floor, which partook at once of the nature of an office and of that of a harness-room (it could not have been called in any degree a library), he went straight to the point in these terms: 'Well now, Lord Canterville, I feel as if I ought to let you know without more delay that I am in love with Lady Barb, and that I should like to marry her.' So he spoke, puffing his cigarette, with his conscious but unextenuating eye fixed on his host.

No man, as I have intimated, bore better being looked at than this noble personage; he seemed to bloom in the envious warmth of human contemplation, and never appeared so faultless as when he was most exposed. 'My dear fellow, my dear fellow,' he murmured, almost in disparagement, stroking his ambrosial beard from before the empty fireplace. He lifted his eyebrows, but he looked perfectly good-natured.

'Are you surprised, sir?' Jackson Lemon asked.

'Why, I suppose any one is surprised at a man wanting one of his children. He sometimes feels the weight of that sort of thing so much, you know. He wonders what the devil another man wants of them.' And Lord Canterville laughed pleasantly out of the copious fringe of his lips.

'I only want one of them,' said Jackson Lemon, laughing too, but with a lighter organ.

'Polygamy would be rather good for the parents. However, Louisa told me the other night that she thought you were looking the way you speak of.'

'Yes, I told Lady Beauchemin that I love Lady Barb, and she seemed to think it was natural.'

'Oh yes, I suppose there's no want of nature in it! But, my dear fellow, I really don't know what to say.'

'Of course you'll have to think of it.' Jackson Lemon, in saying this, felt that he was making the most liberal concession to the point of view of his interlocutor; being perfectly aware that in his own country it was not left much to the parents to think of.

'I shall have to talk it over with my wife.'

'Lady Canterville has been very kind to me; I hope she will continue.'

'My dear fellow, we are excellent friends. No one could appreciate you more than Lady Canterville. Of course we can only consider such a question on the – a – the highest grounds. You would never want to marry without knowing, as it were, exactly what you are doing. I, on my side, naturally, you know, am bound to do the best I can for my own child. At the same time, of course, we don't want to spend our time in – a – walking round the horse. We want to keep to the main line.' It was settled between them after a little that the main line was that Jackson Lemon knew to a certainty the state of his affections and was in a position to pretend to the hand of a young lady who, Lord Canterville might say – of course, you know, without any swagger – had a right to expect to do well, as the women call it.

'I should think she had,' Jackson Lemon said; 'she's a beautiful type.'

Lord Canterville stared a moment. 'She is a clever, well-grown girl, and she takes her fences like a grasshopper. Does she know all this, by the way?' he added.

'Oh yes, I told her last night.'

Again Lord Canterville had the air, unusual with him, of returning his companion's scrutiny. 'I am not sure that you ought to have done that, you know.'

'I couldn't have spoken to you first – I couldn't,' said Jackson Lemon. 'I meant to, but it stuck in my crop.'

'They don't in your country, I guess,' his lordship returned, smiling.

'Well, not as a general thing; however, I find it very pleasant to discuss with you now.' And in truth it was very pleasant. Nothing could be easier, friendlier, more informal, than Lord

Canterville's manner, which implied all sorts of equality, especially that of age and fortune, and made Jackson Lemon feel at the end of three minutes almost as if he too were a beautifully preserved and somewhat straitened nobleman of sixty, with the views of a man of the world about his own marriage. The young American perceived that Lord Canterville waived the point of his having spoken first to the girl herself, and saw in this indulgence a just concession to the ardour of young affection. For Lord Canterville seemed perfectly to appreciate the sentimental side – at least so far as it was embodied in his visitor – when he said, without deprecation: 'Did she give you any encouragement?'

'Well, she didn't box my ears. She told me that she would think of it, but that I must speak to you. But, naturally, I shouldn't have said what I did to her if I hadn't made up my mind during the last fortnight that I am not disagreeable to her.'

'Ah, my dear young man, women are odd cattle!' Lord Canterville exclaimed, rather unexpectedly. 'But of course you know all that,' he added in an instant; 'you take the general risk.'

'I am perfectly willing to take the general risk; the particular risk is small.'

'Well, upon my honour I don't really know my girls. You see a man's time, in England, is tremendously taken up; but I dare say it's the same in your country. Their mother knows them – I think I had better send for their mother. If you don't mind I'll just suggest that she join us here.'

'I'm rather afraid of you both together, but if it will settle it any quicker—' said Jackson Lemon. Lord Canterville rang the bell, and, when a servant appeared, despatched him with a message to her ladyship. While they were waiting, the young man remembered that it was in his power to give a more definite account of his pecuniary basis. He had simply said before that he was abundantly able to marry; he shrank from putting himself forward as a billionaire. He had a fine taste, and he wished to appeal to Lord Canterville primarily as a gentleman. But now that he had to make a double impression, he bethought himself of his millions, for millions were always impressive. 'I think it only fair to let you know that my fortune is really very considerable,' he remarked.

'Yes, I daresay you are beastly rich,' said Lord Canterville.

'I have about seven millions.'

'Seven millions?'

'I count in dollars; upwards of a million and a half sterling.'

Lord Canterville looked at him from head to foot, with an air of cheerful resignation to a form of grossness which threatened to become common. Then he said, with a touch of that inconsequence of which he had already given a glimpse: 'What the deuce, then, possessed you to turn doctor?'

Jackson Lemon coloured a little, hesitated, and then replied, quickly: 'Because I had the talent for it.'

'Of course, I don't for a moment doubt of your ability; but don't you find it rather a bore?'

'I don't practise much. I am rather ashamed to say that.'

'Ah, well, of course, in your country it's different. I daresay you've got a door-plate, eh?'

'Oh yes, and a tin sign tied to the balcony!' said Jackson Lemon, smiling.

'What did your father say to it?'

'To my going into medicine? He said he would be hanged if he'd take any of my doses. He didn't think I should succeed; he wanted me to go into the house.'

'Into the House – a—' said Lord Canterville, hesitating a little. 'Into your Congress – yes, exactly.'

'Ah, no, not so bad as that. Into the store,' Jackson Lemon replied, in the candid tone in which he expressed himself when, for reasons of his own, he wished to be perfectly national.

Lord Canterville stared, not venturing, even for the moment, to hazard an interpretation; and before a solution had presented itself Lady Canterville came into the room.

'My dear, I thought we had better see you. Do you know he wants to marry our second girl?' It was in these simple terms that her husband acquainted her with the question.

Lady Canterville expressed neither surprise nor elation; she simply stood there, smiling, with her head a little inclined to the side, with all her customary graciousness. Her charming eyes rested on those of Jackson Lemon, and though they seemed to show that she had to think a little of so serious a proposition, his own discovered in them none of the coldness of calculation. 'Are you talking about Barberina?' she asked in a moment, as if her thoughts had been far away.

Of course they were talking about Barberina, and Jackson Lemon repeated to her ladyship what he had said to the girl's father. He had thought it all over, and his mind was quite made up. Moreover, he had spoken to Lady Barb.

'Did she tell you that, my dear?' asked Lord Canterville, while he lighted another cigar.

She gave no heed to this inquiry, which had been vague and accidental on his lordship's part, but simply said to Jackson Lemon that the thing was very serious, and that they had better sit down for a moment. In an instant he was near her on the sofa on which she had placed herself, still smiling and looking up at her husband with an air of general meditation, in which a sweet compassion for every one concerned was apparent.

'Barberina has told me nothing,' she said, after a little.

'That proves she cares for me!' Jackson Lemon exclaimed eagerly.

Lady Canterville looked as if she thought this almost too ingenious, almost professional; but her husband said cheerfully, jovially: 'Ah, well, if she cares for you, I don't object.'

This was a little ambiguous; but before Jackson Lemon had time to look into it, Lady Canterville asked gently: 'Should you expect her to live in America?'

'Oh, yes; that's my home, you know.'

'Shouldn't you be living sometimes in England?'

'Oh, yes, we'll come over and see you.' The young man was in love, he wanted to marry, he wanted to be genial, and to commend himself to the parents of Lady Barb; at the same time it was in his nature not to accept conditions, save in so far as they exactly suited him, to tie himself, or, as they said in New York, to give himself away. In any transaction he preferred his own terms to those of any one else. Therefore, the moment Lady Canterville gave signs of wishing to extract a promise, he was on his guard.

'She'll find it very different; perhaps she won't like it,' her ladyship suggested.

'If she likes me, she'll like my country,' said Jackson Lemon, with decision.

'He tells me he has got a plate on his door,' Lord Canterville remarked humorously.

'We must talk to her, of course; we must understand how she feels,' said his wife, looking more serious than she had done as yet.

'Please don't discourage her, Lady Canterville,' the young man begged; 'and give me a chance to talk to her a little more myself. You haven't given me much chance, you know.'

'We don't offer our daughters to people, Mr Lemon.' Lady Canterville was always gentle, but now she was a little majestic.

'She isn't like some women in London, you know,' said Jackson Lemon's host, who seemed to remember that to a discussion of such importance he ought from time to time to contribute a word of wisdom. And Jackson Lemon, certainly, if the idea had been presented to him, would have said that, No, decidedly, Lady Barberina had not been thrown at him.

'Of course not,' he declared, in answer to her mother's remark. 'But, you know, you mustn't refuse them too much, either; you mustn't make a poor fellow wait too long. I admire her, I love her, more than I can say; I give you my word of honour for that.'

'He seems to think that settles it,' said Lord Canterville, smiling down at the young American, very indulgently, from his place before the cold chimney-piece.

'Of course that's what we desire, Philip,' her ladyship returned, very nobly.

'Lady Barb believes it; I am sure she does!' Jackson Lemon exclaimed. 'Why should I pretend to be in love with her if I am not?'

Lady Canterville received this inquiry in silence, and her husband, with just the least air in the world of repressed impatience, began to walk up and down the room. He was a man of many engagements, and he had been closeted for more than a quarter of an hour with the young American doctor. 'Do you imagine you should come often to England?' Lady Canterville demanded, with a certain abruptness, returning to that important point.

'I'm afraid I can't tell you that; of course we shall do whatever seems best.' He was prepared to suppose they should cross the Atlantic every summer: that prospect was by no means displeasing to him; but he was not prepared to give any such pledge to Lady Canterville, especially as he did not believe it would really be necessary. It was in his mind, not as an overt pretension, but as a tacit implication, that he should treat with Barberina's parents on a footing of perfect equality and there would somehow be nothing equal if he should begin to enter into engagements which didn't belong to the essence of the matter. They were to give their daughter, and he was to take her: in this arrangement there would be as much on one side as on the other. But beyond this he had nothing to ask of them; there was nothing he wished them to promise, and his own pledges, therefore, would have no equivalent. Whenever his wife should wish it, she should come over and see her people. Her home was to be in New York; but he was tacitly conscious that on the question of absences he should be very liberal. Nevertheless, there was something in the very grain of his character which forbade that he should commit himself at present in respect to times and dates.

Lady Canterville looked at her husband, but her husband was not attentive; he was taking a peep at his watch. In a moment, however, he threw out a remark to the effect that he thought it a capital thing that the two countries should become more united, and there was nothing that would bring it about better than a few of the best people on both sides pairing off together. The English, indeed, had begun it; a lot of fellows had brought over a lot of pretty girls, and it was quite fair play that the Americans should take their pick. They were all one race, after all; and why shouldn't they make one society – the best on both sides, of course? Jackson Lemon smiled as he recognised Lady Marmaduke's philosophy, and he was pleased to think that Lady Beauchemin had some influence with her father; for he was sure the old gentleman (as he mentally designated his host) had got all this from her, though he expressed himself less happily than the cleverest of his daughters. Our hero had no objection to make to it, especially if there was anything in it that would really help his case. But it was not in the least on these high grounds that he had sought the hand of Lady Barb. He wanted her not in order that her people and his (the best on both sides!) should make one society; he wanted her simply because he wanted her. Lady Canterville smiled; but she seemed to have another thought.

'I quite appreciate what my husband says; but I don't see why poor Barb should be the one to begin.'

'I daresay she'll like it,' said Lord Canterville, as if he were attempting a short cut. 'They say you spoil your women awfully.'

'She's not one of their women yet,' her ladyship remarked, in the sweetest tone in the world; and then she added, without Jackson Lemon's knowing exactly what she meant, 'It seems so strange.'

He was a little irritated; and perhaps these simple words added to the feeling. There had been no positive opposition to his suit, and Lord and Lady Canterville were most kind; but he felt that they held back a little, and though he had not expected them to throw themselves on his neck, he was rather disappointed, his pride was touched. Why should they hesitate? He considered himself such a good *parti*. It was not so much the old gentleman, it was Lady Canterville. As he saw the old gentleman look, covertly, a second time at his watch, he could have believed he would have been glad to settle the matter on the spot. Lady Canterville seemed to wish her daughter's lover to come forward more, to give certain assurances and guarantees. He felt that he was ready to say or do anything that was a matter of proper form; but he couldn't take the tone of trying to purchase her ladyship's consent, penetrated as he was with the conviction that such a man as he could be trusted to care for his wife rather more than an impecunious British peer and *his* wife could be supposed (with the lights he had acquired in English society) to care even for the handsomest of a dozen children. It was a mistake on Lady Canterville's part not to recognise that. He humoured her mistake to the extent of saying, just a little drily, 'My wife shall certainly have everything she wants.'

'He tells me he is disgustingly rich,' Lord Canterville added, pausing before their companion with his hands in his pockets.

'I am glad to hear it; but it isn't so much that,' she answered, sinking back a little on her sofa. If it was not that, she did not say what it was, though she had looked for a moment as if she were going to. She only raised her eyes to her husband's face, as if to ask for inspiration. I know not whether she found it, but in a moment she said to Jackson Lemon, seeming to imply that it was quite another point: 'Do you expect to continue your profession?'

He had no such intention, so far as his profession meant getting up at three o'clock in the morning to assuage the ills of humanity; but here, as before, the touch of such a question instantly stiffened him. 'Oh, my profession! I am rather ashamed of that matter. I have neglected my work so much, I don't know what I shall be able to do, once I am really settled at home.'

Lady Canterville received these remarks in silence; fixing her eyes again upon her husband's face. But this nobleman was really not helpful; still with his hands in his pockets, save when he needed to remove his cigar from his lips, he went and looked out of the window. 'Of course we know you don't practise, and when you're a married man you will have less time even than now. But I should really like to know if they call you Doctor over there.'

'Oh yes, universally. We are nearly as fond of titles as your people.'

'I don't call that a title.'

'It's not so good as duke or marquis, I admit; but we have to take what we have got.'

'Oh, bother, what does it signify?' Lord Canterville demanded, from his place at the window. 'I used to have a horse named Doctor, and a devilish good one too.'

'You may call me bishop, if you like,' said Jackson Lemon, laughing.

Lady Canterville looked grave, as if she did not enjoy this pleasantry. 'I don't care for any titles,' she observed; 'I don't see why a gentleman shouldn't be called Mr.'

It suddenly appeared to Jackson Lemon that there was something helpless, confused, and even slightly comical, in the position of this noble and amiable lady. The impression made him feel kindly; he too, like Lord Canterville, had begun to long for a short cut. He relaxed a moment, and leaning toward his hostess, with a smile and his hands on his little knees, he said softly, 'It seems to me a question of no importance; all I desire is that you should call me your son-in-law.'

Lady Canterville gave him her hand, and he pressed it almost affectionately. Then she got up, remarking that before anything was decided she must see her daughter, she must learn from her own lips the state of her feelings. 'I don't like at all her not having spoken to me already,' she added.

'Where has she gone – to Roehampton? I daresay she has told it all to her godmother,' said Lord Canterville.

'She won't have much to tell, poor girl!' Jackson Lemon exclaimed. 'I must really insist upon seeing with more freedom the person I wish to marry.'

'You shall have all the freedom you want, in two or three days,' said Lady Canterville. She smiled with all her sweetness; she appeared to have accepted him, and yet still to be making tacit assumptions. 'Are there not certain things to be talked of first?'

'Certain things, dear lady?'

Lady Canterville looked at her husband, and though he was still at his window, this time he felt it in her silence, and had to come away and speak. 'Oh, she means settlements, and that kind of thing.' This was an allusion which came with a much better grace from him.

Jackson Lemon looked from one of his companions to the other; he coloured a little, and gave a smile that was perhaps a trifle fixed. 'Settlements? We don't make them in the United States. You may be sure I shall make a proper provision for my wife.'

'My dear fellow, over here – in our class, you know, it's the custom,' said Lord Canterville, with a richer brightness in his face at the thought that the discussion was over.

'I have my own ideas,' Jackson answered, smiling.

'It seems to me it's a question for the solicitors to discuss,' Lady Canterville suggested.

'They may discuss it as much as they please,' said Jackson Lemon, with a laugh. He thought he saw his solicitors discussing it! He had indeed his own ideas. He opened the door for Lady Canterville, and the three passed out of the room together, walking into the hall in a silence in which there was just a tinge of awkwardness. A note had been struck which grated and scratched a little. A pair of brilliant footmen, at their approach, rose from a bench to a great altitude, and stood there like sentinels presenting arms. Jackson Lemon stopped, looking for a moment into the interior of his hat, which he had in his hand. Then, raising his keen eyes, he fixed them a moment on those of Lady Canterville, addressing her, instinctively, rather than her husband. 'I guess you and Lord Canterville had better leave it to me!'

'We have our traditions, Mr Lemon,' said her ladyship, with nobleness. 'I imagine you don't know—' she murmured.

Lord Canterville laid his hand on the young man's shoulder. 'My dear boy, those fellows will settle it in three minutes.'

'Very likely they will!' said Jackson Lemon. Then he asked of Lady Canterville when he might see Lady Barb.

She hesitated a moment, in her gracious way. 'I will write you a note.'

One of the tall footmen, at the end of the impressive vista, had opened wide the portals, as if even he were aware of the dignity to which the little visitor had virtually been raised. But Jackson lingered a moment; he was visibly unsatisfied, though apparently so little unconscious that he was unsatisfying. 'I don't think you understand me.'

'Your ideas are certainly different,' said Lady Canterville.

'If the girl understands you, that's enough!' Lord Canterville exclaimed in a jovial, detached, irrelevant way.

'May not *she* write to me?' Jackson asked of her mother. 'I certainly must write to her, you know, if you won't let me see her.'

'Oh yes, you may write to her, Mr Lemon.'

There was a point for a moment in the look that he gave Lady Canterville, while he said to himself that if it were necessary he would transmit his notes through the old lady at Roehampton. 'All right, good-bye; you know what I want, at any rate.' Then, as he was going, he turned and added: 'You needn't be afraid that I won't bring her over in the hot weather!'

'In the hot weather?' Lady Canterville murmured, with vague visions of the torrid zone, while the young American quitted the house with the sense that he had made great concessions.

His host and hostess passed into a small morning-room, and (Lord Canterville having taken up his hat and stick to go out again) stood there a moment, face to face.

'It's clear enough he wants her,' said his lordship, in a summary manner.

'There's something so odd about him,' Lady Canterville answered. 'Fancy his speaking so about settlements!'

'You had better give him his head; he'll go much quieter.'

'He's so obstinate – very obstinate; it's easy to see that. And he seems to think a girl in your daughter's position can be married from one day to the other – with a ring and a new frock – like a housemaid.'

'Well, of course, over there, that's the kind of thing. But he seems really to have a most extraordinary fortune; and every one does say their women have *carte blanche*.'

'*Carte blanche* is not what Barb wishes; she wishes a settlement. She wants a definite income; she wants to be safe.'

Lord Canterville stared a moment. 'Has she told you so? I thought you said—' And then he stopped. 'I beg your pardon,' he added.

Lady Canterville gave no explanation of her inconsistency. She went on to remark that American fortunes were notoriously insecure; one heard of nothing else; they melted away like smoke. It was their duty to their child to demand that something should be fixed.

'He has a million and a half sterling,' said Lord Canterville. 'I can't make out what he does with it.'

'She ought to have something very handsome,' his wife remarked.

'Well, my dear, you must settle it: you must consider it; you must send for Hilary. Only take care you don't put him off; it may be a very good opening, you know. There is a great deal to be done out there; I believe in all that,' Lord Canterville went on, in the tone of a conscientious parent.

'There is no doubt that he *is* a doctor – in those places,' said Lady Canterville, musingly.

'He may be a pedlar for all I care.'

'If they should go out, I think Agatha might go with them,' her ladyship continued, in the same tone, a little disconnectedly.

'You may send them all out if you like. Good-bye!' And Lord Canterville kissed his wife.

But she detained him a moment, with her hand on his arm. 'Don't you think he is very much in love?'

'Oh yes, he's very bad; but he's a clever little beggar.'

'She likes him very much,' Lady Canterville announced, rather formally, as they separated.

IV

JACKSON LEMON had said to Sidney Feeder in the Park that he would call on Mr and Mrs Freer; but three weeks elapsed before he knocked at their door in Jermyn Street. In the meantime he had met them at dinner, and Mrs Freer had told him that she hoped very much he would find time to come and see her. She had not reproached him, nor shaken her finger at him; and her clemency, which was calculated, and very characteristic of her, touched him so much (for he was in fault; she was one of his mother's oldest and best friends), that he very soon presented himself. It was on a fine Sunday afternoon, rather late, and the region of Jermyn Street looked forsaken and inanimate; the native dullness of the landscape appeared in all its purity. Mrs Freer, however, was at home, resting on a lodging-house sofa – an angular couch, draped in faded chintz – before she went to dress for dinner. She made the young man very welcome; she told him she had been thinking of him a great deal; she had wished to have a chance to talk with him. He immediately perceived what she had in mind, and then he remembered that Sidney Feeder had told him what it was that Mr and Mrs Freer took upon themselves to say. This had provoked him at the time, but he had forgotten it afterward; partly because he became aware, that same evening, that he did wish to marry the 'young marchioness', and partly because since then he had had much greater annoyances. Yes, the poor young man, so conscious of liberal intentions, of a large way of looking at the future, had had much to irritate and disgust him. He had seen the mistress of his affections but three or four times, and he had received letters from Mr Hilary, Lord Canterville's solicitor, asking him, in terms the most obsequious, it is true, to designate some gentleman of the law with whom the preliminaries of his marriage to Lady Barberina Clement might be arranged. He had given Mr Hilary the name of such a functionary, but he had written by the same post to his own solicitor (for whose services in other matters he had had much occasion, Jackson Lemon being distinctly contentious), instructing him that he was at liberty to meet Mr Hilary, but not at liberty to entertain any proposals as to this odious English idea of a settlement. If marrying Jackson Lemon were not settlement enough, then Lord and Lady Canterville had better alter their point of view. It was quite out of the question that he should alter his. It would perhaps be difficult to explain the strong aversion that he entertained to the introduction into his prospective union of this harsh diplomatic element; it was as if they mistrusted him, suspected him; as if his hands were to be tied, so that he could not handle his own fortune as he thought best. It was not the idea of parting with his money that displeased him, for he flattered himself that he had plans of expenditure for his wife beyond even the imagination of her distinguished parents. It struck him even that they were fools not to have perceived that they should make a much better thing of it by leaving him perfectly free. This intervention of the solicitor was a nasty little English tradition – totally at variance with the large spirit of American habits – to which he would not submit. It was not his way to submit when he disapproved: why should he change his way on this occasion, when the matter lay so near him? These reflections, and a hundred more, had flowed freely through his mind for several days before he called in Jermyn Street, and they had engendered a lively indignation and a really bitter sense of wrong. As may be imagined, they had infused a certain awkwardness into his relations with the house of Canterville, and it may be said of these relations that they were for the moment virtually suspended. His first interview with Lady Barb, after his conference with the old couple, as he called her august elders, had been as tender as he could have desired. Lady Canterville, at the end of three days, had sent him an invitation – five words on a card – asking him to dine with them to-morrow, quite *en famille*. This had been the only formal intimation that his engagement to Lady Barb was recognised; for even at the family banquet, which included half a dozen outsiders, there had been no allusion on the part either of his host or his hostess to the subject of their conversation in Lord Canterville's den. The only allusion was a wandering ray, once or twice, in Lady Barberina's eyes. When, however, after dinner, she strolled away with him into the music-room, which was lighted and empty, to play for him something out of *Carmen*, of which he had spoken at table, and when the young couple were allowed to enjoy for upwards of an hour, unmolested, the comparative privacy of this rich apartment, he felt that Lady Canterville definitely counted upon him. She didn't believe in any serious difficulties. Neither did he, then; and that was why it was a nuisance there should be a vain appearance of them. The arrangements, he supposed Lady Canterville would have said, were pending, and indeed they were; for he had already given orders in Bond Street for the setting of an extraordinary number of diamonds. Lady Barb, at any rate, during that hour he spent with her, had had nothing to say about arrangements; and it had been an hour of pure satisfaction. She had seated herself at the piano and had played perpetually, in a soft incoherent manner, while he leaned over the instrument, very close to her, and said everything that came into his head. She was very bright and serene, and she looked at him as if she liked him very much.

This was all he expected of her, for it did not belong to the cast of her beauty to betray a vulgar infatuation. That beauty was more delightful to him than ever; and there was a softness about her which seemed to say to him that from this moment she was quite his own. He felt more than ever the value of such a possession; it came over him more than ever that it had taken a great social outlay to produce such a mixture. Simple and girlish as she was, and not particularly quick in the give and take of conversation, she seemed to him to have a part of the history of England in her blood; she was a *résumé* of generations of privileged people, and of centuries of rich country-life. Between these two, of course, there was no allusion to the question which had been put into the hands of Mr Hilary, and the last thing that occurred to Jackson Lemon was that Lady Barb had views as to his settling a fortune upon her before their marriage. It may appear singular, but he had not asked himself whether his money operated upon her in any degree as a bribe; and this was because, instinctively, he felt that such a speculation was idle, – the point was not to be ascertained, – and because he was willing to assume that it was agreeable to her that she should continue to live in luxury. It was eminently agreeable to him that he might enable her to do so. He was acquainted with the mingled character of human motives, and he was glad that he was rich enough to pretend to the hand of a young woman who, for the best of reasons, would be very expensive. After that happy hour in the music-room he had ridden with her twice; but he had not found her otherwise accessible. She had let him know, the second time they rode, that Lady Canterville had directed her to make, for the moment, no further appointment with him; and on his presenting himself, more than once at the house, he had been told that neither the mother nor the daughter was at home; it had been added that Lady Barberina was staying at Roehampton. On giving him that information in the Park, Lady Barb had looked at him with a mute reproach – there was always a certain superior dumbness in her eyes – as if he were exposing her to an annoyance that she ought to be spared; as if he were taking an eccentric line on a question that all well-bred people treated in the conventional way. His induction from this was not that she wished to be secure about his money, but that, like a dutiful English daughter, she received her opinions (on points that were indifferent to her) ready-made from a mamma whose fallibility had never been exposed. He knew by this that his solicitor had answered Mr Hilary's letter, and that Lady Canterville's coolness was the fruit of this correspondence. The effect of it was not in the least to make him come round, as he phrased it; he had not the smallest intention of doing that. Lady Canterville had spoken of the traditions of her family; but he had no need to go to his family for his own. They resided within himself; anything that he had definitely made up his mind to, acquired in an hour a kind of legendary force. Meanwhile, he was in the detestable position of not knowing whether or no he were engaged. He wrote to Lady Barb to inquire – it being so strange that she should not receive him; and she answered in a very pretty little letter, which had to his mind a sort of bygone quality, an old-fashioned freshness, as if it might have been written in the last century by Clarissa or Amelia: she answered that she did not in the least understand the situation; that, of course, she would never give him up; that her mother had said that there were the best reasons for their not going too fast; that, thank God, she was yet young, and could wait as long as he would; but that she begged he wouldn't write her anything about money-matters, as she could never comprehend them. Jackson felt that he was in no danger whatever of making this last mistake; he only noted how Lady Barb thought it natural that there should be a discussion; and this made it vivid to him afresh that he had got hold of a daughter of the Crusaders. His ingenious mind could appreciate this hereditary assumption perfectly, at the same time that, to light his own footsteps, it remained entirely modern. He believed – or he thought he believed – that in the end he should marry Barberina Clement on his own terms; but in the interval there was a sensible indignity in being challenged and checked. One effect of it, indeed, was to make him desire the girl more keenly. When she was not before his eyes in the flesh, she hovered before him as an image; and this image had reasons of its own for being a radiant picture. There were moments, however, when he wearied of looking at it; it was so impalpable and thankless, and then Jackson Lemon, for the first time in his life, was melancholy. He felt alone in London, and very much out of it, in spite of all the acquaintances he had made, and the bills he had paid; he felt the need of a greater intimacy than any he had formed (save, of course, in the case of Lady Barb). He wanted to vent his disgust, to relieve himself, from the American point of view. He felt that in engaging in a contest with the great house of Canterville he was, after all, rather single. That singleness was, of course, in a great measure an inspiration; but it pinched him a little at moments. Then he wished his mother had been in London, for he used to talk of his affairs a great deal with this delightful parent, who had a soothing way of advising him in the sense he liked best. He had even gone so far as to wish he had never laid eyes on Lady Barb and had fallen in love with some transatlantic maiden of a similar composition. He presently came back, of course, to the knowledge that in the United States there was – and there could be – nothing similar to Lady Barb; for was it not precisely as a product of the English climate and the British constitution that he valued her? He had relieved himself, from his American point of view, by speaking his mind to Lady Beauchemin, who confessed that she was very much vexed with her parents. She agreed with him that they had made a great mistake; they ought to have left him free; and she expressed her confidence that that freedom would be for her family, as it were, like the silence of the sage, golden. He must excuse them; he must remember that what was asked of him had been their custom for centuries. She did not mention her authority as to the origin of customs, but she assured him that she would say three words to her father and mother which would make it all right. Jackson answered that customs were all

very well, but that intelligent people recognised, when they saw
it, the right occasion for departing from them; and with this he
awaited the result of Lady Beauchemin's remonstrance. It had
not as yet been perceptible, and it must be said that this charming woman was herself much bothered. When, on her venturing to say to her mother that she thought a wrong line had been
taken with regard to her sister's *prétendant*, Lady Canterville
had replied that Mr Lemon's unwillingness to settle anything
was in itself a proof of what they had feared, the unstable nature
of his fortune (for it was useless to talk – this gracious lady could
be very decided – there could be no serious reason but that
one): on meeting this argument, as I say, Jackson's protectress
felt considerably baffled. It was perhaps true, as her mother
said, that if they didn't insist upon proper guarantees Barberina
might be left in a few years with nothing but the stars and stripes
(this odd phrase was a quotation from Mr Lemon) to cover her.
Lady Beauchemin tried to reason it out with Lady Marmaduke;
but these were complications unforeseen by Lady Marmaduke
in her project of an Anglo-American society. She was obliged to
confess that Mr Lemon's fortune could not have the solidity of
long-established things; it was a very new fortune indeed. His
father had made the greater part of it all in a lump, a few years
before his death, in the extraordinary way in which people
made money in America; that, of course, was why the son had
those singular professional attributes. He had begun to study to
be a doctor very young, before his expectations were so great.
Then he had found he was very clever, and very fond of it; and
he had kept on, because, after all, in America, where there were
no country-gentlemen, a young man had to have something to
do, don't you know? And Lady Marmaduke, like an enlightened woman, intimated that in such a case she thought it in
much better taste not to try to sink anything. 'Because, in
America, don't you see,' she reasoned, 'you can't sink it –
nothing *will* sink. Everything is floating about – in the newspapers.' And she tried to console her friend by remarking that if
Mr Lemon's fortune was precarious, it was at all events so big.
That was just the trouble for Lady Beauchemin; it was so big,
and yet they were going to lose it. He was as obstinate as a mule;

she was sure he would never come round. Lady Marmaduke declared that he would come round; she even offered to bet a dozen pair of *gants de Suède* on it; and she added that this consummation lay quite in the hands of Barberina. Lady Beauchemin promised herself to converse with her sister; for it was not for nothing that she herself had felt the international contagion.

Jackson Lemon, to dissipate his chagrin, had returned to the sessions of the medical congress, where, inevitably, he had fallen into the hands of Sidney Feeder, who enjoyed in this disinterested assembly a high popularity. It was Doctor Feeder's earnest desire that his old friend should share it, which was all the more easy as the medical congress was really, as the young physician observed, a perpetual symposium. Jackson Lemon entertained the whole body – entertained it profusely, and in a manner befitting one of the patrons of science rather than its humbler votaries; but these dissipations only made him forget for a moment that his relations with the house of Canterville were anomalous. His great difficulty punctually came back to him, and Sidney Feeder saw it stamped upon his brow. Jackson Lemon, with his acute inclination to open himself, was on the point, more than once, of taking the sympathetic Sidney into his confidence. His friend gave him easy opportunity; he asked him what it was he was thinking of all the time, and whether the young marchioness had concluded she couldn't swallow a doctor. These forms of speech were displeasing to Jackson Lemon, whose fastidiousness was nothing new; but it was for even deeper reasons that he said to himself that, for such complicated cases as his, there was no assistance in Sidney Feeder. To understand his situation one must know the world; and the child of Cincinnati didn't know the world – at least the world with which his friend was now concerned.

'Is there a hitch in your marriage? Just tell me that,' Sidney Feeder had said, taking everything for granted, in a manner which was in itself a proof of great innocence. It is true he had added that he supposed he had no business to ask; but he had been anxious about it ever since hearing from Mr and

Mrs Freer that the British aristocracy was down on the medical profession. 'Do they want you to give it up? Is that what the hitch is about? Don't desert your colours, Jackson. The elimination of pain, the mitigation of misery, constitute surely the noblest profession in the world.'

'My dear fellow, you don't know what you are talking about,' Jackson observed, for answer to this. 'I haven't told any one I was going to be married; still less have I told any one that any one objected to my profession. I should like to see them do it. I have got out of the swim to-day, but I don't regard myself as the sort of person that people object to. And I do expect to do something, yet.'

'Come home, then, and do it. And excuse me if I say that the facilities for getting married are much greater over there.'

'You don't seem to have found them very great.'

'I have never had time. Wait till my next vacation, and you will see.'

'The facilities over there are too great. Nothing is good but what is difficult,' said Jackson Lemon, in a tone of artificial sententiousness that quite tormented his interlocutor.

'Well, they have got their backs up, I can see that. I'm glad you like it. Only if they despise your profession, what will they say to that of your friends? If they think you are queer, what would they think of me?' asked Sidney Feeder, the turn of whose mind was not, as a general thing, in the least sarcastic, but who was pushed to this sharpness by a conviction that (in spite of declarations which seemed half an admission and half a denial) his friend was suffering himself to be bothered for the sake of a good which might be obtained elsewhere without bother. It had come over him that the bother was of an unworthy kind.

'My dear fellow, all that is idiotic.' That had been Jackson Lemon's reply; but it expressed but a portion of his thoughts. The rest was inexpressible, or almost; being connected with a sentiment of rage at its having struck even so genial a mind as Sidney Feeder's that, in proposing to marry a daughter of the highest civilisation, he was going out of his way – departing from his natural line. Was he then so ignoble, so pledged to inferior things, that when he saw a girl who (putting aside the fact that she had not genius, which was rare, and which, though he prized rarity, he didn't want) seemed to him the most complete feminine nature he had known, he was to think himself too different, too incongruous, to mate with her? He would mate with whom he chose; that was the upshot of Jackson Lemon's reflections. Several days elapsed, during which everybody – even the pure-minded, like Sidney Feeder – seemed to him very abject.

I relate all this to show why it was that in going to see Mrs Freer he was prepared much less to be angry with people who, like the Dexter Freers, a month before, had given it out that he was engaged to a peer's daughter, than to resent the insinuation that there were obstacles to such a prospect. He sat with Mrs Freer alone for half an hour in the sabbatical stillness of Jermyn Street. Her husband had gone for a walk in the Park; he always walked in the Park on Sunday. All the world might have been there, and Jackson and Mrs Freer in sole possession of the district of St James's. This perhaps had something to do with making him at last rather confidential; the influences were conciliatory, persuasive. Mrs Freer was extremely sympathetic; she treated him like a person she had known from the age of ten; asked his leave to continue recumbent; talked a great deal about his mother; and seemed almost for a while to perform the kindly functions of that lady. It had been wise of her from the first not to allude, even indirectly, to his having neglected so long to call; her silence on this point was in the best taste. Jackson Lemon had forgotten that it was a habit with her, and indeed a high accomplishment, never to reproach people with these omissions. You might have left her alone for two years, her greeting was always the same; she was never either too delighted to see you or not delighted enough. After a while, however, he perceived that her silence had been to a certain extent a reference; she appeared to take for granted that he devoted all his hours to a certain young lady. It came over him for a moment that his country people took a great deal for granted; but when Mrs Freer, rather abruptly, sitting up on her sofa, said to him, half simply, half solemnly, 'And now, my dear Jackson, I want you to tell me something!' – he perceived that after all she didn't pretend to know more about the impending matter than he himself did. In the course of a quarter of an hour – so appreciatively she listened – he had told her a good deal about it. It was the first time he had said so much to any one, and the process relieved him even more than he would have supposed. It made certain things clear to him, by bringing them to a point – above all, the fact that he had been wronged. He made no allusion whatever to its being out of the usual way that, as an American doctor, he should sue for the hand of a marquis's daughter; and this reserve was not voluntary, it was quite unconscious. His mind was too full of the offensive conduct of the Cantervilles, and the sordid side of their want of confidence. He could not imagine that while he talked to Mrs Freer – and it amazed him afterward that he should have chattered so; he could account for it only by the state of his nerves – she should be thinking only of the strangeness of the situation he sketched for her. She thought Americans as good as other people, but she didn't see where, in American life, the daughter of a marquis would, as she phrased it, work in. To take a simple instance, – they coursed through Mrs Freer's mind with extraordinary speed – would she not always expect to go in to dinner first? As a novelty, over there, they might like to see her do it, at first; there might be even a pressure for places for the spectacle. But with the increase of every kind of sophistication that was taking place in America, the humorous view to which she would owe her safety might not continue to be taken; and then where would Lady Barberina be? This was but a small instance; but Mrs Freer's vivid imagination – much as she lived in Europe, she knew her native land so well – saw a host of others massing themselves behind it. The consequence of all of which was that after listening to him in the most engaging silence, she raised her clasped hands, pressed them against her breast, lowered her voice to a tone of entreaty, and, with her perpetual little smile, uttered three words: 'My dear Jackson, don't – don't – don't.'

'Don't what?' he asked, staring.

'Don't neglect the chance you have of getting out of it; it would never do.'

He knew what she meant by his chance of getting out of it; in his many meditations he had, of course, not overlooked that. The ground the old couple had taken about settlements (and the fact that Lady Beauchemin had not come back to him to tell him, as she promised, that she had moved them, proved how firmly they were rooted) would have offered an all-sufficient pretext to a man who should have repented of his advances. Jackson Lemon knew that; but he knew at the same time that he had not repented. The old couple's want of imagination did not in the least alter the fact that Barberina was, as he had told her father, a beautiful type. Therefore he simply said to Mrs Freer that he didn't in the least wish to get out of it; he was as much in it as ever, and he intended to remain there. But what did she mean, he inquired in a moment, by her statement that it would never do? Why wouldn't it do? Mrs Freer replied by another inquiry – Should he really like her to tell him? It wouldn't do, because Lady Barb would not be satisfied with her place at dinner. She would not be content – in a society of commoners – with any but the best; and the best she could not expect (and it was to be supposed that he did not expect her) always to have.

'What do you mean by commoners?' Jackson Lemon demanded, looking very serious.

'I mean you, and me, and my poor husband, and Dr Feeder,' said Mrs Freer.

'I don't see how there can be commoners where there are not lords. It is the lord that makes the commoner; and *vice versa*.'

'Won't a lady do as well? Lady Barberina – a single English girl – can make a million inferiors.'

'She will be, before anything else, my wife; and she will not talk about inferiors any more than I do. I never do; it's very vulgar.'

'I don't know what she'll talk about, my dear Jackson, but she will think; and her thoughts won't be pleasant – I mean for others. Do you expect to sink her to your own rank?'

Jackson Lemon's bright little eyes were fixed more brightly than ever upon his hostess. 'I don't understand you; and I don't think you understand yourself.' This was not absolutely candid, for he did understand Mrs Freer to a certain extent; it has been related that, before he asked Lady Barb's hand of her parents, there had been moments when he himself was not very sure that the flower of the British aristocracy would flourish in American soil. But an intimation from another person that it was beyond his power to pass off his wife – whether she were the daughter of a peer or of a shoemaker – set all his blood on fire. It quenched on the instant his own perception of difficulties of detail, and made him feel only that he was dishonoured – he, the heir of all the ages – by such insinuations. It was his belief – though he had never before had occasion to put it forward – that his position, one of the best in the world, was one of those positions that make everything possible. He had had the best education the age could offer, for if he had rather wasted his time at Harvard, where he entered very young, he had, as he believed, been tremendously serious at Heidelberg and at Vienna. He had devoted himself to one of the noblest of professions – a profession recognised as such everywhere but in England – and he had inherited a fortune far beyond the expectation of his earlier years, the years when he cultivated habits of work which alone – or rather in combination with talents that he neither exaggerated nor minimised – would have conduced to distinction. He was one of the most fortunate inhabitants of an immense, fresh, rich country, a country whose future was admitted to be incalculable, and he moved with perfect ease in a society in which he was not overshadowed by others. It seemed to him, therefore, beneath his dignity to wonder whether he could afford, socially speaking, to marry according to his taste. Jackson Lemon pretended to be strong; and what was the use of being strong if you were not prepared to undertake things that timid people might find difficult? It was his plan to marry the woman he liked, and not to be afraid of her afterward. The effect of Mrs Freer's doubt of his success was to represent to him that his own character would not cover his wife's; she couldn't have made him feel otherwise if she had told him that he was marrying beneath him, and would have to ask for indulgence. 'I don't believe you know how much I think that any woman who marries me will be doing very well,' he added, directly.

'I am very sure of that; but it isn't so simple – one's being an American,' Mrs Freer rejoined, with a little philosophic sigh.

'It's whatever one chooses to make it.'

'Well, you'll make it what no one has done yet, if you take that young lady to America and make her happy there.'

'Do you think it's such a very dreadful place?'

'No, indeed; but she will.'

Jackson Lemon got up from his chair, and took up his hat and stick. He had actually turned a little pale, with the force of his emotion; it had made him really quiver that his marriage to Lady Barberina should be looked at as too high a flight. He stood a moment leaning against the mantelpiece, and very much tempted to say to Mrs Freer that she was a vulgar-minded old woman. But he said something that was really more to the point: 'You forget that she will have her consolations.'

'Don't go away, or I shall think I have offended you. You can't console a wounded marchioness.'

'How will she be wounded? People will be charming to her.'

'They will be charming to her – charming to her!' These words fell from the lips of Dexter Freer, who had opened the door of the room and stood with the knob in his hand, putting himself into relation to his wife's talk with their visitor. This was accomplished in an instant. 'Of course I know whom you mean,' he said, while he exchanged greetings with Jackson Lemon. 'My wife and I – of course you know we are great busybodies – have talked of your affair, and we differ about it completely: she sees only the dangers, and I see the advantages.'

'By the advantages he means the fun for us,' Mrs Freer remarked, settling her sofa-cushions.

Jackson looked with a certain sharp blankness from one of these disinterested judges to the other; and even yet they did not perceive how their misdirected familiarities wrought upon him. It was hardly more agreeable to him to know that the husband wished to see Lady Barb in America, than to know that the wife had a dread of such a vision; for there was that in Dexter Freer's face which seemed to say that the thing would take place somehow for the benefit of the spectators. 'I think you both see too much – a great deal too much,' he answered, rather coldly.

'My dear young man, at my age I can take certain liberties,' said Dexter Freer. 'Do it – I beseech you to do it; it has never been done before.' And then, as if Jackson's glance had challenged this last assertion, he went on: 'Never, I assure you, this particular thing. Young female members of the British aristocracy have married coachmen and fishmongers, and all that sort of thing; but they have never married you and me.'

'They certainly haven't married you,' said Mrs Freer.

'I am much obliged to you for your advice.' It may be thought that Jackson Lemon took himself rather seriously; and indeed I am afraid that if he had not done so there would have been no occasion for my writing this little history. But it made him almost sick to hear his engagement spoken of as a curious and ambiguous phenomenon. He might have his own ideas about it – one always had about one's engagement; but the ideas that appeared to have peopled the imagination of his friends ended by kindling a little hot spot in each of his cheeks. 'I would rather not talk any more about my little plans,' he added to Dexter Freer. 'I have been saying all sorts of absurd things to Mrs Freer.'

'They have been most interesting,' that lady declared. 'You have been very stupidly treated.'

'May she tell me when you go?' her husband asked of the young man.

'I am going now; she may tell you whatever she likes.'

'I am afraid we have displeased you,' said Mrs Freer; 'I have said too much what I think. You must excuse me, it's all for your mother.'

'It's she whom I want Lady Barberina to see!' Jackson Lemon exclaimed, with the inconsequence of filial affection.

'Deary me!' murmured Mrs Freer.

'We shall go back to America to see how you get on,' her husband said; 'and if you succeed, it will be a great precedent.'

'Oh, I shall succeed!' And with this he took his departure. He walked away with the quick step of a man labouring under a certain excitement; walked up to Piccadilly and down past Hyde Park Corner. It relieved him to traverse these distances, for he was thinking hard, under the influence of irritation; and locomotion helped him to think. Certain suggestions that had been made him in the last half hour rankled in his mind, all the more that they seemed to have a kind of representative value, to be an echo of the common voice. If his prospects wore that face to Mrs Freer, they would probably wear it to others; and he felt a sudden need of showing such others that they took a pitiful measure of his position. Jackson Lemon walked and walked till he found himself on the highway of Hammersmith. I have represented him as a young man of much strength of purpose, and I may appear to undermine this plea when I relate that he wrote that evening to his solicitor that Mr Hilary was to be informed that he would agree to any proposals for settlements that Mr Hilary should make. Jackson's strength of purpose was shown in his deciding to marry Lady Barberina on any terms. It seemed to him, under the influence of his desire to prove that he was not afraid – so odious was the imputation – that terms of any kind were very superficial things. What was fundamental, and of the essence of the matter, would be to marry Lady Barb and carry everything out.

V

'ON Sundays, now, you might be at home,' Jackson Lemon said to his wife in the following month of March, more than six months after his marriage.

'Are the people any nicer on Sundays than they are on other days?' Lady Barberina replied, from the depths of her chair, without looking up from a stiff little book.

He hesitated a single instant before answering: 'I don't know whether they are, but I think you might be.'

'I am as nice as I know how to be. You must take me as I am. You knew when you married me that I was not an American.'

Jackson Lemon stood before the fire, towards which his wife's face was turned and her feet were extended; stood there some time, with his hands behind him and his eyes dropped a little obliquely upon the bent head and richly-draped figure of Lady Barberina. It may be said without delay that he was irritated, and it may be added that he had a double cause. He felt himself to be on the verge of the first crisis that had occurred between himself and his wife – the reader will perceive that it had occurred rather promptly – and he was annoyed at his annoyance. A glimpse of his state of mind before his marriage has been given to the reader, who will remember that at that period Jackson Lemon somehow regarded himself as lifted above possibilities of irritation. When one was strong, one was not irritable; and a union with a kind of goddess would of course be an element of strength. Lady Barb was a goddess still, and Jackson Lemon admired his wife as much as the day he led her to the altar; but I am not sure that he felt so strong.

'How do you know what people are?' he said in a moment. 'You have seen so few; you are perpetually denying yourself. If you should leave New York to-morrow you would know wonderfully little about it.'

'It's all the same,' said Lady Barb; 'the people are all exactly alike.'

'How can you tell? You never see them.'

'Didn't I go out every night for the first two months we were here?'

'It was only to about a dozen houses – always the same; people, moreover, you had already met in London. You have got no general impressions.'

'That's just what I have got; I had them before I came. Every one is just the same; they have just the same names – just the same manners.'

Again, for an instant, Jackson Lemon hesitated; then he said, in that apparently artless tone of which mention has already been made, and which he sometimes used in London during his wooing: 'Don't you like it over here?'

Lady Barb raised her eyes from her book. 'Did you expect me to like it?'

'I hoped you would, of course. I think I told you so.'

'I don't remember. You said very little about it; you seemed to make a kind of mystery. I knew, of course, you expected me to live here, but I didn't know you expected me to like it.'

'You thought I asked of you the sacrifice, as it were.'

'I am sure I don't know,' said Lady Barb. She got up from her chair and tossed the volume she had been reading into the empty seat. 'I recommend you to read that book,' she added.

'Is it interesting?'

'It's an American novel.'

'I never read novels.'

'You had better look at that one; it will show you the kind of people you want me to know.'

'I have no doubt it's very vulgar,' said Jackson Lemon; 'I don't see why you read it.'

'What else can I do? I can't always be riding in the Park; I hate the Park,' Lady Barb remarked.

'It's quite as good as your own,' said her husband.

She glanced at him with a certain quickness, her eyebrows slightly lifted. 'Do you mean the park at Pasterns?'

'No; I mean the park in London.'

'I don't care about London. One was only in London a few weeks.'

'I suppose you miss the country,' said Jackson Lemon. It was his idea of life that he should not be afraid of anything, not be afraid, in any situation, of knowing the worst that was to be known about it; and the demon of a courage with which discretion was not properly commingled prompted him to take soundings which were perhaps not absolutely necessary for safety, and yet which revealed unmistakable rocks. It was useless to know about rocks if he couldn't avoid them; the only thing was to trust to the wind.

'I don't know what I miss. I think I miss everything!' This was his wife's answer to his too curious inquiry. It was not peevish, for that is not the tone of a goddess; but it expressed a good deal – a good deal more than Lady Barb, who was rarely eloquent, had expressed before. Nevertheless, though his question had been precipitate, Jackson Lemon said to himself that he might take his time to think over what his wife's little speech contained; he could not help seeing that the future would give him abundant opportunity for that. He was in no hurry to ask himself whether poor Mrs Freer, in Jermyn Street, might not, after all, have been right in saying that, in regard to marrying the product of an English caste, it was not so simple to be an American doctor – might avail little even, in such a case, to be the heir of all the ages. The transition was complicated, but in his bright mind it was rapid, from the brush of a momentary contact with such ideas to certain considerations which led him to say, after an instant, to his wife, 'Should you like to go down into Connecticut?'

'Into Connecticut?'

'That's one of our States; it's about as large as Ireland. I'll take you there if you like.'

'What does one do there?'

'We can try and get some hunting.'

'You and I alone?'

'Perhaps we can get a party to join us.'

'The people in the State?'

'Yes; we might propose it to them.'

'The tradespeople in the towns?'

'Very true; they will have to mind their shops,' said Jackson Lemon. 'But we might hunt alone.'

'Are there any foxes?'

'No; but there are a few old cows.'

Lady Barb had already perceived that her husband took it into his head once in a while to laugh at her, and she was aware that the present occasion was neither worse nor better than some others. She didn't mind it particularly now, though in England it would have disgusted her; she had the consciousness of virtue – an immense comfort – and flattered herself that she had learned the lesson of an altered standard of fitness; there were, moreover, so many more disagreeable things in

America than being laughed at by one's husband. But she
pretended to mind it, because it made him stop, and above all
it stopped discussion, which with Jackson was so often jocular,
and none the less tiresome for that. 'I only want to be left alone,'
she said, in answer – though, indeed, it had not the manner of
an answer – to his speech about the cows. With this she wandered away to one of the windows which looked out on the
Fifth Avenue. She was very fond of these windows, and she had
taken a great fancy to the Fifth Avenue, which, in the high-
pitched winter weather, when everything sparkled, was a spectacle full of novelty. It will be seen that she was not wholly
unjust to her adoptive country: she found it delightful to look
out of the window. This was a pleasure she had enjoyed in
London only in the most furtive manner; it was not the kind
of thing that girls did in England. Besides, in London, in Hill
Street, there was nothing particular to see; but in the Fifth
Avenue everything and every one went by, and observation
was made consistent with dignity by the masses of brocade
and lace in which the windows were draped, which, somehow,
would not have been tidy in England, and which made an
ambush without concealing the brilliant day. Hundreds of
women – the curious women of New York, who were unlike
any that Lady Barb had hitherto seen – passed the house every
hour, and her ladyship was infinitely entertained and mystified
by the sight of their clothes. She spent a good deal more time
than she was aware of in this amusement; and if she had been
addicted to returning upon herself, or asking herself for an
account of her conduct – an inquiry which she did not, indeed,
completely neglect, but treated very cursorily – it would
have made her smile sadly to think what she appeared mainly
to have come to America for, conscious though she was that her
tastes were very simple, and that so long as she didn't hunt, it
didn't much matter what she did.

Her husband turned about to the fire, giving a push with his
foot to a log that had fallen out of its place. Then he said – and
the connection with the words she had just uttered was apparent enough – 'You really must be at home on Sundays, you
know. I used to like that so much in London. All the best

women here do it. You had better begin to-day. I am going to see my mother; if I meet any one I will tell them to come.'

'Tell them not to talk so much,' said Lady Barb, among her lace curtains.

'Ah, my dear,' her husband replied, 'it isn't every one that has your concision!' And he went and stood behind her in the window, putting his arm round her waist. It was as much of a satisfaction to him as it had been six months before, at the time the solicitors were settling the matter, that this flower of an ancient stem should be worn upon his own breast; he still thought its fragrance a thing quite apart, and it was as clear as day to him that his wife was the handsomest woman in New York. He had begun, after their arrival, by telling her this very often; but the assurance brought no colour to her cheek, no light to her eyes; to be the handsomest woman in New York evidently did not seem to her a position in life. Moreover, the reader may be informed that, oddly enough, Lady Barb did not particularly believe this assertion. There were some very pretty women in New York, and without in the least wishing to be like them – she had seen no woman in America whom she desired to resemble – she envied some of their elements. It is probable that her own finest points were those of which she was most unconscious. But her husband was aware of all of them; nothing could exceed the minuteness of his appreciation of his wife. It was a sign of this that after he had stood behind her a moment he kissed her very tenderly. 'Have you any message for my mother?' he asked.

'Please give her my love. And you might take her that book.'

'What book?'

'That nasty one I have been reading.'

'Oh, bother your books,' said Jackson Lemon, with a certain irritation, as he went out of the room.

There had been a good many things in her life in New York that cost Lady Barb an effort; but sending her love to her mother-in-law was not one of these. She liked Mrs Lemon better than any one she had seen in America; she was the only person who seemed to Lady Barb really simple, as she understood that quality. Many people had struck her as homely and rustic, and many others as pretentious and vulgar; but in Jackson's mother she had found the golden mean of a simplicity which, as she would have said, was really nice. Her sister, Lady Agatha, was even fonder of Mrs Lemon; but then Lady Agatha had taken the most extraordinary fancy to every one and everything, and talked as if America were the most delightful country in the world. She was having a lovely time (she already spoke the most beautiful American), and had been, during the winter that was just drawing to a close, the most prominent girl in New York. She had gone out at first with her sister; but for some weeks past Lady Barb had let so many occasions pass, that Agatha threw herself into the arms of Mrs Lemon, who found her extraordinarily quaint and amusing and was delighted to take her into society. Mrs Lemon, as an old woman, had given up such vanities; but she only wanted a motive, and in her good nature she ordered a dozen new caps and sat smiling against the wall while her little English maid, on polished floors, to the sound of music, cultivated the American step as well as the American tone. There was no trouble, in New York, about going out, and the winter was not half over before the little English maid found herself an accomplished diner, rolling about, without any chaperone at all, to banquets where she could count upon a bouquet at her plate. She had had a great deal of correspondence with her mother on this point, and Lady Canterville at last withdrew her protest, which in the meantime had been perfectly useless. It was ultimately Lady Canterville's feeling that if she had married the handsomest of her daughters to an American doctor, she might let another become a professional *raconteuse* (Agatha had written to her that she was expected to talk so much), strange as such a destiny seemed for a girl of nineteen. Mrs Lemon was even a much simpler woman than Lady Barberina thought her; for she had not noticed that Lady Agatha danced much oftener with Herman Longstraw than with any one else. Jackson Lemon, though he went little to balls, had discovered this truth, and he looked slightly preoccupied when, after he had sat five minutes with his mother on the Sunday afternoon through which I have invited the reader to trace so much more than (I am afraid) is easily apparent of the progress of this simple story, he learned that his sister-in-law was entertaining Mr Longstraw in the library. He had called half an hour before, and she had taken him into the other room to show him the seal of the Cantervilles, which she had fastened to one of her numerous trinkets (she was adorned with a hundred bangles and chains), and the proper exhibition of which required a taper and a stick of wax. Apparently he was examining it very carefully, for they had been absent a good while. Mrs Lemon's simplicity was further shown by the fact that she had not measured their absence; it was only when Jackson questioned her that she remembered.

Herman Longstraw was a young Californian who had turned up in New York the winter before, and who travelled on his moustache, as they were understood to say in his native State. This moustache, and some of the accompanying features, were very ornamental; several ladies in New York had been known to declare that they were as beautiful as a dream. Taken in connection with his tall stature, his familiar goodnature, and his remarkable Western vocabulary, they constituted his only social capital; for of the two great divisions, the rich Californians and the poor Californians, it was well known to which he belonged. Jackson Lemon looked at him as a slightly mitigated cowboy, and was somewhat vexed at his dear mother, though he was aware that she could scarcely figure to herself what an effect such an accent as that would produce in the halls of Canterville. He had no desire whatever to play a trick on the house to which he was allied, and knew perfectly that Lady Agatha had not been sent to America to become entangled with a Californian of the wrong denomination. He had been perfectly willing to bring her; he thought, a little vindictively, that this would operate as a hint to her parents as to what he might have been inclined to do if they had not sent Mr Hilary after him. Herman Longstraw, according to the legend, had been a trapper, a squatter, a miner, a pioneer – had been everything that one could be in the romantic parts of America, and had accumulated masses of experience before the age of thirty. He had shot bears in the Rockies and buffaloes on the plains; and it was even believed that he had brought down animals of a still more dangerous kind, among the haunts of men. There had been a story that he owned a cattle-ranch in Arizona; but a later and apparently more authentic version of it, though it represented him as looking after the cattle, did not depict him as their proprietor. Many of the stories told about him were false; but there is no doubt that his moustache, his good-nature and his accent were genuine. He danced very badly; but Lady Agatha had frankly told several persons that that was nothing new to her; and she liked (this, however, she did not tell) Mr Herman Longstraw. What she enjoyed in America was the revelation of freedom; and there was no such proof of freedom as conversation with a gentleman who dressed in skins when he was not in New York, and who, in his usual pursuits, carried his life (as well as that of other people) in his hand. A gentleman whom she had sat next to at a dinner in the early part of her stay in New York, remarked to her that the United States were the paradise of women and mechanics; and this had seemed to her at the time very abstract, for she was not conscious, as yet, of belonging to either class. In England she had been only a girl; and the principal idea connected with that was simply that, for one's misfortune, one was not a boy. But presently she perceived that New York was a paradise; and this helped her to know that she must be one of the people mentioned in the axiom of her neighbour – people who could do whatever they wanted, had a voice in everything, and made their taste and their ideas felt. She saw that it was great fun to be a woman in America, and that this was the best way to enjoy the New York winter – the wonderful, brilliant New York winter, the queer, long-shaped, glittering city, the heterogeneous hours, among which you couldn't tell the morning from the afternoon or the night from either of them, the perpetual liberties and walks, the rushings-out and the droppings-in, the intimacies, the endearments, the comicalities, the sleigh-bells, the cutters, the sunsets on the snow, the ice-parties in the frosty clearness, the bright, hot, velvety houses, the bouquets, the bonbons, the little cakes, the big cakes, the irrepressible inspirations of shopping, the innumerable luncheons and dinners that were offered to youth and innocence, the quantities of

chatter of quantities of girls, the perpetual motion of the German, the suppers at restaurants after the play, the way in which
life was pervaded by Delmonico and Delmonico by the sense
that though one's hunting was lost and this so different, it was
almost as good – and in all, through all, a kind of suffusion of
bright, loud, friendly sound, which was very local, but very
human.

Lady Agatha at present was staying, for a little change, with
Mrs Lemon, and such adventures as that were part of the
pleasure of her American season. The house was too close;
but physically the girl could bear anything, and it was all she
had to complain of; for Mrs Lemon, as we know, thought her a
bonnie little damsel, and had none of those old-world scruples
in regard to spoiling young people to which Lady Agatha now
perceived that she herself, in the past, had been unduly sacrificed. In her own way – it was not at all her sister's way – she
liked to be of importance; and this was assuredly the case when
she saw that Mrs Lemon had apparently nothing in the world to
do (after spending a part of the morning with her servants) but
invent little distractions (many of them of the edible sort) for
her guest. She appeared to have certain friends, but she had no
society to speak of, and the people who came into her house
came principally to see Lady Agatha. This, as we have seen, was
strikingly the case with Herman Longstraw. The whole situation gave Lady Agatha a great feeling of success – success of a
new and unexpected kind. Of course, in England, she had been
born successful, in a manner, in coming into the world in one of
the most beautiful rooms at Pasterns; but her present triumph
was achieved more by her own effort (not that she had tried very
hard) and by her merit. It was not so much what she said (for
she could never say half as much as the girls in New York), as
the spirit of enjoyment that played in her fresh young face, with
its pointless curves, and shone in her grey English eyes. She
enjoyed everything, even the street-cars, of which she made
liberal use; and more than everything she enjoyed Mr Longstraw and his talk about buffaloes and bears. Mrs Lemon
promised to be very careful, as soon as her son had begun to
warn her; and this time she had a certain understanding of what

she promised. She thought people ought to make the matches they liked; she had given proof of this in her later behaviour to Jackson, whose own union was, in her opinion, marked with all the arbitrariness of pure love. Nevertheless, she could see that Herman Longstraw would probably be thought rough in England; and it was not simply that he was so inferior to Jackson, for, after all, certain things were not to be expected. Jackson Lemon was not oppressed with his mother-in-law, having taken his precautions against such a danger; but he was aware that he should give Lady Canterville a permanent advantage over him if, while she was in America, her daughter Agatha should attach herself to a mere moustache.

It was not always, as I have hinted, that Mrs Lemon entered completely into the views of her son, though in form she never failed to subscribe to them devoutly. She had never yet, for instance, apprehended his reason for marrying Lady Barberina Clement. This was a great secret, and Mrs Lemon was determined that no one should ever know it. For herself, she was sure that, to the end of time, she should not discover Jackson's reason. She could never ask about it, for that of course would betray her. From the first she had told him she was delighted; there being no need of asking for explanations then, as the young lady herself, when she should come to know her, would explain. But the young lady had not yet explained; and after this, evidently, she never would. She was very tall, very handsome, she answered exactly to Mrs Lemon's prefigurement of the daughter of a lord, and she wore her clothes, which were peculiar, but, to her, remarkably becoming, very well. But she did not elucidate; we know ourselves that there was very little that was explanatory about Lady Barb. So Mrs Lemon continued to wonder, to ask herself, 'Why that one, more than so many others, who would have been more natural?' The choice appeared to her, as I have said, very arbitrary. She found Lady Barb very different from other girls she had known, and this led her almost immediately to feel sorry for her daughter-in-law. She said to herself that Barb was to be pitied if she found her husband's people as peculiar as his mother found *her*; for the result of that would be to make her very lonesome. Lady Agatha was different, because she seemed to keep nothing back; you saw all there was of her, and she was evidently not homesick. Mrs Lemon could see that Barberina was ravaged by this last passion and was too proud to show it. She even had a glimpse of the ultimate truth; namely, that Jackson's wife had not the comfort of crying, because that would have amounted to a confession that she had been idiotic enough to believe in advance that, in an American town, in the society of doctors, she should escape such pangs. Mrs Lemon treated her with the greatest gentleness – all the gentleness that was due to a young woman who was in the unfortunate position of having been married one couldn't tell why. The world, to Mrs Lemon's view, contained two great departments – that of persons, and that of things; and she believed that you must take an interest either in one or the other. The incomprehensible thing in Lady Barb was that she cared for neither side of the show. Her house apparently inspired her with no curiosity and no enthusiasm, though it had been thought magnificent enough to be described in successive columns of the American newspapers; and she never spoke of her furniture or her domestics, though she had a prodigious supply of such possessions. She was the same with regard to her acquaintance, which was immense, inasmuch as every one in the place had called on her. Mrs Lemon was the least critical woman in the world; but it had sometimes exasperated her just a little that her daughter-in-law should receive every one in New York in exactly the same way. There were differences, Mrs Lemon knew, and some of them were of the highest importance; but poor Lady Barb appeared never to suspect them. She accepted every one and everything, and asked no questions. She had no curiosity about her fellow-citizens, and as she never assumed it for a moment, she gave Mrs Lemon no opportunity to enlighten her. Lady Barb was a person with whom you could do nothing unless she gave you an opening; and nothing would have been more difficult than to enlighten her against her will. Of course she picked up a little knowledge; but she confounded and transposed American attributes in the most extraordinary way. She had a way of calling every one Doctor; and Mrs Lemon could scarcely convince her that this distinction was too precious to be so freely bestowed. She had once said to her mother-in-law that in New York there was nothing to know people by, their names were so very monotonous; and Mrs Lemon had entered into this enough to see that there was something that stood out a good deal in Barberina's own prefix. It is probable that during her short stay in New York complete justice was not done Lady Barb; she never got credit, for instance, for repressing her annoyance at the aridity of the social nomenclature, which seemed to her hideous. That little speech to her mother was the most reckless sign she gave of it; and there were few things that contributed more to the good conscience she habitually enjoyed, than her self-control on this particular point.

Jackson Lemon was making some researches, just now, which took up a great deal of his time; and, for the rest, he passed his hours abundantly with his wife. For the last three months, therefore, he had seen his mother scarcely more than once a week. In spite of researches, in spite of medical societies, where Jackson, to her knowledge, read papers, Lady Barb had more of her husband's company than she had counted upon at the time she married. She had never known a married pair to be so much together as she and Jackson; he appeared to expect her to sit with him in the library in the morning. He had none of the occupations of gentlemen and noblemen in England, for the element of politics appeared to be as absent as the hunting. There were politics in Washington, she had been told, and even at Albany, and Jackson had proposed to introduce her to these cities; but the proposal, made to her once at dinner before several people, had excited such cries of horror that it fell dead on the spot. 'We don't want you to see anything of that kind,' one of the ladies had said, and Jackson had appeared to be discouraged – that is if, in regard to Jackson, one could really tell.

'Pray, what is it you want me to see?' Lady Barb had asked on this occasion.

'Well, New York; and Boston, if you want to very much – but not otherwise; and Niagara; and, more than anything, New-port.'

Lady Barb was tired of their eternal Newport; she had heard of it a thousand times, and felt already as if she had lived there half her life; she was sure, moreover, that she should hate it. This is perhaps as near as she came to having a lively conviction on any American subject. She asked herself whether she was then to spend her life in the Fifth Avenue, with alternations of a city of villas (she detested villas), and wondered whether that was all the great American country had to offer her. There were times when she thought that she should like the backwoods, and that the Far West might be a resource; for she had analysed her feelings just deep enough to discover that when she had – hesitating a good deal – turned over the question of marrying Jackson Lemon, it was not in the least of American barbarism that she was afraid; her dread was of American civilisation. She believed the little lady I have just quoted was a goose; but that did not make New York any more interesting. It would be reckless to say that she suffered from an overdose of Jackson's company, because she had a view of the fact that he was much her most important social resource. She could talk to him about England; about her own England, and he understood more or less what she wished to say, when she wished to say anything, which was not frequent. There were plenty of other people who talked about England; but with them the range of allusion was always the hotels, of which she knew nothing, and the shops, and the opera, and the photographs: they had a mania for photographs. There were other people who were always want-ing her to tell them about Pasterns, and the manner of life there, and the parties; but if there was one thing Lady Barb disliked more than another, it was describing Pasterns. She had always lived with people who knew, of themselves, what such a place would be, without demanding these pictorial efforts, proper only, as she vaguely felt, to persons belonging to the classes whose trade was the arts of expression. Lady Barb, of course, had never gone into it; but she knew that in her own class the business was not to express, but to enjoy; not to represent, but to be represented – though, indeed, this latter liability might convey offence; for it may be noted that even for an aristocrat Jackson Lemon's wife was aristocratic.

Lady Agatha and her visitor came back from the library in course of time, and Jackson Lemon felt it his duty to be rather cold to Herman Longstraw. It was not clear to him what sort of a husband his sister-in-law would do well to look for in America – if there were to be any question of husbands; but as to this he was not bound to be definite, provided he should rule out Mr Longstraw. This gentleman, however, was not given to perceive shades of manner; he had little observation, but very great confidence.

'I think you had better come home with me,' Jackson said to Lady Agatha; 'I guess you have stayed here long enough.'

'Don't let him say that, Mrs Lemon!' the girl cried. 'I like being with you so very much.'

'I try to make it pleasant,' said Mrs Lemon. 'I should really miss you now; but perhaps it's your mother's wish.' If it was a question of defending her guest from ineligible suitors, Mrs Lemon felt, of course, that her son was more competent than she; though she had a lurking kindness for Herman Longstraw, and a vague idea that he was a gallant, genial specimen of young America.

'Oh, mamma wouldn't see any difference!' Lady Agatha exclaimed, looking at Jackson with pleading blue eyes. 'Mamma wants me to see every one; you know she does. That's what she sent me to America for; she knew it was not like England. She wouldn't like it if I didn't sometimes stay with people; she always wanted us to stay at other houses. And she knows all about you, Mrs Lemon, and she likes you immensely. She sent you a message the other day, and I am afraid I forgot to give it you – to thank you for being so kind to me and taking such a lot of trouble. Really she did, but I forgot it. If she wants me to see as much as possible of America, it's much better I should be here than always with Barb – it's much less like one's own country. I mean it's much nicer – for a girl,' said Lady Agatha, affectionately, to Mrs Lemon, who began also to look at Jackson with a kind of tender argumentativeness.

'If you want the genuine thing, you ought to come out on the plains,' Mr Longstraw interposed, with smiling sincerity. 'I guess that was your mother's idea. Why don't you all come out?' He had been looking intently at Lady Agatha while the remarks I have just repeated succeeded each other on her lips – looking at her with a kind of fascinated approbation, for all the world as if he had been a slightly slow-witted English gentleman and the girl had been a flower of the West – a flower that knew how to talk. He made no secret of the fact that Lady Agatha's voice was music to him, his ear being much more susceptible than his own inflections would have indicated. To Lady Agatha those inflections were not displeasing, partly because, like Mr Herman himself, in general, she had not a perception of shades; and partly because it never occurred to her to compare them with any other tones. He seemed to her to speak a foreign language altogether – a romantic dialect, through which the most comical meanings gleamed here and there.

'I should like it above all things,' she said, in answer to his last observation.

'The scenery's superior to anything round here,' Mr Long-straw went on.

Mrs Lemon, as we know, was the softest of women; but, as an old New Yorker, she had no patience with some of the new fashions. Chief among these was the perpetual reference, which had become common only within a few years, to the outlying parts of the country, the States and Territories of which children, in her time, used to learn the names, in their order, at school, but which no one ever thought of going to or talking about. Such places, in Mrs Lemon's opinion, belonged to the geography-books, or at most to the literature of newspapers, but not to society nor to conversation; and the change – which, so far as it lay in people's talk, she thought at bottom a mere affectation – threatened to make her native land appear vulgar and vague. For this amiable daughter of Manhattan, the normal existence of man, and, still more, of woman, had been 'located', as she would have said, between Trinity Church and the beautiful Reservoir at the top of the Fifth Avenue – monuments of which she was personally proud; and if we could look into the deeper parts of her mind, I am afraid we should discover there an impression that both the countries of Europe and the remainder of her own continent were equally far from the centre and the light.

'Well, scenery isn't everything,' she remarked, mildly, to Mr Longstraw; 'and if Lady Agatha should wish to see anything of that kind, all she has got to do is to take the boat up the Hudson.'

Mrs Lemon's recognition of this river, I should say, was all that it need have been; she thought that it existed for the purpose of supplying New Yorkers with poetical feelings, helping them to face comfortably occasions like the present, and, in general, meet foreigners with confidence – part of the oddity of foreigners being their conceit about their own places.

'That's a good idea, Lady Agatha; let's take the boat,' said Mr Longstraw. 'I've had great times on the boats.'

Lady Agatha looked at her cavalier a little with those singular, charming eyes of hers – eyes of which it was impossible to say, at any moment, whether they were the shyest or the frankest in the world; and she was not aware, while this contemplation lasted, that her brother-in-law was observing her. He was thinking of certain things while he did so, of things he had heard about the English; who still, in spite of his having married into a family of that nation, appeared to him very much through the medium of hearsay. They were more passionate than the Americans, and they did things that would never have been expected; though they seemed steadier and less excitable, there was much social evidence to show that they were more impulsive.

'It's so very kind of you to propose that,' Lady Agatha said in a moment to Mrs Lemon. 'I think I have never been in a ship – except, of course, coming from England. I am sure mamma would wish me to see the Hudson. We used to go in immensely for boating in England.'

'Did you boat in a ship?' Herman Longstraw asked, showing his teeth hilariously, and pulling his moustaches.

'Lots of my mother's people have been in the navy.' Lady Agatha perceived vaguely and good-naturedly that she had said something which the odd Americans thought odd, and that she must justify herself. Her standard of oddity was getting dreadfully dislocated.

'I really think you had better come back to us,' said Jackson; 'your sister is very lonely without you.'

'She is much more lonely with me. We are perpetually having differences. Barb is dreadfully vexed because I like America, instead of – instead of—' And Lady Agatha paused a moment; for it just occurred to her that this might be a betrayal.

'Instead of what?' Jackson Lemon inquired.

'Instead of perpetually wanting to go to England, as she does,' she went on, only giving her phrase a little softer turn; for she felt the next moment that her sister could have nothing to hide, and must, of course, have the courage of her opinions. 'Of course England's best, but I daresay I like to be bad,' said Lady Agatha, artlessly.

'Oh, there's no doubt you are awfully bad!' Mr Longstraw exclaimed, with joyous eagerness. Of course he could not know that what she had principally in mind was an exchange of opinions that had taken place between her sister and herself just before she came to stay with Mrs Lemon. This incident, of which Longstraw was the occasion, might indeed have been called a discussion, for it had carried them quite into the realms of the abstract. Lady Barb had said she didn't see how Agatha could look at such a creature as that – an odious, familiar, vulgar being, who had not about him the rudiments of a gentle-man. Lady Agatha had replied that Mr Longstraw was familiar and rough, and that he had a twang, and thought it amusing to talk of her as 'the Princess'; but that he was a gentleman for all that, and that at any rate he was tremendous fun. Her sister to this had rejoined that if he was rough and familiar he couldn't be a gentleman, inasmuch as that was just what a gentleman meant – a man who was civil, and well-bred, and well-born. Lady Agatha had argued that this was just where she differed; that a man might perfectly be a gentleman, and yet be rough, and even ignorant, so long as he was really nice. The only thing was that he should be really nice, which was the case with Mr Longstraw, who, moreover, was quite extraordinarily civil – as civil as a man could be. And then Lady Agatha made the strongest point she had ever made in her life (she had never been so inspired) in saying that Mr Longstraw was rough, perhaps, but not rude – a distinction altogether wasted on her sister, who declared that she had not come to America, of all places, to learn what a gentleman was. The discussion, in short, had been lively. I know not whether it was the tonic effect on them, too, of the fine winter weather, or, on the other hand, that of Lady Barb's being bored and having nothing else to do; but Lord Canterville's daughters went into the question with the moral earnestness of a pair of Bostonians. It was part of Lady Agatha's view of her admirer that he, after all, much resembled other tall people, with smiling eyes and moustaches, who had ridden a good deal in rough countries, and whom she had seen in other places. If he was more familiar, he was also more alert; still, the difference was not in himself, but in the way she saw him – the way she saw everybody in America. If she should see the others in the same way, no doubt they would be quite the same; and Lady Agatha sighed a little over the possibilities of life; for this peculiar way, especially regarded in connection with gentlemen, had become very pleasant to her.

She had betrayed her sister more than she thought, even though Jackson Lemon did not particularly show it in the tone in which he said: 'Of course she knows that she is going to see your mother in the summer.' His tone, rather, was that of irritation at the repetition of a familiar idea.

'Oh, it isn't only mamma,' replied Lady Agatha.

'I know she likes a cool house,' said Mrs Lemon, suggestively.

'When she goes, you had better bid her good-bye,' the girl went on.

'Of course I shall bid her good-bye,' said Mrs Lemon, to whom, apparently, this remark was addressed.

'I shall never bid you good-bye, Princess,' Herman Longstraw interposed. 'I can tell you that you never will see the last of me.'

'Oh, it doesn't matter about me, for I shall come back; but if Barb once gets to England she will never come back.'

'Oh, my dear child,' murmured Mrs Lemon, addressing Lady Agatha, but looking at her son.

Jackson looked at the ceiling, at the floor; above all, he looked very conscious.

'I hope you don't mind my saying that, Jackson dear,' Lady Agatha said to him, for she was very fond of her brother-in-law.

'Ah, well, then, she shan't go, then,' he remarked, after a moment, with a dry little laugh.

'But you promised mamma, you know,' said the girl, with the confidence of her affection.

Jackson looked at her with an eye which expressed none even of his very moderate hilarity. 'Your mother, then, must bring her back.'

'Get some of your navy people to supply an ironclad!' cried Mr Longstraw.

'It would be very pleasant if the Marchioness could come over,' said Mrs Lemon.

'Oh, she would hate it more than poor Barb,' Lady Agatha quickly replied. It did not suit her mood at all to see a marchioness inserted into the field of her vision.

'Doesn't she feel interested, from what you have told her?' Herman Longstraw asked of Lady Agatha. But Jackson Lemon did not heed his sister-in-law's answer; he was thinking of something else. He said nothing more, however, about the subject of his thought, and before ten minutes were over he took his departure, having, meanwhile, neglected also to revert to the question of Lady Agatha's bringing her visit to his mother to a close. It was not to speak to him of this (for, as we know, she wished to keep the girl, and somehow could not bring herself to be afraid of Herman Longstraw) that when Jackson took leave she went with him to the door of the house, detaining him a little, while she stood on the steps, as people had always done in New York in her time, though it was another of the new fashions she did not like, not to come out of the parlour. She placed her hand on his arm to keep him on the 'stoop', and looked up and down into the brilliant afternoon and the beautiful city – its chocolate-coloured houses, so extraordinarily smooth – in which it seemed to her that even the most fastidious people ought to be glad to live. It was useless to attempt to conceal it; her son's marriage had made a difference, had put up a kind of barrier. It had brought with it a problem much more difficult than his old problem of how to make his mother feel that she was still, as she had been in his childhood, the dispenser of his rewards. The old problem had been easily solved; the new one was a visible preoccupation. Mrs Lemon felt that her daughter-in-law did not take her seriously; and that was a part of the barrier. Even if Barberina liked her better than any one else, this was mostly because she liked every one else so little. Mrs Lemon had not a grain of resentment in her nature; and it was not to feed a sense of wrong that she permitted herself to criticise her son's wife. She could not help feeling that his marriage was not altogether fortunate if his wife didn't take his mother seriously. She knew she was not otherwise remarkable than as being his mother; but that position, which was no merit of hers (the merit was all Jackson's, in being her son), seemed to her one which, familiar as Lady Barb appeared to have been in England with positions of various kinds, would naturally strike the girl as a very high one, to be accepted as freely as a fine morning. If she didn't think of his mother as an indivisible part of him, perhaps she didn't think of other things either; and Mrs Lemon vaguely felt that, remarkable as Jackson was, he was made up of parts, and that it would never do that these parts should depreciate one by one, for there was no knowing what that might end in. She feared that things were rather cold for him at home when he had to explain so much to his wife – explain to her, for instance, all the sources of happiness that were to be found in New York. This struck her as a new kind of problem altogether for a husband. She had never thought of matrimony without a community of feeling in regard to religion and country; one took those great conditions for granted, just as one assumed that one's food was to be cooked; and if Jackson should have to discuss them with his wife, he might, in spite of his great abilities, be carried into regions where he would get entangled and embroiled – from which, even, possibly, he would not come back at all. Mrs Lemon had a horror of losing him in some way; and this fear was in her eyes as she stood on the steps of her house, and, after she had glanced up and down the street, looked at him a moment in silence. He simply kissed her again, and said she would take cold.

'I am not afraid of that, I have a shawl!' Mrs Lemon, who was very small and very fair, with pointed features and an elaborate cap, passed her life in a shawl, and owed to this habit her reputation for being an invalid – an idea which she scorned, naturally enough, inasmuch as it was precisely her shawl that (as she believed) kept her from being one. 'Is it true Barberina won't come back?' she asked of her son.

'I don't know that we shall ever find out; I don't know that I shall take her to England.'

'Didn't you promise, dear?'

'I don't know that I promised; not absolutely.'

'But you wouldn't keep her here against her will?' said Mrs Lemon, inconsequently.

'I guess she'll get used to it,' Jackson answered, with a lightness he did not altogether feel.

Mrs Lemon looked up and down the street again, and gave a little sigh. 'What a pity she isn't American!' She did not mean this as a reproach, a hint of what might have been; it was simply embarrassment resolved into speech.

'She couldn't have been American,' said Jackson, with decision.

'Couldn't she, dear?' Mrs Lemon spoke with a kind of respect; she felt that there were imperceptible reasons in this.

'It was just as she is that I wanted her,' Jackson added.

'Even if she won't come back?' his mother asked, with a certain wonder.

'Oh, she has got to come back!' Jackson said, going down the steps.

VI

LADY BARB, after this, did not decline to see her New York acquaintances on Sunday afternoons, though she refused for the present to enter into a project of her husband's, who thought it would be a pleasant thing that she should entertain his friends on the evening of that day. Like all good Americans,

Jackson Lemon devoted much consideration to the great question how, in his native land, society should be brought into being. It seemed to him that it would help the good cause, for which so many Americans are ready to lay down their lives, if his wife should, as he jocularly called it, open a saloon. He believed, or he tried to believe, the *salon* now possible in New York, on condition of its being reserved entirely for adults; and in having taken a wife out of a country in which social traditions were rich and ancient, he had done something towards qualifying his own house – so splendidly qualified in all strictly material respects – to be the scene of such an effort. A charming woman, accustomed only to the best in each country, as Lady Beauchemin said, what might she not achieve by being at home (to the elder generation) in an easy, early, inspiring, comprehensive way, on the evening in the week on which worldly engagements were least numerous? He laid this philosophy before Lady Barb, in pursuance of a theory that if she disliked New York on a short acquaintance, she could not fail to like it on a long one. Jackson Lemon believed in the New York mind – not so much, indeed, in its literary, artistic, or political achievements, as in its general quickness and nascent adaptability. He clung to this belief, for it was a very important piece of material in the structure that he was attempting to rear. The New York mind would throw its glamour over Lady Barb if she would only give it a chance; for it was exceedingly bright, entertaining, and sympathetic. If she would only have a *salon*, where this charming organ might expand, and where she might inhale its fragrance in the most convenient and luxurious way, without, as it were, getting up from her chair; if she would only just try this graceful, good-natured experiment (which would make every one like *her* so much, too), he was sure that all the wrinkles in the gilded scroll of his fate would be smoothed out. But Lady Barb did not rise at all to his conception, and had not the least curiosity about the New York mind. She thought it would be extremely disagreeable to have a lot of people tumbling in on Sunday evening without being invited; and altogether her husband's sketch of the Anglo-American saloon seemed to her to suggest familiarity, high-pitched talk (she had already made a remark to him about 'screeching women'), and exaggerated laughter. She did not tell him – for this, somehow, it was not in her power to express, and, strangely enough, he never completely guessed it – that she was singularly deficient in any natural, or indeed acquired, understanding of what a saloon might be. She had never seen one, and for the most part she never thought of things she had not seen. She had seen great dinners, and balls, and meets, and runs, and races; she had seen garden-parties, and a lot of people, mainly women (who, however, didn't screech), at dull, stuffy teas, and distinguished companies collected in splendid castles; but all this gave her no idea of a tradition of conversation, of a social agreement that the continuity of talk, its accumulations from season to season, should not be lost. Conversation, in Lady Barb's experience, had never been continuous; in such a case it would surely have been a bore. It had been occasional and fragmentary, a trifle jerky, with allusions that were never explained; it had a dread of detail; it seldom pursued anything very far, or kept hold of it very long.

There was something else that she did not say to her husband in reference to his visions of hospitality, which was, that if she should open a saloon (she had taken up the joke as well, for Lady Barb was eminently good-natured), Mrs Vanderdecken would straightway open another, and Mrs Vanderdecken's would be the more successful of the two. This lady, for reasons that Lady Barb had not yet explored, was supposed to be the great personage in New York; there were legends of her husband's family having behind them a fabulous antiquity. When this was alluded to, it was spoken of as something incalculable, and lost in the dimness of time. Mrs Vanderdecken was young, pretty, clever, absurdly pretentious (Lady Barb thought), and had a wonderfully artistic house. Ambition, also, was expressed in every rustle of her garments; and if she was the first person in America (this had an immense sound), it was plain that she intended to remain so. It was not till after she had been several months in New York that it came over Lady Barb that this brilliant, bristling native had flung down the glove; and when the idea presented itself, lighted up by an incident which I have no space to relate, she simply blushed a little (for Mrs Vander-decken), and held her tongue. She had not come to America to bandy words about precedence with such a woman as that. She had ceased to think about it much (of course one thought about it in England); but an instinct of self-preservation led her not to expose herself to occasions on which her claim might be tested. This, at bottom, had much to do with her having, very soon after the first flush of the honours paid her on her arrival, and which seemed to her rather grossly overdone, taken the line of scarcely going out. 'They can't keep *that* up!' she had said to herself; and, in short, she would stay at home. She had a feeling that whenever she should go forth she would meet Mrs Van-derdecken, who would withhold, or deny, or contest something – poor Lady Barb could never imagine what. She did not try to, and gave little thought to all this; for she was not prone to confess to herself fears, especially fears from which terror was absent. But, as I have said, it abode within her as a presentiment that if she should set up a drawing-room in the foreign style (it was curious, in New York, how they tried to be foreign), Mrs Vanderdecken would be beforehand with her. The continuity of conversation, oh! that idea she would certainly have; there was no one so continuous as Mrs Vanderdecken. Lady Barb, as I have related, did not give her husband the surprise of telling him of these thoughts, though she had given him some other surprises. He would have been very much astonished, and perhaps, after a bit, a little encouraged, at finding that she was liable to this particular form of irritation.

On the Sunday afternoon she was visible; and on one of these occasions, going into her drawing-room late, he found her entertaining two ladies and a gentleman. The gentleman was Sidney Feeder, and one of the ladies was Mrs Vander-decken, whose ostensible relations with Lady Barb were of the most cordial nature. If she intended to crush her (as two or three persons, not conspicuous for a narrow accuracy, gave out that she privately declared), Mrs Vanderdecken wished at least to study the weak points of the invader, to penetrate herself with the character of the English girl. Lady Barb, indeed, appeared to have a mysterious fascination for the representative of the American patriciate. Mrs Vanderdecken could not take her eyes off her victim; and whatever might be her estimate of her importance, she at least could not let her alone. 'Why does she come to see me?' poor Lady Barb asked herself. 'I am sure I don't want to see her; she has done enough for civility long ago.' Mrs Vanderdecken had her own reasons; and one of them was simply the pleasure of looking at the Doctor's wife, as she habitually called the daughter of the Cantervilles. She was not guilty of the folly of depreciating this lady's appearance, and professed an unbounded admiration for it, defending it on many occasions against superficial people who said there were fifty women in New York that were handsomer. Whatever might have been Lady Barb's weak points, they were not the curve of her cheek and chin, the setting of her head on her throat, or the quietness of her deep eyes, which were as beautiful as if they had been blank, like those of antique busts. 'The head is enchanting – perfectly enchanting,' Mrs Vanderdecken used to say irrelevantly, as if there were only one head in the place. She always used to ask about the Doctor; and that was another reason why she came. She brought up the Doctor at every turn; asked if he were often called up at night; found it the greatest of luxuries, in a word, to address Lady Barb as the wife of a medical man, more or less *au courant* of her husband's patients. The other lady, on this Sunday afternoon, was a certain little Mrs Chew, whose clothes looked so new that she had the air of a walking advertisement issued by a great shop, and who was always asking Lady Barb about England, which Mrs Vanderdecken never did. The latter visitor conversed with Lady Barb on a purely American basis, with that continuity (on her own side) of which mention has already been made, while Mrs Chew engaged Sidney Feeder on topics equally local. Lady Barb liked Sidney Feeder; she only hated his name, which was constantly in her ears during the half-hour the ladies sat with her, Mrs Chew having the habit, which annoyed Lady Barb, of repeating perpetually the appellation of her interlocutor.

Lady Barb's relations with Mrs Vanderdecken consisted mainly in wondering, while she talked, what she wanted of her, and in looking, with her sculptured eyes, at her visitor's clothes, in which there was always much to examine. 'Oh, Doctor Feeder!' 'Now, Doctor Feeder!' 'Well, Doctor Feeder,' – these exclamations, on the lips of Mrs Chew, were an undertone in Lady Barb's consciousness. When I say that she liked her husband's *confrère*, as he used to call himself, I mean that she smiled at him when he came, and gave him her hand, and asked him if he would have some tea. There was nothing nasty (as they said in London) in Lady Barb, and she would have been incapable of inflicting a deliberate snub upon a man who had the air of standing up so squarely to any work that he might have in hand. But she had nothing to say to Sidney Feeder. He apparently had the art of making her shy, more shy than usual; for she was always a little so; she discouraged him, discouraged him completely. He was not a man who wanted drawing out, there was nothing of that in him, he was remarkably copious; but Lady Barb appeared unable to follow him, and half the time, evidently, did not know what he was saying. He tried to adapt his conversation to her needs; but when he spoke of the world, of what was going on in society, she was more at sea even than when he spoke of hospitals and labouratories, and the health of the city, and the progress of science. She appeared, indeed, after her first smile, when he came in, which was always charming, scarcely to see him, looking past him, and above him, and below him, and everywhere but at him, until he got up to go again, when she gave him another smile, as expressive of pleasure and of casual acquaintance as that with which she had greeted his entry; it seemed to imply that they had been having delightful talk for an hour. He wondered what the deuce Jackson Lemon could find interesting in such a woman, and he believed that his perverse, though gifted colleague, was not destined to feel that she illuminated his life. He pitied Jackson, he saw that Lady Barb, in New York, would neither assimilate nor be assimilated; and yet he was afraid to betray his incredulity, thinking it might be depressing to poor Lemon to show him how his marriage – now so dreadfully irrevocable – struck others. Sidney Feeder was a man of a strenuous conscience, and he did his duty overmuch by his old friend and his wife, from the simple fear that he should not do it enough. In order not to appear to neglect them, he called upon Lady Barb heroically, in spite of pressing engagements, week after week, enjoying his virtue himself as little as he made it fruitful for his hostess, who wondered at last what she had done to deserve these visitations. She spoke of them to her husband, who wondered also what poor Sidney had in his head, and yet was unable, of course, to hint to him that he need not think it necessary to come so often. Between Doctor Feeder's wish not to let Jackson see that his marriage had made a difference, and Jackson's hesitation to reveal to Sidney that his standard of friendship was too high, Lady Barb passed a good many of those numerous hours during which she asked herself if she had come to America for that. Very little had ever passed between her and her husband on the subject of Sidney Feeder; for an instinct told her that if they were ever to have scenes, she must choose the occasion well; and this odd person was not an occasion. Jackson had tacitly admitted that his friend Feeder was anything she chose to think him; he was not a man to be guilty, in a discussion, of the disloyalty of damning him with praise that was faint. If Lady Agatha had usually been with her sister, Doctor Feeder would have been better entertained; for the younger of the English visitors prided herself, after several months of New York, on understanding everything that was said, and catching every allusion, it mattered not from what lips it fell. But Lady Agatha was never at home; she had learned how to describe herself perfectly by the time she wrote to her mother that she was always 'on the go'. None of the innumerable victims of old-world tyranny who have fled to the United States as to a land of freedom, have ever offered more lavish incense to that goddess than this emancipated London *débutante*. She had enrolled herself in an amiable band which was known by the humorous name of 'the Tearers' – a dozen young ladies of agreeable appearance, high spirits and good wind, whose most general characteristic was that, when wanted, they were to be sought anywhere in the world but under the roof that was supposed to shelter them. They were never at home; and when Sidney

Feeder, as sometimes happened, met Lady Agatha at other houses, she was in the hands of the irrepressible Longstraw. She had come back to her sister, but Mr Longstraw had followed her to the door. As to passing it, he had received direct discouragement from her brother-in-law; but he could at least hang about and wait for her. It may be confided to the reader, at the risk of diminishing the effect of the only incident which in the course of this very level narrative may startle him, that he never had to wait very long.

When Jackson Lemon came in, his wife's visitors were on the point of leaving her; and he did not ask even Sidney Feeder to remain, for he had something particular to say to Lady Barb.

'I haven't asked you half what I wanted – I have been talking so much to Doctor Feeder,' the dressy Mrs Chew said, holding the hand of her hostess in one of her own, and toying with one of Lady Barb's ribbons with the other.

'I don't think I have anything to tell you; I think I have told people everything,' Lady Barb answered, rather wearily.

'You haven't told *me* much!' Mrs Vanderdecken said, smiling brightly.

'What could one tell you? – you know everything,' Jackson Lemon interposed.

'Ah, no; there are some things that are great mysteries for me,' the lady returned. 'I hope you are coming to me on the 17th,' she added, to Lady Barb.

'On the 17th? I think we are going somewhere.'

'Do go to Mrs Vanderdecken's,' said Mrs Chew; 'you will see the cream of the cream.'

'Oh, gracious!' Mrs Vanderdecken exclaimed.

'Well, I don't care; she will, won't she, Doctor Feeder? – the very pick of American society.' Mrs Chew stuck to her point.

'Well, I have no doubt Lady Barb will have a good time,' said Sidney Feeder. 'I'm afraid you miss the bran,' he went on, with irrelevant jocosity, to Lady Barb. He always tried the jocose when other elements had failed.

'The bran?' asked Lady Barb, staring.

'Where you used to ride, in the Park.'

'My dear fellow, you speak as if it were the circus,' Jackson Lemon said, smiling; 'I haven't married a mountebank!'

'Well, they put some stuff on the road,' Sidney Feeder explained, not holding much to his joke.

'You must miss a great many things,' said Mrs Chew, tenderly.

'I don't see what,' Mrs Vanderdecken remarked, 'except the fogs and the Queen. New York is getting more and more like London. It's a pity; you ought to have known us thirty years ago.'

'You are the queen, here,' said Jackson Lemon; 'but I don't know what you know about thirty years ago.'

'Do you think she doesn't go back? – she goes back to the last century!' cried Mrs Chew.

'I daresay I should have liked that,' said Lady Barb; 'but I can't imagine.' And she looked at her husband – a look she often had – as if she vaguely wished him to do something.

He was not called upon, however, to take any violent steps, for Mrs Chew presently said: 'Well, Lady Barberina, good-bye'; and Mrs Vanderdecken smiled in silence at her hostess, and addressed a farewell, accompanied very audibly with his title, to her host; and Sidney Feeder made a joke about stepping on the trains of the ladies' dresses as he accompanied them to the door. Mrs Chew had always a great deal to say at the last; she talked till she was in the street, and then she did not cease. But at the end of five minutes Jackson Lemon was alone with his wife; and then he told her a piece of news. He prefaced it, however, by an inquiry as he came back from the hall.

'Where is Agatha, my dear?'

'I haven't the least idea. In the streets somewhere, I suppose.'

'I think you ought to know a little more.'

'How can I know about things here? I have given her up; I can do nothing with her. I don't care what she does.'

'She ought to go back to England,' Jackson Lemon said, after a pause.

'She ought never to have come.'

'It was not my proposal, God knows!' Jackson answered, rather sharply.

'Mamma could never know what it really is,' said his wife.

'No, it has not been as yet what your mother supposed! Herman Longstraw wants to marry her. He has made me a formal proposal. I met him half an hour ago in Madison Avenue, and he asked me to come with him into the Columbia Club. There, in the billiard-room, which to-day is empty, he opened himself – thinking evidently that in laying the matter before me he was behaving with extraordinary propriety. He tells me he is dying of love, and that she is perfectly willing to go and live in Arizona.'

'So she is,' said Lady Barb. 'And what did you tell him?'

'I told him that I was sure it would never do, and that at any rate I could have nothing to say to it. I told him explicitly, in short, what I had told him virtually before. I said that we should send Agatha straight back to England, and that if they have the courage they must themselves broach the question over there.'

'When shall you send her back?' asked Lady Barb.

'Immediately; by the very first steamer.'

'Alone, like an American girl?'

'Don't be rough, Barb,' said Jackson Lemon. 'I shall easily find some people; lots of people are sailing now.'

'I must take her myself,' Lady Barb declared in a moment. 'I brought her out, and I must restore her to my mother's hands.'

Jackson Lemon had expected this, and he believed he was prepared for it. But when it came he found his preparation was not complete; for he had no answer to make – none, at least, that seemed to him to go to the point. During these last weeks it had come over him, with a quiet, irresistible, unmerciful force, that Mrs Dexter Freer had been right when she said to him, that Sunday afternoon in Jermyn Street, the summer before, that he would find it was not so simple to be an American. Such an identity was complicated, in just the measure that she had foretold, by the difficulty of domesticating one's wife. The difficulty was not dissipated by his having taken a high tone about it; it pinched him from morning till night, like a misfitting shoe. His high tone had given him courage when he took the great step; but he began to perceive that the highest tone in the world cannot change the nature of things. His ears tingled when he reflected that if the Dexter Freers, whom he had thought alike ignoble in their hopes and their fears, had been by ill-luck spending the winter in New York, they would have found his predicament as entertaining as they could desire. Drop by drop the conviction had entered his mind – the first drop had come in the form of a word from Lady Agatha – that if his wife should return to England she would never again cross the Atlantic to the West. That word from Lady Agatha had been the touch from the outside, at which, often, one's fears crystallise. What she would do, how she would resist – this he was not yet prepared to tell himself; but he felt, every time he looked at her, that this beautiful woman whom he had adored was filled with a dumb, insuperable, ineradicable purpose. He knew that if she should plant herself, no power on earth would move her; and her blooming, antique beauty, and the general loftiness of her breeding, came to seem to him – rapidly – but the magnificent expression of a dense, patient, imperturbable obstinacy. She was not light, she was not supple, and after six months of marriage he had made up his mind that she was not clever; but nevertheless she would elude him. She had married him, she had come into his fortune and his consideration – for who was she, after all? Jackson Lemon was once so angry as to ask himself, reminding himself that in England Lady Claras and Lady Florences were as thick as blackberries – but she would have nothing to do, if she could help it, with his country. She had gone in to dinner first in every house in the place, but this had not satisfied her. It *had* been simple to be an American, in this sense that no one else in New York had made any difficulties; the difficulties had sprung from her peculiar feelings, which were after all what he had married her for, thinking they would be a fine temperamental heritage for his brood. So they would, doubtless, in the coming years, after the brood should have appeared; but meanwhile they interfered with the best heritage of all – the nationality of his possible children. Lady Barb would do nothing violent; he was tolerably certain of that. She would not return to England without his consent; only, when she should return, it would be once for all. His only possible line, then, was not to take her back – a position replete with difficulties, because, of course, he had, in a manner, given his word, while she had given no word at all, beyond the general promise she murmured at the altar. She had been general, but he had been specific; the settlements he had made were a part of that. His difficulties were such as he could not directly face. He must tack in approaching so uncertain a coast. He said to Lady Barb presently that it would be very inconvenient for him to leave New York at that moment: she must remember that their plans had been laid for a later departure. He could not think of letting her make the voyage without him, and, on the other hand, they must pack her sister off without delay. He would therefore make instant inquiry for a chaperone, and he relieved his irritation by expressing considerable disgust at Herman Longstraw.

Lady Barb did not trouble herself to denounce this gentleman; her manner was that of having for a long time expected the worst. She simply remarked drily, after having listened to her husband for some minutes in silence: 'I would as lief she should marry Doctor Feeder!'

The day after this, Jackson Lemon closeted himself for an hour with Lady Agatha, taking great pains to set forth to her the reasons why she should not unite herself with her Californian. Jackson was kind, he was affectionate; he kissed her and put his arm round her waist, he reminded her that he and she were the best of friends, and that she had always been awfully nice to him; therefore he counted upon her. She would break her mother's heart, she would deserve her father's curse, and she would get him, Jackson, into a pickle from which no human power could ever disembroil him. Lady Agatha listened and cried, and returned his kiss very affectionately, and admitted that her father and mother would never consent to such a marriage; and when he told her that he had made arrangements for her to sail for Liverpool (with some charming people) the next day but one, she embraced him again and assured him that she could never thank him enough for all the trouble he had taken about her. He flattered himself that he had convinced, and in some degree comforted her, and reflected with complacency that even should his wife take it into her head, Barberina would never get ready to embark for her native land between a Monday and a Wednesday. The next morning Lady Agatha did not appear at breakfast; but as she usually rose very late, her absence excited no alarm. She had not rung her bell, and she was supposed still to be sleeping. But she had never yet slept later than midday; and as this hour approached her sister went to her room. Lady Barb then discovered that she had left the house at seven o'clock in the morning, and had gone to meet Herman Longstraw at a neighbouring corner. A little note on the table explained it very succinctly, and put beyond the power of Jackson Lemon and his wife to doubt that by the time this news reached them their wayward sister had been united to the man of her preference as closely as the laws of the State of New York could bind her. Her little note set forth that as she knew she should never be permitted to marry him, she had determined to marry him without permission, and that directly after the ceremony, which would be of the simplest kind, they were to take a train for the far West. Our history is concerned only with the remote consequences of this incident, which made, of course, a great deal of trouble for Jackson Lemon. He went to the far West in pursuit of the fugitives, and overtook them in California; but he had not the audacity to propose to them to separate, as it was easy for him to see that Herman Longstraw was at least as well married as himself. Lady Agatha was already popular in the new States, where the history of her elopement, emblazoned in enormous capitals, was circulated in a thousand newspapers. This question of the newspapers had been for Jackson Lemon one of the most definite results of his sister-in-law's *coup de tête*. His first thought had been of the public prints, and his first exclamation a prayer that they should not get hold of the story. But they did get hold of it, and they treated the affair with their customary energy and eloquence. Lady Barb never saw them; but an affectionate friend of the family, travelling at that time in the United States, made a parcel of some of the leading journals, and sent them to Lord Canterville. This missive elicited from her ladyship a letter addressed to Jackson Lemon which shook the young man's position to the base. The phials of an unnameable vulgarity had been opened upon the house of Canterville, and his mother-in-law demanded that in compensation for the affronts and injuries that were being heaped upon her family, and bereaved and dishonoured as she was, she should at least be allowed to look on the face of her other daughter. 'I suppose you will not, for very pity, be deaf to such a prayer as that,' said Lady Barb; and though shrinking from recording a second act of weakness on the part of a man who had such pretensions to be strong, I must relate that poor Jackson, who blushed dreadfully over the newspapers, and felt afresh, as he read them, the force of Mrs Freer's terrible axiom – poor Jackson paid a visit to the office of the Cunarders. He said to himself afterward that it was the newspapers that had done it; he could not bear to appear to be on their side; they made it so hard to deny that the country was vulgar, at a time when one was in such need of all one's arguments. Lady Barb, before sailing, definitely refused to mention any week or month as the date of their pre-arranged return to New York. Very many weeks and months have elapsed since then, and she gives no sign of coming back. She will never fix a date. She is much missed by Mrs Vanderdecken, who still alludes to her – still says the line of the shoulders was superb; putting the statement, pensively, in the past tense. Lady Beauchemin and Lady Marmaduke are much disconcerted; the international project has not, in their view, received an impetus.

Jackson Lemon has a house in London, and he rides in the park with his wife, who is as beautiful as the day, and a year ago presented him with a little girl, with features that Jackson already scans for the look of race – whether in hope or fear, to-day, is more than my muse has revealed. He has occasional scenes with Lady Barb, during which the look of race is very visible in her own countenance; but they never terminate in a visit to the Cunarders. He is exceedingly restless, and is constantly crossing to the Continent; but he returns with a certain abruptness, for he cannot bear to meet the Dexter Freers, and they seem to pervade the more comfortable parts of Europe. He dodges them in every town. Sidney Feeder feels very badly about him; it is months since Jackson has sent him any 'results'. The excellent fellow goes very often, in a consolatory spirit, to see Mrs Lemon; but he has not yet been able to answer her standing question: 'Why that girl more than another?' Lady Agatha Longstraw and her husband arrived a year ago in England, and Mr Longstraw's personality had immense success during the last London season. It is not exactly known what they live on, though it is perfectly known that he is looking for something to do. Meanwhile it is as good as known that Jackson Lemon supports them.

THE AUTHOR OF 'BELTRAFFIO'

I

MUCH as I wished to see him, I had kept my letter of introduction for three weeks in my pocket-book. I was nervous and timid about meeting him – conscious of youth and ignorance, convinced that he was tormented by strangers, and especially by my country-people, and not exempt from the suspicion that he had the irritability as well as the brilliancy of genius. Moreover, the pleasure, if it should occur (for I could scarcely believe it was really at hand), would be so great that I wished to think of it in advance, to feel that it was in my pocket, not to mix it with satisfactions more superficial and usual. In the little game of new sensations that I was playing with my ingenuous mind, I wished to keep my visit to the author of *Beltraffio* as a trump-card. It was three years after the publication of that fascinating work, which I had read over five times, and which now, with my riper judgement, I admire on the whole as much as ever. This will give you about the date of my first visit (of any duration) to England; for you will not have forgotten the commotion – I may even say the scandal – produced by Mark Ambient's master-piece. It was the most complete presentation that had yet been made of the gospel of art; it was a kind of aesthetic war-cry. People had endeavoured to sail nearer to 'truth' in the cut of their sleeves and the shape of their sideboards; but there had not as yet been, among English novels, such an example of beauty of execution and value of subject. Nothing had been done in that line from the point of view of art for art. This was my own point of view, I may mention, when I was twenty-five; whether it is altered now I won't take upon myself to say – especially as the discerning reader will be able to judge for himself. I had been in England a twelvemonth before the time to which I began by alluding, and had learned then that Mr Ambient was in distant lands – was making a considerable tour in the East. So there was nothing to do but to keep my letter till I should be in London again. It was of little use to me to hear that his wife had not left England and, with her little boy, their only child, was spending the period of her husband's absence – a good many months – at a small place they had down in Surrey. They had a house in London which was let. All this I learned, and also that Mrs Ambient was charming (my friend, the American poet, from whom I had my introduction, had never seen her, his relations with the great man being only epistolary); but she was not, after all, though she had lived so near the rose, the author of *Beltraffio*, and I did not go down into Surrey to call on her. I went to the Continent, spent the following winter in Italy, and returned to London in May. My visit to Italy opened my eyes to a good many things, but to nothing more than the beauty of certain pages in the works of Mark Ambient. I had every one of his productions in my portmanteau – they are not, as you know, very numerous, but he had preluded to *Beltraffio* by some exquisite things – and I used to read them over in the evening at the inn. I used to say to myself that the man who drew those characters and wrote that style understood what he saw and knew what he was doing. This is my only reason for mentioning my winter in Italy. He had been there much in former years, and he was saturated with what painters call the 'feeling' of that classic land. He expressed the charm of the old hill-cities of Tuscany, the look of certain lonely grass-grown places which, in the past, had echoed with life; he understood the great artists, he understood the spirit of the Renaissance, he understood everything. The scene of one of his earlier novels was laid in Rome, the scene of another in Florence, and I moved through these cities in company with the figures whom Mark Ambient had set so firmly upon their feet. This is why I was now so much happier even than before in the prospect of making his acquaintance.

At last, when I had dallied with this privilege long enough, I despatched to him the missive of the American poet. He had already gone out of town; he shrank from the rigour of the London season, and it was his habit to migrate on the first of June. Moreover, I had heard that this year he was hard at work on a new book, into which some of his impressions of the East were to be wrought, so that he desired nothing so much as quiet days. This knowledge, however, did not prevent me – *cet âge est sans pitié* – from sending with my friend's letter a note of my own, in which I asked Mr Ambient's leave to come down and see him for an hour or two, on a day to be designated by himself. My proposal was accompanied with a very frank expression of my sentiments, and the effect of the whole projectile was to elicit from the great man the kindest possible invitation. He would be delighted to see me, especially if I should turn up on the following Saturday and could remain till the Monday morning. We would take a walk over the Surrey commons, and I should tell him all about the other great man, the one in America. He indicated to me the best train, and it may be imagined whether on the Saturday afternoon I was punctual at Waterloo. He carried his benevolence to the point of coming to meet me at the little station at which I was to alight, and my heart beat very fast as I saw his handsome face, surmounted with a soft wide-awake, and which I knew by a photograph long since enshrined upon my mantel-shelf, scanning the carriage-windows as the train rolled up. He recognised me as infallibly as I had recognised him; he appeared to know by instinct how a young American of an aesthetic turn would look when much divided between eagerness and modesty. He took me by the hand, and smiled at me, and said, 'You must be – a – *you*, I think!' and asked if I should mind going on foot to his house, which would take but a few minutes. I remember thinking it a piece of extraordinary affability that he should give directions about the conveyance of my bag, and feeling altogether very happy and rosy, in fact quite transported, when he laid his hand on my shoulder as we came out of the station. I surveyed him, askance, as we walked together; I had already – I had indeed instantly – seen that he was a delightful creature. His face is so well known that I needn't describe it; he looked to me at once an English gentleman and a man of genius, and I thought that a happy combination. There was just a little of the Bohemian in his appearance; you would easily have guessed that he belonged to the guild of artists and men of letters. He was addicted to velvet jackets, to cigarettes, to loose shirt-collars, to looking a little dishevelled. His features, which

were fine but not perfectly regular, are fairly enough represented in his portraits; but no portrait that I have seen gives
any idea of his expression. There were so many things in it, and
they chased each other in and out of his face. I have seen people
who were grave and gay in quick alternation; but Mark Ambient was grave and gay at one and the same moment. There were
other strange oppositions and contradictions in his slightly
faded and fatigued countenance. He seemed both young and
old, both anxious and indifferent. He had evidently had an
active past, which inspired one with curiosity, and yet it was
impossible not to be more curious still about his future. He was
just enough above middle height to be spoken of as tall, and
rather lean and long in the flank. He had the friendliest, frankest manner possible, and yet I could see that he was shy. He was
thirty-eight years old at the time *Beltraffio* was published. He
asked me about his friend in America, about the length of my
stay in England, about the last news in London and the people
I had seen there; and I remember looking for the signs of genius
in the very form of his questions – and thinking I found it. I liked
his voice. There was genius in his house, too, I thought, when
we got there; there was imagination in the carpets and curtains,
in the pictures and books, in the garden behind it, where certain
old brown walls were muffled in creepers that appeared to me
to have been copied from a masterpiece of one of the pre-
Raphaelites. That was the way many things struck me at that
time, in England; as if they were reproductions of something
that existed primarily in art or literature. It was not the picture,
the poem, the fictive page, that seemed to me a copy; these
things were the originals, and the life of happy and distinguished people was fashioned in their image. Mark Ambient
called his house a cottage, and I perceived afterwards that he
was right; for if it had not been a cottage it must have been a
villa, and a villa, in England at least, was not a place in which
one could fancy him at home. But it was, to my vision, a cottage
glorified and translated; it was a palace of art, on a slightly
reduced scale – it was an old English demesne. It nestled
under a cluster of magnificent beeches, it had little creaking
lattices that opened out of, or into, pendent mats of ivy, and

gables, and old red tiles, as well as a general aspect of being painted in water-colours and inhabited by people whose lives would go on in chapters and volumes. The lawn seemed to me of extraordinary extent, the garden-walls of incalculable height, the whole air of the place delightfully still, and private, and proper to itself. 'My wife must be somewhere about,' Mark Ambient said, as we went in. 'We shall find her perhaps; we have got about an hour before dinner. She may be in the garden. I will show you my little place.'

We passed through the house, and into the grounds, as I should have called them, which extended into the rear. They covered but three or four acres, but, like the house, they were very old and crooked, and full of traces of long habitation, with inequalities of level and little steps – mossy and cracked were these – which connected the different parts with each other. The limits of the place, cleverly dissimulated, were muffled in the deepest verdure. They made, as I remember, a kind of curtain at the farther end, in one of the folds of which, as it were, we presently perceived, from afar, a little group. 'Ah, there she is!' said Mark Ambient; 'and she has got the boy.' He made this last remark in a tone slightly different from any in which he yet had spoken. I was not fully aware of it at the time, but it lingered in my ear and I afterwards understood it.

'Is it your son?' I inquired, feeling the question not to be brilliant.

'Yes, my only child. He is always in his mother's pocket. She coddles him too much.' It came back to me afterwards, too – the manner in which he spoke these words. They were not petulant; they expressed rather a sudden coldness, a kind of mechanical submission. We went a few steps further, and then he stopped short, and called the boy, beckoning to him repeatedly.

'Dolcino, come and see your daddy!' There was something in the way he stood still and waited that made me think he did it for a purpose. Mrs Ambient had her arm round the child's waist, and he was leaning against her knee; but though he looked up at the sound of his father's voice, she gave no sign of releasing him. A lady, apparently a neighbour, was seated near her, and before them was a garden-table, on which a tea-service had been placed.

Mark Ambient called again, and Dolcino struggled in the maternal embrace, but he was too tightly held, and after two or three fruitless efforts he suddenly turned round and buried his head deep in his mother's lap. There was a certain awkwardness in the scene; I thought it rather odd that Mrs Ambient should pay so little attention to her husband. But I would not for the world have betrayed my thought, and, to conceal it, I observed that it must be such a pleasant thing to have tea in the garden. 'Ah, she won't let him come!' said Mark Ambient, with a sigh; and we went our way till we reached the two ladies. He mentioned my name to his wife, and I noticed that he addressed her as 'My dear', very genially, without any trace of resentment at her detention of the child. The quickness of the transition made me vaguely ask myself whether he were hen-pecked – a shocking conjecture, which I instantly dismissed. Mrs Ambient was quite such a wife as I should have expected him to have; slim and fair, with a long neck and pretty eyes and an air of great refinement. She was a little cold, and a little shy; but she was very sweet, and she had a certain look of race, justified by my afterwards learning that she was 'connected' with two or three great families. I have seen poets married to women of whom it was difficult to conceive that they should gratify the poetic fancy – women with dull faces and glutinous minds, who were none the less, however, excellent wives. But there was no obvious incongruity in Mark Ambient's union. Mrs Ambient, delicate and quiet, in a white dress, with her beautiful child at her side, was worthy of the author of a work so distinguished as *Beltraffio*. Round her neck she wore a black velvet ribbon, of which the long ends, tied behind, hung down her back, and to which, in front, was attached a miniature portrait of her little boy. Her smooth, shining hair was confined in a net. She gave me a very pleasant greeting, and Dolcino – I thought this little name of endearment delightful – took advantage of her getting up to slip away from her and go to his father, who said nothing to him, but simply seized him and held him high in his arms for a moment, kissing him several times. I had lost no time in observing that the child, who was not more than seven years old, was extraordinarily beautiful. He had the face of an angel – the eyes, the hair, the more than mortal bloom, the smile of innocence. There was something touching, almost alarming, in his beauty, which seemed to be composed of elements too fine and pure for the breath of this world. When I spoke to him, and he came and held out his hand and smiled at me, I felt a sudden pity for him, as if he had been an orphan, or a changeling, or stamped with some social stigma. It was imposs- ible to be, in fact, more exempt from these misfortunes, and yet, as one kissed him, it was hard to keep from murmuring 'Poor little devil!' though why one should have applied this epithet to a living cherub is more than I can say. Afterwards, indeed, I knew a little better; I simply discovered that he was too charming to live, wondering at the same time that his parents should not have perceived it, and should not be in proportionate grief and despair. For myself, I had no doubt of his evanescence, having already noticed that there is a kind of charm which is like a death-warrant. The lady who had been sitting with Mrs Ambient was a jolly, ruddy personage, dressed in velveteen and rather limp feathers, whom I guessed to be the vicar's wife – our hostess did not introduce me – and who immediately began to talk to Ambient about chrysanthemums. This was a safe subject, and yet there was a certain surprise for me in seeing the author of *Beltraffio* even in such superficial communion with the Church of England. His writings implied so much detachment from that institution, expressed a view of life so profane, as it were, so independent, and so little likely, in general, to be thought edifying, that I should have expected to find him an object of horror to vicars and their ladies – of horror repaid on his own part by good-natured but brilliant mockery. This proves how little I knew as yet of the English people and their extraordinary talent for keeping up their forms, as well as of some of the mysteries of Mark Ambient's hearth and home. I found afterwards that he had, in his study, between smiles and cigar-smoke, some wonderful comparisons for his clerical neighbours; but meanwhile the chrysanthemums were a source of harmony, for he and the vicaress were equally fond of them, and I was surprised at the knowledge they exhibited of this interesting plant. The lady's visit, however, had presumably already been long, and she presently got up, saying she must go, and kissed Mrs Ambient. Mark started to walk with her to the gate of the grounds, holding Dolcino by the hand.

'Stay with me, my darling,' Mrs Ambient said to the boy, who was wandering away with his father.

Mark Ambient paid no attention to the summons, but Dolcino turned round and looked with eyes of shy entreaty at his mother. 'Can't I go with papa?'

'Not when I ask you to stay with me.'

'But please don't ask me, mamma,' said the child, in his little clear, new voice.

'I must ask you when I want you. Come to me, my darling.' And Mrs Ambient, who had seated herself again, held out her long, slender hands.

Her husband stopped, with his back turned to her, but without releasing the child. He was still talking to the vicaress, but this good lady, I think, had lost the thread of her attention. She looked at Mrs Ambient and at Dolcino, and then she looked at me, smiling very hard, in an extremely fixed, cheerful manner.

'Papa,' said the child, 'mamma wants me not to go with you.'

'He's very tired – he has run about all day. He ought to be quiet till he goes to bed. Otherwise he won't sleep.' These declarations fell successively and gravely from Mrs Ambient's lips.

Her husband, still without turning round, bent over the boy and looked at him in silence. The vicaress gave a genial, irrelevant laugh, and observed that he was a precious little pet. 'Let him choose,' said Mark Ambient. 'My dear little boy, will you go with me or will you stay with your mother?'

'Oh, it's a shame!' cried the vicar's lady, with increased hilarity.

'Papa, I don't think I can choose,' the child answered, making his voice very low and confidential. 'But I have been a great deal with mamma to-day,' he added in a moment.

'And very little with papa! My dear fellow, I think you have chosen!' And Mark Ambient walked off with his son, accompanied by re-echoing but inarticulate comments from my fellow-visitor.

His wife had seated herself again, and her fixed eyes, bent upon the ground, expressed for a few moments so much mute agitation that I felt as if almost any remark from my own lips would be a false note. But Mrs Ambient quickly recovered herself, and said to me civilly enough that she hoped I didn't mind having had to walk from the station. I reassured her on this point, and she went on, 'We have got a thing that might have gone for you, but my husband wouldn't order it.'

'That gave me the pleasure of a walk with him,' I rejoined.

She was silent a minute, and then she said, 'I believe the Americans walk very little.'

'Yes, we always run,' I answered, laughingly.

She looked at me seriously, and I began to perceive a certain coldness in her pretty eyes. 'I suppose your distances are so great.'

'Yes; but we break our marches! I can't tell you what a pleasure it is for me to find myself here,' I added. 'I have the greatest admiration for Mr Ambient.'

'He will like that. He likes being admired.'

'He must have a very happy life, then. He has many worshippers.'

'Oh yes, I have seen some of them,' said Mrs Ambient, looking away, very far from me, rather as if such a vision were before her at the moment. Something in her tone seemed to indicate that the vision was scarcely edifying, and I guessed very quickly that she was not in sympathy with the author of *Beltraffio*. I thought the fact strange, but, somehow, in the glow of my own enthusiasm, I didn't think it important; it only made me wish to be rather explicit about that enthusiasm.

'For me, you know,' I remarked, 'he is quite the greatest of living writers.'

'Of course I can't judge. Of course he's very clever,' said Mrs Ambient, smiling a little.

'He's magnificent, Mrs Ambient! There are pages in each of his books that have a perfection that classes them with the greatest things. Therefore, for me to see him in this familiar way – in his habit as he lives – and to find, apparently, the man as delightful as the artist, I can't tell you how much too good to be true it seems, and how great a privilege I think it.' I knew that I was gushing, but I couldn't help it, and what I said was a good deal less than what I felt. I was by no means sure that I should dare to say even so much as this to Ambient himself, and there was a kind of rapture in speaking it out to his wife, which was not affected by the fact that, as a wife, she appeared peculiar. She listened to me with her face grave again, and with her lips a little compressed, as if there were no doubt, of course, that her husband was remarkable, but at the same time she had heard all this before and couldn't be expected to be particularly interested in it. There was even in her manner an intimation that I was rather young, and that people usually got over that sort of thing. 'I assure you that for me this is a red-letter day,' I added.

She made no response, until after a pause, looking round her, she said abruptly, though gently, 'We are very much afraid about the fruit this year.'

My eyes wandered to the mossy, mottled, garden-walls, where plum-trees and pear-trees, flattered and fastened upon the rusty bricks, looked like crucified figures with many arms. 'Doesn't it promise well?' I inquired.

'No, the trees look very dull. We had such late frosts.'

Then there was another pause. Mrs Ambient kept her eyes fixed on the opposite end of the grounds, as if she were watching for her husband's return with the child. 'Is Mr Ambient fond of gardening?' it occurred to me to inquire, irresistibly impelled as I felt myself, moreover, to bring the conversation constantly back to him.

'He is very fond of plums,' said his wife.

'Ah, well then, I hope your crop will be better than you fear. It's a lovely old place,' I continued. 'The whole character of it is that of certain places that he describes. Your house is like one of his pictures.'

'It's a pleasant little place. There are hundreds like it.'

'Oh, it has got his tone,' I said laughing, and insisting on my point the more that Mrs Ambient appeared to see in my appreciation of her simple establishment a sign of limited experience.

It was evident that I insisted too much. 'His tone?' she repeated, with a quick look at me and as lightly heightened colour.

'Surely he has a tone, Mrs Ambient.'

'Oh yes, he has indeed! But I don't in the least consider that I am living in one of his books; I shouldn't care for that, at all,' she went on, with a smile which had in some degree the effect of converting my slightly sharp protest into a joke deficient in point. 'I am afraid I am not very literary,' said Mrs Ambient. 'And I am not artistic.'

'I am very sure you are not stupid nor *bornée*,' I ventured to reply, with the accompaniment of feeling immediately afterwards that I had been both familiar and patronising. My only consolation was in the reflection that it was she, and not I, who had begun it. She had brought her idiosyncrasies into the discussion.

'Well, whatever I am, I am very different from my husband. If you like him, you won't like me. You needn't say anything. Your liking me isn't in the least necessary.'

'Don't defy me!' I exclaimed.

She looked as if she had not heard me, which was the best thing she could do; and we sat some time without further speech. Mrs Ambient had evidently the enviable English quality of being able to be silent without being restless. But at last she spoke; she asked me if there seemed to be many people in town. I gave her what satisfaction I could on this point, and we talked a little about London and of some pictures it presented at that time of the year. At the end of this I came back, irrepressibly, to Mark Ambient.

'Doesn't he like to be there now? I suppose he doesn't find the proper quiet for his work. I should think his things had been written, for the most part, in a very still place. They suggest a great stillness, following on a kind of tumult – don't you think so? I suppose London is a tremendous place to collect impressions, but a refuge like this, in the country, must be much better for working them up. Does he get many of his impressions in London, do you think?' I proceeded from point to point, in this malign inquiry, simply because my hostess, who probably thought me a very pushing and talkative young man, gave me time; for when I paused – I have not represented my pauses – she simply continued to let her eyes wander, and, with her long fair fingers, played with the medallion on her neck. When I stopped altogether, however, she was obliged to say something, and what she said was that she had not the least idea where her husband got his impressions. This made me think her, for a moment, positively disagreeable; delicate and proper and rather aristocratically dry as she sat there. But I must either have lost the impression a moment later, or been goaded by it to further aggression, for I remember asking her whether Mr Ambient was in a good vein of work, and when we might look for the appearance of the book on which he was engaged. I have every reason now to know that she thought me an odious person.

She gave a strange, small laugh as she said, 'I'm afraid you think I know a great deal more about my husband's work than I do. I haven't the least idea what he is doing,' she added presently, in a slightly different, that is, a more explanatory, tone; as if she recognised in some degree the enormity of her confession. 'I don't read what he writes!'

She did not succeed (and would not, even had she tried much harder) in making it seem to me anything less than monstrous. I stared at her, and I think I blushed. 'Don't you admire his genius? Don't you admire *Beltraffio*?'

She hesitated a moment, and I wondered what she could possibly say. She did not speak – I could see – the first words that rose to her lips; she repeated what she had said a few minutes before. 'Oh, of course he's very clever!' And with this she got up; her husband and little boy had reappeared. Mrs Ambient left me and went to meet them; she stopped and had a few words with her husband, which I did not hear, and which ended in her taking the child by the hand and returning to the house with him. Her husband joined me in a moment, looking, I thought, the least bit conscious and constrained, and said that if I would come in with him he would show me my room. In looking back upon these first moments of my visit to him, I find it important to avoid the error of appearing to have understood his situation from the first, and to have seen in him the signs of things which I learnt only afterwards. This later knowledge throws a backward light, and makes me forget that at least on the occasion of which I am speaking now (I mean that first afternoon), Mark Ambient struck me as a fortunate man. Allowing for this, I think he was rather silent and irresponsive as we walked back to the house – though I remember well the answer he made to a remark of mine in relation to his child.

'That's an extraordinary little boy of yours,' I said. 'I have never seen such a child.'

'Why do you call him extraordinary?'

'He's so beautiful – so fascinating. He's like a little work of art.'

He turned quickly, grasping my arm an instant. 'Oh, don't call him that, or you'll – you'll—!' And in his hesitation he broke off, suddenly, laughing at my surprise. But immediately afterwards he added, 'You will make his little future very difficult.'

I declared that I wouldn't for the world take any liberties with his little future – it seemed to me to hang by threads of such delicacy. I should only be highly interested in watching it. 'You Americans are very sharp,' said Ambient. 'You notice more things than we do.'

'Ah, if you want visitors who are not struck with you, you shouldn't ask me down here!'

He showed me my room, a little bower of chintz, with open windows where the light was green, and before he left me he said irrelevantly, 'As for my little boy, you know, we shall probably kill him between us, before we have done with him!' And he made this assertion as if he really believed it, without any appearance of jest, with his fine, near-sighted, expressive eyes looking straight into mine.

'Do you mean by spoiling him?'

'No – by fighting for him!'

'You had better give him to me to keep for you,' I said. 'Let me remove the apple of discord.'

I laughed, of course, but he had the air of being perfectly serious. 'It would be quite the best thing we could do. I should be quite ready to do it.'

'I am greatly obliged to you for your confidence.'

Mark Ambient lingered there, with his hands in his pockets. I felt, within a few moments, as if I had, morally speaking, taken several steps nearer to him. He looked weary, just as he faced me then, looked preoccupied, and as if there were something one might do for him. I was terribly conscious of the limits of my own ability, but I wondered what such a service might be – feeling at bottom, however, that the only thing I could do for him was to like him. I suppose he guessed this, and was grateful for what was in my mind; for he went on presently, 'I haven't the advantage of being an American. But I also notice a little, and I have an idea that – a—' here he smiled and laid his hand on my shoulder, 'that even apart from your nationality, you are not destitute of intelligence! I have only known you half an hour, but – a—' And here he hesitated again. 'You are very young, after all.'

'But you may treat me as if I could understand you!' I said; and before he left me to dress for dinner he had virtually given me a promise that he would.

When I went down into the drawing-room – I was very punctual – I found that neither my hostess nor my host had appeared. A lady rose from a sofa, however, and inclined her head as I rather surprisedly gazed at her. 'I daresay you don't know me,' she said, with a modern laugh. 'I am Mark Ambient's sister.' Whereupon I shook hands with her – saluting her very low. Her laugh was modern – by which I mean that it consisted of the vocal agitation which, between people who meet in drawing-rooms, serves as the solvent of social mysteries, the medium of transitions; but her appearance was – what shall I call it? – mediaeval. She was pale and angular, with a long, thin face, inhabited by sad, dark eyes, and black hair intertwined with golden fillets and curious chains. She wore a faded velvet robe, which clung to her when she moved,

fashioned, as to the neck and sleeves, like the garments of old
Venetians and Florentines. She looked pictorial and melancholy, and was so perfect an image of a type which I – in my
ignorance – supposed to be extinct, that while she rose before
me I was almost as much startled as if I had seen a ghost.
I afterwards perceived that Miss Ambient was not incapable
of deriving pleasure from the effect she produced, and I think
this sentiment had something to do with her sinking again into
her seat, with her long, lean, but not ungraceful arms locked
together in an archaic manner on her knees, and her mournful
eyes addressing themselves to me with an intentness which was
an earnest of what they were destined subsequently to inflict
upon me. She was a singular, self-conscious, artificial creature,
and I never, subsequently, more than half penetrated her
motives and mysteries. Of one thing I am sure, however: that
they were considerably less extraordinary than her appearance
announced. Miss Ambient was a restless, yearning spinster,
consumed with the love of Michael-Angelesque attitudes and
mystical robes; but I am pretty sure she had not in her nature
those depths of unutterable thought which, when you first
knew her, seemed to look out from her eyes and to prompt
her complicated gestures. Those features, in especial, had a
misleading eloquence; they rested upon you with a far-off
dimness, an air of obstructed sympathy, which was certainly
not always a key to the spirit of their owner; and I suspect that a
young lady could not really have been so dejected and disillusioned as Miss Ambient looked, without having committed a
crime for which she was consumed with remorse or parted with
a hope which she could not sanely have entertained. She had,
I believe, the usual allowance of vulgar impulses; she wished to
be looked at, she wished to be married, she wished to be
thought original. It costs me something to speak in this irreverent manner of Mark Ambient's sister, but I shall have still more
disagreeable things to say before I have finished my little anecdote, and moreover – I confess it – I owe the young lady a sort of
grudge. Putting aside the curious cast of her face, she had no
natural aptitude for an artistic development – she had little real
intelligence. But her affectations rubbed off on her brother's

renown, and as there were plenty of people who disapproved of him totally, they could easily point to his sister as a person formed by his influence. It was quite possible to regard her as a warning, and she had done him but little good with the world at large. He was the original, and she was the inevitable imitation. I think he was scarcely aware of the impression she produced – beyond having a general idea that she made up very well as a Rossetti; he was used to her, and he was sorry for her – wishing she would marry and observing that she didn't. Doubtless I take her too seriously, for she did me no harm – though I am bound to add that I feel I can only half account for her. She was not so mystical as she looked, but she was a strange, indirect, uncomfortable, embarrassing woman. My story will give the reader at best so very small a knot to untie that I need not hope to excite his curiosity by delaying to remark that Mrs Ambient hated her sister-in-law. This I only found out afterwards, when I found out some other things. But I mention it at once, for I shall perhaps not seem to count too much on having enlisted the imagination of the reader if I say that he will already have guessed it. Mrs Ambient was a person of conscience, and she endeavoured to behave properly to her kinswoman, who spent a month with her twice a year; but it required no great insight to discover that the two ladies were made of a very different paste, and that the usual feminine hypocrisies must have cost them, on either side, much more than the usual effort. Mrs Ambient, smooth-haired, thin-lipped, perpetually fresh, must have regarded her crumpled and dishevelled visitor as a very stale joke; she herself was not a Rossetti, but a Gainsborough or a Lawrence, and she had in her appearance no elements more romantic than a cold, ladylike candour, and a well-starched muslin dress. It was in a garment, and with an expression, of this kind, that she made her entrance, after I had exchanged a few words with Miss Ambient. Her husband presently followed her, and there being no other company we went to dinner. The impression I received from that repast is present to me still. There were elements of oddity in my companions, but they were vague and latent, and didn't interfere with my delight. It came mainly, of course, from Ambient's

talk, which was the most brilliant and interesting I had ever
heard. I know not whether he laid himself out to dazzle a rather
juvenile pilgrim from over the sea; but it matters little, for it was
very easy for him to shine. He was almost better as a talker than
as a writer; that is, if the extraordinary finish of his written prose
be really, as some people have maintained, a fault. There was
such a kindness in him, however, that I have no doubt it gave
him ideas to see me sit open-mouthed, as I suppose I did. Not
so the two ladies, who not only were very nearly dumb from
beginning to the end of the meal, but who had not the air of
being struck with such an exhibition of wit and knowledge. Mrs
Ambient, placid and detached, met neither my eye nor her
husband's; she attended to her dinner, watched the servants,
arranged the puckers in her dress, exchanged at wide intervals a
remark with her sister-in-law, and while she slowly rubbed her
white hands, between the courses, looked out of the window at
the first signs of twilight – the long June day allowing us to dine
without candles. Miss Ambient appeared to give little direct
heed to her brother's discourse; but, on the other hand, she was
much engaged in watching its effect upon me. Her lustreless
pupils continued to attach themselves to my countenance,
and it was only her air of belonging to another century that
kept them from being importunate. She seemed to look at
me across the ages, and the interval of time diminished the
realism of the performance. It was as if she knew in a general
way that her brother must be talking very well, but she herself
was so rich in ideas that she had no need to pick them up,
and was at liberty to see what would become of a young
American when subjected to a high aesthetic temperature.
The temperature was aesthetic, certainly, but it was less so
than I could have desired, for I was unsuccessful in certain little
attempts to make Mark Ambient talk about himself. I tried to
put him on the ground of his own writings, but he slipped
through my fingers every time and shifted the saddle to one of
his contemporaries. He talked about Balzac and Browning, and
what was being done in foreign countries, and about his recent
tour in the East, and the extraordinary forms of life that one saw
in that part of the world. I perceived that he had reasons for not

wishing to descant upon literature, and suffered him without
protest to deliver himself on certain social topics, which he
treated with extraordinary humour and with constant revelations of that power of ironical portraiture of which his books are
full. He had a great deal to say about London, as London
appears to the observer who doesn't fear the accusation of
cynicism, during the high-pressure time – from April to July –
of its peculiarities. He flashed his faculty of making the fanciful
real and the real fanciful over the perfunctory pleasures and
desperate exertions of so many of his compatriots, among
whom there were evidently not a few types for which he had
little love. London bored him, and he made capital sport of it;
his only allusion, that I can remember, to his own work was his
saying that he meant some day to write an immense grotesque
epic of London society. Miss Ambient's perpetual gaze seemed
to say to me, 'Do you perceive how artistic we are? frankly now,
is it possible to be more artistic than this? You surely won't deny
that we are remarkable.' I was irritated by her use of the plural
pronoun, for she had no right to pair herself with her brother;
and moreover, of course, I could not see my way to include
Mrs Ambient. But there was no doubt that (for that matter)
they were all remarkable, and, with all allowances, I had never
heard anything so artistic. Mark Ambient's conversation
seemed to play over the whole field of knowledge and taste; it
made me feel that this at last was real talk, that this was
distinction, culture, experience.

After the ladies had left us he took me into his study, to
smoke, and here I led him on to gossip freely enough about
himself. I was bent upon proving to him that I was worthy to
listen to him, upon repaying him (for what he had said to me
before dinner) by showing him how perfectly I understood. He
liked to talk, he liked to defend his ideas (not that I attacked
them), he liked a little perhaps – it was a pardonable weakness –
to astonish the youthful mind and to feel its admiration and
sympathy. I confess that my own youthful mind was considerably astonished at some of his speeches; he startled me and he
made me wince. He could not help forgetting, or rather he
couldn't know, how little personal contact I had had with the

school in which he was master; and he promoted me at a jump, as it were, to the study of its innermost mysteries. My trepidations, however, were delightful; they were just what I had hoped for, and their only fault was that they passed away too quickly, for I found that, as regards most things, I very soon seized Mark Ambient's point of view. It was the point of view of the artist to whom every manifestation of human energy was a thrilling spectacle, and who felt for ever the desire to resolve his experience of life into a literary form. On this matter of the passion for form – the attempt at perfection, the quest for which was to his mind the real search for the holy grail, he said the most interesting, the most inspiring things. He mixed with them a thousand illustrations from his own life, from other lives that he had known, from history and fiction, and, above all, from the annals of the time that was dear to him beyond all periods – the Italian *cinque-cento*. I saw that in his books he had only said half of his thought, and what he had kept back – from motives that I deplored when I learnt them later – was the richer part. It was his fortune to shock a great many people, but there was not a grain of bravado in his pages (I have always maintained it, though often contradicted), and at bottom the poor fellow, an artist to his finger-tips, and regarding a failure of completeness as a crime, had an extreme dread of scandal. There are people who regret that having gone so far he did not go further; but I regret nothing (putting aside two or three of the motives I just mentioned), for he arrived at perfection, and I don't see how you can go beyond that. The hours I spent in his study – this first one and the few that followed it; they were not, after all, so numerous – seem to glow, as I look back on them, with a tone which is partly that of the brown old room, rich, under the shaded candlelight where we sat and smoked, with the dusky, delicate bindings of valuable books; partly that of his voice, of which I still catch the echo, charged with the images that came at his command. When we went back to the drawing-room we found Miss Ambient alone in possession of it; and she informed us that her sister-in-law had a quarter of an hour before been called by the nurse to see Dolcino, who appeared to be a little feverish.

'Feverish! how in the world does he come to be feverish?' Ambient asked. 'He was perfectly well this afternoon.'

'Beatrice says you walked him about too much – you almost killed him.'

'Beatrice must be very happy – she has an opportunity to triumph!' Mark Ambient said, with a laugh of which the bitterness was just perceptible.

'Surely not if the child is ill,' I ventured to remark, by way of pleading for Mrs Ambient.

'My dear fellow, you are not married – you don't know the nature of wives!' my host exclaimed.

'Possibly not; but I know the nature of mothers.'

'Beatrice is perfect as a mother,' said Miss Ambient, with a tremendous sigh and her fingers interlaced on her embroidered knees.

'I shall go up and see the child,' her brother went on. 'Do you suppose he's asleep?'

'Beatrice won't let you see him, Mark,' said the young lady, looking at me, though she addressed our companion.

'Do you call that being perfect as a mother?' Ambient inquired.

'Yes, from her point of view.'

'Damn her point of view!' cried the author of Beltraffio. And he left the room; after which we heard him ascend the stairs.

I sat there for some ten minutes with Miss Ambient, and we, naturally, had some conversation, which was begun, I think, by my asking her what the point of view of her sister-in-law could be.

'Oh, it's so very odd,' she said. 'But we are so very odd, altogether. Don't you find us so? We have lived so much abroad. Have you people like us in America?'

'You are not all alike, surely; so that I don't think I understand your question. We have no one like your brother – I may go so far as that.'

'You have probably more persons like his wife,' said Miss Ambient, smiling.

'I can tell you that better when you have told me about her point of view.'

'Oh yes – oh yes. Well, she doesn't like his ideas. She doesn't like them for the little boy. She thinks them undesirable.'

Being quite fresh from the contemplation of some of Mark Ambient's *arcana*, I was particularly in a position to appreciate this announcement. But the effect of it was to make me (after staring a moment) burst into laughter, which I instantly checked when I remembered that there was a sick child above.

'What has that infant to do with ideas?' I asked. 'Surely, he can't tell one from another. Has he read his father's novels?'

'He's very precocious and very sensitive, and his mother thinks she can't begin to guard him too early.' Miss Ambient's head drooped a little to one side, and her eyes fixed themselves on futurity. Then, suddenly, there was a strange alteration in her face; she gave a smile that was more joyless than her gravity – a conscious, insincere smile, and added, 'When one has children, it's a great responsibility – what one writes.'

'Children are terrible critics,' I answered. 'I am rather glad I haven't got any.'

'Do you also write then? And in the same style as my brother? And do you like that style? And do people appreciate it in America? I don't write, but I think I feel.' To these and various other inquiries and remarks the young lady treated me, till we heard her brother's step in the hall again and Mark Ambient reappeared. He looked flushed and serious, and I supposed that he had seen something to alarm him in the condition of his child. His sister apparently had another idea; she gazed at him a moment as if he were a burning ship on the horizon, and simply murmured – 'Poor old Mark!'

'I hope you are not anxious,' I said.

'No, but I am disappointed. She won't let me in. She has locked the door, and I'm afraid to make a noise.' I suppose there might have been something ridiculous in a confession of this kind, but I liked my new friend so much that for me it didn't detract from his dignity. 'She tells me – from behind the door – that she will let me know if he is worse.'

'It's very good of her,' said Miss Ambient.

I had exchanged a glance with Mark in which it is possible that he read that my pity for him was untinged with contempt –

though I know not why he should have cared; and as, presently,
his sister got up and took her bedroom candlestick, he proposed that we should go back to his study. We sat there till after
midnight; he put himself into his slippers, into an old velvet
jacket, lighted an ancient pipe and talked considerably less than
he had done before. There were longish pauses in our communion, but they only made me feel that we had advanced in
intimacy. They helped me, too, to understand my friend's
personal situation, and to perceive that it was by no means
the happiest possible. When his face was quiet, it was vaguely
troubled; it seemed to me to show that for him, too, life was a
struggle, as it has been for many other men of genius. At last
I prepared to leave him, and then, to my ineffable joy, he gave
me some of the sheets of his forthcoming book – it was not
finished, but he had indulged in the luxury, so dear to writers of
deliberation, of having it 'set up', from chapter to chapter, as he
advanced – he gave me, I say, the early pages, the *prémices*, as
the French have it, of this new fruit of his imagination, to take to
my room and look over at my leisure. I was just quitting him
when the door of his study was noiselessly pushed open, and
Mrs Ambient stood before us. She looked at us a moment with
her candle in her hand, and then she said to her husband that as
she supposed he had not gone to bed she had come down to tell
him that Dolcino was more quiet and would probably be better
in the morning. Mark Ambient made no reply; he simply
slipped past her, in the doorway, as if he were afraid she
would seize him in his passage, and bounded upstairs, to
judge for himself of his child's condition. Mrs Ambient looked
slightly discomfited, and for a moment I thought she was going
to give chase to her husband. But she resigned herself, with a
sigh, while her eyes wandered over the lamp-lit room, where
various books, at which I had been looking, were pulled out of
their places on the shelves, and the fumes of tobacco seemed to
hang in mid-air. I bade her good-night, and then, without
intention, by a kind of fatality, the perversity which had already
made me insist unduly on talking with her about her husband's
achievements, I alluded to the precious proof-sheets with
which Ambient had entrusted me, and which I was nursing

there under my arm. 'It is the opening chapters of his new book,' I said. 'Fancy my satisfaction at being allowed to carry them to my room!'

She turned away, leaving me to take my candlestick from the table in the hall; but before we separated, thinking it apparently a good occasion to let me know once for all – since I was beginning, it would seem, to be quite 'thick' with my host – that there was no fitness in my appealing to her for sympathy in such a case; before we separated, I say, she remarked to me, with her quick, round, well-bred utterance, 'I daresay you attribute to me ideas that I haven't got. I don't take that sort of interest in my husband's proof-sheets. I consider his writings most objectionable!'

II

I HAD some curious conversation the next morning with Miss Ambient, whom I found strolling in the garden before breakfast. The whole place looked as fresh and trim, amid the twitter of the birds, as if, an hour before, the housemaids had been turned into it with their dustpans and feather-brushes. I almost hesitated to light a cigarette, and was doubly startled when, in the act of doing so, I suddenly perceived the sister of my host, who had, in any case, something of the oddity of an apparition, standing before me. She might have been posing for her photograph. Her sad-coloured robe arranged itself in serpentine folds at her feet; her hands locked themselves listlessly together in front; and her chin rested upon a *cinque-cento* ruff. The first thing I did, after bidding her good morning, was to ask her for news of her little nephew – to express the hope that she had heard he was better. She was able to gratify this hope, and spoke as if we might expect to see him during the day. We walked through the shrubberies together, and she gave me a great deal of information about her brother's ménage, which offered me an opportunity to mention to her that his wife had told me, the night before, that she thought his productions objectionable.

'She doesn't usually come out with that so soon!' Miss Ambient exclaimed, in answer to this piece of gossip.

'Poor lady, she saw that I am a fanatic.'

'Yes, she won't like you for that. But you mustn't mind, if the rest of us like you! Beatrice thinks a work of art ought to have a "purpose". But she's a charming woman – don't you think her charming? – she's such a type of the lady.'

'She's very beautiful,' I answered; while I reflected that though it was true, apparently, that Mark Ambient was mismated, it was also perceptible that his sister was perfidious. She told me that her brother and his wife had no other difference but this one, that she thought his writings immoral and his influence pernicious. It was a fixed idea; she was afraid of these things for the child. I answered that it was not a trifle – a woman's regarding her husband's mind as a well of corruption; and she looked quite struck with the novelty of my remark. 'But there hasn't been any of the sort of trouble that there so often is among married people,' she said. 'I suppose you can judge for yourself that Beatrice isn't at all – well, whatever they call it when a woman misbehaves herself. And Mark doesn't make love to other people, either. I assure you he doesn't! All the same, of course, from her point of view, you know, she has a dread of my brother's influence on the child – on the formation of his character, of his principles. It is as if it were a subtle poison, or a contagion, or something that would rub off on Dolcino when his father kisses him or holds him on his knee. If she could, she would prevent Mark from ever touching him. Every one knows it; visitors see it for themselves; so there is no harm in my telling you. Isn't it excessively odd? It comes from Beatrice's being so religious, and so tremendously moral, and all that. And then, of course, we mustn't forget,' my companion added, unexpectedly, 'that some of Mark's ideas are – well, really – rather queer!'

I reflected, as we went into the house, where we found Ambient unfolding the *Observer* at the breakfast-table, that none of them were probably quite so queer as his sister. Mrs Ambient did not appear at breakfast, being rather tired with her ministrations, during the night, to Dolcino. Her husband mentioned, however, that she was hoping to go to church. I afterwards learned that she did go, but I may as well announce without delay that he and I did not accompany her. It was while the church-bell was murmuring in the distance that the author of *Beltraffio* led me forth for the ramble he had spoken of in his note. I will not attempt to say where we went, or to describe what we saw. We kept to the fields and copses and commons, and breathed the same sweet air as the nibbling donkeys and the browsing sheep, whose woolliness seemed to me, in those early days of my acquaintance with English objects, but a part of the general texture of the small, dense landscape, which looked as if the harvest were gathered by the shears. Everything was full of expression for Mark Ambient's visitor – from the big, bandy-legged geese, whose whiteness was a 'note', amid all the tones of green, as they wandered beside a neat little oval pool, the foreground of a thatched and white-washed inn, with a grassy approach and a pictorial sign – from these humble way-side animals to the crests of high woods which let a gable or a pinnacle peep here and there, and looked, even at a distance, like trees of good company, conscious of an individual profile. I admired the hedgerows, I plucked the faint-hued heather, and I was for ever stopping to say how charming I thought the thread-like footpaths across the fields, which wandered, in a diagonal of finer grain, from one smooth stile to another. Mark Ambient was abundantly good-natured, and was as much entertained with my observations as I was with the literary allusions of the landscape. We sat and smoked upon stiles, broaching paradoxes in the decent English air; we took short cuts across a park or two, where the bracken was deep, and my companion nodded to the old woman at the gate; we skirted rank covers, which rustled here and there as we passed, and we stretched ourselves at last on a heathery hillside where, if the sun was not too hot, neither was the earth too cold, and where the country lay beneath us in a rich blue mist. Of course I had already told Ambient what I thought of his new novel, having the previous night read every word of the opening chapters before I went to bed.

'I am not without hope of being able to make it my best,' he said, as I went back to the subject, while we turned up our heels to the sky. 'At least the people who dislike my prose – and there

are a great many of them, I believe – will dislike this work most.'
This was the first time I had heard him allude to the people
who couldn't read him – a class which is supposed always to
sit heavy upon the consciousness of the man of letters. A
man organised for literature, as Mark Ambient was, must
certainly have had the normal proportion of sensitiveness,
of irritability; the artistic *ego*, capable in some cases of such
monstrous development, must have been, in his composition,
sufficiently erect and definite. I will not therefore go so far as
to say that he never thought of his detractors, or that he had
any illusions with regard to the number of his admirers (he
could never so far have deceived himself as to believe he was
popular); but I may at least affirm that adverse criticism, as
I had occasion to perceive later, ruffled him visibly but little,
that he had an air of thinking it quite natural he should be
offensive to many minds, and that he very seldom talked
about the newspapers – which, by the way, were always very
stupid in regard to the author of *Beltraffio*. Of course he may
have thought about them – the newspapers – night and day; the
only point I wish to make is that he didn't show it; while, at the
same time, he didn't strike one as a man who was on his guard.
I may add that, as regards his hope of making the work on
which he was then engaged the best of his books, it was only
partly carried out. That place belongs, incontestably, to
Beltraffio, in spite of the beauty of certain parts of its successor.
I am pretty sure, however, that he had, at the moment of which
I speak, no sense of failure; he was in love with his idea, which
was indeed magnificent, and though for him, as (I suppose) for
every artist, the act of execution had in it as much torment as
joy, he saw his work growing a little every day and filling out the
largest plan he had yet conceived. 'I want to be truer than I have
ever been,' he said, settling himself on his back, with his
hands clasped behind his head; 'I want to give an impression
of life itself. No, you may say what you will. I have always
arranged things too much, always smoothed them down and
rounded them off and tucked them in – done everything to
them that life doesn't do. I have been a slave to the old superstitions.'

'You a slave, my dear Mark Ambient? You have the freest imagination of our day!'

'All the more shame to me to have done some of the things I have! The reconciliation of the two women in *Ginistrella*, for instance – which could never really have taken place. That sort of thing is ignoble; I blush when I think of it! This new affair must be a golden vessel, filled with the purest distillation of the actual; and oh, how it bothers me, the shaping of the vase – the hammering of the metal! I have to hammer it so fine, so smooth; I don't do more than an inch or two a day. And all the while I have to be so careful not to let a drop of the liquor escape! When I see the kind of things that Life does, I despair of ever catching her peculiar trick. She has an impudence, Life! If one risked a fiftieth part of the effects she risks! It takes ever so long to believe it. You don't know yet, my dear fellow. It isn't till one has been watching Life for forty years that one finds out half of what she's up to! Therefore one's earlier things must inevitably contain a mass of rot. And with what one sees, on one side, with its tongue in its cheek, defying one to be real enough, and on the other the *bonnes gens* rolling up their eyes at one's cynicism, the situation has elements of the ludicrous which the artist himself is doubtless in a position to appreciate better than any one else. Of course one mustn't bother about the *bonnes gens*,' Mark Ambient went on, while my thoughts reverted to his ladylike wife, as interpreted by his remarkable sister.

'To sink your shaft deep, and polish the plate through which people look into it – that's what your work consists of,' I remember remarking.

'Ah, polishing one's plate – that is the torment of execution!' he exclaimed, jerking himself up and sitting forward. 'The effort to arrive at a surface – if you think a surface necessary – some people don't, happily for them! My dear fellow, if you could see the surface I dream of – as compared with the one with which I have to content myself. Life is really too short for art – one hasn't time to make one's shell ideally hard. Firm and bright – firm and bright! – the devilish thing has a way, some-times, of being bright without being firm. When I rap it with my knuckles it doesn't give the right sound. There are horrible little flabby spots where I have taken the second-best word, because I couldn't for the life of me think of the best. If you knew how stupid I am sometimes! They look to me now like pimples and ulcers on the brow of beauty!'

'That's very bad – very bad,' I said, as gravely as I could.

'Very bad? It's the highest social offence I know; it ought – it absolutely ought – I'm quite serious – to be capital. If I knew I should be hanged else, I should manage to find the best word. The people who couldn't – some of them don't know it when they see it – would shut their inkstands, and we shouldn't be deluged by this flood of rubbish!'

I will not attempt to repeat everything that passed between us or to explain just how it was that, every moment I spent in his company, Mark Ambient revealed to me more and more that he looked at all things from the standpoint of the artist, felt all life as literary material. There are people who will tell me that this is a poor way of feeling it, and I am not concerned to defend my statement – having space merely to remark that there is something to be said for any interest which makes a man feel so much. If Mark Ambient did really, as I suggested above, have imaginative contact with 'all life', I, for my part, envy him his *arrière-pensée*. At any rate it was through the receipt of this impression of him that by the time we returned I had acquired the feeling of intimacy I have noted. Before we got up for the homeward stretch he alluded to his wife's having once – or perhaps more than once – asked him whether he should like Dolcino to read *Beltraffio*. I think he was unconscious at the moment of all that this conveyed to me – as well, doubtless, of my extreme curiosity to hear what he had replied. He had said that he hoped very much Dolcino would read all his works – when he was twenty; he should like him to know what his father had done. Before twenty it would be useless – he wouldn't understand them.

'And meanwhile do you propose to hide them – to lock them up in a drawer?' Mrs Ambient had inquired.

'Oh no; we must simply tell him that they are not intended for small boys. If you bring him up properly, after that he won't touch them.'

To this Mrs Ambient had made answer that it would be very awkward when he was about fifteen, and I asked her husband if it was his opinion in general, then, that young people should not read novels.

'Good ones – certainly not!' said my companion. I suppose I had had other views, for I remember saying that, for myself, I was not sure it was bad for them – if the novels were 'good' enough. 'Bad for *them*, I don't say so much!' Ambient exclaimed. 'But very bad, I am afraid, for the novel.' That oblique, accidental allusion to his wife's attitude was followed by a franker style of reference as we walked home. 'The difference between us is simply the opposition between two distinct ways of looking at the world, which have never succeeded in getting on together, or making any kind of common ménage, since the beginning of time. They have borne all sorts of names, and my wife would tell you it's the difference between Christian and Pagan. I may be a pagan, but I don't like the name – it sounds sectarian. She thinks me, at any rate, no better than an ancient Greek. It's the difference between making the most of life and making the least – so that you'll get another better one in some other time and place. Will it be a sin to make the most of that one too, I wonder? and shall we have to be bribed off in the future state, as well as in the present? Perhaps I care too much for beauty – I don't know; I delight in it, I adore it, I think of it continually, I try to produce it, to reproduce it. My wife holds that we shouldn't think too much about it. She's always afraid of that – always on her guard. I don't know what she has got on her back! And she's so pretty, too, herself! Don't you think she's lovely? She was, at any rate, when I married her. At that time I wasn't aware of that difference I speak of – I thought it all came to the same thing: in the end, as they say. Well, perhaps it will in the end. I don't know what the end will be. Moreover, I care for seeing things as they are; that's the way I try to show them in my novels. But you mustn't talk to Mrs Ambient about things as they are. She has a mortal dread of things as they are.'

'She's afraid of them for Dolcino,' I said: surprised a moment afterwards at being in a position – thanks to Miss Ambient – to be so explanatory; and surprised even now that

Mark shouldn't have shown visibly that he wondered what the deuce I knew about it. But he didn't; he simply exclaimed, with a tenderness that touched me –

'Ah, nothing shall ever hurt *him*!' He told me more about his wife before we arrived at the gate of his house, and if it be thought that he was querulous, I am afraid I must admit that he had some of the foibles as well as the gifts of the artistic temperament; adding, however, instantly, that hitherto, to the best of my belief, he had very rarely complained. 'She thinks me immoral – that's the long and short of it,' he said, as we paused outside a moment, and his hand rested on one of the bars of his gate; while his conscious, expressive, perceptive eyes – the eyes of a foreigner, I had begun to account them, much more than of the usual Englishman – viewing me now evidently as quite a familiar friend, took part in the declaration. 'It's very strange, when one thinks it all over, and there's a grand comicality in it which I should like to bring out. She is a very nice woman, extraordinarily well behaved, upright, and clever, and with a tremendous lot of good sense about a good many matters. Yet her conception of a novel – she has explained it to me once or twice, and she doesn't do it badly, as exposition – is a thing so false that it makes me blush. It is a thing so hollow, so dishonest, so lying, in which life is so blinked and blinded, so dodged and disfigured, that it makes my ears burn. It's two different ways of looking at the whole affair,' he repeated, pushing open the gate. 'And they are irreconcilable!' he added with a sigh. We went forward to the house, but on the walk, half way to the door, he stopped, and said to me, 'If you are going into this kind of thing, there's a fact you should know beforehand; it may save you some disappointment. There's a hatred of art – there's a hatred of literature!' I looked up at the charming house, with its genial colour and crookedness, and I answered with a smile that those evil passions might exist, but that I should never have expected to find them there. 'Oh, it doesn't matter, after all,' he said, laughing; which I was glad to hear, for I was reproaching myself with having excited him.

If I had, his excitement soon passed off, for at lunch he was delightful; strangely delightful, considering that the difference between himself and his wife was, as he had said, irreconcilable. He had the art, by his manner, by his smile, by his natural kindliness, of reducing the importance of it in the common concerns of life, and Mrs Ambient, I must add, lent herself to this transaction with a very good grace. I watched her, at table, for further illustrations of that fixed idea of which Miss Ambient had spoken to me; for in the light of the united revelations of her sister-in-law and her husband, she had come to seem to me a very singular personage. I am obliged to say that the signs of a fanatical temperament were not more striking in my hostess than before; it was only after a while that her air of incorruptible conformity, her tapering, monosyllabic correctness, began to appear to be themselves a cold, thin flame. Certainly, at first, she looked like a woman with as few passions as possible; but if she had a passion at all, it would be that of Philistinism. She might have been, for there are guardian-spirits, I suppose, of all great principles – the angel of propriety. Mark Ambient, apparently, ten years before, had simply perceived that she was an angel, without asking himself of what. He had been quite right in calling my attention to her beauty. In looking for the reason why he should have married her, I saw, more than before, that she was, physically speaking, a wonderfully cultivated human plant – that she must have given him many ideas and images. It was impossible to be more pencilled, more garden-like, more delicately tinted and petalled.

If I had had it in my heart to think Ambient a little of a hypocrite for appearing to forget at table everything he had said to me during our walk, I should instantly have cancelled such a judgement on reflecting that the good news his wife was able to give him about their little boy was reason enough for his sudden air of happiness. It may have come partly, too, from a certain remorse at having complained to me of the fair lady who sat there – a desire to show me that he was after all not so miserable. Dolcino continued to be much better, and he had been promised he should come down stairs after he had had his dinner. As soon as we had risen from our own meal Ambient slipped away, evidently for the purpose of going to his child; and no sooner had I observed this than I became aware that his

wife had simultaneously vanished. It happened that Miss
Ambient and I, both at the same moment, saw the tail of her
dress whisk out of a doorway – which led the young lady to
smile at me, as if I now knew all the secrets of the place. I passed
with her into the garden, and we sat down on a dear old bench
which rested against the west wall of the house. It was a perfect
spot for the middle period of a Sunday in June, and its felicity
seemed to come partly from an antique sun-dial which, rising in
front of us and forming the centre of a small, intricate parterre,
measured the moments ever so slowly, and made them safe for
leisure and talk. The garden bloomed in the suffused afternoon, the tall beeches stood still for an example, and, behind
and above us, a rose-tree of many seasons, clinging to the faded
grain of the brick, expressed the whole character of the scene in
a familiar, exquisite smell. It seemed to me a place for genius to
have every sanction, and not to encounter challenges and
checks. Miss Ambient asked me if I had enjoyed my walk
with her brother, and whether we had talked of many things.

'Well, of most things,' I said, smiling, though I remembered
that we had not talked of Miss Ambient.

'And don't you think some of his theories are very peculiar?'

'Oh, I guess I agree with them all.' I was very particular, for
Miss Ambient's entertainment, to guess.

'Do you think art is everything?' she inquired in a moment.

'In art, of course I do!'

'And do you think beauty is everything?'

'I don't know about its being everything. But it's very
delightful.'

'Of course it is difficult for a woman to know how far to go,'
said my companion. 'I adore everything that gives a charm to
life. I am intensely sensitive to form. But sometimes I draw
back – don't you see what I mean? – I don't quite see where
I shall be landed. I only want to be quiet, after all,' Miss
Ambient continued, in a tone of stifled yearning which seemed
to indicate that she had not yet arrived at her desire. 'And one
must be good, at any rate, must not one?' she inquired, with a
cadence apparently intended for an assurance that my answer
would settle this recondite question for her. It was difficult for

me to make it very original, and I am afraid I repaid her confidence with an unblushing platitude. I remember, moreover, appending to it an inquiry, equally destitute of freshness, and still more wanting perhaps in tact, as to whether she did not mean to go to church, as that was an obvious way of being good. She replied that she had performed this duty in the morning, and that for her, on Sunday afternoon, supreme virtue consisted in answering the week's letters. Then suddenly, without transition, she said to me, 'It's quite a mistake about Dolcino being better. I have seen him, and he's not at all right.'

'Surely his mother would know, wouldn't she?' I suggested.

She appeared for a moment to be counting the leaves on one of the great beeches. 'As regards most matters, one can easily say what, in a given situation, my sister-in-law would do. But as regards this one, there are strange elements at work.'

'Strange elements? Do you mean in the constitution of the child?'

'No, I mean in my sister-in-law's feelings.'

'Elements of affection, of course; elements of anxiety. Why do you call them strange?'

She repeated my words. 'Elements of affection, elements of anxiety. She is very anxious.'

Miss Ambient made me vaguely uneasy – she almost frightened me, and I wished she would go and write her letters. 'His father will have seen him now,' I said, 'and if he is not satisfied he will send for the doctor.'

'The doctor ought to have been here this morning. He lives only two miles away.'

I reflected that all this was very possibly only a part of the general tragedy of Miss Ambient's view of things; but I asked her why she hadn't urged such a necessity upon her sister-in-law. She answered me with a smile of extraordinary significance, and told me that I must have very little idea of what her relations with Beatrice were; but I must do her the justice to add that she went on to make herself a little more comprehensible by saying that it was quite reason enough for her sister not to be alarmed that Mark would be sure to be. He was always nervous about the child, and as they were predestined by nature to take opposite views, the only thing for Beatrice was to cultivate a false optimism. If Mark were not there, she would not be at all easy. I remembered what he had said to me about their dealings with Dolcino – that between them they would put an end to him; but I did not repeat this to Miss Ambient: the less so that just then her brother emerged from the house, carrying his child in his arms. Close behind him moved his wife, grave and pale; the boy's face was turned over Ambient's shoulder, towards his mother. We got up to receive the group, and as they came near us Dolcino turned round. I caught, on his enchanting little countenance, a smile of recognition, and for the moment would have been quite content with it. Miss Ambient, however, received another impression, and I make haste to say that her quick sensibility, in which there was something maternal, argues that in spite of her affectations there was a strain of kindness in her. 'It won't do at all – it won't do at all,' she said to me under her breath. 'I shall speak to Mark about the doctor.'

The child was rather white, but the main difference I saw in him was that he was even more beautiful than the day before. He had been dressed in his festal garments – a velvet suit and a crimson sash – and he looked like a little invalid prince, too young to know condescension, and smiling familiarly on his subjects.

'Put him down, Mark, he's not comfortable,' Mrs Ambient said.

'Should you like to stand on your feet, my boy?' his father asked.

'Oh yes; I'm remarkably well,' said the child.

Mark placed him on the ground; he had shining, pointed slippers, with enormous bows. 'Are you happy now, Mr Ambient?'

'Oh yes, I am particularly happy,' Dolcino replied. The words were scarcely out of his mouth when his mother caught him up, and in a moment, holding him on her knees, she took her place on the bench where Miss Ambient and I had been sitting. This young lady said something to her brother, in consequence of which the two wandered away into the garden together. I remained with Mrs Ambient; but as a servant had brought out a couple of chairs I was not obliged to seat myself beside her. Our conversation was not animated, and I, for my part, felt there would be a kind of hypocrisy in my trying to make myself agreeable to Mrs Ambient. I didn't dislike her – I rather admired her; but I was aware that I differed from her inexpressibly. Then I suspected, what I afterwards definitely knew and have already intimated, that the poor lady had taken a dislike to me; and this of course was not encouraging. She thought me an obtrusive and even depraved young man, whom a perverse Providence had dropped upon their quiet lawn to flatter her husband's worst tendencies. She did me the honour to say to Miss Ambient, who repeated the speech, that she didn't know when she had seen her husband take such a fancy to a visitor; and she measured, apparently, my evil influence by Mark's appreciation of my society. I had a consciousness, not yet acute, but quite sufficient, of all this; but I must say that if it chilled my flow of small-talk, it didn't prevent me from thinking that the beautiful mother and beautiful child, interlaced there against their background of roses, made a picture such as I perhaps should not soon see again. I was free, I supposed, to go into the house and write letters, to sit in the drawing-room, to repair to my own apartment and take a nap; but the only use I made of my freedom was to linger still in my chair and say to myself that the light hand of Sir Joshua might have painted Mark Ambient's wife and son. I found myself looking perpetually at Dolcino, and Dolcino looked back at me, and that was enough to detain me. When he looked at me he smiled, and I felt it was an absolute impossibility to abandon a child who was smiling at one like that. His eyes never wandered; they attached themselves to mine, as if among all the small incipient things of his nature there was a desire to say something to me. If I could have taken him upon my own knee he perhaps would have managed to say it; but it would have been far too delicate a matter to ask his mother to give him up, and it has remained a constant regret for me that on that Sunday afternoon I did not, even for a moment, hold Dolcino in my arms. He had said that he felt remarkably well, and that he was especially happy; but though he may have been happy, with his charming head pillowed on his mother's breast and his little crimson silk legs depending from her lap, I did not think he looked well. He made no attempt to walk about; he was content to swing his legs softly and strike one as languid and angelic.

Mark came back to us with his sister; and Miss Ambient, making some remark about having to attend to her correspondence, passed into the house. Mark came and stood in front of his wife, looking down at the child, who immediately took hold of his hand, keeping it while he remained. 'I think Allingham ought to see him,' Ambient said; 'I think I will walk over and fetch him.'

'That's Gwendolen's idea, I suppose,' Mrs Ambient replied, very sweetly.

'It's not such an out-of-the-way idea, when one's child is ill.'

'I'm not ill, papa; I'm much better now,' Dolcino remarked.

'Is that the truth, or are you only saying it to be agreeable? You have a great idea of being agreeable, you know.'

The boy seemed to meditate on this distinction, this imputation, for a moment; then his exaggerated eyes, which had wandered, caught my own as I watched him, 'Do *you* think me agreeable?' he inquired, with the candour of his age and with a smile that made his father turn round to me, laughing, and ask, mutely, with a glance, 'Isn't he adorable?'

'Then why don't you hop about, if you feel so lusty?' Ambient went on, while the boy swung his hand.

'Because mamma is holding me close!'

'Oh yes; I know how mamma holds you when I come near!' Ambient exclaimed, looking at his wife.

She turned her charming eyes up to him, without deprecation or concession, and after a moment she said, 'You can go for Allingham if you like. I think myself it would be better. You ought to drive.'

'She says that to get me away,' Ambient remarked to me, laughing; after which he started for the doctor's.

I remained there with Mrs Ambient, though our conversation had more pauses than speeches. The boy's little fixed white face seemed, as before, to plead with me to stay, and after a while it produced still another effect, a very curious one, which I shall find it difficult to express. Of course I expose myself to the charge of attempting to give fantastic reasons for an act which may have been simply the fruit of a native want of discretion; and indeed the traceable consequences of that perversity were too lamentable to leave me any desire to trifle with the question. All I can say is that I acted in perfect good faith, and that Dolcino's friendly little gaze gradually kindled the spark of my inspiration. What helped it to glow were the other influences – the silent, suggestive garden-nook, the perfect opportunity (if it was not an opportunity for that, it was an opportunity for nothing), and the plea that I speak of, which issued from the child's eyes and seemed to make him say, 'The mother that bore me and that presses me here to her bosom – sympathetic little organism that I am – has really the kind of sensibility which she has been represented to you as lacking; if you only look for it patiently and respectfully. How is it possible that she shouldn't have it? how is it possible that *I* should have so much of it (for I am quite full of it, dear strange gentleman), if it were not also in some degree in her? I am my father's child, but I am also my mother's, and I am sorry for the difference between them!' So it shaped itself before me, the vision of reconciling Mrs Ambient with her husband, of putting an end to their great disagreement. The project was absurd, of course, for had I not had his word for it – spoken with all the bitterness of experience – that the gulf that divided them was well-nigh bottomless? Nevertheless, a quarter of an hour after Mark had left us, I said to his wife that I couldn't get over what she told me the night before about her thinking her husband's writings 'objectionable'. I had been so very sorry to hear it, had thought of it constantly, and wondered whether it were not possible to make her change her mind. Mrs Ambient gave me rather a cold stare – she seemed to be recommending me to mind my own business. I wish I had taken this mute counsel, but I did not. I went on to remark that it seemed an immense pity so much that was beautiful should be lost upon her.

'Nothing is lost upon me,' said Mrs Ambient. 'I know they are very beautiful.'

'Don't you like papa's books?' Dolcino asked, addressing his mother, but still looking at me. Then he added to me, 'Won't you read them to me, American gentleman?'

'I would rather tell you some stories of my own,' I said. 'I know some that are very interesting.'

'When will you tell them – to-morrow?'

'To-morrow, with pleasure, if that suits you.'

Mrs Ambient was silent at this. Her husband, during our walk, had asked me to remain another day; my promise to her son was an implication that I had consented; and it is not probable that the prospect was agreeable to her. This ought, doubtless, to have made me more careful as to what I said next; but all I can say is that it didn't. I presently observed that just after leaving her, the evening before, and after hearing her apply to her husband's writings the epithet I had already quoted, I had, on going up to my room, sat down to the perusal of those sheets of his new book which he had been so good as to lend me. I had sat entranced till nearly three in the morning – I had read them twice over. 'You say you haven't looked at them. I think it's such a pity you shouldn't. Do let me beg you to take them up. They are so very remarkable. I'm sure they will convert you. They place him in – really – such a dazzling light. All that is best in him is there. I have no doubt it's a great liberty, my saying all this; but excuse me, and *do* read them!'

'Do read them, mamma!' Dolcino repeated. 'Do read them!'

She bent her head and closed his lips with a kiss. 'Of course I know he has worked immensely over them,' she said; and after this she made no remark, but sat there looking thoughtful, with her eyes on the ground. The tone of these last words was such as to leave me no spirit for further aggression, and after expressing a fear that her husband had not found the doctor at home, I got up and took a turn about the grounds. When I came back ten minutes later, she was still in her place, watching her boy, who had fallen asleep in her lap. As I drew near she put her finger to her lips, and a moment afterwards she rose, holding the child, and murmured something about its being better that he should go up stairs. I offered to carry him, and held out my hands to take him; but she thanked me and turned away, with the child seated on her arm, his head on her shoulder. 'I am very strong,' she said, as she passed into the house, and her slim, flexible figure bent backwards with the filial weight. So I never touched Dolcino.

I betook myself to Ambient's study, delighted to have a quiet hour to look over his books by myself. The windows were open into the garden, the sunny stillness, the mild light of the English summer, filled the room, without quite chasing away the rich, dusky air which was a part of its charm, and which abode in the serried shelves where old morocco exhaled the fragrance of curious learning, and in the brighter intervals where medals and prints and miniatures were suspended upon a surface of faded stuff. The place had both colour and quiet; I thought it a perfect room for work, and went so far as to say to myself that if it were mine, to sit and scribble in, there was no knowing but that I might learn to write as well as the author of *Beltraffio*. This distinguished man did not turn up, and I rummaged freely among his treasures. At last I took down a book that detained me a while, and seated myself in a fine old leather chair, by the window, to turn it over. I had been occupied in this way for half an hour – a good part of the afternoon had waned – when I become conscious of another presence in the room, and, looking up from my quarto, saw that Mrs Ambient, having pushed open the door in the same noiseless way that marked – or disguised – her entrance the night before, had advanced across the threshold. On seeing me she stopped; she had not, I think, expected to find me. But her hesitation was only of a moment; she came straight to her husband's writing-table, as if she were looking for something. I got up and asked her if I could help her. She glanced about an instant, and then put her hand upon a roll of papers which I recognised, as I had placed it in that spot in the morning, on coming down from my room.

'Is this the new book?' she asked, holding it up.

'The very sheets, with precious annotations.'

'I mean to take your advice.' And she tucked the little bundle under her arm. I congratulated her cordially, and ventured to make of my triumph, as I presumed to call it, a subject of pleasantry. But she was perfectly grave, and turned away from me, as she had presented herself, without a smile; after which I settled down to my quarto again, with the reflection that Mrs Ambient was a queer woman. My triumph, too, suddenly seemed to me rather vain. A woman who couldn't smile in the right place would never understand Mark Ambient. He came in at last in person, having brought the doctor back with him. 'He was away from home,' Mark said, 'and I went after him – to where he was supposed to be. He had left the place, and I followed him to two or three others, which accounts for my delay.' He was now with Mrs Ambient, looking at the child, and was to see Mark again before leaving the house. My host noticed, at the end of ten minutes, that the proof-sheets of his new book had been removed from the table, and when I told him, in reply to his question as to what I knew about them, that Mrs Ambient had carried them off to read, he turned almost pale for an instant with surprise. 'What has suddenly made her so curious?' he exclaimed; and I was obliged to tell him that I was at the bottom of the mystery. I had had it on my conscience to assure her that she really ought to know of what her husband was capable. 'Of what I am capable? *Elle ne s'en doute que trop!*' said Ambient, with a laugh; but he took my meddling very good-naturedly, and contented himself with adding that he was very much afraid she would burn up the sheets, with his emendations, of which he had no duplicate. The doctor paid a long visit in the nursery, and before he came down I retired to my own quarters, where I remained till dinner-time. On entering the drawing-room at this hour I found Miss Ambient in possession, as she had been the evening before.

'I was right about Dolcino,' she said as soon as she saw me, with a strange little air of triumph. 'He is really very ill.'

'Very ill! Why, when I last saw him, at four o'clock, he was in fairly good form.'

'There has been a change for the worse – very sudden and rapid – and when the doctor got here he found diphtheritic symptoms. He ought to have been called, as I knew, in the morning, and the child oughtn't to have been brought into the garden.'

'My dear lady, he was very happy there,' I answered, much appalled.

'He would be happy anywhere. I have no doubt he is happy now, with his poor little throat in a state—' She dropped her voice as her brother came in, and Mark let us know that, as a matter of course, Mrs Ambient would not appear. It was true that Dolcino had developed diphtheritic symptoms, but he was quiet for the present, and his mother was earnestly watching him. She was a perfect nurse, Mark said, and the doctor was coming back at ten o'clock. Our dinner was not very gay; Ambient was anxious and alarmed, and his sister irritated me by her constant tacit assumption, conveyed in the very way she nibbled her bread and sipped her wine, of having 'told me so'. I had had no disposition to deny anything she told me, and I could not see that her satisfaction in being justified by the event made poor Dolcino's throat any better. The truth is that, as the sequel proved, Miss Ambient had some of the qualities of the sibyl, and had therefore, perhaps, a right to the sibylline contortions. Her brother was so preoccupied that I felt my presence to be an indiscretion, and was sorry I had promised to remain over the morrow. I said to Mark that, evidently, I had better leave them in the morning; to which he replied that, on the contrary, if he was to pass the next days in the fidgets my company would be an extreme relief to him. The fidgets had already begun for him, poor fellow, and as we sat in his study with our cigars, after dinner, he wandered to the door whenever he heard the sound of the doctor's wheels. Miss Ambient, who shared this apartment with us, gave me at such moments significant glances; she had gone up stairs before rejoining us, to ask after the child. His mother and his nurse gave a tolerable account of him; but Miss Ambient found his fever high and his symptoms very grave. The doctor came at ten o'clock, and I went to bed after hearing from Mark that he saw no present cause for alarm. He had made every provision for the night, and was to return early in the morning.

I quitted my room at eight o'clock the next day, and as I came down stairs saw, through the open door of the house, Mrs Ambient standing at the front gate of the grounds, in colloquy with the physician. She wore a white dressing-gown, but her shining hair was carefully tucked away in its net, and in the freshness of the morning, after a night of watching, she looked as much 'the type of the lady' as her sister-in-law had described her. Her appearance, I suppose, ought to have reassured me; but I was still nervous and uneasy, so that I shrank from meeting her with the necessary question about Dolcino. None the less, however, was I impatient to learn how the morning found him; and as Mrs Ambient had not seen me, I passed into the grounds by a roundabout way, and, stopping at a further gate, hailed the doctor just as he was driving away. Mrs Ambient had returned to the house before he got into his gig.

'Excuse me – but, as a friend of the family, I should like very much to hear about the little boy.'

The doctor, who was a stout, sharp man, looked at me from head to foot, and then he said, 'I'm sorry to say I haven't seen him.'

'Haven't seen him?'

'Mrs Ambient came down to meet me as I alighted, and told me that he was sleeping so soundly, after a restless night, that she didn't wish him disturbed. I assured her I wouldn't disturb him, but she said he was quite safe now and she could look after him herself.'

'Thank you very much. Are you coming back?'

'No, sir; I'll be hanged if I come back!' exclaimed Dr Allingham, who was evidently very angry. And he started his horse again with the whip.

I wandered back into the garden, and five minutes later Miss Ambient came forth from the house to greet me. She explained that breakfast would not be served for some time, and that she wished to catch the doctor before he went away. I informed her that this functionary had come and departed, and I repeated to her what he had told me about his dismissal. This made Miss Ambient very serious – very serious indeed – and she sank into a bench, with dilated eyes, hugging her elbows with crossed arms. She indulged in many ejaculations, she confessed that she was infinitely perplexed, and she finally told me what her own last news of her nephew had been. She had sat up very late

– after me, after Mark – and before going to bed had knocked at
the door of the child's room, which was opened to her by the
nurse. This good woman had admitted her, and she had found
Dolcino quiet, but flushed and 'unnatural', with his mother
sitting beside his bed. 'She held his hand in one of hers,' said
Miss Ambient, 'and in the other – what do you think? – the
proof-sheets of Mark's new book! She was reading them there,
intently: did you ever hear of anything so extraordinary? Such a
very odd time to be reading an author whom she never could
abide!' In her agitation Miss Ambient was guilty of this vulgar-
ism of speech, and I was so impressed by her narrative that it
was only in recalling her words later that I noticed the lapse.
Mrs Ambient had looked up from her reading with her finger
on her lips – I recognised the gesture she had addressed to me in
the afternoon – and, though the nurse was about to go to rest,
had not encouraged her sister-in-law to relieve her of any part
of her vigil. But certainly, then, Dolcino's condition was far
from reassuring – his poor little breathing was most painful;
and what change could have taken place in him in those few
hours that would justify Beatrice in denying the physician
access to him? This was the moral of Miss Ambient's anecdote
– the moral for herself at least. The moral for me, rather, was
that it *was* a very singular time for Mrs Ambient to be going into
a novelist she had never appreciated and who had simply happened to be recommended to her by a young American she
disliked. I thought of her sitting there in the sick-chamber in
the still hours of the night, after the nurse had left her, turning
over those pages of genius and wrestling with their magical
influence.

I must relate very briefly the circumstances of the rest of my
visit to Mark Ambient – it lasted but a few hours longer – and
devote but three words to my later acquaintance with him.
That lasted five years – till his death – and was full of interest,
of satisfaction, and, I may add, of sadness. The main thing to be
said with regard to it is, that I had a secret from him. I believe he
never suspected it, though of this I am not absolutely sure. If he
did, the line he had taken, the line of absolute negation of the
matter to himself, shows an immense effort of the will. I may tell

my secret now, giving it for what it is worth, now that Mark
Ambient has gone, that he has begun to be alluded to as one of
the famous early dead, and that his wife does not survive him;
now, too, that Miss Ambient, whom I also saw at intervals
during the years that followed, has, with her embroideries and
her attitudes, her necromantic glances and strange intuitions,
retired to a Sisterhood, where, as I am told, she is deeply
immured and quite lost to the world.

Mark came into breakfast after his sister and I had for some
time been seated there. He shook hands with me in silence,
kissed his sister, opened his letters and newspapers, and pretended to drink his coffee. But I could see that these movements were mechanical, and I was little surprised when,
suddenly he pushed away everything that was before him, and
with his head in his hands and his elbows on the table, sat
staring strangely at the cloth.

'What is the matter *fratello mio*?' Miss Ambient inquired,
peeping from behind the urn.

He answered nothing, but got up with a certain violence and
strode to the window. We rose to our feet, his sister and I, by a
common impulse, exchanging a glance of some alarm, while he
stared for a moment into the garden. 'In Heaven's name, what
has got possession of Beatrice?' he cried at last, turning round
with an almost haggard face. And he looked from one of us to
the other; the appeal was addressed to me as well as to his sister.

Miss Ambient gave a shrug. 'My poor Mark, Beatrice is
always – Beatrice!'

'She has locked herself up with the boy – bolted and barred
the door – she refuses to let me come near him!' Ambient
went on.

'She refused to let the doctor see him an hour ago!' Miss
Ambient remarked, with intention, as they say on the stage.

'Refused to let the doctor see him? By Heaven, I'll smash in
the door!' And Mark brought his fist down upon the table, so
that all the breakfast-service rang.

I begged Miss Ambient to go up and try to have speech of
her sister-in-law, and I drew Mark out into the garden. 'You're
exceedingly nervous, and Mrs Ambient is probably right,' I said

to him. 'Women know – women should be supreme in such a situation. Trust a mother – a devoted mother, my dear friend!' With such words as these I tried to soothe and comfort him, and, marvellous to relate, I succeeded, with the help of many cigarettes, in making him walk about the garden and talk, or listen at least to my own ingenuous chatter, for nearly an hour. At the end of this time Miss Ambient returned to us, with a very rapid step, holding her hand to her heart.

'Go for the doctor, Mark; go for the doctor this moment!'

'Is he dying – has she killed him?' poor Ambient cried, flinging away his cigarette.

'I don't know what she has done! But she's frightened, and now she wants the doctor.'

'He told me he would be hanged if he came back,' I felt myself obliged to announce.

'Precisely – therefore Mark himself must go for him, and not a messenger. You must see him and tell him it's to save your child. The trap has been ordered – it's ready.'

'To save him? I'll save him, please God!' Ambient cried, bounding with his great strides across the lawn.

As soon as he had gone I felt that I ought to have volunteered in his place, and I said as much to Miss Ambient; but she checked me by grasping my arm quickly, while we heard the wheels of the dog-cart rattle away from the gate. 'He's off – he's off – and now I can think! To get him away – while I think – while I think!'

'While you think of what, Miss Ambient?'

'Of the unspeakable thing that has happened under this roof!'

Her manner was habitually that of such a prophetess of ill that my first impulse was to believe I must allow here for a great exaggeration. But in a moment I saw that her emotion was real. 'Dolcino *is* dying then – he is dead?'

'It's too late to save him. His mother has let him die! I tell you that, because you are sympathetic, because you have imagination,' Miss Ambient was good enough to add, interrupting my expression of horror. 'That's why you had the idea of making her read Mark's new book!'

'What has that to do with it? I don't understand you – your accusation is monstrous.'

'I see it all – I'm not stupid,' Miss Ambient went on, heedless of the harshness of my tone. 'It was the book that finished her – it was that decided her!'

'Decided her? Do you mean she has murdered her child?' I demanded, trembling at my own words.

'She sacrificed him – she determined to do nothing to make him live. Why else did she lock herself up – why else did she turn away the doctor? The book gave her a horror, she determined to rescue him – to prevent him from ever being touched. He had a crisis at two o'clock in the morning. I know this from the nurse, who had left her then, but whom, for a short time, she called back. Dolcino got much worse, but she insisted on the nurse's going back to bed, and after that she was alone with him for hours.'

'Do you pretend that she has no pity – that she's insane?'

'She held him in her arms – she pressed him to her breast, not to see him; but she gave him no remedies – she did nothing the doctor ordered. Everything is there, untouched. She has had the honesty not even to throw the drugs away!'

I dropped upon the nearest bench, overcome with wonder and agitation: quite as much at Miss Ambient's terrible lucidity as at the charge she made against her sister-in-law. There was an amazing coherency in her story, and it was dreadful to me to see myself figuring in it as so proximate a cause. 'You are a very strange woman, and you say strange things.'

'You think it necessary to protest – but you are quite ready to believe me. You have received an impression of my sister-in-law, you have guessed of what she is capable.'

I do not feel bound to say what concession on this point I made to Miss Ambient, who went on to relate to me that within the last half-hour Beatrice had had a revulsion; that she was tremendously frightened at what she had done; that her fright itself betrayed her; and that she would now give heaven and earth to save the child. 'Let us hope she will!' I said, looking at my watch and trying to time poor Ambient; whereupon my companion repeated, in a singular tone, 'Let us hope so!' When

I asked her if she herself could do nothing, and whether she ought not to be with her sister-in-law, she replied, 'You had better go and judge; she is like a wounded tigress!' I never saw Mrs Ambient till six months after this, and therefore cannot pretend to have verified the comparison. At the latter period she was again the type of the lady. 'She'll be nicer to him after this,' I remember Miss Ambient saying, in response to some quick outburst (on my part) of compassion for her brother. Although I had been in the house but thirty-six hours this young lady had treated me with extraordinary confidence, and there was therefore a certain demand which, as an intimate, I might make of her. I extracted from her a pledge that she would never say to her brother what she had just said to me; she would leave him to form his own theory of his wife's conduct. She agreed with me that there was misery enough in the house without her contributing a new anguish, and that Mrs Ambient's proceedings might be explained, to her husband's mind, by the extravagance of a jealous devotion. Poor Mark came back with the doctor much sooner than we could have hoped, but we knew, five minutes afterward, that they arrived too late. Poor little Dolcino was more exquisitely beautiful in death than he had been in life. Mrs Ambient's grief was frantic; she lost her head and said strange things. As for Mark's – but I will not speak of that. *Basta*, as he used to say. Miss Ambient kept her secret – I have already had occasion to say that she had her good points – but it rankled in her conscience like a guilty participation, and, I imagine, had something to do with her retiring ultimately to a Sisterhood. And, *à propos* of consciences, the reader is now in a position to judge of my compunction for my effort to convert Mrs Ambient. I ought to mention that the death of her child in some degree converted her. When the new book came out – it was long delayed – she read it over as a whole, and her husband told me that a few months before her death – she failed rapidly after losing her son, sank into a consumption, and faded away at Mentone – during those few supreme weeks she even dipped into *Beltraffio*.

LOUISA PALLANT

I

NEVER say you know the last word about any human heart! I was once treated to a revelation which startled and touched me, in the nature of a person with whom I had been acquainted (well, as I supposed) for years, whose character I had had good reasons, heaven knows, to appreciate and in regard to whom I flattered myself that I had nothing more to learn.

It was on the terrace of the Kursaal at Homburg, nearly ten years ago, one lovely night toward the end of July. I had come to the place that day from Frankfort, with vague intentions, and was mainly occupied in waiting for my young nephew, the only son of my sister, who had been entrusted to my care by a very fond mother for the summer (I was expected to show him Europe – only the very best of it), and was on his way from Paris to join me. The excellent band discoursed music not too abstruse, and the air was filled besides with the murmur of different languages, the smoke of many cigars, the creak on the gravel of the gardens of strolling shoes and the thick tinkle of beer-glasses. There were a hundred people walking about, there were some in clusters at little tables and many on benches and rows of chairs, watching the others as if they had paid for the privilege and were rather disappointed. I was among these last; I sat by myself, smoking my cigar and thinking of nothing very particular while families and couples passed and repassed me.

I scarcely know how long I had sat there when I became aware of a recognition which made my meditations definite. It was on my own part, and the object of it was a lady who moved to and fro, unconscious of my observation, with a young girl at her side. I had not seen her for ten years, and what first struck me was the fact not that she was Mrs Henry Pallant but that the girl who was with her was remarkably pretty – or rather first of all that every one who passed her turned round to look at her. This led me to look at the young lady myself, and her charming

777

face diverted my attention for some time from that of her companion. The latter, moreover, though it was night, wore a thin, light veil which made her features vague. The couple walked and walked, slowly, but though they were very quiet and decorous, and also very well dressed, they seemed to have no friends. Every one looked at them but no one spoke; they appeared even to talk very little to each other. Moreover they bore with extreme composure and as if they were thoroughly used to it the attention they excited. I am afraid it occurred to me to take for granted that they were not altogether honourable and that if they had been the elder lady would have covered the younger up a little more from the public stare and not have been so ashamed to exhibit her own face. Perhaps this question came into my mind too easily just then – in view of my prospective mentorship to my nephew. If I was to show him only the best of Europe I should have to be very careful about the people he should meet – especially the ladies – and the relations he should form. I suspected him of knowing very little of life and I was rather uneasy about my responsibilities. Was I completely relieved and reassured when I perceived that I simply had Louisa Pallant before me and that the girl was her daughter Linda, whom I had known as a child – Linda grown up into a regular beauty?

The question is delicate and the proof that I was not very sure is perhaps that I forbore to speak to the ladies immediately. I watched them awhile – I wondered what they would do. No great harm, assuredly; but I was anxious to see if they were really isolated. Homburg is a great resort of the English – the London season takes up its tale there toward the first of August – and I had an idea that in such a company as that Louisa would naturally know people. It was my impression that she 'cultivated' the English, that she had been much in London and would be likely to have views in regard to a permanent settlement there. This supposition was quickened by the sight of Linda's beauty, for I knew there is no country in which a handsome person is more appreciated. You will see that I took time, and I confess that as I finished my cigar I thought it all over. There was no good reason in fact why I should have

rushed into Mrs Pallant's arms. She had not treated me well
and we had never really made it up. Somehow even the circumstance that (after the first soreness) I was glad to have lost her
had never put us quite right with each other; nor, for herself,
had it made her less ashamed of her heartless behaviour that
poor Pallant after all turned out no great catch. I had forgiven
her; I had not felt that it was anything but an escape not to have
married a girl who had it in her to take back her given word and
break a fellow's heart, for mere flesh-pots – or the shallow
promise, as it pitifully proved, of flesh-pots; moreover we had
met since then, on the occasion of my former visit to Europe;
we had looked each other in the eyes, we had pretended to be
free friends and had talked of the wickedness of the world as
composedly as if we were the only just, the only pure. I knew
then what she had given out – that I had driven her off by my
insane jealousy before she ever thought of Henry Pallant,
before she had ever seen him. This had not been then and it
could not be to-day a ground of real reunion, especially if you
add to it that she knew perfectly what I thought of her. It is my
belief that it does not often minister to friendship that your
friend shall know your real opinion, for he knows it mainly
when it is unfavourable, and this is especially the case when
(if the solecism may pass) he is a woman. I had not followed
Mrs Pallant's fortunes; the years elapsed, for me, in my own
country, whereas she led her life, which I vaguely believed to be
difficult after her husband's death – virtually that of a bankrupt
– in foreign lands. I heard of her from time to time; always as
'established' somewhere, but on each occasion in a different
place. She drifted from country to country, and if she had been
of a hard composition at the beginning it could never occur to
me that her struggle with society, as it might be called, would
have softened the paste. Whenever I heard a woman spoken of
as 'horribly worldly' I thought immediately of the object of my
early passion. I imagined she had debts, and when I now at last
made up my mind to recall myself to her it was present to me
that she might ask me to lend her money. More than anything
else, at this time of day, I was sorry for her, so that such an idea
did not operate as a deterrent.

She pretended afterwards that she had not noticed me – expressing great surprise and wishing to know where I had dropped from; but I think the corner of her eye had taken me in and she was waiting to see what I would do. She had ended by sitting down with her girl on the same row of chairs with myself, and after a little, on the seat next to her becoming vacant, I went and stood before her. She looked up at me a moment, staring, as if she could not imagine who I was or what I wanted; then, smiling and extending her hands, she broke out, 'Ah, my dear old friend – what a delight!' If she had waited to see what I would do, in order to choose her own line, she at least carried out this line with the utmost grace. She was cordial, friendly, artless, interested, and indeed I am sure she was very glad to see me. I may as well say immediately, however, that she gave neither then nor later any sign of a disposition to borrow money. She had none too much – that I learned – but for the moment she seemed able to pay her way. I took the empty chair and we remained talking for an hour. After a while she made me sit on the other side of her, next to her daughter, whom she wished to know me – to love me – as one of their oldest friends. 'It goes back, back, back, doesn't it?' said Mrs Pallant; 'and of course she remembers you as a child.' Linda smiled very sweetly and indefinitely, and I saw she remembered me not at all. When her mother intimated that they had often talked about me she failed to take it up, though she looked extremely nice. Looking nice was her strong point; she was prettier even than her mother had been. She was such a little lady that she made me ashamed of having doubted, however vaguely and for a moment, of her position in the scale of propriety. Her appearance seemed to say that if she had no acquaintances, it was because she did not want to – because there was nobody there who struck her as attractive: there was not the slightest difficulty about her choosing her friends. Linda Pallant, young as she was, and fresh and fair and charming and gentle and sufficiently shy, looked somehow exclusive – as if the dust of the common world had never been meant to settle upon her. She was simpler than her mother and was evidently not a young woman of professions – except in so far as she was committed to an interest in you by her bright, pure, intelligent smile. A girl who had such a lovely way of showing her teeth could never pass for heartless.

As I sat between the pair I felt that I had been taken possession of and that for better or worse my stay at Homburg would be intimately associated with theirs. We gave each other a great deal of news and expressed unlimited interest in each other's history since our last meeting. I know not what Mrs Pallant kept back, but for myself I was frank enough. She let me see at any rate that her life had been a good deal what I supposed, though the terms she used to describe it were less crude than those of my thought. She confessed that they had drifted and that they were drifting still. Her narrative rambled and got what is vulgarly called somewhat mixed, as I thought Linda perceived while she sat watching the passers in a manner which betrayed no consciousness of their attention, without coming to her mother's aid. Once or twice Mrs Pallant made me feel like a cross-questioner, which I had no intention of being. I took it that if the girl never put in a word it was because she had perfect confidence in her mother's ability to come out straight. It was suggested to me, I scarcely knew how, that this confidence between the two ladies went to a great length; that their union of thought, their system of reciprocal divination, was remarkable, and that they probably seldom needed to resort to the clumsy and in some cases dangerous expedient of putting their ideas into words. I suppose I made this reflection not all at once – it was not wholly the result of that first meeting. I was with them constantly for the next several days and my impressions had time to clarify.

I do remember however that it was on this first evening that Archie's name came up. She attributed her own stay at Homburg to no refined nor exalted motive – did not say that she was there because she always came or because a high medical authority had ordered her to drink the waters; she frankly admitted that the reason of her visit had been simply that she did not know where else to turn. But she appeared to assume that my behaviour rested on higher grounds and even that it required explanation, the place being frivolous and modern – devoid of that interest of antiquity which I used to value. 'Don't you remember – ever so long ago – that you wouldn't look at anything in Europe that was not a thousand years old? Well, as we advance in life I suppose we don't think that's quite such a charm.' And when I told her that I had come to Homburg because it was as good a place as another to wait for my nephew, she exclaimed: 'Your nephew – what nephew? He must have come up of late.' I answered that he was a youth named Archer Pringle and very modern indeed; he was coming of age in a few months and was in Europe for the first time. My last news of him had been from Paris and I was expecting to hear from him from one day to the other. His father was dead, and though a selfish bachelor, little versed in the care of children, I was considerably counted on by his mother to see that he did not smoke too much nor fall off an Alp.

Mrs Pallant immediately guessed that his mother was my sister Charlotte, whom she spoke of familiarly, though I knew she had seen her but once or twice. Then in a moment it came to her which of the Pringles Charlotte had married; she remembered the family perfectly, in the old New York days – 'that disgustingly rich lot'. She said it was very nice having the boy come out that way to my care; to which I replied that it was very nice for him. She declared that she meant for me – I ought to have had children; there was something so parental about me and I would have brought them up so well. She could make an allusion like that – to all that might have been and had not been – without a gleam of guilt in her eye; and I foresaw that before I left the place I should have confided to her that though I detested her and was very glad we had fallen out, yet our old relations had left me no heart for marrying another woman. If I was a maundering old bachelor to-day it was no one's fault but hers. She asked me what I meant to do with my nephew and I said it was much more a question of what he would do with me. She inquired whether he were a nice young man and had brothers and sisters and any particular profession. I told her that I had really seen but little of him; I believed him to be six feet high and of tolerable parts. He was an only son, but there was a little sister at home, a delicate, unsuccessful child, demanding all the mother's care.

'So that makes your responsibility greater, as it were, about the boy, doesn't it?' said Mrs Pallant.

'Greater? I'm sure I don't know.'

'Why, if the girl's life is uncertain he may be, some moment, all the mother has. So that being in your hands—'

'Oh, I shall keep him alive, I suppose, if you mean that,' I rejoined.

'Well, *we* won't kill him, shall we, Linda?' Mrs Pallant went on, with a laugh.

'I don't know – perhaps we shall!' said the girl, smiling.

II

I CALLED on them the next day at their lodgings, the modesty of which was enhanced by a hundred pretty feminine devices – flowers and photographs and portable knick-knacks and a hired piano and morsels of old brocade flung over angular sofas. I asked them to drive; I met them again at the Kursaal; I arranged that we should dine together, after the Homburg fashion, at the same *table d'hôte*; and during several days this revived familiar intercourse continued, imitating intimacy if it did not quite achieve it. I liked it, for my companions passed my time for me and the conditions of our life were soothing – the feeling of summer and shade and music and leisure, in the German gardens and woods, where we strolled and sat and gossiped; to which may be added a kind of sociable sense that among people whose challenge to the curiosity was mainly not irresistible we kept quite to ourselves. We were on the footing of old friends who, with regard to each other, still had discoveries to make. We knew each other's nature but we did not know each other's experience; so that when Mrs Pallant related to me what she had been 'up to' (as I called it) for so many years, the former knowledge attached a hundred interpretative footnotes (as if I had been editing an author who presented difficulties) to the interesting page. There was nothing new to me in the fact that I did not esteem her, but there was a sort of refreshment in finding that this was not necessary at Homburg and that I could like her in spite of it. She seemed to me, in the oddest way, both improved and degenerate, as if in her nature the two processes had gone on together. She was battered and world-worn and, spiritually speaking, vulgarised; something fresh had rubbed off her (it even included the vivacity of her early desire to do the best thing for herself), and something very stale had rubbed on. On the other hand she betrayed a scepticism, and that was rather becoming, as it quenched the eagerness of her prime, which had taken a form so unfortunate for me. She had grown weary and indifferent, and as she struck me as having seen more of the evil of the world than of the good, that was a gain; in other words the cynicism that had formed itself in her nature had a softer surface than some of her old ambitions. And then I had to recognise that her devotion to her daughter had been a kind of religion; she had done the very best possible for Linda.

Linda was curious – Linda was interesting; I have seen girls I liked better (charming as she was), but I have never seen one who for the time I was with her (the impression passed, some-how, when she was out of sight) occupied me more. I can best describe the sort of attention that she excited by saying that she struck one above all things as a final product – just as some plant or fruit does, some waxen orchid or some perfect peach. More than any girl I ever saw she was the result of a process of calculation; a process patiently educative; a pressure exerted in order that she should reach a high point. This high point had been the star of her mother's heaven (it hung before her so definitely), and had been the source of the only light – in default of a better – that shone upon the poor lady's path. It stood her in stead of every other religion. The very most and the very best – that was what the girl had been led on to achieve; I mean, of course (for no real miracle had been wrought), the most and the best that she was capable of. She was as pretty, as graceful, as intelligent, as well-bred, as well-informed, as well-dressed, as it would have been possible for her to be; her music, her singing, her German, her French, her English, her step, her tone, her glance, her manner, and everything in her person and move-ment, from the shade and twist of her hair to the way you saw her finger-nails were pink when she raised her hand, had been carried so far that one found one's self accepting them as a kind of standard. I regarded her as a model, and yet it was a part of her perfection that she had none of the stiffness of a pattern. If she held the observation it was because one wondered where and when she would break down; but she never did, either in her French accent or in her *rôle* of educated angel.

After Archie had come the ladies were manifestly a great resource to him, and all the world knows that a party of four is more convenient than a party of three. My nephew kept me waiting a week, with a placidity all his own; but this same placidity was an element of success in our personal relations – so long, that is, as I did not lose my temper with it. I did not, for the most part, because my young man's unsurprised acceptance of the most various forms of good fortune had more than anything else the effect of amusing me. I had seen little of him for the last three or four years. I knew not what his impending majority would have made of him (he did not look himself in the least as if the wind were rising), and I watched him with a solicitude which usually ended in a joke. He was a tall, fresh-coloured youth, with a candid circular countenance and a love of cigarettes, horses and boats which had not been sacrificed to more transcendent studies. He was refreshingly natural, in a supercivilised age, and I soon made up my mind that the formula of his character was a certain simplifying serenity. After that I had time to meditate on the line which divides the serene from the inane and simplification from death. Archie was not clever – that theory it was not possible to maintain, though Mrs Pallant tried it once or twice; but on the other hand it seemed to me that his want of wit was a good defensive weapon. It was not the sort of density that would let him in, but the sort that would keep him out. By which I don't mean that he had shortsighted suspicions, but on the contrary that imagination would never be needed to save him, because she would never put him in danger. In short he was a well-grown, well-washed, muscular young American, whose extreme good-nature might have made him pass for conceited. If he looked pleased with himself it was only because he was pleased with life (as well he might be, with the money he was on the point of stepping into), and his big healthy, independent person was an inevitable part of that. I am bound to add that he was accommodating – for which I was grateful. His own habits were active, but he did not insist on my adopting them and he made noteworthy sacrifices for the sake of my society. When I say for the sake of mine I must of course remember that mine and that of Mrs Pallant and Linda were now very much the same thing. He was willing to sit and smoke for hours under the trees or, regulating his long legs to the pace of his three companions, stroll through the nearer woods of the charming little hill-range of the Taunus to those rustic *Wirthschaften* where coffee might be drunk under a trellis.

Mrs Pallant took a great interest in him; she talked a great deal about him and thought him a delightful specimen, as a young gentleman of his period and country. She even asked me the sort of 'figure' that his fortune might really amount to and expressed the most hungry envy when I told her what I sup-posed it to be. While we talked together Archie, on his side, could not do less than converse with Linda, nor to tell the truth did he manifest the least inclination for any different exercise. They strolled away together while their elders rested; two or three times, in the evening, when the ballroom of the Kursaal was lighted and dance-music played, they whirled over the smooth floor in a waltz that made me remember. Whether it had the same effect on Mrs Pallant I know not, for she held her peace. We had on certain occasions our moments, almost our half-hours, of unembarrassed silence while our young com-panions disported themselves. But if at other times her inquiries and comments were numerous on the subject of my ingenuous kinsman this might very well have passed for a courteous recognition of the frequent admiration that I expressed for Linda – an admiration to which I noticed that she was apt to give but a small direct response. I was struck with something anomalous in her way of taking my remarks about her daughter – they produced so little of a maternal flutter. Her detachment, her air of having no fatuous illusions and not being blinded by prejudice seemed to me at times to amount to an affectation. Either she answered me with a vague, slightly impatient sigh and changed the subject, or else she said before doing so: 'Oh yes, yes, she's a very brilliant creature. She ought to be; God knows what I have done for her!'

The reader will have perceived that I am fond of looking at the explanations of things, and in regard to this I had my theory that she was disappointed in the girl. What had been her particular disappointment? As she could not possibly have wished her prettier or more pleasing it could only be that Linda had not made a successful use of her gifts. Had she expected her to capture a prince the day after she left the schoolroom? After all there was plenty of time for this, as Linda was only two and twenty. It did not occur to me to wonder whether the source of her mother's tepidity was that the young lady had not turned out so nice a nature as she had hoped, because in the first place Linda struck me as perfectly innocent and in the second I was not paid, as the French say, for thinking that Louisa Pallant would much mind whether she were or not. The last hypothesis I should have resorted to was that of private despair at bad moral symptoms. And in relation to Linda's nature I had before me the daily spectacle of her manner with my nephew. It was as charming as it could be, without the smallest indication of a desire to lead him on. She was as familiar as a cousin, but as a distant one – a cousin who had been brought up to observe degrees. She was so much cleverer than Archie that she could not help laughing at him, but she did not laugh enough to exclude variety, being well aware, no doubt, that a woman's cleverness most shines in contrast with a man's stupidity when she pretends to take that stupidity for wisdom. Linda Pallant moreover was not a chatterbox; as she knew the value of many things she knew the value of intervals. There were a good many in the conversation of these young persons; my nephew's own speech, to say nothing of his thought, being not exempt from periods of repose; so that I sometimes wondered how their association was kept at that pitch of friendliness of which it certainly bore the stamp.

It was friendly enough, evidently, when Archie sat near her – near enough for low murmurs, if they had risen to his lips – and watched her with interested eyes and with liberty not to try too hard to make himself agreeable. She was always doing something – finishing a flower in a piece of tapestry, cutting the leaves of a magazine, sewing a button on her glove (she carried a little work-bag in her pocket and was a person of the daintiest habits), or plying her pencil in a sketchbook which she rested on her knee. When we were indoors, at her mother's house, she had always the resource of her piano, of which she was of course a perfect mistress. These avocations enabled her to bear such close inspection with composure (I ended by rebuking Archie for it – I told him he stared at the poor girl too much), and she sought further relief in smiling all over the place. When my young man's eyes shone at her those of Miss Pallant addressed themselves brightly to the trees and clouds and other surrounding objects, including her mother and me. Sometimes she broke out into a sudden embarrassed, happy, pointless laugh. When she wandered away from us she looked back at us in a manner which said that it was not for long – that she was with us still in spirit. If I was pleased with her it was for a good reason: it was many a day since any pretty girl had had the air of taking me so much into account. Sometimes, when they were so far away as not to disturb us, she read aloud a little to Mr Archie. I don't know where she got her books – I never provided them, and certainly he did not. He was no reader and I daresay he went to sleep.

III

I REMEMBER well the first time – it was at the end of about ten days of this – that Mrs Pallant remarked to me: 'My dear friend, you are quite amazing! You behave for all the world as if you were perfectly ready to accept certain consequences.' She nodded in the direction of our young companions, but I nevertheless put her at the pains of saying what consequences she meant. 'What consequences?' she repeated. 'Why, the consequences that ensued when you and I first became acquainted.'

I hesitated a moment and then, looking her in the eyes, I said, 'Do you mean that she would throw him over?'

'You are not kind, you are not generous,' she replied, colouring quickly. 'I am giving you a warning.'

'You mean that my boy may fall in love with her?'

'Certainly. It looks even as if the harm might be already done.'

'Then your warning is too late,' I said, smiling. 'But why do you call it a harm?'

'Haven't you any sense of responsibility?' she asked. 'Is that what his mother sent him out to you for – that you should find him a wife – let him put his head into a noose the day after his arrival?'

'Heaven forbid I should do anything of the kind! I know moreover that his mother doesn't want him to marry young. She thinks it's a mistake and that at that age a man never really chooses. He doesn't choose till he has lived awhile – till he has looked about and compared.'

'And what do you think yourself?'

'I should like to say I consider that love itself, however young, is a sufficient choice. But my being a bachelor at this time of day would contradict me too much.'

'Well then, you're too primitive. You ought to leave this place to-morrow.'

'So as not to see Archie tumble in?'

'You ought to fish him out now and take him with you.'

'Do you think he is in very far?' I inquired.

'If I were his mother I know what I should think. I can put myself in her place – I am not narrow – I know perfectly well how she must regard such a question.'

'And don't you know that in America that's not thought important – the way the mother regards it?'

Mrs Pallant was silent a moment, as if I partly mystified and partly vexed her. 'Well, we are not in America; we happen to be here.'

'No; my poor sister is up to her neck in New York.'

'I am almost capable of writing to her to come out,' said Mrs Pallant.

'You *are* warning me,' I exclaimed, 'but I hardly know of what. It seems to me that my responsibility would begin only at the moment when it should appear that your daughter herself was in danger.'

'Oh, you needn't mind that; I'll take care of her.'

'If you think she is in danger already I'll take him away to-morrow,' I went on.

'It would be the best thing you could do.'

'I don't know. I should be very sorry to act on a false alarm. I am very well here; I like the place and the life and your society. Besides, it doesn't strike me that – on her side – there is any-thing.'

She looked at me with an expression that I had never seen in her face, and if I had puzzled her she repaid me in kind. 'You are very annoying; you don't deserve what I would do for you.'

What she would do for me she did not tell me that day, but we took up the subject again. I said to her that I did not really see why we should assume that a girl like Linda – brilliant enough to make one of the greatest matches – would fall into my nephew's arms. Might I inquire whether her mother had won a confession from her – whether she had stammered out her secret? Mrs Pallant answered that they did not need to tell each other such things – they had not lived together twenty years in such intimacy for nothing. To this I rejoined that I had guessed as much but that there might be an exception for a great occasion like the present. If Linda had shown nothing it was a sign that for her the occasion was not great; and I men-tioned that Archie had not once spoken to me of the young lady, save to remark casually and rather patronisingly, after his first encounter with her, that she was a regular little flower. (The little flower was nearly three years older than himself.) Apart from this he had not alluded to her and had taken up no allusion of mine. Mrs Pallant informed me again (for which I was prepared) that I was quite too primitive; and then she said: 'We needn't discuss the matter if you don't wish to, but I happen to know – how I obtained my knowledge is not important – that the moment Mr Pringle should propose to my daughter she would gobble him down. Surely it's a detail worth mentioning to you.'

'Very good. I will sound him. I will look into the matter to-night.'

'Don't, don't; you will spoil everything!' she murmured, in a peculiar tone of discouragement. 'Take him off – that's the only thing.'

I did not at all like the idea of taking him off; it seemed too summary, unnecessarily violent, even if presented to him on specious grounds; and, moreover, as I had told Mrs Pallant, I really had no wish to move. I did not consider it a part of my bargain with my sister that, with my middle-aged habits, I should duck and dodge about Europe. So I said: 'Should you really object to the boy so much as a son-in-law? After all he's a good fellow and a gentleman.'

'My poor friend, you are too superficial – too frivolous,' Mrs Pallant rejoined, with considerable bitterness.

There was a vibration of contempt in this which nettled me, so that I exclaimed, 'Possibly; but it seems odd that a lesson in consistency should come from you.'

I had no retort from her; but at last she said, quietly: 'I think Linda and I had better go away. We have been here a month – that's enough.'

'Dear me, that will be a bore!' I ejaculated; and for the rest of the evening, until we separated (our conversation had taken place after dinner, at the Kursaal), she remained almost silent, with a subdued, injured air. This, somehow, did not soothe me, as it ought to have done, for it was too absurd that Louisa Pallant, of all women, should propose to put me in the wrong. If ever a woman had been in the wrong herself—! Archie and I usually attended the ladies back to their own door – they lived in a street of minor accommodation, at a certain distance from the Rooms – and we parted for the night late, on the big cobble-stones, in the little sleeping German town, under the closed windows of which, suggesting stuffy interiors, our English farewells sounded gay. On this occasion however they were not gay, for the difficulty that had come up, for me, with Mrs Pallant appeared to have extended by a mysterious sympathy to the young couple. They too were rather conscious and dumb.

As I walked back to our hotel with my nephew I passed my hand into his arm and asked him, by no roundabout approach to the question, whether he were in serious peril of love.

'I don't know, I don't know – really, uncle, I don't know!' – this was all the satisfaction I could extract from the youth, who had not the smallest vein of introspection. He might not know, but before we reached the inn (we had a few more words on the subject), it seemed to me that I did. His mind was not made to contain many objects at once, but Linda Pallant for the moment certainly constituted its principal furniture. She pervaded his consciousness, she solicited his curiosity, she associated herself, in a manner as yet undefined and unformulated, with his future. I could see that she was the first intensely agreeable impression of his life. I did not betray to him, however, how much I saw, and I slept not particularly well, for thinking that, after all, it had been none of my business to provide him with intensely agreeable impressions. To find him a wife was the last thing that his mother had expected of me or that I had expected of myself. Moreover it was quite my opinion that he himself was too young to be a judge of wives. Mrs Pallant was right and I had been strangely superficial in regarding her, with her beautiful daughter, as a 'resource'. There were other resources and one of them would be most decidedly to go away. What did I know after all about the girl except that I was very glad to have escaped from marrying her mother? That mother, it was true, was a singular person, and it was strange that her conscience should have begun to fidget before my own did and that she was more anxious on my nephew's behalf than I was. The ways of women were mysterious and it was not a novelty to me that one never knew where one would find them. As I have not hesitated in this narrative to reveal the irritable side of my own nature I will confess that I even wondered whether Mrs Pallant's solicitude had not been a deeper artifice. Was it not possibly a plan of her own for making sure of my young man – though I did not quite see the logic of it? If she regarded him, as she might in view of his large fortune, as a great catch, might she not have arranged this little comedy, in their personal interest, with the girl?

That possibility at any rate only made it a happier thought that I should carry the boy away to visit other cities. There were many assuredly much more worthy of his attention than Homburg. In the course of the morning (it was after our early luncheon) I walked round to Mrs Pallant's, to let her know that this truth had come over me with force; and while I did so I again felt the unlikelihood of the part attributed by my fears and by the mother's own, if they were real, to Linda. Certainly if she was such a girl as these fears represented her she would fly at higher game. It was with an eye to high game, Mrs Pallant had frankly admitted to me, that she had been trained, and such an education, to say nothing of such a subject, justified a hope of greater returns. A young American who could give her nothing but pocket-money was a very moderate prize, and if she were prepared to marry for ambition (there was no such hardness in her face or tone, but then there never is), her mark would be at the least an English duke. I was received at Mrs Pallant's lodgings with the announcement that she had left Homburg with her daughter half an hour before. The good woman who had entertained the pair professed to know nothing of their movements beyond the fact that they had gone to Frankfort, where however it was her belief that they did not intend to remain. They were evidently travelling beyond. Sudden? Oh yes, tremendously sudden. They must have spent the night in packing, they had so many things and such pretty ones; and their poor maid all the morning had scarcely had time to swallow her coffee. But they evidently were ladies accustomed to come and go. It did not matter: with such rooms as hers she never wanted; there was a new family coming in at three o'clock.

IV

THIS piece of strategy left me staring and I confess it made me rather angry. My only consolation was that Archie, when I told him, looked as blank as myself and that the trick touched him more nearly, for I was not in love with Louisa. We agreed that we required an explanation and we pretended to expect one the next day in the shape of a letter satisfactory even to the point of being apologetic. When I say 'we' pretended I mean that I did, for my suspicion that he knew (through an arrangement with Linda) what had become of our friends lasted only a moment. If his resentment was less than my own his surprise was equally great. I had been willing to bolt, but I felt rather slighted by the facility with which Mrs Pallant had shown that she could part with us. Archie was not angry, because in the first place he was good-natured and in the second it was evidently not definite to him that he had been encouraged, having, I think, no very particular idea of what constituted encouragement. He was fresh from the wonderful country in which between the ingenuous young there may be so little question of 'intentions'. He was but dimly conscious of his own and would have had no opinion as to whether he had been provoked or jilted. I had no wish to exasperate him, but when at the end of three days more we were still without news of our late companions I remarked that it was very simple; it was plain they were just hiding from us; they thought us dangerous; they wished to avoid entanglements. They had found us too attentive and wished not to raise false hopes. He appeared to accept this explanation and even had the air (so at least I judged from his asking me no questions) of thinking that the matter might be delicate for myself. The poor youth was altogether much mystified, and I smiled at the image in his mind of Mrs Pallant fleeing from his uncle's importunities.

We decided to leave Homburg, but if we did not pursue her it was not simply that we were ignorant of where she was. I could have found that out with a little trouble, but I was deterred by the reflection that this would be her own reasoning. She was dishonest and her departure was a provocation – I am afraid that it was in that stupid conviction that I made out a little independent itinerary with Archie. I even said to myself that we should learn where they were quite soon enough and that our patience – even my young man's – would be longer than theirs. Therefore I uttered a small private cry of triumph when three weeks later (we happened to be at Interlaken) he told me that he had received a note from Miss Pallant. His

manner of telling me was to inquire whether there were any
particular reasons why we should longer delay our projected
visit to the Italian lakes; was not the fear of the hot weather,
which was moreover in summer our native temperature, at an
end, as it was already the middle of September? I answered that
we would start on the morrow if he liked, and then, pleased
apparently that I was so easy to deal with, he revealed his little
secret. He showed me the letter, which was a graceful, natural
document – it covered with a few flowing strokes but a single
page of notepaper – not at all compromising to the young lady.
If however it was almost the apology I had looked for (save that
that should have come from the mother), it was not ostensibly
in the least an invitation. It mentioned casually (the mention
was mainly in the date) that they were on the Lago Maggiore, at
Baveno; but it consisted mainly of the expression of a regret
that they had to leave us at Homburg without giving notice.
Linda did not say under what necessity they had found themselves; she only hoped we had not judged them too harshly and
would accept 'these few hasty words' as a substitute for the
omitted good-bye. She also hoped we were passing our time in
an interesting manner and having the same lovely weather that
prevailed south of the Alps; and she remained very sincerely,
with the kindest remembrances to me.

The note contained no message from her mother and it was
open to me to suppose, as I should judge, either that Mrs
Pallant had not known she was writing or that they wished to
make us think she had not known. The letter might pass as a
common civility of the girl's to a person with whom she had
been on very familiar terms. It was however as something more
than this that my nephew took it; at least so I was warranted in
inferring from the very distinct nature of his determination to
go to Baveno. I saw it was useless to drag him another way; he
had money in his own pocket and was quite capable of giving
me the slip. Yet – such are the sweet incongruities of youth –
when I asked him if he had been thinking of Linda Pallant ever
since they left us in the lurch he replied, 'Oh dear no; why
should I?' This fib was accompanied by an exorbitant blush.
Since he must obey the young lady's call I must also go and see

where it would take him, and one splendid morning we started over the Simplon in a post-chaise.

I represented to him successfully that it would be in much better taste for us to alight at Stresa, which as every one knows is a resort of tourists, also on the shore of the major lake, at about a mile's distance from Baveno. If we stayed at the latter place we should have to inhabit the same hotel as our friends, and this would be indiscreet, considering our peculiar relations with them. Nothing would be easier than to go and come between the two points, especially by the water, which would give Archie a chance for unlimited paddling. His face lighted up at the vision of a pair of oars; he pretended to take my plea for discretion very seriously and I could see that he immediately began to calculate opportunities for being afloat with Linda. Our post-chaise (I had insisted on easy stages and we were three days on the way) deposited us at Stresa toward the middle of the afternoon, and it was within an amazingly short time that I found myself in a small boat with my nephew, who pulled us over to Baveno with vigorous strokes. I remember the sweetness of the whole impression (I had had it before, but to my companion it was new and he thought it as pretty as the opera); the enchanting beauty of the place and hour, the stillness of the air and water, with the romantic, fantastic Borromean Islands in the midst of them. We disembarked at the steps at the garden-foot of the hotel, and somehow it seemed a perfectly natural part of the lovely situation that I should immediately become conscious Mrs Pallant and her daughter were sitting there – on the terrace – quietly watching us. They had all the air of expecting us and I think we looked for it in them. I had not even asked Archie if he had answered Linda's note; that was between themselves and in the way of supervision I had done enough in coming with him.

There is no doubt there was something very odd in our meeting with our friends – at least as between Louisa and me. I was too much taken up with that part of it to notice very much what was the manner of the encounter of the young people. I have sufficiently indicated that I could not get it out of my head that Mrs Pallant was 'up to' something, and I am afraid she saw in my face that this suspicion had been the motive of my journey. I had come there to find her out. The knowledge of my purpose could not help her to make me very welcome, and that is why I say we met in strange conditions. However, on this occasion we observed all forms and the admirable scene gave us plenty to talk about. I made no reference before Linda to the retreat from Homburg. She looked even prettier than she had done on the eve of that manoeuvre and gave no sign of an awkward consciousness. She struck me so, afresh, as a charming, clever girl that I was puzzled afresh to know why we should get – or should have got – into a tangle about her. People had to want to complicate a situation to do it on so simple a pretext as that Linda was admirable. So she was, and why should not the consequences be equally so? One of them, on the spot, was that at the end of a very short time Archie proposed to her to take a turn with him in his boat, which awaited us at the foot of the steps. She looked at her mother with a smiling 'May I, mamma?' and Mrs Pallant answered, 'Certainly, darling, if you are not afraid.' At this – I scarcely knew why – I burst out laughing; it seemed so droll to me somehow that timidity should be imputed to this competent young lady. She gave me a quick, slightly sharp look as she turned away with my nephew; it appeared to challenge me a little – to say, 'Pray what is the matter with *you*?' It was the first expression of the kind I had ever seen in her face. Mrs Pallant's eyes, on the other hand, were not turned to mine; after we had been left there together she sat silent, not heeding me, looking at the lake and mountains – at the snowy crests which wore the flush of evening. She seemed not even to watch our young companions as they got into their boat and pushed off. For some minutes I respected her reverie; I walked slowly up and down the terrace and lighted a cigar, as she had always permitted me to do at Homburg. I noticed that she had an expression of weariness which I had never seen before; her delicate, agreeable face was pale; I made out that there were new lines of fatigue, almost of age, in it. At last I stopped in front of her and asked her, since she looked so sad, if she had any bad news.

'The only bad news was when I learned – through your nephew's note to Linda – that you were coming to us.'

'Ah, then he wrote?' I exclaimed.

'Certainly he wrote.'

'You take it all harder than I do,' I remarked, sitting down beside her. And then I added, smiling, 'Have you written to his mother?'

She slowly turned her face to me and rested her eyes on mine. 'Take care, take care, or you'll insult me,' she said, with an air of patience before the inevitable.

'Never, never! Unless you think I do so if I ask you if you knew when Linda wrote.'

She hesitated a moment. 'Yes; she showed me her letter. She wouldn't have done anything else. I let it go because I didn't know what it was best to do. I am afraid to oppose her, to her face.'

'Afraid, my dear friend, with that girl?'

'That girl? Much you know about her! It didn't follow that you would come – I didn't think it need follow.'

'I am like you,' I said – 'I am afraid of my nephew. I don't venture to oppose him to his face. The only thing I could do under the circumstances was to come with him.'

'I see; I'm glad you have done it,' said Mrs Pallant, thoughtfully.

'Oh, I was conscientious about that! But I have no authority; I can't order him nor forbid him – I can use no force. Look at the way he is pulling that boat and see if you can fancy me.'

'You could tell him she's a bad, hard girl, who would poison any good man's life!' my companion suddenly broke out, with a kind of passion.

'Dear Mrs Pallant, what do you mean?' I murmured, staring.

She bent her face into her hands, covering it over with them, and remained so for a minute; then she went on, in a different manner, as if she had not heard my question: 'I hoped you were too disgusted with us, after the way we left you planted.'

'It was disconcerting, assuredly, and it might have served if Linda hadn't written. That patched it up,' I said, laughing. But my laughter was hollow, for I had been exceedingly impressed with her little explosion of a moment before. 'Do you really mean she is bad?' I added.

Mrs Pallant made no immediate answer to this; she only said that it did not matter after all whether the crisis should come a few weeks sooner or a few weeks later, since it was destined to come at the first opening. Linda had marked my young man – and when Linda had marked a thing!

'Bless my soul – how very grim! Do you mean she's in love with him?' I demanded, incredulous.

'It's enough if she makes him think she is – though even that isn't essential.'

'If she makes him think so? Dearest lady, what do you mean? I have observed her, I have watched her, and after all what has she done? She has been nice to him, but it would have been much more marked if she hadn't. She has really shown him nothing but the common friendliness of a bright, good-natured girl. Her note was nothing; he showed it to me.'

'I don't think you have heard every word that she has said to him,' Mrs Pallant rejoined, with a persistence that struck me as unnatural.

'No more have you, I take it!' I exclaimed. She evidently meant more than she said, and this impression chilled me, made me really uncomfortable.

'No, but I know my own daughter. She's a very rare young woman.'

'You have a singular tone about her,' I responded – 'such a tone as I think I have never heard on a mother's lips. I have observed it before, but never so accentuated.'

At this Mrs Pallant got up; she stood there an instant, looking down at me. 'You make my reparation – my expiation – difficult!' And leaving me rather startled, she began to move along the terrace.

I overtook her presently and repeated her words. 'Your reparation – your expiation? What on earth do you mean by that?'

'You know perfectly what I mean – it is too magnanimous of you to pretend you don't.'

'Well, at any rate I don't see what good it does me or what it makes up to me for that you should abuse your daughter.'

'Oh, I don't care; I shall save him!' she exclaimed, as we went, with a kind of perverse cheerfulness. At the same moment two ladies, apparently English, came toward us (scattered groups had been sitting there and the inmates of the hotel were moving to and fro), and I observed the immediate charming transition (it seemed to me to show such years of social practice), by which, as they greeted us, she exchanged her excited, almost fevered expression for an air of recognition and pleasure. They stopped to speak to her and she asked with eagerness whether their mother were better. I strolled on and she presently rejoined me; after which she said impatiently, 'Come away from this – come down into the garden.' We descended into the garden, strolled through it and paused on the border of the lake.

V

THE charm of the evening had deepened, the stillness was like a solemn expression on a beautiful face and the whole air of the place divine. In the fading light my nephew's boat was too far out to be perceived. I looked for it a little and then, as I gave it up, I remarked that from such an excursion as that, on such a lake, at such an hour, a young man and a young woman of ordinary sensibility could only come back doubly pledged to each other. To this observation Mrs Pallant's answer was, superficially at least, irrelevant; she said after a pause:

'With you, my dear sir, one has certainly to dot one's "i's". Haven't you discovered, and didn't I tell you at Homburg, that we are miserably poor?'

'Isn't "miserably" rather too much, when you are living at an expensive hotel?'

'They take us *en pension*, for ever so little a day. I have been knocking about Europe long enough to learn there are certain ways of doing things. Besides, don't speak of hotels; we have spent half our life in them and Linda told me only last night that she hoped never to put her foot into one again. She thinks that when she comes to such a place as this it's the least that she should find a villa of her own.'

'Well, her companion there is perfectly competent to give her one. Don't think I have the least desire to push them into each other's arms; I only ask to wash my hands of them. But I should like to know why you want, as you said just now, to save him. When you speak as if your daughter were a monster I take it that you are not serious.'

She was facing me there in the twilight, and to let me know that she was more serious perhaps than she had ever been in her life she had only to look at me awhile without protestation. 'It's Linda's standard. God knows I myself could get on! She is ambitious, luxurious, determined to have what she wants, more than any one I have ever seen. Of course it's open to you to tell me that it's my fault, that I was so before her and have made her so. But does that make me like it any better?'

'Dear Mrs Pallant, you are most extraordinary,' I stammered, infinitely surprised and not a little pained.

'Oh yes, you have made up your mind about me; you see me in a certain way and you don't like the trouble of changing. *Votre siège est fait.* But you will have to change – if you have any generosity!' Her eyes shone in the summer dusk and she looked remarkably handsome.

'Is this a part of the reparation, of the expiation?' I inquired. 'I don't see what you ever did to Archie.'

'It's enough that he belongs to you. But it isn't for you that I do it; it's for myself,' she went on.

'Doubtless you have your own reasons, which I can't penetrate. But can't you sacrifice something else? – must you sacrifice your child?'

'She's my punishment and she's my stigma!' cried Louisa Pallant, with veritable exaltation.

'It seems to me rather that you are hers.'

'Hers? What does *she* know of such things? – what can she ever feel? She's cased in steel; she has a heart of marble. It's true – it's true. She appals me!'

I laid my hand upon the poor lady's; I uttered, with the intention of checking and soothing her, the first incoherent words that came into my head and I drew her toward a bench which I perceived a few yards away. She dropped upon it; I placed myself near her and besought her to consider well what she was saying. She owed me nothing and I wished no one injured, no one denounced or exposed for my sake.

'For your sake? Oh, I am not thinking of you!' she answered; and indeed the next moment I thought my words rather fatuous. 'It's a satisfaction to my own conscience – for I have one, little as you think I have a right to speak of it. I have been punished by my sin itself. I have been hideously worldly, I have thought only of that, and I have taught her to be so – to do the same. That's the only instruction I have ever given her, and she has learned the lesson so well that now that I see it printed there in all her nature I am horrified at my work. For years we have lived that way; we have thought of nothing else. She has learned it so well that she has gone far beyond me. I say I am horrified, because she is horrible.'

'My poor extravagant friend,' I pleaded, 'isn't it still more so to hear a mother say such things?'

'Why so, if they are abominably true? Besides, I don't care what I say, if I save him.'

'Do you expect me to repeat to him—?'

'Not in the least,' she broke in; 'I will do it myself.' At this I uttered some strong inarticulate protest, and she went on with a sort of simplicity: 'I was very glad at first, but it would have been better if we hadn't met.'

'I don't agree to that, for you interest me immensely.'

'I don't care for that – if I can interest him.'

'You must remember then that your charges are strangely vague, considering how violent they are. Never had a girl a more innocent appearance. You know how I have admired it.'

'You know nothing about her. *I* do, for she is the work of my hand!' Mrs Pallant declared, with a bitter laugh. 'I have watched her for years and little by little, for the last two or three, it has come over me. There is not a tender spot in her whole composition. To arrive at a brilliant social position, if it were necessary, she would see me drown in this lake without lifting a finger, she would stand there and see it – she would push me in – and never feel a pang. That's my young lady! To climb up to the top and be splendid and envied there – to do it at any cost or by any meanness and cruelty, is the only thing she has a heart for. She would lie for it, she would steal for it, she would kill for it!' My companion brought out these words with a tremendous low distinctness and an air of sincerity that was really solemn. I watched her pale face and glowing eyes; she held me in a kind of stupor, but her strange, almost vindictive earnestness imposed itself. I found myself believing her, pitying her more than I pitied the girl. It was as if she had been bottled up for longer than she could bear, suffering more and more from the ferment of her knowledge. It relieved her to warn and denounce and expose. 'God has let me see it in time, in his mercy,' she continued; 'but his ways are strange, that he has let me see it in my daughter. It is myself that he has let me see, myself as I was for years. But she's worse – she is, I assure you; she's worse than I ever intended or dreamed.' Her hands were clasped tightly together in her lap; her low voice quavered and her breath came short; she looked up at the faint stars with religious perversity.

'Have you ever spoken to her as you speak to me?' I asked. 'Have you ever admonished her, reproached her?'

'Reproached her? How can I? when all she would have to say would be, "You – *you* – you base one – who made me!"'

'Then why do you want to play her a trick?'

'I'm not bound to tell you and you wouldn't understand if I did. I should play that boy a far worse trick if I were to hold my tongue.'

'If he loves her he won't believe a word you say.'

'Very possibly, but I shall have done my duty.'

'And shall you say to him simply what you have said to me?'

'Never mind what I shall say to him. It will be something that will perhaps affect him, if I lose no time.'

'If you are so bent on gaining time,' I said, 'why did you let her go out in the boat with him?'

'Let her? how could I prevent it?'

'But she asked your permission.'

'That's a part of all the comedy!'

We were silent a moment, after which I resumed: 'Then she doesn't know you hate her?'

'I don't know what she knows. She has depths and depths, and all of them bad. Besides, I don't hate her in the least; I pity her simply, for what I have made of her. But I pity still more the man who may find himself married to her.'

'There's not much danger of there being any such person, at the rate you go on.'

'Oh, perfectly; she'll marry some one. She'll marry a title as well as a fortune.'

'It's a pity my nephew hasn't a title,' I murmured, smiling.

She hesitated a moment. 'I see you think I want that and that I am acting a part. God forgive you! Your suspicion is perfectly natural: how can any one tell, with people like us?'

The way she uttered these last words brought tears to my eyes. I laid my hand on her arm, holding her awhile, and we looked at each other through the dusk. 'You couldn't do more if he were my son,' I said at last.

'Oh, if he had been your son he would have kept out of it! I like him for himself; he's simple and honest – he needs affection.'

'He would have an admirable, a devoted, mother-in-law,' I went on.

Mrs Pallant gave a little impatient sigh and replied that she was not joking. We sat there some time longer, while I thought over what she had said to me and she apparently did the same. I confess that even close at her side, with the echo of her passionate, broken voice still in the air, some queer ideas came into my head. Was the comedy on *her* side and not on the girl's, and was she posturing as a magnanimous woman at poor Linda's expense? Was she determined, in spite of the young lady's preference, to keep her daughter for a grander personage than a young American whose dollars were not numerous enough (numerous as they were) to make up for his want of high relationships, and had she brought forth these cruel imputations to help her to her end? If she was prepared really to denounce the girl to Archie she would have to go very far to overcome the suspicion he would be sure to feel at so unnatural a proceeding. Was she prepared to go far enough? The answer to these doubts was simply the way I had been touched – it came back to me the next moment – when she used the words, 'people like us'. The effect of them was poignant. She made herself humble indeed and I felt in a manner ashamed, on my own side, that I saw her in the dust. She said to me at last that I must wait no longer; I must go away before the young people came back. They were staying very long, too long; all the more reason that she should deal with Archie that evening. I must drive back to Stresa or, if I liked, I could go on foot: it was not far – for a man. She disposed of me freely, she was so full of her purpose; and after we had quitted the garden and returned to the terrace of the hotel she seemed almost to push me to leave her – I felt her fine hands, quivering a little, on my shoulders. I was ready to do what she liked: she affected me painfully and I wanted to get away from her. Before I went I asked her why Linda should regard my young man as such a *parti*; it did not square after all with her account of the girl's fierce ambitions. By that picture it would seem that a reigning prince was the least she would look at.

'Oh, she has reflected well; she has regarded the question in every light,' said Mrs Pallant. 'If she has made up her mind it is because she sees what she can do.'

'Do you mean that she has talked it over with you?'

'Lord! for what do you take us? We don't talk over things to-day. We know each other's point of view and we only have to act. We can take reasons, which are awkward things, for granted.'

'But in this case she certainly doesn't know your point of view, poor thing.'

'No – that's because I haven't played fair. Of course she couldn't expect I would cheat. There ought to be honour among thieves. But it was open to her to do the same.'

'How do you mean, to do the same?'

'She might have fallen in love with a poor man; then I should have been done.'

'A rich one is better; he can do more,' I replied, with conviction.

'So you would have reason to know if you had led the life that we have! Never to have had really enough – I mean to do just the few simple things we have wanted; never to have had the sinews of war, I suppose you would call them – the funds for a campaign; to have felt every day and every hour the hard, monotonous pinch and found the question of dollars and cents (and so horridly few of them) mixed up with every experience, with every impulse – that *does* make one mercenary, it does make money seem a good beyond all others, and it's quite natural it should. That is why Linda is of the opinion that a fortune is always a fortune. She knows all about that of your nephew, how it's invested, how it may be expected to increase, exactly on what sort of footing it would enable her to live. She has decided that it's enough, and enough is as good as a feast. She thinks she could lead him by the nose, and I daresay she could. She will make him live here: she has not the least intention of settling in America. I think she has views upon London, because in England he can hunt and shoot, and that will make him let her alone.'

'It strikes me that he would like that very much,' I interposed; 'that's not at all a bad programme, even from Archie's point of view.'

'It's no use of talking about princes,' Mrs Pallant pursued, as if she had not heard me. 'Yes, they are most of them more in want of money even than we are. Therefore a title is out of the question, and we recognised that at an early stage. Your nephew is exactly the sort of young man we had constructed in advance – he was made on purpose. Dear Linda was her mother's own daughter when she recognised him on the spot! It's enough of a title to-day to be an American – with the way they have come up. It does as well as anything and it's a great simplification. If you don't believe me go to London and see.'

She had come with me out to the road. I had said I would walk back to Stresa and we stood there in the complete evening. As I took her hand, bidding her good-night, I exclaimed, 'Poor Linda – poor Linda!'

'Oh, she'll live to do better,' said Mrs Pallant.

'How can she do better, since you have described this as perfection?'

She hesitated a moment. 'I mean better for Mr Pringle.'

I still had her hand – I remained looking at her. 'How came it that you could throw me over – such a woman as you?'

'Ah, my friend, if I hadn't thrown you over I couldn't do this for you.' And disengaging herself she turned away quickly and went back to the hotel.

VI

I DON'T know whether she blushed as she made this avowal, which was a retraction of a former denial and the real truth, as I permitted myself to believe; but I did, while I took my way to Stresa – it is a walk of half an hour – in the darkness. The new and singular character in which she had appeared to me produced an effect of excitement which would have made it impossible for me to sit still in a carriage. This same agitation kept me up late after I had reached my hotel; as I knew that I should not sleep it was useless to go to bed. Long, however, as I deferred this ceremony Archie had not turned up when the lights in the hotel began to be put out. I felt even slightly nervous about him and wondered whether he had had an accident on the lake. I reflected that in this case – if he had not brought his companion back to Baveno – Mrs Pallant would already have sent after me. It was foolish moreover to suppose that anything could have happened to him after putting off from Baveno by water to rejoin me, for the evening was absolutely windless and more than sufficiently clear and the lake as calm as glass. Besides I had unlimited confidence in his power to take care of himself in circumstances much more difficult. I went to my room at last; his own was at some distance, the people of the hotel not having been able – it was the height of the autumn season – to place us together. Before I went to bed I had occasion to ring for a servant, and then I learned by a chance inquiry that my nephew had returned an hour before and had gone straight to his own apartment. I had not supposed he could come in without my seeing him – I was wandering about the saloons and terraces –

and it had not occurred to me to knock at his door. I had half a mind to do so then – I had such a curiosity as to how I should find him; but I checked myself, for evidently he had not wished to see me. This did not diminish my curiosity, and I slept even less than I had expected. His dodging me that way (for if he had not perceived me downstairs he might have looked for me in my room) was a sign that Mrs Pallant's interview with him had really come off. What had she said to him? What strong measures had she taken? The impression of almost morbid eagerness of purpose that she had given me suggested possibilities that I was afraid to think of. She had spoken of these things as we parted there as something she would do for me; but I had made the mental comment, as I walked away from her, that she had not done it yet. It would not really be done till Archie had backed out. Perhaps it was done by this time; his avoiding me seemed almost a proof. That was what I thought of most of the night. I spent a considerable part of it at my window, looking out at the sleeping mountains. *Had* he backed out? – was he making up his mind to back out? There was a strange contradiction in it; there were in fact more contradictions than ever. I believed what Mrs Pallant had told me about Linda, and yet that other idea made me ashamed of my nephew. I was sorry for the girl; I regretted her loss of a great chance, if loss it was to be; and yet I hoped that the manner in which her mother had betrayed her (there was no other word) to her lover had been thoroughgoing. It would need very radical measures on Mrs Pallant's part to excuse Archie. For him too I was sorry, if she had made an impression on him – the impression she desired. Once or twice I was on the point of going in to condole with him, in my dressing-gown; I was sure he too had jumped up from his bed and was looking out of his window at the everlasting hills.

I am bound to say that he showed few symptoms when we met in the morning and breakfasted together. Youth is strange; it has resources that experience seems only to take away from us. One of these is simply (in the given case) to do nothing – to say nothing. As we grow older and cleverer we think that is too simple, too crude; we dissimulate more elaborately, but with an

effect much less baffling. My young man looked not in the least
as if he had lain awake or had something on his mind; and when
I asked him what he had done after my premature departure
(I explained this by saying I had been tired of waiting for him –
I was weary with my journey and wanted to go to bed), he
replied: 'Oh, nothing in particular. I hung about the place; I like
it better than this. We had an awfully jolly time on the water.
I wasn't in the least tired.' I did not worry him with questions; it
seemed to me indelicate to try to probe his secret. The only
indication he gave was on my saying after breakfast that I should
go over again to see our friends and my appearing to take for
granted that he would be glad to accompany me. Then he
remarked that he would stop at Stresa – he had paid them
such a tremendous visit; also he had some letters to write.
There was a freshness in his scruples about the length of his
visits, and I knew something about his correspondence, which
consisted entirely of twenty pages every week from his mother.
But he satisfied my curiosity so little that it was really this
sentiment that carried me back to Baveno. This time I ordered
a conveyance, and as I got into it he stood watching me in the
porch of the hotel with his hands in his pockets. Then it was for
the first time that I saw in this young man's face the expression
of a person slightly dazed, slightly foolish even, to whom something disagreeable has happened. Our eyes met as I observed
him, and I was on the point of saying, 'You had really better
come with me,' when he turned away. He went into the house
as if he wished to escape from my call. I said to myself that Mrs
Pallant had warned him off but that it would not take much to
bring him back.

The servant to whom I spoke at Baveno told me that my
friends were in a certain summer-house in the garden, to which
he led the way. The place had an empty air; most of the inmates
of the hotel were dispersed on the lake, on the hills, in picnics,
excursions, visits to the Borromean Islands. My guide was so
far right as that Linda was in the summer-house, but she was
there alone. On finding this to be the case I stopped short,
rather awkwardly, for I had a sudden sense of being an
unmasked hypocrite – a conspirator against her security and

honour. But there was no awkwardness about Linda Pallant;
she looked up with a little cry of pleasure from the book she was
reading and held out her hand with the most engaging frankness. I felt as if I had no right to touch her hand and I pretended
not to see it. But this gave no chill to her pretty manner; she
moved a roll of tapestry off the bench, so that I might sit down,
and praised the place as a delightful shady corner. She had
never been fresher, fairer, kinder; she made her mother's damning talk about her seem a hideous dream. She told me Mrs
Pallant was coming to join her; she had remained indoors to
write a letter. One could not write out there, though it was so
nice in other respects: the table was too rickety. They too then
had pretexts between them in the way of letters: I judged this to
be a token that the situation was tense. It was the only one
however that Linda gave: like Archie she was young enough to
carry it off. She had been used to seeing us always together and
she made no comment on my having come over without him.
I waited in vain for her to say something about it; this would
only be natural – it was almost unfriendly to omit it. At last
I observed that my nephew was very unsociable that morning;
I had expected him to join me but he had left me to come alone.

'I am very glad,' she answered. 'You can tell him that if you
like.'

'If I tell him that he will come immediately.'

'Then don't tell him; I don't want him to come. He stayed
too long last night,' Linda went on, 'and kept me out on the
water till the most dreadful hours. That isn't done here, you
know, and every one was shocked when we came back – or
rather when we didn't come back. I begged him to bring me in,
but he wouldn't. When we did return – I almost had to take the
oars myself – I felt as if every one had been sitting up to time us,
to stare at us. It was very embarrassing.'

These words made an impression upon me; and as I have
treated the reader to most of the reflections – some of them
perhaps rather morbid – in which I indulged on the subject of
this young lady and her mother I may as well complete the
record and let him know that I now wondered whether Linda –
candid and accomplished maiden – had conceived the fine idea

of strengthening her hold of Archie by attempting to prove that he had 'compromised' her. 'Ah, no doubt that was the reason he had a bad conscience last evening!' I exclaimed. 'When he came back to Stresa he sneaked off to his room; he wouldn't look me in the face.'

'Mamma was so vexed that she took him apart and gave him a scolding,' the girl went on. 'And to punish *me* she sent me straight to bed. She has very old-fashioned ideas – haven't you, mamma?' she added, looking over my head at Mrs Pallant, who had just come in behind me.

I forget what answer Mrs Pallant made to Linda's appeal; she stood there with two letters, sealed and addressed, in her hand. She greeted me gaily and then asked her daughter if she had any postage-stamps. Linda consulted a somewhat shabby pocket-book and confessed that she was destitute; whereupon her mother gave her the letters, with the request that she would go into the hotel, buy the proper stamps at the office, carefully affix them and put the letters into the box. She was to pay for the stamps, not have them put on the bill – a preference for which Mrs Pallant gave her reasons. I had bought some at Stresa that morning and I was on the point of offering them, when, apparently having guessed my intention, the older lady silenced me with a look. Linda told her she had no money and she fumbled in her pocket for a franc. When she had found it and the girl had taken it Linda kissed her before going off with the letters.

'Darling mother, you haven't any too many of them, have you?' she murmured; and she gave me, sidelong, as she left us, the prettiest half comical, half pitiful smile.

'She's amazing – she's amazing,' said Mrs Pallant, as we looked at each other.

'Does she know what you have done?'

'She knows I have done something and she is making up her mind what it is – or she will in the course of the next twenty-four hours, if your nephew doesn't come back. I think I can promise you he won't.'

'And won't she ask you?'

'Never!'

'Shall you not tell her? Can you sit down together in this summer-house, this divine day, with such a dreadful thing as that between you?'

'Don't you remember what I told you about our relations – that everything was implied between us and nothing expressed? The ideas we have had in common – our perpetual worldliness, our always looking out for chances – are not the sort of thing that can be uttered gracefully between persons who like to keep up forms, as we both do: so that if we understood each other it was enough. We shall understand each other now, as we have always done, and nothing will be changed, because there has always been something between us that couldn't be talked about.'

'Certainly, she is amazing – she is amazing,' I repeated; 'but so are you.' And then I asked her what she had said to my boy.

She seemed surprised. 'Hasn't he told you?'

'No, and he never will.'

'I am glad of that,' she said, simply.

'But I am not sure he won't come back. He didn't this morning, but he had already half a mind to.'

'That's your imagination,' said Mrs Pallant, decisively. 'If you knew what I told him you would be sure.'

'And you won't let me know?'

'Never, my near friend.'

'And did he believe you?'

'Time will show; but I think so.'

'And how did you make it plausible to him that you should take so unnatural a course?'

For a moment she said nothing, only looking at me. Then at last – 'I told him the truth.'

'The truth?' I repeated.

'Take him away – take him away!' she broke out. 'That's why I got rid of Linda, to tell you that you musn't stay – you must leave Stresa to-morrow. This time it's you that must do it; I can't fly from you again – it costs too much!' And she smiled strangely.

'Don't be afraid; don't be afraid. We will leave to-morrow; I want to go myself.' I took her hand in farewell, and while

I held it I said, 'The way you put it, about Linda, was very bad?'

'It was horrible.'

I turned away – I felt indeed that I wanted to leave the neighbourhood. She kept me from going to the hotel, as I might meet Linda coming back, which I was far from wishing to do, and showed me another way into the road. Then she turned round to meet her daughter and spend the rest of the morning in the summer-house with her, looking at the bright blue lake and the snowy crests of the Alps. When I reached Stresa again I found that Archie had gone off to Milan (to see the cathedral, the servant said), leaving a message for me to the effect that, as he should not be back for a day or two (though there were numerous trains), he had taken a small portmanteau with him. The next day I got a telegram from him notifying me that he had determined to go on to Venice and requesting me to forward the rest of his luggage. 'Please don't come after me,' this missive added; 'I want to be alone; I shall do no harm.' That sounded pathetic to me, in the light of what I knew, and I was glad to leave the poor boy to his own devices. He proceeded to Venice and I recrossed the Alps. For several weeks after this I expected to discover that he had rejoined Mrs Pallant; but when we met in Paris, in November, I saw that he had nothing to hide from me, except indeed the secret of what that lady had told him. This he concealed from me then and has concealed ever since. He returned to America before Christmas and then I felt that the crisis had passed. I have never seen my old friend since. About a year after the time to which my story refers, Linda married, in London, a young Englishman, the possessor of a large fortune, a fortune acquired by his father in some useful industry. Mrs Gimingham's photographs (such is her present name) may be obtained from the principal stationers. I am convinced her mother was sincere. My nephew has not changed his state yet, and now even my sister is beginning, for the first time, to desire it. I related to her as soon as I saw her the substance of the story I have written here, and (such is the inconsequence of women) nothing can exceed her reprobation of Louisa Pallant.

THE ASPERN PAPERS

I

I HAD taken Mrs Prest into my confidence; in truth without her I should have made but little advance, for the fruitful idea in the whole business dropped from her friendly lips. It was she who invented the short cut, who severed the Gordian knot. It is not supposed to be the nature of women to rise as a general thing to the largest and most liberal view – I mean of a practical scheme; but it has struck me that they sometimes throw off a bold conception – such as a man would not have risen to – with singular serenity. 'Simply ask them to take you in on the footing of a lodger' – I don't think that unaided I should have risen to that. I was beating about the bush, trying to be ingenious, wondering by what combination of arts I might become an acquaintance, when she offered this happy suggestion that the way to become an acquaintance was first to become an inmate. Her actual knowledge of the Misses Bordereau was scarcely larger than mine, and indeed I had brought with me from England some definite facts which were new to her. Their name had been mixed up ages before with one of the greatest names of the century, and they lived now in Venice in obscurity, on very small means, unvisited, unapproachable, in a dilapidated old palace on an out-of-the-way canal: this was the substance of my friend's impression of them. She herself had been established in Venice for fifteen years and had done a great deal of good there; but the circle of her benevolence did not include the two shy, mysterious and, as it was somehow supposed, scarcely respectable Americans (they were believed to have lost in their long exile all national quality, besides having had, as their name implied, some French strain in their origin), who asked no favours and desired no attention. In the early years of her residence she had made an attempt to see them, but this had been successful only as regards the little one, as Mrs Prest called the niece; though in reality, as I afterwards learned, she was considerably the bigger of the two. She had heard Miss

Bordereau was ill and had a suspicion that she was in want; and she had gone to the house to offer assistance, so that if there were suffering (and American suffering), she should at least not have it on her conscience. The 'little one' received her in the great cold, tarnished Venetian sala, the central hall of the house, paved with marble and roofed with dim cross-beams, and did not even ask her to sit down. This was not encouraging for me, who wished to sit so fast, and I remarked as much to Mrs Prest. She however replied with profundity, 'Ah, but there's all the difference: I went to confer a favour and you will go to ask one. If they are proud you will be on the right side.' And she offered to show me their house to begin with – to row me thither in her gondola. I let her know that I had already been to look at it half a dozen times; but I accepted her invitation, for it charmed me to hover about the place. I had made my way to it the day after my arrival in Venice (it had been described to me in advance by the friend in England to whom I owed definite information as to their possession of the papers), and I had besieged it with my eyes while I considered my plan of campaign. Jeffrey Aspern had never been in it that I knew of; but some note of his voice seemed to abide there by a roundabout implication, a faint reverberation.

Mrs Prest knew nothing about the papers, but she was interested in my curiosity, as she was always interested in the joys and sorrows of her friends. As we went, however, in her gondola, gliding there under the sociable hood with the bright Venetian picture framed on either side by the movable window, I could see that she was amused by my infatuation, the way my interest in the papers had become a fixed idea. 'One would think you expected to find in them the answer to the riddle of the universe,' she said; and I denied the impeachment only by replying that if I had to choose between that precious solution and a bundle of Jeffrey Aspern's letters I knew indeed which would appear to me the greater boon. She pretended to make light of his genius and I took no pains to defend him. One doesn't defend one's god: one's god is in himself a defence. Besides, to-day, after his long comparative obscuration, he hangs high in the heaven of our literature, for all the world to see; he is a part of the light by which we walk. The most I said was that he was no doubt not a woman's poet: to which she rejoined aptly enough that he had been at least Miss Bordereau's. The strange thing had been for me to discover in England that she was still alive: it was as if I had been told Mrs Siddons was, or Queen Caroline, or the famous Lady Hamilton, for it seemed to me that she belonged to a generation as extinct. 'Why, she must be tremendously old – at least a hundred,' I had said; but on coming to consider dates I saw that it was not strictly necessary that she should have exceeded by very much the common span. None the less she was very far advanced in life and her relations with Jeffrey Aspern had occurred in her early womanhood. 'That is her excuse,' said Mrs Prest, half sententiously and yet also somewhat as if she were ashamed of making a speech so little in the real tone of Venice. As if a woman needed an excuse for having loved the divine poet! He had been not only one of the most brilliant minds of his day (and in those years, when the century was young, there were, as every one knows, many), but one of the most genial men and one of the handsomest.

The niece, according to Mrs Prest, was not so old, and she risked the conjecture that she was only a grand-niece. This was possible; I had nothing but my share in the very limited knowledge of my English fellow-worshipper John Cumnor, who had never seen the couple. The world, as I say, had recognised Jeffrey Aspern, but Cumnor and I had recognised him most. The multitude, to-day, flocked to his temple, but of that temple he and I regarded ourselves as the ministers. We held, justly, as I think, that we had done more for his memory than any one else, and we had done it by opening lights into his life. He had nothing to fear from us because he had nothing to fear from the truth, which alone at such a distance of time we could be interested in establishing. His early death had been the only dark spot in his life, unless the papers in Miss Bordereau's hands should perversely bring out others. There had been an impression about 1825 that he had 'treated her badly', just as there had been an impression that he had 'served', as the London populace says, several other ladies in the same way.

Each of these cases Cumnor and I had been able to investigate, and we had never failed to acquit him conscientiously of shabby behaviour. I judged him perhaps more indulgently than my friend; certainly, at any rate, it appeared to me that no man could have walked straighter in the given circumstances. These were almost always awkward. Half the women of his time, to speak liberally, had flung themselves at his head, and out of this pernicious fashion many complications, some of them grave, had not failed to arise. He was not a woman's poet, as I had said to Mrs Prest, in the modern phase of his reputation; but the situation had been different when the man's own voice was mingled with his song. That voice, by every testimony, was one of the sweetest ever heard. 'Orpheus and the Maenads!' was the exclamation that rose to my lips when I first turned over his correspondence. Almost all the Maenads were unreasonable and many of them insupportable; it struck me in short that he was kinder, more considerate than, in his place (if I could imagine myself in such a place!) I should have been.

It was certainly strange beyond all strangeness, and I shall not take up space with attempting to explain it, that whereas in all these other lines of research we had to deal with phantoms and dust, the mere echoes of echoes, the one living source of information that had lingered on into our time had been unheeded by us. Every one of Aspern's contemporaries had, according to our belief, passed away; we had not been able to look into a single pair of eyes into which his had looked and feel a transmitted contact in any aged hand that his had touched. Most dead of all did poor Miss Bordereau appear, and yet she alone had survived. We exhausted in the course of months our wonder that we had not found her out sooner, and the substance of our explanation was that she had kept so quiet. The poor lady on the whole had had reason for doing so. But it was a revelation to us that it was possible to keep so quiet as that in the latter half of the nineteenth century – the age of newspapers and telegrams and photographs and interviewers. And she had taken no great trouble about it either: she had not hidden herself away in an undiscoverable hole; she had boldly settled down in a city of exhibition. The only secret of her safety that

we could perceive was that Venice contained so many curiosities that were greater than she. And then accident had somehow favoured her, as was shown for example in the fact that
Mrs Prest had never happened to mention her to me, though
I had spent three weeks in Venice – under her nose, as it were –
five years before. Mrs Prest had not mentioned this much to
any one; she appeared almost to have forgotten she was there.
Of course she had not the responsibilities of an editor. It was no
explanation of the old woman's having eluded us to say that she
lived abroad, for our researches had again and again taken us
(not only by correspondence but by personal inquiry) to
France, to Germany, to Italy, in which countries, not counting
his important stay in England, so many of the too few years of
Aspern's career were spent. We were glad to think at least that
in all our publishings (some people consider I believe that we
have overdone them), we had only touched in passing and in
the most discreet manner on Miss Bordereau's connection.
Oddly enough, even if we had had the material (and we often
wondered what had become of it), it would have been the most
difficult episode to handle.

The gondola stopped, the old palace was there; it was a
house of the class which in Venice carries even in extreme
dilapidation the dignified name. 'How charming! It's grey and
pink!' my companion exclaimed; and that is the most comprehensive description of it. It was not particularly old, only two or
three centuries; and it had an air not so much of decay as of
quiet discouragement, as if it had rather missed its career. But
its wide front, with a stone balcony from end to end of the *piano
nobile* or most important floor, was architectural enough,
with the aid of various pilasters and arches; and the stucco
with which in the intervals it had long ago been endued was
rosy in the April afternoon. It overlooked a clean, melancholy,
unfrequented canal, which had a narrow *riva* or convenient
footway on either side. 'I don't know why – there are no brick
gables,' said Mrs Prest, 'but this corner has seemed to me
before more Dutch than Italian, more like Amsterdam than
like Venice. It's perversely clean, for reasons of its own; and
though you can pass on foot scarcely any one ever thinks of

doing so. It has the air of a Protestant Sunday. Perhaps the people are afraid of the Misses Bordereau. I daresay they have the reputation of witches.'

I forget what answer I made to this – I was given up to two other reflections. The first of these was that if the old lady lived in such a big, imposing house she could not be in any sort of misery and therefore would not be tempted by a chance to let a couple of rooms. I expressed this idea to Mrs Prest, who gave me a very logical reply. 'If she didn't live in a big house how could it be a question of her having rooms to spare? If she were not amply lodged herself you would lack ground to approach her. Besides, a big house here, and especially in this *quartier perdu*, proves nothing at all: it is perfectly compatible with a state of penury. Dilapidated old palazzi, if you will go out of the way for them, are to be had for five shillings a year. And as for the people who live in them – no, until you have explored Venice socially as much as I have you can form no idea of their domestic desolation. They live on nothing, for they have nothing to live on.' The other idea that had come into my head was connected with a high blank wall which appeared to confine an expanse of ground on one side of the house. Blank I call it, but it was figured over with the patches that please a painter, repaired breaches, crumblings of plaster, extrusions of brick that had turned pink with time; and a few thin trees, with the poles of certain rickety trellises, were visible over the top. The place was a garden and apparently it belonged to the house. It suddenly occurred to me that if it did belong to the house I had my pretext.

I sat looking out on all this with Mrs Prest (it was covered with the golden glow of Venice) from the shade of our *felze*, and she asked me if I would go in then, while she waited for me, or come back another time. At first I could not decide – it was doubtless very weak of me. I wanted still to think I *might* get a footing, and I was afraid to meet failure, for it would leave me, as I remarked to my companion, without another arrow for my bow. 'Why not another?' she inquired, as I sat there hesitating and thinking it over; and she wished to know why even now and before taking the trouble of becoming an inmate (which might be wretchedly uncomfortable after all, even if it succeeded), I had not the resource of simply offering them a sum of money down. In that way I might obtain the documents without bad nights.

'Dearest lady,' I exclaimed, 'excuse the impatience of my tone when I suggest that you must have forgotten the very fact (surely I communicated it to you) which pushed me to throw myself upon your ingenuity. The old woman won't have the documents spoken of; they are personal, delicate, intimate, and she hasn't modern notions, God bless her! If I should sound that note first I should certainly spoil the game. I can arrive at the papers only by putting her off her guard, and I can put her off her guard only by ingratiating diplomatic practices. Hypocrisy, duplicity are my only chance. I am sorry for it, but for Jeffrey Aspern's sake I would do worse still. First I must take tea with her; then tackle the main job.' And I told over what had happened to John Cumnor when he wrote to her. No notice whatever had been taken of his first letter, and the second had been answered very sharply, in six lines, by the niece. 'Miss Bordereau requested her to say that she could not imagine what he meant by troubling them. They had none of Mr Aspern's papers, and if they had should never think of showing them to any one on any account whatever. She didn't know what he was talking about and begged he would let her alone.' I certainly did not want to be met that way.

'Well,' said Mrs Prest, after a moment, provokingly, 'perhaps after all they haven't any of his things. If they deny it flat how are you sure?'

'John Cumnor is sure, and it would take me long to tell you how his conviction, or his very strong presumption – strong enough to stand against the old lady's not unnatural fib – has built itself up. Besides, he makes much of the internal evidence of the niece's letter.'

'The internal evidence?'

'Her calling him "Mr Aspern".'

'I don't see what that proves.'

'It proves familiarity, and familiarity implies the possession of mementos, of relics. I can't tell you how that "Mr" touches me – how it bridges over the gulf of time and brings our hero near to me – nor what an edge it gives to my desire to see Juliana. You don't say "Mr" Shakespeare.'

'Would I, any more, if I had a box full of his letters?'

'Yes, if he had been your lover and some one wanted them!' And I added that John Cumnor was so convinced, and so all the more convinced by Miss Bordereau's tone, that he would have come himself to Venice on the business were it not that for him there was the obstacle that it would be difficult to disprove his identity with the person who had written to them, which the old ladies would be sure to suspect in spite of dissimulation and a change of name. If they were to ask him point-blank if he were not their correspondent it would be too awkward for him to lie; whereas I was fortunately not tied in that way. I was a fresh hand and could say no without lying.

'But you will have to change your name,' said Mrs Prest. 'Juliana lives out of the world as much as it is possible to live, but none the less she has probably heard of Mr Aspern's editors; she perhaps possesses what you have published.'

'I have thought of that,' I returned; and I drew out of my pocket-book a visiting-card, neatly engraved with a name that was not my own.

'You are very extravagant; you might have written it,' said my companion.

'This looks more genuine.'

'Certainly, you are prepared to go far! But it will be awkward about your letters; they won't come to you in that mask.'

'My banker will take them in and I will go every day to fetch them. It will give me a little walk.'

'Shall you only depend upon that?' asked Mrs Prest. 'Aren't you coming to see me?'

'Oh, you will have left Venice, for the hot months, long before there are any results. I am prepared to roast all summer – as well as hereafter, perhaps you'll say! Meanwhile, John Cumnor will bombard me with letters addressed, in my feigned name, to the care of the *padrona*.'

'She will recognise his hand,' my companion suggested.

'On the envelope he can disguise it.'

'Well, you're a precious pair! Doesn't it occur to you that even if you are able to say you are not Mr Cumnor in person they may still suspect you of being his emissary?'

'Certainly, and I see only one way to parry that.'

'And what may that be?'

I hesitated a moment. 'To make love to the niece.'

'Ah,' cried Mrs Prest, 'wait till you see her!'

II

'I MUST work the garden – I must work the garden,' I said to myself, five minutes later, as I waited, upstairs, in the long, dusky sala, where the bare scagliola floor gleamed vaguely in a chink of the closed shutters. The place was impressive but it looked cold and cautious. Mrs Prest had floated away, giving me a rendezvous at the end of half an hour by some neighbouring watersteps; and I had been let into the house, after pulling the rusty bell-wire, by a little red-headed, white-faced maidservant, who was very young and not ugly and wore clicking pattens and a shawl in the fashion of a hood. She had not contented herself with opening the door from above by the usual arrangement of a creaking pulley, though she had looked down at me first from an upper window, dropping the inevitable challenge which in Italy precedes the hospitable act. As a general thing I was irritated by this survival of mediaeval manners, though as I liked the old I suppose I ought to have liked it; but I was so determined to be genial that I took my false card out of my pocket and held it up to her, smiling as if it were a magic token. It had the effect of one indeed, for it brought her, as I say, all the way down. I begged her to hand it to her mistress, having first written on it in Italian the words, 'Could you very kindly see a gentleman, an American, for a moment?' The little maid was not hostile, and I reflected that even that was perhaps something gained. She coloured, she smiled and looked both frightened and pleased. I could see that my arrival was a great affair, that visits were rare in that house, and that she was a person who would have liked a sociable place. When she pushed forward the heavy door behind me I felt that I had a foot in the citadel. She pattered across the damp, stony lower hall and I followed her up the high staircase – stonier still, as it seemed – without an invitation. I think she had meant I should wait for her below, but such was not my idea, and I took up my station in the sala. She flitted, at the far end of it, into impenetrable regions, and I looked at the place with my heart beating as I had known it to do in the dentist's parlour. It was gloomy and stately, but it owed its character almost entirely to its noble shape and to the fine architectural doors – as high as the doors of houses – which, leading into the various rooms, repeated themselves on either side at intervals. They were surmounted with old faded painted escutcheons, and here and there, in the spaces between them, brown pictures, which I perceived to be bad, in battered frames, were suspended. With the exception of several straw-bottomed chairs with their backs to the wall, the grand obscure vista contained nothing else to minister to effect. It was evidently never used save as a passage, and little even as that. I may add that by the time the door opened again through which the maid-servant had escaped, my eyes had grown used to the want of light.

I had not meant by my private ejaculation that I must myself cultivate the soil of the tangled enclosure which lay beneath the windows, but the lady who came toward me from the distance over the hard, shining floor might have supposed as much from the way in which, as I went rapidly to meet her, I exclaimed, taking care to speak Italian: 'The garden, the garden – do me the pleasure to tell me if it's yours!'

She stopped short, looking at me with wonder; and then, 'Nothing here is mine,' she answered in English, coldly and sadly.

'Oh, you are English; how delightful!' I remarked, ingenuously. 'But surely the garden belongs to the house?'

'Yes, but the house doesn't belong to me.' She was a long, lean, pale person, habited apparently in a dull-coloured dressing-gown, and she spoke with a kind of mild literalness. She did not ask me to sit down, any more than years before (if she were the niece) she had asked Mrs Prest, and we stood face to face in the empty pompous hall.

'Well then, would you kindly tell me to whom I must address myself? I'm afraid you'll think me odiously intrusive, but you know I *must* have a garden – upon my honour I must!'

Her face was not young, but it was simple; it was not fresh, but it was mild. She had large eyes which were not bright, and a great deal of hair which was not 'dressed', and long fine hands which were – possibly – not clean. She clasped these members almost convulsively as, with a confused, alarmed look, she broke out, 'Oh, don't take it away from us; we like it ourselves!'

'You have the use of it then?'

'Oh yes. If it wasn't for that!' And she gave a shy, melancholy smile.

'Isn't it a luxury, precisely? That's why, intending to be in Venice some weeks, possibly all summer, and having some literary work, some reading and writing to do, so that I must be quiet, and yet if possible a great deal in the open air – that's why I have felt that a garden is really indispensable. I appeal to your own experience,' I went on, smiling. 'Now can't I look at yours?'

'I don't know, I don't understand,' the poor woman murmured, planted there and letting her embarrassed eyes wander all over my strangeness.

'I mean only from one of those windows – such grand ones as you have here – if you will let me open the shutters.' And I walked toward the back of the house. When I had advanced half-way I stopped and waited, as if I took it for granted she would accompany me. I had been of necessity very abrupt, but I strove at the same time to give her the impression of extreme courtesy. 'I have been looking at furnished rooms all over the place, and it seems impossible to find any with a garden attached. Naturally in a place like Venice gardens are rare. It's absurd if you like, for a man, but I can't live without flowers.'

'There are none to speak of down there.' She came nearer to me, as if, though she mistrusted me, I had drawn her by an invisible thread. I went on again, and she continued as she followed me: 'We have a few, but they are very common. It costs too much to cultivate them; one has to have a man.'

'Why shouldn't I be the man?' I asked. 'I'll work without wages; or rather I'll put in a gardener. You shall have the sweetest flowers in Venice.'

She protested at this, with a queer little sigh which might also have been a gush of rapture at the picture I presented. Then she observed, 'We don't know you – we don't know you.'

'You know me as much as I know you; that is much more, because you know my name. And if you are English I am almost a countryman.'

'We are not English,' said my companion, watching me helplessly while I threw open the shutters of one of the divisions of the wide high window.

'You speak the language so beautifully: might I ask what you are?' Seen from above the garden was certainly shabby; but I perceived at a glance that it had great capabilities. She made no rejoinder, she was so lost in staring at me, and I exclaimed, 'You don't mean to say you are also by chance American?'

'I don't know; we used to be.'

'Used to be? Surely you haven't changed?'

'It's so many years ago – we are nothing.'

'So many years that you have been living here? Well, I don't wonder at that; it's a grand old house. I suppose you all use the garden,' I went on, 'but I assure you I shouldn't be in your way. I would be very quiet and stay in one corner.'

'We all use it?' she repeated after me, vaguely, not coming close to the window but looking at my shoes. She appeared to think me capable of throwing her out.

'I mean all your family, as many as you are.'

'There is only one other; she is very old – she never goes down.'

'Only one other, in all this great house!' I feigned to be not only amazed but almost scandalised. 'Dear lady, you must have space then to spare!'

'To spare?' she repeated, in the same dazed way.

'Why, you surely don't live (two quiet women – I see *you* are quiet, at any rate) in fifty rooms!' Then with a burst of hope and cheer I demanded: 'Couldn't you let me two or three? That would set me up!'

I had now struck the note that translated my purpose and I need not reproduce the whole of the tune I played. I ended by making my interlocutress believe that I was an honourable person, though of course I did not even attempt to persuade her that I was not an eccentric one. I repeated that I had studies to pursue; that I wanted quiet; that I delighted in a garden and had vainly sought one up and down the city; that I would undertake that before another month was over the dear old house should be smothered in flowers. I think it was the flowers that won my suit, for I afterwards found that Miss Tita (for such the name of this high tremulous spinster proved somewhat incongruously to be) had an insatiable appetite for them. When I speak of my suit as won I mean that before I left her she had promised that she would refer the question to her aunt. I inquired who her aunt might be and she answered, 'Why, Miss Bordereau!' with an air of surprise, as if I might have been expected to know. There were contradictions like this in Tita Bordereau which, as I observed later, contributed to make her an odd and affecting person. It was the study of the two ladies to live so that the world should not touch them, and yet they had never altogether accepted the idea that it never heard of them. In Tita at any rate a grateful suscept-ibility to human contact had not died out, and contact of a limited order there would be if I should come to live in the house.

'We have never done anything of the sort; we have never had a lodger or any kind of inmate.' So much as this she made a point of saying to me. 'We are very poor, we live very badly. The rooms are very bare – that you might take; they have nothing in them. I don't know how you would sleep, how you would eat.'

'With your permission, I could easily put in a bed and a few tables and chairs. *C'est la moindre des choses* and the affair of an hour or two. I know a little man from whom I can hire what I should want for a few months, for a trifle, and my gondolier can bring the things round in his boat. Of course in this great house you must have a second kitchen, and my servant, who is a wonderfully handy fellow' (this personage was an evocation of the moment), 'can easily cook me a chop there. My tastes and habits are of the simplest; I live on flowers!' And then I ventured to add that if they were very poor it was all the more reason they should let their rooms. They were bad economists – I had never heard of such a waste of material.

I saw in a moment that the good lady had never before been spoken to in that way, with a kind of humorous firmness which did not exclude sympathy but was on the contrary founded on it. She might easily have told me that my sympathy was impertinent, but this by good fortune did not occur to her. I left her with the understanding that she would consider the matter with her aunt and that I might come back the next day for their decision.

'The aunt will refuse; she will think the whole proceeding very *louche*!' Mrs Prest declared shortly after this, when I had resumed my place in her gondola. She had put the idea into my head and now (so little are women to be counted on) she appeared to take a despondent view of it. Her pessimism provoked me and I pretended to have the best hopes; I went so far as to say that I had a distinct presentiment that I should succeed. Upon this Mrs Prest broke out, 'Oh, I see what's in your head! You fancy you have made such an impression in a quarter of an hour that she is dying for you to come and can be depended upon to bring the old one round. If you do get in you'll count it as a triumph.'

I did count it as a triumph, but only for the editor (in the last analysis), not for the man, who had not the tradition of personal conquest. When I went back on the morrow the little maidservant conducted me straight through the long sala (it opened there as before in perfect perspective and was lighter now, which I thought a good omen) into the apartment from which the recipient of my former visit had emerged on that occasion. It was a large shabby parlour, with a fine old painted ceiling and a strange figure sitting alone at one of the windows. They come back to me now almost with the palpitation they caused, the successive feelings that accompanied my consciousness that as the door of the room closed behind me I was really face to face with the Juliana of some of Aspern's most exquisite and most renowned lyrics. I grew used to her afterwards, though never completely; but as she sat there before me my heart beat as fast as if the miracle of resurrection had taken place for my benefit. Her presence seemed somehow to contain his, and I felt nearer to him at that first moment of seeing her than I ever had been before or ever have been since. Yes, I remember my emotions in their order, even including a curious little tremor that took me when I saw that the niece was not there. With her, the day before, I had become sufficiently familiar, but it almost exceeded my courage (much as I had longed for the event) to be left alone with such a terrible relic as the aunt. She was too strange, too literally resurgent. Then came a check, with the perception that we were not really face to face, inasmuch as she had over her eyes a horrible green shade which, for her, served already as a mask. I believed for the instant that she had put it on expressly, so that from underneath it she might scrutinise me without being scrutinised herself. At the same time it increased the presumption that there was a ghastly death's-head lurking behind it. The divine Juliana as a grinning skull – the vision hung there until it passed. Then it came to me that she *was* tremendously old – so old that death might take her at any moment, before I had time to get what I wanted from her. The next thought was a correction to that; it lighted up the situation. She would die next week, she would die to-morrow – then I could seize her papers. Meanwhile she sat there neither moving nor speaking. She was very small and shrunken, bent forward, with her hands in her lap. She was dressed in black and her head was wrapped in a piece of old black lace which showed no hair.

My emotion keeping me silent she spoke first, and the remark she made was exactly the most unexpected.

III

'Our house is very far from the centre, but the little canal is very *comme il faut*.'

'It's the sweetest corner of Venice and I can imagine nothing more charming,' I hastened to reply. The old lady's voice was very thin and weak, but it had an agreeable, cultivated murmur and there was wonder in the thought that that individual note had been in Jeffrey Aspern's ear.

'Please to sit down there. I hear very well,' she said quietly, as if perhaps I had been shouting at her; and the chair she pointed to was at a certain distance. I took possession of it, telling her that I was perfectly aware that I had intruded, that I had not been properly introduced and could only throw myself upon her indulgence. Perhaps the other lady, the one I had had the honour of seeing the day before, would have explained to her about the garden. That was literally what had given me courage to take a step so unconventional. I had fallen in love at sight with the whole place (she herself probably was so used to it that she did not know the impression it was capable of making on a stranger), and I had felt it was really a case to risk something. Was her own kindness in receiving me a sign that I was not wholly out in my calculation? It would render me extremely happy to think so. I could give her my word of honour that I was a most respectable, inoffensive person and that as an inmate they would be barely conscious of my existence. I would conform to any regulations, any restrictions if they would only let me enjoy the garden. Moreover I should be delighted to give her references, guarantees; they would be of the very best, both in Venice and in England as well as in America.

She listened to me in perfect stillness and I felt that she was looking at me with great attention, though I could see only the lower part of her bleached and shrivelled face. Independently of the refining process of old age it had a delicacy which once must have been great. She had been very fair, she had had a wonderful complexion. She was silent a little after I had ceased speaking; then she inquired, 'If you are so fond of a garden why don't you go to *terra firma*, where there are so many far better than this?'

'Oh, it's the combination!' I answered, smiling; and then, with rather a flight of fancy, 'It's the idea of a garden in the middle of the sea.'

'It's not in the middle of the sea; you can't see the water.'

I stared a moment, wondering whether she wished to convict me of fraud. 'Can't see the water? Why, dear madam, I can come up to the very gate in my boat.'

She appeared inconsequent, for she said vaguely in reply to this, 'Yes, if you have got a boat. I haven't any; it's many years since I have been in one of the gondolas.' She uttered these words as if the gondolas were a curious far-away craft which she knew only by hearsay.

'Let me assure you of the pleasure with which I would put mine at your service!' I exclaimed. I had scarcely said this however before I became aware that the speech was in questionable taste and might also do me the injury of making me appear too eager, too possessed of a hidden motive. But the old woman remained impenetrable and her attitude bothered me by suggesting that she had a fuller vision of me than I had of her. She gave me no thanks for my somewhat extravagant offer but remarked that the lady I had seen the day before was her niece; she would presently come in. She had asked her to stay away a little on purpose, because she herself wished to see me at first alone. She relapsed into silence and I asked myself why she had judged this necessary and what was coming yet; also whether I might venture on some judicious remark in praise of her companion. I went so far as to say that I should be delighted to see her again: she had been so very courteous to me, considering how odd she must have thought me – a declaration which drew from Miss Bordereau another of her whimsical speeches.

'She has very good manners; I bred her up myself!' I was on the point of saying that that accounted for the easy grace of the niece, but I arrested myself in time, and the next moment the old woman went on: 'I don't care who you may be – I don't want to know; it signifies very little to-day.' This had all the air of being a formula of dismissal, as if her next words would be that I might take myself off now that she had had the amusement of looking on the face of such a monster of indiscretion. Therefore I was all the more surprised when she added, with her soft, venerable quaver, 'You may have as many rooms as you like – if you will pay a good deal of money.'

I hesitated but for a single instant, long enough to ask myself what she meant in particular by this condition. First it struck me that she must have really a large sum in her mind; then I reasoned quickly that her idea of a large sum would probably not correspond to my own. My deliberation, I think, was not so visible as to diminish the promptitude with which I replied, 'I will pay with pleasure and of course in advance whatever you may think it proper to ask me.'

'Well then, a thousand francs a month,' she rejoined instantly, while her baffling green shade continued to cover her attitude.

The figure, as they say, was startling and my logic had been at fault. The sum she had mentioned was, by the Venetian measure of such matters, exceedingly large; there was many an old palace in an out-of-the-way corner that I might on such terms have enjoyed by the year. But so far as my small means allowed I was prepared to spend money, and my decision was quickly taken. I would pay her with a smiling face what she asked, but in that case I would give myself the compensation of extracting the papers from her for nothing. Moreover if she had asked five times as much I should have risen to the occasion; so odious would it have appeared to me to stand chaffering with Aspern's Juliana. It was queer enough to have a question of money with her at all. I assured her that her views perfectly met my own and that on the morrow I should have the pleasure of putting three months' rent into her hand. She received this announcement with serenity and with no apparent sense that after all it would be becoming of her to say that I ought to see the rooms first. This did not occur to her and indeed her serenity was mainly what I wanted. Our little bargain was just concluded when the door opened and the younger lady appeared on the threshold. As soon as Miss Bordereau saw her niece she cried out almost gaily, 'He will give three thousand – three thousand to-morrow!'

Miss Tita stood still, with her patient eyes turning from one of us to the other; then she inquired, scarcely above her breath, 'Do you mean francs?'

'Did you mean francs or dollars?' the old woman asked of me at this.

'I think francs were what you said,' I answered, smiling.

'That is very good,' said Miss Tita, as if she had become conscious that her own question might have looked over-reaching.

'What do *you* know? You are ignorant,' Miss Bordereau remarked; not with acerbity but with a strange, soft coldness.

'Yes, of money – certainly of money!' Miss Tita hastened to exclaim.

'I am sure you have your own branches of knowledge,' I took the liberty of saying, genially. There was something painful to me, somehow, in the turn the conversation had taken, in the discussion of the rent.

'She had a very good education when she was young. I looked into that myself,' said Miss Bordereau. Then she added, 'But she has learned nothing since.'

'I have always been with you,' Miss Tita rejoined very mildly, and evidently with no intention of making an epigram.

'Yes, but for that!' her aunt declared, with more satirical force. She evidently meant that but for this her niece would never have got on at all; the point of the observation however being lost on Miss Tita, though she blushed at hearing her history revealed to a stranger. Miss Bordereau went on, addressing herself to me: 'And what time will you come to-morrow with the money?'

'The sooner the better. If it suits you I will come at noon.'

'I am always here but I have my hours,' said the old woman, as if her convenience were not to be taken for granted.

'You mean the times when you receive?'

'I never receive. But I will see you at noon, when you come with the money.'

'Very good, I shall be punctual'; and I added, 'May I shake hands with you, on our contract?' I thought there ought to be some little form, it would make me really feel easier, for I foresaw that there would be no other. Besides, though Miss Bordereau could not to-day be called personally attractive and there was something even in her wasted antiquity that bade one stand at one's distance, I felt an irresistible desire to hold in my own for a moment the hand that Jeffrey Aspern had pressed.

For a minute she made no answer and I saw that my proposal failed to meet with her approbation. She indulged in no movement of withdrawal, which I half expected; she only said coldly, 'I belong to a time when that was not the custom.'

I felt rather snubbed but I exclaimed good-humouredly to Miss Tita, 'Oh, you will do as well!' I shook hands with her while she replied, with a small flutter, 'Yes, yes, to show it's all arranged!'

'Shall you bring the money in gold?' Miss Bordereau demanded, as I was turning to the door.

I looked at her a moment. 'Aren't you a little afraid, after all, of keeping such a sum as that in the house?' It was not that I was annoyed at her avidity but I was really struck with the disparity between such a treasure and such scanty means of guarding it.

'Whom should I be afraid of if I am not afraid of you?' she asked with her shrunken grimness.

'Ah well,' said I, laughing, 'I shall be in point of fact a protector and I will bring gold if you prefer.'

'Thank you,' the old woman returned with dignity and with an inclination of her head which evidently signified that I might depart. I passed out of the room, reflecting that it would not be easy to circumvent her. As I stood in the sala again I saw that Miss Tita had followed me and I supposed that as her aunt had neglected to suggest that I should take a look at my quarters it was her purpose to repair the omission. But she made no such suggestion; she only stood there with a dim, though not a languid smile, and with an effect of irresponsible, incompetent youth which was almost comically at variance with the faded facts of her person. She was not infirm, like her aunt, but she struck me as still more helpless, because her inefficiency was spiritual, which was not the case with Miss Bordereau's. I waited to see if she would offer to show me the rest of the house, but I did not precipitate the question, inasmuch as my plan was from this moment to spend as much of my time as possible in her society. I only observed at the end of a minute:

'I have had better fortune than I hoped. It was very kind of her to see me. Perhaps you said a good word for me.'

'It was the idea of the money,' said Miss Tita.

'And did you suggest that?'

'I told her that you would perhaps give a good deal.'

'What made you think that?'

'I told her I thought you were rich.'

'And what put that idea into your head?'

'I don't know; the way you talked.'

'Dear me, I must talk differently now,' I declared. 'I'm sorry to say it's not the case.'

'Well,' said Miss Tita, 'I think that in Venice the *forestieri*, in general, often give a great deal for something that after all isn't much.' She appeared to make this remark with a comforting intention, to wish to remind me that if I had been extravagant I was not really foolishly singular. We walked together along the sala, and as I took its magnificent measure I said to her that I was afraid it would not form a part of my *quartiere*. Were my rooms by chance to be among those that opened into it? 'Not if you go above, on the second floor,' she answered with a little startled air, as if she had rather taken for granted I would know my proper place.

'And I infer that that's where your aunt would like me to be.'

'She said your apartments ought to be very distinct.'

'That certainly would be best.' And I listened with respect while she told me that up above I was free to take whatever I liked; that there was another staircase, but only from the floor on which we stood, and that to pass from it to the garden-storey or to come up to my lodging I should have in effect to cross the great hall. This was an immense point gained; I foresaw that it would constitute my whole leverage in my relations with the two ladies. When I asked Miss Tita how I was to manage at present to find my way up she replied with an access of that sociable shyness which constantly marked her manner.

'Perhaps you can't. I don't see – unless I should go with you.' She evidently had not thought of this before.

We ascended to the upper floor and visited a long succession of empty rooms. The best of them looked over the garden;

some of the others had a view of the blue lagoon, above the opposite rough-tiled housetops. They were all dusty and even a little disfigured with long neglect, but I saw that by spending a few hundred francs I should be able to convert three or four of them into a convenient habitation. My experiment was turning out costly, yet now that I had all but taken possession I ceased to allow this to trouble me. I mentioned to my companion a few of the things that I should put in, but she replied rather more precipitately than usual that I might do exactly what I liked; she seemed to wish to notify me that the Misses Bordereau would take no overt interest in my proceedings. I guessed that her aunt had instructed her to adopt this tone, and I may as well say now that I came afterwards to distinguish perfectly (as I believed) between the speeches she made on her own responsibility and those the old lady imposed upon her. She took no notice of the unswept condition of the rooms and indulged in no explanations nor apologies. I said to myself that this was a sign that Juliana and her niece (disenchanting idea!) were untidy persons, with a low Italian standard; but I afterwards recognised that a lodger who had forced an entrance had no *locus standi* as a critic. We looked out of a good many windows, for there was nothing within the rooms to look at, and still I wanted to linger. I asked her what several different objects in the prospect might be, but in no case did she appear to know. She was evidently not familiar with the view – it was as if she had not looked at it for years – and I presently saw that she was too preoccupied with something else to pretend to care for it. Suddenly she said – the remark was not suggested:

'I don't know whether it will make any difference to you, but the money is for me.'

'The money?'

'The money you are going to bring.'

'Why, you'll make me wish to stay here two or three years.' I spoke as benevolently as possible, though it had begun to act on my nerves that with these women so associated with Aspern the pecuniary question should constantly come back.

'That would be very good for me,' she replied, smiling.

'You put me on my honour!'

She looked as if she failed to understand this, but went on: 'She wants me to have more. She thinks she is going to die.'

'Ah, not soon, I hope!' I exclaimed, with genuine feeling. I had perfectly considered the possibility that she would destroy her papers on the day she should feel her end really approach. I believed that she would cling to them till then and I think I had an idea that she read Aspern's letters over every night or at least pressed them to her withered lips. I would have given a good deal to have a glimpse of the latter spectacle. I asked Miss Tita if the old lady were seriously ill and she replied that she was only very tired – she had lived so very, very long. That was what she said herself – she wanted to die for a change. Besides, all her friends were dead long ago; either they ought to have remained or she ought to have gone. That was another thing her aunt often said – she was not at all content.

'But people don't die when they like, do they?' Miss Tita inquired. I took the liberty of asking why, if there was actually enough money to maintain both of them, there would not be more than enough in case of her being left alone. She considered this difficult problem a moment and then she said, 'Oh, well, you know, she takes care of me. She thinks that when I'm alone I shall be a great fool, I shall not know how to manage.'

'I should have supposed rather that you took care of her. I'm afraid she is very proud.'

'Why, have you discovered that already?' Miss Tita cried, with the glimmer of an illumination in her face.

'I was shut up with her there for a considerable time, and she struck me, she interested me extremely. It didn't take me long to make my discovery. She won't have much to say to me while I'm here.'

'No, I don't think she will,' my companion averred.

'Do you suppose she has some suspicion of me?'

Miss Tita's honest eyes gave me no sign that I had touched a mark. 'I shouldn't think so – letting you in after all so easily.'

'Oh, so easily! she has covered her risk. But where is it that one could take an advantage of her?'

'I oughtn't to tell you if I knew, ought I?' And Miss Tita added, before I had time to reply to this, smiling dolefully, 'Do you think we have any weak points?'

'That's exactly what I'm asking. You would only have to mention them for me to respect them religiously.'

She looked at me, at this, with that air of timid but candid and even gratified curiosity with which she had confronted me from the first; and then she said, 'There is nothing to tell. We are terribly quiet. I don't know how the days pass. We have no life.'

'I wish I might think that I should bring you a little.'

'Oh, we know what we want,' she went on. 'It's all right.'

There were various things I desired to ask her: how in the world they did live; whether they had any friends or visitors, any relations in America or in other countries. But I judged such an inquiry would be premature; I must leave it to a later chance. 'Well, don't *you* be proud,' I contented myself with saying. 'Don't hide from me altogether.'

'Oh, I must stay with my aunt,' she returned, without looking at me. And at the same moment, abruptly, without any ceremony of parting, she quitted me and disappeared, leaving me to make my own way downstairs. I remained a while longer, wandering about the bright desert (the sun was pouring in) of the old house, thinking the situation over on the spot. Not even the pattering little *serva* came to look after me and I reflected that after all this treatment showed confidence.

IV

PERHAPS it did, but all the same, six weeks later, towards the middle of June, the moment when Mrs Prest undertook her annual migration, I had made no measurable advance. I was obliged to confess to her that I had no results to speak of. My first step had been unexpectedly rapid, but there was no appearance that it would be followed by a second. I was a thousand miles from taking tea with my hostesses – that privilege of which, as I reminded Mrs Prest, we both had had a vision. She reproached me with wanting boldness and

I answered that even to be bold you must have an opportunity: you may push on through a breach but you can't batter down a dead wall. She answered that the breach I had already made was big enough to admit an army and accused me of wasting precious hours in whimpering in her salon when I ought to have been carrying on the struggle in the field. It is true that I went to see her very often, on the theory that it would console me (I freely expressed my discouragement) for my want of success on my own premises. But I began to perceive that it did not console me to be perpetually chaffed for my scruples, especially when I was really so vigilant; and I was rather glad when my derisive friend closed her house for the summer. She had expected to gather amusement from the drama of my inter-course with the Misses Bordereau and she was disappointed that the intercourse, and consequently the drama, had not come off. 'They'll lead you on to your ruin,' she said before she left Venice. 'They'll get all your money without showing you a scrap.' I think I settled down to my business with more concentration after she had gone away.

It was a fact that up to that time I had not, save on a single brief occasion, had even a moment's contact with my queer hostesses. The exception had occurred when I carried them according to my promise the terrible three thousand francs. Then I found Miss Tita waiting for me in the hall, and she took the money from my hand so that I did not see her aunt. The old lady had promised to receive me, but she apparently thought nothing of breaking that vow. The money was contained in a bag of chamois leather, of respectable dimensions, which my banker had given me, and Miss Tita had to make a big fist to receive it. This she did with extreme solemnity, though I tried to treat the affair a little as a joke. It was in no jocular strain, yet it was with simplicity, that she inquired, weighing the money in her two palms: 'Don't you think it's too much?' To which I replied that that would depend upon the amount of pleasure I should get for it. Hereupon she turned away from me quickly, as she had done the day before, murmuring in a tone different from any she had used hitherto: 'Oh, pleasure, pleasure – there's no pleasure in this house!'

After this, for a long time, I never saw her, and I wondered that the common chances of the day should not have helped us to meet. It could only be evident that she was immensely on her guard against them; and in addition to this the house was so big that for each other we were lost in it. I used to look out for her hopefully as I crossed the sala in my comings and goings, but I was not rewarded with a glimpse of the tail of her dress. It was as if she never peeped out of her aunt's apartment. I used to wonder what she did there week after week and year after year. I had never encountered such a violent *parti pris* of seclusion; it was more than keeping quiet – it was like hunted creatures feigning death. The two ladies appeared to have no visitors whatever and no sort of contact with the world. I judged at least that people could not have come to the house and that Miss Tita could not have gone out without my having some observation of it. I did what I disliked myself for doing (reflecting that it was only once in a way): I questioned my servant about their habits and let him divine that I should be interested in any information he could pick up. But he picked up amazingly little for a knowing Venetian: it must be added that where there is a perpetual fast there are very few crumbs on the floor. His cleverness in other ways was sufficient if it was not quite all that I had attributed to him on the occasion of my first interview with Miss Tita. He had helped my gondolier to bring me round a boat-load of furniture; and when these articles had been carried to the top of the palace and distributed according to our associated wisdom he organised my household with such promptitude as was consistent with the fact that it was composed exclusively of himself. He made me in short as comfortable as I could be with my indifferent prospects. I should have been glad if he had fallen in love with Miss Bordereau's maid or, failing this, had taken her in aversion; either event might have brought about some kind of catastrophe and a catastrophe might have led to some parley. It was my idea that she would have been sociable, and I myself on various occasions saw her flit to and fro on domestic errands, so that I was sure she was accessible. But I tasted of no gossip from that fountain, and I afterwards learned that Pasquale's affections were fixed upon an object that made him heedless of other women. This was a young lady with a powdered face, a yellow cotton gown and much leisure, who used often to come to see him. She practised, at her convenience, the art of a stringer of beads (these ornaments are made in Venice, in profusion; she had her pocket full of them and I used to find them on the floor of my apartment), and kept an eye on the maiden in the house. It was not for me of course to make the domestics tattle, and I never said a word to Miss Bordereau's cook.

It seemed to me a proof of the old lady's determination to have nothing to do with me that she should never have sent me a receipt for my three months' rent. For some days I looked out for it and then, when I had given it up, I wasted a good deal of time in wondering what her reason had been for neglecting so indispensable and familiar a form. At first I was tempted to send her a reminder, after which I relinquished the idea (against my judgement as to what was right in the particular case), on the general ground of wishing to keep quiet. If Miss Bordereau suspected me of ulterior aims, she would suspect me less if I should be businesslike, and yet I consented not to be so. It was possible she intended her omission as an impertinence, a visible irony, to show how she could overreach people who attempted to overreach her. On that hypothesis it was well to let her see that one did not notice her little tricks. The real reading of the matter, I afterwards perceived, was simply the poor old woman's desire to emphasise the fact that I was in the enjoyment of a favour as rigidly limited as it had been liberally bestowed. She had given me part of her house and now she would not give me even a morsel of paper with her name on it. Let me say that even at first this did not make me too miserable, for the whole episode was essentially delightful to me. I foresaw that I should have a summer after my own literary heart, and the sense of holding my opportunity was much greater than the sense of losing it. There could be no Venetian business without patience, and since I adored the place I was much more in the spirit of it for having laid in a large provision. That spirit kept me perpetual company and seemed to look out at me from the revived immortal face – in which all his genius shone – of the great poet who was my prompter. I had invoked him and he had come; he hovered before me half the time; it was as if his bright ghost had returned to earth to tell me that he regarded the affair as his own no less than mine and that we should see it fraternally, cheerfully to a conclusion. It was as if he had said, 'Poor dear, be easy with her; she has some natural prejudices; only give her time. Strange as it may appear to you she was very attractive in 1820. Meanwhile are we not in Venice together, and what better place is there for the meeting of dear friends? See how it glows with the advancing summer; how the sky and the sea and the rosy air and the marble of the palaces all shimmer and melt together.' My eccentric private errand became a part of the general romance and the general glory – I felt even a mystic companionship, a moral fraternity with all those who in the past had been in the service of art. They had worked for beauty, for a devotion; and what else was I doing? That element was in everything that Jeffrey Aspern had written and I was only bringing it to the light.

I lingered in the sala when I went to and fro; I used to watch – as long as I thought decent – the door that led to Miss Bordereau's part of the house. A person observing me might have supposed I was trying to cast a spell upon it or attempting some odd experiment in hypnotism. But I was only praying it would open or thinking what treasure probably lurked behind it. I hold it singular, as I look back, that I should never have doubted for a moment that the sacred relics were there; never have failed to feel a certain joy at being under the same roof with them. After all they were under my hand – they had not escaped me yet; and they made my life continuous, in a fashion, with the illustrious life they had touched at the other end. I lost myself in this satisfaction to the point of assuming – in my quiet extravagance – that poor Miss Tita also went back, went back, as I used to phrase it. She did indeed, the gentle spinster, but not quite so far as Jeffrey Aspern, who was simple hearsay to her, quite as he was to me. Only she had lived for years with Juliana, she had seen and handled the papers and (even though she was stupid) some esoteric knowledge had rubbed off on her. That was what the old woman represented – esoteric knowledge; and this was the idea with which my editorial heart used to thrill. It literally beat faster often, of an evening, when I had been out, as I stopped with my candle in the re-echoing hall on my way up to bed. It was as if at such a moment as that, in the stillness, after the long contradiction of the day, Miss Bordereau's secrets were in the air, the wonder of her survival more palpable. These were the acute impressions. I had them in another form, with more of a certain sort of reciprocity, during the hours that I sat in the garden looking up over the top of my book at the closed windows of my hostess. In these windows no sign of life ever appeared; it was as if, for fear of my catching a glimpse of them, the two ladies passed their days in the dark. But this only proved to me that they had something to conceal; which was what I had wished to demonstrate. Their motionless shutters became as expressive as eyes consciously closed, and I took comfort in thinking that at all events though invisible themselves they saw me between the lashes.

I made a point of spending as much time as possible in the garden, to justify the picture I had originally given of my horticultural passion. And I not only spent time, but (hang it! as I said) I spent money. As soon as I had got my rooms arranged and could give the proper thought to the matter I surveyed the place with a clever expert and made terms for having it put in order. I was sorry to do this, for personally I liked it better as it was, with its weeds and its wild, rough tangle, its sweet, characteristic Venetian shabbiness. I had to be consistent, to keep my promise that I would smother the house in flowers. Moreover I formed this graceful project that by flowers I would make my way – I would succeed by big nosegays. I would batter the old women with lilies – I would bombard their citadel with roses. Their door would have to yield to the pressure when a mountain of carnations should be piled up against it. The place in truth had been brutally neglected. The Venetian capacity for dawdling is of the largest, and for a good many days unlimited litter was all my gardener had to show for his ministrations. There was a great digging of holes and carting about of earth, and after a while I grew so impatient that I had thoughts of sending for my bouquets to the nearest stand. But I reflected

that the ladies would see through the chinks of their
shutters that they must have been bought and might make up
their minds from this that I was a humbug. So I composed
myself and finally, though the delay was long, perceived some
appearances of bloom. This encouraged me and I waited serenely enough till they multiplied. Meanwhile the real summer
days arrived and began to pass, and as I look back upon them
they seem to me almost the happiest of my life. I took more and
more care to be in the garden whenever it was not too hot. I had
an arbour arranged and a low table and an armchair put into it;
and I carried out books and portfolios (I had always some
business of writing in hand), and worked and waited and
mused and hoped, while the golden hours elapsed and the
plants drank in the light and the inscrutable old palace turned
pale and then, as the day waned, began to flush in it and my
papers rustled in the wandering breeze of the Adriatic.

Considering how little satisfaction I got from it at first it is
remarkable that I should not have grown more tired of wondering what mystic rites of ennui the Misses Bordereau celebrated
in their darkened rooms; whether this had always been the
tenor of their life and how in previous years they had escaped
elbowing their neighbours. It was clear that they must have had
other habits and other circumstances; that they must once have
been young or at least middle-aged. There was no end to
the questions it was possible to ask about them and no end
to the answers it was not possible to frame. I had known many
of my country-people in Europe and was familiar with the
strange ways they were liable to take up there; but the Misses
Bordereau formed altogether a new type of the American
absentee. Indeed it was plain that the American name had
ceased to have any application to them – I had seen this in the
ten minutes I spent in the old woman's room. You could never
have said whence they came, from the appearance of either of
them; wherever it was they had long ago dropped the local
accent and fashion. There was nothing in them that one recognised, and putting the question of speech aside they might have
been Norwegians or Spaniards. Miss Bordereau, after all,
had been in Europe nearly three-quarters of a century; it

appeared by some verses addressed to her by Aspern on the occasion of his own second absence from America – verses of which Cumnor and I had after infinite conjecture established solidly enough the date – that she was even then, as a girl of twenty, on the foreign side of the sea. There was an implication in the poem (I hope not just for the phrase) that he had come back for her sake. We had no real light upon her circumstances at that moment, any more than we had upon her origin, which we believed to be of the sort usually spoken of as modest. Cumnor had a theory that she had been a governess in some family in which the poet visited and that, in consequence of her position, there was from the first something unavowed, or rather something positively clandestine, in their relations. I on the other hand had hatched a little romance according to which she was the daughter of an artist, a painter or a sculptor, who had left the western world when the century was fresh, to study in the ancient schools. It was essential to my hypothesis that this amiable man should have lost his wife, should have been poor and unsuccessful and should have had a second daughter, of a disposition quite different from Juliana's. It was also indispensable that he should have been accompanied to Europe by these young ladies and should have established himself there for the remainder of a struggling, saddened life. There was a further implication that Miss Bordereau had had in her youth a perverse and adventurous, albeit a generous and fascinating character, and that she had passed through some singular vicissitudes. By what passions had she been ravaged, by what sufferings had she been blanched, what store of memories had she laid away for the monotonous future?

I asked myself these things as I sat spinning theories about her in my arbour and the bees droned in the flowers. It was incontestable that, whether for right or for wrong, most readers of certain of Aspern's poems (poems not as ambiguous as the sonnets – scarcely more divine, I think – of Shakespeare) had taken for granted that Juliana had not always adhered to the steep footway of renunciation. There hovered about her name a perfume of reckless passion, an intimation that she had not been exactly as the respectable young person in general. Was this a sign that her singer had betrayed her, had given her away, as we say nowadays, to posterity? Certain it is that it would have been difficult to put one's finger on the passage in which her fair fame suffered an imputation. Moreover was not any fame fair enough that was so sure of duration and was associated with works immortal through their beauty? It was a part of my idea that the young lady had had a foreign lover (and an unedifying tragical rupture) before her meeting with Jeffrey Aspern. She had lived with her father and sister in a queer old-fashioned, expatriated, artistic Bohemia, in the days when the aesthetic was only the academic and the painters who knew the best models for a *contadina* and *pifferaro* wore peaked hats and long hair. It was a society less furnished than the coteries of to-day (in its ignorance of the wonderful chances, the opportunities of the early bird, with which its path was strewn), with tatters of old stuff and fragments of old crockery; so that Miss Bordereau appeared not to have picked up or have inherited many objects of importance. There was no enviable *bric-à-brac*, with its provoking legend of cheapness, in the room in which I had seen her. Such a fact as that suggested bareness, but none the less it worked happily into the sentimental interest I had always taken in the early movements of my countrymen as visitors to Europe. When Americans went abroad in 1820 there was something romantic, almost heroic in it, as compared with the perpetual ferryings of the present hour, when photography and other conveniences have annihilated surprise. Miss Bordereau sailed with her family on a tossing brig, in the days of long voyages and sharp differences; she had her emotions on the top of yellow diligences, passed the night at inns where she dreamed of travellers' tales, and was struck, on reaching the eternal city, with the elegance of Roman pearls and scarfs. There was something touching to me in all that and my imagination frequently went back to the period. If Miss Bordereau carried it there of course Jeffrey Aspern at other times had done so a great deal more. It was a much more important fact, if one were looking at his genius critically, that he had lived in the days before the general transfusion. It had happened to me to regret that he had known Europe at all; I should have liked to see what he would have written without that experience, by which he had incontestably been enriched. But as his fate had ordered otherwise I went with him – I tried to judge how the old world would have struck him. It was not only there, however, that I watched him; the relations he had entertained with the new had even a livelier interest. His own country after all had had more of his life, and his muse, as they said at that time, was essentially American. That was originally what I had loved him for: that at a period when our native land was nude and crude and provincial, when the famous 'atmosphere' it is supposed to lack was not even missed, when literature was lonely there and art and form almost impossible, he had found means to live and write like one of the first; to be free and general and not at all afraid; to feel, understand and express everything.

V

I was seldom at home in the evening, for when I attempted to occupy myself in my apartments the lamplight brought in a swarm of noxious insects, and it was too hot for closed windows. Accordingly I spent the late hours either on the water (the moonlight of Venice is famous), or in the splendid square which serves as a vast forecourt to the strange old basilica of Saint Mark. I sat in front of Florian's *café*, eating ices, listening to music, talking with acquaintances: the traveller will remember how the immense cluster of tables and little chairs stretches like a promontory into the smooth lake of the Piazza. The whole place, of a summer's evening, under the stars and with all the lamps, all the voices and light footsteps on marble (the only sounds of the arcades that enclose it), is like an open-air saloon dedicated to cooling drinks and to a still finer degustation – that of the exquisite impressions received during the day. When I did not prefer to keep mine to myself there was always a stray tourist, disencumbered of his Bädeker, to discuss them with, or some domesticated painter rejoicing in the return of the season of strong effects. The wonderful church, with its low domes and bristling embroideries, the mystery of its mosaic and sculpture, looked ghostly in the tempered gloom, and the sea-breeze passed between the twin columns of the Piazzetta, the lintels of a door no longer guarded, as gently as if a rich curtain were swaying there. I used sometimes on these occasions to think of the Misses Bordereau and of the pity of their being shut up in apartments which in the Venetian July even Venetian vastness did not prevent from being stuffy. Their life seemed miles away from the life of the Piazza, and no doubt it was really too late to make the austere Juliana change her habits. But poor Miss Tita would have enjoyed one of Florian's ices, I was sure; sometimes I even had thoughts of carrying one home to her. Fortunately my patience bore fruit and I was not obliged to do anything so ridiculous.

One evening about the middle of July I came in earlier than usual – I forget what chance had led to this – and instead of going up to my quarters made my way into the garden. The temperature was very high; it was such a night as one would gladly have spent in the open air and I was in no hurry to go to bed. I had floated home in my gondola, listening to the slow splash of the oar in the narrow dark canals, and now the only thought that solicited me was the vague reflection that it would be pleasant to recline at one's length in the fragrant darkness on a garden bench. The odour of the canal was doubtless at the bottom of that aspiration and the breath of the garden, as I entered it, gave consistency to my purpose. It was delicious – just such an air as must have trembled with Romeo's vows when he stood among the flowers and raised his arms to his mistress's balcony. I looked at the windows of the palace to see if by chance the example of Verona (Verona being not far off) had been followed; but everything was dim, as usual, and everything was still. Juliana, on summer nights in her youth, might have murmured down from open windows at Jeffrey Aspern, but Miss Tita was not a poet's mistress any more than I was a poet. This however did not prevent my gratification from being great as I became aware on reaching the end of the garden that Miss Tita was seated in my little bower. At first I only made out an indistinct figure, not in the least counting on such an overture from one of my hostesses; it even occurred to me that some sentimental maid-servant had stolen in to keep a

tryst with her sweetheart. I was going to turn away, not to
frighten her, when the figure rose to its height and I recognised
Miss Bordereau's niece. I must do myself the justice to say that
I did not wish to frighten her either, and much as I had longed
for some such accident I should have been capable of retreating. It was as if I had laid a trap for her by coming home earlier
than usual and adding to that eccentricity by creeping into the
garden. As she rose she spoke to me, and then I reflected that
perhaps, secure in my almost inveterate absence, it was her
nightly practice to take a lonely airing. There was no trap, in
truth, because I had had no suspicion. At first I took for granted
that the words she uttered expressed discomfiture at my arrival;
but as she repeated them – I had not caught them clearly – I had
the surprise of hearing her say, 'Oh, dear, I'm so very glad
you've come!' She and her aunt had in common the property
of unexpected speeches. She came out of the arbour almost as if
she were going to throw herself into my arms.

I hasten to add that she did nothing of the kind; she did not
even shake hands with me. It was a gratification to her to see me
and presently she told me why – because she was nervous when
she was out-of-doors at night alone. The plants and bushes
looked so strange in the dark, and there were all sorts of queer
sounds – she could not tell what they were – like the noises of
animals. She stood close to me, looking about her with an air of
greater security but without any demonstration of interest in
me as an individual. Then I guessed that nocturnal prowlings
were not in the least her habit, and I was also reminded (I had
been struck with the circumstance in talking with her before
I took possession) that it was impossible to over-estimate her
simplicity.

'You speak as if you were lost in the backwoods,' I said,
laughing. 'How you manage to keep out of this charming place
when you have only three steps to take to get into it, is more
than I have yet been able to discover. You hide away mighty well
so long as I am on the premises, I know; but I had a hope that
you peeped out a little at other times. You and your poor aunt
are worse off than Carmelite nuns in their cells. Should you
mind telling me how you exist without air, without exercise,

without any sort of human contact? I don't see how you carry
on the common business of life.'

She looked at me as if I were talking some strange tongue
and her answer was so little of an answer that I was considerably
irritated. 'We go to bed very early – earlier than you would
believe.' I was on the point of saying that this only deepened
the mystery when she gave me some relief by adding, 'Before
you came we were not so private. But I never have been out at
night.'

'Never in these fragrant alleys, blooming here under your
nose?'

'Ah,' said Miss Tita, 'they were never nice till now!' There
was an unmistakable reference in this and a flattering comparison, so that it seemed to me I had gained a small advantage. As
it would help me to follow it up to establish a sort of grievance I
asked her why, since she thought my garden nice, she had never
thanked me in any way for the flowers I had been sending up in
such quantities for the previous three weeks. I had not been
discouraged – there had been, as she would have observed, a
daily armful; but I had been brought up in the common forms
and a word of recognition now and then would have touched
me in the right place.

'Why I didn't know they were for me!'

'They were for both of you. Why should I make a difference?'

Miss Tita reflected as if she might be thinking of a reason for
that, but she failed to produce one. Instead of this she asked
abruptly, 'Why in the world do you want to know us?'

'I ought after all to make a difference,' I replied. 'That
question is your aunt's; it isn't yours. You wouldn't ask it if
you hadn't been put up to it.'

'She didn't tell me to ask you,' Miss Tita replied, without
confusion; she was the oddest mixture of the shrinking and the
direct.

'Well, she has often wondered about it herself and expressed
her wonder to you. She has insisted on it, so that she has put the
idea into your head that I am unsufferably pushing. Upon my
word I think I have been very discreet. And how completely

your aunt must have lost every tradition of sociability, to see anything out of the way in the idea that respectable intelligent people, living as we do under the same roof, should occasionally exchange a remark! What could be more natural? We are of the same country and we have at least some of the same tastes, since, like you, I am intensely fond of Venice.'

My interlocutress appeared incapable of grasping more than one clause in any proposition, and she declared quickly, eagerly, as if she were answering my whole speech: 'I am not in the least fond of Venice. I should like to go far away!'

'Has she always kept you back so?' I went on, to show her that I could be as irrelevant as herself.

'She told me to come out to-night; she has told me very often,' said Miss Tita. 'It is I who wouldn't come. I don't like to leave her.'

'Is she too weak, is she failing?' I demanded, with more emotion, I think, than I intended to show. I judged this by the way her eyes rested upon me in the darkness. It embarrassed me a little, and to turn the matter off I continued genially: 'Do let us sit down together comfortably somewhere and you will tell me all about her.'

Miss Tita made no resistance to this. We found a bench less secluded, less confidential, as it were, than the one in the arbour; and we were still sitting there when I heard midnight ring out from those clear bells of Venice which vibrate with a solemnity of their own over the lagoon and hold the air so much more than the chimes of other places. We were together more than an hour and our interview gave, as it struck me, a great lift to my undertaking. Miss Tita accepted the situation without a protest; she had avoided me for three months, yet now she treated me almost as if these three months had made me an old friend. If I had chosen I might have inferred from this that though she had avoided me she had given a good deal of consideration to doing so. She paid no attention to the flight of time – never worried at my keeping her so long away from her aunt. She talked freely, answering questions and asking them and not even taking advantage of certain longish pauses with which they inevitably alternated to say she thought she had better go in. It was almost as if she were waiting for something – something I might say to her – and intended to give me my opportunity. I was the more struck by this as she told me that her aunt had been less well for a good many days and in a way that was rather new. She was weaker; at moments it seemed as if she had no strength at all; yet more than ever before she wished to be left alone. That was why she had told her to come out – not even to remain in her own room, which was alongside; she said her niece irritated her, made her nervous. She sat still for hours together, as if she were asleep; she had always done that, musing and dozing; but at such times formerly she gave at intervals some small sign of life, of interest, liking her companion to be near her with her work. Miss Tita confided to me that at present her aunt was so motionless that she sometimes feared she was dead; moreover she took hardly any food – one couldn't see what she lived on. The great thing was that she still on most days got up; the serious job was to dress her, to wheel her out of her bedroom. She clung to as many of her old habits as possible and she had always, little company as they had received for years, made a point of sitting in the parlour.

I scarcely knew what to think of all this – of Miss Tita's sudden conversion to sociability and of the strange circumstance that the more the old lady appeared to decline toward her end the less she should desire to be looked after. The story did not hang together, and I even asked myself whether it were not a trap laid for me, the result of a design to make me show my hand. I could not have told why my companions (as they could only by courtesy be called) should have this purpose – why they should try to trip up so lucrative a lodger. At any rate I kept on my guard, so that Miss Tita should not have occasion again to ask me if I had an *arrière-pensée*. Poor woman, before we parted for the night my mind was at rest as to *her* capacity for entertaining one.

She told me more about their affairs than I had hoped; there was no need to be prying, for it evidently drew her out simply to feel that I listened, that I cared. She ceased wondering why I cared, and at last, as she spoke of the brilliant life they had led years before, she almost chattered. It was Miss Tita who judged it brilliant; she said that when they first came to live in Venice, years and years before (I saw that her mind was essentially vague about dates and the order in which events had occurred), there was scarcely a week that they had not some visitor or did not make some delightful *passeggio* in the city. They had seen all the curiosities; they had even been to the Lido in a boat (she spoke as if I might think there was a way on foot); they had had a collation there, brought in three baskets and spread out on the grass. I asked her what people they had known and she said, Oh! very nice ones – the Cavaliere Bombicci and the Contessa Altemura, with whom they had had a great friendship. Also English people – the Churtons and the Goldies and Mrs Stock-Stock, whom they had loved dearly; she was dead and gone, poor dear. That was the case with most of their pleasant circle (this expression was Miss Tita's own), though a few were left, which was a wonder considering how they had neglected them. She mentioned the names of two or three Venetian old women; of a certain doctor, very clever, who was so kind – he came as a friend, he had really given up practice; of the *avvocato* Pochin-testa, who wrote beautiful poems and had addressed one to her aunt. These people came to see them without fail every year, usually at the *capo d'anno*, and of old her aunt used to make them some little present – her aunt and she together: small things that she, Miss Tita, made herself, like paper lamp-shades or mats for the decanters of wine at dinner or those wollen things that in cold weather were worn on the wrists. The last few years there had not been many presents; she could not think what to make and her aunt had lost her interest and never suggested. But the people came all the same; if the Venetians liked you once they liked you for ever.

There was something affecting in the good faith of this sketch of former social glories; the picnic at the Lido had remained vivid through the ages and poor Miss Tita evidently was of the impression that she had had a brilliant youth. She had in fact had a glimpse of the Venetian world in its gossiping, home-keeping, parsimonious, professional walks; for I observed for the first time that she had acquired by contact something of the trick of the familiar, soft-sounding, almost infantile speech of the place. I judged that she had imbibed this invertebrate dialect, from the natural way the names of things and people – mostly purely local – rose to her lips. If she knew little of what they represented she knew still less of anything else. Her aunt had drawn in – her failing interest in the table-mats and lamp-shades was a sign of that – and she had not been able to mingle in society or to entertain it alone; so that the matter of her reminiscences struck one as an old world altogether. If she had not been so decent her references would have seemed to carry one back to the queer rococo Venice of Casanova. I found myself falling into the error of thinking of her too as one of Jeffrey Aspern's contemporaries; this came from her having so little in common with my own. It was possible, I said to myself, that she had not even heard of him; it might very well be that Juliana had not cared to lift even for her the veil that covered the temple of her youth. In this case she perhaps would not know of the existence of the papers, and I welcomed that presumption – it made me feel more safe with her – until I remembered that we had believed the letter of disavowal received by Cumnor to be in the handwriting of the niece. If it had been dictated to her she had of course to know what it was about; yet after all the effect of it was to repudiate the idea of any connection with the poet. I held it probable at all events that Miss Tita had not read a word of his poetry. Moreover if, with her companion, she had always escaped the interviewer there was little occasion for her having got it into her head that people were 'after' the letters. People had not been after them, inasmuch as they had not heard of them; and Cumnor's fruitless feeler would have been a solitary accident.

When midnight sounded Miss Tita got up; but she stopped at the door of the house only after she had wandered two or three times with me round the garden. 'When shall I see you again?' I asked, before she went in; to which she replied with promptness that she should like to come out the next night. She added however that she should not come – she was so far from doing everything she liked.

'You might do a few things that *I* like,' I said with a sigh.

'Oh, you – I don't believe you!' she murmured, at this, looking at me with her simple solemnity.

'Why don't you believe me?'

'Because I don't understand you.'

'That is just the sort of occasion to have faith.' I could not say more, though I should have liked to, as I saw that I only mystified her; for I had no wish to have it on my conscience that I might pass for having made love to her. Nothing less should I have seemed to do had I continued to beg a lady to 'believe in me' in an Italian garden on a mid-summer night. There was some merit in my scruples, for Miss Tita lingered and lingered: I perceived that she felt that she should not really soon come down again and wished therefore to protract the present. She insisted too on making the talk between us personal to ourselves; and altogether her behaviour was such as would have been possible only to a completely innocent woman.

'I shall like the flowers better now that I know they are also meant for me.'

'How could you have doubted it? If you will tell me the kind you like best I will send a double lot of them.'

'Oh, I like them all best!' Then she went on, familiarly: 'Shall you study – shall you read and write – when you go up to your rooms?'

'I don't do that at night, at this season. The lamplight brings in the animals.'

'You might have known that when you came.'

'I did know it!'

'And in winter do you work at night?'

'I read a good deal, but I don't often write.' She listened as if these details had a rare interest, and suddenly a temptation quite at variance with the prudence I had been teaching myself associated itself with her plain, mild face. Ah yes, she was safe and I could make her safer! It seemed to me from one moment to another that I could not wait longer – that I really must take a sounding. So I went on: 'In general before I go to sleep – very often in bed (it's a bad habit, but I confess to it), I read some great poet. In nine cases out of ten it's a volume of Jeffrey Aspern.'

I watched her well as I pronounced that name but I saw nothing wonderful. Why should I indeed – was not Jeffrey Aspern the property of the human race?

'Oh, we read him – we *have* read him,' she quietly replied.

'He is my poet of poets – I know him almost by heart.'

For an instant Miss Tita hesitated; then her sociability was too much for her.

'Oh, by heart – that's nothing!' she murmured, smiling. 'My aunt used to know him – to know him' – she paused an instant and I wondered what she was going to say – 'to know him as a visitor.'

'As a visitor?' I repeated, staring.

'He used to call on her and take her out.'

I continued to stare. 'My dear lady, he died a hundred years ago!'

'Well,' she said, mirthfully, 'my aunt is a hundred and fifty.'

'Mercy on us!' I exclaimed; 'why didn't you tell me before? I should like so to ask her about him.'

'She wouldn't care for that – she wouldn't tell you,' Miss Tita replied.

'I don't care what she cares for! She *must* tell me – it's not a chance to be lost.'

'Oh, you should have come twenty years ago: then she still talked about him.'

'And what did she say?' I asked, eagerly.

'I don't know – that he liked her immensely.'

'And she – didn't she like him?'

'She said he was a god.' Miss Tita gave me this information flatly, without expression; her tone might have made it a piece of trivial gossip. But it stirred me deeply as she dropped the words into the summer night; it seemed such a direct testimony.

'Fancy, fancy!' I murmured. And then, 'Tell me this, please – has she got a portrait of him? They are distressingly rare.'

'A portrait? I don't know,' said Miss Tita; and now there was discomfiture in her face. 'Well, good-night!' she added; and she turned into the house.

I accompanied her into the wide, dusky, stone-paved passage which on the ground floor corresponded with our grand sala. It opened at one end into the garden, at the other upon the canal, and was lighted now only by the small lamp that was always left for me to take up as I went to bed. An extinguished candle which Miss Tita apparently had brought down with her stood on the same table with it. 'Good-night, good-night!' I replied, keeping beside her as she went to get her light. 'Surely you would know, shouldn't you, if she had one?'

'If she had what?' the poor lady asked, looking at me queerly over the flame of her candle.

'A portrait of the god. I don't know what I wouldn't give to see it.'

'I don't know what she has got. She keeps her things locked up.' And Miss Tita went away, toward the staircase, with the sense evidently that she had said too much.

I let her go – I wished not to frighten her – and I contented myself with remarking that Miss Bordereau would not have locked up such a glorious possession as that – a thing a person would be proud of and hang up in a prominent place on the parlour-wall. Therefore of course she had not any portrait. Miss Tita made no direct answer to this and candle in hand, with her back to me, ascended two or three stairs. Then she stopped short and turned round looking at me across the dusky space.

'Do you write – do you write?' There was a shake in her voice – she could scarcely bring out what she wanted to ask.

'Do I write? Oh, don't speak of my writing on the same day with Aspern's!'

'Do you write about *him* – do you pry into his life?'

'Ah, that's your aunt's question; it can't be yours!' I said, in a tone of slightly wounded sensibility.

'All the more reason then that you should answer it. Do you, please?'

I thought I had allowed for the falsehoods I should have to tell; but I found that in fact when it came to the point I had not. Besides, now that I had an opening there was a kind of relief in being frank. Lastly (it was perhaps fanciful, even fatuous),

I guessed that Miss Tita personally would not in the last resort be less my friend. So after a moment's hesitation I answered, 'Yes, I have written about him and I am looking for more material. In Heaven's name have you got any?'

'*Santo Dio!*' she exclaimed, without heeding my question; and she hurried upstairs and out of sight. I might count upon her in the last resort, but for the present she was visibly alarmed. The proof of it was that she began to hide again, so that for a fortnight I never beheld her. I found my patience ebbing and after four or five days of this I told the gardener to stop the flowers.

VI

ONE afternoon, as I came down from my quarters to go out, I found Miss Tita in the sala: it was our first encounter on that ground since I had come to the house. She put on no air of being there by accident; there was an ignorance of such arts in her angular, diffident directness. That I might be quite sure she was waiting for me she informed me of the fact and told me that Miss Bordereau wished to see me: she would take me into the room at that moment if I had time. If I had been late for a love-tryst I would have stayed for this, and I quickly signified that I should be delighted to wait upon the old lady. 'She wants to talk with you – to know you,' Miss Tita said, smiling as if she herself appreciated that idea; and she led me to the door of her aunt's apartment. I stopped her a moment before she had opened it, looking at her with some curiosity.

I told her that this was a great satisfaction to me and a great honour; but all the same I should like to ask what had made Miss Bordereau change so suddenly. It was only the other day that she wouldn't suffer me near her. Miss Tita was not embarrassed by my question; she had as many little unexpected serenities as if she told fibs, but the odd part of them was that they had on the contrary their source in her truthfulness. 'Oh, my aunt changes,' she answered; 'it's so terribly dull – I suppose she's tired.'

'But you told me that she wanted more and more to be alone.'

Poor Miss Tita coloured, as if she found me over-insistent. 'Well, if you don't believe she wants to see you – I haven't invented it! I think people often are capricious when they are very old.'

'That's perfectly true. I only wanted to be clear as to whether you have repeated to her what I told you the other night.'

'What you told me?'

'About Jeffrey Aspern – that I am looking for materials.'

'If I had told her do you think she would have sent for you?'

'That's exactly what I want to know. If she wants to keep him to herself she might have sent for me to tell me so.'

'She won't speak of him,' said Miss Tita. Then as she opened the door she added in a lower tone, 'I have told her nothing.'

The old woman was sitting in the same place in which I had seen her last, in the same position, with the same mystifying bandage over her eyes. Her welcome was to turn her almost invisible face to me and show me that while she sat silent she saw me clearly. I made no motion to shake hands with her; I felt too well on this occasion that that was out of place for ever. It had been sufficiently enjoined upon me that she was too sacred for that sort of reciprocity – too venerable to touch. There was something so grim in her aspect (it was partly the accident of her green shade), as I stood there to be measured, that I ceased on the spot to feel any doubt as to her knowing my secret, though I did not in the least suspect that Miss Tita had not just spoken the truth. She had not betrayed me, but the old woman's brooding instinct had served her; she had turned me over and over in the long, still hours and she had guessed. The worst of it was that she looked terribly like an old woman who at a pinch would burn her papers. Miss Tita pushed a chair forward, saying to me, 'This will be a good place for you to sit.' As I took possession of it I asked after Miss Bordereau's health; expressed the hope that in spite of the very hot weather it was satisfactory. She replied that it was good enough – good enough; that it was a great thing to be alive.

'Oh, as to that, it depends upon what you compare it with!' I exclaimed, laughing.

'I don't compare – I don't compare. If I did that I should have given everything up long ago.'

I liked to think that this was a subtle allusion to the rapture she had known in the society of Jeffrey Aspern – though it was true that such an allusion would have accorded ill with the wish I imputed to her to keep him buried in her soul. What it accorded with was my constant conviction that no human being had ever had a more delightful social gift than his, and what it seemed to convey was that nothing in the world was worth speaking of if one pretended to speak of that. But one did not! Miss Tita sat down beside her aunt, looking as if she had reason to believe some very remarkable conversation would come off between us.

'It's about the beautiful flowers,' said the old lady; 'you sent us so many – I ought to have thanked you for them before. But I don't write letters and I receive only at long intervals.'

She had not thanked me while the flowers continued to come, but she departed from her custom so far as to send for me as soon as she began to fear that they would not come any more. I noted this; I remembered what an acquisitive propensity she had shown when it was a question of extracting gold from me, and I privately rejoiced at the happy thought I had had in suspending my tribute. She had missed it and she was willing to make a concession to bring it back. At the first sign of this concession I could only go to meet her. 'I am afraid you have not had many, of late, but they shall begin again immediately – to-morrow, to-night.'

'Oh, do send us some to-night!' Miss Tita cried, as if it were an immense circumstance.

'What else should you do with them? It isn't a manly taste to make a bower of your room,' the old woman remarked.

'I don't make a bower of my room, but I am exceedingly fond of growing flowers, of watching their ways. There is nothing unmanly in that: it has been the amusement of philosophers, of statesmen in retirement; even I think of great captains.'

'I suppose you know you can sell them – those you don't use,' Miss Bordereau went on. 'I daresay they wouldn't give you much for them; still, you could make a bargain.'

'Oh, I have never made a bargain, as you ought to know. My gardener disposes of them and I ask no questions.'

'I would ask a few, I can promise you!' said Miss Bordereau; and it was the first time I had heard her laugh. I could not get used to the idea that this vision of pecuniary profit was what drew out the divine Juliana most.

'Come into the garden yourself and pick them; come as often as you like; come every day. They are all for you,' I pursued, addressing Miss Tita and carrying off this veracious statement by treating it as an innocent joke. 'I can't imagine why she doesn't come down,' I added, for Miss Bordereau's benefit.

'You must make her come; you must come up and fetch her,' said the old woman, to my stupefaction. 'That odd thing you have made in the corner would be a capital place for her to sit.'

The allusion to my arbour was irreverent; it confirmed the impression I had already received that there was a flicker of impertinence in Miss Bordereau's talk, a strange mocking lambency which must have been a part of her adventurous youth and which had outlived passions and faculties. None the less I asked, 'Wouldn't it be possible for you to come down there yourself? Wouldn't it do you good to sit there in the shade, in the sweet air?'

'Oh, sir, when I move out of this it won't be to sit in the air, and I'm afraid that any that may be stirring around me won't be particularly sweet! It will be a very dark shade indeed. But that won't be just yet,' Miss Bordereau continued, cannily, as if to correct any hopes that this courageous allusion to the last receptacle of her mortality might lead me to entertain. 'I have sat here many a day and I have had enough of arbours in my time. But I'm not afraid to wait till I'm called.'

Miss Tita had expected some interesting talk, but perhaps she found it less genial on her aunt's side (considering that I had been sent for with a civil intention) than she had hoped. As if to give the conversation a turn that would put our companion in a light more favourable she said to me, 'Didn't I tell you the other night that she had sent me out? You see that I can do what I like!'

'Do you pity her – do you teach her to pity herself?' Miss Bordereau demanded, before I had time to answer this appeal. 'She has a much easier life than I had when I was her age.'

'You must remember that it has been quite open to me to think you rather inhuman.'

'Inhuman? That's what the poets used to call the women a hundred years ago. Don't try that; you won't do as well as they!' Juliana declared. 'There is no more poetry in the world – that I know of at least. But I won't bandy words with you,' she pursued, and I well remember the old-fashioned, artificial sound she gave to the speech. 'You have made me talk, talk! It isn't good for me at all.' I got up at this and told her I would take no more of her time; but she detained me to ask, 'Do you remember, the day I saw you about the rooms, that you offered us the use of your gondola?' And when I assented, promptly, struck again with her disposition to make a 'good thing' of being there and wondering what she now had in her eye, she broke out, 'Why don't you take that girl out in it and show her the place?'

'Oh dear aunt, what do you want to do with me?' cried the 'girl', with a piteous quaver. 'I know all about the place!'

'Well then, go with him as a cicerone!' said Miss Bordereau, with an effect of something like cruelty in her implacable power of retort – an incongruous suggestion that she was a sarcastic, profane, cynical old woman. 'Haven't we heard that there have been all sorts of changes in all these years? You ought to see them and at your age (I don't mean because you're so young), you ought to take the chances that come. You're old enough, my dear, and this gentleman won't hurt you. He will show you the famous sunsets, if they still go on – *do* they go on? The sun set for me so long ago. But that's not a reason. Besides, I shall never miss you; you think you are too important. Take her to the Piazza; it used to be very pretty,' Miss Bordereau continued, addressing herself to me. 'What have they done with the funny old church? I hope it hasn't tumbled down. Let her look at the shops; she may take some money, she may buy what she likes.'

Poor Miss Tita had got up, discountenanced and helpless, and as we stood there before her aunt it would certainly have seemed to a spectator of the scene that the old woman was amusing herself at our expense. Miss Tita protested, in a confusion of exclamations and murmurs; but I lost no time in saying that if she would do me the honour to accept the hospitality of my boat I would engage that she should not be bored. Or if she did not want so much of my company the boat itself, with the gondolier, was at her service; he was a capital oar and she might have every confidence. Miss Tita, without definitely answering this speech, looked away from me, out of the window, as if she were going to cry; and I remarked that once we had Miss Bordereau's approval we could easily come to an understanding. We would take an hour, whichever she liked, one of the very next days. As I made my obeisance to the old lady I asked her if she would kindly permit me to see her again.

For a moment she said nothing; then she inquired, 'Is it very necessary to your happiness?'

'It diverts me more than I can say.'

'You are wonderfully civil. Don't you know it almost kills *me*?'

'How can I believe that when I see you more animated, more brilliant than when I came in?'

'That is very true, aunt,' said Miss Tita. 'I think it does you good.'

'Isn't it touching, the solicitude we each have that the other shall enjoy herself?' sneered Miss Bordereau. 'If you think me brilliant to-day you don't know what you are talking about; you have never seen an agreeable woman. Don't try to pay me a compliment; I have been spoiled,' she went on. 'My door is shut, but you may sometimes knock.'

With this she dismissed me and I left the room. The latch closed behind me, but Miss Tita, contrary to my hope, had remained within. I passed slowly across the hall and before taking my way down-stairs I waited a little. My hope was answered; after a minute Miss Tita followed me. 'That's a

delightful idea about the Piazza,' I said. 'When will you go –
to-night, to-morrow?'

She had been disconcerted, as I have mentioned, but I had
already perceived and I was to observe again that when Miss
Tita was embarrassed she did not (as most women would have
done) turn away from you and try to escape, but came closer, as
it were, with a deprecating, clinging appeal to be spared, to be
protected. Her attitude was perpetually a sort of prayer for
assistance, for explanation; and yet no woman in the world
could have been less of a comedian. From the moment you
were kind to her she depended on you absolutely; her self-
consciousness dropped from her and she took the greatest
intimacy, the innocent intimacy which was the only thing she
could conceive, for granted. She told me she did not know
what had got into her aunt; she had changed so quickly, she
had got some idea. I replied that she must find out what the idea
was and then let me know; we would go and have an ice
together at Florian's and she should tell me while we listened
to the band.

'Oh, it will take me a long time to find out!' she said, rather
ruefully; and she could promise me this satisfaction neither for
that night nor for the next. I was patient now, however, for
I felt that I had only to wait; and in fact at the end of the week,
one lovely evening after dinner, she stepped into my gondola, to
which in honour of the occasion I had attached a second oar.

We swept in the course of five minutes into the Grand Canal;
whereupon she uttered a murmur of ecstasy as fresh as if she
had been a tourist just arrived. She had forgotten how splendid
the great water-way looked on a clear, hot summer evening, and
how the sense of floating between marble palaces and reflected
lights disposed the mind to sympathetic talk. We floated long
and far, and though Miss Tita gave no high-pitched voice to her
satisfaction I felt that she surrendered herself. She was more
than pleased, she was transported; the whole thing was an
immense liberation. The gondola moved with slow strokes, to
give her time to enjoy it, and she listened to the plash of the
oars, which grew louder and more musically liquid as we passed
into narrow canals, as if it were a revelation of Venice. When

I asked her how long it was since she had been in a boat she answered, 'Oh, I don't know; a long time – not since my aunt began to be ill.' This was not the only example she gave me of her extreme vagueness about the previous years and the line which marked off the period when Miss Bordereau flourished. I was not at liberty to keep her out too long, but we took a considerable *giro* before going to the Piazza. I asked her no questions, keeping the conversation on purpose away from her domestic situation and the things I wanted to know; I poured treasures of information about Venice into her ears, described Florence and Rome, discoursed to her on the charms and advantages of travel. She reclined, receptive, on the deep leather cushions, turned her eyes conscientiously to everything I pointed out to her, and never mentioned to me till some time afterwards that she might be supposed to know Florence better than I, as she had lived there for years with Miss Bordereau. At last she asked, with the shy impatience of a child, 'Are we not really going to the Piazza? That's what I want to see!' I immediately gave the order that we should go straight; and then we sat silent with the expectation of arrival. As some time still passed, however, she said suddenly, of her own movement, 'I have found out what is the matter with my aunt: she is afraid you will go!'

'What has put that into her head?'

'She has had an idea you have not been happy. That is why she is different now.'

'You mean she wants to make me happier?'

'Well, she wants you not to go; she wants you to stay.'

'I suppose you mean on account of the rent,' I remarked candidly.

Miss Tita's candour showed itself a match for my own. 'Yes, you know; so that I shall have more.'

'How much does she want you to have?' I asked, laughing. 'She ought to fix the sum, so that I may stay till it's made up.'

'Oh, that wouldn't please me,' said Miss Tita. 'It would be unheard of, your taking that trouble.'

'But suppose I should have my own reasons for staying in Venice?'

'Then it would be better for you to stay in some other house.'

'And what would your aunt say to that?'

'She wouldn't like it at all. But I should think you would do well to give up your reasons and go away altogether.'

'Dear Miss Tita,' I said, 'it's not so easy to give them up!'

She made no immediate answer to this, but after a moment she broke out: 'I think I know what your reasons are!'

'I daresay, because the other night I almost told you how I wish you would help me to make them good.'

'I can't do that without being false to my aunt.'

'What do you mean, being false to her?'

'Why, she would never consent to what you want. She has been asked, she has been written to. It made her fearfully angry.'

'Then she *has* got papers of value?' I demanded, quickly.

'Oh, she has got everything!' sighed Miss Tita, with a curious weariness, a sudden lapse into gloom.

These words caused all my pulses to throb, for I regarded them as precious evidence. For some minutes I was too agitated to speak, and in the interval the gondola approached the Piazzetta. After we had disembarked I asked my companion whether she would rather walk round the square or go and sit at the door of the café; to which she replied that she would do whichever I liked best – I must only remember again how little time she had. I assured her there was plenty to do both, and we made the circuit of the long arcades. Her spirits revived at the sight of the bright shop-windows, and she lingered and stopped, admiring or disapproving of their contents, asking me what I thought of things, theorising about prices. My attention wandered from her; her words of a while before, 'Oh, she has got everything!' echoed so in my consciousness. We sat down at last in the crowded circle at Florian's, finding an unoccupied table among those that were ranged in the square. It was a splendid night and all the world was out-of-doors; Miss Tita could not have wished the elements more auspicious for her return to society. I saw that she enjoyed it even more than she told; she was agitated with the multitude of her impressions. She had forgotten what an attractive thing the world is, and it was coming over her that somehow she had for the best years of her life been cheated of it. This did not make her angry; but as she looked all over the charming scene her face had, in spite of its smile of appreciation, the flush of a sort of wounded surprise. She became silent, as if she were thinking with a secret sadness of opportunities, for ever lost, which ought to have been easy; and this gave me a chance to say to her, 'Did you mean a while ago that your aunt has a plan of keeping me on by admitting me occasionally to her presence?'

'She thinks it will make a difference with you if you some-times see her. She wants you so much to stay that she is willing to make that concession.'

'And what good does she consider that I think it will do me to see her?'

'I don't know; she thinks it's interesting,' said Miss Tita, simply. 'You told her you found it so.'

'So I did; but every one doesn't think so.'

'No, of course not, or more people would try.'

'Well, if she is capable of making that reflection she is cap-able also of making this further one,' I went on: 'that I must have a particular reason for not doing as others do, in spite of the interest she offers – for not leaving her alone.' Miss Tita looked as if she failed to grasp this rather complicated proposi-tion; so I continued, 'If you have not told her what I said to you the other night may she not at least have guessed it?'

'I don't know; she is very suspicious.'

'But she has not been made so by indiscreet curiosity, by persecution?'

'No, no; it isn't that,' said Miss Tita, turning on me a some-what troubled face. 'I don't know how to say it: it's on account of something – ages ago, before I was born – in her life.'

'Something? What sort of thing?' I asked, as if I myself could have no idea.

'Oh, she has never told me,' Miss Tita answered; and I was sure she was speaking the truth.

Her extreme limpidity was almost provoking, and I felt for the moment that she would have been more satisfactory if she had been less ingenuous. 'Do you suppose it's something to which Jeffrey Aspern's letters and papers – I mean the things in her possession – have reference?'

'I daresay it is!' my companion exclaimed, as if this were a very happy suggestion. 'I have never looked at any of those things.'

'None of them? Then how do you know what they are?'

'I don't,' said Miss Tita, placidly. 'I have never had them in my hands. But I have seen them when she has had them out.'

'Does she have them out often?'

'Not now, but she used to. She is very fond of them.'

'In spite of their being compromising?'

'Compromising?' Miss Tita repeated, as if she was ignorant of the meaning of the word. I felt almost as one who corrupts the innocence of youth.

'I mean their containing painful memories.'

'Oh, I don't think they are painful.'

'You mean you don't think they affect her reputation?'

At this a singular look came into the face of Miss Bordereau's niece – a kind of confession of helplessness, an appeal to me to deal fairly, generously with her. I had brought her to the Piazza, placed her among charming influences, paid her an attention she appreciated, and now I seemed to let her perceive that all this had been a bribe – a bribe to make her turn in some way against her aunt. She was of a yielding nature and capable of doing almost anything to please a person who was kind to her; but the greatest kindness of all would be not to presume too much on this. It was strange enough, as I afterwards thought, that she had not the least air of resenting my want of consideration for her aunt's character, which would have been in the worst possible taste if anything less vital (from my point of view) had been at stake. I don't think she really measured it. 'Do you mean that she did something bad?' she asked in a moment.

'Heaven forbid I should say so, and it's none of my business. Besides, if she did,' I added, laughing, 'it was in other ages, in another world. But why should she not destroy her papers?'

'Oh, she loves them too much.'

'Even now, when she may be near her end?'

'Perhaps when she's sure of that she will.'

'Well, Miss Tita,' I said, 'it's just what I should like you to prevent.'

'How can I prevent it?'

'Couldn't you get them away from her?'

'And give them to you?'

This put the case very crudely, though I am sure there was no irony in her intention. 'Oh, I mean that you might let me see them and look them over. It isn't for myself; there is no personal avidity in my desire. It is simply that they would be of such immense interest to the public, such immeasurable importance as a contribution to Jeffrey Aspern's history.'

She listened to me in her usual manner, as if my speech were full of reference to things she had never heard of, and I felt particularly like the reporter of a newspaper who forces his way into a house of mourning. This was especially the case when after a moment she said, 'There was a gentleman who some time ago wrote to her in very much those words. He also wanted her papers.'

'And did she answer him?' I asked, rather ashamed of myself for not having her rectitude.

'Only when he had written two or three times. He made her very angry.'

'And what did she say?'

'She said he was a devil,' Miss Tita replied, simply.

'She used that expression in her letter?'

'Oh no; she said it to me. She made me write to him.'

'And what did you say?'

'I told him there were no papers at all.'

'Ah, poor gentleman!' I exclaimed.

'I knew there were, but I wrote what she bade me.'

'Of course you had to do that. But I hope I shall not pass for a devil.'

'It will depend upon what you ask me to do for you,' said Miss Tita, smiling.

'Oh, if there is a chance of *your* thinking so my affair is in a bad way! I sha'n't ask you to steal for me, nor even to fib – for you can't fib, unless on paper. But the principal thing is this – to prevent her from destroying the papers.'

'Why, I have no control of her,' said Miss Tita. 'It's she who controls me.'

'But she doesn't control her own arms and legs, does she? The way she would naturally destroy her letters would be to burn them. Now she can't burn them without fire, and she can't get fire unless you give it to her.'

'I have always done everything she has asked,' my companion rejoined. 'Besides, there's Olimpia.'

I was on the point of saying that Olimpia was probably corruptible, but I thought it best not to sound that note. So I simply inquired if that faithful domestic could not be managed.

'Every one can be managed by my aunt,' said Miss Tita. And then she observed that her holiday was over; she must go home.

I laid my hand on her arm, across the table, to stay her a moment. 'What I want of you is a general promise to help me.'

'Oh, how can I – how can I?' she asked, wondering and troubled. She was half surprised, half frightened at my wishing to make her play an active part.

'This is the main thing: to watch her carefully and warn me in time, before she commits that horrible sacrilege.'

'I can't watch her when she makes me go out.'

'That's very true.'

'And when you do too.'

'Mercy on us; do you think she will have done anything to-night?'

'I don't know; she is very cunning.'

'Are you trying to frighten me?' I asked.

I felt this inquiry sufficiently answered when my companion murmured in a musing, almost envious way, 'Oh, but she loves them – she loves them!'

This reflection, repeated with such emphasis, gave me great comfort; but to obtain more of that balm I said, 'If she shouldn't intend to destroy the objects we speak of before her death she will probably have made some disposition by will.'

'By will?'

'Hasn't she made a will for your benefit?'

'Why, she has so little to leave. That's why she likes money,' said Miss Tita.

'Might I ask, since we are really talking things over, what you and she live on?'

'On some money that comes from America, from a lawyer. He sends it every quarter. It isn't much!'

'And won't she have disposed of that?'

My companion hesitated – I saw she was blushing. 'I believe it's mine,' she said; and the look and tone which accompanied these words betrayed so the absence of the habit of thinking of herself that I almost thought her charming. The next instant she added, 'But she had a lawyer once, ever so long ago. And some people came and signed something.'

'They were probably witnesses. And you were not asked to sign? Well then,' I argued, rapidly and hopefully, 'it is because you are the legatee; she has left all her documents to you!'

'If she has it's with very strict conditions,' Miss Tita responded, rising quickly, while the movement gave the words a little character of decision. They seemed to imply that the bequest would be accompanied with a command that the articles bequeathed should remain concealed from every inquisitive eye and that I was very much mistaken if I thought she was the person to depart from an injunction so solemn.

'Oh, of course you will have to abide by the terms,' I said; and she uttered nothing to mitigate the severity of this conclusion. None the less, later, just before we disembarked at her own door, on our return, which had taken place almost in silence, she said to me abruptly, 'I will do what I can to help you.' I was grateful for this – it was very well so far as it went; but it did not keep me from remembering that night in a worried waking hour that I now had her word for it to reinforce my own impression that the old woman was very cunning.

VII

THE fear of what this side of her character might have led her to do made me nervous for days afterwards. I waited for an intimation from Miss Tita; I almost figured to myself that it was her duty to keep me informed, to let me know definitely whether or no Miss Bordereau had sacrificed her treasures. But as she gave no sign I lost patience and determined to judge so far as was possible with my own senses. I sent late one afternoon to ask if I might pay the ladies a visit, and my servant came back with surprising news. Miss Bordereau could be approached without the least difficulty; she had been moved out into the sala and was sitting by the window that overlooked the garden. I descended and found this picture correct; the old lady had been wheeled forth into the world and had a certain air, which came mainly perhaps from some brighter element in her dress, of being prepared again to have converse with it. It had not yet, however, begun to flock about her; she was perfectly alone and, though the door leading to her own quarters stood open, I had at first no glimpse of Miss Tita. The window at which she sat had the afternoon shade and, one of the shutters having been pushed back, she could see the pleasant garden, where the summer sun had by this time dried up too many of the plants – she could see the yellow light and the long shadows.

'Have you come to tell me that you will take the rooms for six months more?' she asked, as I approached her, startling me by something coarse in her cupidity almost as much as if she had not already given me a specimen of it. Juliana's desire to make our acquaintance lucrative had been, as I have sufficiently indicated, a false note in my image of the woman who had inspired a great poet with immortal lines; but I may say here definitely that I recognised after all that it behoved me to make a large allowance for her. It was I who had kindled the unholy flame; it was I who had put into her head that she had the means of making money. She appeared never to have thought of that; she had been living wastefully for years, in a house five times too big for her, on a footing that I could explain only by the presumption that, excessive as it was, the space she enjoyed cost her next to nothing and that small as were her revenues they left her, for Venice, an appreciable margin. I had descended on her one day and taught her to calculate, and my almost extravagant comedy on the subject of the garden had presented me irresistibly in the light of a victim. Like all persons who achieve the miracle of changing their point of view when they are old she had been intensely converted; she had seized my hint with a desperate, tremulous clutch.

I invited myself to go and get one of the chairs that stood, at a distance, against the wall (she had given herself no concern as to whether I should sit or stand); and while I placed it near her I began, gaily, 'Oh, dear madam, what an imagination you have, what an intellectual sweep! I am a poor devil of a man of letters who lives from day to day. How can I take palaces by the year? My existence is precarious. I don't know whether six months hence I shall have bread to put in my mouth. I have treated myself for once; it has been an immense luxury. But when it comes to going on—!'

'Are your rooms too dear? if they are you can have more for the same money,' Juliana responded. 'We can arrange, we can combinare, as they say here.'

'Well yes, since you ask me, they are too dear,' I said. 'Evidently you suppose me richer than I am.'

She looked at me in her barricaded way. 'If you write books don't you sell them?'

'Do you mean don't people buy them? A little – not so much as I could wish. Writing books, unless one be a great genius – and even then! – is the last road to fortune. I think there is no more money to be made by literature.'

'Perhaps you don't choose good subjects. What do you write about?' Miss Bordereau inquired.

'About the books of other people. I'm a critic, an historian, in a small way.' I wondered what she was coming to.

'And what other people, now?'

'Oh, better ones than myself: the great writers mainly – the great philosophers and poets of the past; those who are dead and gone and can't speak for themselves.'

'And what do you say about them?'

'I say they sometimes attached themselves to very clever women!' I answered, laughing. I spoke with great deliberation, but as my words fell upon the air they struck me as imprudent.

However, I risked them and I was not sorry, for perhaps after all
the old woman would be willing to treat. It seemed to be
tolerably obvious that she knew my secret: why therefore drag
the matter out? But she did not take what I had said as a
confession: she only asked:

'Do you think it's right to rake up the past?'

'I don't know that I know what you mean by raking it up; but
how can we get at it unless we dig a little? The present has such
a rough way of treading it down.'

'Oh, I like the past, but I don't like critics,' the old woman
declared, with her fine tranquillity.

'Neither do I, but I like their discoveries.'

'Aren't they mostly lies?'

'The lies are what they sometimes discover,' I said, smiling
at the quiet impertinence of this. 'They often lay bare the truth.'

'The truth is God's, it isn't man's; we had better leave it
alone. Who can judge of it – who can say?'

'We are terribly in the dark, I know,' I admitted; 'but if we
give up trying what becomes of all the fine things? What
becomes of the work I just mentioned, that of the great philosophers and poets? It is all vain words if there is nothing to
measure it by.'

'You talk as if you were a tailor,' said Miss Bordereau,
whimsically; and then she added quickly, in a different manner,
'This house is very fine; the proportions are magnificent. To-
day I wanted to look at this place again. I made them bring me
out here. When your man came, just now, to learn if I would see
you, I was on the point of sending for you, to ask if you didn't
mean to go on. I wanted to judge what I'm letting you have.
This sala is very grand,' she pursued, like an auctioneer, moving
a little, as I guessed, her invisible eyes. 'I don't believe you often
have lived in such a house, eh?'

'I can't often afford to!' I said.

'Well then, how much will you give for six months?'

I was on the point of exclaiming – and the air of excruciation
in my face would have denoted a moral fact – 'Don't, Juliana;
for *his* sake, don't!' But I controlled myself and asked less
passionately: 'Why should I remain so long as that?'

'I thought you liked it,' said Miss Bordereau, with her shrivelled dignity.

'So I thought I should.'

For a moment she said nothing more, and I left my own words to suggest to her what they might. I half expected her to say, coldly enough, that if I had been disappointed we need not continue the discussion, and this in spite of the fact that I believed her now to have in her mind (however it had come there), what would have told her that my disappointment was natural. But to my extreme surprise she ended by observing: 'If you don't think we have treated you well enough perhaps we can discover some way of treating you better.' This speech was somehow so incongruous that it made me laugh again, and I excused myself by saying that she talked as if I were a sulky boy, pouting in the corner, to be 'brought round'. I had not a grain of complaint to make; and could anything have exceeded Miss Tita's graciousness in accompanying me a few nights before to the Piazza? At this the old woman went on: 'Well, you brought it on yourself!' And then in a different tone, 'She is a very nice girl.' I assented cordially to this proposition, and she expressed the hope that I did so not merely to be obliging, but that I really liked her. Meanwhile I wondered still more what Miss Bordereau was coming to. 'Except for me, to-day,' she said, 'she has not a relation in the world.' Did she by describing her niece as amiable and unencumbered wish to represent her as a *parti*?

It was perfectly true that I could not afford to go on with my rooms at a fancy price and that I had already devoted to my undertaking almost all the hard cash I had set apart for it. My patience and my time were by no means exhausted, but I should be able to draw upon them only on a more usual Venetian basis. I was willing to pay the venerable woman with whom my pecuniary dealings were such a discord twice as much as any other *padrona di casa* would have asked, but I was not willing to pay her twenty times as much. I told her so plainly, and my plainness appeared to have some success, for she exclaimed, 'Very good; you have done what I asked – you have made an offer!'

'Yes, but not for half a year. Only by the month.'

'Oh, I must think of that then.' She seemed disappointed that I would not tie myself to a period, and I guessed that she wished both to secure me and to discourage me; to say, severely, 'Do you dream that you can get off with less than six months? Do you dream that even by the end of that time you will be appreciably nearer your victory?' What was more in my mind was that she had a fancy to play me the trick of making me engage myself when in fact she had annihilated the papers. There was a moment when my suspense on this point was so acute that I all but broke out with the question, and what kept it back was but a kind of instinctive recoil (lest it should be a mistake), from the last violence of self-exposure. She was such a subtle old witch that one could never tell where one stood with her. You may imagine whether it cleared up the puzzle when, just after she had said she would think of my proposal and without any formal transition, she drew out of her pocket with an embarrassed hand a small object wrapped in crumpled white paper. She held it there a moment and then she asked, 'Do you know much about curiosities?'

'About curiosities?'

'About antiquities, the old gimcracks that people pay so much for to-day. Do you know the kind of price they bring?'

I thought I saw what was coming, but I said ingenuously, 'Do you want to buy something?'

'No, I want to sell. What would an amateur give me for that?' She unfolded the white paper and made a motion for me to take from her a small oval portrait. I possessed myself of it with a hand of which I could only hope that she did not perceive the tremor, and she added, 'I would part with it only for a good price.'

At the first glance I recognised Jeffrey Aspern, and I was well aware that I flushed with the act. As she was watching me however I had the consistency to exclaim, 'What a striking face! Do tell me who it is.'

'It's an old friend of mine, a very distinguished man in his day. He gave it to me himself, but I'm afraid to mention his name, lest you never should have heard of him, critic and historian as you are. I know the world goes fast and one generation forgets another. He was all the fashion when I was young.'

She was perhaps amazed at my assurance, but I was surprised at hers; at her having the energy, in her state of health and at her time of life, to wish to sport with me that way simply for her private entertainment – the humour to test me and practise on me. This, at least, was the interpretation that I put upon her production of the portrait, for I could not believe that she really desired to sell it or cared for any information I might give her. What she wished was to dangle it before my eyes and put a prohibitive price on it. 'The face comes back to me, it torments me,' I said, turning the object this way and that and looking at it very critically. It was a careful but not a supreme work of art, larger than the ordinary miniature and representing a young man with a remarkably handsome face, in a high-collared green coat and a buff waistcoat. I judged the picture to have a valuable quality of resemblance and to have been painted when the model was about twenty-five years old. There are, as all the world knows, three other portraits of the poet in existence, but none of them is of so early a date as this elegant production. 'I have never seen the original but I have seen other likenesses,' I went on. 'You expressed doubt of this generation having heard of the gentleman, but he strikes me for all the world as a celebrity. Now who is he? I can't put my finger on him – I can't give him a label. Wasn't he a writer? Surely he's a poet.' I was determined that it should be she, not I, who should first pronounce Jeffrey Aspern's name.

My resolution was taken in ignorance of Miss Bordereau's extremely resolute character, and her lips never formed in my hearing the syllables that meant so much for her. She neglected to answer my question but raised her hand to take back the picture, with a gesture which though ineffectual was in a high degree peremptory. 'It's only a person who should know for himself that would give me my price,' she said with a certain dryness.

'Oh, then, you have a price?' I did not restore the precious thing; not from any vindictive purpose but because

I instinctively clung to it. We looked at each other hard while I retained it.

'I know the least I would take. What it occurred to me to ask you about is the most I shall be able to get.'

She made a movement, drawing herself together as if, in a spasm of dread at having lost her treasure, she were going to attempt the immense effort of rising to snatch it from me. I instantly placed it in her hand again, saying as I did so, 'I should like to have it myself, but with your ideas I could never afford it.'

She turned the small oval plate over in her lap, with its face down, and I thought I saw her catch her breath a little, as if she had had a strain or an escape. This however did not prevent her saying in a moment, 'You would buy a likeness of a person you don't know, by an artist who has no reputation?'

'The artist may have no reputation, but that thing is wonderfully well painted,' I replied, to give myself a reason.

'It's lucky you thought of saying that, because the painter was my father.'

'That makes the picture indeed precious!' I exclaimed, laughing; and I may add that a part of my laughter came from my satisfaction in finding that I had been right in my theory of Miss Bordereau's origin. Aspern had of course met the young lady when he went to her father's studio as a sitter. I observed to Miss Bordereau that if she would entrust me with her property for twenty-four hours I should be happy to take advice upon it; but she made no answer to this save to slip it in silence into her pocket. This convinced me still more that she had no sincere intention of selling it during her lifetime, though she may have desired to satisfy herself as to the sum her niece, should she leave it to her, might expect eventually to obtain for it. 'Well, at any rate I hope you will not offer it without giving me notice,' I said, as she remained irresponsive. 'Remember that I am a possible purchaser.'

'I should want your money first!' she returned, with unexpected rudeness; and then, as if she bethought herself that I had just cause to complain of such an insinuation and wished to turn the matter off, asked abruptly what I talked about with her niece when I went out with her that way in the evening.

'You speak as if we had set up the habit,' I replied. 'Certainly I should be very glad if it were to become a habit. But in that case I should feel a still greater scruple at betraying a lady's confidence.'

'Her confidence? Has she got confidence?'

'Here she is – she can tell you herself,' I said; for Miss Tita now appeared on the threshold of the old woman's parlour. 'Have you got confidence, Miss Tita? Your aunt wants very much to know.'

'Not in her, not in her!' the younger lady declared, shaking her head with a dolefulness that was neither jocular nor affected. 'I don't know what to do with her; she has fits of horrid imprudence. She is so easily tired – and yet she has begun to roam – to drag herself about the house.' And she stood looking down at her immemorial companion with a sort of helpless wonder, as if all their years of familiarity had not made her perversities, on occasion, any more easy to follow.

'I know what I'm about. I'm not losing my mind. I daresay you would like to think so,' said Miss Bordereau, with a cynical little sigh.

'I don't suppose you came out here yourself. Miss Tita must have had to lend you a hand,' I interposed, with a pacifying intention.

'Oh, she insisted that we should push her; and when she insists!' said Miss Tita, in the same tone of apprehension; as if there were no knowing what service that she disapproved of her aunt might force her next to render.

'I have always got most things done I wanted, thank God! The people I have lived with have humoured me,' the old woman continued, speaking out of the grey ashes of her vanity.

'I suppose you mean that they have obeyed you.'

'Well, whatever it is, when they like you.'

'It's just because I like you that I want to resist,' said Miss Tita, with a nervous laugh.

'Oh, I suspect you'll bring Miss Bordereau upstairs next, to pay me a visit,' I went on; to which the old lady replied:

'Oh no; I can keep an eye on you from here!'

'You are very tired; you will certainly be ill to-night!' cried Miss Tita.

'Nonsense, my dear; I feel better at this moment than I have done for a month. To-morrow I shall come out again. I want to be where I can see this clever gentleman.'

'Shouldn't you perhaps see me better in your sitting-room?' I inquired.

'Don't you mean shouldn't you have a better chance at me?' she returned, fixing me a moment with her green shade.

'Ah, I haven't that anywhere! I look at you but I don't see you.'

'You excite her dreadfully – and that is not good,' said Miss Tita, giving me a reproachful, appealing look.

'I want to watch you – I want to watch you!' the old lady went on.

'Well then, let us spend as much of our time together as possible – I don't care where – and that will give you every facility.'

'Oh, I've seen you enough for to-day. I'm satisfied. Now I'll go home.' Miss Tita laid her hands on the back of her aunt's chair and began to push, but I begged her to let me take her place. 'Oh yes, you may move me this way – you sha'n't in any other!' Miss Bordereau exclaimed, as she felt herself propelled firmly and easily over the smooth, hard floor. Before we reached the door of her own apartment she commanded me to stop, and she took a long, last look up and down the noble sala. 'Oh, it's a magnificent house!' she murmured; after which I pushed her forward. When we had entered the parlour Miss Tita told me that she should now be able to manage, and at the same moment the little red-haired *donna* came to meet her mistress. Miss Tita's idea was evidently to get her aunt immediately back to bed. I confess that in spite of this urgency I was guilty of the indiscretion of lingering; it held me there to think that I was nearer the documents I coveted – that they were probably put away somewhere in the faded, unsociable room. The place had indeed a bareness which did not suggest hidden treasures; there were no dusky nooks nor curtained corners, no massive cabinets nor chests with iron bands. Moreover it was possible, it was perhaps even probable that the old lady had consigned her relics to her bedroom, to some battered box that was shoved under the bed, to the drawer of some lame dressing-table, where they would be in the range of vision by the dim night-lamp. None the less I scrutinised every article of furniture, every conceivable cover for a hoard, and noticed that there were half a dozen things with drawers, and in particular a tall old secretary, with brass ornaments of the style of the Empire – a receptacle somewhat rickety but still capable of keeping a great many secrets. I don't know why this article fascinated me so, inasmuch as I certainly had no definite purpose of breaking into it; but I stared at it so hard that Miss Tita noticed me and changed colour. Her doing this made me think I was right and that wherever they might have been before the Aspern papers at that moment languished behind the peevish little lock of the secretary. It was hard to remove my eyes from the dull mahogany front when I reflected that a simple panel divided me from the goal of my hopes; but I remembered my prudence and with an effort took leave of Miss Bordereau. To make the effort graceful I said to her that I should certainly bring her an opinion about the little picture.

'The little picture?' Miss Tita asked, surprised.

'What do *you* know about it, my dear?' the old woman demanded. 'You needn't mind. I have fixed my price.'

'And what may that be?'

'A thousand pounds.'

'Oh Lord!' cried poor Miss Tita, irrepressibly.

'Is that what she talks to you about?' said Miss Bordereau.

'Imagine your aunt's wanting to know!' I had to separate from Miss Tita with only those words, though I should have liked immensely to add, 'For Heaven's sake meet me to-night in the garden!'

VIII

As it turned out the precaution had not been needed, for three hours later, just as I had finished my dinner, Miss Bordereau's niece appeared, unannounced, in the open doorway of the room in which my simple repasts were served. I remember well that I felt no surprise at seeing her; which is not a proof that I did not believe in her timidity. It was immense, but in a case in which there was a particular reason for boldness it never would have prevented her from running up to my rooms. I saw that she was now quite full of a particular reason; it threw her forward – made her seize me, as I rose to meet her, by the arm.

'My aunt is very ill; I think she is dying!'

'Never in the world,' I answered, bitterly. 'Don't you be afraid!'

'Do go for a doctor – do, do! Olimpia is gone for the one we always have, but she doesn't come back; I don't know what has happened to her. I told her that if he was not at home she was to follow him where he had gone; but apparently she is following him all over Venice. I don't know what to do – she looks so as if she were sinking.'

'May I see her, may I judge?' I asked. 'Of course I shall be delighted to bring some one; but hadn't we better send my man instead, so that I may stay with you?'

Miss Tita assented to this and I despatched my servant for the best doctor in the neighbourhood. I hurried downstairs with her, and on the way she told me that an hour after I quitted them in the afternoon Miss Bordereau had had an attack of 'oppression', a terrible difficulty in breathing. This had subsided but had left her so exhausted that she did not come up: she seemed all gone. I repeated that she was not gone, that she would not go yet; whereupon Miss Tita gave me a sharper sidelong glance than she had ever directed at me and said, 'Really, what do you mean? I suppose you don't accuse her of making-believe!' I forget what reply I made to this, but I grant that in my heart I thought the old woman capable of any weird manoeuvre. Miss Tita wanted to know what I had done to her; her aunt had told her that I had made her so angry. I declared I had done nothing – I had been exceedingly careful; to which my companion rejoined that Miss Bordereau had assured her she had had a scene with me – a scene that had upset her. I answered with some resentment that it was a scene of her own making – that I couldn't think what she was angry with me for unless for not seeing my way to give a thousand pounds for the portrait of Jeffrey Aspern. 'And did she show you that? Oh gracious – oh deary me!' groaned Miss Tita, who appeared to feel that the situation was passing out of her control and that the elements of her fate were thickening around her. I said that I would give anything to possess it, yet that I had not a thousand pounds; but I stopped when we came to the door of Miss Bordereau's room. I had an immense curiosity to pass it, but I thought it my duty to represent to Miss Tita that if I made the invalid angry she ought perhaps to be spared the sight of me. 'The sight of you? Do you think she can *see*?' my companion demanded, almost with indignation. I did think so but forbore to say it, and I softly followed my conductress.

I remember that what I said to her as I stood for a moment beside the old woman's bed was, 'Does she never show you her eyes then? Have you never seen them?' Miss Bordereau had been divested of her green shade, but (it was not my fortune to behold Juliana in her nightcap) the upper half of her face was covered by the fall of a piece of dingy lacelike muslin, a sort of extemporised hood which, wound round her head, descended to the end of her nose, leaving nothing visible but her white withered cheeks and puckered mouth, closed tightly and, as it were, consciously. Miss Tita gave me a glance of surprise, evidently not seeing a reason for my impatience. 'You mean that she always wears something? She does it to preserve them.'

'Because they are so fine?'

'Oh, to-day, to-day!' And Miss Tita shook her head, speaking very low. 'But they used to be magnificent!'

'Yes indeed, we have Aspern's word for that.' And as I looked again at the old woman's wrappings I could imagine that she had not wished to allow people a reason to say that the great poet had overdone it. But I did not waste my time in considering Miss Bordereau, in whom the appearance of respiration was so slight as to suggest that no human attention could ever help her more. I turned my eyes all over the room, rummaging with them the closets, the chests of drawers, the tables. Miss Tita met them quickly and read, I think, what was in them; but she did not answer it, turning away restlessly, anxiously, so that I felt rebuked, with reason, for a preoccupation that was almost profane in the presence of our dying companion. All the same I took another look, endeavouring to pick out mentally the place to try first, for a person who should wish to put his hand on Miss Bordereau's papers directly after her death. The room was a dire confusion; it looked like the room of an old actress. There were clothes hanging over chairs, odd-looking, shabby bundles here and there, and various pasteboard boxes piled together, battered, bulging and discoloured, which might have been fifty years old. Miss Tita after a moment noticed the direction of my eyes again and, as if she guessed how I judged the air of the place (forgetting I had no business to judge it at all), said, perhaps to defend herself from the imputation of complicity in such untidiness:

'She likes it this way; we can't move things. There are old bandboxes she has had most of her life.' Then she added, half taking pity on my real thought, 'Those things were *there*.' And she pointed to a small, low trunk which stood under a sofa where there was just room for it. It appeared to be a queer, superannuated coffer, of painted wood, with elaborate handles and shrivelled straps and with the colour (it had last been endued with a coat of light green) much rubbed off. It evidently had travelled with Juliana in the olden time – in the days of her adventures, which it had shared. It would have made a strange figure arriving at a modern hotel.

'*Were* there – they aren't now?' I asked, startled by Miss Tita's implication.

She was going to answer, but at that moment the doctor came in – the doctor whom the little maid had been sent to fetch and whom she had at last overtaken. My servant, going on his own errand, had met her with her companion in tow, and in the sociable Venetian spirit, retracing his steps with them, had also come up to the threshold of Miss Bordereau's room, where I saw him peeping over the doctor's shoulder. I motioned him away the more instantly that the sight of his prying face reminded me that I myself had almost as little to do there – an admonition confirmed by the sharp way the little doctor looked at me, appearing to take me for a rival who had the field before him. He was a short, fat, brisk gentleman who wore the tall hat of his profession and seemed to look at everything but his patient. He looked particularly at me, as if it struck him that I should be better for a dose, so that I bowed to him and left him with the women, going down to smoke a cigar in the garden. I was nervous; I could not go further; I could not leave the place. I don't know exactly what I thought might happen, but it seemed to me important to be there. I wandered about in the alleys – the warm night had come on – smoking cigar after cigar and looking at the light in Miss Bordereau's windows. They were open now, I could see; the situation was different. Sometimes the light moved, but not quickly; it did not suggest the hurry of a crisis. Was the old woman dying or was she already dead? Had the doctor said that there was nothing to be done at her tremendous age but to let her quietly pass away; or had he simply announced with a look a little more conventional that the end of the end had come? Were the other two women moving about to perform the offices that follow in such a case? It made me uneasy not to be nearer, as if I thought the doctor himself might carry away the papers with him. I bit my cigar hard as it came over me again that perhaps there were now no papers to carry!

I wandered about for an hour – for an hour and a half. I looked out for Miss Tita at one of the windows, having a vague idea that she might come there to give me some sign. Would she not see the red tip of my cigar moving about in the dark and feel that I wanted eminently to know what the doctor had said? I am afraid it is a proof my anxieties had made me gross that I should have taken in some degree for granted that at such an hour, in the midst of the greatest change that could take place in her life, they were uppermost also in poor Miss Tita's mind. My servant came down and spoke to me; he knew nothing save that the doctor had gone after a visit of half an hour. If he had stayed half an hour then Miss Bordereau was still alive: it could not have taken so much time as that to enunciate the contrary. I sent the man out of the house; there were moments when the sense of his curiosity annoyed me and this was one of them. *He* had been watching my cigar-tip from an upper window, if Miss Tita had not; he could not know what I was after and I could not tell him, though I was conscious he had fantastic private theories about me which he thought fine and which I, had I known them, should have thought offensive.

I went upstairs at last but I ascended no higher than the sala. The door of Miss Bordereau's apartment was open, showing from the parlour the dimness of a poor candle. I went toward it with a light tread and at the same moment Miss Tita appeared and stood looking at me as I approached. 'She's better – she's better,' she said, even before I had asked. 'The doctor has given her something; she woke up, came back to life while he was there. He says there is no immediate danger.'

'No immediate danger? Surely he thinks her condition strange!'

'Yes, because she had been excited. That affects her dreadfully.'

'It will do so again then, because she excites herself. She did so this afternoon.'

'Yes; she mustn't come out any more,' said Miss Tita, with one of her lapses into a deeper placidity.

'What is the use of making such a remark as that if you begin to rattle her about again the first time she bids you?'

'I won't – I won't do it any more.'

'You must learn to resist her,' I went on.

'Oh yes, I shall; I shall do so better if you tell me it's right.'

'You mustn't do it for me; you must do it for yourself. It all comes back to you, if you are frightened.'

'Well, I am not frightened now,' said Miss Tita, cheerfully. 'She is very quiet.'

'Is she conscious again – does she speak?'

'No, she doesn't speak, but she takes my hand. She holds it fast.'

'Yes,' I rejoined, 'I can see what force she still has by the way she grabbed that picture this afternoon. But if she holds you fast how comes it that you are here?'

Miss Tita hesitated a moment; though her face was in deep shadow (she had her back to the light in the parlour and I had put down my own candle far off, near the door of the sala), I thought I saw her smile ingenuously. 'I came on purpose – I heard your step.'

'Why, I came on tiptoe, as inaudibly as possible.'

'Well, I heard you,' said Miss Tita.

'And is your aunt alone now?'

'Oh no; Olimpia is sitting there.'

On my side I hesitated. 'Shall we then step in there?' And I nodded at the parlour; I wanted more and more to be on the spot.

'We can't talk there – she will hear us.'

I was on the point of replying that in that case we would sit silent, but I was too conscious that this would not do, as there was something I desired immensely to ask her. So I proposed that we should walk a little in the sala, keeping more at the other end, where we should not disturb the old lady. Miss Tita assented unconditionally; the doctor was coming again, she said, and she would be there to meet him at the door. We strolled through the fine superfluous hall, where on the marble floor – particularly as at first we said nothing – our footsteps were more audible than I had expected. When we reached the other end – the wide window, inveterately closed, connecting with the balcony that overhung the canal – I suggested that we should remain there, as she would see the doctor arrive still better. I opened the window and we passed out on the balcony. The air of the canal seemed even heavier, hotter than that of the sala. The place was hushed and void; the quiet neighbourhood had gone to sleep. A lamp, here and there, over the narrow black water, glimmered in double; the voice of a man going homeward singing, with his jacket on his shoulder and his hat on his ear, came to us from a distance. This did not prevent the scene from being very *comme il faut*, as Miss Bordereau had called it the first time I saw her. Presently a gondola passed along the canal with its slow rhythmical plash, and as we listened we watched it in silence. It did not stop, it did not carry the doctor; and after it had gone on I said to Miss Tita:

'And where are they now – the things that were in the trunk?'

'In the trunk?'

'That green box you pointed out to me in her room. You said her papers had been there; you seemed to imply that she had transferred them.'

'Oh yes; they are not in the trunk,' said Miss Tita.

'May I ask if you have looked?'

'Yes, I have looked – for you.'

'How for me, dear Miss Tita? Do you mean you would have given them to me if you had found them?' I asked, almost trembling.

She delayed to reply and I waited. Suddenly she broke out, 'I don't know what I would do – what I wouldn't!'

'Would you look again – somewhere else?'

She had spoken with a strange, unexpected emotion, and she went on in the same tone: 'I can't – I can't – while she lies there. It isn't decent.'

'No, it isn't decent,' I replied, gravely. 'Let the poor lady rest in peace.' And the words, on my lips, were not hypocritical, for I felt reprimanded and shamed.

Miss Tita added in a moment, as if she had guessed this and were sorry for me, but at the same time wished to explain that I did drive her on or at least did insist too much: 'I can't deceive her that way. I can't deceive her – perhaps on her deathbed.'

'Heaven forbid I should ask you, though I have been guilty myself!'

'You have been guilty?'

'I have sailed under false colours.' I felt now as if I must tell her that I had given her an invented name, on account of my fear that her aunt would have heard of me and would refuse to take me in. I explained this and also that I had really been a party to the letter written to them by John Cumnor months before.

She listened with great attention, looking at me with parted lips, and when I had made my confession she said, 'Then your real name – what is it?' She repeated it over twice when I had told her, accompanying it with the exclamation 'Gracious, gracious!' Then she added, 'I like your own best.'

'So do I,' I said, laughing. 'Ouf! it's a relief to get rid of the other.'

'So it was a regular plot – a kind of conspiracy?'

'Oh, a conspiracy – we were only two,' I replied, leaving out Mrs Prest of course.

She hesitated; I thought she was perhaps going to say that we had been very base. But she remarked after a moment, in a candid, wondering way, 'How much you must want them!'

'Oh, I do, passionately!' I conceded, smiling. And this chance made me go on, forgetting my compunction of a moment before. 'How can she possibly have changed their place herself? How can she walk? How can she arrive at that sort of muscular exertion? How can she lift and carry things?'

'Oh, when one wants and when one has so much will!' said Miss Tita, as if she had thought over my question already herself and had simply had no choice but that answer – the idea that in the dead of night, or at some moment when the coast was clear, the old woman had been capable of a miraculous effort.

'Have you questioned Olimpia? Hasn't she helped her – hasn't she done it for her?' I asked; to which Miss Tita replied promptly and positively that their servant had had nothing to do with the matter, though without admitting definitely that she had spoken to her. It was as if she were a little shy, a little ashamed now of letting me see how much she had entered into my uneasiness and had me on her mind. Suddenly she said to me, without any immediate relevance:

'I feel as if you were a new person, now that you have got a new name.'

'It isn't a new one; it is a very good old one, thank Heaven!'

She looked at me a moment. 'I do like it better.'

'Oh, if you didn't I would almost go on with the other!'

'Would you really?'

I laughed again, but for all answer to this inquiry I said, 'Of course if she can rummage about that way she can perfectly have burnt them.'

'You must wait – you must wait,' Miss Tita moralised mournfully; and her tone ministered little to my patience, for it seemed after all to accept that wretched possibility. I would teach myself to wait, I declared nevertheless; because in the first place I could not do otherwise and in the second I had her promise, given me the other night, that she would help me.

'Of course if the papers are gone that's no use,' she said; not as if she wished to recede, but only to be conscientious.

'Naturally. But if you could only find out!' I groaned, quivering again.

'I thought you said you would wait.'

'Oh, you mean wait even for that?'

'For what then?'

'Oh, nothing,' I replied, rather foolishly, being ashamed to tell her what had been implied in my submission to delay – the idea that she would do more than merely find out. I know not whether she guessed this; at all events she appeared to become aware of the necessity for being a little more rigid.

'I didn't promise to deceive, did I? I don't think I did.'

'It doesn't much matter whether you did or not, for you couldn't!'

I don't think Miss Tita would have contested this even had she not been diverted by our seeing the doctor's gondola shoot into the little canal and approach the house. I noted that he came as fast as if he believed that Miss Bordereau was still in danger. We looked down at him while he disembarked and then went back into the sala to meet him. When he came up however I naturally left Miss Tita to go off with him alone, only asking her leave to come back later for news.

I went out of the house and took a long walk, as far as the Piazza, where my restlessness declined to quit me. I was unable to sit down (it was very late now but there were people still at the little tables in front of the cafés); I could only walk round and round, and I did so half a dozen times. I was uncomfortable, but it gave me a certain pleasure to have told Miss Tita who I really was. At last I took my way home again, slowly getting all but inextricably lost, as I did whenever I went out in Venice: so that it was considerably past midnight when I reached my door. The sala, upstairs, was as dark as usual and my lamp as I crossed it found nothing satisfactory to show me. I was disappointed, for I had notified Miss Tita that I would come back for a report, and I thought she might have left a light there as a sign. The door of the ladies' apartment was closed; which seemed an intimation that my faltering friend had gone to bed, tired of waiting for me. I stood in the middle of the place, considering, hoping she would hear me and perhaps peep out, saying to myself too that she would never go to bed with her aunt in a state so critical; she would sit up and watch – she would be in a chair, in her dressing-gown. I went nearer the door; I stopped there and listened. I heard nothing at all and at last I tapped gently. No answer came and after another minute I turned the handle. There was no light in the room; this ought to have prevented me from going in, but it had no such effect. If I have candidly narrated the importunities, the indelicacies, of which my desire to possess myself of Jeffrey Aspern's papers had rendered me capable I need not shrink from confessing this last indiscretion. I think it was the worst thing I did; yet there were extenuating circumstances. I was deeply though doubtless not disinterestedly anxious for more news of the old lady, and Miss Tita had accepted from me, as it were, a rendezvous which it might have been a point of honour with me to keep. It may be said that her leaving the place dark was a positive sign that she released me, and to this I can only reply that I desired not to be released.

The door of Miss Bordereau's room was open and I could see beyond it the faintness of a taper. There was no sound – my footstep caused no one to stir. I came further into the room; I lingered there with my lamp in my hand. I wanted to give Miss Tita a chance to come to me if she were with her aunt, as she must be. I made no noise to call her; I only waited to see if she would not notice my light. She did not, and I explained this (I found afterwards I was right) by the idea that she had fallen asleep. If she had fallen asleep her aunt was not on her mind, and my explanation ought to have led me to go out as I had come. I must repeat again that it did not, for I found myself at the same moment thinking of something else. I had no definite purpose, no bad intention, but I felt myself held to the spot by an acute, though absurd, sense of opportunity. For what, I could not have said, inasmuch as it was not in my mind that I might commit a theft. Even if it had been, I was confronted with the evident fact that Miss Bordereau did not leave her secretary, her cupboard and the drawers of her tables gaping. I had no keys, no tools and no ambition to smash her furniture. None the less it came to me that I was now, perhaps alone, unmolested, at the hour of temptation and secrecy, nearer to the tormenting treasure than I had ever been. I held up my lamp, let the light play on the different objects as if it could tell me something. Still there came no movement from the other room. If Miss Tita was sleeping she was sleeping sound. Was she doing so – generous creature – on purpose to leave me the field? Did she know I was there and was she just keeping quiet to see what I would do – what I *could* do? But what could I do, when it came to that? She herself knew even better than I how little.

I stopped in front of the secretary, looking at it very idiotically; for what had it to say to me after all? In the first place it was locked, and in the second it almost surely contained nothing in which I was interested. Ten to one the papers had been destroyed; and even if they had not been destroyed the old woman would not have put them in such a place as that after removing them from the green trunk – would not have transferred them, if she had the idea of their safety on her brain, from the better hiding-place to the worse. The secretary was more conspicuous, more accessible in a room in which she could no longer mount guard. It opened with a key, but there was a little brass handle, like a button, as well; I saw this as I played my lamp over it. I did something more than this at that moment: I caught a glimpse of the possibility that Miss Tita wished me really to understand. If she did not wish me to understand, if she wished me to keep away, why had she not locked the door of communication between the sitting-room and the sala? That would have been a definite sign that I was to leave them alone. If I did not leave them alone she meant me to come for a purpose – a purpose now indicated by the quick, fantastic idea that to oblige me she had unlocked the secretary. She had not left the key, but the lid would probably move if I touched the button. This theory fascinated me, and I bent over very close to judge. I did not propose to do anything, not even – not in the least – to let down the lid; I only wanted to test my theory, to see if the cover *would* move. I touched the button with my hand – a mere touch would tell me; and as I did so (it is embarrassing for me to relate it), I looked over my shoulder. It was a chance, an instinct, for I had not heard anything. I almost let my luminary drop and certainly I stepped back, straightening myself up at what I saw. Miss Bordereau stood there in her night-dress, in the doorway of her room, watching me; her hands were raised, she had lifted the everlasting curtain that covered half her face, and for the first, the last, the only time I beheld her extraordinary eyes. They glared at me, they made me horribly ashamed. I never shall forget her strange little bent white tottering figure, with its lifted head, her attitude, her expression; neither shall I forget the tone in which as I turned, looking at her, she hissed out passionately, furiously:

'Ah, you publishing scoundrel!'

I know not what I stammered, to excuse myself, to explain; but I went towards her, to tell her I meant no harm. She waved me off with her old hands, retreating before me in horror; and the next thing I knew she had fallen back with a quick spasm, as if death had descended on her, into Miss Tita's arms.

IX

I LEFT Venice the next morning, as soon as I learnt that the old lady had not succumbed, as I feared at the moment, to the shock I had given her – the shock I may also say she had given me. How in the world could I have supposed her capable of getting out of bed by herself? I failed to see Miss Tita before going; I only saw the *donna*, whom I entrusted with a note for her younger mistress. In this note I mentioned that I should be absent but for a few days. I went to Treviso, to Bassano, to Castelfranco; I took walks and drives and looked at musty old churches with ill-lighted pictures and spent hours seated smoking at the doors of cafés, where there were flies and yellow curtains, on the shady side of sleepy little squares. In spite of these pastimes, which were mechanical and perfunctory, I scantily enjoyed my journey: there was too strong a taste of the disagreeable in my life. It had been devilish awkward, as the young men say, to be found by Miss Bordereau in the dead of

night examining the attachment of her bureau; and it had not
been less so to have to believe for a good many hours afterward
that it was highly probable I had killed her. In writing to Miss
Tita I attempted to minimise these irregularities; but as she
gave me no word of answer I could not know what impression
I made upon her. It rankled in my mind that I had been called a
publishing scoundrel, for certainly I did publish and certainly
I had not been very delicate. There was a moment when I stood
convinced that the only way to make up for this latter fault was
to take myself away altogether on the instant; to sacrifice my
hopes and relieve the two poor women for ever of the oppression of my intercourse. Then I reflected that I had better try a
short absence first, for I must already have had a sense (unexpressed and dim) that in disappearing completely it would not
be merely my own hopes that I should condemn to extinction.
It would perhaps be sufficient if I stayed away long enough to
give the elder lady time to think she was rid of me. That she
would wish to be rid of me after this (if I was not rid of her) was
now not to be doubted: that nocturnal scene would have cured
her of the disposition to put up with my company for the sake of
my dollars. I said to myself that after all I could not abandon
Miss Tita, and I continued to say this even while I observed that
she quite failed to comply with my earnest request (I had given
her two or three addresses, at little towns, *poste restante*) that she
would let me know how she was getting on. I would have made
my servant write to me but that he was unable to manage a pen.
It struck me there was a kind of scorn in Miss Tita's silence
(little disdainful as she had ever been), so that I was uncomfortable and sore. I had scruples about going back and yet I had
others about not doing so, for I wanted to put myself on a better
footing. The end of it was that I did return to Venice on the
twelfth day; and as my gondola gently bumped against Miss
Bordereau's steps a certain palpitation of suspense told me that
I had done myself a violence in holding off so long.

I had faced about so abruptly that I had not telegraphed to
my servant. He was therefore not at the station to meet me, but
he poked out his head from an upper window when I reached
the house. 'They have put her into the earth, *la vecchia*,' he said

to me in the lower hall, while he shouldered my valise; and he grinned and almost winked, as if he knew I should be pleased at the news.

'She's dead!' I exclaimed, giving him a very different look.

'So it appears, since they have buried her.'

'It's all over? When was the funeral?'

'The other yesterday. But a funeral you could scarcely call it, signore; it was a dull little passeggio of two gondolas. Poveretta!' the man continued, referring apparently to Miss Tita. His conception of funerals was apparently that they were mainly to amuse the living.

I wanted to know about Miss Tita – how she was and where she was – but I asked him no more questions till we had got upstairs. Now that the fact had met me I took a bad view of it, especially of the idea that poor Miss Tita had had to manage by herself after the end. What did she know about arrangements, about the steps to take in such a case? Poveretta indeed! I could only hope that the doctor had given her assistance and that she had not been neglected by the old friends of whom she had told me, the little band of the faithful whose fidelity consisted in coming to the house once a year. I elicited from my servant that two old ladies and an old gentleman had in fact rallied round Miss Tita and had supported her (they had come for her in a gondola of their own) during the journey to the cemetery, the little red-walled island of tombs which lies to the north of the town, on the way to Murano. It appeared from these circumstances that the Misses Bordereau were Catholics, a discovery I had never made, as the old woman could not go to church and her niece, so far as I perceived, either did not or went only to early mass in the parish, before I was stirring. Certainly even the priests respected their seclusion; I had never caught the whisk of the curato's skirt. That evening, an hour later, I sent my servant down with five words written on a card, to ask Miss Tita if she would see me for a few moments. She was not in the house, where he had sought her, he told me when he came back, but in the garden walking about to refresh herself and gathering flowers. He had found her there and she would be very happy to see me.

I went down and passed half an hour with poor Miss Tita. She had always had a look of musty mourning (as if she were wearing out old robes of sorrow that would not come to an end), and in this respect there was no appreciable change in her appearance. But she evidently had been crying, crying a great deal – simply, satisfyingly, refreshingly, with a sort of primitive, retarded sense of loneliness and violence. But she had none of the formalism or the self-consciousness of grief, and I was almost surprised to see her standing there in the first dusk with her hands full of flowers, smiling at me with her reddened eyes. Her white face, in the frame of her mantilla, looked longer, leaner than usual. I had had an idea that she would be a good deal disgusted with me – would consider that I ought to have been on the spot to advise her, to help her; and, though I was sure there was no rancour in her composition and no great conviction of the importance of her affairs, I had prepared myself for a difference in her manner, for some little injured look, half familiar, half estranged, which should say to my conscience, 'Well, you are a nice person to have professed things!' But historic truth compels me to declare that Tita Bordereau's countenance expressed unqualified pleasure in seeing her late aunt's lodger. That touched him extremely and he thought it simplified his situation until he found it did not. I was as kind to her that evening as I knew how to be, and I walked about the garden with her for half an hour. There was no explanation of any sort between us; I did not ask her why she had not answered my letter. Still less did I repeat what I had said to her in that communication; if she chose to let me suppose that she had forgotten the position in which Miss Bordereau surprised me that night and the effect of the discovery on the old woman I was quite willing to take it that way: I was grateful to her for not treating me as if I had killed her aunt.

We strolled and strolled and really not much passed between us save the recognition of her bereavement, conveyed in my manner and in a visible air that she had of depending on me now, since I let her see that I took an interest in her. Miss Tita had none of the pride that makes a person wish to preserve the look of independence; she did not in the least pretend that she knew at present what would become of her. I forbore to touch particularly on that however, for I certainly was not prepared to say that I would take charge of her. I was cautious; not ignobly, I think, for I felt that her knowledge of life was so small that in her unsophisticated vision there would be no reason why – since I seemed to pity her – I should not look after her. She told me how her aunt had died, very peacefully at the last, and how everything had been done afterwards by the care of her good friends (fortunately, thanks to me, she said, smiling, there was money in the house; and she repeated that when once the Italians like you they are your friends for life); and when we had gone into this she asked me about my *giro*, my impressions, the places I had seen. I told her what I could, making it up partly, I am afraid, as in my depression I had not seen much; and after she had heard me she exclaimed, quite as if she had forgotten her aunt and her sorrow, 'Dear, dear, how much I should like to do such things – to take a little journey!' It came over me for the moment that I ought to propose some tour, say I would take her anywhere she liked; and I remarked at any rate that some excursion – to give her a change – might be managed: we would think of it, talk it over. I said never a word to her about the Aspern documents; asked no questions as to what she had ascertained or what had otherwise happened with regard to them before Miss Bordereau's death. It was not that I was not on pins and needles to know, but that I thought it more decent not to betray my anxiety so soon after the catastrophe. I hoped she herself would say something, but she never glanced that way, and I thought this natural at the time. Later however, that night, it occurred to me that her silence was somewhat strange; for if she had talked of my movements, of anything so detached as the Giorgione at Castelfranco, she might have alluded to what she could easily remember was in my mind. It was not to be supposed that the emotion produced by her aunt's death had blotted out the recollection that I was inter-ested in that lady's relics, and I fidgeted afterwards as it came to me that her reticence might very possibly mean simply that nothing had been found. We separated in the garden (it was she who said she must go in); now that she was alone in the rooms I felt that (judged, at any rate, by Venetian ideas) I was on rather a different footing in regard to visiting her there. As I shook hands with her for good-night I asked her if she had any general plan – had thought over what she had better do. 'Oh yes, oh yes, but I haven't settled anything yet,' she replied, quite cheerfully. Was her cheerfulness explained by the impression that I would settle for her?

I was glad the next morning that we had neglected practical questions, for this gave me a pretext for seeing her again immediately. There was a very practical question to be touched upon. I owed it to her to let her know formally that of course I did not expect her to keep me on as a lodger, and also to show some interest in her own tenure, what she might have on her hands in the way of a lease. But I was not destined, as it happened, to converse with her for more than an instant on either of these points. I sent her no message; I simply went down to the sala and walked to and fro there. I knew she would come out; she would very soon discover I was there. Somehow I preferred not to be shut up with her; gardens and big halls seemed better places to talk. It was a splendid morning, with something in the air that told of the waning of the long Venetian summer; a freshness from the sea which stirred the flowers in the garden and made a pleasant draught in the house, less shuttered and darkened now than when the old woman was alive. It was the beginning of autumn, of the end of the golden months. With this it was the end of my experiment – or would be in the course of half an hour, when I should really have learned that the papers had been reduced to ashes. After that there would be nothing left for me but to go to the station; for seriously (and as it struck me in the morning light) I could not linger there to act as guardian to a piece of middle-aged female helplessness. If she had not saved the papers wherein should I be indebted to her? I think I winced a little as I asked myself how much, if she *had* saved them, I should have to recognise and, as it were, to reward such a courtesy. Might not that circumstance after all saddle me with a guardianship? If this idea did not make me more uncomfortable as I walked up and down it was because I was convinced I had nothing to look to. If the old woman had not destroyed everything before she pounced upon me in the parlour she had done so afterwards.

It took Miss Tita rather longer than I had expected to guess that I was there; but when at last she came out she looked at me without surprise. I said to her that I had been waiting for her and she asked why I had not let her know. I was glad the next day that I had checked myself before remarking that I had wished to see if a friendly intuition would not tell her: it became a satisfaction to me that I had not indulged in that rather tender joke. What I did say was virtually the truth – that I was too nervous, since I expected her now to settle my fate.

'Your fate?' said Miss Tita, giving me a queer look; and as she spoke I noticed a rare change in her. She was different from what she had been the evening before – less natural, less quiet. She had been crying the day before and she was not crying now, and yet she struck me as less confident. It was as if something had happened to her during the night, or at least as if she had thought of something that troubled her – something in particular that affected her relations with me, made them more embarrassing and complicated. Had she simply perceived that her aunt's not being there now altered my position?

'I mean about our papers. *Are* there any? You must know now.'

'Yes, there are a great many; more than I supposed.' I was struck with the way her voice trembled as she told me this.

'Do you mean that you have got them in there – and that I may see them?'

'I don't think you can see them,' said Miss Tita, with an extraordinary expression of entreaty in her eyes, as if the dearest hope she had in the world now was that I would not take them from her. But how could she expect me to make such a sacrifice as that after all that had passed between us? What had I come back to Venice for but to see them, to take them? My delight at learning they were still in existence was such that if the poor woman had gone down on her knees to beseech me never to mention them again I would have treated the proceeding as a bad joke. 'I have got them but I can't show them,' she added.

'Not even to me? Ah, Miss Tita!' I groaned, with a voice of infinite remonstrance and reproach.

She coloured and the tears came back to her eyes; I saw that it cost her a kind of anguish to take such a stand but that a dreadful sense of duty had descended upon her. It made me quite sick to find myself confronted with that particular obstacle; all the more that it appeared to me I had been extremely encouraged to leave it out of account. I almost considered that Miss Tita had assured me that if she had no greater hindrance than that—! 'You don't mean to say you made her a deathbed promise? It was precisely against your doing anything of that sort that I thought I was safe. Oh, I would rather she had burned the papers outright than that!'

'No, it isn't a promise,' said Miss Tita.

'Pray what is it then?'

She hesitated and then she said, 'She tried to burn them, but I prevented it. She had hid them in her bed.'

'In her bed?'

'Between the mattresses. That's where she put them when she took them out of the trunk. I can't understand how she did it, because Olimpia didn't help her. She tells me so and I believe her. My aunt only told her afterwards, so that she shouldn't touch the bed – anything but the sheets. So it was badly made,' added Miss Tita, simply.

'I should think so! And how did she try to burn them?'

'She didn't try much; she was too weak, those last days. But she told me – she charged me. Oh, it was terrible! She couldn't speak after that night; she could only make signs.'

'And what did you do?'

'I took them away. I locked them up.'

'In the secretary?'

'Yes, in the secretary,' said Miss Tita, reddening again.

'Did you tell her you would burn them?'

'No, I didn't – on purpose.'

'On purpose to gratify me?'

'Yes, only for that.'

'And what good will you have done me if after all you won't show them?'

'Oh, none; I know that – I know that.'

'And did she believe you had destroyed them?'

'I don't know what she believed at the last. I couldn't tell – she was too far gone.'

'Then if there was no promise and no assurance I can't see what ties you.'

'Oh, she hated it so – she hated it so! She was so jealous. But here's the portrait – you may have that,' Miss Tita announced, taking the little picture, wrapped up in the same manner in which her aunt had wrapped it, out of her pocket.

'I may have it – do you mean you give it to me?' I questioned, staring, as it passed into my hand.

'Oh yes.'

'But it's worth money – a large sum.'

'Well!' said Miss Tita, still with her strange look.

I did not know what to make of it, for it could scarcely mean that she wanted to bargain like her aunt. She spoke as if she wished to make me a present. 'I can't take it from you as a gift,' I said, 'and yet I can't afford to pay you for it according to the ideas Miss Bordereau had of its value. She rated it at a thousand pounds.'

'Couldn't we sell it?' asked Miss Tita.

'God forbid! I prefer the picture to the money.'

'Well then keep it.'

'You are very generous.'

'So are you.'

'I don't know why you should think so,' I replied, and this was a truthful speech, for the singular creature appeared to have some very fine reference in her mind, which I did not in the least seize.

'Well, you have made a great difference for me,' said Miss Tita.

I looked at Jeffrey Aspern's face in the little picture, partly in order not to look at that of my interlocutress, which had begun to trouble me, even to frighten me a little – it was so self-conscious, so unnatural. I made no answer to this last declaration; I only privately consulted Jeffrey Aspern's delightful eyes with my own (they were so young and brilliant, and yet so wise, so full of vision); I asked him what on earth was the matter with Miss Tita. He seemed to smile at me with friendly mockery, as if he were amused at my case. I had got into a pickle for him – as if he needed it! He was unsatisfactory, for the only moment since I had known him. Nevertheless, now that I held the little picture in my hand I felt that it would be a precious possession. 'Is this a bribe to make me give up the papers?' I demanded in a moment, perversely. 'Much as I value it, if I were to be obliged to choose, the papers are what I should prefer. Ah, but ever so much!'

'How can you choose – how can you choose?' Miss Tita asked, slowly, lamentably.

'I see! Of course there is nothing to be said, if you regard the interdiction that rests upon you as quite insurmountable. In this case it must seem to you that to part with them would be an impiety of the worst kind, a simple sacrilege!'

Miss Tita shook her head, full of her dolefulness. 'You would understand if you had known her. I'm afraid,' she quavered suddenly – 'I'm afraid! She was terrible when she was angry.'

'Yes, I saw something of that, that night. She was terrible. Then I saw her eyes. Lord, they were fine!'

'I see them – they stare at me in the dark!' said Miss Tita.

'You are nervous, with all you have been through.'

'Oh yes, very – very!'

'You mustn't mind; that will pass away,' I said, kindly. Then I added, resignedly, for it really seemed to me that I must accept the situation, 'Well, so it is, and it can't be helped. I must renounce.' Miss Tita, at this, looking at me, gave a low, soft moan, and I went on: 'I only wish to heaven she had destroyed them; then there would be nothing more to say. And I can't understand why, with her ideas, she didn't.'

'Oh, she lived on them!' said Miss Tita.

'You can imagine whether that makes me want less to see them,' I answered, smiling. 'But don't let me stand here as if I had it in my soul to tempt you to do anything base. Naturally you will understand I give up my rooms. I leave Venice immediately.' And I took up my hat, which I had placed on a chair.

We were still there rather awkwardly, on our feet, in the middle of the sala. She had left the door of the apartments open behind her but she had not led me that way.

A kind of spasm came into her face as she saw me take my hat. 'Immediately – do you mean to-day?' The tone of the words was tragical – they were a cry of desolation.

'Oh no; not so long as I can be of the least service to you.'

'Well, just a day or two more – just two or three days,' she panted. Then controlling herself she added in another manner, 'She wanted to say something to me – the last day – something very particular, but she couldn't.'

'Something very particular?'

'Something more about the papers.'

'And did you guess – have you any idea?'

'No, I have thought – but I don't know. I have thought all kinds of things.'

'And for instance?'

'Well, that if you were a relation it would be different.'

'If I were a relation?'

'If you were not a stranger. Then it would be the same for you as for me. Anything that is mine – would be yours, and you could do what you like. I couldn't prevent you – and you would have no responsibility.'

She brought out this droll explanation with a little nervous rush, as if she were speaking words she had got by heart. They gave me an impression of subtlety and at first I failed to follow. But after a moment her face helped me to see further, and then a light came into my mind. It was embarrassing, and I bent my head over Jeffrey Aspern's portrait. What an odd expression was in his face! 'Get out of it as you can, my dear fellow!' I put the picture into the pocket of my coat and said to Miss Tita, 'Yes, I'll sell it for you. I sha'n't get a thousand pounds by any means, but I shall get something good.'

She looked at me with tears in her eyes, but she seemed to try to smile as she remarked, 'We can divide the money.'

'No, no, it shall be all yours.' Then I went on, 'I think I know what your poor aunt wanted to say. She wanted to give directions that her papers should be buried with her.'

Miss Tita appeared to consider this suggestion for a moment; after which she declared, with striking decision, 'Oh no, she wouldn't have thought that safe!'

'It seems to me nothing could be safer.'

'She had an idea that when people want to publish they are capable—' And she paused, blushing.

'Of violating a tomb? Mercy on us, what must she have thought of me!'

'She was not just, she was not generous!' Miss Tita cried with sudden passion.

The light that had come into my mind a moment before increased. 'Ah, don't say that, for we *are* a dreadful race.' Then I pursued, 'If she left a will, that may give you some idea.'

'I have found nothing of the sort – she destroyed it. She was very fond of me,' Miss Tita added, incongruously. 'She wanted me to be happy. And if any person should be kind to me – she wanted to speak of that.'

I was almost awestricken at the astuteness with which the good lady found herself inspired, transparent astuteness as it was and sewn, as the phrase is, with white thread. 'Depend upon it she didn't want to make any provision that would be agreeable to me.'

'No, not to you but to me. She knew I should like it if you could carry out your idea. Not because she cared for you but because she did think of me,' Miss Tita went on, with her unexpected, persuasive volubility. 'You could see them – you could use them.' She stopped, seeing that I perceived the sense of that conditional – stopped long enough for me to give some sign which I did not give. She must have been conscious however that though my face showed the greatest embarrassment that was ever painted on a human countenance it was not set as a stone, it was also full of compassion. It was a comfort to me a long time afterwards to consider that she could not have seen in me the smallest symptom of disrespect. 'I don't know what to do; I'm too tormented, I'm too ashamed!' she continued, with vehemence. Then turning away from me and burying her face in her hands she burst into a flood of tears. If she did not know what to do it may be imagined whether I did any better. I stood there dumb, watching her while her sobs resounded in the great empty hall. In a moment she was facing me again, with her streaming eyes. 'I would give you everything – she would understand, where she is – she would forgive me!'

'Ah, Miss Tita – ah, Miss Tita,' I stammered, for all reply. I did not know what to do, as I say, but at a venture I made a wild, vague movement, in consequence of which I found myself at the door. I remember standing there and saying, 'It wouldn't do – it wouldn't do!' pensively, awkwardly, grotesquely, while I looked away to the opposite end of the sala as if there were a beautiful view there. The next thing I remember is that I was downstairs and out of the house. My gondola was there and my gondolier, reclining on the cushions, sprang up as soon as he saw me. I jumped in and to his usual '*Dove commanda?*' I replied, in a tone that made him stare, 'Anywhere, anywhere; out into the lagoon!'

He rowed me away and I sat there prostrate, groaning softly to myself, with my hat pulled over my face. What in the name of the preposterous did she mean if she did not mean to offer me her hand? That was the price – that was the price! And did she think I wanted it, poor deluded, infatuated, extravagant lady? My gondolier, behind me, must have seen my ears red as I wondered, sitting there under the fluttering *tenda*, with my hidden face, noticing nothing as we passed – wondered whether her delusion, her infatuation had been my own reckless work. Did she think I had made love to her, even to get the papers? I had not, I had not; I repeated that over to myself for an hour, for two hours, till I was wearied if not convinced. I don't know where my gondolier took me; we floated aimlessly about on the lagoon, with slow, rare strokes. At last I became conscious that we were near the Lido, far up, on the right hand, as you turn your back to Venice, and I made him put me ashore. I wanted to walk, to move, to shed some of my bewilderment. I crossed the narrow strip and got to the sea-beach – I took my way toward Malamocco. But presently I flung myself down again on the warm sand, in the breeze, on the coarse dry grass. It took it out of me to think I had been so much at fault, that I had unwittingly but none the less deplorably trifled.

But I had not given her cause – distinctly I had not. I had said to Mrs Prest that I would make love to her; but it had been a joke without consequences and I had never said it to Tita Bordereau. I had been as kind as possible, because I really liked her; but since when had that become a crime where a woman of such an age and such an appearance was concerned? I am far from remembering clearly the succession of events and feelings during this long day of confusion, which I spent entirely in wandering about, without going home, until late at night; it only comes back to me that there were moments when I pacified my conscience and others when I lashed it into pain. I did not laugh all day – that I do recollect; the case, however it might have struck others, seemed to me so little amusing. It would have been better perhaps for me to feel the comic side of it. At any rate, whether I had given cause or not it went without saying that I could not pay the price. I could not accept. I could not, for a bundle of tattered papers, marry a ridiculous, pathetic, provincial old woman. It was a proof that she did not think the idea would come to me, her having determined to suggest it herself in that practical, argumentative, heroic way, in which the timidity however had been so much more striking than the boldness that her reasons appeared to come first and her feelings afterward.

As the day went on I grew to wish that I had never heard of Aspern's relics, and I cursed the extravagant curiosity that had put John Cumnor on the scent of them. We had more than enough material without them and my predicament was the just punishment of that most fatal of human follies, our not having known when to stop. It was very well to say it was no predicament, that the way out was simple, that I had only to leave Venice by the first train in the morning, after writing a note to Miss Tita, to be placed in her hand as soon as I got clear of the house; for it was a strong sign that I was embarrassed that when I tried to make up the note in my mind in advance (I would put it on paper as soon as I got home, before going to bed), I could not think of anything but 'How can I thank you for the rare confidence you have placed in me?' That would never do; it sounded exactly as if an acceptance were to follow.

Of course I might go away without writing a word, but that would be brutal and my idea was still to exclude brutal solutions. As my confusion cooled I was lost in wonder at the importance I had attached to Miss Bordereau's crumpled scraps; the thought of them became odious to me and I was as vexed with the old witch for the superstition that had prevented her from destroying them as I was with myself for having already spent more money than I could afford in attempting to control their fate. I forget what I did, where I went after leaving the Lido and at what hour or with what recovery of composure I made my way back to my boat. I only know that in the afternoon, when the air was aglow with the sunset, I was standing before the church of Saints John and Paul and looking up at the small square-jawed face of Bartolommeo Colleoni, the terrible *condottiere* who sits so sturdily astride of his huge bronze horse, on the high pedestal on which Venetian gratitude maintains him. The statue is incomparable, the finest of all mounted figures, unless that of Marcus Aurelius, who rides benignant before the Roman Capitol, be finer: but I was not thinking of that; I only found myself staring at the triumphant captain as if he had an oracle on his lips. The western light shines into all his grimness at that hour and makes it wonderfully personal. But he continued to look far over my head, at the red immersion of another day – he had seen so many go down into the lagoon through the centuries – and if he were thinking of battles and stratagems they were of a different quality from any I had to tell him of. He could not direct me what to do, gaze up at him as I might. Was it before this or after that I wandered about for an hour in the small canals, to the continued stupefaction of my gondolier, who had never seen me so restless and yet so void of a purpose and could extract from me no order but 'Go anywhere – everywhere – all over the place'? He reminded me that I had not lunched and expressed therefore respectfully the hope that I would dine earlier. He had had long periods of leisure during the day, when I had left the boat and rambled, so that I was not obliged to consider him, and I told him that that day, for a change, I would touch no meat. It was an effect of poor Miss Tita's proposal, not altogether auspicious, that I had quite

lost my appetite. I don't know why it happened that on this
occasion I was more than ever struck with that queer air of
sociability, of cousinship and family life, which makes up half
the expression of Venice. Without streets and vehicles, the
uproar of wheels, the brutality of horses, and with its little
winding ways where people crowd together, where voices
sound as in the corridors of a house, where the human step
circulates as if it skirted the angles of furniture and shoes never
wear out, the place has the character of an immense collective
apartment, in which Piazza San Marco is the most ornamented
corner and palaces and churches, for the rest, play the part of
great divans of repose, tables of entertainment, expanses of
decoration. And somehow the splendid common domicile,
familiar, domestic and resonant, also resembles a theatre,
with actors clicking over bridges and, in straggling processions,
tripping along fondamentas. As you sit in your gondola the
footways that in certain parts edge the canals assume to the
eye the importance of a stage, meeting it at the same angle, and
the Venetian figures, moving to and fro against the battered
scenery of their little houses of comedy, strike you as members
of an endless dramatic troupe.

I went to bed that night very tired, without being able to
compose a letter to Miss Tita. Was this failure the reason why
I became conscious the next morning as soon as I awoke of a
determination to see the poor lady again the first moment she
would receive me? That had something to do with it, but what
had still more was the fact that during my sleep a very odd
revulsion had taken place in my spirit. I found myself aware of
this almost as soon as I opened my eyes; it made me jump out of
my bed with the movement of a man who remembers that he
has left the house-door ajar or a candle burning under a shelf.
Was I still in time to save my goods? That question was in my
heart; for what had now come to pass was that in the unconscious cerebration of sleep I had swung back to a passionate
appreciation of Miss Bordereau's papers. They were now more
precious than ever and a kind of ferocity had come into my
desire to possess them. The condition Miss Tita had attached
to the possession of them no longer appeared an obstacle worth

thinking of, and for an hour, that morning, my repentant imagination brushed it aside. It was absurd that I should be able to invent nothing; absurd to renounce so easily and turn away helpless from the idea that the only way to get hold of the papers was to unite myself to her for life. I would not unite myself and yet I would have them. I must add that by the time I sent down to ask if she would see me I had invented no alternative, though to do so I had had all the time that I was dressing. This failure was humiliating, yet what could the alternative be? Miss Tita sent back word that I might come; and as I descended the stairs and crossed the sala to her door – this time she received me in her aunt's forlorn parlour – I hoped she would not think my errand was to tell her I accepted her hand. She certainly would have made the day before the reflection that I declined it.

As soon as I came into the room I saw that she had drawn this inference, but I also saw something which had not been in my forecast. Poor Miss Tita's sense of her failure had produced an extraordinary alteration in her, but I had been too full of my literary concupiscence to think of that. Now I perceived it; I can scarcely tell how it startled me. She stood in the middle of the room with a face of mildness bent upon me, and her look of forgiveness, of absolution made her angelic. It beautified her; she was younger; she was not a ridiculous old woman. This optical trick gave her a sort of phantasmagoric brightness, and while I was still the victim of it I heard a whisper somewhere in the depths of my conscience: 'Why not, after all – why not?' It seemed to me I was ready to pay the price. Still more distinctly however than the whisper I heard Miss Tita's own voice. I was so struck with the different effect she made upon me that at first I was not clearly aware of what she was saying; then I perceived she had bade me good-bye – she said something about hoping I should be very happy.

'Good-bye – good-bye?' I repeated, with an inflection interrogative and probably foolish.

I saw she did not feel the interrogation, she only heard the words; she had strung herself up to accepting our separation and they fell upon her ear as a proof. 'Are you going today?' she asked. 'But it doesn't matter, for whenever you go I shall not see

you again. I don't want to.' And she smiled strangely, with an
infinite gentleness. She had never doubted that I had left her
the day before in horror. How could she, since I had not come
back before night to contradict, even as a simple form, such an
idea? And now she had the force of soul – Miss Tita with force
of soul was a new conception – to smile at me in her humiliation.

'What shall you do – where shall you go?' I asked.

'Oh, I don't know. I have done the great thing. I have
destroyed the papers.'

'Destroyed them?' I faltered.

'Yes; what was I to keep them for? I burnt them last night,
one by one, in the kitchen.'

'One by one?' I repeated, mechanically.

'It took a long time – there were so many.' The room seemed
to go round me as she said this and a real darkness for a moment
descended upon my eyes. When it passed Miss Tita was there
still, but the transfiguration was over and she had changed back
to a plain, dingy, elderly person. It was in this character she
spoke as she said, 'I can't stay with you longer, I can't'; and it
was in this character that she turned her back upon me, as I had
turned mine upon her twenty-four hours before, and moved to
the door of her room. Here she did what I had not done when
I quitted her – she paused long enough to give me one look.
I have never forgotten it and I sometimes still suffer from it,
though it was not resentful. No, there was no resentment,
nothing hard or vindictive in poor Miss Tita; for when, later,
I sent her in exchange for the portrait of Jeffrey Aspern a larger
sum of money than I had hoped to be able to gather for her,
writing to her that I had sold the picture, she kept it with thanks;
she never sent it back. I wrote to her that I had sold the picture,
but I admitted to Mrs Prest, at the time (I met her in London, in
the autumn), that it hangs above my writing-table. When I look
at it my chagrin at the loss of the letters becomes almost intolerable.

THE LIAR

I

THE train was half an hour late and the drive from the station longer than he had supposed, so that when he reached the house its inmates had dispersed to dress for dinner and he was conducted straight to his room. The curtains were drawn in this asylum, the candles were lighted, the fire was bright, and when the servant had quickly put out his clothes the comfortable little place became suggestive – seemed to promise a pleasant house, a various party, talks, acquaintances, affinities, to say nothing of very good cheer. He was too occupied with his profession to pay many country visits, but he had heard people who had more time for them speak of establishments where 'they do you very well'. He foresaw that the proprietors of Stayes would do him very well. In his bedroom at a country-house he always looked first at the books on the shelf and the prints on the walls; he considered that these things gave a sort of measure of the culture and even of the character of his hosts. Though he had but little time to devote to them on this occasion a cursory inspection assured him that if the literature, as usual, was mainly American and humorous the art consisted neither of the water-colour studies of the children nor of 'goody' engravings. The walls were adorned with old-fashioned lithographs, principally portraits of country gentlemen with high collars and riding-gloves: this suggested – and it was encouraging – that the tradition of portraiture was held in esteem. There was the customary novel of Mr Le Fanu, for the bedside; the ideal reading in a country-house for the hours after midnight. Oliver Lyon could scarcely forbear beginning it while he buttoned his shirt.

Perhaps that is why he not only found every one assembled in the hall when he went down, but perceived from the way the move to dinner was instantly made that they had been waiting for him. There was no delay, to introduce him to a lady, for he went out in a group of unmatched men, without this appendage. The men, straggling behind, sidled and edged as usual at the door of the dining-room, and the *dénouement* of this little comedy was that he came to his place last of all. This made him think that he was in a sufficiently distinguished company, for if he had been humiliated (which he was not), he could not have consoled himself with the reflection that such a fate was natural to an obscure, struggling young artist. He could no longer think of himself as very young, alas, and if his position was not so brilliant as it ought to be he could no longer justify it by calling it a struggle. He was something of a celebrity and he was apparently in a society of celebrities. This idea added to the curiosity with which he looked up and down the long table as he settled himself in his place.

It was a numerous party – five and twenty people; rather an odd occasion to have proposed to him, as he thought. He would not be surrounded by the quiet that ministers to good work; however, it had never interfered with his work to see the spectacle of human life before him in the intervals. And though he did not know it, it was never quiet at Stayes. When he was working well he found himself in that happy state – the happiest of all for an artist – in which things in general contribute to the particular idea and fall in with it, help it on and justify it, so that he feels for the hour as if nothing in the world can happen to him, even if it come in the guise of disaster or suffering, that will not be an enhancement of his subject. Moreover there was an exhilaration (he had felt it before) in the rapid change of scene – the jump, in the dusk of the afternoon, from foggy London and his familiar studio to a centre of festivity in the middle of Hertfordshire and a drama half acted, a drama of pretty women and noted men and wonderful orchids in silver jars. He observed as a not unimportant fact that one of the pretty women was beside him: a gentleman sat on his other hand. But he went into his neighbours little as yet: he was busy looking out for Sir David, whom he had never seen and about whom he naturally was curious.

Evidently, however, Sir David was not at dinner, a circumstance sufficiently explained by the other circumstance which constituted our friend's principal knowledge of him – his being ninety years of age. Oliver Lyon had looked forward with great pleasure to the chance of painting a nonagenarian, and though the old man's absence from table was something of a disappointment (it was an opportunity the less to observe him before going to work), it seemed a sign that he was rather a sacred and perhaps therefore an impressive relic. Lyon looked at his son with the greater interest – wondered whether the glazed bloom of his cheek had been transmitted from Sir David. That would be jolly to paint, in the old man – the withered ruddiness of a winter apple, especially if the eye were still alive and the white hair carried out the frosty look. Arthur Ashmore's hair had a midsummer glow, but Lyon was glad his commission had been to delineate the father rather than the son, in spite of his never having seen the one and of the other being seated there before him now in the happy expansion of liberal hospitality.

Arthur Ashmore was a fresh-coloured, thick-necked English gentleman, but he was just not a subject; he might have been a farmer and he might have been a banker: you could scarcely paint him in characters. His wife did not make up the amount; she was a large, bright, negative woman, who had the same air as her husband of being somehow tremendously new; a sort of appearance of fresh varnish (Lyon could scarcely tell whether it came from her complexion or from her clothes), so that one felt she ought to sit in a gilt frame, suggesting reference to a catalogue or a price-list. It was as if she were already rather a bad though expensive portrait, knocked off by an eminent hand, and Lyon had no wish to copy that work. The pretty woman on his right was engaged with her neighbour and the gentleman on his other side looked shrinking and scared, so that he had time to lose himself in his favourite diversion of watching face after face. This amusement gave him the greatest pleasure he knew, and he often thought it a mercy that the human mask did interest him and that it was not less vivid than it was (sometimes it ran its success in this line very close), since he was to make his living by reproducing it. Even if Arthur Ashmore would not be inspiring to paint (a certain anxiety rose in him lest, if he should make a hit with her father-in-law, Mrs Arthur should take it into her head that he had now proved himself worthy to *aborder* her husband); even if he had looked a little less like a page (fine as to print and margin) without punctuation, he would still be a refreshing, iridescent surface. But the gentleman four persons off – what was he? Would he be a subject, or was his face only the legible door-plate of his identity, burnished with punctual washing and shaving – the least thing that was decent that you would know him by?

This face arrested Oliver Lyon: it struck him at first as very handsome. The gentleman might still be called young, and his features were regular: he had a plentiful, fair moustache that curled up at the ends, a brilliant, gallant, almost adventurous air, and a big shining breastpin in the middle of his shirt. He appeared a fine satisfied soul, and Lyon perceived that wherever he rested his friendly eye there fell an influence as pleasant as the September sun – as if he could make grapes and pears or even human affection ripen by looking at them. What was odd in him was a certain mixture of the correct and the extravagant: as if he were an adventurer imitating a gentleman with rare perfection or a gentleman who had taken a fancy to go about with hidden arms. He might have been a dethroned prince or the war-correspondent of a newspaper: he represented both enterprise and tradition, good manners and bad taste. Lyon at length fell into conversation with the lady beside him – they dispensed, as he had had to dispense at dinner-parties before, with an introduction – by asking who this personage might be.

'Oh, he's Colonel Capadose, don't you know?' Lyon didn't know and he asked for further information. His neighbour had a sociable manner and evidently was accustomed to quick transitions; she turned from her other interlocutor with a methodical air, as a good cook lifts the cover of the next sauce-pan. 'He has been a great deal in India – isn't he rather celebrated?' she inquired. Lyon confessed he had never heard of him, and she went on, 'Well, perhaps he isn't; but he says he is, and if you think it, that's just the same, isn't it?'

'If *you* think it?'

'I mean if he thinks it – that's just as good, I suppose.'

'Do you mean that he says that which is not?'

'Oh dear, no – because I never know. He is exceedingly clever and amusing – quite the cleverest person in the house, unless indeed you are more so. But that I can't tell yet, can I? I only know about the people I know; I think that's celebrity enough!'

'Enough for them?'

'Oh, I see you're clever. Enough for me! But I have heard of you,' the lady went on. 'I know your pictures; I admire them. But I don't think you look like them.'

'They are mostly portraits,' Lyon said; 'and what I usually try for is not my own resemblance.'

'I see what you mean. But they have much more colour. And now you are going to do some one here?'

'I have been invited to do Sir David. I'm rather disappointed at not seeing him this evening.'

'Oh, he goes to bed at some unnatural hour – eight o'clock or something of that sort. You know he's rather an old mummy.'

'An old mummy?' Oliver Lyon repeated.

'I mean he wears half a dozen waistcoats, and that sort of thing. He's always cold.'

'I have never seen him and never seen any portrait or photograph of him,' Lyon said. 'I'm surprised at his never having had anything done – at their waiting all these years.'

'Ah, that's because he was afraid, you know; it was a kind of superstition. He was sure that if anything were done he would die directly afterwards. He has only consented to-day.'

'He's ready to die then?'

'Oh, now he's so old he doesn't care.'

'Well, I hope I shan't kill him,' said Lyon. 'It was rather unnatural in his son to send for me.'

'Oh, they have nothing to gain – everything is theirs already!' his companion rejoined, as if she took this speech quite literally. Her talkativeness was systematic – she fraternised as seriously as she might have played whist. 'They do as they like – they fill the house with people – they have *carte blanche*.'

'I see – but there's still the title.'

'Yes, but what is it?'

Our artist broke into laughter at this, whereas his companion stared. Before he had recovered himself she was scouring the plain with her other neighbour. The gentleman on his left at last risked an observation, and they had some fragmentary talk. This personage played his part with difficulty: he uttered a remark as a lady fires a pistol, looking the other way. To catch the ball Lyon had to bend his ear, and this movement led to his observing a handsome creature who was seated on the same side, beyond his interlocutor. Her profile was presented to him and at first he was only struck with its beauty; then it produced an impression still more agreeable – a sense of undimmed remembrance and intimate association. He had not recognised her on the instant only because he had so little expected to see her there; he had not seen her anywhere for so long, and no news of her ever came to him. She was often in his thoughts, but she had passed out of his life. He thought of her twice a week; that may be called often in relation to a person one has not seen for twelve years. The moment after he recognised her he felt how true it was that it was only she who could look like that: of the most charming head in the world (and this lady had it) there could never be a replica. She was leaning forward a little; she remained in profile, apparently listening to some one on the other side of her. She was listening, but she was also looking, and after a moment Lyon followed the direction of her eyes. They rested upon the gentleman who had been described to him as Colonel Capadose – rested, as it appeared to him, with a kind of habitual, visible complacency. This was not strange, for the Colonel was unmistakably formed to attract the sympathetic gaze of woman; but Lyon was slightly disappointed that she could let *him* look at her so long without giving him a glance. There was nothing between them to-day and he had no rights, but she must have known he was coming (it was of course not such a tremendous event, but she could not have been staying in the house without hearing of it), and it was not natural that that should absolutely fail to affect her.

She was looking at Colonel Capadose as if she were in love with him – a queer accident for the proudest, most reserved of women. But doubtless it was all right, if her husband liked it or didn't notice it: he had heard indefinitely, years before, that she was married, and he took for granted (as he had not heard that she had become a widow) the presence of the happy man on whom she had conferred what she had refused to *him*, the poor art-student at Munich. Colonel Capadose appeared to be aware of nothing, and this circumstance, incongruously enough, rather irritated Lyon than gratified him. Suddenly the lady turned her head, showing her full face to our hero. He was so prepared with a greeting that he instantly smiled, as a shaken jug overflows; but she gave him no response, turned away again and sank back in her chair. All that her face said in that instant was, 'You see I'm as handsome as ever.' To which he mentally subjoined, 'Yes, and as much good it does me!' He asked the young man beside him if he knew who that beautiful being was – the fifth person beyond him. The young man leaned forward, considered and then said, 'I think she's Mrs Capadose.'

'Do you mean his wife – that fellow's?' And Lyon indicated the subject of the information given him by his other neighbour.

'Oh, is *he* Mr Capadose?' said the young man, who appeared very vague. He admitted his vagueness and explained it by saying that there were so many people and he had come only the day before. What was definite to Lyon was that Mrs Capadose was in love with her husband; so that he wished more than ever that he had married her.

'She's very faithful,' he found himself saying three minutes later to the lady on his right. He added that he meant Mrs Capadose.

'Ah, you know her then?'

'I knew her once upon a time – when I was living abroad.'

'Why then were you asking me about her husband?'

'Precisely for that reason. She married after that – I didn't even know her present name.'

'How then do you know it now?'

'This gentleman has just told me – he appears to know.'

'I didn't know he knew anything,' said the lady, glancing forward.

'I don't think he knows anything but that.'

'Then you have found out for yourself that she is faithful. What do you mean by that?'

'Ah, you mustn't question me – I want to question you,' Lyon said. 'How do you all like her here?'

'You ask too much! I can only speak for myself. I think she's hard.'

'That's only because she's honest and straightforward.'

'Do you mean I like people in proportion as they deceive?'

'I think we all do, so long as we don't find them out,' Lyon said. 'And then there's something in her face – a sort of Roman type, in spite of her having such an English eye. In fact, she's English down to the ground; but her complexion, her low forehead and that beautiful close little wave in her dark hair make her look like a glorified *contadina*.'

'Yes, and she always sticks pins and daggers into her head, to increase that effect. I must say I like her husband better: he is so clever.'

'Well, when I knew her there was no comparison that could injure her. She was altogether the most delightful thing in Munich.'

'In Munich?'

'Her people lived there; they were not rich – in pursuit of economy in fact, and Munich was very cheap. Her father was the younger son of some noble house; he had married a second time and had a lot of little mouths to feed. She was the child of the first wife and she didn't like her stepmother, but she was charming to her little brothers and sisters. I once made a sketch of her as Werther's Charlotte, cutting bread and butter while they clustered all round her. All the artists in the place were in love with her but she wouldn't look at "the likes" of us. She was too proud – I grant you that; but she wasn't stuck up nor young ladyish; she was simple and frank and kind about it. She used to remind me of Thackeray's Ethel Newcome. She told me she must marry well: it was the one thing she could do for her family. I suppose you would say that she *has* married well.'

'She told *you*?' smiled Lyon's neighbour.

'Oh, of course I proposed to her too. But she evidently thinks so herself!' he added.

When the ladies left the table the host as usual bade the gentlemen draw together, so that Lyon found himself opposite to Colonel Capadose. The conversation was mainly about the 'run', for it had apparently been a great day in the hunting-field. Most of the gentlemen communicated their adventures and opinions, but Colonel Capadose's pleasant voice was the most audible in the chorus. It was a bright and fresh but masculine organ, just such a voice as, to Lyon's sense, such a 'fine man' ought to have had. It appeared from his remarks that he was a very straight rider, which was also very much what Lyon would have expected. Not that he swaggered, for his allusions were very quietly and casually made; but they were all to dangerous experiments and close shaves. Lyon perceived after a little that the attention paid by the company to the Colonel's remarks was not in direct relation to the interest they seemed to offer; the result of which was that the speaker, who noticed that *he* at least was listening, began to treat him as his particular auditor and to fix his eyes on him as he talked. Lyon had nothing to do but to look sympathetic and assent – Colonel Capadose appeared to take so much sympathy and assent for granted. A neighbouring squire had had an accident; he had come a cropper in an awkward place – just at the finish – with consequences that looked grave. He had struck his head; he remained insensible, up to the last accounts: there had evidently been concussion of the brain. There was some exchange of views as to his recovery – how soon it would take place or whether it would take place at all; which led the Colonel to confide to our artist across the table that *he* shouldn't despair of a fellow even if he didn't come round for weeks – for weeks and weeks and weeks – for months, almost for years. He leaned forward; Lyon leaned forward to listen, and Colonel Capadose mentioned that he knew from personal experience that there was really no limit to the time one might lie unconscious without being any the worse for it. It had happened to him in Ireland, years before; he had been pitched out of a dogcart, had turned a sheer somersault and landed on his head. They thought he was dead, but he wasn't; they carried him first to the nearest cabin, where he lay for some days with the pigs, and then to an inn in a neighbouring town – it was a near thing they didn't put him under ground. He had been completely insensible – without a ray of recognition of any human thing – for three whole months; had not a glimmer of consciousness of any blessed thing. It was touch and go to that degree that they couldn't come near him, they couldn't feed him, they could scarcely look at him. Then one day he had opened his eyes – as fit as a flea!

'I give you my honour it had done me good – it rested my brain.' He appeared to intimate that with an intelligence so active as his these periods of repose were providential. Lyon thought his story very striking, but he wanted to ask him whether he had not shammed a little – not in relating it, but in keeping so quiet. He hesitated however, in time, to imply a doubt – he was so impressed with the tone in which Colonel Capadose said that it was the turn of a hair that they hadn't buried him alive. That had happened to a friend of his in India – a fellow who was supposed to have died of jungle fever – they clapped him into a coffin. He was going on to recite the further fate of this unfortunate gentleman when Mr Ashmore made a move and every one got up to adjourn to the drawing-room. Lyon noticed that by this time no one was heeding what his new friend said to him. They came round on either side of the table and met while the gentlemen dawdled before going out.

'And do you mean that your friend was literally buried alive?' asked Lyon, in some suspense.

Colonel Capadose looked at him a moment, as if he had already lost the thread of the conversation. Then his face brightened – and when it brightened it was doubly handsome. 'Upon my soul he was chucked into the ground!'

'And was he left there?'

'He was left there till I came and hauled him out.'

'*You* came?'

'I dreamed about him – it's the most extraordinary story: I heard him calling to me in the night. I took upon myself to dig him up. You know there are people in India – a kind of beastly race, the ghouls – who violate graves. I had a sort of presentiment that they would get at him first. I rode straight, I can tell you; and, by Jove, a couple of them had just broken ground! Crack – crack, from a couple of barrels, and they showed me their heels, as you may believe. Would you credit that I took him out myself? The air brought him to and he was none the worse. He has got his pension – he came home the other day; he would do anything for me.'

'He called to you in the night?' said Lyon, much startled.

'That's the interesting point. Now *what was it*? It wasn't his ghost, because he wasn't dead. It wasn't himself, because he couldn't. It was something or other! You see India's a strange country – there's an element of the mysterious: the air is full of things you can't explain.'

They passed out of the dining-room, and Colonel Capadose, who went among the first, was separated from Lyon; but a minute later, before they reached the drawing-room, he joined him again. 'Ashmore tells me who you are. Of course I have often heard of you – I'm very glad to make your acquaintance; my wife used to know you.'

'I'm glad she remembers me. I recognised her at dinner and I was afraid she didn't.'

'Ah, I daresay she was ashamed,' said the Colonel, with indulgent humour.

'Ashamed of me?' Lyon replied, in the same key.

'Wasn't there something about a picture? Yes; you painted her portrait.'

'Many times,' said the artist; 'and she may very well have been ashamed of what I made of her.'

'Well, I wasn't, my dear sir; it was the sight of that picture, which you were so good as to present to her, that made me first fall in love with her.'

'Do you mean that one with the children – cutting bread and butter?'

'Bread and butter? Bless me, no – vine leaves and a leopard skin – a kind of Bacchante.'

'Ah, yes,' said Lyon; 'I remember. It was the first decent portrait I painted. I should be curious to see it to-day.'

'Don't ask her to show it to you – she'll be mortified!' the Colonel exclaimed.

'Mortified?'

'We parted with it – in the most disinterested manner,' he laughed. 'An old friend of my wife's – her family had known him intimately when they lived in Germany – took the most extraordinary fancy to it: the Grand Duke of Silberstadt-Schreckenstein, don't you know? He came out to Bombay while we were there and he spotted your picture (you know he's one of the greatest collectors in Europe), and made such eyes at it that, upon my word – it happened to be his birthday – she told him he might have it, to get rid of him. He was perfectly enchanted – but we miss the picture.'

'It is very good of you,' Lyon said. 'If it's in a great collection – a work of my incompetent youth – I am infinitely honoured.'

'Oh, he has got it in one of his castles; I don't know which – you know he has so many. He sent us, before he left India – to return the compliment – a magnificent old vase.'

'That was more than the thing was worth,' Lyon remarked.

Colonel Capadose gave no heed to this observation; he seemed to be thinking of something. After a moment he said, 'If you'll come and see us in town she'll show you the vase.' And as they passed into the drawing-room he gave the artist a friendly propulsion. 'Go and speak to her; there she is – she'll be delighted.'

Oliver Lyon took but a few steps into the wide saloon; he stood there a moment looking at the bright composition of the lamplit group of fair women, the single figures, the great setting of white and gold, the panels of old damask, in the centre of each of which was a single celebrated picture. There was a subdued lustre in the scene and an air as of the shining trains of dresses tumbled over the carpet. At the furthest end of the room sat Mrs Capadose, rather isolated; she was on a small sofa, with an empty place beside her. Lyon could not flatter himself she had been keeping it for him; her failure to respond to his recognition at table contradicted that, but he felt an extreme desire to go and occupy it. Moreover he had her husband's sanction; so he crossed the room, stepping over the tails of gowns, and stood before his old friend.

'I hope you don't mean to repudiate me,' he said.

She looked up at him with an expression of unalloyed pleasure. 'I am so glad to see you. I was delighted when I heard you were coming.'

'I tried to get a smile from you at dinner – but I couldn't.'

'I didn't see – I didn't understand. Besides, I hate smirking and telegraphing. Also I'm very shy – you won't have forgotten that. Now we can communicate comfortably.' And she made a better place for him on the little sofa. He sat down and they had a talk that he enjoyed, while the reason for which he used to like her so came back to him, as well as a good deal of the very same old liking. She was still the least spoiled beauty he had ever seen, with an absence of coquetry or any insinuating art that seemed almost like an omitted faculty; there were moments when she struck her interlocutor as some fine creature from an asylum – a surprising deaf-mute or one of the operative blind. Her noble pagan head gave her privileges that she neglected, and when people were admiring her brow she was wondering whether there were a good fire in her bedroom. She was simple, kind and good; inexpressive but not inhuman or stupid. Now and again she dropped something that had a sifted, selected air – the sound of an impression at first hand. She had no imagination, but she had added up her feelings, some of her reflections, about life. Lyon talked of the old days in Munich, reminded her of incidents, pleasures and pains, asked her about her father and the others; and she told him in return that she was so impressed with his own fame, his brilliant position in the world, that she had not felt very sure he would speak to her or that his little sign at table was meant for her. This was plainly a perfectly truthful speech – she was incapable of any other – and he was affected by such humility on the part of a woman whose grand line was unique. Her father was dead; one of her brothers was in the navy and the other on a ranch in America; two of her sisters were married and the youngest was just coming out and very pretty. She didn't mention her step-mother. She asked him about his own personal history and he

said that the principal thing that had happened to him was that
he had never married.

'Oh, you ought to,' she answered. 'It's the best thing.'

'I like that – from you!' he returned.

'Why not from me? I am very happy.'

'That's just why I can't be. It's cruel of you to praise
your state. But I have had the pleasure of making the acquaintance of your husband. We had a good bit of talk in the other
room.'

'You must know him better – you must know him really
well,' said Mrs Capadose.

'I am sure that the further you go the more you find. But he
makes a fine show, too.'

She rested her good grey eyes on Lyon. 'Don't you think he's
handsome?'

'Handsome and clever and entertaining. You see I'm generous.'

'Yes; you must know him well,' Mrs Capadose repeated.

'He has seen a great deal of life,' said her companion.

'Yes, we have been in so many places. You must see my little
girl. She is nine years old – she's too beautiful.'

'You must bring her to my studio some day – I should like to
paint her.'

'Ah, don't speak of that,' said Mrs Capadose. 'It reminds me
of something so distressing.'

'I hope you don't mean when *you* used to sit to me – though
that may well have bored you.'

'It's not what you did – it's what we have done. It's a confession I must make – it's a weight on my mind! I mean about
that beautiful picture you gave me – it used to be so much
admired. When you come to see me in London (I count on
your doing that very soon) I shall see you looking all round.
I can't tell you I keep it in my own room because I love it so,
for the simple reason—' And she paused a moment.

'Because you can't tell wicked lies,' said Lyon.

'No, I can't. So before you ask for it—'

'Oh, I know you parted with it – the blow has already fallen,'
Lyon interrupted.

'Ah then, you have heard? I was sure you would! But do you know what we got for it? Two hundred pounds.'

'You might have got much more,' said Lyon, smiling.

'That seemed a great deal at the time. We were in want of the money – it was a good while ago, when we first married. Our means were very small then, but fortunately that has changed rather for the better. We had the chance; it really seemed a big sum, and I am afraid we jumped at it. My husband had expectations which have partly come into effect, so that now we do well enough. But meanwhile the picture went.'

'Fortunately the original remained. But do you mean that two hundred was the value of the vase?' Lyon asked.

'Of the vase?'

'The beautiful old Indian vase – the Grand Duke's offering.'

'The Grand Duke?'

'What's his name? – Silberstadt-Schreckenstein. Your husband mentioned the transaction.'

'Oh, my husband,' said Mrs Capadose; and Lyon saw that she coloured a little.

Not to add to her embarrassment, but to clear up the ambiguity, which he perceived the next moment he had better have left alone, he went on: 'He tells me it's now in his collection.'

'In the Grand Duke's? Ah, you know its reputation? I believe it contains treasures.' She was bewildered, but she recovered herself, and Lyon made the mental reflection that for some reason which would seem good when he knew it the husband and the wife had prepared different versions of the same incident. It was true that he did not exactly see Everina Brant preparing a version; that was not her line of old, and indeed it was not in her eyes to-day. At any rate they both had the matter too much on their conscience. He changed the subject, said Mrs Capadose must really bring the little girl. He sat with her some time longer and thought – perhaps it was only a fancy – that she was rather absent, as if she were annoyed at their having been even for a moment at cross-purposes. This did not prevent him from saying to her at the last, just as the ladies began to gather themselves together to go to bed: 'You seem much impressed, from what you say, with my renown and my prosperity, and you are so good as greatly to exaggerate them. Would you have married me if you had known that I was destined to success?'

'I did know it.'

'Well, I didn't.'

'You were too modest.'

'You didn't think so when I proposed to you.'

'Well, if I had married you I couldn't have married *him* – and he's so nice,' Mrs Capadose said. Lyon knew she thought it – he had learned that at dinner – but it vexed him a little to hear her say it. The gentleman designated by the pronoun came up, amid the prolonged hand-shaking for good-night, and Mrs Capadose remarked to her husband as she turned away, 'He wants to paint Amy.'

'Ah, she's a charming child, a most interesting little creature,' the Colonel said to Lyon. 'She does the most remarkable things.'

Mrs Capadose stopped, in the rustling procession that followed the hostess out of the room. 'Don't tell him, please don't,' she said.

'Don't tell him what?'

'Why, what she does. Let him find out for himself.' And she passed on.

'She thinks I swagger about the child – that I bore people,' said the Colonel. 'I hope you smoke.' He appeared ten minutes later in the smoking-room, in a brilliant equipment, a suit of crimson foulard covered with little white spots. He gratified Lyon's eye, made him feel that the modern age has its splendour too and its opportunities for costume. If his wife was an antique he was a fine specimen of the period of colour: he might have passed for a Venetian of the sixteenth century. They were a remarkable couple, Lyon thought, and as he looked at the Colonel standing in bright erectness before the chimney-piece while he emitted great smoke-puffs he did not wonder that Everina could not regret she had not married *him*. All the gentlemen collected at Stayes were not smokers and some of them had gone to bed. Colonel Capadose remarked that there probably would be a smallish muster, they had had such a hard day's work. That was the worst of a hunting house – the men were so sleepy after dinner; it was devilish stupid for the ladies, even for those who hunted themselves – for women were so extraordinary, they never showed it. But most fellows revived under the stimulating influences of the smoking-room, and some of them, in this confidence, would turn up yet. Some of the grounds of their confidence – not all of them – might have been seen in a cluster of glasses and bottles on a table near the fire, which made the great salver and its contents twinkle sociably. The others lurked as yet in various improper corners of the minds of the most loquacious. Lyon was alone with Colonel Capadose for some moments before their companions, in varied eccentricities of uniform, straggled in, and he perceived that this wonderful man had but little loss of vital tissue to repair.

They talked about the house, Lyon having noticed an oddity of construction in the smoking-room; and the Colonel explained that it consisted of two distinct parts, one of which was of very great antiquity. They were two complete houses in short, the old one and the new, each of great extent and each very fine in its way. The two formed together an enormous structure – Lyon must make a point of going all over it. The modern portion had been erected by the old man when he bought the property; oh yes, he had bought it, forty years before – it hadn't been in the family: there hadn't been any particular family for it to be in. He had had the good taste not to spoil the original house – he had not touched it beyond what was just necessary for joining it on. It was very curious indeed – a most irregular, rambling, mysterious pile, where they every now and then discovered a walled-up room or a secret staircase. To his mind it was essentially gloomy, however; even the modern additions, splendid as they were, failed to make it cheerful. There was some story about a skeleton having been found years before, during some repairs under a stone slab of the floor of one of the passages; but the family were rather shy of its being talked about. The place they were in was of course in the old part, which contained after all some of the best rooms: he had an idea it had been the primitive kitchen, half modernised at some intermediate period.

'My room is in the old part too then – I'm very glad,' Lyon said. 'It's very comfortable and contains all the latest conveniences, but I observed the depth of the recess of the door and the evident antiquity of the corridor and staircase – the first short one – after I came out. That panelled corridor is admirable; it looks as if it stretched away, in its brown dimness (the lamps didn't seem to me to make much impression on it), for half a mile.'

'Oh, don't go to the end of it!' exclaimed the Colonel, smiling.

'Does it lead to the haunted room?' Lyon asked.

His companion looked at him a moment. 'Ah, you know about that?'

'No, I don't speak from knowledge, only from hope. I have never had any luck – I have never stayed in a dangerous house. The places I go to are always as safe as Charing Cross. I want to see – whatever there is, the regular thing. *Is* there a ghost here?'

'Of course there is – a rattling good one.'

'And have you seen him?'

'Oh, don't ask me what *I've* seen – I should tax your credulity. I don't like to talk of these things. But there are two or three as bad – that is, as good! – rooms as you'll find anywhere.'

'Do you mean in my corridor?' Lyon asked.

'I believe the worst is at the far end. But you would be ill-advised to sleep there.'

'Ill-advised?'

'Until you've finished your job. You'll get letters of importance the next morning, and you'll take the 10.20.'

'Do you mean I will invent a pretext for running away?'

'Unless you are braver than almost any one has ever been. They don't often put people to sleep there, but sometimes the house is so crowded that they have to. The same thing always happens – ill-concealed agitation at the breakfast-table and letters of the greatest importance. Of course it's a bachelor's room, and my wife and I are at the other end of the house. But we saw the comedy three days ago – the day after we got here. A young fellow had been put there – I forget his name – the house was so full; and the usual consequence followed. Letters at breakfast – an awfully queer face – an urgent call to town – so very sorry his visit was cut short. Ashmore and his wife looked at each other, and off the poor devil went.'

'Ah, that wouldn't suit me; I must paint my picture,' said Lyon. 'But do they mind your speaking of it? Some people who have a good ghost are very proud of it, you know.'

What answer Colonel Capadose was on the point of making to this inquiry our hero was not to learn, for at that moment their host had walked into the room accompanied by three or four gentlemen. Lyon was conscious that he was partly answered by the Colonel's not going on with the subject. This however on the other hand was rendered natural by the fact that one of the gentlemen appealed to him for an opinion on a point under discussion, something to do with the everlasting history of the day's run. To Lyon himself Mr Ashmore began to talk, expressing his regret at having had so little direct conversation with him as yet. The topic that suggested itself was naturally that most closely connected with the motive of the artist's visit. Lyon remarked that it was a great disadvantage to him not to have had some preliminary acquaintance with Sir David – in most cases he found that so important. But the present sitter was so far advanced in life that there was doubtless no time to lose. 'Oh, I can tell you all about him,' said Mr Ashmore; and for half an hour he told him a good deal. It was very interesting as well as very eulogistic, and Lyon could see that he was a very nice old man, to have endeared himself so to a son who was evidently not a gusher. At last he got up – he said he must go to bed if he wished to be fresh for his work in the morning. To which his host replied, 'Then you must take your candle; the lights are out; I don't keep my servants up.'

In a moment Lyon had his glimmering taper in hand, and as he was leaving the room (he did not disturb the others with a good-night; they were absorbed in the lemon-squeezer and the soda-water cork) he remembered other occasions on which he had made his way to bed alone through a darkened country-house; such occasions had not been rare, for he was almost always the first to leave the smoking-room. If he had not stayed in houses conspicuously haunted he had, none the less (having the artistic temperament), sometimes found the great black halls and staircases rather 'creepy': there had been often a sinister effect, to his imagination, in the sound of his tread in the long passages or the way the winter moon peeped into tall windows on landings. It occurred to him that if houses without supernatural pretensions could look so wicked at night, the old corridors of Stayes would certainly give him a sensation. He didn't know whether the proprietors were sensitive; very often, as he had said to Colonel Capadose, people enjoyed the impeachment. What determined him to speak, with a certain sense of the risk, was the impression that the Colonel told queer stories. As he had his hand on the door he said to Arthur Ashmore, 'I hope I shan't meet any ghosts.'

'Any ghosts?'

'You ought to have some – in this fine old part.'

'We do our best, but *que voulez-vous?* said Mr Ashmore. 'I don't think they like the hot-water pipes.'

'They remind them too much of their own climate? But haven't you a haunted room – at the end of my passage?'

'Oh, there are stories – we try to keep them up.'

'I should like very much to sleep there,' Lyon said.

'Well, you can move there to-morrow if you like.'

'Perhaps I had better wait till I have done my work.'

'Very good; but you won't work there, you know. My father will sit to you in his own apartments.'

'Oh, it isn't that; it's the fear of running away, like that gentleman three days ago.'

'Three days ago? What gentleman?' Mr Ashmore asked.

'The one who got urgent letters at breakfast and fled by the 10.20. Did he stand more than one night?'

'I don't know what you are talking about. There was no such gentleman – three days ago.'

'Ah, so much the better,' said Lyon, nodding good-night and departing. He took his course, as he remembered it, with his wavering candle, and, though he encountered a great many gruesome objects, safely reached the passage out of which his room opened. In the complete darkness it seemed to stretch away still further, but he followed it, for the curiosity of the thing, to the end. He passed several doors with the name of the room painted upon them, but he found nothing else. He was tempted to try the last door – to look into the room of evil fame; but he reflected that this would be indiscreet, since Colonel Capadose handled the brush – as a *raconteur* – with such freedom. There might be a ghost and there might not; but the Colonel himself, he inclined to think, was the most mystifying figure in the house.

II

LYON found Sir David Ashmore a capital subject and a very comfortable sitter into the bargain. Moreover he was a very agreeable old man, tremendously puckered but not in the least dim; and he wore exactly the furred dressing-gown that Lyon would have chosen. He was proud of his age but ashamed of his infirmities, which however he greatly exaggerated and which did not prevent him from sitting there as submissive as if portraiture in oils had been a branch of surgery. He demolished the legend of his having feared the operation would be fatal, giving an explanation which pleased our friend much better. He held that a gentleman should be painted but once in his life – that it was eager and fatuous to be hung up all over the place. That was good for women, who made a pretty wall-pattern; but the male face didn't lend itself to decorative repetition. The proper time for the likeness was at the last, when the whole man was there – you got the totality of his experience. Lyon could not reply that that period was not a real compendium – you had to allow so for leakage; for there had been no crack in Sir David's crystallisation. He spoke of his portrait as a plain map of the country, to be consulted by his children in a case of uncertainty. A proper map could be drawn up only when the country had been travelled. He gave Lyon his mornings, till luncheon, and they talked of many things, not neglecting, as a stimulus to gossip, the people in the house. Now that he did not 'go out', as he said, he saw much less of the visitors at Stayes: people came and went whom he knew nothing about, and he liked to hear Lyon describe them. The artist sketched

with a fine point and did not caricature, and it usually befell
that when Sir David did not know the sons and daughters he
had known the fathers and mothers. He was one of those
terrible old gentlemen who are a repository of antecedents.
But in the case of the Capadose family, at whom they arrived
by an easy stage, his knowledge embraced two, or even three,
generations. General Capadose was an old crony, and he
remembered his father before him. The general was rather a
smart soldier, but in private life of too speculative a turn –
always sneaking into the City to put his money into some rotten
thing. He married a girl who brought him something and
they had half a dozen children. He scarcely knew what had
become of the rest of them, except that one was in the Church
and had found preferment – wasn't he Dean of Rockingham?
Clement, the fellow who was at Stayes, had some military
talent; he had served in the East, he had married a pretty girl.
He had been at Eton with his son, and he used to come to
Stayes in his holidays. Lately, coming back to England, he had
turned up with his wife again; that was before he – the old man –
had been put to grass. He was a taking dog, but he had a
monstrous foible.

'A monstrous foible?' said Lyon.

'He's a thumping liar.'

Lyon's brush stopped short, while he repeated, for somehow
the formula startled him, 'A thumping liar?'

'You are very lucky not to have found it out.'

'Well, I confess I have noticed a romantic tinge—'

'Oh, it isn't always romantic. He'll lie about the time of day,
about the name of his hatter. It appears there are people like
that.'

'Well, they are precious scoundrels,' Lyon declared, his
voice trembling a little with the thought of what Everina
Brant had done with herself.

'Oh, not always,' said the old man. 'This fellow isn't in the
least a scoundrel. There is no harm in him and no bad intention; he doesn't steal nor cheat nor gamble nor drink; he's very
kind – he sticks to his wife, is fond of his children. He simply
can't give you a straight answer.'

'Then everything he told me last night, I suppose, was mendacious: he delivered himself of a series of the stiffest statements. They stuck, when I tried to swallow them, but I never thought of so simple an explanation.'

'No doubt he was in the vein,' Sir David went on. 'It's a natural peculiarity – as you might limp or stutter or be left-handed. I believe it comes and goes, like intermittent fever. My son tells me that his friends usually understand it and don't haul him up – for the sake of his wife.'

'Oh, his wife – his wife!' Lyon murmured, painting fast.

'I daresay she's used to it.'

'Never in the world, Sir David. How can she be used to it?'

'Why, my dear sir, when a woman's fond! – And don't they mostly handle the long bow themselves? They are connoisseurs – they have a sympathy for a fellow performer.'

Lyon was silent a moment; he had no ground for denying that Mrs Capadose was attached to her husband. But after a little he rejoined: 'Oh, not this one! I knew her years ago – before her marriage; knew her well and admired her. She was as clear as a bell.'

'I like her very much,' Sir David said, 'but I have seen her back him up.'

Lyon considered Sir David for a moment, not in the light of a model. 'Are you very sure?'

The old man hesitated; then he answered, smiling, 'You're in love with her.'

'Very likely. God knows I used to be!'

'She must help him out – she can't expose him.'

'She can hold her tongue,' Lyon remarked.

'Well, before you probably she will.'

'That's what I am curious to see.' And Lyon added, privately, 'Mercy on us, what he must have made of her!' He kept this reflection to himself, for he considered that he had sufficiently betrayed his state of mind with regard to Mrs Capadose. None the less it occupied him now immensely, the question of how such a woman would arrange herself in such a predicament. He watched her with an interest deeply quickened when he mingled with the company; he had had his own troubles in life, but he had rarely been so anxious about anything as he was now to see what the loyalty of a wife and the infection of an example would have made of an absolutely truthful mind. Oh, he held it as immutably established that whatever other women might be prone to do she, of old, had been perfectly incapable of a deviation. Even if she had not been too simple to deceive she would have been too proud; and if she had not had too much conscience she would have had too little eagerness. It was the last thing she would have endured or condoned – the particular thing she would not have forgiven. Did she sit in torment while her husband turned his somersaults, or was she now too so perverse that she thought it a fine thing to be striking at the expense of one's honour? It would have taken a wondrous alchemy – working backwards, as it were – to produce this latter result. Besides these two alternatives (that she suffered tortures in silence and that she was so much in love that her husband's humiliating idiosyncrasy seemed to her only an added richness – a proof of life and talent), there was still the possibility that she had not found him out, that she took his false pieces at his own valuation. A little reflection rendered this hypothesis untenable; it was too evident that the account he gave of things must repeatedly have contradicted her own knowledge. Within an hour or two of his meeting them Lyon had seen her confronted with that perfectly gratuitous invention about the profit they had made off his early picture. Even then indeed she had not, so far as he could see, smarted, and – but for the present he could only contemplate the case.

Even if it had not been interfused, through his uneradicated tenderness for Mrs Capadose, with an element of suspense, the question would still have presented itself to him as a very curious problem, for he had not painted portraits during so many years without becoming something of a psychologist. His inquiry was limited for the moment to the opportunity that the following three days might yield, as the Colonel and his wife were going on to another house. It fixed itself largely of course upon the Colonel too – this gentleman was such a rare anomaly. Moreover it had to go on very quickly. Lyon was too scrupulous to ask other people what they thought of the business – he was too afraid of exposing the woman he once had loved. It was probable also that light would come to him from the talk of the rest of the company: the Colonel's queer habit, both as it affected his own situation and as it affected his wife, would be a familiar theme in any house in which he was in the habit of staying. Lyon had not observed in the circles in which he visited any marked abstention from comment on the singularities of their members. It interfered with his progress that the Colonel hunted all day, while he plied his brushes and chatted with Sir David; but a Sunday intervened and that partly made it up. Mrs Capadose fortunately did not hunt, and when his work was over she was not inaccessible. He took a couple of longish walks with her (she was fond of that), and beguiled her at tea into a friendly nook in the hall. Regard her as he might he could not make out to himself that she was consumed by a hidden shame; the sense of being married to a man whose word had no worth was not, in her spirit, so far as he could guess, the canker within the rose. Her mind appeared to have nothing on it but its own placid frankness, and when he looked into her eyes (deeply, as he occasionally permitted himself to do), they had no uncomfortable consciousness. He talked to her again and still again of the dear old days – reminded her of things that he had not (before this reunion) the least idea that he remembered. Then he spoke to her of her husband, praised his appearance, his talent for conversation, professed to have felt a quick friendship for him and asked (with an inward audacity at which he trembled a little) what manner of man he was. 'What manner?' said Mrs Capadose. 'Dear me, how can one describe one's husband? I like him very much.'

'Ah, you have told me that already!' Lyon exclaimed, with exaggerated ruefulness.

'Then why do you ask me again?' She added in a moment, as if she were so happy that she could afford to take pity on him, 'He is everything that's good and kind. He's a soldier – and a gentleman – and a dear! He hasn't a fault. And he has great ability.'

'Yes; he strikes one as having great ability. But of course I can't think him a dear.'

'I don't care what you think him!' said Mrs Capadose, looking, it seemed to him, as she smiled, handsomer than he had ever seen her. She was either deeply cynical or still more deeply impenetrable, and he had little prospect of winning from her the intimation that he longed for – some hint that it had come over her that after all she had better have married a man who was not a by-word for the most contemptible, the least heroic, of vices. Had she not seen – had she not felt – the smile go round when her husband executed some especially characteristic conversational caper? How could a woman of her quality endure that day after day, year after year, except by her quality's altering? But he would believe in the alteration only when he should have heard *her* lie. He was fascinated by his problem and yet half exasperated, and he asked himself all kinds of questions. Did she not lie, after all, when she let his falsehoods pass without a protest? Was not her life a perpetual complicity, and did she not aid and abet him by the simple fact that she was not disgusted with him? Then again perhaps she *was* disgusted and it was the mere desperation of her pride that had given her an inscrutable mask. Perhaps she protested in private, passionately; perhaps every night, in their own apartments, after the day's hideous performance, she made him the most scorching scene. But if such scenes were of no avail and he took no more trouble to cure himself, how could she regard him, and after so many years of marriage too, with the perfectly artless complacency that Lyon had surprised in her in the course of the first day's dinner? If our friend had not been in love with her he could have taken the diverting view of the Colonel's delinquencies; but as it was they turned to the tragical in his mind, even while he had a sense that his solicitude might also have been laughed at.

The observation of these three days showed him that if Capadose was an abundant he was not a malignant liar and that his fine faculty exercised itself mainly on subjects of small direct importance. 'He is the liar platonic,' he said to himself; 'he is disinterested, he doesn't operate with a hope of gain or with a desire to injure. It is art for art and he is prompted by the love of beauty. He has an inner vision of what might have been, of what ought to be, and he helps on the good cause by the simple substitution of a *nuance*. He paints, as it were, and so do I!' His manifestations had a considerable variety, but a family likeness ran through them, which consisted mainly of their singular futility. It was this that made them offensive; they encumbered the field of conversation, took up valuable space, converted it into a sort of brilliant sun-shot fog. For a fib told under pressure a convenient place can usually be found, as for a person who presents himself with an author's order at the first night of a play. But the supererogatory lie is the gentleman without a voucher or a ticket who accommodates himself with a stool in the passage.

In one particular Lyon acquitted his successful rival; it had puzzled him that irrepressible as he was he had not got into a mess in the service. But he perceived that he respected the service – that august institution was sacred from his depredations. Moreover, though there was a great deal of swagger in his talk it was, oddly enough, rarely swagger about his military exploits. He had a passion for the chase, he had followed it in far countries and some of his finest flowers were reminiscences of lonely danger and escape. The more solitary the scene the bigger of course the flower. A new acquaintance, with the Colonel, always received the tribute of a bouquet: that generalisation Lyon very promptly made. And this extraordinary man had inconsistencies and unexpected lapses – lapses into flat veracity. Lyon recognised what Sir David had told him, that his aberrations came in fits or periods – that he would sometimes keep the truce of God for a month at a time. The muse breathed upon him at her pleasure; she often left him alone. He would neglect the finest openings and then set sail in the teeth of the breeze. As a general thing he affirmed the false rather than denied the true; yet this proportion was sometimes strikingly reversed. Very often he joined in the laugh against himself – he admitted that he was trying it on and that a good many of his anecdotes had an experimental character. Still he never completely retracted nor retreated – he dived and came up in another place. Lyon divined that he was capable at intervals of defending his position with violence, but only when it was a very bad one. Then he might easily be dangerous – then he would hit out and become calumnious. Such occasions would test his wife's equanimity – Lyon would have liked to see her there. In the smoking-room and elsewhere the company, so far as it was composed of his familiars, had an hilarious protest always at hand; but among the men who had known him long his rich tone was an old story, so old that they had ceased to talk about it, and Lyon did not care, as I have said, to elicit the judgement of those who might have shared his own surprise.

The oddest thing of all was that neither surprise nor familiarity prevented the Colonel's being liked; his largest drafts on a sceptical attention passed for an overflow of life and gaiety – almost of good looks. He was fond of portraying his bravery and used a very big brush, and yet he was unmistakably brave. He was a capital rider and shot, in spite of his fund of anecdote illustrating these accomplishments: in short he was very nearly as clever and his career had been very nearly as wonderful as he pretended. His best quality however remained that indiscriminate sociability which took interest and credulity for granted and about which he bragged least. It made him cheap, it made him even in a manner vulgar; but it was so contagious that his listener was more or less on his side as against the probabilities. It was a private reflection of Oliver Lyon's that he not only lied but made one feel one's self a bit of a liar, even (or especially) if one contradicted him. In the evening, at dinner and afterwards, our friend watched his wife's face to see if some faint shade or spasm never passed over it. But she showed nothing, and the wonder was that when he spoke she almost always listened. That was her pride: she wished not to be even suspected of not facing the music. Lyon had none the less an importunate vision of a veiled figure coming the next day in the dusk to certain places to repair the Colonel's ravages, as the relatives of kleptomaniacs punctually call at the shops that have suffered from their pilferings.

'I must apologise, of course it wasn't true, I hope no harm is done, it is only his incorrigible—' Oh, to hear that woman's voice in that deep abasement! Lyon had no nefarious plan, no conscious wish to practise upon her shame or her loyalty; but he did say to himself that he should like to bring her round to feel that there would have been more dignity in a union with a certain other person. He even dreamed of the hour when, with a burning face, she would ask *him* not to take it up. Then he should be almost consoled – he would be magnanimous.

Lyon finished his picture and took his departure, after having worked in a glow of interest which made him believe in his success, until he found he had pleased every one, especially Mr and Mrs Ashmore, when he began to be sceptical. The party at any rate changed: Colonel and Mrs Capadose went their way. He was able to say to himself however that his separation from the lady was not so much an end as a beginning, and he called on her soon after his return to town. She had told him the hours she was at home – she seemed to like him. If she liked him why had she not married him or at any rate why was she not sorry she had not? If she was sorry she concealed it too well. Lyon's curiosity on this point may strike the reader as fatuous, but something must be allowed to a disappointed man. He did not ask much after all; not that she should love him to-day or that she should allow him to tell her that he loved her, but only that she should give him some sign she was sorry. Instead of this, for the present, she contented herself with exhibiting her little daughter to him. The child was beautiful and had the prettiest eyes of innocence he had ever seen: which did not prevent him from wondering whether she told horrid fibs. This idea gave him much entertainment – the picture of the anxiety with which her mother would watch as she grew older for the symptoms of heredity. That was a nice occupation for Everina Brant! Did she lie to the child herself, about her father – was that necessary, when she pressed her daughter to her bosom, to cover up his tracks? Did he control himself before the little girl – so that she might not hear him say things she knew to be other than he said? Lyon doubted this: his genius would be too strong for him, and the only safety for the child would be in her being too stupid to analyse. One couldn't judge yet – she was too young. If she should grow up clever she would be sure to tread in his steps – a delightful improvement in her mother's situation! Her little face was not shifty, but neither was her father's big one: so that proved nothing.

Lyon reminded his friends more than once of their promise that Amy should sit to him, and it was only a question of his leisure. The desire grew in him to paint the Colonel also – an operation from which he promised himself a rich private satisfaction. He would draw him out, he would set him up in that totality about which he had talked with Sir David, and none but the initiated would know. They, however, would rank the picture high, and it would be indeed six rows deep – a masterpiece of subtle characterisation, of legitimate treachery. He had dreamed for years of producing something which should bear the stamp of the psychologist as well as of the painter, and here at last was his subject. It was a pity it was not better, but that was not *his* fault. It was his impression that already no one drew the Colonel out more than he, and he did it not only by instinct but on a plan. There were moments when he was almost frightened at the success of his plan – the poor gentleman went so terribly far. He would pull up some day, look at Lyon between the eyes – guess he was being played upon – which would lead to his wife's guessing it also. Not that Lyon cared much for that however, so long as she failed to suppose (as she must) that *she* was a part of his joke. He formed such a habit now of going to see her of a Sunday afternoon that he was angry when she went out of town. This occurred often, as the couple were great visitors and the Colonel was always looking for sport, which he liked best when it could be had at other people's expense. Lyon would have supposed that this sort of life was particularly little to her taste, for he had an idea that it was in country-houses that her husband came out strongest. To let him go off without her, not to see him expose himself – that ought properly to have been a relief and a luxury to her. She told Lyon in fact that she preferred staying at home; but she neglected to say it was because in other people's houses she was on the rack: the reason she gave was that she liked so to be with the child. It was not perhaps criminal to draw such a bow, but it was vulgar: poor Lyon was delighted when he arrived at that formula. Certainly some day too he would cross the line –

he would become a noxious animal. Yes, in the meantime he was vulgar, in spite of his talents, his fine person, his impunity. Twice, by exception, toward the end of the winter, when he left town for a few days' hunting, his wife remained at home. Lyon had not yet reached the point of asking himself whether the desire not to miss two of his visits had something to do with her immobility. That inquiry would perhaps have been more in place later, when he began to paint the child and she always came with her. But it was not in her to give the wrong name, to pretend, and Lyon could see that she had the maternal passion, in spite of the bad blood in the little girl's veins.

She came inveterately, though Lyon multiplied the sittings: Amy was never entrusted to the governess or the maid. He had knocked off poor old Sir David in ten days, but the portrait of the simple-faced child bade fair to stretch over into the following year. He asked for sitting after sitting, and it would have struck any one who might have witnessed the affair that he was wearing the little girl out. He knew better however and Mrs Capadose also knew: they were present together at the long intermissions he gave her, when she left her pose and roamed about the great studio, amusing herself with its curiosities, playing with the old draperies and costumes, having unlimited leave to handle. Then her mother and Mr Lyon sat and talked; he laid aside his brushes and leaned back in his chair; he always gave her tea. What Mrs Capadose did not know was the way that during these weeks he neglected other orders: women have no faculty of imagination with regard to a man's work beyond a vague idea that it doesn't matter. In fact Lyon put off everything and made several celebrities wait. There were half-hours of silence, when he plied his brushes, during which he was mainly conscious that Everina was sitting there. She easily fell into that if he did not insist on talking, and she was not embarrassed nor bored by it. Sometimes she took up a book – there were plenty of them about; sometimes, a little way off, in her chair, she watched his progress (though without in the least advising or correcting), as if she cared for every stroke that represented her daughter. These strokes were occasionally a little wild; he was thinking so much more of his heart than of his hand. He was not more embarrassed than she was, but he was agitated: it was as if in the sittings (for the child, too, was beautifully quiet) something was growing between them or had already grown – a tacit confidence, an inexpressible secret. He felt it that way; but after all he could not be sure that she did. What he wanted her to do for him was very little; it was not even to confess that she was unhappy. He would be superabundantly gratified if she should simply let him know, even by a silent sign, that she recognised that with him her life would have been finer. Sometimes he guessed – his presumption went so far – that he might see this sign in her contentedly sitting there.

III

AT last he broached the question of painting the Colonel: it was now very late in the season – there would be little time before the general dispersal. He said they must make the most of it; the great thing was to begin; then in the autumn, with the resumption of their London life, they could go forward. Mrs Capadose objected to this that she really could not consent to accept another present of such value. Lyon had given her the portrait of herself of old, and he had seen what they had had the indelicacy to do with it. Now he had offered her this beautiful memorial of the child – beautiful it would evidently be when it was finished, if he could ever satisfy himself; a precious possession which they would cherish for ever. But his generosity must stop there – they couldn't be so tremendously 'beholden' to him. They couldn't order the picture – of course he would understand that, without her explaining: it was a luxury beyond their reach, for they knew the great prices he received. Besides, what had they ever done – what above all had *she* ever done, that he should overload them with benefits? No, he was too dreadfully good; it was really impossible that Clement should sit. Lyon listened to her without protest, without interruption, while he bent forward at his work, and at last he said: 'Well, if you won't take it why not let him sit for me for my own pleasure and profit? Let it be a favour, a service I ask of him. It will do me a lot of good to paint him and the picture will remain in my hands.'

'How will it do you a lot of good?' Mrs Capadose asked.

'Why, he's such a rare model – such an interesting subject. He has such an expressive face. It will teach me no end of things.'

'Expressive of what?' said Mrs Capadose.

'Why, of his nature.'

'And do you want to paint his nature?'

'Of course I do. That's what a great portrait gives you, and I shall make the Colonel's a great one. It will put me up high. So you see my request is eminently interested.'

'How can you be higher than you are?'

'Oh, I'm insatiable! Do consent,' said Lyon.

'Well, his nature is very noble,' Mrs Capadose remarked.

'Ah, trust me, I shall bring it out!' Lyon exclaimed, feeling a little ashamed of himself.

Mrs Capadose said before she went away that her husband would probably comply with his invitation, but she added, 'Nothing would induce me to let you pry into *me* that way!'

'Oh, you,' Lyon laughed – 'I could do you in the dark!'

The Colonel shortly afterwards placed his leisure at the painter's disposal and by the end of July had paid him several visits. Lyon was disappointed neither in the quality of his sitter nor in the degree to which he himself rose to the occasion; he felt really confident that he should produce a fine thing. He was in the humour; he was charmed with his *motif* and deeply interested in his problem. The only point that troubled him was the idea that when he should send his picture to the Academy he should not be able to give the title, for the catalogue, simply as 'The Liar'. However, it little mattered, for he had now determined that this character should be perceptible even to the meanest intelligence – as overtopping as it had become to his own sense in the living man. As he saw nothing else in the Colonel to-day, so he gave himself up to the joy of painting nothing else. How he did it he could not have told you, but it seemed to him that the mystery of how to do it was revealed to him afresh every time he sat down to his work. It was in the eyes and it was in the mouth, it was in every line of the face and every fact of the attitude, in the indentation of the chin, in the way the hair was planted, the moustache was twisted, the smile came and went, the breath rose and fell. It was in the way he looked out at a bamboozled world in short – the way he would look out for ever. There were half a dozen portraits in Europe that Lyon rated as supreme; he regarded them as immortal, for they were as perfectly preserved as they were consummately painted. It was to this small exemplary group that he aspired to annex the canvas on which he was now engaged. One of the productions that helped to compose it was the magnificent Moroni of the National Gallery – the young tailor, in the white jacket, at his board with his shears. The Colonel was not a tailor, nor was Moroni's model, unlike many tailors, a liar; but as regards the masterly clearness with which the individual should be rendered his work would be on the same line as that. He had to a degree in which he had rarely had it before the satisfaction of feeling life grow and grow under his brush. The Colonel, as it turned out, liked to sit and he liked to talk while he was sitting: which was very fortunate, as his talk largely constituted Lyon's inspiration. Lyon put into practice that idea of drawing him out which he had been nursing for so many weeks: he could not possibly have been in a better relation to him for the purpose. He encouraged, beguiled, excited him, manifested an unfathomable credulity, and his only interruptions were when the Colonel did not respond to it. He had his intermissions, his hours of sterility, and then Lyon felt that the picture also languished. The higher his companion soared, the more gyrations he executed, in the blue, the better he painted; he couldn't make his flights long enough. He lashed him on when he flagged; his apprehension became great at moments that the Colonel would discover his game. But he never did, apparently; he basked and expanded in the fine steady light of the painter's attention. In this way the picture grew very fast; it was astonishing what a short business it was, compared with the little girl's. By the fifth of August it was pretty well finished: that was the date of the last sitting the Colonel was for the present able to give, as he was leaving town the next day with his wife. Lyon was amply content – he saw his way so clear: he should be able to do at his convenience what remained, with or without his friend's attendance. At any rate, as there was no hurry, he would let the thing stand over till his own return to London, in November, when he would come back to it with a fresh eye. On the Colonel's asking him if his wife might come and see it the next day, if she should find a minute – this was so greatly her desire – Lyon begged as a special favour that she would wait: he was so far from satisfied as yet. This was the repetition of a proposal Mrs Capadose had made on the occasion of his last visit to her, and he had then asked for a delay – declared that he was by no means content. He was really delighted, and he was again a little ashamed of himself.

By the fifth of August the weather was very warm, and on that day, while the Colonel sat straight and gossiped, Lyon opened for the sake of ventilation a little subsidiary door which led directly from his studio into the garden and sometimes served as an entrance and an exit for models and for visitors of the humbler sort, and as a passage for canvases, frames, packing-boxes, and other professional gear. The main entrance was through the house and his own apartments, and this approach had the charming effect of admitting you first to a high gallery, from which a crooked picturesque staircase enabled you to descend to the wide, decorated, encumbered room. The view of this room, beneath them, with all its artistic ingenuities and the objects of value that Lyon had collected, never failed to elicit exclamations of delight from persons stepping into the gallery. The way from the garden was plainer and at once more practicable and more private. Lyon's domain, in St John's Wood, was not vast, but when the door stood open of a summer's day it offered a glimpse of flowers and trees, you smelt something sweet and you heard the birds. On this particular morning the side-door had been found convenient by an unannounced visitor, a youngish woman who stood in the room before the Colonel perceived her and whom he perceived before she was noticed by his friend. She was very quiet, and she looked from one of the men to the other. 'Oh, dear, here's another!' Lyon exclaimed, as soon as his eyes rested on her. She belonged, in fact, to a somewhat importunate class – the model in search of employment, and she explained that she had ventured to come straight in, that way, because very often when she went to call upon gentlemen the servants played her tricks, turned her off and wouldn't take in her name.

'But how did you get into the garden?' Lyon asked.

'The gate was open, sir – the servants' gate. The butcher's cart was there.'

'The butcher ought to have closed it,' said Lyon.

'Then you don't require me, sir?' the lady continued.

Lyon went on with his painting; he had given her a sharp look at first, but now his eyes lighted on her no more. The Colonel, however, examined her with interest. She was a person of whom you could scarcely say whether being young she looked old or old she looked young; she had at any rate evidently rounded several of the corners of life and had a face that was rosy but that somehow failed to suggest freshness. Nevertheless she was pretty and even looked as if at one time she might have sat for the complexion. She wore a hat with many feathers, a dress with many bugles, long black gloves, encircled with silver bracelets, and very bad shoes. There was something about her that was not exactly of the governess out of place nor completely of the actress seeking an engagement, but that savoured of an interrupted profession or even of a blighted career. She was rather soiled and tarnished, and after she had been in the room a few moments the air, or at any rate the nostril, became acquainted with a certain alcoholic waft. She was unpractised in the *h*, and when Lyon at last thanked her and said he didn't want her – he was doing nothing for which she could be useful – she replied with rather a wounded manner, 'Well, you know you *'ave* 'ad me!'

'I don't remember you,' Lyon answered.

'Well, I daresay the people that saw your pictures do! I haven't much time, but I thought I would look in.'

'I am much obliged to you.'

'If ever you should require me, if you just send me a post-card—'

'I never send postcards,' said Lyon.

'Oh well, I should value a private letter! Anything to Miss Geraldine, Mortimer Terrace Mews, Notting 'ill—'

'Very good; I'll remember,' said Lyon.

Miss Geraldine lingered. 'I thought I'd just stop, on the chance.'

'I'm afraid I can't hold out hopes, I'm so busy with portraits,' Lyon continued.

'Yes; I see you are. I wish I was in the gentleman's place.'

'I'm afraid in that case it wouldn't look like me,' said the Colonel, laughing.

'Oh, of course it couldn't compare – it wouldn't be so 'andsome! But I do hate them portraits!' Miss Geraldine declared. 'It's so much bread out of our mouths.'

'Well, there are many who can't paint them,' Lyon suggested, comfortingly.

'Oh, I've sat to the very first – and only to the first! There's many that couldn't do anything without me.'

'I'm glad you're in such demand.' Lyon was beginning to be bored and he added that he wouldn't detain her – he would send for her in case of need.

'Very well; remember it's the Mews – more's the pity! You don't sit so well as *us*!' Miss Geraldine pursued, looking at the Colonel. 'If *you* should require me, sir—'

'You put him out; you embarrass him,' said Lyon.

'Embarrass him, oh gracious!' the visitor cried, with a laugh which diffused a fragrance. 'Perhaps *you* send postcards, eh?' she went on to the Colonel; and then she retreated with a wavering step. She passed out into the garden as she had come.

'How very dreadful – she's drunk!' said Lyon. He was painting hard, but he looked up, checking himself: Miss Geraldine, in the open doorway, had thrust back her head.

'Yes, I do hate it – that sort of thing!' she cried with an explosion of mirth which confirmed Lyon's declaration. And then she disappeared.

'What sort of thing – what does she mean?' the Colonel asked.

'Oh, my painting you, when I might be painting her.'

'And have you ever painted her?'

'Never in the world; I have never seen her. She is quite mistaken.'

The Colonel was silent a moment; then he remarked, 'She was very pretty – ten years ago.'

'I daresay, but she's quite ruined. For me the least drop too much spoils them; I shouldn't care for her at all.'

'My dear fellow, she's not a model,' said the Colonel, laughing.

'To-day, no doubt, she's not worthy of the name; but she has been one.'

'*Jamais de la vie*! That's all a pretext.'

'A pretext?' Lyon pricked up his ears – he began to wonder what was coming now.

'She didn't want you – she wanted me.'

'I noticed she paid you some attention. What does she want of you?'

'Oh, to do me an ill turn. She hates me – lots of women do. She's watching me – she follows me.'

Lyon leaned back in his chair – he didn't believe a word of this. He was all the more delighted with it and with the Colonel's bright, candid manner. The story had bloomed, fragrant, on the spot. 'My dear Colonel!' he murmured, with friendly interest and commiseration.

'I was annoyed when she came in – but I wasn't startled,' his sitter continued.

'You concealed it very well, if you were.'

'Ah, when one has been through what I have! To-day how-ever I confess I was half prepared. I have seen her hanging about – she knows my movements. She was near my house this morning – she must have followed me.'

'But who is she then – with such a *toupet*?'

'Yes, she has that,' said the Colonel; 'but as you observe she was primed. Still, there was a cheek, as they say, in her coming in. Oh, she's a bad one! She isn't a model and she never was; no doubt she has known some of those women and picked up their form. She had hold of a friend of mine ten years ago – a stupid young gander who might have been left to be plucked but whom I was obliged to take an interest in for family reasons.

It's a long story – I had really forgotten all about it. She's thirty-seven if she's a day. I cut in and made him get rid of her – I sent her about her business. She knew it was me she had to thank. She has never forgiven me – I think she's off her head. Her name isn't Geraldine at all and I doubt very much if that's her address.'

'Ah, what is her name?' Lyon asked, most attentive. The details always began to multiply, to abound, when once his companion was well launched – they flowed forth in battalions.

'It's Pearson – Harriet Pearson; but she used to call herself Grenadine – wasn't that a rum appellation? Grenadine – Geraldine – the jump was easy.' Lyon was charmed with the promptitude of this response, and his interlocutor went on: 'I hadn't thought of her for years – I had quite lost sight of her. I don't know what her idea is, but practically she's harmless. As I came in I thought I saw her a little way up the road. She must have found out I come here and have arrived before me. I daresay – or rather I'm sure – she is waiting for me there now.'

'Hadn't you better have protection?' Lyon asked, laughing.

'The best protection is five shillings – I'm willing to go that length. Unless indeed she has a bottle of vitriol. But they only throw vitriol on the men who have deceived them, and I never deceived her – I told her the first time I saw her that it wouldn't do. Oh, if she's there we'll walk a little way together and talk it over and, as I say, I'll go as far as five shillings.'

'Well,' said Lyon, 'I'll contribute another five.' He felt that this was little to pay for his entertainment.

That entertainment was interrupted however for the time by the Colonel's departure. Lyon hoped for a letter recounting the fictive sequel; but apparently his brilliant sitter did not operate with the pen. At any rate he left town without writing; they had taken a rendezvous for three months later. Oliver Lyon always passed the holidays in the same way; during the first weeks he paid a visit to his elder brother, the happy possessor, in the south of England, of a rambling old house with formal gardens, in which he delighted, and then he went abroad – usually to Italy or Spain. This year he carried out his custom after taking a last

look at his all but finished work and feeling as nearly pleased
with it as he ever felt with the translation of the idea by the hand
– always, as it seemed to him, a pitiful compromise. One yellow
afternoon, in the country, as he was smoking his pipe on one of
the old terraces he was seized with the desire to see it again and
do two or three things more to it: he had thought of it so often
while he lounged there. The impulse was too strong to be
dismissed, and though he expected to return to town in the
course of another week he was unable to face the delay. To look
at the picture for five minutes would be enough – it would clear
up certain questions which hummed in his brain; so that the
next morning, to give himself this luxury, he took the train for
London. He sent no word in advance; he would lunch at his
club and probably return into Sussex by the 5.45.

In St John's Wood the tide of human life flows at no time
very fast, and in the first days of September Lyon found unmi-
tigated emptiness in the straight sunny roads where the little
plastered garden-walls, with their incommunicative doors,
looked slightly Oriental. There was definite stillness in his
own house, to which he admitted himself by his pass-key,
having a theory that it was well sometimes to take servants
unprepared. The good woman who was mainly in charge and
who cumulated the functions of cook and housekeeper was,
however, quickly summoned by his step, and (he cultivated
frankness of intercourse with his domestics) received him without the confusion of surprise. He told her that she needn't mind
the place being not quite straight, he had only come up for a few
hours – he should be busy in the studio. To this she replied that
he was just in time to see a lady and a gentleman who were there
at the moment – they had arrived five minutes before. She had
told them he was away from home but they said it was all right;
they only wanted to look at a picture and would be very careful
of everything. 'I hope it is all right, sir,' the housekeeper concluded. 'The gentleman says he's a sitter and he gave me his
name – rather an odd name; I think it's military. The lady's a
very fine lady, sir; at any rate there they are.'

'Oh, it's all right,' Lyon said, the identity of his visitors being
clear. The good woman couldn't know, for she usually had little

to do with the comings and goings; his man, who showed
people in and out, had accompanied him to the country. He
was a good deal surprised at Mrs Capadose's having come to
see her husband's portrait when she knew that the artist himself
wished her to forbear; but it was a familiar truth to him that she
was a woman of a high spirit. Besides, perhaps the lady was not
Mrs Capadose; the Colonel might have brought some inquisitive friend, a person who wanted a portrait of *her* husband.
What were they doing in town, at any rate, at that moment?
Lyon made his way to the studio with a certain curiosity; he
wondered vaguely what his friends were 'up to'. He pushed
aside the curtain that hung in the door of communication – the
door opening upon the gallery which it had been found convenient to construct at the time the studio was added to the
house. When I say he pushed it aside I should amend my
phrase; he laid his hand upon it, but at that moment he was
arrested by a very singular sound. It came from the floor of the
room beneath him and it startled him extremely, consisting
apparently as it did of a passionate wail – a sort of smothered
shriek – accompanied by a violent burst of tears. Oliver Lyon
listened intently a moment, and then he passed out upon the
balcony, which was covered with an old thick Moorish rug. His
step was noiseless, though he had not endeavoured to make it
so, and after that first instant he found himself profiting irresistibly by the accident of his not having attracted the attention
of the two persons in the studio, who were some twenty feet
below him. In truth they were so deeply and so strangely
engaged that their unconsciousness of observation was
explained. The scene that took place before Lyon's eyes was
one of the most extraordinary they had ever rested upon. Delicacy and the failure to comprehend kept him at first from
interrupting it – for what he saw was a woman who had thrown
herself in a flood of tears on her companion's bosom – and these
influences were succeeded after a minute (the minutes were
very few and very short) by a definite motive which presently
had the force to make him step back behind the curtain. I may
add that it also had the force to make him avail himself for
further contemplation of a crevice formed by his gathering

together the two halves of the *portière*. He was perfectly aware of what he was about – he was for the moment an eavesdropper, a spy; but he was also aware that a very odd business, in which his confidence had been trifled with, was going forward, and that if in a measure it didn't concern him, in a measure it very definitely did. His observation, his reflections, accomplished themselves in a flash.

His visitors were in the middle of the room; Mrs Capadose clung to her husband, weeping, sobbing as if her heart would break. Her distress was horrible to Oliver Lyon but his astonishment was greater than his horror when he heard the Colonel respond to it by the words, vehemently uttered, 'Damn him, damn him, damn him!' What in the world had happened? why was she sobbing and whom was he damning? What had happened, Lyon saw the next instant, was that the Colonel had finally rummaged out his unfinished portrait (he knew the corner where the artist usually placed it, out of the way, with its face to the wall) and had set it up before his wife on an empty easel. She had looked at it a few moments and then – apparently – what she saw in it had produced an explosion of dismay and resentment. She was too busy sobbing and the Colonel was too busy holding her and reiterating his objurgation, to look round or look up. The scene was so unexpected to Lyon that he could not take it, on the spot, as a proof of the triumph of his hand – of a tremendous hit: he could only wonder what on earth was the matter. The idea of the triumph came a little later. Yet he could see the portrait from where he stood; he was startled with its look of life – he had not thought it so masterly. Mrs Capadose flung herself away from her husband – she dropped into the nearest chair, buried her face in her arms, leaning on a table. Her weeping suddenly ceased to be audible, but she shuddered there as if she were overwhelmed with anguish and shame. Her husband remained a moment staring at the picture; then he went to her, bent over her, took hold of her again, soothed her. 'What is it, darling, what the devil is it?' he demanded.

Lyon heard her answer. 'It's cruel – oh, it's too cruel!'

'Damn him – damn him – damn him!' the Colonel repeated.

'It's all there – it's all there!' Mrs Capadose went on.

'Hang it, what's all there?'

'Everything there oughtn't to be – everything he has seen – it's too dreadful!'

'Everything he has seen? Why, ain't I a good-looking fellow? He has made me rather handsome.'

Mrs Capadose had sprung up again; she had darted another glance at the painted betrayal. 'Handsome? Hideous, hideous! Not that – never, never!'

'Not *what*, in Heaven's name?' the Colonel almost shouted. Lyon could see his flushed, bewildered face.

'What he has made of you – what you know! *He* knows – he has seen. Every one will know – every one will see. Fancy that thing in the Academy!'

'You're going wild, darling; but if you hate it so it needn't go.'

'Oh, he'll send it – it's so good! Come away – come away!' Mrs Capadose wailed, seizing her husband.

'It's so good?' the poor man cried.

'Come away – come away,' she only repeated; and she turned toward the staircase that ascended to the gallery.

'Not that way – not through the house, in the state you're in,' Lyon heard the Colonel object. 'This way – we can pass,' he added; and he drew his wife to the small door that opened into the garden. It was bolted, but he pushed the bolt and opened the door. She passed out quickly, but he stood there looking back into the room. 'Wait for me a moment!' he cried out to her; and with an excited stride he re-entered the studio. He came up to the picture again, and again he stood looking at it. 'Damn him – damn him – damn him!' he broke out once more. It was not clear to Lyon whether this malediction had for its object the original or the painter of the portrait. The Colonel turned away and moved rapidly about the room, as if he were looking for something; Lyon was unable for the instant to guess his intention. Then the artist said to himself, below his breath, 'He's going to do it a harm!' His first impulse was to rush down and stop him; but he paused, with the sound of Everina Brant's sobs still in his ears. The Colonel found what he was looking for – found it among some odds and ends on a small table and

rushed back with it to the easel. At one and the same moment
Lyon perceived that the object he had seized was a small Eastern dagger and that he had plunged it into the canvas. He
seemed animated by a sudden fury, for with extreme vigour of
hand he dragged the instrument down (Lyon knew it to have no
very fine edge) making a long, abominable gash. Then he
plucked it out and dashed it again several times into the face
of the likeness, exactly as if he were stabbing a human victim: it
had the oddest effect – that of a sort of figurative suicide. In a
few seconds more the Colonel had tossed the dagger away – he
looked at it as he did so, as if he expected it to reek with blood –
and hurried out of the place, closing the door after him.

The strangest part of all was – as will doubtless appear – that
Oliver Lyon made no movement to save his picture. But he did
not feel as if he were losing it or cared not if he were, so much
more did he feel that he was gaining a certitude. His old friend
was ashamed of her husband, and he had made her so, and he
had scored a great success, even though the picture had been
reduced to rags. The revelation excited him so – as indeed the
whole scene did – that when he came down the steps after the
Colonel had gone he trembled with his happy agitation; he was
dizzy and had to sit down a moment. The portrait had a dozen
jagged wounds – the Colonel literally had hacked it to death.
Lyon left it where it was, never touched it, scarcely looked at it;
he only walked up and down his studio, still excited, for an
hour. At the end of this time his good woman came to recommend that he should have some luncheon; there was a passage
under the staircase from the offices.

'Ah, the lady and gentleman have gone, sir? I didn't hear
them.'

'Yes; they went by the garden.'

But she had stopped, staring at the picture on the easel.
'Gracious, how you *'ave* served it, sir!'

Lyon imitated the Colonel. 'Yes, I cut it up – in a fit of
disgust.'

'Mercy, after all your trouble! Because they weren't pleased,
sir?'

'Yes; they weren't pleased.'

'Well, they must be very grand! Blessed if I would!'

'Have it chopped up; it will do to light fires,' Lyon said.

He returned to the country by the 3.30 and a few days later passed over to France. During the two months that he was absent from England he expected something – he could hardly have said what; a manifestation of some sort on the Colonel's part. Wouldn't he write, wouldn't he explain, wouldn't he take for granted Lyon had discovered the way he had, as the cook said, served him and deem it only decent to take pity in some fashion or other on his mystification? Would he plead guilty or would he repudiate suspicion? The latter course would be difficult and make a considerable draft upon his genius, in view of the certain testimony of Lyon's housekeeper, who had admitted the visitors and would establish the connection between their presence and the violence wrought. Would the Colonel proffer some apology or some amends, or would any word from him be only a further expression of that destructive petulance which our friend had seen his wife so suddenly and so potently communicate to him? He would have either to declare that he had not touched the picture or to admit that he had, and in either case he would have to tell a fine story. Lyon was impatient for the story and, as no letter came, disappointed that it was not produced. His impatience however was much greater in respect to Mrs Capadose's version, if version there was to be; for certainly that would be the real test, would show how far she would go for her husband, on the one side, or for him, Oliver Lyon, on the other. He could scarcely wait to see what line she would take; whether she would simply adopt the Colonel's, whatever it might be. He wanted to draw her out without waiting, to get an idea in advance. He wrote to her, to this end, from Venice, in the tone of their established friendship, asking for news, narrating his wanderings, hoping they should soon meet in town and not saying a word about the picture. Day followed day, after the time, and he received no answer; upon which he reflected that she couldn't trust herself to write – was still too much under the influence of the emotion produced by his 'betrayal'. Her husband had espoused that emotion and she had espoused the action he had taken in consequence of it, and it was a complete rupture and everything was at an end. Lyon considered this prospect rather ruefully, at the same time that he thought it deplorable that such charming people should have put themselves so grossly in the wrong. He was at last cheered, though little further enlightened, by the arrival of a letter, brief but breathing good-humour and hinting neither at a grievance nor at a bad conscience. The most interesting part of it to Lyon was the postscript, which consisted of these words: 'I have a confession to make to you. We were in town for a couple of days, the 1st of September, and I took the occasion to defy your authority – it was very bad of me but I couldn't help it. I made Clement take me to your studio – I wanted so dreadfully to see what you had done with him, your wishes to the contrary notwithstanding. We made your servants let us in and I took a good look at the picture. It is really wonderful!' 'Wonderful' was non-committal, but at least with this letter there was no rupture.

The third day after Lyon's return to London was a Sunday, so that he could go and ask Mrs Capadose for luncheon. She had given him in the spring a general invitation to do so and he had availed himself of it several times. These had been the occasions (before he sat to him) when he saw the Colonel most familiarly. Directly after the meal his host disappeared (he went out, as he said, to call on *his* women) and the second half-hour was the best, even when there were other people. Now, in the first days of December, Lyon had the luck to find the pair alone, without even Amy, who appeared but little in public. They were in the drawing-room, waiting for the repast to be announced, and as soon as he came in the Colonel broke out, 'My dear fellow, I'm delighted to see you! I'm so keen to begin again.'

'Oh, do go on, it's so beautiful,' Mrs Capadose said, as she gave him her hand.

Lyon looked from one to the other; he didn't know what he had expected, but he had not expected this. 'Ah, then, you think I've got something?'

'You've got everything,' said Mrs Capadose, smiling from her golden-brown eyes.

'She wrote you of our little crime?' her husband asked. 'She dragged me there – I had to go.' Lyon wondered for a moment whether he meant by their little crime the assault on the canvas; but the Colonel's next words didn't confirm this interpretation. 'You know I like to sit – it gives such a chance to my *bavardise*. And just now I have time.'

'You must remember I had almost finished,' Lyon remarked.

'So you had. More's the pity. I should like you to begin again.'

'My dear fellow, I shall have to begin again!' said Oliver Lyon with a laugh, looking at Mrs Capadose. She did not meet his eyes – she had got up to ring for luncheon. 'The picture has been smashed,' Lyon continued.

'Smashed? Ah, what did you do that for?' Mrs Capadose asked, standing there before him in all her clear, rich beauty. Now that she looked at him she was impenetrable.

'I didn't – I found it so – with a dozen holes punched in it!'

'I say!' cried the Colonel.

Lyon turned his eyes to him, smiling. 'I hope *you* didn't do it?'

'Is it ruined?' the Colonel inquired. He was as brightly true as his wife and he looked simply as if Lyon's question could not be serious. 'For the love of sitting to you? My dear fellow, if I had thought of it I would!'

'Nor you either?' the painter demanded of Mrs Capadose.

Before she had time to reply her husband had seized her arm, as if a highly suggestive idea had come to him. 'I say, my dear, that woman – that woman!'

'That woman?' Mrs Capadose repeated; and Lyon too wondered what woman he meant.

'Don't you remember when we came out, she was at the door – or a little way from it? I spoke to you of her – I told you about her. Geraldine – Grenadine – the one who burst in that day,' he explained to Lyon. 'We saw her hanging about – I called Everina's attention to her.'

'Do you mean she got at my picture?'

'Ah yes, I remember,' said Mrs Capadose, with a sigh.

'She burst in again – she had learned the way – she was waiting for her chance,' the Colonel continued. 'Ah, the little brute!'

Lyon looked down; he felt himself colouring. This was what he had been waiting for – the day the Colonel should wantonly sacrifice some innocent person. And could his wife be a party to that final atrocity? Lyon had reminded himself repeatedly during the previous weeks that when the Colonel perpetrated his misdeed she had already quitted the room; but he had argued none the less – it was a virtual certainty – that he had on rejoining her immediately made his achievement plain to her. He was in the flush of performance; and even if he had not mentioned what he had done she would have guessed it. He did not for an instant believe that poor Miss Geraldine had been hovering about his door, nor had the account given by the Colonel the summer before of his relations with this lady deceived him in the slightest degree. Lyon had never seen her before the day she planted herself in his studio; but he knew her and classified her as if he had made her. He was acquainted with the London female model in all her varieties – in every phase of her development and every step of her decay. When he entered his house that September morning just after the arrival of his two friends there had been no symptoms whatever, up and down the road, of Miss Geraldine's reappearance. That fact had been fixed in his mind by his recollecting the vacancy of the prospect when his cook told him that a lady and a gentleman were in his studio: he had wondered there was not a carriage nor a cab at his door. Then he had reflected that they would have come by the underground railway; he was close to the Marlborough Road station and he knew the Colonel, coming to his sittings, more than once had availed himself of that convenience. 'How in the world did she get in?' He addressed the question to his companions indifferently.

'Let us go down to luncheon,' said Mrs Capadose, passing out of the room.

'We went by the garden – without troubling your servant – I wanted to show my wife.' Lyon followed his hostess with her husband and the Colonel stopped him at the top of the stairs. 'My dear fellow, I *can't* have been guilty of the folly of not fastening the door?'

'I am sure I don't know, Colonel,' Lyon said as they went down. 'It was a very determined hand – a perfect wild-cat.'

'Well, she *is* a wild-cat – confound her! That's why I wanted to get him away from her.'

'But I don't understand her motive.'

'She's off her head – and she hates me; that was her motive.'

'But she doesn't hate me, my dear fellow!' Lyon said, laughing.

'She hated the picture – don't you remember she said so? The more portraits there are the less employment for such as her.'

'Yes; but if she is not really the model she pretends to be, how can that hurt her?' Lyon asked.

The inquiry baffled the Colonel an instant – but only an instant. 'Ah, she was in a vicious muddle! As I say, she's off her head.'

They went into the dining-room, where Mrs Capadose was taking her place. 'It's too bad, it's too horrid!' she said. 'You see the fates are against you. Providence won't let you be so disinterested – painting masterpieces for nothing.'

'Did *you* see the woman?' Lyon demanded, with something like a sternness that he could not mitigate.

Mrs Capadose appeared not to perceive it or not to heed it if she did. 'There was a person, not far from your door, whom Clement called my attention to. He told me something about her but we were going the other way.'

'And do you think she did it?'

'How can I tell? If she did she was mad, poor wretch.'

'I should like very much to get hold of her,' said Lyon. This was a false statement, for he had no desire for any further conversation with Miss Geraldine. He had exposed his friends to himself, but he had no desire to expose them to any one else, least of all to themselves.

'Oh, depend upon it she will never show again. You're safe!' the Colonel exclaimed.

'But I remember her address – Mortimer Terrace Mews, Notting Hill.'

'Oh, that's pure humbug; there isn't any such place.'

'Lord, what a deceiver!' said Lyon.

'Is there any one else you suspect?' the Colonel went on.

'Not a creature.'

'And what do your servants say?'

'They say it wasn't *them*, and I reply that I never said it was. That's about the substance of our conferences.'

'And when did they discover the havoc?'

'They never discovered it at all. I noticed it first – when I came back.'

'Well, she could easily have stepped in,' said the Colonel. 'Don't you remember how she turned up that day, like the clown in the ring?'

'Yes, yes; she could have done the job in three seconds, except that the picture wasn't out.'

'My dear fellow, don't curse me! – but of course I dragged it out.'

'You didn't put it back?' Lyon asked tragically.

'Ah, Clement, Clement, didn't I tell you to?' Mrs Capadose exclaimed in a tone of exquisite reproach.

The Colonel groaned, dramatically; he covered his face with his hands. His wife's words were for Lyon the finishing touch; they made his whole vision crumble – his theory that she had secretly kept herself true. Even to her old lover she wouldn't be so! He was sick; he couldn't eat; he knew that he looked very strange. He murmured something about it being useless to cry over spilled milk – he tried to turn the conversation to other things. But it was a horrid effort and he wondered whether they felt it as much as he. He wondered all sorts of things: whether they guessed he disbelieved them (that he had seen them of course they would never guess); whether they had arranged their story in advance or it was only an inspiration of the moment; whether she had resisted, protested, when the Colonel proposed it to her, and then had been borne down by him; whether in short she didn't loathe herself as she sat there. The cruelty, the cowardice of fastening their unholy act upon

the wretched woman struck him as monstrous – no less monstrous indeed than the levity that could make them run the risk of
her giving them, in her righteous indignation, the lie. Of course
that risk could only exculpate her and not inculpate them – the
probabilities protected them so perfectly; and what the Colonel
counted on (what he would have counted upon the day he
delivered himself, after first seeing her, at the studio, if he had
thought about the matter then at all and not spoken from the
pure spontaneity of his genius) was simply that Miss Geraldine
had really vanished for ever into her native unknown. Lyon
wanted so much to quit the subject that when after a little Mrs
Capadose said to him, 'But can nothing be done, can't the
picture be repaired? You know they do such wonders in that
way now,' he only replied, 'I don't know, I don't care, it's all over,
n'en parlons plus!' Her hypocrisy revolted him. And yet, by way of
plucking off the last veil of her shame, he broke out to her again,
shortly afterward, 'And you *did* like it, really?' To which she
returned, looking him straight in his face, without a blush, a
pallor, an evasion, 'Oh, I loved it!' Truly her husband had
trained her well. After that Lyon said no more and his companions forbore temporarily to insist, like people of tact and
sympathy aware that the odious accident had made him sore.

When they quitted the table the Colonel went away without
coming upstairs; but Lyon returned to the drawing-room with
his hostess, remarking to her however on the way that he could
remain but a moment. He spent that moment – it prolonged
itself a little – standing with her before the chimney-piece. She
neither sat down nor asked him to; her manner denoted that
she intended to go out. Yes, her husband had trained her well;
yet Lyon dreamed for a moment that now he was alone with her
she would perhaps break down, retract, apologise, confide, say
to him, 'My dear old friend, forgive this hideous comedy – you
understand!' And then how he would have loved her and pitied
her, guarded her, helped her always! If she were not ready to do
something of that sort why had she treated him as if he were a
dear old friend; why had she let him for months suppose certain
things – or almost; why had she come to his studio day after day
to sit near him on the pretext of her child's portrait, as if she

liked to think what might have been? Why had she come so near a tacit confession, in a word, if she was not willing to go an inch further? And she was not willing – she was not; he could see that as he lingered there. She moved about the room a little, rearranging two or three objects on the tables, but she did nothing more. Suddenly he said to her: 'Which way was she going, when you came out?'

'She – the woman we saw?'

'Yes, your husband's strange friend. It's a clue worth following.' He had no desire to frighten her; he only wanted to communicate the impulse which would make her say, 'Ah, spare me – and spare *him*! There was no such person.'

Instead of this Mrs Capadose replied, 'She was going away from us – she crossed the road. We were coming towards the station.'

'And did she appear to recognise the Colonel – did she look round?'

'Yes; she looked round, but I didn't notice much. A hansom came along and we got into it. It was not till then that Clement told me who she was: I remember he said that she was there for no good. I suppose we ought to have gone back.'

'Yes; you would have saved the picture.'

For a moment she said nothing; then she smiled. 'For you, I am very sorry. But you must remember that I possess the original!'

At this Lyon turned away. 'Well, I must go,' he said; and he left her without any other farewell and made his way out of the house. As he went slowly up the street the sense came back to him of that first glimpse of her he had had at Stayes – the way he had seen her gaze across the table at her husband. Lyon stopped at the corner, looking vaguely up and down. He would never go back – he couldn't. She was still in love with the Colonel – he had trained her too well.

THE LESSON OF THE MASTER

I

HE had been informed that the ladies were at church, but that was corrected by what he saw from the top of the steps (they descended from a great height in two arms, with a circular sweep of the most charming effect) at the threshold of the door which, from the long, bright gallery, overlooked the immense lawn. Three gentlemen, on the grass, at a distance, sat under the great trees; but the fourth figure was not a gentleman, the one in the crimson dress which made so vivid a spot, told so as a 'bit of colour' amid the fresh, rich green. The servant had come so far with Paul Overt to show him the way and had asked him if he wished first to go to his room. The young man declined this privilege, having no disorder to repair after so short and easy a journey and liking to take a general perceptive possession of the new scene immediately, as he always did. He stood there a little with his eyes on the group and on the admirable picture – the wide grounds of an old country-house near London (that only made it better) on a splendid Sunday in June. 'But that lady, who is she?' he said to the servant before the man went away.

'I think it's Mrs St George, sir.'

'Mrs St George, the wife of the distinguished—' Then Paul Overt checked himself, doubting whether the footman would know.

'Yes, sir – probably, sir,' said the servant, who appeared to wish to intimate that a person staying at Summersoft would naturally be, if only by alliance, distinguished. His manner, however, made poor Overt feel for the moment as if he himself were but little so.

'And the gentlemen?' he inquired.

'Well, sir, one of them is General Fancourt.'

'Ah yes, I know; thank you.' General Fancourt was distinguished, there was no doubt of that, for something he had done, or perhaps even had not done (the young man could not remember which) some years before in India. The servant went away, leaving the glass doors open into the gallery, and Paul Overt remained at the head of the wide double staircase, saying to himself that the place was sweet and promised a pleasant visit, while he leaned on the balustrade of fine old ironwork which, like all the other details, was of the same period as the house. It all went together and spoke in one voice – a rich English voice of the early part of the eighteenth century. It might have been church-time on a summer's day in the reign of Queen Anne; the stillness was too perfect to be modern, the nearness counted so as distance and there was something so fresh and sound in the originality of the large smooth house, the expanse of whose beautiful brickwork, which had been kept clear of messy creepers (as a woman with a rare complexion disdains a veil), was pink rather than red. When Paul Overt perceived that the people under the trees were noticing him he turned back through the open doors into the great gallery which was the pride of the place. It traversed the mansion from end to end and seemed – with its bright colours, its high panelled windows, its faded, flowered chintzes, its quickly-recognised portraits and pictures, the blue and white china of its cabinets and the attenuated festoons and rosettes of its ceiling – a cheerful upholstered avenue into the other century.

The young man was slightly nervous; that belonged in general to his disposition as a student of fine prose, with his dose of the artist's restlessness; and there was a particular excitement in the idea that Henry St George might be a member of the party. For the younger writer he had remained a high literary figure, in spite of the lower range of production to which he had fallen after his three first great successes, the comparative absence of quality in his later work. There had been moments when Paul Overt almost shed tears upon this; but now that he was near him (he had never met him), he was conscious only of the fine original source and of his own immense debt. After he had taken a turn or two up and down the gallery he came out again and descended the steps. He was but slenderly supplied with a certain social boldness (it was really a weakness in him), so that, conscious of a want of acquaintance with the four persons in the distance, he indulged in a movement as to which he had a certain safety in feeling that it did not necessarily appear to commit him to an attempt to join them. There was a fine English awkwardness in it – he felt this too as he sauntered vaguely and obliquely across the lawn, as if to take an independent line. Fortunately there was an equally fine English directness in the way one of the gentlemen presently rose and made as if to approach him, with an air of conciliation and reassurance. To this demonstration Paul Overt instantly responded, though he knew the gentleman was not his host. He was tall, straight and elderly, and had a pink, smiling face and a white moustache. Our young man met him half-way while he laughed and said: 'A— Lady Watermouth told us you were coming; she asked me just to look after you.' Paul Overt thanked him (he liked him without delay) and turned round with him, walking toward the others. 'They've all gone to church – all except us,' the stranger continued as they went; 'we're just sitting here – it's so jolly.' Overt rejoined that it was jolly indeed – it was such a lovely place; he mentioned that he had not seen it before – it was a charming impression.

'Ah, you've not been here before?' said his companion. 'It's a nice little place – not much to *do*, you know.' Overt wondered what he wanted to 'do' – he felt as if he himself were doing a good deal. By the time they came to where the others sat he had guessed his initiator was a military man, and (such was the turn of Overt's imagination) this made him still more sympathetic. He would naturally have a passion for activity – for deeds at variance with the pacific, pastoral scene. He was evidently so good-natured, however, that he accepted the inglorious hour for what it was worth. Paul Overt shared it with him and with his companions for the next twenty minutes; the latter looked at him and he looked at them without knowing much who they were, while the talk went on without enlightening him much as to what it was about. It was indeed about nothing in particular, and wandered, with casual, pointless pauses and short terrestrial flights, amid the names of persons and places – names which, for him, had no great power of evocation. It was all sociable and slow, as was right and natural on a warm Sunday morning.

Overt's first attention was given to the question, privately considered, of whether one of the two younger men would be Henry St George. He knew many of his distinguished contemporaries by their photographs, but he had never, as it happened, seen a portrait of the great misguided novelist. One of the gentlemen was out of the question – he was too young; and the other scarcely looked clever enough, with such mild, undiscriminating eyes. If those eyes were St George's, the problem presented by the ill-matched parts of his genius was still more difficult of solution. Besides, the deportment of the personage possessing them was not, as regards the lady in the red dress, such as could be natural, towards his wife, even to a writer accused by several critics of sacrificing too much to manner. Lastly, Paul Overt had an indefinite feeling that if the gentleman with the sightless eyes bore the name that had set his heart beating faster (he also had contradictory, conventional whiskers – the young admirer of the celebrity had never in a mental vision seen *his* face in so vulgar a frame), he would have given him a sign of recognition or of friendliness – would have heard of him a little, would know something about *Ginistrella*, would have gathered at least that that recent work of fiction had made an impression on the discerning. Paul Overt had a dread of being grossly proud, but it seemed to him that his self-consciousness took no undue licence in thinking that the authorship of *Ginistrella* constituted a degree of identity. His soldierly friend became clear enough; he was 'Fancourt', but he was also the General; and he mentioned to our young man in the course of a few moments that he had but lately returned from twenty years' service abroad.

'And do you mean to remain in England?' Overt asked.

'Oh yes, I have bought a little house in London.'

'And I hope you like it,' said Overt, looking at Mrs St George.

'Well, a little house in Manchester Square – there's a limit to the enthusiasm that that inspires.'

'Oh, I meant being at home again – being in London.'

'My daughter likes it – that's the main thing. She's very fond of art and music and literature and all that kind of thing. She missed it in India and she finds it in London, or she hopes she will find it. Mr St George has promised to help her – he has been awfully kind to her. She has gone to church – she's fond of that too – but they'll all be back in a quarter of an hour. You must let me introduce you to her – she will be so glad to know you. I daresay she has read every word you have written.'

'I shall be delighted – I haven't written very many,' said Overt, who felt without resentment that the General at least was very vague about that. But he wondered a little why, since he expressed this friendly disposition, it did not occur to him to pronounce the word which would put him in relation with Mrs St George. If it was a question of introductions Miss Fancourt (apparently she was unmarried) was far away and the wife of his illustrious *confrère* was almost between them. This lady struck Paul Overt as a very pretty woman, with a surprising air of youth and a high smartness of aspect which seemed to him (he could scarcely have said why) a sort of mystification. St George certainly had every right to a charming wife, but he himself would never have taken the important little woman in the aggressively Parisian dress for the domestic partner of a man of letters. That partner in general, he knew, was far from presenting herself in a single type: his observation had instructed him that she was not inveterately, not necessarily dreary. But he had never before seen her look so much as if her prosperity had deeper foundations than an ink-spotted study-table littered with proof-sheets. Mrs St George might have been the wife of a gentleman who 'kept' books rather than wrote them, who carried on great affairs in the City and made better bargains than those that poets make with publishers. With this she hinted at a success more personal, as if she had been the most characteristic product of an age in which society, the world of conversation, is a great drawing-room with the City for its antechamber. Overt judged her at first to be about thirty years of age; then, after a while, he perceived that she was much nearer fifty. But she juggled away the twenty years some-how – you only saw them in a rare glimpse, like the rabbit in the conjurer's sleeve. She was extraordinarily white, and every-thing about her was pretty – her eyes, her ears, her hair, her voice, her hands, her feet (to which her relaxed attitude in her wicker chair gave a great publicity), and the numerous ribbons and trinkets with which she was bedecked. She looked as if she had put on her best clothes to go to church and then had decided that they were too good for that and had stayed at home. She told a story of some length about the shabby way Lady Jane had treated the Duchess, as well as an anecdote in relation to a purchase she had made in Paris (on her way back from Cannes) for Lady Egbert, who had never refunded the money. Paul Overt suspected her of a tendency to figure great people as larger than life, until he noticed the manner in which she handled Lady Egbert, which was so subversive that it reassured him. He felt that he should have understood her better if he might have met her eye; but she scarcely looked at him. 'Ah, here they come – all the good ones!' she said at last; and Paul Overt saw in the distance the return of the church-goers – several persons, in couples and threes, advancing in a flicker of sun and shade at the end of a large green vista formed by the level grass and the overarching boughs.

'If you mean to imply that we are bad, I protest,' said one of the gentlemen – 'after making oneself agreeable all the morn-ing!'

'Ah, if they've found you agreeable!' Mrs St George exclaimed, smiling. 'But if we are good the others are better.'

'They must be angels then,' observed the General.

'Your husband was an angel, the way he went off at your bidding,' the gentleman who had first spoken said to Mrs St George.

'At my bidding?'

'Didn't you make him go to church?'

'I never made him do anything in my life but once, when I made him burn up a bad book. That's all!' At her 'That's all!' Paul broke into an irrepressible laugh; it lasted only a second, but it drew her eyes to him. His own met them, but not long enough to help him to understand her; unless it were a step towards this that he felt sure on the instant that the burnt book (the way she alluded to it!) was one of her husband's finest things.

'A bad book?' her interlocutor repeated.

'I didn't like it. He went to church because your daughter went,' she continued, to General Fancourt. 'I think it my duty to call your attention to his demeanour to your daughter.'

'Well, if you don't mind it, I don't,' the General laughed.

'*Il s'attache à ses pas.* But I don't wonder – she's so charming.'

'I hope she won't make him burn any books!' Paul Overt ventured to exclaim.

'If she would make him write a few it would be more to the purpose,' said Mrs St George. 'He has been of an indolence this year!'

Our young man stared – he was so struck with the lady's phraseology. Her 'Write a few' seemed to him almost as good as her 'That's all'. Didn't she, as the wife of a rare artist, know what it was to produce *one* perfect work of art? How in the world did she think they were turned off? His private conviction was that admirably as Henry St George wrote, he had written for the last ten years, and especially for the last five, only too much, and there was an instant during which he felt the temptation to make this public. But before he had spoken a diversion was effected by the return of the absent guests. They strolled up dispersedly – there were eight or ten of them – and the circle under the trees rearranged itself as they took their place in it. They made it much larger; so that Paul Overt could feel (he was always feeling that sort of thing, as he said to himself) that if the company had already been interesting to watch it would now become a great deal more so. He shook hands with his hostess, who welcomed him without many words, in the manner of a woman able to trust him to understand – conscious that, in every way, so pleasant an occasion would speak for itself. She offered him no particular facility for sitting by her, and when they had all subsided again he found himself still next General Fancourt, with an unknown lady on his other flank.

'That's my daughter – that one opposite,' the General said to him without loss of time. Overt saw a tall girl, with magnificent red hair, in a dress of a pretty grey-green tint and of a limp silken texture, in which every modern effect had been avoided. It had therefore somehow the stamp of the latest thing, so that Overt quickly perceived she was eminently a contemporary young lady.

'She's very handsome – very handsome,' he repeated, looking at her. There was something noble in her head, and she appeared fresh and strong.

Her father surveyed her with complacency; then he said: 'She looks too hot – that's her walk. But she'll be all right presently. Then I'll make her come over and speak to you.'

'I should be sorry to give you that trouble; if you were to take me over there –' the young man murmured.

'My dear sir, do you suppose I put myself out that way? I don't mean for you, but for Marian,' the General added.

'*I* would put myself out for her, soon enough,' Overt replied; after which he went on: 'Will you be so good as to tell me which of those gentlemen is Henry St George?'

'The fellow talking to my girl. By Jove, he *is* making up to her – they're going off for another walk.'

'Ah, is that he, really?' The young man felt a certain surprise, for the personage before him contradicted a preconception which had been vague only till it was confronted with the reality. As soon as this happened the mental image, retiring with a sigh, became substantial enough to suffer a slight wrong. Overt, who had spent a considerable part of his short life in foreign lands, made now, but not for the first time, the reflection that whereas in those countries he had almost always recognised the artist and the man of letters by his personal 'type', the mould of his face, the character of his head, the expression of his figure and even the indications of his dress, in England this identification was as little as possible a matter of course, thanks to the greater conformity, the habit of sinking the profession instead of advertising it, the general diffusion of the air of the gentleman – the gentleman committed to no particular set of ideas. More than once, on returning to his own country, he had said to himself in regard to the people whom he met in society: 'One sees them about and one even talks with them; but to find out what they *do* one would really have to be a detective.' In respect to several individuals whose work he was unable to like (perhaps he was wrong) he found himself adding, 'No wonder they conceal it – it's so bad!' He observed that oftener than in France and in Germany his artist looked like a gentleman (that is, like an English one), while he perceived that outside of a few exceptions his gentleman didn't look like an artist. St George was not one of the exceptions; that circumstance he definitely apprehended before the great man had turned his back to walk off with Miss Fancourt. He certainly looked better behind than any foreign man of letters, and beautifully correct in his tall black hat and his superior frock coat. Somehow, all the same, these very garments (he wouldn't have minded them so much on a weekday) were disconcerting to Paul Overt, who forgot for the moment that the head of the profession was not a bit better dressed than himself. He had caught a glimpse of a regular face, with a fresh colour, a brown moustache and a pair of eyes surely never visited by a fine frenzy, and he promised himself to study it on the first occasion. His temporary opinion was that St George looked like a lucky stockbroker – a gentleman driving eastward every morning from a sanitary suburb in a smart dog-cart. That carried out the impression already derived from his wife. Paul Overt's glance, after a moment, travelled back to this lady, and he saw that her own had followed her husband as he moved off with Miss Fancourt. Overt permitted himself to wonder a little whether she were jealous when another woman took him away. Then he seemed to perceive that Mrs St George was not glaring at the indifferent maiden – her eyes rested only on her husband, and with unmistakable serenity. That was the way she wanted him to be – she liked his conventional uniform. Overt had a great desire to hear more about the book she had induced him to destroy.

II

As they all came out from luncheon General Fancourt took hold of Paul Overt and exclaimed, 'I say, I want you to know my girl!' as if the idea had just occurred to him and he had not spoken of it before. With the other hand he possessed himself of the young lady and said: 'You know all about him. I've seen you with his books. She reads everything – everything!' he added to the young man. The girl smiled at him and then laughed at her father. The General turned away and his daughter said:

'Isn't papa delightful?'

'He is indeed, Miss Fancourt.'

'As if I read you because I read "everything"!'

'Oh, I don't mean for saying that,' said Paul Overt. 'I liked him from the moment he spoke to me. Then he promised me this privilege.'

'It isn't for you he means it, it's for me. If you flatter yourself that he thinks of anything in life but me you'll find you are mistaken. He introduces every one to me. He thinks me insatiable.'

'You speak like him,' said Paul Overt, laughing.

'Ah, but sometimes I want to,' the girl replied, colouring. 'I don't read everything – I read very little. But I *have* read you.'

'Suppose we go into the gallery,' said Paul Overt. She pleased him greatly, not so much because of this last remark (though that of course was not disagreeable to him), as because, seated opposite to him at luncheon, she had given him for half an hour the impression of her beautiful face. Something else had come with it – a sense of generosity, of an enthusiasm which, unlike many enthusiasms, was not all manner. That was not spoiled for him by the circumstance that the repast had placed her again in familiar contact with Henry St George. Sitting next to her he was also opposite to our young man, who had been able to observe that he multiplied the attentions which his wife had brought to the General's notice. Paul Overt had been able to observe further that this lady was not in the least discomposed by these demonstrations and that she gave every sign of an unclouded spirit. She had Lord Masham on one side of her and on the other the accomplished Mr Mulliner, editor of the new high-class, lively evening paper which was expected to meet a want felt in circles increasingly conscious that Conservatism must be made amusing, and unconvinced when assured by those of another political colour that it was already amusing enough. At the end of an hour spent in her company Paul Overt thought her still prettier than she had appeared to him at first, and if her profane allusions to her husband's work had not still rung in his ears he should have liked her – so far as it could be a question of that in connection with a woman to whom he had not yet spoken and to whom probably he should never speak if it were left to her. Pretty women evidently were necessary to Henry St George, and for the moment it was Miss Fancourt who was most indispensable. If Overt had promised himself to take a better look at him the opportunity now was of the best, and it brought consequences which the young man felt to be important. He saw more in his face, and he liked it the better for its not telling its whole story in the first three minutes. That story came out as one read, in little instalments (it was excusable that Overt's mental comparisons should be somewhat professional), and the text was a style considerably involved – a language not easy to translate at sight. There were shades of meaning in it and a vague perspective of history which receded as you advanced. Of two facts Paul Overt had taken especial notice. The first of these was that he liked the countenance of the illustrious novelist much better when it was in repose than when it smiled; the smile displeased him (as much as anything from that source could), whereas the quiet face had a charm which increased in proportion as it became completely quiet. The change to the expression of gaiety excited on Overt's part a private protest which resembled that of a person sitting in the twilight and enjoying it, when the lamp is brought in too soon. His second reflection was that, though generally he disliked the sight of a man of that age using arts to make himself agreeable to a pretty girl, he was not struck in this case by the ugliness of the thing, which seemed to prove that St George had a light hand or the air of being younger than he was, or else that Miss Fancourt showed that *she* was not conscious of an anomaly.

Overt walked with her into the gallery, and they strolled to the end of it, looking at the pictures, the cabinets, the charming vista, which harmonised with the prospect of the summer afternoon, resembling it in its long brightness, with great divans and old chairs like hours of rest. Such a place as that had the added merit of giving persons who came into it plenty to talk about. Miss Fancourt sat down with Paul Overt on a flowered sofa, the cushions of which, very numerous, were tight, ancient cubes, of many sizes, and presently she said: 'I'm so glad to have a chance to thank you.'

'To thank me?'

'I liked your book so much. I think it's splendid.'

She sat there smiling at him, and he never asked himself which book she meant; for after all he had written three or four. That seemed a vulgar detail, and he was not even gratified by the idea of the pleasure she told him – her bright, handsome face told him – he had given her. The feeling she appealed to, or at any rate the feeling she excited, was something larger – something that had little to do with any quickened pulsation of his own vanity. It was responsive admiration of the life she embodied, the young purity and richness of which appeared to imply that real success was to resemble *that*, to live, to bloom, to present the perfection of a fine type, not to have hammered out headachy fancies with a bent back at an ink-stained table. While her grey eyes rested on him (there was a wideish space between them, and the division of her rich-coloured hair, which was so thick that it ventured to be smooth, made a free arch above them), he was almost ashamed of that exercise of the pen which it was her present inclination to eulogise. He was conscious that he should have liked better to please her in some other way. The lines of her face were those of a woman grown, but there was something childish in her complexion and the sweetness of her mouth. Above all she was natural – that was indubitable now – more natural than he had supposed at first, perhaps on account of her aesthetic drapery, which was conventionally unconventional, suggesting a tortuous spontaneity. He had feared that sort of thing in other cases, and his fears had been justified; though he was an artist to the essence, the modern reactionary nymph, with the brambles of the woodland caught in her folds and a look as if the satyrs had toyed with her hair, was apt to make him uncomfortable. Miss Fancourt was really more candid than her costume, and the best proof of it was her supposing that such garments suited her liberal character. She was robed like a pessimist, but Overt was sure she liked the taste of life. He thanked her for her appreciation – aware at the same time that he didn't appear to thank her enough and that she might think him ungracious. He was afraid she would ask him to explain something that he had written, and he always shrank from that (perhaps too timidly), for to his own ear the explanation of a work of art sounded fatuous. But he liked her so much as to feel a confidence that in the long run he should be able to show her that he was not rudely evasive. Moreover it was very certain that she was not quick to take offence; she was not irritable, she could be trusted to wait. So when he said to her, 'Ah! don't talk of anything I have done, *here*; there is another man in the house who is the actuality!' when he uttered this short, sincere protest, it was with the sense that she would see in the words neither mock humility nor the ungraciousness of a successful man bored with praise.

'You mean Mr St George – isn't he delightful?'

Paul Overt looked at her a moment; there was a species of morning-light in her eyes.

'Alas, I don't know him. I only admire him at a distance.'

'Oh, you must know him – he wants so to talk to you,' rejoined Miss Fancourt, who evidently had the habit of saying the things that, by her quick calculation, would give people pleasure. Overt divined that she would always calculate on everything's being simple between others.

'I shouldn't have supposed he knew anything about me,' Paul said, smiling.

'He does then – everything. And if he didn't, I should be able to tell him.'

'To tell him everything?'

'You talk just like the people in your book!' the girl exclaimed.

'Then they must all talk alike.'

'Well, it must be so difficult. Mr St George tells me it is, terribly. I've tried too and I find it so. I've tried to write a novel.'

'Mr St George oughtn't to discourage you,' said Paul Overt. 'You do much more – when you wear that expression.'

'Well, after all, why try to be an artist?' the young man went on. 'It's so poor – so poor!'

'I don't know what you mean,' said Marian Fancourt, looking grave.

'I mean as compared with being a person of action – as living your works.'

'But what is art but a life – if it be real?' asked the girl. 'I think it's the only one – everything else is so clumsy!' Paul Overt laughed, and she continued: 'It's so interesting, meeting so many celebrated people.'

'So I should think; but surely it isn't new to you.'

'Why, I have never seen any one – any one: living always in Asia.'

'But doesn't Asia swarm with personages? Haven't you administered provinces in India and had captive rajahs and tributary princes chained to your car?'

'I was with my father, after I left school to go out there. It was delightful being with him – we are alone together in the world, he and I – but there was none of the society I like best. One never heard of a picture – never of a book, except bad ones.'

'Never of a picture? Why, wasn't all life a picture?'

Miss Fancourt looked over the delightful place where they sat. 'Nothing to compare with this. I adore England!' she exclaimed.

'Ah, of course I don't deny that we must do something with it yet.'

'It hasn't been touched, really,' said the girl.

'Did Henry St George say that?'

There was a small and, as he felt it, venial intention of irony in his question; which, however, the girl took very simply, not noticing the insinuation. 'Yes, he says it has not been touched – not touched comparatively,' she answered, eagerly. 'He's so interesting about it. To listen to him makes one want so to do something.'

'It would make me want to,' said Paul Overt, feeling strongly, on the instant, the suggestion of what she said and of the emotion with which she said it, and what an incentive, on St George's lips, such a speech might be.

'Oh, you – as if you hadn't! I should like so to hear you talk together,' the girl added, ardently.

'That's very genial of you; but he would have it all his own way. I'm prostrate before him.'

Marian Fancourt looked earnest for a moment. 'Do you think then he's so perfect?'

'Far from it. Some of his later books seem to me awfully queer.'

'Yes, yes – he knows that.'

Paul Overt stared. 'That they seem to me awfully queer?'

'Well yes, or at any rate that they are not what they should be. He told me he didn't esteem them. He has told me such wonderful things – he's so interesting.'

There was a certain shock for Paul Overt in the knowledge that the fine genius they were talking of had been reduced to so explicit a confession and had made it, in his misery, to the first comer; for though Miss Fancourt was charming, what was she after all but an immature girl encountered at a country-house? Yet precisely this was a part of the sentiment that he himself had just expressed; he would make way completely for the poor peccable great man, not because he didn't read him clear, but altogether because he did. His consideration was half composed of tenderness for superficialities which he was sure St George judged privately with supreme sternness and which denoted some tragic intellectual secret. He would have his reasons for his psychology à fleur de peau, and these reasons could only be cruel ones, such as would make him dearer to those who already were fond of him. 'You excite my envy. I judge him, I discriminate – but I love him,' Overt said in a moment. 'And seeing him for the first time this way is a great event for me.'

'How momentous – how magnificent!' cried the girl. 'How delicious to bring you together!'

'*Your* doing it – that makes it perfect,' Overt responded.

'He's as eager as you,' Miss Fancourt went on. 'But it's so odd you shouldn't have met.'

'It's not so odd as it seems. I've been out of England so much
– repeated absences during all these last years.'

'And yet you write of it as well as if you were always here.'

'It's just the being away perhaps. At any rate the best bits,
I suspect, are those that were done in dreary places abroad.'

'And why were they dreary?'

'Because they were health-resorts – where my poor mother
was dying.'

'Your poor mother?' the girl murmured, kindly.

'We went from place to place to help her to get better.
But she never did. To the deadly Riviera (I hate it!) to the
high Alps, to Algiers, and far away – a hideous journey – to
Colorado.'

'And she isn't better?' Miss Fancourt went on.

'She died a year ago.'

'Really? – like mine! Only that is far away. Some day you
must tell me about your mother,' she added.

Overt looked at her a moment. 'What right things you say! If
you say them to St George I don't wonder he's in bondage.'

'I don't know what you mean. He doesn't make speeches
and professions at all – he isn't ridiculous.'

'I'm afraid you consider that I am.'

'No, I don't,' the girl replied, rather shortly. 'He under-
stands everything.'

Overt was on the point of saying jocosely: 'And I don't – is
that it?' But these words, before he had spoken, changed themselves into others slightly less trivial: 'Do you suppose he under-
stands his wife?'

Miss Fancourt made no direct answer to his question; but
after a moment's hesitation she exclaimed: 'Isn't she charming?'

'Not in the least!'

'Here he comes. Now you must know him,' the girl went on.
A small group of visitors had gathered at the other end of the
gallery and they had been joined for a moment by Henry St
George, who strolled in from a neighbouring room. He stood
near them a moment, not, apparently, falling into the conversation, but taking up an old miniature from a table and vaguely

examining it. At the end of a minute he seemed to perceive Miss Fancourt and her companion in the distance; whereupon, laying down his miniature, he approached them with the same procrastinating air, with his hands in his pockets, looking to right and left at the pictures. The gallery was so long that this transit took some little time, especially as there was a moment when he stopped to admire the fine Gainsborough. 'He says she has been the making of him,' Miss Fancourt continued, in a voice slightly lowered.

'Ah, he's often obscure!' laughed Paul Overt.

'Obscure?' she repeated, interrogatively. Her eyes rested upon her other friend, and it was not lost upon Paul that they appeared to send out great shafts of softness. 'He is going to speak to us!' she exclaimed, almost breathlessly. There was a sort of rapture in her voice; Paul Overt was startled. 'Bless my soul, is she so fond of him as that – is she in love with him?' he mentally inquired. 'Didn't I tell you he was eager?' she added, to her companion.

'It's eagerness dissimulated,' the young man rejoined, as the subject of their observation lingered before his Gainsborough. 'He edges toward us shyly. Does he mean that she saved him by burning that book?'

'That book? what book did she burn?' The girl turned her face quickly upon him.

'Hasn't he told you, then?'

'Not a word.'

'Then he doesn't tell you everything!' Paul Overt had guessed that Miss Fancourt pretty much supposed he did. The great man had now resumed his course and come nearer; nevertheless Overt risked the profane observation: 'St George and the dragon, the anecdote suggests!'

Miss Fancourt, however, did not hear it; she was smiling at her approaching friend. 'He *is* eager – he is!' she repeated.

'Eager for you – yes.'

The girl called out frankly, joyously: 'I know you want to know Mr Overt. You'll be great friends, and it will always be delightful to me to think that I was here when you first met and that I had something to do with it.'

There was a freshness of intention in this speech which carried it off; nevertheless our young man was sorry for Henry St George, as he was sorry at any time for any one who was publicly invited to be responsive and delightful. He would have been so contented to believe that a man he deeply admired attached an importance to him that he was determined not to play with such a presumption if it possibly were vain. In a single glance of the eye of the pardonable master he discovered (having the sort of divination that belonged to his talent) that this personage was full of general good-will, but had not read a word he had written. There was even a relief, a simplification, in that: liking him so much already for what he had done, how could he like him more for having been struck with a certain promise? He got up, trying to show his compassion, but at the same instant he found himself encompassed by St George's happy personal art – a manner of which it was the essence to conjure away false positions. It all took place in a moment. He was conscious that he knew him now, conscious of his handshake and of the very quality of his hand; of his face, seen nearer and consequently seen better, of a general fraternising assurance, and in particular of the circumstance that St George didn't dislike him (as yet at least) for being imposed by a charming but too gushing girl, valuable enough without such danglers. At any rate no irritation was reflected in the voice with which he questioned Miss Fancourt in respect to some project of a walk – a general walk of the company round the park. He had said something to Overt about a talk – 'We must have a tremendous lot of talk; there are so many things, aren't there?' – but Paul perceived that this idea would not in the present case take very immediate effect. All the same he was extremely happy, even after the matter of the walk had been settled (the three presently passed back to the other part of the gallery, where it was discussed with several members of the party), even when, after they had all gone out together, he found himself for half an hour in contact with Mrs St George. Her husband had taken the advance with Miss Fancourt, and this pair were quite out of sight. It was the prettiest of rambles for a summer afternoon – a grassy circuit, of immense extent, skirting the limit of the park within. The park was completely surrounded by its old mottled but perfect red wall, which, all the way on their left, made a picturesque accompaniment. Mrs St George mentioned to him the surprising number of acres that were thus enclosed, together with numerous other facts relating to the property and the family, and its other properties: she could not too strongly urge upon him the importance of seeing their other houses. She ran over the names of these and rang the changes on them with the facility of practice, making them appear an almost endless list. She had received Paul Overt very amiably when he broke ground with her by telling her that he had just had the joy of making her husband's acquaintance, and struck him as so alert and so accommodating a little woman that he was rather ashamed of his *mot* about her to Miss Fancourt; though he reflected that a hundred other people, on a hundred occasions, would have been sure to make it. He got on with Mrs St George, in short, better than he expected; but this did not prevent her from suddenly becoming aware that she was faint with fatigue and must take her way back to the house by the shortest cut. She hadn't the strength of a kitten, she said – she was awfully seedy; a state of things that Overt had been too preoccupied to perceive – preoccupied with a private effort to ascertain in what sense she could be held to have been the making of her husband. He had arrived at a glimmering of the answer when she announced that she must leave him, though this perception was of course provisional. While he was in the very act of placing himself at her disposal for the return the situation underwent a change; Lord Masham suddenly turned up, coming back to them, overtaking them, emerging from the shrubbery – Overt could scarcely have said how he appeared, and Mrs St George had protested that she wanted to be left alone and not to break up the party. A moment later she was walking off with Lord Masham. Paul Overt fell back and joined Lady Watermouth, to whom he presently mentioned that Mrs St George had been obliged to renounce the attempt to go further.

'She oughtn't to have come out at all,' her ladyship remarked, rather grumpily.

'Is she so very much of an invalid?'

'Very bad indeed.' And his hostess added, with still greater austerity: 'She oughtn't to come to stay with one!' He wondered what was implied by this, and presently gathered that it was not a reflection on the lady's conduct or her moral nature: it only represented that her strength was not equal to her aspirations.

III

THE smoking-room at Summersoft was on the scale of the rest of the place; that is it was high and light and commodious, and decorated with such refined old carvings and mouldings that it seemed rather a bower for ladies who should sit at work at fading crewels than a parliament of gentlemen smoking strong cigars. The gentlemen mustered there in considerable force on the Sunday evening, collecting mainly at one end, in front of one of the cool fair fireplaces of white marble, the entablature of which was adorned with a delicate little Italian 'subject'. There was another in the wall that faced it, and, thanks to the mild summer night, there was no fire in either; but a nucleus for aggregation was furnished on one side by a table in the chimney-corner laden with bottles, decanters and tall tumblers. Paul Overt was an insincere smoker; he puffed cigarettes occasionally for reasons with which tobacco had nothing to do. This was particularly the case on the occasion of which I speak; his motive was the vision of a little direct talk with Henry St George. The 'tremendous' communion of which the great man had held out hopes to him earlier in the day had not yet come off, and this saddened him considerably, for the party was to go its several ways immediately after breakfast on the morrow. He had, however, the disappointment of finding that apparently the author of *Shadowmere* was not disposed to prolong his vigil. He was not among the gentlemen assembled in the smoking-room when Overt entered it, nor was he one of those who turned up, in bright habiliments, during the next ten minutes. The young man waited a little, wondering whether he had only gone to put on something extraordinary; this would account for his delay as well as contribute further to Overt's observation of his tendency to do the approved superficial thing. But he didn't arrive – he must have been putting on something more extraordinary than was probable. Paul gave him up, feeling a little injured, a little wounded at his not having managed to say twenty words to him. He was not angry, but he puffed his cigarette sighingly, with the sense of having lost a precious chance. He wandered away with his regret, moved slowly round the room, looking at the old prints on the walls. In this attitude he presently felt a hand laid on his shoulder and a friendly voice in his ear. 'This is good. I hoped I should find you. I came down on purpose.' St George was there, without a change of dress and with a kind face – his graver one – to which Overt eagerly responded. He explained that it was only for the Master – the idea of a little talk – that he had sat up and that, not finding him, he had been on the point of going to bed.

'Well, you know, I don't smoke – my wife doesn't let me,' said St George, looking for a place to sit down. 'It's very good for me – very good for me. Let us take that sofa.'

'Do you mean smoking is good for you?'

'No, no, her not letting me. It's a great thing to have a wife who proves to one all the things one can do without. One might never find them out for oneself. She doesn't allow me to touch a cigarette.'

They took possession of the sofa, which was at a distance from the group of smokers, and St George went on: 'Have you got one yourself?'

'Do you mean a cigarette?'

'Dear no! a wife.'

'No; and yet I would give up my cigarette for one.'

'You would give up a good deal more than that,' said St George. 'However, you would get a great deal in return. There is a great deal to be said for wives,' he added, folding his arms and crossing his outstretched legs. He declined tobacco altogether and sat there without returning fire. Paul Overt stopped smoking, touched by his courtesy; and after all they were out of the fumes, their sofa was in a far-away corner. It would have been a mistake, St George went on, a great mistake for them to have separated without a little chat; 'for I know all about you,' he said, 'I know you're very remarkable. You've written a very distinguished book.'

'And how do you know it?' Overt asked.

'Why, my dear fellow, it's in the air, it's in the papers, it's everywhere,' St George replied, with the immediate familiarity of a *confrère* – a tone that seemed to his companion the very rustle of the laurel. 'You're on all men's lips and, what's better, you're on all women's. And I've just been reading your book.'

'Just? You hadn't read it this afternoon,' said Overt.

'How do you know that?'

'You know how I know it,' the young man answered, laughing.

'I suppose Miss Fancourt told you.'

'No, indeed; she led me rather to suppose that you had.'

'Yes; that's much more what she would do. Doesn't she shed a rosy glow over life? But you didn't believe her?' asked St George.

'No, not when you came to us there.'

'Did I pretend? did I pretend badly?' But without waiting for an answer to this St George went on: 'You ought always to believe such a girl as that – always, always. Some women are meant to be taken with allowances and reserves; but you must take *her* just as she is.'

'I like her very much,' said Paul Overt.

Something in his tone appeared to excite on his companion's part a momentary sense of the absurd; perhaps it was the air of deliberation attending this judgement. St George broke into a laugh and returned: 'It's the best thing you can do with her. She's a rare young lady! In point of fact, however, I confess I hadn't read you this afternoon.'

'Then you see how right I was in this particular case not to believe Miss Fancourt.'

'How right? how can I agree to that, when I lost credit by it?'

'Do you wish to pass for exactly what she represents you? Certainly you needn't be afraid,' Paul said.

'Ah, my dear young man, don't talk about passing – for the likes of me! I'm passing away – nothing else than that. She has a better use for her young imagination (isn't it fine?) than in "representing" in any way such a weary, wasted, used-up animal!' St George spoke with a sudden sadness which produced a protest on Paul's part; but before the protest could be uttered he went on, reverting to the latter's successful novel: 'I had no idea you were so good – one hears of so many things. But you're surprisingly good.'

'I'm going to be surprisingly better,' said Overt.

'I see that and it's what fetches me. I don't see so much else – as one looks about – that's going to be surprisingly better. They're going to be consistently worse – most of the things. It's so much easier to be worse – heaven knows I've found it so. I'm not in a great glow, you know, about what's being attempted, what's being done. But you *must* be better – you must keep it up. I haven't, of course. It's very difficult – that's the devil of the whole thing; but I see you can. It will be a great disgrace if you don't.'

'It's very interesting to hear you speak of yourself; but I don't know what you mean by your allusions to your having fallen off,' Paul Overt remarked, with pardonable hypocrisy. He liked his companion so much now that it had ceased for the moment to be vivid to him that there had been any decline.

'Don't say that – don't say that,' St George replied gravely, with his head resting on the top of the back of the sofa and his eyes on the ceiling. 'You know perfectly what I mean. I haven't read twenty pages of your book without seeing that you can't help it.'

'You make me very miserable,' Paul murmured.

'I'm glad of that, for it may serve as a kind of warning. Shocking enough it must be, especially to a young, fresh mind, full of faith, – the spectacle of a man meant for better things sunk at my age in such dishonour.' St George, in the same contemplative attitude, spoke softly but deliberately, and without perceptible emotion. His tone indeed suggested an impersonal lucidity which was cruel – cruel to himself – and which made Paul lay an argumentative hand on his arm. But he went on, while his eyes seemed to follow the ingenuities of the beautiful Adam ceiling: 'Look at me well and take my lesson to heart, for it *is* a lesson. Let that good come of it at least that you shudder with your pitiful impression and that this may help to keep you straight in the future. Don't become in your old age what I am in mine – the depressing, the deplorable illustration of the worship of false gods!'

'What do you mean by your old age?' Paul Overt asked.

'It has made me old. But I like your youth.'

Overt answered nothing – they sat for a minute in silence. They heard the others talking about the governmental majority. Then, 'What do you mean by false gods?' Paul inquired.

'The idols of the market – money and luxury and "the world", placing one's children and dressing one's wife – everything that drives one to the short and easy way. Ah, the vile things they make one do!'

'But surely one is right to want to place one's children.'

'One has no business to have any children,' St George declared, placidly. 'I mean of course if one wants to do something good.'

'But aren't they an inspiration – an incentive?'

'An incentive to damnation, artistically speaking.'

'You touch on very deep things – things I should like to discuss with you,' Paul Overt said. 'I should like you to tell me volumes about yourself. This is a festival for *me*!'

'Of course it is, cruel youth. But to show you that I'm still not incapable, degraded as I am, of an act of faith, I'll tie my vanity to the stake for you and burn it to ashes. You must come and see me – you must come and see us. Mrs St George is charming; I don't know whether you have had any opportunity to talk with her. She will be delighted to see you; she likes great celebrities, whether incipient or predominant. You must come and dine – my wife will write to you. Where are you to be found?'

'This is my little address' – and Overt drew out his pocket-book and extracted a visiting-card. On second thoughts, however, he kept it back, remarking that he would not trouble his friend to take charge of it but would come and see him straightway in London and leave it at his door if he should fail to obtain admittance.

'Ah! you probably will fail; my wife's always out, or when she isn't out she's knocked up from having been out. You must come and dine – though that won't do much good either, for my wife insists on big dinners. You must come down and see us in the country, that's the best way; we have plenty of room, and it isn't bad.'

'You have a house in the country?' Paul asked, enviously.

'Ah, not like this! But we have a sort of place we go to – an hour from Euston. That's one of the reasons.'

'One of the reasons?'

'Why my books are so bad.'

'You must tell me all the others!' Paul exclaimed, laughing.

St George made no direct rejoinder to this; he only inquired rather abruptly: 'Why have I never seen you before?'

The tone of the question was singularly flattering to his new comrade; it seemed to imply that he perceived now that for years he had missed something. 'Partly, I suppose, because there has been no particular reason why you should see me. I haven't lived in the world – in your world. I have spent many years out of England, in different places abroad.'

'Well, please don't do it any more. You must do England – there's such a lot of it.'

'Do you mean I must write about it?' Paul asked, in a voice which had the note of the listening candour of a child.

'Of course you must. And tremendously well, do you mind? That takes off a little of my esteem for this thing of yours – that it goes on abroad. Hang abroad! Stay at home and do things here – do subjects we can measure.'

'I'll do whatever you tell me,' said Paul Overt, deeply attentive. 'But excuse me if I say I don't understand how you have been reading my book,' he subjoined. 'I've had you before me all the afternoon, first in that long walk, then at tea on the lawn, till we went to dress for dinner, and all the evening at dinner and in this place.'

St George turned his face round with a smile. 'I only read for a quarter of an hour.'

'A quarter of an hour is liberal, but I don't understand where you put it in. In the drawing-room, after dinner, you were not reading, you were talking to Miss Fancourt.'

'It comes to the same thing, because we talked about *Ginistrella*. She described it to me – she lent it to me.'

'Lent it to you?'

'She travels with it.'

'It's incredible,' Paul Overt murmured, blushing.

'It's glorious for you; but it also turned out very well for me. When the ladies went off to bed she kindly offered to send the book down to me. Her maid brought it to me in the hall and I went to my room with it. I hadn't thought of coming here, I do that so little. But I don't sleep early, I always have to read for an hour or two. I sat down to your novel on the spot, without undressing, without taking off anything but my coat. I think that's a sign that my curiosity had been strongly roused about it. I read a quarter of an hour, as I tell you, and even in a quarter of an hour I was greatly struck.'

'Ah, the beginning isn't very good – it's the whole thing!' said Overt, who had listened to this recital with extreme interest. 'And you laid down the book and came after me?' he asked.

'That's the way it moved me. I said to myself, "I see it's off his own bat, and he's there, by the way, and the day's over and I haven't said twenty words to him." It occurred to me that you would probably be in the smoking-room and that it wouldn't be too late to repair my omission. I wanted to do something civil to you, so I put on my coat and came down. I shall read your book again when I go up.'

Paul Overt turned round in his place – he was exceedingly touched by the picture of such a demonstration in his favour. 'You're really the kindest of men. *Cela s'est passé comme ça?* and I have been sitting here with you all this time and never apprehended it and never thanked you!'

'Thank Miss Fancourt – it was she who wound me up. She has made me feel as if I had read your novel.'

'She's an angel from heaven!' Paul Overt exclaimed.

'She is indeed. I have never seen anyone like her. Her interest in literature is touching – something quite peculiar to herself; she takes it all so seriously. She feels the arts and she wants to feel them more. To those who practise them it's almost humiliating – her curiosity, her sympathy, her good faith. How can anything be as fine as she supposes it?'

'She's a rare organisation,' Paul Overt sighed.

'The richest I have ever seen – an artistic intelligence really of the first order. And lodged in such a form!' St George exclaimed.

'One would like to paint such a girl as that,' Overt continued.

'Ah, there it is – there's nothing like life! When you're finished, squeezed dry and used up and you think the sack's empty, you're still spoken to, you still get touches and thrills, the idea springs up – out of the lap of the actual – and shows you there's always something to be done. But I shan't do it – she's not for me!'

'How do you mean, not for you?'

'Oh, it's all over – she's for you, if you like.'

'Ah, much less!' said Paul Overt. 'She's not for a dingy little man of letters; she's for the world, the bright rich world of bribes and rewards. And the world will take hold of her – it will carry her away.'

'It will try; but it's just a case in which there may be a fight. It would be worth fighting, for a man who had it in him, with youth and talent on his side.'

These words rang not a little in Paul Overt's consciousness – they held him silent a moment. 'It's a wonder she has remained as she is – giving herself away so, with so much to give away.'

'Do you mean so ingenuous – so natural? Oh, she doesn't care a straw – she gives away because she overflows. She has her own feelings, her own standards; she doesn't keep remembering that she must be proud. And then she hasn't been here long enough to be spoiled; she has picked up a fashion or two, but only the amusing ones. She's a provincial – a provincial of genius; her very blunders are charming, her mistakes are interesting. She has come back from Asia with all sorts of excited curiosities and unappeased appetites. She's first-rate herself and she expends herself on the second-rate. She's life herself and she takes a rare interest in imitations. She mixes all things up, but there are none in regard to which she hasn't perceptions. She sees things in a perspective – as if from the top of the Himalayas – and she enlarges everything she touches. Above all, she exaggerates – to herself, I mean. She exaggerates you and me!'

There was nothing in this description to allay the excitement produced in the mind of our younger friend by such a sketch of a fine subject. It seemed to him to show the art of St George's admired hand, and he lost himself in it, gazing at the vision (it hovered there before him) of a woman's figure which should be part of the perfection of a novel. At the end of a moment he became aware that it had turned into smoke, and out of the smoke – the last puff of a big cigar – proceeded the voice of General Fancourt, who had left the others and come and planted himself before the gentlemen on the sofa. 'I suppose that when you fellows get talking you sit up half the night.'

'Half the night? – *jamais de la vie*! I follow a hygiene,' St George replied, rising to his feet.

'I see, you're hothouse plants,' laughed the General. 'That's the way you produce your flowers.'

'I produce mine between ten and one every morning; I bloom with a regularity!' St George went on.

'And with a splendour!' added the polite General, while Paul Overt noted how little the author of *Shadowmere* minded, as he phrased it to himself, when he was addressed as a celebrated story-teller. The young man had an idea that *he* should never get used to that – it would always make him uncomfortable (from the suspicion that people would think they had to), and he would want to prevent it. Evidently his more illustrious congener had toughened and hardened – had made himself a surface. The group of men had finished their cigars and taken up their bedroom candlesticks; but before they all passed out Lord Watermouth invited St George and Paul Overt to drink something. It happened that they both declined, upon which General Fancourt said: 'Is that the hygiene? You don't sprinkle the flowers?'

'Oh, I should drown them!' St George replied; but leaving the room beside Overt he added whimsically, for the latter's benefit, in a lower tone: 'My wife doesn't let me.'

'Well, I'm glad I'm not one of you fellows!' the General exclaimed.

The nearness of Summersoft to London had this consequence, chilling to a person who had had a vision of sociability in a railway-carriage, that most of the company, after breakfast, drove back to town, entering their own vehicles, which had come out to fetch them, while their servants returned by train with their luggage. Three or four young men, among whom was Paul Overt, also availed themselves of the common convenience; but they stood in the portico of the house and saw the others roll away. Miss Fancourt got into a victoria with her father, after she had shaken hands with Paul Overt and said, smiling in the frankest way in the world – 'I *must* see you more. Mrs St George is so nice: she has promised to ask us both to dinner together.' This lady and her husband took their places in a perfectly-appointed brougham (she required a closed carriage), and as our young man waved his hat to them in response to their nods and flourishes he reflected that, taken together, they were an honourable image of success, of the material rewards and the social credit of literature. Such things were not the full measure, but all the same he felt a little proud for literature.

IV

BEFORE a week had elapsed Paul Overt met Miss Fancourt in Bond Street, at a private view of the works of a young artist in 'black and white' who had been so good as to invite him to the stuffy scene. The drawings were admirable, but the crowd in the one little room was so dense that he felt as if he were up to his neck in a big sack of wool. A fringe of people at the outer edge endeavoured by curving forward their backs and presenting, below them, a still more convex surface of resistance to the pressure of the mass, to preserve an interval between their noses and the glazed mounts of the pictures; while the central body, in the comparative gloom projected by a wide horizontal screen, hung under the sky-light and allowing only a margin for the day, remained upright, dense and vague, lost in the contemplation of its own ingredients. This contemplation sat especially in the sad eyes of certain female heads, surmounted with hats of strange convolution and plumage, which rose on long necks above the others. One of the heads, Paul Overt perceived, was much the most beautiful of the collection, and his next discovery was that it belonged to Miss Fancourt. Its beauty was enhanced by the glad smile that she sent him across surrounding obstructions, a smile which drew him to her as fast as he could make his way. He had divined at Summersoft that the last thing her nature contained was an affectation of indifference; yet even with this circumspection he had a freshness of pleasure in seeing that she did not pretend to await his arrival with composure. She smiled as radiantly as if she wished to make him hurry, and as soon as he came within earshot she said to him, in her voice of joy: 'He's here – he's here – he's coming back in a moment!'

'Ah, your father?' Paul responded, as she offered him her hand.

'Oh dear no, this isn't in my poor father's line. I mean Mr St George. He has just left me to speak to some one – he's coming back. It's he who brought me – wasn't it charming?'

'Ah, that gives him a pull over me – I couldn't have "brought" you, could I?'

'If you had been so kind as to propose it – why not you as well as he?' the girl asked, with a face which expressed no cheap coquetry, but simply affirmed a happy fact.

'Why, he's a *père de famille*. They have privileges,' Paul Overt explained. And then, quickly: 'Will you go to see places with *me*?' he broke out.

'Anything you like!' she smiled. 'I know what you mean, that girls have to have a lot of people—' She interrupted herself to say: 'I don't know; I'm free. I have always been like that,' she went on; 'I can go anywhere with any one. I'm so glad to meet you,' she added, with a sweet distinctness that made the people near her turn round.

'Let me at least repay that speech by taking you out of this squash,' said Paul Overt. 'Surely people are not happy here!'

'No, they are *mornes*, aren't they? But I am very happy indeed, and I promised Mr St George to remain in this spot till he comes back. He's going to take me away. They send him invitations for things of this sort – more than he wants. It was so kind of him to think of me.'

'They also send me invitations of this kind – more than I want. And if thinking of *you* will do it—!' Paul went on.

'Oh, I delight in them – everything that's life – everything that's London!'

'They don't have private views in Asia, I suppose. But what a pity that for this year, in this fertile city, they are pretty well over.'

'Well, next year will do, for I hope you believe we are going to be friends always. Here he comes!' Miss Fancourt continued, before Paul had time to respond.

He made out St George in the gaps of the crowd, and this perhaps led to his hurrying a little to say: 'I hope that doesn't mean that I'm to wait till next year to see you.'

'No, no; are we not to meet at dinner on the 25th?' she answered, with an eagerness greater even than his own.

'That's almost next year. Is there no means of seeing you before?'

She stared, with all her brightness. 'Do you mean that you would *come*?'

'Like a shot, if you'll be so good as to ask me!'

'On Sunday, then – this next Sunday?'

'What have I done that you should doubt it?' the young man demanded, smiling.

Miss Fancourt turned instantly to St George, who had now joined them, and announced triumphantly: 'He's coming on Sunday – this next Sunday!'

'Ah, my day – my day too!' said the famous novelist, laughing at Paul Overt.

'Yes, but not yours only. You shall meet in Manchester Square; you shall talk – you shall be wonderful!'

'We don't meet often enough,' St George remarked, shaking hands with his disciple. 'Too many things – ah, too many things! But we must make it up in the country in September. You won't forget that you've promised me that?'

'Why, he's coming on the 25th; you'll see him then,' said Marian Fancourt.

'On the 25th?' St George asked, vaguely.

'We dine with you; I hope you haven't forgotten. He's dining out,' she added gaily to Paul Overt.

'Oh, bless me, yes; that's charming! And you're coming? My wife didn't tell me,' St George said to Paul. 'Too many things – too many things!' he repeated.

'Too many people – too many people!' Paul exclaimed, giving ground before the penetration of an elbow.

'You oughtn't to say that; they all read you.'

'Me? I should like to see them! Only two or three at most,' the young man rejoined.

'Did you ever hear anything like that? he knows how good he is!' St George exclaimed, laughing, to Miss Fancourt. 'They read *me*, but that doesn't make me like them any better. Come away from them, come away!' And he led the way out of the exhibition.

'He's going to take me to the Park,' the girl said, with elation, to Paul Overt, as they passed along the corridor which led to the street.

'Ah, does he go there?' Paul asked, wondering at the idea as a somewhat unexpected illustration of St George's *moeurs*.

'It's a beautiful day; there will be a great crowd. We're going to look at the people, to look at types,' the girl went on. 'We shall sit under the trees; we shall walk by the Row.'

'I go once a year, on business,' said St George, who had overheard Paul's question.

'Or with a country cousin, didn't you tell me? I'm the country cousin!' she went on, over her shoulder, to Paul, as her companion drew her toward a hansom to which he had signalled. The young man watched them get in; he returned, as he stood there, the friendly wave of the hand with which, ensconced in the vehicle beside Miss Fancourt, St George took leave of him. He even lingered to see the vehicle start away and lose itself in the confusion of Bond Street. He followed it with his eyes; it was embarrassingly suggestive. 'She's not for me!' the great novelist had said emphatically at Summersoft; but his manner of conducting himself toward her appeared not exactly in harmony with such a conviction. How could he have behaved differently if she *had* been for him? An indefinite envy rose in Paul Overt's heart as he took his way on foot alone, and the singular part of it was that it was directed to each of the occupants of the hansom. How much he should like to rattle about London with such a girl! How much he should like to go and look at 'types' with St George!

The next Sunday, at four o'clock, he called in Manchester Square, where his secret wish was gratified by his finding Miss Fancourt alone. She was in a large, bright, friendly, occupied room, which was painted red all over, draped with the quaint, cheap, florid stuffs that are represented as coming from south-ern and eastern countries, where they are fabled to serve as the counterpanes of the peasantry, and bedecked with pottery of vivid hues, ranged on casual shelves, and with many water-colour drawings from the hand (as the visitor learned) of the young lady, commemorating, with courage and skill, the sun-sets, the mountains, the temples and palaces of India. Overt sat there an hour – more than an hour, two hours – and all the while no one came in. Miss Fancourt was so good as to remark, with her liberal humanity, that it was delightful they were not inter-rupted; it was so rare in London, especially at that season, that people got a good talk. But fortunately now, of a fine Sunday, half the world went out of town, and that made it better for those who didn't go, when they were in sympathy. It was the defect of London (one of two or three, the very short list of those she recognised in the teeming world-city that she adored) that there were too few good chances for talk; one never had time to carry anything far.

'Too many things – too many things!' Paul Overt said, quoting St George's exclamation of a few days before.

'Ah yes, for him there are too many; his life is too compli-cated.'

'Have you seen it *near*? That's what I should like to do; it might explain some mysteries,' Paul Overt went on. The girl asked him what mysteries he meant, and he said: 'Oh, peculiarities of his work, inequalities, superficialities. For one who looks at it from the artistic point of view it contains a bottomless ambiguity.'

'Oh, do describe that more – it's so interesting. There are no such suggestive questions. I'm so fond of them. He thinks he's a failure – fancy!' Miss Fancourt added.

'That depends upon what his ideal may have been. Ah, with his gifts it ought to have been high. But till one knows what he really proposed to himself – – Do *you* know, by chance?' the young man asked, breaking off.

'Oh, he doesn't talk to me about himself. I can't make him. It's too provoking.'

Paul Overt was on the point of asking what then he did talk about; but discretion checked this inquiry, and he said instead: 'Do you think he's unhappy at home?'

'At home?'

'I mean in his relations with his wife. He has a mystifying little way of alluding to her.'

'Not to me,' said Marian Fancourt, with her clear eyes. 'That wouldn't be right, would it?' she asked, seriously.

'Not particularly; so I am glad he doesn't mention her to you. To praise her might bore you, and he has no business to do anything else. Yet he knows you better than me.'

'Ah, but he respects *you*!' the girl exclaimed, enviously.

Her visitor stared a moment; then he broke into a laugh. 'Doesn't he respect you?'

'Of course, but not in the same way. He respects what you've done – he told me so, the other day.'

'When you went to look at types?'

'Ah, we found so many – he has such an observation of them! He talked a great deal about your book. He says it's really important.'

'Important! Ah! the grand creature,' Paul murmured, hilarious.

'He was wonderfully amusing, he was inexpressibly droll, while we walked about. He sees everything; he has so many comparisons, and they are always exactly right. *C'est d'un trouvé!* as they say.'

'Yes, with his gifts, such things as he ought to have done!' Paul Overt remarked.

'And don't you think he *has* done them?'

He hesitated a moment. 'A part of them – and of course even that part is immense. But he might have been one of the greatest! However, let us not make this an hour of qualifications. Even as they stand, his writings are a mine of gold.'

To this proposition Marian Fancourt ardently responded, and for half an hour the pair talked over the master's principal productions. She knew them well – she knew them even better than her visitor, who was struck with her critical intelligence and with something large and bold in the movement in her mind. She said things that startled him and that evidently had come to her directly; they were not picked-up phrases, she placed them too well. St George had been right about her being first-rate, about her not being afraid to gush, not remembering that she must be proud. Suddenly something reminded her, and she said: 'I recollect that he did speak of Mrs St George to me once. He said, *à propos* of something or other, that she didn't care for perfection.'

'That's a great crime, for an artist's wife,' said Paul Overt.

'Yes, poor thing!' and the young lady sighed, with a suggestion of many reflections, some of them mitigating. But she added in a moment, 'Ah, perfection, perfection – how one ought to go in for it! I wish I could.'

'Every one can, in his way,' said Paul Overt.

'In *his* way, yes; but not in hers. Women are so hampered – so condemned! But it's a kind of dishonour if you don't, when you want to *do* something, isn't it?' Miss Fancourt pursued, dropping one train in her quickness to take up another, an accident that was common with her. So these two young persons sat discussing high themes in their eclectic drawing-room, in their London season – discussing, with extreme seriousness, the high theme of perfection. And it must be said, in extenuation of this eccentricity, that they were interested in the business; their tone was genuine, their emotion real; they were not posturing for each other or for some one else.

The subject was so wide that they found it necessary to contract it; the perfection to which for the moment they agreed to confine their speculations was that of which the valid work of art is susceptible. Miss Fancourt's imagination, it appeared, had wandered far in that direction, and her visitor had the rare delight of feeling that their conversation was a full interchange. This episode will have lived for years in his memory and even in his wonder; it had the quality that fortune distils in a single drop at a time – the quality that lubricates ensuing weeks and months. He has still a vision of the room, whenever he likes – the bright, red, sociable, talkative room, with the curtains that, by a stroke of successful audacity, had the note of vivid blue. He remembers where certain things stood, the book that was open on the table and the particular odour of the flowers that were placed on the left, somewhere behind him. These facts were the fringe, as it were, of a particular consciousness which had its birth in those two hours and of which perhaps the most general description would be to mention that it led him to say over and over again to himself: 'I had no idea there was any one like this – I had no idea there was any one like this!' Her freedom amazed him and charmed him – it seemed so to simplify the practical question. She was on the footing of an independent personage – a motherless girl who had passed out of her teens and had a position, responsibilities, and was not held down to the limitations of a little miss. She came and went without the clumsiness of a chaperone; she received people alone and, though she was totally without hardness, the question of protection or patronage had no relevancy in regard to her. She gave such an impression of purity combined with naturalness that, in spite of her eminently modern situation, she suggested no sort of sisterhood with the 'fast' girl. Modern she was, indeed, and made Paul Overt, who loved old colour, the golden glaze of time, think with some alarm of the muddled palette of the future. He couldn't get used to her interest in the arts he cared for; it seemed too good to be real – it was so unlikely an adventure to tumble into such a well of sympathy. One might stray into the desert easily – that was on the cards and that was the law of life; but it was too rare an accident to stumble on a crystal well. Yet if her aspirations seemed at one moment too extravagant to be real, they struck him at the next as too intelligent to be false. They were both noble and crude, and whims for whims, he liked them better than any he had met. It was probable enough she would leave them behind – exchange them for politics, or 'smartness', or mere prolific maternity, as was the custom of scribbling, daubing, educated, flattered girls, in an age of luxury and a society of leisure. He noted that the water-colours on the walls of the room she sat in had mainly the quality of being *naïves*, and reflected that *naïveté* in art is like a cipher in a number: its importance depends upon the figure it is united with. But meanwhile he had fallen in love with her.

Before he went away he said to Miss Fancourt: 'I thought St George was coming to see you to-day – but he doesn't turn up.'

For a moment he supposed she was going to reply, '*Comment donc?* Did you come here only to meet him?' But the next he became aware of how little such a speech would have fallen in with any flirtatious element he had as yet perceived in her. She only replied: 'Ah yes, but I don't think he'll come. He recommended me not to expect him.' Then she added, laughing: 'He said it wasn't fair to you. But I think I could manage two.'

'So could I,' Paul Overt rejoined, stretching the point a little to be humorous. In reality his appreciation of the occasion was so completely an appreciation of the woman before him that another figure in the scene, even so esteemed a one as St George, might for the hour have appealed to him vainly. As he went away he wondered what the great man had meant by its not being fair to him; and, still more than that, whether he had actually stayed away out of the delicacy of such an idea. As he took his course, swinging his stick, through the Sunday solitude of Manchester Square, with a good deal of emotion fermenting in his soul, it appeared to him that he was living in a world really magnanimous. Miss Fancourt had told him that there was an uncertainty about her being, and her father's being, in town on the following Sunday, but that she had the hope of a visit from him if they should not go away. She promised to let him know if they stayed at home, then he could act accordingly. After he had passed into one of the streets that lead out of the square, he stopped, without definite intentions, looking sceptically for a cab. In a moment he saw a hansom roll through the square from the other side and come a part of the way toward him. He was on the point of hailing the driver when he perceived that he carried a fare; then he waited, seeing him prepare to deposit his passenger by pulling up at one of the houses. The house was apparently the one he himself had just quitted; at least he drew that inference as he saw that the person who stepped out of the hansom was Henry St George. Paul Overt turned away quickly, as if he had been caught in the act of spying. He gave up his cab – he preferred to walk; he would go nowhere else. He was glad St George had not given up his visit altogether – that would have been too absurd. Yes, the world was magnanimous, and Overt felt so too as, on looking at his watch, he found it was only six o'clock, so that he could mentally congratulate his successor on having an hour still to sit in Miss Fancourt's drawing-room. He himself might use that hour for another visit, but by the time he reached the Marble Arch the idea of another visit had become incongruous to him. He passed beneath that architectural effort and walked into the Park till he got upon the grass. Here he continued to walk; he took his way across the elastic turf and came out by the Serpentine. He watched with a friendly eye the diversions of the London people, and bent a glance almost encouraging upon the young ladies paddling their sweethearts on the lake, and the guardsmen tickling tenderly with their bearskins the artificial flowers in the Sunday hats of their partners. He prolonged his meditative walk; he went into Kensington Gardens – he sat upon the penny chairs – he looked at the little sail-boats launched upon the round pond – he was glad he had no engagement to dine. He repaired for this purpose, very late, to his club, where he found himself unable to order a repast and told the waiter to bring whatever he would. He did not even observe what he was served with, and he spent the evening in the library of the establishment, pretending to read an article in an American magazine. He failed to discover what it was about; it appeared in a dim way to be about Marian Fancourt.

Quite late in the week she wrote to him that she was not to go into the country – it had only just been settled. Her father, she added, would never settle anything – he put it all on her. She felt her responsibility – she had to – and since she was forced that was the way she had decided. She mentioned no reasons, which gave Paul Overt all the clearer field for bold conjecture about them. In Manchester Square, on this second Sunday, he esteemed his fortune less good, for she had three or four other visitors. But there were three or four compensations; the greatest, perhaps, of which was that, learning from her that her father had, after all, at the last hour, gone out of town alone, the bold conjecture I just now spoke of found itself becoming a shade more bold. And then her presence was her presence, and the personal red room was there and was full of it, whatever phantoms passed and vanished, emitting incomprehensible sounds. Lastly, he had the resource of staying till every one had come and gone and of supposing that this pleased her, though she gave no particular sign. When they were alone together he said to her: 'But St George did come – last Sunday. I saw him as I looked back.'

'Yes; but it was the last time.'

'The last time?'

'He said he would never come again.'

Paul Overt stared. 'Does he mean that he wishes to cease to see you?'

'I don't know what he means,' the girl replied, smiling. 'He won't, at any rate, see me here.'

'And, pray, why not?'

'I don't know,' said Marian Fancourt; and her visitor thought he had not yet seen her more beautiful than in uttering these unsatisfactory words.

V

'OH, I say, I want you to remain,' Henry St George said to him at eleven o'clock, the night he dined with the head of the

profession. The company had been numerous and they were
taking their leave; our young man, after bidding good-night to
his hostess, had put out his hand in farewell to the master of the
house. Besides eliciting from St George the protest I have
quoted this movement provoked a further observation about
such a chance to have a talk, their going into his room, his
having still everything to say. Paul Overt was delighted to be
asked to stay; nevertheless he mentioned jocularly the literal
fact that he had promised to go to another place, at a distance.

'Well then, you'll break your promise, that's all. You humbug!' St George exclaimed, in a tone that added to Overt's
contentment.

'Certainly, I'll break it; but it was a real promise.'

'Do you mean to Miss Fancourt? You're following her?' St
George asked.

Paul Overt answered by a question. 'Oh, is *she* going?'

'Base impostor!' his ironic host went on; 'I've treated you
handsomely on the article of that young lady: I won't make
another concession. Wait three minutes – I'll be with you.' He
gave himself to his departing guests, went with the long-trained
ladies to the door. It was a hot night, the windows were open,
the sound of the quick carriages and of the linkmen's call came
into the house. The company had been brilliant; a sense of
festal things was in the heavy air: not only the influence of
that particular entertainment, but the suggestion of the wide
hurry of pleasure which, in London, on summer nights, fills so
many of the happier quarters of the complicated town. Gradually Mrs St George's drawing-room emptied itself; Paul Overt
was left alone with his hostess, to whom he explained the
motive of his waiting. 'Ah yes, some intellectual, some *professional*, talk,' she smiled; 'at this season doesn't one miss it? Poor
dear Henry, I'm so glad!' The young man looked out of the
window a moment, at the called hansoms that lurched up, at
the smooth broughams that rolled away. When he turned
round Mrs St George had disappeared; her husband's voice
came up to him from below – he was laughing and talking, in
the portico, with some lady who awaited her carriage. Paul had
solitary possession, for some minutes, of the warm, deserted

rooms, where the covered, tinted lamplight was soft, the seats had been pushed about and the odour of flowers lingered. They were large, they were pretty, they contained objects of value; everything in the picture told of a 'good house'. At the end of five minutes a servant came in with a request from Mr St George that he would join him downstairs; upon which, descending, he followed his conductor through a long passage to an apartment thrown out, in the rear of the habitation, for the special requirements, as he guessed, of a busy man of letters.

St George was in his shirt-sleeves in the middle of a large, high room – a room without windows, but with a wide skylight at the top, like a place of exhibition. It was furnished as a library, and the serried bookshelves rose to the ceiling, a surface of incomparable tone, produced by dimly-gilt 'backs', which was interrupted here and there by the suspension of old prints and drawings. At the end furthest from the door of admission was a tall desk, of great extent, at which the person using it could only write standing, like a clerk in a counting-house; and stretching from the door to this structure was a large plain band of crimson cloth, as straight as a garden-path and almost as long, where, in his mind's eye, Paul Overt immediately saw his host pace to and fro during his hours of composition. The servant gave him a coat, an old jacket with an air of experience, from a cupboard in the wall, retiring afterwards with the garment he had taken off. Paul Overt welcomed the coat; it was a coat for talk and promised confidences – it must have received so many – and had pathetic literary elbows. 'Ah, we're practical – we're practical!' St George said, as he saw his visitor looking the place over. 'Isn't it a good big cage, to go round and round? My wife invented it and she locks me up here every morning.'

'You don't miss a window – a place to look out?'

'I did at first, awfully; but her calculation was just. It saves time, it has saved me many months in these ten years. Here I stand, under the eye of day – in London of course, very often, it's rather a bleared old eye – walled in to my trade. I can't get away, and the room is a fine lesson in concentration. I've learned the lesson, I think; look at that big bundle of proofs and admit that I have.' He pointed to a fat roll of papers, on one of the tables, which had not been undone.

'Are you bringing out another—?' Paul Overt asked, in a tone of whose deficiencies he was not conscious till his companion burst out laughing, and indeed not even then.

'You humbug – you humbug! Don't I know what you think of them?' St George inquired, standing before him with his hands in his pockets and with a new kind of smile. It was as if he were going to let his young votary know him well now.

'Upon my word, in that case you know more than I do!' Paul ventured to respond, revealing a part of the torment of being able neither clearly to esteem him nor distinctly to renounce him.

'My dear fellow,' said his companion, 'don't imagine I talk about my books, specifically; it isn't a decent subject – *il ne manquerait plus que ça* – I'm not so bad as you may apprehend! About myself, a little, if you like; though it wasn't for that I brought you down here. I want to ask you something – very much indeed – I value this chance. Therefore sit down. We are practical, but there *is* a sofa, you see, for she does humour me a little, after all. Like all really great administrators she knows when to.' Paul Overt sank into the corner of a deep leathern couch, but his interlocutor remained standing and said: 'If you don't mind, in this room this is my habit. From the door to the desk and from the desk to the door. That shakes up my imagination, gently; and don't you see what a good thing it is that there's no window for her to fly out of? The eternal standing as I write (I stop at that bureau and put it down, when anything comes, and so we go on) was rather wearisome at first, but we adopted it with an eye to the long run; you're in better order (if your legs don't break down!) and you can keep it up for more years. Oh, we're practical – we're practical!' St George repeated, going to the table and taking up, mechanically, the bundle of proofs. He pulled off the wrapper, he turned the papers over with a sudden change of attention which only made him more interesting to Paul Overt. He lost himself a moment, examining the sheets of his new book, while the younger man's eyes wandered over the room again.

'Lord, what good things I should do if I had such a charming place as this to do them in!' Paul reflected. The outer world, the world of accident and ugliness was so successfully excluded, and within the rich, protecting square, beneath the patronising sky, the figures projected for an artistic purpose could hold their particular revel. It was a prevision of Paul Overt's rather than an observation on actual data, for which the occasions had been too few, that his new friend would have the quality, the charming quality, of surprising him by flashing out in personal intercourse, at moments of suspended, or perhaps even of diminished expectation. A happy relation with him would be a thing proceeding by jumps, not by traceable stages.

'Do you read them – really?' he asked, laying down the proofs on Paul's inquiring of him how soon the work would be published. And when the young man answered, 'Oh yes, always,' he was moved to mirth again by something he caught in his manner of saying that. 'You go to see your grandmother on her birthday – and very proper it is, especially as she won't last for ever. She has lost every faculty and every sense; she neither sees, nor hears, nor speaks; but all customary pieties and kindly habits are respectable. But you're strong if you *do* read 'em! *I* couldn't, my dear fellow. You *are* strong, I know; and that's just a part of what I wanted to say to you. You're very strong indeed. I've been going into your other things – they've interested me exceedingly. Some one ought to have told me about them before – some one I could believe. But whom can one believe? You're wonderfully in the good direction – it's extremely curious work. Now do you mean to keep it up? – that's what I want to ask you.'

'Do I mean to do others?' Paul Overt asked, looking up from his sofa at his erect inquisitor and feeling partly like a happy little boy when the schoolmaster is gay and partly like some pilgrim of old who might have consulted the oracle. St George's own performance had been infirm, but as an adviser he would be infallible.

'Others – others? Ah, the number won't matter; one other would do, if it were really a further step – a throb of the same effort. What I mean is, have you it in your mind to go in for some sort of little perfection?'

'Ah, perfection!' Overt sighed, 'I talked of that the other Sunday with Miss Fancourt.'

'Oh yes, they'll talk of it, as much as you like! But they do mighty little to help one to it. There's no obligation, of course; only you strike me as capable,' St George went on. 'You must have thought it all over. I can't believe you're without a plan. That's the sensation you give me, and it's so rare that it really stirs up one; it makes you remarkable. If you haven't a plan and you don't mean to keep it up, of course it's all right, it's no one's business, no one can force you, and not more than two or three people will notice that you don't go straight. The others – *all* the rest, every blessed soul in England, will think you do – will think you *are* keeping it up: upon my honour they will! I shall be one of the two or three who know better. Now the question is whether you can do it for two or three. Is that the stuff you're made of?'

'I could do it for one, if you were the one.'

'Don't say that – I don't deserve it; it scorches me,' St George exclaimed, with eyes suddenly grave and glowing. 'The "one" is of course oneself – one's conscience, one's idea, the singleness of one's aim. I think of that pure spirit as a man thinks of a woman whom, in some detested hour of his youth, he has loved and forsaken. She haunts him with reproachful eyes, she lives for ever before him. As an artist, you know, I've married for money.' Paul stared and even blushed a little, confounded by this avowal; whereupon his host, observing the expression of his face, dropped a quick laugh and went on: 'You don't follow my figure. I'm not speaking of my dear wife, who had a small fortune, which, however, was not my bribe. I fell in love with her, as many other people have done. I refer to the mercenary muse whom I led to the altar of literature. Don't do that, my boy. She'll lead you a life!'

'Haven't you been happy?'

'Happy? It's a kind of hell.'

'There are things I should like to ask you,' Paul Overt said, hesitating.

'Ask me anything in all the world. I'd turn myself inside out to save you.'

'To save me?' Paul repeated.

'To make you stick to it – to make you see it through. As I said to you the other night at Summersoft, let my example be vivid to you.'

'Why, your books are not so bad as that,' said Paul, laughing and feeling that he breathed the air of art.

'So bad as what?'

'Your talent is so great that it is in everything you do, in what's less good as well as in what's best. You've some forty volumes to show for it – forty volumes of life, of observation, of magnificent ability.'

'I'm very clever, of course I know that,' St George replied, quietly. 'Lord, what rot they'd all be if I hadn't been! I'm a successful charlatan – I've been able to pass off my system. But do you know what it is? It's *carton-pierre*.'

'*Carton-pierre*?'

'Lincrusta-Walton!'

'Ah, don't say such things – you make me bleed!' the younger man protested. 'I see you in a beautiful, fortunate home, living in comfort and honour.'

'Do you call it honour?' St George interrupted, with an intonation that often comes back to his companion. 'That's what I want *you* to go in for. I mean the real thing. This is brummagem.'

'Brummagem?' Paul ejaculated, while his eyes wandered, by a movement natural at the moment, over the luxurious room.

'Ah, they make it so well to-day; it's wonderfully deceptive!'

'Is it deceptive that I find you living with every appearance of domestic felicity – blessed with a devoted, accomplished wife, with children whose acquaintance I haven't yet had the pleasure of making, but who *must* be delightful young people, from what I know of their parents?'

'It's all excellent, my dear fellow – Heaven forbid I should deny it. I've made a great deal of money; my wife has known how to take care of it, to use it without wasting it, to put a good bit of it by, to make it fructify. I've got a loaf on the shelf; I've got everything, in fact, but the great thing—'

'The great thing?'

'The sense of having done the best – the sense, which is the real life of the artist and the absence of which is his death, of having drawn from his intellectual instrument the finest music that nature had hidden in it, of having played it as it should be played. He either does that or he doesn't – and if he doesn't he isn't worth speaking of. And precisely those who really know don't speak of him. He may still hear a great chatter, but what he hears most is the incorruptible silence of Fame. I have squared her, you may say, for my little hour – but what is my little hour? Don't imagine for a moment I'm such a cad as to have brought you down here to abuse or to complain of my wife to you. She is a woman of very distinguished qualities, to whom my obligations are immense; so that, if you please, we will say nothing about her. My boys – my children are all boys – are straight and strong, thank God! and have no poverty of growth about them, no penury of needs. I receive, periodically, the most satisfactory attestation from Harrow, from Oxford, from Sandhurst (oh, we have done the best for them!) of their being living, thriving, consuming organisms.'

'It must be delightful to feel that the son of one's loins is at Sandhurst,' Paul remarked, enthusiastically.

'It is – it's charming. Oh, I'm a patriot!'

'Then what did you mean – the other night at Summersoft – by saying that children are a curse?'

'My dear fellow, on what basis are we talking?' St George asked, dropping upon the sofa, at a short distance from his visitor. Sitting a little sideways he leaned back against the opposite arm with his hands raised and interlocked behind his head. 'On the supposition that a certain perfection is possible and even desirable – isn't it so? Well, all I say is that one's children interfere with perfection. One's wife interferes. Marriage interferes.'

'You think then the artist shouldn't marry?'

'He does so at his peril – he does so at his cost.'

'Not even when his wife is in sympathy with his work?'

'She never is – she can't be! Women don't know what work is.'

'Surely, they work themselves,' Paul Overt objected.

'Yes, very badly. Oh, of course, often, they think they understand, they think they sympathise. Then it is that they are most dangerous. Their idea is that you shall do a great lot and get a great lot of money. Their great nobleness and virtue, their exemplary conscientiousness as British females, is in keeping you up to that. My wife makes all my bargains with my publishers for me, and she has done so for twenty years. She does it consummately well; that's why I'm really pretty well off. Are you not the father of their innocent babes, and will you withhold from them their natural sustenance? You asked me the other night if they were not an immense incentive. Of course they are – there's no doubt of that!'

'For myself, I have an idea I need incentives,' Paul Overt dropped.

'Ah well, then, *n'en parlons plus*!' said his companion, smiling.

'You are an incentive, I maintain,' the young man went on. 'You don't affect me in the way you apparently would like to. Your great success is what I see – the pomp of Ennismore Gardens!'

'Success? – do you call it success to be spoken of as you would speak of me if you were sitting here with another artist – a young man intelligent and sincere like yourself? Do you call it success to make you blush – as you would blush – if some foreign critic (some fellow, of course, I mean, who should know what he was talking about and should have shown you he did, as foreign critics like to show it!) were to say to you: "He's the one, in this country, whom they consider the most perfect, isn't he?" Is it success to be the occasion of a young Englishman's having to stammer as you would have to stammer at such a moment for old England? No, no; success is to have made people tremble after another fashion. Do try it!'

'Try it?'

'Try to do some really good work.'

'Oh, I want to, Heaven knows!'

'Well, you can't do it without sacrifices; don't believe that for a moment,' said Henry St George. 'I've made none. I've had everything. In other words, I've missed everything.'

'You've had the full, rich, masculine, human, general life, with all the responsibilities and duties and burdens and sorrows and joys – all the domestic and social initiations and complications. They must be immensely suggestive, immensely amusing.'

'Amusing?'

'For a strong man – yes.'

'They've given me subjects without number, if that's what you mean; but they've taken away at the same time the power to use them. I've touched a thousand things, but which one of them have I turned into gold? The artist has to do only with that – he knows nothing of any baser metal. I've led the life of the world, with my wife and my progeny; the clumsy, expensive, materialised, brutalised, Philistine, snobbish life of London. We've got everything handsome, even a carriage – we are prosperous, hospitable, eminent people. But, my dear fellow, don't try to stultify yourself and pretend you don't know what we *haven't* got. It's bigger than all the rest. Between artists – come! You know as well as you sit there that you would put a pistol-ball into your brain if you had written my books!'

It appeared to Paul Overt that the tremendous talk promised by the master at Summersoft had indeed come off, and with a promptitude, a fullness, with which his young imagination had scarcely reckoned. His companion made an immense impression on him and he throbbed with the excitement of such deep soundings and such strange confidences. He throbbed indeed with the conflict of his feelings – bewilderment and recognition and alarm, enjoyment and protest and assent, all commingled with tenderness (and a kind of shame in the participation) for the sores and bruises exhibited by so fine a creature, and with a sense of the tragic secret that he nursed under his trappings. The idea of *his* being made the occasion of such an act of humility made him flush and pant, at the same time that his perception, in certain directions, had been too much awakened to conceal from him anything that St George really meant. It had been his odd fortune to blow upon the deep waters, to make them surge and break in waves of strange eloquence. He launched himself into a passionate contradiction of his host's last declaration; tried to enumerate to him the parts of his work he loved, the splendid things he had found in it, beyond the compass of any other writer of the day. St George listened awhile, courteously; then he said, laying his hand on Paul Overt's:

'That's all very well; and if your idea is to do nothing better there is no reason why you shouldn't have as many good things as I – as many human and material appendages, as many sons or daughters, a wife with as many gowns, a house with as many servants, a stable with as many horses, a heart with as many aches.' He got up when he had spoken thus, and then stood a moment near the sofa, looking down on his agitated pupil. 'Are you possessed of any money?' it occurred to him to ask.

'None to speak of.'

'Oh, well, there's no reason why you shouldn't make a goodish income – if you set about it the right way. Study *me* for that – study me well. You may really have a carriage.'

Paul Overt sat there for some moments without speaking. He looked straight before him – he turned over many things. His friend had wandered away from him, taking up a parcel of letters that were on the table where the roll of proofs had lain. 'What was the book Mrs St George made you burn – the one she didn't like?' he abruptly inquired.

'The book she made me burn – how did you know that?' St George looked up from his letters.

'I heard her speak of it at Summersoft.'

'Ah, yes; she's proud of it. I don't know – it was rather good.'

'What was it about?'

'Let me see.' And St George appeared to make an effort to remember. 'Oh, yes, it was about myself.' Paul Overt gave an irrepressible groan for the disappearance of such a production, and the elder man went on: 'Oh, but *you* should write it – *you* should do me. There's a subject, my boy: no end of stuff in it!'

Again Paul was silent, but after a little he spoke. 'Are there no women that really understand – that can take part in a sacrifice?'

'How can they take part? They themselves are the sacrifice. They're the idol and the altar and the flame.'

'Isn't there even *one* who sees further?' Paul continued.

For a moment St George made no answer to this; then, having torn up his letters, he stood before his disciple again, ironic. 'Of course I know the one you mean. But not even Miss Fancourt.'

'I thought you admired her so much.'

'It's impossible to admire her more. Are you in love with her?' St George asked.

'Yes,' said Paul Overt.

'Well, then, give it up.'

Paul stared. 'Give up my love?'

'Bless me, no; your idea.'

'My idea?'

'The one you talked with her about. The idea of perfection.'

'She would help it – she would help it!' cried the young man.

'For about a year – the first year, yes. After that she would be as a millstone round its neck.'

'Why, she has a passion for completeness, for good work – for everything you and I care for most.'

' "You and I" is charming, my dear fellow! She has it indeed, but she would have a still greater passion for her children; and very proper too. She would insist upon everything's being made comfortable, advantageous, propitious for them. That isn't the artist's business.'

'The artist – the artist! Isn't he a man all the same?'

St George hesitated. 'Sometimes I really think not. You know as well as I what he has to do: the concentration, the finish, the independence that he must strive for, from the moment that he begins to respect his work. Ah, my young friend, his relation to women, especially in matrimony, is at the mercy of this damning fact – that whereas he can in the nature of things have but one standard, they have about fifty.

That's what makes them so superior,' St George added, laughing. 'Fancy an artist with a plurality of standards,' he went on. 'To *do* it – to do it and make it divine is the only thing he has to think about. "Is it done or not?" is his only question. Not "Is it done as well as a proper solicitude for my dear little family will allow?" He has nothing to do with the relative, nothing to do with a dear little family!'

'Then you don't allow him the common passions and affections of men?'

'Hasn't he a passion, an affection, which includes all the rest? Besides, let him have all the passions he likes – if he only keeps his independence. He must afford to be poor.'

Paul Overt slowly got up. 'Why did you advise me to make up to her, then?'

St George laid his hand on his shoulder. 'Because she would make an adorable wife! And I hadn't read you then.'

'I wish you had left me alone!' murmured the young man.

'I didn't know that that wasn't good enough for you,' St George continued.

'What a false position, what a condemnation of the artist, that he's a mere disfranchised monk and can produce his effect only by giving up personal happiness. What an arraignment of art!' Paul Overt pursued, with a trembling voice.

'Ah, you don't imagine, by chance, that I'm defending art? Arraignment, I should think so! Happy the societies in which it hasn't made its appearance; for from the moment it comes they have a consuming ache, they have an incurable corruption in their bosom. Assuredly, the artist is in a false position. But I thought we were taking him for granted. Pardon me,' St George continued; '*Ginistrella* made me!'

Paul Overt stood looking at the floor – one o'clock struck, in the stillness, from a neighbouring church-tower. 'Do you think she would ever look at me?' he asked at last.

'Miss Fancourt – as a suitor? Why shouldn't I think it? That's why I've tried to favour you – I have had a little chance or two of bettering your opportunity.'

'Excuse my asking you, but do you mean by keeping away yourself?' Paul said, blushing.

'I'm an old idiot – my place isn't there,' St George replied, gravely.

'I'm nothing, yet; I've no fortune; and there must be so many others.'

'You're a gentleman and a man of genius. I think you might do something.'

'But if I must give that up – the genius?'

'Lots of people, you know, think I've kept mine.'

'You have a genius for torment!' Paul Overt exclaimed; but taking his companion's hand in farewell as a mitigation of this judgement.

'Poor child, I do bother you. Try, try, then! I think your chances are good, and you'll win a great prize.'

Paul held the other's hand a minute; he looked into his face. 'No, I *am* an artist – I can't help it!'

'Ah, show it then!' St George broke out – 'let me see before I die the thing I most want, the thing I yearn for – a life in which the passion is really intense. If you can be rare, don't fail of it! Think what it is – how it counts – how it lives!' They had moved to the door and St George had closed both his own hands over that of his companion. Here they paused again and Paul Overt ejaculated – 'I want to live!'

'In what sense?'

'In the greatest sense.'

'Well then, stick to it – see it through.'

'With your sympathy – your help?'

'Count on that – you'll be a great figure to me. Count on my highest appreciation, my devotion. You'll give me satisfaction! – if that has any weight with you.' And as Paul appeared still to waver, St George added: 'Do you remember what you said to me at Summersoft?'

'Something infatuated, no doubt!'

'"I'll do anything in the world you tell me." You said that.'

'And you hold me to it?'

'Ah, what am I?' sighed the master, shaking his head.

'Lord, what things I shall have to do!' Paul almost moaned as he turned away.

VI

'IT goes on too much abroad – hang abroad!' These, or something like them, had been St George's remarkable words in relation to the action of *Ginistrella*; and yet, though they had made a sharp impression on Paul Overt, like almost all the master's spoken words, the young man, a week after the conversation I have narrated, left England for a long absence and full of projects of work. It is not a perversion of the truth to say that that conversation was the direct cause of his departure. If the oral utterance of the eminent writer had the privilege of moving him deeply it was especially on his turning it over at leisure, hours and days afterward, that it appeared to yield its full meaning and exhibit its extreme importance. He spent the summer in Switzerland, and having, in September, begun a new task, he determined not to cross the Alps till he should have made a good start. To this end he returned to a quiet corner that he knew well, on the edge of the Lake of Geneva, within sight of the towers of Chillon: a region and a view for which he had an affection springing from old associations, capable of mysterious little revivals and refreshments. Here he lingered late, till the snow was on the nearer hills, almost down to the limit to which he could climb when his stint was done, on the shortening afternoons. The autumn was fine, the lake was blue, and his book took form and direction. These circumstances, for the time, embroidered his life, and he suffered it to cover him with its mantle. At the end of six weeks he appeared to himself to have learned St George's lesson by heart – to have tested and proved its doctrine. Nevertheless he did a very inconsistent thing: before crossing the Alps he wrote to Marian Fancourt. He was aware of the perversity of this act, and it was only as a luxury, an amusement, the reward of a strenuous autumn, that he justified it. She had not asked any such favour of him when he went to see her three days before he left London – three days after their dinner in Ennismore Gardens. It is true that she had no reason to, for he had not mentioned that he was on the eve of such an excursion. He hadn't mentioned it because he didn't know it; it was that particular visit that made the matter clear. He had paid the visit to see how much he really cared for her, and quick departure, without so much as a farewell, was the sequel to this inquiry, the answer to which had been a distinct superlative. When he wrote to her from Clarens he noted that he owed her an explanation (more than three months after!) for the omission of such a form.

She answered him briefly but very promptly, and gave him a striking piece of news: the death, a week before, of Mrs St George. This exemplary woman had succumbed, in the country, to a violent attack of inflammation of the lungs – he would remember that for a long time she had been delicate. Miss Fancourt added that she heard her husband was over-whelmed with the blow; he would miss her unspeakably – she had been everything to him. Paul Overt immediately wrote to St George. He had wished to remain in communication with him, but had hitherto lacked the right excuse for troubling so busy a man. Their long nocturnal talk came back to him in every detail, but this did not prevent his expressing a cordial sympathy with the head of the profession, for had not that very talk made it clear that the accomplished lady was the influence that ruled his life? What catastrophe could be more cruel than the extinction of such an influence? This was exactly the tone that St George took in answering his young friend, upwards of a month later. He made no allusion, of course, to their important discussion. He spoke of his wife as frankly and generously as if he had quite forgotten that occasion, and the feeling of deep bereavement was visible in his words. 'She took every thing off my hands – off my mind. She carried on our life with the greatest art, the rarest devotion, and I was free, as few men can have been, to drive my pen, to shut myself up with my trade. This was a rare service – the highest she could have rendered me. Would I could have acknowledged it more fitly!'

A certain bewilderment, for Paul Overt, disengaged itself from these remarks: they struck him as a contradiction, a retraction. He had certainly not expected his correspondent to rejoice in the death of his wife, and it was perfectly in order that the rupture of a tie of more than twenty years should have left him sore. But if she was such a benefactress as that, what in the name of consistency had St George meant by turning *him* upside down that night – by dosing him to that degree, at the most sensitive hour of his life, with the doctrine of renunciation? If Mrs St George was an irreparable loss, then her husband's inspired advice had been a bad joke and renunciation was a mistake. Overt was on the point of rushing back to London to show that, for his part, he was perfectly willing to consider it so, and he went so far as to take the manuscript of the first chapters of his new book out of his table-drawer, to insert it into a pocket of his portmanteau. This led to his catching a glimpse of some pages he had not looked at for months, and that accident, in turn, to his being struck with the high promise they contained – a rare result of such retrospections, which it was his habit to avoid as much as possible. They usually made him feel that the glow of composition might be a purely subjective and a very barren emotion. On this occasion a certain belief in himself disengaged itself whimsically from the serried erasures of his first draft, making him think it best after all to carry out his present experiment to the end. If he could write as well as that under the influence of renunciation, it would be a pity to change the conditions before the termination of the work. He would go back to London of course, but he would go back only when he should have finished his book. This was the vow he privately made, restoring his manuscript to the table-drawer. It may be added that it took him a long time to finish his book, for the subject was as difficult as it was fine and he was literally embarrassed by the fullness of his notes. Something within him told him that he must make it supremely good – otherwise he should lack, as regards his private behaviour, a handsome excuse. He had a horror of this deficiency and found himself as firm as need be on the question of the lamp and the file. He crossed the Alps at last and spent the winter, the spring, the ensuing summer, in Italy, where still, at the end of a twelvemonth, his task was unachieved. 'Stick to it – see it through': this general injunction of St George's was good also for the particular case. He applied it to the utmost, with the result that when in its slow order, the summer had come round again he felt that he had given all that was in him. This time he put his papers into his portmanteau, with the address of his publisher attached, and took his way northward.

He had been absent from London for two years – two years which were a long period and had made such a difference in his own life (through the production of a novel far stronger, he believed, than *Ginistrella*) that he turned out into Piccadilly, the morning after his arrival, with an indefinite expectation of changes, of finding that things had happened. But there were few transformations in Piccadilly (only three or four big red houses where there had been low black ones), and the brightness of the end of June peeped through the rusty railings of the Green Park and glittered in the varnish of the rolling carriages as he had seen it in other, more cursory Junes. It was a greeting that he appreciated; it seemed friendly and pointed, added to the exhilaration of his finished book, of his having his own country and the huge, oppressive, amusing city that suggested everything, that contained everything, under his hand again. 'Stay at home and do things here – do subjects we can measure,' St George had said; and now it appeared to him that he should ask nothing better than to stay at home for ever. Late in the afternoon he took his way to Manchester Square, looking out for a number he had not forgotten. Miss Fancourt, however, was not within, so that he turned, rather dejectedly, from the door. This movement brought him face to face with a gentleman who was approaching it and whom he promptly perceived to be Miss Fancourt's father. Paul saluted this personage, and the General returned his greeting with his customary good manner – a manner so good, however, that you could never tell whether it meant that he placed you. Paul Overt felt the impulse to speak to him; then, hesitating, became conscious both that he had nothing particular to say and that though the old soldier remembered him he remembered him wrong. He therefore passed on, without calculating on the irresistible effect that his own evident recognition would have upon the General, who never neglected a chance to gossip. Our young man's face was expressive, and observation seldom let it pass. He had not taken ten steps before he heard himself called after with a friendly, semi-articulate 'A – I beg your pardon!' He turned round and the General, smiling at him from the steps, said: 'Won't you come in? I won't leave you the advantage of me!' Paul declined to come in, and then was sorry he had done so, for Miss Fancourt, so late in the afternoon, might return at any moment. But her father gave him no second chance; he appeared mainly to wish not to have struck him as inhospitable. A further look at the visitor told him more about him, enough at least to enable him to say – 'You've come back, you've come back?' Paul was on the point of replying that he had come back the night before, but he bethought himself to suppress this strong light on the immediacy of his visit, and, giving merely a general assent, remarked that he was extremely sorry not to have found Miss Fancourt. He had come late, in the hope that she would be in. 'I'll tell her – I'll tell her,' said the old man; and then he added quickly, gallantly, 'You'll be giving us something new? It's a long time, isn't it?' Now he remembered him right.

'Rather long. I'm very slow,' said Paul. 'I met you at Summersoft a long time ago.'

'Oh, yes, with Henry St George. I remember very well. Before his poor wife—' General Fancourt paused a moment, smiling a little less. 'I daresay you know.'

'About Mrs St George's death? Oh yes, I heard at the time.'

'Oh no; I mean – I mean he's to be married.'

'Ah! I've not heard that.' Just as Paul was about to add, 'To whom?' the General crossed his intention with a question.

'When did you come back? I know you've been away – from my daughter. She was very sorry. You ought to give her something new.'

'I came back last night,' said our young man, to whom something had occurred which made his speech, for the moment, a little thick.

'Ah, most kind of you to come so soon. Couldn't you turn up at dinner?'

'At dinner?' Paul Overt repeated, not liking to ask whom St George was going to marry, but thinking only of that.

'There are several people, I believe. Certainly St George. Or afterwards, if you like better. I believe my daughter expects——.' He appeared to notice something in Overt's upward face (on his steps he stood higher) which led him to interrupt himself, and the interruption gave him a momentary sense of awkwardness, from which he sought a quick issue. 'Perhaps then you haven't heard she's to be married.'

'To be married?' Paul stared.

'To Mr St George – it has just been settled. Odd marriage, isn't it?' Paul uttered no opinion on this point: he only continued to stare. 'But I daresay it will do – she's so awfully literary!' said the General.

Paul had turned very red. 'Oh, it's a surprise – very interesting, very charming! I'm afraid I can't dine – so many thanks!'

'Well, you must come to the wedding!' cried the General. 'Oh, I remember that day at Summersoft. He's a very good fellow.'

'Charming – charming!' Paul stammered, retreating. He shook hands with the General and got off. His face was red and he had the sense of its growing more and more crimson. All the evening at home – he went straight to his rooms and remained there dinnerless – his cheek burned at intervals as if it had been smitten. He didn't understand what had happened to him, what trick had been played him, what treachery practised. 'None, none,' he said to himself. 'I've nothing to do with it. I'm out of it – it's none of my business.' But that bewildered murmur was followed again and again by the incongruous ejaculation – 'Was it a plan – was it a plan?' Sometimes he cried to himself, breathless, 'Am I a dupe – am I a dupe?' If he was, he was an absurd and abject one. It seemed to him he had never lost her till now. He had renounced her, yes; but that was another affair – that was a closed but not a locked door. Now he felt as if the door had been slammed in his face. Did he expect her to wait – was she to give him his time like that: two years at a stretch? He didn't know what he had expected – he only knew what he hadn't. It wasn't this – it wasn't this. Mystification, bitterness and wrath rose and boiled in him when he thought of the deference, the devotion, the credulity with which he had listened to St George. The evening wore on and the light was long; but even when it had darkened he remained without a lamp. He had flung himself on the sofa, and he lay there through the hours with his eyes either closed or gazing into the gloom, in the attitude of a man teaching himself to bear something, to bear having been made a fool of. He had made it too easy – that idea passed over him like a hot wave. Suddenly, as he heard eleven o'clock strike, he jumped up, remembering what General Fancourt had said about his coming after dinner. He would go – he would see her at least; perhaps he should see what it meant. He felt as if some of the elements of a hard sum had been given him and the others were wanting: he couldn't do his sum till he was in possession of them all.

He dressed quickly, so that by half-past eleven he was at Manchester Square. There were a good many carriages at the door – a party was going on; a circumstance which at the last gave him a slight relief, for now he would rather see her in a crowd. People passed him on the staircase; they were going away, going 'on', with the hunted, herdlike movement of London society at night. But sundry groups remained in the drawing-room, and it was some minutes, as she didn't hear him announced, before he discovered her and spoke to her. In this short interval he had perceived that St George was there, talking to a lady before the fireplace; but he looked away from him, for the moment, and therefore failed to see whether the author of *Shadowmere* noticed him. At all events he didn't come to him. Miss Fancourt did, as soon as she saw him; she almost rushed at him, smiling, rustling, radiant, beautiful. He had forgotten what her head, what her face offered to the sight; she was in white, there were gold figures on her dress, and her hair was like a casque of gold. In a single moment he saw she was happy, happy with a kind of aggressiveness, of splendour. But she would not speak to him of that, she would speak only of himself.

'I'm so delighted; my father told me. How kind of you to come!' She struck him as so fresh and brave, while his eyes moved over her, that he said to himself, irresistibly: 'Why to *him*, why not to youth, to strength, to ambition, to a future?

Why, in her rich young capacity, to failure, to abdication, to superannuation?' In his thought, at that sharp moment, he blasphemed even against all that had been left of his faith in the peccable master. 'I'm so sorry I missed you,' she went on. 'My father told me. How charming of you to have come so soon!'

'Does that surprise you?' Paul Overt asked.

'The first day? No, from you – nothing that's nice.' She was interrupted by a lady who bade her good-night, and he seemed to read that it cost her nothing to speak to one in that tone; it was her old bounteous, demonstrative way, with a certain added amplitude that time had brought; and if it began to operate on the spot, at such a juncture in her history, perhaps in the other days too it had meant just as little or as much – a sort of mechanical charity, with the difference now that she was satisfied, ready to give but asking nothing. Oh, she was satisfied – and why shouldn't she be? Why shouldn't she have been surprised at his coming the first day – for all the good she had ever got from him? As the lady continued to hold her attention Paul Overt turned from her with a strange irritation in his complicated artistic soul and a kind of disinterested disappointment. She was so happy that it was almost stupid – it seemed to deny the extraordinary intelligence he had formerly found in her. Didn't she know how bad St George could be, hadn't she perceived the deplorable thinness—? If she didn't she was nothing, and if she did why such an insolence of serenity? This question expired as our young man's eyes settled at last upon the genius who had advised him in a great crisis. St George was still before the chimney-piece, but now he was alone (fixed, waiting, as if he meant to remain after every one), and he met the clouded gaze of the young friend who was tormented with uncertainty as to whether he had the right (which his resentment would have enjoyed) to regard himself as his victim. Somehow, the fantastic inquiry I have just noted was answered by St George's aspect. It was as fine in its way as Marian Fancourt's – it denoted the happy human being; but somehow it represented to Paul Overt that the author of *Shadowmere* had now definitively ceased to count – ceased to count as a writer. As he smiled a welcome across the room he was almost *banal*, he was almost smug. Paul had the impression that for a moment he hesitated to make a movement forward, as if he had a bad conscience; but the next they had met in the middle of the room and had shaken hands, expressively, cordially on St George's part. Then they had passed together to where the elder man had been standing, while St George said: 'I hope you are never going away again. I have been dining here; the General told me.' He was handsome, he was young, he looked as if he had still a great fund of life. He bent the friendliest, most unconfessing eyes upon Paul Overt; asked him about everything, his health, his plans, his late occupations, the new book. 'When will it be out – soon, soon, I hope? Splendid, eh? That's right; you're a comfort! I've read you all over again, the last six months.' Paul waited to see if he would tell him what the General had told him in the afternoon, and what Miss Fancourt, verbally at least, of course had not. But as it didn't come out he asked at last: 'Is it true, the great news I hear, that you're to be married?'

'Ah, you *have* heard it then?'

'Didn't the General tell you?' Paul Overt went on.

'Tell me what?'

'That he mentioned it to me this afternoon?'

'My dear fellow, I don't remember. We've been in the midst of people. I'm sorry, in that case, that I lose the pleasure, myself, of announcing to you a fact that touches me so nearly. It *is* a fact, strange as it may appear. It has only just become one. Isn't it ridiculous?' St George made this speech without confusion, but on the other hand, so far as Paul could see, without latent impudence. It appeared to his interlocutor that, to talk so comfortably and coolly, he must simply have forgotten what had passed between them. His next words, however, showed that he had not, and they had, as an appeal to Paul's own memory, an effect which would have been ludicrous if it had not been cruel. 'Do you recollect the talk we had at my house that night, into which Miss Fancourt's name entered? I've often thought of it since.'

'Yes – no wonder you said what you did,' said Paul, looking at him.

'In the light of the present occasion? Ah! but there was no light then. How could I have foreseen this hour?'

'Didn't you think it probable?'

'Upon my honour, no,' said Henry St George. 'Certainly, I owe you that assurance. Think how my situation has changed.'

'I see – I see,' Paul murmured.

His companion went on, as if, now that the subject had been broached, he was, as a man of imagination and tact, perfectly ready to give every satisfaction – being able to enter fully into everything another might feel. 'But it's not only that – for honestly, at my age, I never dreamed – a widower, with big boys and with so little else! It has turned out differently from any possible calculation, and I am fortunate beyond all measure. She has been so free, and yet she consents. Better than any one else perhaps – for I remember how you liked her, before you went away, and how she liked you – you can intelligently congratulate me.'

'She has been so free!' Those words made a great impression on Paul Overt, and he almost writhed under that irony in them as to which it little mattered whether it was intentional or casual. Of course she had been free and, appreciably perhaps, by his own act; for was not St George's allusion to her having liked him a part of the irony too? 'I thought that by your theory you disapproved of a writer's marrying.'

'Surely – surely. But you don't call me a writer?'

'You ought to be ashamed,' said Paul.

'Ashamed of marrying again?'

'I won't say that – but ashamed of your reasons.'

'You must let me judge of them, my friend.'

'Yes; why not? For you judged wonderfully of mine.'

The tone of these words appeared suddenly, for Henry St George, to suggest the unsuspected. He stared as if he read a bitterness in them. 'Don't you think I have acted fair?'

'You might have told me at the time, perhaps.'

'My dear fellow, when I say I couldn't pierce futurity!'

'I mean afterwards.'

St George hesitated. 'After my wife's death?'

'When this idea came to you.'

'Ah, never, never! I wanted to save you, rare and precious as you are.'

'Are you marrying Miss Fancourt to save me?'

'Not absolutely, but it adds to the pleasure. I shall be the making of you,' said St George, smiling. 'I was greatly struck, after our talk, with the resolute way you quitted the country and still more, perhaps, with your force of character in remaining abroad. You're very strong – you're wonderfully strong.'

Paul Overt tried to sound his pleasant eyes; the strange thing was that he appeared sincere – not a mocking fiend. He turned away, and as he did so he heard St George say something about his giving them the proof, being the joy of his old age. He faced him again, taking another look. 'Do you mean to say you've stopped writing?'

'My dear fellow, of course I have. It's too late. Didn't I tell you?'

'I can't believe it!'

'Of course you can't – with your own talent! No, no; for the rest of my life I shall only read you.'

'Does she know that – Miss Fancourt?'

'She will – she will.' Our young man wondered whether St George meant this as a covert intimation that the assistance he should derive from that young lady's fortune, moderate as it was, would make the difference of putting it in his power to cease to work, ungratefully, an exhausted vein. Somehow, standing there in the ripeness of his successful manhood, he did not suggest that any of his veins were exhausted. 'Don't you remember the moral I offered myself to you – that night – as pointing?' St George continued. 'Consider, at any rate, the warning I am at present.'

This was too much – he *was* the mocking fiend. Paul separated from him with a mere nod for good-night; the sense that he might come back to him some time in the far future but could not fraternise with him now. It was necessary to his sore spirit to believe for the hour that he had a grievance – all the more cruel for not being a legal one. It was doubtless in the attitude of hugging this wrong that he descended the stairs without taking leave of Miss Fancourt, who had not been in view at the moment he quitted the room. He was glad to get out into the honest, dusky, unsophisticating night, to move fast, to take his way home on foot. He walked a long time, missing his way, not thinking of it. He was thinking of too many other things. His steps recovered their direction, however, and at the end of an hour he found himself before his door, in the small, inexpensive, empty street. He lingered, questioning himself still, before going in, with nothing around and above him but moonless blackness, a bad lamp or two and a few far-away dim stars. To these last faint features he raised his eyes; he had been saying to himself that there would have been mockery indeed if now, on his new foundation, at the end of a year, St George should put forth something with his early quality – something of the type of *Shadowmere* and finer than his finest. Greatly as he admired his talent Paul literally hoped such an incident would not occur; it seemed to him just then that he scarcely should be able to endure it. St George's words were still in his ears, 'You're very strong – wonderfully strong.' Was he really? Certainly, he would have to be; and it would be a sort of revenge. *Is* he? the reader may ask in turn, if his interest has followed the perplexed young man so far. The best answer to that perhaps is that he is doing his best but that it is too soon to say. When the new book came out in the autumn Mr and Mrs St George found it really magnificent. The former still has published nothing, but Paul Overt does not even yet feel safe. I may say for him, however, that if this event were to befall he would really be the very first to appreciate it: which is perhaps a proof that St George was essentially right and that Nature dedicated him to intellectual, not to personal passion.

THE PATAGONIA

I

THE houses were dark in the August night and the perspective of Beacon Street, with its double chain of lamps, was a foreshortened desert. The club on the hill alone, from its semicylindrical front, projected a glow upon the dusky vagueness of the Common, and as I passed it I heard in the hot stillness the click of a pair of billiard balls. As 'every one' was out of town perhaps the servants, in the extravagance of their leisure, were profaning the tables. The heat was insufferable and I thought with joy of the morrow, of the deck of the steamer, the freshening breeze, the sense of getting out to sea. I was even glad of what I had learned in the afternoon at the office of the company – that at the eleventh hour an old ship with a lower standard of speed had been put on in place of the vessel in which I had taken my passage. America was roasting, England might very well be stuffy, and a slow passage (which at that season of the year would probably also be a fine one) was a guarantee of ten or twelve days of fresh air.

I strolled down the hill without meeting a creature, though I could see through the palings of the Common that that recreative expanse was peopled with dim forms. I remembered Mrs Nettlepoint's house – she lived in those days (they are not so distant, but there have been changes) on the waterside, a little way beyond the spot at which the Public Garden terminates; and I reflected that like myself she would be spending the night in Boston if it were true that, as had been mentioned to me a few days before at Mount Desert, she was to embark on the morrow for Liverpool. I presently saw this appearance confirmed by a light above her door and in two or three of her windows, and I determined to ask for her, having nothing to do till bedtime. I had come out simply to pass an hour, leaving my hotel to the blaze of its gas and the perspiration of its porters; but it occurred to me that my old friend might very well not know of the substitution of the *Patagonia* for the *Scandinavia*, so that it would be an act of consideration to prepare her mind. Besides, I could offer to help her, to look after her in the morning: lone women are grateful for support in taking ship for far countries.

As I stood on her doorstep I remembered that as she had a son she might not after all be so lone; yet at the same time it was present to me that Jasper Nettlepoint was not quite a young man to lean upon, having (as I at least supposed) a life of his own and tastes and habits which had long since drawn him away from the maternal side. If he did happen just now to be at home my solicitude would of course seem officious; for in his many wanderings – I believed he had roamed all over the globe – he would certainly have learned how to manage. None the less I was very glad to show Mrs Nettlepoint I thought of her. With my long absence I had lost sight of her; but I had liked her of old; she had been a close friend of my sisters; and I had in regard to her that sense which is pleasant to those who, in general, have grown strange or detached – the feeling that she at least knew all about me. I could trust her at any time to tell people what a respectable person I was. Perhaps I was conscious of how little I deserved this indulgence when it came over me that for years I had not communicated with her. The measure of this neglect was given by my vagueness of mind about her son. However, I really belonged nowadays to a different generation: I was more the old lady's contemporary than Jasper's.

Mrs Nettlepoint was at home: I found her in her back drawing-room, where the wide windows opened upon the water. The room was dusky – it was too hot for lamps – and she sat slowly moving her fan and looking out on the little arm of the sea which is so pretty at night, reflecting the lights of Cambridgeport and Charlestown. I supposed she was musing upon the loved ones she was to leave behind, her married daughters, her grandchildren; but she struck a note more specifically Bostonian as she said to me, pointing with her fan to the Back Bay – 'I shall see nothing more charming than that over there, you know!' She made me very welcome, but her son had told her about the *Patagonia*, for which she was sorry, as this would mean a longer voyage. She was a poor creature on shipboard and mainly confined to her cabin, even in weather extravagantly termed fine – as if any weather could be fine at sea.

'Ah, then your son's going with you?' I asked.

'Here he comes, he will tell you for himself much better than I am able to do.'

Jasper Nettlepoint came into the room at that moment, dressed in white flannel and carrying a large fan.

'Well, my dear, have you decided?' his mother continued, with some irony in her tone. 'He hasn't yet made up his mind, and we sail at ten o'clock!'

'What does it matter, when my things are put up?' said the young man. 'There is no crowd at this moment; there will be cabins to spare. I'm waiting for a telegram – that will settle it. I just walked up to the club to see if it was come – they'll send it there because they think the house is closed. Not yet, but I shall go back in twenty minutes.'

'Mercy, how you rush about in this temperature!' his mother exclaimed, while I reflected that it was perhaps *his* billiard-balls I had heard ten minutes before. I was sure he was fond of billiards.

'Rush? not in the least. I take it uncommonly easy.'

'Ah, I'm bound to say you do,' Mrs Nettlepoint exclaimed, inconsequently. I divined that there was a certain tension between the pair and a want of consideration on the young man's part, arising perhaps from selfishness. His mother was nervous, in suspense, wanting to be at rest as to whether she should have his company on the voyage or be obliged to make it alone. But as he stood there smiling and slowly moving his fan he struck me somehow as a person on whom this fact would not sit very heavily. He was of the type of those whom other people worry about, not of those who worry about other people. Tall and strong, he had a handsome face, with a round head and close-curling hair; the whites of his eyes and the enamel of his teeth, under his brown moustache gleamed vaguely in the lights of the Back Bay. I made out that he was sunburnt, as if he lived much in the open air, and that he looked intelligent but also slightly brutal, though not in a morose way. His brutality, if he had any, was bright and finished. I had to tell him who I was, but even then I saw that he failed to place me and that my explanations gave me in his mind no great identity or at any rate no great importance. I foresaw that he would in intercourse make me feel sometimes very young and sometimes very old. He mentioned, as if to show his mother that he might safely be left to his own devices, that he had once started from London to Bombay at three-quarters of an hour's notice.

'Yes, and it must have been pleasant for the people you were with!'

'Oh, the people I was with—!' he rejoined; and his tone appeared to signify that such people would always have to come off as they could. He asked if there were no cold drinks in the house, no lemonade, no iced syrups; in such weather something of that sort ought always to be kept going. When his mother remarked that surely at the club they *were* going he went on, 'Oh, yes, I had various things there; but you know I have walked down the hill since. One should have something at either end. May I ring and see?' He rang while Mrs Nettlepoint observed that with the people they had in the house – an establishment reduced naturally at such a moment to its simplest expression (they were burning-up candle-ends and there were no luxuries) she would not answer for the service. The matter ended in the old lady's going out of the room in quest of syrup with the female domestic who had appeared in response to the bell and in whom Jasper's appeal aroused no visible intelligence.

She remained away some time and I talked with her son, who was sociable but desultory and kept moving about the room, always with his fan, as if he were impatient. Sometimes he seated himself for an instant on the window-sill, and then I saw that he was in fact very good-looking; a fine brown, clean young athlete. He never told me on what special contingency his decision depended; he only alluded familiarly to an expected telegram, and I perceived that he was probably not addicted to copious explanations. His mother's absence was an indication that when it was a question of gratifying him she had grown used to spare no pains, and I fancied her rummaging in some close store-room, among old preserve-pots, while the dull maid-servant held the candle awry. I know not whether this same vision was in his own eyes; at all events it did not prevent him from saying suddenly, as he looked at his watch, that I must excuse him, as he had to go back to the club. He would return in half an hour – or in less. He walked away and I sat there alone, conscious, in the dark, dismantled, simplified room, in the deep silence that rests on American towns during the hot season (there was now and then a far cry or a plash in the water, and at intervals the tinkle of the bells of the horse-cars on the long bridge, slow in the suffocating night), of the strange influence, half sweet, half sad, that abides in houses uninhabited or about to become so – in places muffled and bereaved, where the unheeded sofas and patient belittered tables seem to know (like the disconcerted dogs) that it is the eve of a journey.

After a while I heard the sound of voices, of steps, the rustle of dresses, and I looked round, supposing these things to be the sign of the return of Mrs Nettlepoint and her handmaiden, bearing the refreshment prepared for her son. What I saw however was two other female forms, visitors just admitted apparently, who were ushered into the room. They were not announced – the servant turned her back on them and rambled off to our hostess. They came forward in a wavering, tentative, unintroduced way – partly, I could see, because the place was dark and partly because their visit was in its nature experimental, a stretch of confidence. One of the ladies was stout and the other was slim, and I perceived in a moment that one was talkative and the other silent. I made out further that one was elderly and the other young and that the fact that they were so unlike did not prevent their being mother and daughter. Mrs Nettlepoint reappeared in a very few minutes, but the interval had sufficed to establish a communication (really copious for the occasion) between the strangers and the unknown gentleman whom they found in possession, hat and stick in hand. This was not my doing (for what had I to go upon?) and still less was it the doing of the person whom I supposed and whom I indeed quickly and definitely learned to be the daughter. She spoke but once – when her companion informed me that she was going out to Europe the next day to be married. Then she said, 'Oh, mother!' protestingly, in a tone which struck me in the darkness as doubly strange, exciting my curiosity to see her face.

It had taken her mother but a moment to come to that and to other things besides, after I had explained that I myself was waiting for Mrs Nettlepoint, who would doubtless soon come back.

'Well, she won't know me – I guess she hasn't ever heard much about me,' the good lady said; 'but I have come from Mrs Allen and I guess that will make it all right. I presume you know Mrs Allen?'

I was unacquainted with this influential personage, but I assented vaguely to the proposition. Mrs Allen's emissary was good-humoured and familiar, but rather appealing than insistent (she remarked that if her friend *had* found time to come in the afternoon – she had so much to do, being just up for the day, that she couldn't be sure – it would be all right); and somehow even before she mentioned Merrimac Avenue (they had come all the way from there) my imagination had associated her with that indefinite social limbo known to the properly-constituted Boston mind as the South End – a nebulous region which condenses here and there into a pretty face, in which the daughters are an 'improvement' on the mothers and are sometimes acquainted with gentlemen resident in more distinguished districts of the New England capital – gentlemen whose wives and sisters in turn are not acquainted with them.

When at last Mrs Nettlepoint came in, accompanied by candles and by a tray laden with glasses of coloured fluid which emitted a cool tinkling, I was in a position to officiate as master of the ceremonies, to introduce Mrs Mavis and Miss Grace Mavis, to represent that Mrs Allen had recommended them – nay, had urged them – to come that way, informally, and had been prevented only by the pressure of occupations so characteristic of her (especially when she was up from Mattapoisett just for a few hours' shopping) from herself calling in the course of the day to explain who they were and what was the favour they had to ask of Mrs Nettlepoint. Good-natured women understand each other even when divided by the line of topographical fashion, and our hostess had quickly mastered the main facts: Mrs Allen's visit in the morning in Merrimac Avenue to talk of Mrs Amber's great idea, the classes at the public schools in vacation (she was interested with an equal charity to that of Mrs Mavis – even in such weather! – in those of the South End) for games and exercises and music, to keep the poor unoccupied children out of the streets; then the revelation that it had suddenly been settled almost from one hour to the other that Grace should sail for Liverpool, Mr Porterfield at last being ready. He was taking a little holiday; his mother was with him, they had come over from Paris to see some of the celebrated old buildings in England, and he had telegraphed to say that if Grace would start right off they would just finish it up and be married. It often happened that when things had dragged on that way for years they were all huddled up at the end. Of course in such a case she, Mrs Mavis, had had to fly round. Her daughter's passage was taken, but it seemed too dreadful that she should make her journey all alone, the first time she had ever been at sea, without any companion or escort. *She* couldn't go – Mr Mavis was too sick: she hadn't even been able to get him off to the seaside.

'Well, Mrs Nettlepoint is going in that ship,' Mrs Allen had said; and she had represented that nothing was simpler than to put the girl in her charge. When Mrs Mavis had replied that that was all very well but that she didn't know the lady, Mrs Allen had declared that that didn't make a speck of difference, for Mrs Nettlepoint was kind enough for anything. It was easy enough to know her, if that was all the trouble. All Mrs Mavis would have to do would be to go up to her the next morning when she took her daughter to the ship (she would see her there on the deck with her party) and tell her what she wanted. Mrs Nettlepoint had daughters herself and she would easily understand. Very likely she would even look after Grace a little on the other side, in such a queer situation, going out alone to the gentleman she was engaged to; she would just help her to turn round before she was married. Mr Porterfield seemed to think

they wouldn't wait long, once she was there: they would have it
right over at the American consul's. Mrs Allen had said it would
perhaps be better still to go and see Mrs Nettlepoint beforehand, that day, to tell her what they wanted: then they wouldn't
seem to spring it on her just as she was leaving. She herself (Mrs
Allen) would call and say a word for them if she could save ten
minutes before catching her train. If she hadn't come it was
because she hadn't saved her ten minutes; but she had made
them feel that they must come all the same. Mrs Mavis liked
that better, because on the ship in the morning there would be
such a confusion. She didn't think her daughter would be any
trouble – conscientiously she didn't. It was just to have some
one to speak to her and not sally forth like a servant-girl going to
a situation.

'I see, I am to act as a sort of bridesmaid and to give her
away,' said Mrs Nettlepoint. She was in fact kind enough for
anything and she showed on this occasion that it was easy
enough to know her. There is nothing more tiresome than
complications at sea, but she accepted without a protest the
burden of the young lady's dependence and allowed her, as Mrs
Mavis said, to hook herself on. She evidently had the habit of
patience, and her reception of her visitors' story reminded me
afresh (I was reminded of it whenever I returned to my native
land) that my dear compatriots are the people in the world who
most freely take mutual accommodation for granted. They
have always had to help themselves, and by a magnanimous
extension they confound helping each other with that. In no
country are there fewer forms and more reciprocities.

It was doubtless not singular that the ladies from Merrimac
Avenue should not feel that they were importunate: what was
striking was that Mrs Nettlepoint did not appear to suspect it.
However, she would in any case have thought it inhuman to
show that – though I could see that under the surface she was
amused at everything the lady from the South End took for
granted. I know not whether the attitude of the younger visitor
added or not to the merit of her good-nature. Mr Porterfield's
intended took no part in her mother's appeal, scarcely spoke,
sat looking at the Back Bay and the lights on the long bridge.

She declined the lemonade and the other mixtures which, at Mrs Nettlepoint's request, I offered her, while her mother partook freely of everything and I reflected (for I as freely consumed the reviving liquid) that Mr Jasper had better hurry back if he wished to profit by the refreshment prepared for him.

Was the effect of the young woman's reserve ungracious, or was it only natural that in her particular situation she should not have a flow of compliment at her command? I noticed that Mrs Nettlepoint looked at her often, and certainly though she was undemonstrative Miss Mavis was interesting. The candle-light enabled me to see that if she was not in the very first flower of her youth she was still a handsome girl. Her eyes and hair were dark, her face was pale and she held up her head as if, with its thick braids, it were an appurtenance she was not ashamed of. If her mother was excellent and common she was not common (not flagrantly so) and perhaps not excellent. At all events she would not be, in appearance at least, a dreary appendage, and (in the case of a person 'hooking on') that was always something gained. Is it because something of a romantic or pathetic interest usually attaches to a good creature who has been the victim of a 'long engagement' that this young lady made an impression on me from the first – favoured as I had been so quickly with this glimpse of her history? Certainly she made no positive appeal; she only held her tongue and smiled, and her smile corrected whatever suggestion might have forced itself upon me that the spirit was dead – the spirit of that promise of which she found herself doomed to carry out the letter.

What corrected it less, I must add, was an odd recollection which gathered vividness as I listened to it – a mental association which the name of Mr Porterfield had evoked. Surely I had a personal impression, over-smeared and confused, of the gentleman who was waiting at Liverpool, or who would be, for Mrs Nettlepoint's *protégée*. I had met him, known him, some time, somewhere, somehow, in Europe. Was he not studying something – very hard – somewhere, probably in Paris, ten years before, and did he not make extraordinarily neat drawings, linear and architectural? Didn't he go to a *table d'hôte*, at two francs twenty-five, in the Rue Bonaparte, which I then frequented, and didn't he wear spectacles and a Scotch plaid arranged in a manner which seemed to say, 'I have trustworthy information that that is the way they do it in the Highlands'? Was he not exemplary and very poor, so that I supposed he had no overcoat and his tartan was what he slept under at night? Was he not working very hard still, and wouldn't he be in the natural course, not yet satisfied that he knew enough to launch out? He would be a man of long preparations – Miss Mavis's white face seemed to speak to one of that. It appeared to me that if I had been in love with her I should not have needed to lay such a train to marry her. Architecture was his line and he was a pupil of the Ecole des Beaux Arts. This reminiscence grew so much more vivid with me that at the end of ten minutes I had a curious sense of knowing – by implication – a good deal about the young lady.

Even after it was settled that Mrs Nettlepoint would do everything for her that she could her mother sat a little, sipping her syrup and telling how 'low' Mr Mavis had been. At this period the girl's silence struck me as still more conscious, partly perhaps because she deprecated her mother's loquacity (she was enough of an 'improvement' to measure that) and partly because she was too full of pain at the idea of leaving her infirm, her perhaps dying father. I divined that they were poor and that she would take out a very small purse for her trousseau. Moreover for Mr Porterfield to make up the sum his own case would have had to change. If he had enriched himself by the successful practice of his profession I had not encountered the buildings he had reared – his reputation had not come to my ears.

Mrs Nettlepoint notified her new friends that she was a very inactive person at sea: she was prepared to suffer to the full with Miss Mavis, but she was not prepared to walk with her, to struggle with her, to accompany her to the table. To this the girl replied that she would trouble her little, she was sure: she had a belief that she should prove a wretched sailor and spend the voyage on her back. Her mother scoffed at this picture, prophesying perfect weather and a lovely time, and I said that if I might be trusted, as a tame old bachelor fairly sea-seasoned, I should be delighted to give the new member of our party an arm or any other countenance whenever she should require it. Both the ladies thanked me for this (taking my description only too literally), and the elder one declared that we were evidently going to be such a sociable group that it was too bad to have to stay at home. She inquired of Mrs Nettlepoint if there were any one else – if she were to be accompanied by some of her family; and when our hostess mentioned her son – there was a chance of his embarking but (wasn't it absurd?) he had not decided yet, she rejoined with extraordinary candour – 'Oh dear, I do hope he'll go: that would be so pleasant for Grace.'

Somehow the words made me think of poor Mr Porterfield's tartan, especially as Jasper Nettlepoint strolled in again at that moment. His mother instantly challenged him: it was ten o'clock; had he by chance made up his great mind? Apparently he failed to hear her, being in the first place surprised at the strange ladies and then struck with the fact that one of them was not strange. The young man, after a slight hesitation, greeted Miss Mavis with a handshake and an 'Oh, good evening, how do you do?' He did not utter her name, and I could see that he had forgotten it; but she immediately pronounced his, availing herself of an American girl's discretion to introduce him to her mother.

'Well, you might have told me you knew him all this time!' Mrs Mavis exclaimed. Then smiling at Mrs Nettlepoint she added, 'It would have saved me a worry, an acquaintance already begun.'

'Ah, my son's acquaintances—!' Mrs Nettlepoint murmured.

'Yes, and my daughter's too!' cried Mrs Mavis, jovially. 'Mrs Allen didn't tell us you were going,' she continued, to the young man.

'She would have been clever if she had been able to!' Mrs Nettlepoint ejaculated.

'Dear mother, I have my telegram,' Jasper remarked, looking at Grace Mavis.

'I know you very little,' the girl said, returning his observation.

'I've danced with you at some ball – for some sufferers by something or other.'

'I think it was an inundation,' she replied, smiling. 'But it was a long time ago – and I haven't seen you since.'

'I have been in far countries – to my loss. I should have said it was for a big fire.'

'It was at the Horticultural Hall. I didn't remember your name,' said Grace Mavis.

'That is very unkind of you, when I recall vividly that you had a pink dress.'

'Oh, I remember that dress – you looked lovely in it!' Mrs Mavis broke out. 'You must get another just like it – on the other side.'

'Yes, your daughter looked charming in it,' said Jasper Nettlepoint. Then he added to the girl – 'Yet you mentioned my name to your mother.'

'It came back to me – seeing you here. I had no idea this was your home.'

'Well, I confess it isn't, much. Oh, there are some drinks!' Jasper went on, approaching the tray and its glasses.

'Indeed there are and quite delicious,' Mrs Mavis declared.

'Won't you have another then? – a pink one, like your daughter's gown.'

'With pleasure, sir. Oh, do see them over,' Mrs Mavis continued, accepting from the young man's hand a third tumbler.

'My mother and that gentleman? Surely they can take care of themselves,' said Jasper Nettlepoint.

'But my daughter – she has a claim as an old friend.'

'Jasper, what does your telegram say?' his mother interposed.

He gave no heed to her question: he stood there with his glass in his hand, looking from Mrs Mavis to Miss Grace.

'Ah, leave her to me, madam; I'm quite competent,' I said to Mrs Mavis.

Then the young man looked at me. The next minute he asked of the young lady – 'Do you mean you are going to Europe?'

'Yes, to-morrow; in the same ship as your mother.'

'That's what we've come here for, to see all about it,' said Mrs Mavis.

'My son, take pity on me and tell me what light your telegram throws,' Mrs Nettlepoint went on.

'I will, dearest, when I've quenched my thirst.' And Jasper slowly drained his glass.

'Well, you're worse than Gracie,' Mrs Mavis commented. 'She was first one thing and then the other – but only about up to three o'clock yesterday.'

'Excuse me – won't you take something?' Jasper inquired of Gracie; who however declined, as if to make up for her mother's copious *consommation*. I made privately the reflection that the two ladies ought to take leave, the question of Mrs Nettlepoint's goodwill being so satisfactorily settled and the meeting of the morrow at the ship so near at hand; and I went so far as to judge that their protracted stay, with their hostess visibly in a fidget, was a sign of a want of breeding. Miss Grace after all then was not such an improvement on her mother, for she easily might have taken the initiative of departure, in spite of Mrs Mavis's imbibing her glass of syrup in little interspaced sips, as if to make it last as long as possible. I watched the girl with an increasing curiosity; I could not help asking myself a question or two about her and even perceiving already (in a dim and general way) that there were some complications in her position. Was it not a complication that she should have wished to remain long enough to assuage a certain suspense, to learn whether or no Jasper were going to sail? Had not something particular passed between them on the occasion or at the period to which they had covertly alluded, and did she really not know that her mother was bringing her to *his* mother's, though she apparently had thought it well not to mention the circumstance? Such things were complications on the part of a young lady betrothed to that curious cross-barred phantom of a Mr Porterfield. But I am bound to add that she gave me no further warrant for suspecting them than by the simple fact of her encouraging her mother, by her immobility, to linger. Somehow I had a sense that *she* knew better. I got up myself to go, but

Mrs Nettlepoint detained me after seeing that my movement would not be taken as a hint, and I perceived she wished me not to leave my fellow-visitors on her hands. Jasper complained of the closeness of the room, said that it was not a night to sit in a room – one ought to be out in the air, under the sky. He denounced the windows that overlooked the water for not opening upon a balcony or a terrace, until his mother, whom he had not yet satisfied about his telegram, reminded him that there was a beautiful balcony in front, with room for a dozen people. She assured him we would go and sit there if it would please him.

'It will be nice and cool to-morrow, when we steam into the great ocean,' said Miss Mavis, expressing with more vivacity than she had yet thrown into any of her utterances my own thought of half an hour before. Mrs Nettlepoint replied that it would probably be freezing cold, and her son murmured that he would go and try the drawing-room balcony and report upon it. Just as he was turning away he said, smiling, to Miss Mavis – 'Won't you come with me and see if it's pleasant?'

'Oh, well, we had better not stay all night!' her mother exclaimed, but without moving. The girl moved, after a moment's hesitation; she rose and accompanied Jasper into the other room. I observed that her slim tallness showed to advantage as she walked and that she looked well as she passed, with her head thrown back, into the darkness of the other part of the house. There was something rather marked, rather surprising (I scarcely knew why, for the act was simple enough) in her doing so, and perhaps it was our sense of this that held the rest of us somewhat stiffly silent as she remained away. I was waiting for Mrs Mavis to go, so that I myself might go; and Mrs Nettlepoint was waiting for her to go so that I might not. This doubtless made the young lady's absence appear to us longer than it really was – it was probably very brief. Her mother moreover, I think, had a vague consciousness of embarrassment. Jasper Nettlepoint presently returned to the back drawing-room to get a glass of syrup for his companion, and he took occasion to remark that it was lovely on the balcony: one really got some air, the breeze was from that quarter. I remembered, as he went away with his tinkling tumbler, that from *my* hand, a few minutes before, Miss Mavis had not been willing to accept this innocent offering. A little later Mrs Nettlepoint said – 'Well, if it's so pleasant there we had better go ourselves.' So we passed to the front and in the other room met the two young people coming in from the balcony. I wondered in the light of subsequent events exactly how long they had been sitting there together. (There were three or four cane chairs which had been placed there for the summer.) If it had been but five minutes, that only made subsequent events more curious. 'We must go, mother,' Miss Mavis immediately said; and a moment later, with a little renewal of chatter as to our general meeting on the ship, the visitors had taken leave. Jasper went down with them to the door and as soon as they had gone out Mrs Nettlepoint exclaimed – 'Ah, but she'll be a bore – she'll be a bore!'

'Not through talking too much – surely.'

'An affectation of silence is as bad. I hate that particular *pose*; it's coming up very much now; an imitation of the English, like everything else. A girl who tries to be statuesque at sea – that will act on one's nerves!'

'I don't know what she tries to be, but she succeeds in being very handsome.'

'So much the better for you. I'll leave her to you, for I shall be shut up. I like her being placed under my "care".'

'She will be under Jasper's,' I remarked.

'Ah, he won't go – I want it too much.'

'I have an idea he will go.'

'Why didn't he tell me so then – when he came in?'

'He was diverted by Miss Mavis – a beautiful unexpected girl sitting there.'

'Diverted from his mother – trembling for his decision?'

'She's an old friend; it was a meeting after a long separation.'

'Yes, such a lot of them as he knows!' said Mrs Nettlepoint.

'Such a lot of them?'

'He has so many female friends – in the most varied circles.'

'Well, we can close round her then – for I on my side knew, or used to know, her young man.'

'Her young man?'

'The *fiancé*, the intended, the one she is going out to. He can't by the way be very young now.'

'How odd it sounds!' said Mrs Nettlepoint.

I was going to reply that it was not odd if you knew Mr Porterfield, but I reflected that that perhaps only made it odder. I told my companion briefly who he was – that I had met him in the old days in Paris, when I believed for a fleeting hour that I could learn to paint, when I lived with the *jeunesse des écoles*, and her comment on this was simply – 'Well, he had better have come out for her!'

'Perhaps so. She looked to me as she sat there as if she might change her mind at the last moment.'

'About her marriage?'

'About sailing. But she won't change now.'

Jasper came back, and his mother instantly challenged him. 'Well, *are* you going?'

'Yes, I shall go,' he said, smiling. 'I have got my telegram.'

'Oh, your telegram!' I ventured to exclaim. 'That charming girl is your telegram.'

He gave me a look, but in the dusk I could not make out very well what it conveyed. Then he bent over his mother, kissing her. 'My news isn't particularly satisfactory. I am going for *you*.'

'Oh, you humbug!' she rejoined. But of course she was delighted.

II

PEOPLE usually spend the first hours of a voyage in squeezing themselves into their cabins, taking their little precautions, either so excessive or so inadequate, wondering how they can pass so many days in such a hole and asking idiotic questions of the stewards, who appear in comparison such men of the world. My own initiations were rapid, as became an old sailor, and so it seemed were Miss Mavis's, for when I mounted to the deck at the end of half an hour I found her there alone, in the stern of the ship, looking back at the dwindling continent. It dwindled very fast for so big a place. I accosted her, having had no conversation with her amid the crowd of leave-takers and the muddle of farewells before we put off; we talked a little about the boat, our fellow-passengers and our prospects, and then I said – 'I think you mentioned last night a name I know – that of Mr Porterfield.'

'Oh no, I never uttered it,' she replied, smiling at me through her closely-drawn veil.

'Then it was your mother.'

'Very likely it was my mother.' And she continued to smile, as if I ought to have known the difference.

'I venture to allude to him because I have an idea I used to know him,' I went on.

'Oh, I see.' Beyond this remark she manifested no interest in my having known him.

'That is if it's the same one.' It seemed to me it would be silly to say nothing more; so I added, 'My Mr Porterfield was called David.'

'Well, so is ours.' 'Ours' struck me as clever.

'I suppose I shall see him again if he is to meet you at Liverpool,' I continued.

'Well, it will be bad if he doesn't.'

It was too soon for me to have the idea that it would be bad if he did: that only came later. So I remarked that I had not seen him for so many years that it was very possible I should not know him.

'Well, I have not seen him for a great many years, but I expect I shall know him all the same.'

'Oh, with you it's different,' I rejoined, smiling at her. 'Hasn't he been back since those days?'

'I don't know what days you mean.'

'When I knew him in Paris – ages ago. He was a pupil of the Ecole des Beaux Arts. He was studying architecture.'

'Well, he is studying it still,' said Grace Mavis.

'Hasn't he learned it yet?'

'I don't know what he has learned. I shall see.' Then she added: 'Architecture is very difficult and he is tremendously thorough.'

'Oh, yes, I remember that. He was an admirable worker. But he must have become quite a foreigner, if it's so many years since he has been at home.'

'Oh, he is not changeable. If he were changeable—' But here my interlocutress paused. I suspect she had been going to say that if he were changeable he would have given her up long ago. After an instant she went on: 'He wouldn't have stuck so to his profession. You can't make much by it.'

'You can't make much?'

'It doesn't make you rich.'

'Oh, of course you have got to practise it – and to practise it long.'

'Yes – so Mr Porterfield says.'

Something in the way she uttered these words made me laugh – they were so serene an implication that the gentleman in question did not live up to his principles. But I checked myself, asking my companion if she expected to remain in Europe long – to live there.

'Well, it will be a good while if it takes me as long to come back as it has taken me to go out.'

'And I think your mother said last night that it was your first visit.'

Miss Mavis looked at me a moment. 'Didn't mother talk!'

'It was all very interesting.'

She continued to look at me. 'You don't think that.'

'What have I to gain by saying it if I don't?'

'Oh, men have always something to gain.'

'You make me feel a terrible failure, then! I hope at any rate that it gives you pleasure – the idea of seeing foreign lands.'

'Mercy – I should think so.'

'It's a pity our ship is not one of the fast ones, if you are impatient.'

She was silent a moment; then she exclaimed, 'Oh, I guess it will be fast enough!'

That evening I went in to see Mrs Nettlepoint and sat on her sea-trunk, which was pulled out from under the berth to accommodate me. It was nine o'clock but not quite dark, as our northward course had already taken us into the latitude of the longer days. She had made her nest admirably and lay upon her sofa in a becoming dressing-gown and cap, resting from her labours. It was her regular practice to spend the voyage in her cabin, which smelt good (such was the refinement of her art), and she had a secret peculiar to herself for keeping her port open without shipping seas. She hated what she called the mess of the ship and the idea, if she should go above, of meeting stewards with plates of supererogatory food. She professed to be content with her situation (we promised to lend each other books and I assured her familiarly that I should be in and out of her room a dozen times a day), and pitied me for having to mingle in society. She judged this to be a limited privilege, for on the deck before we left the wharf she had taken a view of our fellow-passengers.

'Oh, I'm an inveterate, almost a professional observer,' I replied, 'and with that vice I am as well occupied as an old woman in the sun with her knitting. It puts it in my power, in any situation, to *see* things. I shall see them even here and I shall come down very often and tell you about them. You are not interested to-day, but you will be to-morrow, for a ship is a great school of gossip. You won't believe the number of researches and problems you will be engaged in by the middle of the voyage.'

'I? Never in the world – lying here with my nose in a book and never seeing any thing.'

'You will participate at second hand. You will see through my eyes, hang upon my lips, take sides, feel passions, all sorts of sympathies and indignations. I have an idea that your young lady is the person on board who will interest me most.'

'Mine, indeed! She has not been near me since we left the dock.'

'Well, she is very curious.'

'You have such cold-blooded terms,' Mrs Nettlepoint murmured. '*Elle ne sait pas se conduire*; she ought to have come to ask about me.'

'Yes, since you are under her care,' I said, smiling. 'As for her not knowing how to behave – well, that's exactly what we shall see.'

'You will, but not I! I wash my hands of her.'

'Don't say that – don't say that.'

Mrs Nettlepoint looked at me a moment. 'Why do you speak so solemnly?'

In return I considered her. 'I will tell you before we land. And have you seen much of your son?'

'Oh yes, he has come in several times. He seems very much pleased. He has got a cabin to himself.'

'That's great luck,' I said, 'but I have an idea he is always in luck. I was sure I should have to offer him the second berth in my room.'

'And you wouldn't have enjoyed that, because you don't like him,' Mrs Nettlepoint took upon herself to say.

'What put that into your head?'

'It isn't in my head – it's in my heart, my *cœur de mère*. We guess those things. You think he's selfish – I could see it last night.'

'Dear lady,' I said, 'I have no general ideas about him at all. He is just one of the phenomena I am going to observe. He seems to me a very fine young man. However,' I added, 'since you have mentioned last night I will admit that I thought he rather tantalised you. He played with your suspense.'

'Why, he came at the last just to please me,' said Mrs Nettlepoint.

I was silent a moment. 'Are you sure it was for your sake?'

'Ah, perhaps it was for yours!'

'When he went out on the balcony with that girl perhaps she asked him to come,' I continued.

'Perhaps she did. But why should he do everything she asks him?'

'I don't know yet, but perhaps I shall know later. Not that he will tell me – for he will never tell me anything: he is not one of those who tell.'

'If she didn't ask him, what you say is a great wrong to her,' said Mrs Nettlepoint.

'Yes, if she didn't. But you say that to protect Jasper, not to protect her,' I continued, smiling.

'You *are* cold-blooded – it's uncanny!' my companion exclaimed.

'Ah, this is nothing yet! Wait a while – you'll see. At sea in general I'm awful – I pass the limits. If I have outraged her in thought I will jump overboard. There are ways of asking (a man doesn't need to tell a woman that) without the crude words.'

'I don't know what you suppose between them,' said Mrs Nettlepoint.

'Nothing but what was visible on the surface. It transpired, as the newspapers say, that they were old friends.'

'He met her at some promiscuous party – I asked him about it afterwards. She is not a person he could ever think of seriously.'

'That's exactly what I believe.'

'You don't observe – you imagine,' Mrs Nettlepoint pursued. 'How do you reconcile her laying a trap for Jasper with her going out to Liverpool on an errand of love?'

'I don't for an instant suppose she laid a trap; I believe she acted on the impulse of the moment. She is going out to Liverpool on an errand of marriage; that is not necessarily the same thing as an errand of love, especially for one who happens to have had a personal impression of the gentleman she is engaged to.'

'Well, there are certain decencies which in such a situation the most abandoned of her sex would still observe. You apparently judge her capable – on no evidence – of violating them.'

'Ah, you don't understand the shades of things,' I rejoined. 'Decencies and violations – there is no need for such heavy artillery! I can perfectly imagine that without the least immodesty she should have said to Jasper on the balcony, in fact if not in words – "I'm in dreadful spirits, but if you come I shall feel better, and that will be pleasant for you too."'

'And why is she in dreadful spirits?'

'She isn't!' I replied, laughing.

'What is she doing?'

'She is walking with your son.'

Mrs Nettlepoint said nothing for a moment, then she broke out, inconsequently – 'Ah, she's horrid!'

'No, she's charming!' I protested.

'You mean she's "curious"?'

'Well, for me it's the same thing!'

This led my friend of course to declare once more that I was cold-blooded. On the afternoon of the morrow we had another talk, and she told me that in the morning Miss Mavis had paid her a long visit. She knew nothing about anything, but her intentions were good and she was evidently in her own eyes conscientious and decorous. And Mrs Nettlepoint concluded these remarks with the exclamation 'Poor young thing!'

'You think she is a good deal to be pitied, then?'

'Well, her story sounds dreary – she told me a great deal of it. She fell to talking little by little and went from one thing to another. She's in that situation when a girl *must* open herself – to some woman.'

'Hasn't she got Jasper?' I inquired.

'He isn't a woman. You strike me as jealous of him,' my companion added.

'I daresay *he* thinks so – or will before the end. Ah no – ah no!' And I asked Mrs Nettlepoint if our young lady struck her as a flirt. She gave me no answer, but went on to remark that it was odd and interesting to her to see the way a girl like Grace Mavis resembled the girls of the kind she herself knew better, the girls of 'society', at the same time that she differed from them; and the way the differences and resemblances were mixed up, so that on certain questions you couldn't tell where you would find her. You would think she would feel as you did because you had found her feeling so, and then suddenly, in regard to some other matter (which was yet quite the same) she would be terribly wanting. Mrs Nettlepoint proceeded to observe (to such idle speculations does the vanity of a sea-voyage give encouragement) that she wondered whether it were better to be an ordinary girl very well brought up or an extraordinary girl not brought up at all.

'Oh, I go in for the extraordinary girl under all circumstances.'

'It is true that if you are *very* well brought up you are not ordinary,' said Mrs Nettlepoint, smelling her strong salts. 'You are a lady, at any rate. *C'est toujours ça.*'

'And Miss Mavis isn't one – is that what you mean?'

'Well – you have seen her mother.'

'Yes, but I think your contention would be that among such people the mother doesn't count.'

'Precisely; and that's bad.'

'I see what you mean. But isn't it rather hard? If your mother doesn't know anything it is better you should be independent of her, and yet if you are that constitutes a bad note.' I added that Mrs Mavis had appeared to count sufficiently two nights before. She had said and done everything she wanted, while the girl sat silent and respectful. Grace's attitude (so far as her mother was concerned) had been eminently decent.

'Yes, but she couldn't bear it,' said Mrs Nettlepoint.

'Ah, if you know it I may confess that she has told me as much.'

Mrs Nettlepoint stared. 'Told you? There's one of the things they do!'

'Well, it was only a word. Won't you let me know whether you think she's a flirt?'

'Find out for yourself, since you pretend to study folks.'

'Oh, your judgement would probably not at all determine mine. It's in regard to yourself that I ask it.'

'In regard to myself?'

'To see the length of maternal immorality.'

Mrs Nettlepoint continued to repeat my words. 'Maternal immorality?'

'You desire your son to have every possible distraction on his voyage, and if you can make up your mind in the sense I refer to that will make it all right. He will have no responsibility.'

'Heavens, how you analyse! I haven't in the least your passion for making up my mind.'

'Then if you chance it you'll be more immoral still.'

'Your reasoning is strange,' said the poor lady; 'when it was you who tried to put it into my head yesterday that she had asked him to come.'

'Yes, but in good faith.'

'How do you mean in good faith?'

'Why, as girls of that sort do. Their allowance and measure in such matters is much larger than that of young ladies who have been, as you say, *very* well brought up; and yet I am not sure that on the whole I don't think them the more innocent. Miss Mavis is engaged, and she's to be married next week, but it's an old, old story, and there's no more romance in it than if she were going to be photographed. So her usual life goes on, and her usual life consists (and that of ces demoiselles in general) in having plenty of gentlemen's society. Having it I mean without having any harm from it.'

'Well, if there is no harm from it what are you talking about and why am I immoral?'

I hesitated, laughing. 'I retract – you are sane and clear. I am sure she thinks there won't be any harm,' I added. 'That's the great point.'

'The great point?'

'I mean, to be settled.'

'Mercy, we are not trying them! How can *we* settle it?'

'I mean of course in our minds. There will be nothing more interesting for the next ten days for our minds to exercise themselves upon.'

'They will get very tired of it,' said Mrs Nettlepoint.

'No, no, because the interest will increase and the plot will thicken. It can't help it.' She looked at me as if she thought me slightly Mephistophelean, and I went on – 'So she told you everything in her life was dreary?'

'Not everything but most things. And she didn't tell me so much as I guessed it. She'll tell me more the next time. She will behave properly now about coming in to see me; I told her she ought to.'

'I am glad of that,' I said. 'Keep her with you as much as possible.'

'I don't follow you much,' Mrs Nettlepoint replied, 'but so far as I do I don't think your remarks are in very good taste.'

'I'm too excited, I lose my head, cold-blooded as you think me. Doesn't she like Mr Porterfield?'

'Yes, that's the worst of it.'

'The worst of it?'

'He's so good – there's no fault to be found with him. Otherwise she would have thrown it all up. It has dragged on since she was eighteen: she became engaged to him before he went abroad to study. It was one of those childish muddles which parents in America might prevent so much more than they do. The thing is to insist on one's daughter's waiting, on the engagement's being long; and then after you have got that started to take it on every occasion as little seriously as possible – to make it die out. You can easily tire it out. However, Mr Porterfield has taken it seriously for some years. He has done his part to keep it alive. She says he adores her.'

'His part? Surely his part would have been to marry her by this time.'

'He has absolutely no money.'

'He ought to have got some, in seven years.'

'So I think she thinks. There are some sorts of poverty that are contemptible. But he has a little more now. That's why he won't wait any longer. His mother has come out, she has something – a little – and she is able to help him. She will live with them and bear some of the expenses, and after her death the son will have what there is.'

'How old is she?' I asked, cynically.

'I haven't the least idea. But it doesn't sound very inspiring. He has not been to America since he first went out.'

'That's an odd way of adoring her.'

'I made that objection mentally, but I didn't express it to her. She met it indeed a little by telling me that he had had other chances to marry.'

'That surprises me,' I remarked. 'And did she say that *she* had had?'

'No, and that's one of the things I thought nice in her; for she must have had. She didn't try to make out that he had spoiled her life. She has three other sisters and there is very little money at home. She has tried to make money; she has written little things and painted little things, but her talent is apparently not in that direction. Her father has had a long illness and has lost his place – he was in receipt of a salary in connection with some waterworks – and one of her sisters has lately become a widow, with children and without means. And so as in fact she never has married any one else, whatever opportunities she may have encountered, she appears to have just made up her mind to go out to Mr Porterfield as the least of her evils. But it isn't very amusing.'

'That only makes it the more honourable. She will go through with it, whatever it costs, rather than disappoint him after he has waited so long. It is true,' I continued, 'that when a woman acts from a sense of honour—'

'Well, when she does?' said Mrs Nettlepoint, for I hesitated perceptibly.

'It is so extravagant a course that some one has to pay for it.'

'You are very impertinent. We all have to pay for each other, all the while; and for each other's virtues as well as vices.'

'That's precisely why I shall be sorry for Mr Porterfield when she steps off the ship with her little bill. I mean with her teeth clenched.'

'Her teeth are not in the least clenched. She is in perfect good-humour.'

'Well, we must try and keep her so,' I said. 'You must take care that Jasper neglects nothing.'

I know not what reflections this innocent pleasantry of mine provoked on the good lady's part; the upshot of them at all events was to make her say – 'Well, I never asked her to come; I'm very glad of that. It is all their own doing.'

'Their own – you mean Jasper's and hers?'

'No indeed. I mean her mother's and Mrs Allen's; the girl's too of course. They put themselves upon us.'

'Oh yes, I can testify to that. Therefore I'm glad too. We should have missed it, I think.'

'How seriously you take it!' Mrs Nettlepoint exclaimed.

'Ah, wait a few days!' I replied, getting up to leave her.

III

THE *Patagonia* was slow, but she was spacious and comfortable, and there was a kind of motherly decency in her long, nursing rock and her rustling, old-fashioned gait. It was as if she wished not to present herself in port with the splashed eagerness of a young creature. We were not numerous enough to squeeze each other and yet we were not too few to entertain – with that familiarity and relief which figures and objects acquire on the great bare field of the ocean, beneath the great bright glass of the sky. I had never liked the sea so much before, indeed I had never liked it at all; but now I had a revelation of how, in a midsummer mood, it could please. It was darkly and magnificently blue and imperturbably quiet – save for the great regular swell of its heart-beats, the pulse of its life, and there grew to be something so agreeable in the sense of floating there in infinite isolation and leisure that it was a positive satisfaction the *Patagonia* was not a racer. One had never thought of the sea as the great place of safety, but now it came over one that there is no place so safe from the land. When it does not give you trouble it takes it away – takes away letters and telegrams and newspapers and visits and duties and efforts, all the complications, all the superfluities and superstitions that we have stuffed into our terrene life. The simple absence of the post, when the particular conditions enable you to enjoy the great fact by which it is produced, becomes in itself a kind of bliss, and the clean stage of the deck shows you a play that amuses, the personal drama of the voyage, the movement and interaction, in the strong sea-light, of figures that end by representing something – something moreover of which the interest is never, even in its keenness, too great to suffer you to go to sleep. I, at any rate, dozed a great deal, lying on my rug with a French novel, and when I opened my eyes I generally saw Jasper Nettlepoint passing with his mother's *protégée* on his arm. Somehow at these moments, between sleeping and waking, I had an inconsequent sense that they were a part of the French novel. Perhaps this was because I had fallen into the trick, at the start, of regarding Grace Mavis almost as a married woman, which, as every one knows, is the necessary status of the heroine of such a work. Every revolution of our engine at any rate would contribute to the effect of making her one.

In the saloon, at meals, my neighbour on the right was a certain little Mrs Peck, a very short and very round person whose head was enveloped in a 'cloud' (a cloud of dirty white wool) and who promptly let me know that she was going to Europe for the education of her children. I had already perceived (an hour after we left the dock) that some energetic step was required in their interest, but as we were not in Europe yet the business could not be said to have begun. The four little Pecks, in the enjoyment of untrammelled leisure, swarmed about the ship as if they had been pirates boarding her, and their mother was as powerless to check their licence as if she had been gagged and stowed away in the hold. They were especially to be trusted to run between the legs of the stewards when these attendants arrived with bowls of soup for the languid ladies. Their mother was too busy recounting to her fellow-passengers how many years Miss Mavis had been engaged. In the blank of a marine existence things that are nobody's business very soon become everybody's, and this was just one of those facts that are propagated with a mysterious and ridiculous rapidity. The whisper that carries them is very small, in the great scale of things, of air and space and progress, but it is also very safe, for there is no compression, no sounding-board, to make speakers responsible. And then repetition at sea is somehow not repetition; monotony is in the air, the mind is flat and everything recurs – the bells, the meals, the stewards' faces, the romp of children, the walk, the clothes, the very shoes and buttons of passengers taking their exercise. These things grow at last so insipid that, in comparison, revelations as to the personal history of one's companions have a taste even when one cares little about the people.

Jasper Nettlepoint sat on my left hand when he was not upstairs seeing that Miss Mavis had her repast comfortably on deck. His mother's place would have been next mine had she shown herself, and then that of the young lady under her care. The two ladies, in other words, would have been between us, Jasper marking the limit of the party on that side. Miss Mavis was present at luncheon the first day, but dinner passed without her coming in, and when it was half over Jasper remarked that he would go up and look after her.

'Isn't that young lady coming – the one who was here to lunch?' Mrs Peck asked of me as he left the saloon.

'Apparently not. My friend tells me she doesn't like the saloon.'

'You don't mean to say she's sick, do you?'

'Oh no, not in this weather. But she likes to be above.'

'And is that gentleman gone up to her?'

'Yes, she's under his mother's care.'

'And is his mother up there, too?' asked Mrs Peck, whose processes were homely and direct.

'No, she remains in her cabin. People have different tastes. Perhaps that's one reason why Miss Mavis doesn't come to table,' I added – 'her chaperone not being able to accompany her.'

'Her chaperone?'

'Mrs Nettlepoint – the lady under whose protection she is.'

'Protection?' Mrs Peck stared at me a moment, moving some valued morsel in her mouth; then she exclaimed, familiarly, 'Pshaw!' I was struck with this and I was on the point of asking her what she meant by it when she continued: 'Are we not going to see Mrs Nettlepoint?'

'I am afraid not. She vows that she won't stir from her sofa.'

'Pshaw!' said Mrs Peck again. 'That's quite a disappointment.'

'Do you know her then?'

'No, but I know all about her.' Then my companion added – 'You don't mean to say she's any relation?'

'Do you mean to me?'

'No, to Grace Mavis.'

'None at all. They are very new friends, as I happen to know. Then you are acquainted with our young lady?' I had not noticed that any recognition passed between them at luncheon.

'Is she yours too?' asked Mrs Peck, smiling at me.

'Ah, when people are in the same boat – literally – they belong a little to each other.'

'That's so,' said Mrs Peck. 'I don't know Miss Mavis but I know all about her – I live opposite to her on Merrimac Avenue. I don't know whether you know that part.'

'Oh yes – it's very beautiful.'

The consequence of this remark was another 'Pshaw!' But Mrs Peck went on – 'When you've lived opposite to people like that for a long time you feel as if you were acquainted. But she didn't take it up to-day; she didn't speak to me. She knows who I am as well as she knows her own mother.'

'You had better speak to her first – she's shy,' I remarked.

'Shy? Why she's nearly thirty years old. I suppose you know where she's going.'

'Oh yes – we all take an interest in that.'

'That young man, I suppose, particularly.'

'That young man?'

'The handsome one, who sits there. Didn't you tell me he is Mrs Nettlepoint's son?'

'Oh yes; he acts as her deputy. No doubt he does all he can to carry out her function.'

Mrs Peck was silent a moment. I had spoken jocosely, but she received my pleasantry with a serious face. 'Well, she might let him eat his dinner in peace!' she presently exclaimed.

'Oh, he'll come back!' I said, glancing at his place. The repast continued and when it was finished I screwed my chair round to leave the table. Mrs Peck performed the same movement and we quitted the saloon together. Outside of it was a kind of vestibule, with several seats, from which you could descend to the lower cabins or mount to the promenade-deck. Mrs Peck appeared to hesitate as to her course and then solved the problem by going neither way. She dropped upon one of the benches and looked up at me.

'I thought you said he would come back.'

'Young Nettlepoint? I see he didn't. Miss Mavis then has given him half of her dinner.'

'It's very kind of her! She has been engaged for ages.'

'Yes, but that will soon be over.'

'So I suppose – as quick as we land. Every one knows it on Merrimac Avenue. Every one there takes a great interest in it.'

'Ah, of course, a girl like that: she has many friends.'

'I mean even people who don't know her.'

'I see,' I went on: 'she is so handsome that she attracts attention, people enter into her affairs.'

'She *used* to be pretty, but I can't say I think she's anything remarkable to-day. Anyhow, if she attracts attention she ought to be all the more careful what she does. You had better tell her that.'

'Oh, it's none of my business!' I replied, leaving Mrs Peck and going above. The exclamation, I confess, was not perfectly in accordance with my feeling, or rather my feeling was not perfectly in harmony with the exclamation. The very first thing I did on reaching the deck was to notice that Miss Mavis was pacing it on Jasper Nettlepoint's arm and that whatever beauty she might have lost, according to Mrs Peck's insinuation, she still kept enough to make one's eyes follow her. She had put on a sort of crimson hood, which was very becoming to her and which she wore for the rest of the voyage. She walked very well, with long steps, and I remember that at this moment the ocean had a gentle evening swell which made the great ship dip slowly, rhythmically, giving a movement that was graceful to graceful pedestrians and a more awkward one to the awkward. It was the loveliest hour of a fine day, the clear early evening, with the glow of the sunset in the air and a purple colour in the sea. I always thought that the waters ploughed by the Homeric heroes must have looked like that. I perceived on that particular occasion moreover that Grace Mavis would for the rest of the voyage be the most visible thing on the ship; the figure that would count most in the composition of groups. She couldn't help it, poor girl; nature had made her conspicuous – important as the painters say. She paid for it by the exposure it brought with it – the danger that people would, as I had said to Mrs Peck, enter into her affairs.

Jasper Nettlepoint went down at certain times to see his mother, and I watched for one of these occasions (on the third day out) and took advantage of it to go and sit by Miss Mavis. She wore a blue veil drawn tightly over her face, so that if the smile with which she greeted me was dim I could account for it partly by that.

'Well, we are getting on – we are getting on,' I said, cheerfully, looking at the friendly, twinkling sea.

'Are we going very fast?'

'Not fast, but steadily. *Ohne Hast, ohne Rast* – do you know German?'

'Well, I've studied it – some.'

'It will be useful to you over there when you travel.'

'Well yes, if we do. But I don't suppose we shall much. Mr Nettlepoint says we ought,' my interlocutress added in a moment.

'Ah, of course *he* thinks so. He has been all over the world.'

'Yes, he has described some of the places. That's what I should like. I didn't know I should like it so much.'

'Like what so much?'

'Going on this way. I could go on for ever, for ever and ever.'

'Ah, you know it's not always like this,' I rejoined.

'Well, it's better than Boston.'

'It isn't so good as Paris,' I said, smiling.

'Oh, I know all about Paris. There is no freshness in that. I feel as if I had been there.'

'You mean you have heard so much about it?'

'Oh yes, nothing else for ten years.'

I had come to talk with Miss Mavis because she was attractive, but I had been rather conscious of the absence of a good topic, not feeling at liberty to revert to Mr Porterfield. She had not encouraged me, when I spoke to her as we were leaving Boston, to go on with the history of my acquaintance with this gentleman; and yet now, unexpectedly, she appeared to imply (it was doubtless one of the disparities mentioned by Mrs Nettlepoint) that he might be glanced at without indelicacy.

'I see, you mean by letters,' I remarked.

'I shan't live in a good part. I know enough to know that,' she went on.

'Dear young lady, there are no bad parts,' I answered, reassuringly.

'Why, Mr Nettlepoint says it's horrid.'

'It's horrid?'

'Up there in the Batignolles. It's worse than Merrimac Avenue.'

'Worse – in what way?'

'Why, even less where the nice people live.'

'He oughtn't to say that,' I returned. 'Don't you call Mr Porterfield a nice person?' I ventured to subjoin.

'Oh, it doesn't make any difference.' She rested her eyes on me a moment through her veil, the texture of which gave them a suffused prettiness. 'Do you know him very well?' she asked.

'Mr Porterfield?'

'No, Mr Nettlepoint.'

'Ah, very little. He's a good deal younger than I.'

She was silent a moment; after which she said: 'He's younger than me, too.' I know not what drollery there was in this but it was unexpected and it made me laugh. Neither do I know whether Miss Mavis took offence at my laughter, though I remember thinking at the moment with compunction that it had brought a certain colour to her cheek. At all events she got up, gathering her shawl and her books into her arm. 'I'm going down – I'm tired.'

'Tired of me, I'm afraid.'

'No, not yet.'

'I'm like you,' I pursued. 'I should like it to go on and on.'

She had begun to walk along the deck to the companion-way and I went with her. 'Oh, no, I shouldn't, after all!'

I had taken her shawl from her to carry it, but at the top of the steps that led down to the cabins I had to give it back. 'Your mother would be glad if she could know,' I observed as we parted.

'If she could know?'

'How well you are getting on. And that good Mrs Allen.'

'Oh, mother, mother! She made me come, she pushed me off.' And almost as if not to say more she went quickly below.

I paid Mrs Nettlepoint a morning visit after luncheon and another in the evening, before she 'turned in'. That same day, in the evening, she said to me suddenly, 'Do you know what I have done? I have asked Jasper.'

'Asked him what?'

'Why, if *she* asked him, you know.'

'I don't understand.'

'You do perfectly. If that girl really asked him – on the balcony – to sail with us.'

'My dear friend, do you suppose that if she did he would tell you?'

'That's just what he says. But he says she didn't.'

'And do you consider the statement valuable?' I asked, laughing out. 'You had better ask Miss Gracie herself.'

Mrs Nettlepoint stared. 'I couldn't do that.'

'Incomparable friend, I am only joking. What does it signify now?'

'I thought you thought everything signified. You were so full of signification!'

'Yes, but we are farther out now, and somehow in mid-ocean everything becomes absolute.'

'What else *can* he do with decency?' Mrs Nettlepoint went on. 'If, as my son, he were never to speak to her it would be very rude and you would think that stranger still. Then *you* would do what he does, and where would be the difference?'

'How do you know what he does? I haven't mentioned him for twenty-four hours.'

'Why, she told me herself: she came in this afternoon.'

'What an odd thing to tell you!' I exclaimed.

'Not as she says it. She says he's full of attention, perfectly devoted – looks after her all the while. She seems to want me to know it, so that I may commend him for it.'

'That's charming; it shows her good conscience.'

'Yes, or her great cleverness.'

Something in the tone in which Mrs Nettlepoint said this caused me to exclaim in real surprise, 'Why, what do you suppose she has in her mind?'

'To get hold of him, to make him go so far that he can't retreat, to marry him, perhaps.'

'To marry him? And what will she do with Mr Porterfield?'

'She'll ask me just to explain to him – or perhaps you.'

'Yes, as an old friend!' I replied, laughing. But I asked more seriously, 'Do you see Jasper caught like that?'

'Well, he's only a boy – he's younger at least than she.'

'Precisely; she regards him as a child.'

'As a child?'

'She remarked to me herself to-day that he is so much younger.'

Mrs Nettlepoint stared. 'Does she talk of it with you? That shows she has a plan, that she has thought it over!'

I have sufficiently betrayed that I deemed Grace Mavis a singular girl, but I was far from judging her capable of laying a trap for our young companion. Moreover my reading of Jasper was not in the least that he was catchable – could be made to do a thing if he didn't want to do it. Of course it was not impossible that he might be inclined, that he might take it (or already have taken it) into his head to marry Miss Mavis; but to believe this I should require still more proof than his always being with her. He wanted at most to marry her for the voyage. 'If you have questioned him perhaps you have tried to make him feel responsible,' I said to his mother.

'A little, but it's very difficult. Interference makes him perverse. One has to go gently. Besides, it's too absurd – think of her age. If she can't take care of herself!' cried Mrs Nettlepoint.

'Yes, let us keep thinking of her age, though it's not so prodigious. And if things get very bad you have one resource left,' I added.

'What is that?'

'You can go upstairs.'

'Ah, never, never! If it takes that to save her she must be lost. Besides, what good would it do? If I were to go up she could come down here.'

'Yes, but you could keep Jasper with you.'

'Could I?' Mrs Nettlepoint demanded, in the manner of a woman who knew her son.

In the saloon the next day, after dinner, over the red cloth of the tables, beneath the swinging lamps and the racks of tumblers, decanters and wineglasses, we sat down to whist, Mrs Peck, among others, taking a hand in the game. She played very badly and talked too much, and when the rubber was over assuaged her discomfiture (though not mine – we had been partners) with a Welsh rabbit and a tumbler of something hot. We had done with the cards, but while she waited for this refreshment she sat with her elbows on the table shuffling a pack.

'She hasn't spoken to me yet – she won't do it,' she remarked in a moment.

'Is it possible there is any one on the ship who hasn't spoken to you?'

'Not that girl – she knows too well!' Mrs Peck looked round our little circle with a smile of intelligence – she had familiar, communicative eyes. Several of our company had assembled, according to the wont, the last thing in the evening, of those who are cheerful at sea, for the consumption of grilled sardines and devilled bones.

'What then does she know?'

'Oh, she knows that I know.'

'Well, we know what Mrs Peck knows,' one of the ladies of the group observed to me, with an air of privilege.

'Well, you wouldn't know if I hadn't told you – from the way she acts,' said Mrs Peck, with a small laugh.

'She is going out to a gentleman who lives over there – he's waiting there to marry her,' the other lady went on, in the tone of authentic information. I remember that her name was Mrs Gotch and that her mouth looked always as if she were whistling.

'Oh, he knows – I've told him,' said Mrs Peck.

'Well, I presume every one knows,' Mrs Gotch reflected.

'Dear madam, is it every one's business?' I asked.

'Why, don't you think it's a peculiar way to act?' Mrs Gotch was evidently surprised at my little protest.

'Why, it's right there – straight in front of you, like a play at the theatre – as if you had paid to see it,' said Mrs Peck. 'If you don't call it public—!'

'Aren't you mixing things up? What do you call public?'

'Why, the way they go on. They are up there now.'

'They cuddle up there half the night,' said Mrs Gotch. 'I don't know when they come down. Any hour you like – when all the lights are out they are up there still.'

'Oh, you can't tire them out. They don't want relief – like the watch!' laughed one of the gentlemen.

'Well, if they enjoy each other's society what's the harm?' another asked. 'They'd do just the same on land.'

'They wouldn't do it on the public streets, I suppose,' said Mrs Peck. 'And they wouldn't do it if Mr Porterfield was round!'

'Isn't that just where your confusion comes in?' I inquired. 'It's public enough that Miss Mavis and Mr Nettlepoint are always together, but it isn't in the least public that she is going to be married.'

'Why, how can you say – when the very sailors know it! The captain knows it and all the officers know it; they see them there – especially at night, when they're sailing the ship.'

'I thought there was some rule—' said Mrs Gotch.

'Well, there is – that you've got to behave yourself,' Mrs Peck rejoined. 'So the captain told me – he said they have some rule. He said they have to have, when people are too demonstrative.'

'Too demonstrative?'

'When they attract so much attention.'

'Ah, it's we who attract the attention – by talking about what doesn't concern us and about what we really don't know,' I ventured to declare.

'She said the captain said he would tell on her as soon as we arrive,' Mrs Gotch interposed.

'*She* said—?' I repeated, bewildered.

'Well, he did say so, that he would think it his duty to inform Mr Porterfield, when he comes on to meet her – if they keep it up in the same way,' said Mrs Peck.

'Oh, they'll keep it up, don't you fear!' one of the gentlemen exclaimed.

'Dear madam, the captain is laughing at you.'

'No, he ain't – he's right down scandalised. He says he regards us all as a real family and wants the family to be properly behaved.' I could see Mrs Peck was irritated by my controversial tone: she challenged me with considerable spirit. 'How can you say I don't know it when all the street knows it and has known it for years – for years and years?' She spoke as if the girl had been engaged at least for twenty. 'What is she going out for, if not to marry him?'

'Perhaps she is going to see how he looks,' suggested one of the gentlemen.

'He'd look queer – if he knew.'

'Well, I guess he'll know,' said Mrs Gotch.

'She'd tell him herself – she wouldn't be afraid,' the gentleman went on.

'Well, she might as well kill him. He'll jump overboard.'

'Jump overboard?' cried Mrs Gotch, as if she hoped then that Mr Porterfield would be told.

'He has just been waiting for this – for years,' said Mrs Peck.

'Do you happen to know him?' I inquired.

Mrs Peck hesitated a moment. 'No, but I know a lady who does. Are you going up?'

I had risen from my place – I had not ordered supper. 'I'm going to take a turn before going to bed.'

'Well then, you'll see!'

Outside the saloon I hesitated, for Mrs Peck's admonition made me feel for a moment that if I ascended to the deck I should have entered in a manner into her little conspiracy. But the night was so warm and splendid that I had been intending to smoke a cigar in the air before going below, and I did not see why I should deprive myself of this pleasure in order to seem not to mind Mrs Peck. I went up and saw a few figures sitting or moving about in the darkness. The ocean looked black and small, as it is apt to do at night, and the long mass of the ship, with its vague dim wings, seemed to take up a great part of it. There were more stars than one saw on land and the heavens struck one more than ever as larger than the earth. Grace Mavis and her companion were not, so far as I perceived at first, among the few passengers who were lingering late, and I was glad, because I hated to hear her talked about in the manner of the gossips I had left at supper. I wished there had been some way to prevent it, but I could think of no way but to recommend her privately to change her habits. That would be a very delicate business, and perhaps it would be better to begin with Jasper, though that would be delicate too. At any rate one might let him know, in a friendly spirit, to how much remark he exposed the young lady – leaving this revelation to work its way upon him. Unfortunately I could not altogether believe that the pair were unconscious of the observation and the opinion of the passengers. They were not a boy and a girl; they had a certain social perspective in their eye. I was not very clear as to the details of that behaviour which had made them (according to the version of my good friends in the saloon) a scandal to the ship, for though I looked at them a good deal I evidently had not looked at them so continuously and so hungrily as Mrs Peck. Nevertheless the probability was that they knew what was thought of them – what naturally would be – and simply didn't care. That made Miss Mavis out rather cynical and even a little immodest; and yet, somehow, if she had such qualities I did not dislike her for them. I don't know what strange, secret excuses I found for her. I presently indeed encountered a need for them on the spot, for just as I was on the point of going below again, after several restless turns and (within the limit where smoking was allowed) as many puffs at a cigar as I cared for, I became aware that a couple of figures were seated behind one of the lifeboats that rested on the deck. They were so placed as to be visible only to a person going close to the rail and peering a little sidewise. I don't think I peered, but as I stood a moment beside the rail my eye was attracted by a dusky object which protruded beyond the boat and which, as I saw at a second glance, was the tail of a lady's dress. I bent forward an instant, but even then I saw very little more; that scarcely mattered, however, for I took for granted on the spot that the persons concealed in so snug a corner were Jasper Nettlepoint and Mr Porterfield's intended. Concealed was the word, and I thought it a real pity; there was bad taste in it. I immediately turned away and the next moment I found myself face to face with the captain of the ship. I had already had some conversation with him (he had been so good as to invite me, as he had invited Mrs

Nettlepoint and her son and the young lady travelling with them, and also Mrs Peck, to sit at his table) and had observed with pleasure that he had the art, not universal on the Atlantic liners, of mingling urbanity with seamanship.

'They don't waste much time – your friends in there,' he said, nodding in the direction in which he had seen me looking.

'Ah well, they haven't much to lose.'

'That's what I mean. I'm told *she* hasn't.'

I wanted to say something exculpatory but I scarcely knew what note to strike. I could only look vaguely about me at the starry darkness and the sea that seemed to sleep. 'Well, with these splendid nights, this perfection of weather, people are beguiled into late hours.'

'Yes. We want a nice little blow,' the captain said.

'A nice little blow?'

'That would clear the decks!'

The captain was rather dry and he went about his business. He had made me uneasy and instead of going below I walked a few steps more. The other walkers dropped off pair by pair (they were all men) till at last I was alone. Then, after a little, I quitted the field. Jasper and his companion were still behind their lifeboat. Personally I greatly preferred good weather, but as I went down I found myself vaguely wishing, in the interest of I scarcely knew what, unless of decorum, that we might have half a gale.

Miss Mavis turned out, in sea-phrase, early; for the next morning I saw her come up only a little while after I had finished my breakfast, a ceremony over which I contrived not to dawdle. She was alone and Jasper Nettlepoint, by a rare accident, was not on deck to help her. I went to meet her (she was encumbered as usual with her shawl, her sun-umbrella and a book) and laid my hands on her chair, placing it near the stern of the ship, where she liked best to be. But I proposed to her to walk a little before she sat down and she took my arm after I had put her accessories into the chair. The deck was clear at that hour and the morning light was gay; one got a sort of exhilarated impression of fair conditions and an absence of hindrance. I forget what we spoke of first, but it was because I felt these things pleasantly, and not to torment my companion nor to test her, that I could not help exclaiming cheerfully, after a moment, as I have mentioned having done the first day, 'Well, we are getting on, we are getting on!'

'Oh yes, I count every hour.'

'The last days always go quicker,' I said, 'and the last hours—'

'Well, the last hours?' she asked; for I had instinctively checked myself.

'Oh, one is so glad then that it is almost the same as if one had arrived. But we ought to be grateful when the elements have been so kind to us,' I added. 'I hope you will have enjoyed the voyage.'

She hesitated a moment, then she said, 'Yes, much more than I expected.'

'Did you think it would be very bad?'

'Horrible, horrible!'

The tone of these words was strange but I had not much time to reflect upon it, for turning round at that moment I saw Jasper Nettlepoint come towards us. He was separated from us by the expanse of the white deck and I could not help looking at him from head to foot as he drew nearer. I know not what rendered me on this occasion particularly sensitive to the impression, but it seemed to me that I saw him as I had never seen him before – saw him inside and out, in the intense sea-light, in his personal, his moral totality. It was a quick, vivid revelation; if it only lasted a moment it had a simplifying, certifying effect. He was intrinsically a pleasing apparition, with his handsome young face and a certain absence of com-promise in his personal arrangements which, more than any one I have ever seen, he managed to exhibit on shipboard. He had none of the appearance of wearing out old clothes that usually prevails there, but dressed straight, as I heard some one say. This gave him a practical, successful air, as of a young man who would come best out of any predicament. I expected to feel my companion's hand loosen itself on my arm, as indication that now she must go to him, and was almost surprised she did not drop me. We stopped as we met and Jasper bade us a friendly good-morning. Of course the remark was not slow to be made that we had another lovely day, which led him to exclaim, in the manner of one to whom criticism came easily, 'Yes, but with this sort of thing consider what one of the others would do!'

'One of the other ships?'

'We should be there now, or at any rate to-morrow.'

'Well then, I'm glad it isn't one of the others,' I said, smiling at the young lady on my arm. My remark offered her a chance to say something appreciative and gave him one even more; but neither Jasper nor Grace Mavis took advantage of the opportunity. What they did do, I perceived, was to look at each other for an instant; after which Miss Mavis turned her eyes silently to the sea. She made no movement and uttered no word, contriving to give me the sense that she had all at once become perfectly passive, that she somehow declined responsibility. We remained standing there with Jasper in front of us, and if the touch of her arm did not suggest that I should give her up, neither did it intimate that we had better pass on. I had no idea of giving her up, albeit one of the things that I seemed to discover just then in Jasper's physiognomy was an imperturbable implication that she was his property. His eye met mine for a moment, and it was exactly as if he had said to me, 'I know what you think, but I don't care a rap.' What I really thought was that he was selfish beyond the limits: that was the substance of my little revelation. Youth is almost always selfish, just as it is almost always conceited, and, after all, when it is combined with health and good parts, good looks and good spirits, it has a right to be, and I easily forgive it if it be really youth. Still, it is a question of degree, and what stuck out of Jasper Nettlepoint (if one felt that sort of thing) was that his egotism had a hardness, his love of his own way an avidity. These elements were jaunty and prosperous, they were accustomed to triumph. He was fond, very fond, of women; they were necessary to him and that was in his type; but he was not in the least in love with Grace Mavis. Among the reflections I quickly made this was the one that was most to the point. There was a degree of awkwardness, after a minute, in the way we were planted there, though the apprehension of it was doubtless not in the least with him.

'How is your mother this morning?' I asked.

'You had better go down and see.'

'Not till Miss Mavis is tired of me.'

She said nothing to this and I made her walk again. For some minutes she remained silent; then, rather unexpectedly, she began: 'I've seen you talking to that lady who sits at our table – the one who has so many children.'

'Mrs Peck? Oh yes, I have talked with her.'

'Do you know her very well?'

'Only as one knows people at sea. An acquaintance makes itself. It doesn't mean very much.'

'She doesn't speak to me – she might if she wanted.'

'That's just what she says of you – that you might speak to her.'

'Oh, if she's waiting for that—!' said my companion, with a laugh. Then she added – 'She lives in our street, nearly opposite.'

'Precisely. That's the reason why she thinks you might speak; she has seen you so often and seems to know so much about you.'

'What does she know about me?'

'Ah, you must ask her – I can't tell you!'

'I don't care what she knows,' said my young lady. After a moment she went on – 'She must have seen that I'm not very sociable.' And then – 'What are you laughing at?'

My laughter was for an instant irrepressible – there was something so droll in the way she had said that.

'Well, you are not sociable and yet you are. Mrs Peck is, at any rate, and thought that ought to make it easy for you to enter into conversation with her.'

'Oh, I don't care for her conversation – I know what it amounts to.' I made no rejoinder – I scarcely knew what rejoinder to make – and the girl went on, 'I know what she thinks and I know what she says.' Still I was silent, but the next moment I saw that my delicacy had been wasted, for Miss

Mavis asked, 'Does she make out that she knows Mr Porterfield?'

'No, she only says that she knows a lady who knows him.'

'Yes, I know – Mrs Jeremie. Mrs Jeremie's an idiot!' I was not
in a position to controvert this, and presently my young lady
said she would sit down. I left her in her chair – I saw that she
preferred it – and wandered to a distance. A few minutes later
I met Jasper again, and he stopped of his own accord and said
to me –

'We shall be in about six in the evening, on the eleventh day –
they promise it.'

'If nothing happens, of course.'

'Well, what's going to happen?'

'That's just what I'm wondering!' And I turned away and
went below with the foolish but innocent satisfaction of thinking that I had mystified him.

IV

'I DON´T know what to do, and you must help me,' Mrs
Nettlepoint said to me that evening, as soon as I went in to
see her.

'I'll do what I can – but what's the matter?'

'She has been crying here and going on – she has quite
upset me.'

'Crying? She doesn't look like that.'

'Exactly, and that's what startled me. She came in to see me
this afternoon, as she has done before, and we talked about the
weather and the run of the ship and the manners of the stewardess and little commonplaces like that, and then suddenly, in
the midst of it, as she sat there, *à propos* of nothing, she burst
into tears. I asked her what ailed her and tried to comfort her,
but she didn't explain; she only said it was nothing, the effect of
the sea, of leaving home. I asked her if it had anything to do with
her prospects, with her marriage; whether she found as that
drew near that her heart was not in it; I told her that she mustn't
be nervous, that I could enter into that – in short I said what
I could. All that she replied was that she *was* nervous, very

nervous, but that it was already over; and then she jumped up and kissed me and went away. Does she look as if she had been crying?' Mrs Nettlepoint asked.

'How can I tell, when she never quits that horrid veil? It's as if she were ashamed to show her face.'

'She's keeping it for Liverpool. But I don't like such incidents,' said Mrs Nettlepoint. 'I shall go upstairs.'

'And is that where you want me to help you?'

'Oh, your arm and that sort of thing, yes. But something more. I feel as if something were going to happen.'

'That's exactly what I said to Jasper this morning.'

'And what did he say?'

'He only looked innocent, as if he thought I meant a fog or a storm.'

'Heaven forbid – it isn't that! I shall never be good-natured again,' Mrs Nettlepoint went on; 'never have a girl put upon me that way. You always pay for it, there are always tiresome complications. What I am afraid of is after we get there. She'll throw up her engagement; there will be dreadful scenes; I shall be mixed up with them and have to look after her and keep her with me. I shall have to stay there with her till she can be sent back, or even take her up to London. *Voyez-vous ça?*'

I listened respectfully to this and then I said: 'You are afraid of your son.'

'Afraid of him?'

'There are things you might say to him – and with your manner; because you have one when you choose.'

'Very likely, but what is my manner to his? Besides, I have said everything to him. That is I have said the great thing, that he is making her immensely talked about.'

'And of course in answer to that he has asked you how you know, and you have told him I have told you.'

'I had to; and he says it's none of your business.'

'I wish he would say that to my face.'

'He'll do so perfectly, if you give him a chance. That's where you can help me. Quarrel with him – he's rather good at a quarrel, and that will divert him and draw him off.'

'Then I'm ready to discuss the matter with him for the rest of the voyage.'

'Very well; I count on you. But he'll ask you, as he asks me, what the deuce you want him to do.'

'To go to bed,' I replied, laughing.

'Oh, it isn't a joke.'

'That's exactly what I told you at first.'

'Yes, but don't exult; I hate people who exult. Jasper wants to know why he should mind her being talked about if she doesn't mind it herself.'

'I'll tell him why,' I replied; and Mrs Nettlepoint said she should be exceedingly obliged to me and repeated that she would come upstairs.

I looked for Jasper above that same evening, but circumstances did not favour my quest. I found him – that is I discovered that he was again ensconced behind the lifeboat with Miss Mavis; but there was a needless violence in breaking into their communion, and I put off our interview till the next day. Then I took the first opportunity, at breakfast, to make sure of it. He was in the saloon when I went in and was preparing to leave the table; but I stopped him and asked if he would give me a quarter of an hour on deck a little later – there was something particular I wanted to say to him. He said, 'Oh yes, if you like,' with just a visible surprise, but no look of an uncomfortable consciousness. When I had finished my breakfast I found him smoking on the forward-deck and I immediately began: 'I am going to say something that you won't at all like; to ask you a question that you will think impertinent.'

'Impertinent? that's bad.'

'I am a good deal older than you and I am a friend – of many years – of your mother. There's nothing I like less than to be meddlesome, but I think these things give me a certain right – a sort of privilege. For the rest, my inquiry will speak for itself.'

'Why so many preliminaries?' the young man asked, smiling.

We looked into each other's eyes a moment. What indeed was his mother's manner – her best manner – compared with his? 'Are you prepared to be responsible?'

'To you?'

'Dear no – to the young lady herself. I am speaking of course of Miss Mavis.'

'Ah yes, my mother tells me you have her greatly on your mind.'

'So has your mother herself – now.'

'She is so good as to say so – to oblige you.'

'She would oblige me a great deal more by reassuring me. I am aware that you know I have told her that Miss Mavis is greatly talked about.'

'Yes, but what on earth does it matter?'

'It matters as a sign.'

'A sign of what?'

'That she is in a false position.'

Jasper puffed his cigar, with his eyes on the horizon. 'I don't know whether it's *your* business, what you are attempting to discuss; but it really appears to me it is none of mine. What have I to do with the tattle with which a pack of old women console themselves for not being sea-sick?'

'Do you call it tattle that Miss Mavis is in love with you?'

'Drivelling.'

'Then you are very ungrateful. The tattle of a pack of old women has this importance, that she suspects or knows that it exists, and that nice girls are for the most part very sensitive to that sort of thing. To be prepared not to heed it in this case she must have a reason, and the reason must be the one I have taken the liberty to call your attention to.'

'In love with me in six days, just like that?' said Jasper, smoking.

'There is no accounting for tastes, and six days at sea are equivalent to sixty on land. I don't want to make you too proud. Of course if you recognise your responsibility it's all right and I have nothing to say.'

'I don't see what you mean,' Jasper went on.

'Surely you ought to have thought of that by this time. She's engaged to be married and the gentleman she is engaged to is to meet her at Liverpool. The whole ship knows it (I didn't tell them!) and the whole ship is watching her. It's impertinent if you like, just as I am, but we make a little world here together and we can't blink its conditions. What I ask you is whether you are prepared to allow her to give up the gentleman I have just mentioned for your sake.'

'For my sake?'

'To marry her if she breaks with him.'

Jasper turned his eyes from the horizon to my own, and I found a strange expression in them. 'Has Miss Mavis commissioned you to make this inquiry?'

'Never in the world.'

'Well then, I don't understand it.'

'It isn't from another I make it. Let it come from yourself – *to* yourself.'

'Lord, you must think I lead myself a life! That's a question the young lady may put to me any moment that it pleases her.'

'Let me then express the hope that she will. But what will you answer?'

'My dear sir, it seems to me that in spite of all the titles you have enumerated you have no reason to expect I will tell you.' He turned away and I exclaimed, sincerely, 'Poor girl!' At this he faced me again and, looking at me from head to foot, demanded: 'What is it you want me to do?'

'I told your mother that you ought to go to bed.'

'You had better do that yourself!'

This time he walked off, and I reflected rather dolefully that the only clear result of my experiment would probably have been to make it vivid to him that she was in love with him. Mrs Nettlepoint came up as she had announced, but the day was half over: it was nearly three o'clock. She was accompanied by her son, who established her on deck, arranged her chair and her shawls, saw that she was protected from sun and wind, and for an hour was very properly attentive. While this went on Grace Mavis was not visible, nor did she reappear during the whole afternoon. I had not observed that she had as yet been absent from the deck for so long a period. Jasper went away, but he came back at intervals to see how his mother got on, and when she asked him where Miss Mavis was he said he had not the least idea. I sat with Mrs Nettlepoint at her particular request: she told me she knew that if I left her Mrs Peck and Mrs Gotch would come to speak to her. She was flurried and fatigued at having to make an effort, and I think that Grace Mavis's choosing this occasion for retirement suggested to her a little that she had been made a fool of. She remarked that the girl's not being there showed her complete want of breeding and that she was really very good to have put herself out for her so; she was a common creature and that was the end of it. I could see that Mrs Nettlepoint's advent quickened the speculative activity of the other ladies; they watched her from the opposite side of the deck, keeping their eyes fixed on her very much as the man at the wheel kept his on the course of the ship. Mrs Peck plainly meditated an approach, and it was from this danger that Mrs Nettlepoint averted her face.

'It's just as we said,' she remarked to me as we sat there. 'It is like the bucket in the well. When I come up that girl goes down.'

'Yes, but you've succeeded, since Jasper remains here.'

'Remains? I don't see him.'

'He comes and goes – it's the same thing.'

'He goes more than he comes. But *n'en parlons plus*; I haven't gained anything. I don't admire the sea at all – what is it but a magnified water-tank? I shan't come up again.'

'I have an idea she'll stay in her cabin now,' I said. 'She tells me she has one to herself.' Mrs Nettlepoint replied that she might do as she liked, and I repeated to her the little conversation I had had with Jasper.

She listened with interest, but 'Marry her? mercy!' she exclaimed. 'I like the manner in which you give my son away.'

'You wouldn't accept that?'

'Never in the world.'

'Then I don't understand your position.'

'Good Heavens, I have none! It isn't a position to be bored to death.'

'You wouldn't accept it even in the case I put to him – that of her believing she had been encouraged to throw over poor Porterfield?'

'Not even – not even. Who knows what she believes?'

'Then you do exactly what I said you would – you show me a fine example of maternal immorality.'

'Maternal fiddlesticks! It was she began it.'

'Then why did you come up to-day?'

'To keep you quiet.'

Mrs Nettlepoint's dinner was served on deck, but I went into the saloon. Jasper was there but not Grace Mavis, as I had half expected. I asked him what had become of her, if she were ill (he must have thought I had an ignoble pertinacity), and he replied that he knew nothing whatever about her. Mrs Peck talked to me about Mrs Nettlepoint and said it had been a great interest to her to see her; only it was a pity she didn't seem more sociable. To this I replied that she had to beg to be excused – she was not well.

'You don't mean to say she's sick, on this pond?'

'No, she's unwell in another way.'

'I guess I know the way!' Mrs Peck laughed. And then she added, 'I suppose she came up to look after her charge.'

'Her charge?'

'Why, Miss Mavis. We've talked enough about that.'

'Quite enough. I don't know what that had to do with it. Miss Mavis hasn't been there to-day.'

'Oh, it goes on all the same.'

'It goes on?'

'Well, it's too late.'

'Too late?'

'Well, you'll see. There'll be a row.'

This was not comforting, but I did not repeat it above. Mrs Nettlepoint returned early to her cabin, professing herself much tired. I know not what 'went on', but Grace Mavis continued not to show. I went in late, to bid Mrs Nettlepoint good-night, and learned from her that the girl had not been to her. She had sent the stewardess to her room for news, to see if she were ill and needed assistance, and the stewardess came back with the information that she was not there. I went above after this; the night was not quite so fair and the deck was almost empty. In a moment Jasper Nettlepoint and our young lady moved past me together. 'I hope you are better!' I called after her; and she replied, over her shoulder –

'Oh, yes, I had a headache; but the air now does me good!'

I went down again – I was the only person there but they, and I wished to not appear to be watching them – and returning to Mrs Nettlepoint's room found (her door was open into the little passage) that she was still sitting up.

'She's all right!' I said. 'She's on the deck with Jasper.'

The old lady looked up at me from her book. 'I didn't know you called that all right.'

'Well, it's better than something else.'

'Something else?'

'Something I was a little afraid of.' Mrs Nettlepoint continued to look at me; she asked me what that was. 'I'll tell you when we are ashore,' I said.

The next day I went to see her, at the usual hour of my morning visit, and found her in considerable agitation. 'The scenes have begun,' she said; 'you know I told you I shouldn't get through without them! You made me nervous last night – I haven't the least idea what you meant; but you made me nervous. She came in to see me an hour ago, and I had the courage to say to her, "I don't know why I shouldn't tell you frankly that I have been scolding my son about you." Of course she asked me what I meant by that, and I said – "It seems to me he drags you about the ship too much, for a girl in your position. He has the air of not remembering that you belong to some one else. There is a kind of want of taste and even of want of respect in it." That produced an explosion; she became very violent.'

'Do you mean angry?'

'Not exactly angry, but very hot and excited – at my presuming to think her relations with my son were not the simplest in the world. I might scold him as much as I liked – that was between ourselves; but she didn't see why I should tell her that I had done so. Did I think she allowed him to treat her with disrespect? That idea was not very complimentary to her! He had treated her better and been kinder to her than most other people – there were very few on the ship that hadn't been insulting. She should be glad enough when she got off it, to her own people, to some one whom no one would have a right to say anything about. What was there in her position that was not perfectly natural? what was the idea of making a fuss about her position? Did I mean that she took it too easily – that she didn't think as much as she ought about Mr Porterfield? Didn't I believe she was attached to him – didn't I believe she was just counting the hours until she saw him? That would be the happiest moment of her life. It showed how little I knew her, if I thought anything else.'

'All that must have been rather fine – I should have liked to hear it,' I said. 'And what did you reply?'

'Oh, I grovelled; I told her that I accused her (as regards my son) of nothing worse than an excess of good nature. She helped him to pass his time – he ought to be immensely obliged. Also that it would be a very happy moment for me too when I should hand her over to Mr Porterfield.'

'And will you come up to-day?'

'No indeed – she'll do very well now.'

I gave a sigh of relief. 'All's well that ends well!'

Jasper, that day, spent a great deal of time with his mother. She had told me that she really had had no proper opportunity to talk over with him their movements after disembarking. Everything changes a little, the last two or three days of a voyage; the spell is broken and new combinations take place. Grace Mavis was neither on deck nor at dinner, and I drew Mrs Peck's attention to the extreme propriety with which she now conducted herself. She had spent the day in meditation and she judged it best to continue to meditate.

'Ah, she's afraid,' said my implacable neighbour.

'Afraid of what?'

'Well, that we'll tell tales when we get there.'

'Whom do you mean by "we"?'

'Well, there are plenty, on a ship like this.'

'Well then, we won't.'

'Maybe we won't have the chance,' said the dreadful little woman.

'Oh, at that moment a universal geniality reigns.'

'Well, she's afraid, all the same.'

'So much the better.'

'Yes, so much the better.'

All the next day, too, the girl remained invisible and Mrs Nettlepoint told me that she had not been in to see her. She had inquired by the stewardess if she would receive her in her own cabin, and Grace Mavis had replied that it was littered up with things and unfit for visitors: she was packing a trunk over. Jasper made up for his devotion to his mother the day before by now spending a great deal of his time in the smoking-room. I wanted to say to him 'This is much better,' but I thought it wiser to hold my tongue. Indeed I had begun to feel the emotion of prospective arrival (I was delighted to be almost back in my dear old Europe again) and had less to spare for other matters. It will doubtless appear to the critical reader that I had already devoted far too much to the little episode of which my story gives an account, but to this I can only reply that the event justified me. We sighted land, the dim yet rich coast of Ireland, about sunset and I leaned on the edge of the ship and looked at it. 'It doesn't look like much, does it?' I heard a voice say, beside me; and turning, I found Grace Mavis was there. Almost for the first time she had her veil up, and I thought her very pale.

'It will be more to-morrow,' I said.

'Oh yes, a great deal more.'

'The first sight of land, at sea, changes everything,' I went on. 'I always think it's like waking up from a dream. It's a return to reality.'

For a moment she made no response to this; then she said, 'It doesn't look very real yet.'

'No, and meanwhile, this lovely evening, the dream is still present.'

She looked up at the sky, which had a brightness, though the light of the sun had left it and that of the stars had not come out. 'It *is* a lovely evening.'

'Oh yes, with this we shall do.'

She stood there a while longer, while the growing dusk effaced the line of the land more rapidly than our progress made it distinct. She said nothing more, she only looked in front of her; but her very quietness made me want to say some-thing suggestive of sympathy and service. I was unable to think what to say – some things seemed too wide of the mark and others too importunate. At last, unexpectedly, she appeared to give me my chance. Irrelevantly, abruptly she broke out:

'Didn't you tell me that you knew Mr Porterfield?'

'Dear me, yes – I used to see him. I have often wanted to talk to you about him.'

She turned her face upon me and in the deepened evening I fancied she looked whiter. 'What good would that do?'

'Why, it would be a pleasure,' I replied, rather foolishly.

'Do you mean for you?'

'Well, yes – call it that,' I said, smiling.

'Did you know him so well?'

My smile became a laugh and I said – 'You are not easy to make speeches to.'

'I hate speeches!' The words came from her lips with a violence that surprised me; they were loud and hard. But before I had time to wonder at it she went on – 'Shall you know him when you see him?'

'Perfectly, I think.' Her manner was so strange that one had to notice it in some way, and it appeared to me the best way was to notice it jocularly; so I added, 'Shan't you?'

'Oh, perhaps you'll point him out!' And she walked quickly away. As I looked after her I had a singular, a perverse and rather an embarrassed sense of having, during the previous days, and especially in speaking to Jasper Nettlepoint, inter-fered with her situation to her loss. I had a sort of pang in seeing her move about alone; I felt somehow responsible for it and asked myself why I could not have kept my hands off. I had seen Jasper in the smoking-room more than once that day, as I passed it, and half an hour before this I had observed, through the open door, that he was there. He had been with her so much that without him she had a bereaved, forsaken air. It was better, no doubt, but superficially it made her rather pitiable. Mrs Peck would have told me that their separation was gammon; they didn't show together on deck and in the saloon, but they made it up elsewhere. The secret places on shipboard are not numerous; Mrs Peck's 'elsewhere' would have been vague and I know not what licence her imagination took. It was distinct that Jasper had fallen off, but of course what had passed between them on this subject was not so and could never be. Later, through his mother, I had *his* version of that, but I may remark that I didn't believe it. Poor Mrs Nettlepoint did, of course. I was almost capable, after the girl had left me, of going to my young man and saying, 'After all, do return to her a little, just till we get in! It won't make any difference after we land.' And I don't think it was the fear he would tell me I was an idiot that prevented me. At any rate the next time I passed the door of the smoking-room I saw that he had left it. I paid my usual visit to Mrs Nettlepoint that night, but I troubled her no further about Miss Mavis. She had made up her mind that everything was smooth and settled now, and it seemed to me that I had worried her and that she had worried herself enough. I left her to enjoy the foretaste of arrival, which had taken possession of her mind. Before turning in I went above and found more passengers on deck than I had ever seen so late. Jasper was walking about among them alone, but I forebore to join him. The coast of Ireland had disappeared, but the night and the sea were perfect. On the way to my cabin, when I came down, I met the stewardess in one of the passages and the idea entered my head to say to her – 'Do you happen to know where Miss Mavis is?'

'Why, she's in her room, sir, at this hour.'

'Do you suppose I could speak to her?' It had come into my mind to ask her why she had inquired of me whether I should recognise Mr Porterfield.

'No, sir,' said the stewardess; 'she has gone to bed.'

'That's all right.' And I followed the young lady's excellent example.

The next morning, while I was dressing, the steward of my side of the ship came to me as usual to see what I wanted. But the first thing he said to me was – 'Rather a bad job, sir – a passenger missing.'

'A passenger – missing?'

'A lady, sir. I think you knew her. Miss Mavis, sir.'

'*Missing*?' I cried – staring at him, horror-stricken.

'She's not on the ship. They can't find her.'

'Then where to God is she?'

I remember his queer face. 'Well sir, I suppose you know that as well as I.'

'Do you mean she has jumped overboard?'

'Some time in the night, sir – on the quiet. But it's beyond every one, the way she escaped notice. They usually sees 'em, sir. It must have been about half-past two. Lord, but she was clever, sir. She didn't so much as make a splash. They say she '*ad* come against her will, sir.'

I had dropped upon my sofa – I felt faint. The man went on, liking to talk, as persons of his class do when they have something horrible to tell. She usually rang for the stewardess early, but this morning of course there had been no ring. The stewardess had gone in all the same about eight o'clock and found the cabin empty. That was about an hour ago. Her things were there in confusion – the things she usually wore when she went above. The stewardess thought she had been rather strange last night, but she waited a little and then went back. Miss Mavis hadn't turned up – and she didn't turn up. The stewardess began to look for her – she hadn't been seen on deck or in the saloon. Besides, she wasn't dressed – not to show herself; all her clothes were in her room. There was another lady, an old lady, Mrs Nettlepoint – I would know her – that she was sometimes with, but the stewardess had been with *her* and she knew Miss Mavis had not come near her that morning. She had spoken to *him* and they had taken a quiet look – they had hunted everywhere. A ship's a big place, but you do come to the end of it, and if a person ain't there why they ain't. In short an hour had passed and the young lady was not accounted for: from which I might judge if she ever would be. The watch couldn't account for her, but no doubt the fishes in the sea could – poor miserable lady! The stewardess and he, they had of course thought it their duty very soon to speak to the doctor, and the doctor had spoken immediately to the captain. The captain didn't like it – they never did. But he would try to keep it quiet – they always did.

By the time I succeeded in pulling myself together and getting on, after a fashion, the rest of my clothes I had learned that Mrs Nettlepoint had not yet been informed, unless the stewardess had broken it to her within the previous few minutes. Her son knew, the young gentleman on the other side of the ship (he had the other steward); my man had seen him come out of his cabin and rush above, just before he came in to me. He *had* gone above, my man was sure; he had not gone to the old lady's cabin. I remember a queer vision when the steward told me this – the wild flash of a picture of Jasper Nettlepoint leaping with a mad compunction in his young agility over the side of the ship. I hasten to add that no such incident was destined to contribute its horror to poor Grace Mavis's mysterious tragic act. What followed was miserable enough, but I can only glance at it. When I got to Mrs Nettlepoint's door she was there in her dressing-gown; the stewardess had just told her and she was rushing out to come to me. I made her go back – I said I would go for Jasper. I went for him but I missed him, partly no doubt because it was really, at first, the captain I was after. I found this personage and found him highly scandalised, but he gave me no hope that we were in error, and his displeasure, expressed with seamanlike plainness, was a definite settlement of the question. From the deck, where I merely turned round and looked, I saw the light of another summer day, the coast of Ireland green and near and the sea a more charming colour than it had been at all. When I came below again Jasper had passed back; he had gone to his cabin and his mother had joined him there. He remained there till we reached Liverpool – I never saw him. His mother, after a little, at his request, left him alone. All the world went above to look at the land and chatter about our tragedy, but the poor lady spent the day, dismally enough, in her room. It seemed to me intolerably long; I was thinking so of vague Porterfield and of my prospect of having to face him on the morrow. Now of course I knew why she had asked me if I should recognise him; she had delegated to me mentally a certain pleasant office. I gave Mrs Peck and Mrs Gotch a wide berth – I couldn't talk to them. I could, or at least I did a little, to Mrs Nettlepoint, but with too many reserves for comfort on either side, for I foresaw that it would not in the least do now to mention Jasper to her. I was obliged to assume by my silence that he had had nothing to do with what had happened; and of course I never really ascertained what he *had* had to do. The secret of what passed between him and the strange girl who would have sacrificed her marriage to him on so short an acquaintance remains shut up in his breast. His mother, I know, went to his door from time to time, but he refused her admission. That evening, to be human at a venture, I requested the steward to go in and ask him if he should care to see me, and the attendant returned with an answer which he candidly transmitted. 'Not in the least!' Jasper apparently was almost as scandalised as the captain.

At Liverpool, at the dock, when we had touched, twenty people came on board, and I had already made out Mr Porterfield at a distance. He was looking up at the side of the great vessel with disappointment written (to my eyes) in his face – disappointment at not seeing the woman he loved lean over it and wave her handkerchief to him. Every one was looking at him, every one but she (his identity flew about in a moment) and I wondered if he did not observe it. He used to be lean, he had grown almost fat. The interval between us diminished – he was on the plank and then on the deck with the jostling officers of the customs – all too soon for my equanimity. I met him instantly however, laid my hand on him and drew him away, though I perceived that he had no impression of having seen me before. It was not till afterwards that I thought this a little stupid of him. I drew him far away (I was conscious of Mrs Peck and Mrs Gotch looking at us as we passed) into the empty, stale smoking-room; he remained speechless, and that struck me as like him. I had to speak first, he could not even relieve me by saying 'Is anything the matter?' I told him first that she was ill. It was an odious moment.

THE PUPIL

I

THE poor young man hesitated and procrastinated: it cost him such an effort to broach the subject of terms, to speak of money to a person who spoke only of feelings and, as it were, of the aristocracy. Yet he was unwilling to take leave, treating his engagement as settled, without some more conventional glance in that direction than he could find an opening for in the manner of the large, affable lady who sat there drawing a pair of soiled *gants de Suède* through a fat, jewelled hand and, at once pressing and gliding, repeated over and over everything but the thing he would have liked to hear. He would have liked to hear the figure of his salary; but just as he was nervously about to sound that note the little boy came back – the little boy Mrs Moreen had sent out of the room to fetch her fan. He came back without the fan, only with the casual observation that he couldn't find it. As he dropped this cynical confession he looked straight and hard at the candidate for the honour of taking his education in hand. This personage reflected, somewhat grimly, that the first thing he should have to teach his little charge would be to appear to address himself to his mother when he spoke to her – especially not to make her such an improper answer as that.

When Mrs Moreen bethought herself of this pretext for getting rid of their companion, Pemberton supposed it was precisely to approach the delicate subject of his remuneration. But it had been only to say some things about her son which it was better that a boy of eleven shouldn't catch. They were extravagantly to his advantage, save when she lowered her voice to sigh, tapping her left side familiarly: 'And all over-clouded by *this*, you know – all at the mercy of a weakness –!' Pemberton gathered that the weakness was in the region of the heart. He had known the poor child was not robust: this was the basis on which he had been invited to treat, through an English lady, an Oxford acquaintance, then at Nice, who happened to know both his needs and those of the amiable American family looking out for something really superior in the way of a resident tutor.

The young man's impression of his prospective pupil, who had first come into the room, as if to see for himself, as soon as Pemberton was admitted, was not quite the soft solicitation the visitor had taken for granted. Morgan Moreen was, somehow, sickly without being delicate, and that he looked intelligent (it is true Pemberton wouldn't have enjoyed his being stupid), only added to the suggestion that, as with his big mouth and big ears he really couldn't be called pretty, he might be unpleasant. Pemberton was modest – he was even timid; and the chance that his small scholar might prove cleverer than himself had quite figured, to his nervousness, among the dangers of an untried experiment. He reflected, however, that these were risks one had to run when one accepted a position, as it was called, in a private family; when as yet one's University honours had, pecuniarily speaking, remained barren. At any rate, when Mrs Moreen got up as if to intimate that, since it was understood he would enter upon his duties within the week she would let him off now, he succeeded, in spite of the presence of the child, in squeezing out a phrase about the rate of payment. It was not the fault of the conscious smile which seemed a reference to the lady's expensive identity, if the allusion did not sound rather vulgar. This was exactly because she became still more gracious to reply: 'Oh! I can assure you that all that will be quite regular.'

Pemberton only wondered, while he took up his hat, what 'all that' was to amount to – people had such different ideas. Mrs Moreen's words, however, seemed to commit the family to a pledge definite enough to elicit from the child a strange little comment, in the shape of the mocking, foreign ejaculation, 'Oh, là-là!'

Pemberton, in some confusion, glanced at him as he walked slowly to the window with his back turned, his hands in his pockets and the air in his elderly shoulders of a boy who didn't play. The young man wondered if he could teach him to play, though his mother had said it would never do and that this was why school was impossible. Mrs Moreen exhibited no discomfiture; she only continued blandly: 'Mr Moreen will be delighted to meet your wishes. As I told you, he has been called to London for a week. As soon as he comes back you shall have it out with him.'

This was so frank and friendly that the young man could only reply, laughing as his hostess laughed: 'Oh! I don't imagine we shall have much of a battle.'

'They'll give you anything you like,' the boy remarked unexpectedly, returning from the window. 'We don't mind what anything costs – we live awfully well.'

'My darling, you're too quaint!' his mother exclaimed, putting out to caress him a practised but ineffectual hand. He slipped out of it, but looked with intelligent, innocent eyes at Pemberton, who had already had time to notice that from one moment to the other his small satiric face seemed to change its time of life. At this moment it was infantine; yet it appeared also to be under the influence of curious intuitions and knowledges. Pemberton rather disliked precocity, and he was disappointed to find gleams of it in a disciple not yet in his teens. Nevertheless he divined on the spot that Morgan wouldn't prove a bore. He would prove on the contrary a kind of excitement. This idea held the young man, in spite of a certain repulsion.

'You pompous little person! We're not extravagant!' Mrs Moreen gaily protested, making another unsuccessful attempt to draw the boy to her side. 'You must know what to expect,' she went on to Pemberton.

'The less you expect the better!' her companion interposed. 'But we *are* people of fashion.'

'Only so far as *you* make us so!' Mrs Moreen mocked, tenderly. 'Well, then, on Friday – don't tell me you're superstitious – and mind you don't fail us. Then you'll see us all. I'm so sorry the girls are out. I guess you'll like the girls. And, you know, I've another son, quite different from this one.'

'He tries to imitate me,' said Morgan to Pemberton.

'He tries? Why, he's twenty years old!' cried Mrs Moreen.

'You're very witty,' Pemberton remarked to the child – a proposition that his mother echoed with enthusiasm, declaring that Morgan's sallies were the delight of the house. The boy paid no heed to this; he only inquired abruptly of the visitor, who was surprised afterwards that he hadn't struck him as offensively forward: 'Do you *want* very much to come?'

'Can you doubt it, after such a description of what I shall hear?' Pemberton replied. Yet he didn't want to come at all; he was coming because he had to go somewhere, thanks to the collapse of his fortune at the end of a year abroad, spent on the system of putting his tiny patrimony into a single full wave of experience. He had had his full wave, but he couldn't pay his hotel bill. Moreover, he had caught in the boy's eyes the glimpse of a far-off appeal.

'Well, I'll do the best I can for you,' said Morgan; with which he turned away again. He passed out of one of the long windows; Pemberton saw him go and lean on the parapet of the terrace. He remained there while the young man took leave of his mother, who, on Pemberton's looking as if he expected a farewell from him, interposed with: 'Leave him, leave him; he's so strange!' Pemberton suspected she was afraid of something he might say. 'He's a genius – you'll love him!' she added. 'He's much the most interesting person in the family.' And before he could invent some civility to oppose to this, she wound up with: 'But we're all good, you know!'

'He's a genius – you'll love him!' were words that recurred to Pemberton before the Friday, suggesting, among other things that geniuses were not invariably lovable. However, it was all the better if there was an element that would make tutorship absorbing: he had perhaps taken too much for granted that it would be dreary. As he left the villa after his interview, he looked up at the balcony and saw the child leaning over it. 'We shall have great larks!' he called up.

Morgan hesitated a moment: then he answered, laughing: 'By the time you come back I shall have thought of something witty!'

This made Pemberton say to himself: 'After all he's rather nice.'

II

ON the Friday he saw them all, as Mrs Moreen had promised, for her husband had come back and the girls and the other son were at home. Mr Moreen had a white moustache, a confiding manner and, in his buttonhole, the ribbon of a foreign order – bestowed, as Pemberton eventually learned, for services. For what services he never clearly ascertained: this was a point – one of a large number – that Mr Moreen's manner never confided. What it emphatically did confide was that he was a man of the world. Ulick, the firstborn, was in visible training for the same profession – under the disadvantage as yet, however, of a buttonhole only feebly floral and a moustache with no pretensions to type. The girls had hair and figures and manners and small fat feet, but had never been out alone. As for Mrs Moreen, Pemberton saw on a nearer view that her elegance was intermittent and her parts didn't always match. Her husband, as she had promised, met with enthusiasm Pemberton's ideas in regard to a salary. The young man had endeavoured to make them modest, and Mr Moreen confided to him that *he* found them positively meagre. He further assured him that he aspired to be intimate with his children, to be their best friend, and that he was always looking out for them. That was what he went off for, to London and other places – to look out; and this vigilance was the theory of life, as well as the real occupation, of the whole family. They all looked out, for they were very frank on the subject of its being necessary. They desired it to be understood that they were earnest people, and also that their fortune, though quite adequate for earnest people, required the most careful admin- istration. Mr Moreen, as the parent bird, sought sustenance for the nest. Ulick found sustenance mainly at the club, where Pemberton guessed that it was usually served on green cloth. The girls used to do up their hair and their frocks themselves, and our young man felt appealed to to be glad, in regard to Morgan's education, that, though it must naturally be of the best, it didn't cost too much. After a little he *was* glad, forgetting at times his own needs in the interest inspired by the child's nature and education and the pleasure of making easy terms for him.

During the first weeks of their acquaintance Morgan had been as puzzling as a page in an unknown language – altogether different from the obvious little Anglo-Saxons who had misrepresented childhood to Pemberton. Indeed the whole mystic volume in which the boy had been bound demanded some practice in translation. To-day, after a considerable interval, there is something phantasmagoric, like a prismatic reflection or a serial novel, in Pemberton's memory of the queerness of the Moreens. If it were not for a few tangible tokens – a lock of Morgan's hair, cut by his own hand, and the half-dozen letters he got from him when they were separated – the whole episode and the figures peopling it would seem too inconsequent for anything but dreamland. The queerest thing about them was their success (as it appeared to him for a while at the time), for he had never seen a family so brilliantly equipped for failure. Wasn't it success to have kept him so hatefully long? Wasn't it success to have drawn him in that first morning at *déjeuner*, the Friday he came – it was enough to *make* one superstitious – so that he utterly committed himself, and this not by calculation or a *mot d'ordre*, but by a happy instinct which made them, like a band of gipsies, work so neatly together? They amused him as much as if they had really been a band of gipsies. He was still young and had not seen much of the world – his English years had been intensely usual; therefore the reversed conventions of the Moreens (for they had their standards), struck him as topsyturvy. He had encountered nothing like them at Oxford; still less had any such note been struck to his younger American ear during the four years at Yale in which he had richly supposed himself to be reacting against Puritanism. The reaction of the Moreens, at any rate, went ever so much further. He had thought himself very clever that first day in hitting them all off in his mind with the term 'cosmopolite'. Later, it seemed feeble and colourless enough – confessedly, helplessly provisional.

However, when he first applied it to them he had a degree of joy – for an instructor he was still empirical – as if from the apprehension that to live with them would really be to see life.

Their sociable strangeness was an intimation of that – their chatter of tongues, their gaiety and good humour, their infinite dawdling (they were always getting themselves up, but it took forever, and Pemberton had once found Mr Moreen shaving in the drawing-room), their French, their Italian and, in the spiced fluency, their cold, tough slices of American. They lived on macaroni and coffee (they had these articles prepared in perfection), but they knew recipes for a hundred other dishes. They overflowed with music and song, were always humming and catching each other up, and had a kind of professional acquaintance with continental cities. They talked of 'good places' as if they had been strolling players. They had at Nice a villa, a carriage, a piano and a banjo, and they went to official parties. They were a perfect calendar of the 'days' of their friends, which Pemberton knew them, when they were indisposed, to get out of bed to go to, and which made the week larger than life when Mrs Moreen talked of them with Paula and Amy. Their romantic initiations gave their new inmate at first an almost dazzling sense of culture. Mrs Moreen had translated something, at some former period – an author whom it made Pemberton feel *borné* never to have heard of. They could imitate Venetian and sing Neapolitan, and when they wanted to say something very particular they communicated with each other in an ingenious dialect of their own – a sort of spoken cipher, which Pemberton at first took for Volapuk, but which he learned to understand as he would not have understood Volapuk.

'It's the family language – Ultramoreen,' Morgan explained to him drolly enough; but the boy rarely condescended to use it himself, though he attempted colloquial Latin as if he had been a little prelate.

Among all the 'days' with which Mrs Moreen's memory was taxed she managed to squeeze in one of her own, which her friends sometimes forgot. But the house derived a frequented air from the number of fine people who were freely named there and from several mysterious men with foreign titles and English clothes whom Morgan called the princes and who, on sofas with the girls, talked French very loud, as if to show they were saying nothing improper. Pemberton wondered how the princes could ever propose in that tone and so publicly: he took for granted cynically that this was what was desired of them. Then he acknowledged that even for the chance of such an advantage Mrs Moreen would never allow Paula and Amy to receive alone. These young ladies were not at all timid, but it was just the safeguards that made them so graceful. It was a houseful of Bohemians who wanted tremendously to be Philistines.

In one respect, however, certainly, they achieved no rigour – they were wonderfully amiable and ecstatic about Morgan. It was a genuine tenderness, an artless admiration, equally strong in each. They even praised his beauty, which was small, and were rather afraid of him, as if they recognised that he was of a finer clay. They called him a little angel and a little prodigy and pitied his want of health effusively. Pemberton feared at first that their extravagance would make him hate the boy, but before this happened he had become extravagant himself. Later, when he had grown rather to hate the others, it was a bribe to patience for him that they were at any rate nice about Morgan, going on tiptoe if they fancied he was showing symptoms, and even giving up somebody's 'day' to procure him a pleasure. But mixed with this was the oddest wish to make him independent, as if they felt that they were not good enough for him. They passed him over to Pemberton very much as if they wished to force a constructive adoption on the obliging bachelor and shirk altogether a responsibility. They were delighted when they perceived that Morgan liked his preceptor, and could think of no higher praise for the young man. It was strange how they contrived to reconcile the appearance, and indeed the essential fact, of adoring the child with their eagerness to wash their hands of him. Did they want to get rid of him before he should find them out? Pemberton was finding them out month by month. At any rate, the boy's relations turned their backs with exaggerated delicacy, as if to escape the charge of interfering. Seeing in time how little he had in common with them (it was by *them* he first observed it – they proclaimed it with complete humility), his preceptor was moved to speculate on the mysteries of transmission, the far jumps of heredity. Where his detachment from most of the things they represented had come from was more than an observer could say – it certainly had burrowed under two or three generations.

As for Pemberton's own estimate of his pupil, it was a good while before he got the point of view, so little had he been prepared for it by the smug young barbarians to whom the tradition of tutorship, as hitherto revealed to him, had been adjusted. Morgan was scrappy and surprising, deficient in many properties supposed common to the *genus* and abounding in others that were the portion only of the supernaturally clever. One day Pemberton made a great stride: it cleared up the question to perceive that Morgan *was* supernaturally clever and that, though the formula was temporarily meagre, this would be the only assumption on which one could successfully deal with him. He had the general quality of a child for whom life had not been simplified by school, a kind of home-bred sensibility which might have been bad for himself but was charming for others, and a whole range of refinement and perception – little musical vibrations as taking as picked-up airs – begotten by wandering about Europe at the tail of his migratory tribe. This might not have been an education to recommend in advance, but its results with Morgan were as palpable as a fine texture. At the same time he had in his composition a sharp spice of stoicism, doubtless the fruit of having had to begin early to bear pain, which produced the impression of pluck and made it of less consequence that he might have been thought at school rather a polyglot little beast. Pemberton indeed quickly found himself rejoicing that school was out of the question: in any million of boys it was probably good for all but one, and Morgan was that millionth. It would have made him comparative and superior – it might have made him priggish. Pemberton would try to be school himself – a bigger seminary than five hundred grazing donkeys; so that, winning no prizes, the boy would remain unconscious and irresponsible and amusing – amusing, because, though life was already intense in his childish nature, freshness still made there a strong draught for jokes. It turned out that even in the still air of Morgan's various disabilities jokes flourished greatly. He was a pale, lean, acute, undeveloped little cosmopolite, who liked intellectual gymnastics and who, also, as regards the behaviour of mankind, had noticed more things than you might suppose, but who nevertheless had his proper playroom of superstitions, where he smashed a dozen toys a day.

III

At Nice once, towards evening, as the pair sat resting in the open air after a walk, looking over the sea at the pink western lights, Morgan said suddenly to his companion: 'Do you like it – you know, being with us all in this intimate way?'

'My dear fellow, why should I stay if I didn't?'

'How do I know you will stay? I'm almost sure you won't, very long.'

'I hope you don't mean to dismiss me,' said Pemberton.

Morgan considered a moment, looking at the sunset. 'I think if I did right I ought to.'

'Well, I know I'm supposed to instruct you in virtue; but in that case don't do right.'

'You're very young – fortunately,' Morgan went on, turning to him again.

'Oh yes, compared with you!'

'Therefore, it won't matter so much if you do lose a lot of time.'

'That's the way to look at it,' said Pemberton accommodatingly.

They were silent a minute; after which the boy asked: 'Do you like my father and mother very much?'

'Dear me, yes. They're charming people.'

Morgan received this with another silence; then, unexpectedly, familiarly, but at the same time affectionately, he remarked: 'You're a jolly old humbug!'

For a particular reason the words made Pemberton change colour. The boy noticed in an instant that he had turned red, whereupon he turned red himself and the pupil and the master exchanged a longish glance in which there was a consciousness of many more things than are usually touched upon, even tacitly, in such a relation. It produced for Pemberton an embarrassment; it raised, in a shadowy form, a question (this was the first glimpse of it), which was destined to play a singular and, as he imagined, owing to the altogether peculiar conditions, an unprecedented part in his intercourse with his little companion. Later, when he found himself talking with this small boy in a way in which few small boys could ever have been talked with, he thought of that clumsy moment on the bench at Nice as the dawn of an understanding that had broadened. What had added to the clumsiness then was that he thought it his duty to declare to Morgan that he might abuse him (Pemberton) as much as he liked, but must never abuse his parents. To this Morgan had the easy reply that he hadn't dreamed of abusing them; which appeared to be true: it put Pemberton in the wrong.

'Then why am I a humbug for saying *I* think them charming?' the young man asked, conscious of a certain rashness.

'Well – they're not *your* parents.'

'They love you better than anything in the world – never forget that,' said Pemberton.

'Is that why you like them so much?'

'They're very kind to me,' Pemberton replied, evasively.

'You *are* a humbug!' laughed Morgan, passing an arm into his tutor's. He leaned against him, looking off at the sea again and swinging his long, thin legs.

'Don't kick my shins,' said Pemberton, while he reflected: 'Hang it, I can't complain of them to the child!'

'There's another reason, too,' Morgan went on, keeping his legs still.

'Another reason for what?'

'Besides their not being your parents.'

'I don't understand you,' said Pemberton.

'Well, you will before long. All right!'

Pemberton did understand, fully, before long; but he made a fight even with himself before he confessed it. He thought it the oddest thing to have a struggle with the child about. He wondered he didn't detest the child for launching him in such a struggle. But by the time it began the resource of detesting the child was closed to him. Morgan was a special case, but to know him was to accept him on his own odd terms. Pemberton had spent his aversion to special cases before arriving at knowledge. When at last he did arrive he felt that he was in an extreme predicament. Against every interest he had attached himself. They would have to meet things together. Before they went home that evening, at Nice, the boy had said, clinging to his arm:

'Well, at any rate you'll hang on to the last.'

'To the last?'

'Till you're fairly beaten.'

'*You* ought to be fairly beaten!' cried the young man, drawing him closer.

IV

A YEAR after Pemberton had come to live with them Mr and Mrs Moreen suddenly gave up the villa at Nice. Pemberton had got used to suddenness, having seen it practised on a considerable scale during two jerky little tours – one in Switzerland the first summer, and the other late in the winter, when they all ran down to Florence and then, at the end of ten days, liking it much less than they had intended, straggled back in mysterious depression. They had returned to Nice 'for ever', as they said; but this didn't prevent them from squeezing, one rainy, muggy May night, into a second-class railway-carriage – you could never tell by which class they would travel – where Pemberton helped them to stow away a wonderful collection of bundles and bags. The explanation of this manoeuvre was that they had determined to spend the summer 'in some bracing place'; but in Paris they dropped into a small furnished apartment – a fourth floor in a third-rate avenue, where there was a smell on the staircase and the *portier* was hateful – and passed the next four months in blank indigence.

The better part of this baffled sojourn was for the preceptor and his pupil, who, visiting the Invalides and Notre Dame, the

Conciergerie and all the museums, took a hundred remunerative rambles. They learned to know their Paris, which was useful, for they came back another year for a longer stay, the general character of which in Pemberton's memory to-day mixes pitiably and confusedly with that of the first. He sees Morgan's shabby knickerbockers – the everlasting pair that didn't match his blouse and that as he grew longer could only grow faded. He remembers the particular holes in his three or four pair of coloured stockings.

Morgan was dear to his mother, but he never was better dressed than was absolutely necessary – partly, no doubt, by his own fault, for he was as indifferent to his appearance as a German philosopher. 'My dear fellow, you *are* coming to pieces,' Pemberton would say to him in sceptical remonstrance; to which the child would reply, looking at him serenely up and down: 'My dear fellow, so are you! I don't want to cast you in the shade.' Pemberton could have no rejoinder for this – the assertion so closely represented the fact. If, however, the deficiencies of his own wardrobe were a chapter by themselves he didn't like his little charge to look too poor. Later he used to say: 'Well, if we are poor, why, after all, shouldn't we look it?' and he consoled himself with thinking there was something rather elderly and gentlemanly in Morgan's seediness – it differed from the untidiness of the urchin who plays and spoils his things. He could trace perfectly the degrees by which, in proportion as her little son confined himself to his tutor for society, Mrs Moreen shrewdly forbore to renew his garments. She did nothing that didn't show, neglected him because he escaped notice, and then, as he illustrated this clever policy, discouraged at home his public appearances. Her position was logical enough – those members of her family who did show had to be showy.

During this period and several others Pemberton was quite aware of how he and his comrade might strike people; wandering languidly through the Jardin des Plantes as if they had nowhere to go, sitting, on the winter days, in the galleries of the Louvre, so splendidly ironical to the homeless, as if for the advantage of the *calorifère*. They joked about it sometimes: it was the sort of joke that was perfectly within the boy's compass. They figured themselves as part of the vast, vague, hand-to-mouth multitude of the enormous city and pretended they were proud of their position in it – it showed them such a lot of life and made them conscious of a sort of democratic brotherhood. If Pemberton could not feel a sympathy in destitution with his small companion (for after all Morgan's fond parents would never have let him really suffer), the boy would at least feel it with him, so it came to the same thing. He used sometimes to wonder what people would think they were – fancy they were looked askance at, as if it might be a suspected case of kidnapping. Morgan wouldn't be taken for a young patrician with a preceptor – he wasn't smart enough; though he might pass for his companion's sickly little brother. Now and then he had a five-franc piece, and except once, when they bought a couple of lovely neckties, one of which he made Pemberton accept, they laid it out scientifically in old books. It was a great day, always spent on the quays, rummaging among the dusty boxes that garnish the parapets. These were occasions that helped them to live, for their books ran low very soon after the beginning of their acquaintance. Pemberton had a good many in England, but he was obliged to write to a friend and ask him kindly to get some fellow to give him something for them.

If the bracing climate was untasted that summer the young man had an idea that at the moment they were about to make a push the cup had been dashed from their lips by a movement of his own. It had been his first blow-out, as he called it, with his patrons; his first successful attempt (though there was little other success about it), to bring them to a consideration of his impossible position. As the ostensible eve of a costly journey the moment struck him as a good one to put in a signal protest – to present an ultimatum. Ridiculous as it sounded he had never yet been able to compass an uninterrupted private interview with the elder pair or with either of them singly. They were always flanked by their elder children, and poor Pemberton usually had his own little charge at his side. He was conscious of its being a house in which the surface of one's delicacy got rather smudged; nevertheless he had kept the bloom of his scruple against announcing to Mr and Mrs Moreen with publicity that he couldn't go on longer without a little money. He was still simple enough to suppose Ulick and Paula and Amy might not know that since his arrival he had only had a hundred and forty francs; and he was magnanimous enough to wish not to compromise their parents in their eyes. Mr Moreen now listened to him, as he listened to every one and to everything, like a man of the world, and seemed to appeal to him – though not of course too grossly – to try and be a little more of one himself. Pemberton recognised the importance of the character from the advantage it gave Mr Moreen. He was not even confused, whereas poor Pemberton was more so than there was any reason for. Neither was he surprised – at least any more than a gentleman had to be who freely confessed himself a little shocked, though not, strictly, at Pemberton.

'We must go into this, mustn't we, dear?' he said to his wife. He assured his young friend that the matter should have his very best attention; and he melted into space as elusively as if, at the door, he were taking an inevitable but deprecatory precedence. When, the next moment, Pemberton found himself alone with Mrs Moreen it was to hear her say: 'I see, I see,' stroking the roundness of her chin and looking as if she were only hesitating between a dozen easy remedies. If they didn't make their push Mr Moreen could at least disappear for several days. During his absence his wife took up the subject again spontaneously, but her contribution to it was merely that she had thought all the while they were getting on so beautifully. Pemberton's reply to this revelation was that unless they immediately handed him a substantial sum he would leave them for ever. He knew she would wonder how he would get away, and for a moment expected her to inquire. She didn't, for which he was almost grateful to her, so little was he in a position to tell.

'You won't, you know you won't – you're too interested,' she said. 'You *are* interested, you know you are, you dear, kind man!' She laughed, with almost condemnatory archness, as if it were a reproach (but she wouldn't insist), while she flirted a soiled pocket-handkerchief at him.

Pemberton's mind was fully made up to quit the house the following week. This would give him time to get an answer to a letter he had despatched to England. If he did nothing of the sort – that is, if he stayed another year and then went away only for three months – it was not merely because before the answer to his letter came (most unsatisfactory when it did arrive), Mr Moreen generously presented him – again with all the precautions of a man of the world – three hundred francs. He was exasperated to find that Mrs Moreen was right, that he couldn't bear to leave the child. This stood out clearer for the very reason that, the night of his desperate appeal to his patrons, he had seen fully for the first time where he was. Wasn't it another proof of the success with which those patrons practised their arts that they had managed to avert for so long the illuminating flash? It descended upon Pemberton with a luridness which perhaps would have struck a spectator as comically excessive, after he had returned to his little servile room, which looked into a close court where a bare, dirty opposite wall took, with the sound of shrill clatter, the reflection of lighted back-windows. He had simply given himself away to a band of adventurers. The idea, the word itself, had a sort of romantic horror for him – he had always lived on such safe lines. Later it assumed a more interesting, almost a soothing, sense: it pointed a moral, and Pemberton could enjoy a moral. The Moreens were adventurers not merely because they didn't pay their debts, because they lived on society, but because their whole view of life, dim and confused and instinctive, like that of clever colour-blind animals, was speculative and rapacious and mean. Oh! they were 'respectable', and that only made them more *immondes*. The young man's analysis of them put it at last very simply – they were adventurers because they were abject snobs. That was the completest account of them – it was the law of their being. Even when this truth became vivid to their ingenious inmate he remained unconscious of how much his mind had been prepared for it by the extraordinary little boy who had now become such a complication in his life. Much less could he then calculate on the information he was still to owe to the extraordinary little boy.

V

BUT it was during the ensuing time that the real problem came up – the problem of how far it was excusable to discuss the turpitude of parents with a child of twelve, of thirteen, of fourteen. Absolutely inexcusable and quite impossible it of course at first appeared; and indeed the question didn't press for a while after Pemberton had received his three hundred francs. They produced a sort of lull, a relief from the sharpest pressure. Pemberton frugally amended his wardrobe and even had a few francs in his pocket. He thought the Moreens looked at him as if he were almost too smart, as if they ought to take care not to spoil him. If Mr Moreen hadn't been such a man of the world he would perhaps have said something to him about his neckties. But Mr Moreen was always enough a man of the world to let things pass – he had certainly shown that. It was singular how Pemberton guessed that Morgan, though saying nothing about it, knew something had happened. But three hundred francs, especially when one owed money, couldn't last for ever; and when they were gone – the boy knew when they were gone – Morgan did say something. The party had returned to Nice at the beginning of the winter, but not to the charming villa. They went to an hotel, where they stayed three months, and then they went to another hotel, explaining that they had left the first because they had waited and waited and couldn't get the rooms they wanted. These apartments, the rooms they wanted, were generally very splendid; but fortunately they never *could* get them – fortunately, I mean, for Pemberton, who reflected always that if they had got them there would have been still less for educational expenses. What Morgan said at last was said suddenly, irrelevantly, when the moment came, in the middle of a lesson, and consisted of the apparently unfeeling words: 'You ought to *filer*, you know – you really ought.'

Pemberton stared. He had learnt enough French slang from Morgan to know that to *filer* meant to go away. 'Ah, my dear fellow, don't turn me off!'

Morgan pulled a Greek lexicon toward him (he used a Greek–German), to look out a word, instead of asking it of Pemberton. 'You can't go on like this, you know.'

'Like what, my boy?'

'You know they don't pay you up,' said Morgan, blushing and turning his leaves.

'Don't pay me?' Pemberton stared again and feigned amazement. 'What on earth put that into your head?'

'It has been there a long time,' the boy replied, continuing his search.

Pemberton was silent, then he went on: 'I say, what are you hunting for? They pay me beautifully.'

'I'm hunting for the Greek for transparent fiction,' Morgan dropped.

'Find that rather for gross impertinence, and disabuse your mind. What do I want of money?'

'Oh, that's another question!'

Pemberton hesitated – he was drawn in different ways. The severely correct thing would have been to tell the boy that such a matter was none of his business and bid him go on with his lines. But they were really too intimate for that; it was not the way he was in the habit of treating him; there had been no reason it should be. On the other hand Morgan had quite lighted on the truth – he really shouldn't be able to keep it up much longer; therefore why not let him know one's real motive for forsaking him? At the same time it wasn't decent to abuse to one's pupil the family of one's pupil; it was better to misrepresent than to do that. So in reply to Morgan's last exclamation he just declared, to dismiss the subject, that he had received several payments.

'I say – I say!' the boy ejaculated, laughing.

'That's all right,' Pemberton insisted. 'Give me your written rendering.'

Morgan pushed a copybook across the table, and his companion began to read the page, but with something running in his head that made it no sense. Looking up after a minute or two he found the child's eyes fixed on him, and he saw something strange in them. Then Morgan said: 'I'm not afraid of the reality.'

'I haven't yet seen the thing that you *are* afraid of – I'll do you that justice!'

This came out with a jump (it was perfectly true), and evidently gave Morgan pleasure. 'I've thought of it a long time,' he presently resumed.

'Well, don't think of it any more.'

The child appeared to comply, and they had a comfortable and even an amusing hour. They had a theory that they were very thorough, and yet they seemed always to be in the amusing part of lessons, the intervals between the tunnels, where there were waysides and views. Yet the morning was brought to a violent end by Morgan's suddenly leaning his arms on the table, burying his head in them and bursting into tears. Pemberton would have been startled at any rate; but he was doubly startled because, as it then occurred to him, it was the first time he had ever seen the boy cry. It was rather awful.

The next day, after much thought, he took a decision and, believing it to be just, immediately acted upon it. He cornered Mr and Mrs Moreen again and informed them that if, on the spot, they didn't pay him all they owed him, he would not only leave their house, but would tell Morgan exactly what had brought him to it.

'Oh, you *haven't* told him?' cried Mrs Moreen, with a pacifying hand on her well-dressed bosom.

'Without warning you? For what do you take me?'

Mr and Mrs Moreen looked at each other, and Pemberton could see both that they were relieved and that there was a certain alarm in their relief. 'My dear fellow,' Mr Moreen demanded, 'what use *can* you have, leading the quiet life we all do, for such a lot of money?' – an inquiry to which Pemberton made no answer, occupied as he was in perceiving that what passed in the mind of his patrons was something like: 'Oh, then, if we've felt that the child, dear little angel, has judged us and how he regards us, and we haven't been betrayed, he must have guessed – and, in short, it's *general*!' an idea that rather stirred up Mr and Mrs Moreen, as Pemberton had desired that it should. At the same time, if he had thought that his threat would do something towards bringing them round, he was disappointed to find they had taken for granted (how little they appreciated his delicacy!) that he had already given them away to his pupil. There was a mystic uneasiness in their parental breasts, and that was the way they had accounted for it. None the less his threat did touch them; for if they had escaped it was only to meet a new danger. Mr Moreen appealed to Pemberton, as usual, as a man of the world; but his wife had recourse, for the first time since the arrival of their inmate, to a fine *hauteur*, reminding him that a devoted mother, with her child, had arts that protected her against gross misrepresentation.

'I should misrepresent you grossly if I accused you of common honesty!' the young man replied; but as he closed the door behind him sharply, thinking he had not done himself much good, while Mr Moreen lighted another cigarette, he heard Mrs Moreen shout after him, more touchingly:

'Oh, you do, you *do*, put the knife to one's throat!'

The next morning, very early, she came to his room. He recognised her knock, but he had no hope that she brought him money; as to which he was wrong, for she had fifty francs in her hand. She squeezed forward in her dressing-gown, and he received her in his own, between his bath-tub and his bed. He had been tolerably schooled by this time to the 'foreign ways' of his hosts. Mrs Moreen was zealous, and when she was zealous she didn't care what she did; so she now sat down on his bed, his clothes being on the chairs, and, in her preoccupation, forgot, as she glanced round, to be ashamed of giving him such a nasty room. What Mrs Moreen was zealous about on this occasion was to persuade him that in the first place she was very good-natured to bring him fifty francs, and, in the second, if he would only see it, he was really too absurd to expect to be *paid*. Wasn't he paid enough, without perpetual money – wasn't he paid by the comfortable, luxurious home that he enjoyed with them all, without a care, an anxiety, a solitary want?

Wasn't he sure of his position, and wasn't that everything to a young man like him, quite unknown, with singularly little to show, the ground of whose exorbitant pretensions it was not easy to discover? Wasn't he paid, above all, by the delightful relation he had established with Morgan – quite ideal, as from master to pupil – and by the simple privilege of knowing and living with so amazingly gifted a child, than whom really – she meant literally what she said – there was no better company in Europe? Mrs Moreen herself took to appealing to him as a man of the world; she said 'Voyons, mon cher', and 'My dear sir, look here now'; and urged him to be reasonable, putting it before him that it was really a chance for him. She spoke as if, according as he *should* be reasonable, he would prove himself worthy to be her son's tutor and of the extraordinary confidence they had placed in him.

After all, Pemberton reflected, it was only a difference of theory, and the theory didn't matter much. They had hitherto gone on that of remunerated, as now they would go on that of gratuitous, service; but why should they have so many words about it? Mrs Moreen, however, continued to be convincing; sitting there with her fifty francs she talked and repeated, as women repeat, and bored and irritated him, while he leaned against the wall with his hands in the pockets of his wrapper, drawing it together round his legs and looking over the head of his visitor at the grey negations of his window. She wound up with saying: 'You see I bring you a definite proposal.'

'A definite proposal?'

'To make our relations regular, as it were – to put them on a comfortable footing.'

'I see – it's a system,' said Pemberton. 'A kind of blackmail.'

Mrs Moreen bounded up, which was what the young man wanted.

'What do you mean by that?'

'You practise on one's fears – one's fears about the child if one should go away.'

'And, pray, what would happen to him in that event?' demanded Mrs Moreen, with majesty.

'Why, he'd be alone with *you*.'

'And pray, with whom *should* a child be but with those whom he loves most?'

'If you think that, why don't you dismiss me?'

'Do you pretend that he loves you more than he loves *us*?' cried Mrs Moreen.

'I think he ought to. I make sacrifices for him. Though I've heard of those *you* make, I don't see them.'

Mrs Moreen stared a moment; then, with emotion, she grasped Pemberton's hand. '*Will* you make it – the sacrifice?'

Pemberton burst out laughing. 'I'll see – I'll do what I can – I'll stay a little longer. Your calculation is just – I *do* hate intensely to give him up; I'm fond of him and he interests me deeply, in spite of the inconvenience I suffer. You know my situation perfectly; I haven't a penny in the world, and, occupied as I am with Morgan, I'm unable to earn money.'

Mrs Moreen tapped her undressed arm with her folded bank-note. 'Can't you write articles? Can't you translate, as *I* do?'

'I don't know about translating; it's wretchedly paid.'

'I am glad to earn what I can,' said Mrs Moreen virtuously, with her head high.

'You ought to tell me who you do it for.' Pemberton paused a moment, and she said nothing; so he added: 'I've tried to turn off some little sketches, but the magazines won't have them – they're declined with thanks.'

'You see then you're not such a phoenix – to have such pretensions,' smiled his interlocutress.

'I haven't time to do things properly,' Pemberton went on. Then as it came over him that he was almost abjectly good-natured to give these explanations he added: 'If I stay on longer it must be on one condition – that Morgan shall know distinctly on what footing I am.'

Mrs Moreen hesitated. 'Surely you don't want to show off to a child?'

'To show *you* off, do you mean?'

Again Mrs Moreen hesitated, but this time it was to produce a still finer flower. 'And *you* talk of blackmail!'

'You can easily prevent it,' said Pemberton.

'And *you* talk of practising on fears,' Mrs Moreen continued.

'Yes, there's no doubt I'm a great scoundrel.'

His visitor looked at him a moment – it was evident that she was sorely bothered. Then she thrust out her money at him. 'Mr Moreen desired me to give you this on account.'

'I'm much obliged to Mr Moreen; but we have no account.'

'You won't take it?'

'That leaves me more free,' said Pemberton.

'To poison my darling's mind?' groaned Mrs Moreen.

'Oh, your darling's mind!' laughed the young man.

She fixed him a moment, and he thought she was going to break out tormentedly, pleadingly: 'For God's sake, tell me what *is* in it!' But she checked this impulse – another was stronger. She pocketed the money – the crudity of the alternative was comical – and swept out of the room with the desperate concession: 'You may tell him any horror you like!'

VI

A COUPLE of days after this, during which Pemberton had delayed to profit by Mrs Moreen's permission to tell her son any horror, the two had been for a quarter of an hour walking together in silence when the boy became sociable again with the remark: 'I'll tell you how I know it; I know it through Zénobie.'

'Zénobie? Who in the world is *she*?'

'A nurse I used to have – ever so many years ago. A charming woman. I liked her awfully, and she liked me.'

'There's no accounting for tastes. What is it you know through her?'

'Why, what their idea is. She went away because they didn't pay her. She did like me awfully, and she stayed two years. She told me all about it – that at last she could never get her wages. As soon as they saw how much she liked me they stopped giving her anything. They thought she'd stay for nothing, out of devotion. And she did stay ever so long – as long as she could. She was only a poor girl. She used to send money to her mother. At last she couldn't afford it any longer, and she went away in a fearful rage one night – I mean of course in a rage against *them*. She cried over me tremendously, she hugged me nearly to death. She told me all about it,' Morgan repeated. 'She told me it was their idea. So I guessed, ever so long ago, that they have had the same idea with you.'

'Zénobie was very shrewd,' said Pemberton. 'And she made you so.'

'Oh, that wasn't Zénobie; that was nature. And experience!' Morgan laughed.

'Well, Zénobie was a part of your experience.'

'Certainly I was a part of hers, poor dear!' the boy exclaimed. 'And I'm a part of yours.'

'A very important part. But I don't see how you know that I've been treated like Zénobie.'

'Do you take me for an idiot?' Morgan asked. 'Haven't I been conscious of what we've been through together?'

'What we've been through?'

'Our privations – our dark days.'

'Oh, our days have been bright enough.'

Morgan went on in silence for a moment. Then he said: 'My dear fellow, you're a hero!'

'Well, you're another!' Pemberton retorted.

'No, I'm not; but I'm not a baby. I won't stand it any longer. You must get some occupation that pays. I'm ashamed, I'm ashamed!' quavered the boy in a little passionate voice that was very touching to Pemberton.

'We ought to go off and live somewhere together,' said the young man.

'I'll go like a shot if you'll take me.'

'I'd get some work that would keep us both afloat,' Pemberton continued.

'So would I. Why shouldn't *I* work? I ain't such a *crétin*!'

'The difficulty is that your parents wouldn't hear of it,' said Pemberton. 'They would never part with you; they worship the ground you tread on. Don't you see the proof of it? They don't dislike me; they wish me no harm; they've very amiable people; but they're perfectly ready to treat me badly for your sake.'

The silence in which Morgan received this graceful sophistry struck Pemberton somehow as expressive. After a moment Morgan repeated: 'You *are* a hero!' Then he added: 'They leave me with you altogether. You've all the responsibility. They put me off on you from morning till night. Why, then, should they object to my taking up with you completely? I'd help you.'

'They're not particularly keen about my being helped, and they delight in thinking of you as *theirs*. They're tremendously proud of you.'

'I'm not proud of them. But you know *that*,' Morgan returned.

'Except for the little matter we speak of, they're charming people,' said Pemberton, not taking up the imputation of lucidity, but wondering greatly at the child's own, and especially at this fresh reminder of something he had been conscious of from the first – the strangest thing in the boy's large little composition, a temper, a sensibility, even a sort of ideal, which made him privately resent the general quality of his kinsfolk. Morgan had in secret a small loftiness which begot an element of reflection, a domestic scorn not imperceptible to his companion (though they never had any talk about it), and absolutely anomalous in a juvenile nature, especially when one noted that it had not made this nature 'old-fashioned', as the word is of children – quaint or wizened or offensive. It was as if he had been a little gentleman and had paid the penalty by discovering that he was the only such person in the family. This comparison didn't make him vain; but it could make him melancholy and a trifle austere. When Pemberton guessed at these young dimnesses he saw him serious and gallant, and was partly drawn on and partly checked, as if with a scruple, by the charm of attempting to sound the little cool shallows which were quickly growing deeper. When he tried to figure to himself the morning twilight of childhood, so as to deal with it safely, he perceived that it was never fixed, never arrested, that ignorance, at the instant one touched it, was already flushing faintly into knowledge, that there was nothing that at a given moment you could say a clever child didn't know. It seemed to him that *he* both knew too much to imagine Morgan's simplicity and too little to disembroil his tangle.

The boy paid no heed to his last remark; he only went on: 'I should have spoken to them about their idea, as I call it, long ago, if I hadn't been sure what they would say.'

'And what would they say?'

'Just what they said about what poor Zénobie told me – that it was a horrid, dreadful story, that they had paid her every penny they owed her.'

'Well, perhaps they had,' said Pemberton.

'Perhaps they've paid you!'

'Let us pretend they have, and *n'en parlons plus*.'

'They accused her of lying and cheating,' Morgan insisted perversely. 'That's why I don't want to speak to them.'

'Lest they should accuse me, too?'

To this Morgan made no answer, and his companion, looking down at him (the boy turned his eyes, which had filled, away), saw that he couldn't have trusted himself to utter.

'You're right. Don't squeeze them,' Pemberton pursued. 'Except for that, they *are* charming people.'

'Except for *their* lying and *their* cheating?'

'I say – I say!' cried Pemberton, imitating a little tone of the lad's which was itself an imitation.

'We must be frank, at the last; we *must* come to an understanding,' said Morgan, with the importance of the small boy who lets himself think he is arranging great affairs – almost playing at shipwreck or at Indians. 'I know all about everything,' he added.

'I daresay your father has his reasons,' Pemberton observed, too vaguely, as he was aware.

'For lying and cheating?'

'For saving and managing and turning his means to the best account. He has plenty to do with his money. You're an expensive family.'

'Yes, I'm very expensive,' Morgan rejoined, in a manner which made his preceptor burst out laughing.

'He's saving for *you*,' said Pemberton. 'They think of you in everything they do.'

'He might save a little—' The boy paused. Pemberton waited to hear what. Then Morgan brought out oddly: 'A little reputation.'

'Oh, there's plenty of that. That's all right!'

'Enough of it for the people they know, no doubt. The people they know are awful.'

'Do you mean the princes? We mustn't abuse the princes.'

'Why not? They haven't married Paula – they haven't married Amy. They only clean out Ulick.'

'You *do* know everything!' Pemberton exclaimed.

'No, I don't, after all. I don't know what they live on, or how they live, or *why* they live! What have they got and how did they get it? Are they rich, are they poor, or have they a *modeste aisance*? Why are they always chiveying about – living one year like ambassadors and the next like paupers? Who are they, any way, and what are they? I've thought of all that – I've thought of a lot of things. They're so beastly worldly. That's what I hate most – oh, I've *seen* it! All they care about is to make an appearance and to pass for something or other. What do they want to pass for? What *do* they, Mr Pemberton?'

'You pause for a reply,' said Pemberton, treating the inquiry as a joke, yet wondering too, and greatly struck with the boy's intense, if imperfect, vision. 'I haven't the least idea.'

'And what good does it do? Haven't I seen the way people treat them – the "nice" people, the ones they want to know? They'll take anything from them – they'll lie down and be trampled on. The nice ones hate that – they just sicken them. You're the only really nice person we know.'

'Are you sure? They don't lie down for me!'

'Well, you shan't lie down for them. You've got to go – that's what you've got to do,' said Morgan.

'And what will become of you?'

'Oh, I'm growing up. I shall get off before long. I'll see you later.'

'You had better let me finish you,' Pemberton urged, lending himself to the child's extraordinarily competent attitude.

Morgan stopped in their walk, looking up at him. He had to look up much less than a couple of years before – he had grown, in his loose leanness, so long and high. 'Finish me?' he echoed.

'There are such a lot of jolly things we can do together yet. I want to turn you out – I want you to do me credit.'

Morgan continued to look at him. 'To give you credit – do you mean?'

'My dear fellow, you're too clever to live.'

'That's just what I'm afraid you think. No, no; it isn't fair – I can't endure it. We'll part next week. The sooner it's over the sooner to sleep.'

'If I hear of anything – any other chance, I promise to go,' said Pemberton.

Morgan consented to consider this. 'But you'll be honest,' he demanded; 'you won't pretend you haven't heard?'

'I'm much more likely to pretend I have.'

'But what can you hear of, this way, stuck in a hole with us? You ought to be on the spot, to go to England – you ought to go to America.'

'One would think you were *my* tutor!' said Pemberton.

Morgan walked on, and after a moment he began again: 'Well, now that you know that I know and that we look at the facts and keep nothing back – it's much more comfortable, isn't it?'

'My dear boy, it's so amusing, so interesting, that it surely will be quite impossible for me to forgo such hours as these.'

This made Morgan stop once more. 'You *do* keep something back. Oh, you're not straight – *I* am!'

'Why am I not straight?'

'Oh, you've got your idea!'

'My idea?'

'Why, that I probably sha'n't live, and that you can stick it out till I'm removed.'

'You *are* too clever to live!' Pemberton repeated.

'I call it a mean idea,' Morgan pursued. 'But I shall punish you by the way I hang on.'

'Look out or I'll poison you!' Pemberton laughed.

'I'm stronger and better every year. Haven't you noticed that there hasn't been a doctor near me since you came?'

'*I'm* your doctor,' said the young man, taking his arm and drawing him on again.

Morgan proceeded, and after a few steps he gave a sigh of mingled weariness and relief. 'Ah, now that we look at the facts, it's all right!'

VII

THEY looked at the facts a good deal after this; and one of the first consequences of their doing so was that Pemberton stuck it out, as it were, for the purpose. Morgan made the facts so vivid and so droll, and at the same time so bald and so ugly, that there was fascination in talking them over with him, just as there would have been heartlessness in leaving him alone with them. Now that they had such a number of perceptions in common it was useless for the pair to pretend that they didn't judge such people; but the very judgement, and the exchange of perceptions, created another tie. Morgan had never been so interesting as now that he himself was made plainer by the sidelight of these confidences. What came out in it most was the soreness of his characteristic pride. He had plenty of that, Pemberton felt – so much that it was perhaps well it should have had to take some early bruises. He would have liked his people to be gallant, and he had waked up too soon to the sense that they were perpetually swallowing humble-pie. His mother would consume any amount, and his father would consume even more than his mother. He had a theory that Ulick had wriggled out of an 'affair' at Nice: there had once been a flurry at home, a regular panic, after which they all went to bed and took medicine, not to be accounted for on any other supposition. Morgan had a romantic imagination, fed by poetry and history, and he would have liked those who 'bore his name' (as he used to say to Pemberton with the humour that made his sensitiveness manly), to have a proper spirit. But their one idea was to get in with people who didn't want them and to take snubs as if they were honourable scars. Why people didn't want them more he didn't know – that was people's own affair; after all they were not superficially repulsive – they were a hundred times cleverer than most of the dreary grandees, the 'poor swells' they rushed about Europe to catch up with. 'After all, they *are* amusing – they are!' Morgan used to say, with the wisdom of the ages. To which Pemberton always replied: 'Amusing – the great Moreen troupe? Why, they're altogether delightful; and if it were not for the hitch that you and I (feeble performers!) make in the *ensemble*, they would carry everything before them.'

What the boy couldn't get over was that this particular blight seemed, in a tradition of self-respect, so undeserved and so arbitrary. No doubt people had a right to take the line they liked; but why should *his* people have liked the line of pushing and toadying and lying and cheating? What had their forefathers – all decent folk, so far as he knew – done to them, or what had *he* done to them? Who had poisoned their blood with the fifth-rate social ideal, the fixed idea of making smart acquaintances and getting into the *monde chic*, especially when it was foredoomed to failure and exposure? They showed so what they were after; that was what made the people they wanted not want *them*. And never a movement of dignity, never a throb of shame at looking each other in the face, never any independence or resentment or disgust. If his father or his brother would only knock some one down once or twice a year! Clever as they were they never guessed how they appeared. They were good-natured, yes – as good-natured as Jews at the doors of clothing-shops! But was that the model one wanted one's family to follow? Morgan had dim memories of an old grandfather, the maternal, in New York, whom he had been taken across the ocean to see, at the age of five: a gentleman with a high neckcloth and a good deal of pronunciation, who wore a dress-coat in the morning, which made one wonder what he wore in the evening, and had, or was supposed to have, 'property' and something to do with the Bible Society. It couldn't have been but that *he* was a good type. Pemberton himself remembered Mrs Clancy, a widowed sister of Mr Moreen's, who was as irritating as a moral tale and had paid a fortnight's visit to the family at Nice shortly after he came to live with them. She was

'pure and refined', as Amy said, over the banjo, and had the air
of not knowing what they meant and of keeping something
back. Pemberton judged that what she kept back was an
approval of many of their ways; therefore it was to be supposed
that she too was of a good type, and that Mr and Mrs Moreen
and Ulick and Paula and Amy might easily have been better if
they would.

But that they wouldn't was more and more perceptible from
day to day. They continued to 'chivey', as Morgan called it, and
in due time became aware of a variety of reasons for proceeding
to Venice. They mentioned a great many of them – they were
always strikingly frank, and had the brightest friendly chatter, at
the late foreign breakfast in especial, before the ladies had made
up their faces, when they leaned their arms on the table, had
something to follow the *demi-tasse*, and, in the heat of familiar
discussion as to what they 'really ought' to do, fell inevitably
into the languages in which they could *tutoyer*. Even Pemberton
liked them, then; he could endure even Ulick when he heard
him give his little flat voice for the 'sweet sea-city'. That was
what made him have a sneaking kindness for them – that they
were so out of the workaday world and kept him so out of it.
The summer had waned when, with cries of ecstasy, they all
passed out on the balcony that overhung the Grand Canal; the
sunsets were splendid – the Dorringtons had arrived. The
Dorringtons were the only reason they had not talked of at
breakfast; but the reasons that they didn't talk of at breakfast
always came out in the end. The Dorringtons, on the other
hand, came out very little; or else, when they did, they stayed –
as was natural – for hours, during which periods Mrs Moreen
and the girls sometimes called at their hotel (to see if they had
returned) as many as three times running. The gondola was for
the ladies; for in Venice too there were 'days', which Mrs
Moreen knew in their order an hour after she arrived. She
immediately took one herself, to which the Dorringtons never
came, though on a certain occasion when Pemberton and his
pupil were together at St Mark's – where, taking the best walks
they had ever had and haunting a hundred churches, they spent
a great deal of time – they saw the old lord turn up with Mr

Moreen and Ulick, who showed him the dim basilica as if it belonged to them. Pemberton noted how much less, among its curiosities, Lord Dorrington carried himself as a man of the world; wondering too whether, for such services, his companions took a fee from him. The autumn, at any rate, waned, the Dorringtons departed, and Lord Verschoyle, the eldest son, had proposed neither for Amy nor for Paula.

One sad November day, while the wind roared round the old palace and the rain lashed the lagoon, Pemberton, for exercise and even somewhat for warmth (the Moreens were horribly frugal about fires – it was a cause of suffering to their inmate), walked up and down the big bare *sala* with his pupil. The scagliola floor was cold, the high battered casements shook in the storm, and the stately decay of the place was unrelieved by a particle of furniture. Pemberton's spirits were low, and it came over him that the fortune of the Moreens was now even lower. A blast of desolation, a prophecy of disaster and disgrace, seemed to draw through the comfortless hall. Mr Moreen and Ulick were in the Piazza, looking out for something, strolling drearily, in mackintoshes, under the arcades; but still, in spite of mackintoshes, unmistakable men of the world. Paula and Amy were in bed – it might have been thought they were staying there to keep warm. Pemberton looked askance at the boy at his side, to see to what extent he was conscious of these portents. But Morgan, luckily for him, was now mainly conscious of growing taller and stronger and indeed of being in his fifteenth year. This fact was intensely interesting to him – it was the basis of a private theory (which, however, he had imparted to his tutor) that in a little while he should stand on his own feet. He considered that the situation would change – that, in short, he should be 'finished', grown up, producible in the world of affairs and ready to prove himself of sterling ability. Sharply as he was capable, at times, of questioning his circumstances, there were happy hours when he was as superficial as a child; the proof of which was his fundamental assumption that he should presently go to Oxford, to Pemberton's college, and, aided and abetted by Pemberton, do the most wonderful things. It vexed Pemberton to see how little, in such a project, he took account of ways and means: on other matters he was so sceptical about them. Pemberton tried to imagine the Moreens at Oxford, and fortunately failed; yet unless they were to remove there as a family there would be no *modus vivendi* for Morgan. How could he live without an allowance, and where was the allowance to come from? He (Pemberton) might live on Morgan; but how could Morgan live on him? What was to become of him anyhow? Somehow, the fact that he was a big boy now, with better prospects of health, made the question of his future more difficult. So long as he was frail the consideration that he inspired seemed enough of an answer to it. But at the bottom of Pemberton's heart was the recognition of his probably being strong enough to live and not strong enough to thrive. He himself, at any rate, was in a period of natural, boyish rosiness about all this, so that the beating of the tempest seemed to him only the voice of life and the challenge of fate. He had on his shabby little overcoat, with the collar up, but he was enjoying his walk.

It was interrupted at last by the appearance of his mother at the end of the *sala*. She beckoned to Morgan to come to her, and while Pemberton saw him, complacent, pass down the long vista, over the damp false marble, he wondered what was in the air. Mrs Moreen said a word to the boy and made him go into the room she had quitted. Then, having closed the door after him, she directed her steps swiftly to Pemberton. There *was* something in the air, but his wildest flight of fancy wouldn't have suggested what it proved to be. She signified that she had made a pretext to get Morgan out of the way, and then she inquired – without hesitation – if the young man could lend her sixty francs. While, before bursting into a laugh, he stared at her with surprise, she declared that she was awfully pressed for the money; she was desperate for it – it would save her life.

'Dear lady, *c'est trop fort!*' Pemberton laughed. 'Where in the world do you suppose I should get sixty francs, *du train dont vous allez?*'

'I thought you worked – wrote things; don't they pay you?'

'Not a penny.'

'Are you such a fool as to work for nothing?'

'You ought surely to know that.'

Mrs Moreen stared an instant, then she coloured a little. Pemberton saw she had quite forgotten the terms – if 'terms' they could be called – that he had ended by accepting from herself; they had burdened her memory as little as her conscience. 'Oh, yes, I see what you mean – you have been very nice about that; but why go back to it so often?' She had been perfectly urbane with him ever since the rough scene of explanation in his room, the morning he made her accept *his* 'terms' – the necessity of his making his case known to Morgan. She had felt no resentment, after seeing that there was no danger of Morgan's taking the matter up with her. Indeed, attributing this immunity to the good taste of his influence with the boy, she had once said to Pemberton: 'My dear fellow; it's an immense comfort you're a gentleman.' She repeated this, in substance, now. 'Of course you're a gentleman – that's a bother the less!' Pemberton reminded her that he had not 'gone back' to anything; and she also repeated her prayer that, somewhere and somehow, he would find her sixty francs. He took the liberty of declaring that if he could find them it wouldn't be to lend them to *her* – as to which he consciously did himself injustice, knowing that if he had them he would certainly place them in her hand. He accused himself, at bottom and with some truth, of a fantastic, demoralised sympathy with her. If misery made strange bed-fellows it also made strange sentiments. It was moreover a part of the demoralisation and of the general bad effect of living with such people that one had to make rough retorts, quite out of the tradition of good manners. 'Morgan, Morgan, to what pass have I come for you?' he privately exclaimed, while Mrs Moreen floated voluminously down the *sala* again, to liberate the boy; groaning, as she went, that everything was too odious.

Before the boy was liberated there came a thump at the door communicating with the staircase, followed by the apparition of a dripping youth who poked in his head. Pemberton recognised him as the bearer of a telegram and recognised the telegram as addressed to himself. Morgan came back as, after glancing at the signature (that of a friend in London), he was reading the words: 'Found jolly job for you – engagement to coach opulent youth on own terms. Come immediately.' The answer, happily, was paid, and the messenger waited. Morgan, who had drawn near, waited too, and looked hard at Pemberton; and Pemberton, after a moment, having met his look, handed him the telegram. It was really by wise looks (they knew each other so well), that, while the tele-graph-boy, in his waterproof cape, made a great puddle on the floor, the thing was settled between them. Pemberton wrote the answer with a pencil against the frescoed wall, and the messenger departed. When he had gone Pemberton said to Morgan:

'I'll make a tremendous charge; I'll earn a lot of money in a short time, and we'll live on it.'

'Well, I hope the opulent youth will be stupid – he probably will –' Morgan parenthesised, 'and keep you a long time.'

'Of course, the longer he keeps me the more we shall have for our old age.'

'But suppose *they* don't pay you!' Morgan awfully sug-gested.

'Oh, there are not two such –!' Pemberton paused, he was on the point of using an invidious term. Instead of this he said 'two such chances'.

Morgan flushed – the tears came to his eyes. '*Dites toujours,* two such rascally crews!' Then, in a different tone, he added: 'Happy opulent youth!'

'Not if he's stupid!'

'Oh, they're happier then. But you can't have everything, can you?' the boy smiled.

Pemberton held him, his hands on his shoulders. 'What will become of *you*, what will you do?' He thought of Mrs Moreen, desperate for sixty francs.

'I shall turn into a man.' And then, as if he recognised all the bearings of Pemberton's allusion: 'I shall get on with them better when you're not here.'

'Ah, don't say that – it sounds as if I set you against them!'

'You do – the sight of you. It's all right; you know what I mean. I shall be beautiful. I'll take their affairs in hand; I'll marry my sisters.'

'You'll marry yourself!' joked Pemberton; as high, rather tense pleasantry would evidently be the right, or the safest, tone for their separation.

It was, however, not purely in this strain that Morgan suddenly asked: 'But I say – how will you get to your jolly job? You'll have to telegraph to the opulent youth for money to come on.'

Pemberton bethought himself. 'They won't like that, will they?'

'Oh, look out for them!'

Then Pemberton brought out his remedy. 'I'll go to the American Consul; I'll borrow some money of him – just for the few days, on the strength of the telegram.'

Morgan was hilarious. 'Show him the telegram – then stay and keep the money!'

Pemberton entered into the joke enough to reply that, for Morgan, he was really capable of that; but the boy, growing more serious, and to prove that he hadn't meant what he said, not only hurried him off to the Consulate (since he was to start that evening, as he had wired to his friend), but insisted on going with him. They splashed through the tortuous perforations and over the humpbacked bridges, and they passed through the Piazza, where they saw Mr Moreen and Ulick go into a jeweller's shop. The Consul proved accommodating (Pemberton said it wasn't the letter, but Morgan's grand air), and on their way back they went into St Mark's for a hushed ten minutes. Later they took up and kept up the fun of it to the very end; and it seemed to Pemberton a part of that fun that Mrs Moreen, who was very angry when he had announced to her his intention, should charge him, grotesquely and vulgarly, and in reference to the loan she had vainly endeavoured to effect, with bolting lest they should 'get something out' of him. On the other hand he had to do Mr Moreen and Ulick the justice to recognise that when, on coming in, *they* heard the cruel news, they took it like perfect men of the world.

VIII

When Pemberton got at work with the opulent youth, who was to be taken in hand for Balliol, he found himself unable to say whether he was really an idiot or it was only, on his own part, the long association with an intensely living little mind that made him seem so. From Morgan he heard half-a-dozen times: the boy wrote charming young letters, a patchwork of tongues, with indulgent postscripts in the family Volapuk and, in little squares and rounds and crannies of the text, the drollest illustrations – letters that he was divided between the impulse to show his present disciple, as a kind of wasted incentive, and the sense of something in them that was profanable by publicity. The opulent youth went up, in due course, and failed to pass; but it seemed to add to the presumption that brilliancy was not expected of him all at once that his parents, condoning the lapse, which they good-naturedly treated as little as possible as if it were Pemberton's, should have sounded the rally again, begged the young coach to keep his pupil in hand another year.

The young coach was now in a position to lend Mrs Moreen sixty francs, and he sent her a post-office order for the amount. In return for this favour he received a frantic, scribbled line from her: 'Implore you to come back instantly – Morgan dreadfully ill.' They were on the rebound, once more in Paris – often as Pemberton had seen them depressed he had never seen them crushed – and communication was therefore rapid. He wrote to the boy to ascertain the state of his health, but he received no answer to his letter. Accordingly he took an abrupt leave of the opulent youth and, crossing the Channel, alighted at the small hotel, in the quarter of the Champs Elysées, of which Mrs Moreen had given him the address. A deep if dumb dissatisfaction with this lady and her companions bore him company: they couldn't be vulgarly honest, but they could live at hotels, in velvety *entresols*, amid a smell of burnt pastilles, in the most expensive city in Europe. When he had left them, in Venice, it was with an irrepressible suspicion that something was going to happen; but the only thing that had happened was that they succeeded in getting away. 'How is he? where is he?' he asked of

Mrs Moreen; but before she could speak, these questions were answered by the pressure round his neck of a pair of arms, in shrunken sleeves, which were perfectly capable of an effusive young foreign squeeze.

'Dreadfully ill – I don't see it!' the young man cried. And then, to Morgan: 'Why on earth didn't you relieve me? Why didn't you answer my letter?'

Mrs Moreen declared that when she wrote he was very bad, and Pemberton learned at the same time from the boy that he had answered every letter he had received. This led to the demonstration that Pemberton's note had been intercepted. Mrs Moreen was prepared to see the fact exposed, as Pemberton perceived, the moment he faced her, that she was prepared for a good many other things. She was prepared above all to maintain that she had acted from a sense of duty, that she was enchanted she had got him over, whatever they might say; and that it was useless of him to pretend that he didn't *know*, in all his bones, that his place at such a time was with Morgan. He had taken the boy away from them, and now he had no right to abandon him. He had created for himself the gravest responsibilities; he must at least abide by what he had done.

'Taken him away from you?' Pemberton exclaimed indignantly.

'Do it – do it, for pity's sake; that's just what I want. I can't stand *this* – and such scenes. They're treacherous!' These words broke from Morgan, who had intermitted his embrace, in a key which made Pemberton turn quickly to him, to see that he had suddenly seated himself, was breathing with evident difficulty and was very pale.

'*Now* do you say he's not ill – my precious pet?' shouted his mother, dropping on her knees before him with clasped hands, but touching him no more than if he had been a gilded idol. 'It will pass – it's only for an instant; but don't say such dreadful things!'

'I'm all right – all right,' Morgan panted to Pemberton, whom he sat looking up at with a strange smile, his hands resting on either side of the sofa.

'Now do you pretend I've been treacherous – that I've deceived?' Mrs Moreen flashed at Pemberton as she got up.

'It isn't *he* says it, it's I!' the boy returned, apparently easier, but sinking back against the wall; while Pemberton, who had sat down beside him, taking his hand, bent over him.

'Darling child, one does what one can; there are so many things to consider,' urged Mrs Moreen. 'It's his *place* – his only place. You see *you* think it is now.'

'Take me away – take me away,' Morgan went on, smiling to Pemberton from his white face.

'Where shall I take you, and how – oh, *how*, my boy?' the young man stammered, thinking of the rude way in which his friends in London held that, for his convenience, and without a pledge of instantaneous return, he had thrown them over; of the just resentment with which they would already have called in a successor, and of the little help as regarded finding fresh employment that resided for him in the flatness of his having failed to pass his pupil.

'Oh, we'll settle that. You used to talk about it,' said Morgan. 'If we can only go, all the rest's a detail.'

'Talk about it as much as you like, but don't think you can attempt it. Mr Moreen would never consent – it would be so precarious,' Pemberton's hostess explained to him. Then to Morgan she explained: 'It would destroy our peace, it would break our hearts. Now that he's back it will be all the same again. You'll have your life, your work and your freedom, and we'll all be happy as we used to be. You'll bloom and grow perfectly well, and we won't have any more silly experiments, will we? They're too absurd. It's Mr Pemberton's place – every one in his place. You in yours, your papa in his, me in mine – *n'est-ce pas, chéri*? We'll all forget how foolish we've been, and we'll have lovely times.'

She continued to talk and to surge vaguely about the little draped, stuffy *salon*, while Pemberton sat with the boy, whose colour gradually came back; and she mixed up her reasons, dropping that there were going to be changes, that the other children might scatter (who knew? – Paula had her ideas), and that then it might be fancied how much the poor old

parent-birds would want the little nestling. Morgan looked at
Pemberton, who wouldn't let him move; and Pemberton knew
exactly how he felt at hearing himself called a little nestling. He
admitted that he had had one or two bad days, but he protested
afresh against the iniquity of his mother's having made them
the ground of an appeal to poor Pemberton. Poor Pemberton
could laugh now, apart from the comicality of Mrs Moreen's
producing so much philosophy for her defence (she seemed to
shake it out of her agitated petticoats, which knocked over the
light gilt chairs), so little did the sick boy strike him as qualified
to repudiate any advantage.

He himself was in for it, at any rate. He should have Morgan
on his hands again indefinitely; though indeed he saw the lad
had a private theory to produce which would be intended to
smooth this down. He was obliged to him for it in advance; but
the suggested amendment didn't keep his heart from sinking a
little, any more than it prevented him from accepting the prospect on the spot, with some confidence moreover that he
would do so even better if he could have a little supper. Mrs
Moreen threw out more hints about the changes that were to be
looked for, but she was such a mixture of smiles and shudders
(she confessed she was very nervous), that he couldn't tell
whether she were in high feather or only in hysterics. If the
family were really at last going to pieces why shouldn't she
recognise the necessity of pitching Morgan into some sort of
lifeboat? This presumption was fostered by the fact that
they were established in luxurious quarters in the capital of
pleasure; that was exactly where they naturally *would* be established in view of going to pieces. Moreover didn't she
mention that Mr Moreen and the others were enjoying themselves at the opera with Mr Granger, and wasn't *that* also
precisely where one would look for them on the eve of a
smash? Pemberton gathered that Mr Granger was a rich,
vacant American – a big bill with a flourishy heading and no
items; so that one of Paula's 'ideas' was probably that this time
she had really done it, which was indeed an unprecedented
blow to the general cohesion. And if the cohesion was to
terminate what was to become of poor Pemberton? He felt

quite enough bound up with them to figure, to his alarm, as a floating spar in case of a wreck.

It was Morgan who eventually asked if no supper had been ordered for him; sitting with him below, later, at the dim, delayed meal, in the presence of a great deal of corded green plush, a plate of ornamental biscuit and a languor marked on the part of the waiter. Mrs Moreen had explained that they had been obliged to secure a room for the visitor out of the house; and Morgan's consolation (he offered it while Pemberton reflected on the nastiness of lukewarm sauces) proved to be, largely, that this circumstance would facilitate their escape. He talked of their escape (recurring to it often afterwards) as if they were making up a 'boy's book' together. But he likewise expressed his sense that there was something in the air, that the Moreens couldn't keep it up much longer. In point of fact, as Pemberton was to see, they kept it up for five or six months. All the while, however, Morgan's contention was designed to cheer him. Mr Moreen and Ulick, whom he had met the day after his return, accepted that return like perfect men of the world. If Paula and Amy treated it even with less formality an allowance was to be made for them, inasmuch as Mr Granger had not come to the opera after all. He had only placed his box at their service, with a bouquet for each of the party; there was even one apiece, embittering the thought of his profusion, for Mr Moreen and Ulick. 'They're all like that,' was Morgan's comment; 'at the very last, just when we think we've got them fast, we're chucked!'

Morgan's comments, in these days, were more and more free; they even included a large recognition of the extra-ordinary tenderness with which he had been treated while Pemberton was away. Oh, yes, they couldn't do enough to be nice to him, to show him they had him on their mind and make up for his loss. That was just what made the whole thing so sad, and him so glad, after all, of Pemberton's return – he had to keep thinking of their affection less, had less sense of obligation. Pemberton laughed out at this last reason, and Morgan blushed and said: 'You know what I mean.' Pemberton knew perfectly what he meant; but there were a good many things it

didn't make any clearer. This episode of his second sojourn in
Paris stretched itself out wearily, with their resumed readings
and wanderings and maunderings, their potterings on the
quays, their hauntings of the museums, their occasional linger-
ings in the Palais Royal, when the first sharp weather came on
and there was a comfort in warm emanations, before Chevet's
wonderful succulent window. Morgan wanted to hear a great
deal about the opulent youth – he took an immense interest in
him. Some of the details of his opulence – Pemberton could
spare him none of them – evidently intensified the boy's appreciation of all his friend had given up to come back to him; but in
addition to the greater reciprocity established by such a renunciation he had always his little brooding theory, in which there
was a frivolous gaiety too, that their long probation was drawing to a close. Morgan's conviction that the Moreens couldn't
go on much longer kept pace with the unexpended impetus
with which, from month to month, they did go on. Three weeks
after Pemberton had rejoined them they went on to another
hotel, a dingier one than the first; but Morgan rejoiced that his
tutor had at least still not sacrificed the advantage of a room
outside. He clung to the romantic utility of this when the day, or
rather the night, should arrive for their escape.

For the first time, in this complicated connection, Pemberton felt sore and exasperated. It was, as he had said to Mrs
Moreen in Venice, *trop fort* – everything was *trop fort*. He could
neither really throw off his blighting burden nor find in it the
benefit of a pacified conscience or of a rewarded affection. He
had spent all the money that he had earned in England, and he
felt that his youth was going and that he was getting nothing
back for it. It was all very well for Morgan to seem to consider
that he would make up to him for all inconveniences by settling
himself upon him permanently – there was an irritating flaw in
such a view. He saw what the boy had in his mind; the conception that as his friend had had the generosity to come back to
him he must show his gratitude by giving him his life. But the
poor friend didn't desire the gift – what could he do with
Morgan's life? Of course at the same time that Pemberton
was irritated he remembered the reason, which was very

honourable to Morgan and which consisted simply of the fact
that he was perpetually making one forget that he was after all
only a child. If one dealt with him on a different basis one's
misadventures were one's own fault. So Pemberton waited in a
queer confusion of yearning and alarm for the catastrophe
which was held to hang over the house of Moreen, of which
he certainly at moments felt the symptoms brush his cheek and
as to which he wondered much in what form it would come.

Perhaps it would take the form of dispersal – a frightened
sauve qui peut, a scuttling into selfish corners. Certainly they
were less elastic than of yore; they were evidently looking for
something they didn't find. The Dorringtons hadn't reappeared, the princes had scattered; wasn't that the beginning
of the end? Mrs Moreen had lost her reckoning of the famous
'days'; her social calendar was blurred – it had turned its face to
the wall. Pemberton suspected that the great, the cruel, discomfiture had been the extraordinary behaviour of Mr Granger, who seemed not to know what he wanted, or, what was
much worse, what *they* wanted. He kept sending flowers, as if to
bestrew the path of his retreat, which was never the path of
return. Flowers were all very well, but – Pemberton could
complete the proposition. It was now positively conspicuous
that in the long run the Moreens were a failure; so that the
young man was almost grateful the run had not been short. Mr
Moreen, indeed, was still occasionally able to get away on
business, and, what was more surprising, he was also able to
get back. Ulick had no club, but you could not have discovered
it from his appearance, which was as much as ever that of a
person looking at life from the window of such an institution;
therefore Pemberton was doubly astonished at an answer he
once heard him make to his mother, in the desperate tone of a
man familiar with the worst privations. Her question Pemberton had not quite caught; it appeared to be an appeal for a
suggestion as to whom they could get to take Amy. 'Let the
devil take her!' Ulick snapped; so that Pemberton could see
that not only they had lost their amiability, but had ceased to
believe in themselves. He could also see that if Mrs Moreen was
trying to get people to take her children she might be regarded

as closing the hatches for the storm. But Morgan would be the last she would part with.

One winter afternoon – it was a Sunday – he and the boy walked far together in the Bois de Boulogne. The evening was so splendid, the cold lemon-coloured sunset so clear, the stream of carriages and pedestrians so amusing and the fascination of Paris so great, that they stayed out later than usual and became aware that they would have to hurry home to arrive in time for dinner. They hurried accordingly, arm-in-arm, good-humoured and hungry, agreeing that there was nothing like Paris after all and that after all, too, that had come and gone they were not yet sated with innocent pleasures. When they reached the hotel they found that, though scandalously late, they were in time for all the dinner they were likely to sit down to. Confusion reigned in the apartments of the Moreens (very shabby ones this time, but the best in the house), and before the interrupted service of the table (with objects displaced almost as if there had been a scuffle, and a great wine stain from an overturned bottle), Pemberton could not blink the fact that there had been a scene of proprietary mutiny. The storm had come – they were all seeking refuge. The hatches were down – Paula and Amy were invisible (they had never tried the most casual art upon Pemberton, but he felt that they had enough of an eye to him not to wish to meet him as young ladies whose frocks had been confiscated), and Ulick appeared to have jumped overboard. In a word, the host and his staff had ceased to 'go on' at the pace of their guests, and the air of embarrassed detention, thanks to a pile of gaping trunks in the passage, was strangely commingled with the air of indignant withdrawal.

When Morgan took in all this – and he took it in very quickly – he blushed to the roots of his hair. He had walked, from his infancy, among difficulties and dangers, but he had never seen a public exposure. Pemberton noticed, in a second glance at him, that the tears had rushed into his eyes and that they were tears of bitter shame. He wondered for an instant, for the boy's sake, whether he might successfully pretend not to understand. Not successfully, he felt, as Mr and Mrs Moreen, dinnerless by their extinguished hearth, rose before him in their little dishonoured *salon*, considering apparently with much intensity what lively capital would be next on their list. They were not prostrate, but they were very pale, and Mrs Moreen had evidently been crying. Pemberton quickly learned however that her grief was not for the loss of her dinner, much as she usually enjoyed it, but on account of a necessity much more tragic. She lost no time in laying this necessity bare, in telling him how the change had come, the bolt had fallen, and how they would all have to turn themselves about. Therefore, cruel as it was to them to part with their darling, she must look to him to carry a little further the influence he had so fortunately acquired with the boy – to induce his young charge to follow him into some modest retreat. They depended upon him, in a word, to take their delightful child temporarily under his protection – it would leave Mr Moreen and herself so much more free to give the proper attention (too little, alas! had been given), to the readjustment of their affairs.

'We trust you – we feel that we can,' said Mrs Moreen, slowly rubbing her plump white hands and looking, with compunction, hard at Morgan, whose chin, not to take liberties, her husband stroked with a tentative paternal forefinger.

'Oh, yes; we feel that we can. We trust Mr Pemberton fully, Morgan,' Mr Moreen conceded.

Pemberton wondered again if he might pretend not to understand; but the idea was painfully complicated by the immediate perception that Morgan had understood.

'Do you mean that he may take me to live with him – for ever and ever?' cried the boy. 'Away, away, anywhere he likes?'

'For ever and ever? *Comme vous-y-allez!*' Mr Moreen laughed indulgently. 'For as long as Mr Pemberton may be so good.'

'We've struggled, we've suffered,' his wife went on; 'but you've made him so your own that we've already been through the worst of the sacrifice.'

Morgan had turned away from his father – he stood looking at Pemberton with a light in his face. His blush had died out, but something had come that was brighter and more vivid. He had a moment of boyish joy, scarcely mitigated by the reflection that, with this unexpected consecration of his hope – too sudden and too violent; the thing was a good deal less like a boy's book – the 'escape' was left on their hands. The boyish joy was there for an instant, and Pemberton was almost frightened at the revelation of gratitude and affection that shone through his humiliation. When Morgan stammered 'My dear fellow, what do you say to *that*?' he felt that he should say something enthusiastic. But he was still more frightened at something else that immediately followed and that made the lad sit down quickly on the nearest chair. He had turned very white and had raised his hand to his left side. They were all three looking at him, but Mrs Moreen was the first to bound forward. 'Ah, his darling little heart!' she broke out; and this time, on her knees before him and without respect for the idol, she caught him ardently in her arms. 'You walked him too far, you hurried him too fast!' she tossed over her shoulder at Pemberton. The boy made no protest, and the next instant his mother, still holding him, sprang up with her face convulsed and with the terrified cry 'Help, help! he's going, he's gone!' Pemberton saw, with equal horror, by Morgan's own stricken face, that he *was* gone. He pulled him half out of his mother's hands, and for a moment, while they held him together, they looked, in their dismay, into each other's eyes. 'He couldn't stand it, with his infirmity,' said Pemberton – 'the shock, the whole scene, the violent emotion.'

'But I thought he *wanted* to go to you!' wailed Mrs Moreen.

'I *told* you he didn't, my dear,' argued Mr Moreen. He was trembling all over, and he was, in his way, as deeply affected as his wife. But, after the first, he took his bereavement like a man of the world.

THE MARRIAGES

I

'Won't you stay a little longer?' the hostess said, holding the girl's hand and smiling. 'It's too early for every one to go; it's too absurd.' Mrs Churchley inclined her head to one side and looked gracious; she held up to her face, in a vague, protecting, sheltering way, an enormous fan of red feathers. Everything about her, to Adela Chart, was enormous. She had big eyes, big teeth, big shoulders, big hands, big rings and bracelets, big jewels of every sort and many of them. The train of her crimson dress was longer than any other; her house was huge; her drawing-room, especially now that the company had left it, looked vast, and it offered to the girl's eyes a collection of the largest sofas and chairs, pictures, mirrors, and clocks that she had ever beheld. Was Mrs Churchley's fortune also large, to account for so many immensities? Of this Adela could know nothing, but she reflected, while she smiled sweetly back at their entertainer, that she had better try to find out. Mrs Churchley had at least a high-hung carriage drawn by the tallest horses, and in the Row she was to be seen perched on a mighty hunter. She was high and expansive herself, though not exactly fat; her bones were big, her limbs were long, and she had a loud, hurrying voice, like the bell of a steamboat. While she spoke to his daughter she had the air of hiding from Colonel Chart, a little shyly, behind the wide ostrich fan. But Colonel Chart was not a man to be either ignored or eluded.

'Of course every one is going on to something else,' he said. 'I believe there are a lot of things to-night.'

'And where are *you* going?' Mrs Churchley asked, dropping her fan and turning her bright, hard eyes on the Colonel.

'Oh, I don't do that sort of thing!' he replied, in a tone of resentment just perceptible to his daughter. She saw in it that he thought Mrs Churchley might have done him a little more justice. But what made the honest soul think that she was a person to look to for a perception of fine shades? Indeed the

shade was one that it might have been a little difficult to seize –
the difference between 'going on' and coming to a dinner of
twenty people. The pair were in mourning; the second year had
not lightened it for Adela, but the Colonel had not objected to
dining with Mrs Churchley, any more than he had objected, at
Easter, to going down to the Millwards', where he had met her,
and where the girl had her reasons for believing him to have
known he should meet her. Adela was not clear about the
occasion of their original meeting, to which a certain mystery
attached. In Mrs Churchley's exclamation now there was the
fullest concurrence in Colonel Chart's idea; she didn't say, 'Ah,
yes, dear friend, I understand!' but this was the note of sympathy she plainly wished to sound. It immediately made Adela
say to her, 'Surely you must be going on somewhere yourself.'

'Yes, you must have a lot of places,' the Colonel observed,
looking at her shining raiment with a sort of invidious directness. Adela could read the tacit implication: 'You're not in
sorrow, in desolation.'

Mrs Churchley turned away from her at this, waiting just a
moment before answering. The red fan was up again, and this
time it sheltered her from Adela. 'I'll give everything up – for
you,' were the words that issued from behind it. '*Do* stay a little.
I always think this is such a nice hour. One can really talk,' Mrs
Churchley went on. The Colonel laughed; he said it wasn't fair.
But their hostess continued, to Adela, 'Do sit down; it's the
only time to have any talk.' The girl saw her father sit down, but
she wandered away, turning her back and pretending to look at
a picture. She was so far from agreeing with Mrs Churchley that
it was an hour she particularly disliked. She was conscious of
the queerness, the shyness, in London, of the gregarious flight
of guests, after a dinner, the general *sauve qui peut* and panic
fear of being left with the host and hostess. But personally she
always felt the contagion, always conformed to the flurry.
Besides, she felt herself turning red now, flushed with a conviction that had come over her and that she wished not to show.

Her father sat down on one of the big sofas with Mrs
Churchley; fortunately he was also a person with a presence
that could hold its own. Adela didn't care to sit and watch them

while they made love, as she crudely formulated it, and she cared still less to join in their conversation. She wandered further away, went into another of the bright, 'handsome', rather nude rooms – they were like women dressed for a ball – where the displaced chairs, at awkward angles to each other, seemed to retain the attitudes of bored talkers. Her heart beat strangely, but she continued to make a pretence of looking at the pictures on the walls and the ornaments on the tables, while she hoped that, as she preferred it, it would be also the course that her father would like best. She hoped 'awfully', as she would have said, that he wouldn't think her rude. She was a person of courage, and he was a kind, an intensely good-natured man; nevertheless, she was a good deal afraid of him. At home it had always been a religion with them to be nice to the people he liked. How, in the old days, her mother, her incomparable mother, so clever, so unerring, so perfect – how in the precious days her mother had practised that art! Oh, her mother, her irrecoverable mother! One of the pictures that she was looking at swam before her eyes. Mrs Churchley, in the natural course, would have begun immediately to climb stair-cases. Adela could see the high bony shoulders and the long crimson tail and the universal coruscating nod wriggle their business-like way through the rest of the night. Therefore she *must* have had her reasons for detaining them. There were mothers who thought every one wanted to marry their eldest son, and the girl asked herself if *she* belonged to the class of daughters who thought every one wanted to marry their father. Her companions left her alone; and though she didn't want to be near them, it angered her that Mrs Churchley didn't call her. That proved that she was conscious of the situation. She would have called her, only Colonel Chart had probably murmured, 'Don't.' That proved that he also was conscious. The time was really not long – ten minutes at the most elapsed – when he cried out, gaily, pleasantly, as if with a little jocular reproach, 'I say, Adela, we must release this dear lady!' He spoke, of course, as if it had been Adela's fault that they lingered. When they took leave she gave Mrs Churchley, without intention and without defiance, but from the simple sincerity of her anxiety, a longer look into the eyes than she had ever given her before. Mrs Churchley's onyx pupils reflected the question; they seemed to say: 'Yes, I *am*, if that's what you want to know!'

What made the case worse, what made the girl more sure, was the silence preserved by her companion in the brougham, on their way home. They rolled along in the June darkness from Prince's Gate to Seymour Street, each looking out of a window in conscious dumbness; watching without seeing the hurry of the London night, the flash of lamps, the quick roll on the wood of hansoms and other broughams. Adela had expected that her father would say something about Mrs Churchley; but when he said nothing, it was, strangely, still more as if he had spoken. In Seymour Street he asked the footman if Mr Godfrey had come in, to which the servant replied that he had come in early and gone straight to his room. Adela had perceived as much, without saying so, by a lighted window in the third storey; but she contributed no remark to the question. At the foot of the stairs her father halted a moment, hesitating, as if he had something on his mind; but what it amounted to, apparently, was only the dry 'Good-night' with which he presently ascended. It was the first time since her mother's death that he had bidden her good-night without kissing her. They were a kissing family, and after her mother's death the habit had taken a fresh spring. She had left behind her such a general passion of regret that in kissing each other they seemed to themselves a little to be kissing her. Now, as, standing in the hall, with the stiff watching footman (she could have said to him angrily, 'Go away!') planted near her, she looked with unspeakable pain at her father's back while he mounted, the effect was of his having withheld from other and still more sensitive lips the touch of his own.

He was going to his room, and after a moment she heard his door close. Then she said to the servant, 'Shut up the house' (she tried to do everything her mother had done, to be a little of what she had been, conscious only of mediocrity), and took her own way upstairs. After she had reached her room she waited, listening, shaken by the apprehension that she should hear her father come out again and go up to Godfrey. He would go up to tell him, to have it over without delay, precisely because it would be so difficult. She asked herself, indeed, why he should tell Godfrey when he had not taken the occasion – their drive home was an occasion – to tell herself. However, she wanted no announcing, no telling; there was such a horrible clearness in her mind that what she now waited for was only to be sure her father wouldn't leave his room. At the end of ten minutes she saw that this particular danger was over, upon which she came out and made her way to Godfrey. Exactly what she wanted to say to him first, if her father counted on the boy's greater indulgence, and before he could say anything, was, 'Don't forgive him; don't, don't!'

He was to go up for an examination, poor fellow, and during these weeks his lamp burned till the small hours. It was for the diplomatic service, and there was to be some frightful number of competitors; but Adela had great hopes of him – she believed so in his talents, and she saw, with pity, how hard he worked. This would have made her spare him, not trouble his night, his scanty rest, if anything less dreadful had been at stake. It was a blessing, however, that one could count upon his coolness, young as he was – his bright, good-looking discretion. Moreover he was the one who would care most. If Leonard was the eldest son – he had, as a matter of course, gone into the army and was in India, on the staff, by good luck, of a governor-general – it was exactly this that would make him comparatively indifferent. His life was elsewhere, and his father and he had been in a measure military comrades, so that he would be deterred by a certain delicacy from protesting; he wouldn't have liked his father to protest in an affair of *his*. Beatrice and Muriel would care, but they were too young to speak, and this was just why her own responsibility was so great.

Godfrey was in working-gear – shirt and trousers and slippers and a beautiful silk jacket. His room felt hot, though a window was open to the summer night; the lamp on the table shed its studious light over a formidable heap of text books and papers, and the bed showed that he had flung himself down to think out a problem. As soon as she got in she said to him: 'Father's going to marry Mrs Churchley!'

She saw the poor boy's pink face turn pale. 'How do you know?'

'I've seen with my eyes. We've been dining there – we've just come home. He's in love with her – she's in love with him; they'll arrange it.'

'Oh, I say!' Godfrey exclaimed, incredulous.

'He will, he will, he will!' cried the girl; and with this she burst into tears.

Godfrey, who had a cigarette in his hand, lighted it at one of the candles on the mantelpiece as if he were embarrassed. As Adela, who had dropped into his armchair, continued to sob, he said, after a moment: 'He oughtn't to – he oughtn't to.'

'Oh, think of mamma – think of mamma!' the girl went on.

'Yes, he ought to think of mamma'; and Godfrey looked at the tip of his cigarette.

'To such a woman as that, after *her*!'

'Dear old mamma!' said Godfrey, smoking.

Adela rose again, drying her eyes. 'It's like an insult to her; it's as if he denied her.' Now that she spoke of it, she felt herself tremendously exalted. 'It's as if he rubbed out at a stroke all the years of their happiness.'

'They were awfully happy,' said Godfrey.

'Think what she was – think how no one else will ever again be like her!' the girl cried.

'I suppose he's not very happy now,' Godfrey continued vaguely.

'Of course he isn't, any more than you and I are; and it's dreadful of him to want to be.'

'Well, don't make yourself miserable till you're sure,' the young man said.

But his sister showed him confidently that she *was* sure, from the way the pair had behaved together and from her father's attitude on the drive home. If Godfrey had been there he would have seen everything; it couldn't be explained, but he would have felt. When he asked at what moment the girl had first had her suspicion, she replied that it had all come at once, that evening; or that at least she had had no conscious fear till then. There had been signs for two or three weeks, but she hadn't understood them – ever since the day Mrs Churchley had dined in Seymour Street. Adela had thought it odd then that her father had wished to invite her, in the quiet way they were living; she was a person they knew so little. He had said something about her having been very civil to him, and that evening, already, she had guessed that he had been to Mrs Churchley's oftener than she had supposed. Tonight it had come to her clearly that he had been to see her every day since the day she dined with them; every afternoon, about the hour she thought he was at his club. Mrs Churchley was his club, – she was just like a club. At this Godfrey laughed; he wanted to know what his sister knew about clubs. She was slightly disappointed in his laugh, slightly wounded by it, but she knew perfectly what she meant: she meant that Mrs Churchley was public and florid, promiscuous and mannish.

'Oh, I daresay she's all right,' said Godfrey, as if he wanted to get on with his work. He looked at the clock on the mantelshelf; he would have to put in another hour.

'All right to come and take darling mamma's place – to sit where *she* used to sit, to lay her horrible hands on *her* things?' Adela was appalled – all the more that she had not expected it – at her brother's apparent acceptance of such a prospect.

He coloured; there was something in her passionate piety that scorched him. She glared at him with her tragic eyes as if he had profaned an altar. 'Oh, I mean nothing will come of it.'

'Not if we do our duty,' said Adela.

'Our duty?'

'You must speak to him – tell him how we feel; that we shall never forgive him, that we can't endure it.'

'He'll think I'm cheeky,' returned Godfrey, looking down at his papers, with his back to her and his hands in his pockets.

'Cheeky, to plead for *her* memory?'

'He'll say it's none of my business.'

'Then you believe he'll do it?' cried the girl.

'Not a bit. Go to bed!'

'*I'*ll speak to him,' said Adela, as pale as a young priestess.

'Don't cry out till you're hurt; wait till he speaks to *you*.'

'He won't, he won't!' the girl declared. 'He'll do it without telling us.'

Her brother had faced round to her again; he started a little at this, and again, at one of the candles, lighted his cigarette, which had gone out. She looked at him a moment; then he said something that surprised her.

'Is Mrs Churchley very rich?'

'I haven't the least idea. What has that to do with it?'

Godfrey puffed his cigarette. 'Does she live as if she were?'

'She has got a lot of showy things.'

'Well, we must keep our eyes open,' said Godfrey. 'And now you *must* let me get on.' He kissed his sister, as if to make up for dismissing her, or for his failure to take fire; and she held him a moment, burying her head on his shoulder. A wave of emotion surged through her; she broke out with a wail:

'Ah, why did she leave us? Why did she leave us?'

'Yes, why indeed?' the young man sighed, disengaging himself with a movement of oppression.

II

ADELA was so far right as that by the end of the week, though she remained certain, her father had not made the announcement she dreaded. What made her certain was the sense of her changed relations with him – of there being between them something unexpressed, something of which she was as conscious as she would have been of an unhealed wound. When she spoke of this to Godfrey, he said the change was of her own making, that she was cruelly unjust to the governor. She suffered even more from her brother's unexpected perversity; she had had so different a theory about him that her disappointment was almost an humiliation and she needed all her fortitude to pitch her faith lower. She wondered what had happened to him and why he had changed. She would have trusted him to feel right about anything, above all about such a matter as this. Their worship of their mother's memory, their recognition of her sacred place in their past, her exquisite influence in their father's life, his fortunes, his career, in the whole history of the family and welfare of the house – accomplished, clever, gentle, good, beautiful and capable as she had been, a woman whose soft distinction was universally proclaimed, so that on her death one of the Princesses, the most august of her friends, had written Adela such a note about her as princesses were understood very seldom to write: their hushed tenderness over all this was a kind of religion, and also a sort of honour, in falling away from which there was a semblance of treachery. This was not the way people usually felt in London, she knew; but, strenuous, ardent, observant girl as she was, with secrecies of sentiment and dim originalities of attitude, she had already made up her mind that London was no place to look for delicacies. Remembrance there was hammered thin, and to be faithful was to be a bore. The patient dead were sacrificed; they had no shrines, for people were literally ashamed of mourning. When they had hustled all sensibility out of their lives, they invented the fiction that they felt too much to utter. Adela said nothing to her sisters; this reticence was part of the virtue it was her system to exercise for them. *She* was to be their mother, a direct deputy and representative. Before the vision of that other woman parading in such a character, she felt capable of ingenuities and subtleties. The foremost of these was tremulously to watch her father. Five days after they had dined together at Mrs Churchley's he asked her if she had been to see that lady.

'No indeed, why should I?' Adela knew that he knew she had not been, since Mrs Churchley would have told him.

'Don't you call on people after you dine with them?' said Colonel Chart.

'Yes, in the course of time. I don't rush off within the week.'

Her father looked at her, and his eyes were colder than she had ever seen them, which was probably, she reflected, just the way her own appeared to him. 'Then you'll please rush off tomorrow. She's to dine with us on the 12th, and I shall expect your sisters to come down.'

Adela stared. 'To a dinner party?'

'It's not to be a dinner party. I want them to know Mrs Churchley.'

'Is there to be nobody else?'

'Godfrey, of course. A family party.'

The girl asked her brother that evening if *that* was not tantamount to an announcement. He looked at her queerly, and then he said, '*I've* been to see her.'

'What on earth did you do that for?'

'Father told me he wished it.'

'Then he *has* told you?'

'Told me what?' Godfrey asked, while her heart sank with the sense that he was making difficulties for her.

'That they're engaged, of course. What else can all this mean?'

'He didn't tell me that, but I like her.'

'*Like* her!' the girl shrieked.

'She's very kind, very good.'

'To thrust herself upon us when we hate her? Is that what you call kind? Is that what you call decent?'

'Oh, *I* don't hate her,' Godfrey rejoined, turning away as if his sister bored him.

She went the next day to see Mrs Churchley, with a vague plan of breaking out to her, appealing to her, saying, 'Oh, spare us! have mercy on us! let him alone! go away!' But that was not easy when they were face to face. Mrs Churchley had every intention of getting, as she would have said – she was perpetually using the expression – into touch; but her good intentions were as depressing as a tailor's misfits. She could never understand that they had no place for her vulgar charity; that their life was filled with a fragrance of perfection for which she had no sense fine enough. She was as undomestic as a shopfront and as out of tune as a parrot. She would make them live in the streets, or bring the streets into their lives – it was the same thing. She had evidently never read a book, and she used intonations that Adela had never heard, as if she had been an Australian or an American. She understood everything in a vulgar sense; speaking of Godfrey's visit to her and praising him according to her idea, saying horrid things about him – that he was awfully good-looking, a perfect gentleman, the kind she liked. How could her father, who was after all, in everything else, such a dear, listen to a woman, or endure her, who thought she was pleasing when she called the son of his dead wife a perfect gentleman? What would he have been, pray? Much she knew about what any of them were! When she told Adela she wanted her to like her, the girl thought for an instant her opportunity had come – the chance to plead with her and beg her off. But she presented such an impenetrable surface that it would have been like giving a message to a varnished door. She wasn't a woman, said Adela; she was an address.

When she dined in Seymour Street, the 'children', as the girl called the others, including Godfrey, liked her. Beatrice and Muriel stared shyly and silently at the wonders of her apparel (she was brutally overdressed!) without, of course, guessing the danger that tainted the air. They supposed her, in their innocence, to be amusing, and they didn't know, any more than she did herself, that she patronised them. When she was upstairs with them, after dinner, Adela could see her looking round the room at the things she meant to alter; their mother's things, not a bit like her own and not good enough for her. After a quarter of an hour of this, our young lady felt sure she was deciding that Seymour Street wouldn't do at all, the dear old home that had done for their mother for twenty years. Was she plotting to transport them all to her horrible Prince's Gate? Of one thing, at any rate, Adela was certain: her father, at that moment, alone in the dining-room with Godfrey, pretending to drink another glass of wine to make time, was coming to the point, was telling the news. When they came upstairs, they both, to her eyes, looked strange: the news had been told.

She had it from Godfrey before Mrs Churchley left the house, when, after a brief interval, he followed her out of the drawing-room on her taking her sisters to bed. She was waiting for him at the door of her room. Her father was then alone with his *fiancée* (the word was grotesque to Adela); it was already as if it were her home.

'What did you say to him?' the girl asked, when her brother had told her.

'I said nothing.' Then he added, colouring (the expression of her face was such), 'There was nothing to say.'

'Is that how it strikes you?' said Adela, staring at the lamp.

'He asked me to speak to her,' Godfrey went on.

'To speak to her?'

'To tell her I was glad.'

'And did you?' Adela panted.

'I don't know. I said something. She kissed me.'

'Oh, how *could* you?' shuddered the girl, covering her face with her hands.

'He says she's very rich,' said Godfrey simply.

'Is that why you kissed her?'

'I didn't kiss her. Good-night,' and the young man, turning his back upon her, went out.

When her brother was gone Adela locked herself in, as if with the fear that she should be overtaken or invaded, and during a sleepless, feverish, memorable night she took counsel of her uncompromising spirit. She saw things as they were, in all the indignity of life. The levity, the mockery, the infidelity, the ugliness, lay as plain as a map before her; it was a world *pour rire*, but she cried about it, all the same. The morning dawned early, or rather it seemed to her that there had been no night, nothing but a sickly, creeping day. But by the time she heard the house stirring again she had determined what to do. When she came down to the breakfast-room her father was already in his place, with newspapers and letters; and she expected the first words he would utter to be a rebuke to her for having disappeared, the night before, without taking leave of Mrs Churchley. Then she saw that he wished to be intensely kind, to make every allowance, to conciliate and console her. He knew that she knew from Godfrey, and he got up and kissed her. He told her as quickly as possible, to have it over, stammering a little, with an 'I've a piece of news for you that will probably shock you,' yet looking even exaggeratedly grave and rather pompous, to inspire the respect he didn't deserve. When he kissed her she melted, she burst into tears. He held her against him, kissing her again and again, saying tenderly, 'Yes, yes, I know, I know.' But he didn't know, or he could never have done it. Beatrice and Muriel came in, frightened when they saw her crying, and still more scared when she turned to them with words and an air that were terrible in their comfortable little lives: 'Papa's going to be married; he's going to marry Mrs Churchley!' After staring a moment and seeing their father look as strange, on his side, as Adela, though in a different way, the children also began to cry, so that when the servants arrived, with tea and boiled eggs, these functionaries were greatly embarrassed with their burden, not knowing whether to come in or hang back. They all scraped together a decorum, and as soon as the things had been put on the table the Colonel banished the men with a glance. Then he made a little affectionate speech to Beatrice and Muriel, in which he assured them that Mrs Churchley was the kindest, the most delightful, of women, only wanting to make them happy, only wanting to make him happy, and convinced that he would be if they were and that they would be if he was.

'What do such words mean?' Adela asked herself. She declared privately that they meant nothing, but she was silent, and every one was silent, on account of the advent of Miss Flynn, the governess, before whom Colonel Chart preferred not to discuss the situation. Adela recognised on the spot that, if things were to go as he wished, his children would practically never again be alone with him. He would spend all his time with Mrs Churchley till they were married, and then Mrs Churchley would spend all her time with him. Adela was ashamed of him, and that was horrible – all the more that every one else would be, all his other friends, every one who had known her mother. But the public dishonour to that high memory should not be enacted; he should not do as he wished.

After breakfast her father told her that it would give him pleasure if, in a day or two, she would take her sisters to see Mrs Churchley, and she replied that he should be obeyed. He held her hand a moment, looking at her with an appeal in his eyes which presently hardened into sternness. He wanted to know that she forgave him, but he also wanted to say to her that he expected her to mind what she did, to go straight. She turned away her eyes; she was indeed ashamed of him.

She waited three days, and then she took her sisters to see Mrs Churchley. That lady was surrounded with callers, as

Adela knew she would be; it was her 'day' and the occasion the girl preferred. Before this she had spent all her time with her sisters, talking to them about their mother, playing upon their memory of her, making them cry and making them laugh, reminding them of certain hours of their early childhood, telling them anecdotes of her own. None the less she assured them that she believed there was no harm at all in Mrs Churchley, and that when the time should come she would probably take them out immensely. She saw with smothered irritation that they enjoyed their visit in Prince's Gate; they had never been at anything so 'grown up', nor seen so many smart bonnets and brilliant complexions. Moreover, they were considered with interest, as if, as features of Mrs Churchley's new life, they had been described in advance and were the heroines of the occasion. There were so many ladies present that Mrs Churchley didn't talk to them much; but she called them her 'chicks' and asked them to hand about tea-cups and bread and butter. All this was highly agreeable and indeed intensely exciting to Beatrice and Muriel, who had little round red spots in *their* cheeks when they came away. Adela quivered with the sense that her mother's children were now Mrs Churchley's 'chicks' and features of Mrs Churchley's life.

It was one thing to have made up her mind, however; it was another thing to make her attempt. It was when she learned from Godfrey that the day was fixed, the 20th of July, only six weeks removed, that she felt the importance of prompt action. She learned everything from Godfrey now, having determined that it would be hypocrisy to question her father. Even her silence was hypocritical, but she couldn't weep and wail. Her father showed extreme tact; taking no notice of her detachment, treating her as if it were a moment of *bouderie* which he was bound to allow her and which would pout itself away. She debated much as to whether she should take Godfrey into her confidence; she would have done so without hesitation if he had not disappointed her. He was so strange and so perversely preoccupied that she could explain it only by the high pressure at which he was living, his anxiety about his 'exam'. He was in a fidget, in a fever, putting on a spurt to come in first; sceptical moreover about his success and cynical about everything else. He appeared to agree to the general axiom that they didn't want a strange woman thrust into their home, but he found Mrs Churchley 'very jolly as a person to know'. He had been to see her by himself; he had been to see her three times. He said to his sister that he would make the most of her now; he should probably be so little in Seymour Street after these days. What Adela at last determined to say to him was that the marriage would never take place. When he asked her what she meant and who was to prevent it, she replied that the interesting couple would give it up themselves, or that Mrs Churchley at least would after a week or two back out of it.

'That will be really horrid then,' Godfrey rejoined. 'The only respectable thing, at the point they've come to, is to put it through. Charming for poor father to have the air of being "chucked".'

This made her hesitate two days more, but she found answers more valid than any objections. The many-voiced answer to everything – it was like the autumn wind around the house – was the backward affront to her mother. Her mother was dead, but it killed her again. So one morning, at eleven o'clock, when Adela knew her father was writing letters, she went out quietly and, stopping the first hansom she met, drove to Prince's Gate. Mrs Churchley was at home, and she was shown into the drawing-room with the request that she would wait five minutes. She waited, without the sense of breaking down at the last, the impulse to run away, which was what she had expected to have. In the cab and at the door her heart had beat terribly, but now, suddenly, with the game really to play, she found herself lucid and calm. It was a joy to her to feel later that this was the way Mrs Churchley found her; not confused, not stammering nor prevaricating, only a little amazed at her own courage, conscious of the immense responsibility of her step and wonderfully older than her years. Her hostess fixed her at first with the waiting eyes of a cashier, but after a little, to Adela's surprise, she burst into tears. At this the girl cried herself, but with the secret happiness of believing they were saved. Mrs Churchley said she would think over what she had been told, and she promised Adela, freely enough and very firmly, not to betray the secret of her visit to the Colonel. They were saved – they were saved: the words sung themselves in the girl's soul as she came downstairs. When the door was opened for her she saw her brother on the step, and they looked at each other in surprise, each finding it on the part of the other an odd hour for Prince's Gate. Godfrey remarked that Mrs Churchley would have enough of the family, and Adela answered that she would perhaps have too much. None the less the young man went in, while his sister took her way home.

III

ADELA CHART saw nothing of her brother for nearly a week; he had more and more his own time and hours, adjusted to his tremendous responsibilities, and he spent whole days at his crammer's. When she knocked at his door, late in the evening, he was not in his room. It was known in the house that he was greatly worried; he was horribly nervous about his ordeal. It was to begin on the 23d of June, and his father was as worried as himself. The wedding had been arranged in relation to this; they wished poor Godfrey's fate settled first, though it was felt that the nuptials would be darkened if it should not be settled right.

Ten days after her morning visit to Mrs Churchley Adela began to perceive that there was a difference in the air; but as yet she was afraid to exult. It was not a difference for the better, so that there might be still many hours of pain. Her father, since the announcement of his intended marriage, had been visibly pleased with himself, but that pleasure appeared to have undergone a check. Adela had the impression which the passengers on a great steamer receive when, in the middle of the night, they hear the engines stop. As this impression resolves itself into the general sense that something serious has happened, so the girl asked herself what had happened now. She had expected something serious; but it was as if she couldn't keep still in her cabin – she wanted to go up and see. On the 20th, just before breakfast, her maid brought her a message from her brother. Mr

Godfrey would be obliged if she would speak to him in his room. She went straight up to him, dreading to find him ill, broken down on the eve of his formidable week. This was not the case, however, inasmuch as he appeared to be already at work, to have been at work since dawn. But he was very white, and his eyes had a strange and new expression. Her beautiful young brother looked older; he looked haggard and hard. He met her there as if he had been waiting for her, and he said immediately: 'Please to tell me this, Adela: what was the purpose of your visit, the other morning, to Mrs Churchley – the day I met you at her door?'

She stared – she hesitated. 'The purpose? What's the matter? Why do you ask?'

'They've put it off – they've put it off a month.'

'Ah, thank God!' said Adela.

'Why do you thank God?' Godfrey exclaimed roughly.

His sister gave a strained, intense smile. 'You know I think it's all wrong.'

He stood looking at her up and down. 'What did you do there? How did you interfere?'

'Who told you I interfered?' she asked, flushing.

'You said something – you did something. I knew you had done it when I saw you come out.'

'What I did was my own business.'

'Damn your own business!' cried the young man.

She had never in her life been so spoken to, and in advance, if she had been given the choice, she would have said that she would rather die than be so spoken to by Godfrey. But her spirit was high, and for a moment she was as angry as if some one had cut at her with a whip. She escaped the blow, but she felt the insult. 'And *your* business, then?' she asked. 'I wondered what that was when I saw *you*.'

He stood a moment longer frowning at her; then, with the exclamation 'You've made a pretty mess!' he turned away from her and sat down to his books.

They had put it off, as he said; her father was dry and stiff and official about it. 'I suppose I had better let you know that we have thought it best to postpone our marriage till the end of the summer – Mrs Churchley has so many arrangements to make': he was not more expansive than that. She neither knew nor greatly cared whether it was her fancy or a reality that he watched her obliquely, to see how she would take these words. She flattered herself that, thanks to Godfrey's preparation, cruel as the form of it had been, she took them very cleverly. She had a perfectly good conscience, for she was now able to judge what odious elements Mrs Churchley, whom she had not seen since the morning in Prince's Gate, had already introduced into their relations with each other. She was able to infer that her father had not concurred in the postponement, for he was more restless than before, more absent, and distinctly irritable. There was of course still the question of how much of this condition was to be attributed to his solicitude about Godfrey. That young man took occasion to say a horrible thing to his sister: 'If I don't pass it will be your fault.' These were dreadful days for the girl, and she asked herself how she could have borne them if the hovering spirit of her mother had not been at her side. Fortunately, she always felt it there, sustaining, commending, sanctifying. Suddenly her father announced to her that he wished her to go immediately, with her sisters, down to Overland, where there was always part of a household and where for a few weeks they would be sufficiently comfortable. The only explanation he gave of this desire was that he wanted them out of the way. 'Out of the way of what?' she queried, since, for the time, there were to be no preparations in Seymour Street. She was willing to believe that it was out of the way of his nerves.

She never needed urging, however, to go to Overland, the dearest old house in the world, where the happiest days of her young life had been spent and the silent nearness of her mother always seemed greatest. She was happy again, with Beatrice and Muriel and Miss Flynn, and the air of summer, and the haunted rooms, and her mother's garden, and the talking oaks and the nightingales. She wrote briefly to her father, to give him, as he had requested, an account of things; and he wrote back that, since she was so contented (she didn't remember telling him that), she had better not return to town at all. The rest of the season was not important for her, and he was getting on very well. He mentioned that Godfrey had finished his exam; but, as she knew, there would be a tiresome wait before they could learn the result. Godfrey was going abroad for a month with young Sherard – he had earned a little rest and a little fun. He went abroad without a word to Adela, but in his beautiful little hand he took a chaffing leave of Beatrice. The child showed her sister the letter, of which she was very proud and which contained no message for Adela. This was the worst bitterness of the whole crisis for that young lady – that it exhibited so strangely the creature in the world whom, after her mother, she had loved best.

Colonel Chart had said he would 'run down' while his children were at Overland, but they heard no more about it. He only wrote two or three times to Miss Flynn, upon matters in regard to which Adela was surprised that he should not have communicated with herself. Muriel accomplished an upright little letter to Mrs Churchley – her eldest sister neither fostered nor discouraged the performance – to which Mrs Churchley replied, after a fortnight, in a meagre and, as Adela thought, illiterate fashion, making no allusion to the approach of any closer tie. Evidently the situation had changed; the question of the marriage was dropped, at any rate for the time. This idea gave the girl a singular and almost intoxicating sense of power; she felt as if she were riding a great wave of responsibility. She had chosen and acted, and the greatest could do no more than that. The grand thing was to see one's results, and what else was she doing? These results were in important and opulent lives; the stage was large on which she moved her figures. Such a vision was exciting, and as they had the use of a couple of ponies at Overland she worked off her excitement by a long gallop. A day or two after this, however, came news of which the effect was to rekindle it. Godfrey had come back, the list had been published, he had passed first. These happy tidings proceeded from the young man himself; he announced them by a telegram to Beatrice, who had never in her life before received such a missive and was proportionately inflated. Adela reflected that she herself ought to have felt snubbed, but she was too happy.

They were free again, they were themselves, the nightmare of the previous weeks was blown away, the unity and dignity of her father's life were restored, and, to round off her sense of success, Godfrey had achieved his first step toward high distinction. She wrote to him the next day, as frankly and affectionately as if there had been no estrangement between them; and besides telling him that she rejoiced in his triumph, she begged him in charity to let them know exactly how the case stood with regard to Mrs Churchley.

Late in the summer afternoon she walked through the park to the village with her letter, posted it and came back. Suddenly, at one of the turns of the avenue, half-way to the house, she saw a young man looking toward her and waiting for her – a young man who proved to be Godfrey, on his march, on foot, across from the station. He had seen her, as he took his short cut, and if he had come down to Overland it was not, apparently, to avoid her. There was none of the joy of his triumph in his face, however, as he came a very few steps to meet her; and although, stiffly enough, he let her kiss him and say, 'I'm so glad – I'm so glad!' she felt that this tolerance was not quite the calmness of the rising diplomatist. He turned toward the house with her and walked on a short distance, while she uttered the hope that he had come to stay some days.

'Only till to-morrow morning. They are sending me straight to Madrid. I came down to say good-by; there's a fellow bringing my portmanteau.'

'To Madrid? How awfully nice! And it's awfully nice of you to have come,' Adela said, passing her hand into his arm.

The movement made him stop, and, stopping, he turned on her, in a flash, a face of something more than suspicion – of passionate reprobation. 'What I really came for – you might as well know without more delay – is to ask you a question.'

'A question?' Adela repeated with a beating heart.

They stood there, under the old trees, in the lingering light, and, young and fine and fair as they both were, they were in complete superficial accord with the peaceful English scene. A near view, however, would have shown that Godfrey Chart had not come down to Overland to be superficial. He looked deep into his sister's eyes and demanded: 'What was it you said that morning to Mrs Churchley?'

Adela gazed at the ground a moment; then, raising her eyes: 'If she has told you, why do you ask?'

'She has told me nothing. I've seen for myself.'

'What have you seen?'

'She has broken it off – everything's over – father's in the depths.'

'In the depths?' the girl quavered.

'Did you think it would make him jolly?' asked her brother. 'He'll get over it; he'll be glad.'

'That remains to be seen. You interfered, you invented something, you got round her. I insist on knowing what you did.'

Adela felt that she could be obstinate if she wished, and that if it should be a question of organising a defence she should find treasures of perversity under her hand. She stood looking down again a moment, and saying to herself, 'I could be dumb and dogged if I chose, but I scorn to be.' She was not ashamed of what she had done, but she wanted to be clear. 'Are you absolutely certain it's broken off?'

'He is, and she is; so that's as good.'

'What reason has she given?'

'None at all – or half a dozen; it's the same thing. She has changed her mind – she mistook her feelings – she can't part with her independence; moreover, he has too many children.'

'Did he tell you this?' said Adela.

'Mrs Churchley told me. She has gone abroad for a year.'

'And she didn't tell you what I said to her?'

'Why should I take this trouble if she had?'

'You might have taken it to make me suffer,' said Adela. 'That appears to be what you want to do.'

'No, I leave that to *you*; it's the good turn you've done me!' cried the young man, with hot tears in his eyes.

She stared, aghast with the perception that there was some dreadful thing she didn't know; but he walked on, dropping the question angrily and turning his back to her as if he couldn't trust himself. She read his disgust in his averted face, in the way he squared his shoulders and smote the ground with his stick, and she hurried after him and presently overtook him. She accompanied him for a moment in silence; then she pleaded: 'What do you mean? What in the world have I done to you?'

'She would have helped me; she was all ready to do it,' said Godfrey.

'Helped you in what?' She wondered what he meant; if he had made debts that he was afraid to confess to his father and – of all horrible things – had been looking to Mrs Churchley to pay. She turned red with the mere apprehension of this and, on the heels of her guess, exulted again at having perhaps averted such a shame.

'Can't you see that I'm in trouble? Where are your eyes, your senses, your sympathy, that you talk so much about? Haven't you seen these six months that I've a cursed worry in my life?'

She seized his arm, she made him stop, she stood looking up at him like a frightened little girl. 'What's the matter, Godfrey – what *is* the matter?'

'You've vexed me so – I could strangle you!' he growled. This idea added nothing to her dread; her dread was that he had done some wrong, was stained with some guilt. She uttered it to him with clasped hands, begging him to tell her the worst; but, still more passionately, he cut her short with his own cry: 'In God's name, satisfy me! What infernal thing did you do?'

'It was not infernal; it was right. I told her mamma had been wretched,' said Adela.

'Wretched? You told her such a lie?'

'It was the only way, and she believed me.'

'Wretched how – wretched when – wretched where?' the young man stammered.

'I told her papa had made her so, and that *she* ought to know it. I told her the question troubled me unspeakably, but that I had made up my mind it was my duty to initiate her.' Adela paused, with the light of bravado in her face, as if, though struck while she phrased it, with the monstrosity of what she had done, she was incapable of abating a jot of it. 'I notified her that he had faults and peculiarities that made mamma's life a long worry – a martyrdom that she hid wonderfully from the world, but that we saw and that I had often pitied. I told her what they were, these faults and peculiarities; I put the dots on the *i*'s. I said it wasn't fair to let another person marry him without a warning. I warned her; I satisfied my conscience. She could do as she liked. My responsibility was over.'

Godfrey gazed at her; he listened, with parted lips, incredulous and appalled. 'You invented such a tissue of falsities and calumnies, and you talk about your conscience? You stand there in your senses and proclaim your crime?'

'I would have committed any crime that would have rescued us.'

'You insult and defame your own father?' Godfrey continued.

'He'll never know it; she took a vow she wouldn't tell him.'

'I'll be damned if *I* won't tell him!' Godfrey cried.

Adela felt sick at this, but she flamed up to resent the treachery, as it struck her, of such a menace. 'I did right – I did right!' she vehemently declared. 'I went down on my knees to pray for guidance, and I saved mamma's memory from outrage. But if I hadn't, if I hadn't' – she faltered for an instant – 'I'm not worse than you, and I'm not so bad, for you've done something that you're ashamed to tell me.'

Godfrey had taken out his watch; he looked at it with quick intensity, as if he were not hearing nor heeding her. Then, glancing up with his calculating eye, he fixed her long enough to exclaim, with unsurpassable horror and contempt: 'You raving maniac!' He turned away from her; he bounded down the avenue in the direction from which they had come, and, while she watched him, strode away across the grass, toward the short cut to the station.

IV

GODFREY'S portmanteau, by the time Adela got home, had been brought to the house, but Beatrice and Muriel, who had been informed of this, waited for their brother in vain. Their sister said nothing to them about having seen him, and she accepted, after a little, with a calmness that surprised herself,

the idea that he had returned to town to denounce her. She
believed that would make no difference now – she had done
what she had done. She had somehow a faith in Mrs Churchley.
If Mrs Churchley had broken off she wouldn't renew. She was a
heavy-footed person, incapable of further agility. Adela recognised too that it might well have come over her that there were
too many children. Lastly the girl fortified herself with the
reflection, grotesque under the circumstances and tending to
prove that her sense of humour was not high, that her father,
after all, was not a man to be played with. It seemed to her,
at any rate, that if she *had* prevented his marriage she could
bear anything – bear imprisonment and bread and water, bear
lashes and torture, bear even his lifelong reproach. What she
could bear least was the wonder of the inconvenience she had
inflicted on Godfrey. She had time to turn this over, very vainly,
for a succession of days – days more numerous than she had
expected, which passed without bringing her from London any
summons to come up and take her punishment. She sounded
the possible, she compared the degrees of the probable; feeling
however that, as a cloistered girl she was poorly equipped for
speculation. She tried to imagine the calamitous things young
men might do, and could only feel that such things would
naturally be connected either with money or with women.
She became conscious that after all she knew almost nothing
about either subject. Meanwhile there was no reverberation
from Seymour Street – only a sultry silence.

At Overland she spent hours in her mother's garden, where
she had grown up, where she considered that she was training
for old age, for she meant not to depend upon whist. She loved
the place as, had she been a good Catholic, she would have
loved the smell of her parish church; and indeed there was in
her passion for flowers something of the respect of a religion.
They seemed to her the only things in the world that really
respected themselves, unless one made an exception for Nutkins, who had been in command all through her mother's time,
with whom she had had a real friendship, and who had been
affected by their pure example. He was the person left in the
world with whom, on the whole, she could talk most intimately

about her mother. They never had to name her together – they only said 'she'; and Nutkins freely conceded that she had taught him everything he knew. When Beatrice and Muriel said 'she' they referred to Mrs Churchley. Adela had reason to believe that she should never marry, and that some day she should have about a thousand a year. This made her see in the far future a little garden of her own, under a hill, full of rare and exquisite things, where she would spend most of her old age on her knees, with an apron and stout gloves, a pair of shears and a trowel, steeped in the comfort of being thought mad.

One morning, ten days after her scene with Godfrey, upon coming back into the house shortly before lunch, she was met by Miss Flynn with the notification that a lady in the drawing-room had been waiting for her for some minutes. 'A lady' suggested immediately Mrs Churchley. It came over Adela that the form in which her penalty was to descend would be a personal explanation with that misdirected woman. The lady had not given her name, and Miss Flynn had not seen Mrs Churchley; nevertheless the governess was certain that Adela's surmise was wrong.

'Is she big and dreadful?' the girl asked.

Miss Flynn, who was circumspection itself, hesitated a moment. 'She's dreadful, but she's not big.' She added that she was not sure she ought to let Adela go in alone; but this young lady felt throughout like a heroine, and it was not for a heroine to shrink from any encounter. Was she not, every instant, in transcendent contact with her mother? The visitor might have no connection whatever with the drama of her father's frustrated marriage; but everything, to-day, to Adela, was a part of that.

Miss Flynn's description had prepared her for a considerable shock, but she was not agitated by her first glimpse of the person who awaited her. A youngish, well-dressed woman stood there, and silence was between them while they looked at each other. Before either of them had spoken, however, Adela began to see what Miss Flynn had intended. In the light of the drawing-room window the lady was five-and-thirty years of age and had vivid yellow hair. She also had a blue cloth suit with brass buttons, a stick-up collar like a gentleman's, a necktie arranged in a sailor's knot, with a golden pin in the shape of a little lawn-tennis racket, and pearl-grey gloves with big black stitchings. Adela's second impression was that she was an actress; her third was that no such person had ever before crossed that threshold.

'I'll tell you what I've come for,' said the apparition. 'I've come to ask you to intercede.' She was not an actress; an actress would have had a nicer voice.

'To intercede?' Adela was too bewildered to ask her to sit down.

'With your father, you know. He doesn't know, but he'll have to.' Her 'have' sounded like ''ave'. She explained, with many more such sounds, that she was Mrs Godfrey, that they had been married seven mortal months. If Godfrey was going abroad she must go with him, and the only way she could go with him would be for his father to do something. He was afraid of his father – that was clear; he was afraid even to tell him. What she had come down for was to see some other member of the family face to face ('fice to fice' Mrs Godfrey called it), and try if he couldn't be approached by another side. If no one else would act, then she would just have to act herself. The Colonel would have to do something – that was the only way out of it.

What really happened Adela never quite understood; what seemed to be happening was that the room went round and round. Through the blur of perception accompanying this effect the sharp stabs of her visitor's revelation came to her like the words heard by a patient 'going off' under either. She denied passionately, afterwards, even to herself, that she had done anything so abject as to faint; but there was a lapse in her consciousness in relation to Miss Flynn's intervention. This intervention had evidently been active, for when they talked the matter over, later in the day, with bated breath and infinite dissimulation for the schoolroom quarter, the governess had more information, and still stranger, to impart than to receive. She was at any rate under the impression that she had athletic-ally contended, in the drawing-room, with the yellow hair, after removing Adela from the scene and before inducing Mrs

Godfrey to withdraw. Miss Flynn had never known a more thrilling day, for all the rest of it too was pervaded with agitations and conversations, precautions and alarms. It was given out to Beatrice and Muriel that their sister had been taken suddenly ill, and the governess ministered to her in her room. Indeed Adela had never found herself less at ease; for this time she had received a blow that she couldn't return. There was nothing to do but to take it, to endure the humiliation of her wound.

At first she declined to take it; it was much easier to consider that her visitor was a monstrous masquerader. On the face of the matter, moreover, it was not fair to believe till one heard; and to hear in such a case was to hear Godfrey himself. Whatever his sister had tried to imagine about him she had not arrived at anything so belittling as an idiotic secret marriage with a dyed and painted hag. Adela repeated this last word as if it gave her some comfort; and indeed where everything was so bad fifteen years of seniority made the case little worse. Miss Flynn was portentous, for Miss Flynn had had it out with the wretch. She had cross-questioned her and had not broken her down. This was the most important hour of Miss Flynn's life; for whereas she usually had to content herself with being humbly and gloomily in the right, she could now be magnanimously and showily so. Her only perplexity was as to what she ought to do – write to Colonel Chart or go up to town to see him. She bloomed with alternatives, never having known the like before. Toward evening Adela was obliged to recognise that Godfrey's worry, of which he had spoken to her, had appeared bad enough to consist even of a low wife, and to remember that, so far from its being inconceivable that a young man in his position should clandestinely take one, she had been present, years before, during her mother's lifetime, when Lady Molesley declared gaily, over a cup of tea, that this was precisely what she expected of her eldest son. The next morning it was the worst possibilities that seemed the clearest; the only thing left with a tatter of dusky comfort being the ambiguity of Godfrey's charge that his sister's action had 'done' for him. That was a matter by itself, and she racked her brains for a connecting link between Mrs Churchley and Mrs Godfrey. At last she made up her mind that they were related by blood; very likely, though differing in fortune, they were cousins or even sisters. But even then what did her brother mean?

Arrested by the unnatural fascination of opportunity, Miss Flynn received before lunch a telegram from Colonel Chart – an order for dinner and a vehicle; he and Godfrey were to arrive at six o'clock. Adela had plenty of occupation for the interval, for she was pitying her father when she was not rejoicing that her mother had gone too soon to know. She flattered herself she discerned the providential reason of that cruelty now. She found time however still to wonder for what purpose, under the circumstances, Godfrey was to be brought down. She was not unconscious, it is true, that she had little general knowledge of what usually was done with young men in that predicament. One talked about the circumstances, but the circumstances were an abyss. She felt this still more when she found, on her father's arrival, that nothing, apparently, was to happen as she had taken for granted it would. There was a kind of inviolable hush over the whole affair, but no tragedy, no publicity, nothing ugly. The tragedy had been in town, and the faces of the two men spoke of it, in spite of themselves; so that at present there was only a family dinner, with Beatrice and Muriel and the governess, and almost a company tone, the result of the desire to avoid publicity. Adela admired her father; she knew what he was feeling, if Mrs Godfrey had been at him, and yet she saw him positively gallant. He was very gentle, he never looked at his son, and there were moments when he seemed almost sick with sadness. Godfrey was equally inscrutable and therefore wholly different from what he had been as he stood before her in the park. If he was to start on his career (with such a wife! – wouldn't she utterly blight it?) he was already professional enough to know how to wear a mask.

Before they rose from table the girl was wholly bewildered, so little could she perceive the effects of such large causes. She had nerved herself for a great ordeal, but the air was as sweet as an anodyne. It was constantly plain to her that her father was deadly sad – as pathetic as a creature jilted. He was broken, but he showed no resentment; there was a weight on his heart, but he had lightened it by dressing as immaculately as usual for dinner. She asked herself what immensity of a row there could have been in town to have left his anger so spent. He went through everything, even to sitting with his son after dinner. When they came out together he invited Beatrice and Muriel to the billiard-room; and as Miss Flynn discreetly withdrew Adela was left alone with Godfrey, who was completely changed and not in a rage any more. He was broken, too, but he was not so pathetic as his father. He was only very correct and apologetic; he said to his sister, 'I'm awfully sorry *you* were annoyed; it was something I never dreamed of.'

She couldn't think immediately what he meant; then she grasped the reference to the yellow hair. She was uncertain, however, what tone to take; perhaps his father had arranged with him that they were to make the best of it. But she spoke her own despair in the way she murmured: 'O Godfrey, Godfrey, is it true?'

'I've been the most unutterable donkey – you can say what you like to me. You can't say anything worse than I've said to myself.'

'My brother, my brother!' his words made her moan. He hushed her with a movement, and she asked, 'What has father said?'

Godfrey looked over her head. 'He'll give her six hundred a year.'

'Ah, the angel!'

'On condition she never comes near me. She has solemnly promised; and she'll probably leave me alone, to get the money. If she doesn't – in diplomacy – I'm lost.' The young man had been turning his eyes vaguely about, this way and that, to avoid meeting hers; but after another instant he gave up the effort, and she had the miserable confession of his glance. 'I've been living in hell,' he said.

'My brother, my brother!' she repeated.

'I'm not an idiot; yet for her I've behaved like one. Don't ask me – you mustn't know. It was all done in a day, and since then, fancy my condition – fancy my work!'

'Thank God you passed!' cried Adela.

'I would have shot myself if I hadn't. I had an awful day yesterday with father; it was late at night before it was over. I leave England next week. He brought me down here for it to look well – so that the children sha'n't know.'

'He's wonderful!' she murmured.

'He's wonderful!' said Godfrey.

'Did *she* tell him?' the girl asked.

'She came straight to Seymour Street from here. She saw him alone first; then he called me in. *That* luxury lasted about an hour.'

Adela said, 'Poor, poor father!' to this; on which her brother remained silent. Then, after he had remarked that it had been the scene he had lived in terror of all through his cramming, and she had stammered her pity and admiration at such a mixture of anxieties and such a triumph of talent, she demanded: 'Have you told him?'

'Told him what?'

'What you said you would – what *I* did.'

Godfrey turned away as if at present he had very little interest in that inferior tribulation. 'I was angry with you, but I cooled off. I held my tongue.'

Adela clasped her hands. 'You thought of mamma!'

'Oh, don't speak of mamma,' said the young man tenderly.

It was indeed not a happy moment; and she murmured: 'No; if you *had* thought of her –'

This made Godfrey turn back at her, with a little flare in his eyes. 'Oh, *then* it didn't prevent. I thought that woman was good. I believed in her.'

'Is she *very* bad?' his sister inquired.

'I shall never mention her to you again,' Godfrey answered, with dignity.

'You may believe that *I* won't speak of her. So father doesn't know?' she added.

'Doesn't know what?'

'That I said that to Mrs Churchley.'

'I don't think so, but you must find out for yourself.'

'I shall find out,' said Adela. 'But what had Mrs Churchley to do with it?'

'With *my* misery? I told her. I had to tell some one.'

'Why didn't you tell me?'

Godfrey hesitated. 'Oh, you take things so beastly hard – you make such rows.' Adela covered her face with her hands, and he went on: 'What I wanted was comfort – not to be lashed up. I thought I should go mad. I wanted Mrs Churchley to break it to father, to intercede for me and help him to meet it. She was awfully kind to me; she listened and she understood; she could fancy how it had happened. Without her I shouldn't have pulled through. She liked me, you know,' Godfrey dropped. 'She said she would do what she could for me; she was full of sympathy and resource; I really leaned on her. But when you cut in, of course it spoiled everything. That's why I was so angry with you. She couldn't do anything then.'

Adela dropped her hands, staring; she felt that she had walked in darkness. 'So that he had to meet it alone?'

'*Dame!*' said Godfrey, who had got up his French tremendously.

Muriel came to the door to say papa wished the two others to join them, and the next day Godfrey returned to town. His father remained at Overland, without an intermission, the rest of the summer and the whole of the autumn, and Adela had a chance to find out, as she had said, whether he knew that she had interfered. But in spite of her chance she never found out. He knew that Mrs Churchley had thrown him over and he knew that his daughter rejoiced in it, but he appeared not to have divined the relation between the two facts. It was strange that one of the matters he was clearest about – Adela's secret triumph – should have been just the thing which, from this time on, justified less and less such a confidence. She was too sorry for him to be consistently glad. She watched his attempts to wind himself up on the subject of shorthorns and drainage, and she favoured to the utmost of her ability his intermittent disposition to make a figure in orchids. She wondered whether they mightn't have a few people at Overland; but when she mentioned the idea her father asked what in the world there would be to attract them. It was a confoundedly stupid house, he remarked, with all respect to *her* cleverness. Beatrice and Muriel were mystified; the prospect of going out immensely had faded so utterly away. They were apparently not to go out at all. Colonel Chart was aimless and bored; he paced up and down and went back to smoking, which was bad for him, and looked drearily out of windows, as if on the bare chance that something might arrive. Did he expect Mrs Churchley to arrive, to relent? It was Adela's belief that she gave no sign. But the girl thought it really remarkable of her not to have betrayed her ingenious young visitor. Adela's judgement of human nature was perhaps harsh, but she believed that many women, under the circumstances, would not have been so forbearing. This lady's conception of the point of honour presented her as rather a higher type than one might have supposed.

Adela knew her father found the burden of Godfrey's folly very heavy to bear and was incommoded at having to pay the horrible woman six hundred a year. Doubtless he was having dreadful letters from her; doubtless she threatened them all with a hideous exposure. If the matter should be bruited Godfrey's prospects would collapse on the spot. He thought Madrid very charming and curious, but Mrs Godfrey was in England, so that his father had to face the music. Adela took a dolorous comfort in thinking that her mother was out of *that* – it would have killed her; but this didn't blind her to the fact that the comfort for her father would perhaps have been greater if he had had some one to talk to about his trouble. He never dreamed of doing so to her, and she felt that she couldn't ask him. In the family life he wanted utter silence about it. Early in the winter he went abroad for ten weeks, leaving her with her sisters in the country, where it was not to be denied that at this time existence had very little savour. She half expected that her sister-in-law would descend upon her again; but the fear was not justified, and the quietude of such a personage savoured terribly of expense. There were sure to be extras. Colonel Chart went to Paris and to Monte Carlo and then to Madrid to see his boy. Adela wondered whether he would meet Mrs Churchley somewhere, since, if she had gone for a year, she would still be on the Continent. If he should meet her perhaps the affair would come on again: she caught herself musing over this. Her father brought back no news of her, and seeing him after an interval, she was struck afresh with his jilted and wasted air. She didn't like it; she resented it. A little more and she would have said that that was no way to treat such a man.

They all went up to town in March, and on one of the first days of April she saw Mrs Churchley in the park. She herself remained apparently invisible to that lady – she herself and Beatrice and Muriel, who sat with her in their mother's old bottle-green landau. Mrs Churchley, perched higher than ever, rode by without a recognition; but this didn't prevent Adela from going to her before the month was over. As on her great previous occasion she went in the morning, and she again had the good fortune to be admitted. But this time her visit was shorter, and a week after making it – the week was a desolation – she addressed to her brother at Madrid a letter which contained these words:

'I could endure it no longer – I confessed and retracted; I explained to her as well as I could the falsity of what I said to her ten months ago and the benighted purity of my motives for saying it. I besought her to regard it as unsaid, to forgive me, not to despise me too much, to take pity on poor *perfect* papa and come back to him. She was more good-natured than you might have expected; indeed, she laughed extravagantly. She had never believed me – it was too absurd; she had only, at the time, disliked me. She found me utterly false (she was very frank with me about this), and she told papa that she thought I was horrid. She said she could never live with such a girl, and as I would certainly never marry I must be sent away; in short she quite loathed me. Papa defended me, he refused to sacrifice me, and this led practically to their rupture. Papa gave her up, as it were, for me. Fancy the angel, and fancy what I must try to be to him for the rest of his life! Mrs Churchley can never come back – she's going to marry Lord Dovedale.'

THE CHAPERON

I

An old lady, in a high drawing-room, had had her chair moved close to the fire, where she sat knitting and warming her knees. She was dressed in deep mourning; her face had a faded nobleness, tempered, however, by the somewhat illiberal compression assumed by her lips in obedience to something that was passing in her mind. She was far from the lamp, but though her eyes were fixed upon her active needles she was not looking at them. What she really saw was quite another train of affairs. The room was spacious and dim; the thick London fog had oozed into it even through its superior defences. It was full of dusky, massive, valuable things. The old lady sat motionless save for the regularity of her clicking needles, which seemed as personal to her and as expressive as prolonged fingers. If she was thinking something out, she was thinking it thoroughly.

When she looked up, on the entrance of a girl of twenty, it might have been guessed that the appearance of this young lady was not an interruption of her meditation, but rather a contribution to it. The young lady, who was charming to behold, was also in deep mourning, which had a freshness, if mourning can be fresh, an air of having been lately put on. She went straight to the bell beside the chimney-piece and pulled it, while in her other hand she held a sealed and directed letter. Her companion glanced in silence at the letter; then she looked still harder at her work. The girl hovered near the fireplace, without speaking, and after a due, a dignified interval the butler appeared in response to the bell. The time had been sufficient to make the silence between the ladies seem long. The younger one asked the butler to see that her letter should be posted; and after he had gone out she moved vaguely about the room, as if to give her grandmother – for such was the elder personage – a chance to begin a colloquy of which she herself preferred not to strike the first note. As equally with herself her companion was on the face of it capable of holding out, the tension, though it was already late in the evening, might have lasted long. But the old lady after a little appeared to recognise, a trifle ungraciously, the girl's superior resources.

'Have you written to your mother?'

'Yes, but only a few lines, to tell her I shall come and see her in the morning.'

'Is that all you've got to say?' asked the grandmother.

'I don't quite know what you want me to say.'

'I want you to say that you've made up your mind.'

'Yes, I've done that, granny.'

'You intend to respect your father's wishes?'

'It depends upon what you mean by respecting them. I do justice to the feelings by which they were dictated.'

'What do you mean by justice?' the old lady retorted.

The girl was silent a moment; then she said: 'You'll see my idea of it.'

'I see it already! You'll go and live with her.'

'I shall talk the situation over with her to-morrow and tell her that I think that will be best.'

'Best for her, no doubt!'

'What's best for her is best for me.'

'And for your brother and sister?' As the girl made no reply to this her grandmother went on: 'What's best for them is that you should acknowledge some responsibility in regard to them and, considering how young they are, try and do something for them.'

'They must do as I've done – they must act for themselves. They have their means now, and they're free.'

'Free? They're mere children.'

'Let me remind you that Eric is older than I.'

'He doesn't like his mother,' said the old lady, as if that were an answer.

'I never said he did. And she adores him.'

'Oh, your mother's adorations!'

'Don't abuse her now,' the girl rejoined, after a pause.

The old lady forbore to abuse her, but she made up for it the next moment by saying: 'It will be dreadful for Edith.'

'What will be dreadful?'

'Your desertion of her.'

'The desertion's on her side.'

'Her consideration for her father does her honour.'

'Of course I'm a brute, *n'en parlons plus*,' said the girl. 'We must go our respective ways,' she added, in a tone of extreme wisdom and philosophy.

Her grandmother straightened out her knitting and began to roll it up. 'Be so good as to ring for my maid,' she said, after a minute. The young lady rang, and there was another wait and another conscious hush. Before the maid came her mistress remarked: 'Of course then you'll not come to *me*, you know.'

'What do you mean by "coming" to you?'

'I can't receive you on that footing.'

'She'll not come *with* me, if you mean that.'

'I don't mean that,' said the old lady, getting up as her maid came in. This attendant took her work from her, gave her an arm and helped her out of the room, while Rose Tramore, standing before the fire and looking into it, faced the idea that her grandmother's door would now under all circumstances be closed to her. She lost no time however in brooding over this anomaly: it only added energy to her determination to act. All she could do to-night was to go to bed, for she felt utterly weary. She had been living, in imagination, in a prospective struggle, and it had left her as exhausted as a real fight. Moreover this was the culmination of a crisis, of weeks of suspense, of a long, hard strain. Her father had been laid in his grave five days before, and that morning his will had been read. In the afternoon she had got Edith off to St Leonard's with their aunt Julia, and then she had had a wretched talk with Eric. Lastly, she had made up her mind to act in opposition to the formidable will, to a clause which embodied if not exactly a provision, a recommendation singularly emphatic. She went to bed and slept the sleep of the just.

'Oh, my dear, how charming! I must take another house!' It was in these words that her mother responded to the announcement Rose had just formally made and with which she had vaguely expected to produce a certain dignity of effect. In the way of emotion there was apparently no effect at all, and the girl was wise enough to know that this was not simply on account of the general line of non-allusion taken by the extremely pretty woman before her, who looked like her elder sister. Mrs Tramore had never manifested, to her daughter, the slightest consciousness that her position was peculiar; but the recollection of something more than that fine policy was required to explain such a failure to appreciate Rose's sacrifice. It was simply a fresh reminder that she had never appreciated anything, that she was nothing but a tinted and stippled surface. Her situation was peculiar indeed. She had been the heroine of a scandal which had grown dim only because, in the eyes of the London world, it paled in the lurid light of the contemporaneous. That attention had been fixed on it for several days, fifteen years before; there had been a high relish of the vivid evidence as to his wife's misconduct with which, in the divorce-court, Charles Tramore had judged well to regale a cynical public. The case was pronounced awfully bad, and he obtained his decree. The folly of the wife had been inconceivable, in spite of other examples: she had quitted her children, she had followed the 'other fellow' abroad. The other fellow hadn't married her, not having had time: he had lost his life in the Mediterranean by the capsizing of a boat, before the prohibitory term had expired.

Mrs Tramore had striven to extract from this accident something of the austerity of widowhood; but her mourning only made her deviation more public, she was a widow whose husband was awkwardly alive. She had not prowled about the Continent on the classic lines; she had come back to London to take her chance. But London would give her no chance, would have nothing to say to her; as many persons had remarked, you could never tell how London would behave. It would not receive Mrs Tramore again on any terms, and when she was spoken of, which now was not often, it was inveterately said of her that she went nowhere. Apparently she had not the qualities for which London compounds; though in the cases in which it does compound you may often wonder what these qualities are. She had not at any rate been successful: her lover was dead, her husband was liked and her children were pitied, for in payment for a topic London will parenthetically pity. It was thought interesting and magnanimous that Charles Tramore had not married again. The disadvantage to his children of the miserable story was thus left uncorrected, and this, rather oddly, was counted as *his* sacrifice. His mother, whose arrangements were elaborate, looked after them a great deal, and they enjoyed a mixture of laxity and discipline under the roof of their aunt, Miss Tramore, who was independent, having, for reasons that the two ladies had exhaustively discussed, determined to lead her own life. She had set up a home at St Leonard's, and that contracted shore had played a considerable part in the upbringing of the little Tramores. They knew about their mother, as the phrase was, but they didn't know her; which was naturally deemed more pathetic for them than for her. She had a house in Chester Square and an income and a victoria – it served all purposes, as she never went out in the evening – and flowers on her window-sills, and a remarkable appearance of youth. The income was supposed to be in part the result of a bequest from the man for whose sake she had committed the error of her life, and in the appearance of youth there was a slightly impertinent implication that it was a sort of afterglow of the same connection.

Her children, as they grew older, fortunately showed signs of some individuality of disposition. Edith, the second girl, clung to her aunt Julia; Eric, the son, clung frantically to polo; while Rose, the elder daughter, appeared to cling mainly to herself. Collectively, of course, they clung to their father, whose attitude in the family group, however, was casual and intermittent. He was charming and vague; he was like a clever actor who often didn't come to rehearsal. Fortune, which but for that one stroke had been generous to him, had provided him with deputies and trouble-takers, as well as with whimsical opinions, and a reputation for excellent taste, and whist at his club, and perpetual cigars on morocco sofas, and a beautiful absence of purpose. Nature had thrown in a remarkably fine hand, which he sometimes passed over his children's heads when they were glossy from the nursery brush. On Rose's eighteenth birthday he said to her that she might go to see her mother, on condition that her visits should be limited to an hour each time and to four

in the year. She was to go alone; the other children were not
included in the arrangement. This was the result of a visit that
he himself had paid his repudiated wife at her urgent request,
their only encounter during the fifteen years. The girl knew as
much as this from her aunt Julia, who was full of tell-tale
secrecies. She availed herself eagerly of the licence, and in
course of the period that elapsed before her father's death she
spent with Mrs Tramore exactly eight hours by the watch. Her
father, who was as inconsistent and disappointing as he was
amiable, spoke to her of her mother only once afterwards. This
occasion had been the sequel of her first visit, and he had made
no use of it to ask what she thought of the personality in Chester
Square or how she liked it. He had only said 'Did she take you
out?' and when Rose answered 'Yes, she put me straight into a
carriage and drove me up and down Bond Street,' had rejoined
sharply 'See that that never occurs again.' It never did, but once
was enough, every one they knew having happened to be in
Bond Street at that particular hour.

After this the periodical interview took place in private, in
Mrs Tramore's beautiful little wasted drawing-room. Rose
knew that, rare as these occasions were, her mother would
not have kept her 'all to herself' had there been anybody she
could have shown her to. But in the poor lady's social void there
was no one; she had after all her own correctness and she
consistently preferred isolation to inferior contacts. So her
daughter was subjected only to the maternal; it was not necessary to be definite in qualifying that. The girl had by this time a
collection of ideas, gathered by impenetrable processes; she
had tasted, in the ostracism of her ambiguous parent, of the
acrid fruit of the tree of knowledge. She not only had an
approximate vision of what every one had done, but she had a
private judgement for each case. She had a particular vision of
her father, which did not interfere with his being dear to her,
but which was directly concerned in her resolution, after his
death, to do the special thing he had expressed the wish she
should not do. In the general estimate her grandmother and her
grandmother's money had their place, and the strong probability that any enjoyment of the latter commodity would now be

withheld from her. It included Edith's marked inclination to receive the law, and doubtless eventually a more substantial memento, from Miss Tramore, and opened the question whether her own course might not contribute to make her sister's appear heartless. The answer to this question however would depend on the success that might attend her own, which would very possibly be small. Eric's attitude was eminently simple; he didn't care to know people who didn't know *his* people. If his mother should ever get back into society perhaps he would take her up. Rose Tramore had decided to do what she could to bring this consummation about; and strangely enough – so mixed were her superstitions and her heresies – a large part of her motive lay in the value she attached to such a consecration.

Of her mother intrinsically she thought very little now, and if her eyes were fixed on a special achievement it was much more for the sake of that achievement and to satisfy a latent energy that was in her than because her heart was wrung by this sufferer. Her heart had not been wrung at all, though she had quite held it out for the experience. Her purpose was a pious game, but it was still essentially a game. Among the ideas I have mentioned she had her idea of triumph. She had caught the inevitable note, the pitch, on her very first visit to Chester Square. She had arrived there in intense excitement, and her excitement was left on her hands in a manner that reminded her of a difficult air she had once heard sung at the opera when no one applauded the performer. That flatness had made her sick, and so did this, in another way. A part of her agitation proceeded from the fact that her aunt Julia had told her, in the manner of a burst of confidence, something she was not to repeat, that she was in appearance the very image of the lady in Chester Square. The motive that prompted this declaration was between aunt Julia and her conscience; but it was a great emotion to the girl to find her entertainer so beautiful. She was tall and exquisitely slim; she had hair more exactly to Rose Tramore's taste than any other she had ever seen, even to every detail in the way it was dressed, and a complexion and a figure of the kind that are always spoken of as 'lovely'. Her eyes were irresistible, and so were her clothes, though the clothes were perhaps a little more precisely the right thing than the eyes. Her appearance was marked to her daughter's sense by the highest distinction; though it may be mentioned that this had never been the opinion of all the world. It was a revelation to Rose that she herself might look a little like that. She knew however that aunt Julia had not seen her deposed sister-in-law for a long time, and she had a general impression that Mrs Tramore was to-day a more complete production – for instance as regarded her air of youth – than she had ever been. There was no excitement on her side – that was all her visitor's; there was no emotion – that was excluded by the plan, to say nothing of conditions more primal. Rose had from the first a glimpse of her mother's plan. It was to mention nothing and imply nothing, neither to acknowledge, to explain nor to extenuate. She would leave everything to her child; with her child she was secure. She only wanted to get back into society; she would leave even that to her child, whom she treated not as a high-strung and heroic daughter, a creature of exaltation, of devotion, but as a new, charming, clever, useful friend, a little younger than herself. Already on that first day she had talked about dressmakers. Of course, poor thing, it was to be remembered that in her circumstances there were not many things she *could* talk about. 'She wants to go out again; that's the only thing in the wide world she wants,' Rose had promptly, compendiously said to herself. There had been a sequel to this observation, uttered, in intense engrossment, in her own room half an hour before she had, on the important evening, made known her decision to her grandmother: 'Then I'll *take* her out!'

'She'll drag you down, she'll drag you down!' Julia Tramore permitted herself to remark to her niece, the next day, in a tone of feverish prophecy.

As the girl's own theory was that all the dragging there might be would be upward, and moreover administered by herself, she could look at her aunt with a cold and inscrutable eye.

'Very well, then, I shall be out of your sight, from the pinnacle you occupy, and I sha'n't trouble you.'

'Do you reproach me for my disinterested exertions, for the way I've toiled over you, the way I've lived for you?' Miss Tramore demanded.

'Don't reproach *me* for being kind to my mother and I won't reproach you for anything.'

'She'll keep you out of everything – she'll make you miss everything,' Miss Tramore continued.

'Then she'll make me miss a great deal that's odious,' said the girl.

'You're too young for such extravagances,' her aunt declared.

'And yet Edith, who is younger than I, seems to be too old for them: how do you arrange that? My mother's society will make me older,' Rose replied.

'Don't speak to me of your mother; you *have* no mother.'

'Then if I'm an orphan I must settle things for myself.'

'Do you justify her, do you approve of her?' cried Miss Tramore, who was inferior to her niece in capacity for retort and whose limitations made the girl appear pert.

Rose looked at her a moment in silence; then she said, turning away: 'I think she's charming.'

'And do you propose to become charming in the same manner?'

'Her manner is perfect; it would be an excellent model. But I can't discuss my mother with you.'

'You'll have to discuss her with some other people!' Miss Tramore proclaimed, going out of the room.

Rose wondered whether this were a general or a particular vaticination. There was something her aunt might have meant by it, but her aunt rarely meant the best thing she might have meant. Miss Tramore had come up from St Leonard's in response to a telegram from her own parent, for an occasion like the present brought with it, for a few hours, a certain relaxation of their dissent. 'Do what you can to stop her,' the old lady had said; but her daughter found that the most she could do was not much. They both had a baffled sense that Rose had thought the question out a good deal further than they; and this was particularly irritating to Mrs Tramore, as consciously the cleverer of the two. A question thought out as far as *she* could think it had always appeared to her to have performed its human uses; she had never encountered a ghost emerging from that extinction. Their great contention was that Rose would cut herself off; and certainly if she wasn't afraid of that she wasn't afraid of anything. Julia Tramore could only tell her mother how little the girl was afraid. She was already prepared to leave the house, taking with her the possessions, or her share of them, that had accumulated there during her father's illness. There had been a going and coming of her maid, a thumping about of boxes, an ordering of four-wheelers; it appeared to old Mrs Tramore that something of the objectionableness, the indecency, of her granddaughter's prospective connection had already gathered about the place. It was a violation of the decorum of bereavement which was still fresh there, and from the indignant gloom of the mistress of the house you might have inferred not so much that the daughter was about to depart as that the mother was about to arrive. There had been no conversation on the dreadful subject at luncheon; for at luncheon at Mrs Tramore's (her son never came to it) there were always, even after funerals and other miseries, stray guests of both sexes whose policy it was to be cheerful and superficial. Rose had sat down as if nothing had happened – nothing worse, that is, than her father's death; but no one had spoken of anything that any one else was thinking of.

Before she left the house a servant brought her a message from her grandmother – the old lady desired to see her in the drawing-room. She had on her bonnet, and she went down as if she were about to step into her cab. Mrs Tramore sat there with her eternal knitting, from which she forebore even to raise her eyes as, after a silence that seemed to express the fullness of her reprobation, while Rose stood motionless, she began: 'I wonder if you really understand what you're doing.'

'I think so. I'm not so stupid.'

'I never thought you were; but I don't know what to make of you now. You're giving up everything.'

The girl was tempted to inquire whether her grandmother called herself 'everything'; but she checked this question, answering instead that she knew she was giving up much.

'You're taking a step of which you will feel the effect to the end of your days,' Mrs Tramore went on.

'In a good conscience, I heartily hope,' said Rose.

'Your father's conscience was good enough for his mother; it ought to be good enough for his daughter.'

Rose sat down – she could afford to – as if she wished to be very attentive and were still accessible to argument. But this demonstration only ushered in, after a moment, the surprising words 'I don't think papa had any conscience.'

'What in the name of all that's unnatural do you mean?' Mrs Tramore cried, over her glasses. 'The dearest and best creature that ever lived!'

'He was kind, he had charming impulses, he was delightful. But he never reflected.'

Mrs Tramore stared, as if at a language she had never heard, a farrago, a *galimatias*. Her life was made up of items, but she had never had to deal, intellectually, with a fine shade. Then while her needles, which had paused an instant, began to fly again, she rejoined: 'Do you know what you are, my dear? You're a dreadful little prig. Where do you pick up such talk?'

'Of course I don't mean to judge between them,' Rose pursued. 'I can only judge between my mother and myself. Papa couldn't judge for me.' And with this she got up.

'One would think you were horrid. I never thought so before.'

'Thank you for that.'

'You're embarking on a struggle with society,' continued Mrs Tramore, indulging in an unusual flight of oratory. 'Society will put you in your place.'

'Hasn't it too many other things to do?' asked the girl.

This question had an ingenuity which led her grandmother to meet it with a merely provisional and somewhat sketchy answer. 'Your ignorance would be melancholy if your behaviour were not so insane.'

'Oh, no; I know perfectly what she'll do!' Rose replied, almost gaily. 'She'll drag me down.'

'She won't even do that,' the old lady declared contradictiously. 'She'll keep you forever in the same dull hole.'

'I shall come and see *you*, granny, when I want something more lively.'

'You may come if you like, but you'll come no further than the door. If you leave this house now you don't enter it again.'

Rose hesitated a moment. 'Do you really mean that?'

'You may judge whether I choose such a time to joke.'

'Good-bye, then,' said the girl.

'Good-bye.'

Rose quitted the room successfully enough; but on the other side of the door, on the landing, she sank into a chair and buried her face in her hands. She had burst into tears, and she sobbed there for a moment, trying hard to recover herself, so as to go downstairs without showing any traces of emotion, passing before the servants and again perhaps before aunt Julia. Mrs Tramore was too old to cry; she could only drop her knitting and, for a long time, sit with her head bowed and her eyes closed.

Rose had reckoned justly with her aunt Julia; there were no footmen, but this vigilant virgin was posted at the foot of the stairs. She offered no challenge however; she only said: 'There's some one in the parlour who wants to see you.' The girl demanded a name, but Miss Tramore only mouthed inaudibly and winked and waved. Rose instantly reflected that there was only one man in the world her aunt would look such deep things about. 'Captain Jay?' her own eyes asked, while Miss Tramore's were those of a conspirator: they were, for a moment, the only embarrassed eyes Rose had encountered that day. They contributed to make aunt Julia's further response evasive, after her niece inquired if she had communicated in advance with this visitor. Miss Tramore merely said that he had been upstairs with her mother – hadn't she mentioned it? – and had been waiting for her. She thought herself acute in not putting the question of the girl's seeing him before her as a favour to him or to herself; she presented it as a duty, and wound up with the proposition: 'It's not fair to him, it's not kind, not to let him speak to you before you go.'

'What does he want to say?' Rose demanded.

'Go in and find out.'

She really knew, for she had found out before; but after standing uncertain an instant she went in. 'The parlour' was the name that had always been borne by a spacious sitting-room downstairs, an apartment occupied by her father during his frequent phases of residence in Hill Street – episodes increasingly frequent after his house in the country had, in consequence, as Rose perfectly knew, of his spending too much money, been disposed of at a sacrifice which he always characterised as horrid. He had been left with the place in Hertfordshire and his mother with the London house, on the general understanding that they would change about; but during the last years the community had grown more rigid, mainly at his mother's expense. The parlour was full of his memory and his habits and his things – his books and pictures and *bibelots*, objects that belonged now to Eric. Rose had sat in it for hours since his death; it was the place in which she could still be nearest to him. But she felt far from him as Captain Jay rose erect on her opening the door. This was a very different presence. He had not liked Captain Jay. She herself had, but not enough to make a great complication of her father's coldness. This afternoon however she foresaw complications. At the very outset for instance she was not pleased with his having arranged such a surprise for her with her grandmother and her aunt. It was probably aunt Julia who had sent for him; her grandmother wouldn't have done it. It placed him immediately on their side, and Rose was almost as disappointed at this as if she had not known it was quite where he would naturally be. He had never paid her a special visit, but if that was what he wished to do why shouldn't he have waited till she should be under her mother's roof? She knew the reason, but she had an angry prospect of enjoyment in making him express it. She liked him enough, after all, if it were measured by the idea of what she could make him do.

In Bertram Jay the elements were surprisingly mingled; you would have gone astray, in reading him, if you had counted on finding the complements of some of his qualities. He would not however have struck you in the least as incomplete, for in every case in which you didn't find the complement you would have found the contradiction. He was in the Royal Engineers, and was tall, lean and high-shouldered. He looked every inch a soldier, yet there were people who considered that he had missed his vocation in not becoming a parson. He took a public interest in the spiritual life of the army. Other persons still, on closer observation, would have felt that his most appropriate field was neither the army nor the church, but simply the world – the social, successful, worldly world. If he had a sword in one hand and a Bible in the other he had a Court Guide concealed somewhere about his person. His profile was hard and handsome, his eyes were both cold and kind, his dark straight hair was imperturbably smooth and prematurely streaked with grey. There was nothing in existence that he didn't take seriously. He had a first-rate power of work and an ambition as minutely organised as a German plan of invasion. His only real recreation was to go to church, but he went to parties when he had time. If he was in love with Rose Tramore this was distracting to him only in the same sense as his religion, and it was included in that department of his extremely sub-divided life. His religion indeed was of an encroaching, annexing sort. Seen from in front he looked diffident and blank, but he was capable of exposing himself in a way (to speak only of the paths of peace) wholly inconsistent with shyness. He had a passion for instance for open-air speaking, but was not thought on the whole to excel in it unless he could help himself out with a hymn. In conversation he kept his eyes on you with a kind of colourless candour, as if he had not understood what you were saying and, in a fashion that made many people turn red, waited before answering. This was only because he was considering their remarks in more relations than they had intended. He had in his face no expression whatever save the one just mentioned, and was, in his profession, already very distinguished.

He had seen Rose Tramore for the first time on a Sunday of the previous March, at a house in the country at which she was staying with her father, and five weeks later he had made her, by letter, an offer of marriage. She showed her father the letter of course, and he told her that it would give him great pleasure that she should send Captain Jay about his business. 'My dear child,' he said, 'we must really have some one who will be better fun than that.' Rose had declined the honour, very considerately and kindly, but not simply because her father wished it. She didn't herself wish to detach this flower from the stem, though when the young man wrote again, to express the hope that he *might* hope – so long was he willing to wait – and ask if he might not still sometimes see her, she answered even more indulgently than at first. She had shown her father her former letter, but she didn't show him this one; she only told him what it contained, submitting to him also that of her correspondent. Captain Jay moreover wrote to Mr Tramore, who replied sociably, but so vaguely that he almost neglected the subject under discussion – a communication that made poor Bertram ponder long. He could never get to the bottom of the superficial, and all the proprieties and conventions of life were profound to him. Fortunately for him old Mrs Tramore liked him, he was satisfactory to her long-sightedness; so that a relation was established under cover of which he still occasionally presented himself in Hill Street – presented himself nominally to the mistress of the house. He had had scruples about the veracity of his visits, but he had disposed of them; he had scruples about so many things that he had had to invent a general way, to dig a central drain. Julia Tramore happened to meet him when she came up to town, and she took a view of him more benevolent than her usual estimate of people encouraged by her mother. The fear of agreeing with that lady was a motive, but there was a stronger one, in this particular case, in the fear of agreeing with her niece, who had rejected him. His situation might be held to have improved when Mr Tramore was taken so gravely ill that with regard to his recovery those about him left their eyes to speak for their lips; and in the light of the poor gentleman's recent death it was doubtless better than it had ever been.

He was only a quarter of an hour with the girl, but this gave him time to take the measure of it. After he had spoken to her about her bereavement, very much as an especially mild missionary might have spoken to a beautiful Polynesian, he let her know that he had learned from her companions the very strong step she was about to take. This led to their spending together ten minutes which, to her mind, threw more light on his character than anything that had ever passed between them. She had always felt with him as if she were standing on an edge, looking down into something decidedly deep. Today the impression of the perpendicular shaft was there, but it was rather an abyss of confusion and disorder than the large bright space in which she had figured everything as ranged and pigeon-holed, presenting the appearance of the labelled shelves and drawers at a chemist's. He discussed without an invitation to discuss, he appealed without a right to appeal. He was nothing but a suitor tolerated after dismissal, but he took strangely for granted a participation in her affairs. He assumed all sorts of things that made her draw back. He implied that there was everything now to assist them in arriving at an agreement, since she had never informed him that he was positively objectionable; but that this symmetry would be spoiled if she should not be willing to take a little longer to think of certain consequences. She was greatly disconcerted when she saw what consequences he meant and at his reminding her of them. What on earth was the use of a lover if he was to speak only like one's grandmother and one's aunt? He struck her as much in love with her and as particularly careful at the same time as to what he might say. He never mentioned her mother; he only alluded, indirectly but earnestly, to the 'step'. He disapproved of it altogether, took an unexpectedly prudent, politic view of it. He evidently also believed that she would be dragged down; in other words that she would not be asked out. It was his idea that her mother would contaminate her, so that he should find himself interested in a young person discredited and virtually unmarriageable. All this was more obvious to him than the consideration that a daughter should be merciful. Where was his religion if he understood mercy so little, and where were his talent and his courage if he were so miserably afraid of trumpery social penalties? Rose's heart sank when she reflected that a man supposed to be first-rate hadn't guessed that rather than not do what she could for her mother she would give up all the Engineers in the world. She became aware that she probably would have been moved to place her hand in his on the spot if he had come to her saying 'Your idea is the right one; put it through at every cost.' She couldn't discuss this with him, though he impressed her as having too much at stake for her to treat him with mere disdain. She sickened at the revelation that a gentleman could see so much in mere vulgarities of opinion, and though she uttered as few words as possible, conversing only in sad smiles and headshakes and in intercepted movements toward the door, she happened, in some unguarded lapse from her reticence, to use the expression that she was disappointed in him. He caught at it and, seeming to drop his field-glass, pressed upon her with nearer, tenderer eyes.

'Can I be so happy as to believe, then, that you had thought of me with some confidence, with some faith?'

'If you didn't suppose so, what is the sense of this visit?' Rose asked.

'One can be faithful without reciprocity,' said the young man. 'I regard you in a light which makes me want to protect you even if I have nothing to gain by it.'

'Yet you speak as if you thought you might keep me for yourself.'

'For *yourself*. I don't want you to suffer.'

'Nor to suffer yourself by my doing so,' said Rose, looking down.

'Ah, if you would only marry me next month!' he broke out inconsequently.

'And give up going to mamma?' Rose waited to see if he would say 'What need that matter? Can't your mother come to us?' But he said nothing of the sort; he only answered –

'She surely would be sorry to interfere with the exercise of any other affection which I might have the bliss of believing that you are now free, in however small a degree, to entertain.'

Rose knew that her mother wouldn't be sorry at all; but she contented herself with rejoining, her hand on the door: 'Good-bye. I sha'n't suffer. I'm not afraid.'

'You don't know how terrible, how cruel, the world can be.'

'Yes, I do know. I know everything!'

The declaration sprang from her lips in a tone which made him look at her as he had never looked before, as if he saw something new in her face, as if he had never yet known her. He hadn't displeased her so much but that she would like to give him that impression, and since she felt that she was doing so she lingered an instant for the purpose. It enabled her to see, further, that he turned red; then to become aware that a carriage had stopped at the door. Captain Jay's eyes, from where he stood, fell upon this arrival, and the nature of their glance made Rose step forward to look. Her mother sat there, brilliant, conspicuous, in the eternal victoria, and the footman was already sounding the knocker. It had been no part of the arrangement that she should come to fetch her; it had been out of the question – a stroke in such bad taste as would have put Rose in the wrong. The girl had never dreamed of it, but somehow, suddenly, perversely, she was glad of it now; she even hoped that her grandmother and her aunt were looking out upstairs.

'My mother has come for me. Good-bye,' she repeated; but this time her visitor had got between her and the door.

'Listen to me before you go. I will give you a life's devotion,' the young man pleaded. He really barred the way.

She wondered whether her grandmother had told him that if her flight were not prevented she would forfeit money. Then, vividly, it came over her that this would be what he was occupied with. 'I shall never think of you – let me go!' she cried, with passion.

Captain Jay opened the door, but Rose didn't see his face, and in a moment she was out of the house. Aunt Julia, who was sure to have been hovering, had taken flight before the profanity of the knock.

'Heavens, dear, where did you get your mourning?' the lady in the victoria asked of her daughter as they drove away.

II

LADY MARESFIELD had given her boy a push in his plump back and had said to him, 'Go and speak to her now; it's your chance.' She had for a long time wanted this scion to make himself audible to Rose Tramore, but the opportunity was not easy to come by. The case was complicated. Lady Maresfield had four daughters, of whom only one was married. It so happened moreover that this one, Mrs Vaughan-Vesey, the only person in the world her mother was afraid of, was the most to be reckoned with. The Honourable Guy was in appearance all his mother's child, though he was really a simpler soul. He was large and pink; large, that is, as to everything but the eyes, which were diminishing points, and pink as to everything but the hair, which was comparable, faintly, to the hue of the richer rose. He had also, it must be conceded, very small neat teeth, which made his smile look like a young lady's. He had no wish to resemble any such person, but he was perpetually smiling, and he smiled more than ever as he approached Rose Tramore, who, looking altogether, to his mind, as a pretty girl should, and wearing a soft white opera-cloak over a softer black dress, leaned alone against the wall of the vestibule at Covent Garden while, a few paces off, an old gentleman engaged her mother in conversation. Madame Patti had been singing, and they were all waiting for their carriages. To their ears at present came a vociferation of names and a rattle of wheels. The air, through banging doors, entered in damp, warm gusts, heavy with the stale, slightly sweet taste of the London season when the London season is overripe and spoiling.

Guy Mangler had only three minutes to re-establish an interrupted acquaintance with our young lady. He reminded her that he had danced with her the year before, and he mentioned that he knew her brother. His mother had lately been to see old Mrs Tramore, but this he did not mention, not being aware of it. That visit had produced, on Lady Maresfield's part, a private crisis, engendered ideas. One of them was that the grandmother in Hill Street had really forgiven the wilful girl much more than she admitted. Another was that there would still be some money for Rose when the others should come into theirs. Still another was that the others would come into theirs at no distant date; the old lady was so visibly going to pieces. There were several more besides, as for instance that Rose had already fifteen hundred a year from her father. The figure had been betrayed in Hill Street; it was part of the proof of Mrs Tramore's decrepitude. Then there was an equal amount that her mother had to dispose of and on which the girl could absolutely count, though of course it might involve much waiting, as the mother, a person of gross insensibility, evidently wouldn't die of cold-shouldering. Equally definite, to do it justice, was the conception that Rose was in truth remarkably good-looking, and that what she had undertaken to do showed, and would show even should it fail, cleverness of the right sort. Cleverness of the right sort was exactly the quality that Lady Maresfield prefigured as indispensable in a young lady to whom she should marry her second son, over whose own deficiencies she flung the veil of a maternal theory that *his* cleverness was of a sort that was wrong. Those who knew him less well were content to wish that he might not conceal it for such a scruple. This enumeration of his mother's views does not exhaust the list, and it was in obedience to one too profound to be uttered even by the historian that, after a very brief delay, she decided to move across the crowded lobby. Her daughter Bessie was the only one with her; Maggie was dining with the Vaughan-Veseys, and Fanny was not of an age. Mrs Tramore the younger showed only an admirable back – her face was to her old gentleman – and Bessie had drifted to some other people; so that it was comparatively easy for Lady Maresfield to say to Rose, in a moment: 'My dear child, are you never coming to see us?'

'We shall be delighted to come if you'll ask us,' Rose smiled.

Lady Maresfield had been prepared for the plural number, and she was a woman whom it took many plurals to disconcert. 'I'm sure Guy is longing for another dance with you,' she rejoined, with the most unblinking irrelevance.

'I'm afraid we're not dancing again quite yet,' said Rose, glancing at her mother's exposed shoulders, but speaking as if they were muffled in crape.

Lady Maresfield leaned her head on one side and seemed almost wistful. 'Not even at my sister's ball? She's to have something next week. She'll write to you.'

Rose Tramore, on the spot, looking bright but vague, turned three or four things over in her mind. She remembered that the sister of her interlocutress was the proverbially rich Mrs Bray, a bankeress or a breweress or a builderess, who had so big a house that she couldn't fill it unless she opened her doors, or her mouth, very wide. Rose had learnt more about London society during these lonely months with her mother than she had ever picked up in Hill Street. The younger Mrs Tramore was a mine of *commérages*, and she had no need to go out to bring home the latest intelligence. At any rate Mrs Bray might serve as the end of a wedge. 'Oh, I daresay we might think of that,' Rose said. 'It would be very kind of your sister.'

'Guy'll think of it, won't you, Guy?' asked Lady Maresfield.

'Rather!' Guy responded, with an intonation as fine as if he had learnt it at a music hall; while at the same moment the name of his mother's carriage was bawled through the place. Mrs Tramore had parted with her old gentleman; she turned again to her daughter. Nothing occurred but what always occurred, which was exactly this absence of everything – a universal lapse. She didn't exist, even for a second, to any recognising eye. The people who looked at her – of course there were plenty of those – were only the people who didn't exist for hers. Lady Maresfield surged away on her son's arm.

It was this noble matron herself who wrote, the next day, enclosing a card of invitation from Mrs Bray and expressing the hope that Rose would come and dine and let her ladyship take her. She should have only one of her own girls; Gwendolen Vesey was to take the other. Rose handed both the note and the card in silence to her mother; the latter exhibited only the name of Miss Tramore. 'You had much better go, dear,' her mother said; in answer to which Miss Tramore slowly tore up the documents, looking with clear, meditative eyes out of the window. Her mother always said 'You had better go' – there had been other incidents – and Rose had never even once taken account of the observation. She would make no first advances, only plenty of second ones, and, condoning no discrimination, would treat no omission as venial. She would keep all concessions till afterwards; then she would make them one by one. Fighting society was quite as hard as her grandmother had said it would be; but there was a tension in it which made the dreariness vibrate – the dreariness of such a winter as she had just passed. Her companion had cried at the end of it, and she had cried all through; only her tears had been private, while her mother's had fallen once for all, at luncheon on the bleak Easter Monday – produced by the way a silent survey of the deadly square brought home to her that every creature but themselves was out of town and having tremendous fun. Rose felt that it was useless to attempt to explain simply by her mourning this severity of solitude; for if people didn't go to parties (at least a few didn't) for six months after their father died, this was the very time other people took for coming to see them. It was not too much to say that during this first winter of Rose's period with her mother she had no communication whatever with the world. It had the effect of making her take to reading the new American books: she wanted to see how girls got on by themselves. She had never read so much before, and there was a legitimate indifference in it when topics failed with her mother. They often failed after the first days, and then, while she bent over instructive volumes, this lady, dressed as if for an impending function, sat on the sofa and watched her. Rose was not embarrassed by such an appearance, for she could reflect that, a little before, her companion had not even a girl who had taken refuge in queer researches to look at. She was moreover used to her mother's attitude by this time. She had her own description of it: it was the attitude of waiting for the carriage. If they didn't go out it was not that Mrs Tramore was not ready in time, and Rose had even an alarmed prevision of their some day always arriving first. Mrs Tramore's conversation at such moments was abrupt, inconsequent and personal. She sat on the edge of sofas and chairs and glanced occasionally at the fit of her gloves (she was perpetually gloved, and the fit was a thing it was melancholy to see wasted), as people do who are expecting guests to dinner. Rose used almost to fancy herself at times a perfunctory husband on the other side of the fire.

What she was not yet used to – there was still a charm in it – was her mother's extraordinary tact. During the years they lived together they never had a discussion; a circumstance all the more remarkable since if the girl had a reason for sparing her companion (that of being sorry for her) Mrs Tramore had none for sparing her child. She only showed in doing so a happy instinct – the happiest thing about her. She took in perfection a course which represented everything and covered everything; she utterly abjured all authority. She testified to her abjuration in hourly ingenious, touching ways. In this manner nothing had to be talked over, which was a mercy all round. The tears on Easter Monday were merely a nervous gust, to help show she was not a Christmas doll from the Burlington Arcade; and there was no lifting up of the repentant Magdalen, no uttered remorse for the former abandonment of children. Of the way she could treat her children her demeanour to this one was an example; it was an uninterrupted appeal to her eldest daughter for direction. She took the law from Rose in every circumstance, and if you had noticed these ladies without knowing their history you would have wondered what tie was fine enough to make maturity so respectful to youth. No mother was ever so filial as Mrs Tramore, and there had never been such a difference of position between sisters. Not that the elder one fawned, which would have been fearful; she only renounced – whatever she had to renounce. If the amount was not much she at any rate made no scene over it. Her hand was so light that Rose said of her secretly, in vague glances at the past, 'No wonder people liked her!' She never characterised the old element of interference with her mother's respectability more definitely than as 'people'. They were people, it was true, for whom gentleness must have been everything and who didn't demand a variety of interests. The desire to 'go out' was the one passion that even a closer acquaintance with her parent revealed to Rose Tramore. She marvelled at its strength, in the light of the poor lady's history: there was comedy enough in this unquenchable flame on the part of a woman who had known such misery. She had drunk deep of every dishonour, but the bitter cup had left her with a taste for lighted candles, for squeezing up staircases and hooking herself to the human elbow. Rose had a vision of the future years in which this taste would grow with restored exercise – of her mother, in a long-tailed dress, jogging on and on and on, jogging further and further from her sins, through a century of the 'Morning Post' and down the fashionable avenue of time. She herself would then be very old – she herself would be dead. Mrs Tramore would cover a span of life for which such an allowance of sin was small. The girl could laugh indeed now at that theory of her being dragged down. If one thing were more present to her than another it was the very desolation of their propriety. As she glanced at her companion, it sometimes seemed to her that if she had been a bad woman she would have been worse than that. There were compensations for being 'cut' which Mrs Tramore too much neglected.

The lonely old lady in Hill Street – Rose thought of her that way now – was the one person to whom she was ready to say that she would come to her on any terms. She wrote this to her three times over, and she knocked still oftener at her door. But the old lady answered no letters; if Rose had remained in Hill Street it would have been her own function to answer them; and at the door, the butler, whom the girl had known for ten years, considered her, when he told her his mistress was not at home, quite as he might have considered a young person who had come about a place and of whose eligibility he took a negative view. That was Rose's one pang, that she probably appeared rather heartless. Her aunt Julia had gone to Florence with Edith for the winter, on purpose to make her appear more so; for Miss Tramore was still the person most scandalised by her secession. Edith and she, doubtless, often talked over in Florence the destitution of the aged victim in Hill Street. Eric never came to see his sister, because, being full both of family and of personal feeling, he thought she really ought to have stayed with his grandmother. If she had had such an appurten- ance all to herself she might have done what she liked with it;

but he couldn't forgive such a want of consideration for anything of his. There were moments when Rose would have been
ready to take her hand from the plough and insist upon reinte-
gration, if only the fierce voice of the old house had allowed
people to look her up. But she read, ever so clearly, that her
grandmother had made this a question of loyalty to seventy
years of virtue. Mrs Tramore's forlornness didn't prevent her
drawing-room from being a very public place, in which Rose
could hear certain words reverberate: 'Leave her alone; it's the
only way to see how long she'll hold out.' The old woman's
visitors were people who didn't wish to quarrel, and the girl was
conscious that if they had not let her alone – that is if they had
come to her from her grandmother – she might perhaps not
have held out. She had no friends quite of her own; she had not
been brought up to have them, and it would not have been easy
in a house which two such persons as her father and his mother
divided between them. Her father disapproved of crude intimacies, and all the intimacies of youth were crude. He had
married at five-and-twenty and could testify to such a truth.
Rose felt that she shared even Captain Jay with her grandmother; she had seen what *he* was worth. Moreover, she had
spoken to him at that last moment in Hill Street in a way which,
taken with her former refusal, made it impossible that he
should come near her again. She hoped he went to see his
protectress: he could be a kind of substitute and administer
comfort.

It so happened, however, that the day after she threw Lady
Maresfield's invitation into the waste-paper basket she received
a visit from a certain Mrs Donovan, whom she had occasionally
seen in Hill Street. She vaguely knew this lady for a busybody,
but she was in a situation which even busybodies might alle-
viate. Mrs Donovan was poor, but honest – so scrupulously
honest that she was perpetually returning visits she had never
received. She was always clad in weather-beaten sealskin, and
had an odd air of being prepared for the worst, which was borne
out by her denying that she was Irish. She was of the English
Donovans.

'Dear child, won't you go out with me?' she asked.

Rose looked at her a moment and then rang the bell. She spoke of something else, without answering the question, and when the servant came she said: 'Please tell Mrs Tramore that Mrs Donovan has come to see her.'

'Oh, that'll be delightful; only you mustn't tell your grandmother!' the visitor exclaimed.

'Tell her what?'

'That I come to see your mamma.'

'You don't,' said Rose.

'Sure I hoped you'd introduce me!' cried Mrs Donovan, compromising herself in her embarrassment.

'It's not necessary; you knew her once.'

'Indeed and I've known every one once,' the visitor confessed.

Mrs Tramore, when she came in, was charming and exactly right; she greeted Mrs Donovan as if she had met her the week before last, giving her daughter such a new illustration of her tact that Rose again had the idea that it was no wonder 'people' had liked her. The girl grudged Mrs Donovan so fresh a morsel as a description of her mother at home, rejoicing that she would be inconvenienced by having to keep the story out of Hill Street. Her mother went away before Mrs Donovan departed, and Rose was touched by guessing her reason – the thought that since even this circuitous personage had been moved to come, the two might, if left together, invent some remedy. Rose waited to see what Mrs Donovan had in fact invented.

'You won't come out with me then?'

'Come out with you?'

'My daughters are married. You know I'm a lone woman. It would be an immense pleasure to me to have so charming a creature as yourself to present to the world.'

'I go out with my mother,' said Rose, after a moment.

'Yes, but sometimes when she's not inclined?'

'She goes everywhere she wants to go,' Rose continued, uttering the biggest fib of her life and only regretting it should be wasted on Mrs Donovan.

'Ah, but do you go everywhere *you* want?' the lady asked sociably.

'One goes even to places one hates. Every one does that.'

'Oh, what *I* go through!' this social martyr cried. Then she laid a persuasive hand on the girl's arm. 'Let me show you at a few places first, and then we'll see. I'll bring them all here.'

'I don't think I understand you,' replied Rose, though in Mrs Donovan's words she perfectly saw her own theory of the case reflected. For a quarter of a minute she asked herself whether she might not, after all, do so much evil that good might come. Mrs Donovan would take her out the next day, and be thankful enough to annex such an attraction as a pretty girl. Various consequences would ensue and the long delay would be shortened; her mother's drawing-room would resound with the clatter of teacups.

'Mrs Bray's having some big thing next week; come with me there and I'll show you what I mane,' Mrs Donovan pleaded.

'I see what you mane,' Rose answered, brushing away her temptation and getting up. 'I'm much obliged to you.'

'You know you're wrong, my dear,' said her interlocutress, with angry little eyes.

'I'm not going to Mrs Bray's.'

'I'll get you a kyard; it'll only cost me a penny stamp.'

'I've got one,' said the girl, smiling.

'Do you mean a penny stamp?' Mrs Donovan, especially at departure, always observed all the forms of amity. 'You can't do it alone, my darling,' she declared.

'Shall they call you a cab?' Rose asked.

'I'll pick one up. I choose my horse. You know you require your start,' her visitor went on.

'Excuse my mother,' was Rose's only reply.

'Don't mention it. Come to me when you need me. You'll find me in the Red Book.'

'It's awfully kind of you.'

Mrs Donovan lingered a moment on the threshold. 'Who will you *have* now, my child?' she appealed.

'I won't have any one!' Rose turned away, blushing for her. 'She came on speculation,' she said afterwards to Mrs Tramore.

Her mother looked at her a moment in silence. 'You can do it if you like, you know.'

Rose made no direct answer to this observation; she remarked instead: 'See what our quiet life allows us to escape.'

'We don't escape it. She has been here an hour.'

'Once in twenty years! We might meet her three times a day.'

'Oh, I'd take her with the rest!' sighed Mrs Tramore; while her daughter recognised that what her companion wanted to do was just what Mrs Donovan was doing. Mrs Donovan's life was her ideal.

On a Sunday, ten days later, Rose went to see one of her old governesses, of whom she had lost sight for some time and who had written to her that she was in London, unoccupied and ill. This was just the sort of relation into which she could throw herself now with inordinate zeal; the idea of it, however, not preventing a foretaste of the queer expression in the excellent lady's face when she should mention with whom she was living. While she smiled at this picture she threw in another joke, asking herself if Miss Hack could be held in any degree to constitute the nucleus of a circle. She would come to see her, in any event – come the more the further she was dragged down. Sunday was always a difficult day with the two ladies – the afternoons made it so apparent that they were not frequented. Her mother, it is true, was comprised in the habits of two or three old gentlemen – she had for a long time avoided male friends of less than seventy – who disliked each other enough to make the room, when they were there at once, crack with pressure. Rose sat for a long time with Miss Hack, doing conscientious justice to the conception that there could be troubles in the world worse than her own; and when she came back her mother was alone, but with a story to tell of a long visit from Mr Guy Mangler, who had waited and waited for her return. 'He's in love with you; he's coming again on Tuesday,' Mrs Tramore announced.

'Did he say so?'

'That he's coming back on Tuesday?'

'No, that he's in love with me.'

'He didn't need, when he stayed two hours.'

'With you? It's you he's in love with, mamma!'

'That will do as well,' laughed Mrs Tramore. 'For all the use we shall make of him!' she added in a moment.

'We shall make great use of him. His mother sent him.'

'Oh, she'll never come!'

'Then *he* sha'n't,' said Rose. Yet he was admitted on the Tuesday, and after she had given him his tea Mrs Tramore left the young people alone. Rose wished she hadn't – she herself had another view. At any rate she disliked her mother's view, which she had easily guessed. Mr Mangler did nothing but say how charming he thought his hostess of the Sunday, and what a tremendously jolly visit he had had. He didn't remark in so many words 'I had no idea your mother was such a good sort'; but this was the spirit of his simple discourse. Rose liked it at first – a little of it gratified her; then she thought there was too much of it for good taste. She had to reflect that one does what one can and that Mr Mangler probably thought he was delicate. He wished to convey that he desired to make up to her for the injustice of society. Why shouldn't her mother receive gracefully, she asked (not audibly) and who had ever said she didn't? Mr Mangler had a great deal to say about the disappointment of his own parent over Miss Tramore's not having come to dine with them the night of his aunt's ball.

'Lady Maresfield knows why I didn't come,' Rose answered at last.

'Ah, now, but *I* don't, you know; can't you tell *me*?' asked the young man.

'It doesn't matter, if your mother's clear about it.'

'Oh, but why make such an awful mystery of it, when I'm dying to know?'

He talked about this, he chaffed her about it for the rest of his visit: he had at last found a topic after his own heart. If her mother considered that he might be the emblem of their redemption he was an engine of the most primitive construction. He stayed and stayed; he struck Rose as on the point of bringing out something for which he had not quite, as he would have said, the cheek. Sometimes she thought he was going to begin: 'By the way, my mother told me to propose to you.' At other moments he seemed charged with the admission: 'I say, of course I really know what you're trying to do for her,' nodding at the door: 'therefore hadn't we better speak of it frankly, so that I can help you with my mother, and more particularly with my sister Gwendolen, who's the difficult one? The fact is, you see, they won't do anything for nothing. If you'll accept me they'll call, but they won't call without something "down".' Mr Mangler departed without their speaking frankly, and Rose Tramore had a hot hour during which she almost entertained, vindictively, the project of 'accepting' the limpid youth until after she should have got her mother into circulation. The cream of the vision was that she might break with him later. She could read that this was what her mother would have liked, but the next time he came the door was closed to him, and the next and the next.

In August there was nothing to do but to go abroad, with the sense on Rose's part that the battle was still all to fight; for a round of country visits was not in prospect, and English watering-places constituted one of the few subjects on which the girl had heard her mother express herself with disgust. Continental autumns had been indeed for years, one of the various forms of Mrs Tramore's atonement, but Rose could only infer that such fruit as they had borne was bitter. The stony stare of Belgravia could be practised at Homburg; and somehow it was inveterately only gentlemen who sat next to her at the *table d'hôte* at Cadenabbia. Gentlemen had never been of any use to Mrs Tramore for getting back into society; they had only helped her effectually to get out of it. She once dropped, to her daughter, in a moralising mood, the remark that it was astonishing how many of them one could know without its doing one any good. Fifty of them – even very clever ones – represented a value inferior to that of one stupid woman. Rose wondered at the offhand way in which her mother could talk of fifty clever men; it seemed to her that the whole world couldn't contain such a number. She had a sombre sense that mankind must be dull and mean. These cogitations took place in a cold hotel, in an eternal Swiss rain, and they had a flat echo in the transalpine valleys, as the lonely ladies went vaguely down to the Italian lakes and cities. Rose guided their course, at moments, with a kind of aimless ferocity; she moved abruptly, feeling vulgar and hating their life, though destitute of any definite vision of another life that would have been open to her. She had set herself a task and she clung to it; but she appeared to herself despicably idle. She had succeeded in not going to Homburg waters, where London was trying to wash away some of its stains; that would be too staring an advertisement of their situation. The main difference in situations to her now was the difference of being more or less pitied, at the best an intolerable danger; so that the places she preferred were the unsuspicious ones. She wanted to triumph with contempt, not with submission.

One morning in September, coming with her mother out of the marble church at Milan, she perceived that a gentleman who had just passed her on his way into the cathedral and whose face she had not noticed, had quickly raised his hat, with a suppressed ejaculation. She involuntarily glanced back; the gentleman had paused, again uncovering, and Captain Jay stood saluting her in the Italian sunshine. 'Oh, good-morning!' she said, and walked on, pursuing her course; her mother was a little in front. She overtook her in a moment, with an unreasonable sense, like a gust of cold air, that men were worse than ever, for Captain Jay had apparently moved into the church. Her mother turned as they met, and suddenly, as she looked back, an expression of peculiar sweetness came into this lady's eyes. It made Rose's take the same direction and rest a second time on Captain Jay, who was planted just where he had stood a minute before. He immediately came forward, asking Rose with great gravity if he might speak to her a moment, while Mrs Tramore went her way again. He had the expression of a man who wished to say something very important; yet his next words were simple enough and consisted of the remark that he had not seen her for a year.

'Is it really so much as that?' asked Rose.

'Very nearly. I would have looked you up, but in the first place I have been very little in London, and in the second I believed it wouldn't have done any good.'

'You should have put that first,' said the girl. 'It wouldn't have done any good.'

He was silent over this a moment, in his customary deciphering way; but the view he took of it did not prevent him from inquiring, as she slowly followed her mother, if he mightn't walk with her now. She answered with a laugh that it wouldn't do any good but that he might do as he liked. He replied without the slightest manifestation of levity that it would do more good than if he didn't, and they strolled together, with Mrs Tramore well before them, across the big, amusing piazza, where the front of the cathedral makes a sort of builded light. He asked a question or two and he explained his own presence: having a month's holiday, the first clear time for several years, he had just popped over the Alps. He inquired if Rose had recent news of the old lady in Hill Street, and it was the only tortuous thing she had ever heard him say.

'I have had no communication of any kind from her since I parted with you under her roof. Hasn't she mentioned that?' said Rose.

'I haven't seen her.'

'I thought you were such great friends.'

Bertram Jay hesitated a moment. 'Well, not so much now.'

'What has she done to you?' Rose demanded.

He fidgeted a little, as if he were thinking of something that made him unconscious of her question; then, with mild violence, he brought out the inquiry: 'Miss Tramore, are you happy?'

She was startled by the words, for she on her side had been reflecting – reflecting that he had broken with her grandmother and that this pointed to a reason. It suggested at least that he wouldn't now be so much like a mouthpiece for that cold ancestral tone. She turned off his question – said it never was a fair one, as you gave yourself away however you answered it. When he repeated 'You give yourself away?' as if he didn't understand, she remembered that he had not read the funny American books. This brought them to a silence, for she had enlightened him only by another laugh, and he was evidently preparing another question, which he wished carefully to disconnect from the former. Presently, just as they were coming near Mrs Tramore, it arrived in the words 'Is this lady your mother?' On Rose's assenting, with the addition that she was travelling with her, he said: 'Will you be so kind as to introduce me to her?' They were so close to Mrs Tramore that she probably heard, but she floated away with a single stroke of her paddle and an inattentive poise of her head. It was a striking exhibition of the famous tact, for Rose delayed to answer, which was exactly what might have made her mother wish to turn; and indeed when at last the girl spoke she only said to her companion:

'Why do you ask me that?'

'Because I desire the pleasure of making her acquaintance.'

Rose had stopped, and in the middle of the square they stood looking at each other. 'Do you remember what you said to me the last time I saw you?'

'Oh, don't speak of that!'

'It's better to speak of it now than to speak of it later.'

Bertram Jay looked round him, as if to see whether any one would hear; but the bright foreignness gave him a sense of safety, and he unexpectedly exclaimed:

'Miss Tramore, I love you more than ever!'

'Then you ought to have come to see us,' declared the girl, quickly walking on.

'You treated me the last time as if I were positively offensive to you.'

'So I did, but you know my reason.'

'Because I protested against the course you were taking? I did, I did!' the young man rang out, as if he still, a little, stuck to that.

His tone made Rose say gaily: 'Perhaps you do so yet?'

'I can't tell till I've seen more of your circumstances,' he replied with eminent honesty.

The girl stared; her light laugh filled the air. 'And it's in order to see more of them and judge that you wish to make my mother's acquaintance?'

He coloured at this and he evaded; then he broke out with a confused 'Miss Tramore, let me stay with you a little!' which made her stop again.

'Your company will do us great honour, but there must be a rigid condition attached to our acceptance of it.'

'Kindly mention it,' said Captain Jay, staring at the façade of the cathedral.

'You don't take us on trial.'

'On trial?'

'You don't make an observation to me – not a single one, ever, ever! – on the matter that, in Hill Street, we had our last words about.'

Captain Jay appeared to be counting the thousand pinnacles of the church. 'I think you really must be right,' he remarked at last.

'There you are!' cried Rose Tramore, and walked rapidly away.

He caught up with her, he laid his hand upon her arm to stay her. 'If you're going to Venice, let me go to Venice with you!'

'You don't even understand my condition.'

'I'm sure you're right, then: you must be right about everything.'

'That's not in the least true, and I don't care a fig whether you're sure or not. Please let me go.'

He had barred her way, he kept her longer. 'I'll go and speak to your mother myself!'

Even in the midst of another emotion she was amused at the air of audacity accompanying this declaration. Poor Captain Jay might have been on the point of marching up to a battery. She looked at him a moment; then she said: 'You'll be disappointed!'

'Disappointed?'

'She's much more proper than grandmamma, because she's much more amiable!'

'Dear Miss Tramore – dear Miss Tramore!' the young man murmured helplessly.

'You'll see for yourself. Only there's another condition,' Rose went on.

'Another?' he cried, with discouragement and alarm.

'You must understand thoroughly, before you throw in your lot with us even for a few days, what our position really is.'

'Is it very bad?' asked Bertram Jay artlessly.

'No one has anything to do with us, no one speaks to us, no one looks at us.'

'Really?' stared the young man.

'We've no social existence, we're utterly despised.'

'Oh, Miss Tramore!' Captain Jay interposed. He added quickly, vaguely, and with a want of presence of mind of which he as quickly felt ashamed: 'Do none of your family –?' The question collapsed; the brilliant girl was looking at him.

'We're extraordinarily happy,' she threw out.

'Now that's all I wanted to know!' he exclaimed, with a kind of exaggerated cheery reproach, walking on with her briskly to overtake her mother.

He was not dining at their inn, but he insisted on coming that evening to their *table d'hôte*. He sat next Mrs Tramore, and in the evening he accompanied them gallantly to the opera, at a third-rate theatre where they were almost the only ladies in the boxes. The next day they went together by rail to the Charterhouse of Pavia, and while he strolled with the girl, as they waited for the homeward train, he said to her candidly: 'Your mother's remarkably pretty.' She remembered the words and the feeling they gave her: they were the first note of a new era. The feeling was somewhat that of an anxious, gratified matron who has 'presented' her child and is thinking of the matrimonial market. Men might be of no use, as Mrs Tramore said, yet it was from this moment Rose dated the rosy dawn of her confidence that her *protégée* would go off; and when later, in crowded assemblies, the phrase, or something like it behind a hat or a fan, fell repeatedly on her anxious ear, 'Your mother *is* in beauty!' or 'I've never seen her look better!' she had a faint vision of the yellow sunshine and the afternoon shadows on the dusty Italian platform.

Mrs Tramore's behaviour at this period was a revelation of her native understanding of delicate situations. She needed no account of this one from her daughter – it was one of the things for which she had a scent; and there was a kind of loyalty to the rules of a game in the silent sweetness with which she smoothed the path of Bertram Jay. It was clear that she was in her element in fostering the exercise of the affections, and if she ever spoke without thinking twice it is probable that she would have exclaimed, with some gaiety, 'Oh, I know all about *love*!' Rose could see that she thought their companion would be a help, in spite of his being no dispenser of patronage. The key to the gates of fashion had not been placed in his hand, and no one had ever heard of the ladies of his family, who lived in some vague hollow of the Yorkshire moors; but none the less he might administer a muscular push. Yes indeed, men in general were broken reeds, but Captain Jay was peculiarly representative. Respectability was the woman's maximum, as honour was the man's, but this distinguished young soldier inspired more than one kind of confidence. Rose had a great deal of attention for the use to which his respectability was put; and there mingled with this attention some amusement and much compassion. She saw that after a couple of days he decidedly liked her mother, and that he was yet not in the least aware of it. He took for granted that he believed in her but little; notwithstanding which he would have trusted her with anything except Rose herself. His trusting her with Rose would come very soon. He never spoke to her daughter about her qualities of character, but two or three of them (and indeed these were all the poor lady had, and they made the best show) were what he had in mind in praising her appearance. When he remarked: 'What attention Mrs Tramore seems to attract everywhere!' he meant: 'What a beautifully simple nature it is!' and when he said: 'There's something extraordinarily harmonious in the colours she wears,' it signified: 'Upon my word, I never saw such a sweet temper in my life!' She lost one of her boxes at Verona, and made the prettiest joke of it to Captain Jay. When Rose saw this she said to herself, 'Next season we shall have only to choose.' Rose knew what was in the box.

By the time they reached Venice (they had stopped at half a dozen little old romantic cities in the most frolicsome aesthetic way) she liked their companion better than she had ever liked him before. She did him the justice to recognise that if he was not quite honest with himself he was at least wholly honest with *her*. She reckoned up everything he had been since he joined them, and put upon it all an interpretation so favourable to his devotion that, catching herself in the act of glossing over one or two episodes that had not struck her at the time as disinterested she exclaimed, beneath her breath, 'Look out – you're falling in love!' But if he liked correctness wasn't he quite right? Could any one possibly like it more than *she* did? And if he had protested against her throwing in her lot with her mother, this was not because of the benefit conferred but because of the injury received. He exaggerated that injury, but this was the privilege of a lover perfectly willing to be selfish on behalf of his mistress. He might have wanted her grandmother's money for her, but if he had given her up on first discovering that she was throwing away her chance of it (oh, this was *her* doing too!) he had given up her grandmother as much: not keeping well with the old woman, as some men would have done; not waiting to see how the perverse experiment would turn out and appeasing her, if it should promise tolerably, with a view to future operations. He had had a simple-minded, evangelical, lurid view of what the girl he loved would find herself in for. She could see this now – she could see it from his present bewilderment and mystification, and she liked him and pitied him, with the kindest smile, for the original *naïveté* as well as for the actual meekness. No wonder he hadn't known what she was in for, since he now didn't even known what he was in for himself. Were there not moments when he thought his companions almost unnaturally good, almost suspiciously safe? He had lost all power to verify that sketch of their isolation and *déclassement* to which she had treated him on the great square at Milan. The last thing he noticed was that they were neglected, and he had never, for himself, had such an impression of society.

It could scarcely be enhanced even by the apparition of a large, fair, hot, red-haired young man, carrying a lady's fan in his hand, who suddenly stood before their little party as, on the third evening after their arrival in Venice, it partook of ices at one of the tables before the celebrated Café Florian. The lamp-lit Venetian dusk appeared to have revealed them to this gentleman as he sat with other friends at a neighbouring table, and he had sprung up, with unsophisticated glee, to shake hands with Mrs Tramore and her daughter. Rose recalled him to her mother, who looked at first as though she didn't remember him but presently bestowed a sufficiently gracious smile on Mr Guy Mangler. He gave with youthful candour the history of his movements and indicated the where-abouts of his family: he was with his mother and sisters; they had met the Bob Veseys, who had taken Lord Whiteroy's yacht and were going to Constantinople. His mother and the girls, poor things, were at the Grand Hotel, but he was on the yacht with the Veseys, where they had Lord Whiteroy's cook. Wasn't the food in Venice filthy, and wouldn't they come and look at the yacht? She wasn't very fast, but she was awfully jolly. His mother might have come if she would, but she wouldn't at first, and now, when she wanted to, there were other people, who naturally wouldn't turn out for her. Mr Mangler sat down; he alluded with artless resentment to the way, in July, the door of his friends had been closed to him. He was going to Constantinople, but he didn't care – if *they* were going anywhere; meanwhile his mother hoped awfully they would look her up.

Lady Maresfield, if she had given her son any such message, which Rose disbelieved, entertained her hope in a manner compatible with her sitting for half an hour, surrounded by her little retinue, without glancing in the direction of Mrs Tramore. The girl, however, was aware that this was not a good enough instance of their humiliation; inasmuch as it was rather she who, on the occasion of their last contact, had held off from Lady Maresfield. She was a little ashamed now of not having answered the note in which this affable personage ignored her mother. She couldn't help perceiving indeed a dim movement on the part of some of the other members of the group; she made out an attitude of observation in the high-plumed head of Mrs Vaughan-Vesey. Mrs Vesey, perhaps, might have been looking at Captain Jay, for as this gentleman walked back to the hotel with our young lady (they were at the 'Britannia', and young Mangler, who clung to them, went in front with Mrs Tramore) he revealed to Rose that he had some acquaintance with Lady Maresfield's eldest daughter, though he didn't know and didn't particularly want to know, her ladyship. He expressed himself with more acerbity than she had ever heard him use (Christian charity so generally governed his speech) about the young donkey who had been prattling to them. They separated at the door of the hotel. Mrs Tramore had got rid of Mr Mangler, and Bertram Jay was in other quarters.

'If you know Mrs Vesey, why didn't you go and speak to her? I'm sure she saw you,' Rose said.

Captain Jay replied even more circumspectly than usual. 'Because I didn't want to leave you.'

'Well, you can go now; you're free,' Rose rejoined.

'Thank you. I shall never go again.'

'That won't be civil,' said Rose.

'I don't care to be civil. I don't like her.'

'Why don't you like her?'

'You ask too many questions.'

'I know I do,' the girl acknowledged.

Captain Jay had already shaken hands with her, but at this he put out his hand again. 'She's too worldly,' he murmured, while he held Rose Tramore's a moment.

'Ah, you dear!' Rose exclaimed almost audibly as, with her mother, she turned away.

The next morning, upon the Grand Canal, the gondola of our three friends encountered a stately barge which, though it contained several persons, seemed pervaded mainly by one majestic presence. During the instant the gondolas were passing each other it was impossible either for Rose Tramore or for her companions not to become conscious that this distinguished identity had markedly inclined itself – a circumstance commemorated the next moment, almost within earshot of the other boat, by the most spontaneous cry that had issued for many a day from the lips of Mrs Tramore. 'Fancy, my dear, Lady Maresfield has bowed to us!'

'We ought to have returned it,' Rose answered; but she looked at Bertram Jay, who was opposite to her. He blushed, and she blushed, and during this moment was born a deeper understanding than had yet existed between these associated spirits. It had something to do with their going together that afternoon, without her mother, to look at certain out-of-the-way pictures as to which Ruskin had inspired her with a desire to see sincerely. Mrs Tramore expressed the wish to stay at home, and the motive of this wish – a finer shade than any that even Ruskin had ever found a phrase for – was not translated into misrepresenting words by either the mother or the daughter. At San Giovanni in Bragora the girl and her companion came upon Mrs Vaughan-Vesey, who, with one of her sisters, was also endeavouring to do the earnest thing. She did it to Rose, she did it to Captain Jay, as well as to Gianbellini; she was a handsome, long-necked, aquiline person, of a different type from the rest of her family, and she did it remarkably well. She secured our friends – it was her own expression – for luncheon, on the morrow, on the yacht, and she made it public to Rose that she would come that afternoon to invite her mother. When the girl returned to the hotel, Mrs Tramore mentioned, before Captain Jay, who had come up to their sitting-room, that Lady Maresfield had called. 'She stayed a long time – at least it seemed long!' laughed Mrs Tramore.

The poor lady could laugh freely now; yet there was some grimness in a colloquy that she had with her daughter after Bertram Jay had departed. Before this happened Mrs Vesey's card, scrawled over in pencil and referring to the morrow's luncheon, was brought up to Mrs Tramore.

'They mean it all as a bribe,' said the principal recipient of these civilities.

'As a bribe?' Rose repeated.

'She wants to marry you to that boy; they've seen Captain Jay and they're frightened.'

'Well, dear mamma, I can't take Mr Mangler for a husband.'

'Of course not. But oughtn't we to go to the luncheon?'

'Certainly we'll go to the luncheon,' Rose said; and when the affair took place, on the morrow, she could feel for the first time that she was taking her mother out. This appearance was some-how brought home to every one else, and it was really the agent of her success. For it is of the essence of this simple history that, in the first place, her success dated from Mrs Vesey's Venetian *déjeuner*, and in the second reposed, by a subtle social logic, on the very anomaly that had made it dubious. There is always a chance in things, and Rose Tramore's chance was in the fact that Gwendolen Vesey was, as some one had said, awfully modern, an immense improvement on the exploded science of her mother, and capable of seeing what a 'draw' there would be in the comedy, if properly brought out, of the reversed positions of Mrs Tramore and Mrs Tramore's diplomatic daughter. With a first-rate managerial eye she perceived that people would flock into any room – and all the more into one of hers – to see Rose bring in her dreadful mother. She treated the cream of English society to this thrilling spectacle later in the autumn, when she once more 'secured' both the performers for a week at Brimble. It made a hit on the spot, the very first evening – the girl was felt to play her part so well. The rumour of the performance spread; every one wanted to see it. It was an entertainment of which, that winter in the country, and the next season in town, persons of taste desired to give their friends the freshness. The thing was to make the Tramores come late, after every one had arrived. They were engaged for a fixed hour, like the American imitator and the Patagonian contralto. Mrs Vesey had been the first to say the girl was awfully original, but that became the general view.

Gwendolen Vesey had with her mother one of the few quar-rels in which Lady Maresfield had really stood up to such an antagonist (the elder woman had to recognise in general in whose veins it was that the blood of the Manglers flowed) on account of this very circumstance of her attaching more importance to Miss Tramore's originality ('Her originality be hanged!' her ladyship had gone so far as unintelligently to exclaim) than to the prospects of the unfortunate Guy. Mrs Vesey actually lost sight of these pressing problems in her admiration of the way the mother and the daughter, or rather the daughter and the mother (it was slightly confusing) 'drew'.

It was Lady Maresfield's version of the case that the brazen girl (she was shockingly coarse) had treated poor Guy abominably. At any rate it was made known, just after Easter, that Miss Tramore was to be married to Captain Jay. The marriage was not to take place till the summer; but Rose felt that before this the field would practically be won. There had been some bad moments, there had been several warm corners and a certain number of cold shoulders and closed doors and stony stares; but the breach was effectually made – the rest was only a question of time. Mrs Tramore could be trusted to keep what she had gained, and it was the dowagers, the old dragons with prominent fangs and glittering scales, whom the trick had already mainly caught. By this time there were several houses into which the liberated lady had crept alone. Her daughter had been expected with her, but they couldn't turn her out because the girl had stayed behind, and she was fast acquiring a new identity, that of a parental connection with the heroine of such a romantic story. She was at least the next best thing to her daughter, and Rose foresaw the day when she would be valued principally as a memento of one of the prettiest episodes in the annals of London. At a big official party, in June, Rose had the joy of introducing Eric to his mother. She was a little sorry it was an official party – there were some other such queer people there; but Eric called, observing the shade, the next day but one.

No observer, probably, would have been acute enough to fix exactly the moment at which the girl ceased to take out her mother and began to be taken out by her. A later phase was more distinguishable – that at which Rose forbore to inflict on her companion a duality that might become oppressive. She began to economise her force, she went only when the particular effect was required. Her marriage was delayed by the period of mourning consequent upon the death of her grandmother, who, the younger Mrs Tramore averred, was killed by the rumour of her own new birth. She was the only one of the dragons who had not been tamed. Julia Tramore knew the truth about this – she was determined such things should not kill *her*. She would live to do something – she hardly knew what. The provisions of her mother's will were published in the 'Illustrated News'; from which it appeared that everything that was not to go to Eric and to Julia was to go to the fortunate Edith. Miss Tramore makes no secret of her own intentions as regards this favourite. Edith is not pretty, but Lady Maresfield is waiting for her; she is determined Gwendolen Vesey shall not get hold of her. Mrs Vesey however takes no interest in her at all. She is whimsical, as befits a woman of her fashion; but there are two persons she is still very fond of, the delightful Bertram Jays. The fondness of this pair, it must be added, is not wholly expended in return. They are extremely united, but their life is more domestic than might have been expected from the pre-liminary signs. It owes a portion of its concentration to the fact that Mrs Tramore has now so many places to go to that she has almost no time to come to her daughter's. She is, under her son-in-law's roof, a brilliant but a rare apparition, and the other day he remarked upon the circumstance to his wife.

'If it hadn't been for you,' she replied, smiling, 'she might have had her regular place at our fireside.'

'Good heavens, how did I prevent it?' cried Captain Jay, with all the consciousness of virtue.

'You ordered it otherwise, you goose!' And she says, in the same spirit, whenever her husband commends her (which he does, sometimes, extravagantly) for the way she launched her mother: 'Nonsense, my dear – practically it was *you*!'

SIR EDMUND ORME

THE statement appears to have been written, though the fragment is undated, long after the death of his wife, whom I take to
have been one of the persons referred to. There is, however,
nothing in the strange story to establish this point, which is,
perhaps, not of importance. When I took possession of his
effects I found these pages, in a locked drawer, among papers
relating to the unfortunate lady's too brief career (she died in
childbirth a year after her marriage), letters, memoranda,
accounts, faded photographs, cards of invitation. That is the
only connection I can point to, and you may easily and will
probably say that the tale is too extravagant to have had a
demonstrable origin. I cannot, I admit, vouch for his having
intended it as a report of real occurrence – I can only vouch for
his general veracity. In any case it was written for himself, not
for others. I offer it to others – having full option – precisely
because it is so singular. Let them, in respect to the form of the
thing, bear in mind that it was written quite for himself. I have
altered nothing but the names.

If there's a story in the matter I recognise the exact moment at
which it began. This was on a soft, still Sunday noon in November, just after church, on the sunny Parade. Brighton was full of
people; it was the height of the season, and the day was even
more respectable than lovely – which helped to account for the
multitude of walkers. The blue sea itself was decorous; it
seemed to doze, with a gentle snore (if that *be* decorum), as if
nature were preaching a sermon. After writing letters all the
morning I had come out to take a look at it before luncheon. I
was leaning over the rail which separates the King's Road from
the beach, and I think I was smoking a cigarette, when I became
conscious of an intended joke in the shape of a light walking-
stick laid across my shoulders. The idea, I found, had been
thrown off by Teddy Bostwick, of the Rifles, and was intended

as a contribution to talk. Our talk came off as we strolled together – he always took your arm to show you he forgave your obtuseness about his humour – and looked at the people, and bowed to some of them, and wondered who others were, and differed in opinion as to the prettiness of the girls. About Charlotte Marden we agreed, however, as we saw her coming toward us with her mother; and there surely could have been no one who wouldn't have agreed with us. The Brighton air, of old, used to make plain girls pretty and pretty girls prettier still – I don't know whether it works the spell now. The place, at any rate, was rare for complexions, and Miss Marden's was one that made people turn round. It made *us* stop, heaven knows – at least, it was one of the things, for we already knew the ladies.

We turned with them, we joined them, we went where they were going. They were only going to the end and back – they had just come out of church. It was another manifestation of Teddy's humour that he got immediate possession of Charlotte, leaving me to walk with her mother. However, I was not unhappy; the girl was before me and I had her to talk about. We prolonged our walk, Mrs Marden kept me, and presently she said she was tired and must sit down. We found a place on a sheltered bench – we gossiped as the people passed. It had already struck me, in this pair, that the resemblance between the mother and the daughter was wonderful even among such resemblances – the more so that it took so little account of a difference of nature. One often hears mature mothers spoken of as warnings – signposts, more or less discouraging, of the way daughters may go. But there was nothing deterrent in the idea that Charlotte, at fifty-five, should be as beautiful, even though it were conditioned on her being as pale and preoccupied, as Mrs Marden. At twenty-two she had a kind of rosy blankness and she was admirably handsome. Her head had the charming shape of her mother's, and her features the same fine order. Then there were looks and movements and tones (moments when you could scarcely say whether it were aspect or sound), which, between the two personalities, were a reflection, a recall.

These ladies had a small fortune and a cheerful little house at Brighton, full of portraits and tokens and trophies (stuffed animals on the top of bookcases, and sallow, varnished fish under glass), to which Mrs Marden professed herself attached by pious memories. Her husband had been 'ordered' there in ill-health, to spend the last years of his life, and she had already mentioned to me that it was a place in which she felt herself still under the protection of his goodness. His goodness appeared to have been great, and she sometimes had the air of defending it against mysterious imputations. Some sense of protection, of an influence invoked and cherished, was evidently necessary to her; she had a dim wistfulness, a longing for security. She wanted friends and she had a good many. She was kind to me on our first meeting, and I never suspected her of the vulgar purpose of 'making up' to me – a suspicion, of course, unduly frequent in conceited young men. It never struck me that she wanted me for her daughter, nor yet, like some unnatural mammas, for herself. It was as if they had had a common deep, shy need and had been ready to say: 'Oh, be friendly to us and be trustful! Don't be afraid, you won't be expected to marry us.' 'Of course there's something about mamma; that's really what makes her such a dear!' Charlotte said to me, confidentially, at an early stage of our acquaintance. She worshipped her mother's appearance. It was the only thing she was vain of; she accepted the raised eyebrows as a charming ultimate fact. 'She looks as if she were waiting for the doctor, dear mamma,' she said on another occasion. 'Perhaps *you're* the doctor; do you think you are?' It appeared in the event that I had some healing power. At any rate when I learned, for she once dropped the remark, that Mrs Marden also thought there was something 'awfully strange' about Charlotte, the relation between the two ladies became extremely interesting. It was happy enough, at bottom; each had the other so much on her mind.

On the Parade the stream of strollers held its course, and Charlotte presently went by with Teddy Bostwick. She smiled and nodded and continued, but when she came back she stopped and spoke to us. Captain Bostwick positively declined to go in, he said the occasion was too jolly: might they therefore take another turn? Her mother dropped a 'Do as you like,' and the girl gave me an impertinent smile over her shoulder as they quitted us. Teddy looked at me with his glass in one eye; but I didn't mind that; it was only of Miss Marden I was thinking as I observed to my companion, laughing:

'She's a bit of a coquette, you know.'

'Don't say that – don't say that!' Mrs Marden murmured.

'The nicest girls always are – just a little,' I was magnanimous enough to plead.

'Then why are they always punished?'

The intensity of the question startled me – it had come out in such a vivid flash. Therefore I had to think a moment before I inquired: 'What do you know about it?'

'I was a bad girl myself.'

'And were you punished?'

'I carry it through life,' said Mrs Marden, looking away from me. 'Ah!' she suddenly panted, in the next breath, rising to her feet and staring at her daughter, who had reappeared again with Captain Bostwick. She stood a few seconds, with the queerest expression in her face; then she sank upon the seat again and I saw that she had blushed crimson. Charlotte, who had observed her movement, came straight up to her and, taking her hand with quick tenderness, seated herself on the other side of her. The girl had turned pale – she gave her mother a fixed, frightened look. Mrs Marden, who had had some shock which escaped our detection, recovered herself; that is she sat quiet and inexpressive, gazing at the indifferent crowd, the sunny air, the slumbering sea. My eye happened to fall, however, on the interlocked hands of the two ladies, and I quickly guessed that the grasp of the elder one was violent. Bostwick stood before them, wondering what was the matter and asking me from his little vacant disc if *I* knew; which led Charlotte to say to him after a moment, with a certain irritation:

'Don't stand there that way, Captain Bostwick; go away – *please* go away.'

I got up at this, hoping that Mrs Marden wasn't ill; but she immediately begged that we would *not* go away, that we would particularly stay and that we would presently come home to lunch. She drew me down beside her and for a moment I felt her hand pressing my arm in a way that might have been an involuntary betrayal of distress and might have been a private signal. What she might have wished to point out to me I couldn't divine: perhaps she had seen somebody or something abnormal in the crowd. She explained to us in a few minutes that she was all right; that she was only liable to palpitations – they came as quickly as they went. It was time to move, and we moved. The incident was felt to be closed. Bostwick and I lunched with our sociable friends, and when I walked away with him he declared that he had never seen such dear kind creatures.

Mrs Marden had made us promise to come back the next day to tea, and had exhorted us in general to come as often as we could. Yet the next day, when at five o'clock I knocked at the door of the pretty house, it was to learn that the ladies had gone up to town. They had left a message for us with the butler: he was to say that they had suddenly been called – were very sorry. They would be absent a few days. This was all I could extract from the dumb domestic. I went again three days later, but they were still away; and it was not till the end of a week that I got a note from Mrs Marden, saying 'We are back; do come and forgive us.' It was on this occasion, I remember (the occasion of my going just after getting the note), that she told me she had intuitions. I don't know how many people there were in England at that time in that predicament, but there were very few who would have mentioned it; so that the announcement struck me as original, especially as her point was that some of these uncanny promptings were connected with me. There were other people present – idle Brighton folk, old women with frightened eyes and irrelevant interjections – and I had but a few minutes' talk with Charlotte; but the day after this I met them both at dinner and had the satisfaction of sitting next to Miss Marden. I recall that hour as the hour on which it first completely came over me that she was a beautiful, liberal creature. I had seen her personality in patches and gleams, like a song sung in snatches, but now it was before me in a large rosy glow, as if it had been a full volume of sound – I heard the whole of the air. It was sweet, fresh music – I was often to hum it over.

After dinner I had a few words with Mrs Marden; it was at the moment, late in the evening, when tea was handed about. A servant passed near us with a tray, I asked her if she would have a cup, and, on her assenting, took one and handed it to her. She put out her hand for it and I gave it to her, safely as I supposed; but as she was in the act of receiving it she started and faltered, so that the cup and saucer dropped with a crash of porcelain and without, on the part of my interlocutress, the usual woman's movement to save her dress. I stooped to pick up the fragments and when I raised myself Mrs Marden was look-ing across the room at her daughter, who looked back at her smiling, but with an anxious light in her eyes. 'Dear mamma, what on earth *is* the matter with you?' the silent question seemed to say. Mrs Marden coloured, just as she had done after her strange movement on the Parade the other week, and I was therefore surprised when she said to me with unexpected assurance: 'You should really have a steadier hand!' I had begun to stammer a defence of my hand when I became aware that she had fixed her eyes upon me with an intense appeal. It was ambiguous at first and only added to my confu-sion; then suddenly I understood, as plainly as if she had murmured 'Make believe it was you – make believe it was you.' The servant came back to take the morsels of the cup and wipe up the spilt tea, and while I was in the midst of making believe Mrs Marden abruptly brushed away from me and from her daughter's attention and went into another room. I noticed that she gave no heed to the state of her dress.

I saw nothing more of either of them that evening, but the next morning, in the King's Road, I met Miss Marden with a roll of music in her muff. She told me she had been a little way alone, to practise duets with a friend, and I asked her if she would go a little way further in company. She gave me leave to attend her to her door, and as we stood before it I inquired if I might go in. 'No, not to-day – I don't want you,' she said, candidly, though not roughly; while the words caused me to direct a wistful, disconcerted gaze at one of the windows of the house. It fell upon the white face of Mrs Marden, who was looking out at us from the drawing-room. She stood there long enough for me to see that it *was* she and not an apparition, as I had thought for a second, and then she vanished before her daughter had observed her. The girl, during our walk, had said nothing about her. As I had been told they didn't want me I left them alone a little, after which circumstances supervened that kept us still longer apart. I finally went up to London, and while there I received a pressing invitation to come immediately down to Tranton, a pretty old place in Sussex belonging to a couple whose acquaintance I had lately made.

I went to Tranton from town, and on arriving found the Mardens, with a dozen other people, in the house. The first thing Mrs Marden said was: 'Will you forgive me?' and when I asked what I had to forgive she answered: 'My throwing my tea over you.' I replied that it had gone over herself; whereupon she said: 'At any rate I was very rude; but some day I think you'll understand, and then you'll make allowances for me.' The first day I was there she dropped two or three of these references (she had already indulged in more than one), to the mystic initiation that was in store for me; so that I began, as the phrase is, to chaff her about it, to say I would rather it were less wonderful and take it out at once. She answered that when it should come to me I would have to take it out – there would be little enough option. That it *would* come was privately clear to her, a deep presentiment, which was the only reason she had ever mentioned the matter. Didn't I remember she had told me she had intuitions? From the first time of her seeing me she had been sure there were things I should not escape knowing. Meanwhile there was nothing to do but wait and keep cool, not to be precipitate. She particularly wished not to be any more nervous than she was. And I was above all not to be nervous myself – one got used to everything. I declared that though I couldn't make out what she was talking about I was terribly frightened; the absence of a clue gave such a range to one's imagination. I exaggerated on purpose; for if Mrs Marden was mystifying I can scarcely say she was alarming. I couldn't imagine what she meant, but I wondered more than I shuddered. I might have said to myself that she was a little wrong in the upper storey; but that never occurred to me. She struck me as hopelessly right.

There were other girls in the house, but Charlotte Marden was the most charming; which was so generally felt to be the case that she really interfered with the slaughter of ground game. There were two or three men, and I was of the number, who actually preferred her to the society of the beaters. In short she was recognised as a form of sport superior and exquisite. She was kind to all of us – she made us go out late and come in early. I don't know whether she flirted, but several other members of the party thought *they* did. Indeed, as regards himself, Teddy Bostwick, who had come over from Brighton, was visibly sure.

The third day I was at Tranton was a Sunday, and there was a very pretty walk to morning service over the fields. It was grey, windless weather, and the bell of the little old church that nestled in the hollow of the Sussex down sounded near and domestic. We were a straggling procession, in the mild damp air (which, as always at that season, gave one the feeling that after the trees were bare there was more of it – a larger sky), and I managed to fall a good way behind with Miss Marden. I remember entertaining, as we moved together over the turf, a strong impulse to say something intensely personal, something violent and important – important for *me*, such as that I had never seen her so lovely, or that that particular moment was the sweetest of my life. But always, in youth, such words have been on the lips many times before they are spoken; and I had the sense, not that I didn't know her well enough (I cared little for that), but that she didn't know *me* well enough. In the church, where there were old Tranton tombs and brasses, the big Tranton pew was full. Several of us were scattered, and I found a seat for Miss Marden, and another for myself beside it, at a distance from her mother and from most of our friends. There were two or three decent rustics on the bench, who moved in further to make room for us, and I took my place first, to cut off my companion from our neighbours. After she was seated there was still a space left, which remained empty till service was about half over.

This at least was the moment at which I became aware that another person had entered and had taken the seat. When I noticed him he had apparently been for some minutes in the pew, for he had settled himself and put down his hat beside him, and, with his hands crossed on the nob of his cane, was gazing before him at the altar. He was a pale young man in black, with the air of a gentleman. I was slightly startled on perceiving him, for Miss Marden had not attracted my attention to his entrance by moving to make room for him. After a few minutes, observing that he had no prayer-book, I reached across my neighbour and placed mine before him, on the ledge of the pew; a manoeuvre the motive of which was not unconnected with the possibility that, in my own destitution, Miss Marden would give me one side of *her* velvet volume to hold. The pretext, however, was destined to fail, for at the moment I offered him the book the intruder – whose intrusion I had so condoned – rose from his place without thanking me, stepped noiselessly out of the pew (it had no door), and, so discreetly as to attract no attention, passed down the centre of the church. A few minutes had sufficed for his devotions. His behaviour was unbecoming, his early departure even more than his late arrival; but he managed so quietly that we were not incommoded, and I perceived, on turning a little to glance after him, that nobody was disturbed by his withdrawal. I only noticed, and with surprise, that Mrs Marden had been so affected by it as to rise, involuntarily, an instant, in her place. She stared at him as he passed, but he passed very quickly, and she as quickly dropped down again, though not too soon to catch my eye across the church. Five minutes later I asked Miss Marden, in a low voice, if she would kindly pass me back my prayer-book – I had waited to see if she would spontaneously perform the act. She restored this aid to devotion, but had been so far from troubling herself about it that she could say to me as she did so: 'Why on earth did you put it there?' I was on the point of answering her when she dropped on her knees, and I held my tongue. I had only been going to say: 'To be decently civil.'

After the benediction, as we were leaving our places, I was slightly surprised, again, to see that Mrs Marden, instead of going out with her companions, had come up the aisle to join us, having apparently something to say to her daughter. She said it, but in an instant I observed that it was only a pretext –

her real business was with me. She pushed Charlotte forward and suddenly murmured to me: 'Did you see him?'

'The gentleman who sat down here? How could I help seeing him?'

'Hush!' she said, with the intensest excitement; 'don't *speak* to her – don't tell her!' She slipped her hand into my arm, to keep me near her, to keep me, it seemed, away from her daughter. The precaution was unnecessary, for Teddy Bostwick had already taken possession of Miss Marden, and as they passed out of church in front of me I saw one of the other men close up on her other hand. It appeared to be considered that I had had my turn. Mrs Marden withdrew her hand from my arm as soon as we got out, but not before I felt that she had really needed the support. 'Don't speak to any one – don't tell any one!' she went on.

'I don't understand. Tell them what?'

'Why, that you saw him.'

'Surely they saw him for themselves.'

'Not one of them, not one of them.' She spoke in a tone of such passionate decision that I glanced at her – she was staring straight before her. But she felt the challenge of my eyes and she stopped short, in the old brown timber porch of the church, with the others well in advance of us, and said, looking at me now and in a quite extraordinary manner: 'You're the only person, the only person in the world.'

'But *you*, dear madam?'

'Oh me – of course. That's my curse!' And with this she moved rapidly away from me to join the body of the party. I hovered on its outskirts on the way home, for I had food for rumination. Whom had I seen and why was the apparition – it rose before my mind's eye very vividly again – invisible to the others? If an exception had been made for Mrs Marden, why did it constitute a curse, and why was I to share so questionable an advantage? This inquiry, carried on in my own locked breast, kept me doubtless silent enough during luncheon. After luncheon I went out on the old terrace to smoke a cigarette, but I had only taken a couple of turns when I perceived Mrs Marden's moulded mask at the window of one of the rooms which opened on the crooked flags. It reminded me of the same flitting presence at the window at Brighton the day I met Charlotte and walked home with her. But this time my ambiguous friend didn't vanish; she tapped on the pane and motioned me to come in. She was in a queer little apartment, one of the many reception-rooms of which the ground-floor at Tranton consisted; it was known as the Indian room and had a decoration vaguely Oriental – bamboo lounges, lacquered screens, lanterns with long fringes and strange idols in cabinets, objects not held to conduce to sociability. The place was little used, and when I went round to her we had it to ourselves. As soon as I entered she said to me: 'Please tell me this; are you in love with my daughter?'

I hesitated a moment. 'Before I answer your question will you kindly tell me what gives you the idea? I don't consider that I have been very forward.'

Mrs Marden, contradicting me with her beautiful anxious eyes, gave me no satisfaction on the point I mentioned; she only went on strenuously:

'Did you say nothing to her on the way to church?'

'What makes you think I said anything?'

'The fact that you saw him.'

'Saw whom, dear Mrs Marden?'

'Oh, you know,' she answered, gravely, even a little reproachfully, as if I were trying to humiliate her by making her phrase the unphraseable.

'Do you mean the gentleman who formed the subject of your strange statement in church – the one who came into the pew?'

'You saw him, you saw him!' Mrs Marden panted, with a strange mixture of dismay and relief.

'Of course I saw him; and so did you.'

'It didn't follow. Did you feel it to be inevitable?'

I was puzzled again. 'Inevitable?'

'That you *should* see him?'

'Certainly, since I'm not blind.'

'You might have been; every one else is.' I was wonderfully at sea, and I frankly confessed it to my interlocutress; but the case was not made clearer by her presently exclaiming: 'I knew you would, from the moment you should be really in love with her! I knew it would be the test – what do I mean? – the proof.'

'Are there such strange bewilderments attached to that high state?' I asked, smiling.

'You perceive there are. You see him, you see him!' Mrs Marden announced, with tremendous exaltation. 'You'll see him again.'

'I've no objection; but I shall take more interest in him if you'll kindly tell me who he is.'

She hesitated, looking down a moment; then she said, raising her eyes: 'I'll tell you if you'll tell me first what you said to her on the way to church.'

'Has she told you I said anything?'

'Do I need that?' smiled Mrs Marden.

'Oh yes, I remember – your intuitions! But I'm sorry to see they're at fault this time; because I really said nothing to your daughter that was the least out of the way.'

'Are you very sure?'

'On my honour, Mrs Marden.'

'Then you consider that you're not in love with her?'

'That's another affair!' I laughed.

'You are – you *are*! You wouldn't have seen him if you hadn't been.'

'Who the deuce *is* he, then, madam?' I inquired with some irritation.

She would still only answer me with another question. 'Didn't you at least *want* to say something to her – didn't you come very near it?'

The question was much to the point; it justified the famous intuitions. 'Very near it – it was the turn of a hair. I don't know what kept me quiet.'

'That was quite enough,' said Mrs Marden. 'It isn't what you say that determines it; it's what you feel. *That's* what he goes by.'

I was annoyed, at last, by her reiterated reference to an identity yet to be established, and I clasped my hands with an air of supplication which covered much real impatience, a sharper curiosity and even the first short throbs of a certain sacred dread. 'I entreat you to tell me whom you're talking about.'

She threw up her arms, looking away from me, as if to shake off both reserve and responsibility. 'Sir Edmund Orme.'

'And who is Sir Edmund Orme?'

At the moment I spoke she gave a start. 'Hush, here they come.' Then as, following the direction of her eyes, I saw Charlotte Marden on the terrace, at the window, she added, with an intensity of warning: 'Don't notice him – *never*!'

Charlotte, who had had her hands beside her eyes, peering into the room and smiling, made a sign that she was to be admitted, on which I went and opened the long window. Her mother turned away, and the girl came in with a laughing challenge: 'What plot in the world are you two hatching here?' Some plan – I forget what – was in prospect for the afternoon, as to which Mrs Marden's participation or consent was solicited – *my* adhesion was taken for granted – and she had been half over the place in her quest. I was flurried, because I saw that Mrs Marden was flurried (when she turned round to meet her daughter she covered it by a kind of extravagance, throwing herself on the girl's neck and embracing her), and to pass it off I said, fancifully, to Charlotte:

'I've been asking your mother for your hand.'

'Oh, indeed, and has she given it?' Miss Marden answered, gaily.

'She was just going to when you appeared there.'

'Well, it's only for a moment – I'll leave you free.'

'Do you like him, Charlotte?' Mrs Marden asked, with a candour I scarcely expected.

'It's difficult to say it *before* him isn't it?' the girl replied, entering into the humour of the thing, but looking at me as if she didn't like me.

She would have had to say it before another person as well, for at that moment there stepped into the room from the terrace (the window had been left open), a gentleman who had come into sight, at least into mine, only within the instant. Mrs Marden had said 'Here *they* come,' but he appeared to have followed her daughter at a certain distance. I immediately recognised him as the personage who had sat beside us in church. This time I saw him better, saw that his face and his whole air were strange. I speak of him as a personage, because one felt, indescribably, as if a reigning prince had come into the room. He held himself with a kind of habitual majesty, as if he were different from us. Yet he looked fixedly and gravely at me, till I wondered what he expected of me. Did he consider that I should bend my knee or kiss his hand? He turned his eyes in the same way on Mrs Marden, but she knew what to do. After the first agitation produced by his approach she took no notice of him whatever; it made me remember her passionate adjuration to me. I had to achieve a great effort to imitate her, for though I knew nothing about him but that he was Sir Edmund Orme I felt his presence as a strong appeal, almost as an oppression. He stood there without speaking – young, pale, handsome, clean-shaven, decorous, with extraordinary light blue eyes and something old-fashioned, like a portrait of years ago, in his head, his manner of wearing his hair. He was in complete mourning (one immediately felt that he was very well dressed), and he carried his hat in his hand. He looked again strangely hard at me, harder than any one in the world had ever looked before; and I remember feeling rather cold and wishing he would say something. No silence had ever seemed to me so soundless. All this was of course an impression intensely rapid; but that it had consumed some instants was proved to me suddenly by the aspect of Charlotte Marden, who stared from her mother to me and back again (he never looked at her, and she had no appearance of looking at him), and then broke out with: 'What on earth is the matter with you? You've such odd faces!' I felt the colour come back to mine, and when she went on in the same tone: 'One would think you had seen a ghost!' I was conscious that I had turned very red. Sir Edmund Orme never blushed, and I could see that he had no capacity for embarrassment. One had met people of that sort, but never any one with such a grand indifference.

'Don't be impertinent; and go and tell them all that I'll join them,' said Mrs Marden with much dignity, but with a quaver in her voice.

'And will you come – *you*?' the girl asked, turning away. I made no answer, taking the question, somehow, as meant for her companion. But he was more silent than I, and when she reached the door (she was going out that way), she stopped, with her hand on the knob, and looked at me, repeating it. I assented, springing forward to open the door for her, and as she passed out she exclaimed to me mockingly: 'You haven't got your wits about you – you sha'n't have my hand!'

I closed the door and turned round to find that Sir Edmund Orme had during the moment my back was presented to him retired by the window. Mrs Marden stood there and we looked at each other long. It had only then – as the girl flitted away – come home to me that her daughter was unconscious of what had happened. It was *that*, oddly enough, that gave me a sudden, sharp shake, and not my own perception of our visitor, which appeared perfectly natural. It made the fact vivid to me that she had been equally unaware of him in church, and the two facts together – now that they were over – set my heart more sensibly beating. I wiped my forehead, and Mrs Marden broke out with a low distressful wail: 'Now you know my life – now you know my life!'

'In God's name who is he – *what* is he?'

'He's a man I wronged.'

'How did you wrong him?'

'Oh, awfully – years ago.'

'Years ago? Why, he's very young.'

'Young – young?' cried Mrs Marden. 'He was born before *I* was!'

'Then why does he look so?'

She came nearer to me, she laid her hand on my arm, and there was something in her face that made me shrink a little. 'Don't you understand – don't you *feel*?' she murmured, reproachfully.

'I feel very queer!' I laughed; and I was conscious that my laugh betrayed it.

'He's dead!' said Mrs Marden, from her white face.

'Dead?' I panted. 'Then that gentleman was –?' I couldn't even say the word.

'Call him what you like – there are twenty vulgar names. He's a perfect presence.'

'He's a splendid presence!' I cried. 'The place is haunted – *haunted*!' I exulted in the word as if it represented the fulfilment of my dearest dream.

'It isn't the place – more's the pity! That has nothing to do with it!'

'Then it's you, dear lady?' I said, as if this were still better.

'No, nor me either – I wish it were!'

'Perhaps it's me,' I suggested with a sickly smile.

'It's nobody but my child – my innocent, innocent child!' And with this Mrs Marden broke down – she dropped into a chair and burst into tears. I stammered some question – I pressed on her some bewildered appeal, but she waved me off, unexpectedly and passionately. I persisted – couldn't I help her, couldn't I intervene? 'You *have* intervened,' she sobbed; 'you're *in* it, you're *in* it.'

'I'm very glad to be in anything so curious,' I boldly declared.

'Glad or not, you can't get out of it.'

'I don't want to get out of it – it's too interesting.'

'I'm glad you like it. Go away.'

'But I want to know more about it.'

'You'll see all you want – go away!'

'But I want to understand what I see.'

'How can you – when I don't understand myself?'

'We'll do so together – we'll make it out.'

At this she got up, doing what she could to obliterate her tears. 'Yes, it will be better together – that's why I've liked you.'

'Oh, we'll see it through!' I declared.

'Then you must control yourself better.'

'I will, I will – with practice.'

'You'll get used to it,' said Mrs Marden, in a tone I never forgot. 'But go and join them – I'll come in a moment.'

I passed out to the terrace and I felt that I had a part to play. So far from dreading another encounter with the 'perfect presence', as Mrs Marden called it, I was filled with an excitement that was positively joyous. I desired a renewal of the sensation –

I opened myself wide to the impression, I went round the house as quickly as if I expected to overtake Sir Edmund Orme. I didn't overtake him just then, but the day was not to close without my recognising that, as Mrs Marden had said, I should see all I wanted of him.

We took, or most of us took, the collective sociable walk which, in the English country-house, is the consecrated pastime on Sunday afternoons. We were restricted to such a regulated ramble as the ladies were good for; the afternoons, moreover, were short, and by five o'clock we were restored to the fireside in the hall, with a sense, on my part at least, that we might have done a little more for our tea. Mrs Marden had said she would join us, but she had not appeared; her daughter, who had seen her again before we went out, only explained that she was tired. She remained invisible all the afternoon, but this was a detail to which I gave as little heed as I had given to the circumstance of my not having Miss Marden to myself during all our walk. I was too much taken up with another emotion to care; I felt beneath my feet the threshold of the strange door, in my life, which had suddenly been thrown open and out of which unspeakable vibrations played up through me like a fountain. I had heard all my days of apparitions, but it was a different thing to have seen one and to know that I should in all probability see it familiarly, as it were, again. I was on the look-out for it, as a pilot for the flash of a revolving light, and I was ready to generalise on the sinister subject, to declare that ghosts were much less alarming and much more amusing than was commonly supposed. There is no doubt that I was extremely nervous. I couldn't get over the distinction conferred upon me – the exception (in the way of mystic enlargement of vision), made in my favour. At the same time I think I did justice to Mrs Marden's absence; it was a commentary on what she had said to me – 'Now you know my life.' She had probably been seeing Sir Edmund Orme for years, and, not having my firm fibre, she had broken down under him. Her nerve was gone, though she had also been able to attest that, in a degree, one got used to him. She had got used to breaking down.

Afternoon tea, when the dusk fell early, was a friendly hour at Tranton; the firelight played into the wide, white last-century hall; sympathies almost confessed themselves, lingering together, before dressing, on deep sofas, in muddy boots, for last words, after walks; and even solitary absorption in the third volume of a novel that was wanted by some one else seemed a form of geniality. I watched my moment and went over to Charlotte Marden when I saw she was about to withdraw. The ladies had left the place one by one, and after I had addressed myself particularly to Miss Marden the three men who were near her gradually dispersed. We had a little vague talk – she appeared preoccupied, and heaven knows *I* was – after which she said she must go: she should be late for dinner. I proved to her by book that she had plenty of time, and she objected that she must at any rate go up to see her mother: she was afraid she was unwell.

'On the contrary, she's better than she has been for a long time – I'll guarantee that,' I said. 'She has found out that she can have confidence in me, and that has done her good.' Miss Marden had dropped into her chair again. I was standing before her, and she looked up at me without a smile – with a dim distress in her beautiful eyes; not exactly as if I were hurting her, but as if she were no longer disposed to treat as a joke what had passed (whatever it was, it was at the same time difficult to be serious about it) between her mother and myself. But I could answer her inquiry in all kindness and candour, for I was really conscious that the poor lady had put off a part of her burden on me and was proportionately relieved and eased. 'I'm sure she has slept all the afternoon as she hasn't slept for years,' I went on. 'You have only to ask her.'

Charlotte got up again. 'You make yourself out very useful.'

'You've a good quarter of an hour,' I said. 'Haven't I a right to talk to you a little this way, alone, when your mother has given me your hand?'

'And is it *your* mother who has given me yours? I'm much obliged to her, but I don't want it. I think our hands are not our mothers' – they happen to be our own!' laughed the girl.

'Sit down, sit down and let me tell you!' I pleaded.

I still stood before her, urgently, to see if she wouldn't oblige me. She hesitated a moment, looking vaguely this way and that, as if under a compulsion that was slightly painful. The empty hall was quiet – we heard the loud ticking of the great clock. Then she slowly sank down and I drew a chair close to her. This made me face round to the fire again, and with the movement I perceived, disconcertedly, that we were not alone. The next instant, more strangely than I can say, my discomposure, instead of increasing, dropped, for the person before the fire was Sir Edmund Orme. He stood there as I had seen him in the Indian room, looking at me with the expressionless attention which borrowed its sternness from his sombre distinction. I knew so much more about him now that I had to check a movement of recognition, an acknowledgement of his presence. When once I was aware of it, and that it lasted, the sense that we had company, Charlotte and I, quitted me; it was impressed on me on the contrary that I was more intensely alone with Miss Marden. She evidently saw nothing to look at, and I made a tremendous and very nearly successful effort to conceal from her that my own situation was different. I say 'very nearly', because she watched me an instant – while my words were arrested – in a way that made me fear she was going to say again, as she had said in the Indian room: 'What on earth is the matter with you?'

What the matter with me was I quickly told her, for the full knowledge of it rolled over me with the touching spectacle of her unconsciousness. It was touching that she became, in the presence of this extraordinary portent. What was portended, danger or sorrow, bliss or bane, was a minor question; all I saw, as she sat there, was that, innocent and charming, she was close to a horror, as she might have thought it, that happened to be veiled from her but that might at any moment be disclosed. I didn't mind it now, as I found, but nothing was more possible than she should, and if it wasn't curious and interesting it might easily be very dreadful. If I didn't mind it for myself, as I afterwards saw, this was largely because I was so taken up with the idea of protecting *her*. My heart beat high with this idea, on the spot; I determined to do everything I could to keep her sense sealed. What I could do might have been very obscure to me if I had not, in all this, become more aware than of anything else that I loved her. The way to save her was to love her, and the way to love her was to tell her, now and here, that I did so. Sir Edmund Orme didn't prevent me, especially as after a moment he turned his back to us and stood looking discreetly at the fire. At the end of another moment he leaned his head on his arm, against the chimney-piece, with an air of gradual dejection, like a spirit still more weary than discreet. Charlotte Marden was startled by what I said to her, and she jumped up to escape it; but she took no offence – my tenderness was too real. She only moved about the room with a deprecating murmur, and I was so busy following up any little advantage that I might have obtained that I didn't notice in what manner Sir Edmund Orme disappeared. I only observed presently that he had gone. This made no difference – he had been so small a hindrance; I only remember being struck, suddenly, with something inexorable in the slow, sweet, sad headshake that Miss Marden gave me.

'I don't ask for an answer now,' I said; 'I only want you to be sure – to know how much depends on it.'

'Oh, I don't want to give it to you, now or ever!' she replied. 'I hate the subject, please – I wish one could be let alone.' And then, as if I might have found something harsh in this irrepressible, artless cry of beauty beset, she added quickly, vaguely, kindly, as she left the room: 'Thank you, thank you – thank you so much!'

At dinner I could be generous enough to be glad, for her, that I was placed on the same side of the table with her, where she couldn't see me. Her mother was nearly opposite to me, and just after we had sat down Mrs Marden gave me one long, deep look, in which all our strange communion was expressed. It meant of course 'She has told me,' but it meant other things beside. At any rate I know what my answering look to her conveyed: 'I've seen him again – I've seen him again!' This didn't prevent Mrs Marden from treating her neighbours with her usual scrupulous blandness. After dinner, when, in the drawing-room, the men joined the ladies and I went straight up to her to tell her how I wished we could have some private conversation, she said immediately, in a low tone, looking down at her fan while she opened and shut it:

'He's here – he's here.'

'Here?' I looked round the room, but I was disappointed.

'Look where *she* is,' said Mrs Marden, with just the faintest asperity. Charlotte was in fact not in the main saloon, but in an apartment into which it opened and which was known as the morning-room. I took a few steps and saw her, through a doorway, upright in the middle of the room, talking with three gentlemen whose backs were practically turned to me. For a moment my quest seemed vain; then I recognised that one of the gentlemen – the middle one – was Sir Edmund Orme. This time it *was* surprising that the others didn't see him. Charlotte seemed to be looking straight at him, addressing her conversation to him. She saw me after an instant, however, and immediately turned her eyes away. I went back to her mother with an annoyed sense that the girl would think I was watching *her*, which would be unjust. Mrs Marden had found a small sofa – a little apart – and I sat down beside her. There were some questions I had so wanted to go into that I wished we were once more in the Indian room. I presently gathered, however, that our privacy was all-sufficient. We communicated so closely and completely now, and with such silent reciprocities, that it would in every circumstance be adequate.

'Oh, yes, he's there,' I said; 'and at about a quarter-past seven he was in the hall.'

'I knew it at the time, and I was so glad!'

'So glad?'

'That it was your affair, this time, and not mine. It's a rest for me.'

'Did you sleep all the afternoon?' I asked.

'As I haven't done for months. But how did you know that?'

'As *you* knew, I take it, that Sir Edmund was in the hall. We shall evidently each of us know things now – where the other is concerned.'

'Where *he* is concerned,' Mrs Marden amended. 'It's a blessing, the way you take it,' she added, with a long, mild sigh.

'I take it as a man who's in love with your daughter.'

'Of course – of course.' Intense as I now felt my desire for the girl to be, I couldn't help laughing a little at the tone of these words; and it led my companion immediately to say: 'Otherwise you wouldn't have seen him.'

'But every one doesn't see him who's in love with her, or there would be dozens.'

'They're not in love with her as you are.'

'I can, of course, only speak for myself; and I found a moment, before dinner, to do so.'

'She told me immediately.'

'And have I any hope – any chance?'

'That's what *I* long for, what I pray for.'

'Ah, how can I thank you enough?' I murmured.

'I believe it will all pass – if she loves you,' Mrs Marden continued.

'It will all pass?'

'We shall never see him again.'

'Oh, if she loves me I don't care how often I see him!'

'Ah, you take it better than I could,' said my companion. 'You have the happiness not to know – not to understand.'

'I don't indeed. What on earth does he want?'

'He wants to make me suffer.' She turned her wan face upon me with this, and I saw now for the first time, fully, how perfectly, if this had been Sir Edmund Orme's purpose, he had succeeded. 'For what I did to him,' Mrs Marden explained.

'And what did you do to him?'

She looked at me a moment. 'I killed him.' As I had seen him fifty yards away only five minutes before the words gave me a start. 'Yes, I make you jump; be careful. He's there still, but he killed himself. I broke his heart – he thought me awfully bad. We were to have been married, but I broke it off – just at the last. I saw some one I liked better; I had no reason but that. It wasn't for interest, or money, or position, or anything of that sort. All *those* things were his. It was simply that I fell in love with Captain Marden. When I saw him I felt that I couldn't marry any one else. I wasn't in love with Edmund Orme – my mother, my elder sister had brought it about. But he did love me. I told him I didn't care – that I couldn't, that I *wouldn't*. I threw him over, and he took something, some abominable drug or draught that proved fatal. It was dreadful, it was horrible, he was found that way – he died in agony. I married Captain Marden, but not for five years. I was happy, perfectly happy; time obliterates. But when my husband died I began to see him.'

I had listened intently, but I wondered. 'To see your husband?'

'Never, never *that* way, thank God! To see *him*, with Chartie – always with Chartie. The first time it nearly killed me – about seven years ago, when she first came out. Never when I'm by myself – only with her. Sometimes not for months, then every day for a week. I've tried everything to break the spell – doctors and *régimes* and climates; I've prayed to God on my knees. That day at Brighton, on the Parade with you, when you thought I was ill, that was the first for an age. And then, in the evening, when I knocked my tea over you, and the day you were at the door with Charlotte and I saw you from the window – each time he was there.'

'I see, I see.' I was more thrilled than I could say. 'It's an apparition like another.'

'Like another? Have you ever seen another?'

'No, I mean the sort of thing one has heard of. It's tremendously interesting to encounter a case.'

'Do you call me a "case"?' Mrs Marden asked, with exquisite resentment.

'I mean myself.'

'Oh, you're the right one!' she exclaimed. 'I was right when I trusted you.'

'I'm devoutly grateful you did; but what made you do it?'

'I had thought the whole thing out – I had had time to in those dreadful years, while he was punishing me in my daughter.'

'Hardly that,' I objected, 'if she never knew.'

'That has been my terror, that she *will*, from one occasion to another. I've an unspeakable dread of the effect on her.'

'She sha'n't, she sha'n't!' I declared, so loud that several people looked round. Mrs Marden made me get up, and I had no more talk with her that evening. The next day I told her I must take my departure from Tranton – it was neither comfortable nor considerate to remain as a rejected suitor. She was disconcerted, but she accepted my reasons, only saying to me out of her mournful eyes: 'You'll leave me alone then with my burden?' It was of course understood between us that for many weeks to come there would be no discretion in 'worrying poor Charlotte': such were the terms in which, with odd feminine and maternal inconsistency, she alluded to an attitude on my part that she favoured. I was prepared to be heroically considerate, but it seemed to me that even this delicacy permitted me to say a word to Miss Marden before I went. I begged her, after breakfast, to take a turn with me on the terrace, and as she hesitated, looking at me distantly, I informed her that it was only to ask her a question and to say good-bye – I was leaving Tranton for *her*.

She came out with me, and we passed slowly round the house three or four times. Nothing is finer than this great airy platform, from which every look is a sweep of the country, with the sea on the furthest edge. It might have been that as we passed the windows we were conspicuous to our friends in the house, who would divine, sarcastically, why I was so significantly bolting. But I didn't care; I only wondered whether they wouldn't really this time make out Sir Edmund Orme, who joined us on one of our turns and strolled slowly on the other side of my companion. Of what transcendent essence he was composed I knew not; I have no theory about him (leaving that to others), any more than I have one about such or such another of my fellow-mortals whom I have elbowed in life. He was as positive, as individual, as ultimate a fact as any of these. Above all he was as respectable, as sensitive a fact; so that I should no more have thought of taking a liberty, of practising an experiment with him, of touching him, for instance, or speaking to him, since he set the example of silence, than I should have thought of committing any other social grossness. He had always, as I saw more fully later, the perfect propriety of his position – had always the appearance of being dressed and, in attitude and aspect, of comporting himself, as the occasion demanded. He looked strange, incontestably, but somehow he always looked *right*. I very soon came to attach an idea of beauty to his unmentionable presence, the beauty of an old story of love and pain. What I ended by feeling was that he was on my side, that he was watching over my interest, that he was looking to it that my heart shouldn't be broken. Oh, he had taken it seriously, his own catastrophe – he had certainly proved that in his day. If poor Mrs Marden, as she told me, had thought it out, I also subjected the case to the finest analysis of which my intellect was capable. It was a case of retributive justice. The mother was to pay, in suffering, for the suffering she had inflicted, and as the disposition to jilt a lover might have been transmitted to the daughter, the daughter was to be watched, so that *she* might be made to suffer should she do an equal wrong. She might repro-duce her mother in character as vividly as she did in face. On the day she should transgress, in other words, her eyes would be opened suddenly and unpitiedly to the 'perfect presence', which she would have to work as she could into her conception of a young lady's universe. I had no great fear for her, because I didn't believe she was, in any cruel degree, a coquette. We should have a good deal of ground to get over before I, at least, should be in a position to be sacrificed by her. She couldn't throw me over before she had made a little more of me.

The question I asked her on the terrace that morning was whether I might continue, during the winter, to come to Mrs Marden's house. I promised not to come too often and not to speak to her for three months of the question I had raised the day before. She replied that I might do as I liked, and on this we parted.

I carried out the vow I had made her; I held my tongue for my three months. Unexpectedly to myself there were moments of this time when she struck me as capable of playing with a man. I wanted so to make her like me that I became subtle and ingenious, wonderfully alert, patiently diplomatic. Sometimes I thought I had earned my reward, brought her to the point of saying: 'Well, well, you're the best of them all – you may speak to me now.' Then there was a greater blankness than ever in her beauty, and on certain days a mocking light in her eyes, of which the meaning seemed to be: 'If you don't take care, I *will* accept you, to have done with you the more effectually.' Mrs Marden was a great help to me simply by believing in me, and I valued her faith all the more that it continued even though there was a sudden intermission of the miracle that had been wrought for me. After our visit to Tranton Sir Edmund Orme gave us a holiday, and I confess it was at first a disappointment to me. I felt less designated, less connected with Charlotte. 'Oh, don't cry till you're out of the wood,' her mother said; 'he has let me off sometimes for six months. He'll break out again when you least expect it – he knows what he's about.' For her these weeks were happy, and she was wise enough not to talk about me to the girl. She was so good as to assure me that I was taking the right way, that I looked as if I felt secure and that in the long run women give way to that. She had known them do it even when the man was a fool for looking so – or was a fool on any terms. For herself she felt it to be a good time, a sort of St Martin's summer of the soul. She was better than she had been for years, and she had me to thank for it. The sense of visitation was light upon her – she wasn't in anguish every time she looked round. Charlotte contradicted me very often, but she contradicted herself still more. That winter was a wonder of mildness, and we often sat out in the sun. I walked up and down with Charlotte, and Mrs Marden, sometimes on a bench, sometimes in a bath-chair, waited for us and smiled at us as we passed. I always looked out for a sign in her face – 'He's with you, he's with you' (she would see him before I should), but nothing came; the season had brought us also a sort of spiritual softness. Toward the end of April the air was so like June that, meeting my two friends one night at some Brighton sociability – an evening party with amateur music – I drew Miss Marden unresistingly out upon a balcony to which a window in one of the rooms stood open. The night was close and thick, the stars were dim, and below us, under the cliff, we heard the regular rumble of the sea. We listened to it a little and we heard mixed with it, from within the house, the sound of a violin accompanied by a piano – a performance which had been our pretext for passing out.

'Do you like me a little better?' I asked, abruptly, after a minute. 'Could you listen to me again?'

I had no sooner spoken than she laid her hand quickly, with a certain force, on my arm. 'Hush! – isn't there some one there?' She was looking into the gloom of the far end of the balcony. This balcony ran the whole width of the house, a width very great in the best of the old houses at Brighton. We were lighted a little by the open window behind us, but the other windows, curtained within, left the darkness undiminished, so that I made out but dimly the figure of a gentleman standing there and looking at us. He was in evening dress, like a guest – I saw the vague shine of his white shirt and the pale oval of his face – and he might perfectly have been a guest who had stepped out in advance of us to take the air. Miss Marden took him for one at first – then evidently, even in a few seconds, she saw that the intensity of his gaze was unconventional. What else she saw I couldn't determine; I was too taken up with my own impression to do more than feel the quick contact of her uneasiness. My own impression was in fact the strongest of sensations, a sensation of horror; for what could the thing mean but that the girl at last *saw*? I heard her give a sudden, gasping 'Ah!' and move quickly into the house. It was only afterwards that I knew that I myself had had a totally new emotion – my horror passing into anger, and my anger into a stride along the balcony with a gesture of reprobation. The case was simplified to the vision of a frightened girl whom I loved. I advanced to vindicate her security, but I found nothing there to meet me. It was either all a mistake or Sir Edmund Orme had vanished.

I followed Miss Marden immediately, but there were symptoms of confusion in the drawing-room when I passed in. A lady had fainted, the music had stopped; there was a shuffling of chairs and a pressing forward. The lady was not Charlotte, as I feared, but Mrs Marden, who had suddenly been taken ill. I remember the relief with which I learned this, for to see Charlotte stricken would have been anguish, and her mother's condition gave a channel to her agitation. It was of course all a matter for the people of the house and for the ladies, and I could have no share in attending to my friends or in conducting them to their carriage. Mrs Marden revived and insisted on going home, after which I uneasily withdrew.

I called the next morning to ask about her and was informed that she was better, but when I asked if Miss Marden would see me the message sent down was that it was impossible. There was nothing for me to do all day but to roam about with a beating heart. But toward evening I received a line in pencil, brought by hand – 'Please come; mother wishes you.' Five minutes afterward I was at the door again and ushered into the drawing-room. Mrs Marden lay upon the sofa, and as soon as I looked at her I saw the shadow of death in her face. But the first thing she said was that she was better, ever so much better; her poor old heart had been behaving queerly again, but now it was quiet. She gave me her hand and I bent over her with my eyes in hers, and in this way I was able to read what she didn't speak – 'I'm really very ill, but appear to take what I say exactly as I say it.' Charlotte stood there beside her, looking not frightened now, but intensely grave, and not meeting my eyes. 'She has told me – she has told me!' her mother went on.

'She has told you?' I stared from one of them to the other, wondering if Mrs Marden meant that the girl had spoken to her of the circumstances on the balcony.

'That you spoke to her again – that you're admirably faithful.'

I felt a thrill of joy at this; it showed me that that memory had been uppermost, and also that Charlotte had wished to say the thing that would soothe her mother most, not the thing that would alarm her. Yet I now knew, myself, as well as if Mrs Marden had told me, that she knew and had known at the moment what her daughter had seen. 'I spoke – I spoke, but she gave me no answer,' I said.

'She will now, won't you, Chartie? I want it so, I want it!' the poor lady murmured, with ineffable wistfulness.

'You're very good to me,' Charlotte said to me, seriously and sweetly, looking fixedly on the carpet. There was something different in her, different from all the past. She had recognised something, she felt a coercion. I could see that she was trembling.

'Ah, if you would let me show you *how* good I can be!' I exclaimed, holding out my hands to her. As I uttered the words I was touched with the knowledge that something had happened. A form had constituted itself on the other side of the bed, and the form leaned over Mrs Marden. My whole being went forth into a mute prayer that Charlotte shouldn't see it and that I should be able to betray nothing. The impulse to glance toward Mrs Marden was even stronger than the involuntary movement of taking in Sir Edmund Orme; but I could resist even that, and Mrs Marden was perfectly still. Charlotte got up to give me her hand, and with the definite act she saw. She gave, with a shriek, one stare of dismay, and another sound, like a wail of one of the lost, fell at the same instant on my ear. But I had already sprung toward the girl to cover her, to veil her face. She had already thrown herself into my arms. I held her there a moment – bending over her, given up to her, feeling each of her throbs with my own and not knowing which was which; then, all of a sudden, coldly, I gathered that we were alone. She released herself. The figure beside the sofa had vanished; but Mrs Marden lay in her place with closed eyes, with something in her stillness that gave us both another terror. Charlotte expressed it in the cry of 'Mother, mother!' with which she flung herself down. I fell on my knees beside her. Mrs Marden had passed away.

Was the sound I heard when Chartie shrieked – the other and still more tragic sound I mean – the despairing cry of the poor lady's death-shock or the articulate sob (it was like a waft from a great tempest), of the exorcised and pacified spirit? Possibly the latter, for that was, mercifully, the last of Sir Edmund Orme.

ABOUT THE INTRODUCER

JOHN BAYLEY is former Thomas Warton Professor of English Literature at the University of Oxford. His many books include *The Short Story: Henry James to Elizabeth Bowen*; *An Essay on Hardy, Shakespeare and Tragedy*; *Tolstoy and the Novel*; *Pushkin: A Comparative Commentary* and a detailed study of A. E. Housman's poems. He has also written several novels.

TITLES IN EVERYMAN'S LIBRARY

This book is set in PLANTIN, designed by the great French printer and typographer Christopher Plantin (*c.* 1520–89), who began as a bookbinder in Antwerp. Plantin was instrumental in establishing the pre-eminence of Flemish printing during the sixteenth century, although in the elegance of his fonts he remained quintessentially French.